*The*

# NORTON
# ANTHOLOGY
*of*
# SHORT
# FICTION

SHORTER EIGHTH EDITION

# The
# NORTON
# ANTHOLOGY
## of
# SHORT
# FICTION

---

SHORTER EIGHTH EDITION

---

## RICHARD BAUSCH
### Chapman University

## R. V. CASSILL
### Late of Brown University

W. W. NORTON & COMPANY | NEW YORK | LONDON

W. W. Norton & Company has been independent since its founding in 1923, when William Warder Norton and Mary D. Herter Norton first published lectures delivered at the People's Institute, the adult education division of New York City's Cooper Union. The firm soon expanded its program beyond the Institute, publishing books by celebrated academics from America and abroad. By midcentury, the two major pillars of Norton's publishing program—trade books and college texts—were firmly established. In the 1950s, the Norton family transferred control of the company to its employees, and today—with a staff of four hundred and a comparable number of trade, college, and professional titles published each year—W. W. Norton & Company stands as the largest and oldest publishing house owned wholly by its employees.

Editor: Spencer Richardson-Jones
Project Editor: Linda Feldman
Assistant Editor: Emily Stuart
Managing Editor, College: Marian Johnson
Managing Editor, College Digital Media: Kim Yi
Production Manager: Sean Mintus
Marketing Manager, Literature: Kimberly Bowers
Designer: Charlotte Straub
Photo Editor: Evan Luberger
Permissions Manager: Megan Jackson
Permissions Clearing: Margaret Gorenstein
Composition: Westchester Book Composition
Manufacturing: LSC Communications Crawfordsville

Permission to use copyrighted material is included in the credits section of this book, which begins on page 988.

The Library of Congress has catalogued the full edition as follows:

The Norton anthology of short fiction / [compiled by] Richard Bausch, Chapman University; R . V. Cassill, Late of Brown University. —Eighth edition.
    pages cm
    Includes bibliographical references and index.
    ISBN 978-0-393-93775-6 (pbk.)
    1. Short stories. I. Bausch, Richard, date. II. Cassill, R. V. (Ronald Verlin), date.
PN6120.2.N59 2015
808.83'1—dc23

                                                            2014044145

This edition:
ISBN: 978-0-393-93776-3 (pbk.)

W. W. Norton & Company, Inc., 500 Fifth Avenue, New York, NY 10110-0017
wwnorton.com

W. W. Norton & Company Ltd., 15 Carlisle Street, London W1D 3BS

3   4   5   6   7   8   9   0

# CONTENTS

## Writers on Writing  871

# Chronological Table of Contents

The date given for each story is that of first book publication; if, however, the story was published earlier in a journal or magazine, the date of first periodical publication is given instead.

# PREFACE

In the preface to the Seventh Edition of this ongoing enterprise, the teaching of what is one of the oldest and still most vibrant forms of human expression, I said that the work of *continuing* was what I had been about. We had lost R. V. Cassill, who built the anthology and maintained it through six editions, changing and expanding as he went along, always concerned with filling the book with stories that "discriminating readers liked most." Because as a reader I had a long history of reading the anthology (really from my first days of trying to be what Cassill was: a practicing writer of fiction, short or long) it seemed the wildest good fortune to wind up being the editor of the very volume I cut my literary teeth on in my twenties. The *Norton Anthology of Short Fiction* was what led me to the reading I have since done in the world's store of great stories, and that happy accident is really what all this work, this immense collaboration, is about: the leading of youthful readers and writers on the journey outward, to the treasures that are there. For of course the fact is that no one book can come near representing the whole of the form, or all of its greatest practitioners, yet it can indeed be a generous sampling of the abundance that exists.

The present volume, in that spirit, contains 73 stories, including 9 authors new to the gathering, and 12 new stories. There are several more authors with two or more stories included, since this gives students a sense of the range of expression, even in one career. Also, we have a new section concerned with creative writing and an expanded section of writers on writing.

As I said in the preface to the previous edition, the idea is to help college-level teaching of the short story and, by providing a wide selection of work, to help demonstrate the continuing vigor of the form itself. My whole writing life, people—some of them writers, too—have spoken glibly about the death of this superior form of entertainment. My answer has been that the short story as a form will be at all of their funerals. Indeed I'm convinced that there are more first-rate writers of stories at work now than there ever has been. A few years back, sitting in a car with Grace Paley, that old fighter, talking about stories and story writers, I had the realization that, at that very time, alive and still writing, we had Eudora Welty, William Maxwell, John Cheever, John Updike, George Garrett, Elizabeth Spencer, Saul Bellow, Bernard Malamud, Peter Taylor, Ruth Jhabvala, Joyce Carol Oates, Philip Roth, and Alice Munro, to name only a few. Well, they are all here, with many of the worthy others of their kind.

Riches. And Alice Munro just became the first writer of short stories to receive the Nobel Prize for Literature. So quite obviously the form is as fresh and alive and vibrant as it ever was, and of course the great old examples of it still stand, continuing to amaze and enrich our lives. Enrichment is indeed the word. And we want always as teachers to remember that one of the greatest gifts coming from good stories and good writing is pleasure.

Humbly, then, with a sense of gratitude and with the perdurable hope of every committed teacher, I offer this book of treasures, understanding that even in its hoped-for capaciousness, it is still only a small fraction of the continuing, vast expression John Updike called the "human news."

## Features of the Shorter Eighth Edition

—The Eighth Edition now offers 73 stories by 69 authors. It is perhaps the most generous collection of short fiction available. Twelve of the stories are new to this edition, as are nine of the authors.

—A new "Authors in Depth" section brings together excerpts from essays, criticism, speeches, interviews, and more to offer students even more insight into the works and writing processes of three influential authors featured in the anthology: William Faulkner, Alice Munro, and Flannery O'Connor.

—A new section, "A Local Habitation and a Name: Meditations on Writing," draws upon advice, ideas, encouragements, and conversations had among the community of writers and readers found at Richard Bausch's Facebook page. You are invited to join the conversation at www.facebook.com/RichardBausch Writer.

## Acknowledgments

Lisa Cupolo provided advice, love, patience, and also time and space; my editor, Spencer Richardson-Jones was simply amazing as colleague, adviser, and finally as friend; the book wouldn't exist without his continual and tireless effort to bring it about. And Peter Simon, senior editor at Norton, was, as old friends are, quietly and, with great humor and encouragement, instrumental. I send each of them a line from a lovely prayer by John Berryman: "Bless everyone in the world, especially some, thou knowest whom." Thanks also to Cynthia Shearer for all her wonderful work on the new "Authors in Depth" section and the Instructor's Manual for the Eighth Edition.

I would also like to thank the many teachers whose comments on the Seventh Edition have helped me plan the Eighth:

Jose Aparicio (University of South Florida), Mark Armstrong (Austin Community College), Martha Bayless (University of Oregon), Carl Bloom (Southeast Missouri State University), J. T. Bushnell (Oregon State University), Ben Cartwright (University of Kansas), Gabrielle Ceraldi (University of Western Ontario), Jean Lee Cole (Loyola University Maryland), Patrick Collins (Austin Community College), Bonnie Costello (Boston University), Lutgarda Cowan (Portland Community College), Tamas Dobozy (Wilfrid Laurier University), David H. Evans (Dalhousie University), Jonathan Foltz (Boston University), Dorritta Fong (Douglas College), James Freeman (Bucks County Community College), Lawrence Garber (University of Western Ontario), Ibis Gomez-Vega (Northern Illinois University), Andrew E. J. Gutteridge (University of the Fraser Valley), Sarah Harwell (Syracuse University), Tim Houghton (Loyola University Maryland), Mark Jarman (University of New Brunswick), Debbie Killingsworth (Clark College), Ellen Lansky (Inver Hills Community College), Christine Lasek (University of South Florida), Jane Lim (University of North Carolina at Chapel Hill), Wendy Lym (Austin Community College), Tanis MacDonald (Wilfrid Laurier University), Nicholas Mainieri (Nicholls State University),

Micheline Maylor (Mount Royal University), Gayla McGlamery (Loyola University Maryland), Jose-Luis Moctezuma (University of Chicago), Paul Moffett (Memorial University of Newfoundland), Lawrence Naumoff (University of North Carolina at Chapel Hill), Roger Ploude (University of New Brunswick), Anne Sandor (Orange County Community College), F. J. Schaack (Austin Community College), James Thompson (University of North Carolina at Chapel Hill), John Witte (University of Oregon), and Charles Wukasch (Austin Community College).

# WRITING ABOUT FICTION

The American poet and translator John Ciardi used to be fond of telling a story about going around to schools and speaking to groups of students as part of a poets-in-the-schools program. The idea was and is a good one: to expose young people to writers, the actual practitioners of the craft or art. One morning, as Ciardi would tell it, he was scheduled to visit an elementary school, so he brought along a poem he had written for children called "The Stranger Inside the Pumpkin." The poem begins like this:

> The stranger inside the pumpkin said,
> "It's only dark inside your head."

After he had read the poem aloud to a crowded room of fifth graders, he asked, "Who's speaking in this poem?" Every hand in the room went up, and he chose a girl in front who, without the slightest hesitation, said, "Jack O'Lantern." Ciardi then asked, "What is Jack O'Lantern telling us?" Again, there was a clamor to get his attention, hands waving, little voices saying, "Me, me." Ciardi chose a boy this time. "Jack O'Lantern thinks we don't have any light inside us because there's no candle showing out our eyes," the boy said. And after this, the whole class began to talk about the truth, or lack of it, in that idea. There was even some talk about the quality of light, ordinary candlelight as opposed to the light of imagination.

At the end of the session, as Ciardi and his escort were leaving the school, the escort said, "There's a high school nearby, we have some extra time, would you mind visiting with a class there?"

Ciardi felt slightly ill-prepared, because all he had with him was this children's poem, "The Stranger Inside the Pumpkin." But he agreed to visit the high school, deciding that he would simply read the same poem, and talk about writing children's poems. To a large group of twelfth graders—young men and women, really—he read those same lines:

> The stranger inside the pumpkin said,
> "It's only dark inside your head."

When he finished reading, he asked the same question he had asked the fifth grade children. "Who's speaking in this poem?"

Silence.

He waited, intending—as he put it, telling the story—to keep waiting until the sun went down if it took that long, for someone, anyone, to gather the courage to speak. Finally one brave young man in the back of the room raised his hand. "Yes?" Ciardi said.

"Is that, symbolism?"

Ciardi would go on to say that it had taken a mere seven years of schooling to reduce this young reader to that level of stupidity about the written word.

Now, of course, this is a story, and John Ciardi used it with delight, and to great effect, as an illustration of how students learning to think critically about what they read often learn to look past the words of a piece of writing and, in so doing, miss what is obvious and quite simple. What follows here are a few general principles to help you in the task of writing papers about the fiction you'll be reading, to alleviate some of your anxiety about the undertaking, and to suggest some ways of approaching the problem of how to write a critical paper about fiction.

The matters discussed in this section are meant to suggest some ways to formulate a critical response and express it in a paper. These are not part of a list or catalog and cannot be set down like a set of commandments or rules, but they do apply to what most students face when the first paper comes due.

And perhaps the thing to be emphasized here is that how much and how well you are able to express yourself about the fiction you are studying depends to a large extent on your own attitude toward the task.

The first thing to remember when you begin to write a paper about fiction is that you must allow for what is direct and *literal* in the words on the page. A work of fiction, in spite of what you may already have internalized about it, is not a code, not something that needs deciphering, particularly, or translation into some other form of expression. One misleading question about fiction, and one of the easiest and, therefore, most often asked questions about it, is "What is the writer *trying* to say?" If the story is any good at all, the writer is in fact *saying* it, whatever it is, and the story itself makes up the terms of that saying. The writer of a good story is almost never trying to be obscure or even difficult; the experience the writer is exploring may be filled with difficulty and ambiguity, but the writer is always striving for *clarity,* trying to be *perfectly* clear.

Therefore, to read a story intelligently, you need bring only your own experience to it and strive to be *open* to what transpires literally on the page. The story will either interest you or it won't. If the story doesn't interest you, the fault may lie with you, in that you are not yet emotionally or intellectually ready for it; it is also possible that the particular story will *never* interest you, and that is one of the reasons why conversations and commentary and friendly arguments about fiction have been going on for as long as fiction has existed. But if the story does *not* interest you, if it does nothing to you, if you feel nothing reading it, I do not recommend that you choose it to write about. When you *do* find a story that interests you—and it is hard to imagine that in an anthology of this variety and size you would not find at least *one* that did so—your first order of business is to read it again. Read it several times, in fact, and you will find with each reading that you notice more about it, that its architecture becomes a bit more readily visible to you, its nature more clear.

But let me go back for a moment.

The difficulty for any new student of fiction is that while you are *reading* stories you are asked to *write* criticism. That is like entering a room full of strangers among whom an animated and widely various conversation has been going on for centuries and being asked to add something to the conversation. You read a story that you think you might be able to say something about; you even like the story. Yet even though you could sense it breaking down into its component parts as you were reading it and rereading it, when you actually come to thinking about it as a subject for a paper, your mind goes blank. There the story is, like a painting or a piece of sculpture. It is made out of words, but it is just as mute as a statue, just as much a silent, existing, created thing, insisting on its own wholeness, resisting all your efforts to take it apart.

You must understand that this is not an unusual feeling for *any* reader of a truly good story. You are not being confronted with some deficiency in your own ability to *understand* or *get* it; you are simply experiencing the territory, and if you allow yourself a little confusion and uncertainty, you might find that the exploration of the inner workings of the story is fun, that it enhances your enjoyment of it. And though we live in a highly politicized time, we must never lose sight of the fact that one of the most important functions of fictive art is *pleasure*. And so the first rule of thumb for anyone assigned to write a paper about fiction is to *find something that truly does engage you,* something about which you can express yourself in terms other than the artificial, forced, exhausting phrases of false interest—that awful feeling of trying to guess what you believe your professor wants to hear, of trying to say something as if you had the slightest interest in it, when in fact the whole enterprise seems only a little less painful than a dental procedure involving a drill.

Having found a story that does engage you—and by this I mean it has caused some reaction in you, even if that reaction is at first negative—and having read the story again and decided that you will write about it, the next order of business is to locate some aspect of it that especially interests you: its use of language, the presence in it—or lack of presence in it—of one facet or another, the nature of its characters, some element of conflict or treatment of theme, the way any of its internal aspects contrasts or compares to some other story or stories, or how it reflects the values of its time and place or may be applied to the values of our own time and place or even how it may seem *not* to reflect such values, distant or near. You may discover an element of the story that speaks to you on some deeper level about yourself, about something you are afraid of, or ache for, or love. Any element of a story is worth writing about if you have some stake in it, some actual connection to it. And writing about it is how you explore this connection.

It has been said that the best preparation for the reading of any story is to have read all other stories. That is to say that the more you read, the better able you are to respond. But even having read dozens of stories, you may feel at a loss when the time comes to write about one. So let us take the logic a step further and say that the best preparation for writing a piece of criticism is having read all other criticism.

Obviously, you can do no such thing in either case: no one *ever* gets to all there is that is worth reading and remembering. Geoffrey Chaucer was one of the most learned men of his time, and his library contained ninety books. I am a practicing writer of prose fiction, I read both for the love of it and as a profession, and my personal library—a modest one by modern standards—contains more than seventy-five hundred volumes. The remark about preparation is simply to suggest a truth, though; and writing your paper you will have to address the problem of what we can call "The Customs of Critical Speech."

How do you begin to express yourself in the language of criticism if you have not been reading criticism? If you have had no real taste of how it is done? It is no accident that people who write poetry *read* a great deal of poetry, that people who write fiction read thousands of stories and novels (poets also read novels, of course; and novelists, most of them anyway, also read poetry); but the fact is that one reads a great deal in the form in which one primarily works. That is how we all learn to write; indeed, it is usually the thing that *leads* us to writing. Yet new students of literature are regularly asked to write criticism without having ever really been exposed to any critical writing.

To extend the metaphor of the conversation, then: you have entered this room, people have been discussing a story. The simplest, first strategy, is to familiarize yourself as quickly as possible with the manner and nature of the conversation. You do this by listening in, as it were. By reading some criticism of stories, or of any work of literary art that you already know, have already read. When I teach sophomore literature, before I give any other assignments, I ask my students to do an annotated bibliography about *Hamlet*. They must find ten critical essays about the play, read them, and then summarize them for me, merely to show that they have indeed read the essays. This is less to teach them about *Hamlet* than to expose them to the ways and means of critical speech about that great play and, by extension, about any other work of literature.

What you will find, reading in criticism, is that the work being discussed is rarely considered in its entire form or shape; that the critical writer, in nearly every case, has chosen—or discovered—some vital or crucial but always quite specific aspect of the work and is concentrating on that, tracing its use and the ramifications of its use through the story (or its similarity or difference to some aspect of another story from the same writer, or a contemporary, or even someone far away in time or place). Notice, too, how the critical writer *uses the words of the story itself* to support what he has to say about it. The use of plot summary is always to underscore or illustrate the point, and quotations from the story follow from assertions about it as *demonstrations* of the truth of those assertions.

Too often, student papers about fiction end up merely summarizing the story's plot and recounting the names of its characters. For teachers of literature, there is nothing so dull as having to read twenty-seven versions of the same plot summary in a single afternoon. And falling into mere plot summary is the most common mistake students make when writing papers, mostly because they do not feel confident talking about the story in any other way, and they have seldom if ever experienced stories being talked about in any other way. (Much of this goes back, no doubt, to the old high school "book report," in which students are asked to recount book plots more or less as proof that they have done the assigned reading.)

Mere plot summary is likely to be a habit you will have to work to break. And one rather simple way to break it, though at first you may find it difficult to do, is to keep in mind the fact that the audience for your paper about a given story is made up of people who are *familiar* with it.

Here, for instance, is one facet of a story you probably already know; it is a play rather than a work of short fiction, but it will serve to illustrate my point. To audiences in ancient Greece who went to see Sophocles' great *Oedipus Rex,* the story of Oedipus was at least as familiar as the story of Christ is to us (there is a reference to the Oedipus story in Homer, who predates Sophocles by hundreds of years, and the tone of that reference is that it was an *old* story, even then); hence, one of the most interesting elements of that play is the irony in which it is soaked—this mystery story, in which the detective searching for a murderer finds that the murderer is himself, actually contained no mystery at all to the audiences of its time. Instead, there was the excruciating spectacle of Oedipus moving ever closer to the discovery of the truth that everyone in the theater already knew. To write a paper about this, you would use those lines Oedipus speaks that, given the nature of the audience's knowledge, contain the most irony. You might explore how that irony carries the play forward and informs the action; you might show how it extends to other characters in the play and how it shapes the emotions created by the spectacle of the tragedy.

The same approach works when you write criticism about fiction. Your audience is made up of participants in the appreciation of some *part* of a thing with which everyone is acquainted.

So, you choose something *inside* the story, some specific element of its workings that you have noticed, and you present that to your audience, all of whom know the plot of the story, and you move through your discussion of this thing you have noticed, following your assertions about it with proof out of the material of the story, using the words of the story itself to support what you say.

But suppose you cannot find anything in the story that seems worth writing about? Suppose that, even having found a story with which you feel a connection, you are still unable to settle on some specific element of it? On page xxiii you'll find a list of general questions including a wide range of approaches for exploring the details of any good story. You need only look over the list and then turn to your story and think through some of these questions in relation to the story. If that fails to spark something, try looking at what some of the contemporary writers in this book have had to say about stories by other writers, living and dead. You might even find one that you wish to add to, or take issue with. But as you read, see how often these contemporary writers *use the words of the stories themselves* to make their observations about those stories. Pay close attention to the ways in which they move from assertion to quotations, from the exploration of something *about* the story to the use of details *from* the story to support their claims.

To write a paper about a work of fiction is simply to take part in a civilized and polite conversation about it with others who have read the same story, to say something meaningful about a matter of importance to you. If the story has moved you in some way, then you will be saying something meaningful as it applies to your own life, your own experience, your own interests. And in the act of expressing this, of working through the story, you become a sharper reader, you develop a more sophisticated sense of language as it is used by artists, and you become less likely to be fooled by empty rhetoric and cant, by the flood of falsity and hype all around you, by the ways in which society names you and places you and makes assumptions about you and tries to control you—for whatever purpose, even if only to sell you something you don't need. By reading good short fiction, and thinking critically about it, you not only gain the deeper pleasures there are in the contemplation of this superior art form but become more free. No less than that.

Finally, remember that fiction is about *experience*, that its truths are not necessarily—they are not even very often—merely philosophical truths, but contain the truths of *felt life;* that good stories break down the barriers between peoples and times and cultures; that fiction speaks to us across boundaries as distant as the centuries and as unbridgeable as death itself. The editors of this anthology hope you will find something that engages you, something about which you can speak passionately, in terms of the pleasure that reading good stories provides. As fiction writers—as practicing short-story writers—we take issue with the idea that the study of literature is a science; literature is far too disruptive and unruly and filled with human contradiction to be any such thing, and writers have never been in the business of engineering better human beings. Thus we encourage you to think about the stories in this book as works of art that relate to life most consistently as an *enhancement* of being—and perhaps only a momentary one at that—and that they resemble more closely all the other good stories that you may happen to be reading, or have read, than they resemble the life we actually lead, even though, in that momentary shapeliness that always obtains when a story is told, they somehow make us feel life more vividly. We hope you will make *connections,* not theories or ideology. We hope you will consider the poetry you read and hear in these prose pieces as elements of the lovely songs that exist in them, concentrating on the art of the expression rather than what you may have already been taught to search out in terms of social constructs or political "stances."

Politics is politics, and everything else is everything else.

The study of fiction is mostly the study of everything else, and politics is no more nor less important to storytelling than botany or history or psychology or religion. Most good writers are steeped in all of these things and more, without being in thrall to any of them. And by the phrase *everything else,* we mean what it is like to be alive on the planet earth at widely various points in the human journey. What it feels like being new, being crowded or alone, being in love or out of it, worrying, trying, failing; succeeding, growing old, or wishing one were older; missing lost friends, lost loved ones, or being reunited with them; fearing for one's children; living with regret, with the hope of revenge, or with an obsession; being weak or timid or confused, or consumed with fury; hating something or dreading it; wanting something and not being able to have it; grieving or gathering strength; bearing the remorseless facts of existence with some kind of dignity and with some kind of grace; facing damnation or achieving redemption. Absurdity, foolishness. Folly and heroism. What it means to be alive, engaged in the struggle to be decent, and prosperous, too. In other words, the nature of the human family in all its complexity, its age-old refusal to conform to any reductive idea about itself.

# General Questions

*The following questions are designed to guide your approaches to your reading and to preparing papers or notes for classroom discussion. It is by no means necessary to prepare systematic answers for all or any of the stories. Obviously not all questions need to be answered in relation to any particular story.*

## EXPOSITION AND SETTING

1. How and when has the author introduced the main characters?
2. How much background information or history has the author provided for the main characters? At what point in the story, and by what means, is this background information brought in? What makes such background-ing necessary or (in cases in which it is scanty or lacking altogether) unnecessary? Are the characters made quickly comprehensible by representing them as familiar types?
3. To what extent is a prevailing and preexisting conflict used as a jumping-off place for the present action of the story? How has the author made us aware of this situation or conflict?
4. What is there of special interest or significance in the setting of the story? By what means are we informed about the details of the setting? At what point in the story? How is its relation to the significance of the action expressed?
5. Is the setting vividly represented or merely implied by the way in which events unfold? Has the author assumed that readers would be familiar with the significant qualities to be found in this setting?
6. How is the setting exploited to enhance or control the mood of the story? How does it help to bring out the feelings or emotions experienced by the characters?
7. In stories told in the first person, do we learn essential things about the narrator by the feelings or attention the narrator devotes to the setting?
8. Could the action take place meaningfully in another setting? That is—has the setting been chosen arbitrarily, for its own sake, or because it has an integral connection with the action?

## PLOT

1. Do the meaning and emotional impact of this story heavily depend on the working out of the plot? Or is the plot—if it is noticeable at all—subordinate to the other elements?
2. To what extent does the action of the plot arise from the kinds of characters depicted in the story and their relation to each other?
3. Are there any major breaks or omissions in the chain of events or episodes of the plot? Is the outcome of the plot consistent with the actions that initiated it? If there is a surprise ending, does it emerge from some unforeseen but plausible change in direction of the plot line?
4. How is the plot related to the chronology of the story? That is, have some decisive actions, necessary to the plot, taken place before the narration begins? Is the narration halted with an implication that some event still to come will round out the plot?

5. Test the plot for meaning and credibility by imagining alternative events which, at any point, might have made for a different outcome.
6. What motivations in the characters are necessary to move the plot along?

## CHARACTER AND CONFLICT

1. Who is the central character, or who are the central characters? What means has the author used to demonstrate their qualities? To what extent are the characters defined by contrast with minor characters?
2. Do we understand the characters as types or as individuals? By their actions? Their speech? Their thoughts? (It may be useful for you to pick a single instance of action, speech, or thought and ask in what ways it represents the character to whom it is attributed.)
3. Which characters are active and which passive within the pattern of the story?
4. Does the story show growth or change of character? How much of the story's meaning depends on such growth or change?
5. How much of the conflict in the story arises from an opposition between the central character and his or her environment?
6. Is the conflict inherent in the personality of the characters assembled by the author, or in the backgrounds they represent?
7. How has the author worked to involve the reader's sympathies for certain characters, and how does this contribute to the reader's assessment of the issues of the conflict?
8. How much are the characters (or their representation) conditioned by their time and place?

## POINT OF VIEW AND PERSON OF NARRATION

1. Has the author confined the narration to a single point of view? Taking into account the nature of the material in the story, what apparent advantages lie in telling it from the point of view actually chosen?
2. What potentially interesting aspects of the subject matter have been subordinated or omitted by the choice of point of view?
3. In first-person narration, to what extent does the author appear to have identified himself with the narrator? What has the author gained by keeping a distinction between himself and the personality of the narrator?
4. What would be gained or lost by changing the narration from first to third person, or vice versa?
5. How is the point of view complemented by the style and diction? How do self-imposed limits of diction reinforce the emotional impact of a story or focus its meaning?
6. Is an illusion of reality enhanced by choice of point of view? A sense of immediacy?

## THEME

1. Does the story make a general statement about life or experience? Can this be stated in the form of a maxim? Does the so-called maxim really provide a complete statement of the story?

2. Is the thematic statement accomplished chiefly by the outcome of the action? What qualifications and shadings are given to it by the characters' awareness of what has happened to them?
3. What values and ideas are reflected in the conflict from which the thematic statement comes?
4. Is the theme a traditional one? Has the story given a new twist to traditional wisdom? Where else—in literature, history, or religion—have you encountered a similar theme? Can you recall a poem or another story that makes a comparable thematic statement?

## DESCRIPTION, REPRESENTATION, AND SYMBOL

1. Pick out some examples of language used by the author to stimulate and control the reader's visualization of the scene. Consider not only individual words and phrases but the accumulations and combinations of nouns, verbs, and their modifiers in paragraph structures.
2. How have the details chosen by the author given the essential appearance of characters or scene? Is the story fully presented to your senses? Comment on the adequacy of the description.
3. Has the author relied on your familiarity with certain scenes, characters, and situations to fill in what has been omitted from the actual text of the story?
4. How has the objectively rendered action of the story helped you to understand the thoughts, emotions, and motivations of the characters? Can you fill in the thought processes of those characters whose thoughts are not described?
5. What objects, acts, or situations have a symbolic meaning? Are the characters aware of these symbolic meanings? Has the author used symbols as a means of communicating to the reader some meanings not implicit in the action and not understood by any character in the story?

## MODE (AS IT APPLIES)

1. What devices or instances has the author relied on to heighten the comic (or pathetic, tragic, satiric, elegiac) effect of the story?
2. What exaggerations or distortions of reality have been used to shape the material of the story to a particular purpose? Could the same material serve another purpose? (For example, in the case of comedy, could the material have been treated in a way that would produce a tragic effect?)
3. To what extent has the author manipulated the tone of the story to give a special flavor to the material?
4. With what views of life does this story fit best?
5. What satiric or ironic elements can you distinguish in the story? Do these dominate the whole story? Are they consistent with the overall quality of the story, or do they provide tension, variety, and suspense as you wait to learn what the author is really driving at?
6. Does the story appeal chiefly to a romantic or realistic sensibility? Does it tend to stir up pity, contempt, amusement, awe, dismay, admiration, or a desire that life should be different?

*The*

# NORTON
# ANTHOLOGY
*of*
# SHORT
# FICTION

SHORTER EIGHTH EDITION

# CONRAD AIKEN
## (1889–1973)

Conrad Aiken was born in Savannah, Georgia to socially prominent parents from New York and Boston. When Aiken was eleven years old, his father shot and killed Aiken's mother and then himself. This traumatic event undoubtedly had a tremendous impact on his life and writing, which is often deeply psychological. Aiken relates the events surrounding the tragic incident in his autobiography, *Ushant* (1952). Following the death of his parents, Aiken went to live with an aunt in Massachusetts. He knew from an early age that he wanted to be a poet and attended Harvard University determined to become one. While at Harvard, Aiken made a lifelong friend of T. S. Eliot and studied under George Santayana, both of whom greatly influenced his work. Two years after graduating, he published his first book of poetry, *Earth Triumphant* (1914). Aiken spent most of the 1920s and '30s in England—a prolific time for him, despite multiple divorces and a suicide attempt. Aiken has said that his short story "Silent Snow, Secret Snow," below, is "a projection of [his] own inclination to insanity." He returned to the United States in the early 1940s, settling in New England until the last years of his life, when he returned to Savannah, Georgia. Aiken's dozens of publications include collections of poetry and short stories, novels, and literary criticism. He was awarded the Pulitzer Prize in 1930 for his *Selected Poems* and the National Book Award in 1954 for his *Collected Poems*. From 1950 to 1952 he was the Consultant in Poetry to the Library of Congress and in 1973 became the Poet Laureate of his home state of Georgia. He also received the National Institute of Arts and Letters Gold Medal, the National Medal for Literature, and the Bollingen Prize for Poetry. Among his collections of short fiction are *Bring! Bring! And Other Stories* (1925), *Costumes by Eros* (1928), *Among the Lost People* (1934), and *The Collected Short Stories of Conrad Aiken* (1960).

## Silent Snow, Secret Snow

### I

Just why it should have happened, or why it should have happened just when it did, he could not, of course, possibly have said; nor perhaps would it even have occurred to him to ask. The thing was above all a secret, something to be preciously concealed from Mother and Father; and to that very fact it owed an enormous part of its deliciousness. It was like a peculiarly beautiful trinket to be carried unmentioned in one's trouser pocket—a rare stamp, an old coin, a few tiny gold links found trodden out of shape on the path in the park, a pebble of carnelian,[1] a seashell distinguishable from all others by an unusual spot or stripe—and, as if it were any one of these, he carried around with him everywhere a warm and persistent and increasingly beautiful sense of possession. Nor was it only a sense of possession—it was also a sense of protection. It was as if, in some delightful way, his secret gave him a fortress, a wall behind which he could retreat into heavenly seclusion. This was almost the first thing he had noticed about it—apart from the oddness of the thing itself—and it was this that now again, for the fiftieth time, occurred to him, as he sat in the little schoolroom. It was the half-hour for geography. Miss Buell was revolving with one finger, slowly, a huge terrestrial globe which had been placed on her desk. The green and yellow continents passed and repassed, questions were asked and answered, and now the little girl in front of him, Deirdre, who had a funny little constellation of freckles on the back of her neck, exactly like the Big Dipper, was standing up and telling Miss Buell that the equator was the line that ran round the middle.

Miss Buell's face, which was old and grayish and kindly, with gray stiff curls beside the cheeks, and eyes that swam very brightly, like little minnows, behind thick glasses, wrinkled itself into a complication of amusements.

"Ah! I see. The earth is wearing a belt, or a sash. Or someone drew a line round it!"

"Oh no—not that—I mean——"

In the general laughter, he did not share, or only a very little. He was thinking about the Arctic and Antarctic regions, which of course, on the globe, were white. Miss Buell was now telling them about the tropics, the jungles, the steamy heat of equatorial swamps, where the birds and butterflies, and even the snakes, were like living jewels. As he listened to these things, he was already, with a pleasant sense of half-effort, putting his secret between himself and the words. Was it really an effort at all? For effort implied something voluntary, and perhaps even something one did not especially want; whereas this was distinctly pleasant, and came almost of its own accord. All he needed to do was to think of that morning, the first one, and then of all the others—

But it was all so absurdly simple! It had amounted to so little. It was nothing, just an idea—and just why it should have become so wonderful, so permanent, was a mystery—a very pleasant one, to be sure, but also, in an amusing way, foolish. However, without ceasing to listen to Miss Buell, who had now moved up to the north temperate zones, he deliberately invited his memory of the first morning. It was only a moment or two after he had waked up—or perhaps the moment itself. But was there, to be exact, an exact moment? Was one awake all at once? or was it gradual? Anyway, it was after he had stretched a lazy hand up toward the headrail, and yawned, and then relaxed again among his warm covers, all the more grateful on a December morning, that the thing had happened. Suddenly, for no reason, he had thought of the postman, he remembered the postman. Perhaps there was nothing so odd in that. After all, he heard the postman almost every morning in his life—his heavy boots could be heard clumping round the corner at the top of the little cobbled hill-street, and then, progressively nearer, progressively louder, the double knock at each

---

1. A reddish-colored semiprecious mineral.

door, the crossings and re-crossings of the street, till finally the clumsy steps came stumbling across to the very door, and the tremendous knock came which shook the house itself.

(Miss Buell was saying, "Vast wheat-growing areas in North America and Siberia."

Deirdre had for the moment placed her left hand across the back of her neck.)

But on this particular morning, the first morning, as he lay there with his eyes closed, he had for some reason *waited* for the postman. He wanted to hear him come round the corner. And that was precisely the joke—he never did. He never came. He never had come—*round the corner*—again. For when at last the steps *were* heard, they had already, he was quite sure, come a little down the hill, to the first house; and even so, the steps were curiously different—they were softer, they had a new secrecy about them, they were muffled and indistinct; and while the rhythm of them was the same, it now said a new thing—it said peace, it said remoteness, it said cold, it said sleep. And he had understood the situation at once—nothing could have seemed simpler—there had been snow in the night, such as all winter he had been longing for; and it was this which had rendered the postman's first footsteps inaudible, and the later ones faint. Of course! How lovely! And even now it must be snowing—it was going to be a snowy day—the long white ragged lines were drifting and sifting across the street, across the faces of the old houses, whispering and hushing, making little triangles of white in the corners between cobblestones, seething a little when the wind blew them over the ground to a drifted corner; and so it would be all day, getting deeper and deeper and silenter and silenter.

(Miss Buell was saying, "Land of perpetual snow.")

All this time, of course (while he lay in bed), he had kept his eyes closed, listening to the nearer progress of the postman, the muffled footsteps thumping and slipping on the snow-sheathed cobbles; and all the other sounds—the double knocks, a frosty far-off voice or two, a bell ringing thinly and softly as if under a sheet of ice—had the same slightly abstracted quality, as if removed by one degree from actuality—as if everything in the world had been insulated by snow. But when at last, pleased, he opened his eyes, and turned them toward the window, to see for himself this long-desired and now so clearly imagined miracle—what he saw instead was brilliant sunlight on a roof; and when, astonished, he jumped out of bed and stared down into the street, expecting to see the cobbles obliterated by the snow, he saw nothing but the bare bright cobbles themselves.

Queer, the effect this extraordinary surprise had had upon him—all the following morning he had kept with him a sense as of snow falling about him, a secret screen of new snow between himself and the world. If he had not dreamed such a thing—and how could he have dreamed it while awake?—how else could one explain it? In any case, the delusion had been so vivid as to affect his entire behavior. He could not now remember whether it was on the first or the second morning—or was it even the third?—that his mother had drawn attention to some oddness in his manner.

"But my darling"—she had said at the breakfast table—"what has come over you? You don't seem to be listening. . . ."

And how often that very thing had happened since!

(Miss Buell was now asking if anyone knew the difference between the North Pole and the Magnetic Pole. Deirdre was holding up her flickering brown hand, and he could see the four white dimples that marked the knuckles.)

Perhaps it hadn't been either the second or third morning—or even the fourth or fifth. How could he be sure? How could he be sure just when the delicious *progress* had become clear? Just when it had really *begun?* The intervals weren't very precise. . . . All he now knew was, that at some point or other— perhaps the second day, perhaps the sixth—he had noticed that the presence of the snow was a little more insistent, the sound of it clearer; and, conversely, the sound of the postman's footsteps more indistinct. Not only could he not hear the steps come round the corner, he could not even hear them at the first house. It was below the first house that he heard them; and then, a few days later, it was below the second house that he heard them; and a few days later again, below the third. Gradually, gradually, the snow was becoming heavier, the sound of its seething louder, the cobblestones more and more muffled. When he found, each morning, on going to the window, after the ritual of listening, that the roofs and cobbles were as bare as ever, it made no difference. This was, after all, only what he had expected. It was even what pleased him, what rewarded him: the thing was his own, belonged to no one else. No one else knew about it, not even his mother and father. There, outside, were the bare cobbles; and here, inside, was the snow. Snow growing heavier each day, muffling the world, hiding the ugly, and deadening increasingly—above all— the steps of the postman.

"But, my darling"—she had said at the luncheon table—"what has come over you? You don't seem to listen when people speak to you. That's the third time I've asked you to pass your plate. . . ."

How was one to explain this to Mother? or to Father? There was, of course, nothing to be done about it: nothing. All one could do was to laugh embarrassedly, pretend to be a little ashamed, apologize, and take a sudden and somewhat disingenuous interest in what was being done or said. The cat had stayed out all night. He had a curious swelling on his left cheek—perhaps somebody had kicked him, or a stone had struck him. Mrs. Kempton was or was not coming to tea. The house was going to be housecleaned, or "turned out," on Wednesday instead of Friday. A new lamp was provided for his evening work— perhaps it was eyestrain which accounted for this new and so peculiar vagueness of his—Mother was looking at him with amusement as she said this, but with something else as well. A new lamp? A new lamp. Yes, Mother, No, Mother, Yes, Mother. School is going very well. The geometry is very easy. The history is very dull. The geography is very interesting—particularly when it takes one to the North Pole. Why the North Pole? Oh, well, it would be fun to be an explorer. Another Peary or Scott or Shackleton. And then abruptly he found his interest in the talk at an end, stared at the pudding on his plate, listened, waited, and began once more—ah, how heavenly, too, the first beginnings—to hear or feel—for could he actually hear it?—the silent snow, the secret snow.

(Miss Buell was telling them about the search for the Northwest Passage, about Hendrik Hudson, the *Half Moon*.)

This had been, indeed, the only distressing feature of the new experience; the fact that it so increasingly had brought him into a kind of mute misunderstanding, or even conflict, with his father and mother. It was as if he were trying to lead a double life. On the one hand, he had to be Paul Hasleman, and keep up the appearance of being that person—dress, wash, and answer intelligently when spoken to—; on the other, he had to explore this new world which had been opened to him. Nor could there be the slightest doubt—not the slightest—that the new world was the profounder and more wonderful of the two. It was irresistible. It was miraculous. Its beauty was simply beyond anything—beyond speech as beyond thought—utterly incommunicable. But how then, between the two worlds, of which he was thus constantly aware, was he to keep a balance? One must get up, one must go to breakfast, one must talk with Mother, go to school, do one's lessons—and, in all this, try not to appear too much of a fool. But if all the while one was also trying to extract the full deliciousness of another and quite separate existence, one which could not easily (if at all) be spoken of—how was one to manage? How was one to explain? Would it be safe to explain? Would it be absurd? Would it merely mean that he would get into some obscure kind of trouble?

These thoughts came and went, came and went, as softly and secretly as the snow; they were not precisely a disturbance, perhaps they were even a pleasure; he liked to have them; their presence was something almost palpable, something he could stroke with his hand, without closing his eyes, and without ceasing to see Miss Buell and the schoolroom and the globe and the freckles on Deirdre's neck; nevertheless he did in a sense cease to see, or to see the obvious external world, and substituted for this vision the vision of snow, the sound of snow, and the slow, almost soundless, approach of the postman. Yesterday, it had been only at the sixth house that the postman had become audible; the snow was much deeper now, it was falling more swiftly and heavily, the sound of its seething was more distinct, more soothing, more persistent. And this morning, it had been—as nearly as he could figure—just above the seventh house—perhaps only a step or two above; at most, he had heard two or three footsteps before the knock had sounded. . . . And with each such narrowing of the sphere, each nearer approach of the limit at which the postman was first audible, it was odd how sharply was increased the amount of illusion which had to be carried into the ordinary business of daily life. Each day, it was harder to get out of bed, to go to the window, to look out at the—as always—perfectly empty and snowless street. Each day it was more difficult to go through the perfunctory motions of greeting Mother and Father at breakfast, to reply to their questions, to put his books together and go to school. And at school, how extraordinarily hard to conduct with success simultaneously the public life and the life that was secret! There were times when he longed—positively ached—to tell everyone about it—to burst out with it—only to be checked almost at once by a far-off feeling as of some faint absurdity which was inherent in it—but *was* it absurd?—and more importantly by a sense of mysterious power in his very secrecy. Yes; it must be kept secret. That, more and more, became clear. At whatever cost to himself, whatever pain to others—

(Miss Buell looked straight at him, smiling, and said, "Perhaps we'll ask Paul. I'm sure Paul will come out of his daydream long enough to be able to tell us. Won't you, Paul?" He rose slowly from his chair, resting one hand on the brightly varnished desk, and deliberately stared through the snow toward the blackboard. It was an effort, but it was amusing to make it. "Yes," he said slowly, "it was what we now call the Hudson River. This he thought to be the

Northwest Passage. He was disappointed." He sat down again, and as he did so Deirdre half turned in her chair and gave him a shy smile, of approval and admiration.)

At whatever pain to others.

This part of it was very puzzling, very puzzling. Mother was very nice, and so was Father. Yes, that was all true enough. He wanted to be nice to them, to tell them everything—and yet, was it really wrong of him to want to have a secret place of his own?

At bed-time, the night before, Mother had said, "If this goes on, my lad, we'll have to see a doctor, we will! We can't have our boy—" But what was it she had said? "Live in another world"? "Live so far away"? The word "far" had been in it, he was sure, and then Mother had taken up a magazine again and laughed a little, but with an expression which wasn't mirthful. He had felt sorry for her. . . .

The bell rang for dismissal. The sound came to him through long curved parallels of falling snow. He saw Deirdre rise, and had himself risen almost as soon—but not quite as soon—as she.

## II

On the walk homeward, which was timeless, it pleased him to see through the accompaniment, or counterpoint, of snow, the items of mere externality on his way. There were many kinds of brick in the sidewalks, and laid in many kinds of pattern. The garden walls, too, were various, some of wooden palings, some of plaster, some of stone. Twigs of bushes leaned over the walls: the little hard green winter-buds of lilac, on gray stems, sheathed and fat; other branches very thin and fine and black and desiccated. Dirty sparrows huddled in the bushes, as dull in color as dead fruit left in leafless trees. A single starling creaked on a weather vane. In the gutter, beside a drain, was a scrap of torn and dirty newspaper, caught in a little delta of filth; the word ECZEMA appeared in large capitals, and below it was a letter from Mrs. Amelia D. Cravath, 2100 Pine Street, Fort Worth, Texas, to the effect that after being a sufferer for years she had been cured by Caley's Ointment. In the little delta, beside the fan-shaped and deeply runneled continent of brown mud, were lost twigs, descended from their parent trees, dead matches, a rusty horse-chestnut burr, a small concentration of eggshell, a streak of yellow sawdust which had been wet and now was dry and congealed, a brown pebble, and a broken feather. Farther on was a cement sidewalk, ruled into geometrical parallelograms, with a brass inlay at one end commemorating the contractors who had laid it, and, halfway across, an irregular and random series of dog-tracks, immortalized in synthetic stone. He knew these well, and always stepped on them; to cover the little hollows with his own foot had always been a queer pleasure; today he did it once more, but perfunctorily and detachedly, all the while thinking of something else. That was a dog, a long time ago, who had made a mistake and walked on the cement while it was still wet. He had probably wagged his tail, but that hadn't been recorded. Now, Paul Hasleman, aged twelve, on his way home from school, crossed the same river, which in the meantime had frozen into rock. Homeward through the snow, the snow falling in bright sunshine. Homeward?

Then came the gateway with the two posts surmounted by egg-shaped stones which had been cunningly balanced on their ends, as if by Columbus, and mortared in the very act of balance; a source of perpetual wonder. On the brick wall just beyond, the letter H had been stenciled, presumably for some purpose. H? H.

The green hydrant, with a little green-painted chain attached to the brass screw-cap.

The elm tree, with the great gray wound in the bark, kidney-shaped, into which he always put his hand—to feel the cold but living wood. The injury, he had been sure, was due to the gnawings of a tethered horse. But now it deserved only a passing palm, a merely tolerant eye. There were more important things. Miracles. Beyond the thoughts of trees, mere elms. Beyond the thoughts of sidewalks, mere stone, mere brick, mere cement. Beyond the thoughts even of his own shoes, which trod these sidewalks obediently, bearing a burden—far above—of elaborate mystery. He watched them. They were not very well polished; he had neglected them, for a very good reason: they were one of the many parts of the increasing difficulty of the daily return to daily life, the morning struggle. To get up, having at last opened one's eyes, to go to the window, and discover no snow, to wash, to dress, to descend the curving stairs to breakfast—

At whatever pain to others, nevertheless, one must persevere in severance, since the incommunicability of the experience demanded it. It was desirable, of course, to be kind to Mother and Father, especially as they seemed to be worried, but it was also desirable to be resolute. If they should decide—as appeared likely—to consult the doctor, Doctor Howells, and have Paul inspected, his heart listened to through a kind of dictaphone, his lungs, his stomach—well, that was all right. He would go through with it. He would give them answer for question, too—perhaps such answers as they hadn't expected? No. That would never do. For the secret world must, at all costs, be preserved.

The bird-house in the apple tree was empty—it was the wrong time of year for wrens. The little round black door had lost its pleasure. The wrens were enjoying other houses, other nests, remoter trees. But this too was a notion which he only vaguely and grazingly entertained—as if, for the moment, he merely touched an edge of it; there was something further on, which was already assuming a sharper importance; something which already teased at the corners of his eyes, teasing also at the corner of his mind. It was funny to think that he so wanted this, so awaited it—and yet found himself enjoying this momentary dalliance with the bird-house, as if for a quite deliberate postponement and enhancement of the approaching pleasure. He was aware of his delay, of his smiling and detached and now almost uncomprehending gaze at the little bird-house; he knew what he was going to look at next: it was his own little cobbled hill-street, his own house, the little river at the bottom of the hill, the grocer's shop with the cardboard man in the window—and now, thinking of all this, he turned his head, still smiling, and looking quickly right and left through the snow-laden sunlight.

And the mist of snow, as he had foreseen, was still on it—a ghost of snow falling in the bright sunlight, softly and steadily floating and turning and pausing, soundlessly meeting the snow that covered, as with a transparent mirage, the bare bright cobbles. He loved it—he stood still and loved it. Its beauty was paralyzing—beyond all words, all experience, all dream. No fairy story he

had ever read could be compared with it—none had ever given him this extraordinary combination of ethereal loveliness with a something else, unname-
able, which was just faintly and deliciously terrifying. What was this thing?
As he thought of it, he looked upward toward his own bedroom window, which
was open—and it was as if he looked straight into the room and saw himself
lying half awake in his bed. There he was—at this very instant he was still perhaps actually there—more truly there than standing here at the edge of the
cobbled hill-street, with one hand lifted to shade his eyes against the snow-
sun. Had he indeed ever left his room, in all this time? since that very first
morning? Was the whole progress still being enacted there, was it still the
same morning, and himself not yet wholly awake? And even now, had the postman not yet come round the corner? . . .

   This idea amused him, and automatically, as he thought of it, he turned
his head and looked toward the top of the hill. There was, of course, nothing
there—nothing and no one. The street was empty and quiet. And all the more
because of its emptiness it occurred to him to count the houses—a thing
which, oddly enough, he hadn't before thought of doing. Of course, he had
known there weren't many—many, that is, on his own side of the street, which
were the ones that figured in the postman's progress—but nevertheless it came
as something of a shock to find that there were precisely *six,* above his own
house—his own house was the seventh.

   Six!

   Astonished, he looked at his own house—looked at the door, on which was
the number thirteen—and then realized that the whole thing was exactly and
logically and absurdly what he ought to have known. Just the same, the realization gave him abruptly, and even a little frighteningly, a sense of hurry. He
was being hurried—he was being rushed. For—he knit his brow—he couldn't
be mistaken—it was just above the *seventh* house, his *own* house, that the postman had first been audible this very morning. But in that case—in that case—
did it mean that tomorrow he would hear nothing? The knock he had heard
must have been the knock of their own door. Did it mean—and this was an
idea which gave him a really extraordinary feeling of surprise—that he would
never hear the postman again?—that tomorrow morning the postman
would already have passed the house, in a snow so deep as to render his
footsteps completely inaudible? That he would have made his approach
down the snow-filled street so soundlessly, so secretly, that he, Paul Hasleman, there lying in bed, would not have waked in time, or waking, would
have heard nothing?

   But how could that be? Unless even the knocker should be muffled in the
snow—frozen tight, perhaps? . . . But in that case—

   A vague feeling of disappointment came over him; a vague sadness as if he
felt himself deprived of something which he had long looked forward to,
something much prized. After all this, all this beautiful progress, the slow
delicious advance of the postman through the silent and secret snow, the
knock creeping closer each day, and the footsteps nearer, the audible compass
of the world thus daily narrowed, narrowed, narrowed, as the snow soothingly
and beautifully encroached and deepened, after all this, was he to be defrauded
of the one thing he had so wanted—to be able to count, as it were, the last two
or three solemn footsteps, as they finally approached his own door? Was it all

going to happen, at the end, so suddenly? or indeed, had it already happened? with no slow and subtle gradations of menace, in which he could luxuriate?

He gazed upward again, toward his own window which flashed in the sun; and this time almost with a feeling that it would be better if he *were* still in bed, in that room; for in that case this must still be the first morning, and there would be six more mornings to come—or, for that matter, seven or eight or nine—how could he be sure?—or even more.

**III**

After supper, the inquisition began. He stood before the doctor, under the lamp, and submitted silently to the usual thumpings and tappings.

"Now will you please say 'Ah!'?"

"Ah!"

"Now again, please, if you don't mind."

"Ah."

"Say it slowly, and hold it if you can——"

"Ah-h-h-h-h-h——"

"Good."

How silly all this was. As if it had anything to do with his throat! Or his heart, or lungs!

Relaxing his mouth, of which the corners, after all this absurd stretching, felt uncomfortable, he avoided the doctor's eyes, and stared toward the fireplace, past his mother's feet (in gray slippers) which projected from the green chair, and his father's feet (in brown slippers) which stood neatly side by side on the hearth rug.

"Hm. There is certainly nothing wrong there . . . ?"

He felt the doctor's eyes fixed upon him, and, as if merely to be polite, returned the look, but with a feeling of justifiable evasiveness.

"Now, young man, tell me—do you feel all right?"

"Yes, sir, quite all right."

"No headaches? no dizziness?"

"No, I don't think so."

"Let me see. Let's get a book, if you don't mind—yes, thank you, that will do splendidly—and now, Paul, if you'll just read it, holding it as you would normally hold it——"

He took the book and read:

"And another praise have I to tell for this the city our mother, the gift of a great god, a glory of the land most high; the might of horses, the might of young horses, the might of the sea. . . . For thou, son of Cronus, our lord Poseidon, hath throned herein this pride, since in these roads first thou didst show forth the curb that cures the rage of steeds. And the shapely oar, apt to men's hands, hath a wondrous speed on the brine, following the hundred-footed Nereids. . . . O land that art praised above all lands, now is it for thee to make those bright praises seen in deeds."

He stopped, tentatively, and lowered the heavy book.

"No—as I thought—there is certainly no superficial sign of eyestrain."

Silence thronged the room, and he was aware of the focused scrutiny of the three people who confronted him. . . .

"We could have his eyes examined—but I believe it is something else."

"What could it be?" That was his father's voice.

"It's only this curious absent-mindedness—" This was his mother's voice. In the presence of the doctor, they both seemed irritatingly apologetic.

"I believe it is something else. Now Paul—I would like very much to ask you a question or two. You will answer them, won't you—you know I'm an old, old friend of yours, eh? That's right! . . ."

His back was thumped twice by the doctor's fat fist—then the doctor was grinning at him with false amiability, while with one fingernail he was scratching the top button of his waistcoat. Beyond the doctor's shoulder was the fire, the fingers of flame making light prestidigitation[2] against the sooty fireback, the soft sound of their random flutter the only sound.

"I would like to know—is there anything that worries you?"

The doctor was again smiling, his eyelids low against the little black pupils, in each of which was a tiny white bead of light. Why answer him? why answer him at all? "At whatever pain to others"—but it was all a nuisance, this necessity for resistance, this necessity for attention; it was as if one had been stood up on a brilliantly lighted stage, under a great round blaze of spotlight; as if one were merely a trained seal, or a performing dog, or a fish, dipped out of an aquarium and held up by the tail. It would serve them right if he were merely to bark or growl. And meanwhile, to miss these last few precious hours, these hours of which each minute was more beautiful than the last, more menacing—! He still looked, as if from a great distance, at the beads of light in the doctor's eyes, at the fixed false smile, and then, beyond, once more at his mother's slippers, his father's slippers, the soft flutter of the fire. Even here, even amongst these hostile presences, and in this arranged light, he could see the snow, he could hear it—it was in the corners of the room, where the shadow was deepest, under the sofa, behind the half-opened door which led to the dining room. It was gentler here, softer, its seethe the quietest of whispers, as if, in deference to a drawing room, it had quite deliberately put on its "manners"; it kept itself out of sight, obliterated itself, but distinctly with an air of saying, "Ah, but just wait! Wait till we are alone together! Then I will begin to tell you something new! Something white! something cold! something sleepy! something of cease, and peace, and the long bright curve of space! Tell them to go away. Banish them. Refuse to speak. Leave them, go upstairs to your room, turn out the light and get into bed—I will go with you, I will be waiting for you, I will tell you a better story than Little Kay of the Skates, or The Snow Ghost—I will surround your bed, I will close the windows, pile a deep drift against the door, so that none will ever again be able to enter. Speak to them! . . ." It seemed as if the little hissing voice came from a slow white spiral of falling flakes in the corner by the front window—but he could not be sure. He felt himself smiling, then, and said to the doctor, but without looking at him, looking beyond him still—

"Oh no, I think not——"

"But are you sure, my boy?"

His father's voice came softly and coldly then—the familiar voice of silken warning.

---

2. Sleight-of-hand tricks.

"You needn't answer at once, Paul—remember we're trying to help you—think it over and be quite sure, won't you?"

He felt himself smiling again, at the notion of being quite sure. What a joke! As if he weren't so sure that reassurance was no longer necessary, and all this cross-examination a ridiculous farce, a grotesque parody! What could they know about it? these gross intelligences, these humdrum minds so bound to the usual, the ordinary? Impossible to tell them about it! Why, even now, even now, with the proof so abundant, so formidable, so imminent, so appallingly present here in this very room, could they believe it?—could even his mother believe it? No—it was only too plain that if anything were said about it, the merest hint given, they would be incredulous—they would laugh—they would say "Absurd!"—think things about him which weren't true. . . .

"Why no, I'm not worried—why should I be?"

He looked then straight at the doctor's low-lidded eyes, looked from one of them to the other, from one bead of light to the other, and gave a little laugh.

The doctor seemed to be disconcerted by this. He drew back in his chair, resting a fat white hand on either knee. The smile faded slowly from his face.

"Well, Paul!" he said, and paused gravely, "I'm afraid you don't take this quite seriously enough. I think you perhaps don't quite realize—don't quite realize—" He took a deep quick breath and turned, as if helplessly, at a loss for words, to the others. But Mother and Father were both silent—no help was forthcoming.

"You must surely know, be aware, that you have not been quite yourself, of late? Don't you know that? . . ."

It was amusing to watch the doctor's renewed attempt at a smile, a queer disorganized look, as of confidential embarrassment.

"I feel all right, sir," he said, and again gave the little laugh.

"And we're trying to help you." The doctor's tone sharpened.

"Yes, sir, I know. But why? I'm all right. I'm just *thinking*, that's all."

His mother made a quick movement forward, resting a hand on the back of the doctor's chair.

"Thinking?" she said. "But my dear, about what?"

This was a direct challenge—and would have to be directly met. But before he met it, he looked again into the corner by the door, as if for reassurance. He smiled again at what he saw, at what he heard. The little spiral was still there, still softly whirling, like the ghost of a white kitten chasing the ghost of a white tail, and making as it did so the faintest of whispers. It was all right! If only he could remain firm, everything was going to be all right.

"Oh, about anything, about nothing—*you* know the way you do!"

"You mean—daydreaming?"

"Oh, no—thinking!"

"But thinking about *what*?"

"Anything."

He laughed a third time—but this time, happening to glance upward toward his mother's face, he was appalled at the effect his laughter seemed to have upon her. Her mouth had opened in an expression of horror. . . . This was too bad! Unfortunate! He had known it would cause pain, of course—but he hadn't expected it to be quite so bad as this. Perhaps—perhaps if he just gave them a tiny gleaming hint——?

"About the snow," he said.

"What on earth?" This was his father's voice. The brown slippers came a step nearer on the hearth-rug.

"But my dear, what do you mean?" This was his mother's voice. The doctor merely stared.

"Just *snow*, that's all. I like to think about it."

"Tell us about it, my boy."

"But that's all it is. There's nothing to tell. *You* know what snow is?"

This he said almost angrily, for he felt that they were trying to corner him. He turned sideways so as no longer to face the doctor, and the better to see the inch of blackness between the window-sill and the lowered curtain—the cold inch of beckoning and delicious night. At once he felt better, more assured.

"Mother—can I go to bed, now, please? I've got a headache."

"But I thought you said——"

"It's just come. It's all these questions—! Can I, mother?"

"You can go as soon as the doctor has finished."

"Don't you think this thing ought to be gone into thoroughly, and *now?*" This was Father's voice. The brown slippers again came a step nearer, the voice was the well-known "punishment" voice, resonant and cruel.

"Oh, what's the use, Norman——"

Quite suddenly, everyone was silent. And without precisely facing them, nevertheless he was aware that all three of them were watching him with an extraordinary intensity—staring hard at him—as if he had done something monstrous, or was himself some kind of monster. He could hear the soft irregular flutter of the flames; the cluck-click-cluck-click of the clock; far and faint, two sudden spurts of laughter from the kitchen, as quickly cut off as begun; a murmur of water in the pipes; and then, the silence seemed to deepen, to spread out, to become world-long and world-wide, to become timeless and shapeless, and to center inevitably and rightly, with a slow and sleepy but enormous concentration of all power, on the beginning of a new sound. What this new sound was going to be, he knew perfectly well. It might begin with a hiss, but it would end with a roar—there was no time to lose—he must escape. It mustn't happen here——

Without another word, he turned and ran up the stairs.

## I V

Not a moment too soon. The darkness was coming in long white waves. A prolonged sibilance filled the night—a great seamless seethe of wild influence went abruptly across it—a cold low humming shook the windows. He shut the door and flung off his clothes in the dark. The bare black door was like a little raft tossed in waves of snow, almost overwhelmed, washed under whitely, up again, smothered in curled billows of feather. The snow was laughing; it spoke from all sides at once; it pressed closer to him as he ran and jumped exulting into his bed.

"Listen to us!" it said. "Listen! We have come to tell you the story we told you about. You remember? Lie down. Shut your eyes, now—you will no longer see much—in this white darkness who could see, or want to see? We will take the place of everything. . . . Listen——"

A beautiful varying dance of snow began at the front of the room, came forward and then retreated, flattened out toward the floor, then rose fountain-like to the ceiling, swayed, recruited itself from a new stream of flakes which poured laughing in through the humming window, advanced again, lifted long white arms. It said peace, it said remoteness, it said cold—it said—

But then a gash of horrible light fell brutally across the room from the opening door—the snow drew back hissing—something alien had come into the room—something hostile. This thing rushed at him, clutched at him, shook him—and he was not merely horrified, he was filled with such a loathing as he had never known. What was this? this cruel disturbance? this act of anger and hate? It was as if he had to reach up a hand toward another world for any understanding of it—an effort of which he was only barely capable. But of that other world he still remembered just enough to know the exorcising words. They tore themselves from his other life suddenly—

"Mother! Mother! Go away! I hate you!"

And with that effort, everything was solved, everything became all right: the seamless hiss advanced once more, the long white wavering lines rose and fell like enormous whispering sea-waves, the whisper becoming louder, the laughter more numerous.

"Listen!" it said. "We'll tell you the last, the most beautiful and secret story—shut your eyes—it is a very small story—a story that gets smaller and smaller—it comes inward instead of opening like a flower—it is a flower becoming a seed—a little cold seed—do you hear? we are leaning closer to you——"

The hiss was now becoming a roar—the whole world was a vast moving screen of snow—but even now it said peace, it said remoteness, it said cold, it said sleep.

1934

# DOROTHY ALLISON

*b. 1949*

Dorothy Allison was born in Greenville, South Carolina to a fifteen-year-old single mother. The first member of her family to graduate from high school, she earned a National Merit Scholarship to Florida Presbyterian (now Eckerd) College. In college Allison became acquainted with the early feminist movement, which she says changed her life. Her semi-autobiographical writing reflects her staunch feminism and addresses topics such as abuse, poverty, and lesbianism. Before becoming known for her fiction, Allison was an award-winning editor for early feminist and lesbian and gay magazines, including *Quest, Conditions,* and *Outlook.* During this time she held a number of jobs—as a waitress, nanny, and substitute teacher, among others—and received an M.A. in Anthropology from The New School in New York City. Allison's first publication was a collection of poems, *The Women Who Hate Me* (1983). Five years later, she published a collection of short fiction, *Trash* (1988), which won her two Lambda Literary Awards and the American Library Association Prize for Lesbian and Gay Writing. *Trash* was reissued in 2002 with a new story, "Compassion," which was selected for *The Best American Short Stories* and *The Best New Stories from the South.* Her 1992 bestselling novel, *Bastard Out of Carolina,* was a finalist for the National Book Award. Since then, Allison has published a book of essays, *Skin: Talking About Sex, Class & Literature* (1992); the memoir *Two or Three Things I Know for Sure* (1995), a *New York Times* Notable Book; and a second novel, *Cavedweller* (1998), another national bestseller.

## Jason Who Will Be Famous

Jason is going to be famous, and the best part is that he knows he will be good at it.

He has this real clear picture of himself, of him being interviewed—not of the place or even when it happens, but of the event itself. What he sees is him and the interviewer, a recording so clear and close up, he can see the reflections sparking off his own pupils. It's hi-def or Blu-ray or something past all that, a rendering that catches the way the soft hairs just forward of his earlobe lift and shine in the light reflecting off his pale cheeks. All he has to do is close his eyes and it begins to play, crisp and crackling with energy as the microphone bumps hollowly against the button on his open collar.

"A lot of it, I can't tell you," he says, and the interviewer nods.

Jason is sitting leaning forward. His features gleam in the bright light, his expression is carefully composed, focused on the interviewer. Jason nods his head and his hair swings down over his forehead. One auburn strand just brushes across the edges of his eyebrows. The interviewer is so close their elbows are almost touching. He is an older man with gray in his hair and an expression of watchful readiness—a man Jason has seen do this kind of thing on the news before, someone to be trusted, someone serious.

That is the word. Serious. The word echoes along Jason's nervous system. He is being taken seriously. Every time he imagines it again, the thought makes him take a deep breath. A little heat flares in his neck as the camera follows his eyes. He looks away from the interviewer, and his face goes still. He looks back and his eyes go dark and sad.

"I'm sorry to have to ask you about something so painful," the interviewer says to him.

"It's all right," Jason says. "I understand." He keeps his expression a mirror of the other man's, careful and composed. He can do this. Piece of cake.

Behind the cameraman, there are other people waiting to speak to Jason, others are standing close by to hear what he has to say. Everyone has questions, questions about what happened, of course, about the kidnapping and all the months in captivity. But they also want to ask him what he thinks about other things, about people, and events. In the interview as Jason sees it, he always has answers—surprising and complicated, wonderful answers.

"That boy is extraordinary," he hears the serious man tell another.

Extraordinary. The heat in his neck moves down into his chest, circles his diaphragm, and filters out to his arms and legs. He hopes it does not show on his face. Better to remain pale and impassive, pretend he does not hear what they say about him. How extraordinary he is, that everyone says so, some kind of genius. He half-smiles and then recomposes his expression. Genius. Jason is not sure what his genius is exactly, but he trusts it. He knows it will be revealed at the right time, in the right circumstances. It is simply that those events have not happened as of yet. But they will.

He opens his eyes. He has stopped at the edge of the road. Dust, white-grey and alkaline, has drifted up from his boots, and he can taste eucalyptus and piney resin. He looks up the road toward the next hill and the curve down into the shade of the redwood stand there. Should have brought a bottle of water, he thinks. Then, extraordinary. How would you know if you were extraordinary? Or a genius? He's pretty good at math, and music—though nothing that special. If he worked more, put more of himself into the work, no telling what he might not do. His dad told him that, once, when he was still living with them. His teachers have said something of the same thing. All of them though, his dad, teachers and his mom, they say it like it's a bad thing—his talents and his waste of them.

"If you worked more. If you worked harder."

They don't understand. No one does.

Jason wipes dust off his mouth and rocks his head from side to side. He knows the problem. It's not that he's lazy or stupid or even scared. No. The problem is that he never has had enough time or focus. There's just always so much that has to be done, and how does anyone do that kind of kung fu stuff anyway? How does anyone become extraordinary? Like Uma Thurman in the Tarantino movie? Years going up and down staircases. It's like that. You do some stupid thing over and over and over, and sometime along in there, you discover you have achieved this enormous talent.

He glares up the road and resumes his pace, boots kicking dust and his hands gripping the straps of his backpack. He could do extraordinary stuff. Given the right circumstances, he has everything in him to do stuff that will startle everyone. It just takes the right circumstances—getting everything out of the way. He nods to himself. He can feel that coming toward him—the opportunity, the time, and the focus.

He has dreamed it so often, he knows it is coming—though he doesn't know all of how it will happen. That too, he sees like a movie, the movie of his life going on all the time. Step in and it is already in motion. Like that. He grins and speeds up slightly. Might be, he will be walking home along the river road from Connie's on a day just like this one. He'll have something in his backpack, after working for Connie all day, doing what he does so well, little baby buds his specialty. Connie always tells him how good he is. He knows exactly how to clip and trim and harvest only what is ready to come away, leave what should be left behind. That shows talent. That shows aptitude. Bonsai killer weed work, he does that all the time. Connie knows she can trust him. Some people she strings along, but him she always pays with a ready smile and a touch along his arm or one quick knuckle push at his hip. Cash or buds, she pays him, and that's all good. Just as it is good no one knows what Jason has in his backpack. No one knows his business.

Still, he knows, the day is coming. Someone is going to snatch him up right off the road or outside the liquor store downtown—some old guy maybe, or even one of them scary old dykes from out the bay side of the Jenner beach. Those bitches are dangerous and he can barely imagine what they would do with a piece of work like him. Everyone knows they all got stuff, guns and money and stuff. Bitches like that stick together. But maybe it will be someone from nowhere nearby, some bunch of crazies with some plan he will never fully understand, that no one will understand.

He nods slowly, his hands gripping the straps tight as he imagines it—the snatch, the basement, the months alone and everything that comes after. He has been seeing it for a long time, the story in his head, the way it will happen. It was a dream the first time, a nightmare, grabby hands and the skin scraped off his knees—a nightmare of sweaty basement walls and dirt in his mouth. But by the third or fourth time he dreamed it, everything receded and it was not so nightmarish. He was fighting back and able to think. Then it was magical how he started thinking about it in the daytime, daydreaming it, planning what he would do, how he would handle things. Then what came after the snatch became more and more important. He had started imagining the person he would be afterward. He didn't think so much about the kidnapping then, or even the kidnappers. It was all about him and the basement and what he did down there, who he would become, who he was meant to become. It was set and in motion. It was coming, Jason was sure of it. Not that he thought he was psychic or anything, it was just that this big thing was coming, so big he could feel it, and he had thought it through and whatever happened, he was going to be ready.

He stumbles and stops. He is almost gasping, smelling the sweat on his neck, the dust on the road, the acrid breeze from the eucalyptus trees past the stand of old-growth stunted apple trees around the curve. He leans forward, stretching his back, and straightens to watch a turkey buzzard circling the hill to his left. No hurry. It is only half a mile to his mom's place, two twists in the road and an uphill grade. Jason shakes his head. He knows this road in its whole length, two and a half miles and every decrepit house along the way, every crumbling garage and leaning fence. Of course, everyone here also knows him, which is sometimes more than he can stand. But somewhere someone who does not know him is coming along, and they will change everything. He nods and resumes a steady pace. Everything will be made over—and he will never know when or why. It will be a mystery.

He thinks of the basement room, that dim space with the windows boarded over. Nothing much will be down there, but he won't need much. He would love a piano, of course, but a guitar is more the kind of thing you might find in a basement. Nothing fancy. Some dented old acoustic. Jason thinks about it, the throwaway object he will use. God knows what he will have to do to tune the thing. Not likely to be any help in the junk people keep in basements. But there will be paper or notebooks. The notebooks will have pages marked up, of course, but he can work around that, use the backs of pages or something. It is what he creates in the silence that will need to be written down, the songs or poems. Lyrics. He will write it all down—easy to imagine that—him singing to himself in the quiet. The pencil marks along the pages. Of course his music notation sucks. He's never been too good at that. He sighs and stops again.

Maybe there will be a recorder—some old thing probably. A little old tape recorder, not a good digital. But hey it will get the job done. He smiles and hears above him the turkey buzzard's awkward call. Ugly sound from an ugly bird. He watches a big white pickup truck drive slowly up and past him. Big metal locks clamp down on the storage bin at the front of the truck bed.

Connie's boyfriend, Grange, told Jason you could bust most of those locks with the right chisel and mallet. "It's all in the angle. Got to hit it right."

Jason has a chisel in his backpack but no mallet. He licks his lips and resumes his slow hike between the ditch and the road. You got to have the right stuff to get anything done. Unless you are lucky or have an edge.

Famous is the way to go, he thinks. You get stuff once you are famous.

Jason wipes sweat off his neck as he walks and imagines it again—the reporter, the camera, the intensity of the lights, the intensity of his genius. It will take time, but he will figure it out. Maybe it won't be music. Maybe it will be words. He's damn good with words, not like those assholes at school who talk all the time. He knows the value of words, keeps them in his head, not always spilling them out like they mean nothing. He doesn't have to tell what he knows. He just knows—lyrics and poetry and all that stuff. Good poetry, he tells himself. Not that crap they want him to read in school. Kind of stuff makes your neck go stiff, that kind of poetry, that's what he likes. He looks at the dust on his hand, sweat-darkened and spotted with little grey-green bits. Little nubbins of weeds and grass flung up with the dust as the trucks pass. He'll get on the computer tonight, look up all the words for grey-green. Emerald, olive-drab, unripe fruit, something or the other. Nothing too hard about getting the words right.

Jason wipes his hands on his jeans, enjoying the feel of the fabric under his palms. Truth is more important than how you tell it, he thinks. And he knows stuff, lots of stuff, secrets and stuff. He has stories.

Maybe that will be it, the stories he tells himself to pass the time. Movie scripts, plays, dialogues between characters that come and go when he is all gaunt and feverish. In the basement, they won't feed him much, so he will get all dramatic skinny and probably have lots of fever dreams. He'll write them down, everything. His hands will cramp and he'll go on writing, get up and pace back and forth and write some more. Pages on pages will pile up. He'll bathe his face in cool water and walk some more. He'll drink so much water his skin will clear up. His mom is always telling him that if he washed his face more, drank more water and yeah, and ate more vegetables, his skin would do that right away. Maybe she has a point. Maybe in the basement that's all they will give him. Vegetables and water—lots of water, 'cause you know they ain't gonna waste no greasy expensive stuff on no captive. No Coke, no potato chips, no Kentucky Fried Chicken.

Pure water and rivers of words. Jason grins and lengthens his stride. Maybe after a while he won't care what he eats, or he will learn to make an apple taste like a pie. That would be the kind of thing might happen. He could learn to eat imaginary meals and taste every bite—donuts and hot barbecue wings—and stay all skinny and pure. That would be something. He could teach people how to do that afterwards maybe. Some day he might run an ashram like the one his mama used to talk about.

The turkey buzzard swoops low and arcs downhill toward the river. Jason stops to watch its flight. A moment in time and the bird disappears. Things can change that fast. Anything could happen and you can't predict what might come along. But what he knows is that there won't be any distractions down in the basement, anything to get in the way. Cold walls and dim light and maybe just a shower. Might be it will only run cold water, but he can handle that. What he hates is tub baths, sitting in dirty water. No way there is not gonna be a shower in the basement, or, all right, maybe only a hose and a drain in the floor. But he knows he will bathe himself a lot 'cause what else will there be to do? 'Cept write what he knows and use the weights set. He laughs out loud. Maybe there won't be no weights, though every shed or garage he knows has some stacked in some corner or the other. If there's nothing like that in his basement, still there will be stuff, something he can use.

He grabs his backpack straps again and begins the uphill grade. His steps slow and he focuses on the notion of making do, figuring out what he will use. Stuff like old cans of paint or bundles of rebar or bricks left lying around. He'll Tarantino it all, laying on the concrete floor and pushing up and down over and over till his arms get all muscled, and his legs too. He'll push off against the wall or doorjamb or something. He's gonna be bored out of his mind. He'll get desperate. He'll be working out, running in place and lifting heavy things—whatever he finds. Yeah, he'll get pretty well muscled. He grins. That is how it will be. He's going to come out just amazing.

Jason looks up the road, quarter of a mile to his mom's turnoff. He's right at the spot where the old firebreak cuts uphill, right up to his dad's place. He can almost see around the redwoods along the hill up to the house. He won't be like his dad, he thinks, he won't waste his chances. He'll grab what comes and run with it. When he comes out of that basement, he'll be slick. That is what it is all gonna be. Slick and sure, and he will know how to manage it, not wind up house-sitting for some crappy old guy wants you to carry stuff and keep an eye on the dogs.

Fuck it. Jason says it out loud. "Fuck it!" He's gonna come out of that basement Brad-Pitt handsome and ready for anything. He'll be ready, all soulful and quirky like that guy from the White Stripes, only he won't take himself too seriously. Everyone else will do that for him. He'll know how to behave.

Jason laughs out loud again. "Yeah," he says. Yeah.

Serious. Yes. That's the word. He is going to be seriously famous.

That's when his mom will realize how shitty she has treated him. Then his dad will hear about it, for sure—and maybe let him come back up to the house and hang out. Of course that creep that owns the property will be around too, but Jason knows it won't be scary like last time. He'll have all those muscles, and he will have gotten past being scared of small shit like grabby old guys and dads that don't give a shit.

It will be different. It will all be different. His mom and his dad will work it all out. His dad will be his manager, his mom will take over the press stuff. You got to have someone handle that stuff, and if the creepy guy comes round to stake some kind of claim, it won't be no big deal. Everyone will know how to handle him—what to believe and what to laugh at. He can almost hear his dad talking loud in his growly hoarse voice. He can hear him finally saying what he wanted him to say before.

"Jason didn't take nothing off you, old man. Look at him. What would he need off you?"

Yeah.

But maybe he will let the old guy hang around. Jason thinks about it, looking uphill and remembering. He gnaws at the nail on his left little finger.

Maybe not.

Why would he want that old bastard around?

He thinks about his dad, what he looks like now, all puffy and grey around the eyes with his hair so thin on top. His dad had this belly on him that he tries to hide under loose shirts, and he's always worried about money and stuff. That kind of old is embarrassing. After the basement though, his dad will be all different. He'll be old, but not so gross. He'll be more like Clint Eastwood old, craggy and wise. That's the notion, and his dad will have figured stuff out all that time worrying about Jason. Things will be different once he sees his son clear. Maybe he'll even own the property by then. The old guy can't live forever. Maybe he'll just give his dad the top of the hill as a kind of death tip. Might be it will turn out like that guy in Forestville a few years back, that black guy who got the thirty acres in the will of the man he worked for all that time.

That could happen. And then if his dad needs someone to help him with things, Jason will be there. That bad leg will hurt his dad a lot by then, even though he will try not to show it. Jason could do stuff—carry things for him and give him a hand. Maybe that is how they work it out—all the anger and guilt and shame and resentment. He can see that too, hear how it will go, them finally talking.

"You had no business running off like that, leaving Mom and me, I was just a little kid."

"You don't know how it was, how desperate I had gotten. I couldn't take care of you the way I wanted to, and you know your mom. She was always telling me I was lazy and the world wasn't gonna wait for me to get myself together."

That was just the kind of thing his mom said all the time. Jason nods. His mom can be a real pain in the ass. He sees himself looking at his dad and trying to imagine how he had felt when he had left. Maybe his dad had left in order to get himself together, to try and make something of himself so he could come back and take good care of them. After all that time cold and miserable and hungry in the basement, he will be able to feel stuff differently. Even standing in the dust of the road he can imagine his dad looking at him with an open face. Maybe they could talk finally, and it would shift all the anger around.

Maybe his dad will get to the point where he can look at him and see Jason clearly, see how he became so strong in that basement. Maybe he will finally see himself in his son. Of course, like everyone, his dad will know the story, how the kidnappers beat him, and starved him, and how Jason endured everything and stood up to them. It will make stuff in his dad shift around. He will get all wet-eyed and ashamed of himself. Jason can see that—the moment between them as real as the interviewer and the cameras, the moment burning him right through to his backbone. He almost sobs out loud, but then stops himself. His eyes are closed. The wind is picking up the way it always does as the afternoon settles toward evening. There is a birdcall somewhere up in the trees, but Jason is inside seeing into what is coming, what has to come.

They will touch each other like men do. Men. Yeah. Maybe his dad will embrace him, say his name. Jason can see that. It is as clear as anything. That is how it is in stories, how it is in his head, how it could be.

Jason sways a little there by the side of the road in the sun's heat. His ears are ringing with electric cricket sounds, the buzzard's cries, and the movement of the wind. Still, he hears a vehicle coming and the sound of its tires on the gritty tarmac. Rock and redwood debris grinding into dust and crackling as the wheels turn into the bend. Jason can see that, the wheels revolving and grinding forward. He imagines the kidnapper's truck, white and thick like one of those big Dodge Fat Boys, but one with a camper on the back—just the thing for snatching a guy off the road. Slowly Jason lets his face relax into a lazy smile. He doesn't look back. He keeps his eyes forward. His mom is always telling him to stop living in a dream, to be in the real world. But this is the real world, the road and the truck and everything that is coming toward him.

Anything can happen any time.

Everything can change, and it is going to, any time now.

Any time.

Any time.

Now.

2009

# SHERWOOD ANDERSON
## *1876–1941*

Anderson was born in Camden, Ohio, the son of a roving, likable, improvident, and talkative man who often appears under one name or another in Anderson's works. After some intermittent schooling, Anderson enlisted in the army for service in Cuba during the Spanish-American War. A few years later—in the spirit of rebellion against industrial and commercial civilization that was to color his writing thereafter—he "left business for literature," as he later put it, when he walked out of his job as manager of an Ohio paint factory. Going to Chicago, then in the ferment of a literary renaissance, he wrote feverishly and soon began to publish his own poetry and fiction. With the appearance in 1919 of *Winesburg, Ohio,* he became famous. As in the collections that followed, the stories of this book show life and desire frustrated by the provincialism of the Midwest. Characteristic of his work is a tone of melancholy reminiscence in which he projects remembered realities on the screen of a philosophic imagination. His autobiography, *A Story-Teller's Story* (1924), is partly fictional, as most of his fiction is partly autobiographical. His novels include *Windy McPherson's Son* (1916), *Poor White* (1920), *Many Marriages* (1923), and *Dark Laughter* (1925). His later collections of stories are *The Triumph of the Egg* (1921), *Horses and Men* (1923), and *Death in the Woods and Other Stories* (1933).

## I Want to Know Why

We got up at four in the morning, that first day in the East. On the evening before, we had climbed off a freight train at the edge of town and with the true instinct of Kentucky boys had found our way across town and to the race track and the stables at once. Then we knew we were all right. Hanley Turner right away found a nigger we knew. It was Bildad Johnson, who in the winter works at Ed Becker's livery barn in our home town, Beckersville. Bildad is a good cook as almost all our niggers are and of course he, like everyone in our part of Kentucky who is anyone at all, likes the horses. In the spring Bildad begins to scratch around. A nigger from our country can flatter and wheedle anyone into letting him do most anything he wants. Bildad wheedles the stable men and the trainers from the horse farms in our country around Lexington. The trainers come into town in the evening to stand around and talk and maybe get into a poker game. Bildad gets in with them. He is always doing little favors and telling about things to eat, chicken browned in a pan, and how is the best way to cook sweet potatoes and corn bread. It makes your mouth water to hear him.

When the racing season comes on and the horses go to the races and there is all the talk on the streets in the evenings about the new colts, and everyone says when they are going over to Lexington or to the spring meeting at Churchill Downs or to Latonia,[1] and the horsemen that have been down to New Orleans or maybe at the winter meeting at Havana in Cuba[2] come home to spend a week before they start out again, at such a time when everything talked about in Beckersville is just horses and nothing else and the outfits start out and horse racing is in every breath of air you breathe, Bildad shows up with a job as cook for some outfit. Often when I think about it, his always going all season to the races and working in the livery barn in the winter where horses are and where men like to come and talk about horses, I wish I was a nigger. It's a foolish thing to say, but that's the way I am about being around horses, just crazy. I can't help it.

Well, I must tell you about what we did and let you in on what I'm talking about. Four of us boys from Beckersville, all whites and sons of men who live in Beckersville regular, made up our minds we were going to the races, not just to Lexington or Louisville, I don't mean, but to the big eastern track we were always hearing our Beckersville men talk about, to Saratoga.[3] We were all pretty young then. I was just turned fifteen and I was the oldest of the four. It was my scheme. I admit that, and I talked the others into trying it. There was Hanley Turner and Henry Rieback and Tom Tumberton and myself. I had thirty-seven dollars I had earned during the winter working nights and Saturdays in Enoch Myer's grocery. Henry Rieback had eleven dollars and the others, Hanley and Tom, had only a dollar or two each. We fixed it all up and laid low until the Kentucky spring meetings were over and some of our men, the sportiest ones, the ones we envied the most, had cut out. Then we cut out too.

I won't tell you the trouble we had beating our way on freights and all. We went through Cleveland and Buffalo and other cities and saw Niagara Falls. We bought things there, souvenirs and spoons and cards and shells with pictures of the falls on them for our sisters and mothers, but thought we had better not send any of the things home. We didn't want to put the folks on our trail and maybe be nabbed. 被捉住

We got into Saratoga as I said at night and went to the track. Bildad fed us up. He showed us a place to sleep in hay over a shed and promised to keep still. Niggers are all right about things like that. They won't squeal on you. Often a white man you might meet, when you had run away from home like that, might appear to be all right and give you a quarter or a half dollar or something, and then go right and give you away. White men will do that, but not a nigger. You can trust them. They are squarer with kids. I don't know why.

At the Saratoga meeting that year there were a lot of men from home. Dave Williams and Arthur Mulford and Jerry Myers and others. Then there was a lot from Louisville and Lexington Henry Rieback knew but I didn't. They were professional gamblers and Henry Rieback's father is one too. He is what is called a sheet writer and goes away most of the year to tracks. In the winter when he is home in Beckersville he don't stay there much but goes away to cit-

**1.** Racetrack in Covington, Kentucky. *Churchill Downs:* the famous track in Louisville, Kentucky, where the Kentucky Derby is run every year.  **2.** That is, the horse-racing season in Havana.  **3.** Famous resort town and site of a racetrack in upstate New York.

ies and deals faro.[4] He is a nice man and generous, is always sending Henry presents, a bicycle and a gold watch and a boy scout suit of clothes and things like that.

My own father is a lawyer. He's all right, but don't make much money and can't buy me things, and anyway I'm getting so old now I don't expect it. He never said nothing to me against Henry, but Hanley Turner and Tom Tumberton's fathers did. They said to their boys that money so come by is no good and they didn't want their boys brought up to hear gamblers' talk and be thinking about such things and maybe embrace them.

That's all right and I guess the men know what they are talking about, but I don't see what it's got to do with Henry or with horses either. That's what I'm writing this story about. I'm puzzled. I'm getting to be a man and want to think straight and be O.K., and there's something I saw at the race meeting at the eastern track I can't figure out.

I can't help it, I'm crazy about thoroughbred horses, I've always been that way. When I was ten years old and saw I was growing to be big and couldn't be a rider I was so sorry I nearly died. Harry Hellinfinger in Beckersville, whose father is Postmaster, is grown up and too lazy to work, but likes to stand around in the street and get up jokes on boys like sending them to a hardware store for a gimlet to bore square holes and other jokes like that. He played one on me. He told me that if I would eat a half a cigar I would be stunted and not grow any more and maybe could be a rider. I did it. When father wasn't looking I took a cigar out of his pocket and gagged it down some way. It made me awful sick and the doctor had to be sent for, and then it did no good. I kept right on growing. It was a joke. When I told what I had done and why, most fathers would have whipped me, but mine didn't.

Well, I didn't get stunted and didn't die. It serves Harry Hellinfinger right. Then I made up my mind I would like to be a stableboy, but had to give that up too. Mostly niggers do that work and I knew father wouldn't let me go into it. No use to ask him.

If you've never been crazy about thoroughbreds, it's because you've never been around where they are much and don't know any better. They're beautiful. There isn't anything so lovely and clean and full of spunk and honest and everything as some race horses. On the big horse farms that are all around our town Beckersville there are tracks, and the horses run in the early morning. More than a thousand times I've got out of bed before daylight and walked two or three miles to the tracks. Mother wouldn't of let me go, but father always says, "Let him alone." So I got some bread out of the breadbox and some butter and jam, gobbled it and lit out.

At the tracks you sit on the fence with men, whites and niggers, and they chew tobacco and talk, and then the colts are brought out. It's early and the grass is covered with shiny dew and in another field a man is plowing and they are frying things in a shed where the track niggers sleep, and you know how a nigger can giggle and laugh and say things that make you laugh. A white man can't do it and some niggers can't, but a track nigger can every time.

And so the colts are brought out and some are just galloped by stableboys, but almost every morning on a big track owned by a rich man who lives maybe

---

4. A card game, favorite of gamblers. *Sheet writer:* a bookmaker.

in New York, there are always, nearly every morning, a few colts and some of the old race horses and geldings and mares that are cut loose.

It brings a lump up into my throat when a horse runs. I don't mean all horses, but some. I can pick them nearly every time. It's in my blood like in the blood of race track niggers and trainers. Even when they just go slop-jogging along with a little nigger on their backs, I can tell a winner. If my throat hurts and it's hard for me to swallow, that's him. He'll run like Sam Hill[5] when you let him out. If he don't win every time it'll be a wonder and because they've got him in a pocket behind another or he was pulled or got off bad at the post or something. If I wanted to be a gambler like Henry Rieback's father I could get rich. I know I could and Henry says so too. All I would have to do is to wait till that hurt comes when I see a horse and then bet every cent. That's what I would do if I wanted to be a gambler, but I don't.

When you're at the tracks in the morning—not the race tracks but the training tracks around Beckersville—you don't see a horse, the kind I've been talking about, very often, but it's nice anyway. Any thoroughbred, that is sired right and out of a good mare and trained by a man that knows how, can run. If he couldn't, what would he be there for and not pulling a plow?

Well, out of the stables they come and the boys are on their backs and it's lovely to be there. You hunch down on top of the fence and itch inside you. Over in the sheds the niggers giggle and sing. Bacon is being fried and coffee made. Everything smells lovely. Nothing smells better than coffee and manure and horses and niggers and bacon frying and pipes being smoked out of doors on a morning like that. It just gets you, that's what it does.

But about Saratoga. We was there six days and not a soul from home seen us and everything came off just as we wanted it to, fine weather and horses and races and all. We beat our way home and Bildad gave us a basket with fried chicken and bread and other eatables in, and I had eighteen dollars when we got back to Beckersville. Mother jawed and cried, but Pop didn't say much. I told everything we done, except one thing. I did and saw that alone. That's what I'm writing about. It got me upset. I think about it at night. Here it is.

At Saratoga we laid up nights in the hay in the shed Bildad had showed us and ate with the niggers early and at night when the race people had all gone away. The men from home stayed mostly in the grandstand and betting field and didn't come out around the places where the horses are kept except to the paddocks just before a race when the horses are saddled. At Saratoga they don't have paddocks under an open shed as at Lexington and Churchill Downs and other tracks down in our country, but saddle the horses right out in an open place under trees on a lawn as smooth and nice as Banker Bohon's front yard here in Beckersville. It's lovely. The horses are sweaty and nervous and shine and the men come out and smoke cigars and look at them and the trainers are there and the owners, and your heart thumps so you can hardly breathe.

Then the bugle blows for post and the boys that ride come running out with their silk clothes on and you run to get a place by the fence with the niggers. I always am wanting to be a trainer or owner, and at the risk of being seen and caught and sent home I went to the paddocks before every race. The other boys didn't, but I did.

We got to Saratoga on a Friday, and on Wednesday the next week the big Mullford Handicap was to be run. Middlestride was in it and Sunstreak. The weather was fine and the track fast. I couldn't sleep the night before.

What had happened was that both these horses are the kind it makes my throat hurt to see. Middlestride is long and looks awkward and is a gelding. He belongs to Joe Thompson, a little owner from home who only has half a dozen horses. The Mullford Handicap is for a mile and Middlestride can't untrack fast. He goes away slow and is always 'way back at the half, then he begins to run and if the race is a mile and a quarter he'll just eat up everything and get there.

Sunstreak is different. He is a stallion and nervous and belongs on the biggest farm we've got in our country, the Van Riddle place that belongs to Mr. Van Riddle of New York. Sunstreak is like a girl you think about sometimes but never see. He is hard all over and lovely too. When you look at his head you want to kiss him. He is trained by Jerry Tillford who knows me and has been good to me lots of times, lets me walk into a horse's stall to look at him close and other things. There isn't anything as sweet as that horse. He stands at the post quiet and not letting on, but he is just burning up inside. Then when the barrier goes up he is off like his name, Sunstreak. It makes you ache to see him. It hurts you. He just lays down and runs like a bird dog. There can't anything I ever see run like him except Middlestride when he gets untracked and stretches himself.

Gee! I ached to see that race and those two horses run, ached and dreaded it too. I didn't want to see either of our horses beaten. We had never sent a pair like that to the races before. Old men in Beckersville said so and the niggers said so. It was a fact.

Before the race, I went over to the paddocks to see. I looked a last look at Middlestride, who isn't such a much standing in a paddock that way, then I went to see Sunstreak.

It was his day. I knew when I see him. I forgot all about being seen myself and walked right up. All the men from Beckersville were there and no one noticed me except Jerry Tillford. He saw me and something happened. I'll tell you about that.

I was standing looking at that horse and aching. In some way, I can't tell how, I knew just how Sunstreak felt inside. He was quiet and letting the niggers rub his legs and Mr. Van Riddle himself put the saddle on, but he was just a raging torrent inside. He was like the water in the river at Niagara Falls just before it goes plunk down. That horse wasn't thinking about running. He don't have to think about that. He was just thinking about holding himself back till the time for the running came. I knew that. I could just in a way see right inside him. He was going to do some awful running and I knew it. He wasn't bragging or letting on much or prancing or making a fuss, but just waiting. I knew it and Jerry Tillford his trainer knew. I looked up, and then that man and I looked into each other's eyes. Something happened to me. I guess I loved the man as much as I did the horse because he knew what I knew. Seemed to me there wasn't anything in the world but that man and the horse and me. I cried and Jerry Tillford had a shine in his eyes. Then I came away to the fence to wait for the race. The horse was better than me, more steadier and, now I know, better than Jerry. He was the quietest and he had to do the running.

Sunstreak ran first of course and he busted the world's record for a mile. I've seen that if I never see anything more. Everything came out just as I expected. Middlestride got left at the post and was 'way back and closed up to be second, just as I knew he would. He'll get a world's record too some day. They can't skin the Beckersville country on horses.

I watched the race calm because I knew what would happen. I was sure. Hanley Turner and Henry Rieback and Tom Tumberton were all more excited than me.

A funny thing that happened to me. I was thinking about Jerry Tillford the trainer and how happy he was all through the race. I liked him that afternoon even more than I ever liked my own father. I almost forgot the horses thinking that way about him. It was because of what I had seen in his eyes as he stood in the paddocks beside Sunstreak before the race started. I knew he had been watching and working with Sunstreak since the horse was a baby colt, had taught him to run and be patient and when to let himself out and not to quit, never. I knew that for him it was like a mother seeing her child do something brave or wonderful. It was the first time I ever felt for a man like that.

After the race that night I cut out from Tom and Hanley and Henry. I wanted to be by myself and I wanted to be near Jerry Tillford if I could work it. Here is what happened.

The track in Saratoga is near the edge of town. It is all polished up and trees around, the evergreen kind, and grass and everything painted and nice. If you go past the track you get to a hard road made of asphalt for automobiles, and if you go along this for a few miles there is a road turns off to a little rummy-looking farmhouse set in a yard.

That night after the race I went along that road because I had seen Jerry and some other men go that way in an automobile. I didn't expect to find them. I walked for a ways and then sat down by a fence to think. It was the direction they went in. I wanted to be as near Jerry as I could. I felt close to him. Pretty soon I went up the side road—I don't know why—and came to the rummy farmhouse. I was just lonesome to see Jerry, like wanting to see your father at night when you are a young kid. Just then an automobile came along and turned in. Jerry was in it and Henry Rieback's father, and Arthur Bedford from home, and Dave Williams and two other men I didn't know. They got out of the car and went into the house, all but Henry Rieback's father who quarreled with them and said he wouldn't go. It was only about nine o'clock, but they were all drunk and the rummy-looking farmhouse was a place for bad women to stay in. That's what it was. I crept up along a fence and looked through a window and saw.

It's what give me the fantods.[6] I can't make it out. The women in the house were all ugly mean-looking women, not nice to look at or be near. They were homely too, except one who was tall and looked a little like the gelding Middlestride, but not clean like him, but with a hard ugly mouth. She had red hair. I saw everything plain. I got up by an old rosebush by an open window and looked. The women had on loose dresses and sat around in chairs. The men came in and some sat on the women's laps. The place smelled rotten and there was rotten talk, the kind a kid hears around a livery stable in a town like Beck-

---

6. Slang for being very shaken and upset.

ersville in the winter but don't ever expect to hear talked when there are women around. It was rotten. A nigger wouldn't go into such a place.

I looked at Jerry Tillford. I've told you how I had been feeling about him on account of his knowing what was going on inside of Sunstreak in the minute before he went to the post for the race in which he made a world's record.

Jerry bragged in that bad woman house as I knew Sunstreak wouldn't never have bragged. He said that he made that horse, that it was him that won the race and made the record. He lied and bragged like a fool. I never heard such silly talk.

And then, what do you suppose he did! He looked at the woman in there, the one that was lean and hard-mouthed and looked a little like the gelding Middlestride but not clean like him, and his eyes began to shine just as they did when he looked at me and at Sunstreak in the paddocks at the track in the afternoon. I stood there by the window—gee!—but I wished I hadn't gone away from the tracks, but had stayed with the boys and the niggers and the horses. The tall rotten-looking woman was between us just as Sunstreak was in the paddocks in the afternoon.

Then, all of a sudden, I began to hate that man. I wanted to scream and rush in the room and kill him. I never had such a feeling before. I was so mad clean through that I cried and my fists were doubled up so my fingernails cut my hands.

And Jerry's eyes kept shining and he waved back and forth, and then he went and kissed that woman and I crept away and went back to the tracks and to bed and didn't sleep hardly any, and then next day I got the other kids to start home with me and never told them anything I seen.

I been thinking about it ever since. I can't make it out. Spring has come again and I'm nearly sixteen and go to the tracks mornings same as always, and I see Sunstreak and Middlestride and a new colt named Strident I'll bet will lay them all out, but no one thinks so but me and two or three niggers.

But things are different. At the tracks the air don't taste as good or smell as good. It's because a man like Jerry Tillford, who knows what he does, could see a horse like Sunstreak run, and kiss a woman like that the same day. I can't make it out. Darn him, what did he want to do like that for? I kept thinking about it and it spoils looking at horses and smelling things and hearing niggers laugh and everything. Sometimes I'm so mad about it I want to fight someone. It gives me the fantods. What did he do it for? I want to know why.

1921

# MARGARET ATWOOD
## *b. 1939*

Atwood was born in Ottawa, Ontario, the daughter of an entomologist. Much of her childhood was spent in isolated wilderness areas of northern Ontario and Quebec, where she grew to love nature and the companionship of books. After her education at the University of Toronto, Radcliffe, and Harvard, she held various jobs as cashier, waitress, market-research writer, and writer of screenplays. Atwood's poetry and fiction have garnered many awards, including—twice—Canada's highest literary honor, the Governor General's Award. Her novels include *The Edible Woman* (1969), *Surfacing* (1972), *Lady Oracle* (1976), *Life before Man* (1979), *The Handmaid's Tale* (1985), *Cat's Eye* (1988), *The Robber Bride* (1993), *The Blind Assassin* (winner of Britain's prestigious Booker Prize, 2000), *Oryx and Crake* (2003), *The Penelopiad* (2005), *The Year of the Flood* (2009), and *MaddAddam* (2013). Many of her stories have been collected in *Dancing Girls and Other Stories* (1978), *Murder in the Dark* (1983), *Bluebeard's Egg* (1983), *Wilderness Tips* (1991), *Good Bones* (1992), *Curious Pursuits* (2005), *The Tent* (2006), *Moral Disorder* (2006), and *Stone Mattress* (2014).

## Death by Landscape

Now that the boys are grown up and Rob is dead, Lois has moved to a condominium apartment in one of the new waterfront developments. She is relieved not to have to worry about the lawn, or about the ivy pushing its muscular little suckers into the brickwork, or the squirrels gnawing their way into the attic and eating the insulation off the wiring, or about strange noises. This building has a security system, and the only plant life is in pots in the solarium.

Lois is glad she's been able to find an apartment big enough for her pictures. They are more crowded together than they were in the house, but this arrangement gives the walls a European look: blocks of pictures, above and beside one another, rather than one over the chesterfield, one over the fireplace, one in the front hall, in the old acceptable manner of sprinkling art around so it does not get too intrusive. This way has more of an impact. You know it's not supposed to be furniture.

None of the pictures is very large, which doesn't mean they aren't valuable. They are paintings, or sketches and drawings, by artists who were not nearly as well known when Lois began to buy them as they are now. Their work later turned up on stamps, or as silk-screen reproductions hung in the principals' offices of high schools, or as jigsaw puzzles, or on beautifully printed calendars sent out by corporations as Christmas gifts, to their less important clients. These artists painted mostly in the twenties and thirties and forties; they painted landscapes. Lois has two Tom Thomsons, three A. Y. Jacksons, a Lawren Harris. She has an Arthur Lismer, she has a J. E. H. MacDonald. She has a David Milne. They are pictures of convoluted tree trunks on an island of pink wave-smoothed stone, with more islands behind; of a lake with rough, bright, sparsely wooded cliffs; of a vivid river shore with a tangle of bush and two beached canoes, one red, one gray; of a yellow autumn woods with the ice-blue gleam of a pond half-seen through the interlaced branches.

It was Lois who'd chosen them. Rob had no interest in art, although he could see the necessity of having something on the walls. He left all the decorating decisions to her, while providing the money, of course. Because of this collection of hers, Lois's friends—especially the men—have given her the reputation of having a good nose for art investments.

But this is not why she bought the pictures, way back then. She bought them because she wanted them. She wanted something that was in them, although she could not have said at the time what it was. It was not peace: she does not find them peaceful in the least. Looking at them fills her with a wordless unease. Despite the fact that there are no people in them or even animals, it's as if there is something, or someone, looking back out.

When she was thirteen, Lois went on a canoe trip. She'd only been on overnights before. This was to be a long one, into the trackless wilderness, as Cappie put it. It was Lois's first canoe trip, and her last.

Cappie was the head of the summer camp to which Lois had been sent ever since she was nine. Camp Manitou, it was called; it was one of the better ones, for girls, though not the best. Girls of her age whose parents could afford it were routinely packed off to such camps, which bore a generic resemblance to one another. They favored Indian names and had hearty, energetic leaders, who were called Cappie or Skip or Scottie. At these camps you learned to swim well and sail, and paddle a canoe, and perhaps ride a horse or play tennis. When you weren't doing these things you could do Arts and Crafts and turn out dingy, lumpish clay ashtrays for your mother—mothers smoked more, then—or bracelets made of colored braided string.

Cheerfulness was required at all times, even at breakfast. Loud shouting and the banging of spoons on the tables were allowed, and even encouraged, at ritual intervals. Chocolate bars were rationed, to control tooth decay and pimples. At night, after supper, in the dining hall or outside around a mosquito-infested campfire ring for special treats, there were singsongs. Lois can still remember all the words to "My Darling Clementine," and "My Bonnie Lies over the Ocean," with acting-out gestures: a rippling of the hands for "the ocean," two hands together under the cheek for "lies." She will never be able to forget them, which is a sad thought.

Lois thinks she can recognize women who went to these camps, and were good at it. They have a hardness to their handshakes, even now; a way of standing, legs planted firmly and farther apart than usual; a way of sizing you up, to see if you'd be any good in a canoe—the front, not the back. They themselves would be in the back. They would call it the stern.

She knows that such camps still exist, although Camp Manitou does not. They are one of the few things that haven't changed much. They now offer copper enameling, and functionless pieces of stained glass baked in electric ovens, though judging from the productions of her friends' grandchildren the artistic standards have not improved.

To Lois, encountering it in the first year after the war, Camp Manitou seemed ancient. Its log-sided buildings with the white cement in between the half-logs, its flagpole ringed with whitewashed stones, its weathered gray dock jutting out into Lake Prospect, with its woven rope bumpers and its rusty rings for tying up, its prim round flowerbed of petunias near the office door, must surely have been there always. In truth it dated only from the first decade of the century; it had been founded by Cappie's parents, who'd thought of camping as bracing to the character, like cold showers, and had been passed along to her as an inheritance, and an obligation.

Lois realized, later, that it must have been a struggle for Cappie to keep Camp Manitou going, during the Depression and then the war, when money did not flow freely. If it had been a camp for the very rich, instead of the merely well off, there would have been fewer problems. But there must have been enough Old Girls, ones with daughters, to keep the thing in operation, though not entirely shipshape: furniture was battered, painted trim was peeling, roofs leaked. There were dim photographs of these Old Girls dotted around the dining hall, wearing ample woolen bathing suits and showing their fat, dimpled legs, or standing, arms twined, in odd tennis outfits with baggy skirts.

In the dining hall, over the stone fireplace that was never used, there was a huge molting stuffed moosehead, which looked somehow carnivorous. It was a sort of mascot; its name was Monty Manitou. The older campers spread the story that it was haunted, and came to life in the dark, when the feeble and undependable lights had been turned off or, due to yet another generator failure, had gone out. Lois was afraid of it at first, but not after she got used to it.

Cappie was the same: you had to get used to her. Possibly she was forty, or thirty-five, or fifty. She had fawn-colored hair that looked as if it was cut with a bowl. Her head jutted forward, jigging like a chicken's as she strode around the camp, clutching notebooks and checking things off in them. She was like their minister in church: both of them smiled a lot and were anxious because they wanted things to go well; they both had the same overwashed skins and stringy necks. But all this disappeared when Cappie was leading a singsong, or otherwise leading. Then she was happy, sure of herself, her plain face almost luminous. She wanted to cause joy. At these times she was loved, at others merely trusted.

There were many things Lois didn't like about Camp Manitou, at first. She hated the noisy chaos and spoon-banging of the dining hall, the rowdy singsongs at which you were expected to yell in order to show that you were enjoying yourself. Hers was not a household that encouraged yelling. She hated the necessity of having to write dutiful letters to her parents claiming she was having fun. She could not complain, because camp cost so much money.

She didn't much like having to undress in a roomful of other girls, even in the dim light, although nobody paid any attention, or sleeping in a cabin with seven other girls, some of whom snored because they had adenoids or colds, some of whom had nightmares, or wet their beds and cried about it. Bottom bunks made her feel closed in, and she was afraid of falling out of top ones;

she was afraid of heights. She got homesick, and suspected her parents of having a better time when she wasn't there than when she was, although her mother wrote to her every week saying how much they missed her. All this was when she was nine. By the time she was thirteen she liked it. She was an old hand by then.

Lucy was her best friend at camp. Lois had other friends in winter, when there was school and itchy woolen clothing and darkness in the afternoons, but Lucy was her summer friend.

She turned up the second year, when Lois was ten, and a Bluejay. (Chickadees, Bluejays, Ravens, and Kingfishers—these were the names Camp Manitou assigned to the different age groups, a sort of totemic clan system. In those days, thinks Lois, it was birds for girls, animals for boys: wolves, and so forth. Though some animals and birds were suitable and some were not. Never vultures, for instance; never skunks, or rats.)

Lois helped Lucy to unpack her tin trunk and place the folded clothes on the wooden shelves, and to make up her bed. She put her in the top bunk right above her, where she could keep an eye on her. Already she knew that Lucy was an exception to a good many rules; already she felt proprietorial.

Lucy was from the United States, where the comic books came from, and the movies. She wasn't from New York or Hollywood or Buffalo, the only American cities Lois knew the names of, but from Chicago. Her house was on the lake shore and had gates to it, and grounds. They had a maid, all of the time. Lois's family only had a cleaning lady twice a week.

The only reason Lucy was being sent to *this* camp (she cast a look of minor scorn around the cabin, diminishing it and also offending Lois, while at the same time daunting her) was that her mother had been a camper here. Her mother had been a Canadian once, but had married her father, who had a patch over one eye, like a pirate. She showed Lois the picture of him in her wallet. He got the patch in the war. "Shrapnel," said Lucy. Lois, who was unsure about shrapnel, was so impressed she could only grunt. Her own two-eyed, unwounded father was tame by comparison.

"My father plays golf," she ventured at last.

"*Everyone* plays golf," said Lucy. "My *mother* plays golf."

Lois's mother did not. Lois took Lucy to see the outhouses and the swimming dock and the dining hall with Monty Manitou's baleful head, knowing in advance they would not measure up.

This was a bad beginning; but Lucy was good-natured, and accepted Camp Manitou with the same casual shrug with which she seemed to accept everything. She would make the best of it, without letting Lois forget that this was what she was doing.

However, there were things Lois knew that Lucy did not. Lucy scratched the tops off all her mosquito bites and had to be taken to the infirmary to be daubed with Ozonol. She took her T-shirt off while sailing, and although the counselor spotted her after a while and made her put it back on, she burnt spectacularly, bright red, with the X of her bathing-suit straps standing out in alarming white; she let Lois peel the sheets of whispery-thin burned skin off her shoulders. When they sang "Alouette" around the campfire, she did not know any of the French words. The difference was that Lucy did not care about the things she didn't know, whereas Lois did.

During the next winter, and subsequent winters, Lucy and Lois wrote to each other. They were both only children, at a time when this was thought to be a disadvantage, so in their letters they pretended to be sisters, or even twins. Lois had to strain a little over this, because Lucy was so blond, with translucent skin and large blue eyes like a doll's, and Lois was nothing out of the ordinary—just a tallish, thinnish, brownish person with freckles. They signed their letters LL, with the L's entwined together like the monograms on a towel. (Lois and Lucy, thinks Lois. How our names date us. Lois Lane, Superman's girlfriend, enterprising female reporter; "I Love Lucy." Now we are obsolete, and it's little Jennifers, little Emilys, little Alexandras and Carolines and Tiffanys.)

They were more effusive in their letters than they ever were in person. They bordered their pages with X's and O's, but when they met again in the summers it was always a shock. They had changed so much, or Lucy had. It was like watching someone grow up in jolts. At first it would be hard to think up things to say.

But Lucy always had a surprise or two, or something to show, some marvel to reveal. The first year she had a picture of herself in a tutu, her hair in a ballerina's knot on the top of her head; she pirouetted around the swimming dock, to show Lois how it was done, and almost fell off. The next year she had given that up and was taking horseback riding. (Camp Manitou did not have horses.) The next year her mother and father had been divorced, and she had a new stepfather, one with both eyes, and a new house, although the maid was the same. The next year when they had graduated from Bluejays and entered Ravens, she got her period, right in the first week of camp. The two of them snitched some matches from their counselor, who smoked illegally, and made a small fire out behind the farthest outhouse, at dusk, using their flashlights. They could set all kinds of fires by now; they had learned how in Campcraft. On this fire they burned one of Lucy's used sanitary napkins. Lois is not sure why they did this, or whose idea it was. But she can remember the feeling of deep satisfaction it gave her as the white fluff singed and the blood sizzled, as if some wordless ritual had been fulfilled.

They did not get caught, but then they rarely got caught at any of their camp transgressions. Lucy had such large eyes, and was such an accomplished liar.

This year Lucy is different again: slower, more languorous. She is no longer interested in sneaking around after dark, purloining cigarettes from the counselor, dealing in black-market candy bars. She is pensive, and hard to wake in the mornings. She doesn't like her stepfather, but she doesn't want to live with her real father either, who has a new wife. She thinks her mother may be having a love affair with a doctor; she doesn't know for sure, but she's seen them smooching in his car, out on the driveway, when her stepfather wasn't there. It serves him right. She hates her private school. She has a boyfriend, who is sixteen and works as a gardener's assistant. This is how she met him: in the garden. She describes to Lois what it is like when he kisses her—rubbery at first, but then your knees go limp. She has been forbidden to see him, and threatened with boarding school. She wants to run away from home.

Lois has little to offer in return. Her own life is placid and satisfactory, but there is nothing much that can be said about happiness. "You're so lucky,"

Lucy tells her, a little smugly. She might as well say *boring* because this is how it makes Lois feel.

Lucy is apathetic about the canoe trip, so Lois has to disguise her own excitement. The evening before they are to leave, she slouches into the campfire ring as if coerced, and sits down with a sigh of endurance, just as Lucy does.

Every canoe trip that went out of camp was given a special send-off by Cappie and the section leader and counselors, with the whole section in attendance. Cappie painted three streaks of red across each of her cheeks with a lipstick. They looked like three-fingered claw marks. She put a blue circle on her forehead with fountain-pen ink, and tied a twisted bandanna around her head and stuck a row of frazzle-ended feathers around it, and wrapped herself in a red-and-black Hudson's Bay blanket. The counselors, also in blankets but with only two streaks of red, beat on tom-toms made of round wooden cheese boxes with leather stretched over the top and nailed in place. Cappie was Chief Cappeosota. They all had to say "How!" when she walked into the circle and stood there with one hand raised.

Looking back on this, Lois finds it disquieting. She knows too much about Indians: this is why. She knows, for instance, that they should not even be called Indians, and that they have enough worries without other people taking their names and dressing up as them. It has all been a form of stealing.

But she remembers, too, that she was once ignorant of this. Once she loved the campfire, the flickering of light on the ring of faces, the sound of the fake tom-toms, heavy and fast like a scared heartbeat; she loved Cappie in a red blanket and feathers, solemn, as a chief should be, raising her hand and saying, "Greetings, my Ravens." It was not funny, it was not making fun. She wanted to be an Indian. She wanted to be adventurous and pure, and aboriginal.

"You go on big water," says Cappie. This is her idea—all their ideas—of how Indians talk. "You go where no man has ever trod. You go many moons." This is not true. They are only going for a week, not many moons. The canoe route is clearly marked, they have gone over it on a map, and there are prepared campsites with names which are used year after year. But when Cappie says this—and despite the way Lucy rolls up her eyes—Lois can feel the water stretching out, with the shores twisting away on either side, immense and a little frightening.

"You bring back much wampum," says Cappie. "Do good in war, my braves, and capture many scalps." This is another of her pretenses: that they are boys, and bloodthirsty. But such a game cannot be played by substituting the word "squaw." It would not work at all.

Each of them has to stand up and step forward and have a red line drawn across her cheeks by Cappie. She tells them they must follow the paths of their ancestors (who most certainly, thinks Lois, looking out the window of her apartment and remembering the family stash of daguerreotypes and sepia-colored portraits on her mother's dressing table, the stiff-shirted, black-coated, grim-faced men and the beflounced women with their severe hair and their corseted respectability, would never have considered heading off onto an open lake, in a canoe, just for fun).

At the end of the ceremony they all stood and held hands around the circle, and sang taps. They did not sound very Indian, thinks Lois. It sounded like a bugle call at a military post, in a movie. But Cappie was never one to be much concerned with consistency, or with archeology.

After breakfast the next morning they set out from the main dock, in four canoes, three in each. The lipstick stripes have not come off completely, and still show faintly pink, like healing burns. They wear their white denim sailing hats, because of the sun, and thin-striped T-shirts, and pale baggy shorts with the cuffs rolled up. The middle one kneels, propping her rear end against the rolled sleeping bags. The counselors going with them are Pat and Kip. Kip is no-nonsense; Pat is easier to wheedle, or fool.

There are white puffy clouds and a small breeze. Glints come from the little waves. Lois is in the bow of Kip's canoe. She still can't do a J-stroke very well, and she will have to be in the bow or the middle for the whole trip. Lucy is behind her; her own J-stroke is even worse. She splashes Lois with her paddle, quite a big splash.

"I'll get you back," says Lois.

"There was a stable fly on your shoulder," Lucy says.

Lois turns to look at her, to see if she's grinning. They're in the habit of splashing each other. Back there, the camp has vanished behind the first long point of rock and rough trees. Lois feels as if an invisible rope has broken. They're floating free, on their own, cut loose. Beneath the canoe the lake goes down, deeper and colder than it was a minute before.

"No horsing around in the canoe," says Kip. She's rolled her T-shirt sleeves up to the shoulder; her arms are brown and sinewy, her jaw determined, her stroke perfect. She looks as if she knows exactly what she is doing.

The four canoes keep close together. They sing, raucously and with defiance; they sing "The Quartermaster's Store," and "Clementine," and "Alouette." It is more like bellowing than singing.

After that the wind grows stronger, blowing slantwise against the bows, and they have to put all their energy into shoving themselves through the water.

Was there anything important, anything that would provide some sort of reason or clue to what happened next? Lois can remember everything, every detail; but it does her no good.

They stopped at noon for a swim and lunch, and went on in the afternoon. At last they reached Little Birch, which was the first campsite for overnight. Lois and Lucy made the fire, while the others pitched the heavy canvas tents. The fireplace was already there, flat stones piled into a U. A burned tin can and a beer bottle had been left in it. Their fire went out, and they had to restart it. "Hustle your bustle," said Kip. "We're starving."

The sun went down, and in the pink sunset light they brushed their teeth and spat the toothpaste froth into the lake. Kip and Pat put all the food that wasn't in cans into a packsack and slung it into a tree, in case of bears.

Lois and Lucy weren't sleeping in a tent. They'd begged to be allowed to sleep out; that way they could talk without others hearing. If it rained, they told Kip, they promised not to crawl dripping into the tent over everyone's legs: they would get under the canoes. So they were out on the point.

Lois tried to get comfortable inside her sleeping bag, which smelled of musty storage and of earlier campers, a stale salty sweetness. She curled herself up, with her sweater rolled up under her head for a pillow and her flashlight inside her sleeping bag so it wouldn't roll away. The muscles of her sore arms were making small pings, like rubber bands breaking.

Beside her Lucy was rustling around. Lois could see the glimmering oval of her white face.

"I've got a rock poking into my back," said Lucy.

"So do I," said Lois. "You want to go into the tent?" She herself didn't, but it was right to ask.

"No," said Lucy. She subsided into her sleeping bag. After a moment she said, "It would be nice not to go back."

"To camp?" said Lois.

"To Chicago," said Lucy. "I hate it there."

"What about your boyfriend?" said Lois. Lucy didn't answer. She was either asleep or pretending to be.

There was a moon, and a movement of the trees. In the sky there were stars, layers of stars that went down and down. Kip said that when the stars were bright like that instead of hazy it meant bad weather later on. Out on the lake there were two loons, calling to each other in their insane, mournful voices. At the time it did not sound like grief. It was just background.

The lake in the morning was flat calm. They skimmed along over the glassy surface, leaving V-shaped trails behind them; it felt like flying. As the sun rose higher it got hot, almost too hot. There were stable flies in the canoes, landing on a bare arm or leg for a quick sting. Lois hoped for wind.

They stopped for lunch at the next of the named campsites, Lookout Point. It was called this because, although the site itself was down near the water on a flat shelf of rock, there was a sheer cliff nearby and a trail that led up to the top. The top was the lookout, although what you were supposed to see from there was not clear. Kip said it was just a view.

Lois and Lucy decided to make the climb anyway. They didn't want to hang around waiting for lunch. It wasn't their turn to cook, though they hadn't avoided much by not doing it, because cooking lunch was no big deal, it was just unwrapping the cheese and getting out the bread and peanut butter, but Pat and Kip always had to do their woodsy act and boil up a billy tin for their own tea.

They told Kip where they were going. You had to tell Kip where you were going, even if it was only a little way into the woods to get dry twigs for kindling. You could never go anywhere without a buddy.

"Sure," said Kip, who was crouching over the fire, feeding driftwood into it. "Fifteen minutes to lunch."

"Where are they off to?" said Pat. She was bringing their billy tin of water from the lake.

"Lookout," said Kip.

"Be careful," said Pat. She said it as an afterthought, because it was what she always said.

"They're old hands," Kip said.

Lois looks at her watch: it's ten to twelve. She is the watchminder; Lucy is careless of time. They walk up the path, which is dry earth and rocks, big rounded pinky-gray boulders or split-open ones with jagged edges. Spindly balsam and spruce trees grow to either side, the lake is blue fragments to the left. The sun is right overhead; there are no shadows anywhere. The heat comes up at them as well as down. The forest is dry and crackly.

It isn't far, but it's a steep climb and they're sweating when they reach the top. They wipe their faces with their bare arms, sit gingerly down on a scorching-hot rock, five feet from the edge but too close for Lois. It's a lookout all right, a sheer drop to the lake and a long view over the water, back the way they've come. It's amazing to Lois that they've traveled so far, over all that water, with nothing to propel them but their own arms. It makes her feel strong. There are all kinds of things she is capable of doing.

"It would be quite a dive off here," says Lucy.

"You'd have to be nuts," says Lois.

"Why?" says Lucy. "It's really deep. It goes straight down." She stands up and takes a step nearer the edge. Lois gets a stab in her midriff, the kind she gets when a car goes too fast over a bump. "Don't," she says.

"Don't what?" says Lucy, glancing around at her mischievously. She knows how Lois feels about heights. But she turns back. "I really have to pee," she says.

"You have toilet paper?" says Lois, who is never without it. She digs in her shorts pocket.

"Thanks," says Lucy.

They are both adept at peeing in the woods: doing it fast so the mosquitoes don't get you, the underwear pulled up between the knees, the squat with the feet apart so you don't wet your legs, facing downhill. The exposed feeling of your bum, as if someone is looking at you from behind. The etiquette when you're with someone else is not to look. Lois stands up and starts to walk back down the path, to be out of sight.

"Wait for me?" says Lucy.

Lois climbed down, over and around the boulders, until she could not see Lucy; she waited. She could hear the voices of the others, talking and laughing, down near the shore. One voice was yelling, "Ants! Ants!" Someone must have sat on an ant hill. Off to the side, in the woods, a raven was croaking, a hoarse single note.

She looked at her watch: it was noon. This is when she heard the shout.

She has gone over and over it in her mind since, so many times that the first, real shout has been obliterated, like a footprint trampled by other footprints. But she is sure (she is almost positive, she is nearly certain) that it was not a shout of fear. Not a scream. More like a cry of surprise, cut off too soon. Short, like a dog's bark.

"Lucy?" Lois said. Then she called "Lucy!" By now she was clambering back up, over the stones of the path. Lucy was not up there. Or she was not in sight.

"Stop fooling around," Lois said. "It's lunchtime." But Lucy did not rise from behind a rock or step out, smiling, from behind a tree. The sunlight was all around; the rocks looked white. "This isn't funny!" Lois said, and it wasn't, panic was rising in her, the panic of a small child who does not know where the bigger ones are hidden. She could hear her own heart. She looked quickly around; she lay down on the ground and looked over the edge of the cliff. It made her feel cold. There was nothing.

She went back down the path, stumbling; she was breathing too quickly; she was too frightened to cry. She felt terrible—guilty and dismayed, as if she had done something very bad, by mistake. Something that could never be repaired. "Lucy's gone," she told Kip.

Kip looked up from the fire, annoyed. The water in the billy can was boiling. "What do you mean, gone?" she said. "Where did she go?"

"I don't know," said Lois. "She's just gone."

No one had heard the shout, but then no one had heard Lois calling, either. They had been talking among themselves, by the water.

Kip and Pat went up to the lookout and searched and called, and blew their whistles. Nothing answered.

Then they came back down, and Lois had to tell exactly what had happened. The other girls all sat in a circle and listened to her. Nobody said anything. They all looked frightened, especially Pat and Kip. They were the leaders. You did not just lose a camper like this, for no reason at all.

"Why did you leave her alone?" said Kip.

"I was just down the path," said Lois. "I told you. She had to go to the bathroom." She did not say *pee* in front of people older than herself.

Kip looked disgusted.

"Maybe she just walked off into the woods and got turned around," said one of the girls.

"Maybe she's doing it on purpose," said another.

Nobody believed either of these theories.

They took the canoes and searched around the base of the cliff, and peered down into the water. But there had been no sound of falling rock; there had been no splash. There was no clue, nothing at all. Lucy had simply vanished.

That was the end of the canoe trip. It took them the same two days to go back that it had taken coming in, even though they were short a paddler. They did not sing.

After that, the police went in a motorboat, with dogs; they were the Mounties and the dogs were German shepherds, trained to follow trails in the woods. But it had rained since, and they could find nothing.

Lois is sitting in Cappie's office. Her face is bloated with crying, she's seen that in the mirror. By now she feels numbed; she feels as if she has drowned. She can't stay here. It has been too much of a shock. Tomorrow her parents are coming to take her away. Several of the other girls who were on the canoe trip are also being collected. The others will have to stay, because their parents are in Europe, or cannot be reached.

Cappie is grim. They've tried to hush it up, but of course everyone in camp knows. Soon the papers will know too. You can't keep it quiet, but what can be said? What can be said that makes any sense? "Girl vanishes in broad daylight, without a trace." It can't be believed. Other things, worse things, will be suspected. Negligence, at the very least. But they have always taken such care. Bad luck will gather around Camp Manitou like a fog; parents will avoid it, in favor of other, luckier places. Lois can see Cappie thinking all this, even through her numbness. It's what anyone would think.

Lois sits on the hard wooden chair in Cappie's office, beside the old wooden desk, over which hangs the thumbtacked bulletin board of normal camp routine, and gazes at Cappie through her puffy eyelids. Cappie is now smiling what is supposed to be a reassuring smile. Her manner is too casual: she's after something. Lois has seen this look on Cappie's face when she's been sniffing out contraband chocolate bars, hunting down those rumored to have snuck out of their cabins at night.

"Tell me again," says Cappie, "from the beginning."

Lois has told her story so many times by now, to Pat and Kip, to Cappie, to the police, that she knows it word for word. She knows it, but she no longer believes it. It has become a story. "I told you," she said. "She wanted to go to the bathroom. I gave her my toilet paper. I went down the path, I waited for her. I heard this kind of shout . . ."

"Yes," says Cappie, smiling confidingly, "but before that. What did you say to one another?"

Lois thinks. Nobody has asked her this before. "She said you could dive off there. She said it went straight down."

"And what did you say?"

"I said you'd have to be nuts."

"Were you mad at Lucy?" says Cappie, in an encouraging voice.

"No," says Lois. "Why would I be mad at Lucy? I wasn't ever mad at Lucy." She feels like crying again. The times when she has in fact been mad at Lucy have been erased already. Lucy was always perfect.

"Sometimes we're angry when we don't know we're angry," says Cappie, as if to herself. "Sometimes we get really mad and we don't even know it. Sometimes we might do a thing without meaning to, or without knowing what will happen. We lose our tempers."

Lois is only thirteen, but it doesn't take her long to figure out that Cappie is not including herself in any of this. By *we* she means Lois. She is accusing Lois of pushing Lucy off the cliff. The unfairness of this hits her like a slap. "I didn't!" she says.

"Didn't what?" says Cappie softly. "Didn't what, Lois?"

Lois does the worst thing, she begins to cry. Cappie gives her a look like a pounce. She's got what she wanted.

Later, when she was grown up, Lois was able to understand what this interview had been about. She could see Cappie's desperation, her need for a story, a real story with a reason in it; anything but the senseless vacancy Lucy had left for her to deal with. Cappie wanted Lois to supply the reason, to be the reason. It wasn't even for the newspapers or the parents, because she could never make such an accusation without proof. It was for herself: something to explain the loss of Camp Manitou and of all she had worked for, the years of entertaining spoiled children and buttering up parents and making a fool of herself with feathers stuck in her hair. Camp Manitou was in fact lost. It did not survive.

Lois worked all this out, twenty years later. But it was far too late. It was too late even ten minutes afterwards, when she'd left Cappie's office and was walking slowly back to her cabin to pack. Lucy's clothes were still there, folded on the shelves, as if waiting. She felt the other girls in the cabin watching her with speculation in their eyes. *Could she have done it? She must have done it.* For the rest of her life, she has caught people watching her in this way.

Maybe they weren't thinking this. Maybe they were merely sorry for her. But she felt she had been tried and sentenced, and this is what has stayed with her: the knowledge that she had been singled out, condemned for something that was not her fault.

Lois sits in the living room of her apartment, drinking a cup of tea. Through the knee-to-ceiling window she has a wide view of Lake Ontario, with its skin of wrinkled blue-gray light, and of the willows of Centre Island shaken by a wind, which is silent at this distance, and on this side of the glass. When there isn't too much pollution she can see the far shore, the foreign shore; though today it is obscured.

Possibly she could go out, go downstairs, do some shopping; there isn't much in the refrigerator. The boys say she doesn't get out enough. But she isn't hungry, and moving, stirring from this space, is increasingly an effort.

She can hardly remember, now, having her two boys in the hospital, nursing them as babies; she can hardly remember getting married, or what Rob looked like. Even at the time she never felt she was paying full attention. She was tired a lot, as if she was living not one life but two: her own, and another, shadowy life that hovered around her and would not let itself be realized—the life of what would have happened if Lucy had not stepped sideways, and disappeared from time.

She would never go up north, to Rob's family cottage or to any place with wild lakes and wild trees and the calls of loons. She would never go anywhere near. Still, it was as if she was always listening for another voice, the voice of a person who should have been there but was not. An echo.

While Rob was alive, while the boys were growing up, she could pretend she didn't hear it, this empty space in sound. But now there is nothing much left to distract her.

She turns away from the window and looks at her pictures. There is the pinkish island, in the lake, with the intertwisted trees. It's the same landscape they paddled through, that distant summer. She's seen travelogues of this country, aerial photographs; it looks different from above, bigger, more hopeless: lake after lake, random blue puddles in dark green bush, the trees like bristles.

How could you ever find anything there, once it was lost? Maybe if they cut it all down, drained it all away, they might find Lucy's bones, some time, wherever they are hidden. A few bones, some buttons, the buckle from her shorts.

But a dead person is a body; a body occupies space, it exists somewhere. You can see it; you put it in a box and bury it in the ground, and then it's in a box in the ground. But Lucy is not in a box, or in the ground. Because she is nowhere definite, she could be anywhere.

And these paintings are not landscape paintings. Because there aren't any landscapes up there, not in the old, tidy European sense, with a gentle hill, a curving river, a cottage, a mountain in the background, a golden evening sky. Instead there's a tangle, a receding maze, in which you can become lost almost as soon as you step off the path. There are no backgrounds in any of these paintings, no vistas; only a great deal of foreground that goes back and back, endlessly, involving you in its twists and turns of trees and branch and rock.

No matter how far back in you go, there will be more. And the trees themselves are hardly trees; they are currents of energy, charged with violent color.

Who knows how many trees there were on the cliff just before Lucy disappeared? Who counted? Maybe there was one more, afterwards.

Lois sits in her chair and does not move. Her hand with the cup is raised halfway to her mouth. She hears something, almost hears it: a shout of recognition, or of joy.

She looks at the paintings, she looks into them. Every one of them is a picture of Lucy. You can't see her exactly, but she's there, in behind the pink stone island or the one behind that. In the picture of the cliff she is hidden by the clutch of fallen rocks towards the bottom, in the one of the river shore she is crouching beneath the overturned canoe. In the yellow autumn woods she's behind the tree that cannot be seen because of the other trees, over beside the blue sliver of pond; but if you walked into the picture and found the tree, it would be the wrong one, because the right one would be further on.

Everyone has to be somewhere, and this is where Lucy is. She is in Lois's apartment, in the holes that open inwards on the wall, not like windows but like doors. She is here. She is entirely alive.

1989

---

RELATED:

—Atwood, "Why Do You Write?" p. 872

# JAMES BALDWIN
## 1924–1987

Baldwin was born in New York City. Stepson of a revivalist minister and himself active in the ministry for three years, he drew on and refined the passionate eloquence of religious oratory as one ingredient of his style. He began his literary career while living in Paris, during a time when he had to support himself by a variety of odd jobs to supplement his income from writing. Recognition of his talents as a novelist and short-story writer was paralleled by the attention paid to him as an essayist who confronted the American conscience with his fierce indictment of the racial inequities that blight the country. Much of his work aimed at unraveling the repressive myths of white society and at healing the disastrous estrangement he found in the lives of black people in America. His novels include *Go Tell It on the Mountain* (1953), *Giovanni's Room* (1957), *Another Country* (1962), *Tell Me How Long the Train's Been Gone* (1968), *If Beale Street Could Talk* (1974), and *Just Above My Head* (1979). His books of essays are *Notes of a Native Son* (1955), *Nobody Knows My Name* (1961), *The Fire Next Time* (1963), and *No Name in the Street* (1972). His short stories are collected in *Going to Meet the Man* (1965).

## Sonny's Blues

I read about it in the paper, in the subway, on my way to work. I read it, and I couldn't believe it, and I read it again. Then perhaps I just stared at it, at the newsprint spelling out his name, spelling out the story. I stared at it in the swinging lights of the subway car, and in the faces and bodies of the people, and in my own face, trapped in the darkness which roared outside.

It was not to be believed and I kept telling myself that, as I walked from the subway station to the high school. And at the same time I couldn't doubt it. I was scared, scared for Sonny. He became real to me again. A great block of ice got settled in my belly and kept melting there slowly all day long, while I taught my classes algebra. It was a special kind of ice. It kept melting, sending trickles of ice water all up and down my veins, but it never got less. Sometimes it hardened and seemed to expand until I felt my guts were going to come spilling out or that I was going to choke or scream. This would always be at a moment when I was remembering some specific thing Sonny had once said or done.

When he was about as old as the boys in my classes his face had been bright and open, there was a lot of copper in it; and he'd had wonderfully direct brown eyes, and great gentleness and privacy. I wondered what he looked like now. He had been picked up, the evening before, in a raid on an apartment downtown, for peddling and using heroin.

I couldn't believe it: but what I mean by that is that I couldn't find any room for it anywhere inside me. I had kept it outside me for a long time. I hadn't wanted to know. I had had suspicions, but I didn't name them, I kept putting them away. I told myself that Sonny was wild, but he wasn't crazy. And he'd always been a good boy, he hadn't ever turned hard or evil or disrespectful, the way kids can, so quick, so quick, especially in Harlem. I didn't want to believe that I'd ever see my brother going down, coming to nothing, all that light in his face gone out, in the condition I'd already seen so many others. Yet it had happened and here I was, talking about algebra to a lot of boys who might, every one of them for all I knew, be popping off needles every time they went to the head.[1] Maybe it did more for them than algebra could.

I was sure that the first time Sonny had ever had horse,[2] he couldn't have been much older than these boys were now. These boys, now, were living as we'd been living then, they were growing up with a rush and their heads bumped abruptly against the low ceiling of their actual possibilities. They were filled with rage. All they really knew were two darknesses, the darkness of their lives, which was now closing in on them, and the darkness of the movies, which had blinded them to that other darkness, and in which they now, vindictively, dreamed, at once more together than they were at any other time, and more alone.

When the last bell rang, the last class ended, I let out my breath. It seemed I'd been holding it for all that time. My clothes were wet—I may have looked as though I'd been sitting in a steam bath, all dressed up, all afternoon. I sat alone in the classroom a long time. I listened to the boys outside, downstairs, shouting and cursing and laughing. Their laughter struck me for perhaps the first time. It was not the joyous laughter which—God knows why—one associates with children. It was mocking and insular, its intent was to denigrate. It was disenchanted, and in this, also, lay the authority of their curses. Perhaps I was listening to them because I was thinking about my brother and in them I heard my brother. And myself.

One boy was whistling a tune, at once very complicated and very simple, it seemed to be pouring out of him as though he were a bird, and it sounded very cool and moving through all that harsh, bright air, only just holding its own through all those other sounds.

I stood up and walked over to the window and looked down into the courtyard. It was the beginning of the spring and the sap was rising in the boys. A teacher passed through them every now and again, quickly, as though he or she couldn't wait to get out of that courtyard, to get those boys out of their sight and off their minds. I started collecting my stuff. I thought I'd better get home and talk to Isabel.

The courtyard was almost deserted by the time I got downstairs. I saw this boy standing in the shadow of a doorway, looking just like Sonny. I almost called his name. Then I saw that it wasn't Sonny, but somebody we used to know, a boy from around our block. He'd been Sonny's friend. He'd never been mine, having been too young for me, and, anyway, I'd never liked him. And now, even though he was a grown-up man, he still hung around that block, still

1. Toilet.  2. Heroin.

spent hours on the street corners, was always high and raggy. I used to run into him from time to time and he'd often work around to asking me for a quarter or fifty cents. He always had some real good excuse, too, and I always gave it to him. I don't know why.

But now, abruptly, I hated him. I couldn't stand the way he looked at me, partly like a dog, partly like a cunning child. I wanted to ask him what the hell he was doing in the school courtyard.

He sort of shuffled over to me, and he said, "I see you got the papers. So you already know about it."

"You mean about Sonny? Yes, I already know about it. How come they didn't get you?"

He grinned. It made him repulsive and it also brought to mind what he'd looked like as a kid. "I wasn't there. I stay away from them people."

"Good for you." I offered him a cigarette and I watched him through the smoke. "You come all the way down here just to tell me about Sonny?"

"That's right." He was sort of shaking his head and his eyes looked strange, as though they were about to cross. The bright sun deadened his damp dark brown skin and it made his eyes look yellow and showed up the dirt in his kinked hair. He smelled funky.[3] I moved a little away from him and I said, "Well, thanks. But I already know about it and I got to get home."

"I'll walk you a little ways," he said. We started walking. There were a couple of kids still loitering in the courtyard and one of them said goodnight to me and looked strangely at the boy beside me.

"What're you going to do?" he asked me. "I mean, about Sonny?"

"Look. I haven't seen Sonny for over a year, I'm not sure I'm going to do anything. Anyway, what the hell *can* I do?"

"That's right," he said quickly, "ain't nothing you can do. Can't much help old Sonny no more, I guess."

It was what I was thinking and so it seemed to me he had no right to say it.

"I'm surprised at Sonny, though," he went on—he had a funny way of talking, he looked straight ahead as though he were talking to himself—"I thought Sonny was a smart boy, I thought he was too smart to get hung."

"I guess he thought so too," I said sharply, "and that's how he got hung. And how about you? You're pretty goddamn smart, I bet."

Then he looked directly at me, just for a minute. "I ain't smart," he said. "If I was smart, I'd have reached for a pistol a long time ago."

"Look. Don't tell *me* your sad story, if it was up to me, I'd give you one." Then I felt guilty—guilty, probably, for never having supposed that the poor bastard *had* a story of his own, much less a sad one, and I asked, quickly, "What's going to happen to him now?"

He didn't answer this. He was off by himself some place.

"Funny thing," he said, and from his tone we might have been discussing the quickest way to get to Brooklyn, "when I saw the papers this morning, the first thing I asked myself was if I had anything to do with it. I felt sort of responsible."

I began to listen more carefully. The subway station was on the corner, just before us, and I stopped. He stopped, too. We were in front of a bar and he

**3.** Unwashed.

ducked slightly, peering in, but whoever he was looking for didn't seem to be there. The juke box was blasting away with something black and bouncy and I half watched the barmaid as she danced her way from the juke box to her place behind the bar. And I watched her face as she laughingly responded to something someone said to her, still keeping time to the music. When she smiled one saw the little girl, one sensed the doomed, still-struggling woman beneath the battered face of the semi-whore.

"I never *give* Sonny nothing," the boy said finally, "but a long time ago I come to school high and Sonny asked me how it felt." He paused, I couldn't bear to watch him, I watched the barmaid, and I listened to the music which seemed to be causing the pavement to shake. "I told him it felt great." The music stopped, the barmaid paused and watched the juke box until the music began again. "It did."

All this was carrying me some place I didn't want to go. I certainly didn't want to know how it felt. It filled everything, the people, the houses, the music, the dark, quicksilver barmaid, with menace; and this menace was their reality.

"What's going to happen to him now?" I asked again.

"They'll send him away some place and they'll try to cure him." He shook his head. "Maybe he'll even think he's kicked the habit. Then they'll let him loose"—he gestured, throwing his cigarette into the gutter. "That's all."

"What do you mean, that's *all?*"

But I knew what he meant.

"I *mean*, that's *all*." He turned his head and looked at me, pulling down the corners of his mouth. "Don't you know what I mean?" he asked, softly.

"How the hell *would* I know what you mean?" I almost whispered it, I don't know why.

"That's right," he said to the air, "how would *he* know what I mean?" He turned toward me again, patient and calm, and yet I somehow felt him shaking, shaking as though he were going to fall apart. I felt that ice in my guts again, the dread I'd felt all afternoon; and again I watched the barmaid, moving about the bar, washing glasses, and singing. "Listen. They'll let him out and then it'll just start all over again. That's what I mean."

"You mean—they'll let him out. And then he'll just start working his way back in again. You mean he'll never kick the habit. Is that what you mean?"

"That's right," he said, cheerfully. "*You* see what I mean."

"Tell me," I said at last, "why does he want to die? He must want to die, he's killing himself, why does he want to die?"

He looked at me in surprise. He licked his lips. "He don't want to die. He wants to live. Don't nobody want to die, ever."

Then I wanted to ask him—too many things. He could not have answered, or if he had, I could not have borne the answers. I started walking. "Well, I guess it's none of my business."

"It's going to be rough on old Sonny," he said. We reached the subway station. "This is your station?" he asked. I nodded. I took one step down. "Damn!" he said, suddenly. I looked up at him. He grinned again. "Damn it if I didn't leave all my money home. You ain't got a dollar on you, have you? Just for a couple of days, is all."

All at once something inside gave and threatened to come pouring out of me. I didn't hate him any more. I felt that in another moment I'd start crying like a child.

"Sure," I said. "Don't sweat." I looked in my wallet and didn't have a dollar, I only had a five. "Here," I said. "That hold you?"

He didn't look at it—he didn't want to look at it. A terrible, closed look came over his face, as though he were keeping the number on the bill a secret from him and me. "Thanks," he said, and now he was dying to see me go. "Don't worry about Sonny. Maybe I'll write him or something."

"Sure," I said. "You do that. So long."

"Be seeing you," he said. I went on down the steps.

And I didn't write Sonny or send him anything for a long time. When I finally did, it was just after my little girl died, and he wrote me back a letter which made me feel like a bastard.

Here's what he said:

Dear brother,

You don't know how much I needed to hear from you. I wanted to write you many a time but I dug how much I must have hurt you and so I didn't write. But now I feel like a man who's been trying to climb up out of some deep, real deep and funky hole and just saw the sun up there, outside. I got to get outside.

I can't tell you much about how I got here. I mean I don't know how to tell you. I guess I was afraid of something or I was trying to escape from something and you know I have never been very strong in the head (smile). I'm glad Mama and Daddy are dead and can't see what's happened to their son and I swear if I'd known what I was doing I would never have hurt you so, you and a lot of other fine people who were nice to me and who believed in me.

I don't want you to think it had anything to do with me being a musician. It's more than that. Or maybe less than that. I can't get anything straight in my head down here and I try not to think about what's going to happen to me when I get outside again. Sometime I think I'm going to flip and *never* get outside and sometime I think I'll come straight back. I tell you one thing, though, I'd rather blow my brains out than go through this again. But that's what they all say, so they tell me. If I tell you when I'm coming to New York and if you could meet me, I sure would appreciate it. Give my love to Isabel and the kids and I was sure sorry to hear about little Gracie. I wish I could be like Mama and say the Lord's will be done, but I don't know it seems to me that trouble is the one thing that never does get stopped and I don't know what good it does to blame it on the Lord. But maybe it does some good if you believe it.

Your brother,
Sonny

Then I kept in constant touch with him and I sent him whatever I could and I went to meet him when he came back to New York. When I saw him many things I thought I had forgotten came flooding back to me. This was because I had begun, finally, to wonder about Sonny, about the life that Sonny lived inside. This life, whatever it was, had made him older and thinner and it had deepened the distant stillness in which he had always moved. He looked very unlike my baby brother. Yet, when he smiled, when we shook hands, the baby brother I'd never known looked out from the depths of his private life, like an animal waiting to be coaxed into the light.

"How you been keeping?" he asked me.

"All right. And you?"

"Just fine." He was smiling all over his face. "It's good to see you again."

"It's good to see you."

The seven years' difference in our ages lay between us like a chasm: I wondered if these years would ever operate between us as a bridge. I was remembering, and it made it hard to catch my breath, that I had been there when he was born; and I had heard the first words he had ever spoken. When he started to walk, he walked from our mother straight to me. I caught him just before he fell when he took the first steps he ever took in this world.

"How's Isabel?"

"Just fine. She's dying to see you."

"And the boys?"

"They're fine, too. They're anxious to see their uncle."

"Oh, come on. You know they don't remember me."

"Are you kidding? Of course they remember you."

He grinned again. We got into a taxi. We had a lot to say to each other, far too much to know how to begin.

As the taxi began to move, I asked, "You still want to go to India?"

He laughed. "You still remember that. Hell, no. This place is Indian enough for me."

"It used to belong to them," I said.

And he laughed again. "They damn sure knew what they were doing when they got rid of it."

Years ago, when he was around fourteen, he'd been all hipped on the idea of going to India. He read books about people sitting on rocks, naked, in all kinds of weather, but mostly bad, naturally, and walking barefoot through hot coals and arriving at wisdom. I used to say that it sounded to me as though they were getting away from wisdom as fast as they could. I think he sort of looked down on me for that.

"Do you mind," he asked, "if we have the driver drive alongside the park? On the west side—I haven't seen the city in so long."

"Of course not," I said. I was afraid that I might sound as though I were humoring him, but I hoped he wouldn't take it that way.

So we drove along, between the green of the park and the stony, lifeless elegance of hotels and apartment buildings, toward the vivid, killing streets of our childhood. These streets hadn't changed, though housing projects jutted up out of them now like rocks in the middle of a boiling sea. Most of the houses in which we had grown up had vanished, as had the stores from which we had stolen, the basements in which we had first tried sex, the rooftops from which we had hurled tin cans and bricks. But houses exactly like the houses of our past yet dominated the landscape, boys exactly like the boys we once had been found themselves smothering in these houses, came down into the streets for light and air and found themselves encircled by disaster. Some escaped the trap, most didn't. Those who got out always left something of themselves behind, as some animals amputate a leg and leave it in the trap. It might be said, perhaps, that I had escaped, after all, I was a school teacher; or that Sonny had, he hadn't lived in Harlem for years. Yet, as the cab moved uptown through streets which seemed, with a rush, to darken with dark people, and as I covertly studied Sonny's face, it came to me that what we both were seeking through our separate cab windows was that part of ourselves which had been left behind. It's always at the hour of trouble and confrontation that the missing member aches.

We hit 110th Street and started rolling up Lenox Avenue. And I'd known this avenue all my life, but it seemed to me again, as it had seemed on the day I'd first heard about Sonny's trouble, filled with a hidden menace which was its very breath of life.

"We almost there," said Sonny.

"Almost." We were both too nervous to say anything more.

We live in a housing project. It hasn't been up long. A few days after it was up it seemed uninhabitably new. Now, of course, it's already rundown. It looks like a parody of the good, clean, faceless life—God knows the people who live in it do their best to make it a parody. The beat-looking grass lying around isn't enough to make their lives green, the hedges will never hold out the streets, and they know it. The big windows fool no one, they aren't big enough to make space out of no space. They don't bother with the windows, they watch the TV screen instead. The playground is most popular with the children who don't play at jacks, or skip rope, or roller skate, or swing, and they can be found in it after dark. We moved in partly because it's not too far from where I teach, and partly for the kids; but it's really just like the houses in which Sonny and I grew up. The same things happen, they'll have the same things to remember. The moment Sonny and I started into the house I had the feeling that I was simply bringing him back into the danger he had almost died trying to escape.

Sonny has never been talkative. So I don't know why I was sure he'd be dying to talk to me when supper was over the first night. Everything went fine, the oldest boy remembered him, and the youngest boy liked him, and Sonny had remembered to bring something for each of them; and Isabel, who is really much nicer than I am, more open and giving, had gone to a lot of trouble about dinner and was genuinely glad to see him. And she's always been able to tease Sonny in a way that I haven't. It was nice to see her face so vivid again and to hear her laugh and watch her make Sonny laugh. She wasn't, or, anyway, she didn't seem to be, at all uneasy or embarrassed. She chatted as though there were no subject which had to be avoided and she got Sonny past his first, faint stiffness. And thank God she was there, for I was filled with that icy dread again. Everything I did seemed awkward to me, and everything I said sounded freighted with hidden meaning. I was trying to remember everything I'd heard about dope addiction and I couldn't help watching Sonny for signs. I wasn't doing it out of malice. I was trying to find out something about my brother. I was dying to hear him tell me he was safe.

"Safe!" my father grunted, whenever Mama suggested trying to move to a neighborhood which might be safer for children. "Safe, hell! Ain't no place safe for kids, nor nobody."

He always went on like this, but he wasn't, ever, really as bad as he sounded, not even on weekends, when he got drunk. As a matter of fact, he was always on the lookout for "something a little better," but he died before he found it. He died suddenly, during a drunken weekend in the middle of the war, when Sonny was fifteen. He and Sonny hadn't ever got on too well. And this was partly because Sonny was the apple of his father's eye. It was because he loved

Sonny so much and was frightened for him, that he was always fighting with him. It doesn't do any good to fight with Sonny. Sonny just moves back, inside himself, where he can't be reached. But the principal reason that they never hit it off is that they were so much alike. Daddy was big and rough and loud-talking, just the opposite of Sonny, but they both had—that same privacy.

Mama tried to tell me something about this, just after Daddy died. I was home on leave from the army.

This was the last time I ever saw my mother alive. Just the same, this picture gets all mixed up in my mind with pictures I had of her when she was younger. The way I always see her is the way she used to be on a Sunday afternoon, say, when the old folks were talking after the big Sunday dinner. I always see her wearing pale blue. She'd be sitting on the sofa. And my father would be sitting in the easy chair, not far from her. And the living room would be full of church folks and relatives. There they sit, in chairs all around the living room, and the night is creeping up outside, but nobody knows it yet. You can see the darkness growing against the windowpanes and you hear the street noises every now and again, or maybe the jangling beat of a tambourine from one of the churches close by, but it's real quiet in the room. For a moment nobody's talking, but every face looks darkening, like the sky outside. And my mother rocks a little from the waist, and my father's eyes are closed. Everyone is looking at something a child can't see. For a minute they've forgotten the children. Maybe a kid is lying on the rug, half asleep. Maybe somebody's got a kid in his lap and is absent-mindedly stroking the kid's head. Maybe there's a kid, quiet and big-eyed, curled up in a big chair in the corner. The silence, the darkness coming, and the darkness in the faces frighten the child obscurely. He hopes that the hand which strokes his forehead will never stop—will never die. He hopes that there will never come a time when the old folks won't be sitting around the living room, talking about where they've come from, and what they've seen, and what's happened to them and their kinfolk.

But something deep and watchful in the child knows that this is bound to end, is already ending. In a moment someone will get up and turn on the light. Then the old folks will remember the children and they won't talk any more that day. And when light fills the room, the child is filled with darkness. He knows that every time this happens he's moved just a little closer to that darkness outside. The darkness outside is what the old folks have been talking about. It's what they've come from. It's what they endure. The child knows that they won't talk any more because if he knows too much about what's happened to *them*, he'll know too much too soon, about what's going to happen to *him*.

The last time I talked to my mother, I remember I was restless. I wanted to get out and see Isabel. We weren't married then and we had a lot to straighten out between us.

There Mama sat, in black, by the window. She was humming an old church song, *Lord, you brought me from a long ways off.* Sonny was out somewhere. Mama kept watching the streets.

"I don't know," she said, "if I'll ever see you again, after you go off from here. But I hope you'll remember the things I tried to teach you."

"Don't talk like that," I said, and smiled. "You'll be here a long time yet."

She smiled, too, but she said nothing. She was quiet for a long time. And I said, "Mama, don't you worry about nothing. I'll be writing all the time, and you be getting the checks. . . ."

"I want to talk to you about your brother," she said, suddenly. "If anything happens to me he ain't going to have nobody to look out for him."

"Mama," I said, "ain't nothing going to happen to you *or* Sonny. Sonny's all right. He's a good boy and he's got good sense."

"It ain't a question of his being a good boy," Mama said, "nor of his having good sense. It ain't only the bad ones, nor yet the dumb ones that gets sucked under." She stopped, looking at me. "Your Daddy once had a brother," she said, and she smiled in a way that made me feel she was in pain. "You didn't never know that, did you?"

"No," I said, "I never knew that," and I watched her face.

"Oh, yes," she said, "your Daddy had a brother." She looked out of the window again. "I know you never saw your Daddy cry. But *I* did—many a time, through all these years."

I asked her, "What happened to his brother? How come nobody's ever talked about him?"

This was the first time I ever saw my mother look old.

"His brother got killed," she said, "when he was just a little younger than you are now. I knew him. He was a fine boy. He was maybe a little full of the devil, but he didn't mean nobody no harm."

Then she stopped and the room was silent, exactly as it had sometimes been on those Sunday afternoons. Mama kept looking out into the streets.

"He used to have a job in the mill," she said, "and, like all young folks, he just liked to perform on Saturday nights. Saturday nights, him and your father would drift around to different places, go to dances and things like that, or just sit around with people they knew, and your father's brother would sing, he had a fine voice, and play along with himself on his guitar. Well, this particular Saturday night, him and your father was coming home from some place, and they were both a little drunk and there was a moon that night, it was bright like day. Your father's brother was feeling kind of good, and he was whistling to himself, and he had his guitar slung over his shoulder. They was coming down a hill and beneath them was a road that turned off from the highway. Well, your father's brother, being always kind of frisky, decided to run down this hill, and he did, with that guitar banging and clanging behind him, and he ran across the road, and he was making water behind a tree. And your father was sort of amused at him and he was still coming down the hill, kind of slow. Then he heard a car motor and that same minute his brother stepped from behind the tree, into the road, in the moonlight. And he started to cross the road. And your father started to run down the hill, he says he don't know why. This car was full of white men. They was all drunk, and when they seen your father's brother they let out a great whoop and holler and they aimed the car straight at him. They was having fun, they just wanted to scare him, the way they do sometimes, you know. But they was drunk. And I guess the boy, being drunk, too, and scared, kind of lost his head. By the time he jumped it was too late. Your father says he heard his brother scream when the car rolled over him, and he heard the wood of that guitar when it give, and he heard them strings go flying, and he heard them white men shouting, and the car kept on a-going and it ain't stopped till this day. And, time your father got down the hill, his brother weren't nothing but blood and pulp."

Tears were gleaming on my mother's face. There wasn't anything I could say.

"He never mentioned it," she said, "because I never let him mention it before you children. Your Daddy was like a crazy man that night and for many a night thereafter. He says he never in his life seen anything as dark as that road after the lights of that car had gone away. Weren't nothing, weren't nobody on that road, just your Daddy and his brother and that busted guitar. Oh, yes. Your Daddy never did really get right again. Till the day he died he weren't sure but that every white man he saw was the man that killed his brother."

She stopped and took out her handkerchief and dried her eyes and looked at me.

"I ain't telling you all this," she said, "to make you scared or bitter or to make you hate nobody. I'm telling you this because you got a brother. And the world ain't changed."

I guess I didn't want to believe this. I guess she saw this in my face. She turned away from me, toward the window again, searching those streets.

"But I praise my Redeemer," she said at last, "that He called your Daddy home before me. I ain't saying it to throw no flowers at myself, but, I declare, it keeps me from feeling too cast down to know I helped your father get safely through this world. Your father always acted like he was the roughest, strongest man on earth. And everybody took him to be like that. But if he hadn't had me there—to see his tears!"

She was crying again. Still, I couldn't move. I said, "Lord, Lord, Mama, I didn't know it was like that."

"Oh, honey," she said, "there's a lot that you don't know. But you are going to find out." She stood up from the window and came over to me. "You got to hold on to your brother," she said, "and don't let him fall, no matter what it looks like is happening to him and no matter how evil you gets with him. You going to be evil with him many a time. But don't you forget what I told you, you hear?"

"I won't forget," I said. "Don't you worry, I won't forget. I won't let nothing happen to Sonny."

My mother smiled as though she was amused at something she saw in my face. Then, "You may not be able to stop nothing from happening. But you got to let him know you's *there*."

Two days later I was married, and then I was gone. And I had a lot of things on my mind and I pretty well forgot my promise to Mama until I got shipped home on a special furlough for her funeral.

And, after the funeral, with just Sonny and me alone in the empty kitchen, I tried to find out something about him.

"What do you want to do?" I asked him.

"I'm going to be a musician," he said.

For he had graduated, in the time I had been away, from dancing to the juke box to finding out who was playing what, and what they were doing with it, and he had bought himself a set of drums.

"You mean, you want to be a drummer?" I somehow had the feeling that being a drummer might be all right for other people but not for my brother Sonny.

"I don't think," he said, looking at me very gravely, "that I'll ever be a good drummer. But I think I can play a piano."

I frowned. I'd never played the role of the oldest brother quite so seriously before, had scarcely ever, in fact, *asked* Sonny a damn thing. I sensed myself in the presence of something I didn't really know how to handle, didn't understand. So I made my frown a little deeper as I asked: "What kind of musician do you want to be?"

He grinned. "How many kinds do you think there are?"

"Be *serious*," I said.

He laughed, throwing his head back, and then looked at me. "I *am* serious."

"Well, then, for Christ's sake, stop kidding around and answer a serious question. I mean, do you want to be a concert pianist, you want to play classical music and all that, or—or what?" Long before I finished he was laughing again. "For Christ's *sake*, Sonny!"

He sobered, but with difficulty. "I'm sorry. But you sound so—*scared!*" and he was off again.

"Well, you may think it's funny now, baby, but it's not going to be so funny when you have to make your living at it, let me tell you *that*." I was furious because I knew he was laughing at me and I didn't know why.

"No," he said, very sober now, and afraid, perhaps, that he'd hurt me, "I don't want to be a classical pianist. That isn't what interests me. I mean"—he paused, looking hard at me, as though his eyes would help me to understand, and then gestured helplessly, as though perhaps his hand would help—"I mean, I'll have a lot of studying to do, and I'll have to study *everything*, but, I mean, I want to play *with*—jazz musicians." He stopped. "I want to play jazz," he said.

Well, the word had never before sounded as heavy, as real, as it sounded that afternoon in Sonny's mouth. I just looked at him and I was probably frowning a real frown by this time. I simply couldn't see why on earth he'd want to spend his time hanging around nightclubs, clowning around on bandstands, while people pushed each other around a dance floor. It seemed—beneath him, somehow. I had never thought about it before, had never been forced to, but I suppose I had always put jazz musicians in a class with what Daddy called "good-time people."

"Are you *serious?*"

"Hell, *yes*, I'm serious."

He looked more helpless than ever, and annoyed, and deeply hurt.

I suggested, helpfully: "You mean—like Louis Armstrong?"

His face closed as though I'd struck him. "No. I'm not talking about none of that old-time, down-home crap."

"Well, look, Sonny, I'm sorry, don't get mad. I just don't altogether get it, that's all. Name somebody—you know, a jazz musician you admire."

"Bird."

"Who?"

"Bird! Charlie Parker![4] Don't they teach you nothing in the goddamn army?"

I lit a cigarette. I was surprised and then a little amused to discover that I was trembling. "I've been out of touch," I said. "You'll have to be patient with me. Now. Who's this Parker character?"

---

4. Charlie "Bird" Parker (1920–1955), saxophone player for whom Birdland jazz club in New York was named. A founder of the new jazz, "bebop," that began to flourish in the 1940s.

"He's just one of the greatest jazz musicians alive," said Sonny, sullenly, his hands in his pockets, his back to me. "Maybe *the* greatest," he added, bitterly. "That's probably why *you* never heard of him."

"All right," I said, "I'm ignorant. I'm sorry. I'll go out and buy all the cat's records right away, all right?"

"It don't," said Sonny, with dignity, "make any difference to me. I don't care what you listen to. Don't do me no favors."

I was beginning to realize that I'd never seen him so upset before. With another part of my mind I was thinking that this would probably turn out to be one of those things kids go through and that I shouldn't make it seem important by pushing it too hard. Still, I didn't think it would do any harm to ask: "Doesn't all this take a lot of time? Can you make a living at it?"

He turned back to me and half leaned, half sat, on the kitchen table. "Everything takes time," he said, "and—well, yes, sure, I can make a living at it. But what I don't seem to be able to make you understand is that it's the only thing I want to do."

"Well, Sonny," I said gently, "you know people can't always do exactly what they *want* to do—"

"*No*, I don't know that," said Sonny, surprising me. "I think people *ought* to do what they want to do, what else are they alive for?"

"You getting to be a big boy," I said desperately, "it's time you started thinking about your future."

"I'm thinking about my future," said Sonny, grimly. "I think about it all the time."

I gave up. I decided, if he didn't change his mind, that we could always talk about it later. "In the meantime," I said, "you got to finish school." We had already decided that he'd have to move in with Isabel and her folks. I knew this wasn't the ideal arrangement because Isabel's folks are inclined to be dicty[5] and they hadn't especially wanted Isabel to marry me. But I didn't know what else to do. "And we have to get you fixed up at Isabel's."

There was a long silence. He moved from the kitchen table to the window. "That's a terrible idea. You know it yourself."

"Do you have a *better* idea?"

He just walked up and down the kitchen for a minute. He was as tall as I was. He had started to shave. I suddenly had the feeling that I didn't know him at all.

He stopped at the kitchen table and picked up my cigarettes. Looking at me with a kind of mocking, amused defiance, he put one between his lips. "You mind?"

"You smoking already?"

He lit the cigarette and nodded, watching me through the smoke. "I just wanted to see if I'd have the courage to smoke in front of you." He grinned and blew a great cloud of smoke to the ceiling. "It was easy." He looked at my face. "Come on, now. I bet you was smoking at my age, tell the truth."

I didn't say anything but the truth was on my face, and he laughed. But now there was something very strained in his laugh. "Sure. And I bet that ain't all you was doing."

5. Dictatorial, overbearing.

He was frightening me a little. "Cut the crap," I said. "We already decided that you was going to go and live at Isabel's. Now what's got into you all of a sudden?"

"*You* decided it," he pointed out. "*I* didn't decide nothing." He stopped in front of me, leaning against the stove, arms loosely folded. "Look, brother. I don't want to stay in Harlem no more, I really don't." He was very earnest. He looked at me, then over toward the kitchen window. There was something in his eyes I'd never seen before, some thoughtfulness, some worry all his own. He rubbed the muscle of one arm. "It's time I was getting out of here."

"Where do you want to *go*, Sonny?"

"I want to join the army. Or the navy, I don't care. If I say I'm old enough, they'll believe me."

Then I got mad. It was because I was so scared. "You must be crazy. You goddamn fool, what the hell do you want to go and join the *army* for?"

"I just told you. To get out of Harlem."

"Sonny, you haven't even finished *school*. And if you really want to be a musician, how do you expect to study if you're in the *army?*"

He looked at me, trapped, and in anguish. "There's ways. I might be able to work out some kind of deal. Anyway, I'll have the G.I. Bill[6] when I come out."

"*If* you come out." We stared at each other. "Sonny, please. Be reasonable. I know the setup is far from perfect. But we got to do the best we can."

"I ain't learning nothing in school," he said. "Even when I go." He turned away from me and opened the window and threw his cigarette out into the narrow alley. I watched his back. "At least, I ain't learning nothing you'd want me to learn." He slammed the window so hard I thought the glass would fly out, and turned back to me. "And I'm sick of the stink of these garbage cans!"

"Sonny," I said, "I know how you feel. But if you don't finish school now, you're going to be sorry later that you didn't." I grabbed him by the shoulders. "And you only got another year. It ain't so bad. And I'll come back and I swear I'll help you do *whatever* you want to do. Just try to put up with it till I come back. Will you please do that? For me?"

He didn't answer and he wouldn't look at me.

"Sonny. You hear me?"

He pulled away. "I hear you. But you never hear anything *I* say."

I didn't know what to say to that. He looked out of the window and then back at me. "OK," he said, and sighed. "I'll try."

Then I said, trying to cheer him up a little, "They got a piano at Isabel's. You can practice on it."

And as a matter of fact, it did cheer him up for a minute. "That's right," he said to himself. "I forgot that." His face relaxed a little. But the worry, the thoughtfulness, played on it still, the way shadows play on a face which is staring into the fire.

But I thought I'd never hear the end of that piano. At first, Isabel would write me, saying how nice it was that Sonny was so serious about his music and how, as soon as he came in from school, or wherever he had been when he

---

6. The G.I. Bill of Rights, established by the Servicemen's Readjustment Act of 1944, which provided a number of veterans' benefits, including tuition assistance.

was supposed to be at school, he went straight to that piano and stayed there until suppertime. And, after supper, he went back to that piano and stayed there until everybody went to bed. He was at the piano all day Saturday and all day Sunday. Then he bought a record player and started playing records. He'd play one record over and over again, all day long sometimes, and he'd improvise along with it on the piano. Or he'd play one section of the record, one chord, one change, one progression, then he'd do it on the piano. Then back to the record. Then back to the piano.

Well, I really don't know how they stood it. Isabel finally confessed that it wasn't like living with a person at all, it was like living with sound. And the sound didn't make any sense to her, didn't make any sense to any of them—naturally. They began, in a way, to be afflicted by this presence that was living in their home. It was as though Sonny were some sort of god, or monster. He moved in an atmosphere which wasn't like theirs at all. They fed him and he ate, he washed himself, he walked in and out of their door; he certainly wasn't nasty or unpleasant or rude, Sonny isn't any of those things; but it was as though he were all wrapped up in some cloud, some fire, some vision all his own; and there wasn't any way to reach him.

At the same time, he wasn't really a man yet, he was still a child, and they had to watch out for him in all kinds of ways. They certainly couldn't throw him out. Neither did they dare to make a great scene about that piano because even they dimly sensed, as I sensed, from so many thousands of miles away, that Sonny was at that piano playing for his life.

But he hadn't been going to school. One day a letter came from the school board and Isabel's mother got it—there had, apparently, been other letters but Sonny had torn them up. This day, when Sonny came in, Isabel's mother showed him the letter and asked where he'd been spending his time. And she finally got it out of him that he'd been down in Greenwich Village, with musicians and other characters, in a white girl's apartment. And this scared her and she started to scream at him and what came up, once she began—though she denies it to this day—was what sacrifices they were making to give Sonny a decent home and how little he appreciated it.

Sonny didn't play the piano that day. By evening, Isabel's mother had calmed down but then there was the old man to deal with, and Isabel herself. Isabel says she did her best to be calm but she broke down and started crying. She says she just watched Sonny's face. She could tell, by watching him, what was happening with him. And what was happening was that they penetrated his cloud, they had reached him. Even if their fingers had been a thousand times more gentle than human fingers ever are, he could hardly help feeling that they had stripped him naked and were spitting on that nakedness. For he also had to see that his presence, that music, which was life or death to him, had been torture for them and that they had endured it, not at all for his sake, but only for mine. And Sonny couldn't take that. He can take it a little better today than he could then but he's still not very good at it and, frankly, I don't know anybody who is.

The silence of the next few days must have been louder than the sound of all the music ever played since time began. One morning, before she went to work, Isabel was in his room for something and she suddenly realized that all of his records were gone. And she knew for certain that he was gone. And he was. He went as far as the navy would carry him. He finally sent me a postcard from some place in Greece and that was the first I knew that Sonny was still alive. I didn't see him any more until we were both back in New York and the war had long been over.

He was a man by then, of course, but I wasn't willing to see it. He came by the house from time to time, but we fought almost every time we met. I didn't like the way he carried himself, loose and dreamlike all the time, and I didn't like his friends, and his music seemed to be merely an excuse for the life he led. It sounded just that weird and disordered.

Then we had a fight, a pretty awful fight, and I didn't see him for months. By and by I looked him up, where he was living, in a furnished room in the Village, and I tried to make it up. But there were lots of other people in the room and Sonny just lay on his bed, and he wouldn't come downstairs with me, and he treated these other people as though they were his family and I weren't. So I got mad and then he got mad, and then I told him that he might just as well be dead as live the way he was living. Then he stood up and he told me not to worry about him any more in life, that he *was* dead as far as I was concerned. Then he pushed me to the door and the other people looked on as though nothing were happening, and he slammed the door behind me. I stood in the hallway, staring at the door. I heard somebody laugh in the room and then the tears came to my eyes. I started down the steps, whistling to keep from crying, I kept whistling to myself, *You going to need me, baby, one of these cold, rainy days.*

I read about Sonny's trouble in the spring. Little Grace died in the fall. She was a beautiful little girl. But she only lived a little over two years. She died of polio and she suffered. She had a slight fever for a couple of days, but it didn't seem like anything and we just kept her in bed. And we would certainly have called the doctor, but the fever dropped, she seemed to be all right. So we thought it had just been a cold. Then, one day, she was up, playing, Isabel was in the kitchen fixing lunch for the two boys when they'd come in from school, and she heard Grace fall down in the living room. When you have a lot of children you don't always start running when one of them falls, unless they start screaming or something. And, this time, Gracie was quiet. Yet, Isabel says that when she heard that *thump* and then that silence, something happened to her to make her afraid. And she ran to the living room and there was little Grace on the floor, all twisted up, and the reason she hadn't screamed was that she couldn't get her breath. And when she did scream, it was the worst sound, Isabel says, that she'd ever heard in all her life, and she still hears it sometimes in her dreams. Isabel will sometimes wake me up with a low, moaning, strangling sound and I have to be quick to awaken her and hold her to me and where Isabel is weeping against me seems a mortal wound.

I think I may have written Sonny the very day that little Grace was buried. I was sitting in the living room in the dark, by myself, and I suddenly thought of Sonny. My trouble made his real.

One Saturday afternoon, when Sonny had been living with us, or anyway, been in our house, for nearly two weeks, I found myself wandering aimlessly about the living room, drinking from a can of beer, and trying to work up courage to search Sonny's room. He was out, he was usually out whenever I was home, and Isabel had taken the children to see their grandparents. Suddenly

I was standing still in front of the living room window, watching Seventh Avenue. The idea of searching Sonny's room made me still. I scarcely dared to admit to myself what I'd be searching for. I didn't know what I'd do if I found it. Or if I didn't.

On the sidewalk across from me, near the entrance to a barbecue joint, some people were holding an old-fashioned revival meeting. The barbecue cook, wearing a dirty white apron, his conked[7] hair reddish and metallic in the pale sun, and a cigarette between his lips, stood in the doorway, watching them. Kids and older people paused in their errands and stood there, along with some older men and a couple of very tough-looking women who watched everything that happened on the avenue, as though they owned it, or were maybe owned by it. Well, they were watching this, too. The revival was being carried on by three sisters in black, and a brother. All they had were their voices and their Bibles and a tambourine. The brother was testifying[8] and while he testified two of the sisters stood together, seeming to say, amen, and the third sister walked around with the tambourine outstretched and a couple of people dropped coins into it. Then the brother's testimony ended and the sister who had been taking up the collection dumped the coins into her palm and transferred them to the pocket of her long black robe. Then she raised both hands, striking the tambourine against the air, and then against one hand, and she started to sing. And the two other sisters and the brother joined in.

It was strange, suddenly, to watch, though I had been seeing these meetings all my life. So, of course, had everybody else down there. Yet, they paused and watched and listened and I stood still at the window. " 'Tis the old ship of Zion," they sang, and the sister with the tambourine kept a steady, jangling beat, "it has rescued many a thousand!" Not a soul under the sound of their voices was hearing this song for the first time, not one of them had been rescued. Nor had they seen much in the way of rescue work being done around them. Neither did they especially believe in the holiness of the three sisters and the brother, they knew too much about them, knew where they lived, and how. The woman with the tambourine, whose voice dominated the air, whose face was bright with joy, was divided by very little from the woman who stood watching her, a cigarette between her heavy, chapped lips, her hair a cuckoo's nest, her face scarred and swollen from many beatings, and her black eyes glittering like coal. Perhaps they both knew this, which was why, when, as rarely, they addressed each other, they addressed each other as Sister. As the singing filled the air the watching, listening faces underwent a change, the eyes focusing on something within; the music seemed to soothe a poison out of them; and time seemed, nearly, to fall away from the sullen, belligerent, battered faces, as though they were fleeing back to their first condition, while dreaming of their last. The barbecue cook half shook his head and smiled, and dropped his cigarette and disappeared into his joint. A man fumbled in his pockets for change and stood holding it in his hand impatiently, as though he had just remembered a pressing appointment further up the avenue. He looked furious. Then I saw Sonny, standing on the edge of the crowd. He was carrying a wide, flat notebook with a green cover, and it made him look, from where I was standing, almost like a schoolboy. The coppery sun

---

7. Straightened and greased. **8.** Proclaiming his religious belief.

brought out the copper in his skin, he was very faintly smiling, standing very still. Then the singing stopped, the tambourine turned into a collection plate again. The furious man dropped in his coins and vanished, so did a couple of the women, and Sonny dropped some change in the plate, looking directly at the woman with a little smile. He started across the avenue, toward the house. He has a slow, loping walk, something like the way Harlem hipsters walk, only he's imposed on this his own half-beat. I had never really noticed it before.

I stayed at the window, both relieved and apprehensive. As Sonny disappeared from my sight, they began singing again. And they were still singing when his key turned in the lock.

"Hey," he said.

"Hey, yourself. You want some beer?"

"No. Well, maybe." But he came up to the window and stood beside me, looking out. "What a warm voice," he said.

They were singing *If I could only hear my mother pray again!*

"Yes," I said, "and she can sure beat that tambourine."

"But what a terrible song," he said, and laughed. He dropped his notebook on the sofa and disappeared into the kitchen. "Where's Isabel and the kids?"

"I think they went to see their grandparents. You hungry?"

"No." He came back into the living room with his can of beer. "You want to come some place with me tonight?"

I sensed, I don't know how, that I couldn't possibly say no. "Sure. Where?"

He sat down on the sofa and picked up his notebook and started leafing through it. "I'm going to sit in with some fellows in a joint in the Village."

"You mean, you're going to play, tonight?"

"That's right." He took a swallow of his beer and moved back to the window. He gave me a sidelong look. "If you can stand it."

"I'll try," I said.

He smiled to himself and we both watched as the meeting across the way broke up. The three sisters and the brother, heads bowed, were singing *God be with you till we meet again.* The faces around them were very quiet. Then the song ended. The small crowd dispersed. We watched the three women and the lone man walk slowly up the avenue.

"When she was singing before," said Sonny, abruptly, "her voice reminded me for a minute of what heroin feels like sometimes—when it's in your veins. It makes you feel sort of warm and cool at the same time. And distant. And—and sure." He sipped his beer, very deliberately not looking at me. I watched his face. "It makes you feel—in control. Sometimes you've got to have that feeling."

"Do you?" I sat down slowly in the easy chair.

"Sometimes." He went to the sofa and picked up his notebook again. "Some people do."

"In order," I asked, "to play?" And my voice was very ugly, full of contempt and anger.

"Well"—he looked at me with great, troubled eyes, as though, in fact, he hoped his eyes would tell me things he could never otherwise say—"they *think* so. And *if* they think so—!"

"And what do *you* think?" I asked.

He sat on the sofa and put his can of beer on the floor. "I don't know," he said, and I couldn't be sure if he were answering my question or pursuing his thoughts. His face didn't tell me. "It's not so much to *play*. It's to *stand* it, to be able to make it at all. On any level." He frowned and smiled: "In order to keep from shaking to pieces."

"But these friends of yours," I said, "they seem to shake themselves to pieces pretty goddamn fast."

"Maybe." He played with the notebook. And something told me that I should curb my tongue, that Sonny was doing his best to talk, that I should listen. "But of course you only know the ones that've gone to pieces. Some don't—or at least they haven't *yet* and that's just about all *any* of us can say." He paused. "And then there are some who just live, really, in hell, and they know it and they see what's happening and they go right on. I don't know." He sighed, dropped the notebook, folded his arms. "Some guys, you can tell from the way they play, they on something *all* the time. And you can see that, well, it makes something real for them. But of course," he picked up his beer from the floor and sipped it and put the can down again, "they *want* to, too, you've got to see that. Even some of them that say they don't—*some*, not all."

"And what about you?" I asked—I couldn't help it. "What about you? Do *you* want to?"

He stood up and walked to the window and I remained silent for a long time. Then he sighed. "Me," he said. Then: "While I was downstairs before, on my way here, listening to that woman sing, it struck me all of a sudden how much suffering she must have had to go through—to sing like that. It's *repulsive* to think you have to suffer that much."

I said: "But there's no way not to suffer—is there, Sonny?"

"I believe not," he said and smiled, "but that's never stopped anyone from trying." He looked at me. "Has it?" I realized, with this mocking look, that there stood between us, forever, beyond the power of time or forgiveness, the fact that I had held silence—so long!—when he had needed human speech to help him. He turned back to the window. "No, there's no way not to suffer. But you try all kinds of ways to keep from drowning in it, to keep on top of it, and to make it seem—well, like *you*. Like you did something, all right, and now you're suffering for it. You know?" I said nothing. "Well you know," he said, impatiently, "why *do* people suffer? Maybe it's better to do something to give it a reason, *any* reason."

"But we just agreed," I said, "that there's no way not to suffer. Isn't it better, then, just to—take it?"

"But nobody just takes it," Sonny cried, "that's what I'm telling you! *Everybody* tries not to. You're just hung up on the *way* some people try—it's not *your* way!"

The hair on my face began to itch, my face felt wet. "That's not true," I said, "that's not true. I don't give a damn what other people do, I don't even care how they suffer. I just care how *you* suffer." And he looked at me. "Please believe me," I said, "I don't want to see you—die—trying not to suffer."

"I won't," he said flatly, "die trying not to suffer. At least, not any faster than anybody else."

"But there's no need," I said, trying to laugh, "is there? in killing yourself."

I wanted to say more, but I couldn't. I wanted to talk about will power and how life could be—well, beautiful. I wanted to say that it was all within; but was it? or, rather, wasn't that exactly the trouble? And I wanted to promise that I would never fail him again. But it would all have sounded—empty words and lies.

So I made the promise to myself and prayed that I would keep it.

"It's terrible sometimes, inside," he said, "that's what's the trouble. You walk these streets, black and funky and cold, and there's not really a living ass to talk to, and there's nothing shaking, and there's no way of getting it out— that storm inside. You can't talk it and you can't make love with it, and when you finally try to get with it and play it, you realize *nobody's* listening. So *you've* got to listen. You got to find a way to listen."

And then he walked away from the window and sat on the sofa again, as though all the wind had suddenly been knocked out of him. "Sometimes you'll do *anything* to play, even cut your mother's throat." He laughed and looked at me. "Or your brother's." Then he sobered. "Or your own." Then: "Don't worry. I'm all right now and I think I'll *be* all right. But I can't forget—where I've been. I don't mean just the physical place I've been, I mean where I've *been*. And *what* I've been."

"What have you been, Sonny?" I asked.

He smiled—but sat sideways on the sofa, his elbow resting on the back, his fingers playing with his mouth and chin, not looking at me. "I've been something I didn't recognize, didn't know I could be. Didn't know anybody could be." He stopped, looking inward, looking helplessly young, looking old. "I'm not talking about it now because I feel *guilty* or anything like that—maybe it would be better if I did, I don't know. Anyway, I can't really talk about it. Not to you, not to anybody," and now he turned and faced me. "Sometimes, you know, and it was actually when I was most *out* of the world, I felt that I was in it, that I was *with* it, really, and I could play or I didn't really have to *play,* it just came out of me, it was there. And I don't know how I played, thinking about it now, but I know I did awful things, those times, sometimes, to people. Or it wasn't that I *did* anything to them—it was that they weren't real." He picked up the beer can; it was empty; he rolled it between his palms: "And other times—well, I needed a fix, I needed to find a place to lean, I needed to clear a space to *listen*—and I couldn't find it, and I—went crazy, I did terrible things to *me,* I was terrible *for* me." He began pressing the beer can between his hands, I watched the metal begin to give. It glittered, as he played with it like a knife, and I was afraid he would cut himself, but I said nothing. "Oh well. I can never tell you. I was all by myself at the bottom of something, stinking and sweating and crying and shaking, and I smelled it, you know? *my* stink, and I thought I'd die if I couldn't get away from it and yet, all the same, I knew that everything I was doing was just locking me in with it. And I didn't know," he paused, still flattening the beer can, "I didn't know, I still *don't* know, something kept telling me that maybe it was good to smell your own stink, but I didn't think that *that* was what I'd been trying to do—and—who can stand it?" and he abruptly dropped the ruined beer can, looking at me with a small, still smile, and then rose, walking to the window as though it were the lodestone rock. I watched his face, he watched the avenue. "I couldn't tell you when Mama died—but the reason I wanted to leave Harlem so bad was to get away from drugs. And then, when I ran away, that's what I was running from—really. When I came back, nothing had changed, *I* hadn't changed, I was just—older." And he stopped, drumming with his fingers on the windowpane. The sun had vanished, soon darkness would fall. I watched his face. "It can come again," he said, almost as though speaking to himself. Then he turned to me. "It can come again," he repeated. "I just want you to know that."

"All right," I said, at last. "So it can come again. All right."

He smiled, but the smile was sorrowful. "I had to try to tell you," he said.

"Yes," I said. "I understand that."

"You're my brother," he said, looking straight at me, and not smiling at all.

"Yes," I repeated, "yes. I understand that."

He turned back to the window, looking out. "All that hatred down there," he said, "all that hatred and misery and love. It's a wonder it doesn't blow the avenue apart."

We went to the only nightclub on a short, dark street, downtown. We squeezed through the narrow, chattering, jampacked bar to the entrance of the big room, where the bandstand was. And we stood there for a moment, for the lights were very dim in this room and we couldn't see. Then, "Hello, boy," said the voice and an enormous black man, much older than Sonny or myself, erupted out of all that atmospheric lighting and put an arm around Sonny's shoulder. "I been sitting right here," he said, "waiting for you."

He had a big voice, too, and heads in the darkness turned toward us.

Sonny grinned and pulled a little away, and said, "Creole, this is my brother. I told you about him."

Creole shook my hand. "I'm glad to meet you, son," he said, and it was clear that he was glad to meet me *there*, for Sonny's sake. And he smiled, "You got a real musician in *your* family," and he took his arm from Sonny's shoulder and slapped him, lightly, affectionately, with the back of his hand.

"Well. Now I've heard it all," said a voice behind us. This was another musician, and a friend of Sonny's, a coal-black, cheerful-looking man, built close to the ground. He immediately began confiding to me, at the top of his lungs, the most terrible things about Sonny, his teeth gleaming like a lighthouse and his laugh coming up out of him like the beginning of an earthquake. And it turned out that everyone at the bar knew Sonny, or almost everyone; some were musicians, working there, or nearby, or not working, some were simply hangers-on, and some were there to hear Sonny play. I was introduced to all of them and they were all very polite to me. Yet, it was clear that, for them, I was only Sonny's brother. Here, I was in Sonny's world. Or, rather: his kingdom. Here, it was not even a question that his veins bore royal blood.

They were going to play soon and Creole installed me, by myself, at a table in a dark corner. Then I watched them, Creole, and the little black man, and Sonny, and the others, while they horsed around, standing just below the bandstand. The light from the bandstand spilled just a little short of them and, watching them laughing and gesturing and moving about, I had the feeling that they, nevertheless, were being most careful not to step into that circle of light too suddenly; that if they moved into the light too suddenly, without thinking, they would perish in flame. Then, while I watched, one of them, the small black man, moved into the light and crossed the bandstand and started fooling around with his drums. Then—being funny and being, also, extremely ceremonious—Creole took Sonny by the arm and led him to the piano. A woman's voice called Sonny's name and a few hands started clapping.

And Sonny, also being funny and being ceremonious, and so touched, I think, that he could have cried, but neither hiding it nor showing it, riding it like a man, grinned, and put both hands to his heart and bowed from the waist.

Creole then went to the bass fiddle and a lean, very bright-skinned brown man jumped up on the bandstand and picked up his horn. So there they were, and the atmosphere on the bandstand and in the room began to change and tighten. Someone stepped up to the microphone and announced them. Then there were all kinds of murmurs. Some people at the bar shushed others. The waitress ran around, frantically getting in the last orders, guys and chicks got closer to each other, and the lights on the bandstand, on the quartet, turned to a kind of indigo. Then they all looked different there. Creole looked about him for the last time, as though he were making certain that all his chickens were in the coop, and then he—jumped and struck the fiddle. And there they were.

All I know about music is that not many people ever really hear it. And even then, on the rare occasions when something opens within, and the music enters, what we mainly hear, or hear corroborated, are personal, private, vanishing evocations. But the man who creates the music is hearing something else, is dealing with the roar rising from the void and imposing order on it as it hits the air. What is evoked in him, then, is of another order, more terrible because it has no words, and triumphant, too, for that same reason. And his triumph, when he triumphs, is ours. I just watched Sonny's face. His face was troubled, he was working hard, but he wasn't with it. And I had the feeling that, in a way, everyone on the bandstand was waiting for him, both waiting for him and pushing him along. But as I began to watch Creole, I realized that it was Creole who held them all back. He had them on a short rein. Up there, keeping the beat with his whole body, wailing on the fiddle, with his eyes half closed, he was listening to everything, but he was listening to Sonny. He was having a dialogue with Sonny. He wanted Sonny to leave the shoreline and strike out for the deep water. He was Sonny's witness that deep water and drowning were not the same thing—he had been there, and he knew. And he wanted Sonny to know. He was waiting for Sonny to do the things on the keys which would let Creole know that Sonny was in the water.

And, while Creole listened, Sonny moved, deep within, exactly like someone in torment. I had never before thought of how awful the relationship must be between the musician and his instrument. He has to fill it, this instrument, with the breath of life, his own. He has to make it do what he wants it to do. And a piano is just a piano. It's made out of so much wood and wires and little hammers and big ones, and ivory. While there's only so much you can do with it, the only way to find this out is to try; to try and make it do everything.

And Sonny hadn't been near a piano for over a year. And he wasn't on much better terms with his life, not the life that stretched before him now. He and the piano stammered, started one way, got scared, stopped; started another way, panicked, marked time, started again; then seemed to have found a direction, panicked again, got stuck. And the face I saw on Sonny I'd never seen before. Everything had been burned out of it, and, at the same time, things usually hidden were being burned in, by the fire and fury of the battle which was occurring in him up there.

Yet, watching Creole's face as they neared the end of the first set, I had the feeling that something had happened, something I hadn't heard. Then they finished, there was scattered applause, and then, without an instant's warning, Creole started into something else, it was almost sardonic, it was *Am I Blue?*[9] And, as though he commanded, Sonny began to play. Something began to happen. And Creole let out the reins. The dry, low, black man said something awful on the drums, Creole answered, and the drums talked back. Then the horn insisted, sweet and high, slightly detached perhaps, and Creole listened, commenting now and then, dry, and driving, beautiful and calm and old. Then they all came together again, and Sonny was part of the family again. I could tell this from his face. He seemed to have found, right there beneath his fingers, a damn brand-new piano. It seemed that he couldn't get over it. Then, for a while, just being happy with Sonny, they seemed to be agreeing with him that brand-new pianos certainly were a gas.

Then Creole stepped forward to remind them that what they were playing was the blues. He hit something in all of them, he hit something in me, myself, and the music tightened and deepened, apprehension began to beat the air. Creole began to tell us what the blues were all about. They were not about anything very new. He and his boys up there were keeping it new, at the risk of ruin, destruction, madness, and death, in order to find new ways to make us listen. For, while the tale of how we suffer, and how we are delighted, and how we may triumph is never new, it always must be heard. There isn't any other tale to tell, it's the only light we've got in all this darkness.

And this tale, according to that face, that body, those strong hands on those strings, has another aspect in every country, and a new depth in every generation. Listen, Creole seemed to be saying, listen. Now these are Sonny's blues. He made the little black man on the drums know it, and the bright, brown man on the horn. Creole wasn't trying any longer to get Sonny in the water. He was wishing him Godspeed. Then he stepped back, very slowly, filling the air with the immense suggestion that Sonny speak for himself.

Then they all gathered around Sonny and Sonny played. Every now and again one of them seemed to say, amen. Sonny's fingers filled the air with life, his life. But that life contained so many others. And Sonny went all the way back, he really began with the spare, flat statement of the opening phrase of the song. Then he began to make it his. It was very beautiful because it wasn't hurried and it was no longer a lament. I seemed to hear with what burning he had made it his, and what burning we had yet to make it ours, how we could cease lamenting. Freedom lurked around us and I understood, at last, that he could help us to be free if we would listen, that he would never be free until we did. Yet, there was no battle in his face now, I heard what he had gone through, and would continue to go through until he came to rest in earth. He had made it his: that long line, of which we knew only Mama and Daddy. And he was giving it back, as everything must be given back, so that, passing through death, it can live forever. I saw my mother's face again, and felt, for the first time, how the stones of the road she had walked on must have bruised her feet. I saw the moonlit road where my father's brother died. And it brought something else back to me, and carried me past it, I saw my little girl again and felt Isabel's tears again, and I felt my own tears begin to rise. And I was yet aware that this was only a moment, that the world waited outside, as hungry as a tiger, and that trouble stretched above us, longer than the sky.

**9.** A jazz tune, by H. Akst and G. Clarke, from *On With the Show* (1929).

Then it was over. Creole and Sonny let out their breath, both soaking wet, and grinning. There was a lot of applause and some of it was real. In the dark, the girl came by and I asked her to take drinks to the bandstand. There was a long pause, while they talked up there in the indigo light and after awhile I saw the girl put a Scotch and milk on top of the piano for Sonny. He didn't seem to notice it, but just before they started playing again, he sipped from it and looked toward me, and nodded. Then he put it back on top of the piano. For me, then, as they began to play again, it glowed and shook above my brother's head like the very cup of trembling.[1]

1957

---

1. Isaiah 51:22: "I have taken out of thine hand the cup of trembling . . . thou shalt no more drink it again."

# TONI CADE BAMBARA
## *1939–1995*

Bambara was born in New York and grew up in two of the city's poorest neighborhoods, Harlem and Bedford-Stuyvesant. Early in life she was drawn to social activism and in high school years learned that writing is a splendid means of doing battle. For years after graduating from Queens College, she wrote fiction in "the predawn in-betweens" while earning her M.A. at the City College of New York and working at a great variety of jobs: dancer, social worker, psychiatric counselor, college English teacher, literary critic, and film producer. She began to publish short stories in 1960, and in 1972 many of these were collected in her first book, *Gorilla, My Love*. This was followed by another collection, *The Sea Birds Are Still Alive* (1977), and two novels: *The Salt Eaters* (1980) and *Those Bones Are Not My Child*, published posthumously in 1999.

## Gorilla, My Love

That was the year Hunca Bubba changed his name. Not a change up, but a change back, since Jefferson Winston Vale was the name in the first place. Which was news to me cause he'd been my Hunca Bubba my whole lifetime, since I couldn't manage Uncle to save my life. So far as I was concerned it was a change completely to somethin soundin very geographical weatherlike to me, like somethin you'd find in a almanac. Or somethin you'd run across when you sittin in the navigator seat with a wet thumb on the map crinkly in your lap, watchin the roads and signs so when Granddaddy Vale say "Which way, Scout," you got sense enough to say take the next exit or take a left or whatever it is. Not that Scout's my name. Just the name Granddaddy call whoever sittin in the navigator seat. Which is usually me cause I don't feature sittin in the back with the pecans. Now, you figure pecans all right to be sittin with. If you thinks so, that's your business. But they dusty sometime and make you cough. And they got a way of slidin around and dippin down sudden, like maybe a rat in the buckets. So if you scary like me, you sleep with the lights on and blame it on Baby Jason and, so as not to waste good electric, you study the maps. And that's how come I'm in the navigator seat most times and get to be called Scout.

So Hunca Bubba in the back with the pecans and Baby Jason, and he in love. And we got to hear all this stuff about this woman he in love with and all. Which really ain't enough to keep the mind alive, though Baby Jason got no better sense than to give his undivided attention and keep grabbin at the photograph which is just a picture of some skinny woman in a countrified dress with her hand shot up to her face like she shame fore cameras. But there's a movie house in the background which I ax about. Cause I am a movie freak from way back, even though it do get me in trouble sometime.

Like when me and Big Brood and Baby Jason was on our own last Easter and couldn't go to the Dorset cause we'd seen all the Three Stooges they was. And the RKO Hamilton was closed readying up for the Easter Pageant that night. And the West End, the Regun and the Sunset was too far, less we had grown-ups with us which we didn't. So we walk up Amsterdam Avenue to the Washington and *Gorilla, My Love* playin, they say, which suit me just fine, though the "my love" part kinda drag Big Brood some. As for Baby Jason, shoot, like Granddaddy say, he'd follow me into the fiery furnace if I say come on. So we go in and get three bags of Havmore potato chips which not only are the best potato chips but the best bags for blowin up and bustin real loud so the matron come trottin down the aisle with her chunky self, flashin that flashlight dead in your eye so you can give her some lip, and if she answer back and you already finish seein the show anyway, why then you just turn the place out. Which I love to do, no lie. With Baby Jason kickin at the seat in front, egging me on, and Big Brood mumblin bout what fiercesome things we goin do. Which means me. Like when the big boys come up on us talkin bout Lemme a nickel. It's me that hide the money. Or when the bad boys in the park take Big Brood's Spaudeen[1] way from him. It's me that jump on they back and fight awhile. And it's me that turns out the show if the matron get too salty.

So the movie come on and right away it's this churchy music and clearly not about no gorilla. Bout Jesus. And I am ready to kill, not cause I got anything gainst Jesus. Just that when you fixed to watch a gorilla picture you don't wanna get messed around with Sunday School stuff. So I am mad. Besides, we see this raggedy old brown film *King of Kings*[2] every year and enough's enough. Grown-ups figure they can treat you just anyhow. Which burns me up. There I am, my feet up and my Havmore potato chips really salty and crispy and two jaw-breakers in my lap and the money safe in my shoe from the big boys, and there comes this Jesus stuff. So we all go wild. Yellin, booin, stompin and carrying on. Really to wake the man in the booth up there who musta went to sleep and put on the wrong reels. But no, cause he holler down to shut up and then he turn the sound up so we really gotta holler like crazy to even hear ourselves good. And the matron ropes off the children section and flashes her light all over the place and we yell some more and some kids slip under the rope and run up and down the aisle just to show it take more than some dusty ole velvet rope to tie us down. And I'm flingin the kid in front of me's popcorn. And Baby Jason kickin seats. And it's really somethin. Then here come the big and bad matron, the one they let out in case of emergency. This here the colored matron Brandy and her friends call Thunderbuns. She do not play. She do not smile. So we shut up and watch the simple ass picture.

Which is not so simple as it is stupid. Cause I realized that just about any-body in my family is better than this god they always talkin about. My daddy wouldn't stand for nobody treatin any of us that way. My mama specially. And I can just see it now, Big Brood up there on the cross talkin bout Forgive

---

**1.** Rubber balls used in stickball, an urban form of baseball.   **2.** Silent movie depicting the life of Christ.

them Daddy cause they don't know what they doin. And my Mama say Get on down from there you big fool, whatcha think this is, playtime? And my Daddy yellin to Granddaddy to get him a ladder cause Big Brood actin the fool, his mother side of the family showin up. And my mama and her sister Daisy jumpin on them Romans beatin them with they pocketbooks. And Hunca Bubba tellin them folks on they knees they better get out the way and go get some help or they goin to get trampled on. And Granddaddy Vale sayin Leave the boy alone, if that's what he wants to do with his life we ain't got nothin to say about it. Then Aunt Daisy givin him a taste of that pocketbook, fussin bout what a damn fool old man Granddaddy is. Then everybody jumpin in his chest like the time Uncle Clayton went in the army and come back with only one leg and Granddaddy say somethin stupid about that's life. And by this time Big Brood off the cross and in the park playin handball or skully or somethin. And the family in the kitchen throwin dishes at each other, screamin bout if you hadn't done this I wouldn't had to do that. And me in the parlor trying to do my arithmetic yellin Shut it off.

Which is what I was yellin all by myself which make me a sittin target for Thunderbuns. But when I yell We want our money back, that gets everybody in chorus. And the movie windin up with this heavenly cloud music and the smart-ass up there in his hole in the wall turns up the sound again to drown us out. Then there comes Bugs Bunny which we already seen so we know we been had. No gorilla my nuthin. And Big Brood say Awwww sheeet, we goin to see the manager and get our money back. And I know from this we business. So I brush the potato chips out of my hair which is where Baby Jason like to put em, and I march myself up the aisle to deal with the manager who is a crook in the first place for lyin out there sayin *Gorilla, My Love* playin. And I never did like the man cause he oily and pasty at the same time like the bad guy in the serial, the one that got a hideout behind a push-button bookcase and play "Moonlight Sonata" with gloves on. I knock on the door and I am furious. And I am alone, too. Cause Big Brood suddenly got to go so bad even though my mama told us bout goin in them nasty bathrooms. And I hear him sigh like he disgusted when he get to the door and see only a little kid there. And now I'm really furious cause I get so tired grownups messin over kids cause they little and can't take em to court. What is it, he say to me like I lost my mittens or wet myself or am somebody's retarded child. When in reality I am the smartest kid P.S. 186 ever had in its whole lifetime and you can ax anybody. Even them teachers that don't like me cause I won't sing them Southern songs or back off when they tell me my questions are out of order. And cause my Mama come up there in a minute when them teachers start playin the dozens[3] behind colored folks. She stalks in with her hat pulled down bad and that Persian lamb coat draped back over one hip on account of she got her fist planted there so she can talk that talk which gets us all hypnotized and teacher be comin undone cause she know this could be her job and her behind cause Mama got pull with the Board and bad by her own self anyhow.

So I kick the door open wider and just walk right by him and sit down and tell the man about himself and that I want my money back and that goes for Baby Jason and Big Brood too. And he still trying to shuffle me out the door

---

3. Trading insults about each other's relatives.

even though I'm sittin which shows him for the fool he is. Just like them teachers do fore they realize Mama like a stone on that spot and ain't backin up. So he ain't gettin up off the money. So I was forced to leave, takin the matches from under his ashtray, and set a fire under the candy stand, which closed the raggedy ole Washington down for a week. My Daddy had the suspect it was me cause Big Brood got a big mouth. But I explained right quick what the whole thing was about and I figured it was even-steven. Cause if you say Gorilla, My Love, you supposed to mean it. Just like when you say you goin to give me a party on my birthday, you gotta mean it. And if you say me and Baby Jason can go South pecan haulin with Granddaddy Vale, you better not be comin up with no stuff about the weather look uncertain or did you mop the bathroom or any other trickified business. I mean even gangsters in the movies say My word is my bond. So don't nobody get away with nothin far as I'm concerned. So Daddy put his belt back on. Cause that's the way I was raised. Like my Mama say in one of them situations when I won't back down, Okay Badbird, you right. Your point is well-taken. Not that Badbird my name, just what she say when she tired arguin and know I'm right. And Aunt Jo, who is the hardest head in the family and worse even than Aunt Daisy, she say, You absolutely right Miss Muffin, which also ain't my real name but the name she gave me one time when I got some medicine shot in my behind and wouldn't get up off her pillows for nothin. And even Granddaddy Vale—who got no memory to speak of, so sometime you can just plain lie to him, if you want to be like that—he say, Well if that's what I said, then that's it. But this name business was different they said. It wasn't like Hunca Bubba had gone back on his word or anything. Just that he was thinkin bout gettin married and was usin his real name now. Which ain't the way I saw it at all.

So there I am in the navigator seat. And I turned to him and just plain ole ax him. I mean I come right on out with it. No sense goin all around that barn the old folks talk about. And like my mama say, Hazel—which is my real name and what she remembers to call me when she bein serious—when you got somethin on your mind, speak up and let the chips fall where they may. And if anybody don't like it, tell em to come see your mama. And Daddy look up from the paper and say, You hear your Mama good, Hazel. And tell em to come see me first. Like that. That's how I was raised.

So I turn clear round in the navigator seat and say, "Look here, Hunca Bubba or Jefferson Windsong Vale or whatever your name is, you gonna marry this girl?"

"Sure am," he say, all grins.

And I say, "Member that time you was baby-sittin me when we lived at four-o-nine and there was this big snow and Mama and Daddy got held up in the country so you had to stay for two days?"

And he say, "Sure do."

"Well. You remember how you told me I was the cutest thing that ever walked the earth?"

"Oh, you were real cute when you were little," he say, which is supposed to be funny. I am not laughin.

"Well. You remember what you said?"

And Granddaddy Vale squintin over the wheel and axin Which way, Scout. But Scout is busy and don't care if we all get lost for days.

"Watcha mean, Peaches?"

"My name is Hazel. And what I mean is you said you were going to marry *me* when I grew up. You were going to wait. That's what I mean, my dear Uncle Jefferson." And he don't say nuthin. Just look at me real strange like he never saw me before in life. Like he lost in some weird town in the middle of night and lookin for directions and there's no one to ask. Like it was me that messed up the maps and turned the road posts round. "Well, you said it, didn't you?" And Baby Jason lookin back and forth like we playin ping-pong. Only I ain't playin. I'm hurtin and I can hear that I am screamin. And Granddaddy Vale mumblin how we never gonna get to where we goin if I don't turn around and take my navigator job serious.

"Well, for cryin out loud, Hazel, you just a little girl. And I was just teasin."

"'And I was just teasin,'" I say back just how he said it so he can hear what a terrible thing it is. Then I don't say nuthin. And he don't say nuthin. And Baby Jason don't say nuthin nohow. Then Granddaddy Vale speak up. "Look here, Precious, it was Hunca Bubba what told you them things. This here, Jefferson Winston Vale." And Hunca Bubba say, "That's right. That was somebody else. I'm a new somebody."

"You a lyin dawg," I say, when I meant to say treacherous dog, but just couldn't get hold of the word. It slipped away from me. And I'm crying and crumplin down in the seat and just don't care. And Granddaddy say to hush and steps on the gas. And I'm losin my bearins and don't even know where to look on the map cause I can't see for cryin. And Baby Jason cryin too. Cause he is my blood brother and understands that we must stick together or be forever lost, what with grown-ups playin change-up and turnin you round every which way so bad. And don't even say they sorry.

1972

---

RELATED:

—Bambara, "What Is It I Think I'm Doing Anyhow?" p. 872

# RICHARD BAUSCH
*b. 1945*

 Born in Fort Benning, Georgia, Richard Bausch served in the air force from 1965 to 1969. After a stint as a singer-songwriter, Bausch attended the Iowa Writer's Workshop in the mid-1970s and has subsequently taught creative writing at the University of Iowa, the University of Virginia, Bread Loaf, the University of the South, George Mason University, the University of Memphis, and now Chapman University. He is the author of twelve novels, including *Good Evening Mr. and Mrs. America and All the Ships at Sea* (1996), *In the Night Season* (1999), *Hello to the Cannibals* (2002), and, most recently, *Before, During, and After* (2014). His stories have appeared in *The Atlantic Monthly*, the *New Yorker, Esquire, Harper's,* and other magazines, and have been anthologized in many publications, including *The Best American Short Stories* and the *O. Henry* and the *Pushcart Prize* series. Bausch was awarded the PEN/Malamud Award for Excellence in the Short Story in 2004, the Dayton Peace Prize for Literature in 2009, and the Rea Award for the Short Story in 2012.

## Letter to the Lady of the House

It's exactly twenty minutes to midnight, on this the eve of my seventieth birthday, and I've decided to address you, for a change, in writing—odd as that might seem. I'm perfectly aware of how many years we've been together, even if I haven't been very good about remembering to commemorate certain dates, certain days of the year. I'm also perfectly aware of how you're going to take the fact that I'm doing this at all, so late at night, with everybody due to arrive tomorrow, and the house still unready. I haven't spent almost five decades with you without learning a few things about you that I can predict and describe with some accuracy, though I admit that, as you put it, lately we've been more like strangers than husband and wife. Well, so if we are like strangers, perhaps there are some things I can tell you that you won't have already figured out about the way I feel.

Tonight, we had another one of those long, silent evenings after an argument (remember?) over pepper. We had been bickering all day, really, but at dinner I put pepper on my potatoes and you said that about how I shouldn't have pepper because it always upsets my stomach. I bothered to remark that I used to eat chili peppers for breakfast and if I wanted to put plain old ordinary black pepper on my potatoes, as I had been doing for more than sixty years, that was my privilege. Writing this now, it sounds far more testy than I meant it, but that isn't really the point.

In any case, you chose to overlook my tone. You simply said, "John, you were up all night the last time you had pepper with your dinner."

I said, "I was up all night because I ate green peppers. Not black pepper, but green peppers."

"A pepper is a pepper, isn't it?" you said. And then I started in on you. I got, as you call it, legal with you—pointing out that green peppers are not black pepper—and from there we moved on to an evening of mutual disregard for each other that ended with your decision to go to bed early. The grand-children will make you tired, and there's still the house to do; you had every reason to want to get some rest, and yet I felt that you were also making a point of getting yourself out of proximity with me, leaving me to my displea-sure, with another ridiculous argument settling between us like a fog.

So, after you went to bed, I got out the whiskey and started pouring drinks, and I had every intention of putting myself into a stupor. It was almost my birthday, after all, and—forgive this, it's the way I felt at the time—you had nagged me into an argument and then gone off to bed; the day had ended as so many of our days end now, and I felt, well, entitled. I had a few drinks, without any appreciable effect (though you might well see this letter as firm evidence to the contrary), and then I decided to do something to shake you up. I would leave. I'd make a lot of noise going out the door; I'd take a walk around the neighborhood and make you wonder where I could be. Perhaps I'd go check into a motel for the night. The thought even crossed my mind that I might leave you altogether. I admit that I entertained the thought, Marie. I saw our life together now as the day-to-day round of petty quarreling and tension that it's mostly been over the past couple of years or so, and I wanted out as sincerely as I ever wanted anything.

My God, I wanted an end to it, and I got up from my seat in front of the tele-vision and walked back down the hall to the entrance of our room to look at you. I suppose I hoped you'd still be awake so I could tell you of this momen-tous decision I felt I'd reached. And maybe you were awake: one of our oldest areas of contention being the noise I make—the feather-thin membrane of your sleep that I am always disturbing with my restlessness in the nights. All right. Assuming you were asleep and don't know that I stood in the doorway of our room, I will say that I stood there for perhaps five minutes, looking at you in the half-dark, the shape of your body under the blanket—you really did look like one of the girls when they were little and I used to stand in the doorway of their rooms; your illness last year made you so small again—and, as I said, I thought I had decided to leave you, for your peace as well as mine. I know you have gone to sleep crying, Marie. I know you've felt sorry about things and wished we could find some way to stop irritating each other so much.

Well, of course I didn't go anywhere. I came back to this room and drank more of the whiskey and watched television. It was like all the other nights. The shows came on and ended, and the whiskey began to wear off. There was a little rain shower. I had a moment of the shock of knowing I was seventy. After the rain ended, I did go outside for a few minutes. I stood on the side-walk and looked at the house. The kids, with their kids, were on the road somewhere between their homes and here. I walked up to the end of the block and back, and a pleasant breeze blew and shook the drops out of the trees. My stomach was bothering me some, and maybe it was the pepper I'd put on my potatoes. It could just as well have been the whiskey. Anyway, as I came back to the house, I began to have the eerie feeling that I had reached the last night of my life. There was this small discomfort in my stomach, and no other physical pang or pain, and I am used to the small ills and side effects of my way of eating and drinking; yet I felt the sense of the end of things more strongly than I can describe. When I stood in the entrance of our room and looked at you again, wondering if I would make it through to the morning, I suddenly found myself trying to think what I would say to you if indeed this *were* the last time I would ever be able to speak to you. And I began to know I would write you this letter.

At least words in a letter aren't blurred by tone of voice, by the old aggravating sound of me talking to you. I began with this and with the idea that, after months of thinking about it, I would at last try to say something to you that wasn't colored by our disaffections. What I have to tell you must be explained in a rather roundabout way.

I've been thinking about my cousin Louise and her husband. When he died and she stayed with us last summer, something brought back to me what is really only the memory of a moment; yet it reached me, that moment, across more than fifty years. As you know, Louise is nine years older than I, and more like an older sister than a cousin. I must have told you at one time or another that I spent some weeks with her, back in 1933, when she was first married. The memory I'm talking about comes from that time, and what I have decided I have to tell you comes from that memory.

Father had been dead four years. We were all used to the fact that times were hard and that there was no man in the house, though I suppose I filled that role in some titular way. In any case, when Mother became ill there was the problem of us, her children. Though I was the oldest, I wasn't old enough to stay in the house alone, or to nurse her, either. My grandfather came up with the solution—and everybody went along with it—that I would go to Louise's for a time, and the two girls would go to stay with Grandfather. You'll remember that people did pretty much what that old man wanted them to do.

So we closed up the house, and I got on a train to Virginia. I was a few weeks shy of fourteen years old. I remember that I was not able to believe that anything truly bad would come of Mother's pleurisy,[1] and was consequently glad of the opportunity it afforded me to travel the hundred miles south to Charlottesville, where cousin Louise had moved with her new husband only a month earlier, after her wedding. Because *we* traveled so much at the beginning, you never got to really know Charles when he was young—in 1933 he was a very tall, imposing fellow, with bright red hair and a graceful way of moving that always made me think of athletics, contests of skill. He had worked at the Navy Yard in Washington, and had been laid off in the first months of Roosevelt's New Deal. Louise was teaching in a day school in Charlottesville so they could make ends meet, and Charles was spending most of his time looking for work and fixing up the house. I had only met Charles once or twice before the wedding, but already I admired him and wanted to emulate him. The prospect of spending time in his house, of perhaps going fishing with him in the small streams of central Virginia, was all I thought about on the way

---

1. A type of lung disease.

down. And I remember that we did go fishing one weekend, that I would end up spending a lot of time with Charles, helping to paint the house and to run water lines under it for indoor plumbing. Oh, I had time with Louise, too—listening to her read from the books she wanted me to be interested in, walking with her around Charlottesville in the evenings and looking at the city as it was then. Or sitting on her small porch and talking about the family, Mother's stubborn illness, the children Louise saw every day at school. But what I want to tell you has to do with the very first day I was there.

I know you think I use far too much energy thinking about and pining away for the past, and I therefore know that I'm taking a risk by talking about this ancient history, and by trying to make you see it. But this all has to do with you and me, my dear, and our late inability to find ourselves in the same room together without bitterness and pain.

That summer, 1933, was unusually warm in Virginia, and the heat, along with my impatience to arrive, made the train almost unbearable. I think it was just past noon when it pulled into the station at Charlottesville, with me hanging out one of the windows, looking for Louise or Charles. It was Charles who had come to meet me. He stood in a crisp-looking seer-sucker suit, with a straw boater cocked at just the angle you'd expect a young, newly married man to wear a straw boater, even in the middle of economic disaster. I waved at him and he waved back, and I might've jumped out the window if the train had slowed even a little more than it had before it stopped in the shade of the platform. I made my way out, carrying the cloth bag my grandfather had given me for the trip—Mother had said through her rheum that I looked like a carpetbagger—and when I stepped down to shake hands with Charles I noticed that what I thought was a new suit was tattered at the ends of the sleeves.

"Well," he said. "Young John."

I smiled at him. I was perceptive enough to see that his cheerfulness was not entirely effortless. He was a man out of work, after all, and so in spite of himself there was worry in his face, the slightest shadow in an otherwise glad and proud countenance. We walked through the station to the street, and on up the steep hill to the house, which was a small clapboard structure, a cottage, really, with a porch at the end of a short sidewalk lined with flowers—they were marigolds, I think—and here was Louise, coming out of the house, her arms already stretched wide to embrace me. "Lord," she said. "I swear you've grown since the wedding, John." Charles took my bag and went inside.

"Let me look at you, young man," Louise said.

I stood for inspection. And as she looked me over I saw that her hair was pulled back, that a few strands of it had come loose, that it was brilliantly auburn in the sun. I suppose I was a little in love with her. She was grown, and married now. She was a part of what seemed a great mystery to me, even as I was about to enter it, and of course you remember how that feels, Marie, when one is on the verge of things—nearly adult, nearly old enough to fall in love. I looked at Louise's happy, flushed face, and felt a deep ache as she ushered me into her house. I wanted so to be older.

Inside, Charles had poured lemonade for us and was sitting in the easy chair by the fireplace, already sipping his. Louise wanted to show me the house and the backyard—which she had tilled and turned into a small vegetable garden—but she must've sensed how thirsty I was, and so she asked me to sit down and have a cool drink before she showed me the upstairs. Now, of course, looking back on it, I remember that those rooms she was so anxious to show me were meager indeed. They were not much bigger than closets, really, and the paint was faded and dull; the furniture she'd arranged so artfully was coming apart; the pictures she'd put on the walls were prints she'd cut out—magazine covers, mostly—and the curtains over the windows were the same ones that had hung in her childhood bedroom for twenty years. ("Recognize these?" she said with a deprecating smile.) Of course, the quality of her pride had nothing to do with the fineness—or lack of it—in these things, but in the fact that they belonged to her, and that she was a married lady in her own house.

On this day in July, in 1933, she and Charles were waiting for the delivery of a fan they had scrounged enough money to buy from Sears, through the catalogue. There were things they would rather have been doing, especially in this heat, and especially with me there. Monticello wasn't far away, the university was within walking distance, and without too much expense one could ride a taxi to one of the lakes nearby. They had hoped that the fan would arrive before I did, but since it hadn't, and since neither Louise nor Charles was willing to leave the other alone while traipsing off with me that day, there wasn't anything to do but wait around for it. Louise had opened the windows and shut the shades, and we sat in her small living room and drank the lemonade, fanning ourselves with folded parts of Charles's morning newspaper. From time to time an anemic breath of air would move the shades slightly, but then everything grew still again. Louise sat on the arm of Charles's chair, and I sat on the sofa. We talked about pleurisy and, I think, about the fact that Thomas Jefferson had invented the dumbwaiter, how the plumbing at Monticello was at least a century ahead of its time. Charles remarked that it was the spirit of invention that would make a man's career in these days. "That's what I'm aiming for, to be inventive in a job. No matter what it winds up being."

When the lemonade ran out, Louise got up and went into the kitchen to make some more. Charles and I talked about taking a weekend to go fishing. He leaned back in his chair and put his hands behind his head, looking satisfied. In the kitchen, Louise was chipping ice for our glasses, and she began singing something low, for her own pleasure, a barely audible lilting, and Charles and I sat listening. It occurred to me that I was very happy. I had the sense that soon I would be embarked on my own life, as Charles was, and that an attractive woman like Louise would be there with me. Charles yawned and said, "God, listen to that. Doesn't Louise have the loveliest voice?"

And that's all I have from that day. I don't even know if the fan arrived later, and I have no clear memory of how we spent the rest of the afternoon and evening. I remember Louise singing a song, her husband leaning back in his chair, folding his hands behind his head, expressing his pleasure in his young wife's voice. I remember that I felt quite extraordinarily content just then. And that's all I remember.

But there are, of course, the things we both know: we know they moved to Colorado to be near Charles's parents; we know they never had any children; we know that Charles fell down a shaft at a construction site in the fall of 1957 and was hurt so badly that he never walked again. And I know that when she came to stay with us last summer she told me she'd learned to hate him, and not for what she'd had to help him do all those years. No, it started earlier and was deeper than that. She hadn't minded the care of him—the washing and feeding and all the numberless small tasks she had to perform each and every day, all day—she hadn't minded this. In fact, she thought there was something in her makeup that liked being needed so completely. The trouble was simply that whatever she had once loved in him she had stopped loving, and for many, many years before he died, she'd felt only suffocation when he was near enough to touch her, only irritation and anxiety when he spoke. She said all this, and then looked at me, her cousin, who had been fortunate enough to have children, and to be in love over time, and said, "John, how have you and Marie managed it?"

And what I wanted to tell you has to do with this fact—that while you and I had had one of our whispering arguments only moments before, I felt quite certain of the simple truth of the matter, which is that whatever our complications, we *have* managed to be in love over time.

"Louise," I said.

"People start out with such high hopes," she said, as if I wasn't there. She looked at me. "Don't they?"

"Yes," I said.

She seemed to consider this a moment. Then she said, "I wonder how it happens."

I said, "You ought to get some rest." Or something equally pointless and admonitory.

As she moved away from me, I had an image of Charles standing on the station platform in Charlottesville that summer, the straw boater set at its cocky angle. It was an image I would see most of the rest of that night, and on many another night since.

I can almost hear your voice as you point out that once again I've managed to dwell too long on the memory of something that's past and gone. The difference is that I'm not grieving over the past now. I'm merely reporting a memory, so that you might understand what I'm about to say to you.

The fact is, we aren't the people we were even then, just a year ago. I know that. As I know things have been slowly eroding between us for a very long time; we are a little tired of each other, and there are annoyances and old scars that won't be obliterated with a letter—even a long one written in the middle of the night in desperate sincerity, under the influence, admittedly, of a considerable portion of bourbon whiskey, but nevertheless with the best intention and hope: that you may know how, over the course of this night, I came to the end of needing an explanation for our difficulty. We have reached this—place. Everything we say seems rather aggravatingly mindless and automatic, like something one stranger might say to another in any of the thousand circumstances where strangers are thrown together for a time, and the silence begins to grow heavy on their minds, and someone has to say something. Darling, we go so long these days without having anything at all to do with each other, and the children are arriving tomorrow, and once more we'll be in the position of making all the gestures that give them back their parents as they think their parents are, and what I wanted to say to you, what came to me as I thought about Louise and Charles on that day so long ago, when they were young and so obviously glad of each other, and I looked at them and knew it and was happy—what came to me was that even the harsh things that happened to them, even the years of anger and silence, even the disappointment and the bitterness and the wanting not to be in the same room anymore, even all that must have been worth it for such loveliness. At least I am here, at seventy years old, hoping so. Tonight, I went back to our room again and stood gazing at you asleep, dreaming whatever you were dreaming, and I had a moment of thinking how we were always friends, too. Because what I wanted finally to say was that I remember well our own sweet times, our own old loveliness, and I would like to think that even if at the very beginning of our lives together I had somehow been shown that we would end up here, with this longing to be away from each other, this feeling of being trapped together, of being tied to each other in a way that makes us wish for other times, some other place—I would have known enough to accept it all freely for the chance at that love. And if I could, I would do it all again, Marie. All of it, even the sorrow. My sweet, my dear adversary. For everything that I remember.

1989

RELATED:

—Bausch, "Letter to a Young Writer," p. 873
—Bausch on Anton Chekhov's "Gusev," p. 918

# ANN BEATTIE
## b. 1947

Beattie was born in Washington, D.C., and attended both American University and the University of Connecticut. Subsequently, she taught at Harvard and the University of Virginia. She has received a Guggenheim Fellowship and has built a broad reputation for the many stories she has published in *The New Yorker,* establishing her as a spokesperson for the generation of the 1960s as her characters adapt—or fail to adapt—to the oncoming years. She writes of those who took the 1960s to be a Golden Age and cannot free themselves from the enchantment of their youth. Her books of short stories include *Distortions* (1976), *The Burning House* (1982), *What Was Mine* (1991), *Selected Stories* (1999), and *Follies* (2005). A collection of her *New Yorker* stories was published in 2011. Her novels include *Chilly Scenes of Winter* (1976), *Falling in Place* (1980), *Love Always* (1985), *Picturing Will* (1990), *My Life, Starring Dara Falcon* (1997), *Perfect Recall* (2000), *The Doctor's House* (2001), and *Mrs. Nixon* (2011). In 2005 Beattie won the Rea Award for the Short Story.

## Snow

I remember the cold night you brought in a pile of logs and a chipmunk jumped off as you lowered your arms. "What do you think *you're* doing in here?" you said, as it ran through the living room. It went through the library and stopped at the front door as though it knew the house well. This would be difficult for anyone to believe, except perhaps as the subject of a poem. Our first week in the house was spent scraping, finding some of the house's secrets, like wallpaper underneath wallpaper. In the kitchen, a pattern of white-gold trellises supported purple grapes as big and round as Ping-Pong balls. When we painted the walls yellow, I thought of the bits of grape that remained underneath and imagined the vine popping through, the way some plants can tenaciously push through anything. The day of the big snow, when you had to shovel the walk and couldn't find your cap and asked me how to wind a towel so that it would stay on your head—you, in the white towel turban, like a crazy king of snow. People liked the idea of our being together, leaving the city for the country. So many people visited, and the fireplace made all of them want to tell amazing stories: the child who happened to be standing on the right corner when the door of the ice-cream truck came open and hundreds of Popsicles crashed out; the man standing on the beach, sand sparkling in the sun, one bit glinting more than the rest, stooping to find a diamond ring. Did they talk about amazing things because they thought we'd turn into one of them? Now I think they probably guessed it wouldn't work. It was as hopeless as giving a child a matched cup and saucer. Remember the night, out on the lawn, knee-deep in snow, chins pointed at the sky as the wind whirled down all that whiteness? It seemed that the world had been turned upside down, and we were looking into an enormous field of Queen Anne's lace.[1] Later, headlights off, our car was the first to ride through the newly fallen snow. The world outside the car looked solarized.

You remember it differently. You remember that the cold settled in stages, that a small curve of light was shaved from the moon night after night, until you were no longer surprised the sky was black, that the chipmunk ran to hide in the dark, not simply to a door that led to its escape. Our visitors told the same stories people always tell. One night, giving me a lesson in storytelling, you said, "Any life will seem dramatic if you omit mention of most of it."

This, then, for drama: I drove back to that house not long ago. It was April, and Allen had died. In spite of all the visitors, Allen, next door, had been the good friend in bad times. I sat with his wife in their living room, looking out the glass doors to the backyard, and there was Allen's pool, still covered with black plastic that had been stretched across it for winter. It had rained, and as the rain fell, the cover collected more and more water until it finally spilled onto the concrete. When I left that day, I drove past what had been our house. Three or four crocuses were blooming in the front—just a few dots of white, no field of snow. I felt embarrassed for them. They couldn't compete.

This is a story, told the way you say stories should be told: Somebody grew up, fell in love, and spent a winter with her lover in the country. This, of course, is the barest outline, and futile to discuss. It's as pointless as throwing birdseed on the ground while snow still falls fast. Who expects small things to survive when even the largest get lost? People forget years and remember moments. Seconds and symbols are left to sum things up: the black shroud over the pool. Love, in its shortest form, becomes a word. What I remember about all that time is one winter. The snow. Even now, saying "snow," my lips move so that they kiss the air.

No mention has been made of the snowplow that seemed always to be there, scraping snow off our narrow road—an artery cleared, though neither of us could have said where the heart was.

1983

---

1. *Daucus carota,* the wild form of the carrot, which has flat clusters of tiny white flowers.

# AMBROSE BIERCE
## *1842–1913?*

Bierce was born on a religious campground at Western Reserve, Ohio. The poverty of his family required him early in life to quit school and begin working as a copyboy for a newspaper before he enlisted with the Indiana Infantry in the Civil War. He rose through the military ranks to become a staff officer and was twice wounded. The horrors of war imbued his attitudes with an enduring cynicism, and his war stories are among the first to treat the subject with detailed realism. In San Francisco after the war he began his literary career by working, along with Mark Twain and Bret Harte, as a journalist. He spent the years between 1872 and 1876 in London, where his boisterous Western mannerisms and savage wit made him a celebrity, earning him the nickname "Bitter Bierce." Poor health forced him to return in 1876 to his journalistic career in California. In 1891 he published *Tales of Soldiers and Civilians,* followed two years later by another volume of short stories, *Can Such Things Be?* The death of his two sons in 1889 and 1901, along with his divorce in 1891, intensified his prevailing pessimism and resulted at length in his disappearance into revolution-torn Mexico, where he is believed to have died in 1913. His sardonic wit can be sampled in *The Devil's Dictionary* (1911). Twelve volumes of his *Collected Works* (prose and poetry) were published in 1909–1912.

## An Occurrence at Owl Creek Bridge

### I

A man stood upon a railroad bridge in Northern Alabama, looking down into the swift waters twenty feet below. The man's hands were behind his back, the wrists bound with a cord. A rope loosely encircled his neck. It was attached to a stout cross-timber above his head, and the slack fell to the level of his knees. Some loose boards laid upon the sleepers[1] supporting the metals of the railway supplied a footing for him and his executioners—two private soldiers of the Federal army, directed by a sergeant, who in civil life may have been a deputy sheriff. At a short remove upon the same temporary platform was an officer in the uniform of his rank, armed. He was a captain. A sentinel at each end of the bridge stood with his rifle in the position known as "support," that is to say, vertical in front of the left shoulder, the hammer resting on the forearm thrown straight across the chest—a formal and unnatural

1. Crossties.

position, enforcing an erect carriage of the body. It did not appear to be the duty of these two men to know what was occurring at the centre of the bridge; they merely blockaded the two ends of the foot plank which traversed it.

Beyond one of the sentinels nobody was in sight; the railroad ran straight away into a forest for a hundred yards, then, curving, was lost to view. Doubtless there was an outpost further along. The other bank of the stream was open ground—a gentle acclivity crowned with a stockade of vertical tree trunks, loop-holed for rifles, with a single embrasure through which protruded the muzzle of a brass cannon commanding the bridge. Midway of the slope between bridge and fort were the spectators—a single company of infantry in line, at "parade rest," the butts of the rifles on the ground, the barrels inclining slightly backward against the right shoulder, the hands crossed upon the stock. A lieutenant stood at the right of the line, the point of his sword upon the ground, his left hand resting upon his right. Excepting the group of four at the centre of the bridge not a man moved. The company faced the bridge, staring stonily, motionless. The sentinels, facing the banks of the stream, might have been statues to adorn the bridge. The captain stood with folded arms, silent, observing the work of his subordinates but making no sign. Death is a dignitary who, when he comes announced, is to be received with formal manifestations of respect, even by those most familiar with him. In the code of military etiquette silence and fixity are forms of deference.

The man who was engaged in being hanged was apparently about thirty-five years of age. He was a civilian, if one might judge from his dress, which was that of a planter. His features were good—a straight nose, firm mouth, broad forehead, from which his long, dark hair was combed straight back, falling behind his ears to the collar of his well-fitting frock coat. He wore a moustache and pointed beard, but no whiskers; his eyes were large and dark grey and had a kindly expression which one would hardly have expected in one whose neck was in the hemp. Evidently this was no vulgar assassin. The liberal military code makes provision for hanging many kinds of people, and gentlemen are not excluded.

The preparations being complete, the two private soldiers stepped aside and each drew away the plank upon which he had been standing. The sergeant turned to the captain, saluted and placed himself immediately behind that officer, who in turn moved apart one pace. These movements left the condemned man and the sergeant standing on the two ends of the same plank, which spanned three of the cross-ties of the bridge. The end upon which the civilian stood almost, but not quite, reached a fourth. This plank had been held in place by the weight of the captain; it was now held by that of the sergeant. At a signal from the former, the latter would step aside, the plank would tilt and the condemned man go down between two ties. The arrangement commended itself to his judgment as simple and effective. His face had not been covered nor his eyes bandaged. He looked a moment at his "unsteadfast footing," then let his gaze wander to the swirling water of the stream racing madly beneath his feet. A piece of dancing driftwood caught his attention and his eyes followed it down the current. How slowly it appeared to move! What a sluggish stream!

He closed his eyes in order to fix his last thoughts upon his wife and children. The water, touched to gold by the early sun, the brooding mists under the banks at some distance down the stream, the fort, the soldiers, the piece of drift—all had distracted him. And now he became conscious of a new disturbance. Striking through the thought of his dear ones was a sound which he could neither ignore nor understand, a sharp, distinct, metallic percussion like the stroke of a blacksmith's hammer upon the anvil; it had the same ringing quality. He wondered what it was, and whether immeasurably distant or near by—it seemed both. Its recurrence was regular, but as slow as the tolling of a death knell. He awaited each stroke with impatience and—he knew not why—apprehension. The intervals of silence grew progressively longer, the delays became maddening. With their greater infrequency the sounds increased in strength and sharpness. They hurt his ear like the thrust of a knife; he feared he would shriek. What he heard was the ticking of his watch.

He unclosed his eyes and saw again the water below him. "If I could free my hands," he thought, "I might throw off the noose and spring into the stream. By diving I could evade the bullets, and, swimming vigorously, reach the bank, take to the woods, and get away home. My home, thank God, is as yet outside their lines; my wife and little ones are still beyond the invader's farthest advance."

As these thoughts, which have here to be set down in words, were flashed into the doomed man's brain rather than evolved from it, the captain nodded to the sergeant. The sergeant stepped aside.

## I I

Peyton Farquhar was a well-to-do planter, of an old and highly-respected Alabama family. Being a slave owner, and, like other slave owners, a politician, he was naturally an original secessionist and ardently devoted to the Southern cause. Circumstances of an imperious nature which it is unnecessary to relate here, had prevented him from taking service with the gallant army which had fought the disastrous campaigns ending with the fall of Corinth,[2] and he chafed under the inglorious restraint, longing for the release of his energies, the larger life of the soldier, the opportunity for distinction. That opportunity, he felt, would come, as it comes to all in war time. Meanwhile he did what he could. No service was too humble for him to perform in aid of the South, no adventure too perilous for him to undertake if consistent with the character of a civilian who was at heart a soldier, and who in good faith and without too much qualification assented to at least a part of the frankly villainous dictum that all is fair in love and war.

One evening while Farquhar and his wife were sitting on a rustic bench near the entrance to his grounds, a grey-clad soldier rode up to the gate and asked for a drink of water. Mrs. Farquhar was only too happy to serve him with her own white hands. While she was gone to fetch the water, her husband approached the dusty horseman and inquired eagerly for news from the front.

"The Yanks are repairing the railroads," said the man, "and are getting ready for another advance. They have reached the Owl Creek bridge, put it in order, and built a stockade on the other bank. The commandant has issued

---

**2.** In Mississippi; the main battle for Corinth occurred in 1862 when the Confederates tried to retake the town and were decisively beaten.

an order, which is posted everywhere, declaring that any civilian caught interfering with the railroad, its bridges, tunnels, or trains, will be summarily hanged. I saw the order."

"How far is it to the Owl Creek bridge?" Farquhar asked.

"About thirty miles."

"Is there no force on this side the creek?"

"Only a picket post half a mile out, on the railroad, and a single sentinel at this end of the bridge."

"Suppose a man—a civilian and student of hanging—should elude the picket post and perhaps get the better of the sentinel," said Farquhar, smiling, "what could he accomplish?"

The soldier reflected. "I was there a month ago," he replied. "I observed that the flood of last winter had lodged a great quantity of driftwood against the wooden pier at this end of the bridge. It is now dry and would burn like tow."

The lady had now brought the water, which the soldier drank. He thanked her ceremoniously, bowed to her husband, and rode away. An hour later, after nightfall he repassed the plantation, going northward in the direction from which he had come. He was a Federal scout.

## III

As Peyton Farquhar fell straight downward through the bridge, he lost consciousness and was as one already dead. From this state he was awakened—ages later, it seemed to him—by the pain of a sharp pressure upon his throat, followed by a sense of suffocation. Keen, poignant agonies seemed to shoot from his neck downward through every fibre of his body and limbs. These pains appeared to flash along well-defined lines of ramification, and to beat with an inconceivably rapid periodicity. They seemed like streams of pulsating fire heating him to an intolerable temperature. As to his head, he was conscious of nothing but a feeling of fullness—of congestion. These sensations were unaccompanied by thought. The intellectual part of his nature was already effaced; he had power only to feel, and feeling was torment. He was conscious of motion. Encompassed in a luminous cloud, of which he was now merely the fiery heart, without material substance, he swung through unthinkable arcs of oscillation, like a vast pendulum. Then all at once, with terrible suddenness, the light about him shot upward with the noise of a loud plash; a frightful roaring was in his ears, and all was cold and dark. The power of thought was restored; he knew that the rope had broken and he had fallen into the stream. There was no additional strangulation; the noose about his neck was already suffocating him, and kept the water from his lungs. To die of hanging at the bottom of a river!—the idea seemed to him ludicrous. He opened his eyes in the blackness and saw above him a gleam of light, but how distant, how inaccessible! He was still sinking, for the light became fainter and fainter until it was a mere glimmer. Then it began to grow and brighten, and he knew that he was rising toward the surface—knew it with reluctance, for he was now very comfortable. "To be hanged and drowned," he thought, "that is not so bad; but I do not wish to be shot. No; I will not be shot; that is not fair."

He was not conscious of an effort, but a sharp pain in his wrist apprised him that he was trying to free his hands. He gave the struggle his attention,

as an idler might observe the feat of a juggler, without interest in the outcome. What splendid effort!—what magnificent, what superhuman strength!
Ah, that was a fine endeavour! Bravo! The cord fell away; his arms parted and
floated upward, the hands dimly seen on each side in the growing light. He
watched them with a new interest as first one and then the other pounced upon
the noose at his neck. They tore it away and thrust it fiercely aside, its undula-
tions resembling those of a water-snake. "Put it back, put it back!" He thought
he shouted these words to his hands, for the undoing of the noose had been
succeeded by the direst pang which he had yet experienced. His neck ached
horribly; his brain was on fire; his heart, which had been fluttering faintly,
gave a great leap, trying to force itself out at his mouth. His whole body was
racked and wrenched with an insupportable anguish! But his disobedient
hands gave no heed to the command. They beat the water vigorously with
quick, downward strokes, forcing him to the surface. He felt his head emerge;
his eyes were blinded by the sunlight; his chest expanded convulsively, and
with a supreme and crowning agony his lungs engulfed a great draught of air,
which instantly he expelled in a shriek!

He was now in full possession of his physical senses. They were, indeed, pre-
ternaturally keen and alert. Something in the awful disturbance of his organic
system had so exalted and refined them that they made record of things never
before perceived. He felt the ripples upon his face and heard their separate
sounds as they struck. He looked at the forest on the bank of the stream, saw
the individual trees, the leaves and the veining of each leaf—the very insects
upon them, the locusts, the brilliant-bodied flies, the grey spiders stretching
their webs from twig to twig. He noted the prismatic colors in all the dewdrops
upon a million blades of grass. The humming of the gnats that danced above
the eddies of the stream, the beating of the dragon flies' wings, the strokes of
the water spiders' legs, like oars which had lifted their boat—all these made
audible music. A fish slid along beneath his eyes and he heard the rush of its
body parting the water.

He had come to the surface facing down the stream; in a moment the visible
world seemed to wheel slowly round, himself the pivotal point, and he saw the
bridge, the fort, the soldiers upon the bridge, the captain, the sergeant, the two
privates, his executioners. They were in silhouette against the blue sky. They
shouted and gesticulated, pointing at him; the captain had drawn his pistol,
but did not fire; the others were unarmed. Their movements were grotesque
and horrible, their forms gigantic.

Suddenly he heard a sharp report and something struck the water smartly
within a few inches of his head, spattering his face with spray. He heard a second report, and saw one of the sentinels with his rifle at his shoulder, a light
cloud of blue smoke rising from the muzzle. The man in the water saw the eye
of the man on the bridge gazing into his own through the sights of the rifle.
He observed that it was a grey eye, and remembered having read that grey eyes
were keenest and that all famous marksmen had them. Nevertheless, this one
had missed.

A counter swirl had caught Farquhar and turned him half round; he was
again looking into the forest on the bank opposite the fort. The sound of a
clear, high voice in a monotonous singsong now rang out behind him and came
across the water with a distinctness that pierced and subdued all other sounds,

even the beating of the ripples in his ears. Although no soldier, he had frequented camps enough to know the dread significance of that deliberate, drawling, aspirated chant; the lieutenant on shore was taking a part in the morning's work. How coldly and pitilessly—with what an even, calm intonation, presaging and enforcing tranquillity in the men—with what accurately-measured intervals fell those cruel words:

"Attention, company.... Shoulder arms.... Ready.... Aim.... Fire."

Farquhar dived—dived as deeply as he could. The water roared in his ears like the voice of Niagara, yet he heard the dulled thunder of the volley, and rising again toward the surface, met shining bits of metal, singularly flattened, oscillating slowly downward. Some of them touched him on the face and hands, then fell away, continuing their descent. One lodged between his collar and neck; it was uncomfortably warm, and he snatched it out.

As he rose to the surface, gasping for breath, he saw that he had been a long time under water; he was perceptibly farther down stream—nearer to safety. The soldiers had almost finished reloading; the metal ramrods flashed all at once in the sunshine as they were drawn from the barrels, turned in the air, and thrust into their sockets. The two sentinels fired again, independently and ineffectually.

The hunted man saw all this over his shoulder; he was now swimming vigorously with the current. His brain was as energetic as his arms and legs; he thought with the rapidity of lightning.

"The officer," he reasoned, "will not make that martinet's error a second time. It is as easy to dodge a volley as a single shot. He has probably already given the command to fire at will. God help me, I cannot dodge them all!"

An appalling plash within two yards of him, followed by a loud rushing sound, *diminuendo*,[3] which seemed to travel back through the air to the fort and died in an explosion which stirred the very river to its deeps! A rising sheet of water, which curved over him, fell down upon him, blinded him, strangled him! The cannon had taken a hand in the game. As he shook his head free from the commotion of the smitten water, he heard the deflected shot humming through the air ahead, and in an instant it was cracking and smashing the branches in the forest beyond.

"They will not do that again," he thought; "the next time they will use a charge of grape.[4] I must keep my eye upon the gun; the smoke will apprise me—the report arrives too late; it lags behind the missile. It is a good gun."

Suddenly he felt himself whirled round and round—spinning like a top. The water, the banks, the forest, the now distant bridge, fort and men—all were commingled and blurred. Objects were represented by their colors only; circular horizontal streaks of color—that was all he saw. He had been caught in a vortex and was being whirled on with a velocity of advance and gyration which made him giddy and sick. In a few moments he was flung upon the gravel at the foot of the left bank of the stream—the southern bank—and behind a projecting point which concealed him from his enemies. The sudden arrest of his motion, the abrasion of one of his hands on the gravel, restored him and he wept with delight. He dug his fingers into the sand, threw it over

---

**3.** Diminishing (generally used for music).　**4.** That is, grapeshot, a cluster of small pellets fired from a cannon.

himself in handfuls and audibly blessed it. It looked like gold, like diamonds, rubies, emeralds; he could think of nothing beautiful which it did not resemble. The trees upon the bank were giant garden plants; he noted a definite order in their arrangement, inhaled the fragrance of their blooms. A strange, rose-ate light shone through the spaces among their trunks, and the wind made in their branches the music of æolian harps. He had no wish to perfect his escape, was content to remain in that enchanting spot until retaken.

A whizz and rattle of grapeshot among the branches high above his head roused him from his dream. The baffled cannoneer had fired him a random farewell. He sprang to his feet, rushed up the sloping bank, and plunged into the forest.

All that day he travelled, laying his course by the rounding sun. The forest seemed interminable; nowhere did he discover a break in it, not even a wood-man's road. He had not known that he lived in so wild a region. There was something uncanny in the revelation.

By nightfall he was fatigued, footsore, famishing. The thought of his wife and children urged him on. At last he found a road which led him in what he knew to be the right direction. It was as wide and straight as a city street, yet it seemed untravelled. No fields bordered it, no dwelling anywhere. Not so much as the barking of a dog suggested human habitation. The black bodies of the great trees formed a straight wall on both sides, terminating on the horizon in a point, like a diagram in a lesson in perspective. Overhead, as he looked up through this rift in the wood, shone great golden stars looking unfamiliar and grouped in strange constellations. He was sure they were arranged in some order which had a secret and malign significance. The wood on either side was full of singular noises, among which—once, twice, and again—he distinctly heard whispers in an unknown tongue.

His neck was in pain, and, lifting his hand to it, he found it horribly swollen. He knew that it had a circle of black where the rope had bruised it. His eyes felt congested; he could no longer close them. His tongue was swollen with thirst; he relieved its fever by thrusting it forward from between his teeth into the cool air. How softly the turf had carpeted the untravelled avenue! He could no longer feel the roadway beneath his feet!

Doubtless, despite his suffering, he fell asleep while walking, for now he sees another scene—perhaps he has merely recovered from a delirium. He stands at the gate of his own home. All is as he left it, and all bright and beautiful in the morning sunshine. He must have travelled the entire night. As he pushes open the gate and passes up the wide white walk, he sees a flutter of female garments; his wife, looking fresh and cool and sweet, steps down from the verandah to meet him. At the bottom of the steps she stands waiting, with a smile of ineffable joy, an attitude of matchless grace and dignity. Ah, how beautiful she is! He springs forward with extended arms. As he is about to clasp her, he feels a stunning blow upon the back of the neck; a blinding white light blazes all about him, with a sound like the shock of a cannon—then all is darkness and silence!

Peyton Farquhar was dead; his body, with a broken neck, swung gently from side to side beneath the timbers of the Owl Creek bridge.

1891

# JORGE LUIS BORGES
## *1899–1986*

Borges was born in Buenos Aires, Argentina, to a family of middle-class intellectuals. After his education in Geneva and some years in Europe, where he associated with avant garde literary groups, he returned to Buenos Aires in 1921 and became the leader of a South American literary movement based on Surrealism and Imagism. In the early phases of his career, he wrote poetry for the most part, turning to prose as his varied intellectual interests came together to suggest new forms. A vastly erudite man, who directed the National Library until the dictator Perón removed him for political reasons, Borges built a "literature about literature"; his typically brief essays and short narratives are miniature encyclopedias of literary history, mingling gravity with absurdity in a constant parade of the complexities of human awareness. Though blind and a partial invalid in his later years, he lectured and taught in the United States. His books available in English include *Labyrinths* (1962), *Ficciones* (1962), *Dreamtigers* (1964), *The Book of Imaginary Beings* (1969), *The Aleph and Other Stories* (1970), *Dr. Brodie's Report* (1977), and *The Book of Sand* (1977).

## Pierre Menard, Author of the *Quixote*[1]

The *visible*[2] work left by this novelist is easily and briefly enumerated. Impardonable, therefore, are the omissions and additions perpetrated by Madame Henri Bachelier in a fallacious catalogue which a certain daily, whose *Protestant* tendency is no secret, has had the inconsideration to inflict upon its deplorable readers—though these be few and Calvinist, if not Masonic and circumcised.[3] The true friends of Menard have viewed this catalogue with alarm and even with a certain melancholy. One might say that only yesterday we gathered before his final monument, amidst the lugubrious cypresses, and already Error tries to tarnish his Memory . . . Decidedly, a brief rectification is unavoidable.

---

**1.** Translated by James E. Irby. This story parodies a scholarly study. It comes complete with footnotes of its own, and these footnotes must be considered an integral part of the parody. So—to avoid confusion—Borges's footnotes are marked with symbols and printed above a ruled line at the bottom of each page. The editor's footnotes are printed below the line. The editor's footnotes are necessarily numerous because Borges's method is to mix an abundance of scholarly allusions to real personalities and literary works with names of fictitious authors and their fictitious works.   **2.** That is, that which actually exists on paper.   **3.** That is, those who are prejudiced by their Protestant, Free Thinking, or Jewish biases.

I am aware that it is quite easy to challenge my slight authority. I hope, however, that I shall not be prohibited from mentioning two eminent testimonies. The Baroness de Bacourt (at whose unforgettable *vendredis*[4] I had the honor of meeting the lamented poet) has seen fit to approve the pages which follow. The Countess de Bagnoregio,[5] one of the most delicate spirits of the Principality of Monaco (and now of Pittsburgh, Pennsylvania, following her recent marriage to the international philanthropist Simon Kautzsch, who has been so inconsiderately slandered, alas! by the victims of his disinterested maneuvers) has sacrificed "to veracity and to death" (such were her words) the stately reserve which is her distinction, and, in an open letter published in the magazine *Luxe*,[6] concedes me her approval as well. These authorizations, I think, are not entirely insufficient.

I have said that Menard's visible work can be easily enumerated. Having examined with care his personal files, I find that they contain the following items:

a) A Symbolist sonnet which appeared twice (with variants) in the review *La conque*[7] (Issues of March and October 1899).

b) A monograph on the possibility of constructing a poetic vocabulary of concepts which would not be synonyms or periphrases of those which make up our everyday language, "but rather ideal objects created according to convention and essentially designed to satisfy poetic needs" (Nîmes,[8] 1901).

c) A monograph on "certain connections or affinities" between the thought of Descartes, Leibniz and John Wilkins[9] (Nîmes, 1903).

d) A monograph on Leibniz's *Characteristica universalis*[1] (Nîmes, 1904).

e) A technical article on the possibility of improving the game of chess, eliminating one of the rook's pawns. Menard proposes, recommends, discusses and finally rejects this innovation.

f) A monograph on Raymond Lully's *Ars magna generalis*[2] (Nîmes, 1906).

g) A translation, with prologue and notes, of Ruy López de Segura's *Libro de la invención liberal y arte del juego del axedrez*[3] (Paris, 1907).

h) The work sheets of a monograph on George Boole's[4] symbolic logic.

i) An examination of the essential metric laws of French prose, illustrated with examples taken from Saint-Simon (*Revue des langues romanes*, Montpellier, October 1909).[5]

j) A reply to Luc Durtain[6] (who had denied the existence of such laws), illustrated with examples from Luc Durtain (*Revue des langues romanes*, Montpellier, December 1909).

---

4. Literally "Fridays" (French), regular Friday meetings devoted to a discussion of the arts.   5. Evidently a fictitious patroness of the arts.   6. "Luxury" (French).   7. "Seashell" (French). In the second half of the 19th century there arose in France what has come to be known as the Symbolist movement. The Symbolists sought to express or suggest ideas and emotions by means of symbols, as by the mention or introduction of things or the use of words and word sounds to convey a meaning, often with mystical or vague effects.   8. A city in southern France.   9. Bishop of Chester (1614–1672). René Descartes (1596–1650), French philosopher and mathematician. Gottfried Wilhelm Leibniz (1646–1716), German philosopher, mathematician, and theologian.   1. "Universal Characteristics" (Latin), written in 1679.   2. "The Great Art of the General" (Latin), Lully (c. 1232–1315).   3. "The Book of Liberal Invention and the Game of Chess," (Spanish), published in 1561.   4. English mathematician, metaphysician, and author (1815–1864).   5. "Review of Romance Languages" (French), published in Montpellier, France. No article on the Duc de Saint-Simon (1675–1755) appears in the issue cited.   6. Durtain (1881–1959) does not appear in the issue cited.

k) A manuscript translation of the *Aguja de navegar cultos* of Quevedo, entitled *La boussole des précieux*.[7]

l) A preface to the Catalogue of an exposition of lithographs by Carolus Hourcade[8] (Nîmes, 1914).

m) The work *Les problèmes d'un problème*[9] (Paris, 1917) which discusses, in chronological order, the different solutions given to the illustrious problem of Achilles and the tortoise.[1] Two editions of this book have appeared so far; the second bears as an epigraph Leibniz's recommendation *"Ne craignez point, monsieur, la tortue"*[2] and revises the chapters dedicated to Russell[3] and Descartes.

n) A determined analysis of the "syntactical customs" of Toulet (N. R. F.,[4] March 1921). Menard—I recall—declared that censure and praise are sentimental operations which have nothing to do with literary criticism.

o) A transposition into alexandrines of Paul Valéry's *Le cimetière marin*[5] (N. R. F., January 1928).

p) An invective against Paul Valéry, in the *Papers for the Suppression of Reality* of Jacques Reboul.[6] (This invective, we might say parenthetically, is the exact opposite of his true opinion of Valéry. The latter understood it as such and their old friendship was not endangered.)

q) A "definition" of the Countess de Bagnoregio, in the "victorious volume"—the locution is Gabriele d'Annunzio's,[7] another of its collaborators—published annually by this lady to rectify the inevitable falsifications of journalists and to present "to the world and to Italy" an authentic image of her person, so often exposed (by very reason of her beauty and her activities) to erroneous or hasty interpretations.

r) A cycle of admirable sonnets for the Baroness de Bacourt (1934).

s) A manuscript list of verses which owe their efficacy to their punctuation.*

This, then, is the *visible* work of Menard, in chronological order (with no omission other than a few vague sonnets of circumstance written for the hospitable, or avid, album of Madame Henri Bachelier). I turn now to his other work: the subterranean, the interminably heroic, the peerless. And—such are the capacities of man!—the unfinished. This work, perhaps the most significant of our time, consists of the ninth and thirty-eighth chapters of the first

---

* Madame Henri Bachelier also lists a literal translation of Quevedo's literal translation of the *Introduction à la vie dévote* of St. Francis of Sales [*Introduction to the Devout Life* of St. Francis of Sales (1567–1622), Bishop and prince of Geneva]. There are no traces of such a work in Menard's library. It must have been a jest of our friend, misunderstood by the lady.

---

7. Each title, in Spanish and French, respectively, means "Guide to (or Compass for) the Euphuists (or Aesthetes)," by Vasco Mousinho Quevedo (d. 1628), Portuguese poet. **8.** Unidentified, probably fictitious. **9.** "Problems of a Problem" (French). **1.** The Eleatic school of philosophers, including most probably Zeno and Parmenides, flourished in Greece in the 5th century B.C.E. It held that being is the only reality and that plurality, change, and motion are illusory. Among Zeno's arguments against motion, e.g., are these paradoxes: motion cannot begin because a body in motion cannot arrive at another place until it has passed through an unlimited number of places intermediate; Achilles cannot overtake a tortoise, because as often as he reaches the place occupied by the tortoise at some previous moment the tortoise has already left it; a flying arrow is at rest, for it is at every moment in only one place. **2.** "Don't fear, sir, the tortoise" (French). **3.** Bertrand Russell (1872–1970), English philosopher and mathematician. **4.** *La Nouvelle revue Française* (New French review). Pierre-Jean Toulet (1867–1920), French poet. **5.** "The Graveyard by the Sea." Valéry (1871–1945), French poet. **6.** Unidentified, probably fictitious. **7.** Italian poet, novelist, and dramatist (1863–1938).

part of *Don Quixote*[8] and a fragment of chapter twenty-two. I know such an affirmation seems an absurdity; to justify this "absurdity" is the primordial object of this note.*

Two texts of unequal value inspired this undertaking. One is that philological fragment by Novalis[9]—the one numbered 2005 in the Dresden edition—which outlines the theme of a *total* identification with a given author. The other is one of those parasitic books which situate Christ on a boulevard, Hamlet on La Cannebière[1] or Don Quixote on Wall Street. Like all men of good taste, Menard abhorred these useless carnivals, fit only—as he would say—to produce the plebeian pleasure of anachronism or (what is worse) to enthrall us with the elementary idea that all epochs are the same or are different. More interesting, though contradictory and superficial of execution, seemed to him the famous plan of Daudet: to conjoin the Ingenious Gentleman and his squire in *one* figure, which was Tartarin[2] . . . Those who have insinuated that Menard dedicated his life to writing a contemporary *Quixote* calumniate his illustrious memory.

He did not want to compose another *Quixote*—which is easy—but *the Quixote itself.* Needless to say, he never contemplated a mechanical transcription of the original; he did not propose to copy it. His admirable intention was to produce a few pages which would coincide—word for word and line for line—with those of Miguel de Cervantes.

"My intent is no more than astonishing," he wrote me the 30th of September, 1934, from Bayonne. "The final term in a theological or metaphysical demonstration—the objective world, God, causality, the forms of the universe—is no less previous and common than my famed novel. The only difference is that the philosophers publish the intermediary stages of their labor in pleasant volumes and I have resolved to do away with those stages." In truth, not one worksheet remains to bear witness to his years of effort.

The first method he conceived was relatively simple. Know Spanish well, recover the Catholic faith, fight against the Moors or the Turk, forget the history of Europe between the years 1602 and 1918, *be* Miguel de Cervantes. Pierre Menard studied this procedure (I know he attained a fairly accurate command of seventeenth-century Spanish) but discarded it as too easy. Rather as impossible! my reader will say. Granted, but the undertaking was impossible from the very beginning and of all the impossible ways of carrying it out, this was the least interesting. To be, in the twentieth century, a popular novelist of the seventeenth seemed to him a diminution. To be, in some way, Cervantes and reach the *Quixote* seemed less arduous to him—and, consequently, less interesting—than to go on being Pierre Menard and reach the *Quixote* through the experiences of Pierre Menard. (This conviction, we might say in

* I also had the secondary intention of sketching a personal portrait of Pierre Menard. But how could I dare to compete with the golden pages which, I am told, the Baroness de Bacourt is preparing or with the delicate and punctual pencil of Carolus Hourcade?

---

**8.** Classic novel by Miguel de Cervantes (1547-1616).    **9.** Friedrich von (Hardenberg) Novalis (1772–1801), German poet and philosopher.    **1.** Street in Paris, an incongruous or absurd setting for Hamlet.   **2.** Chief character in *Tartarin de Tarascon* (1872) and *Tartarin sur les Alpes* (1885), novels by French writer Alphonse Daudet (1840-1897). *Ingenious Gentleman and his squire:* a reference to Don Quixote and Sancho Panza in Cervantes' *Don Quixote*. Tartarin is, in Daudet's treatment, alternately practical—like Sancho Panza—and recklessly idealistic—like Don Quixote.

passing, made him omit the autobiographical prologue to the second part of *Don Quixote.* To include that prologue would have been to create another character—Cervantes—but it would also have meant presenting the *Quixote* in terms of that character and not of Menard. The latter, naturally, declined that facility.) "My undertaking is not difficult, essentially," I read in another part of his letter. "I should only have to be immortal to carry it out." Shall I confess that I often imagine he did finish it and that I read the *Quixote*—all of it—as if Menard had conceived it? Some nights past, while leafing through chapter XXVI—never essayed by him—I recognized our friend's style and something of his voice in this exceptional phrase: "the river nymphs and the dolorous and humid Echo."[3] This happy conjunction of a spiritual and a physical adjective brought to my mind a verse by Shakespeare which we discussed one afternoon:

> Where a malignant and a turbaned Turk[4] . . .

But why precisely the *Quixote?* our reader will ask. Such a preference, in a Spaniard, would not have been inexplicable; but it is, no doubt, in a Symbolist from Nîmes, essentially a dévoté of Poe, who engendered Baudelaire, who engendered Mallarmé, who engendered Valéry, who engendered Edmond Teste.[5] The aforementioned letter illuminates this point. "The *Quixote*," clarifies Menard, "interests me deeply, but it does not seem—how shall I say it?—inevitable. I cannot imagine the universe without Edgar Allan Poe's exclamation:

> Ah, bear in mind this garden was enchanted![6]

or without the *Bateau ivre* or the *Ancient Mariner,*[7] but I am quite capable of imagining it without the *Quixote.* (I speak, naturally, of my personal capacity and not of those works' historical resonance.) The *Quixote* is a contingent book; the *Quixote* is unnecessary. I can premeditate writing it, I can write it, without falling into a tautology. When I was ten or twelve years old, I read it, perhaps in its entirety. Later, I have reread closely certain chapters, those which I shall not attempt for the time being. I have also gone through the interludes, the plays, the *Galatea,* the exemplary novels, the undoubtedly laborious tribulations of Persiles and Segismunda and the *Viaje del Parnaso*[8] . . . My general recollection of the *Quixote,* simplified by forgetfulness and indifference, can well equal the imprecise and prior image of a book not yet written. Once that image (which no one can legitimately deny me) is postulated, it is certain that

---

**3.** In Greek mythology Hera (Juno), the wife and sister of Zeus, condemned the nymph Echo to never use her tongue again except to repeat what was said to her.  **4.** Shakespeare's *Othello* 5.2.  **5.** A fictional character in *Monsieur Teste,* a novel by Valéry. Edgar Allan Poe (1809–1849), American poet and short-story writer. Charles Baudelaire (1821–1867) and Stéphane Mallarmé (1842–1898), French poets. The names in this sequence are said to engender their successors in the sense that they influenced them and, by their work, provided points for new departures. That the sequence ends with a fictional personage, Monsieur Teste, suggests that both Borges and Pierre Menard—his fictional creation—have been "engendered" by the same ancestors.  **6.** From one of Poe's two poems entitled *To Helen.* This, the lesser known one, is dedicated to Mrs. Sarah Helen Whitman.  **7.** *The Rime of the Ancient Mariner* by the English poet Samuel Taylor Coleridge (1772–1834). *Bateau ivre* ("The Drunken Boat"), by Arthur Rimbaud (1854–1891), a French poet. Both poems and both poets are important forerunners of the literary mode that Menard practices.  **8.** "Voyage to Parnassus" (Spanish). *Galatea* is a novel of Cervantes, first published in 1914. Other allusions in the line are to Cervantes' works.

my problem is a good bit more difficult than Cervantes' was. My obliging predecessor did not refuse the collaboration of chance: he composed his immortal work somewhat *à la diable*,[9] carried along by the inertias of language and invention. I have taken on the mysterious duty of reconstructing literally his spontaneous work. My solitary game is governed by two polar laws. The first permits me to essay variations of a formal or psychological type; the second obliges me to sacrifice these variations to the 'original' text and reason out this annihilation in an irrefutable manner . . . To these artificial hindrances, another—of a congenital kind—must be added. To compose the *Quixote* at the beginning of the seventeenth century was a reasonable undertaking, necessary and perhaps even unavoidable; at the beginning of the twentieth, it is almost impossible. It is not in vain that three hundred years have gone by, filled with exceedingly complex events. Amongst them, to mention only one, is the *Quixote* itself."

In spite of these three obstacles, Menard's fragmentary *Quixote* is more subtle than Cervantes'. The latter, in a clumsy fashion, opposes to the fictions of chivalry the tawdry provincial reality of his country; Menard selects as his "reality" the land of Carmen during the century of Lepanto and Lope de Vega.[1] What a series of *espagnolades* that selection would have suggested to Maurice Barrès or Dr. Rodríguez Larreta![2] Menard eludes them with complete naturalness. In his work there are no gypsy flourishes or conquistadors or mystics or Philip the Seconds or *autos da fé*.[3] He neglects or eliminates local color. This disdain points to a new conception of the historical novel. This disdain condemns *Salammbô*,[4] with no possibility of appeal.

It is no less astounding to consider isolated chapters. For example, let us examine Chapter XXXVIII of the first part, "which treats of the curious discourse of Don Quixote on arms and letters." It is well known that Don Quixote (like Quevedo in an analogous and later passage in *La hora de todos*[5]) decided the debate against letters and in favor of arms. Cervantes was a former soldier: his verdict is understandable. But that Pierre Menard's Don Quixote—a contemporary of *La trahison des clercs*[6] and Bertrand Russell—should fall prey to such nebulous sophistries! Madame Bachelier has seen here an admirable and typical subordination on the part of the author to the hero's psychology; others (not at all perspicaciously), a *transcription* of the *Quixote;* the Baroness de Bacourt, the influence of Nietzsche.[7] To this third interpretation

**9.** "Like the devil" (French), i.e., with inspired haste.   **1.** Spanish dramatist (1562–1635). *Lepanto:* 1571 battle in which a largely Spanish fleet destroyed the Turkish naval power. Thus both references are to the century in which Cervantes lived. Carmen is the Gypsy heroine of a novel by Prosper Merimée (1803–1870), French writer. The novel was made into an immensely popular opera by the composer Georges Bizet (1838–1875).   **2.** Unidentified and possibly fictitious. *Espagnolades:* a French term for a literary work heavily saturated with the local color of Spain. Barrès (1862–1923), French novelist.   **3.** "Acts of the faith" (Portuguese), executions by fire of heretics condemned by the Inquisition. Philip the Second (1527–1598) was a Spanish king, sponsor of the Spanish Inquisition and leader of the Counter Reformation, a movement in opposition to the Protestant Reformation.   **4.** A colorful and detailed historical novel by French writer Gustave Flaubert (1821–1880).   **5.** *La hora de todos y la fortuna con seso:* everyone's hour (or time) and the wit of fortune (Spanish, literal trans.), roughly equivalent to "every dog has his day by the turns of fortune."   **6.** "The Treason of the Intellectuals," by Julien Benda (1867–1956), French essayist who in this book attacks European intellectuals for allowing their talents to be exploited for nationalist political ends.   **7.** Friedrich Nietzsche (1844–1900), German philosopher. The allusion is probably to his idea of "eternal recurrence"—a belief that everything that happens will happen again and again within the frame of eternity, as Menard's *Quixote* recurs after that of Cervantes.

(which I judge to be irrefutable) I am not sure I dare to add a fourth, which concords very well with the almost divine modesty of Pierre Menard: his resigned or ironical habit of propagating ideas which were the strict reverse of those he preferred. (Let us recall once more his diatribe against Paul Valéry in Jacques Reboul's ephemeral Surrealist sheet.) Cervantes' text and Menard's are verbally identical, but the second is almost infinitely richer. (More ambiguous, his detractors will say, but ambiguity is richness.)

It is a revelation to compare Menard's *Don Quixote* with Cervantes'. The latter, for example, wrote (part one, chapter nine):

> . . . truth, whose mother is history, rival of time, depository of deeds, witness of the past, exemplar and adviser to the present, and the future's counselor.

Written in the seventeenth century, written by the "lay genius" Cervantes, this enumeration is a mere rhetorical praise of history. Menard, on the other hand, writes:

> . . . truth, whose mother is history, rival of time, depository of deeds, witness of the past, exemplar and adviser to the present, and the future's counselor.

History, the *mother* of truth: the idea is astounding. Menard, a contemporary of William James,[8] does not define history as an inquiry into reality but as its origin. Historical truth, for him, is not what has happened; it is what we judge to have happened. The final phrases—*exemplar and adviser to the present, and the future's counselor*—are brazenly pragmatic.

The contrast in style is also vivid. The archaic style of Menard—quite foreign, after all—suffers from a certain affectation. Not so that of his forerunner, who handles with ease the current Spanish of his time.

There is no exercise of the intellect which is not, in the final analysis, useless. A philosophical doctrine begins as a plausible description of the universe; with the passage of the years it becomes a mere chapter—if not a paragraph or a name—in the history of philosophy. In literature, this eventual caducity is even more notorious. The *Quixote*—Menard told me—was, above all, an entertaining book; now it is the occasion for patriotic toasts, grammatical insolence and obscene de luxe editions. Fame is a form of incomprehension, perhaps the worst.

There is nothing new in these nihilistic verifications; what is singular is the determination Menard derived from them. He decided to anticipate the vanity awaiting all man's efforts; he set himself to an undertaking which was exceedingly complex and, from the very beginning, futile. He dedicated his scruples and his sleepless nights to repeating an already extant book in an alien tongue. He multiplied draft upon draft, revised tenaciously and tore up thousands of manuscript pages.* He did not let anyone examine these drafts and took care they should not survive him. In vain have I tried to reconstruct them.

---

* I remember his quadricular notebooks, his black crossed-out passages, his peculiar typographical symbols and his insect-like handwriting. In the afternoons he liked to go out for a walk around the outskirts of Nîmes; he would take a notebook with him and make a merry bonfire.

**8.** American pragmatist philosopher (1842–1910).

I have reflected that it is permissible to see in this "final" *Quixote* a kind of palimpsest,[9] through which the traces—tenuous but not indecipherable—of our friend's "previous" writing should be translucently visible. Unfortunately, only a second Pierre Menard, inverting the other's work, would be able to exhume and revive those lost Troys[1] . . .

"Thinking, analyzing, inventing (he also wrote me) are not anomalous acts; they are the normal respiration of the intelligence. To glorify the occasional performance of that function, to hoard ancient and alien thoughts, to recall with incredulous stupor that the *doctor universalis*[2] thought, is to confess our laziness or our barbarity. Every man should be capable of all ideas and I understand that in the future this will be the case."

Menard (perhaps without wanting to) has enriched, by means of a new technique, the halting and rudimentary art of reading: this new technique is that of the deliberate anachronism and the erroneous attribution. This technique, whose applications are infinite, prompts us to go through the *Odyssey* as if it were posterior to the *Aeneid*[3] and the book *Le jardin du Centaure*[4] of Madame Henri Bachelier as if it were by Madame Henri Bachelier. This technique fills the most placid works with adventure. To attribute the *Imitatio Christi* to Louis Ferdinand Céline or to James Joyce,[5] is this not a sufficient renovation of its tenuous spiritual indications?

*For Silvina Ocampo*

1944

---

**9.** A parchment document from which writing has been partially erased to make room for another text. Frequently fragments of the original text are inadvertently combined with the new additions. **1.** Troy, which was destroyed by the Greeks in the Trojan War, has become a conventional symbol of lost cultures. **2.** "The universal doctor" (Latin), a term sometimes applied to the philosophers Aristotle and Thomas Aquinas. **3.** Homer's epic poem *The Odyssey* dates from the 7th or 8th century B.C.E., while Virgil's *Aeneid* was written in the 1st century B.C.E. Borges is playing with anachronism. **4.** "The Centaur's Garden," (French), obviously a fictitious work by a fictitious author. **5.** Céline (pen name for Ferdinand Destouches) (1894–1961) and Joyce (1882–1941) are 20th-century writers. *Imitatio Christi* (The Imitation of Christ) was written by Thomas à Kempis (1380–1471). More anachronism.

# TRUMAN CAPOTE
## *1924–1984*

One of America's true masters of the short story, and a sad example of the destruction of a first-rate talent, Capote is best known for his nonfiction novel, *In Cold Blood* (1966), the story of the 1959 murder of a Holcombe, Kansas, family, the Clutters, by two sociopaths. Born Truman Strekfus Persons in New Orleans, he spent his first years in an unhappy household, and when his parents divorced in 1928, he lived for several years with relatives in Monroeville, Alabama. When his mother remarried and moved with him to New York, he took his stepfather's name. Always flamboyant, frequently outrageous, Capote embraced the world of celebrity so wholeheartedly and with such success that many people knew of him without knowing anything about his work—and his work in the short story is just as fresh today as it was when it first appeared. He died in California, at the age of 59, after years of near-silence and excess: drugs, alcohol, too much of everything. But that delicate boy with the deep understanding of human joys and sorrows, the piercing eye for telling detail, and the perfect pitch, is still very much present in the best of his short fiction, which can be found in his *Collected Stories* (2004).

## Miriam

For several years, Mrs. H. T. Miller had lived alone in a pleasant apartment (two rooms with kitchenette) in a remodeled brownstone near the East River. She was a widow: Mr. H. T. Miller had left a reasonable amount of insurance. Her interests were narrow, she had no friends to speak of, and she rarely journeyed farther than the corner grocery. The other people in the house never seemed to notice her: her clothes were matter-of-fact, her hair iron-gray, clipped and casually waved; she did not use cosmetics, her features were plain and inconspicuous, and on her last birthday she was sixty-one. Her activities were seldom spontaneous: she kept the two rooms immaculate, smoked an occasional cigarette, prepared her own meals and tended a canary.

Then she met Miriam. It was snowing that night. Mrs. Miller had finished drying the supper dishes and was thumbing through an afternoon paper when she saw an advertisement of a picture playing at a neighborhood theater. The title sounded good, so she struggled into her beaver coat, laced her galoshes and left the apartment, leaving one light burning in the foyer: she found nothing more disturbing than a sensation of darkness.

The snow was fine, falling gently, not yet making an impression on the pavement. The wind from the river cut only at street crossings. Mrs. Miller hurried, her head bowed, oblivious as a mole burrowing a blind path. She stopped at a drugstore and bought a package of peppermints.

A long line stretched in front of the box office; she took her place at the end. There would be (a tired voice groaned) a short wait for all seats. Mrs. Miller rummaged in her leather handbag till she collected exactly the correct change for admission. The line seemed to be taking its own time and, looking around for some distraction, she suddenly became conscious of a little girl standing under the edge of the marquee.

Her hair was the longest and strangest Mrs. Miller had ever seen: absolutely silver-white, like an albino's. It flowed waist-length in smooth, loose lines. She was thin and fragilely constructed. There was a simple, special elegance in the way she stood with her thumbs in the pockets of a tailored plum-velvet coat.

Mrs. Miller felt oddly excited, and when the little girl glanced toward her, she smiled warmly. The little girl walked over and said, "Would you care to do me a favor?"

"I'd be glad to, if I can," said Mrs. Miller.

"Oh, it's quite easy. I merely want you to buy a ticket for me; they won't let me in otherwise. Here, I have the money." And gracefully she handed Mrs. Miller two dimes and a nickel.

They went over to the theater together. An usherette directed them to a lounge; in twenty minutes the picture would be over.

"I feel just like a genuine criminal," said Mrs. Miller gaily, as she sat down. "I mean, that sort of thing's against the law, isn't it? I do hope I haven't done the wrong thing. Your mother knows where you are, dear? I mean she does, doesn't she?"

The little girl said nothing. She unbuttoned her coat and folded it across her lap. Her dress underneath was prim and dark blue. A gold chain dangled about her neck, and her fingers, sensitive and musical-looking, toyed with it. Examining her more attentively, Mrs. Miller decided the truly distinctive feature was not her hair, but her eyes; they were hazel, steady, lacking any childlike quality whatsoever and, because of their size, seemed to consume her small face.

Mrs. Miller offered a peppermint. "What's your name, dear?"

"Miriam," she said, as though, in some curious way, it were information already familiar.

"Why, isn't that funny—my name's Miriam, too. And it's not a terribly common name either. Now, don't tell me your last name's Miller!"

"Just Miriam."

"But isn't that funny?"

"Moderately," said Miriam, and rolled the peppermint on her tongue.

Mrs. Miller flushed and shifted uncomfortably. "You have such a large vocabulary for such a little girl."

"Do I?"

"Well, yes," said Mrs. Miller, hastily changing the topic to: "Do you like the movies?"

"I really wouldn't know," said Miriam. "I've never been before."

Women began filling the lounge; the rumble of the newsreel bombs exploded in the distance. Mrs. Miller rose, tucking her purse under her arm. "I guess I'd better be running now if I want to get a seat," she said. "It was nice to have met you."

Miriam nodded ever so slightly.

It snowed all week. Wheels and footsteps moved soundlessly on the street, as if the business of living continued secretly behind a pale but impenetrable curtain. In the falling quiet there was no sky or earth, only snow lifting in the wind, frosting the window glass, chilling the rooms, deadening and hushing the city. At all hours it was necessary to keep a lamp lighted, and Mrs. Miller lost track of the days: Friday was no different from Saturday and on Sunday she went to the grocery: closed, of course.

That evening she scrambled eggs and fixed a bowl of tomato soup. Then, after putting on a flannel robe and cold-creaming her face, she propped herself up in bed with a hot-water bottle under her feet. She was reading the *Times* when the doorbell rang. At first she thought it must be a mistake and whoever it was would go away. But it rang and rang and settled to a persistent buzz. She looked at the clock: a little after eleven; it did not seem possible, she was always asleep by ten.

Climbing out of bed, she trotted barefoot across the living room. "I'm coming, please be patient." The latch was caught; she turned it this way and that way and the bell never paused an instant. "Stop it," she cried. The bolt gave way and she opened the door an inch. "What in heaven's name?"

"Hello," said Miriam.

"Oh ... why, hello," said Mrs. Miller, stepping hesitantly into the hall. "You're that little girl."

"I thought you'd never answer, but I kept my finger on the button; I knew you were home. Aren't you glad to see me?"

Mrs. Miller did not know what to say. Miriam, she saw, wore the same plum-velvet coat and now she had also a beret to match; her white hair was braided in two shining plaits and looped at the ends with enormous white ribbons.

"Since I've waited so long, you could at least let me in," she said.

"It's awfully late. . . ."

Miriam regarded her blankly. "What difference does that make? Let me in. It's cold out here and I have on a silk dress." Then, with a gentle gesture, she urged Mrs. Miller aside and passed into the apartment.

She dropped her coat and beret on a chair. She was indeed wearing a silk dress. White silk. White silk in February. The skirt was beautifully pleated and the sleeves long; it made a faint rustle as she strolled about the room. "I like your place," she said. "I like the rug, blue's my favorite color." She touched a paper rose in a vase on the coffee table. "Imitation," she commented wanly. "How sad. Aren't imitations sad?" She seated herself on the sofa, daintily spreading her skirt.

"What do you want?" asked Mrs. Miller.

"Sit down," said Miriam. "It makes me nervous to see people stand."

Mrs. Miller sank to a hassock. "What do you want?" she repeated.

"You know, I don't think you're glad I came."

For a second time Mrs. Miller was without an answer; her hand motioned vaguely. Miriam giggled and pressed back on a mound of chintz pillows. Mrs. Miller observed that the girl was less pale than she remembered; her cheeks were flushed.

"How did you know where I lived?"

Miriam frowned. "That's no question at all. What's your name? What's mine?"

"But I'm not listed in the phone book."

"Oh, let's talk about something else."

Mrs. Miller said, "Your mother must be insane to let a child like you wander around at all hours of the night—and in such ridiculous clothes. She must be out of her mind."

Miriam got up and moved to a corner where a covered birdcage hung from a ceiling chain. She peeked beneath the cover. "It's a canary," she said. "Would you mind if I woke him? I'd like to hear him sing."

"Leave Tommy alone," said Mrs. Miller anxiously. "Don't you dare wake him."

"Certainly," said Miriam. "But I don't see why I can't hear him sing." And then, "Have you anything to eat? I'm starving! Even milk and a jam sandwich would be fine."

"Look," said Mrs. Miller, arising from the hassock, "look—if I make some nice sandwiches will you be a good child and run along home? It's past midnight, I'm sure."

"It's snowing," reproached Miriam. "And cold and dark."

"Well, you shouldn't have come here to begin with," said Mrs. Miller, struggling to control her voice. "I can't help the weather. If you want anything to eat, you'll have to promise to leave."

Miriam brushed a braid against her cheek. Her eyes were thoughtful, as if weighing the proposition. She turned toward the birdcage. "Very well," she said, "I promise."

*How old is she? Ten? Eleven?* Mrs. Miller, in the kitchen, unsealed a jar of strawberry preserves and cut four slices of bread. She poured a glass of milk and paused to light a cigarette. *And why has she come?* Her hand shook as she held the match, fascinated, till it burned her finger. The canary was singing; singing as he did in the morning and at no other time. "Miriam," she called, "Miriam, I told you not to disturb Tommy." There was no answer. She called again; all she heard was the canary. She inhaled the cigarette and discovered she had lighted the cork-tip end and—oh, really, she mustn't lose her temper.

She carried the food in on a tray and set it on the coffee table. She saw first that the birdcage still wore its night cover. And Tommy was singing. It gave her a queer sensation. And no one was in the room. Mrs. Miller went through an alcove leading to her bedroom; at the door she caught her breath.

"What are you doing?" she asked.

Miriam glanced up and in her eyes there was a look that was not ordinary. She was standing by the bureau, a jewel case opened before her. For a minute she studied Mrs. Miller, forcing their eyes to meet, and she smiled. "There's nothing good here," she said. "But I like this." Her hand held a cameo brooch. "It's charming."

"Suppose—perhaps you'd better put it back," said Mrs. Miller, feeling suddenly the need of some support. She leaned against the door frame; her head was unbearably heavy; a pressure weighted the rhythm of her heartbeat. The light seemed to flutter defectively. "Please, child—a gift from my husband . . ."

"But it's beautiful and I want it," said Miriam. *"Give it to me."*

As she stood, striving to shape a sentence which would somehow save the brooch, it came to Mrs. Miller there was no one to whom she might turn; she was alone; a fact that had not been among her thoughts for a long time. Its sheer emphasis was stunning. But here in her own room in the hushed snow-city were evidences she could not ignore or, she knew with startling clarity, resist.

Miriam ate ravenously, and when the sandwiches and milk were gone, her fingers made cobweb movements over the plate, gathering crumbs. The cameo gleamed on her blouse, the blond profile like a trick reflection of its wearer. "That was very nice," she sighed, "though now an almond cake or a cherry would be ideal. Sweets are lovely, don't you think?"

Mrs. Miller was perched precariously on the hassock, smoking a cigarette. Her hairnet had slipped lopsided and loose strands straggled down her face. Her eyes were stupidly concentrated on nothing and her cheeks were mottled in red patches, as though a fierce slap had left permanent marks.

"Is there a candy—a cake?"

Mrs. Miller tapped ash on the rug. Her head swayed slightly as she tried to focus her eyes. "You promised to leave if I made the sandwiches," she said.

"Dear me, did I?"

"It was a promise and I'm tired and I don't feel well at all."

"Mustn't fret," said Miriam. "I'm only teasing."

She picked up her coat, slung it over her arm, and arranged her beret in front of a mirror. Presently she bent close to Mrs. Miller and whispered, "Kiss me good night."

"Please—I'd rather not," said Mrs. Miller.

Miriam lifted a shoulder, arched an eyebrow. "As you like," she said, and went directly to the coffee table, seized the vase containing the paper roses, carried it to where the hard surface of the floor lay bare, and hurled it downward. Glass sprayed in all directions and she stamped her foot on the bouquet.

Then slowly she walked to the door, but before closing it, she looked back at Mrs. Miller with a slyly innocent curiosity.

Mrs. Miller spent the next day in bed, rising once to feed the canary and drink a cup of tea; she took her temperature and had none, yet her dreams were feverishly agitated; their unbalanced mood lingered even as she lay staring wide-eyed at the ceiling. One dream threaded through the others like an elusively mysterious theme in a complicated symphony, and the scenes it depicted were sharply outlined, as though sketched by a hand of gifted intensity: a small girl, wearing a bridal gown and a wreath of leaves, led a gray procession down a mountain path, and among them there was unusual silence till a woman at the rear asked, "Where is she taking us?" "No one knows," said an old man marching in front. "But isn't she pretty?" volunteered a third voice. "Isn't she like a frost flower . . . so shining and white?"

Tuesday morning she woke up feeling better; harsh slats of sunlight, slanting through Venetian blinds, shed a disrupting light on her unwholesome fancies. She opened the window to discover a thawed, mild-as-spring day; a sweep of clean new clouds crumpled against a vastly blue, out-of-season sky; and across the low line of rooftops she could see the river and smoke curving from tugboat stacks in a warm wind. A great silver truck plowed the snow-banked street, its machine sound humming on the air.

After straightening the apartment, she went to the grocer's, cashed a check and continued to Schrafft's, where she ate breakfast and chatted happily with the waitress. Oh, it was a wonderful day—more like a holiday—and it would be so foolish to go home.

She boarded a Lexington Avenue bus and rode up to Eighty-sixth Street; it was here that she had decided to do a little shopping.

She had no idea what she wanted or needed, but she idled along, intent only upon the passers-by, brisk and preoccupied, who gave her a disturbing sense of separateness.

It was while waiting at the corner of Third Avenue that she saw the man: an old man, bowlegged and stooped under an armload of bulging packages; he wore a shabby brown coat and a checkered cap. Suddenly she realized they were exchanging a smile: there was nothing friendly about this smile, it was merely two cold flickers of recognition. But she was certain she had never seen him before.

He was standing next to an El[1] pillar, and as she crossed the street he turned and followed. He kept quite close; from the corner of her eye she watched his reflection wavering on the shopwindows.

Then in the middle of the block she stopped and faced him. He stopped also and cocked his head, grinning. But what could she say? Do? Here, in broad daylight, on Eighty-sixth Street? It was useless and, despising her own helplessness, she quickened her steps.

Now Second Avenue is a dismal street, made from scraps and ends; part cobblestone, part asphalt, part cement; and its atmosphere of desertion is permanent. Mrs. Miller walked five blocks without meeting anyone, and all the while the steady crunch of his footfalls in the snow stayed near. And when she came to a florist's shop, the sound was still with her. She hurried inside and watched through the glass door as the old man passed; he kept his eyes straight ahead and didn't slow his pace, but he did one strange, telling thing: he tipped his cap.

"Six white ones, did you say?" asked the florist. "Yes," she told him, "white roses." From there she went to a glassware store and selected a vase, presumably a replacement for the one Miriam had broken, though the price was intolerable and the vase itself (she thought) grotesquely vulgar. But a series of unaccountable purchases had begun, as if by prearranged plan: a plan of which she had not the least knowledge or control.

She bought a bag of glazed cherries, and at a place called the Knickerbocker Bakery she paid forty cents for six almond cakes.

---

**1.** Elevated railroad.

Within the last hour the weather had turned cold again; like blurred lenses, winter clouds cast a shade over the sun, and the skeleton of an early dusk colored the sky; a damp mist mixed with the wind and the voices of a few children who romped high on mountains of gutter snow seemed lonely and cheerless. Soon the first flake fell, and when Mrs. Miller reached the brownstone house, snow was falling in a swift screen and foot tracks vanished as they were printed.

The white roses were arranged decoratively in the vase. The glazed cherries shone on a ceramic plate. The almond cakes, dusted with sugar, awaited a hand. The canary fluttered on its swing and picked at a bar of seed.

At precisely five the doorbell rang. Mrs. Miller *knew* who it was. The hem of her housecoat trailed as she crossed the floor. "Is that you?" she called.

"Naturally," said Miriam, the word resounding shrilly from the hall. "Open this door."

"Go away," said Mrs. Miller.

"Please hurry . . . I have a heavy package."

"Go away," said Mrs. Miller. She returned to the living room, lighted a cigarette, sat down and calmly listened to the buzzer; on and on and on. "You might as well leave. I have no intention of letting you in."

Shortly the bell stopped. For possibly ten minutes Mrs. Miller did not move. Then, hearing no sound, she concluded Miriam had gone. She tiptoed to the door and opened it a sliver; Miriam was half-reclining atop a cardboard box with a beautiful French doll cradled in her arms.

"Really, I thought you were never coming," she said peevishly. "Here, help me get this in, it's awfully heavy."

It was not spell-like compulsion that Mrs. Miller felt, but rather a curious passivity; she brought in the box, Miriam, the doll. Miriam curled up on the sofa, not troubling to remove her coat or beret, and watched disinterestedly as Mrs. Miller dropped the box and stood trembling, trying to catch her breath.

"Thank you," she said. In the daylight she looked pinched and drawn, her hair less luminous. The French doll she was loving wore an exquisite powdered wig and its idiot glass eyes sought solace in Miriam's. "I have a surprise," she continued. "Look into my box."

Kneeling, Mrs. Miller parted the flaps and lifted out another doll; then a blue dress which she recalled as the one Miriam had worn that first night at the theater; and of the remainder she said, "It's all clothes. Why?"

"Because I've come to live with you," said Miriam, twisting a cherry stem. "Wasn't it nice of you to buy me the cherries . . . ?"

"But you can't! For God's sake go away—go away and leave me alone!"

". . . and the roses and the almond cakes? How really wonderfully generous. You know, these cherries are delicious. The last place I lived was with an old man; he was terribly poor and we never had good things to eat. But I think I'll be happy here." She paused to snuggle her doll closer. "Now, if you'll just show me where to put my things . . ."

Mrs. Miller's face dissolved into a mask of ugly red lines; she began to cry, and it was an unnatural, tearless sort of weeping, as though, not having wept for a long time, she had forgotten how. Carefully she edged backward till she touched the door.

She fumbled through the hall and down the stairs to a landing below. She pounded frantically on the door of the first apartment she came to; a short, redheaded man answered and she pushed past him. "Say, what the hell is this?" he said. "Anything wrong, lover?" asked a young woman who appeared from the kitchen, drying her hands. And it was to her that Mrs. Miller turned.

"Listen," she cried, "I'm ashamed behaving this way but—well, I'm Mrs. H. T. Miller and I live upstairs and . . ." She pressed her hands over her face. "It sounds so absurd. . . ."

The woman guided her to a chair, while the man excitedly rattled pocket change. "Yeah?"

"I live upstairs and there's a little girl visiting me, and I suppose that I'm afraid of her. She won't leave and I can't make her and—she's going to do something terrible. She's already stolen my cameo, but she's about to do something worse—something terrible!"

The man asked, "Is she a relative, huh?"

Mrs. Miller shook her head. "I don't know who she is. Her name's Miriam, but I don't know for certain who she is."

"You gotta calm down, honey," said the woman, stroking Mrs. Miller's arm. "Harry here'll tend to this kid. Go on, lover." And Mrs. Miller said, "The door's open—5A."

After the man left, the woman brought a towel and bathed Mrs. Miller's face. "You're very kind," Mrs. Miller said. "I'm sorry to act like such a fool, only this wicked child . . ."

"Sure, honey," consoled the woman. "Now, you better take it easy."

Mrs. Miller rested her head in the crook of her arm; she was quiet enough to be asleep. The woman turned a radio dial; a piano and a husky voice filled the silence and the woman, tapping her foot, kept excellent time. "Maybe we oughta go up too," she said.

"I don't want to see her again. I don't want to be anywhere near her."

"Uh huh, but what you shoulda done, you shoulda called a cop."

Presently they heard the man on the stairs. He strode into the room frowning and scratching the back of his neck. "Nobody there," he said, honestly embarrassed. "She musta beat it."

"Harry, you're a jerk," announced the woman. "We been sitting here the whole time and we woulda seen . . ." she stopped abruptly, for the man's glance was sharp.

"I looked all over," he said, "and there just ain't nobody there. Nobody, understand?"

"Tell me," said Mrs. Miller, rising, "tell me, did you see a large box? Or a doll?"

"No, ma'am, I didn't."

And the woman, as if delivering a verdict, said, "Well, for cryinout-loud. . . ."

Mrs. Miller entered her apartment softly; she walked to the center of the room and stood quite still. No, in a sense it had not changed: the roses, the cakes, and the cherries were in place. But this was an empty room, emptier than if the furnishings and familiars were not present, lifeless and petrified as a funeral parlor. The sofa loomed before her with a new strangeness: its vacancy had a meaning that would have been less penetrating and terrible had Miriam been curled on it. She gazed fixedly at the space where she remembered setting the box and, for a moment, the hassock spun desperately. And she looked through the window; surely the river was real, surely snow was falling—but then, one could not be certain witness to anything: Miriam, so vividly there—and yet, where was she? Where, where?

As though moving in a dream, she sank to a chair. The room was losing shape; it was dark and getting darker and there was nothing to be done about it; she could not lift her hand to light a lamp.

Suddenly, closing her eyes, she felt an upward surge, like a diver emerging from some deeper, greener depth. In times of terror or immense distress, there are moments when the mind waits, as though for a revelation, while a skein of calm is woven over thought; it is like a sleep, or a supernatural trance; and during this lull one is aware of a force of quiet reasoning: well, what if she had never really known a girl named Miriam? that she had been foolishly frightened on the street? In the end, like everything else, it was of no importance. For the only thing she had lost to Miriam was her identity, but now she knew she had found again the person who lived in this room, who cooked her own meals, who owned a canary, who was someone she could trust and believe in: Mrs. H. T. Miller.

Listening in contentment, she became aware of a double sound: a bureau drawer opening and closing; she seemed to hear it long after completion—opening and closing. Then gradually, the harshness of it was replaced by the murmur of a silk dress and this, delicately faint, was moving nearer and swelling in intensity till the walls trembled with the vibration and the room was caving under a wave of whispers. Mrs. Miller stiffened and opened her eyes to a dull, direct stare.

"Hello," said Miriam.

1945

# RAYMOND CARVER
## 1938–1988

Carver was born in Clatskanie, Oregon, and attended Humboldt State University in California before going on to graduate work at the University of Iowa. For several years he taught writing at Syracuse University. In the late 1970s his poetry and fiction, much of it describing working-class life in the Pacific Northwest, marked him as one of the more noteworthy talents of his generation. Carver's spare, direct "minimalist" style continues to spawn imitators decades after his death from lung cancer at the age of 50. His stories are collected in *Will You Please Be Quiet, Please?* (1978), *What We Talk about When We Talk about Love* (1981), *Cathedral* (1983), and *Where I'm Calling From: New and Selected Stories* (1988).

# Cathedral

This blind man, an old friend of my wife's, he was on his way to spend the night. His wife had died. So he was visiting the dead wife's relatives in Connecticut. He called my wife from his in-laws'. Arrangements were made. He would come by train, a five-hour trip, and my wife would meet him at the station. She hadn't seen him since she worked for him one summer in Seattle ten years ago. But she and the blind man had kept in touch. They made tapes and mailed them back and forth. I wasn't enthusiastic about his visit. He was no one I knew. And his being blind bothered me. My idea of blindness came from the movies. In the movies, the blind moved slowly and never laughed. Sometimes they were led by seeing-eye dogs. A blind man in my house was not something I looked forward to.

That summer in Seattle she had needed a job. She didn't have any money. The man she was going to marry at the end of the summer was in officers' training school. He didn't have any money, either. But she was in love with the guy, and he was in love with her, etc. She'd seen something in the paper: HELP WANTED—*Reading to Blind Man*, and a telephone number. She phoned and went over, was hired on the spot. She'd worked with this blind man all summer. She read stuff to him, case studies, reports, that sort of thing. She helped him organize his little office in the county social-service department. They'd become good friends, my wife and the blind man. How do I know these things? She told me. And she told me something else. On her last day in the office, the blind man asked if he could touch her face. She agreed to this. She told me he touched his fingers to every part of her face, her nose—even her neck! She never forgot it. She even tried to write a poem about it. She was always trying to write a poem. She wrote a poem or two every year, usually after something really important had happened to her.

When we first started going out together, she showed me the poem. In the poem, she recalled his fingers and the way they had moved around over her face. In the poem, she talked about what she had felt at the time, about what went through her mind when the blind man touched her nose and lips. I can remember I didn't think much of the poem. Of course, I didn't tell her that. Maybe I just don't understand poetry. I admit it's not the first thing I reach for when I pick up something to read.

Anyway, this man who'd first enjoyed her favors, the officer-to-be, he'd been her childhood sweetheart. So okay. I'm saying that at the end of the summer she let the blind man run his hands over her face, said goodbye to him, married her childhood etc., who was now a commissioned officer, and she moved away from Seattle. But they'd kept in touch, she and the blind man. She made the first contact after a year or so. She called him up one night from an Air Force base in Alabama. She wanted to talk. They talked. He asked her to send him a tape and tell him about her life. She did this. She sent the tape. On the tape, she told the blind man about her husband and about their life together in the military. She told the blind man she loved her husband but she didn't like it where they lived and she didn't like it that he was a part of the military-industrial thing. She told the blind man she'd written a poem about what it was like to be an Air Force officer's wife. The poem wasn't finished yet. She was still writing it. The blind man made a tape. He sent her the tape. She made a tape. This went on for years. My wife's officer was posted to one base and then another. She sent tapes from Moody AFB, McGuire, McConnell, and finally Travis, near Sacramento, where one night she got to feeling lonely and cut off from people she kept losing in that moving-around life. She got to feeling she couldn't go it another step. She went in and swallowed all the pills and capsules in the medicine chest and washed them down with a bottle of gin. Then she got into a hot bath and passed out.

But instead of dying, she got sick. She threw up. Her officer—why should he have a name? he was the childhood sweetheart, and what more does he want?—came home from somewhere, found her, and called the ambulance. In time, she put it all on a tape and sent the tape to the blind man. Over the years, she put all kinds of stuff on tapes and sent the tapes off lickety-split. Next to writing a poem every year, I think it was her chief means of recreation. On one tape, she told the blind man she'd decided to live away from her officer for a time. On another tape, she told him about her divorce. She and I began going out, and of course she told her blind man about it. She told him everything, or so it seemed to me. Once she asked me if I'd like to hear the latest tape from the blind man. This was a year ago. I was on the tape, she said. So I said okay, I'd listen to it. I got us drinks and we settled down in the living room. We made ready to listen. First she inserted the tape into the player and adjusted a couple of dials. Then she pushed a lever. The tape squeaked and someone began to talk in this loud voice. She lowered the volume. After a few minutes of harmless chitchat, I heard my own name in the mouth of this stranger, this blind man I didn't even know! And then this: "From all you've said about him, I can only conclude—" But we were interrupted, a knock at the door, something, and we didn't ever get back to the tape. Maybe it was just as well. I'd heard all I wanted to.

Now this same blind man was coming to sleep in my house.

"Maybe I could take him bowling," I said to my wife. She was at the draining board doing scalloped potatoes. She put down the knife she was using and turned around.

"If you love me," she said, "you can do this for me. If you don't love me, okay. But if you had a friend, any friend, and the friend came to visit, I'd make him feel comfortable." She wiped her hands with the dish towel.

"I don't have any blind friends," I said.

"You don't have *any* friends," she said. "Period. Besides," she said, "goddamn it, his wife's just died! Don't you understand that? The man's lost his wife!"

I didn't answer. She'd told me a little about the blind man's wife. Her name was Beulah. Beulah! That's a name for a colored woman.

"Was his wife a Negro?" I asked.

"Are you crazy?" my wife said. "Have you just flipped or something?" She picked up a potato. I saw it hit the floor, then roll under the stove. "What's wrong with you?" she said. "Are you drunk?"

"I'm just asking," I said.

Right then my wife filled me in with more detail than I cared to know. I made a drink and sat at the kitchen table to listen. Pieces of the story began to fall into place.

Beulah had gone to work for the blind man the summer after my wife had stopped working for him. Pretty soon Beulah and the blind man had themselves a church wedding. It was a little wedding—who'd want to go to such a wedding in the first place?—just the two of them, plus the minister and the minister's wife. But it was a church wedding just the same. It was what Beulah had wanted, he'd said. But even then Beulah must have been carrying the cancer in her glands. After they had been inseparable for eight years—my wife's word, *inseparable*—Beulah's health went into a rapid decline. She died in a Seattle hospital room, the blind man sitting beside the bed and holding on to her hand. They'd married, lived and worked together, slept together—had sex, sure—and then the blind man had to bury her. All this without his having ever seen what the goddamned woman looked like. It was beyond my understanding. Hearing this, I felt sorry for the blind man for a little bit. And then I found myself thinking what a pitiful life this woman must have led. Imagine a woman who could never see herself as she was seen in the eyes of her loved one. A woman who could go on day after day and never receive the smallest compliment from her beloved. A woman whose husband could never read the expression on her face, be it misery or something better. Someone who could wear makeup or not—what difference to him? She could, if she wanted, wear green eye-shadow around one eye, a straight pin in her nostril, yellow slacks and purple shoes, no matter. And then to slip off into death, the blind man's hand on her hand, his blind eyes streaming tears—I'm imagining now—her last thought maybe this: that he never even knew what she looked like, and she on an express to the grave. Robert was left with a small insurance policy and half of a twenty-peso Mexican coin. The other half of the coin went into the box with her. Pathetic.

So when the time rolled around, my wife went to the depot to pick him up. With nothing to do but wait—sure, I blamed him for that—I was having a drink and watching the TV when I heard the car pull into the drive. I got up from the sofa with my drink and went to the window to have a look.

I saw my wife laughing as she parked the car. I saw her get out of the car and shut the door. She was still wearing a smile. Just amazing. She went around to the other side of the car to where the blind man was already starting to get out. This blind man, feature this, he was wearing a full beard! A beard on a blind man! Too much, I say. The blind man reached into the back seat and dragged out a suitcase. My wife took his arm, shut the car door, and, talking all the way, moved him down the drive and then up the steps to the front porch. I turned off the TV. I finished my drink, rinsed the glass, dried my hands. Then I went to the door.

My wife said, "I want you to meet Robert. Robert, this is my husband. I've told you all about him." She was beaming. She had this blind man by his coat sleeve.

The blind man let go of his suitcase and up came his hand.

I took it. He squeezed hard, held my hand, and then he let it go.

"I feel like we've already met," he boomed.

"Likewise," I said. I didn't know what else to say. Then I said, "Welcome. I've heard a lot about you." We began to move then, a little group, from the porch into the living room, my wife guiding him by the arm. The blind man was carrying his suitcase in his other hand. My wife said things like, "To your left here, Robert. That's right. Now watch it, there's a chair. That's it. Sit down right here. This is the sofa. We just bought this sofa two weeks ago."

I started to say something about the old sofa. I'd liked that old sofa. But I didn't say anything. Then I wanted to say something else, small-talk, about the scenic ride along the Hudson. How going *to* New York, you should sit on the right-hand side of the train, and coming *from* New York, the left-hand side.

"Did you have a good train ride?" I said. "Which side of the train did you sit on, by the way?"

"What a question, which side!" my wife said. "What's it matter which side?" she said.

"I just asked," I said.

"Right side," the blind man said. "I hadn't been on a train in nearly forty years. Not since I was a kid. With my folks. That's been a long time. I'd nearly forgotten the sensation. I have winter in my beard now," he said. "So I've been told, anyway. Do I look distinguished, my dear?" the blind man said to my wife.

"You look distinguished, Robert," she said. "Robert," she said. "Robert, it's just so good to see you."

My wife finally took her eyes off the blind man and looked at me. I had the feeling she didn't like what she saw. I shrugged.

I've never met, or personally known, anyone who was blind. This blind man was late forties, a heavy-set, balding man with stooped shoulders, as if he carried a great weight there. He wore brown slacks, brown shoes, a light-brown shirt, a tie, a sports coat. Spiffy. He also had this full beard. But he didn't use a cane and he didn't wear dark glasses. I'd always thought dark glasses were a must for the blind. Fact was, I wished he had a pair. At first glance, his eyes looked like anyone else's eyes. But if you looked close, there was something different about them. Too much white in the iris, for one thing, and the pupils seemed to move around in the sockets without his knowing it or being able to stop it. Creepy. As I stared at his face, I saw the left pupil turn in toward his nose while the other made an effort to keep in one place. But it was only an effort, for that eye was on the roam without his knowing it or wanting it to be.

I said, "Let me get you a drink. What's your pleasure? We have a little of everything. It's one of our pastimes."

"Bub, I'm a Scotch man myself," he said fast enough in this big voice.

"Right," I said. Bub! "Sure you are. I knew it."

He let his fingers touch his suitcase, which was sitting alongside the sofa. He was taking his bearings. I didn't blame him for that.

"I'll move that up to your room," my wife said.

"No, that's fine," the blind man said loudly. "It can go up when I go up."

"A little water with the Scotch?" I said.

"Very little," he said.

"I knew it," I said.

He said, "Just a tad. The Irish actor, Barry Fitzgerald? I'm like that fellow. When I drink water, Fitzgerald said, I drink water. When I drink whiskey, I drink whiskey." My wife laughed. The blind man brought his hand up under his beard. He lifted his beard slowly and let it drop.

I did the drinks, three big glasses of Scotch with a splash of water in each. Then we made ourselves comfortable and talked about Robert's travels. First the long flight from the West Coast to Connecticut, we covered that. Then from Connecticut up here by train. We had another drink concerning that leg of the trip.

I remembered having read somewhere that the blind didn't smoke because, as speculation had it, they couldn't see the smoke they exhaled. I thought I knew that much and that much only about blind people. But this blind man smoked his cigarette down to the nubbin and then lit another one. This blind man filled his ashtray and my wife emptied it.

When we sat down at the table for dinner, we had another drink. My wife heaped Robert's plate with cube steak, scalloped potatoes, green beans. I buttered him up two slices of bread. I said, "Here's bread and butter for you." I swallowed some of my drink. "Now let us pray," I said, and the blind man lowered his head. My wife looked at me, her mouth agape. "Pray the phone won't ring and the food doesn't get cold," I said.

We dug in. We ate everything there was to eat on the table. We ate like there was no tomorrow. We didn't talk. We ate. We scarfed. We grazed that table. We were into serious eating. The blind man had right away located his foods, he knew just where everything was on his plate. I watched with admiration as he used his knife and fork on the meat. He'd cut two pieces of meat, fork the meat into his mouth, and then go all out for the scalloped potatoes, the beans next, and then he'd tear off a hunk of buttered bread and eat that. He'd follow this up with a big drink of milk. It didn't seem to bother him to use his fingers once in a while, either.

We finished everything, including half a strawberry pie. For a few moments, we sat as if stunned. Sweat beaded on our faces. Finally, we got up from the table and left the dirty plates. We didn't look back. We took ourselves into the living room and sank into our places again. Robert and my wife sat on the sofa. I took the big chair. We had us two or three more drinks while they talked about the major things that had come to pass for them in the past ten years. For the most part, I just listened. Now and then I joined in. I didn't want him to think I'd left the room, and I didn't want her to think I was feeling left out. They talked of things that had happened to them—to them!—these past ten years. I waited in vain to hear my name on my wife's sweet lips: "And then my dear husband came into my life"—something like that. But I heard nothing of the sort. More talk of Robert. Robert had done a little of everything, it seemed, a regular blind jack-of-all-trades. But most recently he and his wife had had an Amway distributorship, from which, I gathered, they'd earned their living, such as it was. The blind man was also a ham radio operator. He talked in his loud voice about conversations he'd had with fellow operators in Guam, in the Philippines, in Alaska, and even in Tahiti. He said he'd have a lot of friends there if he ever wanted to go visit those places. From time to time, he'd turn his blind face toward me, put his hand under his beard, ask me something. How long had I been in my present position? (Three years.) Did I like my work? (I didn't.) Was I going to stay with it? (What were the options?) Finally, when I thought he was beginning to run down, I got up and turned on the TV.

My wife looked at me with irritation. She was heading toward a boil. Then she looked at the blind man and said, "Robert, do you have a TV?"

The blind man said, "My dear, I have two TVs. I have a color set and a black-and-white thing, an old relic. It's funny, but if I turn the TV on, and I'm always turning it on, I turn on the color set. It's funny, don't you think?"

I didn't know what to say to that. I had absolutely nothing to say to that. No opinion. So I watched the news program and tried to listen to what the announcer was saying.

"This is a color TV," the blind man said. "Don't ask me how, but I can tell."

"We traded up a while ago," I said.

The blind man had another taste of his drink. He lifted his beard, sniffed it, and let it fall. He leaned forward on the sofa. He positioned his ashtray on the coffee table, then put the lighter to his cigarette. He leaned back on the sofa and crossed his legs at the ankles.

My wife covered her mouth, and then she yawned. She stretched. She said, "I think I'll go upstairs and put on my robe. I think I'll change into something else. Robert, you make yourself comfortable," she said.

"I'm comfortable," the blind man said.

"I want you to feel comfortable in this house," she said.

"I am comfortable," the blind man said.

After she'd left the room, he and I listened to the weather report and then to the sports roundup. By that time, she'd been gone so long I didn't know if she was going to come back. I thought she might have gone to bed. I wished she'd come back downstairs. I didn't want to be left alone with a blind man. I asked him if he wanted to smoke some dope with me. I said I'd just rolled a number. I hadn't, but I planned to do so in about two shakes.

"I'll try some with you," he said.

"Damn right," I said. "That's the stuff."

I got our drinks and sat down on the sofa with him. Then I rolled us two fat numbers. I lit one and passed it. I brought it to his fingers. He took it and inhaled.

"Hold it as long as you can," I said. I could tell he didn't know the first thing.

My wife came back downstairs wearing her pink robe and her pink slippers.

"What do I smell?" she said.

"We thought we'd have us some cannabis," I said.

My wife gave me a savage look. Then she looked at the blind man and said, "Robert, I didn't know you smoked."

He said, "I do now, my dear. There's a first time for everything. But I don't feel anything yet."

"This stuff is pretty mellow," I said. "This stuff is mild. It's dope you can reason with," I said. "It doesn't mess you up."

"Not much it doesn't, bub," he said, and laughed.

My wife sat on the sofa between the blind man and me. I passed her the number. She took it and toked and then passed it back to me. "Which way is this going?" she said. Then she said, "I shouldn't be smoking this. I can hardly keep my eyes open as it is. That dinner did me in. I shouldn't have eaten so much."

"It was the strawberry pie," the blind man said. "That's what did it," he said, and he laughed his big laugh. Then he shook his head.

"There's more strawberry pie," I said.

"Do you want some more, Robert?" my wife said.

"Maybe in a little while," he said.

We gave our attention to the TV. My wife yawned again. She said, "Your bed is made up when you feel like going to bed, Robert. I know you must have had a long day. When you're ready to go to bed, say so." She pulled his arm. "Robert?"

He came to and said, "I've had a real nice time. This beats tapes, doesn't it?"

I said, "Coming at you," and I put the number between his fingers. He inhaled, held the smoke, and then let it go. It was like he'd been doing it since he was nine years old.

"Thanks, bub," he said. "But I think this is all for me. I think I'm beginning to feel it," he said. He held the burning roach out for my wife.

"Same here," she said. "Ditto. Me, too." She took the roach and passed it to me. "I may just sit here for a while between you two guys with my eyes closed. But don't let me bother you, okay? Either one of you. If it bothers you, say so. Otherwise, I may just sit here with my eyes closed until you're ready to go to bed," she said. "Your bed's made up, Robert, when you're ready. It's right next to our room at the top of the stairs. We'll show you up when you're ready. You wake me up now, you guys, if I fall asleep." She said that and then she closed her eyes and went to sleep.

The news program ended. I got up and changed the channel. I sat back down on the sofa. I wished my wife hadn't pooped out. Her head lay across the back of the sofa, her mouth open. She'd turned so that her robe had slipped away from her legs, exposing a juicy thigh. I reached to draw her robe back over her, and it was then that I glanced at the blind man. What the hell! I flipped the robe open again.

"You say when you want some strawberry pie," I said.

"I will," he said.

I said, "Are you tired? Do you want me to take you up to your bed? Are you ready to hit the hay?"

"Not yet," he said. "No, I'll stay up with you, bub. If that's all right. I'll stay up until you're ready to turn in. We haven't had a chance to talk. Know what I mean? I feel like me and her monopolized the evening." He lifted his beard and he let it fall. He picked up his cigarettes and lighter.

"That's all right," I said. Then I said, "I'm glad for the company."

And I guess I was. Every night I smoked dope and stayed up as long as I could before I fell asleep. My wife and I hardly ever went to bed at the same time. When I did go to sleep, I had these dreams. Sometimes I'd wake up from one of them, my heart going crazy.

Something about the church and the Middle Ages was on the TV. Not your run-of-the-mill TV fare. I wanted to watch something else. I turned to the other channels. But there was nothing on them, either. So I turned back to the first channel and apologized.

"Bub, it's all right," the blind man said. "It's fine with me. Whatever you want to watch is okay. I'm always learning something. Learning never ends. It won't hurt me to learn something tonight. I got ears," he said.

We didn't say anything for a time. He was leaning forward with his head turned at me, his right ear aimed in the direction of the set. Very disconcerting. Now and then his eyelids dropped and then they snapped open again. Now and then he put his fingers into his beard and tugged, like he was thinking about something he was hearing on the television.

On the screen, a group of men wearing cowls was being set upon and tormented by men dressed in skeleton costumes and men dressed as devils. The men dressed as devils wore devil masks, horns, and long tails. This pageant was part of a procession. The Englishman who was narrating the thing said it took place in Spain once a year. I tried to explain to the blind man what was happening.

"Skeletons," he said. "I know about skeletons," he said, and he nodded.

The TV showed this one cathedral. Then there was a long, slow look at another one. Finally, the picture switched to the famous one in Paris,[1] with its flying buttresses and its spires reaching up to the clouds. The camera pulled away to show the whole of the cathedral rising above the skyline.

There were times when the Englishman who was telling the thing would shut up, would simply let the camera move around over the cathedrals. Or else the camera would tour the countryside, men in fields walking behind oxen. I waited as long as I could. Then I felt I had to say something. I said, "They're showing the outside of this cathedral now. Gargoyles. Little statues carved to look like monsters. Now I guess they're in Italy. Yeah, they're in Italy. There's paintings on the walls of this one church."

---

**1.** Notre Dame de Paris, begun in 1163 and completed nearly two centuries later.

"Are those fresco paintings, bub?" he asked, and he sipped from his drink.

I reached for my glass. But it was empty. I tried to remember what I could remember. "You're asking me are those frescoes?" I said. "That's a good question. I don't know."

The camera moved to a cathedral outside Lisbon. The differences in the Portuguese cathedral compared with the French and Italian were not that great. But they were there. Mostly the interior stuff. Then something occurred to me, and I said, "Something has occurred to me. Do you have any idea what a cathedral is? What they look like, that is? Do you follow me? If somebody says cathedral to you, do you have any notion what they're talking about? Do you know the difference between that and a Baptist church, say?"

He let the smoke dribble from his mouth. "I know they took hundreds of workers fifty or a hundred years to build," he said. "I just heard the man say that, of course. I know generations of the same families worked on a cathedral. I heard him say that, too. The men who began their life's work on them, they never lived to see the completion of their work. In that wise, bub, they're no different from the rest of us, right?" He laughed. Then his eyelids drooped again. His head nodded. He seemed to be snoozing. Maybe he was imagining himself in Portugal. The TV was showing another cathedral now. This one was in Germany. The Englishman's voice droned on. "Cathedrals," the blind man said. He sat up and rolled his head back and forth. "If you want the truth, bub, that's about all I know. What I just said. What I heard him say. But maybe you could describe one to me? I wish you'd do it. I'd like that. If you want to know, I really don't have a good idea."

I stared hard at the shot of the cathedral on the TV. How could I even begin to describe it? But say my life depended on it. Say my life was being threatened by an insane guy who said I had to do it or else.

I stared some more at the cathedral before the picture flipped off into the countryside. There was no use. I turned to the blind man and said, "To begin with, they're very tall." I was looking around the room for clues. "They reach way up. Up and up. Toward the sky. They're so big, some of them, they have to have these supports. To help hold them up, so to speak. These supports are called buttresses. They remind me of viaducts, for some reason. But maybe you don't know viaducts, either? Sometimes the cathedrals have devils and such carved into the front. Sometimes lords and ladies. Don't ask me why this is," I said.

He was nodding. The whole upper part of his body seemed to be moving back and forth.

"I'm not doing so good, am I?" I said.

He stopped nodding and leaned forward on the edge of the sofa. As he listened to me, he was running his fingers through his beard. I wasn't getting through to him, I could see that. But he waited for me to go on just the same. He nodded, like he was trying to encourage me. I tried to think what else to say. "They're really big," I said. "They're massive. They're built of stone. Marble, too, sometimes. In those olden days, when they built cathedrals, men wanted to be close to God. In those olden days, God was an important part of everyone's life. You could tell this from their cathedral-building. I'm sorry," I said, "but it looks like that's the best I can do for you. I'm just no good at it."

"That's all right, bub," the blind man said. "Hey, listen. I hope you don't mind my asking you. Can I ask you something? Let me ask you a simple question, yes or no. I'm just curious and there's no offense. You're my host. But let me ask if you are in any way religious? You don't mind my asking?"

I shook my head. He couldn't see that, though. A wink is the same as a nod to a blind man. "I guess I don't believe in it. In anything. Sometimes it's hard. You know what I'm saying?"

"Sure, I do," he said.

"Right," I said.

The Englishman was still holding forth. My wife sighed in her sleep. She drew a long breath and went on with her sleeping.

"You'll have to forgive me," I said. "But I can't tell you what a cathedral looks like. It just isn't in me to do it. I can't do any more than I've done."

The blind man sat very still, his head down, as he listened to me.

I said, "The truth is, cathedrals don't mean anything special to me. Nothing. Cathedrals. They're something to look at on late-night TV. That's all they are."

It was then that the blind man cleared his throat. He brought something up. He took a handkerchief from his back pocket. Then he said, "I get it, bub. It's okay. It happens. Don't worry about it," he said. "Hey, listen to me. Will you do me a favor? I got an idea. Why don't you find us some heavy paper? And a pen. We'll do something. We'll draw one together. Get us a pen and some heavy paper. Go on, bub, get the stuff," he said.

So I went upstairs. My legs felt like they didn't have any strength in them. They felt like they did after I'd done some running. In my wife's room, I looked around. I found some ballpoints in a little basket on her table. And then I tried to think where to look for the kind of paper he was talking about.

Downstairs, in the kitchen, I found a shopping bag with onion skins at the bottom of the bag. I emptied the bag and shook it. I brought it into the living room and sat down with it near his legs. I moved some things, smoothed the wrinkles from the bag, spread it out on the coffee table.

The blind man got down from the sofa and sat next to me on the carpet.

He ran his fingers over the paper. He went up and down the sides of the paper. The edges, even the edges. He fingered the corners.

"All right," he said. "All right, let's do her."

He found my hand, the hand with the pen. He closed his hand over my hand. "Go ahead, bub, draw," he said. "Draw. You'll see. I'll follow along with you. It'll be okay. Just begin now like I'm telling you. You'll see. Draw," the blind man said.

So I began. First I drew a box that looked like a house. It could have been the house I lived in. Then I put a roof on it. At either end of the roof, I drew spires. Crazy.

"Swell," he said. "Terrific. You're doing fine," he said. "Never thought anything like this could happen in your lifetime, did you, bub? Well, it's a strange life, we all know that. Go on now. Keep it up."

I put in windows with arches. I drew flying buttresses. I hung great doors. I couldn't stop. The TV station went off the air. I put down the pen and closed and opened my fingers. The blind man felt around over the paper. He moved the tips of his fingers over the paper, all over what I had drawn, and he nodded.

"Doing fine," the blind man said.

I took up the pen again, and he found my hand. I kept at it. I'm no artist. But I kept drawing just the same.

My wife opened up her eyes and gazed at us. She sat up on the sofa, her robe hanging open. She said, "What are you doing? Tell me, I want to know."

I didn't answer her.

The blind man said, "We're drawing a cathedral. Me and him are working on it. Press hard," he said to me. "That's right. That's good," he said. "Sure. You got it, bub. I can tell. You didn't think you could. But you can, can't you? You're cooking with gas now. You know what I'm saying? We're going to really have us something here in a minute. How's the old arm?" he said. "Put some people in there now. What's a cathedral without people?"

My wife said, "What's going on? Robert, what are you doing? What's going on?"

"It's all right," he said to her. "Close your eyes now," the blind man said to me. I did it. I closed them just like he said.

"Are they closed?" he said. "Don't fudge."

"They're closed," I said.

"Keep them that way," he said. He said, "Don't stop now. Draw."

So we kept on with it. His fingers rode my fingers as my hand went over the paper. It was like nothing else in my life up to now.

Then he said, "I think that's it. I think you got it," he said. "Take a look. What do you think?"

But I had my eyes closed. I thought I'd keep them that way for a little longer. I thought it was something I ought to do.

"Well?" he said. "Are you looking?"

My eyes were still closed. I was in my house. I knew that. But I didn't feel like I was inside anything.

"It's really something," I said.

1983

# WILLA CATHER
## 1873–1947

Cather was born of Anglo-Irish parents in Back Creek Valley, Virginia. At ten she moved with her family to Red Cloud, Nebraska, where she grew up, exploring the prairies on horseback and making friends with the immigrant farmers of the area. While she worked her way through the University of Nebraska, she acquired an enduring passion for music and determined to devote her energies to writing. From 1896 to 1905 she worked for a newspaper in Pittsburgh, and she later held editorial positions in New York, but her poetry and fiction looked to the Midwest and Southwest for their subject matter and to the depths of the American past for their values. She never married. The last part of her life was spent in New York, with occasional European travels that never swayed her from nostalgia or the conservatism of her views. Once she declared that the world had "broken apart" in about 1922; unmistakably, she preferred the manners, styles, and virtues that prevailed before that date—which was, incidentally, the year in which she was awarded the Pulitzer Prize for her novel *One of Ours*. Among her best-known novels are *My Ántonia* (1918), *A Lost Lady* (1923), *The Professor's House* (1925), and *Death Comes for the Archbishop* (1927). *Not under Forty* (1936) contains many of her essays. Her collections of short stories are *Youth and the Bright Medusa* (1920), *Obscure Destinies* (1932), and *The Old Beauty and Others* (1948).

## Paul's Case

### A Study in Temperament

It was Paul's afternoon to appear before the faculty of the Pittsburgh High School to account for his various misdemeanors. He had been suspended a week ago, and his father had called at the Principal's office and confessed his perplexity about his son. Paul entered the faculty room suave and smiling. His clothes were a trifle outgrown, and the tan velvet on the collar of his open overcoat was frayed and worn; but for all that there was something of the dandy about him, and he wore an opal pin in his neatly knotted black four-in-hand,[1] and a red carnation in his buttonhole. This latter adornment the faculty somehow felt was not properly significant of the contrite spirit befitting a boy under the ban of suspension.

Paul was tall for his age and very thin, with high, cramped shoulders and a narrow chest. His eyes were remarkable for a certain hysterical brilliancy, and

---

1. The long necktie we are now familiar with.

he continually used them in a conscious, theatrical sort of way, peculiarly offensive in a boy. The pupils were abnormally large, as though he were addicted to belladonna, but there was a glassy glitter about them which that drug does not produce.

When questioned by the Principal as to why he was there Paul stated, politely enough, that he wanted to come back to school. This was a lie, but Paul was quite accustomed to lying; found it, indeed, indispensable for overcoming friction. His teachers were asked to state their respective charges against him, which they did with such a rancor and aggrievedness as evinced that this was not a usual case. Disorder and impertinence were among the offenses named, yet each of his instructors felt that it was scarcely possible to put into words the real cause of the trouble, which lay in a sort of hysterically defiant manner of the boy's; in the contempt which they all knew he felt for them, and which he seemingly made not the least effort to conceal. Once, when he had been making a synopsis of a paragraph at the blackboard, his English teacher had stepped to his side and attempted to guide his hand. Paul had started back with a shudder and thrust his hands violently behind him. The astonished woman could scarcely have been more hurt and embarrassed had he struck at her. The insult was so involuntary and definitely personal as to be unforgettable. In one way and another he had made all his teachers, men and women alike, conscious of the same feeling of physical aversion. In one class he habitually sat with his hand shading his eyes; in another he always looked out of the window during the recitation; in another he made a running commentary on the lecture, with humorous intention.

His teachers felt this afternoon that his whole attitude was symbolized by his shrug and his flippantly red carnation flower, and they fell upon him without mercy, his English teacher leading the pack. He stood through it smiling, his pale lips parted over his white teeth. (His lips were continually twitching, and he had a habit of raising his eyebrows that was contemptuous and irritating to the last degree.) Older boys than Paul had broken down and shed tears under that baptism of fire, but his set smile did not once desert him, and his only sign of discomfort was the nervous trembling of the fingers that toyed with the buttons of his overcoat, and an occasional jerking of the other hand that held his hat. Paul was always smiling, always glancing about him, seeming to feel that people might be watching him and trying to detect something. This conscious expression, since it was as far as possible from boyish mirthfulness, was usually attributed to insolence or "smartness."

As the inquisition proceeded one of his instructors repeated an impertinent remark of the boy's, and the Principal asked him whether he thought that a courteous speech to have made a woman. Paul shrugged his shoulders slightly and his eyebrows twitched.

"I don't know," he replied. "I didn't mean to be polite or impolite, either. I guess it's a sort of way I have of saying things regardless."

The Principal, who was a sympathetic man, asked him whether he didn't think that a way it would be well to get rid of. Paul grinned and said he guessed so. When he was told that he could go he bowed gracefully and went out. His bow was but a repetition of the scandalous red carnation.

His teachers were in despair, and his drawing master voiced the feeling of them all when he declared there was something about the boy which none of them understood. He added: "I don't really believe that smile of his comes altogether from insolence; there's something sort of haunted about it. The boy is not strong, for one thing. I happen to know that he was born in Colorado, only a few months before his mother died out there of a long illness. There is something wrong about the fellow."

The drawing master had come to realize that, in looking at Paul, one saw only his white teeth and the forced animation of his eyes. One warm afternoon the boy had gone to sleep at his drawing board, and his master had noted with amazement what a white, blue-veined face it was; drawn and wrinkled like an old man's about the eyes, the lips twitching even in his sleep, and stiff with a nervous tension that drew them back from his teeth.

His teachers left the building dissatisfied and unhappy; humiliated to have felt so vindictive toward a mere boy, to have uttered this feeling in cutting terms, and to have set each other on, as it were, in the gruesome game of intemperate reproach. Some of them remembered having seen a miserable street cat set at bay by a ring of tormentors.

As for Paul, he ran down the hill whistling the "Soldiers' Chorus" from *Faust*,[2] looking wildly behind him now and then to see whether some of his teachers were not there to writhe under his lightheartedness. As it was now late in the afternoon and Paul was on duty that evening as usher at Carnegie Hall,[3] he decided that he would not go home to supper. When he reached the concert hall the doors were not yet open and, as it was chilly outside, he decided to go up into the picture gallery—always deserted at this hour— where there were some of Raffaelli's[4] gay studies of Paris streets and an airy blue Venetian scene or two that always exhilarated him. He was delighted to find no one in the gallery but the old guard, who sat in one corner, a newspaper on his knee, a black patch over one eye and the other closed. Paul possessed himself of the place and walked confidently up and down, whistling under his breath. After a while he sat down before a blue Rico[5] and lost himself. When he bethought him to look at his watch, it was after seven o'clock, and he rose with a start and ran downstairs, making a face at Augustus, peering out from the cast room, and an evil gesture at the Venus de Milo[6] as he passed her on the stairway.

When Paul reached the ushers' dressing room half a dozen boys were there already, and he began excitedly to tumble into his uniform. It was one of the few that at all approached fitting, and Paul thought it very becoming—though he knew that the tight, straight coat accentuated his narrow chest, about which he was exceedingly sensitive. He was always considerably excited while he dressed, twanging all over to the tuning of the strings and the preliminary flourishes of the horns in the music room; but tonight he seemed quite beside himself, and he teased and plagued the boys until, telling him that he was crazy, they put him down on the floor and sat on him.

Somewhat calmed by his suppression, Paul dashed out to the front of the house to seat the early comers. He was a model usher; gracious and smiling he ran up and down the aisles; nothing was too much trouble for him; he carried

**2.** Opera by Charles Gounod (1818–1893). **3.** Pittsburgh theater named for Andrew Carnegie (1835– 1919), famous industrialist and philanthropist. **4.** Jean-François Raffaëlli (1850–1924), French painter, sculptor, and etcher. **5.** Andreas Rico (1500–1550), Cretan-Italian painter. **6.** A famous Greek statue; the original is in the Louvre, Paris. Augustus (63 B.C.E.–C.E. 14) was the first Roman emperor.

messages and brought programs as though it were his greatest pleasure in life, and all the people in his section thought him a charming boy, feeling that he remembered and admired them. As the house filled, he grew more and more vivacious and animated, and the color came to his cheeks and lips. It was very much as though this were a great reception and Paul were the host. Just as the musicians came out to take their places, his English teacher arrived with checks for the seats which a prominent manufacturer had taken for the season. She betrayed some embarrassment when she handed Paul the tickets, and a hauteur which subsequently made her feel very foolish. Paul was startled for a moment, and had the feeling of wanting to put her out; what business had she here among all these fine people and gay colors? He looked her over and decided that she was not appropriately dressed and must be a fool to sit downstairs in such togs. The tickets had probably been sent her out of kindness, he reflected as he put down a seat for her, and she had about as much right to sit there as he had.

When the symphony began Paul sank into one of the rear seats with a long sigh of relief, and lost himself, as he had done before the Rico. It was not that symphonies, as such, meant anything in particular to Paul, but the first sigh of the instruments seemed to free some hilarious and potent spirit within him; something that struggled there like the genie in the bottle found by the Arab fisherman.[7] He felt a sudden zest of life; the lights danced before his eyes and the concert hall blazed into unimaginable splendor. When the soprano soloist came on Paul forgot even the nastiness of his teacher's being there and gave himself up to the peculiar stimulus such personages always had for him. The soloist chanced to be a German woman, by no means in her first youth, and the mother of many children; but she wore an elaborate gown and tiara, and above all she had that indefinable air of achievement, that worldshine upon her, which, in Paul's eyes, made her a veritable queen of Romance.

After a concert was over Paul was always irritable and wretched until he got to sleep, and tonight he was even more than usually restless. He had the feeling of not being able to let down, of its being impossible to give up this delicious excitement which was the only thing that could be called living at all. During the last number he withdrew and, after hastily changing his clothes in the dressing room, slipped out to the side door where the soprano's carriage stood. Here he began pacing rapidly up and down the walk, waiting to see her come out.

Over yonder, the Schenley, in its vacant stretch, loomed big and square through the fine rain, the windows of its twelve stories glowing like those of a lighted cardboard house under a Christmas tree. All the actors and singers of the better class stayed there when they were in the city, and a number of the big manufacturers of the place lived there in the winter. Paul had often hung about the hotel, watching the people go in and out, longing to enter and leave schoolmasters and dull care behind him forever.

At last the singer came out, accompanied by the conductor, who helped her into her carriage and closed the door with a cordial *auf wiedersehen*[8] which set Paul to wondering whether she were not an old sweetheart of his. Paul fol-

---

7. In one of the tales of the *Arabian Nights* (also called *Thousand and One Nights*), the fisherman Ali Baba finds a genie imprisoned in a bottle who is able to perform miracles.   8. Good-bye (German).

lowed the carriage over to the hotel, walking so rapidly as not to be far from
the entrance when the singer alighted, and disappeared behind the swinging
glass doors that were opened by a Negro in a tall hat and a long coat. In the
moment that the door was ajar it seemed to Paul that he, too, entered. He
seemed to feel himself go after her up the steps, into the warm, lighted building, into an exotic, tropical world of shiny, glistening surfaces and basking
ease. He reflected upon the mysterious dishes that were brought into the dining room, the green bottles in buckets of ice, as he had seen them in the supper party pictures of the *Sunday World* supplement. A quick gust of wind
brought the rain down with sudden vehemence, and Paul was startled to find
that he was still outside in the slush of the gravel driveway; that his boots
were letting in the water and his scanty overcoat was clinging wet about him;
that the lights in front of the concert hall were out and that the rain was driving in sheets between him and the orange glow of the windows above him.
There it was, what he wanted—tangibly before him, like the fairy world of a
Christmas pantomime—but mocking spirits stood guard at the doors, and,
as the rain beat in his face, Paul wondered whether he were destined always to
shiver in the black night outside, looking up at it.

He turned and walked reluctantly toward the car[9] tracks. The end had to
come sometime; his father in his nightclothes at the top of the stairs, explanations that did not explain, hastily improvised fictions that were forever tripping him up, his upstairs room and its horrible yellow wallpaper, the creaking
bureau with the greasy plush collarbox, and over his painted wooden bed the
pictures of George Washington and John Calvin,[1] and the framed motto,
"Feed my Lambs," which had been worked in red worsted[2] by his mother.

Half an hour later Paul alighted from his car and went slowly down one of
the side streets off the main thoroughfare. It was a highly respectable street,
where all the houses were exactly alike, and where businessmen of moderate
means begot and reared large families of children, all of whom went to Sabbath school and learned the shorter catechism, and were interested in arithmetic; all of whom were as exactly alike as their homes, and of a piece with the
monotony in which they lived. Paul never went up Cordelia Street without a
shudder of loathing. His home was next to the house of the Cumberland[3]
minister. He approached it tonight with the nerveless sense of defeat, the hopeless feeling of sinking back forever into ugliness and commonness that he
had always had when he came home. The moment he turned into Cordelia
Street he felt the waters close above his head. After each of these orgies of living
he experienced all the physical depression which follows a debauch; the loathing of respectable beds, of common food, of a house penetrated by kitchen
odors; a shuddering repulsion for the flavorless, colorless mass of everyday
existence; a morbid desire for cool things and soft lights and fresh flowers.

The nearer he approached the house, the more absolutely unequal Paul felt
to the sight of it all: his ugly sleeping chamber; the cold bathroom with the
grimy zinc tub, the cracked mirror, the dripping spigots; his father, at the top
of the stairs, his hairy legs sticking out from his nightshirt, his feet thrust into
carpet slippers. He was so much later than usual that there would certainly
be inquiries and reproaches. Paul stopped short before the door. He felt that

---

**9.** That is, streetcar.  **1.** French Protestant reformer who lived in Geneva (1509–1564).  **2.** That is,
embroidered with red wool.  **3.** A division of the Presbyterian Church in the United States.

he could not be accosted by his father tonight; that he could not toss again on that miserable bed. He would not go in. He would tell his father that he had no carfare and it was raining so hard he had gone home with one of the boys and stayed all night.

Meanwhile, he was wet and cold. He went around to the back of the house and tried one of the basement windows, found it open, raised it cautiously, and scrambled down the cellar wall to the floor. There he stood, holding his breath, terrified by the noise he had made, but the floor above him was silent, and there was no creak on the stairs. He found a soapbox, and carried it over to the soft ring of light that streamed from the furnace door, and sat down. He was horribly afraid of rats, so he did not try to sleep, but sat looking distrustfully at the dark, still terrified lest he might have awakened his father. In such reactions, after one of the experiences which made days and nights out of the dreary blanks of the calendar, when his senses were deadened, Paul's head was always singularly clear. Suppose his father had heard him getting in at the window and had come down and shot him for a burglar? Then, again, suppose his father had come down, pistol in hand, and he had cried out in time to save himself, and his father had been horrified to think how nearly he had killed him? Then, again, suppose a day should come when his father would remember that night, and wish there had been no warning cry to stay his hand? With this last supposition Paul entertained himself until daybreak.

The following Sunday was fine; the sodden November chill was broken by the last flash of autumnal summer. In the morning Paul had to go to church and Sabbath school, as always. On seasonable Sunday afternoons the burghers of Cordelia Street always sat out on their front stoops and talked to their neighbors on the next stoop, or called to those across the street in neighborly fashion. The men usually sat on gay cushions placed upon the steps that led down to the sidewalk, while the women, in their Sunday "waists,"[4] sat in rockers on the cramped porches, pretending to be greatly at their ease. The children played in the streets; there were so many of them that the place resembled the recreation grounds of a kindergarten. The men on the steps—all in their shirt sleeves their vests unbuttoned—sat with their legs well apart, their stomachs comfortably protruding, and talked of the prices of things, or told anecdotes of the sagacity of their various chiefs and overlords. They occasionally looked over the multitude of squabbling children, listened affectionately to their high-pitched, nasal voices, smiling to see their own proclivities reproduced in their offspring, and interspersed their legends of the iron kings[5] with remarks about their sons' progress at school, their grades in arithmetic, and the amounts they had saved in their toy banks.

On this last Sunday of November Paul sat all the afternoon on the lowest step of his stoop, staring into the street, while his sisters, in their rockers, were talking to the minister's daughters next door about how many shirtwaists they had made in the last week, and how many waffles someone had eaten at the last church supper. When the weather was warm, and his father was in a particularly jovial frame of mind, the girls made lemonade, which was always brought out in a red-glass pitcher, ornamented with forget-me-nots in blue enamel. This the girls thought very fine, and the neighbors always joked about the suspicious color of the pitcher.

---

4. Bodices or blouses.    5. Tycoons of the iron and steel industry.

Today Paul's father sat on the top step, talking to a young man who shifted a restless baby from knee to knee. He happened to be the young man who was daily held up to Paul as a model, and after whom it was his father's dearest hope that he would pattern. This young man was of a ruddy complexion, with a compressed, red mouth, and faded, nearsighted eyes, over which he wore thick spectacles, with gold bows that curved about his ears. He was clerk to one of the magnates of a great steel corporation, and was looked upon in Cordelia Street as a young man with a future. There was a story that, some five years ago—he was now barely twenty-six—he had been a trifle dissipated, but in order to curb his appetites and save the loss of time and strength that a sowing of wild oats might have entailed, he had taken his chief's advice, oft reiterated to his employees, and at twenty-one had married the first woman whom he could persuade to share his fortunes. She happened to be an angular schoolmistress, much older than he, who also wore thick glasses, and who had now borne him four children, all nearsighted, like herself.

The young man was relating how his chief, now cruising in the Mediterranean, kept in touch with all the details of the business, arranging his office hours on his yacht just as though he were at home, and "knocking off work enough to keep two stenographers busy." His father told, in turn, the plan his corporation was considering, of putting in an electric railway plant in Cairo. Paul snapped his teeth; he had an awful apprehension that they might spoil it all before he got there. Yet he rather liked to hear these legends of the iron kings that were told and retold on Sundays and holidays; these stories of palaces in Venice, yachts on the Mediterranean, and high play at Monte Carlo appealed to his fancy, and he was interested in the triumphs of these cash boys who had become famous, though he had no mind for the cash-boy stage.

After supper was over and he had helped to dry the dishes, Paul nervously asked his father whether he could go to George's to get some help in his geometry, and still more nervously asked for carfare. This latter request he had to repeat, as his father, on principle, did not like to hear requests for money, whether much or little. He asked Paul whether he could not go to some boy who lived nearer, and told him that he ought not to leave his schoolwork until Sunday; but he gave him the dime. He was not a poor man, but he had a worthy ambition to come up in the world. His only reason for allowing Paul to usher was that he thought a boy ought to be earning a little.

Paul bounded upstairs, scrubbed the greasy odor of the dishwater from his hands with the ill-smelling soap he hated, and then shook over his fingers a few drops of violet water from the bottle he kept hidden in his drawer. He left the house with his geometry conspicuously under his arm, and the moment he got out of Cordelia Street and boarded a downtown car, he shook off the lethargy of two deadening days and began to live again.

The leading juvenile[6] of the permanent stock company which played at one of the downtown theaters was an acquaintance of Paul's, and the boy had been invited to drop in at the Sunday-night rehearsals whenever he could. For more than a year Paul had spent every available moment loitering about Charley Edwards's dressing room. He had won a place among Edwards's following not only because the young actor, who could not afford to employ a dresser, often

---

**6.** Youthful male actor.

found him useful, but because he recognized in Paul something akin to what churchmen term "vocation."

It was at the theater and at Carnegie Hall that Paul really lived; the rest was but a sleep and a forgetting. This was Paul's fairy tale, and it had for him all the allurement of a secret love. The moment he inhaled the gassy, painty, dusty odor behind the scenes, he breathed like a prisoner set free, and felt within him the possibility of doing or saying splendid, brilliant, poetic things. The moment the cracked orchestra beat out the overture from *Martha*, or jerked at the serenade from *Rigoletto*,[7] all stupid and ugly things slid from him, and his senses were deliciously, yet delicately fired.

Perhaps it was because, in Paul's world, the natural nearly always wore the guise of ugliness, that a certain element of artificiality seemed to him necessary in beauty. Perhaps it was because his experience of life elsewhere was so full of Sabbath-school picnics, petty economies, wholesome advice as to how to succeed in life, and the inescapable odors of cooking, that he found this existence so alluring, these smartly clad men and women so attractive, that he was so moved by these starry apple orchards that bloomed perennially under the limelight.

It would be difficult to put it strongly enough how convincingly the stage entrance of that theater was for Paul the actual portal of Romance. Certainly none of the company ever suspected it, least of all Charley Edwards. It was very like the old stories that used to float about London of fabulously rich Jews, who had subterranean halls there, with palms, and fountains, and soft lamps and richly appareled women who never saw the disenchanting light of London day. So, in the midst of that smoke-palled city, enamored of figures and grimy toil, Paul had his secret temple, his wishing carpet, his bit of blue-and-white Mediterranean shore bathed in perpetual sunshine.

Several of Paul's teachers had a theory that his imagination had been perverted by garish fiction but the truth was that he scarcely ever read at all. The books at home were not such as would either tempt or corrupt a youthful mind, and as for reading the novels that some of his friends urged upon him— well, he got what he wanted much more quickly from music; any sort of music, from an orchestra to a barrel organ. He needed only the spark, the indescribable thrill that made his imagination master of his senses, and he could make plots and pictures enough of his own. It was equally true that he was not stagestruck—not, at any rate, in the usual acceptation of that expression. He had no desire to become an actor, any more than he had to become a musician. He felt no necessity to do any of these things; what he wanted was to see, to be in the atmosphere, float on the wave of it, to be carried out, blue league after blue league, away from everything.

After a night behind the scenes Paul found the schoolroom more than ever repulsive; the bare floors and naked walls; the prosy men who never wore frock coats, or violets in their bottonholes; the women with their dull gowns, shrill voices, and pitiful seriousness about prepositions that govern the dative. He could not bear to have the other pupils think, for a moment, that he took these people seriously; he must convey to them that he considered it all trivial, and was there only by way of a jest, anyway. He had autographed pictures of all the

---

7. Operas by Friedrich von Flotow (1812–1883) and Giuseppe Verdi (1813–1901).

members of the stock company which he showed his classmates, telling them the most incredible stories of his familiarity with these people, of his acquaintance with the soloists who came to Carnegie Hall, his suppers with them and the flowers he sent them. When these stories lost their effect, and his audience grew listless, he became desperate and would bid all the boys good-by, announcing that he was going to travel for a while; going to Naples, to Venice, to Egypt. Then, next Monday, he would slip back, conscious and nervously smiling; his sister was ill, and he should have to defer his voyage until spring.

Matters went steadily worse with Paul at school. In the itch to let his instructors know how heartily he despised them and their homilies, and how thoroughly he was appreciated elsewhere, he mentioned once or twice that he had no time to fool with theorems; adding—with a twitch of the eyebrows and a touch of that nervous bravado which so perplexed them—that he was helping the people down at the stock company; they were old friends of his.

The upshot of the matter was that the Principal went to Paul's father, and Paul was taken out of school and put to work. The manager at Carnegie Hall was told to get another usher in his stead; the doorkeeper at the theater was warned not to admit him to the house; and Charley Edwards remorsefully promised the boy's father not to see him again.

The members of the stock company were vastly amused when some of Paul's stories reached them—especially the women. They were hard-working women, most of them supporting indigent husbands or brothers, and they laughed rather bitterly at having stirred the boy to such fervid and florid inventions. They agreed with the faculty and with his father that Paul's was a bad case.

The eastbound train was plowing through a January snowstorm; the dull dawn was beginning to show gray when the engine whistled a mile out of Newark.[8] Paul started up from the seat where he had lain curled in uneasy slumber, rubbed the breath-misted window glass with his hand, and peered out. The snow was whirling in curling eddies above the white bottom lands, and the drifts lay already deep in the fields and along the fences, while here and there the long dead grass and dried weed stalks protruded black above it. Lights shone from the scattered houses, and a gang of laborers who stood beside the track waved their lanterns.

Paul had slept very little, and he felt grimy and uncomfortable. He had made the all-night journey in a day coach, partly because he was ashamed, dressed as he was, to go into a Pullman, and partly because he was afraid of being seen there by some Pittsburgh businessman, who might have noticed him in Denny & Carson's office. When the whistle awoke him, he clutched quickly at his breast pocket, glancing about him with an uncertain smile. But the little, clay-bespattered Italians were still sleeping, the slatternly women across the aisle were in open-mouthed oblivion, and even the crumby, crying babies were for the nonce stilled. Paul settled back to struggle with his impatience as best he could.

When he arrived at the Jersey City station he hurried through his breakfast, manifestly ill at ease and keeping a sharp eye about him. After he reached the Twenty-third Street station,[9] he consulted a cabman and had himself driven

8. City in New Jersey just outside New York City.  9. Railway terminal in Manhattan.

to a men's-furnishings establishment that was just opening for the day. He spent upward of two hours, buying with endless reconsidering and great care. His new street suit he put on in the fitting room; the frock coat and dress clothes he had bundled into the cab with his linen. Then he drove to a hatter's and a shoe house. His next errand was at Tiffany's, where he selected his silver and a new scarf pin. He would not wait to have his silver marked,[1] he said. Lastly, he stopped at a trunk shop on Broadway and had his purchases packed into various traveling bags.

It was a little after one o'clock when he drove up to the Waldorf,[2] and after settling with the cabman, went into the office. He registered from Washington; said his mother and father had been abroad, and that he had come down to await the arrival of their steamer. He told his story plausibly and had no trouble, since he volunteered to pay for them in advance, in engaging his rooms; a sleeping room, sitting room, and bath.

Not once, but a hundred times, Paul had planned this entry into New York. He had gone over every detail of it with Charley Edwards, and in his scrapbook at home there were pages of description about New York hotels, cut from the Sunday papers. When he was shown to his sitting room on the eighth floor he saw at a glance that everything was as it should be; there was but one detail in his mental picture that the place did not realize, so he rang for the bellboy and sent him down for flowers. He moved about nervously until the boy returned, putting away his new linen and fingering it delightedly as he did so. When the flowers came he put them hastily into water, and then tumbled into a hot bath. Presently he came out of his white bathroom, resplendent in his new silk underwear, and playing with the tassels of his red robe. The snow was whirling so fiercely outside his windows that he could scarcely see across the street, but within the air was deliciously soft and fragrant. He put the violets and jonquils on the taboret beside the couch, and threw himself down, with a long sigh, covering himself with a Roman blanket. He was thoroughly tired; he had been in such haste, he had stood up to such a strain, covered so much ground in the last twenty-four hours, that he wanted to think how it had all come about. Lulled by the sound of the wind, the warm air, and the cool fragrance of the flowers, he sank into deep, drowsy retrospection.

It had been wonderfully simple; when they had shut him out of the theater and concert hall, when they had taken away his bone, the whole thing was virtually determined. The rest was a mere matter of opportunity. The only thing that at all surprised him was his own courage—for he realized well enough that he had always been tormented by fear, a sort of apprehensive dread that, of late years, as the meshes of the lies he had told closed about him, had been pulling the muscles of his body tighter and tighter. Until now he could not remember the time when he had not been dreading something. Even when he was a little boy it was always there—behind him, or before, or on either side. There had always been the shadowed corner, the dark place into which he dared not look, but from which something seemed always to be watching him—and Paul had done things that were not pretty to watch, he knew.

---

1. Monogrammed. Tiffany's is a fashionable jewelry store in Manhattan. *Silver:* a comb and brush set.
2. Fashionable hotel in Manhattan.

But now he had a curious sense of relief, as though he had at last thrown down the gauntlet to the thing in the corner.

Yet it was but a day since he had been sulking in the traces; but yesterday afternoon that he had been sent to the bank with Denny & Carson's deposit, as usual—but this time he was instructed to leave the book to be balanced. There was above two thousand dollars in checks, and nearly a thousand in the bank notes which he had taken from the book and quietly transferred to his pocket. At the bank he had made out a new deposit slip. His nerves had been steady enough to permit of his returning to the office, where he had finished his work and asked for a full day's holiday tomorrow, Saturday, giving a perfectly reasonable pretext. The bankbook, he knew, would not be returned before Monday or Tuesday, and his father would be out of town for the next week. From the time he slipped the bank notes into his pocket until he boarded the night train for New York, he had not known a moment's hesitation. It was not the first time Paul had steered through treacherous waters.

How astonishingly easy it had all been; here he was, the thing done; and this time there would be no awakening, no figure at the top of the stairs. He watched the snowflakes whirling by his window until he fell asleep.

When he awoke, it was three o'clock in the afternoon. He bounded up with a start; half of one of his precious days gone already! He spent more than an hour in dressing, watching every stage of his toilet carefully in the mirror. Everything was quite perfect; he was exactly the kind of boy he had always wanted to be.

When he went downstairs Paul took a carriage and drove up Fifth Avenue toward the Park.[3] The snow had somewhat abated; carriages and tradesmen's wagons were hurrying soundlessly to and fro in the winter twilight; boys in woolen mufflers were shoveling off the doorsteps; the avenue stages[4] made fine spots of color against the white street. Here and there on the corners were stands, with whole flower gardens blooming under glass cases, against the sides of which the snowflakes stuck and melted; violets, roses, carnations, lilies of the valley—somehow vastly more lovely and alluring that they blossomed thus unnaturally in the snow. The Park itself was a wonderful stage winterpiece.

When he returned, the pause of the twilight had ceased and the tune of the streets had changed. The snow was falling faster, lights streamed from the hotels that reared their dozen stories fearlessly up into the storm, defying the raging Atlantic winds. A long, black stream of carriages poured down the avenue, intersected here and there by other streams, tending horizontally. There were a score of cabs about the entrance of this hotel, and his driver had to wait. Boys in livery were running in and out of the awning stretched across the sidewalk, up and down the red velvet carpet laid from the door to the street. Above, about, within it all was the rumble and roar, the hurry and toss of thousands of human beings as hot for pleasure as himself, and on every side of him towered the glaring affirmation of the omnipotence of wealth.

The boy set his teeth and drew his shoulders together in a spasm of realization; the plot of all dramas, the text of all romances, the nerve-stuff of all

---

**3.** That is, Central Park, the principal park in Manhattan.  **4.** Window displays.

sensations was whirling about him like the snowflakes. He burnt like a faggot in a tempest.

When Paul went down to dinner the music of the orchestra came floating up the elevator shaft to greet him. His head whirled as he stepped into the thronged corridor, and he sank back into one of the chairs against the wall to get his breath. The lights, the chatter, the perfumes, the bewildering medley of color—he had, for a moment, the feeling of not being able to stand it. But only for a moment; these were his own people, he told himself. He went slowly about the corridors, through the writing rooms, smoking rooms, reception rooms, as though he were exploring the chambers of an enchanted palace, built and peopled for him alone.

When he reached the dining room he sat down at a table near a window. The flowers, the white linen, the many-colored wineglasses, the gay toilettes of the women, the low popping of corks, the undulating repetitions of the *Blue Danube*[5] from the orchestra, all flooded Paul's dream with bewildering radiance. When the roseate tinge of his champagne was added—that cold, precious, bubbling stuff that creamed and foamed in his glass—Paul wondered that there were honest men in the world at all. This was what all the world was fighting for, he reflected; this was what all the struggle was about. He doubted the reality of his past. Had he ever known a place called Cordelia Street, a place where fagged-looking businessmen got on the early car; mere rivets in a machine they seemed to Paul,—sickening men, with combings of children's hair always hanging to their coats, and the smell of cooking in their clothes. Cordelia Street—Ah, that belonged to another time and country; had he not always been thus, had he not sat here night after night, from as far back as he could remember, looking pensively over just such shimmering textures and slowly twirling the stem of a glass like this one between his thumb and middle finger? He rather thought he had.

He was not the least abashed or lonely. He had no especial desire to meet or to know any of these people; all he demanded was the right to look on and conjecture, to watch the pageant. The mere stage properties were all he contended for. Nor was he lonely later in the evening, in his lodge at the Metropolitan.[6] He was now entirely rid of his nervous misgivings, of his forced aggressiveness, of the imperative desire to show himself different from his surroundings. He felt now that his surroundings explained him. Nobody questioned the purple,[7] he had only to wear it passively. He had only to glance down at his attire to reassure himself that here it would be impossible for anyone to humiliate him.

He found it hard to leave his beautiful sitting room to go to bed that night, and sat long watching the raging storm from his turret window. When he went to sleep it was with the lights turned on in his bedroom; partly because of his old timidity, and partly so that, if he should wake in the night, there would be no wretched moment of doubt, no horrible suspicion of yellow wallpaper, or of Washington and Calvin above his bed.

Sunday morning the city was practically snowbound. Paul breakfasted late, and in the afternoon he fell in with a wild San Francisco boy, a freshman

---

5. Waltz by Johann Strauss II (1825–1899), Austrian composer.   6. His box at the Metropolitan Opera House.   7. That is, his assumption of a royal robe.

at Yale, who said he had run down for a "little flyer" over Sunday. The young man offered to show Paul the night side of the town, and the two boys went out together after dinner, not returning to the hotel until seven o'clock the next morning. They had started out in the confiding warmth of a champagne friendship, but their parting in the elevator was singularly cool. The freshman pulled himself together to make his train, and Paul went to bed. He awoke at two o'clock in the afternoon, very thirsty and dizzy, and rang for ice-water, coffee, and the Pittsburgh papers.

On the part of the hotel management, Paul excited no suspicion. There was this to be said for him, that he wore his spoils with dignity and in no way made himself conspicuous. Even under the glow of his wine he was never boisterous, though he found the stuff like a magician's wand for wonder-building. His chief greediness lay in his ears and eyes, and his excesses were not offensive ones. His dearest pleasures were the gray winter twilights in his sitting room; his quiet enjoyment of his flowers, his clothes, his wide divan, his cigarette, and his sense of power. He could not remember a time when he had felt so at peace with himself. The mere release from the necessity of petty lying, lying every day and every day, restored his self-respect. He had never lied for pleasure, even at school; but to be noticed and admired, to assert his difference from other Cordelia Street boys; and he felt a good deal more manly, more honest, even, now that he had no need for boastful pretensions, now that he could, as his actor friends used to say, "dress the part." It was characteristic that remorse did not occur to him. His golden days went by without a shadow, and he made each as perfect as he could.

On the eighth day after his arrival in New York he found the whole affair exploited in the Pittsburgh papers, exploited with a wealth of detail which indicated that local news of a sensational nature was at a low ebb. The firm of Denny & Carson announced that the boy's father had refunded the full amount of the theft and that they had no intention of prosecuting. The Cumberland minister had been interviewed, and expressed his hope of yet reclaiming the motherless lad, and his Sabbath-school teacher declared that she would spare no effort to that end. The rumor had reached Pittsburgh that the boy had been seen in a New York hotel, and his father had gone East to find him and bring him home.

Paul had just come in to dress for dinner; he sank into a chair, weak to the knees, and clasped his head in his hands. It was to be worse than jail, even; the tepid waters of Cordelia Street were to close over him finally and forever. The gray monotony stretched before him in hopeless, unrelieved years; Sabbath school, Young People's Meeting, the yellow-papered room, the damp dish-towels; it all rushed back upon him with a sickening vividness. He had the old feeling that the orchestra had suddenly stopped, the sinking sensation that the play was over. The sweat broke out on his face, and he sprang to his feet, looked about him with his white, conscious smile, and winked at himself in the mirror. With something of the old childish belief in miracles with which he had so often gone to class, all his lessons unlearned, Paul dressed and dashed whistling down the corridor to the elevator.

He had no sooner entered the dining room and caught the measure of the music than his remembrance was lightened by his old elastic power of claiming the moment, mounting with it, and finding it all-sufficient. The glare and glitter about him, the mere scenic accessories had again, and for the last time, their old potency. He would show himself that he was game, he would finish the thing splendidly. He doubted, more than ever, the existence of Cordelia Street, and for the first time he drank his wine recklessly. Was he not, after all, one of those fortunate beings born to the purple, was he not still himself and in his own place? He drummed a nervous accompaniment to the Pagliacci[8] music and looked about him, telling himself over and over that it had paid.

He reflected drowsily, to the swell of the music and the chill sweetness of his wine, that he might have done it more wisely. He might have caught an outbound steamer and been well out of their clutches before now. But the other side of the world had seemed too far away and too uncertain then; he could not have waited for it; his need had been too sharp. If he had to choose over again, he would do the same thing tomorrow. He looked affectionately about the dining room, now gilded with a soft mist. Ah, it had paid indeed!

Paul was awakened next morning by a painful throbbing in his head and feet. He had thrown himself across the bed without undressing, and had slept with his shoes on. His limbs and hands were lead heavy, and his tongue and throat were parched and burnt. There came upon him one of those fateful attacks of clearheadedness that never occurred except when he was physically exhausted and his nerves hung loose. He lay still, closed his eyes, and let the tide of things wash over him.

His father was in New York; "stopping at some joint or other," he told himself. The memory of successive summers on the front stoop fell upon him like a weight of black water. He had not a hundred dollars left; and he knew now, more than ever, that money was everything, the wall that stood between all he loathed and all he wanted. The thing was winding itself up; he had thought of that on his first glorious day in New York, and had even provided a way to snap the thread. It lay on his dressing table now; he had got it out last night when he came blindly up from dinner, but the shiny metal hurt his eyes, and he disliked the looks of it.

He rose and moved about with a painful effort, succumbing now and again to attacks of nausea. It was the old depression exaggerated; all the world had become Cordelia Street. Yet somehow he was not afraid of anything, was absolutely calm; perhaps because he had looked into the dark corner at last and knew. It was bad enough, what he saw there, but somehow not so bad as his long fear of it had been. He saw everything clearly now. He had a feeling that he had made the best of it, that he had lived the sort of life he was meant to live, and for half an hour he sat staring at the revolver. But he told himself that was not the way, so he went downstairs and took a cab to the ferry.

When Paul arrived in Newark he got off the train and took another cab, directing the driver to follow the Pennsylvania tracks out of the town. The snow lay heavy on the roadways and had drifted deep in the open fields. Only here and there the dead grass or dried weed stalks projected, singularly black, above it. Once well into the country, Paul dismissed the carriage and walked, floundering along the tracks, his mind a medley of irrelevant things. He seemed to hold in his brain an actual picture of everything he had seen that

---

8. Opera by Ruggiero Leoncavallo (1858–1919).

morning. He remembered every feature of both his drivers, of the toothless old woman from whom he had bought the red flowers in his coat, the agent from whom he had got his ticket, and all of his fellow passengers on the ferry. His mind, unable to cope with vital matters near at hand, worked feverishly and deftly at sorting and grouping these images. They made for him a part of the ugliness of the world, of the ache in his head, and the bitter burning on his tongue. He stooped and put a handful of snow into his mouth as he walked, but that, too, seemed hot. When he reached a little hillside, where the tracks ran through a cut some twenty feet below him, he stopped and sat down.

The carnations in his coat were drooping with the cold, he noticed, their red glory all over. It occurred to him that all the flowers he had seen in the glass cases that first night must have gone the same way, long before this. It was only one splendid breath they had, in spite of their brave mockery at the winter outside the glass; and it was a losing game in the end, it seemed, this revolt against the homilies by which the world is run. Paul took one of the blossoms carefully from his coat and scooped a little hole in the snow, where he covered it up. Then he dozed awhile, from his weak condition, seemingly insensible to the cold.

The sound of an approaching train awoke him, and he started to his feet, remembering only his resolution, and afraid lest he should be too late. He stood watching the approaching locomotive, his teeth chattering, his lips drawn away from them in a frightened smile; once or twice he glanced nervously sidewise, as though he were being watched. When the right moment came, he jumped. As he fell, the folly of his haste occurred to him with merciless clearness, the vastness of what he had left undone. There flashed through his brain, clearer than ever before, the blue of Adriatic water, the yellow of Algerian sands.

He felt something strike his chest, and that his body was being thrown swiftly through the air, on and on, immeasurably far and fast, while his limbs were gently relaxed. Then, because the picturemaking mechanism was crushed, the disturbing visions flashed into black, and Paul dropped back into the immense design of things.

1905

RELATED:

—Andrea Barrett on "Paul's Case," p. 917

# JOHN CHEEVER
## *1912–1982*

 Cheever was born in Quincy, Massachusetts. His formal education ended when he was expelled from Thayer Academy at the age of seventeen—a circumstance that gave him subject matter for his first publication. Thereafter, he devoted himself completely to writing, except for brief interludes of teaching at Barnard and the University of Iowa. He wrote television scripts and four novels, but his fame rests on the large number of short stories, many appearing in *The New Yorker,* that he published in a steady stream beginning in the 1940s. Built around a strong moral core and tinged with melancholy nostalgia for the past, these stories form a running commentary on the tensions, manners, and crippled aspirations of urban and suburban life. Many of his stories have been collected in *The Enormous Radio and Other Stories* (1953), *The Housebreaker of Shady Hill and Other Stories* (1958), *The Brigadier and the Golf Widow* (1964), and *The World of Apples* (1973). His novels are *The Wapshot Chronicle* (1957), *The Wapshot Scandal* (1964), *Bullet Park* (1969), and *Falconer* (1977). *The Stories of John Cheever* (1978) won the Pulitzer Prize.

## The Enormous Radio

Jim and Irene Westcott were the kind of people who seem to strike that satisfactory average of income, endeavor, and respectability that is reached by the statistical reports in college alumni bulletins. They were the parents of two young children, they had been married nine years, they lived on the twelfth floor of an apartment house near Sutton Place,[1] they went to the theatre on an average of 10.3 times a year, and they hoped someday to live in Westchester.[2] Irene Westcott was a pleasant, rather plain girl with soft brown hair and a wide, fine forehead upon which nothing at all had been written, and in the cold weather she wore a coat of fitch skins dyed to resemble mink. You could not say that Jim Westcott looked younger than he was, but you could at least say of him that he seemed to feel younger. He wore his graying hair cut very short, he dressed in the kind of clothes his class had worn at Andover,[3] and his manner was earnest, vehement, and intentionally naïve. The Westcotts differed from their friends, their classmates, and their neighbors only in an interest they shared in serious music. They went to a great

---

1. Fashionable area on New York City's East Side.   2. Affluent suburban county to the north of New York City.   3. Phillips Andover Academy, elite boarding school in Andover, Massachusetts.

many concerts—although they seldom mentioned this to anyone—and they spent a good deal of time listening to music on the radio.

Their radio was an old instrument, sensitive, unpredictable, and beyond repair. Neither of them understood the mechanics of radio—or of any of the other appliances that surrounded them—and when the instrument faltered, Jim would strike the side of the cabinet with his hand. This sometimes helped. One Sunday afternoon, in the middle of a Schubert[4] quartet, the music faded away altogether. Jim struck the cabinet repeatedly, but there was no response; the Schubert was lost to them forever. He promised to buy Irene a new radio, and on Monday when he came home from work he told her that he had got one. He refused to describe it, and said it would be a surprise for her when it came.

The radio was delivered at the kitchen door the following afternoon, and with the assistance of her maid and the handyman Irene uncrated it and brought it into the living room. She was struck at once with the physical ugliness of the large gumwood cabinet. Irene was proud of her living room, she had chosen its furnishings and colors as carefully as she chose her clothes, and now it seemed to her that the new radio stood among her intimate possessions like an aggressive intruder. She was confounded by the number of dials and switches on the instrument panel, and she studied them thoroughly before she put the plug into a wall socket and turned the radio on. The dials flooded with a malevolent green light, and in the distance she heard the music of a piano quintet. The quintet was in the distance for only an instant; it bore down upon her with a speed greater than light and filled the apartment with the noise of music amplified so mightily that it knocked a china ornament from a table to the floor. She rushed to the instrument and reduced the volume. The violent forces that were snared in the ugly gumwood cabinet made her uneasy. Her children came home from school then, and she took them to the Park. It was not until later in the afternoon that she was able to return to the radio.

The maid had given the children their suppers and was supervising their baths when Irene turned on the radio, reduced the volume, and sat down to listen to a Mozart[5] quintet that she knew and enjoyed. The music came through clearly. The new instrument had a much purer tone, she thought, than the old one. She decided that tone was most important and that she could conceal the cabinet behind a sofa. But as soon as she had made her peace with the radio, the interference began. A crackling sound like the noise of a burning powder fuse began to accompany the singing of the strings. Beyond the music, there was a rustling that reminded Irene unpleasantly of the sea, and as the quintet progressed, these noises were joined by many others. She tried all the dials and switches but nothing dimmed the interference, and she sat down, disappointed and bewildered, and tried to trace the flight of the melody. The elevator shaft in her building ran beside the living-room wall, and it was the noise of the elevator that gave her a clue to the character of the static. The rattling of the elevator cables and the opening and closing of the elevator doors were reproduced in her loudspeaker, and, realizing that the radio was

---

**4.** Franz Peter Schubert (1797–1828), Austrian composer.   **5.** Wolfgang Amadeus Mozart (1756–1791), Austrian composer.

sensitive to electrical currents of all sorts, she began to discern through the Mozart the ringing of telephone bells, the dialing of phones, and the lamentation of a vacuum cleaner. By listening more carefully, she was able to distinguish doorbells, elevator bells, electric razors, and Waring mixers, whose sounds had been picked up from the apartments that surrounded hers and transmitted through her loudspeaker. The powerful and ugly instrument, with its mistaken sensitivity to discord, was more than she could hope to master, so she turned the thing off and went into the nursery to see her children.

When Jim Westcott came home that night, he went to the radio confidently and worked the controls. He had the same sort of experience Irene had had. A man was speaking on the station Jim had chosen, and his voice swung instantly from the distance into a force so powerful that it shook the apartment. Jim turned the volume control and reduced the voice. Then, a minute or two later, the interference began. The ringing of telephones and doorbells set in, joined by the rasp of the elevator doors and the whir of cooking appliances. The character of the noise had changed since Irene had tried the radio earlier; the last of the electric razors was being unplugged, the vacuum cleaners had all been returned to their closets, and the static reflected that change in pace that overtakes the city after the sun goes down. He fiddled with the knobs but couldn't get rid of the noises, so he turned the radio off and told Irene that in the morning he'd call the people who had sold it to him and give them hell.

The following afternoon, when Irene returned to the apartment from a luncheon date, the maid told her that a man had come and fixed the radio. Irene went into the living room before she took off her hat or her furs and tried the instrument. From the loudspeaker came a recording of the "Missouri Waltz."[6] It reminded her of the thin, scratchy music from an old-fashioned phonograph that she sometimes heard across the lake where she spent her summers. She waited until the waltz had finished, expecting an explanation of the recording, but there was none. The music was followed by silence, and then the plaintive and scratchy record was repeated. She turned the dial and got a satisfactory burst of Caucasian music—the thump of bare feet in the dust and the rattle of coin jewelry—but in the background she could hear the ringing of bells and a confusion of voices. Her children came home from school then, and she turned off the radio and went to the nursery.

When Jim came home that night, he was tired, and he took a bath and changed his clothes. Then he joined Irene in the living room. He had just turned on the radio when the maid announced dinner, so he left it on, and he and Irene went to the table.

Jim was too tired to make even pretense of sociability, and there was nothing about the dinner to hold Irene's interest, so her attention wandered from the food to the deposits of silver polish on the candlesticks and from there to the music in the other room. She listened for a few minutes to a Chopin[7] prelude and then was surprised to hear a man's voice break in. "For Christ's sake, Kathy," he said, "do you always have to play the piano when I get home?"

---

6. Popular tune of 1916 by J. R. Shannon and Frederick Knight Logan. It was made popular again in the 1940s by President Harry Truman.    7. Frédéric François Chopin (1810–1849), Polish-French composer and pianist.

The music stopped abruptly. "It's the only chance I have," a woman said. "I'm at the office all day." "So am I," the man said. He added something obscene about an upright piano, and slammed a door. The passionate and melancholy music began again.

"Did you hear that?" Irene asked.

"What?" Jim was eating his dessert.

"The radio. A man said something while the music was still going on—something dirty."

"It's probably a play."

"I don't think it *is* a play," Irene said.

They left the table and took their coffee into the living room. Irene asked Jim to try another station. He turned the knob. "Have you seen my garters?" a man asked. "Button me up," a woman said. "Have you seen my garters?" the man said again. "Just button me up and I'll find your garters," the woman said. Jim shifted to another station. "I wish you wouldn't leave apple cores in the ashtrays," a man said. "I hate the smell."

"This is strange," Jim said.

"Isn't it?" Irene said.

Jim turned the knob again. "'On the coast of Coromandel where the early pumpkins blow,'" a woman with a pronounced English accent said, "'in the middle of the woods lived the Yonghy-Bonghy-Bò. Two old chairs, and half a candle, one old jug without a handle . . .'"[8]

"My God!" Irene cried. "That's the Sweeneys' nurse."

"'These were all his worldly goods,'" the British voice continued.

"Turn that thing off," Irene said. "Maybe they can hear *us*." Jim switched the radio off. "That was Miss Armstrong, the Sweeneys' nurse," Irene said. "She must be reading to the little girl. They live in 17-B. I've talked with Miss Armstrong in the Park. I know her voice very well. We must be getting other people's apartments."

"That's impossible," Jim said.

"Well, that was the Sweeneys' nurse," Irene said hotly. "I know her voice. I know it very well. I'm wondering if they can hear us."

Jim turned the switch. First from a distance and then nearer, nearer, as if borne on the wind, came the pure accents of the Sweeneys' nurse again: "'*Lady Jingly! Lady Jingly!*'" she said, "'*sitting where the pumpkins blow, will you come and be my wife? said the Yonghy-Bonghy-Bò . . .*'"

Jim went over to the radio and said "Hello" loudly into the speaker.

"'*I am tired of living singly,*'" the nurse went on, "'*on this coast so wild and shingly, I'm a-weary of my life; if you'll come and be my wife, quite serene would be my life . . .*'"

"I guess she can't hear us," Irene said. "Try something else."

Jim turned to another station, and the living room was filled with the uproar of a cocktail party that had overshot its mark. Someone was playing the piano and singing the "Whiffenpoof Song,"[9] and the voices that surrounded the piano were vehement and happy. "Eat some more sandwiches," a woman shrieked. There were screams of laughter and a dish of some sort crashed to the floor.

---

**8.** From *The Courtship of the Yonghy-Bonghy-Bò* by Edward Lear (1812–1888), English nonsense poet.
**9.** Famous Yale drinking song.

"Those must be the Fullers, in 11-E," Irene said. "I knew they were giving a party this afternoon. I saw her in the liquor store. Isn't this too divine? Try something else. See if you can get those people in 18-C."

The Westcotts overheard that evening a monologue on salmon fishing in Canada, a bridge game, running comments on home movies of what had apparently been a fortnight at Sea Island, and a bitter family quarrel about an overdraft at the bank. They turned off their radio at midnight and went to bed, weak with laughter. Sometime in the night, their son began to call for a glass of water and Irene got one and took it to his room. It was very early. All the lights in the neighborhood were extinguished, and from the boy's window she could see the empty street. She went into the living room and tried the radio. There was some faint coughing, a moan, and then a man spoke. "Are you all right, darling?" he asked. "Yes," a woman said wearily. "Yes, I'm all right, I guess," and then she added with great feeling, "But, you know, Charlie, I don't feel like myself any more. Sometimes there are about fifteen or twenty minutes in the week when I feel like myself. I don't like to go to another doctor, because the doctor's bills are so awful already, but I just don't feel like myself, Charlie. I just never feel like myself." They were not young, Irene thought. She guessed from the timbre of their voices that they were middle-aged. The restrained melancholy of the dialogue and the draft from the bedroom window made her shiver, and she went back to bed.

The following morning, Irene cooked breakfast for the family—the maid didn't come up from her room in the basement until ten—braided her daughter's hair, and waited at the door until her children and her husband had been carried away in the elevator. Then she went into the living room and tried the radio. "I don't want to go to school," a child screamed. "I hate school. I won't go to school. I hate school." "You will go to school," an enraged woman said. "We paid eight hundred dollars to get you into that school and you'll go if it kills you." The next number on the dial produced the worn record of the "Missouri Waltz." Irene shifted the control and invaded the privacy of several breakfast tables. She overheard demonstrations of indigestion, carnal love, abysmal vanity, faith, and despair. Irene's life was nearly as simple and sheltered as it appeared to be, and the forthright and sometimes brutal language that came from the loudspeaker that morning astonished and troubled her. She continued to listen until her maid came in. Then she turned off the radio quickly, since this insight, she realized, was a furtive one.

Irene had a luncheon date with a friend that day, and she left her apartment at a little after twelve. There were a number of women in the elevator when it stopped at her floor. She stared at their handsome and impassive faces, their furs, and the cloth flowers in their hats. Which one of them had been to Sea Island? she wondered. Which one had overdrawn her bank account. The elevator stopped at the tenth floor and a woman with a pair of Skye terriers joined them. Her hair was rigged high on her head and she wore a mink cape. She was humming the "Missouri Waltz."

Irene had two Martinis at lunch, and she looked searchingly at her friend and wondered what her secrets were. They had intended to go shopping after lunch, but Irene excused herself and went home. She told the maid that she was not to be disturbed; then she went into the living room, closed the doors, and switched on the radio. She heard, in the course of the afternoon, the halting conversation of a woman entertaining her aunt, the hysterical conclusion of a luncheon party, and a hostess briefing her maid about some cocktail guests. "Don't give the best Scotch to anyone who hasn't white hair," the hostess said. "See if you can get rid of that liver paste before you pass those hot things, and could you lend me five dollars? I want to tip the elevator man."

As the afternoon waned, the conversations increased in intensity. From where Irene sat, she could see the open sky above the East River. There were hundreds of clouds in the sky, as though the south wind had broken the winter into pieces and were blowing it north, and on her radio she could hear the arrival of cocktail guests and the return of children and businessmen from their schools and offices. "I found a good-sized diamond on the bathroom floor this morning," a woman said. "It must have fallen out of that bracelet Mrs. Dunston was wearing last night." "We'll sell it," a man said. "Take it down to the jeweler on Madison Avenue and sell it. Mrs. Dunston won't know the difference, and we could use a couple of hundred bucks . . ." "'Oranges and lemons, say the bells of St. Clement's,'" the Sweeneys' nurse sang. "'Halfpence and farthings, say the bells of St. Martin's. When will you pay me? say the bells at old Bailey . . .'"[1] "It's not a hat," a woman cried, and at her back roared a cocktail party. "It's not a hat, it's a love affair. That's what Walter Florell said. He said it's not a hat, it's a love affair," and then, in a lower voice, the same woman added, "Talk to somebody, for Christ's sake, honey, talk to somebody. If she catches you standing here not talking to anybody, she'll take us off her invitation list, and I love these parties."

The Westcotts were going out for dinner that night, and when Jim came home, Irene was dressing. She seemed sad and vague, and he brought her a drink. They were dining with friends in the neighborhood, and they walked to where they were going. The sky was broad and filled with light. It was one of those splendid spring evenings that excite memory and desire, and the air that touched their hands and faces felt very soft. A Salvation Army band was on the corner playing "Jesus Is Sweeter." Irene drew on her husband's arm and held him there for a minute, to hear the music. "They're really such nice people, aren't they?" she said. "They have such nice faces. Actually, they're so much nicer than a lot of the people we know." She took a bill from her purse and walked over and dropped it into the tambourine. There was in her face, when she returned to her husband, a look of radiant melancholy that he was not familiar with. And her conduct at the dinner party that night seemed strange to him, too. She interrupted her hostess rudely and stared at the people across the table from her with an intensity for which she would have punished her children.

It was still mild when they walked home from the party, and Irene looked up at the spring stars. "'How far that little candle throws its beams,'" she exclaimed. "'So shines a good deed in a naughty world.'"[2] She waited that night until Jim had fallen asleep, and then went into the living room and turned on the radio.

Jim came home at about six the next night. Emma, the maid, let him in, and he had taken off his hat and was taking off his coat when Irene ran into

---

**1.** From a British folk song.   **2.** Shakespeare's *Merchant of Venice* 5.1.

the hall. Her face was shining with tears and her hair was disordered. "Go up to 16-C, Jim!" she screamed. "Don't take off your coat. Go up to 16-C. Mr. Osborn's beating his wife. They've been quarreling since four o'clock, and now he's hitting her. Go up there and stop him."

From the radio in the living room, Jim heard screams, obscenities, and thuds. "You know you don't have to listen to this sort of thing," he said. He strode into the living room and turned the switch. "It's indecent," he said. "It's like looking in windows. You know you don't have to listen to this sort of thing. You can turn it off."

"Oh, it's so horrible, it's so dreadful," Irene was sobbing. "I've been listening all day, and it's so depressing."

"Well, if it's so depressing, why do you listen to it? I bought this damned radio to give you some pleasure," he said. "I paid a great deal of money for it. I thought it might make you happy. I wanted to make you happy."

"Don't, don't, don't, don't quarrel with me," she moaned, and laid her head on his shoulder. "All the others have been quarreling all day. Everybody's been quarreling. They're all worried about money. Mrs. Hutchinson's mother is dying of cancer in Florida and they don't have enough money to send her to the Mayo Clinic.[3] At least, Mr. Hutchinson says they don't have enough money. And some woman in this building is having an affair with the handyman— with that hideous handyman. It's too disgusting. And Mrs. Melville has heart trouble, and Mr. Hendricks is going to lose his job in April and Mrs. Hendricks is horrid about the whole thing and that girl who plays the 'Missouri Waltz' is a whore, a common whore, and the elevator man has tuberculosis and Mr. Osborn has been beating Mrs. Osborn." She wailed, she trembled with grief and checked the stream of tears down her face with the heel of her palm.

"Well, why do you have to listen?" Jim asked again. "Why do you have to listen to this stuff if it makes you so miserable?"

"Oh, don't, don't, don't," she cried. "Life is too terrible, too sordid and awful. But we've never been like that, have we, darling? Have we? I mean, we've always been good and decent and loving to one another, haven't we? And we have two children, two beautiful children. Our lives aren't sordid, are they, darling? Are they?" She flung her arms around his neck and drew his face down to hers. "We're happy, aren't we, darling? We are happy, aren't we?"

"Of course we're happy," he said tiredly. He began to surrender his resentment. "Of course we're happy. I'll have that damned radio fixed or taken away tomorrow." He stroked her soft hair. "My poor girl," he said.

"You love me, don't you?" she asked. "And we're not hypercritical or worried about money or dishonest, are we?"

"No, darling," he said.

A man came in the morning and fixed the radio. Irene turned it on cautiously and was happy to hear a California-wine commercial and a recording of Beethoven's Ninth Symphony, including Schiller's[4] "Ode to Joy." She kept the radio on all day and nothing untoward came from the speaker.

A Spanish suite was being played when Jim came home. "Is everything all right?" he asked. His face was pale, she thought. They had some cocktails and

---

3. Internationally famous hospital and diagnostic center in Rochester, Minnesota. 4. Johann Christoph Friedrich von Schiller (1759-1805), German poet and dramatist. Ludwig van Beethoven (1770-1827), German composer.

went in to dinner to the "Anvil Chorus" from *Il Trovatore*. This was followed by Debussy's[5] "La Mer."

"I paid the bill for the radio today," Jim said. "It cost four hundred dollars. I hope you'll get some enjoyment out of it."

"Oh, I'm sure I will," Irene said.

"Four hundred dollars is a good deal more than I can afford," he went on. "I wanted to get something that you'd enjoy. It's the last extravagance we'll be able to indulge in this year. I see that you haven't paid your clothing bills yet. I saw them on your dressing table." He looked directly at her. "Why did you tell me you'd paid them? Why did you lie to me?"

"I just didn't want you to worry, Jim," she said. She drank some water. "I'll be able to pay my bills out of this month's allowance. There were the slipcovers last month, and that party."

"You've got to learn to handle the money I give you a little more intelligently, Irene," he said. "You've got to understand that we don't have as much money this year as we had last. I had a very sobering talk with Mitchell today. No one is buying anything. We're spending all our time promoting new issues, and you know how long that takes. I'm not getting any younger, you know. I'm thirty-seven. My hair will be gray next year. I haven't done as well as I'd hoped to do. And I don't suppose things will get any better."

"Yes, dear," she said.

"We've got to start cutting down," Jim said. "We've got to think of the children. To be perfectly frank with you, I worry about money a great deal. I'm not at all sure of the future. No one is. If anything should happen to me, there's the insurance, but that wouldn't go very far today. I've worked awfully hard to give you and the children a comfortable life," he said bitterly. "I don't like to see all my energies, all of my youth, wasted in fur coats and radios and slipcovers and—"

"Please, Jim," she said. "Please. They'll hear us."

"*Who'll hear us?* Emma can't hear us."

"The radio."

"Oh, I'm sick!" he shouted. "I'm sick to death of your apprehensiveness. The radio can't hear us. Nobody can hear us. And what if they can hear us? Who cares?"

Irene got up from the table and went into the living room. Jim went to the door and shouted at her from there. "Why are you so Christly all of a sudden? What's turned you overnight into a convent girl? You stole your mother's jewelry before they probated her will. You never gave your sister a cent of that money that was intended for her—not even when she needed it. You made Grace Howland's life miserable, and where was all your piety and your virtue when you went to that abortionist? I'll never forget how cool you were. You packed your bag and went off to have that child murdered as if you were going to Nassau. If you'd had any reasons, if you'd had any good reasons—"

Irene stood for a minute before the hideous cabinet, disgraced and sickened, but she held her hand on the switch before she extinguished the music and the voices, hoping that the instrument might speak to her kindly, that

✓ 人为坚防考

---

5. Claude Achille Debussy (1862–1918), French composer. *Il Trovatore*: opera by Giuseppe Verdi (1813–1901), Italian composer.

she might hear the Sweeneys' nurse. Jim continued to shout at her from the door. The voice on the radio was suave and noncommital. "An early-morning railroad disaster in Tokyo," the loudspeaker said, "killed twenty-nine people. A fire in a Catholic hospital near Buffalo for the care of blind children was extinguished early this morning by nuns. The temperature is forty-seven. The humidity is eighty-nine."

1953

# ANTON CHEKHOV
## *1860–1904*

Chekhov was born in Taganrog, Russia, the son of a despotic, dishonest, and rough-grained father—who was nevertheless eager to impart to his children his love for music and art. Trained as a physician at Moscow University, Chekhov practiced medicine only intermittently, although he credited his scientific training with conditioning him to be a perceptive observer of society and individual behavior. While still a medical student he began to write short pieces for humorous magazines; the popularity of these sketches roused his determination to become a serious artist. In 1890 he visited the Russian penal island of Sakhalin and without fanfare or special pleading wrote a moving account of convict life as he saw it there. He was at the height of his literary powers and his fame in 1901 when he married a young actress, but the state of his health by then was precarious. In the short time remaining to him, he was confined mostly to the house he had built with his literary earnings at Yalta in southern Russia, infrequently able to accompany his wife to Moscow to watch her performances in his plays. Those plays—among them *The Seagull* (1896), *Uncle Vanya* (1899), *The Three Sisters* (1901), and *The Cherry Orchard* (1904)—established him as one of the great dramatists of modern times, while his hundreds of short stories and novellas have immensely influenced the art of fiction since his death. In tribute to the humanity and responsibility of his work, Leo Tolstoy called him "an artist of life."

## Gusev[1]

### I

It is already dark, it will soon be night.

Gusev, a discharged private, half rises in his bunk and says in a low voice:

"Do you hear me, Pavel Ivanych? A soldier in Suchan was telling me: while they were sailing, their ship bumped into a big fish and smashed a hole in its bottom."

The individual of uncertain social status whom he is addressing, and whom everyone in the ship infirmary calls Pavel Ivanych, is silent as though he hasn't heard.

And again all is still. The wind is flirting with the rigging, the screw is throbbing, the waves are lashing, the bunks creak, but the ear has long since become used to these sounds, and everything around seems to slumber in silence. It is

1. Translated by Constance Garnett.

dull. The three invalids—two soldiers and a sailor—who were playing cards all day are dozing and talking deliriously.

The ship is apparently beginning to roll. The bunk slowly rises and falls under Gusev as though it were breathing, and this occurs once, twice, three times . . . Something hits the floor with a clang: a jug must have dropped.

"The wind has broken loose from its chain," says Gusev, straining his ears.

This time Pavel Ivanych coughs and says irritably:

"One minute a vessel bumps into a fish, the next the wind breaks loose from its chain . . . Is the wind a beast that it breaks loose from its chain?"

"That's what Christian folks say."

"They are as ignorant as you . . . They say all sorts of things. One must have one's head on one's shoulders and reason it out. You have no sense."

Pavel Ivanych is subject to seasickness. When the sea is rough he is usually out of sorts, and the merest trifle irritates him. In Gusev's opinion there is absolutely nothing to be irritated about. What is there that is strange or out of the way about that fish, for instance, or about the wind breaking loose from its chain? Suppose the fish were as big as the mountain and its back as hard as a sturgeon's, and supposing, too, that over yonder at the end of the world stood great stone walls and the fierce winds were chained up to the walls. If they haven't broken loose, why then do they rush all over the sea like madmen and strain like hounds tugging at their leash? If they are not chained up what becomes of them when it is calm?

Gusev ponders for a long time about fishes as big as a mountain and about stout, rusty chains. Then he begins to feel bored and falls to thinking about his home, to which he is returning after five years' service in the Far East. He pictures an immense pond covered with drifts. On one side of the pond is the brick-colored building of the pottery with a tall chimney and clouds of black smoke; on the other side is a village. His brother Alexey drives out of the fifth yard from the end in a sleigh; behind him sits his little son Vanka in big felt boots, and his little girl Akulka also wearing felt boots. Alexey has had a drop, Vanka is laughing, Akulka's face cannot be seen, she is muffled up. 取好

"If he doesn't look out, he will have the children frostbitten," Gusev reflects. "Lord send them sense that they may honor their parents and not be any wiser than their father and mother."

"They need new soles," a delirious sailor says in a bass voice. "Yes, yes!"

Gusev's thoughts abruptly break off and suddenly without rhyme or reason the pond is replaced by a huge bull's head without eyes, and the horse and sleigh are no longer going straight ahead but are whirling round and round, wrapped in black smoke. But still he is glad he has had a glimpse of his people. In fact, he is breathless with joy, and his whole body, down to his fingertips, tingles with it. "Thanks be to God we have seen each other again," he mutters deliriously, but at once opens his eyes and looks for water in the dark.

He drinks and lies down, and again the sleigh is gliding along, then again there is the bull's head without eyes, smoke, clouds . . . And so it goes till daybreak.

## II

A blue circle is the first thing to become visible in the darkness—it is the porthole; then, little by little, Gusev makes out the man in the next bunk, Pavel

Ivanych. The man sleeps sitting up, as he cannot breathe lying down. His face is gray, his nose long and sharp, his eyes look huge because he is terribly emaciated, his temples are sunken, his beard skimpy, his hair long. His face does not reveal his social status: you cannot tell whether he is a gentleman, a merchant, or a peasant. Judging from his expression and his long hair, he may be an assiduous churchgoer or a lay brother, but his manner of speaking does not seem to be that of a monk. He is utterly worn out by his cough, by the stifling heat, his illness, and he breathes with difficulty, moving his parched lips. Noticing that Gusev is looking at him he turns his face toward him and says:

"I begin to guess . . . Yes, I understand it all perfectly now."

"What do you understand, Pavel Ivanych?"

"Here's how it is . . . It has always seemed strange to me that terribly ill as you fellows are, you should be on a steamer where the stifling air, the heavy seas, in fact everything, threatens you with death; but now it is all clear to me . . . Yes. . . . The doctors put you on the steamer to get rid of you. They got tired of bothering with you, cattle . . . You don't pay them any money, you are a nuisance, and you spoil their statistics with your deaths . . . So, of course, you are just cattle. And it's not hard to get rid of you . . . All that's necessary is, in the first place, to have no conscience or humanity, and, secondly, to deceive the ship authorities. The first requirement need hardly be given a thought—in that respect we are virtuosos, and as for the second condition, it can always be fulfilled with a little practice. In a crowd of four hundred healthy soldiers and sailors, five sick ones are not conspicuous; well, they got you all onto the steamer, mixed you with the healthy ones, hurriedly counted you over, and in the confusion nothing untoward was noticed, and when the steamer was on the way, people discovered that there were paralytics and consumptives on their last legs lying about the deck . . ."

Gusev does not understand Pavel Ivanych; thinking that he is being reprimanded, he says in self-justification:

"I lay on the deck because I was so sick; when we were being unloaded from the barge onto the steamer, I caught a bad chill."

"It's revolting," Pavel Ivanych continues. "The main thing is, they know perfectly well that you can't stand the long journey and yet they put you here. Suppose you last as far as the Indian Ocean, and then what? It's horrible to think of . . . And that's the gratitude for your faithful, irreproachable service!"

Pavel Ivanych's eyes flash with anger. He frowns fastidiously and says, gasping for breath, "Those are the people who ought to be given a drubbing in the newspapers till the feathers fly in all directions."

The two sick soldiers and the sailor have waked up and are already playing cards. The sailor is half reclining in his bunk, the soldiers are sitting near by on the floor in most uncomfortable positions. One of the soldiers has his right arm bandaged and his wrist is heavily swathed in wrappings that look like a cap, so that he holds his cards under his right arm or in the crook of his elbow while he plays with his left. The ship is rolling heavily. It is impossible to stand up, or have tea, or take medicine.

"Were you an orderly?" Pavel Ivanych asks Gusev.

"Yes, sir, an orderly."

"My God, my God!" says Pavel Ivanych and shakes his head sadly. "To tear a man from his home, drag him a distance of ten thousand miles, then wear him out till he gets consumption and . . . and what is it all for, one asks? To turn him into an orderly for some Captain Kopeykin or Midshipman Dyrka! How reasonable!"

"It's not hard work, Pavel Ivanych. You get up in the morning and polish the boots, start the samovars going, tidy the rooms, and then you have nothing more to do. The lieutenant drafts plans all day, and if you like, you can say your prayers, or read a book or go out on the street. God grant everyone such a life."

"Yes, very good! The lieutenant drafts plans all day long, and you sit in the kitchen and long for home . . . Plans, indeed! . . . It's not plans that matter but human life. You have only one life to live and it mustn't be wronged."

"Of course, Pavel Ivanych, a bad man gets no break anywhere, either at home or in the service, but if you live as you ought and obey orders, who will want to wrong you? The officers are educated gentlemen, they understand . . . In five years I have never once been in the guard house, and I was struck, if I remember right, only once."

"What for?"

"For fighting. I have a heavy hand, Pavel Ivanych. Four Chinks came into our yard; they were bringing firewood or something, I forget. Well, I was bored and I knocked them about a bit, the nose of one of them, damn him, began bleeding . . . The lieutenant saw it all through the window, got angry, and boxed me on the ear."

"You are a poor, foolish fellow . . ." whispers Pavel Ivanych. "You don't understand anything."

He is utterly exhausted by the rolling of the ship and shuts his eyes; now his head drops back, now it sinks forward on his chest. Several times he tries to lie down but nothing comes of it: he finds it difficult to breathe.

"And what did you beat up the four Chinks for?" he asks after a while.

"Oh, just like that. They came into the yard and I hit them."

There is silence . . . The card-players play for two hours, eagerly, swearing sometimes, but the rolling and pitching of the ship overcomes them, too; they throw aside the cards and lie down. Again Gusev has a vision: the big pond, the pottery, the village . . . Once more the sleigh is gliding along, once more Vanka is laughing and Akulka, the silly thing, throws open her fur coat and thrusts out her feet, as much as to say: "Look, good people, my felt boots are not like Vanka's, they're new ones."

"Going on six, and she has no sense yet," Gusev mutters in his delirium. "Instead of showing off your boots you had better come and get your soldier uncle a drink. I'll give you a present."

And here is Andron with a flintlock on his shoulder, carrying a hare he has killed, and behind him is the decrepit old Jew Isaychik, who offers him a piece of soap in exchange for the hare; and here is the black calf in the entry, and Domna sewing a shirt and crying about something, and then again the bull's head without eyes, black smoke . . .

Someone shouts overhead, several sailors run by; it seems that something bulky is being dragged over the deck, something falls with a crash. Again some people run by. . . . Has there been an accident? Gusev raises his head, listens, and sees that the two soldiers and the sailor are playing cards again;

Pavel Ivanych is sitting up and moving his lips. It is stifling, you haven't the strength to breathe, you are thirsty, the water is warm, disgusting. The ship is still rolling and pitching.

Suddenly something strange happens to one of the soldiers playing cards. He calls hearts diamonds, gets muddled over his score, and drops his cards, then with a frightened, foolish smile looks round at all of them.

"I shan't be a minute, fellows . . ." he says, and lies down on the floor.

Everybody is nonplussed. They call to him, he does not answer.

"Stepan, maybe you are feeling bad, eh?" the soldier with the bandaged arm asks him. "Perhaps we had better call the priest, eh?"

"Have a drink of water, Stepan . . ." says the sailor. "Here, brother, drink."

"Why are you knocking the jug against his teeth?" says Gusev angrily. "Don't you see, you cabbage-head?"

"What?"

"What?" Gusev mimics him. "There is no breath in him, he's dead! That's what! Such stupid people, Lord God!"

## III

The ship has stopped rolling and Pavel Ivanych is cheerful. He is no longer cross. His face wears a boastful, challenging, mocking expression. It is as though he wants to say: "Yes, right away I'll tell you something that will make you burst with laughter." The round porthole is open and a soft breeze is blowing on Pavel Ivanych. There is a sound of voices, the splash of oars in the water . . . Just under the porthole someone is droning in a thin, disgusting voice; must be a Chinaman singing.

"Here we are in the harbor," says Pavel Ivanych with a mocking smile. "Only another month or so and we shall be in Russia. M'yes, messieurs of the armed forces! I'll arrive in Odessa and from there go straight to Kharkov. In Kharkov I have a friend, a man of letters. I'll go to him and say, 'Come, brother, put aside your vile subjects, women's amours and the beauties of Nature, and show up the two-legged vermin' . . . There's a subject for you."

For a while he reflects, then says:

"Gusev, do you know how I tricked them?"

"Tricked who, Pavel Ivanych?"

"Why, these people . . . You understand, on this steamer there is only a first class and a third class, and they only allow peasants, that is, the common herd, to go in the third. If you have got a jacket on and even at a distance look like a gentleman or a bourgeois,[2] you have to go first class, if you please. You must fork out five hundred rubles if it kills you. 'Why do you have such a regulation?' I ask them. 'Do you mean to raise the prestige of the Russian intelligentsia thereby?' 'Not a bit of it. We don't let you simply because a decent person can't go third class; it is too horrible and disgusting there.' 'Yes, sir? Thank you for being so solicitous about decent people's welfare. But in any case, whether it's nasty there or nice, I haven't got five hundred rubles. I didn't loot the Treasury, I didn't exploit the natives, I didn't traffic in contraband, I flogged nobody to death, so judge for yourselves if I have the right to occupy a first class cabin and even to reckon myself among the Russian intelligentsia.'

2. A member of the middle class.

But logic means nothing to them. So I had to resort to fraud. I put on a peasant coat and high boots, I pulled a face so that I looked like a common drunk, and went to the agents: 'Give us a little ticket, your Excellency,' said I—"

"You're not of the gentry, are you?" asked the sailor.

"I come of a clerical family. My father was a priest, and an honest one; he always told the high and mighty the truth to their faces and, as a result, he suffered a great deal."

Pavel Ivanych is exhausted from talking and gasps for breath, but still continues:

"Yes, I always tell people the truth to their faces. I'm not afraid of anyone or anything. In this respect, there is a great difference between me and all of you, men. You are dark people, blind, crushed; you see nothing and what you do see, you don't understand . . . You are told that the wind breaks loose from its chain, that you are beasts, savages, and you believe it; someone gives it to you in the neck—you kiss his hand; some animal in a racoon coat robs you and then tosses you a fifteen-kopeck tip and you say: 'Let me kiss your hand, sir.' You are outcasts, pitiful wretches. I am different, my mind is clear. I see it all plainly like a hawk or an eagle when it hovers over the earth, and I understand everything. I am protest personified. I see tyranny—I protest. I see a hypocrite—I protest, I see a triumphant swine—I protest. And I cannot be put down, no Spanish Inquisition[3] can silence me. No. Cut out my tongue and I will protest with gestures. Wall me up in a cellar—I will shout so that you will hear me half a mile away, or will starve myself to death, so that they may have another weight on their black consciences. Kill me and I will haunt them. All my acquaintances say to me: 'You are a most insufferable person, Pavel Ivanych.' I am proud of such a reputation. I served three years in the Far East and I shall be remembered there a hundred years. I had rows there with everybody. My friends wrote to me from Russia: 'Don't come back,' but here I am going back to spite them . . . Yes . . . That's life as I understand it. That's what one can call life."

Gusev is not listening; he is looking at the porthole. A junk, flooded with dazzling hot sunshine, is swaying on the transparent turquoise water. In it stand naked Chinamen, holding up cages with canaries in them and calling out: "It sings, it sings!"

Another boat knocks against it; a steam cutter glides past. Then there is another boat: a fat Chinaman sits in it, eating rice with chopsticks. The water sways lazily, white sea gulls languidly hover over it.

"Would be fine to give that fat fellow one in the neck," reflects Gusev, looking at the stout Chinaman and yawning.

He dozes off and it seems to him that all nature is dozing too. Time flies swiftly by. Imperceptibly the day passes. Imperceptibly darkness descends . . . The steamer is no longer standing still but is on the move again.

## IV

Two days pass. Pavel Ivanych no longer sits up but is lying down. His eyes are closed, his nose seems to have grown sharper.

"Pavel Ivanych," Gusev calls to him. "Hey, Pavel Ivanych."

---

3. The state tribunal of the Roman Catholic Church, established in Spain in 1480 to eradicate heresy, infamous for its cruelty and capriciousness. Joseph Bonaparte abolished it in 1808.

Pavel Ivanych opens his eyes and moves his lips.

"Are you feeling bad?"

"No ... It's nothing ..." answers Pavel Ivanych gasping for breath. "Nothing, on the contrary ... I am better ... You see, I can lie down now ... I have improved ..."

"Well, thank God for that, Pavel Ivanych."

"When I compare myself to you, I am sorry for you, poor fellows. My lungs are healthy, mine is a stomach cough ... I can stand hell, let alone the Red Sea. Besides, I take a critical attitude toward my illness and the medicines. While you—Your minds are dark ... It's hard on you, very, very hard!"

The ship is not rolling, it is quiet, but as hot and stifling as a Turkish bath; it is hard, not only to speak, but even to listen. Gusev hugs his knees, lays his head on them and thinks of his home. God, in this stifling heat, what a relief it is to think of snow and cold! You're driving in a sleigh; all of a sudden, the horses take fright at something and bolt. Careless of the road, the ditches, the gullies, they tear like mad things right through the village, across the pond, past the pottery, across the open fields. "Hold them!" the pottery hands and the peasants they meet shout at the top of their voices. "Hold them!" But why hold them? Let the keen cold wind beat in your face and bite your hands; let the lumps of snow, kicked up by the horses, slide down your collar, your neck, your chest; let the runners sing, and the traces and the whippletrees break, the devil take them. And what delight when the sleigh upsets and you go flying full tilt into a drift, face right in the snow, and then you get up, white all over with icicles on your mustache, no cap, no gloves, your belt undone ... People laugh, dogs bark ...

Pavel Ivanych half opens one eye, fixes Gusev with it and asks softly:

"Gusev, did your commanding officer steal?"

"Who can tell, Pavel Ivanych? We can't say, we didn't hear about it."

And after that, a long time passes in silence. Gusev broods, his mind wanders, and he keeps drinking water: it is hard for him to talk and hard for him to listen, and he is afraid of being talked to. An hour passes, a second, a third; evening comes, then night, but he doesn't notice it; he sits up and keeps dreaming of the frost.

There is a sound as though someone were coming into the infirmary, voices are heard, but five minutes pass and all is quiet again.

"The kingdom of Heaven be his and eternal peace," says the soldier with a bandaged arm. "He was an uneasy chap."

"What?" asks Gusev. "Who?"

"He died, they have just carried him up."

"Oh, well," mutters Gusev, yawning, "the kingdom of Heaven be his."

"What do you think, Gusev?" the soldier with the bandaged arm says after a while. "Will he be in the kingdom of Heaven or not?"

"Who do you mean?"

"Pavel Ivanych."

"He will ... He suffered so long. Then again, he belonged to the clergy and priests have a lot of relatives. Their prayers will get him there."

The soldier with the bandage sits down on Gusev's bunk and says in an undertone:

"You too, Gusev, aren't long for this world. You will never get to Russia."

"Did the doctor or the nurse say so?" asks Gusev.

"It isn't that they said so, but one can see it. It's plain when a man will die soon. You don't eat, you don't drink, you've got so thin it's dreadful to look at you. It's consumption, in a word. I say it not to worry you, but because maybe you would like to receive the sacrament and extreme unction.[4] And if you have any money, you had better turn it over to the senior officer."

"I haven't written home," Gusev sighs: "I shall die and they won't know."

"They will," the sick sailor says in a bass voice. "When you die, they will put it down in the ship's log, in Odessa they will send a copy of the entry to the army authorities, and they will notify your district board or somebody like that."

Such a conversation makes Gusev uneasy and a vague craving begins to torment him. He takes a drink—it isn't that; he drags himself to the porthole and breathes the hot, moist air—it isn't that; he tries to think of home, of the frost—it isn't that . . . At last it seems to him that if he stays in the infirmary another minute, he will certainly choke to death.

"It's stifling, brother," he says. "I'll go on deck. Take me there, for Christ's sake."

"All right," the soldier with the bandage agrees. "You can't walk, I'll carry you. Hold on to my neck."

Gusev puts his arm around the soldier's neck, the latter places his uninjured arm round him and carries him up. On the deck, discharged soldiers and sailors are lying asleep side by side; there are so many of them it is difficult to pass.

"Get down on the floor," the soldier with the bandage says softly. "Follow me quietly, hold on to my shirt."

It is dark, there are no lights on deck or on the masts or anywhere on the sea around. On the prow the seaman on watch stands perfectly still like a statue, and it looks as though he, too, were asleep. The steamer seems to be left to its own devices and to be going where it pleases.

"Now they'll throw Pavel Ivanych into the sea," says the soldier with the bandage, "in a sack and then into the water."

"Yes, that's the regulation."

"At home, it's better to lie in the earth. Anyway, your mother will come to the grave and shed a tear."

"Sure."

There is a smell of dung and hay. With drooping heads, steers stand at the ship's rail. One, two, three—eight of them! And there's a pony. Gusev puts out his hand to stroke it, but it shakes its head, shows its teeth, and tries to bite his sleeve.

"Damn brute!" says Gusev crossly.

The two of them thread their way to the prow, then stand at the rail, peering. Overhead there is deep sky, bright stars, peace and quiet, exactly as at home in the village. But below there is darkness and disorder. Tall waves are making an uproar for no reason. Each one of them as you look at it is trying to rise higher than all the rest and to chase and crush its neighbor; it is thunderously attacked by a third wave that has a gleaming white mane and is just as ferocious and ugly.

4. The sacrament also known as the Anointing of the Sick, or Last Rites.

The sea has neither sense nor pity. If the steamer had been smaller, not made of thick iron plates, the waves would have crushed it without the slightest remorse, and would have devoured all the people in it without distinguishing between saints and sinners. The steamer's expression was equally senseless and cruel. This beaked monster presses forward, cutting millions of waves in its path; it fears neither darkness nor the wind, nor space, nor solitude—it's all child's play for it, and if the ocean had its population, this monster would crush it, too, without distinguishing between saints and sinners.

"Where are we now?" asks Gusev.

"I don't know. Must be the ocean."

"You can't see land . . ."

"No chance of it! They say we'll see it only in seven days."

The two men stare silently at the white phosphorescent foam and brood. Gusev is first to break the silence.

"There is nothing frightening here," he says. "Only you feel queer as if you were in a dark forest; but if, let's say, they lowered the boat this minute and an officer ordered me to go fifty miles across the sea to catch fish, I'll go. Or, let's say, if a Christian were to fall into the water right now, I'd jump in after him. A German or a Chink I wouldn't try to save, but I'd go in after a Christian."

"And are you afraid to die?"

"I am. I am sorry about the farm. My brother at home, you know, isn't steady; he drinks, he beats his wife for no reason, he doesn't honor his father and mother. Without me everything will go to rack and ruin, and before long it's my fear that my father and old mother will be begging their bread. But my legs won't hold me up, brother, and it's stifling here. Let's go to sleep."

V

Gusev goes back to the infirmary and gets into his bunk. He is again tormented by a vague desire and he can't make out what it is that he wants. There is a weight on his chest, a throbbing in his head, his mouth is so dry that it is difficult for him to move his tongue. He dozes and talks in his sleep and, worn out with nightmares, with coughing and the stifling heat, towards morning he falls into a heavy sleep. He dreams that they have just taken the bread out of the oven in the barracks and that he has climbed into the oven and is having a steam bath there, lashing himself with a besom of birch twigs. He sleeps for two days and on the third at noon two sailors come down and carry him out of the infirmary. He is sewn up in sailcloth and to make him heavier, they put two gridirons in with him. Sewn up in sailcloth, he looks like a carrot or a radish: broad at the head and narrow at the feet. Before sunset, they carry him on deck and put him on a plank. One end of the plank lies on the ship's rail, the other on a box placed on a stool. Round him stand the discharged soldiers and the crew with heads bared.

"Blessed is our God," the priest begins, "now, and ever, and unto ages of ages."

"Amen," three sailors chant.

The discharged men and the crew cross themselves and look off at the waves. It is strange that a man should be sewn up in sailcloth and should soon be flying into the sea. Is it possible that such a thing can happen to anyone?

The priest strews earth upon Gusev and makes obeisance to him. The men sing "Memory Eternal."

The seaman on watch duty raises the end of the plank, Gusev slides off it slowly and then flying, head foremost, turns over in the air and—plop! Foam covers him, and for a moment, he seems to be wrapped in lace, but the instant passes and he disappears in the waves.

He plunges rapidly downward. Will he reach the bottom? At this spot the ocean is said to be three miles deep. After sinking sixty or seventy feet, he begins to descend more and more slowly, swaying rhythmically as though in hesitation, and, carried along by the current, moves faster laterally than vertically.

And now he runs into a school of fish called pilot fish. Seeing the dark body, the little fish stop as though petrified and suddenly all turn round together and disappear. In less than a minute they rush back at Gusev, swift as arrows and begin zigzagging round him in the water. Then another dark body appears. It is a shark. With dignity and reluctance, seeming not to notice Gusev, as it were, it swims under him; then while he, moving downward, sinks upon its back, the shark turns, belly upward, basks in the warm transparent water and languidly opens its jaws with two rows of teeth. The pilot fish are in ecstasy; they stop to see what will happen next. After playing a little with the body, the shark nonchalantly puts his jaws under it, cautiously touches it with his teeth and the sailcloth is ripped the full length of the body, from head to foot; one of the gridirons falls out, frightens the pilot fish and striking the shark on the flank, sinks rapidly to the bottom.

Meanwhile, up above, in that part of the sky where the sun is about to set, clouds are massing, one resembling a triumphal arch, another a lion, a third a pair of scissors. A broad shaft of green light issues from the clouds and reaches to the middle of the sky; a while later, a violet beam appears alongside of it and then a golden one and a pink one . . . The heavens turn a soft lilac tint. Looking at this magnificent enchanting sky, the ocean frowns at first, but soon it, too, takes on tender, joyous, passionate colors for which it is hard to find a name in the language of man.

1890

---

RELATED:

—Richard Bausch on "Gusev," p. 918

# KATE CHOPIN
## *1851–1904*

Chopin was born in St. Louis to a prominent Creole-Irish family that prized books and education. On a visit to New Orleans she met her husband-to-be and returned there to live with him when she married at twenty. After her husband's early death, she went back to St. Louis and began to write, largely drawing on the experiences of her years in the Deep South. She contributed to many of the popular periodicals of her time, but her writing career came to an end with the publication of her novel *The Awakening* (1899), which was sharply condemned for its frank representation of adultery and mixed marriage. This book has subsequently been praised for its sensitive portrayal of a woman in quest of her individuality. Many of Chopin's stories were collected in *Bayou Folk* (1894) and *A Night in Acadie* (1899).

## The Story of an Hour

Knowing that Mrs. Mallard was afflicted with a heart trouble, great care was taken to break to her as gently as possible the news of her husband's death.

It was her sister Josephine who told her, in broken sentences; veiled hints that revealed in half concealing. Her husband's friend Richards was there, too, near her. It was he who had been in the newspaper office when intelligence of the railroad disaster was received, with Brently Mallard's name leading the list of "killed." He had only taken the time to assure himself of its truth by a second telegram, and had hastened to forestall any less careful, less tender friend in bearing the sad message.

She did not hear the story as many women have heard the same, with a paralyzed inability to accept its significance. She wept at once, with sudden, wild abandonment, in her sister's arms. When the storm of grief had spent itself she went away to her room alone. She would have no one follow her.

There stood, facing the open window, a comfortable, roomy armchair. Into this she sank, pressed down by a physical exhaustion that haunted her body and seemed to reach into her soul.

She could see in the open square before her house the tops of trees that were all aquiver with the new spring life. The delicious breath of rain was in the air. In the street below a peddler was crying his wares. The notes of a distant song which some one was singing reached her faintly, and countless sparrows were twittering in the eaves.

There were patches of blue sky showing here and there through the clouds that had met and piled one above the other in the west facing her window.

She sat with her head thrown back upon the cushion of the chair, quite motionless, except when a sob came up into her throat and shook her, as a child who has cried itself to sleep continues to sob in its dreams.

She was young, with a fair, calm face, whose lines bespoke repression and even a certain strength. But now there was a dull stare in her eyes, whose gaze was fixed away off yonder on one of those patches of blue sky. It was not a glance of reflection, but rather indicated a suspension of intelligent thought.

There was something coming to her and she was waiting for it, fearfully. What was it? She did not know; it was too subtle and elusive to name. But she felt it, creeping out of the sky, reaching toward her through the sounds, the scents, the color that filled the air.

Now her bosom rose and fell tumultuously. She was beginning to recognize this thing that was approaching to possess her, and she was striving to beat it back with her will—as powerless as her two white slender hands would have been.

When she abandoned herself a little whispered word escaped her slightly parted lips. She said it over and over under her breath: "free, free, free!" The vacant stare and the look of terror that had followed it went from her eyes. They stayed keen and bright. Her pulses beat fast, and the coursing blood warmed and relaxed every inch of her body.

She did not stop to ask if it were or were not a monstrous joy that held her. A clear and exalted perception enabled her to dismiss the suggestion as trivial.

She knew that she would weep again when she saw the kind, tender hands folded in death; the face that had never looked save with love upon her, fixed and gray and dead. But she saw beyond that bitter moment a long procession of years to come that would belong to her absolutely. And she opened and spread her arms out to them in welcome.

There would be no one to live for her during those coming years; she would live for herself. There would be no powerful will bending hers in that blind persistence with which men and women believe they have a right to impose a private will upon a fellow-creature. A kind intention or a cruel intention made the act seem no less a crime as she looked upon it in that brief moment of illumination.

And yet she had loved him—sometimes. Often she had not. What did it matter! What could love, the unsolved mystery, count for in face of this possession of self-assertion which she suddenly recognized as the strongest impulse of her being!

"Free! Body and soul free!" she kept whispering.

Josephine was kneeling before the closed door with her lips to the keyhole, imploring for admission. "Louise, open the door! I beg; open the door—you will make yourself ill. What are you doing, Louise? For heaven's sake open the door."

"Go away. I am not making myself ill." No; she was drinking in a very elixir of life through that open window.

Her fancy was running riot along those days ahead of her. Spring days, and summer days, and all sorts of days that would be her own. She breathed a quick prayer that life might be long. It was only yesterday she had thought with a shudder that life might be long.

She arose at length and opened the door to her sister's importunities. There was a feverish triumph in her eyes, and she carried herself unwittingly like a goddess of Victory. She clasped her sister's waist, and together they descended the stairs. Richards stood waiting for them at the bottom.

Some one was opening the front door with a latchkey. It was Brently Mallard who entered, a little travel-stained, composedly carrying his grip-sack and umbrella. He had been far from the scene of accident, and did not even know there had been one. He stood amazed at Josephine's piercing cry; at Richards' quick motion to screen him from the view of his wife.

But Richards was too late.

When the doctors came they said she had died of heart disease—of joy that kills.

1891

# JOSEPH CONRAD
## *1857–1924*

Conrad (christened Jozef Teodor Konrad Nalecz Korzeniowski) was born in Polish Ukraine to a family of landed gentry. In 1863 his hotheaded father was exiled for revolutionary activities to an area northeast of Moscow. He took his family with him to this inhospitable region, where the climate proved too much for both parents. The orphaned Conrad at seventeen persuaded his guardian uncle to let him join the French merchant navy, and for about twenty years he sailed to many exotic places, surviving shipwrecks and (probably) an attempted suicide, running guns at intervals in his more respectable occupations and rising, finally, to the rank of master (captain) in the British merchant fleet. He began to write before he gave up his seagoing career; and some of his early work led to his friendship with such literary figures as Henry James, Stephen Crane, and Ford Madox Ford. With their encouragement he not only devoted himself full time to fiction but developed the style and form of narration that are so much his own. (One of the marvels is that so fine a stylist should have written in English when Polish was his native tongue and French his "second language.") Though he was respected from the beginning of his writing career and critically acclaimed after the publication of *The Nigger of the "Narcissus"* (1897), he had small popular success before his novel *Chance* was brought out in 1914. In his later years, after World War I, he was one of the most venerated of English novelists. He was working on a novel of Napoleon's escape from Elba when he died. His novels include *Lord Jim* (1900), *Nostromo* (1904), *The Secret Agent* (1907), *Under Western Eyes* (1910), and *Victory* (1915). Three works of medium length, including the novella *Heart of Darkness*, were published in *Youth* (1902).

# Heart of Darkness

## I

The *Nellie,* a cruising yawl, swung to her anchor without a flutter of the sails, and was at rest. The flood had made, the wind was nearly calm, and being bound down the river, the only thing for it was to come to and wait for the turn of the tide.

The sea-reach[1] of the Thames stretched before us like the beginning of an interminable waterway. In the offing[2] the sea and the sky were welded together

---

**1.** Tidal part of the river as it broadens toward the sea.   **2.** Part of the sea visible from the river's mouth.

without a joint, and in the luminous space the tanned sails of the barges drifting up with the tide seemed to stand still in red clusters of canvas sharply peaked, with gleams of varnished sprits. A haze rested on the low shores that ran out to sea in vanishing flatness. The air was dark above Gravesend,[3] and farther back still seemed condensed into a mournful gloom, brooding motionless over the biggest, and the greatest, town on earth.

The Director of Companies was our captain and our host. We four affectionately watched his back as he stood in the bows looking to seaward. On the whole river there was nothing that looked half so nautical. He resembled a pilot, which to a seaman is trustworthiness personified. It was difficult to realize his work was not out there in the luminous estuary, but behind him, within the brooding gloom.

Between us there was, as I have already said somewhere, the bond of the sea. Besides holding our hearts together through long periods of separation, it had the effect of making us tolerant of each other's yarns—and even convictions. The Lawyer—the best of old fellows—had, because of his many years and many virtues, the only cushion on deck, and was lying on the only rug. The accountant had brought out already a box of dominoes, and was toying architecturally with the bones. Marlow sat cross-legged right aft, leaning against the mizzen-mast. He had sunken cheeks, a yellow complexion, a straight back, and ascetic aspect, and, with his arms dropped, the palms of hands outwards, resembled an idol. The director, satisfied the anchor had good hold, made his way aft and sat down amongst us. We exchanged a few words lazily. Afterwards there was silence on board the yacht. For some reason or other we did not begin that game of dominoes. We felt meditative, and fit for nothing but placid staring. The day was ending in a serenity of still and exquisite brilliance. The water shone pacifically; the sky, without a speck, was a benign immensity of unstained light; the very mist on the Essex marshes[4] was like a gauzy and radiant fabric, hung from the wooded rises inland, and draping the low shores in diaphanous folds. Only the gloom to the west, brooding over the upper reaches, became more somber every minute, as if angered by the approach of the sun.

And at last, in its curved and imperceptible fall, the sun sank low, and from glowing white changed to a dull red without rays and without heat, as if about to go out suddenly, stricken to death by the touch of that gloom brooding over a crowd of men.

Forthwith a change came over the waters, and the serenity became less brilliant but more profound. The old river in its broad reach rested unruffled at the decline of day, after ages of good service done to the race that peopled its banks, spread out in the tranquil dignity of a waterway leading to the uttermost ends of the earth. We looked at the venerable stream not in the vivid flush of a short day that comes and departs forever, but in the august light of abiding memories. And indeed nothing is easier for a man who has, as the phrase goes, "followed the sea" with reverence and affection, than to evoke the great spirit of the past upon the lower reaches of the Thames. The tidal current runs to and fro in its unceasing service, crowded with memories of men and ships it had borne to the rest of home or to the battles of the sea. It

---

**3.** City on the Thames, twenty-six miles east of London.  **4.** On the north bank of the Thames.

had known and served all the men of whom the nation is proud, from Sir Francis Drake to Sir John Franklin,[5] knights all, titled and untitled—the great knights-errant of the sea. It had borne all the ships whose names are like jewels flashing in the night of time, from the *Golden Hind* returning with her round flanks full of treasure, to be visited by the Queen's Highness and thus pass out of the gigantic tale, to the *Erebus* and *Terror,* bound on other conquests—and that never returned. It had known the ships and the men. They had sailed from Deptford, from Greenwich, from Erith—the adventurers and the settlers; kings' ships and the ships of men on 'Change; captains, admirals, the dark "interlopers"[6] of the Eastern trade, and the commissioned "Generals" of East India fleets. Hunters for gold or pursuers of fame, they all had gone out on that stream, bearing the sword, and often the torch, messengers of the might within the land, bearers of a spark from the sacred fire. What greatness had not floated on the ebb of that river into the mystery of an unknown earth! . . . The dreams of men, the seed of commonwealths, the germs of empires.

The sun set; the dusk fell on the stream, and lights began to appear along the shore. The Chapman lighthouse, a three-legged thing erect on a mud-flat, shone strongly. Lights of ships moved in the fairway—a great stir of lights going up and going down. And farther west on the upper reaches the place of the monstrous town was still marked ominously on the sky, a brooding gloom in sunshine, a lurid glare under the stars.

"And this also," said Marlow suddenly, "has been one of the dark places on the earth."

.He was the only man of us who still "followed the sea." The worst that could be said of him was that he did not represent his class. He was a seaman, but he was a wanderer, too, while most seamen lead, if one may so express it, a sedentary life. Their minds are of the stay-at-home order, and their home is always with them—the ship; and so is their country—the sea. One ship is very much like another, and the sea is always the same. In the immutability of their surroundings the foreign shores, the foreign faces, the changing immensity of life, glide past, veiled not by a sense of mystery but by a slightly disdainful ignorance; for there is nothing mysterious to a seaman unless it be the sea itself, which is the mistress of his existence and as inscrutable as Destiny. For the rest, after his hours of work, a casual stroll or a casual spree on shore suffices to unfold for him the secret of a whole continent, and generally he finds the secret not worth knowing. The yarns of seamen have a direct simplicity, the whole meaning of which lies within the shell of a cracked nut. But Marlow was not typical (if his propensity to spin yarns be excepted), and to him the meaning of an episode was not inside like a kernel but outside, enveloping the tale which brought it out only as a glow brings out a haze, in the likeness of one of these misty halos that sometimes are made visible by the spectral illumination of moonshine.

**5.** An Arctic explorer (1786–1847) who commanded an expedition, including the ships *Erebus* and *Terror,* and was lost in a search for the Northwest Passage. Drake (1540–1596) sailed around the world aboard the *Golden Hind* (1577–80) and defeated the Spanish Armada (1588). **6.** Unauthorized competitors of the East India Company, chartered by the British Crown, in the reign of Charles II, who were given the right to maintain troops in India and thus to appoint "generals." Deptford, Greenwich, and Erith are seaports on the Thames. 'Change, i.e., Exchange, the financial district of London.

His remark did not seem at all surprising. It was just like Marlow. It was accepted in silence. No one took the trouble to grunt even; and presently he said, very slow—

"I was thinking of very old times, when the Romans first came here, nineteen hundred years ago—the other day. . . . Light came out of this river since—you say Knights? Yes; but it is like a running blaze on a plain, like a flash of lightning in the clouds. We live in the flicker—may it last as long as the old earth keeps rolling! But darkness was here yesterday. Imagine the feelings of a commander of a fine—what d'ye call 'em?—trireme[7] in the Mediterranean, ordered suddenly to the north; run overland across the Gauls[8] in a hurry; put in charge of one of these craft the legionaries—a wonderful lot of handy men they must have been, too—used to build, apparently by the hundred, in a month or two, if we may believe what we read. Imagine him here—the very end of the world, a sea the color of lead, a sky the color of smoke, a kind of ship about as rigid as a concertina—and going up this river with stores, or orders, or what you like. Sand-banks, marshes, forests, savages,—precious little to eat fit for a civilized man, nothing but Thames water to drink. No Falernian wine[9] here, no going ashore. Here and there a military camp lost in a wilderness, like a needle in a bundle of hay—cold, fog, tempests, disease, exile, and death,—death skulking in the air, in the water, in the bush. They must have been dying like flies here. Oh yes—he did it. Did it very well, too, no doubt, and without thinking much about it either, except afterwards to brag of what he had gone through in his time, perhaps. They were men enough to face the darkness. And perhaps he was cheered by keeping his eye on a chance of promotion to the fleet at Ravenna[1] by and by, if he had good friends in Rome and survived the awful climate. Or think of a decent young citizen in a toga—perhaps too much dice, you know—coming out here in the train of some prefect,[2] or taxgatherer, or trader even, to mend his fortunes. Land in a swamp, march through the woods, and in some inland post feel the savagery, the utter savagery, had closed round him,—all that mysterious life of the wilderness that stirs in the forest, in the jungles, in the hearts of wild men. There's no initiation either into such mysteries. He has to live in the midst of the incomprehensible, which is also detestable. And it has a fascination, too, that goes to work upon him. The fascination of the abomination—you know, imagine the growing regrets, the longing to escape, the powerless disgust, the surrender, the hate."

He paused.

"Mind," he began again, lifting one arm from the elbow, the palm of the hand outwards, so that, with his legs folded before him, he had the pose of a Buddha preaching in European clothes and without a lotus-flower—"Mind, none of us would feel exactly like this. What saves us is efficiency—the devotion to efficiency. But these chaps were not much account, really. They were no colonists; their administration was merely a squeeze, and nothing more, I suspect. They were conquerors, and for that you want only brute force—nothing to boast of, when you have it, since your strength is just an accident arising from the weakness of others. They grabbed what they could get for the sake of what was to be got. It was just robbery with violence, aggravated

7. Roman galley propelled by three banks of oars.  **8.** Inhabitants of France in Roman times.  **9.** Legendary Roman wine.  **1.** Base on the Adriatic in northern Italy—a comfortable assignment.  **2.** High official.

murder on a great scale, and men going at it blind—as is very proper for those who tackle a darkness. The conquest of the earth, which mostly means the taking it away from those who have a different complexion or slightly flatter noses than ourselves, is not a pretty thing when you look into it too much. What redeems it is the idea only. An idea at the back of it; not a sentimental pretense but an idea; and an unselfish belief in the idea—something you can set up, and bow down before, and offer a sacrifice to. . . ."

He broke off. Flames glided in the river, small green flames, red flames, white flames, pursuing, overtaking, joining, crossing each other—then separating slowly or hastily. The traffic of the great city went on in the deepening night upon the sleepless river. We looked on, waiting patiently—there was nothing else to do till the end of the flood; but it was only after a long silence, when he said, in a hesitating voice, "I suppose you fellows remember I did once turn fresh-water sailor for a bit," that we knew we were fated, before the ebb began to run, to hear one of Marlow's inconclusive experiences.

"I don't want to bother you much with what happened to me personally," he began, showing in this remark the weakness of many tellers of tales who seem so often unaware of what their audience would best like to hear; "yet to understand the effect of it on me you ought to know how I got out there, what I saw, how I went up that river to the place where I first met the poor chap. It was the farthest point of navigation and the culminating point of my experience. It seemed somehow to throw a kind of light on everything about me—and into my thoughts. It was somber enough, too—and pitiful—not extraordinary in any way—not very clear either. No, not very clear. And yet it seemed to throw a kind of light.

"I had then, as you remember, just returned to London after a lot of Indian Ocean, Pacific, China Seas—a regular dose of the East—six years or so, and I was loafing about, hindering you fellows in your work and invading your homes, just as though I had got a heavenly mission to civilize you. It was very fine for a time, but after a bit I did get tired of resting. Then I began to look for a ship—I should think the hardest work on earth. But the ships wouldn't even look at me. And I got tired of that game too.

"Now when I was a little chap I had a passion for maps. I would look for hours at South America, or Africa, or Australia, and lose myself in all the glories of exploration. At that time there were many blank spaces on the earth, and when I saw one that looked particularly inviting on a map (but they all look that) I would put my finger on it and say, When I grow up I will go there. The North Pole was one of these places, I remember. Well, I haven't been there yet, and shall not try now. The glamour's off. Other places were scattered about the Equator, and in every sort of latitude all over the two hemispheres. I have been in some of them, and . . . well, we won't talk about that. But there was one yet—the biggest, the most blank, so to speak—that I had a hankering after.

"True, by this time it was not a blank space any more. It had got filled since my childhood with rivers and lakes and names. It had ceased to be a blank space of delightful mystery—a white patch for a boy to dream gloriously over. It had become a place of darkness.[3] But there was in it one river especially, a

3. Congo Free State (now Democratic Republic of the Congo). At the time of the story it was a colony owned personally, in effect, by Leopold II, king of Belgium; it consisted of the Congo River basin and some adjacent territories, a total area of nearly a million square miles.

mighty big river, that you could see on the map, resembling an immense snake uncoiled, with its head in the sea, its body at rest curving afar over a vast country, and its tail lost in the depths of the land. And as I looked at the map of it in a shop-window, it fascinated me as a snake would a bird—a silly little bird. Then I remembered there was a big concern, a Company for trade on that river. Dash it all! I thought to myself, they can't trade without using some kind of craft on that lot of fresh water—steamboats! Why shouldn't I try to get charge of one? I went on along Fleet Street, but could not shake off the idea. The snake had charmed me.

"You understand it was a Continental concern, that Trading society; but I have a lot of relations living on the Continent, because it's cheap and not so nasty as it looks, they say.

"I am sorry to own I began to worry them. This was already a fresh departure for me. I was not used to getting things that way, you know. I always went my own road and on my own legs where I had a mind to go. I wouldn't have believed it of myself; but, then—you see—I felt somehow I must get there by hook or by crook. So I worried them. The men said, 'My dear fellow,' and did nothing. Then—would you believe it?—I tried the women. I, Charlie Marlow, set the women to work—to get a job. Heavens! Well, you see, the notion drove me. I had an aunt, a dear enthusiastic soul. She wrote: 'It will be delightful. I am ready to do anything, anything for you. It is a glorious idea. I know the wife of a very high personage in the Administration, and also a man who has lots of influence with,' etc. etc. She was determined to make no end of fuss to get me appointed skipper of a river steamboat, if such was my fancy.

"I got my appointment—of course; and I got it very quick. It appears the Company had received news that one of their captains had been killed in a scuffle with the natives. This was my chance, and it made me the more anxious to go. It was only months and months afterwards, when I made the attempt to recover what was left of the body, that I heard the original quarrel arose from a misunderstanding about some hens. Yes, two black hens. Fresleven—that was the fellow's name, a Dane—thought himself wronged somehow in the bargain, so he went ashore and started to hammer the chief of the village with a stick. Oh, it didn't surprise me in the least to hear this, and at the same time to be told that Fresleven was the gentlest, quietest creature that ever walked on two legs. No doubt he was; but he had been a couple of years already out there engaged in the noble cause, you know, and he probably felt the need at last of asserting his self-respect in some way. Therefore he whacked the old nigger mercilessly, while a big crowd of his people watched him, thunderstruck, till some man—I was told the chief's son—in desperation at hearing the old chap yell, made a tentative jab with a spear at the white man—and of course it went quite easy between the shoulder blades. Then the whole population cleared into the forest, expecting all kinds of calamities to happen, while, on the other hand, the steamer Fresleven commanded left also in a bad panic, in charge of the engineer, I believe. Afterwards nobody seemed to trouble much about Fresleven's remains, till I got out and stepped into his shoes. I couldn't let it rest, though; but when an opportunity offered at last to meet my predecessor, the grass growing through his ribs was tall enough to hide his bones. They were all there. The supernatural being had not been touched after he fell. And the village was deserted, the huts gaped black, rotting, all askew within the fallen enclosures. A calamity had come to it, sure enough. The people had vanished. Mad terror had scattered them, men, women, and children, through the bush, and they had never returned. What became of the hens I don't know either. I should think the cause of progress got them, anyhow. However, through this glorious affair I got my appointment, before I had fairly begun to hope for it.

"I flew around like mad to get ready, and before forty-eight hours I was crossing the Channel to show myself to my employers, and sign the contract. In a very few hours I arrived in a city[4] that always makes me think of a whited sepulcher. Prejudice no doubt. I had no difficulty in finding the Company's offices. It was the biggest thing in the town, and everybody I met was full of it. They were going to run an oversea empire, and make no end of coin by trade.

"A narrow and deserted street in deep shadow, high houses, innumerable windows with venetian blinds, a dead silence, grass sprouting between the stones, imposing carriage archways right and left, immense double doors standing ponderously ajar. I slipped through one of these cracks, went up a swept and unvarnished staircase, as arid as a desert, and opened the first door I came to. Two women, one fat and the other slim, sat on straw-bottomed chairs, knitting black wool. The slim one got up and walked straight at me—still knitting with downcast eyes—and only just as I began to think of getting out of her way, as you would for a somnambulist, stood still, and looked up. Her dress was as plain as an umbrella-cover, and she turned round without a word and preceded me into a waiting-room. I gave my name, and looked about. Deal table in the middle, plain chairs all around the walls, on one end a large shining map, marked with all the colors of a rainbow. There was a vast amount of red—good to see at any time, because one knows that some real work is done in there, a deuce of a lot of blue, a little green, smears of orange, and, on the East Coast, a purple patch,[5] to show where the jolly pioneers of progress drink the jolly lager-beer. However, I wasn't going into any of these. I was going into the yellow. Dead in the center. And the river was there—fascinating—deadly—like a snake. Ough! A door opened, a white-haired secretarial head, but wearing a compassionate expression, appeared, and a skinny forefinger beckoned me into the sanctuary. Its light was dim, and a heavy writing-desk squatted in the middle. From behind that structure came out an impression of pale plumpness in a frock-coat. The great man himself. He was five feet six, I should judge, and had his grip on the handle-end of ever so many millions. He shook hands, I fancy, murmured vaguely, was satisfied with my French. *Bon voyage.*[6]

"In about forty-five seconds I found myself again in the waiting-room with the compassionate secretary, who, full of desolation and sympathy, made me sign some document. I believe I undertook amongst other things not to disclose any trade secrets. Well, I am not going to.

"I began to feel slightly uneasy. You know I am not used to such ceremonies, and there was something ominous in the atmosphere. It was just as though I had been let into some conspiracy—I don't know—something not quite right; and I was glad to get out. In the outer room the two women knit-

---

**4.** Brussels, Belgium. *Whited sepulcher:* hypocrite. (Metaphor attributed to Jesus; cf. Matthew 23: 27.)   **5.** The red areas on the map were British colonies; blue, French; green, Italian; orange, Portuguese; and purple, German East Africa.   **6.** "Have a good trip" (French).

ted black wool feverishly. People were arriving, and the younger one was walking back and forth introducing them. The old one sat on her chair. Her flat cloth slippers were propped up on a footwarmer, and a cat reposed on her lap. She wore a starched white affair on her head, had a wart on one cheek, and silver-rimmed spectacles hung on the tip of her nose. She glanced at me above the glasses. The swift and indifferent placidity of that look troubled me. Two youths with foolish and cheery countenances were being piloted over, and she threw at them the same quick glance of unconcerned wisdom. She seemed to know all about them and about me, too. An eerie feeling came over me. She seemed uncanny and fateful. Often far away there I thought of these two, guarding the door of Darkness, knitting black wool as for a warm pall, one introducing, introducing continuously to the unknown, the other scrutinizing the cheery and foolish faces with unconcerned old eyes. *Ave!* Old knitter of black wool. *Morituri te salutant.*[7] Not many of those she looked at ever saw her again—not half, by a long way.

"There was yet a visit to the doctor. 'A simple formality,' assured me the secretary, with an air of taking an immense part in all my sorrows. Accordingly a young chap wearing his hat over the left eyebrow, some clerk I suppose—there must have been clerks in the business, though the house was as still as a house in a city of the dead—came from somewhere upstairs, and led me forth. He was shabby and careless, with inkstains on the sleeves of his jacket, and his cravat was large and billowy, under a chin shaped like the toe of an old boot. It was a little too early for the doctor, so I proposed a drink, and thereupon he developed a vein of joviality. As we sat over our vermouths he glorified the Company's business, and by and by I expressed casually my surprise at him not going out there. He became very cool and collected all at once. 'I am not such a fool as I look, quoth Plato to his disciples,' he said sententiously, emptied his glass with great resolution, and we rose.

"The old doctor felt my pulse, evidently thinking of something else the while. 'Good, good for there,' he mumbled, and then with a certain eagerness asked me whether I would let him measure my head.[8] Rather surprised, I said Yes, when he produced a thing like calipers and got the dimensions back and front and every way, taking notes carefully. He was an unshaven little man in a threadbare coat like a gaberdine, with his feet in slippers, and I thought him a harmless fool. 'I always ask leave, in the interests of science, to measure the crania of those going out there,' he said. 'And when they come back, too?' I asked. 'Oh, I never see them,' he remarked; 'and, moreover, the changes take place inside, you know.' He smiled, as if at some quiet joke. 'So you are going out there. Famous. Interesting too.' He gave me a searching glance, and made another note. 'Ever any madness in your family?' he asked, in a matter-of-fact tone. I felt very annoyed. 'Is that question in the interests of science, too?' 'It would be,' he said, without taking notice of my irritation, 'interesting for science to watch the mental changes of individuals, on the spot, but . . .' 'Are you an alienist?'[9] I interrupted. 'Every doctor should be—a little,' answered that original, imperturbably. 'I have a little theory which you Messieurs who go

7. "Hail! . . . They who are about to die salute you" (Latin). The traditional salutation of gladiators in ancient Rome.   8. Phrenology, the study of skull conformation as an index of mind and personality, was a more or less respectable part of 19th-century medical study.   9. Doctor who treats mental disease.

out there must help me to prove. This is my share in the advantages my country shall reap from the possession of such a magnificent dependency. The mere wealth I leave to others. Pardon my questions, but you are the first Englishman coming under my observation . . .' I hastened to assure him I was not in the least typical. 'If I were,' said I, 'I wouldn't be talking like this with you.' 'What you say is rather profound, and probably erroneous,' he said, with a laugh. 'Avoid irritation more than exposure to the sun. Adieu. How do you English say, eh? Good-by. Ah! Good-by. Adieu. In the tropics one must before everything keep calm.' . . . He lifted a warning forefinger. . . . *'Du calme, du calme. Adieu.'*[1]

"One thing more remained to do—say good-by to my excellent aunt. I found her triumphant. I had a cup of tea—the last decent cup of tea for many days—and in a room that most soothingly looked just as you would expect a lady's drawing-room to look, we had a long quiet chat by the fireside. In the course of these confidences it became quite plain to me I had been represented to the wife of the high dignitary, and goodness knows to how many more people besides, as an exceptional and gifted creature—a piece of good fortune for the Company—a man you don't get hold of every day. Good heavens! and I was going to take charge of a two-penny-half-penny river-steamboat with a penny whistle attached! It appeared, however, I was also one of the Workers, with a capital—you know. Something like an emissary of light, something like a lower sort of apostle. There had been a lot of such rot let loose in print and talk just about that time, and the excellent woman, living right in the rush of all that humbug, got carried off her feet. She talked about 'weaning those ignorant millions from their horrid ways,' till, upon my word, she made me quite uncomfortable. I ventured to hint that the Company was run for profit.

" 'You forget, dear Charlie, that the laborer is worthy of his hire,'[2] she said, brightly. It's queer how out of touch with truth women are. They live in a world of their own, and there has never been anything like it, and never can be. It is too beautiful altogether, and if they were to set it up it would go to pieces before the first sunset. Some confounded fact we men have been living contentedly with ever since the day of creation would start up and knock the whole thing over.

"After this I got embraced, told to wear flannel, be sure to write often, and so on—and I left. In the street—I don't know why—a queer feeling came to me that I was an impostor. Odd thing that I, who used to clear out for any part of the world at twenty-four hours' notice, with less thought than most men give to the crossing of a street, had a moment—I won't say of hesitation, but of startled pause, before this commonplace affair. The best way I can explain it to you is by saying that, for a second or two, I felt as though, instead of going to the center of a continent, I were about to set off for the center of the earth.

"I left in a French steamer, and she called in every blamed port they have out there,[3] for, as far as I could see, the sole purpose of landing soldiers and custom-house officers. I watched the coast. Watching a coast as it slips by the ship is like thinking about an enigma. There it is before you—smiling, frown-

---

1. "Keep calm, keep calm. Good-bye" (French).   2. Words of Christ (Luke 10.7).   3. French colonies stretched down most of the West African coast to the mouth of the Congo, with major ports at Casablanca and Dakar.

ing, inviting, grand, mean, insipid, or savage, and always mute with an air of whispering, Come and find out. This one was almost featureless, as if still in the making, with an aspect of monotonous grimness. The edge of a colossal jungle, so dark-green as to be almost black, fringed with white surf, ran straight, like a ruled line, far, far away along a blue sea whose glitter was blurred by a creeping mist. The sun was fierce, the land seemed to glisten and drip with steam. Here and there grayish-whitish specks showed up clustered inside the white surf, with a flag flying above them perhaps. Settlements some centuries old, and still no bigger than pinheads on the untouched expanse of their background. We pounded along, stopped, landed soldiers; went on, landed custom-house clerks to levy toll in what looked like a God-forsaken wilderness, with a tin shed and a flag-pole lost in it; landed more soldiers—to take care of the custom-house clerks, presumably. Some, I heard, got drowned in the surf; but whether they did or not, nobody seemed particularly to care. They were just flung out there, and on we went. Every day the coast looked the same, as though we had not moved; but we passed various places—trading places—with names like Gran' Bassam, Little Popo; names that seemed to belong to some sordid farce acted in front of a sinister backcloth. The idleness of a passenger, my isolation amongst all these men with whom I had no point of contact, the oily and languid sea, the uniform somberness of the coast, seemed to keep me away from the truth of things, within the toil of a mournful and senseless delusion. The voice of the surf heard now and then was a positive pleasure, like the speech of a brother. It was something natural, that had its reason, that had a meaning. Now and then a boat from the shore gave one a momentary contact with reality. It was paddled by black fellows. You could see from afar the white of their eyeballs glistening. They shouted, sang; their bodies streamed with perspiration; they had faces like grotesque masks—these chaps; but they had bone, muscle, a wild vitality, an intense energy of movement, that was as natural and true as the surf along their coast. They wanted no excuse for being there. They were a great comfort to look at. For a time I would feel I belonged still to a world of straightforward facts; but the feeling would not last long. Something would turn up to scare it away. Once, I remember, we came upon a man-of-war anchored off the coast. There wasn't even a shed there, and she was shelling the bush. It appears the French had one of their wars going on thereabouts. Her ensign[4] dropped limp like a rag; the muzzles of the long six-inch guns stuck out all over the low hull; the greasy, slimy swell swung her up lazily and let her down, swaying her thin masts. In the empty immensity of earth, sky, and water, there she was, incomprehensible, firing into a continent. Pop, would go one of the six-inch guns; a small flame would dart and vanish, a little white smoke would disappear, a tiny projectile would give a feeble screech—and nothing happened. Nothing could happen. There was a touch of insanity in the proceeding, a sense of lugubrious drollery in the sight; and it was not dissipated by somebody on board assuring me earnestly there was a camp of natives—he called them enemies!—hidden out of sight somewhere.

"We gave her her letters (I heard the men in that lonely ship were dying of fever at the rate of three a day) and went on. We called at some more places

4. Flag.

with farcical names, where the merry dance of death and trade goes on in a still and earthy atmosphere as of an overheated catacomb; all along the formless coast bordered by dangerous surf, as if Nature herself had tried to ward off intruders; in and out of rivers, streams of death in life, whose banks were rotting into mud, whose waters, thickened into slime, invaded the contorted mangroves, that seemed to writhe at us in the extremity of an impotent despair. Nowhere did we stop long enough to get a particularized impression, but the general sense of vague and oppressive wonder grew upon me. It was like a weary pilgrimage amongst hints for nightmares.

"It was upward of thirty days before I saw the mouth of the big river. We anchored off the seat of the government.[5] But my work would not begin till some two hundred miles farther on. So as soon as I could I made a start for a place thirty miles higher up.

"I had my passage on a little sea-going steamer. Her captain was a Swede, and knowing me for a seaman, invited me on the bridge. He was a young man, lean, fair, and morose, with lanky hair and a shuffling gait. As we left the miserable little wharf, he tossed his head contemptuously at the shore. 'Been living there?' he asked. I said, 'Yes.' 'Fine lot these government chaps—are they not?' he went on, speaking English with great precision and considerable bitterness. 'It is funny what some people will do for a few francs a month. I wonder what becomes of that kind when it goes up-country?' I said to him I expected to see that soon. 'So-o-o!' he exclaimed. He shuffled athwart, keeping one eye ahead vigilantly. 'Don't be too sure,' he continued. 'The other day I took up a man who hanged himself on the road. He was a Swede, too.' 'Hanged himself! Why, in God's name?' I cried. He kept on looking out watchfully. 'Who knows? The sun was too much for him, or the country perhaps.'

"At last we opened a reach.[6] A rocky cliff appeared, mounds of turned-up earth by the shore, houses on a hill, others with iron roofs, amongst a waste of excavations, or hanging to the declivity.[7] A continuous noise of the rapids above hovered over this scene of inhabited devastation. A lot of people, mostly black and naked, moved about like ants. A jetty projected into the river. A blinding sunlight drowned all this at times in a sudden recrudescence of glare. 'There's your Company's station,' said the Swede, pointing to three wooden barrack-like structures on the rocky slope. 'I will send your things up. Four boxes did you say? So. Farewell.'

"I came upon a boiler wallowing in the grass, then found a path leading up the hill. It turned aside for the boulders, and also for an undersized railway-truck lying there on its back with its wheels in the air. One was off. The thing looked as dead as the carcass of some animal. I came upon more pieces of decaying machinery, a stack of rusty nails. To the left a clump of trees made a shady spot, where dark things seemed to stir feebly. I blinked, the path was steep. A horn tooted to the right, and I saw the black people run. A heavy and dull detonation shook the ground, a puff of smoke came out of the cliff, and that was all. No change appeared on the face of the rock. They were building a railway. The cliff was not in the way or anything; but this objectless blasting was all the work going on.

---

5. Boma, in the mouth of the Congo River.   6. That is, came to a clear stretch of the river.   7. Town of Matadi.

"A slight clinking behind me made me turn my head. Six black men advanced in a file, toiling up the path. They walked erect and slow, balancing small baskets full of earth on their heads, and the clink kept time with their footsteps. Black rags were wound round their loins, and the short ends behind waggled to and fro like tails. I could see every rib, the joints of their limbs were like knots in a rope; each had an iron collar on his neck, and all were connected together with a chain whose bights[8] swung between them, rhythmically clinking. Another report from the cliff made me think suddenly of that ship of war I had seen firing into a continent. It was the same kind of ominous voice; but these men could by no stretch of imagination be called enemies. They were called criminals, and the outraged law, like the bursting shells, had come to them, an insoluble mystery from the sea. All their meager breasts panted together, the violently dilated nostrils quivered, the eyes stared stonily up-hill. They passed me within six inches, without a glance, with that complete, deathlike indifference of unhappy savages. Behind this raw matter one of the reclaimed, the product of the new forces at work, strolled despondently, carrying a rifle by its middle. He had a uniform jacket with one button off, and seeing a white man on the path, hoisted his weapon to his shoulder with alacrity. This was simple prudence, white men being so much alike at a distance that he could not tell who I might be. He was speedily reassured, and with a large, white, rascally grin, and a glance at his charge, seemed to take me into partnership in his exalted trust. After all, I also was a part of the great cause of these high and just proceedings.

"Instead of going up, I turned and descended to the left. My idea was to let that chain-gang get out of sight before I climbed the hill. You know I am not particularly tender; I've had to strike and to fend off. I've had to resist and to attack sometimes—that's only one way of resisting—without counting the exact cost, according to the demands of such sort of life as I had blundered into. I've seen the devil of violence, and the devil of greed, and the devil of hot desire; but, by all the stars! these were strong, lusty, red-eyed devils, that swayed and drove men—men, I tell you. But as I stood on this hillside, I foresaw that in the blinding sunshine of that land I would become acquainted with a flabby, pretending, weak-eyed devil of a rapacious and pitiless folly. How insidious he could be, too, I was only to find out several months later and a thousand miles farther. For a moment I stood appalled, as though by a warning. Finally I descended the hill, obliquely, towards the trees I had seen.

"I avoided a vast artificial hole somebody had been digging on the slope, the purpose of which I found it impossible to divine. It wasn't a quarry or a sandpit, anyhow. It was just a hole. It might have been connected with the philanthropic desire of giving the criminals something to do. I don't know. Then I nearly fell into a very narrow ravine, almost no more than a scar in the hillside. I discovered that a lot of imported drainage-pipes for the settlement had been tumbled in there. There wasn't one that was not broken. It was a wanton smash-up. At last I got under the trees. My purpose was to stroll into the shade for a moment; but no sooner within than it seemed to me I had stepped into the gloomy circle of some Inferno. The rapids were near, and an uninterrupted, uniform, headlong, rushing noise filled the mournful still-

**8.** Slack sections.

ness of the grove, where not a breath stirred, not a leaf moved, with a mysterious sound—as though the tearing pace of the launched earth had suddenly become audible.

"Black shapes crouched, lay, sat between the trees, leaning against the trunks, clinging to the earth, half coming out, half effaced within the dim light, in all the attitudes of pain, abandonment, and despair. Another mine[9] on the cliff went off, followed by a slight shudder of the soil under my feet. The work was going on. The work! And this was the place where some of the helpers had withdrawn to die.

"They were dying slowly—it was very clear. They were not enemies, they were not criminals, they were nothing earthly now,—nothing but black shadows of disease and starvation, lying confusedly in the greenish gloom. Brought from all the recesses of the coast in all the legality of time contracts, lost in uncongenial surroundings, fed on unfamiliar food, they sickened, became inefficient, and were then allowed to crawl away and rest. These moribund shapes were free as air—and nearly as thin. I began to distinguish the gleam of the eyes under the trees. Then, glancing down, I saw a face near my hand. The black bones reclined at full length with one shoulder against the tree, and slowly the eyelids rose and the sunken eyes looked up at me, enormous and vacant, a kind of blind, white flicker in the depths of the orbs, which died out slowly. The man seemed young—almost a boy—but you know with them it's hard to tell. I found nothing else to do but to offer him one of my good Swede's ship's biscuits I had in my pocket. The fingers closed slowly on it and held—there was no other movement and no other glance. He had tied a bit of white worsted round his neck—Why? Where did he get it? Was it a badge—an ornament—a charm—a propitiatory act? Was there any idea at all connected with it? It looked startling round his black neck, this bit of white thread from beyond the seas.

"Near the same tree two more bundles of acute angles sat with their legs drawn up. One, with his chin propped on his knees, stared at nothing, in an intolerable and appalling manner: his brother phantom rested its forehead, as if overcome with a great weariness; and all about others were scattered in every pose of contorted collapse, as in some picture of a massacre or a pestilence. While I stood horror-struck, one of these creatures rose to his hands and knees, and went off on all-fours towards the river to drink. He lapped out of his hand, then sat up in the sunlight, crossing his shins in front of him, and after a time let his woolly head fall on his breastbone.

"I didn't want any more loitering in the shade, and I made haste towards the station. When near the buildings I met a white man, in such an unexpected elegance of get-up that in the first moment I took him for a sort of vision. I saw a high starched collar, white cuffs, a light alpaca jacket, snowy trousers, a clear necktie, and varnished boots. No hat. Hair parted, brushed, oiled, under a green-lined parasol held in a big white hand. He was amazing, and had a penholder behind his ear.

"I shook hands with this miracle, and I learned he was the Company's chief accountant, and that all the bookkeeping was done at this station. He had come out for a moment, he said, 'to get a breath of fresh air.' The expression

9. Explosive charge.

sounded wonderfully odd, with its suggestion of sedentary desk-life. I wouldn't have mentioned the fellow to you at all, only it was from his lips that I first heard the name of the man who is so indissolubly connected with the memories of that time. Moreover, I respected the fellow. Yes; I respected his collars, his vast cuffs, his brushed hair. His appearance was certainly that of a hairdresser's dummy; but in the great demoralization of the land he kept up his appearance. That's backbone. His starched collars and got-up shirt-fronts were achievements of character. He had been out nearly three years; and, later, I could not help asking him how he managed to sport such linen. He had just the faintest blush, and said modestly, 'I've been teaching one of the native women about the station. It was difficult. She had a distaste for the work.' Thus this man had verily accomplished something. And he was devoted to his books, which were in apple-pie order.

"Everything else in the station was in a muddle,—heads, things, buildings. Strings of dusty niggers with splay feet arrived and departed; a stream of manufactured goods, rubbishy cottons, beads, and brass-wire set into the depths of darkness, and in return came a precious trickle of ivory.[1]

"I had to wait in the station for ten days—an eternity. I lived in a hut in the yard, but to be out of the chaos I would sometimes get into the accountant's office. It was built of horizontal planks, and so badly put together that, as he bent over his high desk, he was barred from neck to heels with narrow strips of sunlight. There was no need to open the big shutter to see. It was hot there, too; big flies buzzed fiendishly, and did not sting, but stabbed. I sat generally on the floor, while, of faultless appearance (and even slightly scented), perching on a high stool, he wrote, he wrote. Sometimes he stood up for exercise. When a trucklebed with a sick man (some invalid agent from up-country) was put in there, he exhibited a gentle annoyance. 'The groans of this sick person,' he said, 'distract my attention. And without that it is extremely difficult to guard against clerical errors in this climate.'

"One day he remarked, without lifting his head, 'In the interior you will no doubt meet Mr. Kurtz.' On my asking who Mr. Kurtz was, he said he was a first-class agent; and seeing my disappointment at this information, he added slowly, laying down his pen, 'He is a very remarkable person.' Further questions elicited from him that Mr. Kurtz was at present in charge of a trading post, a very important one, in the true ivory-country, at 'the very bottom of there. Sends in as much ivory as all the others put together....' He began to write again. The sick man was too ill to groan. The flies buzzed in a great peace.

"Suddenly there was a growing murmur of voices and a great tramping of feet. A caravan had come in. A violent babble of uncouth sounds burst out on the other side of the planks. All the carriers were speaking together, and in the midst of the uproar the lamentable voice of the chief agent was heard 'giving it up' tearfully for the twentieth time that day.... He rose slowly. 'What a frightful row,' he said. He crossed the room gently to look at the sick man, and returning, said to me, 'He does not hear.' 'What! Dead?' I asked, startled. 'No, not yet,' he answered, with great composure. Then, alluding with a toss

---

**1.** Ivory and rubber were the main commercial resources traded from the Congo Free State. Ivory was used for billiard balls, piano keys, and carved art objects.

of the head to the tumult in the station-yard, 'When one has got to make correct entries, one comes to hate those savages—hate them to the death.' He remained thoughtful for a moment. 'When you see Mr. Kurtz,' he went on, 'tell him for me that everything here'—he glanced at the desk—'is very satisfactory. I don't like to write to him—with those messengers of ours you never know who may get hold of your letter—at that Central Station.' He stared at me for a moment with his mild, bulging eyes. 'Oh, he will go far, very far,' he began again. 'He will be a somebody in the Administration before long. They, above—the Council in Europe, you know—mean him to be.'

"He turned to his work. The noise outside had ceased, and presently in going out I stopped at the door. In the steady buzz of flies the homeward-bound agent was lying flushed and insensible; the other, bent over his books, was making correct entries of perfectly correct transactions; and fifty feet below the doorstep I could see the still tree-tops of the grove of death.

"Next day I left that station at last, with a caravan of sixty men, for a two-hundred-mile tramp.

"No use telling you much about that. Paths, paths, everywhere; a stamped-in network of paths spreading over the empty land, through long grass, through burnt grass, through thickets, down and up chilly ravines, up and down stony hills ablaze with heat; and a solitude, a solitude, nobody, not a hut. The population had cleared out a long time ago. Well, if a lot of mysterious niggers armed with all kinds of fearful weapons suddenly took to traveling on the road between Deal and Gravesend,[2] catching the yokels right and left to carry heavy loads for them, I fancy every farm and cottage thereabouts would get empty very soon. Only here the dwellings were gone, too. Still I passed through several abandoned villages. There's something pathetically childish in the ruins of grass walls. Day after day, with the stamp and shuffle of sixty pair of bare feet behind me, each pair under a sixty-pound load. Camp, cook, sleep, strike camp, march. Now and then a carrier dead in harness, at rest in the long grass near the path, with an empty water-gourd and his long staff lying by his side. A great silence around and above. Perhaps on some quiet night the tremor of far-off drums, sinking, swelling, a tremor vast, faint; a sound weird, appealing, suggestive, and wild—and perhaps with as profound a meaning as the sound of bells in a Christian country. Once a white man in an unbuttoned uniform, camping on the path with an armed escort of lank Zanzibaris,[3] very hospitable and festive—not to say drunk. Was looking after the upkeep of the road, he declared. Can't say I saw any road or any upkeep, unless the body of a middle-aged Negro, with a bullet-hole in the forehead, upon which I absolutely stumbled three miles farther on, may be considered as a permanent improvement. I had a white companion, too, not a bad chap, but rather too fleshy and with the exasperating habit of fainting on the hot hillsides, miles away from the least bit of shade and water. Annoying, you know, to hold your own coat like a parasol over a man's head while he is coming-to. I couldn't help asking him once what he meant by coming there at all. 'To make money, of course. What do you think?' he said, scornfully. Then he got fever, and had to be carried in a hammock slung under a pole. As he

---

**2.** English coastal cities in Kent, east of London.  **3.** Mercenary soldiers from Zanzibar, an island off the east coast of Africa.

weighed sixteen stone[4] I had no end of rows with the carriers. They jibbed, ran away, sneaked off with their loads in the night—quite a mutiny. So, one evening, I made a speech in English with gestures, not one of which was lost to the sixty pairs of eyes before me, and the next morning I started the hammock off in front all right. An hour afterwards I came upon the whole concern wrecked in a bush—man, hammock, groans, blankets, horrors. The heavy pole had skinned his poor nose. He was very anxious for me to kill somebody, but there wasn't the shadow of a carrier near. I remembered the old doctor—'It would be interesting for science to watch the mental changes of individuals, on the spot.' I felt I was becoming scientifically interesting. However, all that is to no purpose. On the fifteenth day I came in sight of the big river again, and hobbled into the Central Station. It was on a backwater surrounded by scrub and forest, with a pretty border of smelly mud on one side, and on the three others enclosed by a crazy fence of rushes. A neglected gap was all the gate it had, and the first glance at the place was enough to let you see the flabby devil was running that show. White men with long staves in their hands appeared languidly from amongst the buildings, strolling up to take a look at me, and then retired out of sight somewhere. One of them, a stout, excitable chap with black mustaches, informed me with great volubility and many digressions, as soon as I told him who I was, that my steamer was at the bottom of the river. I was thunderstruck. What, how, why? Oh, it was 'all right.' The 'manager himself' was there. All quite correct. 'Everybody had behaved splendidly! splendidly!'—'you must,' he said in agitation, 'go and see the general manager at once. He is waiting!'

"I did not see the real significance of that wreck at once. I fancy I see it now, but I am not sure—not at all. Certainly the affair was too stupid—when I think of it—to be altogether natural. Still. . . . But at the moment it presented itself simply as a confounded nuisance. The steamer was sunk. They had started two days before in a sudden hurry up the river with the manager on board, in charge of some volunteer skipper, and before they had been out three hours they tore the bottom out of her on stones, and she sank near the south bank. I asked myself what I was to do there, now my boat was lost. As a matter of fact, I had plenty to do in fishing my command out of the river. I had to set about it the very next day. That, and the repairs when I brought the pieces to the station, took some months.

"My first interview with the manager was curious. He did not ask me to sit down after my twenty-mile walk that morning. He was commonplace in complexion, in feature, in manners, and in voice. He was of middle size and of ordinary build. His eyes, of the usual blue, were perhaps remarkably cold, and he certainly could make his glance fall on one as trenchant and heavy as an ax. But even at these times the rest of his person seemed to disclaim the intention. Otherwise there was only an indefinable, faint expression of his lips, something stealthy—a smile—not a smile—I remember it, but I can't explain. It was unconscious, this smile was, though just after he had said something it got intensified for an instant. It came at the end of his speeches like a seal applied on the words to make the meaning of the commonest phrase appear absolutely inscrutable. He was a common trader, from his youth up employed

---

4. British unit of weight equaling 14 pounds—hence he weighed 224 pounds.

in these parts—nothing more. He was obeyed, yet he inspired neither love nor fear, nor even respect. He inspired uneasiness. That was it! Uneasiness. Not a definite mistrust—just uneasiness—nothing more. You have no idea how effective such a . . . a . . . faculty can be. He had no genius for organizing, for initiative, or for order even. That was evident in such things as the deplorable state of the station. He had no learning, and no intelligence. His position had come to him—why? Perhaps because he was never ill. . . . He had served three terms of three years out there. . . . Because triumphant health in the general rout of constitutions is a kind of power in itself. When he went home on leave he rioted on a large scale—pompously. Jack ashore[5]—with a difference—in externals only. This one could gather from his casual talk. He originated nothing, he could keep the routine going—that's all. But he was great. He was great by this little thing that it was impossible to tell what could control such a man. He never gave that secret away. Perhaps there was nothing within him. Such a suspicion made one pause—for out there there were no external checks. Once when various tropical diseases had laid low almost every 'agent' in the station, he was heard to say, 'Men who come out here should have no entrails.' He sealed the utterance with that smile of his, as though it had been a door opening into a darkness he had in his keeping. You fancied you had seen things—but the seal was on. When annoyed at meal-times by the constant quarrels of the white men about precedence, he ordered an immense round table to be made, for which a special house had to be built. This was the station's messroom. Where he sat was the first place—the rest were nowhere. One felt this to be his unalterable conviction. He was neither civil nor uncivil. He was quiet. He allowed his 'boy'—an overfed young Negro from the coast—to treat the white men, under his very eyes, with provoking insolence.

"He began to speak as soon as he saw me. I had been very long on the road. He could not wait. Had to start without me. The upriver stations had to be relieved. There had been so many delays already that he did not know who was dead and who was alive, and how they got on—and so on, and so on. He paid no attention to my explanations, and, playing with a stick of sealing-wax, repeated several times that the situation was 'very grave, very grave.' There were rumors that a very important station was in jeopardy, and its chief, Mr. Kurtz, was ill. Hoped it was not true. Mr. Kurtz was . . . I felt weary and irritable. Hang Kurtz, I thought. I interrupted him by saying I had heard of Mr. Kurtz on the coast. 'Ah! So they talk of him down there,' he murmured to himself. Then he began again, assuring me Mr. Kurtz was the best agent he had, an exceptional man, of the greatest importance to the Company; therefore I could understand his anxiety. He was, he said, 'very, very uneasy.' Certainly he fidgeted on his chair a good deal, exclaimed, 'Ah, Mr. Kurtz!' broke the stick of sealing-wax and seemed dumfounded by the accident. Next thing he wanted to know 'how long it would take to . . .' I interrupted him again. Being hungry, you know, and kept on my feet too, I was getting savage. 'How can I tell?' I said, 'I haven't even seen the wreck yet—some months, no doubt.' All this talk seemed to me so futile. 'Some months,' he said. 'Well, let us say three months before we can make a start. Yes. That ought to do the affair.' I flung out of his hut (he lived all alone in a clay hut with a sort of veranda)

---

5. That is, like a sailor on shore leave.

muttering to myself my opinion of him. He was a chattering idiot. Afterwards I took it back when it was borne in upon me startlingly with what extreme nicety he had estimated the time requisite for the 'affair.'

"I went to work the next day, turning, so to speak, my back on that station. In that way only it seemed to me I could keep my hold on the redeeming facts of life. Still, one must look about sometimes; and then I saw this station, these men strolling aimlessly about in the sunshine of the yard. I asked myself sometimes what it all meant. They wandered here and there with their absurd long staves in their hands, like a lot of faithless pilgrims bewitched inside a rotten fence. The word 'ivory' rang in the air, was whispered, was sighed. You would think they were praying to it. A taint of imbecile rapacity blew through it all, like a whiff from some corpse. By Jove! I've never seen anything so unreal in my life. And outside, the silent wilderness surrounding this cleared speck on the earth struck me as something great and invincible, like evil or truth, waiting patiently for the passing away of this fantastic invasion.

"Oh, these months! Well, never mind. Various things happened. One evening a grass shed full of calico, cotton prints, beads, and I don't know what else, burst into a blaze so suddenly that you would have thought the earth had opened to let an avenging fire consume all that trash. I was smoking my pipe quietly by my dismantled steamer, and saw them all cutting capers in the light, with their arms lifted high, when the stout man with mustaches came tearing down to the river, a tin pail in his hand, assured me that everybody was 'behaving splendidly, splendidly,' dipped about a quart of water and tore back again. I noticed there was a hole in the bottom of his pail.

"I strolled up. There was no hurry. You see the thing had gone off like a box of matches. It had been hopeless from the very first. The flame had leaped high, driven everybody back, lighted up everything—and collapsed. The shed was already a heap of embers glowing fiercely. A nigger was being beaten near by. They said he had caused the fire in some way; be that as it may, he was screeching most horribly. I saw him, later, for several days, sitting in a bit of shade looking very sick and trying to recover himself: afterwards he arose and went out—and the wilderness without a sound took him into its bosom again. As I approached the glow from the dark I found myself at the back of two men, talking. I heard the name of Kurtz pronounced, then the words, 'take advantage of this unfortunate accident.' One of the men was the manager. I wished him a good evening. 'Did you ever see anything like it—eh? it is incredible,' he said, and walked off. The other man remained. He was a first-class agent, young, gentlemanly, a bit reserved, with a forked little beard and a hooked nose. He was standoffish with the other agents, and they on their side said he was the manager's spy among them. As to me, I had hardly ever spoken to him before. We got into talk, and by and by we strolled away from the hissing ruins. Then he asked me to his room, which was in the main building of the station. He struck a match, and I perceived that this young aristocrat had not only a silver-mounted dressing-case but also a whole candle all to himself. Just at that time the manager was the only man supposed to have any right to candles. Native mats covered the clay walls; a collection of spears, assegais,[6] shields, knives was hung up in trophies. The business

---

**6.** Slender southern African throwing spears.

intrusted to this fellow was the making of bricks—so I had been informed; but there wasn't a fragment of a brick anywhere in the station, and he had been there more than a year—waiting. It seems he could not make bricks without something, I don't know what—straw, maybe. Anyways, it could not be found there, and as it was not likely to be sent from Europe, it did not appear clear to me what he was waiting for. An act of special creation perhaps. However, they were all waiting—all the sixteen or twenty pilgrims of them—for something; and upon my word it did not seem an uncongenial occupation, from the way they took it, though the only thing that ever came to them was disease—as far as I could see. They beguiled the time by backbiting and intriguing against each other in a foolish kind of way. There was an air of plotting about that station, but nothing came of it, of course. It was as unreal as everything else—as the philanthropic pretense of the whole concern, as their talk, as their government, as their show of work. The only real feeling was a desire to get appointed to a trading-post where ivory was to be had, so that they could earn percentages. They intrigued and slandered and hated each other only on that account,—but as to effectually lifting a little finger—oh, no. By heavens! there is something after all in the world allowing one man to steal a horse while another must not look at the halter. Steal a horse straight out. Very well. He has done it. Perhaps he can ride. But there is a way of looking at a halter that would provoke the most charitable of saints into a kick.

"I had no idea why he wanted to be sociable, but as we chatted in there it suddenly occurred to me the fellow was trying to get at something—in fact, pumping me. He alluded constantly to Europe, to the people I was supposed to know there—putting leading questions as to my acquaintances in the sepulchral city, and so on. His little eyes glittered like mica discs—with curiosity—though he tried to keep up a bit of superciliousness. At first I was astonished, but very soon I became awfully curious to see what he would find out from me. I couldn't possibly imagine what I had in me to make it worth his while. It was very pretty to see how he baffled himself, for in truth my body was full only of chills, and my head had nothing in it but that wretched steamboat business. It was evident he took me for a perfectly shameless prevaricator. At last he got angry, and, to conceal a movement of furious annoyance, he yawned. I rose. Then I noticed a small sketch in oils, on a panel, representing a woman, draped and blindfolded, carrying a lighted torch. The background was somber—almost black. The movement of the woman was stately, and the effect of the torchlight on the face was sinister.

"It arrested me, and he stood by civilly, holding an empty half-pint champagne bottle (medical comforts) with the candle stuck in it. To my question he said Mr. Kurtz had painted this—in this very station more than a year ago—while waiting for means to go to his trading-post. 'Tell me, pray,' said I, 'who is this Mr. Kurtz?'

"'The chief of the Inner Station,' he answered in a short tone, looking away. 'Much obliged,' I said, laughing. 'And you are the brickmaker of the Central Station. Everyone knows that.' He was silent for a while. 'He is a prodigy,' he said at last. 'He is an emissary of pity, and science, and progress, and devil knows what else. We want,' he began to declaim suddenly, 'for the guidance of the cause intrusted to us by Europe, so to speak, higher intelligence, wide sympathies, a singleness of purpose.' 'Who says that?' I asked. 'Lots of them,' he replied. 'Some even write that; and so *he* comes here, a special being, as you ought to know.' 'Why ought I to know?' I interrupted, really surprised. He paid no attention. 'Yes. Today he is chief of the best station, next year he will be assistant-manager, two years more and . . . but I daresay you know what he will be in two years' time. You are of the new gang—the gang of virtue. The same people who sent him specially also recommended you. Oh, don't say no. I've my own eyes to trust.' Light dawned upon me. My dear aunt's influential acquaintances were producing an unexpected effect upon that young man. I nearly burst into a laugh. 'Do you read the Company's confidential correspondence?' I asked. He hadn't a word to say. It was great fun. 'When Mr. Kurtz,' I continued, severely, 'is General Manager, you won't have the opportunity.'

"He blew the candle out suddenly, and we went outside. The moon had risen. Black figures strolled about listlessly, pouring water on the glow, whence proceeded a sound of hissing; steam ascended in the moonlight, the beaten nigger groaned somewhere. 'What a row the brute makes!' said the indefatigable man with the mustaches, appearing near us. 'Serves him right. Transgression—punishment—bang! Pitiless, pitiless. That's the only way. This will prevent all conflagrations for the future. I was just telling the manager. . . .' He noticed my companion, and became crestfallen all at once. 'Not in bed yet,' he said, with a kind of servile heartiness; 'it's so natural. Ha! Danger—agitation.' He vanished. I went on to the river-side, and the other followed me. I heard a scathing murmur at my ear, 'Heap of muffs[7]—go to.' The pilgrims could be seen in knots gesticulating, discussing. Several had still their staves in their hands. I verily believe they took these sticks to bed with them. Beyond the fence the forest stood up spectrally in the moonlight, and through the dim stir, through the faint sounds of that lamentable courtyard, the silence of the land went home to one's very heart—its mystery, its greatness, the amazing reality of its concealed life. The hurt nigger moaned feebly somewhere near by, and then fetched a deep sigh that made me mend my pace away from there. I felt a hand introducing itself under my arm. 'My dear sir,' said the fellow, 'I don't want to be misunderstood, and especially by you, who will see Mr. Kurtz long before I can have that pleasure. I wouldn't like him to get a false idea of my disposition. . . .'

"I let him run on, this papier-mâché Mephistopheles,[8] and it seemed to me that if I tried I could poke my forefinger through him, and would find nothing inside but a little loose dirt, maybe. He, don't you see, had been planning to be assistant-manager by and by under the present man, and I could see that the coming of that Kurtz had upset them both not a little. He talked precipitately, and I did not try to stop him. I had my shoulders against the wreck of my steamer, hauled up on the slope like a carcass of some big river animal. The smell of mud, of primeval mud, by Jove! was in my nostrils, the high stillness of primeval forest was before my eyes; there were shiny patches on the black creek. The moon had spread over everything a thin layer of silver—over the rank grass, over the mud, upon the wall of matted vegetation standing higher than the wall of a temple, over the great river I could see through a somber gap glittering, glittering, as it flowed broadly by without a

---

**7.** Gang of bunglers.   **8.** That is, devil made of pasteboard.

murmur. All this was great, expectant, mute, while the man jabbered about himself. I wondered whether the stillness on the face of the immensity look-ing at us two were meant as an appeal or as a menace. What were we who had strayed in here? Could we handle that dumb thing, or would it handle us? I felt how big, how confoundedly big, was that thing that couldn't talk, and perhaps was deaf as well. What was in there? I could see a little ivory coming out from there, and I had heard Mr. Kurtz was in there. I had heard enough about it, too—God knows! Yet somehow it didn't bring any image with it—no more than if I had been told an angel or a fiend was in there. I believed it in the same way one of you might believe there are inhabitants in the planet Mars. I knew once a Scotch sailmaker who was certain, dead sure, there were people in Mars. If you asked him for some idea how they looked and behaved, he would get shy and mutter something about 'walking on all-fours.' If you as much as smiled, he would—though a man of sixty—offer to fight you. I would not have gone so far as to fight for Kurtz, but I went for him near enough to a lie. You know I hate, detest, and can't bear a lie, not because I am straighter than the rest of us, but simply because it appalls me. There is a taint of death, a flavor of mortality in lies—which is exactly what I hate and detest in the world—what I want to forget. It makes me miserable and sick, like biting something rotten would do. Temperament, I suppose. Well, I went near enough to it by letting the young fool there believe anything he liked to imag-ine as to my influence in Europe. I became in an instant as much of a pretence as the rest of the bewitched pilgrims. This simply because I had a notion it somehow would be of help to that Kurtz whom at the time I did not see—you understand. He was just a word for me. I did not see the man in the name any more than you do. Do you see him? Do you see the story? Do you see any-thing? It seems to me I am trying to tell you a dream—making a vain attempt, because no relation of a dream can convey the dream-sensation, that com-mingling of absurdity, surprise, and bewilderment in a tremor of struggling revolt, that notion of being captured by the incredible which is of the very essence of dreams...."

He was silent for a while.

"...No, it is impossible; it is impossible to convey the life-sensation of any given epoch of one's existence—that which makes its truth, its meaning—its subtle and penetrating essence. It is impossible. We live, as we dream—alone...."

He paused again as if reflecting, then added—

"Of course in this you fellows see more than I could then. You see me, whom you know...."

It had become so pitch dark that we listeners could hardly see one another. For a long time already he, sitting apart, had been no more to us than a voice. There was not a word from anybody. The others might have been asleep, but I was awake. I listened, I listened on the watch for the sentence, for the word, that would give me the clew to the faint uneasiness inspired by this narra-tive that seemed to shape itself without human lips in the heavy night-air of the river.

"...Yes—I let him run on," Marlow began again, "and think what he pleased about the powers that were behind me. I did! And there was nothing behind me! There was nothing but that wretched, old, mangled steamboat I was leaning against, while he talked fluently about 'the necessity for every man to get on.' 'And when one comes out here, you conceive, it is not to gaze at the moon.' Mr. Kurtz was a 'universal genius,' but even a genius would find it easier to work with 'adequate tools—intelligent men.' He did not make bricks—why, there was a physical impossibility in the way—as I was well aware; and if he did secretarial work for the manager, it was because 'no sensible man rejects wantonly the confidence of his superiors.' Did I see it? I saw it. What more did I want? What I really wanted was rivets, by heaven! Rivets. To get on with the work—to stop the hole. Rivets I wanted. There were cases of them down at the coast—cases—piled up—burst—split! You kicked a loose rivet at every second step in that station yard on the hillside. Rivets had rolled into the grove of death. You could fill your pockets with rivets for the trouble of stooping down—and there wasn't one rivet to be found where it was wanted. We had plates that would do, but nothing to fasten them with. And every week the messenger, a lone Negro, letter-bag on shoulder and staff in hand, left our station for the coast. And several times a week a coast caravan came in with trade goods—ghastly glazed calico that made you shudder only to look at it; glass beads, valued about a penny a quart, confounded spotted cotton handkerchiefs. And no rivets. Three carriers could have brought all that was wanted to set that steamboat afloat.

"He was becoming confidential now, but I fancy my unresponsive attitude must have exasperated him at last, for he judged it necessary to inform me he feared neither God nor devil, let alone any mere man. I said I could see that very well, but what I wanted was a certain quantity of rivets—and rivets were what really Mr. Kurtz wanted, if he had only known it. Now letters went to the coast every week. . . . 'My dear sir,' he cried, 'I write from dictation.' I demanded rivets. There was a way—for an intelligent man. He changed his manner; became very cold, and suddenly began to talk about a hippopotamus; wondered whether sleeping on board the steamer (I stuck to my salvage night and day) I wasn't disturbed. There was an old hippo that had the bad habit of getting out on the bank and roaming at night over the station grounds. The pilgrims used to turn out in a body and empty every rifle they could lay hands on at him. Some even had sat up o' nights for him. All this energy was wasted, though. 'That animal has a charmed life,' he said; 'but you can say this only of brutes in this country. No man—you apprehend me?—no man here bears a charmed life.' He stood there for a moment in the moonlight with his delicate hooked nose set a little askew, and his mica eyes glittering without a wink, then, with a curt good night, he strode off. I could see he was disturbed and considerably puzzled, which made me feel more hopeful than I had been for days. It was a great comfort to turn from that chap to my influential friend, the battered, twisted, ruined, tin-pot steamboat. I clambered on board. She rang under my feet like an empty Huntley & Palmer biscuit-tin kicked along a gutter; she was nothing so solid in make, and rather less pretty in shape, but I had expended enough hard work on her to make me love her. No influential friend would have served me better. She had given me a chance to come out a bit—to find out what I could do. No, I don't like work. I had rather laze about and think of all the fine things that can be done. I don't like work—no man does—but I like what is in the work,—the chance to find yourself. Your own reality—for yourself, not for others—what no other man can ever know. They can only see the mere show, and never can tell what it really means.

"I was not surprised to see somebody sitting aft, on the deck, with his legs dangling over the mud. You see I rather chummed with the few mechanics there were in that station, whom the other pilgrims naturally despised—on account of their imperfect manners, I suppose. This was the foreman—a boiler-maker by trade—a good worker. He was a lank, bony, yellow-faced man, with big intense eyes. His aspect was worried, and his head was as bald as the palm of my hand; but his hair in falling seemed to have stuck to his chin, and had prospered in the new locality, for his beard hung down to his waist. He was a widower with six young children (he had left them in charge of a sister of his to come out there), and the passion of his life was pigeon-flying. He was an enthusiast and a connoisseur. He would rave about pigeons. After work hours he used sometimes to come over from his hut for a talk about his children and his pigeons; at work, when he had to crawl in the mud under the bottom of the steamboat, he would tie up that beard of his in a kind of white serviette[9] he brought for the purpose. It had loops to go over his ears. In the evening he could be seen squatted on the bank rinsing that wrapper in the creek with great care, then spreading it solemnly on a bush to dry.

"I slapped him on the back and shouted, 'We shall have rivets!' He scrambled to his feet exclaiming, 'No! Rivets!' as though he couldn't believe his ears. Then in a low voice, 'You . . . eh?' I don't know why we behaved like lunatics. I put my finger to the side of my nose and nodded mysteriously. 'Good for you!' he cried, snapped his fingers above his head, lifting one foot. I tried a jig. We capered on the iron deck. A frightful clatter came out of that hulk, and the virgin forest on the other bank of the creek sent it back in a thundering roll upon the sleeping station. It must have made some of the pilgrims sit up in their hovels. A dark figure obscured the lighted doorway of the manager's hut, vanished, then, a second or so after, the doorway itself vanished, too. We stopped, and the silence driven away by the stamping of our feet flowed back again from the recesses of the land. The great wall of vegetation, an exuberant and entangled mass of trunks, branches, leaves, boughs, festoons, motionless in the moonlight, was like a rioting invasion of soundless life, a rolling wave of plants, piled up, crested, ready to topple over the creek, to sweep every little man of us out of his little existence. And it moved not. A deadened burst of mighty splashes and snorts reached us from afar as though an ichthyosaurus[1] had been taking a bath of glitter in the great river. 'After all,' said the boiler-maker in a reasonable tone, 'why shouldn't we get the rivets?' Why not, indeed! I did not know of any reason why we shouldn't. 'They'll come in three weeks,' I said, confidently.

"But they didn't. Instead of rivets there came an invasion, an in-fliction, a visitation. It came in sections during the next three weeks, each section headed by a donkey carrying a white man in new clothes and tan shoes, bowing from that elevation right and left to the impressed pilgrims. A quarrelsome band of footsore sulky niggers trod on the heels of the donkeys; a lot of tents, campstools, tin boxes, white cases, brown bales would be shot down in the courtyard, and the air of mystery would deepen a little over the muddle of

---

9. Napkin.    1. Prehistoric marine reptile.

the station. Five such installments came, with their absurd air of disorderly flight with the loot of innumerable outfit shops and provision stores, that, one would think, they were lugging, after a raid, into the wilderness for equitable division. It was an extricable mess of things decent in themselves but that human folly made look like the spoils of thieving.

"This devoted band called itself the Eldorado Exploring Expedition, and I believe they were sworn to secrecy. Their talk, however, was the talk of sordid buccaneers: it was reckless without hardihood, greedy without audacity, and cruel without courage; there was not an atom of foresight or of serious intention in the whole batch of them, and they did not seem aware these things are wanted for the work of the world. To tear treasure out of the bowels of the land was their desire, with no more moral purpose at the back of it than there is in burglars breaking into a safe. Who paid the expenses of the noble enterprise I don't know; but the uncle of our manager was leader of that lot.

"In exterior he resembled a butcher in a poor neighborhood, and his eyes had a look of sleepy cunning. He carried his fat paunch with ostentation on his short legs, and during the time his gang infested the station spoke to no one but his nephew. You could see these two roaming about all day long with their heads close together in an everlasting confab.

"I had given up worrying myself about the rivets. One's capacity for that kind of folly is more limited than you would suppose. I said Hang!—and let things slide. I had plenty of time for meditation, and now and then I would give some thought to Kurtz. I wasn't very interested in him. No. Still, I was curious to see whether this man, who had come out equipped with moral ideas of some sort, would climb to the top after all and how he would set about his work when there."

## II

"One evening as I was lying flat on the deck of my steamboat, I heard voices approaching—and there were the nephew and the uncle strolling along the bank. I laid my head on my arm again, and had nearly lost myself in a doze, when somebody said in my ear, as it were: 'I am as harmless as a little child, but I don't like to be dictated to. Am I the manager—or am I not? I was ordered to send him there. It's incredible.' . . . I became aware that the two were standing on the shore alongside the forepart of the steamboat, just below my head. I did not move; it did not occur to me to move: I was sleepy. 'It *is* unpleasant,' grunted the uncle. 'He has asked the Administration to be sent there,' said the other, 'with the idea of showing what he could do; and I was instructed accordingly. Look at the influence that man must have. Is it not frightful?' They both agreed it was frightful, then made several bizarre remarks: 'Make rain and fine weather—one man—the Council—by the nose'—bits of absurd sentences that got the better of my drowsiness, so that I had pretty near the whole of my wits about me when the uncle said, 'The climate may do away with this difficulty for you. Is he alone there?' 'Yes,' answered the manager; 'he sent his assistant down the river with a note to me in these terms: "Clear this poor devil out of the country, and don't bother sending more of that sort. I had rather be alone than have the kind of men you can dispose of with me." It was more than a year ago. Can you imagine such impudence?' 'Anything since then?' asked the other, hoarsely. 'Ivory,' jerked the nephew; 'lots of it—prime sort—lots—most annoying, from him.' 'And with that?' questioned the heavy rumble. 'Invoice,' was the reply fired out, so to speak. Then silence. They had been talking about Kurtz.

"I was broad awake by this time, but, lying perfectly at ease, remained still, having no inducement to change my position. 'How did that ivory come all this way?' growled the elder man, who seemed very vexed. The other explained that it had come with a fleet of canoes in charge of an English half-caste clerk Kurtz had with him; that Kurtz had apparently intended to return himself, the station being by that time bare of goods and stores, but after coming three hundred miles, had suddenly decided to go back, which he started to do alone in a small dugout with four paddlers, leaving the half-caste to continue down the river with the ivory. The two fellows there seemed astounded at anybody attempting such a thing. They were at a loss for an adequate motive. As to me, I seemed to see Kurtz for the first time. It was a distinct glimpse: the dugout, four paddling savages, and the lone white man turning his back suddenly on the headquarters, on relief, on thoughts of home—perhaps; setting his face towards the depths of the wilderness, towards his empty and desolate station. I did not know the motive. Perhaps he was just simply a fine fellow who stuck to his work for its own sake. His name, you understand, had not been pronounced once. He was 'that man.' The half-caste, who, as far as I could see, had conducted a difficult trip with great prudence and pluck, was invariably alluded to as 'that scoundrel.' The 'scoundrel' had reported that the 'man' had been very ill—had recovered imperfectly.... The two below me moved away then a few paces, and strolled back and forth at some little distance. I heard: 'Military post—doctor—two hundred miles—quite alone now—unavoidable delays—nine months—no news—strange rumors.' They approached again, just as the manager was saying, 'No one, as far as I know, unless a species of wandering trader—a pestilential fellow, snapping ivory from the natives.' Who was it they were talking about now? I gathered in snatches that this was some man supposed to be in Kurtz's district, and of whom the manager did not approve. 'We will not be free from unfair competition till one of these fellows is hanged for an example,' he said. 'Certainly,' grunted the other; 'get him hanged! Why not? Anything—anything can be done in this country. That's what I say; nobody here, you understand, *here*, can endanger your position. And why? You stand the climate—you outlast them all. The danger is in Europe; but there before I left I took care to—' They moved off and whispered, then their voices rose again. 'The extraordinary series of delays is not my fault. I did my best.' The fat man sighed. 'Very sad.' 'And the pestiferous absurdity of his talk,' continued the other; 'he bothered me enough when he was here. "Each station should be like a beacon on the road towards better things, a center for trade, of course, but also for humanizing, improving, instructing." Conceive you—that ass! And he wants to be manager! No, it's—' Here he got choked by excessive indignation, and I lifted my head the least bit. I was surprised to see how near they were—right under me. I could have spat upon their hats. They were looking on the ground, absorbed in thought. The manager was switching his leg with a slender twig: his sagacious relative lifted his head. 'You have been well since you came out this time?' he asked. The other gave a start. 'Who? I? Oh! Like a charm—like a charm. But the rest—oh, my goodness! All sick. They die so quick, too, that I haven't the time to send them out of the country—it's incredible!' 'H'm. Just so,' grunted the uncle. 'Ah! my boy, trust to this—I say, trust to this.' I saw him extend his short flipper of an arm for a gesture that took in the forest, the creek, the mud, the river,—seemed to beckon with a dishonoring flourish before the sunlit face of the land a treacherous appeal to the lurking death, to the hidden evil, to the profound darkness of its heart. It was so startling that I leaped to my feet and looked back at the edge of the forest, as though I had expected an answer of some sort to that black display of confidence. You know the foolish notions that come to one sometimes. The high stillness confronted these two figures with its ominous patience, waiting for the passing away of a fantastic invasion.

"They swore aloud together—out of sheer fright, I believe—then pretending not to know anything of my existence, turned back to the station. The sun was low; and leaning forward side by side, they seemed to be tugging painfully uphill their two ridiculous shadows of unequal length, that trailed behind them slowly over the tall grass without bending a single blade.

"In a few days the Eldorado Expedition went into the patient wilderness, that closed upon it as the sea closes over a diver. Long afterwards the news came that all the donkeys were dead. I know nothing as to the fate of the less valuable animals. They, no doubt, like the rest of us, found what they deserved. I did not inquire. I was then rather excited at the prospect of meeting Kurtz very soon. When I say very soon I mean it comparatively. It was just two months from the day we left the creek when we came to the bank below Kurtz's station.

"Going up that river was like traveling back to the earliest beginnings of the world, when vegetation rioted on the earth and the big trees were kings. An empty stream, a great silence, an impenetrable forest. The air was warm, thick, heavy, sluggish. There was no joy in the brilliance of sunshine. The long stretches of the waterway ran on, deserted, into the gloom of overshadowed distances. On silvery sandbanks hippos and alligators sunned themselves side by side. The broadening waters flowed through a mob of wooded islands; you lost your way on that river as you would in a desert, and butted all day long against shoals, trying to find the channel, till you thought yourself bewitched and cut off forever from everything you had known once—somewhere—far away—in another existence perhaps. There were moments when one's past came back to one, as it will sometimes when you have not a moment to spare to yourself; but it came in the shape of an unrestful and noisy dream, remembered with wonder amongst the overwhelming realities of this strange world of plants, and water, and silence. And this stillness of life did not in the least resemble a peace. It was the stillness of an implacable force brooding over an inscrutable intention. It looked at you with a vengeful aspect. I got used to it afterwards; I did not see it any more; I had no time. I had to keep guessing at the channel; I had to discern, mostly by inspiration, the signs of hidden banks; I watched for sunken stones; I was learning to clap my teeth smartly before my heart flew out, when I shaved by a fluke some infernal sly old snag that would have ripped the life out of the tin-pot steamboat and drowned all the pilgrims; I had to keep a lookout for the signs of dead wood we could cut up in the night for next day's steaming. When you have to attend to things of that sort, to the mere incidents of the surface, the reality—the reality, I tell you—fades. The inner truth is hidden—luckily, luckily. But I felt it all the same; I felt often its mysterious stillness watching me at my monkey tricks, just as it watches you fellows performing on your respective tight-ropes for—what is it? half-a-crown a tumble—"

"Try to be civil, Marlow," growled a voice, and I knew there was at least one listener awake besides myself.

"I beg your pardon. I forgot the heartache which makes up the rest of the price. And indeed what does the price matter, if the trick be well done? You do your tricks very well. And I didn't do badly either, since I managed not to sink that steamboat on my first trip. It's a wonder to me yet. Imagine a blindfolded man set to drive a van over a bad road. I sweated and shivered over that business considerably, I can tell you. After all, for a seaman, to scrape the bottom of the thing that's supposed to float all the time under his care is the unpardonable sin. No one may know of it, but you never forget the thump—eh? A blow on the very heart. You remember it, you dream of it, you wake up at night and think of it—years after—and go hot and cold all over. I don't pretend to say that steamboat floated all the time. More than once she had to wade for a bit, with twenty cannibals splashing around and pushing. We had enlisted some of these chaps on the way for a crew. Fine fellows—cannibals—in their place. They were men one could work with, and I am grateful to them. And, after all, they did not eat each other before my face: they had brought along a provision of hippo-meat which went rotten, and made the mystery of the wilderness stink in my nostrils. Phoo! I can sniff it now. I had the manager on board and three or four pilgrims with their staves—all complete. Sometimes we came upon a station close by the bank, clinging to the skirts of the unknown, and the white men rushing out of a tumble-down hovel, with great gestures of joy and surprise and welcome, seemed very strange—had the appearance of being held there captive by a spell. The word ivory would ring in the air for a while—and on we went again into the silence, along empty reaches, round the still bends, between the high walls of our winding way, reverberating in hollow claps the ponderous beat of the stern-wheel. Trees, trees, millions of trees, massive, immense, running up high; and at their foot, hugging the bank against the stream, crept the little begrimed steamboat, like a sluggish beetle crawling on the floor of a lofty portico. It made you feel very small, very lost, and yet it was not altogether depressing, that feeling. After all, if you were small, the grimy beetle crawled on—which was just what you wanted it to do. Where the pilgrims imagined it crawled to I don't know. To some place where they expected to get something, I bet! For me it crawled towards Kurtz—exclusively; but when the steam-pipes started leaking we crawled very slow. The reaches opened before us and closed behind, as if the forest had stepped leisurely across the water to bar the way for our return. We penetrated deeper and deeper into the heart of darkness. It was very quiet there. At night sometimes the roll of drums behind the curtain of trees would run up the river and remain sustained faintly, as if hovering in the air high over our heads, till the first break of day. Whether it meant war, peace, or prayer we could not tell. The dawns were heralded by the descent of a chill stillness; the woodcutters slept, their fires burned low; the snapping of a twig would make you start. We were wanderers on a prehistoric earth, on an earth that wore the aspect of an unknown planet. We could have fancied ourselves the first men taking possession of an accursed inheritance, to be subdued at the cost of profound anguish and of excessive toil. But suddenly, as we struggled round a bend, there would be a glimpse of rush walls, of peaked grass-roofs, a burst of yells, a whirl of black limbs, a mass of hands clapping, of feet stamping, of bodies swaying, of eyes rolling, under the droop of heavy and motionless foliage. The steamer toiled along slowly on the edge of a black and incomprehensible frenzy. The prehistoric man was cursing us, praying to us, welcoming us—who could tell? We were cut off from the comprehension of our surroundings; we glided past like phantoms, wondering and secretly appalled, as sane men would be before an enthusiastic outbreak in a madhouse. We could not understand because we were too far and could not remember, because we were traveling in the night of first ages, of those ages that are gone, leaving hardly a sign—and no memories.

"The earth seemed unearthly. We are accustomed to look upon the shackled form of a conquered monster, but there—there you could look at a thing monstrous and free. It was unearthly, and the men were—No, they were not inhuman. Well, you know, that was the worst of it—this suspicion of their not being inhuman. It would come slowly to one. They howled and leaped, and spun, and made horrid faces; but what thrilled you was just the thought of their humanity—like yours—the thought of your remote kinship with this wild and passionate uproar. Ugly. Yes, it was ugly enough; but if you were man enough you would admit to yourself that there was in you just the faintest trace of a response to the terrible frankness of that noise, a dim suspicion of there being a meaning in it which you—you so remote from the night of first ages—could comprehend. And why not? The mind of man is capable of anything—because everything is in it, all the past as well as all the future. What was there after all? Joy, fear, sorrow, devotion, valor, rage—who can tell?—but truth—truth stripped of its cloak of time. Let the fool gape and shudder—the man knows, and can look on without a wink. But he must at least be as much of a man as these on the shore. He must meet that truth with his own true stuff—with his own inborn strength. Principles won't do. Acquisitions, clothes, pretty rags—rags that would fly off at the first good shake. No; you want a deliberate belief. An appeal to me in this fiendish row—is there? Very well; I hear; I admit, but I have a voice too, and for good or evil mine is the speech that cannot be silenced. Of course, a fool, what with sheer fright and fine sentiments, is always safe. Who's that grunting? You wonder I didn't go ashore for a howl and a dance? Well, no—I didn't. Fine sentiments, you say? Fine sentiments, be hanged! I had no time. I had to mess about with white-lead and strips of woolen blanket helping to put bandages on those leaky steam-pipes—I tell you. I had to watch the steering, and circumvent those snags, and get the tin-pot along by hook or by crook. There was surface-truth enough in these things to save a wiser man. And between whiles I had to look after the savage who was fireman. He was an improved specimen; he could fire up a vertical boiler.[2] He was there below me, and, upon my word, to look at him was as edifying as seeing a dog in a parody of breeches and a feather hat, walking on his hindlegs. A few months of training had done for that

---

**2.** Simple, easily fired boiler, typical of the primitive machinery on Marlow's "tin-pot" boat.

really fine chap. He squinted at the steam-gauge and at the water-gauge with an evident effort of intrepidity—and he had filed teeth, too, the poor devil, and the wool of his pate shaved into queer patterns, and three ornamental scars on each of his cheeks. He ought to have been clapping his hands and stamping his feet on the bank, instead of which he was hard at work, a thrall to strange witchcraft, full of improving knowledge. He was useful because he had been instructed; and what he knew was this—that should the water in that transparent thing disappear, the evil spirit inside the boiler would get angry through the greatness of his thirst, and take a terrible vengeance. So he sweated and fired up and watched the glass fearfully (with an impromptu charm, made of rags, tied to his arm, and a piece of polished bone, as big as a watch, stuck flatways through his lower lip), while the wooden banks slipped past us slowly, the short noise was left behind, the interminable miles of silence—and we crept on, towards Kurtz. But the snags were thick, the water was treacherous and shallow, the boiler seemed indeed to have a sulky devil in it, and thus neither that fireman nor I had any time to peer into our creepy thoughts.

"Some fifty miles below the Inner Station we came upon a hut of reeds, an inclined and melancholy pole, with the unrecognizable tatters of what had been a flag of some sort flying from it, and a neatly stacked woodpile. This was unexpected. We came to the bank, and on the stack of firewood found a flat piece of board with some faded pencil-writing on it. When deciphered it said: 'Wood for you. Hurry up. Approach cautiously.' There was a signature, but it was illegible—not Kurtz—a much longer word. 'Hurry up.' Where? Up the river? 'Approach cautiously.' We had not done so. But the warning could not have been meant for the place where it could be only found after approach. Something was wrong above. But what—and how much? That was the question. We commented adversely upon the imbecility of that telegraphic style. The bush around said nothing, and would not let us look very far, either. A torn curtain of red twill hung in the doorway of the hut, and flapped sadly in our faces. The dwelling was dismantled; but we could see a white man had lived there not very long ago. There remained a rude table—a plank on two posts; a heap of rubbish reposed in a dark corner, and by the door I picked up a book. It had lost its covers, and the pages had been thumbed into a state of extremely dirty softness; but the back had been lovingly stitched afresh with white cotton thread, which looked clean yet. It was an extraordinary find. Its title was, *An Inquiry into some Points of Seamanship*, by a man Towser, Towson—some such name—Master in his Majesty's Navy. The matter looked dreary reading enough, with illustrative diagrams and repulsive tables of figures, and the copy was sixty years old. I handled this amazing antiquity with the greatest possible tenderness, lest it should dissolve in my hands. Within, Towson or Towser was inquiring earnestly into the breaking strain of ships' chains and tackle, and other such matters. Not a very enthralling book; but at the first glance you could see there a singleness of intention, an honest concern for the right way of going to work, which made these humble pages, thought out so many years ago, luminous with another than a professional light. The simple old sailor, with his talk of chains and purchases,[3] made me forget the jungle and the pilgrims in a delicious sensation of having come

---

3. Leverages.

upon something unmistakably real. Such a book being there was wonderful enough; but still more astounding were the notes penciled in the margin, and plainly referring to the text. I couldn't believe my eyes! They were in cipher! Yes, it looked like cipher. Fancy a man lugging with him a book of that description into this nowhere and studying it—and making notes—in cipher at that! It was an extravagant mystery.

"I had been dimly aware for some time of a worrying noise, and when I lifted my eyes I saw the woodpile was gone, and the manager, aided by all the pilgrims, was shouting at me from the river-side. I slipped the book into my pocket. I assure you to leave off reading was like tearing myself away from the shelter of an old and solid friendship.

"I started the lame engine ahead. 'It must be this miserable trader—this intruder,' exclaimed the manager, looking back malevolently at the place we had left. 'He must be English,' I said. 'It will not save him from getting into trouble if he is not careful,' muttered the manager darkly. I observed with assumed innocence that no man was safe from trouble in this world.

"The current was more rapid now, the steamer seemed at her last gasp, the stern-wheel flopped languidly, and I caught myself listening on tiptoe for the next beat of the float,[4] for in sober truth I expected the wretched thing to give up every moment. It was like watching the last flickers of a life. But still we crawled. Sometimes I would pick out a tree a little way ahead to measure our progress towards Kurtz by, but I lost it invariably before we got abreast. To keep the eyes so long on one thing was too much for human patience. The manager displayed a beautiful resignation. I fretted and fumed and took to arguing with myself whether or no I would talk openly with Kurtz; but before I could come to any conclusion it occurred to me that my speech or my silence, indeed any action of mine, would be a mere futility. What did it matter what anyone knew or ignored? What did it matter who was manager? One gets sometimes such a flash of insight. The essentials of this affair lay deep under the surface, beyond my reach, and beyond my power of meddling.

"Towards the evening of the second day we judged ourselves about eight miles from Kurtz's station. I wanted to push on; but the manager looked grave, and told me the navigation up there was so dangerous that it would be advisable, the sun being very low already, to wait where we were till next morning. Moreover, he pointed out that if the warning to approach cautiously were to be followed, we must approach in daylight—not at dusk, or in the dark. This was sensible enough. Eight miles meant nearly three hours' steaming for us, and I could also see suspicious ripples at the upper end of the reach. Nevertheless, I was annoyed beyond expression at the delay, and most unreasonably, too, since one night more could not matter much after so many months. As we had plenty of wood, and caution was the word, I brought up in the middle of the stream. The reach was narrow, straight, with high sides like a railway cutting. The dusk came gliding into it long before the sun had set. The current ran smooth and swift, but a dumb immobility sat on the banks. The living trees, lashed together by the creepers and every living bush of the undergrowth, might have been changed into stone, even to the slenderest twig, to the lightest leaf. It was not sleep—it seemed unnatural, like a state of

4. A blade of the multibladed paddle wheel.

trance. Not the faintest sound of any kind could be heard. You looked on amazed, and began to suspect yourself of being deaf—then the night came suddenly, and struck you blind as well. About three in the morning some large fish leaped, and the loud splash made me jump as though a gun had been fired. When the sun rose there was a white fog, very warm and clammy, and more blinding than the night. It did not shift or drive; it was just there, standing all around you like something solid. At eight or nine, perhaps, it lifted as a shutter lifts. We had a glimpse of the towering multitude of trees, of the immense matted jungle, with the blazing little ball of the sun hanging over it—all perfectly still—and then the white shutter came down again, smoothly, as if sliding in greased grooves. I ordered the chain, which we had begun to heave in, to be paid out again. Before it stopped running with a muffled rattle, a cry, a very loud cry, as of infinite desolation, soared slowly in the opaque air. It ceased. A complaining clamor, modulated in savage dis-cords, filled our ears. The sheer unexpectedness of it made my hair stir under my cap. I don't know how it struck the others: to me it seemed as though the mist itself had screamed, so suddenly, and apparently from all sides at once, did this tumultuous and mournful uproar arise. It culminated in a hurried outbreak of almost intolerably excessive shrieking, which stopped short, leav-ing us stiffened in a variety of silly attitudes, and obstinately listening to the nearly as appalling and excessive silence. 'Good God! What is the meaning—' stammered at my elbow one of the pilgrims,—a little fat man, with sandy hair and red whiskers, who wore side-spring boots, and pink pajamas tucked into his socks. Two others remained open-mouthed a whole minute, then dashed into the little cabin, to rush out incontinently and stand darting scared glances, with Winchesters[5] at 'ready' in their hands. What we could see was just the steamer we were on, her outlines blurred as though she had been on the point of dissolving, and a misty strip of water, perhaps two feet broad, around her—and that was all. The rest of the world was nowhere, as far as our eyes and ears were concerned. Just nowhere. Gone, disappeared; swept off without leaving a whisper or a shadow behind.

"I went forward, and ordered the chain to be hauled in short, so as to be ready to trip the anchor and move the steamboat at once if necessary. 'Will they attack?' whispered an awed voice. 'We will be all butchered in this fog,' murmured another. The faces twitched with the strain, the hands trembling slightly, the eyes forgot to wink. It was very curious to see the contrast of expressions of the white men and of the black fellows of our crew, who were as much strangers to that part of the river as we, though their homes were only eight hundred miles away. The whites, of course, greatly discomposed, had besides a curious look of being painfully shocked by such an outrageous row. The others had an alert, naturally interested expression; but their faces were essentially quiet, even those of the one or two who grinned as they hauled at the chain. Several exchanged short, grunting phrases, which seemed to settle the matter to their satisfaction. Their headman, a young, broad-chested black, severely draped in dark-blue fringed cloths, with fierce nostrils and his hair all done up artfully in oily ringlets, stood near me. 'Aha!' I said, just for good fellowship's sake. 'Catch 'em,' he snapped, with a bloodshot widening of

5. American repeating rifles.

his eyes and a flash of sharp teeth—'catch 'im. Give 'im to us.' 'To you, eh?' I asked; 'what would you do with them?' 'Eat 'em!' he said, curtly, and, leaning his elbow on the rail, looked out into the fog in a dignified and profoundly pensive attitude. I would no doubt have been properly horrified, had it not occurred to me that he and his chaps must be very hungry: that they must have been growing increasingly hungry for at least this month past. They had been engaged for six months (I don't think a single one of them had any clear idea of time, as we at the end of countless ages have. They still belonged to the beginnings of time—had no inherited experience to teach them as it were), and of course, as long as there was a piece of paper written over in accordance with some farcical law or other made down the river, it didn't enter anybody's head to trouble how they would live. Certainly they had brought with them some rotten hippo-meat, which couldn't have lasted very long, anyway, even if the pilgrims hadn't, in the midst of a shocking hullabaloo, thrown a considerable quantity of it overboard. It looked like a high-handed proceeding; but it was really a case of legitimate self-defense. You can't breathe dead hippo waking, sleeping, and eating, and at the same time keep your precarious grip on existence. Besides that, they had given them every week three pieces of brass wire, each about nine inches long; and the theory was they were to buy their provisions with that currency in riverside villages. You can see how *that* worked. There were either no villages, or the people were hostile, or the director, who like the rest of us fed out of tins, with an occasional old he-goat thrown in, didn't want to stop the steamer for some more or less recondite reason. So, unless they swallowed the wire itself, or made loops of it to snare the fishes with, I don't see what good their extravagant salary could be to them. I must say it was paid with a regularity worthy of a large and honorable trading company. For the rest, the only thing to eat—though it didn't look eatable in the least—I saw in their possession was a few lumps of some stuff like half-cooked dough, of a dirty lavender color, they kept wrapped in leaves, and now and then swallowed a piece of, but so small that it seemed done more for the looks of the thing than for any serious purpose of sustenance. Why in the name of all the gnawing devils of hunger they didn't go for us—they were thirty to five—and have a good tuck-in[6] for once, amazes me now when I think of it. They were big powerful men, with not much capacity to weigh the consequences, with courage, with strength, even yet, though their skins were no longer glossy and their muscles no longer hard. And I saw that something restraining, one of those human secrets that baffle probability, had come into play there. I looked at them with a swift quickening of interest—not because it occurred to me I might be eaten by them before very long, though I own to you that just then I perceived—in a new light, as it were—how unwholesome the pilgrims looked, and I hoped, yes, I positively hoped, that my aspect was not so—what shall I say?—so—unappetizing: a touch of fantastic vanity which fitted well with the dream-sensation that pervaded all my days at that time. Perhaps I had a little fever, too. One can't live with one's finger everlastingly on one's pulse. I had often 'a little fever,' or a little touch of other things— the playful paw-strokes of the wilderness, the preliminary trifling before the more serious onslaught which came in due course. Yes; I looked at them as

6. British slang for a good meal.

you would on any human being, with a curiosity of their impulses, motives, capacities, weaknesses, when brought to the test of an inexorable physical necessity. Restraint! What possible restraint? Was it superstition, disgust, patience, fear—or some kind of primitive honor? No fear can stand up to hunger, no patience can wear it out, disgust simply does not exist where hunger is; and as to superstition, beliefs, and what you may call principles, they are less than chaff in a breeze. Don't you know the devilry of lingering starvation, its exasperating torment, its black thoughts, its somber and brooding ferocity? Well, I do. It takes a man all his inborn strength to fight hunger properly. It's really easier to face bereavement, dishonor, and the perdition of one's soul— than this kind of prolonged hunger. Sad, but true. And these chaps, too, had no earthly reason for any kind of scruple. Restraint! I would just as soon have expected restraint from a hyena prowling amongst the corpses of a battle-field. But there was the fact facing me—the fact dazzling, to be seen, like the foam on the depths of the sea, like a ripple on an unfathomable enigma, a mystery greater—when I thought of it—than the curious, inexplicable note of desperate grief in this savage clamor that had swept by us on the river-bank, behind the blind whiteness of the fog.

"Two pilgrims were quarreling in hurried whispers as to which bank. 'Left.' 'No, no; how can you? Right, right, of course.' 'It is very serious,' said the manager's voice behind me; 'I would be desolated if anything should happen to Mr. Kurtz before we came up.' I looked at him, and had not the slightest doubt he was sincere. He was just the kind of man who would wish to preserve appearances. That was his restraint. But when he muttered something about going on at once, I did not even take the trouble to answer him. I knew, and he knew, that it was impossible. Were we to let go our hold of the bottom, we would be absolutely in the air—in space. We wouldn't be able to tell where we were going to—whether up or down stream, or across—till we fetched against one bank or the other,—and then we wouldn't know at first which it was. Of course I made no move. I had no mind for a smash-up. You couldn't imagine a more deadly place for a shipwreck. Whether drowned at once or not, we were sure to perish speedily in one way or another. 'I authorize you to take all the risks,' he said, after a short silence. 'I refuse to take any,' I said, shortly; which was just the answer he expected, though its tone might have surprised him. 'Well, I must defer to your judgment. You are captain,' he said, with marked civility. I turned my shoulder to him in sign of my appreciation, and looked into the fog. How long would it last? It was the most hopeless lookout. The approach to this Kurtz grubbing for ivory in the wretched bush was beset by as many dangers as though he had been an enchanted princess sleeping in a fabulous castle. 'Will they attack, do you think?' asked the manager, in a confidential tone.

"I did not think they would attack, for several obvious reasons. The thick fog was one. If they left the bank in their canoes they would get lost in it, as we would be if we attempted to move. Still, I had also judged the jungle of both banks quite impenetrable—and yet eyes were in it, eyes that had seen us. The river-side bushes were certainly very thick; but the undergrowth behind was evidently penetrable. However, during the short lift I had seen no canoes anywhere in the reach—certainly not abreast of the steamer. But what made the idea of attack inconceivable to me was the nature of the noise—of the cries we had heard. They had not the fierce character boding immediate hostile intention. Unexpected, wild, and violent as they had been, they had given me an irresistible impression of sorrow. The glimpse of the steamboat had for some reason filled those savages with unrestrained grief. The danger, if any, I expounded, was from our proximity to a great human passion let loose. Even extreme grief may ultimately vent itself in violence—but more generally takes the form of apathy. . . .

"You should have seen the pilgrims stare! They had no heart to grin, or even to revile me: but I believe they thought me gone mad—with fright, maybe. I delivered a regular lecture. My dear boys, it was no good bothering. Keep a look-out? Well, you may guess I watched the fog for the signs of lifting as a cat watches a mouse; but for anything else our eyes were of no more use to us than if we had been buried miles deep in a heap of cotton-wool. It felt like it, too—choking, warm, stifling. Besides, all I said, though it sounded extravagant, was absolutely true to fact. What we afterwards alluded to as an attack was really an attempt at repulse. The action was very far from being aggressive—it was not even defensive, in the usual sense: it was undertaken under the stress of desperation, and in its essence was purely protective.

"It developed itself, I should say, two hours after the fog lifted, and its commencement was at a spot, roughly speaking, about a mile and a half below Kurtz's station. We had just floundered and flopped round a bend, when I saw an islet, a mere grassy hummock of bright green, in the middle of the stream. It was the only thing of the kind; but as we opened the reach more, I perceived it was the head of a long sandbank, or rather of a chain of shallow patches stretching down the middle of the river. They were discolored, just awash, and the whole lot was seen just under the water, exactly as a man's backbone is seen running down the middle of his back under the skin. Now, as far as I did see, I could go to the right or to the left of this. I didn't know either channel, of course. The banks looked pretty well alike, the depth appeared the same; but as I had been informed the station was on the west side, I naturally headed for the western passage.

"No sooner had we fairly entered it than I became aware it was much narrower than I had supposed. To the left of us there was the long uninterrupted shoal, and to the right a high, steep bank heavily overgrown with bushes. Above the bush the trees stood in serried ranks. The twigs overhung the current thickly, and from distance to distance a large limb of some tree projected rigidly over the stream. It was then well on in the afternoon, the face of the forest was gloomy, and a broad strip of shadow had already fallen on the water. In this shadow we steamed up—very slowly, as you may imagine. I sheered her well inshore—the water being deepest near the bank, as the sounding-pole informed me.

"One of my hungry and forbearing friends was sounding[7] in the bows just below me. This steamboat was exactly like a decked scow. On the deck, there were two little teak-wood houses, with doors and windows. The boiler was in the fore-end, and the machinery right astern. Over the whole there was a light roof, supported on stanchions. The funnel projected through that roof, and in front of the funnel a small cabin built of light planks served for a pilot-

---

7. Measuring water depth with a sounding line.

house. It contained a couch, two campstools, a loaded Martini-Henry[8] leaning in one corner, a tiny table, and the steering-wheel. It had a wide door in
front and a broad shutter at each side. All these were always thrown open, of
course. I spent my days perched up there on the extreme fore-end of that roof,
before the door. At night I slept, or tried to, on the couch. An athletic black
belonging to some coast tribe, and educated by my poor predecessor, was the
helmsman. He sported a pair of brass earrings, wore a blue cloth wrapper
from the waist to the ankles, and thought all the world of himself. He was the
most unstable kind of fool I had ever seen. He steered with no end of a swagger while you were by; but if he lost sight of you, he became instantly the prey
of an abject funk, and would let that cripple of a steamboat get the upper
hand of him in a minute.

"I was looking down at the sounding-pole, and feeling much annoyed to
see at each try a little more of it stick out of that river, when I saw my poleman
give up the business suddenly, and stretch himself flat on the deck, without
even taking the trouble to haul his pole in. He kept hold on it though, and it
trailed in the water. At the same time the fireman, whom I could also see
below me, sat down abruptly before his furnace and ducked his head. I was
amazed. Then I had to look at the river mighty quick, because there was a
snag in the fairway. Sticks, little sticks, were flying about—thick: they were
whizzing before my nose, dropping below me, striking behind me against my
pilot-house. All this time the river, the shore, the woods, were very quiet—
perfectly quiet. I could only hear the heavy splashing thump of the stern-
wheel and the patter of these things. We cleared the snag clumsily. Arrows, by
Jove! We were being shot at! I stepped in quickly to close the shutter on the
land-side. That fool-helmsman, his hands on the spokes, was lifting his knees
high, stamping his feet, champing his mouth, like a reined-in horse. Confound him! And we were staggering within ten feet of the bank. I had to lean
right out to swing the heavy shutter, and I saw a face amongst the leaves on
the level with my own, looking at me very fierce and steady; and then suddenly, as though a veil had been removed from my eyes, I made out, deep in
the tangled gloom, naked breasts, arms, legs, glaring eyes,—the bush was
swarming with human limbs in movement, glistening, of bronze color. The
twigs shook, swayed, and rustled, the arrows flew out of them, and then the
shutter came to. 'Steer her straight,' I said to the helmsman. He held his head
rigid, face forward; but his eyes rolled, he kept on lifting and setting down his
feet gently, his mouth foamed a little. 'Keep quiet!' I said in a fury. I might
just as well have ordered a tree not to sway in the wind. I darted out. Below me
there was a great scuffle of feet on the iron deck; confused exclamations; a
voice screamed, 'Can you turn back?' I caught sight of a V-shaped ripple on
the water ahead. What? Another snag! A fusillade burst out under my feet.
The pilgrims had opened with their Winchesters, and were simply squirting
lead into that bush. A deuce of a lot of smoke came up and drove slowly forward. I swore at it. Now I couldn't see the ripple or the snag either. I stood in
the doorway, peering, and the arrows came in swarms. They might have been
poisoned, but they looked as though they wouldn't kill a cat. The bush began
to howl. Our wood-cutters raised a warlike whoop; the report of a rifle just at

8. Heavy military rifle.

my back deafened me. I glanced over my shoulder, and the pilot-house was yet full of noise and smoke when I made a dash at the wheel. The fool-nigger had dropped everything to throw the shutter open and let off[9] that Martini-Henry. He stood before the wide opening, glaring, and I yelled at him to come back, while I straightened the sudden twist out of that steamboat. There was no room to turn even if I had wanted to, the snag was somewhere very near ahead in that confounded smoke, there was no time to lose, so I just crowded her into the bank—right into the bank, where I knew the water was deep.

"We tore slowly along the overhanging bushes in a whirl of broken twigs and flying leaves. The fusillade below stopped short, as I had foreseen it would when the squirts got empty. I threw my head back to a glinting whizz that traversed the pilot-house, in at one shutter-hole and out at the other. Looking past that mad helmsman, who was shaking the empty rifle and yelling at the shore, I saw vague forms of men running bent double, leaping, gliding, distinct, incomplete, evanescent. Something big appeared in the air before the shutter, the rifle went overboard, and the man stepped back swiftly, looked at me over his shoulder in an extraordinary, profound, familiar manner, and fell upon my feet. The side of his head hit the wheel twice, and the end of what appeared a long cane clattered round and knocked over a little campstool. It looked as though after wrenching that thing from somebody ashore he had lost his balance in the effort. The thin smoke had blown away, we were clear of the snag, and looking ahead I could see that in another hundred yards or so I would be free to sheer off, away from the bank; but my feet felt so very warm and wet that I had to look down. The man had rolled on his back and stared straight up at me; both his hands clutched that cane. It was the shaft of a spear that, either thrown or lunged through the opening, had caught him in the side just below the ribs; the blade had gone in out of sight, after making a frightful gash; my shoes were full; a pool of blood lay very still, gleaming dark-red under the wheel; his eyes shone with an amazing luster. The fusillade burst out again. He looked at me anxiously, gripping the spear like something precious, with an air of being afraid I would try to take it away from him. I had to make an effort to free my eyes from his gaze and attend to steering. With one hand I felt above my head for the line of the steam-whistle, and jerked out screech after screech hurriedly. The tumult of angry and war-like yells was checked instantly, and then from the depths of the woods went out such a tremulous and prolonged wail of mournful fear and utter despair as may be imagined to follow the flight of the last hope from the earth. There was a great commotion in the bush; the shower of arrows stopped, a few dropping shots rang out sharply—then silence, in which the languid beat of the stern-wheel came plainly to my ears. I put the helm hard a-starboard at the moment when the pilgrim in pink pajamas, very hot and agitated, appeared in the doorway. 'The manager sends me—' he began in an official tone, and stopped short. 'Good God!' he said, glaring at the wounded man.

"We two whites stood over him, and his lustrous and inquiring glance enveloped us both. I declare it looked as though he would presently put to us some question in an understandable language; but he died without uttering a sound, without moving a limb, without twitching a muscle. Only in the very

**9.** Fire.

last moment, as though in response to some sign we could not see, to some whisper we could not hear, he frowned heavily, and that frown gave to his black death-mask an inconceivably somber, brooding, and menacing expression. The luster of inquiring glance faded swiftly into vacant glassiness. 'Can you steer?' I asked the agent eagerly. He looked very dubious; but I made a grab at his arm, and he understood at once I meant him to steer whether or no. To tell you the truth, I was morbidly anxious to change my shoes and socks. 'He is dead,' murmured the fellow, immensely impressed. 'No doubt about it,' said I tugging like mad at the shoe-laces. 'And by the way, I suppose Mr. Kurtz is dead as well by this time.'

"For the moment that was the dominant thought. There was a sense of extreme disappointment, as though I had found out I had been striving after something altogether without a substance. I couldn't have been more disgusted if I had traveled all this way for the sole purpose of talking with Mr. Kurtz. Talking with . . . I flung one shoe overboard, and became aware that that was exactly what I had been looking forward to—a talk with Kurtz. I made the strange discovery that I had never imagined him as doing, you know, but as discoursing. I didn't say to myself, 'Now I will never see him,' or 'Now I will never shake him by the hand,' but, 'Now I will never hear him.' The man presented himself as a voice. Not of course that I did not connect him with some sort of action. Hadn't I been told in all the tones of jealousy and admiration that he had collected, bartered, swindled, or stolen more ivory than all the other agents together? That was not the point. The point was in his being a gifted creature, and that of all his gifts the one that stood out preeminently, that carried with it a sense of real presence, was his ability to talk, his words—the gift of expression, the bewildering, the illuminating, the most exalted and the most contemptible, the pulsating stream of light, or the deceitful flow from the heart of an impenetrable darkness.

"The other shoe went flying unto the devil-god of that river. I thought, by Jove! it's all over. We are too late; he has vanished—the gift has vanished, by means of some spear, arrow, or club. I will never hear that chap speak after all,—and my sorrow had a startling extravagance of emotion, even such as I had noticed in the howling sorrow of these savages in the bush. I couldn't have felt more lonely desolation somehow, had I been robbed of a belief or had missed my destiny in life. . . . Why do you sigh in this beastly way, somebody? Absurd? Well, absurd. Good Lord! mustn't a man ever—Here, give me some tobacco." . . .

There was a pause of profound stillness, then a match flared, and Marlow's lean face appeared, worn, hollow, with downward folds and drooped eyelids, with an aspect of concentrated attention; and as he took vigorous draws at his pipe, it seemed to retreat and advance out of the night in the regular flicker of the tiny flame. The match went out.

"Absurd!" he cried. "This is the worst of trying to tell. . . . Here you all are, each moored with two good addresses, like a hulk with two anchors, a butcher round one corner, a policeman round another, excellent appetites, and temperature normal—you hear—normal from year's end to year's end. And you say, Absurd! Absurd be—exploded! Absurd! My dear boys, what can you expect from a man who out of sheer nervousness had just flung overboard a pair of new shoes? Now I think of it, it is amazing I did not shed tears. I am, upon the whole, proud of my fortitude. I was cut to the quick at the idea of having lost the inestimable privilege of listening to the gifted Kurtz. Of course I was wrong. The privilege was waiting for me. Oh yes, I heard more than enough. And I was right, too. A voice. He was very little more than a voice. And I heard—him—it—this voice—other voices—all of them were so little more than voices—and the memory of that time itself lingers around me, impalpable, like a dying vibration of one immense jabber, silly, atrocious, sordid, savage, or simply mean, without any kind of sense. Voices, voices—even the girl herself—now—"

He was silent for a long time.

"I laid the ghost of his gifts at last with a lie," he began, suddenly. "Girl! What? Did I mention a girl? Oh, she is out of it—completely. They—the women I mean—are out of it—should be out of it. We must help them to stay in that beautiful world of their own, lest ours gets worse. Oh, she had to be out of it. You should have heard the disinterred body of Mr. Kurtz saying, 'My Intended.' You would have perceived directly then how completely she was out of it. And the lofty frontal bone of Mr. Kurtz! They say the hair goes on growing sometimes, but this—ah—specimen, was impressively bald. The wilderness had patted him on the head, and, behold, it was like a ball—an ivory ball; it had caressed him, and—lo!—he had withered; it had taken him, loved him, embraced him, got into his veins, consumed his flesh, and sealed his soul to its own by the inconceivable ceremonies of some devilish initiation. He was its spoiled and pampered favorite. Ivory? I should think so. Heaps of it, stacks of it. The old mud shanty was bursting with it. You would think here was not a single tusk left either above or below the ground in the whole country. 'Mostly fossil,' the manager had remarked, disparagingly. It was no more fossil than I am; but they call it fossil when it is dug up. It appears these niggers do bury the tusks sometimes—but evidently they couldn't bury this parcel deep enough to save the gifted Mr. Kurtz from his fate. We filled the steamboat with it, and had to pile a lot on the deck. Thus he could see and enjoy as long as he could see, because the appreciation of this favor had remained with him to the last. You should have heard him say, 'My ivory.' Oh yes, I heard him. 'My Intended, my ivory, my station, my river, my—' everything belonged to him. It made me hold my breath in expectation of hearing the wilderness burst into a prodigious peal of laughter that would shake the fixed stars in their places. Everything belonged to him—but that was a trifle. The thing was to know what he belonged to, how many powers of darkness claimed him for their own. That was the reflection that made you creepy all over. It was impossible—it was not good for one either—trying to imagine. He had taken a high seat amongst the devils of the land—I mean literally. You can't understand. How could you?—with solid pavement under your feet, surrounded by kind neighbors ready to cheer you or to fall on you, stepping delicately between the butcher and the policeman, in the holy terror of scandal and gallows and lunatic asylums—how can you imagine what particular region of the first ages a man's untrammeled feet may take him into by the way of solitude—utter solitude without a policeman—by the way of silence—utter silence, where no warning voice of a kind neighbor can be heard whispering of public opinion? These little things make all the great difference. When they are gone you must fall back upon your own innate strength, upon your own capacity for faithfulness. Of course you may be too much of a fool to go wrong—too dull even to know you are being assaulted by the powers of darkness. I take it, no fool ever made a bargain for his soul with the devil: the fool is too much of a fool, or the devil too much of a devil—I don't know which. Or you may be such a thunderingly exalted creature as to be altogether deaf and blind to anything but heavenly sights and sounds. Then the earth for you is only a standing place—and whether to be like this is your loss or your gain I won't pretend to say. But most of us are neither one nor the other. The earth for us is a place to live in, where we must put up with sights, with sounds, with smells, too, by Jove!—breathe dead hippo, so to speak, and not be contaminated. And there, don't you see? your strength comes in, the faith in your ability for the digging of unostentatious holes to bury the stuff in—your power of devotion, not to yourself, but to an obscure, back-breaking business. And that's difficult enough. Mind, I am not trying to excuse or even explain—I am trying to account to myself for—for—Mr. Kurtz—for the shade of Mr. Kurtz. This initiated wraith from the back of Nowhere honored me with its amazing confidence before it vanished altogether. This was because it could speak English to me. The original Kurtz had been educated partly in England, and—as he was good enough to say himself—his sympathies were in the right place. His mother was half-English, his father was half-French. All Europe contributed to the making of Kurtz; and by and by I learned that, most appropriately, the International Society for the Suppression of Savage Customs had intrusted him with the making of a report, for its future guidance. And he had written it, too. I've seen it. I've read it. It was eloquent, vibrating with eloquence, but too high-strung, I think. Seventeen pages of close writing he had found time for! But this must have been before his—let us say—nerves, went wrong, and caused him to preside at certain midnight dances ending with unspeakable rites, which—as far as I reluctantly gathered from what I heard at various times—were offered up to him—do you understand?—to Mr. Kurtz himself. But it was a beautiful piece of writing. The opening paragraph, however, in the light of later information, strikes me now as ominous. He began with the argument that we whites, from the point of development we had arrived at, 'must necessarily appear to them [savages] in the nature of supernatural beings—we approach them with the might as of a deity,' and so on, and so on. 'By the simple exercise of our will we can exert a power for good practically unbounded,' etc., etc. From that point he soared and took me with him. The peroration was magnificent, though difficult to remember, you know. It gave me the notion of an exotic Immensity ruled by an august Benevolence. It made me tingle with enthusiasm. This was the unbounded power of eloquence—of words—of burning noble words. There were no practical hints to interrupt the magic current of phrases, unless a kind of note at the foot of the last page, scrawled evidently much later, in an unsteady hand, may be regarded as the exposition of a method. It was very simple, and at the end of that moving appeal to every altruistic sentiment it blazed at you, luminous and terrifying, like a flash of lightning in a serene sky: 'Exterminate all the brutes!' The curious part was that he had apparently forgotten all about that valuable postscriptum, because, later on, when he in a sense came to himself, he repeatedly entreated me to take good care of 'my pamphlet' (he called it), as it was sure to have in the future a good influence upon his career. I had full information about all these things, and, besides, as it turned out, I was to have the care of his memory. I've done enough for it to give me the indisputable right to lay it, if I choose, for an everlasting rest in the dust-bin of progress, amongst all the sweepings and, figuratively speaking, all the dead cats of civilization. But then, you see, I can't choose. He won't be forgotten. Whatever he was, he was not common. He had the power to charm or frighten rudimentary souls into an aggravated witch-dance in his honor; he could also fill the small souls of the pilgrims with bitter misgivings: he had one devoted friend at least, and he had conquered one soul in the world that was neither rudimentary nor tainted with self-seeking. No; I can't forget him, though I am not prepared to affirm the fellow was exactly worth the life we lost in getting to him. I missed my late helmsman awfully,—I missed him even while his body was still lying in the pilot-house. Perhaps you will think it passing strange this regret for a savage who was no more account than a grain of sand in a black Sahara. Well, don't you see, he had done something, he had steered; for months I had him at my back—a help—an instrument. It was a kind of partnership. He steered for me—I had to look after him, I worried about his deficiencies, and thus a subtle bond had been created, of which I only became aware when it was suddenly broken. And the intimate profundity of that look he gave me when he received his hurt remains to this day in my memory—like a claim of distant kinship affirmed in a supreme moment.

"Poor fool! If he had only left that shutter alone. He had no restraint, no restraint—just like Kurtz—a tree swayed by the wind. As soon as I had put on a dry pair of slippers, I dragged him out, after first jerking the spear out of his side, which operation I confess I performed with my eyes shut tight. His heels leaped together over the little doorstep; his shoulders were pressed to my breast; I hugged him from behind desperately. Oh! he was heavy, heavy; heavier than any man on earth, I should imagine. Then without more ado I tipped him overboard. The current snatched him as though he had been a wisp of grass, and I saw the body roll over twice before I lost sight of it forever. All the pilgrims and the manager were then congregated on the awning-deck about the pilot-house, chattering at each other like a flock of excited magpies, and there was a scandalized murmur at my heartless promptitude. What they wanted to keep that body hanging about for I can't guess. Embalm it, maybe. But I had also heard another, and a very ominous, murmur on the deck below. My friends the wood-cutters were likewise scandalized, and with a better show of reason—though I admit that the reason itself was quite inadmissible. Oh, quite! I had made up my mind that if my late helmsman was to be eaten, the fishes alone should have him. He had been a very second-rate helmsman while alive, but now he was dead he might have become a first-class temptation, and possibly cause some startling trouble. Besides, I was anxious to take the wheel, the man in pink pajamas showing himself a hopeless duffer at the business.

"This I did directly the simple funeral was over. We were going half-speed, keeping right in the middle of the stream, and I listened to the talk about me. They had given up Kurtz, they had given up the station; Kurtz was dead, and the station had been burnt—and so on—and so on. The red-haired pilgrim was beside himself with the thought that at least this poor Kurtz had been properly avenged. 'Say! We must have made a glorious slaughter of them in the bush. Eh? What do you think? Say?' He positively danced, the blood-thirsty little gingery beggar.[1] And he had nearly fainted when he saw the wounded man! I could not help saying, 'You made a glorious lot of smoke, anyhow.' I had seen, from the way the tops of the bushes rustled and flew, that almost all the shots had gone too high. You can't hit anything unless you take aim and fire from the shoulder; but these chaps fired from the hip with their eyes shut. The retreat, I maintained—and I was right—was caused by the screeching of the steam-whistle. Upon this they forgot Kurtz, and began to howl at me with indignant protests.

"The manager stood by the wheel murmuring confidentially about the necessity of getting well away down the river before dark at all events, when I saw in the distance a clearing on the river-side and the outlines of some sort of building. 'What's this?' I asked. He clapped his hands in wonder. 'The station!' he cried. I edged in at once, still going half-speed.

"Through my glasses I saw the slope of a hill interspersed with rare trees and perfectly free from undergrowth. A long decaying building on the summit was half buried in the high grass; the large holes in the peaked roof gaped black from afar; the jungle and the woods made a background. There was no enclosure or fence of any kind; but there had been one apparently, for near the house half-a-dozen slim posts remained in a row, roughly trimmed, and with their upper ends ornamented with round carved balls. The rails, or whatever there had been between, had disappeared. Of course the forest surrounded all that. The river-bank was clear, and on the water-side I saw a white man under a hat like a cart-wheel beckoning persistently with his whole arm. Examining the edge of the forest above and below, I was almost certain I could see movements—human forms gliding here and there. I steamed past prudently, then stopped the engines and let her drift down. The man on the shore began to shout, urging us to land. 'We have been attacked,' screamed the manager. 'I know—I know. It's all right,' yelled back the other, as cheerful as you please. 'Come along. It's all right. I am glad.'

"His aspect reminded me of something I had seen—something funny I had seen somewhere. As I maneuvered to get alongside, I was asking myself, 'What does this fellow look like?' Suddenly I got it. He looked like a harlequin. His clothes had been made of some stuff that was brown holland probably, but it was covered with patches all over, with bright patches, blue, red, and yellow,—patches on the back, patches on the front, patches on elbows, on knees; colored binding around his jacket, scarlet edging at the bottom of his trousers; and the sunshine made him look extremely gay and wonderfully neat withal, because you could see how beautifully all this patching had been done. A beardless, boyish face, very fair, no features to speak of, nose peeling, little blue eyes, smiles and frowns chasing each other over that open countenance like sunshine and shadow on a windswept plain. 'Look out, captain!' he cried; 'there's a snag lodged in here last night.' What! Another snag? I confess I swore shamefully. I had nearly holed my cripple, to finish off that charming trip. The harlequin on the bank turned his little pug-nose up to me. 'You English?' he asked, all smiles. 'Are you?' I shouted from the wheel. The smiles

1. British slang for redheaded rascal.

vanished, and he shook his head as if sorry for my disappointment. Then he brightened up. 'Never mind!' he cried, encouragingly. 'Are we in time?' I asked. 'He is up there,' he replied, with a toss of the head up the hill, and becoming gloomy all of a sudden. His face was like the autumn sky, overcast one moment and bright the next.

"When the manager, escorted by the pilgrims, all of them armed to the teeth, had gone to the house this chap came on board. 'I say, I don't like this. These natives are in the bush,' I said. He assured me earnestly it was all right. 'They are simple people,' he added; 'well, I am glad you came. It took me all my time to keep them off.' 'But you said it was all right,' I cried. 'Oh, they meant no harm,' he said; and as I stared he corrected himself, 'Not exactly.' Then vivaciously, 'My faith, your pilot-house wants a clean-up!' In the next breath he advised me to keep enough steam on the boiler to blow the whistle in case of any trouble. 'One good screech will do more for you than all your rifles. They are simple people,' he repeated. He rattled away at such a rate he quite overwhelmed me. He seemed to be trying to make up for lots of silence, and actually hinted, laughing, that such was the case. 'Don't you talk with Mr. Kurtz?' I said. 'You don't talk with that man—you listen to him,' he exclaimed with severe exaltation. 'But now—' He waved his arm, and in the twinkling of an eye was in the uttermost depths of despondency. In a moment he came up again with a jump, possessed himself of both my hands, shook them continuously, while he gabbled: 'Brother sailor . . . honor . . . pleasure . . . delight . . . introduce myself . . . Russian . . . son of an arch-priest . . . Government of Tambov. . . . What? Tobacco! English tobacco; the excellent English tobacco! Now, that's brotherly. Smoke? Where's a sailor that does not smoke?'

"The pipe soothed him, and gradually I made out he had run away from school, had gone to sea in a Russian ship; ran away again; served some time in English ships; was now reconciled with the arch-priest. He made a point of that. 'But when one is young one must see things, gather experience, ideas; enlarge the mind.' 'Here!' I interrupted. 'You can never tell! Here I met Mr. Kurtz,' he said, youthfully solemn and reproachful. I held my tongue after that. It appears he had persuaded a Dutch trading-house on the coast to fit him out with stores and goods, and had started for the interior with a light heart, and no more idea of what would happen to him than a baby. He had been wandering about that river for nearly two years alone, cut off from everybody and everything. 'I am not so young as I look. I am twenty-five,' he said. 'At first old Van Shuyten would tell me to go to the devil,' he narrated with keen enjoyment; 'but I stuck to him, and talked and talked, till at last he got afraid I would talk the hind-leg off his favorite dog, so he gave me some cheap things and a few guns, and told me he hoped he would never see my face again. Good old Dutchman, Van Shuyten. I've sent him one small lot of ivory a year ago, so that he can't call me a little thief when I get back. I hope he got it. And for the rest I don't care. I had some wood stacked for you. That was my old house. Did you see?'

"I gave him Towson's book. He made as though he would kiss me, but restrained himself. 'The only book I had left, and I thought I had lost it,' he said, looking at it ecstatically. 'So many accidents happen to a man going about alone, you know. Canoes get upset sometimes—and sometimes you've got to clear out so quick when the people get angry.' He thumbed the pages.

'You made notes in Russian?' I asked. He nodded. 'I thought they were written in cipher,' I said. He laughed, then became serious. 'I had lots of trouble to keep these people off,' he said. 'Did they want to kill you?' I asked. 'Oh no!' he cried, and checked himself. 'Why did they attack us?' I pursued. He hesitated, then said shamefacedly, 'They don't want him to go.' 'Don't they?' I said curiously. He nodded a nod full of mystery and wisdom. 'I tell you,' he cried, 'this man has enlarged my mind.' He opened his arms wide, staring at me with his little blue eyes that were perfectly round."

# III

"I looked at him, lost in astonishment. There he was before me, in motley, as though he had absconded from a troupe of mimes, enthusiastic, fabulous. His very existence was improbable, inexplicable, and altogether bewildering. He was an insoluble problem. It was inconceivable how he had existed, how he had succeeded in getting so far, how he had managed to remain—why he did not instantly disappear. 'I went a little farther,' he said, 'then still a little farther—till I had gone so far that I don't know how I'll ever get back. Never mind. Plenty of time. I can manage. You take Kurtz away quick—quick—I tell you.' The glamour of youth enveloped his parti-colored rags, his destitution, his loneliness, the essential desolation of his futile wanderings. For months—for years—his life hadn't been worth a day's purchase; and there he was gallantly, thoughtlessly alive, to all appearance indestructible solely by the virtue of his few years and of his unreflecting audacity. I was seduced into something like admiration—like envy. Glamour urged him on, glamour kept him unscathed. He surely wanted nothing from the wilderness but space to breathe in and to push on through. His need was to exist, and to move onwards at the greatest possible risk, and with a maximum of privation. If the absolutely pure, uncalculating, unpractical spirit of adventure had ever ruled a human being, it ruled this be-patched youth. I almost envied him the possession of this modest and clear flame. It seemed to have consumed all thought of self so completely, that even while he was talking to you, you forgot that it was he—the man before your eyes—who had gone through these things. I did not envy him his devotion to Kurtz, though. He had not meditated over it. It came to him and he accepted it with a sort of eager fatalism. I must say that to me it appeared about the most dangerous thing in every way he had come upon so far.

"They had come together unavoidably, like two ships becalmed near each other, and lay rubbing sides at last. I suppose Kurtz wanted an audience, because on a certain occasion, when encamped in the forest, they had talked all night, or more probably Kurtz had talked. 'We talked of everything,' he said, quite transported at the recollection. 'I forgot there was such a thing as sleep. The night did not seem to last an hour. Everything! Everything! . . . Of love, too.' 'Ah, he talked to you of love!' I said, much amused. 'It isn't what you think,' he cried, almost passionately. 'It was in general. He made me see things—things.'

"He threw his arms up. We were on deck at the time, and the headman of my wood-cutters, lounging near by, turned upon him his heavy and glittering eyes. I looked around, and I don't know why, but I assure you that never, never before, did this land, this river, this jungle, the very arch of this blazing sky, appear to me so hopeless and so dark, so impenetrable to human thought, so pitiless to human weakness. 'And, ever since, you have been with him, of course?' I said.

"On the contrary. It appears their intercourse had been very much broken by various causes. He had, as he informed me proudly, managed to nurse Kurtz through two illnesses (he alluded to it as you would to some risky feat), but as a rule Kurtz wandered alone far in the depths of the forest. 'Very often coming to this station, I had to wait days and days before he would turn up,' he said. 'Ah, it was worth waiting for!—sometimes.' 'What was he doing? exploring or what?' I asked. 'Oh, yes, of course'; he had discovered lots of villages, a lake, too—he did not know exactly in what direction; it was dangerous to inquire too much—but mostly his expeditions had been for ivory. 'But he had no goods to trade with by that time,' I objected. 'There's a good lot of cartridges left even yet,' he answered, looking away. 'To speak plainly, he raided the country,' I said. He nodded. 'Not alone, surely!' He muttered something about the villages round that lake. 'Kurtz got the tribe to follow him, did he?' I suggested. He fidgeted a little. 'They adored him,' he said. The tone of these words was so extraordinary that I looked at him searchingly. It was curious to see his mingled eagerness and reluctance to speak of Kurtz. The man filled his life, occupied his thoughts, swayed his emotions. 'What can you expect?' he burst out; 'he came to them with thunder and lightning, you know—and they had never seen anything like it—and very terrible. He could be very terrible. You can't judge Mr. Kurtz as you would an ordinary man. No, no, no! Now—just to give you an idea—I don't mind telling you, he wanted to shoot me, too, one day—but I don't judge him.' 'Shoot you!' I cried. 'What for?' 'Well, I had a small lot of ivory the chief of that village near my house gave me. You see I used to shoot game for them. Well, he wanted it, and wouldn't hear reason. He declared he would shoot me unless I gave him the ivory and then cleared out of the country, because he could do so, and had a fancy for it, and there was nothing on earth to prevent him killing whom he jolly well pleased. And it was true, too. I gave him the ivory. What did I care! But I didn't clear out. No, no. I couldn't leave him. I had to be careful, of course, till we got friendly again for a time. He had his second illness then. Afterwards I had to keep out of the way; but I didn't mind. He was living for the most part in those villages on the lake. When he came down to the river, sometimes he would take to me, and sometimes it was better for me to be careful. This man suffered too much. He hated all this, and somehow he couldn't get away. When I had a chance I begged him to try and leave while there was time; I offered to go back with him. And he would say yes, and then he would remain; go off on another ivory hunt; disappear for weeks; forget himself amongst these people—forget himself—you know.' 'Why! he's mad,' I said. He protested indignantly. Mr. Kurtz couldn't be mad. If I had heard him talk, only two days ago, I wouldn't dare hint at such a thing. . . . I had taken up my binoculars while we talked, and was looking at the shore, sweeping the limit of the forest at each side and at the back of the house. The consciousness of there being people in that bush, so silent, so quiet—as silent and quiet as the ruined house on the hill—made me uneasy. There was no sign on the face of nature of this amazing tale that was not so much told as suggested to me in desolate exclamations, completed by shrugs, in interrupted phrases, in hints ending in deep sighs. The woods were unmoved, like a mask—heavy, like the closed door of a prison—they looked with their air of hidden knowledge, of patient expectation, of unapproachable silence. The Russian was explaining to me that it was only lately that Mr. Kurtz had come down to the river, bringing along with him all the fighting men of that lake tribe. He had been absent for several months—getting himself adored, I suppose—and had come down unexpectedly, with the intention to all appearance of making a raid either across the river or down stream. Evidently the appetite for more ivory had got the better of the—what shall I say?—less material aspirations. However he had got much worse suddenly. 'I heard he was lying helpless, and so I came up—took my chance,' said the Russian. 'Oh, he is bad, very bad.' I directed my glass to the house. There were no signs of life, but there was the ruined roof, the long mud wall peeping above the grass, with three little square window-holes, no two of the same size; all this brought within reach of my hand, as it were. And then I made a brusque movement, and one of the remaining posts of that vanished fence leaped up in the field of my glass. You remember I told you I had been struck at the distance by certain attempts at ornamentation, rather remarkable in the ruinous aspect of the place. Now I had suddenly a nearer view, and its first result was to make me throw my head back as if before a blow. Then I went carefully from post to post with my glass, and I saw my mistake. These round knobs were not ornamental but symbolic; they were expressive and puzzling, striking and disturbing—food for thought and also for vultures if there had been any looking down from the sky; but at all events for such ants as were industrious enough to ascend the pole. They would have been even more impressive, those heads on the stakes, if their faces had not been turned to the house. Only one, the first I had made out, was facing my way. I was not so shocked as you may think. The start back I had given was really nothing but a movement of surprise. I had expected to see a knob of wood there, you know. I returned deliberately to the first I had seen—and there it was, black, dried, sunken, with closed eyelids,—a head that seemed to sleep at the top of that pole, and with the shrunken dry lips showing a narrow white line of the teeth, was smiling, too, smiling continuously at some endless and jocose dream of that eternal slumber.

"I am not disclosing any trade secrets. In fact, the manager said afterwards that Mr. Kurtz's methods had ruined the district. I have no opinion on that point, but I want you clearly to understand that there was nothing exactly profitable in these heads being there. They only showed that Mr. Kurtz lacked restraint in the gratification of his various lusts, that there was something wanting in him—some small matter which, when the pressing need arose, could not be found under his magnificent eloquence. Whether he knew of this deficiency himself I can't say. I think the knowledge came to him at last—only at the very last. But the wilderness had found him out early, and had taken on him a terrible vengeance for the fantastic invasion. I think it had whispered to him things about himself which he did not know, things of which he had no conception till he took counsel with this great solitude—and the whisper had proved irresistibly fascinating. It echoed loudly within him because he was hollow at the core. . . . I put down the glass, and the head that had appeared near enough to be spoken to seemed at once to have leaped away from me into inaccessible distance.

"The admirer of Mr. Kurtz was a bit crestfallen. In a hurried indistinct voice he began to assure me he had not dared to take these—say, symbols—down. He was not afraid of the natives; they would not stir till Mr. Kurtz gave the word. His ascendancy was extraordinary. The camps of these people surrounded the place, and the chiefs came every day to see him. They would crawl.... 'I don't want to know anything of the ceremonies used when approaching Mr. Kurtz,' I shouted. Curious, this feeling that came over me that such details would be more intolerable than those heads drying on the stakes under Mr. Kurtz's windows. After all, that was only a savage sight, while I seemed at one bound to have been transported into some lightless region of subtle horrors, where pure, uncomplicated savagery was a positive relief, being something that had a right to exist—obviously—in the sunshine. The young man looked at me with surprise. I suppose it did not occur to him that Mr. Kurtz was no idol of mine. He forgot I hadn't heard any of these splendid monologues on, what was it? on love, justice, conduct of life—or what not. If it had come to crawling before Mr. Kurtz, he crawled as much as the veriest savage of them all. I had no idea of the conditions, he said: these heads were the heads of rebels. I shocked him excessively by laughing. Rebels! What would be the next definition I was to hear? There had been enemies, criminals, workers—and these were rebels. Those rebellious heads looked very subdued to me on their sticks. 'You don't know how such a life tries a man like Kurtz,' cried Kurtz's last disciple. 'Well, and you?' I said. 'I! I! I am a simple man. I have no great thoughts. I want nothing from anybody. How can you compare me to ...?' His feelings were too much for speech, and suddenly he broke down. 'I don't understand,' he groaned. 'I've been doing my best to keep him alive, and that's enough. I had no hand in all this. I have no abilities. There hasn't been a drop of medicine or a mouthful of invalid food for months here. He was shamefully abandoned. A man like this, with such ideas. Shamefully! Shamefully! I—I—haven't slept for the last ten nights....'

"His voice lost itself in the calm of the evening. The long shadows of the forest had slipped downhill while we talked, had gone far beyond the ruined hovel, beyond the symbolic row of stakes. All this was in the gloom, while we down there were yet in the sunshine, and the stretch of the river abreast of the clearing glittered in a still and dazzling splendor, with a murky and over-shadowed bend above and below. Not a living soul was seen on the shore. The bushes did not rustle.

"Suddenly round the corner of the house a group of men appeared, as though they had come up from the ground. They waded waist-deep in the grass, in a compact body, bearing an improvised stretcher in their midst. Instantly, in the emptiness of the landscape, a cry arose whose shrillness pierced the still air like a sharp arrow flying straight to the very heart of the land; and, as if by enchantment, streams of human beings—of naked human beings—with spears in their hands, with bows, with shields, with wild glances and savage movements, were poured into the clearing by the dark-faced and pensive forest. The bushes shook, the grass swayed for a time, and then everything stood still in attentive immobility.

"'Now, if he does not say the right thing to them we are all done for,' said the Russian at my elbow. The knot of men with the stretcher had stopped, too, halfway to the steamer, as if petrified. I saw the man on the stretcher sit up, lank and with an uplifted arm, above the shoulders of the bearers. 'Let us hope that the man who can talk so well of love in general will find some particular reason to spare us this time,' I said. I resented bitterly the absurd danger of our situation, as if to be at the mercy of that atrocious phantom had been a dishonoring necessity. I could not hear a sound, but through my glasses I saw the thin arm extended commandingly, the lower jaw moving, the eyes of that apparition shining darkly far in its bony head that nodded with grotesque jerks. Kurtz—Kurtz—that means short in German—don't it? Well, the name was as true as everything else in his life—and death. He looked at least seven feet long. His covering had fallen off, and his body emerged from it pitiful and appalling as from a winding-sheet. I could see the cage of his ribs all astir, the bones of his arm waving. It was as though an animated image of death carved out of old ivory had been shaking its hand with menaces at a motionless crowd of men made of dark and glittering bronze. I saw him open his mouth wide—it gave him a weirdly voracious aspect, as though he had wanted to swallow all the air, all the earth, all the men before him. A deep voice reached me faintly. He must have been shouting. He fell back suddenly. The stretcher shook as the bearers staggered forward again, and almost at the same time I noticed that the crowd of savages was vanishing without any perceptible movement of retreat, as if the forest that had ejected these beings so suddenly had drawn them in again as the breath is drawn in a long aspiration.

"Some of the pilgrims behind the stretcher carried his arms—two shotguns, a heavy rifle, and a light revolver-carbine[2]—the thunderbolts of that pitiful Jupiter. The manager bent over him murmuring as he walked beside his head. They laid him down in one of the little cabins—just a room for a bedplace and a campstool or two, you know. We had brought his belated correspondence, and a lot of torn envelopes and open letters littered his bed. His hand roamed feebly amongst these papers. I was struck by the fire in his eyes and the composed languor of his expression. It was not so much the exhaustion of disease. He did not seem in pain. This shadow looked satiated and calm, as though for the moment it had had its fill of all the emotions.

"He rustled one of the letters, and looking straight in my face said, 'I am glad.' Somebody had been writing to him about me. These special recommendations were turning up again. The volume of tone he emitted without effort, almost without the trouble of moving his lips, amazed me. A voice! a voice! It was grave, profound, vibrating, while the man did not seem capable of a whisper. However, he had enough strength in him—factitious no doubt—to very nearly make an end of us, as you shall hear directly.

"The manager appeared silently in the doorway; I stepped out at once and he drew the curtain after me. The Russian, eyed curiously by the pilgrims, was staring at the shore. I followed the direction of his glance.

"Dark human shapes could be made out in the distance, flitting indistinctly against the gloomy border of the forest, and near the river two bronze figures, leaning on tall spears, stood in the sunlight under fantastic headdresses of spotted skins, war-like and still in statuesque repose. And from right to left along the lighted shore moved a wild and gorgeous apparition of a woman.

2. Short-barreled, lightweight rifle with a revolving, chambered cylinder.

"She walked with measured steps, draped in striped and fringed cloths, treading the earth proudly, with a slight jingle and flash of barbarous ornaments. She carried her head high; her hair was done in the shape of a helmet; she had brass leggings to the knee, brass wire gauntlets to the elbow, a crimson spot on her tawny cheek, innumerable necklaces of glass beads on her neck; bizarre things, charms, gifts of witch-men, that hung about her, glittered and trembled at every step. She must have had the value of several elephant tusks upon her. She was savage and superb, wild-eyed and magnificent; there was something ominous and stately in her deliberate progress. And in the hush that had fallen suddenly upon the whole sorrowful land, the immense wilderness, the colossal body of the fecund and mysterious life seemed to look at her, pensive, as though it had been looking at the image of its own tenebrous and passionate soul.

"She came abreast of the steamer, stood still, and faced us. Her long shadow fell to the water's edge. Her face had a tragic and fierce aspect of wild sorrow and of dumb pain mingled with the fear of some struggling, half-shaped resolve. She stood looking at us without a stir, and like the wilderness itself, with an air of brooding over an inscrutable purpose. A whole minute passed, and then she made a step forward. There was a low jingle, a glint of yellow metal, a sway of fringed draperies, and she stopped as if her heart had failed her. The young fellow by my side growled. The pilgrims murmured at my back. She looked at us all as if her life had depended upon the unswerving steadiness of her glance. Suddenly she opened her bared arms and threw them up rigid above her head, as though in an uncontrollable desire to touch the sky, and at the same time the swift shadows darted out on the earth, swept around on the river, gathering the steamer into a shadowy embrace. A formidable silence hung over the scene.

"She turned away slowly, walked on, following the bank, and passed into the bushes to the left. Once only her eyes gleamed back at us in the dusk of the thickets before she disappeared.

"'If she had offered to come aboard I really think I would have tried to shoot her,' said the man of patches, nervously. 'I have been risking my life every day for the last fortnight to keep her out of the house. She got in one day and kicked up a row about those miserable rags I picked up in the store-room to mend my clothes with. I wasn't decent. At least it must have been that, for she talked like a fury to Kurtz for an hour, pointing at me now and then. I don't understand the dialect of this tribe. Luckily for me, I fancy Kurtz felt too ill that day to care, or there would have been mischief. I don't understand. . . . No—it's too much for me. Ah, well, it's all over now.'

"At this moment I heard Kurtz's deep voice behind the curtain: 'Save me!—save the ivory, you mean. Don't tell me. Save *me!* Why, I've had to save you. You are interrupting my plans now. Sick! Sick! Not so sick as you would like to believe. Never mind. I'll carry my ideas out yet—I will return. I'll show you what can be done. You with your little peddling notions—you are interfering with me. I will return. I . . .'

"The manager came out. He did me the honor to take me under the arm and lead me aside. 'He is very low, very low,' he said. He considered it necessary to sigh, but neglected to be consistently sorrowful. 'We have done all we could for him—haven't we? But there is no disguising the fact, Mr. Kurtz has done more harm than good to the Company. He did not see the time was not ripe for vigorous action. Cautiously, cautiously—that's my principle. We must be cautious yet. The district is closed to us for a time. Deplorable! Upon the whole, the trade will suffer. I don't deny there is a remarkable quantity of ivory—mostly fossil. We must save it, at all events—but look how precarious the position is—and why? Because the method is unsound.' 'Do you,' said I, looking at the shore, 'call it "unsound method"?' 'Without doubt,' he exclaimed hotly. 'Don't you?' . . . 'No method at all,' I murmured after a while. 'Exactly,' he exulted. 'I anticipated this. Shows a complete want of judgment. It is my duty to point it out in the proper quarter.' 'Oh,' said I, 'that fellow—what's his name?—the brick-maker, will make a readable report for you.' He appeared confounded for a moment. It seemed to me I had never breathed an atmosphere so vile, and I turned mentally to Kurtz for relief—positively for relief. 'Nevertheless I think Mr. Kurtz is a remarkable man,' I said with emphasis. He started, dropped on me a cold heavy glance, said very quietly, 'he *was*,' and turned his back on me. My hour of favor was over; I found myself lumped along with Kurtz as a partisan of methods for which the time was not ripe: I was unsound! Ah! but it was something to have at least a choice of nightmares.

"I had turned to the wilderness really, not to Mr. Kurtz, who, I was ready to admit, was as good as buried. And for a moment it seemed to me as if I also were buried in a vast grave full of unspeakable secrets. I felt an intolerable weight oppressing my breast, the smell of the damp earth, the unseen presence of victorious corruption, the darkness of an impenetrable night. . . . The Russian tapped me on the shoulder. I heard him mumbling and stammering something about 'brother seaman—couldn't conceal—knowledge of matters that would affect Mr. Kurtz's reputation.' I waited. For him evidently Mr. Kurtz was not in his grave; I suspect that for him Mr. Kurtz was one of the immortals. 'Well!' said I at last, 'speak out. As it happens, I am Mr. Kurtz's friend—in a way.'

"He stated with a good deal of formality that had we not been 'of the same profession,' he would have kept the matter to himself without regard to consequences. 'He suspected there was an active ill will towards him on the part of these white men that—' 'You are right,' I said, remembering a certain conversation I had overheard. 'The manager thinks you ought to be hanged.' He showed a concern at this intelligence which amused me at first. 'I had better get out of the way quietly,' he said, earnestly. 'I can do no more for Kurtz now, and they would soon find some excuse. What's to stop them? There's a military post three hundred miles from here.' 'Well, upon my word,' said I, 'perhaps you had better go if you have any friends amongst the savages near by.' 'Plenty,' he said. 'They are simple people—and I want nothing, you know.' He stood biting his lip, then: 'I don't want any harm to happen to these whites here, but of course I was thinking of Mr. Kurtz's reputation—but you are a brother seaman and—' 'All right,' said I, after a time. 'Mr. Kurtz's reputation is safe with me.' I did not know how truly I spoke.

"He informed me, lowering his voice, that it was Kurtz who had ordered the attack to be made on the steamer. 'He hated sometimes the idea of being taken away—and then again . . . But I don't understand these matters. I am a simple man. He thought it would scare you away—that you would give it up, thinking him dead. I could not stop him. Oh, I had an awful time of it this last month.' 'Very well,' I said. 'He is all right now.' 'Ye-e-es,' he muttered, not very convinced apparently. 'Thanks,' said I; 'I shall keep my eyes open.' 'But quiet—eh?' he urged, anxiously. 'It would be awful for his reputation if anybody here—' I promised a complete discretion with great gravity. 'I have a canoe and three black fellows waiting not very far. I am off. Could you give me a few Martini-Henry cartridges?' I could, and did, with proper secrecy. He helped himself, with a wink at me, to a handful of my tobacco. 'Between sailors—you know—good English tobacco.' At the door of the pilot-house he turned round—'I say, haven't you a pair of shoes you could spare?' He raised one leg. 'Look.' The soles were tied with knotted strings sandal-wise under his bare feet. I rooted out an old pair, at which he looked with admiration before tucking them under his left arm. One of his pockets (bright red) was bulging with cartridges, from the other (dark blue) peeped 'Towson's Inquiry,' etc., etc. He seemed to think himself excellently well equipped for a renewed encounter with the wilderness. 'Ah! I'll never, never meet such a man again. You ought to have heard him recite poetry—his own, too, it was, he told me. Poetry!' He rolled his eyes at the recollection of these delights. 'Oh, he enlarged my mind!' 'Good-by,' said I. He shook hands and vanished in the night. Sometimes I ask myself whether I had ever really seen him—whether it was possible to meet such a phenomenon! . . .

"When I woke up shortly after midnight his warning came to my mind with its hint of danger that seemed, in the starred darkness, real enough to make me get up for the purpose of having a look round. On the hill a big fire burned, illuminating fitfully a crooked corner of the station-house. One of the agents with a picket of a few of our blacks, armed for the purpose, was keeping guard over the ivory; but deep within the forest, red gleams that wavered, that seemed to sink and rise from the ground amongst confused columnar shapes of intense blackness, showed the exact position of the camp where Mr. Kurtz's adorers were keeping their uneasy vigil. The monotonous beating of a big drum filled the air with muffled shocks and a lingering vibration. A steady droning sound of many men chanting each to himself some weird incantation came out from the black, flat wall of the woods as the humming of bees comes out of a hive, and had a strange narcotic effect upon my half-awake senses. I believe I dozed off leaning over the rail, till an abrupt burst of yells, an overwhelming outbreak of a pent-up and mysterious frenzy, woke me up in a bewildered wonder. It was cut short all at once, and the low droning went on with an effect of audible and soothing silence. I glanced casually into the little cabin. A light was burning within, but Mr. Kurtz was not there.

"I think I would have raised an outcry if I had believed my eyes. But I didn't believe them at first—the thing seemed so impossible. The fact is I was completely unnerved by a sheer blank fright, pure abstract terror, unconnected with any distinct shape of physical danger. What made this emotion so overpowering was—how shall I define it?—the moral shock I received, as if something altogether monstrous, intolerable to thought and odious to the soul, had been thrust upon me unexpectedly. This lasted of course the merest fraction of a second, and then the usual sense of commonplace, deadly danger, the possibility of a sudden onslaught and massacre, or something of the kind, which I saw impending, was positively welcome and composing. It pacified me, in fact, so much, that I did not raise an alarm.

"There was an agent buttoned up inside an ulster and sleeping on a chair on deck within three feet of me. The yells had not awakened him; he snored very slightly; I left him to his slumbers and leaped ashore. I did not betray Mr. Kurtz—it was ordered I should never betray him—it was written I should be loyal to the nightmare of my choice. I was anxious to deal with this shadow by myself alone,—and to this day I don't know why I was so jealous of sharing with anyone the peculiar blackness of that experience.

"As soon as I got on the bank I saw a trail—a broad trail through the grass. I remember the exultation with which I said to myself, 'He can't walk—he is crawling on all-fours—I've got him.' The grass was wet with dew. I strode rapidly with clenched fists. I fancy I had some vague notion of falling upon him and giving him a drubbing. I don't know. I had some imbecile thoughts. The knitting old woman with the cat obtruded herself upon my memory as a most improper person to be sitting at the other end of such an affair. I saw a row of pilgrims squirting lead in the air out of Winchesters held to the hip. I thought I would never get back to the steamer, and imagined myself living alone and unarmed in the woods to an advanced age. Such silly things—you know. And I remember I confounded the beat of the drum with the beating of my heart, and was pleased at its calm regularity.

"I kept to the track though—then stopped to listen. The night was very clear; a dark blue space, sparkling with dew and starlight, in which black things stood very still. I thought I could see a kind of motion ahead of me. I was strangely cocksure of everything that night. I actually left the track and ran in a wide semicircle (I verily believe chuckling to myself) so as to get in front of that stir, of that motion I had seen—if indeed I had seen anything. I was circumventing Kurtz as though it had been a boyish game.

"I came upon him, and, if he had not heard me coming, I would have fallen over him too, but he got up in time. He rose, unsteady, long, pale, indistinct, like a vapor exhaled by the earth, and swayed slightly, misty and silent before me; while at my back the fires loomed between the trees, and the murmur of many voices issued from the forest. I had cut him off cleverly; but when actually confronting him I seemed to come to my senses, I saw the danger in its right proportion. It was by no means over yet. Suppose he began to shout? Though he could hardly stand, there was still plenty of vigor in his voice. 'Go away—hide yourself,' he said, in that profound tone. It was very awful. I glanced back. We were within thirty yards from the nearest fire. A black figure stood up, strode on long black legs, waving long black arms, across the glow. It had horns—antelope horns, I think—on its head. Some sorcerer, some witchman, no doubt: it looked fiend-like enough. 'Do you know what you are doing?' I whispered. 'Perfectly,' he answered, raising his voice for that single word: it sounded to me far off and yet loud, like a hail through a speaking-trumpet. If he makes a row we are lost, I thought to myself. This clearly was not a case for fisticuffs, even apart from the very natural aversion I had to beat that Shadow—this wandering and tormented thing. 'You will be lost,' I said—'utterly lost.' One gets sometimes such a flash of inspiration, you know. I did say the right thing, though indeed he could not have been more irretrievably lost than he was at this very moment, when the foundations of our intimacy were being laid—to endure—to endure—even to the end—even beyond.

"'I had immense plans,' he muttered irresolutely. 'Yes,' said I; 'but if you try to shout I'll smash your head with—' There was not a stick or a stone near. 'I will throttle you for good,' I corrected myself. 'I was on the threshold of great things,' he pleaded, in a voice of longing, with a wistfulness of tone that made my blood run cold. 'And now for this stupid scoundrel—' 'Your success in Europe is assured in any case,' I affirmed, steadily. I did not want to have the throttling of him, you understand—and indeed it would have been very little use for any practical purpose. I tried to break the spell—the heavy, mute spell of the wilderness—that seemed to draw him to its pitiless breast by the awakening of forgotten and brutal instincts, by the memory of gratified and monstrous passions. This alone, I was convinced, had driven him out to the edge of the forest, to the bush, towards the gleam of fires, the throb of drums, the drone of weird incantations; this alone had beguiled his unlawful soul beyond the bounds of permitted aspirations. And, don't you see, the terror of the position was not in being knocked on the head—though I had a very lively sense of that danger, too—but in this, that I had to deal with a being to whom I could not appeal in the name of anything high or low. I had, even like the niggers, to invoke him—himself—his own exalted and incredible degradation. There was nothing either above or below him, and I knew it. He had kicked himself loose of the earth. Confound the man! he had kicked the very earth to pieces. He was alone, and I before him did not know whether I stood on the ground or floated in the air. I've been telling you what we said—repeating the phrases we pronounced—but what's the good? They were common everyday words—the familiar, vague sounds exchanged on every waking day of life. But what of that? They had behind them, to my mind, the terrific suggestiveness of words heard in dreams, of phrases spoken in nightmares. Soul! If anybody had ever struggled with a soul, I am the man. And I wasn't arguing with a lunatic either. Believe me or not, his intelligence was perfectly clear—concentrated, it is true, upon himself with horrible intensity, yet clear; and therein was my only chance—barring, of course, the killing him there and then, which wasn't so good, on account of unavoidable noise. But his soul was mad. Being alone in the wilderness, it had looked within itself, and, by heavens! I tell you, it had gone mad. I had—for my sins, I suppose—to go through the ordeal of looking into it myself. No eloquence could have been so withering to one's belief in mankind as his final burst of sincerity. He struggled with himself, too. I saw it,—I heard it. I saw the inconceivable mystery of a soul that knew no restraint, no faith, and no fear, yet struggling blindly with itself. I kept my head pretty well; but when I had him at last stretched on the couch, I wiped my forehead, while my legs shook under me as though I had carried half a ton on my back down that hill. And yet I had only supported him, his bony arm clasped round my neck—and he was not much heavier than a child.

"When next day we left at noon, the crowd, of whose presence behind the curtain of trees I had been acutely conscious all the time, flowed out of the woods again, filled the clearing, covered the slope with a mass of naked, breathing, quivering, bronze bodies. I steamed up a bit, then swung downstream, and two thousand eyes followed the evolutions of the splashing, thumping, fierce river-demon beating the water with its terrible tail and breathing black smoke into the air. In front of the first rank, along the river, three men, plastered with bright red earth from head to foot, strutted to and fro restlessly. When we came abreast again, they faced the river, stamped their feet, nodded their horned heads, swayed their scarlet bodies; they shook towards the fierce river-demon a bunch of black feathers, a mangy skin with a pendent tail—something that looked like a dried gourd; they shouted periodically together strings of amazing words that resembled no sounds of human language; and the deep murmurs of the crowd, interrupted suddenly, were like the responses of some satanic litany.

"We had carried Kurtz into the pilot-house: there was more air there. Lying on the couch, he stared through the open shutter. There was an eddy in the mass of human bodies, and the woman with helmeted head and tawny cheeks rushed out to the very brink of the stream. She put out her hands, shouted something, and all that wild mob took up the shout in a roaring chorus of articulated, rapid, breathless utterance.

"'Do you understand this?' I asked.

"He kept on looking out past me with fiery, longing eyes, with a mingled expression of wistfulness and hate. He made no answer, but I saw a smile, a smile of indefinable meaning, appear on his colorless lips that a moment after twitched convulsively. 'Do I not?' he said slowly, gasping, as if the words had been torn out of him by a supernatural power.

"I pulled the string of the whistle, and I did this because I saw the pilgrims on deck getting out their rifles with an air of anticipating a jolly lark. At the sudden screech there was a movement of abject terror through that wedged mass of bodies. 'Don't! don't you frighten them away,' cried someone on deck disconsolately. I pulled the string time after time. They broke and ran, they leaped, they crouched, they swerved, they dodged the flying terror of the sound. The three red chaps had fallen flat, face down on the shore, as though they had been shot dead. Only the barbarous and superb woman did not so much as flinch, and stretched tragically her bare arms after us over the somber and glittering river.

"And then that imbecile crowd down on the deck started their little fun, and I could see nothing more for smoke.

"The brown current ran swiftly out of the heart of darkness, bearing us down towards the sea with twice the speed of our upward progress; and Kurtz's life was running swiftly, too, ebbing, ebbing out of his heart into the sea of inexorable time. The manager was very placid, he had no vital anxieties now, he took us both in with a comprehensive and satisfied glance: the 'affair' had come off as well as could be wished. I saw the time approaching when I would be left alone of the party of 'unsound method.' The pilgrims looked upon me with disfavor. I was, so to speak, numbered with the dead. It is strange how I accepted this unforeseen partnership, this choice of nightmares forced upon me in the tenebrous land invaded by these mean and greedy phantoms.

"Kurtz discoursed. A voice! a voice! It rang deep to the very last. It survived his strength to hide in the magnificent folds of eloquence the barren darkness of his heart. Oh, he struggled! he struggled! The wastes of his weary brain were haunted by shadowy images now—images of wealth and fame revolving obsequiously round his unextinguishable gift of noble and lofty expression. My Intended, my station, my career, my ideas—these were the subjects for the occasional utterances of elevated sentiments. The shade of the original Kurtz frequented the bedside of the hollow sham, whose fate it was to be buried presently in the mold of primeval earth. But both the diabolic love and the unearthly hate of the mysteries it had penetrated fought for the possession of that soul satiated with primitive emotions, avid of lying fame, of sham distinction, of all the appearances of success and power.

"Sometimes he was contemptibly childish. He desired to have kings meet him at railway stations on his return from some ghastly Nowhere, where he intended to accomplish great things. 'You show them you have in you something that is really profitable, and then there will be no limits to the recognition of your ability,' he would say. 'Of course you must take care of the motives—right motives—always.' The long reaches that were like one and the same reach, monotonous bends that were exactly alike, slipped past the steamer with their multitude of secular³ trees looking patiently after this grimy fragment of another world, the forerunner of change, of conquest, of trade, of massacres, of blessings. I looked ahead—piloting. 'Close the shutter,' said Kurtz suddenly one day; 'I can't bear to look at this.' I did so. There was a silence. 'Oh, but I will wring your heart yet!' he cried at the invisible wilderness.

"We broke down—as I had expected—and had to lie up for repairs at the head of an island. This delay was the first thing that shook Kurtz's confidence. One morning he gave me a packet of papers and a photograph—the lot tied together with a shoestring. 'Keep this for me,' he said. 'This noxious fool' (meaning the manager) 'is capable of prying into my boxes when I am not looking.' In the afternoon I saw him. He was lying on his back with closed eyes, and I withdrew quietly, but I heard him mutter, 'Live rightly, die, die. . . .' I listened. There was nothing more. Was he rehearsing some speech in his sleep, or was it a fragment of a phrase from some newspaper article? He had been writing for the papers and meant to do so again, 'for the furthering of my ideas. It's a duty.'

"His was an impenetrable darkness. I looked at him as you peer down at a man who is lying at the bottom of a precipice where the sun never shines. But I had not much time to give him, because I was helping the engine-driver to take to pieces the leaky cylinders, to straighten a bent connecting-rod, and in other such matters. I lived in an infernal mess of rust, filings, nuts, bolts, spanners, hammers, ratchet-drills—things I abominate, because I don't get on with them. I tended the little forge we fortunately had aboard; I toiled wearily in a wretched scrap-heap—unless I had the shakes too bad to stand.

"One evening coming in with a candle I was startled to hear him say a little tremulously, 'I am lying here in the dark waiting for death.' The light was within a foot of his eyes. I forced myself to murmur, 'Oh, nonsense!' and stood over him as if transfixed.

"Anything approaching the change that came over his features I have never seen before, and hope never to see again. Oh, I wasn't touched. I was fascinated. It was as though a veil had been rent. I saw on that ivory face the expression of somber pride, of ruthless power, of craven terror—of an intense

**3.** Centuries-old.

and hopeless despair. Did he live his life again in every detail of desire, temptation, and surrender during that supreme moment of complete knowledge? He cried in a whisper at some image, at some vision—he cried out twice, a cry that was no more than a breath—

"'The horror! The horror!'

"I blew the candle out and left the cabin. The pilgrims were dining in the mess-room, and I took my place opposite the manager, who lifted his eyes to give me a questioning glance, which I successfully ignored. He leaned back, serene, with that peculiar smile of his sealing the unexpressed depths of his meanness. A continuous shower of small flies streamed upon the lamp, upon the cloth, upon our hands and faces. Suddenly the manager's boy put his insolent black head in the doorway, and said in a tone of scathing contempt—

"'Mistah Kurtz—he dead.'

"All the pilgrims rushed out to see. I remained, and went on with my dinner. I believe I was considered brutally callous. However, I did not eat much. There was a lamp in there—light, don't you know—and outside it was so beastly, beastly dark. I went no more near the remarkable man who had pronounced a judgment upon the adventures of his soul on this earth. The voice was gone. What else had been there? But I am of course aware that next day the pilgrims buried something in a muddy hole.

"And then they very nearly buried me.

"However, as you see, I did not go to join Kurtz there and then. I did not. I remained to dream the nightmare out to the end, and to show my loyalty to Kurtz once more. Destiny. My destiny! Droll thing life is—that mysterious arrangement of merciless logic for a futile purpose. The most you can hope from it is some knowledge of yourself—that comes too late—a crop of unextinguishable regrets. I have wrestled with death. It is the most unexciting contest you can imagine. It takes place in an impalpable grayness, with nothing underfoot, with nothing around, without spectators, without clamor, without glory, without the great desire of victory, without the great fear of defeat, in a sickly atmosphere of tepid skepticism, without much belief in your own right, and still less in that of your adversary. If such is the form of ultimate wisdom, then life is a greater riddle than some of us think it to be. I was within a hair's breadth of the last opportunity for pronouncement, and I found with humiliation that probably I would have nothing to say. This is the reason why I affirm that Kurtz was a remarkable man. He had something to say. He said it. Since I had peeped over the edge myself, I understand better the meaning of his stare, that could not see the flame of the candle, but was wide enough to embrace the whole universe, piercing enough to penetrate all the hearts that beat in the darkness. He had summed up—he had judged. 'The horror!' He was a remarkable man. After all, this was the expression of some sort of belief; it had candor, it had conviction, it had a vibrating note of revolt in its whisper, it had the appalling face of a glimpsed truth—the strange commingling of desire and hate. And it is not my own extremity I remember best—a vision of grayness without form filled with physical pain, and a careless contempt for the evanescence of all things—even of this pain itself. No! It is his extremity that I seem to have lived through. True, he had made that last stride, he had stepped over the edge, while I had been permitted to draw back my hesitating foot. And perhaps in this is the whole difference; perhaps all the wisdom, and all truth, and all sincerity, are just compressed into that inappreciable moment of time in which we step over the threshold of the invisible. Perhaps! I like to think my summing-up would not have been a word of careless contempt. Better his cry—much better. It was an affirmation, a moral victory paid for by innumerable defeats, by abominable terrors, by abominable satisfactions. But it was a victory! That is why I have remained loyal to Kurtz to the last, and even beyond, when a long time after I heard once more, not his own voice, but the echo of his magnificent eloquence thrown to me from a soul as translucently pure as a cliff of crystal.

"No, they did not bury me, though there is a period of time which I remember mistily, with a shuddering wonder, like a passage through some inconceivable world that had no hope in it and no desire. I found myself back in the sepulchral city resenting the sight of people hurrying through the streets to filch a little money from each other, to devour their infamous cookery, to gulp their unwholesome beer, to dream their insignificant and silly dreams. They trespassed upon my thoughts. They were intruders whose knowledge of life was to me an irritating pretense, because I felt so sure they could not possibly know the things I knew. Their bearing, which was simply the bearing of commonplace individuals going about their business in the assurance of perfect safety, was offensive to me like the outrageous flauntings of folly in the face of a danger it is unable to comprehend. I had no particular desire to enlighten them, but I had some difficulty in restraining myself from laughing in their faces, so full of stupid importance. I daresay I was not very well at that time. I tottered about the streets—there were various affairs to settle—grinning bitterly at perfectly respectable persons. I admit my behavior was inexcusable, but then my temperature was seldom normal in these days. My dear aunt's endeavors to 'nurse up my strength' seemed altogether beside the mark. It was not my strength that wanted nursing, it was my imagination that wanted soothing. I kept the bundle of papers given me by Kurtz, not knowing exactly what to do with it. His mother had died lately, watched over, as I was told, by his Intended. A clean-shaven man, with an official manner and wearing gold-rimmed spectacles, called on me one day and made inquiries, at first circuitous, afterwards suavely pressing, about what he was pleased to denominate certain 'documents.' I was not surprised, because I had had two rows with the manager on the subject out there. I had refused to give up the smallest scrap out of that package, and I took the same attitude with the spectacled man. He became darkly menacing at last, and with much heat argued that the Company had the right to every bit of information about its 'territories.' And said he, 'Mr. Kurtz's knowledge of unexplored regions must have been necessarily extensive and peculiar—owing to his great abilities and to the deplorable circumstances in which he had been placed: therefore—' I assured him Mr. Kurtz's knowledge, however extensive, did not bear upon the problems of commerce or administration. He invoked then the name of science. 'It would be an incalculable loss if,' etc., etc. I offered him the report on the 'Suppression of Savage Customs,' with the postscriptum torn off. He took it up eagerly, but ended by sniffing at it with an air of contempt. 'This is not what we had a right to expect,' he remarked. 'Expect nothing else,' I said. 'There are only private letters.' He withdrew upon some threat of legal proceedings, and I saw him no more; but another fellow, calling himself Kurtz's cousin, appeared two days later, and was anxious to hear all the details about his dear relative's last moments. Incidentally he gave me to understand that Kurtz had been essentially a great musician. 'There was the making of an immense success,' said the man, who was an organist, I believe, with lank gray hair flowing over a greasy coat-collar. I had no reason to doubt his statement; and to this day I am unable to say what was Kurtz's profession, whether he ever had any—which was the greatest of his talents. I had taken him for a painter who wrote for the papers, or else for a journalist who could paint—but even the cousin (who took snuff during the interview) could not tell me what he had been—exactly. He was a universal genius—on that point I agreed with the old chap, who thereupon blew his nose noisily into a large cotton handkerchief and withdrew in senile agitation, bearing off some family letters and memoranda without importance. Ultimately a journalist anxious to know something of the fate of his 'dear colleague' turned up. This visitor informed me Kurtz's proper sphere ought to have been politics 'on the popular side.' He had furry straight eyebrows, bristly hair cropped short, an eyeglass on a broad ribbon, and, becoming expansive, confessed his opinion that Kurtz really couldn't write a bit—'But heavens! how that man could talk. He electrified large meetings. He had faith—don't you see?—he had the faith. He could get himself to believe anything—anything. He would have been a splendid leader of an extreme party.' 'What party?' I asked. 'Any party,' answered the other. 'He was an—an—extremist.' Did I not think so? I assented. Did I know, he asked, with a sudden flash of curiosity, 'what it was that had induced him to go out there?' 'Yes,' said I, and forthwith handed him the famous Report for publication, if he thought fit. He glanced through it hurriedly, mumbling all the time, judged 'it would do,' and took himself off with this plunder.

"Thus I was left at last with a slim packet of letters and the girl's portrait. She struck me as beautiful—I mean she had a beautiful expression. I know that the sunlight can be made to lie, too, yet one felt that no manipulation of light and pose could have conveyed the delicate shade of truthfulness upon those features. She seemed ready to listen without mental reservation, without suspicion, without a thought for herself. I concluded I would go and give her back her portrait and those letters myself. Curiosity? Yes; and also some other feeling perhaps. All that had been Kurtz's had passed out of my hands: his soul, his body, his station, his plans, his ivory, his career. There remained only this memory and his Intended—and I wanted to give that up, too, to the past, in a way—to surrender personally all that remained of him with me to that oblivion which is the last word of our common fate. I don't defend myself. I had no clear perception of what it was I really wanted. Perhaps it was an impulse of unconscious loyalty, or the fulfillment of one of those ironic necessities, that lurk in the facts of human existence. I don't know. I can't tell. But I went.

"I thought his memory was like the other memories of the dead that accumulate in every man's life—a vague impress on the brain of shadows that had fallen on it in their swift and final passage; but before the high and ponderous door, between the tall houses of a street as still and decorous as a well-kept alley in a cemetery, I had a vision of him on the stretcher, opening his mouth voraciously, as if to devour all the earth with all its mankind. He lived then before me; he lived as much as he had ever lived—a shadow insatiable of splendid appearances, of frightful realities; a shadow darker than the shadow of the night, and draped nobly in the folds of a gorgeous eloquence. The vision seemed to enter the house with me—the stretcher, the phantom-bearers, the wild crowd of obedient worshipers, the gloom of the forests, the glitter of the reach between the murky bends, the beat of the drum, regular and muffled like the beating of a heart—the heart of a conquering darkness. It was a moment of triumph for the wilderness, an invading and vengeful rush which, it seemed to me, I would have to keep back alone for the salvation of another soul. And the memory of what I had heard him say afar there, with the horned shapes stirring at my back, in the glow of fires, within the patient woods, those broken phrases came back to me, were heard again in their ominous and terrifying simplicity. I remembered his abject pleading, his abject threats, the colossal scale of his vile desires, the meanness, the torment, the tempestuous anguish of his soul. And later on I seem to see his collected languid manner, when he said one day, 'This lot of ivory now is really mine. The Company did not pay for it. I collected it myself at a very great personal risk. I am afraid they will try to claim it as theirs though. H'm. It is a difficult case. What do you think I ought to do—resist? Eh? I want no more than justice.' . . . He wanted no more than justice—no more than justice. I rang the bell before a mahogany door on the first floor, and while I waited he seemed to stare at me out of the glossy panel—stare with that wide and immense stare embracing, condemning, loathing all the universe. I seemed to hear the whispered cry, 'The horror! The horror!'

"The dusk was falling. I had to wait in a lofty drawing-room with three long windows from floor to ceiling that were like three luminous and bedraped columns. The bent gilt legs and backs of the furniture shone in indistinct curves. The tall marble fireplace had a cold and monumental whiteness. A grand piano stood massively in a corner; with dark gleams on the flat surfaces like a somber and polished sarcophagus. A high door opened—closed. I rose.

"She came forward, all in black, with a pale head, floating towards me in the dusk. She was in mourning. It was more than a year since his death, more than a year since the news came; she seemed as though she would remember and mourn forever. She took both my hands in hers and murmured, 'I had heard you were coming.' I noticed she was not very young—I mean not girlish. She had a mature capacity for fidelity, for belief, for suffering. The room seemed to have grown darker, as if all the sad light of the cloudy evening had taken refuge on her forehead. This fair hair, this pale visage, this pure brow, seemed surrounded by an ashy halo from which the dark eyes looked out at me. Their glance was guileless, profound, confident, and trustful. She carried her sorrowful head as though she were proud of that sorrow, as though she would say, I—I alone know how to mourn him as he deserves. But while we were still shaking hands, such a look of awful desolation came upon her face that I perceived she was one of those creatures that are not the playthings of Time. For her he had died only yesterday. And, by Jove! the impression was so powerful that for me, too, he seemed to have died only yesterday—nay, this very minute. I saw her and him in the same instant of time—his death and her sorrow—I saw her sorrow in the very moment of his death. Do you understand? I saw them together—I heard them together. She had said, with a deep catch of the breath, 'I have survived' while my strained ears seemed to hear distinctly, mingled with her tone of despairing regret, the summing up whisper of his eternal condemnation. I asked myself what I was doing there, with a sensation of panic in my heart as though I had blundered into a place of cruel and absurd mysteries not fit for a human being to behold. She motioned me to a chair. We sat down. I laid the packet gently on the little table, and she put her hand over it.... 'You knew him well,' she murmured, after a moment of mourning silence.

"'Intimacy grows quickly out there,' I said. 'I knew him as well as it is possible for one man to know another.'

"'And you admired him,' she said. 'It was impossible to know him and not to admire him. Was it?'

"'He was a remarkable man,' I said, unsteadily. Then before the appealing fixity of her gaze, that seemed to watch for more words on my lips, I went on, 'It was impossible not to—'

"'Love him,' she finished eagerly, silencing me into an appalled dumbness. 'How true! how true! But when you think that no one knew him so well as I! I had all his noble confidence. I knew him best.'

"'You knew him best,' I repeated. And perhaps she did. But with every word spoken the room was growing darker, and only her forehead, smooth and white, remained illumined by the unextinguishable light of belief and love.

"'You were his friend,' she went on. 'His friend,' she repeated, a little louder. 'You must have been, if he had given you this, and sent you to me. I feel I can speak to you—and oh! I must speak. I want you—you have heard his last words—to know I have been worthy of him.... It is not pride.... Yes! I am proud to know I understood him better than anyone on earth—he told me so himself. And since his mother died I have had no one—no one—to—to—'

"I listened. The darkness deepened. I was not even sure whether he had given me the right bundle. I rather suspect he wanted me to take care of another batch of his papers which, after his death, I saw the manager examining under the lamp. And the girl talked, easing her pain in the certitude of my sympathy; she talked as thirsty men drink. I had heard that her engagement with Kurtz had been disapproved by her people. He wasn't rich enough or something. And indeed I don't know whether he had not been a pauper all his life. He had given me some reason to infer that it was his impatience of comparative poverty that drove him out there.

"'... Who was not his friend who had heard him speak once?' she was saying. 'He drew men towards him by what was best in them.' She looked at me with intensity. 'It is the gift of the great,' she went on, and the sound of her low voice seemed to have the accompaniment of all the other sounds, full of mystery, desolation, and sorrow, I had ever heard—the ripple of the river, the soughing of the trees swayed by the wind, the murmurs of the crowds, the faint ring of incomprehensible words cried from afar, the whisper of a voice speaking from beyond the threshold of an eternal darkness. 'But you have heard him! You know!' she cried.

"'Yes, I know,' I said with something like despair in my heart, but bowing my head before the faith that was in her, before that great and saving illusion that shone with an unearthly glow in the darkness, in the triumphant darkness from which I could not have defended her—from which I could not even defend myself.

"'What a loss to me—to us!'—she corrected herself with beautiful generosity; then added in a murmur, 'To the world.' By the last gleams of twilight I could see the glitter of her eyes, full of tears—of tears that would not fall.

"'I have been very happy—very fortunate—very proud,' she went on. 'Too fortunate. Too happy for a little while. And now I am unhappy for—for life.'

"She stood up; her fair hair seemed to catch all the remaining light in a glimmer of gold. I rose, too.

"'And of all this,' she went on, mournfully, 'of all his promise, and of all his greatness, of his generous mind, of his noble heart, nothing remains—nothing but a memory. You and I—'

"'We shall always remember him,' I said, hastily.

"'No!' she cried. 'It is impossible that all this should be lost—that such a life should be sacrificed to leave nothing—but sorrow. You know what vast plans he had. I knew of them, too—I could not perhaps understand—but others knew of them. Something must remain. His words, at least, have not died.'

"'His words will remain,' I said.

"'And his example,' she whispered to herself. 'Men looked up to him—his goodness shone in every act. His example—'

"'True,' I said; 'his example too. Yes, his example. I forgot that.'

"'But I do not. I cannot—I cannot believe—not yet. I cannot believe that I shall never see him again, that nobody will see him again, never, never, never.'

"She put out her arms as if after a retreating figure, stretching them back and with clasped pale hands across the fading and narrow sheen of the window. Never see him! I saw him clearly enough then. I shall see this eloquent phantom as long as I live, and I shall see her, too, a tragic and familiar Shade, resembling in this gesture another one, tragic also, and bedecked with powerless charms, stretching bare brown arms over the glitter of the infernal stream, the stream of darkness. She said suddenly very low, 'He died as he lived.'

"'His end,' said I, with dull anger stirring in me, 'was in every way worthy of his life.'

"'And I was not with him,' she murmured. My anger subsided before a feeling of infinite pity.

"'Everything that could be done—' I mumbled.

"'Ah, but I believed in him more than anyone on earth—more than his own mother, more than—himself. He needed me! Me! I would have treasured every sigh, every word, every sign, every glance.'

"I felt like a chill grip on my chest. 'Don't,' I said, in a muffled voice.

"'Forgive me. I—I—have mourned so long in silence—in silence. . . . You were with him—to the last? I think of his loneliness. Nobody near to understand him as I would have understood. Perhaps no one to hear. . . .'

"'To the very end,' I said shakily. 'I heard his very last words. . . .' I stopped in a fright.

"'Repeat them,' she murmured in a heart-broken tone. 'I want—I want—something—something—to—live with.'

"I was on the point of crying at her, 'Don't you hear them?' The dusk was repeating them in a persistent whisper all around us, in a whisper that seemed to swell menacingly like the first whisper of a rising wind. 'The horror! The horror!'

"'His last word—to live with,' she insisted. 'Don't you understand I loved him—I loved him—I loved him!'

"I pulled myself together and spoke slowly.

"'The last word he pronounced was—your name.'

"I heard a light sigh and then my heart stood still, stopped dead short by an exulting and terrible cry, by the cry of inconceivable triumph and of unspeakable pain. 'I knew it—I was sure!' . . . She knew. She was sure. I heard her weeping, she had hidden her face in her hands. It seemed to me that the house would collapse before I could escape, that the heavens would fall upon my head. But nothing happened. The heavens do not fall for such a trifle. Would they have fallen, I wonder, if I had rendered Kurtz that justice which was his due? Hadn't he said he wanted only justice? But I couldn't. I could not tell her. It would have been too dark—too dark altogether. . . ."

Marlow ceased, and sat apart, indistinct and silent, in the pose of a meditating Buddha. Nobody moved for a time. "We have lost the first of the ebb," said the Director, suddenly. I raised my head. The offing was barred by a black bank of clouds, and the tranquil waterway leading to the uttermost ends of the earth flowed somber under an overcast sky—seemed to lead into the heart of an immense darkness.

1902

---

RELATED:

—Conrad, Preface to *The Nigger of the "Narcissus,"* p. 877
—Conrad, Letter to Barrett H. Clark, p. 879
—Barry Hannah on *Heart of Darkness,* p. 925
—C. P. Sarvan, "Racism and the *Heart of Darkness,*" p. 936

# STEPHEN CRANE
## 1871–1900

Crane was born in Newark, New Jersey, the son of a Methodist minister. After schooling at Lafayette College and Syracuse University, he worked in New York as a freelance journalist. In 1893 he published at his own expense the novel *Maggie: A Girl of the Streets*, a pioneering work of sociological realism. Two years later he brought out his famous short novel about the Civil War, *The Red Badge of Courage*, which in theme and technique foreshadows the war novels of the twentieth century. His short stories and experimental poetry also anticipate the ironic realism of the decades ahead. In his brief and energetic life he published fourteen books while acting out, in his personal adventures, the legend of the writer as soldier of fortune. On his way to Cuba for the first time he picked up a mistress at the Hotel de Dream in Jacksonville, Florida—a woman who accompanied him when he went on to Greece as a war correspondent. Malicious gossip about his private life subsequently drove him from America to England, where he settled in 1897 and made friends with leading English writers. In his travels he had accumulated a malignant tangle of debts. He was trying to free himself of them by writing when tuberculosis killed him, his promise only partially fulfilled. His short stories were collected in *The Open Boat and Other Tales of Adventure* (1898), *The Monster and Other Stories* (1899), and *Wounds in the Rain* (1900). His complete works in prose and verse were published in 1925–26.

## The Open Boat

*A Tale Intended to Be after the Fact:*[1] *Being the Experience of Four Men from the Sunk Steamer COMMODORE*

### I

None of them knew the color of the sky. Their eyes glanced level and were fastened upon the waves that swept toward them. These waves were of the hue of slate, save for the tops, which were of foaming white, and all of the men knew the colors of the sea. The horizon narrowed and widened, and dipped and rose, and at all times its edge was jagged with waves that seemed thrust up in points like rocks.

---

**1.** Crane underwent the adventure here re-created in fiction. He also wrote a journalistic account of it, published in the *New York Press* (January 7, 1897).

Many a man ought to have a bathtub larger than the boat which here rode upon the sea. These waves were most wrongfully and barbarously abrupt and tall, and each froth-top was a problem in small-boat navigation.

The cook squatted in the bottom, and looked with both eyes at the six inches of gunwale which separated him from the ocean. His sleeves were rolled over his fat forearms, and the two flaps of his unbuttoned vest dangled as he bent to bail out the boat. Often he said, "Gawd! that was a narrow clip." As he remarked it he invariably gazed eastward over the broken sea.

The oiler, steering with one of the two oars in the boat, sometimes raised himself suddenly to keep clear of water that swirled in over the stern. It was a thin little oar, and it seemed often ready to snap.

The correspondent, pulling at the other oar, watched the waves and wondered why he was there.

The injured captain, lying in the bow, was at this time buried in that profound dejection and indifference which comes, temporarily at least, to even the bravest and most enduring when, willy-nilly, the firm fails, the army loses, the ship goes down. The mind of the master of a vessel is rooted deep in the timbers of her, though he command for a day or a decade; and this captain had on him the stern impression of a scene in the grays of dawn of seven turned faces, and later a stump of a topmast with a white ball on it, that slashed to and fro at the waves, went low and lower, and down. Thereafter there was something strange in his voice. Although steady, it was deep with mourning, and of a quality beyond oration or tears.

"Keep 'er a little more south, Billie," said he.

"A little more south, sir," said the oiler in the stern.

A seat in his boat was not unlike a seat upon a bucking broncho, and by the same token a broncho is not much smaller. The craft pranced and reared and plunged like an animal. As each wave came, and she rose for it, she seemed like a horse making at a fence outrageously high. The manner of her scramble over these walls of water is a mystic thing, and, moreover, at the top of them were ordinarily these problems in white water, the foam racing down from the summit of each wave requiring a new leap, and a leap from the air. Then, after scornfully bumping a crest, she would slide and race and splash down a long incline, and arrive bobbing and nodding in front of the next menace.

A singular disadvantage of the sea lies in the fact that after successfully surmounting one wave you discover that there is another behind it just as important and just as nervously anxious to do something effective in the way of swamping boats. In a ten-foot dinghy one can get an idea of the resources of the sea in the line of waves that is not probable to the average experience, which is never at sea in a dinghy. As each slaty wall of water approached, it shut all else from the view of the men in the boat, and it was not difficult to imagine that this particular wave was the final outburst of the ocean, the last effort of the grim water. There was a terrible grace in the move of the waves, and they came in silence, save for the snarling of the crests.

In the wan light the faces of the men must have been gray. Their eyes must have glinted in strange ways as they gazed steadily astern. Viewed from a balcony, the whole thing would, doubtless, have been weirdly picturesque. But the men in the boat had no time to see it, and if they had had leisure, there were other things to occupy their minds. The sun swung steadily up the sky, and they knew it was broad day because the color of the sea changed from slate to emerald-green streaked with amber lights, and the foam was like tumbling snow. The process of the breaking day was unknown to them. They were aware only of this effect upon the color of the waves that rolled toward them.

In disjointed sentences the cook and the correspondent argued as to the difference between a life-saving station and a house of refuge. The cook had said: "There's a house of refuge just north of the Mosquito Inlet Light, and as soon as they see us they'll come off in their boat and pick us up."

"As soon as who see us?" said the correspondent.

"The crew," said the cook.

"Houses of refuge don't have crews," said the correspondent. "As I understand them, they are only places where clothes and grub are stored for the benefit of shipwrecked people. They don't carry crews."

"Oh, yes, they do," said the cook.

"No, they don't," said the correspondent.

"Well, we're not there yet, anyhow," said the oiler, in the stern.

"Well," said the cook, "perhaps it's not a house of refuge that I'm thinking of as being near Mosquito Inlet Light; perhaps it's a life-saving station."

"We're not there yet," said the oiler in the stern.

## II

As the boat bounced from the top of each wave the wind tore through the hair of the hatless men, and as the craft plopped her stern down again the spray slashed past them. The crest of each of these waves was a hill, from the top of which the men surveyed for a moment a broad tumultuous expanse, shining and wind-riven. It was probably splendid, it was probably glorious, this play of the free sea, wild with lights of emerald and white and amber.

"Bully good thing it's an on-shore wind," said the cook. "If not, where would we be? Wouldn't have a show."

"That's right," said the correspondent.

The busy oiler nodded his assent.

Then the captain, in the bow, chuckled in a way that expressed humor, contempt, tragedy, all in one. "Do you think we've got much of a show now, boys?" said he.

Whereupon the three were silent, save for a trifle of hemming and hawing. To express any particular optimism at this time they felt to be childish and stupid, but they all doubtless possessed this sense of the situation in their minds. A young man thinks doggedly at such times. On the other hand, the ethics of their condition was decidedly against any open suggestion of hopelessness. So they were silent.

"Oh, well," said the captain, soothing his children, "we'll get ashore all right."

But there was that in his tone which made them think; so the oiler quoth, "Yes! if this wind holds."

The cook was bailing. "Yes! if we don't catch hell in the surf."

Canton-flannel[2] gulls flew near and far. Sometimes they sat down on the sea, near patches of brown seaweed that rolled over the waves with a movement like carpets on a line in a gale. The birds sat comfortably in groups, and they were envied by some in the dinghy, for the wrath of the sea was no more to them than it was to a covey of prairie chickens a thousand miles inland. Often they came very close and stared at the men with black bead-like eyes. At these times they were uncanny and sinister in their unblinking scrutiny, and the men hooted angrily at them, telling them to be gone. One came, and evidently decided to alight on the top of the captain's head. The bird flew parallel to the boat and did not circle, but made short sidelong jumps in the air in chicken fashion. His black eyes were wistfully fixed upon the captain's head. "Ugly brute," said the oiler to the bird. "You look as if you were made with a jackknife." The cook and the correspondent swore darkly at the creature. The captain naturally wished to knock it away with the end of the heavy painter,[3] but he did not dare do it, because anything resembling an emphatic gesture would have capsized this freighted boat; and so, with his open hand, the captain gently and carefully waved the gull away. After it had been discouraged from the pursuit the captain breathed easier on account of his hair, and others breathed easier because the bird struck their minds at this time as being somehow gruesome and ominous.

In the meantime the oiler and the correspondent rowed; and also they rowed. They sat together in the same seat, and each rowed an oar. Then the oiler took both oars; then the correspondent took both oars, then the oiler; then the correspondent. They rowed and they rowed. The very ticklish part of the business was when the time came for the reclining one in the stern to take his turn at the oars. By the very last star of truth, it is easier to steal eggs from under a hen than it was to change seats in the dinghy. First the man in the stern slid his hand along the thwart and moved with care, as if he were of Sèvres.[4] Then the man in the rowing-seat slid his hand along the other thwart. It was all done with the most extraordinary care. As the two sidled past each other, the whole party kept watchful eyes on the coming wave, and the captain cried: "Look out, now! Steady, there!"

The brown mats of seaweed that appeared from time to time were like islands, bits of earth. They were travelling, apparently, neither one way nor the other. They were, to all intents, stationary. They informed the men in the boat that it was making progress slowly toward the land.

The captain, rearing cautiously in the bow after the dinghy soared on a great swell, said that he had seen the lighthouse at Mosquito Inlet. Presently the cook remarked that he had seen it. The correspondent was at the oars then, and for some reason he too wished to look at the lighthouse; but his back was toward the far shore, and the waves were important, and for some time he could not seize an opportunity to turn his head. But at last there came a wave more gentle than the others, and when at the crest of it he swiftly scoured the western horizon.

"See it?" said the captain.

---

2. Actually a plain-weave cotton fabric.  3. A mooring rope attached to the bow of a boat.  4. A type of fine china.

"No," said the correspondent, slowly; "I didn't see anything."

"Look again," said the captain. He pointed. "It's exactly in that direction."

At the top of another wave the correspondent did as he was bid, and this time his eyes chanced on a small, still thing on the edge of the swaying horizon. It was precisely like the point of a pin. It took an anxious eye to find a lighthouse so tiny.

"Think we'll make it, Captain?"

"If this wind holds and the boat don't swamp, we can't do much else," said the captain.

The little boat, lifted by each towering sea and splashed viciously by the crests, made progress that in the absence of seaweed was not apparent to those in her. She seemed just a wee thing wallowing, miraculously top up, at the mercy of five oceans. Occasionally a great spread of water, like white flames, swarmed into her.

"Bail her, cook," said the captain, serenely.

"All right, Captain," said the cheerful cook.

### III

It would be difficult to describe the subtle brotherhood of men that was here established on the seas. No one said that it was so. No one mentioned it. But it dwelt in the boat, and each man felt it warm him. They were a captain, an oiler, a cook, and a correspondent, and they were friends—friends in a more curiously iron-bound degree than may be common. The hurt captain, lying against the water jar in the bow, spoke always in a low voice and calmly; but he could never command a more ready and swiftly obedient crew than the motley three of the dinghy. It was more than a mere recognition of what was best for the common safety. There was surely in it a quality that was personal and heart-felt. And after this devotion to the commander of the boat, there was this comradeship, that the correspondent, for instance, who had been taught to be cynical of men, knew even at the time was the best experience of his life. But no one said that it was so. No one mentioned it.

"I wish we had a sail," remarked the captain. "We might try my overcoat on the end of an oar, and give you two boys a chance to rest." So the cook and the correspondent held the mast and spread wide the overcoat; the oiler steered; and the little boat made good way with her new rig. Sometimes the oiler had to scull sharply to keep a sea from breaking into the boat, but otherwise sailing was a success.

Meanwhile the lighthouse had been growing slowly larger. It had now almost assumed color, and appeared like a little gray shadow on the sky. The man at the oars could not be prevented from turning his head rather often to try for a glimpse of this little gray shadow.

At last, from the top of each wave, the men in the tossing boat could see land. Even as the lighthouse was an upright shadow on the sky, this land seemed but a long black shadow on the sea. It certainly was thinner than paper. "We must be about opposite New Smyrna,"[5] said the cook, who had

5. Town on the Florida coast.

coasted this shore often in schooners. "Captain, by the way, I believe they abandoned that life-saving station there about a year ago."

"Did they?" said the captain.

The wind slowly died away. The cook and the correspondent were not now obliged to slave in order to hold high the oar. But the waves continued their old impetuous swooping at the dinghy, and the little craft, no longer underway, struggled woundily over them. The oiler or the correspondent took the oars again.

Shipwrecks are *apropos* of nothing. If men could only train for them and have them occur when the men had reached pink condition, there would be less drowning at sea. Of the four in the dinghy none had slept any time worth mentioning for two days and two nights previous to embarking in the dinghy, and in the excitement of clambering about the deck of a foundering ship they had also forgotten to eat heartily.

For these reasons, and for others, neither the oiler nor the correspondent was fond of rowing at this time. The correspondent wondered ingenuously how in the name of all that was sane could there be people who thought it amusing to row a boat. It was not an amusement; it was a diabolical punishment, and even a genius of mental aberrations could never conclude that it was anything but a horror to the muscles and a crime against the back. He mentioned to the boat in general how the amusement of rowing struck him, and the weary-faced oiler smiled in full sympathy. Previously to the foundering, by the way, the oiler had worked a double watch in the engine-room of the ship.

"Take her easy, now, boys," said the captain. "Don't spend yourselves. If we have to run a surf you'll need all your strength, because we'll sure have to swim for it. Take your time."

Slowly the land arose from the sea. From a black line it became a line of black and a line of white—trees and sand. Finally the captain said that he could make out a house on the shore. "That's the house of refuge, sure," said the cook. "They'll see us before long, and come out after us."

The distant lighthouse reared high. "The keeper ought to be able to make us out now, if he's looking through a glass," said the captain. "He'll notify the life-saving people."

"None of those other boats could have got ashore to give word of the wreck," said the oiler, in a low voice, "else the life-boat would be out hunting us."

Slowly and beautifully the land loomed out of the sea. The wind came again. It had veered from the northeast to the southeast. Finally a new sound struck the ears of the men in the boat. It was the low thunder of the surf on the shore. "We'll never be able to make the lighthouse now," said the captain. "Swing her head a little more north, Billie."

"A little more north, sir," said the oiler.

Whereupon the little boat turned her nose once more down the wind, and all but the oarsman watched the shore grow. Under the influence of this expansion doubt and direful apprehension were leaving the minds of the men. The management of the boat was still most absorbing, but it could not prevent a quiet cheerfulness. In an hour, perhaps, they would be ashore.

Their backbones had become thoroughly used to balancing in the boat, and they now rode this wild colt of a dinghy like circus men. The correspondent thought that he had been drenched to the skin, but happening to feel in the top pocket of his coat, he found therein eight cigars. Four of them were soaked with sea-water; four were perfectly scatheless. After a search, somebody produced three dry matches; and thereupon the four waifs rode impudently in their little boat and, with an assurance of an impending rescue shining in their eyes, puffed at the big cigars, and judged well and ill of all men. Everybody took a drink of water.

## I V

"Cook," remarked the captain, "there don't seem to be any signs of life about your house of refuge."

"No," replied the cook. "Funny they don't see us!"

A broad stretch of lowly coast lay before the eyes of the men. It was of low dunes topped with dark vegetation. The roar of the surf was plain, and sometimes they could see the white lip of a wave as it spun up the beach. A tiny house was blocked out black upon the sky. Southward, the slim lighthouse lifted its little gray length.

Tide, wind, and waves were swinging the dinghy northward. "Funny they don't see us," said the men.

The surf's roar was here dulled, but its tone was nevertheless thunderous and mighty. As the boat swam over the great rollers the men sat listening to this roar. "We'll swamp sure," said everybody.

It is fair to say here that there was not a life-saving station within twenty miles in either direction; but the men did not know this fact, and in consequence they made dark and opprobrious remarks concerning the eyesight of the nation's life-savers. Four scowling men sat in the dinghy and surpassed records in the invention of epithets.

"Funny they don't see us."

The light-heartedness of a former time had completely faded. To their sharpened minds it was easy to conjure pictures of all kinds of incompetency and blindness and, indeed, cowardice. There was the shore of the populous land, and it was bitter and bitter to them that from it came no sign.

"Well," said the captain, ultimately, "I suppose we'll have to make a try for ourselves. If we stay out here too long, we'll none of us have strength left to swim after the boat swamps."

And so the oiler, who was at the oars, turned the boat straight for the shore. There was a sudden tightening of muscles. There was some thinking.

"If we don't all get ashore," said the captain—"if we don't all get ashore, I suppose you fellows know where to send news of my finish?"

They then briefly exchanged some addresses and admonitions. As for the reflections of the men, there was a great deal of rage in them. Perchance they might be formulated thus: "If I am going to be drowned—if I am going to be drowned—if I am going to be drowned, why, in the name of the seven mad gods who rule the sea, was I allowed to come thus far and contemplate sand and trees? Was I brought here merely to have my nose dragged away as I was about to nibble the sacred cheese of life? It is preposterous. If this old ninny-woman, Fate, cannot do better than this, she should be deprived of the management of men's fortunes. She is an old hen who knows not her intention. If she has decided to drown me, why did she not do it in the beginning and save me all this trouble? The whole affair is absurd. . . . But no; she cannot mean to drown me. She dare not drown me. She cannot drown me. Not after all this work." Afterward the man might have had an impulse to shake his fist at the clouds. "Just you drown me, now, and then hear what I call you!"

The billows that came at this time were more formidable. They seemed always just about to break and roll over the little boat in a turmoil of foam. There was a preparatory and long growl in the speech of them. No mind unused to the sea would have concluded that the dinghy could ascend these sheer heights in time. The shore was still afar. The oiler was a wily surfman. "Boys," he said, swiftly, "she won't live three minutes more, and we're too far out to swim. Shall I take her to sea again, Captain?"

"Yes; go ahead!" said the captain.

This oiler, by a series of quick miracles and fast and steady oarsmanship, turned the boat in the middle of the surf and took her safely to sea again.

There was a considerable silence as the boat bumped over the furrowed sea to deeper water. Then somebody in gloom spoke: "Well, anyhow, they must have seen us from the shore by now."

The gulls went in slanting flight up the wind toward the gray, desolate east. A squall, marked by dingy clouds and clouds brick-red, like smoke from a burning building, appeared from the southeast.

"What do you think of those life-saving people? Ain't they peaches?"

"Funny they haven't seen us."

"Maybe they think we're out here for sport! Maybe they think we're fishin'. Maybe they think we're damned fools."

It was a long afternoon. A changed tide tried to force them southward, but wind and wave said northward. Far ahead, where coast-line, sea, and sky formed their mighty angle, there were little dots which seemed to indicate a city on the shore.

"St. Augustine?"

The captain shook his head. "Too near Mosquito Inlet."

And the oiler rowed, and then the correspondent rowed; then the oiler rowed. It was a weary business. The human back can become the seat of more aches and pains than are registered in books for the composite anatomy of a regiment. It is a limited area, but it can become the theatre of innumerable muscular conflicts, tangles, wrenches, knots, and other comforts.

"Did you ever like to row, Billie?" asked the correspondent.

"No," said the oiler. "Hang it."

When one exchanged the rowing-seat for a place in the bottom of the boat, he suffered a bodily depression that caused him to be careless of everything save an obligation to wiggle one finger. There was cold sea-water swashing to and fro in the boat, and he lay in it. His head, pillowed on a thwart, was within an inch of the swirl of a wave-crest, and sometimes a particularly obstreperous sea came inboard and drenched him once more. But these matters did not annoy him. It is almost certain that if the boat had capsized he would have tumbled comfortably out upon the ocean as if he felt sure that it was a great soft mattress.

"Look! There's a man on the shore!"

"Where?"

"There? See 'im? See 'im?"

"Yes, sure! He's walking along."

"Now he's stopped. Look! He's facing us!"

"He's waving at us!"

"So he is! By thunder!"

"Ah, now we're all right! Now we're all right! There'll be a boat out here for us in half an hour."

"He's going on. He's running. He's going up to that house there."

The remote beach seemed lower than the sea, and it required a searching glance to discern the little black figure. The captain saw a floating stick, and they rowed to it. A bath towel was by some weird chance in the boat, and, tying this on the stick, the captain waved it. The oarsman did not dare turn his head, so he was obliged to ask questions.

"What's he doing now?"

"He's standing still again. He's looking, I think. . . . There he goes again— toward the house. . . . Now he's stopped again."

"Is he waving at us?"

"No, not now; he was, though."

"Look! There comes another man!"

"He's running."

"Look at him go, would you!"

"Why, he's on a bicycle. Now he's met the other man. They're both waving at us. Look!"

"There comes something up the beach."

"What the devil is that thing?"

"Why, it looks like a boat."

"Why, certainly, it's a boat."

"No; it's on wheels."

"Yes, so it is. Well, that must be the life-boat. They drag them along shore on a wagon."

"That's the life-boat, sure."

"No, by God, it's—it's an omnibus."

"I tell you it's a life-boat."

"It is not! It's an omnibus. I can see it plain. See? One of these big hotel omnibuses."

"By thunder, you're right. It's an omnibus, sure as fate. What do you suppose they are doing with an omnibus? Maybe they are going around collecting the life-crew, hey?"

"That's it, likely. Look! There's a fellow waving a little black flag. He's standing on the steps of the omnibus. There come those other two fellows. Now they're all talking together. Look at the fellow with the flag. Maybe he ain't waving it!"

"That ain't a flag, is it? That's his coat. Why, certainly, that's his coat."

"So it is; it's his coat. He's taken it off and is waving it around his head. But would you look at him swing it!"

"Oh, say, there isn't any life-saving station there. That's just a winter-resort hotel omnibus that has brought over some of the boarders to see us drown."

"What's that idiot with the coat mean? What's he signaling, anyhow?"

"It looks as if he were trying to tell us to go north. There must be a life-saving station up there."

"No; he thinks we're fishing. Just giving us a merry hand. See? Ah, there, Willie!"

"Well, I wish I could make something out of those signals. What do you suppose he means?"

"He don't mean anything; he's just playing."

"Well, if he'd just signal us to try the surf again, or to go to sea and wait, or go north, or go south, or go to hell, there would be some reason in it. But look at him! He just stands there and keeps his coat revolving like a wheel. The ass!"

"There come more people."

"Now there's quite a mob. Look! Isn't that a boat?"

"Where? Oh, I see where you mean. No, that's no boat."

"That fellow is still waving his coat."

"He must think we like to see him do that. Why don't he quit it? It don't mean anything."

"I don't know. I think he is trying to make us go north. It must be that there's a life-saving station there somewhere."

"Say, he ain't tired yet. Look at 'im wave!"

"Wonder how long he can keep that up. He's been revolving his coat ever since he caught sight of us. He's an idiot. Why aren't they getting men to bring a boat out? A fishing boat—one of those big yawls—could come out here all right. Why don't he do something?"

"Oh, it's all right now."

"They'll have a boat out here for us in less than no time, now that they've seen us."

A faint yellow tone came into the sky over the low land. The shadows on the sea slowly deepened. The wind bore coldness with it, and the men began to shiver.

"Holy smoke!" said one, allowing his voice to express his impious mood, "if we keep on monkeying out here! If we've got to flounder out here all night!"

"Oh, we'll never have to stay here all night! Don't you worry. They've seen us now, and it won't be long before they'll come chasing out after us."

The shore grew dusky. The man waving a coat blended gradually into this gloom, and it swallowed in the same manner the omnibus and the group of people. The spray, when it dashed uproariously over the side, made the voyagers shrink and swear like men who were being branded.

"I'd like to catch the chump who waved the coat. I feel like socking him one, just for luck."

"Why? What did he do?"

"Oh, nothing, but then he seemed so damned cheerful."

In the meantime the oiler rowed, and then the correspondent rowed, and then the oiler rowed. Gray-faced and bowed forward, they mechanically, turn by turn, plied the leaden oars. The form of the lighthouse had vanished from the southern horizon, but finally a pale star appeared, just lifting from the sea. The streaked saffron in the west passed before the all-merging darkness, and the sea to the east was black. The land had vanished, and was expressed only by the low and drear thunder of the surf.

"If I am going to be drowned—if I am going to be drowned—if I am going to be drowned, why, in the name of the seven mad gods who rule the sea, was I allowed to come thus far and contemplate sand and trees? Was I brought here merely to have my nose dragged away as I was about to nibble the sacred cheese of life?"

The patient captain, drooped over the water-jar, was sometimes obliged to speak to the oarsman.

"Keep her head up! Keep her head up!"

"Keep her head up, sir." The voices were weary and low.

This was surely a quiet evening. All save the oarsman lay heavily and listlessly in the boat's bottom. As for him, his eyes were just capable of noting the tall black waves that swept forward in a most sinister silence, save for an occasional subdued growl of a crest.

The cook's head was on a thwart, and he looked without interest at the water under his nose. He was deep in other scenes. Finally he spoke. "Billie," he murmured, dreamfully, "what kind of pie do you like best?"

## V

"Pie!" said the oiler and the correspondent, agitatedly. "Don't talk about those things, blast you!"

"Well," said the cook, "I was just thinking about ham sandwiches, and——"

A night on the sea in an open boat is a long night. As darkness settled finally, the shine of the light, lifting from the sea in the south, changed to full gold. On the northern horizon a new light appeared, a small bluish gleam on the edge of the waters. These two lights were the furniture of the world. Otherwise there was nothing but waves.

Two men huddled in the stern, and distances were so magnificent in the dinghy that the rower was enabled to keep his feet partly warm by thrusting them under his companions. Their legs indeed extended far under the rowing-seat until they touched the feet of the captain forward. Sometimes, despite the efforts of the tired oarsman, a wave came piling into the boat, an icy wave of the night, and the chilling water soaked them anew. They would twist their bodies for a moment and groan, and sleep the dead sleep once more, while the water in the boat gurgled about them as the craft rocked.

The plan of the oiler and the correspondent was for one to row until he lost the ability, and then arouse the other from his sea-water couch in the bottom of the boat.

The oiler plied the oars until his head drooped forward and the overpowering sleep blinded him; and he rowed yet afterward. Then he touched a man in the bottom of the boat, and called his name. "Will you spell me for a little while?" he said meekly.

"Sure, Billie," said the correspondent, awaking and dragging himself to a sitting position. They exchanged places carefully, and the oiler, cuddling down in the sea-water at the cook's side, seemed to go to sleep instantly.

The particular violence of the sea had ceased. The waves came without snarling. The obligation of the man at the oars was to keep the boat headed so that the tilt of the rollers would not capsize her, and to preserve her from filling when the crests rushed past. The black waves were silent and hard to be seen in the darkness. Often one was almost upon the boat before the oarsman was aware.

In a low voice the correspondent addressed the captain. He was not sure that the captain was awake, although this iron man seemed to be always awake. "Captain, shall I keep her making for that light north, sir?"

The same steady voice answered him. "Yes. Keep it about two points off the port bow."

The cook had tied a life-belt around himself in order to get even the warmth which this clumsy cork contrivance could donate, and he seemed almost stove-like when a rower, whose teeth invariably chattered wildly as soon as he ceased his labor, dropped down to sleep.

The correspondent, as he rowed, looked down at the two men sleeping underfoot. The cook's arm was around the oiler's shoulders, and, with their fragmentary clothing and haggard faces, they were the babes of the sea—a grotesque rendering of the old babes in the wood.

Later he must have grown stupid at his work, for suddenly there was a growling of water, and a crest came with a roar and a swash into the boat, and it was a wonder that it did not set the cook afloat in his life-belt. The cook continued to sleep, but the oiler sat up, blinking his eyes and shaking with the new cold.

"Oh, I'm awful sorry, Billie," said the correspondent, contritely.

"That's all right, old boy," said the oiler, and lay down again and was asleep.

Presently it seemed that even the captain dozed, and the correspondent thought that he was the one man afloat on all the ocean. The wind had a voice as it came over the waves, and it was sadder than the end.

There was a long, loud swishing astern of the boat, and a gleaming trail of phosphorescence, like blue flame, was furrowed on the black waters. It might have been made by a monstrous knife.

Then there came a stillness, while the correspondent breathed with open mouth and looked at the sea.

Suddenly there was another swish and another long flash of bluish light, and this time it was alongside the boat, and might almost have been reached with an oar. The correspondent saw an enormous fin speed like a shadow through the water, hurling the crystalline spray and leaving the long glowing trail.

The correspondent looked over his shoulder at the captain. His face was hidden, and he seemed to be asleep. He looked at the babes of the sea. They certainly were asleep. So, being bereft of sympathy, he leaned a little way to one side and swore softly into the sea.

But the thing did not then leave the vicinity of the boat. Ahead or astern, on one side or the other, at intervals long or short, fled the long sparkling streak, and there was to be heard the *whirroo* of the dark fin. The speed and power of the thing was greatly to be admired. It cut the water like a gigantic and keen projectile.

The presence of this biding thing did not affect the man with the same horror that it would if he had been a picnicker. He simply looked at the sea dully and swore in an undertone.

Nevertheless, it is true that he did not wish to be alone with the thing. He wished one of his companions to awake by chance and keep him company with it. But the captain hung motionless over the water-jar and the oiler and the cook in the bottom of the boat were plunged in slumber.

# VI

"If I am going to be drowned—if I am going to be drowned—if I am going to be drowned, why, in the name of the seven mad gods who rule the sea, was I allowed to come this far and contemplate sand and trees?"

During this dismal night, it may be remarked that a man would conclude that it was really the intention of the seven mad gods to drown him, despite the abominable injustice of it. For it was certainly an abominable injustice to drown a man who had worked so hard, so hard. The man felt it would be a crime most unnatural. Other people had drowned at sea since galleys swarmed with painted sails, but still——

When it occurs to a man that nature does not regard him as important, and that she feels she would not maim the universe by disposing of him, he at first wishes to throw bricks at the temple, and he hates deeply the fact that there are no bricks and no temples. Any visible expression of nature would surely be pelleted with his jeers.

Then, if there be no tangible thing to hoot, he feels, perhaps, the desire to confront a personification and indulge in pleas, bowed to one knee, and with hands supplicant, saying, "Yes, but I love myself."

A high cold star on a winter's night is the word he feels that she says to him. Thereafter he knows the pathos of his situation.

The men in the dinghy had not discussed these matters, but each had, no doubt, reflected upon them in silence and according to his mind. There was seldom any expression upon their faces save the general one of complete weariness. Speech was devoted to the business of the boat.

To chime the notes of his emotions, a verse mysteriously entered the correspondent's head. He had even forgotten that he had forgotten this verse, but it suddenly was in his mind.

> *A soldier of the Legion lay dying in Algiers;*
> *There was lack of woman's nursing,*
> *   there was dearth of woman's tears;*
> *But a comrade stood beside him,*
> *   and he took the comrade's hand,*
> *And he said, "I never more shall see*
> *   my own, my native land."*[6]

In his childhood the corresponden⸱
that a soldier of the Legion l⸱
as important. Myriads of his s
plight, but the dinning had na
ferent. He had never considered
dying in Algiers, nor had it appea
to him than the breaking of a pen⸱
Now, however, it quaintly came t
longer merely a picture of a few throe⸱

6. From "Bingen on the Rhine," a sentimental poem

ing tea and warming his feet at the grate; it was an actuality—stern, mournful, and fine.

The correspondent plainly saw the soldier. He lay on the sand with his feet out straight and still. While his pale left hand was upon his chest in an attempt to thwart the going of his life, the blood came between his fingers. In the far Algerian distance, a city of low square forms was set against a sky that was faint with the last sunset hues. The correspondent, plying the oars and dreaming of the slow and slower movements of the lips of the soldier, was moved by a profound and perfectly impersonal comprehension. He was sorry for the soldier of the Legion who lay dying in Algiers.

The thing which had followed the boat and waited had evidently grown bored at the delay. There was no longer to be heard the slash of the cutwater, and there was no longer the flame of the long trail. The light in the north still glimmered, but it was apparently no nearer to the boat. Sometimes the boom of the surf rang in the correspondent's ears, and he turned the craft seaward then and rowed harder. Southward, some one had evidently built a watch-fire on the beach. It was too low and too far to be seen, but it made a shimmering, roseate reflection upon the bluff in back of it, and this could be discerned from the boat. The wind came stronger, and sometimes a wave suddenly raged out like a mountain-cat, and there was to be seen the sheen and sparkle of a broken crest.

The captain, in the bow, moved on his water-jar and sat erect. "Pretty long night," he observed to the correspondent. He looked at the shore. "Those life-saving people take their time."

"Did you see that shark playing around?"

"Yes, I saw him. He was a big fellow, all right."

"Wish I had known you were awake."

Later the correspondent spoke into the bottom of the boat. "Billie!" There was a slow and gradual disentanglement. "Billie, will you spell me?"

"Sure," said the oiler.

As soon as the correspondent touched the cold, comfortable seawater in the bottom of the boat and had huddled close to the cook's life-belt he was deep in sleep, despite the fact that his teeth played all the popular airs. This sleep was so good to him that it was but a moment before he heard a voice call his name in a tone that demonstrated the last stages of exhaustion. "Will you spell me?"

"Sure, Billie."

The light in the north had mysteriously vanished, but the correspondent ook his course from the wide-awake captain.

ater in the night they took the boat farther out to sea, and the captain ed the cook to take one oar at the stern and keep the boat facing the was to call out if he should hear the thunder of the surf. This plan he oiler and the correspondent to get respite together. "We'll give a chance to get into shape again," said the captain. They curled er a few preliminary chatterings and trembles, slept once more Neither knew they had bequeathed to the cook the company or perhaps the same shark.

sed on the waves, spray occasionally bumped over the side soaking, but this had no power to break their repose. he wind and the water affected them as it would have

"Boys," said the cook, with the notes of every reluctance in his voice, "she's drifted in pretty close. I guess one of you had better take her to sea again." The correspondent, aroused, heard the crash of the toppled crests.

As he was rowing, the captain gave him some whiskey-and-water, and this steadied the chills out of him. "If I ever get ashore and anybody shows me even a photograph of an oar——"

At last there was a short conversation.

"Billie! . . . Billie, will you spell me?"

"Sure," said the oiler.

## VII

When the correspondent again opened his eyes, the sea and the sky were each of the gray hue of the dawning. Later, carmine and gold was painted upon the waters. The morning appeared finally, in its splendor, with a sky of pure blue, and the sunlight flamed on the tips of the waves.

On the distant dunes were set many little black cottages, and a tall white windmill reared above them. No man, nor dog, nor bicycle appeared on the beach. The cottages might have formed a deserted village.

The voyagers scanned the shore. A conference was held in the boat. "Well," said the captain, "if no help is coming, we might better try a run through the surf right away. If we stay out here much longer we will be too weak to do anything for ourselves at all." The others silently acquiesced in this reasoning. The boat was headed for the beach. The correspondent wondered if none ever ascended the tall wind-tower,[7] and if then they never looked seaward. This tower was a giant, standing with its back to the plight of the ants. It represented in a degree, to the correspondent, the serenity of nature amid the struggles of the individual—nature in the wind, and nature in the vision of men. She did not seem cruel to him then, nor beneficent, nor treacherous, nor wise. But she was indifferent, flatly indifferent. It is, perhaps, plausible that a man in this situation, impressed with the unconcern of the universe, should see the innumerable flaws of his life, and have them taste wickedly in his mind, and wish for another chance. A distinction between right and wrong seems absurdly clear to him, then, in this new ignorance of the grave-edge, and he understands that if he were given another opportunity he would mend his conduct and his words, and be better and brighter during an introduction or at a tea.

"Now, boys," said the captain, "she is going to swamp sure. All we can do is to work her in as far as possible, and then when she swamps, pile out and scramble for the beach. Keep cool now, and don't jump until she swamps sure."

The oiler took the oars. Over his shoulders he scanned the surf. "Captain," he said, "I think I'd better bring her about and keep her head-on to the seas and back her in."

"All right, Billie," said the captain. "Back her in." The oiler swung the boat then, and, seated in the stern, the cook and the correspondent were obliged to look over their shoulders to contemplate the lonely and indifferent shore.

The monstrous inshore rollers heaved the boat high until the men were again enabled to see the white sheets of water scudding up the slanted beach.

7. A watchtower for observing weather.

"We won't get in very close," said the captain. Each time a man could wrest his attention from the rollers, he turned his glance toward the shore, and in the expression of the eyes during this contemplation there was a singular quality. The correspondent, observing the others, knew that they were not afraid, but the full meaning of their glances was shrouded.

As for himself, he was too tired to grapple fundamentally with the fact. He tried to coerce his mind into thinking of it, but the mind was dominated at this time by the muscles, and the muscles said they did not care. It merely occurred to him that if he should drown it would be a shame.

There were no hurried words, no pallor, no plain agitation. The men simply looked at the shore. "Now, remember to get well clear of the boat when you jump," said the captain.

Seaward the crest of a roller suddenly fell with a thunderous crash, and the long white comber came roaring down upon the boat.

"Steady now," said the captain. The men were silent. They turned their eyes from the shore to the comber and waited. The boat slid up the incline, leaped at the furious top, bounced over it, and swung down the long back of the wave. Some water had been shipped, and the cook bailed it out.

But the next crest crashed also. The tumbling, boiling flood of white water caught the boat and whirled it almost perpendicular. Water swarmed in from all sides. The correspondent had his hands on the gunwale at this time, and when the water entered at that place he swiftly withdrew his fingers, as if he objected to wetting them.

The little boat, drunken with this weight of water, reeled and snuggled deeper into the sea.

"Bail her out, cook! Bail her out!" said the captain.

"All right, Captain," said the cook.

"Now, boys, the next one will do for us sure," said the oiler. "Mind to jump clear of the boat."

The third wave moved forward, huge, furious, implacable. It fairly swallowed the dinghy, and almost simultaneously the men tumbled into the sea. A piece of life-belt had lain in the bottom of the boat, and as the correspondent went overboard he held this to his chest with his left hand.

The January water was icy, and reflected immediately that it was colder than he had expected to find it off the coast of Florida. This appeared to his dazed mind as a fact important enough to be noted at the time. The coldness of the water was sad; it was tragic. This fact was somehow mixed and confused with his opinion of his own situation, so that it seemed almost a proper reason for tears. The water was cold.

When he came to the surface he was conscious of little but the noisy water. Afterward he saw his companions in the sea. The oiler was ahead in the race. He was swimming strongly and rapidly. Off to the correspondent's left, the cook's great white and corked back bulged out of the water, and in the rear the captain was hanging with his one good hand to the keel of the overturned dinghy.

There is a certain immovable quality to a shore, and the correspondent wondered at it amid the confusion of the sea.

It seemed also very attractive; but the correspondent knew that it was a long journey, and he paddled leisurely. The piece of life-preserver lay under him, and sometimes he whirled down the incline of a wave as if he were on a hand-sled.

But finally he arrived at a place in the sea where travel was beset with difficulty. He did not pause swimming to inquire what manner of current had caught him, but there his progress ceased. The shore was set before him like a bit of scenery on a stage, and he looked at it and understood with his eyes each detail of it.

As the cook passed, much farther to the left, the captain was calling to him, "Turn over on your back, cook! Turn over on your back and use the oar."

"All right, sir." The cook turned on his back, and, paddling with an oar, went ahead as if he were a canoe.

Presently the boat also passed to the left of the correspondent, with the captain clinging with one hand to the keel. He would have appeared like a man raising himself to look over a board fence if it were not for the extraordinary gymnastics of the boat. The correspondent marvelled that the captain could still hold to it.

They passed on nearer to shore—the oiler, the cook, the captain—and following them went the water-jar, bouncing gaily over the seas.

The correspondent remained in the grip of this strange new enemy, a current. The shore, with its white slope of sand and its green bluff topped with little silent cottages, was spread like a picture before him. It was very near to him then, but he was impressed as one who, in a gallery, looks at a scene from Brittany or Algiers.

He thought: "I am going to drown? Can it be possible? Can it be possible? Can it be possible?" Perhaps an individual must consider his own death to be the final phenomenon of nature.

But later a wave perhaps whirled him out of this small deadly current, for he found suddenly that he could again make progress toward the shore. Later still he was aware that the captain, clinging with one hand to the keel of the dinghy, had his face turned away from the shore and toward him, and was calling his name. "Come to the boat! Come to the boat!"

In his struggle to reach the captain and the boat, he reflected that when one gets properly wearied drowning must really be a comfortable arrangement—a cessation of hostilities accompanied by a large degree of relief; and he was glad of it, for the main thing in his mind for some moments had been horror of the temporary agony; he did not wish to be hurt.

Presently he saw a man running along the shore. He was undressing with most remarkable speed. Coat, trousers, shirt, everything flew magically off him.

"Come to the boat!" called the captain.

"All right, Captain." As the correspondent paddled, he saw the captain let himself down to bottom and leave the boat. Then the correspondent performed his one little marvel of the voyage. A large wave caught him and flung him with ease and supreme speed completely over the boat and far beyond it. It struck him even then as an event in gymnastics and a true miracle of the sea. An overturned boat in the surf is not a plaything to a swimming man.

The correspondent arrived in water that reached only to his waist, but his condition did not enable him to stand for more than a moment. Each wave knocked him into a heap, and the undertow pulled at him.

Then he saw the man who had been running and undressing, and undressing and running, come bounding into the water. He dragged ashore the cook, and then waded toward the captain; but the captain waved him away and sent him to the correspondent. He was naked—naked as a tree in winter; but a halo was about his head, and he shone like a saint. He gave a strong pull, and a long drag, and a bully heave at the correspondent's hand. The correspondent, schooled in the minor formulae, said, "Thanks, old man." But suddenly the man cried, "What's that?" He pointed a swift finger. The correspondent said, "Go."

In the shallows, face downward, lay the oiler. His forehead touched sand that was periodically, between each wave, clear of the sea.

The correspondent did not know all that transpired afterward. When he achieved safe ground he fell, striking the sand with each particular part of his body. It was as if he had dropped from a roof, but the thud was grateful to him.

It seems that instantly the beach was populated with men with blankets, clothes, and flasks, and women with coffee-pots and all the remedies sacred to their minds. The welcome of the land to the men from the sea was warm and generous; but a still and dripping shape was carried slowly up the beach, and the land's welcome for it could only be the different and sinister hospitality of the grave.

When it came night, the white waves paced to and fro in the moonlight, and the wind brought the sound of the great sea's voice to the men on the shore, and they felt that they could then be interpreters.

1897

---

RELATED:

—Crane, Letter to John Northern Hilliard, p. 880
—Allan Gurganus on "The Open Boat," p. 923
—Charles C. Walcutt, "Stephen Crane: Naturalist," p. 940

# EDWIDGE DANTICAT
## *b. 1969*

Edwidge Danticat was born in Port-au-Prince, Haiti, where she was raised by her aunt. At the age of twelve she moved to the United States to join her parents, who were living in a Haitian-American neighborhood in Brooklyn, New York, and she published her first writing in English two years later, a newspaper article about her immigration to the United States that eventually developed into her first novel, *Breath, Eyes, Memory* (1994). Since earning a degree in French literature from Barnard College and an M.F.A. from Brown University, she has focused on writing. Her first collection of stories *Krik? Krak!* (1995) established her as a developing master of the form. Her second novel, *The Farming of Bones* (1998), is based on the 1937 massacre of Haitians at the border of the Dominican Republic. Most recently, Danticat published *After the Dance: A Walk through Carnival in Jacmel, Haiti* (2002), an account of her travels, a second story collection, *The Dew Breaker* (2004), an essay collection, *Create Dangerously* (2010), and a new novel, *Claire of the Sea Light* (2013). She teaches creative writing at New York University.

# A Wall of Fire Rising

Listen to what happened today," Guy said as he barged through the rattling door of his tiny shack.

His wife, Lili, was squatting in the middle of their one-room home, spreading cornmeal mush on banana leaves for their supper.

"Listen to what happened to *me* today!" Guy's seven-year-old son—Little Guy—dashed from a corner and grabbed his father's hand. The boy dropped his composition notebook as he leaped to his father, nearly stepping into the corn mush and herring that his mother had set out in a trio of half gourds on the clay floor.

"Our boy is in a play." Lili quickly robbed Little Guy of the honor of telling his father the news.

"A play?" Guy affectionately stroked the boy's hair.

The boy had such tiny corkscrew curls that no amount of brushing could ever make them all look like a single entity. The other boys at the Lycée Jean-Jacques[1] called him "pepper head" because each separate kinky strand was coiled into a tight tiny ball that looked like small peppercorns.

---

1. The *lycée* (French for "school") is named for Jean-Jacques Dessalines (1758–1806), a former slave who founded independent Haiti and was declared Emperor Jacques I in 1804.

"When is this play?" Guy asked both the boy and his wife. "Are we going to have to buy new clothes for this?"

Lili got up from the floor and inclined her face towards her husband's in order to receive her nightly peck on the cheek.

"What role do you have in the play?" Guy asked, slowly rubbing the tip of his nails across the boy's scalp. His fingers made a soft grating noise with each invisible circle drawn around the perimeters of the boy's head. Guy's fingers finally landed inside the boy's ears, forcing the boy to giggle until he almost gave himself the hiccups.

"Tell me, what is your part in the play?" Guy asked again, pulling his fingers away from his son's ear.

"I am Boukman," the boy huffed out, as though there was some laughter caught in his throat.

"Show Papy your lines," Lili told the boy as she arranged the three open gourds on a piece of plywood raised like a table on two bricks, in the middle of the room. "My love, Boukman is the hero of the play."

The boy went back to the corner where he had been studying and pulled out a thick book carefully covered in brown paper.

"You're going to spend a lifetime learning those." Guy took the book from the boy's hand and flipped through the pages quickly. He had to strain his eyes to see the words by the light of an old kerosene lamp, which that night—like all others—flickered as though it was burning its very last wick.

"All these words seem so long and heavy," Guy said. "You think you can do this, son?"

"He has one very good speech," Lili said. "Page forty, remember, son?"

The boy took back the book from his father. His face was crimped in an of-course-I-remember look as he searched for page forty.

"Bouk-man," Guy struggled with the letters of the slave revolutionary's name as he looked over his son's shoulders. "I see some very hard words here, son."

"He already knows his speech," Lili told her husband.

"Does he now?" asked Guy.

"We've been at it all afternoon," Lili said. "Why don't you go on and recite that speech for your father?"

The boy tipped his head towards the rusting tin on the roof as he prepared to recite his lines.

Lili wiped her hands on an old apron tied around her waist and stopped to listen.

"Remember what you are," Lili said, "a great rebel leader. Remember, it is the revolution."

"Do we want him to be all of that?" Guy asked.

"He is Boukman," Lili said. "What is the only thing on your mind now, Boukman?"

"Supper," Guy whispered, enviously eyeing the food cooling off in the middle of the room. He and the boy looked at each other and began to snicker.

"Tell us the other thing that is on your mind," Lili said, joining in their laughter.

"Freedom!" shouted the boy, as he quickly slipped into his role.

"Louder!" urged Lili.

"Freedom is on my mind!" yelled the boy.

"Why don't you start, son?" said Guy. "If you don't, we'll never get to that other thing that we have on our minds."

The boy closed his eyes and took a deep breath. At first, his lips parted but nothing came out. Lili pushed her head forward as though she were holding her breath. Then like the last burst of lightning out of clearing sky, the boy began.

*"A wall of fire is rising and in the ashes, I see the bones of my people. Not only those people whose dark hollow faces I see daily in the fields, but all those souls who have gone ahead to haunt my dreams. At night I relive once more the last caresses from the hand of a loving father, a valiant love, a beloved friend."*[2]

It was obvious that this was a speech written by a European man, who gave to the slave revolutionary Boukman the kind of European phrasing that might have sent the real Boukman turning in his grave. However, the speech made Lili and Guy stand on the tips of their toes from great pride. As their applause thundered in the small space of their shack that night, they felt as though for a moment they had been given the rare pleasure of hearing the voice of one of the forefathers of Haitian independence in the forced baritone of their only child. The experience left them both with a strange feeling that they could not explain. It left the hair on the back of their necks standing on end. It left them feeling much more love than they ever knew that they could add to their feeling for their son.

"Bravo," Lili cheered, pressing her son into the folds of her apron. "Long live Boukman and long live my boy."

"Long live our supper," Guy said, quickly batting his eyelashes to keep tears from rolling down his face.

The boy kept his eyes on his book as they ate their supper that night. Usually Guy and Lili would not have allowed that, but this was a special occasion. They watched proudly as the boy muttered his lines between swallows of cornmeal.

The boy was still mumbling the same words as the three of them used the last of the rainwater trapped in old gasoline containers and sugarcane pulp from the nearby sugarcane mill to scrub the gourds that they had eaten from.

When things were really bad for the family, they boiled clean sugarcane pulp to make what Lili called her special sweet water tea. It was supposed to suppress gas and kill the vermin in the stomach that made poor children hungry. That and a pinch of salt under the tongue could usually quench hunger until Guy found a day's work or Lili could manage to buy spices on credit and then peddle them for a profit at the marketplace.

That night, anyway, things were good. Everyone had eaten enough to put all their hunger vermin to sleep.

The boy was sitting in front of the shack on an old plastic bucket turned upside down, straining his eyes to find the words on the page. Sometimes when there was no kerosene for the lamp, the boy would have to go sit by the

2. On the night of August 22, 1791, slaves led by a slave foreman named Boukman (secretly a voodoo high priest) built a "wall of fire" that destroyed many plantations in the north of the French colony of Saint-Domingue, marking the beginning of a mass slave revolt that would lead, fourteen years later, to the establishment of independent Haiti.

side of the road and study under the street lamps with the rest of the neighborhood children. Tonight, at least, they had a bit of their own light.

Guy bent down by a small clump of old mushrooms near the boy's feet, trying to get a better look at the plant. He emptied the last drops of rainwater from a gasoline container on the mushroom, wetting the bulging toes sticking out of his sons' sandals, which were already coming apart around his endlessly growing feet.

Guy tried to pluck some of the mushrooms, which were being pushed into the dust as though they wanted to grow beneath the ground as roots. He took one of the mushrooms in his hand, running his smallest finger over the round bulb. He clipped the stem and buried the top in a thick strand of his wife's hair.

The mushroom looked like a dried insect in Lili's hair.

"It sure makes you look special," Guy said, teasing her.

"Thank you so much," Lili said, tapping her husband's arm. "It's nice to know that I deserve these much more than roses."

Taking his wife's hand, Guy said, "Let's go to the sugar mill."

"Can I study my lines there?" the boy asked.

"You know them well enough already," Guy said.

"I need many repetitions," the boy said.

Their feet sounded as though they were playing a wet wind instrument as they slipped in and out of the puddles between the shacks in the shantytown. Near the sugar mill was a large television screen in a iron grill cage that the government had installed so that the shantytown dwellers could watch the state-sponsored news at eight o'clock every night. After the news, a gendarme[3] would come and turn off the television set, taking home the key. On most nights, the people stayed at the site long after this gendarme had gone and told stories to one another beneath the big blank screen. They made bonfires with dried sticks, corn husks, and paper, cursing the authorities under their breath.

There was a crowd already gathering for the nightly news event. The sugar mill workers sat in the front row in chairs or on old buckets.

Lili and Guy passed the group, clinging to their son so that in his childhood naïveté he wouldn't accidentally glance at the wrong person and be called an insolent child. They didn't like the ambiance of the nightly news watch. They spared themselves trouble by going instead to the sugar mill, where in the past year they had discovered their own wonder.

Everyone knew that the family who owned the sugar mill were eccentric "Arabs," Haitians of Lebanese or Palestinian descent whose family had been in the country for generations. The Assad family had a son who, it seems, was into all manner of odd things, the most recent of which was a hot-air balloon, which he had brought to Haiti from America and occasionally flew over the shantytown skies.

As they approached the fence surrounding the field where the large wicker basket and deflated balloon rested on the ground, Guy let go of the hands of both his wife and the boy.

---

3. Policeman or guard (French).

Lili walked on slowly with her son. For the last few weeks, she had been feeling as though Guy was lost to her each time he reached this point, twelve feet away from the balloon. As Guy pushed his hand through the barbed wire, she could tell from the look on his face that he was thinking of sitting inside the square basket while the smooth rainbow surface of the balloon itself floated above his head. During the day, when the field was open, Guy would walk up to the basket, staring at it with the same kind of longing that most men display when they admire very pretty girls.

Lili and the boy stood watching from a distance as Guy tried to push his hand deeper, beyond the chain link fence that separated him from the balloon. He reached into his pants pocket and pulled out a small pocketknife, sharpening the edges on the metal surface of the fence. When his wife and child moved closer, he put the knife back in his pocket, letting his fingers slide across his son's tightly coiled curls.

"I wager you I can make this thing fly," Guy said.

"Why do you think you can do that?" Lili asked.

"I know it," Guy replied.

He followed her as she circled the sugar mill, leading to their favorite spot under a watch light. Little Guy lagged faithfully behind them. From this distance, the hot-air balloon looked like an odd spaceship.

Lili stretched her body out in the knee-high grass in the field. Guy reached over and tried to touch her between her legs.

"You're not one to worry, Lili," he said. "You're not afraid of the frogs, lizards, or snakes that could be hiding in this grass?"

"I am here with my husband," she said. "You are here to protect me if anything happens."

Guy reached into his shirt pocket and pulled out a lighter and a crumpled piece of paper. He lit the paper until it burned to an ashy film. The burning paper floated in the night breeze for a while, landing in fragments on the grass.

"Did you see that, Lili?" Guy asked with a flame in his eyes brighter than the lighter's. "Did you see how the paper floated when it was burned? This is how that balloon flies."

"What did you mean by saying that you could make it fly?" Lili asked.

"You already know all my secrets," Guy said as the boy came charging towards them.

"Papa, could you play *Lago* with me?" the boy asked.

Lili lay peacefully on the grass as her son and husband played hide-and-seek. Guy kept hiding and his son kept finding him as each time Guy made it easier for the boy.

"We rest now." Guy was becoming breathless.

The stars were circling the peaks of the mountains, dipping into the cane fields belonging to the sugar mill. As Guy caught his breath, the boy raced around the fence, running as fast as he could to purposely make himself dizzy.

"Listen to what happened today," Guy whispered softly in Lili's ear.

"I heard you say that when you walked in the house tonight," Lili said. "With the boy's play, I forgot to ask you."

The boy sneaked up behind them, his face lit up, though his brain was spinning. He wrapped his arms around both their necks.

"We will go back home soon," Lili said.

"Can I recite my lines?" asked the boy.

"We have heard them," Guy said. "Don't tire your lips."

The boy mumbled something under his breath. Guy grabbed his ear and twirled it until it was a tiny ball in his hand. The boy's face contorted with agony as Guy made him kneel in the deep grass in punishment.

Lili looked tortured as she watched the boy squirming in the grass, obviously terrified of the crickets, lizards, and small snakes that might be there.

"Perhaps we should take him home to bed," she said.

"He will never learn," Guy said, "if I say one thing and you say another."

Guy got up and angrily started walking home. Lili walked over, took her son's hand, and raised him from his knees.

"You know you must not mumble," she said.

"I was saying my lines," the boy said.

"Next time say them loud," Lili said, "so he knows what is coming out of your mouth."

That night Lili could hear her son muttering his lines as he tucked himself in his corner of the room and drifted off to sleep. The boy still had the book with his monologue in it clasped under his arm as he slept.

Guy stayed outside in front of the shack as Lili undressed for bed. She loosened the ribbon that held the old light blue cotton skirt around her waist and let it drop past her knees. She grabbed half a lemon that she kept in the corner by the folded mat that she and Guy unrolled to sleep on every night. Lili let her blouse drop to the floor as she smoothed the lemon over her ashen legs.

Guy came in just at that moment and saw her bare chest by the light of the smaller castor oil lamp that they used for the later hours of the night. Her skin had coarsened a bit over the years, he thought. Her breasts now drooped from having nursed their son for two years after he was born. It was now easier for him to imagine their son's lips around those breasts than to imagine his anywhere near them.

He turned his face away as she fumbled for her nightgown. He helped her open the mat, tucking the blanket edges underneath.

Fully clothed, Guy dropped onto the mat next to her. He laid his head on her chest, rubbing the spiky edges of his hair against her nipples.

"What was it that happened today?" Lili asked, running her fingers along Guy's hairline, an angular hairline, almost like a triangle, in the middle of his forehead. She nearly didn't marry him because it was said that people with angular hairlines often have very troubled lives.

"I got a few hours' work for tomorrow at the sugar mill," Guy said. "That's what happened today."

"It was such a long time coming," Lili said.

It was almost six months since the last time Guy had gotten work there. The jobs at the sugar mill were few and far between. The people who had them never left, or when they did they would pass the job on to another family member who was already waiting on line.

Guy did not seem overjoyed about the one day's work.

"I wish I had paid more attention when you came in with the news," Lili said. "I was just so happy about the boy."

"I was born in the shadow of that sugar mill," Guy said. "Probably the first thing my mother gave me to drink as a baby was some sweet water tea from the pulp of the sugarcane. If anyone deserves to work there, I should."

"What will you be doing for your day's work?"

"Would you really like to know?"

"There is never any shame in honest work," she said.

"They want me to scrub the latrines."

"It's honest work," Lili said, trying to console him.

"I am still number seventy-eight on the permanent hire list," he said. "I was thinking of putting the boy on the list now, so maybe by the time he becomes a man he can be up for a job."

Lili's body jerked forward, rising straight up in the air. Guy's head dropped with a loud thump onto the mat.

"I don't want him on that list," she said. "For a young boy to be on any list like that might influence his destiny. I don't want him on the list."

"Look at me," Guy said. "If my father had worked there, if he had me on the list, don't you think I would be working?"

"If you have any regard for me," she said, "you will not put him on the list."

She groped for her husband's chest in the dark and laid her head on it. She could hear his heart beating loudly as though it were pumping double, triple its normal rate.

"You won't put the boy on any lists, will you?" she implored.

"Please, Lili, no more about the boy. He will not go on the list."

"Thank you."

"Tonight I was looking at that balloon in the yard behind the sugar mill," he said. "I have been watching it real close."

"I know."

"I have seen the man who owns it," he said. "I've seen him get in it and put it in the sky and go up there like it was some kind of kite and he was the kite master. I see the men who run after it trying to figure out where it will land. Once I was there and I was one of those men who were running and I actually guessed correctly. I picked a spot in the sugarcane fields. I picked the spot from a distance and it actually landed there."

"Let me say something to you, Guy—"

"Pretend that this is the time of miracles and we believed in them. I watched the owner for a long time, and I think I can fly that balloon. The first time I saw him do it, it looked like a miracle, but the more and more I saw it, the more ordinary it became."

"You're probably intelligent enough to do it," she said.

"I am intelligent enough to do it. You're right to say that I can."

"Don't you think about hurting yourself?"

"Think like this. Can't you see yourself up there? Up in the clouds somewhere like some kind of bird?"

"If God wanted people to fly, he would have given us wings on our backs."

"You're right, Lili, you're right. But look what he gave us instead. He gave us reasons to want to fly. He gave us the air, the birds, our son."

"I don't understand you," she said.

"Our son, your son, you do not want him cleaning latrines."

"He can do other things."

"Me too. I can do other things too."

A loud scream came from the corner where the boy was sleeping. Lili and Guy rushed to him and tried to wake him. The boy was trembling when he opened his eyes.

"What is the matter?" Guy asked.

"I cannot remember my lines," the boy said.

Lili tried to string together what she could remember of her son's lines. The words slowly came back to the boy. By the time he fell back to sleep, it was almost dawn.

The light was slowly coming up behind the trees. Lili could hear the whispers of the market women, their hisses and swearing as their sandals dug into the sharp-edged rocks on the road.

She turned her back to her husband as she slipped out of her nightgown, quickly putting on her day clothes.

"Imagine this," Guy said from the mat on the floor. "I have never really seen your entire body in broad daylight."

Lili shut the door behind her, making her way out to the yard. The empty gasoline containers rested easily on her head as she walked a few miles to the public water fountains. It was harder to keep them steady when the containers were full. The water splashed all over her blouse and rippled down her back.

The sky was blue as it was most mornings, a dark indigo-shaded turquoise that would get lighter when the sun was fully risen.

Guy and the boy were standing in the yard waiting for her when she got back.

"You did not get much sleep, my handsome boy," she said, running her wet fingers over the boy's face.

"He'll be late for school if we do not go right now," Guy said. "I want to drop him off before I start work."

"Do we remember our lines this morning?" Lili asked, tucking the boy's shirt down deep into his short pants.

"We just recited them," Guy said. "Even I know them now."

Lili watched them walk down the footpath, her eyes following them until they disappeared.

As soon as they were out of sight, she poured the water she had fetched into a large calabash, letting it stand beside the house.

She went back into the room and slipped into a dry blouse. It was never too early to start looking around, to scrape together that night's meal.

"Listen to what happened again today," Lili said when Guy walked through the door that afternoon.

Guy blotted his face with a dust rag as he prepared to hear the news. After the day he'd had at the factory, he wanted to sit under a tree and have a leisurely smoke, but he did not want to set a bad example for his son by indulging his very small pleasures.

"You tell him, son," Lili urged the boy, who was quietly sitting in a corner, reading.

"I've got more lines," the boy announced, springing up to his feet. "Papy, do you want to hear them?"

"They are giving him more things to say in the play," Lili explained, "because he did such a good job memorizing so fast."

"My compliments, son. Do you have your new lines memorized too?" Guy asked.

"Why don't you recite your new lines for your father?" Lili said.

The boy walked to the middle of the room and prepared to recite. He cleared his throat, raising his eyes towards the ceiling.

*"There is so much sadness in the faces of my people. I have called on their gods, now I call on our gods. I call on our young. I call on our old. I call on our mighty and the weak. I call on everyone and anyone so that we shall all let out one piercing cry that we may either live freely or we should die."*

"I see your new lines have as much drama as the old ones," Guy said. He wiped a tear away, walked over to the chair, and took the boy in his arms. He pressed the boy's body against his chest before lowering him to the ground.

"Your new lines are wonderful, son. They're every bit as affecting as the old." He tapped the boy's shoulder and walked out of the house.

"What's the matter with Papy?" the boy asked as the door slammed shut behind Guy.

"His heart hurts," Lili said.

After supper, Lili took her son to the field where she knew her husband would be. While the boy ran around, she found her husband sitting in his favorite spot behind the sugar mill.

"Nothing, Lili," he said. "Ask me nothing about this day that I have had."

She sat down on the grass next to him, for once feeling the sharp edges of the grass blades against her ankles.

"You're really good with that boy," he said, drawing circles with his smallest finger on her elbow. "You will make a performer of him. I know you will. You can see the best in that whole situation. It's because you have those stars in your eyes. That's the first thing I noticed about you when I met you. It was your eyes, Lili, so dark and deep. They drew me like danger draws a fool."

He turned over on the grass so that he was staring directly at the moon up in the sky. She could tell that he was also watching the hot-air balloon behind the sugar mill fence out of the corner of his eye.

"Sometimes I know you want to believe in me," he said. "I know you're wishing things for me. You want me to work at the mill. You want me to get a pretty house for us. I know you want these things too, but mostly you want me to feel like a man. That's why you're not one to worry about, Lili. I know you can take things as they come."

"I don't like it when you talk this way," she said.

"Listen to this, Lili. I want to tell you a secret. Sometimes, I just want to take that big balloon and ride it up in the air. I'd like to sail off somewhere and keep floating until I got to a really nice place with a nice plot of land where I could be something. I'd build my own house, keep my own garden. Just *be* something new."

"I want you to stay away from there."

"I know you don't think I should take it. That can't keep me from wanting."

"You could be injured. Do you ever think about that?"

"Don't you ever want to be something new?"

"I don't like it," she said.

"Please don't get angry with me," he said, his voice straining almost like the boy's.

"If you were to take that balloon and fly away, would you take me and the boy?"

"First you don't want me to take it and now you want to go?"

"I just want to know that when you dream, me and the boy, we're always in your dreams."

He leaned his head on her shoulders and drifted off to sleep. Her back ached as she sat there with his face pressed against her collar bone. He drooled and the saliva dripped down to her breasts, soaking her frayed polyester bra. She listened to the crickets while watching her son play, muttering his lines to himself as he went in a circle around the field. The moon was glowing above their heads. Winking at them, as Guy liked to say, on its way to brighter shores.

Opening his eyes, Guy asked her, "How do you think a man is judged after he's gone?"

How did he expect her to answer something like that?

"People don't eat riches," she said. "They eat what it can buy."

"What does that mean, Lili? Don't talk to me in parables. Talk to me honestly."

"A man is judged by his deeds," she said. "The boy never goes to bed hungry. For as long as he's been with us, he's always been fed."

Just as if he had heard himself mentioned, the boy came dashing from the other side of the field, crashing in a heap on top of his parents.

"My new lines," he said. "I have forgotten my new lines."

"Is this how you will be the day of this play, son?" Guy asked. "When people give you big responsibilities, you have to try to live up to them."

The boy had relearned his new lines by the time they went to bed.

That night, Guy watched his wife very closely as she undressed for bed.

"I would like to be the one to rub that piece of lemon on your knees tonight," he said.

She handed him the half lemon, then raised her skirt above her knees.

Her body began to tremble as he rubbed his fingers over her skin.

"You know that question I asked you before," he said, "how a man is remembered after he's gone? I know the answer now. I know because I remember my father, who was a very poor struggling man all his life. I remember him as a man that I would never want to be."

Lili got up with the break of dawn the next day. The light came up quickly above the trees. Lili greeted some of the market women as they walked together to the public water fountain.

On her way back, the sun had already melted a few gray clouds. She found the boy standing alone in the yard with a terrified expression on his face, the old withered mushrooms uprooted at his feet. He ran up to meet her, nearly knocking her off balance.

"What happened?" she asked. "Have you forgotten your lines?"

The boy was breathing so heavily that his lips could not form a single word.

"What is it?" Lili asked, almost shaking him with anxiety.

"It's Papa," he said finally, raising a stiff finger in the air.

The boy covered his face as his mother looked up at the sky. A rainbow-colored balloon was floating aimlessly above their heads.

"It's Papa," the boy said. "He is in it."

She wanted to look down at her son and tell him that it wasn't his father, but she immediately recognized the spindly arms, in a bright flowered shirt that she had made, gripping the cables.

From the field behind the sugar mill a group of workers were watching the balloon floating in the air. Many were clapping and cheering, calling out Guy's name. A few of the women were waving their head rags at the sky, shouting, "Go! Beautiful, go!"

Lili edged her way to the front of the crowd. Everyone was waiting, watching the balloon drift higher up into the clouds.

"He seems to be right over our heads," said the factory foreman, a short slender mulatto with large buckteeth.

Just then, Lili noticed young Assad, his thick black hair sticking to the beads of sweat on his forehead. His face had the crumpled expression of disrupted sleep.

"He's further away than he seems," said young Assad. "I still don't understand. How did he get up there? You need a whole crew to fly these things."

"I don't know," the foreman said. "One of my workers just came in saying there was a man flying above the factory."

"But how the hell did he start it?" Young Assad was perplexed.

"He just did it," the foreman said.

"Look, he's trying to get out!" someone hollered.

A chorus of screams broke out among the workers.

The boy was looking up, trying to see if his father was really trying to jump out of the balloon. Guy was climbing over the side of the basket. Lili pressed her son's face into her skirt.

Within seconds, Guy was in the air hurtling down towards the crowd. Lili held her breath as she watched him fall. He crashed not far from where Lili and the boy were standing, his blood immediately soaking the landing spot.

The balloon kept floating free, drifting on its way to brighter shores. Young Assad rushed towards the body. He dropped to his knees and checked the wrist for a pulse, then dropped the arm back to the ground.

"It's over!" The foreman ordered the workers back to work.

Lili tried to keep her son's head pressed against her skirt as she moved closer to the body. The boy yanked himself away and raced to the edge of the field where his father's body was lying on the grass. He reached the body as young Assad still knelt examining the corpse. Lili rushed after him.

"He is mine," she said to young Assad. "He is my family. He belongs to me."

Young Assad got up and raised his head to search the sky for his aimless balloon, trying to guess where it would land. He took one last glance at Guy's bloody corpse, then raced to his car and sped away.

The foreman and another worker carried a cot and blanket from the factory.

Little Guy was breathing quickly as he looked at his father's body on the ground. While the foreman draped a sheet over Guy's corpse, his son began to recite the lines from his play.

*"A wall of fire is rising and in the ashes, I see the bones of my people. Not only those people whose dark hollow faces I see daily in the fields, but all those souls who have gone ahead to haunt my dreams. At night I relive once more the last caresses from the hand of a loving father, a valiant love, a beloved friend."*

"Let me look at him one last time," Lili said, pulling back the sheet.

She leaned in very close to get a better look at Guy's face. There was little left of that countenance that she had loved so much. Those lips that curled when he was teasing her. That large flat nose that felt like a feather when rubbed against hers. And those eyes, those night-colored eyes. Though clouded with blood, Guy's eyes were still bulging open. Lili was searching for some kind of sign—a blink, a smile, a wink—something that would remind her of the man that she had married.

"His eyes aren't closed," the foreman said to Lili. "Do you want to close them, or should I?"

The boy continued reciting his lines, his voice rising to a man's grieving roar. He kept his eyes closed, his fists balled at his side as he continued with his newest lines.

*"There is so much sadness in the faces of my people. I have called on their gods, now I call on our gods. I call on our young. I call on our old. I call on our mighty and the weak. I call on everyone and anyone so that we shall all let out one piercing cry that we may either live freely or we should die."*

"Do you want to close the eyes?" the foreman repeated impatiently.

"No, leave them open," Lili said. "My husband, he likes to look at the sky."

1991

# RALPH ELLISON
## *1914–1994*

Ellison was born in Oklahoma City and studied music at Tuskegee Institute before dropping out to embark on a course that would eventually lead him to chance meetings with Langston Hughes and Richard Wright, which led him to join the Federal Writers' Project. At last he had found his calling. Though his publications were few, his novel *Invisible Man* (1952) became one of the most discussed and praised books published in America since World War II. While it announces no program of black liberation, it starkly bares the moral, political, and psychological aspects of the enduring struggle. In his other writings, including the essay collections *Shadow and Act* (1964) and *Going to the Territory* (1986), as well as the posthumously published novel *Juneteenth* (1999), Ellison continued his exploration of the problem of identity within the context of black culture. He brought to a culmination the double consciousness of blacks who also know themselves to be American.

## King of the Bingo Game

The woman in front of him was eating roasted peanuts that smelled so good that he could barely contain his hunger. He could not even sleep and wished they'd hurry and begin the bingo game. There, on his right, two fellows were drinking wine out of a bottle wrapped in a paper bag, and he could hear soft gurgling in the dark. His stomach gave a low, gnawing growl. "If this was down South," he thought, "all I'd have to do is lean over and say, 'Lady, gimme a few of those peanuts, please ma'am,' and she'd pass me the bag and never think nothing of it." Or he could ask the fellows for a drink in the same way. Folks down South stuck together that way; they didn't even have to know you. But up here it was different. Ask somebody for something, and they'd think you were crazy. Well, I ain't crazy. I'm just broke, 'cause I got no birth certificate to get a job, and Laura 'bout to die 'cause we got no money for a doctor. But I ain't crazy. And yet a pinpoint of doubt was focused in his mind as he glanced toward the screen and saw the hero stealthily entering a dark room and sending the beam of a flashlight along a wall of bookcases. This is where he finds the trapdoor, he remembered. The man would pass abruptly through the wall and find the girl tied to a bed, her legs and arms spread wide, and her clothing torn to rags. He laughed softly to himself. He had seen the picture three times, and this was one of the best scenes.

On his right the fellow whispered wide-eyed to his companion, "Man, look ayonder!"

"Damn!"

"Wouldn't I like to have her tied up like that . . ."

"Hey! That fool's letting her loose!"

"Aw, man, he loves her."

"Love or no love!"

The man moved impatiently beside him, and he tried to involve himself in the scene. But Laura was on his mind. Tiring quickly of watching the picture he looked back to where the white beam filtered from the projection room above the balcony. It started small and grew large, specks of dust dancing in its whiteness as it reached the screen. It was strange how the beam always landed right on the screen and didn't mess up and fall somewhere else. But they had it all fixed. Everything was fixed. Now suppose when they showed that girl with her dress torn the girl started taking off the rest of her clothes, and when the guy came in he didn't untie her but kept her there and went to taking off his own clothes? *That* would be something to see. If a picture got out of hand like that those guys up there would go nuts. Yeah, and there'd be so many folks in here you couldn't find a seat for nine months! A strange sensation played over his skin. He shuddered. Yesterday he'd seen a bedbug on a woman's neck as they walked out into the bright street. But exploring his thigh through a hole in his pocket he found only goose pimples and old scars.

The bottle gurgled again. He closed his eyes. Now a dreamy music was accompanying the film and train whistles were sounding in the distance, and he was a boy again walking along a railroad trestle down South, and seeing the train coming, and running back as fast as he could go, and hearing the whistle blowing, and getting off the trestle to solid ground just in time, with the earth trembling beneath his feet, and feeling relieved as he ran down the cinder-strewn embankment onto the highway, and looking back and seeing with terror that the train had left the track and was following him right down the middle of the street, and all the white people laughing as he ran screaming . . .

"Wake up there, buddy! What the hell do you mean hollering like that? Can't you see we trying to enjoy this here picture?"

He stared at the man with gratitude.

"I'm sorry, old man," he said. "I musta been dreaming."

"Well, here, have a drink. And don't be making no noise like that, damn!"

His hands trembled as he tilted his head. It was not wine, but whiskey. Cold rye whiskey. He took a deep swoller, decided it was better not to take another, and handed the bottle back to its owner.

"Thanks, old man," he said.

Now he felt the cold whiskey breaking a warm path straight through the middle of him, growing hotter and sharper as it moved. He had not eaten all day, and it made him light-headed. The smell of the peanuts stabbed him like a knife, and he got up and found a seat in the middle aisle. But no sooner did he sit than he saw a row of intense-faced young girls, and got up again, thinking, "You chicks musta been Lindy-hopping[1] somewhere." He found a seat several rows ahead as the lights came on, and he saw the screen disappear

1. Dancing.

behind a heavy red and gold curtain; then the curtain rising, and the man with the microphone and a uniformed attendant coming on the stage.

He felt for his bingo cards, smiling. The guy at the door wouldn't like it if he knew about his having *five* cards. Well, not everyone played the bingo game; and even with five cards he didn't have much of a chance. For Laura, though, he had to have faith. He studied the cards, each with its different numerals, punching the free center hole in each and spreading them neatly across his lap; and when the lights faded he sat slouched in his seat so that he could look from his cards to the bingo wheel with but a quick shifting of his eyes.

Ahead, at the end of the darkness, the man with the microphone was pressing a button attached to a long cord and spinning the bingo wheel and calling out the number each time the wheel came to rest. And each time the voice rang out his finger raced over the cards for the number. With five cards he had to move fast. He became nervous; there were too many cards, and the man went too fast with his grating voice. Perhaps he should just select one and throw the others away. But he was afraid. He became warm. Wonder how much Laura's doctor would cost? Damn that, watch the cards! And with despair he heard the man call three in a row which he missed on all five cards. This way he'd never win . . .

When he saw the row of holes punched across the third card, he sat paralyzed and heard the man call three more numbers before he stumbled forward, screaming,

"Bingo! Bingo!"

"Let that fool up there," someone called.

"Get up there, man!"

He stumbled down the aisle and up the steps to the stage into a light so sharp and bright that for a moment it blinded him, and he felt that he had moved into the spell of some strange, mysterious power. Yet it was as familiar as the sun, and he knew it was the perfectly familiar bingo.

The man with the microphone was saying something to the audience as he held out his card. A cold light flashed from the man's finger as the card left his hand. His knees trembled. The man stepped closer, checking the card against the numbers chalked on the board. Suppose he had made a mistake? The pomade on the man's hair made him feel faint, and he backed away. But the man was checking the card over the microphone now, and he had to stay. He stood tense, listening.

"Under the O, forty-four," the man chanted. "Under the I, seven. Under the G, three. Under the B, ninety-six. Under the N, thirteen!"

His breath came easier as the man smiled at the audience.

"Yes sir, ladies and gentlemen, he's one of the chosen people!"

The audience rippled with laughter and applause.

"Step right up to the front of the stage."

He moved slowly forward, wishing that the light was not so bright.

"To win tonight's jackpot of $36.90 the wheel must stop between the double zero, understand?"

He nodded, knowing the ritual from the many days and nights he had watched the winners march across the stage to press the button that controlled the spinning wheel and receive the prizes. And now he followed the instructions as though he'd crossed the slippery stage a million prize-winning times.

The man was making some kind of joke, and he nodded vacantly. So tense had he become that he felt a sudden desire to cry and shook it away. He felt vaguely that his whole life was determined by the bingo wheel; not only that which would happen now that he was at last before it, but all that had gone before, since his birth, and his mother's birth and the birth of his father. It had always been there, even though he had not been aware of it, handing out the unlucky cards and numbers of his days. The feeling persisted, and he started quickly away. I better get down from here before I make a fool of myself, he thought.

"Here, boy," the man called. "You haven't started yet."

Someone laughed as he went hesitantly back.

"Are you all reet?"

He grinned at the man's jive talk, but no words would come, and he knew it was not a convincing grin. For suddenly he knew that he stood on the slippery brink of some terrible embarrassment.

"Where are you from, boy?" the man asked.

"Down South."

"He's from down South, ladies and gentlemen," the man said. "Where from? Speak right into the mike."

"Rocky Mont," he said. "Rock' Mont, North Car'lina."

"So you decided to come down off that mountain to the U.S.," the man laughed. He felt that the man was making a fool of him, but then something cold was placed in his hand, and the lights were no longer behind him.

Standing before the wheel he felt alone, but that was somehow right, and he remembered his plan. He would give the wheel a short quick twirl. Just a touch of the button. He had watched it many times, and always it came close to double zero when it was short and quick. He steeled himself; the fear had left, and he felt a profound sense of promise, as though he were about to be repaid for all the things he'd suffered all his life. Trembling, he pressed the button. There was a whirl of lights, and in a second he realized with finality that though he wanted to, he could not stop. It was as though he held a high-powered line in his naked hand. His nerves tightened. As the wheel increased its speed it seemed to draw him more and more into its power, as though it held his fate; and with it came a deep need to submit, to whirl, to lose himself in its swirl of color. He could not stop it now. So let it be.

The button rested snugly in his palm where the man had placed it. And now he became aware of the man beside him, advising him through the microphone, while behind the shadowy audience hummed with noisy voices. He shifted his feet. There was still that feeling of helplessness within him, making part of him desire to turn back, even now that the jackpot was right in his hand. He squeezed the button until his fist ached. Then, like the sudden shriek of a subway whistle, a doubt tore through his head. Suppose he did not spin the wheel long enough? What could he do, and how could he tell? And then he knew, even as he wondered, that as long as he pressed the button, he could control the jackpot. He and only he could determine whether or not it was to be his. Not even the man with the microphone could do anything about it now. He felt drunk. Then, as though he had come down from a high hill into a valley of people, he heard the audience yelling.

"Come down from there, you jerk!"

"Let somebody else have a chance . . ."

"Ole Jack thinks he done found the end of the rainbow . . ."

The last voice was not unfriendly, and he turned and smiled dreamily into the yelling mouths. Then he turned his back squarely on them.

"Don't take too long, boy," a voice said.

He nodded. They were yelling behind him. Those folks did not understand what had happened to him. They had been playing the bingo game day in and night out for years, trying to win rent money or hamburger change. But not one of those wise guys had discovered this wonderful thing. He watched the wheel whirling past the numbers and experienced a burst of exaltation: This is God! This is the really truly God! He said it aloud, "This is God!"

He said it with such absolute conviction that he feared he would fall fainting into the footlights. But the crowd yelled so loud that they could not hear. These fools, he thought. I'm here trying to tell them the most wonderful secret in the world, and they're yelling like they gone crazy. A hand fell upon his shoulder.

"You'll have to make a choice now, boy. You've taken too long."

He brushed the hand violently away.

"Leave me alone, man. I know what I'm doing!"

The man looked surprised and held on to the microphone for support. And because he did not wish to hurt the man's feelings he smiled, realizing with a sudden pang that there was no way of explaining to the man just why he had to stand there pressing the button forever.

"Come here," he called tiredly.

The man approached, rolling the heavy microphone across the stage.

"Anybody can play this bingo game, right?" he said.

"Sure, but . . ."

He smiled, feeling inclined to be patient with this slick looking white man with his blue shirt and his sharp gabardine suit.

"That's what I thought," he said. "Anybody can win the jackpot as long as they get the lucky number, right?"

"That's the rule, but after all . . ."

"That's what I thought," he said. "And the big prize goes to the man who knows how to win it?"

The man nodded speechlessly.

"Well then, go on over there and watch me win like I want to. I ain't going to hurt nobody," he said, "and I'll show you how to win. I mean to show the whole world how it's got to be done."

And because he understood, he smiled again to let the man know that he held nothing against him for being white and impatient. Then he refused to see the man any longer and stood pressing the button, the voices of the crowd reaching him like sounds in distant streets. Let them yell. All the Negroes down there were just ashamed because he was black like them. He smiled inwardly, knowing how it was. Most of the time he was ashamed of what Negroes did himself. Well, let them be ashamed for something this time. Like him. He was like a long thin black wire that was being stretched and wound upon the bingo wheel; wound until he wanted to scream; wound, but this time himself controlling the winding and the sadness and the shame, and because he did, Laura would be all right. Suddenly the lights flickered. He staggered backwards. Had something gone wrong? All this noise. Didn't they know that although he controlled the wheel, it also controlled him, and unless he pressed the button forever and forever and ever it would stop, leaving him high and dry, dry and high on this hard high slippery hill and Laura dead? There was only one chance; he had to do whatever the wheel demanded. And gripping the button in despair, he discovered with surprise that it imparted a nervous energy. His spine tingled. He felt a certain power.

Now he faced the raging crowd with defiance, its screams penetrating his eardrums like trumpets shrieking from a juke-box. The vague faces glowing in the bingo lights gave him a sense of himself that he had never known before. He was running the show, by God! They had to react to him, for he was their luck. This is *me*, he thought. Let the bastards yell. Then someone was laughing inside him, and he realized that somehow he had forgotten his own name. It was a sad, lost feeling to lose your name, and a crazy thing to do. That name had been given him by the white man who had owned his grandfather a long lost time ago down South. But maybe those wise guys knew his name.

"Who am I?" he screamed.

"Hurry up and bingo, you jerk!"

They didn't know either, he thought sadly. They didn't even know their own names, they were all poor nameless bastards. Well, he didn't need that old name; he was reborn. For as long as he pressed the button he was The-man-who-pressed-the-button-who-held-the-prize-who-was-the-King-of-Bingo. That was the way it was, and he'd have to press the button even if nobody understood, even though Laura did not understand.

"Live!" he shouted.

The audience quieted like the dying of a huge fan.

"Live, Laura, baby. I got holt of it now, sugar. Live!"

He screamed it, tears streaming down his face. "I got nobody but YOU!"

The screams tore from his very guts. He felt as though the rush of blood to his head would burst out in baseball seams of small red droplets, like a head beaten by police clubs. Bending over he saw a trickle of blood splashing the toe of his shoe. With his free hand he searched his head. It was his nose. God, suppose something has gone wrong? He felt that the whole audience had somehow entered him and was stamping its feet in his stomach and he was unable to throw them out. They wanted the prize, that was it. They wanted the secret for themselves. But they'd never get it; he would keep the bingo wheel whirling forever, and Laura would be safe in the wheel. But would she? It had to be, because if she were not safe the wheel would cease to turn; it could not go on. He had to get away, *vomit* all, and his mind formed an image of himself running with Laura in his arms down the tracks of the subway just ahead of an A train,[2] running desperately *vomit* with people screaming for him to come out but knowing no way of leaving the tracks because to stop would bring the train crushing down upon him and to attempt to leave

---

2. New York City subway line.

across the other tracks would mean to run into a hot third rail as high as his waist which threw blue sparks that blinded his eyes until he could hardly see.

He heard singing and the audience was clapping its hands.

> *Shoot the liquor to him, Jim, boy!*
> *Clap-clap-clap*
> *Well a-calla the cop*
> *He's blowing his top!*
> *Shoot the liquor to him, Jim, boy!*

Bitter anger grew within him at the singing. They think I'm crazy. Well let 'em laugh. I'll do what I got to do.

He was standing in an attitude of intense listening when he saw that they were watching something on the stage behind him. He felt weak. But when he turned he saw no one. If only his thumb did not ache so. Now they were applauding. And for a moment he thought that the wheel had stopped. But that was impossible, his thumb still pressed the button. Then he saw them. Two men in uniform beckoned from the end of the stage. They were coming toward him, walking in step, slowly, like a tap-dance team returning for a third encore. But their shoulders shot forward, and he backed away, looking wildly about. There was nothing to fight them with. He had only the long black cord which led to a plug somewhere back stage, and he couldn't use that because it operated the bingo wheel. He backed slowly, fixing the men with his eyes as his lips stretched over his teeth in a tight, fixed grin; moved toward the end of the stage and realizing that he couldn't go much further, for suddenly the cord became taut and he couldn't afford to break the cord. But he had to do something. The audience was howling. Suddenly he stopped dead, seeing the men halt, their legs lifted as in an interrupted step of a slow-motion dance. There was nothing to do but run in the other direction and he dashed forward, slipping and sliding. The men fell back, surprised. He struck out violently going past.

"Grab him!"

He ran, but all too quickly the cord tightened, resistingly, and he turned and ran back again. This time he slipped them, and discovered by running in a circle before the wheel he could keep the cord from tightening. But this way he had to flail his arms to keep the men away. Why couldn't they leave a man alone? He ran, circling.

"Ring down the curtain," someone yelled. But they couldn't do that. If they did the wheel flashing from the projection room would be cut off. But they had him before he could tell them so, trying to pry open his fist, and he was wrestling and trying to bring his knees into the fight and holding on to the button, for it was his life. And now he was down, seeing a foot coming down, crushing his wrist cruelly, down, as he saw the wheel whirling serenely above.

"I can't give it up," he screamed. Then quietly, in a confidential tone, "Boys, I really can't give it up."

It landed hard against his head. And in the blank moment they had it away from him, completely now. He fought them trying to pull him up from the stage as he watched the wheel spin slowly to a stop. Without surprise he saw it rest at double-zero.

"You see," he pointed bitterly.

"Sure, boy, sure, it's O.K.," one of the men said smiling.

And seeing the man bow his head to someone he could not see, he felt very, very happy; he would receive what all the winners received.

But as he warmed in the justice of the man's tight smile he did not see the man's slow wink, nor see the bow-legged man behind him step clear of the swiftly descending curtain and set himself for a blow. He only felt the dull pain exploding in his skull, and he knew even as it slipped out of him that his luck had run out on the stage.

1944

---

RELATED:

—Ellison, An Interview, p. 881

# LOUISE ERDRICH
### b. 1954

Erdrich was born in Little Falls, Minnesota, of German-American and Chippewa descent. She grew up in Wahpeton, North Dakota, and graduated from Dartmouth College. Her thriving literary career has included the publication of three books of poems, *Jacklight* (1984), *Baptism of Desire* (1989), and *Original Fire* (2003), the novels *Love Medicine* (1984), *The Beet Queen* (1986), *Tracks* (1988), *The Bingo Palace* (1994), and *Tales of Burning Love* (1996), as well as *The Crown of Columbus* (1991), which she coauthored with her then-husband, Michael Dorris. Her recent works include the novels *The Painted Drum* (2005), *The Plague of Doves* (2008), *Shadow Tag* (2010), and *The Round House* (2012), which won the National Book Award that year. She has received ample recognition for the quality of her work, including a fellowship from the National Endowment for the Arts and a Guggenheim Fellowship. *Love Medicine* was the winner of the National Book Critics Circle Award for fiction.

## Matchimanito

We started dying before the snow, and, like the snow, we continued to fall. We were surprised that so many of us were left to die. For those who survived the spotted sickness from the south and our long fight west to Dakota land, where we signed the treaty, and then a wind from the east, bringing exile in a storm of government papers, what descended from the north in 1914 seemed terrible, and unjust.

By then we thought disaster must surely have spent its force, that disease must have claimed all of the Anishinabe[1] that the earth could hold and bury.

But along with the first bitter punishments of early winter a new sickness swept down. The consumption, it was called by young Father Damien, who came in that year to replace the priest who had succumbed to the same devastation as his flock. This disease was different from the pox and fever, for it came on slowly. The outcome, however, was just as certain. Whole families of Anishinabe lay ill and helpless in its breath. On the reservation, where we were forced close together, the clans dwindled. Our tribe unraveled like a coarse rope, frayed at either end as the old and new among us were taken. My own family was wiped out one by one. I was the only Nanapush[2] who lived.

---

1. Ojibwa, American Indian tribe of the western Great Lakes region. 2. The narrator's family.

And after, although I had seen no more than fifty winters, I was considered an old man.

I guided the last buffalo hunt. I saw the last bear shot. I trapped the last beaver with a pelt of more than two years' growth. I spoke aloud the words of the government treaty and refused to sign the settlement papers that would take away our woods and lake. I axed the last birch that was older than I, and I saved the last of the Pillager family.

Fleur.[3]

We found her on a cold afternoon in late winter, out in her family's cabin near Matchimanito Lake, where my companion, Edgar Pukwan, of the tribal police, was afraid to go. The water there was surrounded by the highest oaks, by woods inhabited by ghosts and roamed by Pillagers, who knew the secret ways to cure or kill, until their art deserted them. Dragging our sled into the clearing, we saw two things: the smokeless tin chimney spout jutting from the roof, and the empty hole in the door where the string was drawn inside. Pukwan did not want to enter, fearing that the unburied Pillager spirits might seize him by the throat and turn him windigo.[4] So I was the one who broke the thin-scraped hide that made a window. I was the one who lowered himself into the stinking silence, onto the floor. I was also the one to find the old man and woman, the little brother and two sisters, stone cold and wrapped in gray horse blankets, their faces turned to the west.

Afraid as I was, stilled by their quiet forms, I touched each bundle in the gloom of the cabin, and wished each spirit a good journey on the three-day road, the old-time road, so well trampled by our people this deadly season. Then something in the corner knocked. I flung the door wide. It was the eldest daughter, Fleur, so feverish that she'd thrown off her covers. She huddled against the cold wood range, staring and shaking. She was wild as a filthy wolf, a big bony girl whose sudden bursts of strength and snarling cries terrified the listening Pukwan. I was the one who struggled to lash her to the sacks of supplies and to the boards of the sled. I wrapped blankets over her and tied them down as well.

Pukwan kept us back, convinced that he should carry out the agency's instructions to the letter: he carefully nailed up the official quarantine sign, and then, without removing the bodies, he tried to burn down the house. But though he threw kerosene repeatedly against the logs and even started a blaze with birch bark and chips of wood, the flames narrowed and shrank, went out in puffs of smoke. Pukwan cursed and looked desperate, caught between his official duties and his fear of Pillagers. The fear won out. He finally dropped the tinders and helped me drag Fleur along the trail.

And so we left five dead at Matchimanito, frozen behind their cabin door.

Some say that Pukwan and I should have done right and buried the Pillagers first thing. They say the unrest and curse of trouble that struck our people in the years that followed was the doing of dissatisfied spirits. I know what's fact, and have never been afraid of talking. Our trouble came from the living, from liquor and the dollar bill. We stumbled toward the government bait,

---

3. Flower (French).    4. In Algonquin lore someone transformed into a cannibalistic giant by tasting human flesh.

never looking down, never noticing how the land was snatched from under us at every step.

When Edgar Pukwan's turn came to draw the sled, he took off like devils chased him, bounced Fleur over potholes as if she were a log, and tipped her twice into the snow. I followed the sled, encouraged Fleur with songs, cried at Pukwan to watch for hidden branches and deceptive drops, and finally got her to my cabin, a small, tightly tamped box overlooking the crossroads.

"Help me," I cried, cutting at the ropes, not even bothering with knots. Fleur closed her eyes, panted, and tossed her head from side to side. Her chest rattled as she strained for air; she grabbed me around the neck. Still weak from my own bout with the sickness, I staggered, fell, lurched into my cabin, wrestling the strong girl inside with me. I had no wind left over to curse Pukwan, who watched but refused to touch her, turned away, and vanished with the whole sled of supplies. I was neither surprised nor caused enduring sorrow later when Pukwan's son, also named Edgar and also of the tribal police, told me that his father came home, crawled into bed, and took no food from that moment until his last breath passed.

As for Fleur, each day she improved in small changes. First her gaze focused, and the next night her skin was cool and damp. She was clearheaded, and after a week she remembered what had befallen her family, how they had taken sick so suddenly, gone under. With her memory mine came back, only too sharply. I was not prepared to think of the people I had lost, or to speak of them, although we did, carefully, without letting their names loose in the wind that would reach their ears.

We feared that they would hear us and never rest, come back out of pity for the loneliness we felt. They would sit in the snow outside the door, waiting until from longing we joined them. We would all be together on the journey then, our destination the village at the end of the road, where people gamble day and night but never lose their money, eat but never fill their stomachs, drink but never leave their minds.

The snow receded enough for us to dig the ground with picks. As a tribal policeman, Pukwan's son was forced by regulation to help bury the dead. So again we took the dark road to Matchimanito, the son leading rather than the father. We spent the day chipping at the earth until we had a hole long and deep enough to lay the Pillagers shoulder to shoulder. We covered them and built five small board houses. I scratched out their clan markers, four crosshatched bears and a marten; then Pukwan Junior shouldered the government's tools and took off down the path. I settled myself near the graves.

I asked those Pillagers, as I had asked my own children and wives, to leave us now and never come back. I offered tobacco, smoked a pipe of red willow for the old man. I told them not to pester their daughter just because she had survived, or to blame me for finding them, or Pukwan Junior for leaving too soon. I told them that I was sorry, but they must abandon us. I insisted. But the Pillagers were as stubborn as the Nanapush clan and would not leave my thoughts. I think they followed me home. All the way down the trail, just beyond the edges of my sight, they flickered, thin as needles, shadows piercing shadows.

The sun had set by the time I got back, but Fleur was awake, sitting in the dark as if she knew. She never moved to build up the fire, never asked where I had been. I never told her about it either, and as the days passed we spoke rarely, always with roundabout caution. We felt the spirits of the dead so near that at length we just stopped talking.

This made it worse.

Their names grew within us, swelled to the brink of our lips, forced our eyes open in the middle of the night. We were filled with the water of the drowned, cold and black—airless water that lapped against the seal of our tongues or leaked slowly from the corners of our eyes. Within us, like ice shards, their names bobbed and shifted. Then the slivers of ice began to collect and cover us. We became so heavy, weighted down with the lead-gray frost, that we could not move. Our hands lay on the table like cloudy blocks. The blood within us grew thick. We needed no food. And little warmth. Days passed, weeks, and we didn't leave the cabin for fear we'd crack our cold and fragile bodies. We had gone half windigo. I learned later that this was common, that many of our people died in this manner, of the invisible sickness. Some could not swallow another bite of food because the names of their dead thickened on their tongues. Some let their blood stop, took the road west after all.

One day the new priest—just a boy, really—opened our door. A dazzling and painful light flooded through and surrounded Fleur and me. Numb, stupid as bears in a winter den, we blinked at the priest's slight silhouette. Our lips were parched, stuck together. We could hardly utter a greeting, but we were saved by one thought: a guest must eat. Fleur gave Father Damien her chair and put wood on the gray coals. She found flour for gaulette. I went to fetch snow to boil for tea water, but to my amazement the ground was bare. I was so surprised that I bent over and touched the soft, wet earth.

My voice rasped at first when I tried to speak, but then, oiled by strong tea, lard, and bread, I was off and talking. You could not stop me with a sledge-hammer, once I started. Father Damien looked astonished, and then wary, as I began to creak and roll. I gathered speed. I talked both languages in streams that ran alongside each other, over every rock, around every obstacle. The sound of my voice convinced me I was alive. I kept Father Damien listening all night, his green eyes round, his thin face straining to understand, his odd brown hair in curls and clipped knots. Occasionally he took in air, as if to add observations of his own, but I pushed him under with my words.

I don't know when Fleur slipped out.

She was too young and had no stories or depth of life to rely upon. All she had was raw power, and the names of the dead that filled her. I can speak them now. They have no more interest in any of us. Old Pillager. Ogimaakwe, Boss Woman, his wife. Asasaweminikwesens, Chokecherry Girl. Bineshii, Small Bird, also known as Josette. And the last, the boy Ombaashi, He Is Lifted by Wind.

They are gone, but sometimes I don't know where they are anymore—this place of reservation surveys or the other place, boundless, where the dead sit talking, see too much, and regard the living as fools.

And we were. Starvation makes fools of anyone. In the past some had sold their allotment land for a hundred pound weight of flour. Others, who were desperate to hold on, now urged that we get together and buy back our land, or at least pay a tax and refuse the settlement money that would sweep the marks of our boundaries off the map like a pattern of straws. Many were determined not to allow the hired surveyors, or even our own people, to enter the deepest bush.

But that spring outsiders went in as before, permitted by the agent, a short round man with hair blond as chaff. The purpose of these people was to measure the lake. Only now they walked upon the fresh graves of Pillagers, crossed death roads to plot out the deepest water where the lake monster, Misshepeshu, hid and waited.

"Stay here with me," I said to Fleur when she came to visit.

She refused.

"The land will go," I told her. "The land will be sold and measured."

But she tossed back her hair and walked off, down the path, with nothing to eat till thaw but a bag of my onions and a sack of oats.

Who knows what happened? She returned to Matchimanito and stayed there alone in the cabin that even fire did not want. A young girl had never done such a thing before. I heard that in those months she was asked for fee money for the land. The agent went out there and got lost, spent a whole night following the moving lights and lamps of people who would not answer him but talked and laughed among themselves. They let him go, at dawn, only because he was so stupid. Yet he went out there to ask Fleur for money again, and the next thing we heard he was living in the woods and eating roots, gambling with ghosts.

Some had ideas. You know how old chickens scratch and gabble. That's how the tales started, all the gossip, the wondering, all the things people said without knowing and then believed, since they heard it with their own ears, from their own lips, each word.

I am not one to take notice of the talk of those who fatten in the shade of the new agent's storehouse. But I watched the old agent, the one who was never found, take the rutted turnoff to Matchimanito. He was replaced by a darker man who spoke long and hard with many of our own about a money settlement. But nothing changed my mind. I've seen too much go by—unturned grass below my feet, and overhead the great white cranes flung south forever.

I am a holdout, like the Pillagers, and I told the agent, in good English, what I thought of his treaty paper. I could have written my name, and much more too, in script. I had a Jesuit education in the halls of Saint John[5] before I ran back to the woods and forgot all my prayers.

Since I had saved Fleur from the sickness, I was entangled with her. Not that I knew it at first. Only when I look back do I see a pattern. I was the vine of a wild grape that twined the timbers and drew them close. I was a branch that lived long enough to touch the next tree over, which was Pillagers. The story, like all stories, is never visible while it is happening. Only after, when an old man sits dreaming and talking in his chair, does the design spring clear.

There was so much I saw, and never knew.

When Fleur came down onto the reservation, walking right through town, no one guessed what she hid in that green rag of a dress. I do remember that it was too small, split down the back and strained across the front. That's

---

5. Roman Catholic school in Wahpeton, North Dakota.

what I noticed when I greeted her. Not whether she had money in the dress, or a child.

Other people speculated.

They added up the money she used now to buy supplies and how the agent disappeared from his post, and came out betting she would have a baby. He could have paid cash to Fleur and then run off in shame. She could even have stolen cash from him, cursed him dead, and hidden his remains. Everybody would have known, they thought, in nine months or less, if young Eli Kashpaw hadn't gone out and muddied the waters.

This Eli never cared to figure out business, politics, or church. He never applied for a chunk of land or registered himself. Eli hid from authorities, never saw the inside of a classroom, and although his mother, Margaret, got baptized in the church and tried to collar him for Mass, the best he could do was sit outside the big pine door and whittle pegs. For money Eli chopped wood, pitched hay, harvested potatoes or cranberry bark. He wanted to be a hunter, though, like me, and he had asked to partner that winter before the sickness.

I think like animals, have perfect understanding for where they hide. I can track a deer back through time and brush and cleared field to the place where it was born. Only one thing is wrong with teaching these things, however. I showed Eli how to hunt and trap from such an early age that he lived too much in the company of trees and wind. At fifteen he was uncomfortable around human beings. Especially women. So I had to help him out some.

I'm a Nanapush, remember. That's as good as saying I knew what interested Eli Kashpaw. He wanted something other than what I could teach him about the woods. He was no longer curious only about where a mink will fish or burrow, or when pike will lie low or bite. He wanted to hear how, in the days before the priest's ban and the sickness, I had satisfied three wives.

"Nanapush," Eli said, appearing at my door one day, "I have to ask you something."

"Come on in here, then," I said. "I won't bite you like the little girls do."

He was steadier, more serious, than he was the winter we went out together on the trapline. I was going to wonder what the different thing about him was when he said, "Fleur Pillager."

"She's no little girl," I answered, motioning toward the table. He told me his story.

It began when Eli got himself good and lost up near Matchimanito. He was hunting a doe in a light rain, having no luck until he rounded a slough and shot badly, which wasn't unusual. She was wounded to death but not crippled. She might walk all day, which shamed him, so he dabbed a bit of her blood on the barrel of his gun, the charm I taught him, and he followed her trail.

He had a time of it. She sawed through the woods, took the worst way, moved into heavy brush like a ghost. For hours Eli blazed his passage with snapped branches and clumps of leaves, scuffed the ground, or left a bootprint. But the trail and the day wore on, and for some reason that he did not understand, he gave up and quit leaving sign.

"That was when you should have turned back," I told him. "You should have known. It's no accident people don't like to go there. Those trees are too big, thick, and twisted at the top like bent arms. In the wind their limbs cast, creak against each other, snap. The leaves speak a cold language that overfills your brain. You want to lie down. You want never to get up. You hunger. You rake black chokecherries off their stems and stuff them down, and then you shit like a bird. Your blood thins. You're too close to where the Lake Man lives. And you're too close to where I buried the Pillagers during the long sickness that claimed them like it claimed the Nanapush clan."

I said this to Eli Kashpaw: "I understand Fleur. I am alone in this. I know that was no ordinary doe drawing you out there."

But the doe was real enough, he told me, and it was gut-shot and weakening. The blood dropped fresher, darker, until he thought he heard her just ahead and bent to the ground, desperate to see in the falling dusk, and looked ahead to catch a glimpse, and instead saw the glow of fire. He started toward it, then stopped just outside the circle of light. The deer hung, already split, turning back and forth on a rope. When he saw the woman, gutting with long quick movements, her arms bloody and bare, he stepped into the clearing.

"That's mine," he said.

I hid my face, shook my head.

"You should have turned back," I told him. "Stupid! You should have left it."

But he was stubborn, a vein of Kashpaw that held out for what it had coming. He couldn't have taken the carcass home anyway, couldn't have lugged it back, even if he had known his direction. Yet he stood his ground with the woman and said he'd tracked that deer too far to let it go. She did not respond. "Or maybe half," he thought, studying her back, uncomfortable. Even so, that was as generous as he could get.

She kept working. Never noticed him. He was so ignorant that he reached out and tapped her on the shoulder. She never even twitched. He walked around her, watched the knife cut, trespassed into her line of vision.

At last she saw him, he said, but then scorned him as though he were nothing.

"Little fly"—she straightened her back, the knife loose and casual in her hand—"quit buzzing."

Eli said she looked so wild her beauty didn't throw him, and I leaned closer, worried as he said this, worried as he reported how her hair was clumped with dirt, her face thin as a bony bitch's, her dress a rag that hung, and no curve to her except her breasts.

He noticed some things.

"No curve?" I said, thinking of the rumors.

He shook his head, impatient to continue his story. He felt sorry for her, he said. I told him the last man who was interested in Fleur Pillager had vanished, never to be found. She made us all uneasy, out there so alone. I was a friend to the Pillagers before they died off, I said, and I was safe from Fleur because the two of us had mourned the dead together. She was almost a relative. But that wasn't the case with him.

Eli looked at me with an unbelieving frown. Then he said he didn't see where she was so dangerous. After a while he had recognized her manner as exhaustion more than anger. She made no protest when he took out his own knife and helped her work. Halfway through the job she allowed him to finish, and then Eli hoisted most of the meat into the tree. He took the choice parts into the cabin. She let him in, hardly noticed him, and he helped her start the small range and even took it on himself to melt lard. She ate the whole heart, fell on it like a starved animal, and then her eyes shut.

From the way he described her actions, I was sure she was pregnant. I'm familiar with the signs, and I can talk about this since I'm an old man, far past anything a woman can do to weaken me. I was more certain still when Eli said that he took her in his arms, helped her to a pile of blankets on a willow bed. And then—hard to believe, even though it was, for the first time, the right thing to do—Eli rolled up in a coat on the other side of the cabin floor and lay there all night, and slept alone.

"So," I said, "why have you come to me now? You got away, you survived, she even let you find your way home. You learned your lesson and none the worse."

"I want her," Eli said.

I could not believe that I heard right, but we were sitting by the stove, face to face, so there was no doubt. I rose and turned away. Maybe I was less than generous, having lost my own girls. Maybe I wanted to keep Fleur as my daughter, who would visit me, joke with me, beat me at cards. But I believe it was only for Eli's own good that I was harsh.

"Forget that thing so heavy in our pocket," I said, "or put it somewhere else. Go town way and find yourself a tamer woman."

He brooded at my tabletop and then spoke. "I want know-how, not warnings, not my mother's caution."

"You don't want instruction!" I was pushed too far. "Love medicine is what you're after. A Nanapush never needed any, but Old Lady Aintapi or the Pillagers, they sell it. Go ask Moses for a medicine and pay your price."

"I don't want anything that can wear off," the boy said. He was determined. Maybe his new, steady coolness was the thing that turned my mind, the quiet of him. He was different, sitting there so still. It struck me that he had come into his growth, and who was I to hold him back from going to a Pillager, since someone had to, since the whole tribe had got to thinking that she couldn't be left alone out there, a girl ready to go wild, a woman whose family would not leave her, even dead, but stayed close to her, whispered, passed on their power. People said that she had to be harnessed. Maybe, I thought, Eli was the young man to do it, even though he couldn't rub two words together and get a spark.

So I gave in. I told him what he wanted to know. He asked me the old-time way to make a woman love him, and I went into detail so that he would make no disgraceful error. I told him about the first woman who had given herself to me. Sanawashonekek, her name was, The Lying-Down Grass, for the place where a deer has spent the night. I described the finicky taste of Omiimii, The Dove, and the trials I'd gone through to keep my second wife pleasured. Zezikaaikwe, The Unexpected, was a woman whose name was the exact prediction of her desires. I gave him a few things from the French trunk my third wife left—a white woman's fan, bead leggings, a little girl's soft doll made of fawn skin.

When Eli Kashpaw stroked their beauty and asked where these things had come from, I remembered the old days, opened my mouth.

Talk is an old man's last vice.

I wore out the boy's ears, but that is not my fault. I shouldn't have been caused to live so long, been shown so much of death, had to squeeze so many stories into the corners of my brain. They're all attached, and once I start, the telling doesn't end, because they're hooked from one side to the other, mouth to tail.

During the year of sickness, when I was the last one left, I saved myself by starting a story. One night I was ready to bring to the other side the fawn-skin doll I now gave Eli. My wife had sewn it together after our daughter died, and I held it in my hands when I fainted, lost breath so that I could hardly keep moving my lips. But I did continue and recovered. I got well by talking. Death could not get a word in edgewise, grew discouraged, and traveled on.

Eli returned to Fleur, and stopped badgering me, which I took as a sign she liked the fan, the bead leggings, and maybe the rest of Eli, the part where he was on his own. The thing I've found about women is that you must use every instinct to confuse.

"Look here," I told Eli, before he went out my door. "It's like you're a log in a stream. Along comes this bear. She jumps on. Don't let her dig in her claws."

So keeping Fleur off balance was what I presumed Eli was doing. But, as I learned in time, he was further along than that, way off and running beyond the reach of anything I said.

His mother was the one who gave me the news.

Margaret Kashpaw was a woman who had sunk her claws in the log and peeled it to a toothpick, and she wasn't going to let any man forget it. Especially me, her dead husband's partner in some youthful pursuits.

"Aneesh," she said, slamming my door shut. Margaret never knocked, because with warning you might get your breath, or escape. She was headlong, bossy, scared of nobody, and full of vinegar. She was a little woman, but so blinded by irritation that she'd take on anyone. She was thin on the top and plump as a turnip below, with a face like a round molasses cake. On each side of it gray plaits hung. With age her part had widened down the middle so that it looked as though the braids were slipping off her head. Her eyes were harsh, bright, and her tongue was honed keen. She sat right down.

"Would you care to know what you have my son doing?"

I mumbled, kept reading by the window, tucked my spectacles from Father Damien more comfortably around my ears. My newspaper came from Grand Forks once a week, and I wasn't about to let Margaret spoil my pleasure or get past my hiding place.

"*Sah!*" She swiped at the sheets with her hand, grazed the print, but never quite dared to flip it aside. This was not for any fear of me, however. She didn't want the tracks rubbing off on her skin. She never learned to read, and the mystery troubled her.

I took advantage of that, snapped the paper in front of my face and sat for a moment. But she won, of course, because she knew I'd get curious. I felt her eyes glittering beyond the paper, and when I put the pages down, she continued.

"Who learned my Eli to make love standing up? Who learned him to have a woman against a tree in clear daylight? Who learned him to . . ."

"Wait," I said. "How'd you get to know this?"

She shrugged it off, and said in a smaller voice, "Boy Lazarre."

And I, who knew that the dirty Lazarres don't spy for nothing, just smiled. "How much did you pay the fat-bellied dog?"

"The Lazarres are like animals in their season! No sense of shame!" But the wind was out of her. "Against the wall of the cabin," she said. "Down beside it. In grass and up in trees. Who'd he learn that from?"

"Maybe my late partner Kashpaw."

She puffed her cheeks out, fumed. "Not from him!"

"Not that you knew." I put my spectacles carefully upon the windowsill. Her hand could snake out quickly.

She hissed. The words flew like razor grass between her teeth. "Old man," she said with scorn. "Two wrinkled berries and a twig."

"A twig can grow," I offered.

"But only in the spring."

Then she was gone, out the door, leaving my tongue tingling for the last word, and still ignorant of the full effect of my advice. I didn't wonder until later if it didn't go both ways, though—if Fleur had wound her private hairs around the buttons of Eli's shirt, if she had stirred smoky powders or crushed snakeroot into his tea. Perhaps she had bitten his nails in sleep and swallowed the ends, snipped threads from his clothing and made a doll of them to wear between her legs. For they got bolder, until the whole reservation gossiped.

Then one day the big, unsteady Lazarre, an Indian on whose birth certificate was recorded simply "Boy," returned from the woods talking backwards, garbled, mixing his words. At first people thought the sights of passion had cleft his mind. Then they figured otherwise, imagined that Fleur had caught Lazarre watching and tied him up, cut his tongue out, and sewn it in reversed.

The same day I heard this, Margaret burst into my house a second time.

"Take me out to their place, you four-eyes," she said. "And be ready with the boat tomorrow, sunup!"

She stamped through the door and vanished, leaving me with hardly time enough to patch the seams and holes of the old-time boat I kept, dragged up in a brush shelter on the quieter inlet, the south end of the lake. I took some boiled pine gum to the seams that afternoon, and did my best. I was drawn to the situation, curious myself, and though I didn't want to spy either on the girl whose life I'd saved or on the boy I'd advised on courting, I was down by the water with the paddles at dawn.

The light was chill and green, the waves on the lake were small, confused ripples, and no steady wind had gathered. The water could be deceptive, set snares for the careless young or for withered-up and eager fools like ourselves. I put my hand in the current.

"Margaret," I said, "the lake's too cold. I never could swim, either, not that well."

But Margaret had set her mind, and made her peace, too.

"If he wants me"—she was talking about the lake spirit but, out of caution, using no names—"I'll give him good as I get."

"Oh," I said, "has it been that long, Margaret?"

Her eyes lit and I wished I had kept my mouth shut. But she only commented, later, after we had launched, "Not so long that I would consider the dregs."

I handed her the lard can I kept my bait in. "You better take this, Margaret. You better bail."

So at least on that long trip across I had the satisfaction of seeing her bend to the dipping and pouring with a sour but desperate will. We rode low. The water covered our ankles by the time we beached on shore, but Margaret was forced to shut her mouth in a firm line. The whole idea had been hers. She was so relieved to stand finally upon solid ground that she helped me haul the boat and wedge it in a pile of mangled roots. She wrung her skirt and sat beside me, panting. She shared some dried meat from the pocket of her dress, tore at it like a young snapping turtle. How I envied her sharp, strong teeth.

"Go on, eat," she said, "or I'll take an insult."

I put the jerky into my mouth.

"That's right," she sneered. "Suck long enough and it will soften."

I had no choice. I could think of no other way to get any of it down.

"Go now," I said, after a while. "I was thinking. I had this old barren she-dog once. She'd back up to anything. But the only satisfaction she could get was from watching the young."

Margaret jumped to her feet, skirts flapping. I had said too much. Her claws gave my ears too fast, furious jerks that set me whirling, sickening me so that I couldn't balance or even keep track of time. She took herself up the bank and into the Pillager woods, but I don't know when she went there or how long she stayed, and I had barely set myself to rights before she returned.

By then the sky had gone dead gray, the waves rolled white and fitful. Margaret took tobacco from a pouch in her pocket, threw it on the water, and said a few distracted, imploring words. We jumped into the boat, which leaked worse than ever, and pushed off. The wind blew harsh, in heavy circular gusts, and I was hard put. I never saw the bailing can move so fast, before or since. The old woman made it flash and dip, and hardly even broke the rhythm when, halfway across, she reached into her pocket again and this time dumped the whole pouch into the pounding waves. From then on she alternated between working her arms and addressing different Manitous[6] along with the Blessed Virgin and Her heart, the sacred bloody lump that the blue-robed woman held in the awful picture Margaret kept nailed to her wall. We made it back by the time rain poured down, and hoisted ourselves over the edge of the boat. When we got back to my house, after she'd swallowed some warm broth and her clothes had begun to steam dry upon her, Margaret told me what she had seen with her own eyes.

Fleur Pillager was pregnant, going to have a child in spring. At least that's what Margaret had decided with her measuring gaze. I stirred the fire with my walking stick. Maybe I had a shiver, a feeling, a worry. I was close as a relative, closer perhaps. Maybe I knew already that when spring did come, the ice milky, porous, and broken, Margaret and I were the ones who would have to save Fleur a second time.

---

**6.** Great spirits.

Margaret, however, had no such premonition. The child would turn out fork-footed, she predicted, with straw for hair, yellow as the agent's. Its eyes would glow blue, its skin shine white. As she sipped from her cup, Margaret's memory of the agent made a monster, and she savored the variations the child might reveal: red, flapping ears, a strange birthmark, chicken lips, an extra finger, by which the taint of its conception would be certain and people convinced, at last, that it did not belong to her son.

The morning we got word, the water had just opened for a boat, if you dared to travel that way so early in spring. Fleur was in trouble with her baby. That's all I heard, as the women kept the particulars to themselves. Out of desperation Eli had run to Margaret on the way to the midwife's. He wanted us to take the shortcut and stay with Fleur until he brought back the woman whose hands held the wisdom, who wore the dried caul of a rabbit in a little belt around her waist.

Margaret was puffed up, full of satisfaction, until she saw the boat, leaking even more than usual after another winter of neglect. On the ride, bailing for her life, Margaret raged at me between her prayers and muttered strict assurances that her reasons for helping in this matter were not ties of kinship. Her presence did not count as acknowledgment, she said. It was her duty to see the evidence, whatever that turned out to be—the hair gold as straw, the blazing eyes.

But the child had none of those markings.

She was born on the day we shot the last bear, drunk, on the reservation. The midwife was the one who shot it, and the bear was drunk, not her. That she-bear had broken into the trader's wine I had brought across the lake beneath my jacket and then stowed in a rotten stump off in the woods behind the house. She bit the cork and emptied the white clay jug. Then she lost her mind and stumbled into the beaten grass of Fleur's yard.

By then we were a day in the waiting. In all that time we heard not a sound from Fleur's cabin, just crushing silence, like the inside of a drum before the stick drops. Eli and I slumped against the woodpile. We made a fire, swaddled ourselves in blankets. My stomach creaked with the lack of food, for Eli was starving himself from worry and I hated to eat in front of him. His eyes were rimmed with blood as he moaned and talked and prayed beneath the burden, which grew heavier.

On the second day we leaned to the fire, strained for the sound of the cry a baby makes. Our ears picked up everything in the woods, the rustle of birds, the crack of dead spring leaves and twigs. Our hearing had by then grown so keen that we heard the muffled sounds the women made inside the house. Now we heard other activity, which gave us hope. The stove lid clanked, pans rang together. Margaret came to the door and we heard the tear of water splashing on the ground. Eli moved then, fetched more. But not until the afternoon of that second day did the stillness finally break, and then the Manitous all through the woods seemed to speak through Fleur, loose, arguing. I recognized them. Turtle's quavering scratch, Eagle's high shriek, Loon's crazy bitterness, Otter, the howl of Wolf, Bear's low rasp.

Perhaps the bear heard Fleur calling, and answered.

I was alone when it happened, because Eli had broken when the silence shattered, slashed his arm with his hunting knife, and run out of the clearing, straight north. I sat quietly after he was gone, and sampled the food that he had refused. I drew close to the fire, settled my back against the split logs, and was just about to have a second helping when the drunk bear rambled past. She sniffed the ground, rolled over in an odor that pleased her, drew up and sat, addled, on her haunches like a dog. I jumped straight onto the top of the woodpile—I don't know how, since my limbs were so stiff from the wet cold. I crouched, yelled at the house, screamed for the gun, but only attracted the bear. She dragged herself over, gave a drawn-out whine, a cough, and fixed me with a long patient stare.

Margaret flung the door open. "Shoot it, you old fool," she hollered. But I was empty-handed. Margaret was irritated with this trifle, put out that I had not obeyed her, anxious to get rid of the nuisance and go back to Fleur. She marched straight toward us. Her face was pinched with exhaustion, her pace furious. Her arms moved like pistons, and she came so fast that she and the bear were face to face before she realized that she had nothing with which to attack. She was sensible, Margaret Kashpaw, and turned straight around. Fleur kept her gun above the flour cupboard in a rack of antlers. The bear followed, heeling Margaret like a puppy, and at the door to the house, when Margaret turned, arms spread to bar the way, it swatted her aside with one sharp, dreamy blow. Then it ambled in and reared on its hind legs.

I am a man, so I don't know exactly what happened when the bear came into the birth house, but they talk among themselves, the women, and sometimes they forget I'm listening. So I know that when Fleur saw the bear in the house she was filled with such fear and power that she raised herself on the mound of blankets and gave birth. Then the midwife took down the gun and shot point-blank, filling the bear's heart. She says so, anyway. But Margaret says that the lead only gave the bear strength, and I'll support that. For I heard the gun go off and then saw the creature whirl and roar from the house. It barreled past me, crashed through the brush into the woods, and was not seen after. It left no trail, either, so it could have been a spirit bear. I don't know. I was still on the woodpile.

I took the precaution of finishing my meal there. From what I overheard later, they were sure Fleur was dead, she was so cold and still after giving birth. But then the baby cried. That I heard with my own ears. At that sound, they say, Fleur opened her eyes and breathed. That was when the women went to work and saved her, packed moss between her legs, wrapped her in blankets heated with stones, kneaded Fleur's stomach and forced her to drink cup after cup of boiled raspberry leaf, until at last Fleur groaned, drew the baby against her breast, and lived.

1988

# WILLIAM FAULKNER
## 1897–1962

Faulkner was born in New Albany, Mississippi, to a family that had once included wealthy and powerful people ruined by the Civil War. His great-grandfather was a popular novelist, and this ancestor served, like other family members, as a model from whom Faulkner drew traits used in composing the characters in his fiction. He attended the University of Mississippi in Oxford before and after his service in the Royal Canadian Air Force in World War I. Thereafter, he lived in Oxford for most of his life, though he spent much time in Hollywood as a screenwriter. It was in New Orleans, though, that his literary career began. There he met Sherwood Anderson, who encouraged him to turn from poetry to fiction and helped him get his first novel published. His lifetime's work, which eventually won Faulkner a Nobel Prize in 1950, is largely a depiction of life in his fictional Yoknapatawpha County, an imaginative reconstruction of the area adjacent to Oxford. Faulkner was a passionately devoted hunter, and his love of the disappearing wilderness is expressed in many of his tales. He sought out the honor and courage of people thwarted by circumstance, and the sum of his writing testifies to his faith that these virtues will prevail despite the corruptions of modern life. His major novels were mostly the product of a prodigious decade of creative effort. They include *The Sound and the Fury* (1929), *As I Lay Dying* (1930), *Sanctuary* (1931), *Light in August* (1932), *Absalom, Absalom!* (1936), *The Wild Palms* (1939), and *The Hamlet* (1940). His books of short stories include *These Thirteen* (1931), *Go Down, Moses* (1942), and the *Collected Stories of William Faulkner* (1950).

## A Rose for Emily

### I

When Miss Emily Grierson died, our whole town went to her funeral: the men through a sort of respectful affection for a fallen monument, the women mostly out of curiosity to see the inside of her house, which no one save an old man-servant—a combined gardener and cook—had seen in at least ten years.

It was a big, squarish frame house that had once been white, decorated with cupolas and spires and scrolled balconies in the heavily lightsome style of the seventies,[1] set on what had once been our most select street. But garages

---

1. The 1870s, the decade following the American Civil War, mentioned at the end of the paragraph.

and cotton gins had encroached and obliterated even the august names of that neighborhood; only Miss Emily's house was left, lifting its stubborn and coquettish decay above the cotton wagons and the gasoline pumps—an eyesore among eyesores. And now Miss Emily had gone to join the representatives of those august names where they lay in the cedar-bemused cemetery among the ranked and anonymous graves of Union and Confederate soldiers who fell at the battle of Jefferson.[2]

Alive, Miss Emily had been a tradition, a duty, and a care; a sort of hereditary obligation upon the town, dating from that day in 1894 when Colonel Sartoris, the mayor—he who fathered the edict that no Negro woman should appear on the streets without an apron—remitted her taxes, the dispensation dating from the death of her father on into perpetuity. Not that Miss Emily would have accepted charity. Colonel Sartoris invented an involved tale to the effect that Miss Emily's father had loaned money to the town, which the town, as a matter of business, preferred this way of repaying. Only a man of Colonel Sartoris' generation and thought could have invented it, and only a woman could have believed it.

When the next generation, with its more modern ideas, became mayors and aldermen, this arrangement created some little dissatisfaction. On the first of the year they mailed her a tax notice. February came, and there was no reply. They wrote her a formal letter, asking her to call at the sheriff's office at her convenience. A week later the mayor wrote her himself, offering to call or to send his car for her, and received in reply a note on paper of an archaic shape, in a thin, flowing calligraphy in faded ink, to the effect that she no longer went out at all. The tax notice was also enclosed, without comment.

They called a special meeting of the Board of Aldermen. A deputation waited upon her, knocked at the door through which no visitor had passed since she ceased giving china-painting lessons eight or ten years earlier. They were admitted by the old Negro into a dim hall from which a stairway mounted into still more shadow. It smelled of dust and disuse—a close, dank smell. The Negro led them into the parlor. It was furnished in heavy, leather-covered furniture. When the Negro opened the blinds of one window, they could see that the leather was cracked; and when they sat down, a faint dust rose sluggishly about their thighs, spinning with slow motes in the single sun-ray. On a tarnished gilt easel before the fireplace stood a crayon portrait of Miss Emily's father.

They rose when she entered—a small, fat woman in black, with a thin gold chain descending to her waist and vanishing into her belt, leaning on an ebony cane with a tarnished gold head. Her skeleton was small and spare; perhaps that was why what would have been merely plumpness in another was obesity in her. She looked bloated, like a body long submerged in motionless water, and of that pallid hue. Her eyes, lost in the fatty ridges of her face, looked like two small pieces of coal pressed into a lump of dough as they moved from one face to another while the visitors stated their errand.

She did not ask them to sit. She just stood in the door and listened quietly until the spokesman came to a stumbling halt. Then they could hear the invisible watch ticking at the end of the gold chain.

2. The principal town and county seat of Faulkner's fictional Yoknapatawpha County.

Her voice was dry and cold. "I have no taxes in Jefferson. Colonel Sartoris explained it to me. Perhaps one of you can gain access to the city records and satisfy yourselves."

"But we have. We are the city authorities, Miss Emily. Didn't you get a notice from the sheriff, signed by him?"

"I received a paper, yes," Miss Emily said. "Perhaps he considers himself the sheriff . . . I have no taxes in Jefferson."

"But there is nothing on the books to show that, you see. We must go by the—"

"See Colonel Sartoris. I have no taxes in Jefferson."

"But, Miss Emily—"

"See Colonel Sartoris." (Colonel Sartoris had been dead almost ten years.) "I have no taxes in Jefferson. Tobe!" The Negro appeared. "Show these gentlemen out."

## II

So she vanquished them, horse and foot, just as she had vanquished their fathers thirty years before about the smell. That was two years after her father's death and a short time after her sweetheart—the one we believed would marry her—had deserted her. After her father's death she went out very little; after her sweetheart went away, people hardly saw her at all. A few of the ladies had the temerity to call, but were not received, and the only sign of life about the place was the Negro man—a young man then—going in and out with a market basket.

"Just as if a man—any man—could keep a kitchen properly," the ladies said; so they were not surprised when the smell developed. It was another link between the gross, teeming world and the high and mighty Griersons.

A neighbor, a woman, complained to the mayor, Judge Stevens, eighty years old.

"But what will you have me do about it, madam?" he said.

"Why, send her word to stop it," the woman said. "Isn't there a law?"

"I'm sure that won't be necessary," Judge Stevens said. "It's probably just a snake or a rat that nigger of hers killed in the yard. I'll speak to him about it."

The next day he received two more complaints, one from a man who came in diffident deprecation. "We really must do something about it, Judge. I'd be the last one in the world to bother Miss Emily, but we've got to do something." That night the Board of Aldermen met—three graybeards and one younger man, a member of the rising generation.

"It's simple enough," he said. "Send her word to have her place cleaned up. Give her a certain time to do it in, and if she don't . . ."

"Dammit, sir," Judge Stevens said, "will you accuse a lady to her face of smelling bad?"

So the next night, after midnight, four men crossed Miss Emily's lawn and slunk about the house like burglars, sniffing along the base of the brickwork and at the cellar openings while one of them performed a regular sowing motion with his hand out of a sack slung from his shoulder. They broke open the cellar door and sprinkled lime there, and in all the outbuildings. As they recrossed the lawn, a window that had been dark was lighted and Miss Emily sat in it, the light behind her, and her upright torso motionless as that of an idol. They crept quietly across the lawn and into the shadow of the locusts that lined the street. After a week or two the smell went away.

That was when people had begun to feel really sorry for her. People in our town, remembering how old lady Wyatt, her great-aunt, had gone completely crazy at last, believed that the Griersons held themselves a little too high for what they really were. None of the young men were quite good enough for Miss Emily and such. We had long thought of them as a tableau, Miss Emily a slender figure in white in the background, her father a spraddled silhouette in the foreground, his back to her and clutching a horsewhip, the two of them framed by the back-flung front door. So when she got to be thirty and was still single, we were not pleased exactly, but vindicated; even with insanity in the family she wouldn't have turned down all of her chances if they had really materialized.

When her father died, it got about that the house was all that was left to her; and in a way, people were glad. At last they could pity Miss Emily. Being left alone, and a pauper, she had become humanized. Now she too would know the old thrill and the old despair of a penny more or less.

The day after his death all the ladies prepared to call at the house and offer condolence and aid, as is our custom. Miss Emily met them at the door, dressed as usual and with no trace of grief on her face. She told them that her father was not dead. She did that for three days, with the ministers calling on her, and the doctors, trying to persuade her to let them dispose of the body. Just as they were about to resort to law and force, she broke down, and they buried her father quickly.

We did not say she was crazy then. We believed she had to do that. We remembered all the young men her father had driven away, and we knew that with nothing left, she would have to cling to that which had robbed her, as people will.

### III

She was sick for a long time. When we saw her again her hair was cut short, making her look like a girl, with a vague resemblance to those angels in colored church windows—sort of tragic and serene.

The town had just let the contracts for paving the sidewalks, and in the summer after her father's death they began the work. The construction company came with niggers and mules and machinery, and a foreman named Homer Barron, a Yankee—a big, dark, ready man, with a big voice and eyes lighter than his face. The little boys would follow in groups to hear him cuss the niggers, and the niggers singing in time to the rise and fall of picks. Pretty soon he knew everybody in town. Whenever you heard a lot of laughing anywhere about the square, Homer Barron would be in the center of the group. Presently we began to see him and Miss Emily on Sunday afternoons driving in the yellow-wheeled buggy and the matched team of bays from the livery stable.

At first we were glad that Miss Emily would have an interest, because the ladies all said, "Of course a Grierson would not think seriously of a Northerner, a day laborer." But there were still others, older people, who said that even grief could not cause a real lady to forget *noblesse oblige*—without calling it *noblesse oblige*.[3] They just said, "Poor Emily. Her kinsfolk should come to her." She had some kin in Alabama; but years ago her father had fallen out with them over the estate of old lady Wyatt, the crazy woman, and there was no communication between the two families. They had not even been represented at the funeral.

And as soon as the old people said, "Poor Emily," the whispering began. "Do you suppose it's really so?" they said to one another. "Of course it is. What else could . . ." This behind their hands; rustling of craned silk and satin behind jalousies[4] closed upon the sun of Sunday afternoon as the thin, swift clop-clop-clop of the matched team passed: "Poor Emily."

She carried her head high enough—even when we believed that she was fallen. It was as if she demanded more than ever the recognition of her dignity as the last Grierson; as if it had wanted that touch of earthiness to reaffirm her imperviousness. Like when she bought the rat poison, the arsenic. That was over a year after they had begun to say "Poor Emily," and while the two female cousins were visiting her.

"I want some poison," she said to the druggist. She was over thirty then, still a slight woman, though thinner than usual, with cold, haughty black eyes in a face the flesh of which was strained across the temples and about the eyesockets as you imagine a lighthouse-keeper's face ought to look. "I want some poison," she said.

"Yes, Miss Emily. What kind? For rats and such? I'd recom—"

"I want the best you have. I don't care what kind."

The druggist named several. "They'll kill anything up to an elephant. But what you want is—"

"Arsenic," Miss Emily said. "Is that a good one?"

"Is . . . arsenic? Yes, ma'am. But what you want—"

"I want arsenic."

The druggist looked down at her. She looked back at him, erect, her face like a strained flag. "Why, of course," the druggist said. "If that's what you want. But the law requires you to tell what you are going to use it for."

Miss Emily just stared at him, her head tilted back in order to look him eye for eye, until he looked away and went and got the arsenic and wrapped it up. The Negro delivery boy brought her the package; the druggist didn't come back. When she opened the package at home there was written on the box, under the skull and bones: "For rats."

## IV

So the next day we all said, "She will kill herself"; and we said it would be the best thing. When she had first begun to be seen with Homer Barron, we had said, "She will marry him." Then we said, "She will persuade him yet," because Homer himself had remarked—he liked men, and it was known that he drank with the younger men in the Elks' Club—that he was not a marrying man.

---

3. The obligation of the nobility or upper classes to behave with honor and generosity toward those less privileged. 4. Window blinds, made of adjustable horizontal louvers.

Later we said, "Poor Emily" behind the jalousies as they passed on Sunday afternoon in the glittering buggy, Miss Emily with her head high and Homer Barron with his hat cocked and a cigar in his teeth, reins and whip in a yellow glove.

Then some of the ladies began to say that it was a disgrace to the town and a bad example to the young people. The men did not want to interfere, but at last the ladies forced the Baptist minister—Miss Emily's people were Episcopal—to call upon her. He would never divulge what happened during that interview, but he refused to go back again. The next Sunday they again drove about the streets, and the following day the minister's wife wrote to Miss Emily's relations in Alabama.

So she had blood-kin under her roof again and we sat back to watch developments. At first nothing happened. Then we were sure that they were to be married. We learned that Miss Emily had been to the jeweler's and ordered a man's toilet set in silver, with the letters H. B. on each piece. Two days later we learned that she had bought a complete outfit of men's clothing, including a nightshirt, and we said, "They are married." We were really glad. We were glad because the two female cousins were even more Grierson than Miss Emily had ever been.

So we were not surprised when Homer Barron—the streets had been finished some time since—was gone. We were a little disappointed that there was not a public blowing-off, but we believed that he had gone on to prepare for Miss Emily's coming, or to give her a chance to get rid of the cousins. (By that time it was a cabal, and we were all Miss Emily's allies to help circumvent the cousins.) Sure enough, after another week they departed. And, as we had expected all along, within three days Homer Barron was back in town. A neighbor saw the Negro man admit him at the kitchen door at dusk one evening.

And that was the last we saw of Homer Barron. And of Miss Emily for some time. The Negro man went in and out with the market basket, but the front door remained closed. Now and then we would see her at a window for a moment, as the men did that night when they sprinkled the lime; but for almost six months she did not appear on the streets. Then we knew that this was to be expected too; as if that quality of her father which had thwarted her woman's life so many times had been too virulent and too furious to die.

When we next saw Miss Emily, she had grown fat and her hair was turning gray. During the next few years it grew grayer and grayer until it attained an even pepper-and-salt iron-gray, when it ceased turning. Up to the day of her death at seventy-four it was still that vigorous iron-gray, like the hair of an active man.

From that time on her front door remained closed, save for a period of six or seven years, when she was about forty, during which she gave lessons in china-painting. She fitted up a studio in one of the downstairs rooms, where the daughters and granddaughters of Colonel Sartoris' contemporaries were sent to her with the same regularity and in the same spirit that they were sent to church on Sundays with a twenty-five-cent piece for the collection plate. Meanwhile her taxes had been remitted.

Then the newer generation became the backbone and the spirit of the town, and the painting pupils grew up and fell away and did not send their children to her with boxes of color and tedious brushes and pictures cut from the ladies' magazines. The front door closed upon the last one and remained closed for good. When the town got free postal delivery, Miss Emily alone refused to let them fasten the metal numbers above her door and attach a mailbox to it. She would not listen to them.

Daily, monthly, yearly we watched the Negro grow grayer and more stooped, going in and out with the market basket. Each December we sent her a tax notice, which would be returned by the post office a week later, unclaimed. Now and then we would see her in one of the downstairs windows—she had evidently shut up the top floor of the house—like the carven torso of an idol in a niche, looking or not looking at us, we could never tell which. Thus she passed from generation to generation—dear, inescapable, impervious, tranquil, and perverse.

And so she died. Fell ill in the house filled with dust and shadows, with only a doddering Negro man to wait on her. We did not even know she was sick; we had long since given up trying to get any information from the Negro. He talked to no one, probably not even to her, for his voice had grown harsh and rusty, as if from disuse.

She died in one of the downstairs rooms, in a heavy walnut bed with a curtain, her gray head propped on a pillow yellow and moldy with age and lack of sunlight.

## V

The Negro met the first of the ladies at the front door and let them in, with their hushed, sibilant voices and their quick, curious glances, and then he disappeared. He walked right through the house and out the back and was not seen again.

The two female cousins came at once. They held the funeral on the second day, with the town coming to look at Miss Emily beneath a mass of bought flowers, with the crayon face of her father musing profoundly above the bier and the ladies sibilant and macabre; and the very old men—some in their brushed Confederate uniforms—on the porch and the lawn, talking of Miss Emily as if she had been a contemporary of theirs, believing that they had danced with her and courted her perhaps, confusing time with its mathematical progression, as the old do, to whom all the past is not a diminishing road but, instead, a huge meadow which no winter ever quite touches, divided from them now by the narrow bottle-neck of the most recent decade of years.

Already we knew that there was one room in that region above stairs which no one had seen in forty years, and which would have to be forced. They waited until Miss Emily was decently in the ground before they opened it.

The violence of breaking down the door seemed to fill this room with pervading dust. A thin, acrid pall as of the tomb seemed to lie everywhere upon this room decked and furnished as for a bridal: upon the valance curtains of faded rose color, upon the rose-shaded lights, upon the dressing table, upon the delicate array of crystal and the man's toilet things backed with tarnished silver, silver so tarnished that the monogram was obscured. Among them lay a collar and tie, as if they had just been removed, which, lifted, left upon the surface a pale crescent in the dust. Upon a chair hung the suit, carefully folded; beneath it the two mute shoes and the discarded socks.

The man himself lay in the bed.

For a long while we just stood there, looking down at the profound and fleshless grin. The body had apparently once lain in the attitude of an embrace, but now the long sleep that outlasts love, that conquers even the grimace of love, had cuckolded him. What was left of him, rotted beneath what was left of the nightshirt, had become inextricable from the bed in which he lay; and upon him and upon the pillow beside him lay that even coating of the patient and biding dust.

Then we noticed that in the second pillow was the indentation of a head. One of us lifted something from it, and leaning forward, that faint and invisible dust dry and acrid in the nostrils, we saw a long strand of iron-gray hair.

1930

# Barn Burning

The store in which the Justice of the Peace's court was sitting smelled of cheese. The boy, crouched on his nail keg at the back of the crowded room, knew he smelled cheese, and more: from where he sat he could see the ranked shelves close-packed with the solid, squat, dynamic shapes of tin cans whose labels his stomach read, not from the lettering which meant nothing to his mind but from the scarlet devils and the silver curve of fish—this, the cheese which he knew he smelled and the hermetic meat[1] which his intestines believed he smelled coming in intermittent gusts momentary and brief between the other constant one, the smell and sense just a little of fear because mostly of despair and grief, the old fierce pull of blood. He could not see the table where the Justice sat and before which his father and his father's enemy (*our enemy* he thought in that despair; *ourn! mine and hisn both! He's my father!*) stood, but he could hear them, the two of them that is, because his father had said no word yet:

"But what proof have you, Mr. Harris?"

"I told you. The hog got into my corn. I caught it up and sent it back to him. He had no fence that would hold it. I told him so, warned him. The next time I put the hog in my pen. When he came to get it I gave him enough wire to patch up his pen. The next time I put the hog up and kept it. I rode down to his house and saw the wire I gave him still rolled on to the spool in his yard. I told him he could have the hog when he paid me a dollar pound fee. That evening a nigger came with the dollar and got the hog. He was a strange nigger. He said, 'He say to tell you wood and hay kin burn.' I said, 'What?' 'That whut he say to tell you,' the nigger said. 'Wood and hay kin burn.' That night my barn burned. I got the stock out but I lost the barn."

"Where is the nigger? Have you got him?"

"He was a strange nigger, I tell you. I don't know what became of him."

"But that's not proof. Don't you see that's not proof?"

1. Canned meat.

"Get that boy up here. He knows." For a moment the boy thought too that the man meant his older brother until Harris said, "Not him. The little one. The boy," and, crouching, small for his age, small and wiry like his father, in patched and faded jeans even too small for him, with straight, uncombed, brown hair and eyes gray and wild as storm scud, he saw the men between himself and the table part and become a lane of grim faces, at the end of which he saw the Justice, a shabby, collarless, graying man in spectacles, beckoning him. He felt no floor under his bare feet; he seemed to walk beneath the palpable weight of the grim turning faces. His father, stiff in his black Sunday coat donned not for the trial but for the moving, did not even look at him. *He aims for me to lie,* he thought, again with that frantic grief and despair. *And I will have to do hit.*

"What's your name, boy?" the Justice said.

"Colonel Sartoris Snopes,"[2] the boy whispered.

"Hey?" the Justice said. "Talk louder. Colonel Sartoris? I reckon anybody named for Colonel Sartoris in this country can't help but tell the truth, can they?" The boy said nothing. *Enemy! Enemy!* he thought; for a moment he could not even see, could not see that the Justice's face was kindly nor discern that his voice was troubled when he spoke to the man named Harris: "Do you want me to question this boy?" But he could hear, and during those subsequent long seconds while there was absolutely no sound in the crowded little room save that of quiet and intent breathing it was as if he had swung outward at the end of a grape vine, over a ravine, and at the top of the swing had been caught in a prolonged instant of mesmerized gravity, weightless in time.

"No!" Harris said violently, explosively. "Damnation! Send him out of here!" Now time, the fluid world, rushed beneath him again, the voices coming to him again through the smell of cheese and sealed meat, the fear and despair and the old grief of blood:

"This case is closed. I can't find against you, Snopes, but I can give you advice. Leave this country and don't come back to it."

His father spoke for the first time, his voice cold and harsh, level, without emphasis: "I aim to. I don't figure to stay in a country among people who . . ." he said something unprintable and vile, addressed to no one.

"That'll do," the Justice said. "Take your wagon and get out of this country before dark. Case dismissed."

His father turned, and he followed the stiff black coat, the wiry figure walking a little stiffly from where a Confederate provost's man's[3] musket ball had taken him in the heel on a stolen horse thirty years ago, followed the two backs now, since his older brother had appeared from somewhere in the crowd, no taller than the father but thicker, chewing tobacco steadily, between the two lines of grim-faced men and out of the store and across the worn gallery and down the sagging steps and among the dogs and half-grown boys in the mild May dust, where as he passed a voice hissed:

"Barn burner!"

Again he could not see, whirling; there was a face in a red haze, moonlike, bigger than the full moon, the owner of it half again his size, he leaping in the

---

2. The Snopes family figures in many Faulkner stories and novels. Colonel Sartoris is a major personage among Faulkner's fictional inhabitants of Yoknapatawpha County. 3. Military policeman's.

red haze toward the face, feeling no blow, feeling no shock when his head struck the earth, scrabbling up and leaping again, feeling no blow this time either and tasting no blood, scrabbling up to see the other boy in full flight and himself already leaping into pursuit as his father's hand jerked him back, the harsh, cold voice speaking above him: "Go get in the wagon."

It stood in a grove of locusts and mulberries across the road. His two hulking sisters in their Sunday dresses and his mother and her sister in calico and sunbonnets were already in it, sitting on and among the sorry residue of the dozen and more movings which even the boy could remember—the battered stove, the broken beds and chairs, the clock inlaid with mother-of-pearl, which would not run, stopped at some fourteen minutes past two o'clock of a dead and forgotten day and time, which had been his mother's dowry. She was crying, though when she saw him she drew her sleeve across her face and began to descend from the wagon. "Get back," the father said.

"He's hurt. I got to get some water and wash his . . ."

"Get back in the wagon," his father said. He got in too, over the tail-gate. His father mounted to the seat where the older brother already sat and struck the gaunt mules two savage blows with the peeled willow, but without heat. It was not even sadistic; it was exactly that same quality which in later years would cause his descendants to overrun the engine before putting a motor car into motion, striking and reining back in the same movement. The wagon went on, the store with its quiet crowd of grimly watching men dropped behind; a curve in the road hid it. *Forever* he thought. *Maybe he's done satisfied now, now that he has* . . . stopping himself, not to say it aloud even to himself. His mother's hand touched his shoulder.

"Does hit hurt?" she said.

"Naw," he said. "Hit don't hurt. Lemme be."

"Can't you wipe some of the blood off before hit dries?"

"I'll wash to-night," he said. "Lemme be, I tell you."

The wagon went on. He did not know where they were going. None of them ever did or ever asked, because it was always somewhere, always a house of sorts waiting for them a day or two days or even three days away. Likely his father had already arranged to make a crop on another farm before he . . . Again he had to stop himself. He (the father) always did. There was something about his wolf-like independence and even courage when the advantage was at least neutral which impressed strangers, as if they got from his latent ravening ferocity not so much a sense of dependability as a feeling that his ferocious conviction in the rightness of his own actions would be of advantage to all whose interest lay with his.

That night they camped, in a grove of oaks and beeches where a spring ran. The nights were still cool and they had a fire against it, of a rail lifted from a nearby fence and cut into lengths—a small fire, neat, niggard almost, a shrewd fire; such fires were his father's habit and custom always, even in freezing weather. Older, the boy might have remarked this and wondered why not a big one; why should not a man who had not only seen the waste and extravagance of war, but who had in his blood an inherent voracious prodigality with material not his own, have burned everything in sight? Then he might have gone a step farther and thought that that was the reason: that niggard blaze was the living fruit of nights passed during those four years in the woods hiding from all men, blue or gray, with his strings of horses (captured horses, he called them). And older still, he might have divined the true reason: that the element of fire spoke to some deep mainspring of his father's being, as the element of steel or of powder spoke to other men, as the one weapon for the preservation of integrity, else breath were not worth the breathing, and hence to be regarded with respect and used with discretion.

But he did not think this now and he had seen those same niggard blazes all his life. He merely ate his supper beside it and was already half asleep over his iron plate when his father called him, and once more he followed the stiff back, the stiff and ruthless limp, up the slope and on to the starlit road where, turning, he could see his father against the stars but without face or depth—a shape black, flat, and bloodless as though cut from tin in the iron folds of the frockcoat which had not been made for him, the voice harsh like tin and without heat like tin:

"You were fixing to tell them. You would have told him." He didn't answer. His father struck him with the flat of his hand on the side of the head, hard but without heat, exactly as he had struck the two mules at the store, exactly as he would strike either of them with any stick in order to kill a horse fly, his voice still without heat or anger: "You're getting to be a man. You got to learn. You got to learn to stick to your own blood or you ain't going to have any blood to stick to you. Do you think either of them, any man there this morning, would? Don't you know all they wanted was a chance to get at me because they knew I had them beat? Eh?" Later, twenty years later, he was to tell himself, "If I had said they wanted only truth, justice, he would have hit me again." But now he said nothing. He was not crying. He just stood there. "Answer me," his father said.

"Yes," he whispered. His father turned.

"Get on to bed. We'll be there tomorrow."

Tomorrow they were there. In the early afternoon the wagon stopped before a paintless two-room house identical almost with the dozen others it had stopped before even in the boy's ten years, and again, as on the other dozen occasions, his mother and aunt got down and began to unload the wagon, although his two sisters and his father and brother had not moved.

"Likely hit ain't fitten for hawgs," one of the sisters said.

"Nevertheless, fit it will and you'll hog it and like it," his father said. "Get out of them chairs and help your Ma unload."

The two sisters got down, big, bovine, in a flutter of cheap ribbons; one of them drew from the jumbled wagon bed a battered lantern, the other a worn broom. His father handed the reins to the older son and began to climb stiffly over the wheel. "When they get unloaded, take the team to the barn and feed them." Then he said, and at first the boy thought he was still speaking to his brother: "Come with me."

"Me?" he said.

"Yes," his father said. "You."

"Abner," his mother said. His father paused and looked back—the harsh level stare beneath the shaggy, graying, irascible brows.

"I reckon I'll have a word with the man that aims to begin to-morrow owning me body and soul for the next eight months."

They went back up the road. A week ago—or before last night, that is—he would have asked where they were going, but not now. His father had struck him before last night but never before had he paused afterward to explain why; it was as if the blow and the following calm, outrageous voice still rang, repercussed, divulging nothing to him save the terrible handicap of being young, the light weight of his few years, just heavy enough to prevent his soaring free of the world as it seemed to be ordered but not heavy enough to keep him footed solid in it, to resist it and try to change the course of its events.

Presently he could see the grove of oaks and cedars and the other flowering trees and shrubs, where the house would be, though not the house yet. They walked beside a fence massed with honeysuckle and Cherokee roses and came to a gate swinging open between two brick pillars, and now, beyond a sweep of drive, he saw the house for the first time and at that instant he forgot his father and the terror and despair both, and even when he remembered his father again (who had not stopped) the terror and despair did not return. Because, for all the twelve movings, they had sojourned until now in a poor country, a land of small farms and fields and houses, and he had never seen a house like this before. *Hit's big as a courthouse* he thought quietly, with a surge of peace and joy whose reason he could not have thought into words, being too young for that: *They are safe from him. People whose lives are a part of this peace and dignity are beyond his touch, he no more to them than a buzzing wasp: capable of stinging for a little moment but that's all; the spell of this peace and dignity rendering even the barns and stable and cribs which belong to it impervious to the puny flames he might contrive . . .* this, the peace and joy, ebbing for an instant as he looked again at the stiff black back, the stiff and implacable limp of the figure which was not dwarfed by the house, for the reason that it had never looked big anywhere and which now, against the serene columned backdrop, had more than ever that impervious quality of something cut ruthlessly from tin, depthless, as though, sidewise to the sun, it would cast no shadow. Watching him, the boy remarked the absolutely undeviating course which his father held and saw the stiff foot come squarely down in a pile of fresh droppings where a horse had stood in the drive and which his father could have avoided by a simple change of stride. But it ebbed only for a moment, though he could not have thought this into words either, walking on in the spell of the house, which he could even want but without envy, without sorrow, certainly never with that ravening and jealous rage which unknown to him walked in the ironlike black coat before him: *Maybe he will feel it too. Maybe it will even change him now from what maybe he couldn't help but be.*

They crossed the portico. Now he could hear his father's stiff foot as it came down on the boards with clocklike finality, a sound out of all proportion to the displacement of the body it bore and which was not dwarfed either by the white door before it, as though it had attained to a sort of vicious and ravening minimum not to be dwarfed by anything—the flat, wide, black hat, the formal coat of broadcloth which had once been black but which had now that friction-glazed greenish cast of the bodies of old house flies, the lifted sleeve which was too large, the lifted hand like a curled claw. The door opened so promptly that the boy knew the Negro must have been watching them all the time, an old man with neat grizzled hair, in a linen jacket, who stood barring the door with his body, saying, "Wipe yo foots, white man, fo you come in here. Major ain't home nohow."

"Get out of my way, nigger," his father said, without heat too, flinging the door back and the Negro also and entering, his hat still on his head. And now the boy saw the prints of the stiff foot on the doorjamb and saw them appear on the pale rug behind the machinelike deliberation of the foot which seemed to bear (or transmit) twice the weight which the body compassed. The Negro was shouting "Miss Lula! Miss Lula!" somewhere behind them, then the boy, deluged as though by a warm wave by a suave turn of carpeted stair and a pendant glitter of chandeliers and a mute gleam of gold frames, heard the swift feet and saw her too, a lady—perhaps he had never seen her like before either—in a gray, smooth gown with lace at the throat and an apron tied at the waist and the sleeves turned back, wiping cake or biscuit dough from her hands with a towel as she came up the hall, looking not at his father at all but at the tracks on the blond rug with an expression of incredulous amazement.

"I tried," the Negro cried. "I tole him to . . ."

"Will you please go away?" she said in a shaking voice. "Major de Spain is not at home. Will you please go away?"

His father had not spoken again. He did not speak again. He did not even look at her. He just stood stiff in the center of the rug, in his hat, the shaggy iron-gray brows twitching slightly above the pebble-colored eyes as he appeared to examine the house with brief deliberation. Then with the same deliberation he turned; the boy watched him pivot on the good leg and saw the stiff foot drag round the arc of the turning, leaving a final long and fading smear. His father never looked at it, he never once looked down at the rug. The Negro held the door. It closed behind them, upon the hysteric and indistinguishable woman-wail. His father stopped at the top of the steps and scraped his boot clean on the edge of it. At the gate he stopped again. He stood for a moment, planted stiffly on the stiff foot, looking back at the house. "Pretty and white, ain't it?" he said. "That's sweat. Nigger sweat. Maybe it ain't white enough yet to suit him. Maybe he wants to mix some white sweat with it."

Two hours later the boy was chopping wood behind the house within which his mother and aunt and the two sisters (the mother and aunt, not the two girls, he knew that; even at this distance and muffled by walls the flat loud voices of the two girls emanated an incorrigible idle inertia) were setting up the stove to prepare a meal, when he heard the hooves and saw the linen-clad man on a fine sorrel mare, whom he recognized even before he saw the rolled rug in front of the Negro youth following on a fat bay carriage horse—a suffused, angry face vanishing, still at full gallop, beyond the corner of the house where his father and brother were sitting in the two tilted chairs; and a moment later, almost before he could have put the axe down, he heard the hooves again and watched the sorrel mare go back out of the yard, already galloping again. Then his father began to shout one of the sisters' names, who presently emerged backward from the kitchen door dragging the rolled rug along the ground by one end while the other sister walked behind it.

"If you ain't going to tote, go on and set up the wash pot," the first said.

"You, Sarty!" the second shouted. "Set up the wash pot!" His father appeared at the door, framed against that shabbiness, as he had been against that other bland perfection, impervious to either, the mother's anxious face at his shoulder.

"Go on," the father said. "Pick it up." The two sisters stooped, broad, lethargic; stooping, they presented an incredible expanse of pale cloth and a flutter of tawdry ribbons.

"If I thought enough of a rug to have to git hit all the way from France I wouldn't keep hit where folks coming in would have to tromp on hit," the first said. They raised the rug.

"Abner," the mother said. "Let me do it."

"You go back and git dinner," his father said. "I'll tend to this."

From the woodpile through the rest of the afternoon the boy watched them, the rug spread flat in the dust beside the bubbling wash pot, the two sisters stooping over it with that profound and lethargic reluctance, while the father stood over them in turn, implacable and grim, driving them though never raising his voice again. He could smell the harsh homemade lye[4] they were using; he saw his mother come to the door once and look toward them with an expression not anxious now but very like despair; he saw his father turn, and he fell to with the axe and saw from the corner of his eye his father raise from the ground a flattish fragment of field stone and examine it and return to the pot, and this time his mother actually spoke: "Abner. Abner. Please don't. Please, Abner."

Then he was done too. It was dusk; the whippoorwills had already begun. He could smell coffee from the room where they would presently eat the cold food remaining from the mid-afternoon meal, though when he entered the house he realized they were having coffee again probably because there was a fire on the hearth, before which the rug now lay spread over the backs of the two chairs. The tracks of his father's foot were gone. Where they had been were now long, water-cloudy scoriations resembling the sporadic course of a Lilliputian mowing machine.

It still hung there while they ate the cold food and then went to bed, scattered without order or claim up and down the two rooms, his mother in one bed, where his father would later lie, the older brother in the other, himself, the aunt, and the two sisters on pallets on the floor. But his father was not in bed yet. The last thing the boy remembered was the depthless, harsh silhouette of the hat and coat bending over the rug and it seemed to him that he had not even closed his eyes when the silhouette was standing over him, the fire almost dead behind it, the stiff foot prodding him awake. "Catch up the mule," his father said.

When he returned with the mule his father was standing in the black door, the rolled rug over his shoulder. "Ain't you going to ride?" he said.

"No. Give me your foot."

He bent his knee into his father's hand, the wiry, surprising power flowed smoothly, rising, he rising with it, on to the mule's bare back (they had owned a saddle once; the boy could remember it though not when or where) and with the same effortlessness his father swung the rug up in front of him. Now in the starlight they retraced the afternoon's path, up the dusty road rife with honeysuckle, through the gate and up the black tunnel of the drive to the lightless house, where he sat on the mule and felt the rough warp of the rug drag across his thighs and vanish.

---

4. A caustic detergent, unsuitable for cleaning fine fabrics.

"Don't you want me to help?" he whispered. His father did not answer and now he heard again that stiff foot striking the hollow portico with that wooden and clocklike deliberation, that outrageous overstatement of the weight it carried. The rug, hunched, not flung (the boy could tell that even in the darkness) from his father's shoulder struck the angle of wall and floor with a sound unbelievably loud, thunderous, then the foot again, unhurried and enormous; a light came on in the house and the boy sat, tense, breathing steadily and quietly and just a little fast, though the foot itself did not increase its beat at all, descending the steps now; now the boy could see him.

"Don't you want to ride now?" he whispered. "We kin both ride now," the light within the house altering now, flaring up and sinking. *He's coming down the stairs now,* he thought. He had already ridden the mule up beside the horse block; presently his father was up behind him and he doubled the reins over and slashed the mule across the neck, but before the animal could begin to trot the hard, thin arm came round him, the hard, knotted hand jerking the mule back to a walk.

In the first red rays of the sun they were in the lot, putting plow gear on the mules. This time the sorrel mare was in the lot before he heard it at all, the rider collarless and even bareheaded, trembling, speaking in a shaking voice as the woman in the house had done, his father merely looking up once before stooping again to the hame he was buckling, so that the man on the mare spoke to his stooping back:

"You must realize you have ruined that rug. Wasn't there anybody here, any of your women . . ." he ceased, shaking, the boy watching him, the older brother leaning now in the stable door, chewing, blinking slowly and steadily at nothing apparently. "It cost a hundred dollars. But you never had a hundred dollars. You never will. So I'm going to charge you twenty bushels of corn against your crop. I'll add it in your contract and when you come to the commissary you can sign it. That won't keep Mrs. de Spain quiet but maybe it will teach you to wipe your feet off before you enter her house again."

Then he was gone. The boy looked at his father, who still had not spoken or even looked up again, who was now adjusting the logger-head in the hame.

"Pap," he said. His father looked at him—the inscrutable face, the shaggy brows beneath which the gray eyes glinted coldly. Suddenly the boy went toward him, fast, stopping as suddenly. "You done the best you could!" he cried. "If he wanted hit done different why didn't he wait and tell you how? He won't git no twenty bushels! He won't git none! We'll gether hit and hide hit! I kin watch . . ."

"Did you put the cutter back in that straight stock like I told you?"

"No, sir," he said.

"Then go do it."

That was Wednesday. During the rest of that week he worked steadily, at what was within his scope and some which was beyond it, with an industry that did not need to be driven nor even commanded twice; he had this from his mother, with the difference that some at least of what he did he liked to do, such as splitting wood with the half-size axe which his mother and aunt had earned, or saved money somehow, to present him with at Christmas. In company with the two older women (and on one afternoon, even one of the sisters), he built pens for the shoat and the cow which were a part of his father's contract with the landlord, and one afternoon, his father being absent, gone somewhere on one of the mules, he went to the field.

They were running a middle buster[5] now, his brother holding the plow straight while he handled the reins, and walking beside the straining mule, the rich black soil shearing cool and damp against his bare ankles, he thought *Maybe this is the end of it. Maybe even that twenty bushels that seems hard to have to pay for just a rug will be a cheap price for him to stop forever and always from being what he used to be;* thinking, dreaming now, so that his brother had to speak sharply to him to mind the mule: *Maybe he even won't collect the twenty bushels. Maybe it will all add up and balance and vanish—corn, rug, fire; the terror and grief, the being pulled two ways like between two teams of horses—gone, done with for ever and ever.*

Then it was Saturday; he looked up from beneath the mule he was harnessing and saw his father in the black coat and hat. "Not that," his father said. "The wagon gear." And then, two hours later, sitting in the wagon bed behind his father and brother on the seat, the wagon accomplished a final curve, and he saw the weathered paintless store with its tattered tobacco- and patent-medicine posters and the tethered wagons and saddle animals below the gallery. He mounted the gnawed steps behind his father and brother, and there again was the lane of quiet, watching faces for the three of them to walk through. He saw the man in spectacles sitting at the plank table and he did not need to be told this was a Justice of the Peace; he sent one glare of fierce, exultant, partisan defiance at the man in collar and cravat now, whom he had seen but twice before in his life, and that on a galloping horse, who now wore on his face an expression not of rage but of amazed unbelief which the boy could not have known was at the incredible circumstance of being sued by one of his own tenants, and came and stood against his father and cried at the Justice: "He ain't done it! He ain't burnt . . ."

"Go back to the wagon," his father said.

"Burnt?" the Justice said. "Do I understand this rug was burned too?"

"Does anybody here claim it was?" his father said. "Go back to the wagon." But he did not, he merely retreated to the rear of the room, crowded as that other had been, but not to sit down this time, instead, to stand pressing among the motionless bodies, listening to the voices:

"And you claim twenty bushels of corn is too high for the damage you did to the rug?"

"He brought the rug to me and said he wanted the tracks washed out of it. I washed the tracks out and took the rug back to him."

"But you didn't carry the rug back to him in the same condition it was in before you made the tracks on it."

His father did not answer, and now for perhaps half a minute there was no sound at all save that of breathing, the faint, steady suspiration of complete and intent listening.

"You decline to answer that, Mr. Snopes?" Again his father did not answer. "I'm going to find against you, Mr. Snopes. I'm going to find that you were responsible for the injury to Major de Spain's rug and hold you liable for it. But twenty bushels of corn seems a little high for a man in your circumstances to have to pay. Major de Spain claims it cost a hundred dollars. October corn will

---

5. A plow that turns the soil to both sides of the blade.

be worth about fifty cents. I figure that if Major de Spain can stand a ninety-five dollar loss on something he paid cash for, you can stand a five-dollar loss you haven't earned yet. I hold you in damages to Major de Spain to the amount of ten bushels of corn over and above your contract with him, to be paid to him out of your crop at gathering time. Court adjourned."

It had taken no time hardly, the morning was but half begun. He thought they would return home and perhaps back to the field, since they were late, far behind all other farmers. But instead his father passed on behind the wagon, merely indicating with his hand for the older brother to follow with it, and crossed the road toward the blacksmith shop opposite, pressing on after his father, overtaking him, speaking, whispering up at the harsh, calm face beneath the weathered hat: "He won't git no ten bushels neither. He won't git one. We'll . . ." until his father glanced for an instant down at him, the face absolutely calm, the grizzled eyebrows tangled above the cold eyes, the voice almost pleasant, almost gentle:

"You think so? Well, we'll wait till October anyway."

The matter of the wagon—the setting of a spoke or two and the tightening of the tires—did not take long either, the business of the tires accomplished by driving the wagon into the spring branch behind the shop and letting it stand there, the mules nuzzling into the water from time to time, and the boy on the seat with the idle reins, looking up the slope and through the sooty tunnel of the shed where the slow hammer rang and where his father sat on an upended cypress bolt, easily, either talking or listening, still sitting there when the boy brought the dripping wagon up out of the branch and halted it before the door.

"Take them on to the shade and hitch," his father said. He did so and returned. His father and the smith and a third man squatting on his heels inside the door were talking, about crops and animals; the boy, squatting too in the ammoniac dust and hoof-parings and scales of rust, heard his father tell a long and unhurried story out of the time before the birth of the older brother even when he had been a professional horsetrader. And then his father came up beside him where he stood before a tattered last year's circus poster on the other side of the store, gazing rapt and quiet at the scarlet horses, the incredible poisings and convolutions of tulle and tights and the painted leers of comedians, and said, "It's time to eat."

But not at home. Squatting beside his brother against the front wall, he watched his father emerge from the store and produce from a paper sack a segment of cheese and divide it carefully and deliberately into three with his pocket knife and produce crackers from the same sack. They all three squatted on the gallery and ate, slowly, without talking; then in the store again, they drank from a tin dipper tepid water smelling of the cedar bucket and of living beech trees. And still they did not go home. It was a horse lot this time, a tall rail fence upon and along which men stood and sat and out of which one by one horses were led, to be walked and trotted and then cantered back and forth along the road while the slow swapping and buying went on and the sun began to slant westward, they—the three of them—watching and listening, the older brother with his muddy eyes and his steady, inevitable tobacco, the father commenting now and then on certain of the animals, to no one in particular.

It was after sundown when they reached home. They ate supper by lamp-light, then, sitting on the doorstep, the boy watched the night fully accomplish, listening to the whippoorwills and the frogs, when he heard his mother's voice: "Abner! No! No! Oh, God. Oh, God. Abner!" and he rose, whirled, and saw the altered light through the door where a candle stub now burned in a bottle neck on the table and his father, still in the hat and coat, at once formal and burlesque as though dressed carefully for some shabby and ceremonial violence, emptying the reservoir of the lamp back into the five-gallon kerosene can from which it had been filled, while the mother tugged at his arm until he shifted the lamp to the other hand and flung her back, not savagely or viciously, just hard, into the wall, her hands flung out against the wall for balance, her mouth open and in her face the same quality of hopeless despair as had been in her voice. Then his father saw him standing in the door.

"Go to the barn and get that can of oil we were oiling the wagon with," he said. The boy did not move. Then he could speak.

"What . . ." he cried. "What are you . . ."

"Go get that oil," his father said. "Go."

Then he was moving, running, outside the house, toward the stable: this the old habit, the old blood which he had not been permitted to choose for himself, which had been bequeathed him willy nilly and which had run for so long (and who knew where, battening on what of outrage and savagery and lust) before it came to him. *I could keep on,* he thought. *I could run on and on and never look back, never need to see his face again. Only I can't. I can't,* the rusted can in his hand now, the liquid sploshing in it as he ran back to the house and into it, into the sound of his mother's weeping in the next room, and handed the can to his father.

"Ain't you going to even send a nigger?" he cried. "At least you sent a nigger before!"

This time his father didn't strike him. The hand came even faster than the blow had, the same hand which had set the can on the table with almost excruciating care flashing from the can toward him too quick for him to follow it, gripping him by the back of his shirt and on to tiptoe before he had seen it quit the can, the face stooping at him in breathless and frozen ferocity, the cold, dead voice speaking over him to the older brother, who leaned against the table, chewing with that steady, curious, sidewise motion of cows:

"Empty the can into the big one and go on. I'll catch up with you."

"Better tie him up to the bedpost," the brother said.

"Do like I told you," the father said. Then the boy was moving, his bunched shirt and the hard, bony hand between his shoulder-blades, his toes just touching the floor, across the room and into the other one, past the sisters sitting with spread heavy thighs in the two chairs over the cold hearth, and to where his mother and aunt sat side by side on the bed, the aunt's arms about his mother's shoulders.

"Hold him," the father said. The aunt made a startled movement. "Not you," the father said. "Lennie. Take hold of him. I want to see you do it." His mother took him by the wrist. "You'll hold him better than that. If he gets loose don't you know what he is going to do? He will go up yonder." He jerked his head toward the road. "Maybe I'd better tie him."

"I'll hold him," his mother whispered.

"See you do then." Then his father was gone, the stiff foot heavy and measured upon the boards, ceasing at last.

Then he began to struggle. His mother caught him in both arms, he jerking and wrenching at them. He would be stronger in the end, he knew that. But he had no time to wait for it. "Lemme go!" he cried. "I don't want to have to hit you!"

"Let him go!" the aunt said. "If he don't go, before God, I am going up there myself!"

"Don't you see I can't?" his mother cried. "Sarty! Sarty! No! No! Help me, Lizzie!"

Then he was free. His aunt grasped at him but it was too late. He whirled, running, his mother stumbled forward on to her knees behind him, crying to the nearer sister: "Catch him, Net! Catch him!" But that was too late too, the sister (the sisters were twins, born at the same time, yet either of them now gave the impression of being, encompassing as much living meat and volume and weight as any other two of the family) not yet having begun to rise from the chair, her head, face, alone merely turned, presenting to him in the flying instant an astonishing expanse of young female features untroubled by any surprise even, wearing only an expression of bovine interest. Then he was out of the room, out of the house, in the mild dust of the starlit road and the heavy rifeness of honeysuckle, the pale ribbon unspooling with terrific slowness under his running feet, reaching the gate at last and turning in, running, his heart and lungs drumming, on up the drive toward the lighted house, the lighted door. He did not knock, he burst in, sobbing for breath, incapable for the moment of speech; he saw the astonished face of the Negro in the linen jacket without knowing when the Negro had appeared.

"De Spain!" he cried, panted. "Where's . . ." then he saw the white man too emerging from a white door down the hall. "Barn!" he cried. "Barn!"

"What?" the white man said. "Barn?"

"Yes!" the boy cried. "Barn!"

"Catch him!" the white man shouted.

But it was too late this time too. The Negro grasped his shirt, but the entire sleeve, rotten with washing, carried away, and he was out that door too and in the drive again, and had actually never ceased to run even while he was screaming into the white man's face.

Behind him the white man was shouting, "My horse! Fetch my horse!" and he thought for an instant of cutting across the park and climbing the fence into the road, but he did not know the park nor how high the vine-massed fence might be and he dared not risk it. So he ran on down the drive, blood and breath roaring; presently he was in the road again though he could not see it. He could not hear either: the galloping mare was almost upon him before he heard her, and even then he held his course, as if the very urgency of his wild grief and need must in a moment more find his wings, waiting until the ultimate instant to hurl himself aside and into the weed-choked roadside ditch as the horse thundered past and on, for an instant in furious silhouette against the stars, the tranquil early summer night sky which, even before the shape of the horse and rider vanished, stained abruptly and violently upward: a long, swirling roar incredible and soundless, blotting the stars, and he springing up and into the road again, running again, knowing it was too late yet still running even after he heard the shot and, an instant later, two shots, pausing now without knowing he had ceased to run, crying "Pap! Pap!", running again before he knew he had begun to run, stumbling, tripping over something and scrabbling up again without ceasing to run, looking backward over his shoulder at the glare as he got up, running on among the invisible trees, panting, sobbing, "Father! Father!"

At midnight he was sitting on the crest of a hill. He did not know it was midnight and he did not know how far he had come. But there was no glare behind him now and he sat now, his back toward what he had called home for four days anyhow, his face toward the dark woods which he would enter when breath was strong again, small, shaking steadily in the chill darkness, hugging himself into the remainder of his thin, rotten shirt, the grief and despair now no longer terror and fear but just grief and despair. *Father. My father,* he thought. "He was brave!" he cried suddenly, aloud but not loud, no more than a whisper: "He was! He was in the war! He was in Colonel Sartoris' cav'ry!" not knowing that his father had gone to that war a private in the fine old European sense, wearing no uniform, admitting the authority of and giving fidelity to no man or army or flag, going to war as Malbrouck[6] himself did: for booty—it meant nothing and less than nothing to him if it were enemy booty or his own.

The slow constellations wheeled on. It would be dawn and then sun-up after a while and he would be hungry. But that would be to-morrow and now he was only cold, and walking would cure that. His breathing was easier now and he decided to get up and go on, and then he found that he had been asleep because he knew it was almost dawn, the night almost over. He could tell that from the whippoorwills. They were everywhere now among the dark trees below him, constant and inflectioned and ceaseless, so that, as the instant for giving over to the day birds drew nearer and nearer, there was no interval at all between them. He got up. He was a little stiff, but walking would cure that too as it would the cold, and soon there would be the sun. He went on down the hill, toward the dark woods within which the liquid silver voices of the birds called unceasing—the rapid and urgent beating of the urgent and quiring heart of the late spring night. He did not look back.

1939

---

RELATED:
—Author in Depth: William Faulkner, p. 944

---

6. The chief character in a popular and pervasive 18th-century nursery ditty about a legendary warrior. Originally, this warrior figure may have derived from the character and exploits of John Churchill (1650–1722), Duke of Marlborough.

# F. SCOTT FITZGERALD
## *1896–1940*

Fitzgerald was born in St. Paul, Minnesota. After a glamorous but abortive undergraduate career at Princeton, he entered the army as a second lieutenant and while he was in training camp met the beautiful young woman who was to become his wife. He married Zelda Sayre as his literary career got off to a meteoric start in 1920 with the publication of his first novel, *This Side of Paradise*. Through the 1920s, when money seemed plentiful and postwar morality encouraged a reckless pursuit of happiness, he and Zelda traveled with a well-heeled crowd in Europe and New York, acting out the glamorous lifestyle he wrote of in his popular magazine fiction. He was a spokesman for the so-called Jazz Age, setting a personal as well as a literary example for a generation whose first commandment was simply: Do what you will. The tempo of his life slackened as his marriage was shredded by Zelda's insanity and his own self-destructive alcoholism. He fell from literary favor when the indulgent decade of his triumph went down under the impact of the Great Depression. Through years of emotional and physical collapse he struggled to repair his life by writing for Hollywood—producing at the same time a series of stories that exposed his humiliations there. His novels: *The Great Gatsby* (1925), *Tender Is the Night* (1934), and *The Last Tycoon* (1941) amplify the melancholy he discovered beneath the glitter of American-style success. In his pathetically candid collection of essays and letters, *The Crack-up* (1945), Fitzgerald documents the shattering of his personal ambitions. His stories were collected in *Flappers and Philosophers* (1920), *Tales of the Jazz Age* (1922), *All the Sad Young Men* (1926), and *Taps at Reveille* (1935).

## Babylon[1] Revisited

### I

"And where's Mr. Campbell?" Charlie asked.

"Gone to Switzerland. Mr. Campbell's a pretty sick man, Mr. Wales."

"I'm sorry to hear that. And George Hardt?" Charlie inquired.

"Back in America, gone to work."

"And where is the Snow Bird?"

"He was in here last week. Anyway, his friend, Mr. Schaeffer, is in Paris."

---

1. This ancient city is a symbol of orgiastic decadence.

Two familiar names from the long list of a year and a half ago. Charlie scribbled an address in his notebook and tore out the page.

"If you see Mr. Schaeffer, give him this," he said. "It's my brother-in-law's address. I haven't settled on a hotel yet."

He was not really disappointed to find Paris was so empty. But the stillness in the Ritz bar[2] was strange and portentous. It was not an American bar any more—he felt polite in it, and not as if he owned it. It had gone back into France. He felt the stillness from the moment he got out of the taxi and saw the doorman, usually in a frenzy of activity at this hour, gossiping with a *chasseur*[3] by the servants' entrance.

Passing through the corridor, he heard only a single, bored voice in the once-clamorous women's room. When he turned into the bar he traveled the twenty feet of green carpet with his eyes fixed straight ahead by old habit; and then, with his foot firmly on the rail, he turned and surveyed the room, encountering only a single pair of eyes that fluttered up from a newspaper in the corner. Charlie asked for the head barman, Paul, who in the latter days of the bull market[4] had come to work in his own custom-built car—disembarking, however, with due nicety at the nearest corner. But Paul was at his country house today and Alix giving him information.

"No, no more," Charlie said, "I'm going slow these days."

Alix congratulated him: "You were going pretty strong a couple of years ago."

"I'll stick to it all right," Charlie assured him. "I've stuck to it for over a year and a half now."

"How do you find conditions in America?"

"I haven't been to America for months. I'm in business in Prague, representing a couple of concerns there. They don't know about me down there."

Alix smiled.

"Remember the night of George Hardt's bachelor dinner here?" said Charlie. "By the way, what's become of Claude Fessenden?"

Alix lowered his voice confidentially: "He's in Paris, but he doesn't come here anymore. Paul doesn't allow it. He ran up a bill of thirty thousand francs, charging all his drinks and his lunches, and usually his dinner, for more than a year. And when Paul finally told him he had to pay, he gave him a bad check."

Alix shook his head sadly.

"I don't understand it, such a dandy fellow. Now he's all bloated up—" He made a plump apple of his hands.

Charlie watched a group of strident queens installing themselves in a corner.

"Nothing affects them," he thought. "Stocks rise and fall, people loaf or work, but they go on forever." The place oppressed him. He called for the dice and shook with Alix for the drink.

"Here for long, Mr. Wales?"

"I'm here for four or five days to see my little girl."

"Oh-h! You have a little girl?"

Outside, the fire-red, gas-blue, ghost-green signs shone smokily through the tranquil rain. It was late afternoon and the streets were in movement; the *bistros*[5] gleamed. At the corner of the Boulevard des Capucines he took a taxi.

---

**2.** Hangout for wealthy and glamorous Americans.   **3.** Hotel servant who runs various errands (French).   **4.** The period of prosperity for players of the stock market that immediately preceded the crash of 1929, which was the beginning of the Great Depression.   **5.** Small cafés.

The Place de la Concorde moved by in pink majesty; they crossed the logical Seine, and Charlie felt the sudden provincial quality of the Left Bank.[6]

Charlie directed his taxi to the Avenue de l'Opéra, which was out of his way. But he wanted to see the blue hour spread over the magnificent façade, and imagine that the cab horns, playing endlessly the first few bars of *La Plus que Lent,* were the trumpets of the Second Empire.[7] They were closing the iron grill in front of Brentano's Book-store, and people were already at dinner behind the trim little bourgeois hedge of Duval's. He had never eaten at a really cheap restaurant in Paris. Five-course dinner, four francs fifty, eighteen cents, wine included. For some odd reason he wished that he had.

As they rolled on to the Left Bank and he felt its sudden provincialism, he thought, "I spoiled this city for myself. I didn't realize it, but the days came along one after another, and then two years were gone, and everything was gone, and I was gone."

He was thirty-five, and good to look at. The Irish mobility of his face was sobered by a deep wrinkle between his eyes. As he rang his brother-in-law's bell in the Rue Palatine, the wrinkle deepened till it pulled down his brows; he felt a cramping sensation in his belly. From behind the maid who opened the door darted a lovely little girl of nine who shrieked "Daddy!" and flew up, struggling like a fish, into his arms. She pulled his head around by one ear and set her cheek against his.

"My old pie," he said.

"Oh, daddy, daddy, daddy, daddy, dads, dads, dads!"

She drew him into the salon, where the family waited, a boy and a girl his daughter's age, his sister-in-law and her husband. He greeted Marion with his voice pitched carefully to avoid either feigned enthusiasm or dislike, but her response was more frankly tepid, though she minimized her expression of unalterable distrust by directing her regard toward his child. The two men clasped hands in a friendly way and Lincoln Peters rested his for a moment on Charlie's shoulder.

The room was warm and comfortably American. The three children moved intimately about, playing through the yellow oblongs that led to other rooms; the cheer of six o'clock spoke in the eager smacks of the fire and the sounds of French activity in the kitchen. But Charlie did not relax; his heart sat up rigidly in his body and he drew confidence from his daughter, who from time to time came close to him, holding in her arms the doll he had brought.

"Really extremely well," he declared in answer to Lincoln's question. "There's a lot of business there that isn't moving at all, but we're doing even better than ever. In fact, damn well. I'm bringing my sister over from America next month to keep house for me. My income last year was bigger than it was when I had money. You see, the Czechs—"

His boasting was for a specific purpose; but after a moment, seeing a faint restiveness in Lincoln's eye, he changed the subject:

"Those are fine children of yours, well brought up, good manners."

"We think Honoria's a great little girl too."

---

**6.** South side of the Seine River; site of the student quarter and in recent tradition the Bohemian part of Paris. **7.** That is, that of Louis-Napoléon of France (reign, 1852–70), a period of bourgeois ostentation, which seemed, in retrospect, glamorous. *La Plus que Lent:* slower than slow (French); refers to the parodistic piano composition (*La Plus que Lente*) by Claude Debussy (1862–1918).

Marion Peters came back from the kitchen. She was a tall woman with worried eyes, who had once possessed a fresh American loveliness. Charlie had never been sensitive to it and was always surprised when people spoke of how pretty she had been. From the first there had been an instinctive antipathy between them.

"Well, how do you find Honoria?" she asked.

"Wonderful. I was astonished how much she's grown in ten months. All the children are looking well."

"We haven't had a doctor for a year. How do you like being back in Paris?"

"It seems very funny to see so few Americans around."

"I'm delighted," Marion said vehemently. "Now at least you can go into a store without their assuming you're a millionaire. We've suffered like everybody, but on the whole it's a good deal pleasanter."

"But it was nice while it lasted," Charlie said. "We were a sort of royalty, almost infallible, with a sort of magic around us. In the bar this afternoon"—he stumbled, seeing his mistake—"there wasn't a man I knew."

She looked at him keenly. "I should think you'd have had enough of bars."

"I only stayed a minute. I take one drink every afternoon, and no more."

"Don't you want a cocktail before dinner?" Lincoln asked.

"I take only one drink every afternoon, and I've had that."

"I hope you keep to it," said Marion.

Her dislike was evident in the coldness with which she spoke, but Charlie only smiled; he had larger plans. Her very aggressiveness gave him an advantage, and he knew enough to wait. He wanted them to initiate the discussion of what they knew had brought him to Paris.

At dinner he couldn't decide whether Honoria was most like him or her mother. Fortunate if she didn't combine the traits of both that had brought them to disaster. A great wave of protectiveness went over him. He thought he knew what to do for her. He believed in character; he wanted to jump back a whole generation and trust in character again as the eternally valuable element. Everything else wore out.

He left soon after dinner, but not to go home. He was curious to see Paris by night with clearer and more judicious eyes than those of other days. He bought a *strapontin* for the Casino and watched Josephine Baker[8] go through her chocolate arabesques.

After an hour he left and strolled toward Montmartre, up the Rue Pigalle into the Place Blanche. The rain had stopped and there were a few people in evening clothes disembarking from taxis in front of cabarets, and *cocottes*[9] prowling singly or in pairs, and many Negroes. He passed a lighted door from which issued music, and stopped with the sense of familiarity; it was Bricktop's, where he had parted with so many hours and so much money. A few doors farther on he found another ancient rendezvous and incautiously put his head inside. Immediately an eager orchestra burst into sound, a pair of professional dancers leaped to their feet and a maître d'hôtel swooped toward him, crying, "Crowd just arriving, sir!" But he withdrew quickly.

"You have to be damn drunk," he thought.

**8.** A celebrated African American dancer of the epoch. *Strapontin:* a bracket seat in the aisle, cheaper than regular seats. **9.** Prostitutes who flourish on the Boulevard Clichy between Pigalle and the Place Blanche. Montmartre is a district in northern Paris.

Zelli's was closed, the bleak and sinister cheap hotels surrounding it were dark; up in the Rue Blanche there was more light and a local, colloquial French crowd. The Poet's Cave had disappeared, but the two great mouths of the Café of Heaven and the Café of Hell still yawned—even devoured, as he watched, the meager contents of a tourist bus—a German, a Japanese, and an American couple who glanced at him with frightened eyes.

So much for the effort and ingenuity of Montmartre. All the catering to vice and waste was on an utterly childish scale, and he suddenly realized the meaning of the word "dissipate"—to dissipate into thin air; to make nothing out of something. In the little hours of the night every move from place to place was an enormous human jump, an increase of paying for the privilege of slower and slower motion.

He remembered thousand-franc notes given to an orchestra for playing a single number, hundred-franc notes tossed to a doorman for calling a cab.

But it hadn't been given for nothing.

It had been given, even the most wildly squandered sum, as an offering to destiny that he might not remember the things most worth remembering, the things that now he would always remember—his child taken from his control, his wife escaped to a grave in Vermont.

In the glare of a *brasserie*[1] a woman spoke to him. He bought her some eggs and coffee, and then, eluding her encouraging stare, gave her a twenty-franc note and took a taxi to his hotel.

## II

He woke upon a fine fall day—football weather. The depression of yesterday was gone and he liked the people on the streets. At noon he sat opposite Honoria at Le Grand Vatel, the only restaurant he could think of not reminiscent of champagne dinners and long luncheons that began at two and ended in a blurred and vague twilight.

"Now, how about vegetables? Oughtn't you to have some vegetables?"

"Well, yes."

"Here's *épinards* and *chou-fleur* and carrots and *haricots*."[2]

"I'd like *chou-fleur*."

"Wouldn't you like to have two vegetables?"

"I usually only have one at lunch."

The waiter was pretending to be inordinately fond of children. "*Qu'elle est mignonne la petite! Elle parle exactement comme une Française.*"[3]

"How about dessert? Shall we wait and see?"

The waiter disappeared. Honoria looked at her father expectantly.

"What are we going to do?"

"First, we're going to that toy store in the Rue Saint-Honoré and buy you anything you like. And then we're going to the vaudeville at the Empire."

She hesitated. "I like it about the vaudeville, but not the toy store."

"Why not?"

---

**1.** Small restaurant (French) that also serves drinks.   **2.** *Haricots:* beans (French). *Épinards:* spinach (French). *Chou-fleur:* cauliflower (French).   **3.** "What a darling little girl! She speaks exactly like a French girl" (French).

"Well, you brought me this doll." She had it with her. "And I've got lots of things. And we're not rich anymore, are we?"

"We never were. But today you are to have anything you want."

"All right," she agreed resignedly.

When there had been her mother and a French nurse he had been inclined to be strict; now he extended himself, reached out for a new tolerance; he must be both parents to her and not shut any of her out of communication.

"I want to get to know you," he said gravely. "First let me introduce myself. My name is Charles J. Wales, of Prague."

"Oh, daddy!" her voice cracked with laughter.

"And who are you, please?" he persisted, and she accepted a rôle immediately: "Honoria Wales, Rue Palatine, Paris."

"Married or single?"

"No, not married. Single."

He indicated the doll. "But I see you have a child, madame."

Unwilling to disinherit it, she took it to her heart and thought quickly: "Yes, I've been married, but I'm not married now. My husband is dead."

He went on quickly, "And the child's name?"

"Simone. That's after my best friend at school."

"I'm very pleased that you're doing so well at school."

"I'm third this month," she boasted. "Elsie"—that was her cousin—"is only about eighteenth, and Richard is about at the bottom."

"You like Richard and Elsie, don't you?"

"Oh, yes. I like Richard quite well and I like her all right."

Cautiously and casually he asked: "And Aunt Marion and Uncle Lincoln—which do you like best?"

"Oh, Uncle Lincoln, I guess."

He was increasingly aware of her presence. As they came in, a murmur of "... adorable" followed them, and now the people at the next table bent all their silences upon her, staring as if she were something no more conscious than a flower.

"Why don't I live with you?" she asked suddenly. "Because mamma's dead?"

"You must stay here and learn more French. It would have been hard for daddy to take care of you so well."

"I don't really need much taking care of anymore. I do everything for myself."

Going out of the restaurant, a man and a woman unexpectedly hailed him.

"Well, the old Wales!"

"Hello there, Lorraine. . . . Dunc."

Sudden ghosts out of the past: Duncan Schaeffer, a friend from college. Lorraine Quarrles, a lovely, pale blonde of thirty; one of a crowd who had helped them make months into days in the lavish times of three years ago.

"My husband couldn't come this year," she said, in answer to his question. "We're poor as hell. So he gave me two hundred a month and told me I could do my worst on that. . . . This your little girl?"

"What about coming back and sitting down?" Duncan asked.

"Can't do it." He was glad for an excuse. As always, he felt Lorraine's passionate, provocative attraction, but his own rhythm was different now.

"Well, how about dinner?" she asked.

"I'm not free. Give me your address and let me call you."

"Charlie, I believe you're sober," she said judicially. "I honestly believe he's sober, Dunc. Pinch him and see if he's sober."

Charlie indicated Honoria with his head. They both laughed.

"What's your address?" said Duncan skeptically.

He hesitated, unwilling to give the name of his hotel.

"I'm not settled yet. I'd better call you. We're going to see the vaudeville at the Empire."

"There! That's what I want to do," Lorraine said. "I want to see some clowns and acrobats and jugglers. That's just what we'll do, Dunc."

"We've got to do an errand first," said Charlie. "Perhaps we'll see you there."

"All right, you snot. . . . Good-by, beautiful little girl."

"Good-by."

Honoria bobbed politely.

Somehow, an unwelcome encounter. They liked him because he was functioning, because he was serious; they wanted to see him, because he was stronger than they were now, because they wanted to draw a certain sustenance from his strength.

At the Empire, Honoria proudly refused to sit upon her father's folded coat. She was already an individual with a code of her own, and Charlie was more and more absorbed by the desire of putting a little of himself into her before she crystallized utterly. It was hopeless to try to know her in so short a time.

Between the acts they came upon Duncan and Lorraine in the lobby where the band was playing.

"Have a drink?"

"All right, but not up at the bar. We'll take a table."

"The perfect father."

Listening abstractedly to Lorraine, Charlie watched Honoria's eyes leave their table, and he followed them wistfully about the room, wondering what they saw. He met her glance and she smiled.

"I liked that lemonade," she said.

What had she said? What had he expected? Going home in a taxi afterward, he pulled her over until her head rested against his chest.

"Darling, do you ever think about your mother?"

"Yes, sometimes," she answered vaguely.

"I don't want you to forget her. Have you got a picture of her?"

"Yes, I think so. Anyhow, Aunt Marion has. Why don't you want me to forget her?"

"She loved you very much."

"I loved her too."

They were silent for a moment.

"Daddy, I want to come and live with you," she said suddenly.

His heart leaped; he had wanted it to come like this.

"Aren't you perfectly happy?"

"Yes, but I love you better than anybody. And you love me better than anybody, don't you, now that mummy's dead?"

"Of course I do. But you won't always like me best, honey. You'll grow up and meet somebody your own age and go marry him and forget you ever had a daddy."

"Yes, that's true," she agreed tranquilly.

He didn't go in. He was coming back at nine o'clock and he wanted to keep himself fresh and new for the thing he must say then.

"When you're safe inside, just show yourself in that window."

"All right. Good-by, dads, dads, dads, dads."

He waited in the dark street until she appeared, all warm and glowing, in the window above and kissed her fingers out into the night.

<h1 style="text-align:center">III</h1>

They were waiting. Marion sat behind the coffee service in a dignified black dinner dress that just faintly suggested mourning. Lincoln was walking up and down with the animation of one who had already been talking. They were as anxious as he was to get into the question. He opened it almost immediately:

"I suppose you know what I want to see you about—why I really came to Paris."

Marion played with the black stars on her necklace and frowned.

"I'm awfully anxious to have a home," he continued. "And I'm awfully anxious to have Honoria in it. I appreciate your taking in Honoria for her mother's sake, but things have changed now"—he hesitated and then continued more forcibly—"changed radically with me, and I want to ask you to reconsider the matter. It would be silly for me to deny that about three years ago I was acting badly—"

Marion looked up at him with hard eyes.

"—but all that's over. As I told you, I haven't had more than a drink a day for over a year, and I take that drink deliberately, so that the idea of alcohol won't get too big in my imagination. You see the idea?"

"No," said Marion succinctly.

"It's a sort of stunt I set myself. It keeps the matter in proportion."

"I get you," said Lincoln. "You don't want to admit it's got any attraction for you."

"Something like that. Sometimes I forget and don't take it. But I try to take it. Anyhow, I couldn't afford to drink in my position. The people I represent are more than satisfied with what I've done, and I'm bringing my sister over from Burlington to keep house for me, and I want awfully to have Honoria too. You know that even when her mother and I weren't getting along well we never let anything that happened touch Honoria. I know she's fond of me and I know I'm able to take care of her and—well, there you are. How do you feel about it?"

He knew that now he would have to take a beating. It would last an hour or two hours, and it would be difficult, but if he modulated his inevitable resentment to the chastened attitude of the reformed sinner, he might win his point in the end.

Keep your temper, he told himself. You don't want to be justified. You want Honoria.

Lincoln spoke first: "We've been talking it over ever since we got your letter last month. We're happy to have Honoria here. She's a dear little thing, and we're glad to be able to help her, but of course that isn't the question—"

Marion interrupted suddenly. "How long are you going to stay sober, Charlie?" she asked.

"Permanently, I hope."

"How can anybody count on that?"

"You know I never did drink heavily until I gave up business and came over here with nothing to do. Then Helen and I began to run around with——"

"Please leave Helen out of it. I can't bear to hear you talk about her like that."

He stared at her grimly; he had never been certain how fond of each other the sisters were in life.

"My drinking only lasted about a year and a half—from the time we came over until I—collapsed."

"It was time enough."

"It was time enough," he agreed.

"My duty is entirely to Helen," she said. "I try to think what she would have wanted me to do. Frankly, from the night you did that terrible thing you haven't really existed for me. I can't help that. She was my sister."

"Yes."

"When she was dying she asked me to look out for Honoria. If you hadn't been in a sanitarium then, it might have helped matters."

He had no answer.

"I'll never in my life be able to forget the morning when Helen knocked at my door, soaked to the skin and shivering, and said you'd locked her out."

Charlie gripped the sides of the chair. This was more difficult than he expected; he wanted to launch out into a long expostulation and explanation, but he only said: "The night I locked her out—" and she interrupted, "I don't feel up to going over that again."

After a moment's silence Lincoln said: "We're getting off the subject. You want Marion to set aside her legal guardianship and give you Honoria. I think the main point for her is whether she has confidence in you or not."

"I don't blame Marion," Charlie said slowly, "but I think she can have entire confidence in me. I had a good record up to three years ago. Of course, it's within human possibilities I might go wrong any time. But if we wait much longer I'll lose Honoria's childhood and my chance for a home." He shook his head, "I'll simply lose her, don't you see?"

"Yes, I see," said Lincoln.

"Why didn't you think of all this before?" Marion asked.

"I suppose I did, from time to time, but Helen and I were getting along badly. When I consented to the guardianship, I was flat on my back in a sanitarium and the market had cleaned me out. I knew I'd acted badly, and I thought if it would bring any peace to Helen, I'd agree to anything. But now it's different. I'm functioning, I'm behaving damn well, so far as——"

"Please don't swear at me," Marion said.

He looked at her, startled. With each remark the force of her dislike became more and more apparent. She had built up all her fear of life into one wall and faced it toward him. This trivial reproof was possibly the result of some trouble with the cook several hours before. Charlie became increasingly alarmed at leaving Honoria in this atmosphere of hostility against himself; sooner or later it would come out, in a word here, a shake of the head there, and some of that distrust would be irrevocably implanted in Honoria. But he pulled his temper down out of his face and shut it up inside him; he had won a point, for Lincoln realized the absurdity of Marion's remark and asked her lightly since when she had objected to the word "damn."

"Another thing," Charlie said: "I'm able to give her certain advantages now. I'm going to take a French governess to Prague with me. I've got a lease on a new apartment——"

He stopped, realizing that he was blundering. They couldn't be expected to accept with equanimity the fact that his income was again twice as large as their own.

"I suppose you can give her more luxuries than we can," said Marion. "When you were throwing away money we were living along watching every ten francs. . . . I suppose you'll start doing it again."

"Oh, no," he said. "I've learned. I worked hard for ten years, you know— until I got lucky in the market, like so many people. Terribly lucky. It won't happen again."

There was a long silence. All of them felt their nerves straining, and for the first time in a year Charlie wanted a drink. He was sure now that Lincoln Peters wanted him to have his child.

Marion shuddered suddenly; part of her saw that Charlie's feet were planted on the earth now, and her own maternal feeling recognized the naturalness of his desire; but she had lived for a long time with a prejudice—a prejudice founded on a curious disbelief in her sister's happiness, and which, in the shock of one terrible night, had turned to hatred for him. It had all happened at a point in her life where the discouragement of ill health and adverse circumstances made it necessary for her to believe in tangible villainy and a tangible villain.

"I can't help what I think!" she cried out suddenly. "How much you were responsible for Helen's death, I don't know. It's something you'll have to square with your own conscience."

An electric current of agony surged through him; for a moment he was almost on his feet, an unuttered sound echoing in his throat. He hung on to himself for a moment, another moment.

"Hold on there," said Lincoln uncomfortably. "I never thought you were responsible for that."

"Helen died of heart trouble," Charlie said dully.

"Yes, heart trouble." Marion spoke as if the phrase had another meaning for her.

Then, in the flatness that followed her outburst, she saw him plainly and she knew he had somehow arrived at control over the situation. Glancing at her husband, she found no help from him, and as abruptly as if it were a matter of no importance, she threw up the sponge.

"Do what you like!" she cried, springing up from her chair. "She's your child. I'm not the person to stand in your way. I think if it were my child I'd rather see her—" She managed to check herself. "You two decide it. I can't stand this. I'm sick. I'm going to bed."

She hurried from the room; after a moment Lincoln said:

"This has been a hard day for her. You know how strongly she feels—" His voice was almost apologetic: "When a woman gets an idea in her head."

"Of course."

"It's going to be all right. I think she sees now that you—can provide for the child, and so we can't very well stand in your way or Honoria's way."

"Thank you, Lincoln."

"I'd better go along and see how she is."

"I'm going."

He was still trembling when he reached the street, but a walk down the Rue Bonaparte to the *quais*[4] set him up, and as he crossed the Seine, fresh and new by the *quai* lamps, he felt exultant. But back in his room he couldn't sleep. The image of Helen haunted him. Helen whom he had loved so until they had senselessly begun to abuse each other's love, tear it into shreds. On that terrible February night that Marion remembered so vividly, a slow quarrel had gone on for hours. There was a scene at the Florida, and then he attempted to take her home, and then she kissed young Webb at a table; after that there was what she had hysterically said. When he arrived home alone he turned the key in the lock in wild anger. How could he know she would arrive an hour later alone, that there would be a snowstorm in which she wandered about in slippers, too confused to find a taxi? Then the aftermath, her escaping pneumonia by a miracle, and all the attendant horror. They were "reconciled," but that was the beginning of the end, and Marion, who had seen with her own eyes and who imagined it to be one of many scenes from her sister's martyrdom, never forgot.

Going over it again brought Helen nearer, and in the white, soft light that steals upon half sleep near morning he found himself talking to her again. She said that he was perfectly right about Honoria and that she wanted Honoria to be with him. She said she was glad he was being good and doing better. She said a lot of other things—very friendly things—but she was in a swing in a white dress, and swinging faster and faster all the time, so that at the end he could not hear clearly all that she said.

## IV

He woke up feeling happy. The door of the world was open again. He made plans, vistas, futures for Honoria and himself, but suddenly he grew sad, remembering all the plans he and Helen had made. She had not planned to die. The present was the thing—work to do and someone to love. But not to love too much, for he knew the injury that a father can do to a daughter or a mother to a son by attaching them too closely: afterward, out in the world, the child would seek in the marriage partner the same blind tenderness and, failing probably to find it, turn against love and life.

It was another bright, crisp day. He called Lincoln Peters at the bank where he worked and asked if he could count on taking Honoria when he left for Prague. Lincoln agreed that there was no reason for delay. One thing—the legal guardianship. Marion wanted to retain that a while longer. She was upset by the whole matter, and it would oil things if she felt that the situation was still in her control for another year. Charlie agreed, wanting only the tangible, visible child.

4. Paved riverbanks (French).

Then the question of a governess. Charles sat in a gloomy agency and talked to a cross Béarnaise and to a buxom Breton[5] peasant, neither of whom he could have endured. There were others whom he would see tomorrow.

He lunched with Lincoln Peters at Griffons, trying to keep down his exultation.

"There's nothing quite like your own child," Lincoln said. "But you understand how Marion feels too."

"She's forgotten how hard I worked for seven years there," Charlie said. "She just remembers one night."

"There's another thing." Lincoln hesitated. "While you and Helen were tearing around Europe throwing money away, we were just getting along. I didn't touch any of the prosperity because I never got ahead enough to carry anything but my insurance. I think Marion felt there was some kind of injustice in it—you not even working toward the end, and getting richer and richer."

"It went just as quick as it came," said Charlie.

"Yes, a lot of it stayed in the hands of *chasseurs* and saxophone players and maîtres d'hôtel—well, the big party's over now. I just said that to explain Marion's feeling about those crazy years. If you drop in about six o'clock tonight before Marion's too tired, we'll settle the details on the spot."

Back at his hotel, Charlie found a *pneumatique*[6] that had been redirected from the Ritz bar where Charlie had left his address for the purpose of finding a certain man.

> DEAR CHARLIE: You were so strange when we saw you the other day that I wondered if I did something to offend you. If so, I'm not conscious of it. In fact, I have thought about you too much for the last year, and it's always been in the back of my mind that I might see you if I came over here. We *did* have such good times that crazy spring, like the night you and I stole the butcher's tricycle, and the time we tried to call on the president and you had the old derby rim and the wire cane. Everybody seems so old lately, but I don't feel old a bit. Couldn't we get together some time today for old time's sake? I've got a vile hang-over for the moment, but will be feeling better this afternoon and will look for you about five in the sweatshop at the Ritz.
>
> Always devotedly,
> Lorraine

His first feeling was one of awe that he had actually, in his mature years, stolen a tricycle and pedaled Lorraine all over the Étoile[7] between the small hours and dawn. In retrospect it was a nightmare. Locking out Helen didn't fit in with any other act of his life, but the tricycle incident did—it was one of many. How many weeks or months of dissipation to arrive at that condition of utter irresponsibility?

He tried to picture how Lorraine had appeared to him then—very attractive; Helen was unhappy about it, though she said nothing. Yesterday, in the

---

**5.** Native of Brittany, in northwestern France. *Béarnaise:* native of Béarn, in southwestern France. **6.** Message delivered speedily via a system of pneumatic tubes (French). **7.** Intersection of twelve streets at the northwestern end of the Champs-Élysees, forming a "star" (*étoile*).

restaurant, Lorraine had seemed trite, blurred, worn away. He emphatically did not want to see her, and he was glad Alix had not given away his hotel address. It was a relief to think, instead, of Honoria, to think of Sundays spent with her and of saying good morning to her and of knowing she was there in his house at night, drawing her breath in the darkness.

At five he took a taxi and bought presents for all the Peters—a piquant cloth doll, a box of Roman soldiers, flowers for Marion, big linen handkerchiefs for Lincoln.

He saw, when he arrived in the apartment, that Marion had accepted the inevitable. She greeted him now as though he were a recalcitrant member of the family, rather than a menacing outsider. Honoria had been told she was going; Charlie was glad to see that her tact made her conceal her excessive happiness. Only on his lap did she whisper her delight and the question "When?" before she slipped away with the other children.

He and Marion were alone for a minute in the room, and on an impulse he spoke out boldly:

"Family quarrels are bitter things. They don't go according to any rules. They're not like aches or wounds; they're more like splits in the skin that won't heal because there's not enough material. I wish you and I could be on better terms."

"Some things are hard to forget," she answered. "It's a question of confidence." There was no answer to this and presently she asked, "When do you propose to take her?"

"As soon as I can get a governess. I hoped the day after tomorrow."

"That's impossible. I've got to get her things in shape. Not before Saturday."

He yielded. Coming back into the room, Lincoln offered him a drink.

"I'll take my daily whisky," he said.

It was warm here, it was a home, people together by a fire. The children felt very safe and important; the mother and father were serious, watchful. They had things to do for the children more important than his visit here. A spoonful of medicine was, after all, more important than the strained relations between Marion and himself. They were not dull people, but they were very much in the grip of life and circumstances. He wondered if he couldn't do something to get Lincoln out of his rut at the bank.

A long peal at the door-bell; the *bonne à tout faire*[8] passed through and went down the corridor. The door opened upon another long ring, and then voices, and the three in the salon looked up expectantly; Richard moved to bring the corridor within his range of vision, and Marion rose. Then the maid came back along the corridor, closely followed by the voices, which developed under the light into Duncan Schaeffer and Lorraine Quarrles.

They were gay, they were hilarious, they were roaring with laughter. For a moment Charlie was astounded; unable to understand how they ferreted out the Peters' address.

"Ah-h-h!" Duncan wagged his finger roguishly at Charlie. "Ah-h-h!"

They both slid down another cascade of laughter. Anxious and at a loss, Charlie shook hands with them quickly and presented them to Lincoln and Marion. Marion nodded, scarcely speaking. She had drawn back a step toward

8. Maid of all work (French).

the fire; her little girl stood beside her, and Marion put an arm about her shoulder.

With growing annoyance at the intrusion, Charlie waited for them to explain themselves. After some concentration Duncan said:

"We came to invite you out to dinner. Lorraine and I insist that all this shishi, cagy business 'bout your address got to stop."

Charlie came closer to them, as if to force them backward down the corridor.

"Sorry, but I can't. Tell me where you'll be and I'll phone you in half an hour."

This made no impression. Lorraine sat down suddenly on the side of a chair, and focusing her eyes on Richard, cried, "Oh, what a nice little boy! Come here, little boy." Richard glanced at his mother, but did not move. With a perceptible shrug of her shoulders, Lorraine turned back to Charlie:

"Come and dine. Sure your cousins won' mine. See you so sel'om. Or solemn."

"I can't," said Charlie sharply. "You two have dinner and I'll phone you."

Her voice became suddenly unpleasant. "All right, we'll go. But I remember once when you hammered on my door at four A.M. I was enough of a good sport to give you a drink. Come on, Dunc."

Still in slow motion, with blurred, angry faces, with uncertain feet, they retired along the corridor.

"Good night," Charlie said.

"Good night!" responded Lorraine emphatically.

When he went back into the salon Marion had not moved, only now her son was standing in the circle of her other arm. Lincoln was still swinging Honoria back and forth like a pendulum from side to side.

"What an outrage!" Charlie broke out. "What an absolute outrage!"

Neither of them answered. Charlie dropped into an armchair, picked up his drink, set it down again and said:

"People I haven't seen for two years having the colossal nerve——"

He broke off. Marion had made the sound "Oh!" in one swift, furious breath, turned her body from him with a jerk and left the room.

Lincoln set down Honoria carefully.

"You children go in and start your soup," he said, and when they obeyed, he said to Charlie:

"Marion's not well and she can't stand shocks. That kind of people make her really physically sick."

"I didn't tell them to come here. They wormed your name out of somebody. They deliberately——"

"Well, it's too bad. It doesn't help matters. Excuse me a minute."

Left alone, Charlie sat tense in his chair. In the next room he could hear the children eating, talking in monosyllables, already oblivious to the scene between their elders. He heard a murmur of conversation from a farther room and then the ticking bell of a telephone receiver picked up, and in a panic he moved to the other side of the room and out of earshot.

In a minute Lincoln came back. "Look here, Charlie. I think we'd better call off dinner for tonight. Marion's in bad shape."

"Is she angry with me?"

"Sort of," he said, almost roughly. "She's not strong and—"

"You mean she's changed her mind about Honoria?"

"She's pretty bitter right now. I don't know. You phone me at the bank tomorrow."

"I wish you'd explain to her I never dreamed these people would come here. I'm just as sore as you are."

"I couldn't explain anything to her now."

Charlie got up. He took his coat and hat and started down the corridor. Then he opened the door of the dining room and said in a strange voice, "Good night, children."

Honoria rose and ran around the table to hug him.

"Good night, sweetheart," he said vaguely, and then trying to make his voice more tender, trying to conciliate something, "Good night, dear children."

## V

Charlie went directly to the Ritz bar with the furious idea of finding Lorraine and Duncan, but they were not there, and he realized that in any case there was nothing he could do. He had not touched his drink at the Peters', and now he ordered a whisky-and-soda. Paul came over to say hello.

"It's a great change," he said sadly. "We do about half the business we did. So many fellows I hear about back in the States lost everything, maybe not in the first crash, but then in the second. Your friend George Hardt lost every cent, I hear. Are you back in the States?"

"No, I'm in business in Prague."

"I heard that you lost a lot in the crash."

"I did," and he added grimly, "but I lost everything I wanted in the boom."

"Selling short."[9]

"Something like that."

Again the memory of those days swept over him like a nightmare—the people they had met travelling; then people who couldn't add a row of figures or speak a coherent sentence. The little man Helen had consented to dance with at the ship's party, who had insulted her ten feet from the table; the women and girls carried screaming with drink or drugs out of public places—

—The men who locked their wives out in the snow, because the snow of twenty-nine wasn't real snow. If you didn't want it to be snow, you just paid some money.

He went to the phone and called the Peters' apartment; Lincoln answered.

"I called up because this thing is on my mind. Has Marion said anything definite?"

"Marion's sick," Lincoln answered shortly. "I know this thing isn't altogether your fault, but I can't have her go to pieces about it. I'm afraid we'll have to let it slide for six months; I can't take the chance of working her up to this state again."

"I see."

"I'm sorry, Charlie."

**9.** Selling securities, in anticipation of falling prices, that the seller does not actually possess at the time of sale.

He went back to his table. His whisky glass was empty, but he shook his head when Alix looked at it questioningly. There wasn't much he could do now except send Honoria some things; he would send her a lot of things tomorrow. He thought rather angrily that this was just money—he had given so many people money. . . .

"No, no more," he said to another waiter. "What do I owe you?"

He would come back some day; they couldn't make him pay forever. But he wanted his child, and nothing was much good now, beside that fact. He wasn't young anymore, with a lot of nice thoughts and dreams to have by himself. He was absolutely sure Helen wouldn't have wanted him to be so alone.

1935

# RICHARD FORD
## *b. 1944*

Ford was born in Jackson, Mississippi. After a boyhood in Arkansas, he attended Michigan State University, the University of California, and Washington University Law School in St. Louis. He has traveled in the fast lane of American letters since he began to publish stories in *Esquire, The New Yorker,* and *Granta.* For these he has received Guggenheim and National Endowment for the Arts grants, and his reputation puts him in the top rank of contemporary writers. His novels are *A Piece of My Heart* (1976), *The Ultimate Good Luck* (1981), *The Sportswriter* (1986), *Wildlife* (1990), the Pulitzer Prize–winning *Independence Day* (1995), and *Canada* (2012). His stories can be found in *Rock Springs* (1987), *Women with Men* (1997), *A Multitude of Sins* (2002), and *Vintage Ford* (2004).

## Great Falls

This is not a happy story. I warn you.

My father was a man named Jack Russell, and when I was a young boy in my early teens, we lived with my mother in a house to the east of Great Falls, Montana, near the small town of Highwood and the Highwood Mountains and the Missouri River. It is a flat, treeless benchland there, all of it used for wheat farming, though my father was never a farmer, but was brought up near Tacoma, Washington, in a family that worked for Boeing.

He—my father—had been an Air Force sergeant and had taken his discharge in Great Falls. And instead of going home to Tacoma, where my mother wanted to go, he had taken a civilian's job with the Air Force, working on planes, which was what he liked to do. And he had rented the house out of town from a farmer who did not want it left standing empty.

The house itself is gone now—I have been to the spot. But the double row of Russian olive trees and two of the outbuildings are still standing in the milkweeds. It was a plain, two-story house with a porch on the front and no place for the cars. At the time, I rode the school bus to Great Falls every morning, and my father drove in while my mother stayed home.

My mother was a tall pretty woman, thin, with black hair and slightly sharp features that made her seem to smile when she wasn't smiling. She had grown up in Wallace, Idaho, and gone to college a year in Spokane, then moved out to the coast, which is where she met Jack Russell. She was two years older than he was, and married him, she said to me, because he was young and wonderful looking, and because she thought they could leave the sticks and see the world together—which I suppose they did for a while. That was the life she wanted, even before she knew much about wanting anything else or about the future.

When my father wasn't working on airplanes, he was going hunting or fishing, two things he could do as well as anyone. He had learned to fish, he said, in Iceland, and to hunt ducks up on the DEW[1] line—stations he had visited in the Air Force. And during the time of this—it was 1960—he began to take me with him on what he called his "expeditions." I thought even then, with as little as I knew, that these were opportunities other boys would dream of having but probably never would. And I don't think that I was wrong in that.

It is a true thing that my father did not know limits. In the spring, when we would go east to the Judith River Basin and camp up on the banks, he would catch a hundred fish in a weekend, and sometimes more than that. It was all he did from morning until night, and it was never hard for him. He used yellow corn kernels stacked onto a #4 snelled hook, and he would rattle this rig-up along the bottom of a deep pool below a split-shot sinker, and catch fish. And most of the time, because he knew the Judith River and knew how to feel his bait down deep, he would catch fish of good size.

It was the same with ducks, the other thing he liked. When the northern birds were down, usually by mid-October, he would take me and we would build a cattail and wheat-straw blind on one of the tule ponds or sloughs he knew about down the Missouri, where the water was shallow enough to wade. We would set out his decoys to the leeward side of our blind, and he would sprinkle corn on a hunger-line from the decoys to where we were. In the evenings when he came home from the base, we would go and sit out in the blind until the roosting flights came and put down among the decoys—there was never calling involved. And after a while, sometimes it would be an hour and full dark, the ducks would find the corn, and the whole raft of them—sixty, sometimes—would swim in to us. At the moment he judged they were close enough, my father would say to me, "Shine, Jackie," and I would stand and shine a seal-beam car light out onto the pond, and he would stand up beside me and shoot all the ducks that were there, on the water if he could, but flying and getting up as well. He owned a Model 11 Remington with a long-tube magazine that would hold ten shells, and with that many, and shooting straight over the surface rather than down onto it, he could kill or wound thirty ducks in twenty seconds' time. I remember distinctly the report of that gun and the flash of it over the water into the dark air, one shot after another, not even so fast, but measured in a way to hit as many as he could.

What my father did with the ducks he killed, and the fish, too, was sell them. It was against the law then to sell wild game, and it is against the law now. And though he kept some for us, most he would take—his fish laid on ice, or his ducks still wet and bagged in the burlap corn sacks—down to the Great Northern Hotel, which was still open then on Second Street in Great Falls, and sell them to the Negro caterer who bought them for his wealthy customers and for the dining car passengers who came through. We would drive in

---

**1.** The Distant Early Warning line, a system of radar installations established by the United States in northern Canada during the Cold War against the Soviet Union.

my father's Plymouth to the back of the hotel—always this was after dark—to a concrete loading ramp and lighted door that were close enough to the yards that I could sometimes see passenger trains waiting at the station, their car lights yellow and warm inside, the passengers dressed in suits, all bound for someplace far away from Montana—Milwaukee or Chicago or New York City, unimaginable places to me, a boy fourteen years old, with my father in the cold dark selling illegal game.

The caterer was a tall, stooped-back man in a white jacket, who my father called "Professor Ducks" or "Professor Fish," and the Professor referred to my father as "Sarge." He paid a quarter per pound for trout, a dime for whitefish, a dollar for a mallard duck, two for a speckle or a blue goose, and four dollars for a Canada. I have been with my father when he took away a hundred dollars for fish he'd caught and, in the fall, more than that for ducks and geese. When he had sold game in that way, we would drive out 10th Avenue and stop at a bar called The Mermaid which was by the air base, and he would drink with some friends he knew there, and they would laugh about hunting and fishing while I played pinball and wasted money in the jukebox.

It was on such a night as this that the unhappy things came about. It was in late October. I remember the time because Halloween had not been yet, and in the windows of the houses that I passed every day on the bus to Great Falls, people had put pumpkin lanterns, and set scarecrows in their yards in chairs.

My father and I had been shooting ducks in a slough on the Smith River, upstream from where it enters on the Missouri. He had killed thirty ducks, and we'd driven them down to the Great Northern and sold them there, though my father had kept two back in his corn sack. And when we had driven away, he suddenly said, "Jackie, let's us go back home tonight. Who cares about those hard-dicks at The Mermaid. I'll cook these ducks on the grill. We'll do something different tonight." He smiled at me in an odd way. This was not a thing he usually said, or the way he usually talked. He liked The Mermaid, and my mother—as far as I knew—didn't mind it if he went there.

"That sounds good," I said.

"We'll surprise your mother," he said. "We'll make her happy."

We drove out past the air base on Highway 87, past where there were planes taking off into the night. The darkness was dotted by the green and red beacons, and the tower light swept the sky and trapped planes as they disappeared over the flat landscape toward Canada or Alaska and the Pacific.

"Boy-oh-boy," my father said—just out of the dark. I looked at him and his eyes were narrow, and he seemed to be thinking about something. "You know, Jackie," he said, "your mother said something to me once I've never forgotten. She said, 'Nobody dies of a broken heart.' This was somewhat before you were born. We were living down in Texas and we'd had some big blow-up, and that was the idea she had. I don't know why." He shook his head.

He ran his hand under the seat, found a half-pint bottle of whiskey, and held it up to the lights of the car behind us to see what there was left of it. He unscrewed the cap and took a drink, then held the bottle out to me. "Have a drink, son," he said. "Something oughta be good in life." And I felt that something was wrong. Not because of the whiskey, which I had drunk before and he had reason to know about, but because of some sound in his voice, something I didn't recognize and did not know the importance of, though I was certain it was important.

I took a drink and gave the bottle back to him, holding the whiskey in my mouth until it stopped burning and I could swallow it a little at a time. When we turned out the road to Highwood, the lights of Great Falls sank below the horizon, and I could see the small white lights of farms, burning at wide distances in the dark.

"What do you worry about, Jackie," my father said. "Do you worry about girls? Do you worry about your future sex life? Is that some of it?" He glanced at me, then back at the road.

"I don't worry about that," I said.

"Well, what then?" my father said. "What else is there?"

"I worry if you're going to die before I do," I said, though I hated saying that, "or if Mother is. That worries me."

"It'd be a miracle if we didn't," my father said, with the half-pint held in the same hand he held the steering wheel. I had seen him drive that way before. "Things pass too fast in your life, Jackie. Don't worry about that. If I were you, I'd worry we might not." He smiled at me, and it was not the worried, nervous smile from before, but a smile that meant he was pleased. And I don't remember him ever smiling at me that way again.

We drove on out behind the town of Highwood and onto the flat field roads toward our house. I could see, out on the prairie, a moving light where the farmer who rented our house to us was disking his field for winter wheat. "He's waited too late with that business," my father said and took a drink, then threw the bottle right out the window. "He'll lose that," he said, "the cold'll kill it." I did not answer him, but what I thought was that my father knew nothing about farming, and if he was right it would be an accident. He knew about planes and hunting game, and that seemed all to me.

"I want to respect your privacy," he said then, for no reason at all that I understood. I am not even certain he said it, only that it is in my memory that way. I don't know what he was thinking of. Just words. But I said to him, I remember well, "It's all right. Thank you."

We did not go straight out the Geraldine Road to our house. Instead my father went down another mile and turned, went a mile and turned back again so that we came home from the other direction. "I want to stop and listen now," he said. "The geese should be in the stubble." We stopped and he cut the lights and engine, and we opened the car windows and listened. It was eight o'clock at night and it was getting colder, though it was dry. But I could hear nothing, just the sound of air moving lightly through the cut field, and not a goose sound. Though I could smell the whiskey on my father's breath and on mine, could hear the motor ticking, could hear him breathe, hear the sound we made sitting side by side on the car seat, our clothes, our feet, almost our hearts beating. And I could see out in the night the yellow lights of our house, shining through the olive trees south of us like a ship on the sea. "I hear them, by God," my father said, his head stuck out the window. "But they're high up. They won't stop here now, Jackie. They're high flyers, those boys. Long gone geese."

There was a car parked off the road, down the line of wind-break trees, beside a steel thresher the farmer had left there to rust. You could see moonlight off the taillight chrome. It was a Pontiac, a two-door hardtop. My father said nothing about it and I didn't either, though I think now for different reasons.

The floodlight was on over the side door of our house and lights were on inside, upstairs and down. My mother had a pumpkin on the front porch, and the wind chime she had hung by the door was tinkling. My dog, Major, came out of the quonset shed and stood in the car lights when we drove up.

"Let's see what's happening here," my father said, opening the door and stepping out quickly. He looked at me inside the car, and his eyes were wide and his mouth drawn tight.

We walked in the side door and up the basement steps into the kitchen, and a man was standing there—a man I had never seen before, a young man with blond hair, who might've been twenty or twenty-five. He was tall and was wearing a short-sleeved shirt and beige slacks with pleats. He was on the other side of the breakfast table, his fingertips just touching the wooden tabletop. His blue eyes were on my father, who was dressed in hunting clothes.

"Hello," my father said.

"Hello," the young man said, and nothing else. And for some reason I looked at his arms, which were long and pale. They looked like a young man's arms, like my arms. His short sleeves had each been neatly rolled up, and I could see the bottom of a small green tattoo edging out from underneath. There was a glass of whiskey on the table, but no bottle.

"What's your name?" my father said, standing in the kitchen under the bright ceiling light. He sounded like he might be going to laugh.

"Woody," the young man said and cleared his throat. He looked at me, then he touched the glass of whiskey, just the rim of the glass. He wasn't nervous, I could tell that. He did not seem to be afraid of anything.

"Woody," my father said and looked at the glass of whiskey. He looked at me, then sighed and shook his head. "Where's Mrs. Russell, Woody? I guess you aren't robbing my house, are you?"

Woody smiled. "No," he said. "Upstairs. I think she went upstairs."

"Good," my father said, "that's a good place." And he walked straight out of the room, but came back and stood in the doorway. "Jackie, you and Woody step outside and wait on me. Just stay there and I'll come out." He looked at Woody then in a way I would not have liked him to look at me, a look that meant he was studying Woody. "I guess that's your car," he said.

"That Pontiac." Woody nodded.

"Okay. Right," my father said. Then he went out again and up the stairs. At that moment the phone started to ring in the living room, and I heard my mother say, "Who's that?" And my father say, "It's me. It's Jack." And I decided I wouldn't go answer the phone. Woody looked at me, and I understood he wasn't sure what to do. Run, maybe. But he didn't have run in him. Though I thought he would probably do what I said if I would say it.

"Let's just go outside," I said.

And he said, "All right."

Woody and I walked outside and stood in the light of the floodlamp above the side door. I had on my wool jacket, but Woody was cold and stood with his hands in his pockets, and his arms bare, moving from foot to foot. Inside, the phone was ringing again. Once I looked up and saw my mother come to the window and look down at Woody and me. Woody didn't look up or see her, but I did. I waved at her, and she waved back at me and smiled. She was wearing a powder-blue dress. In another minute the phone stopped ringing.

Woody took a cigarette out of his shirt pocket and lit it. Smoke shot through his nose into the cold air, and he sniffed, looked around the ground and threw his match on the gravel. His blond hair was combed backwards and neat on the sides, and I could smell his aftershave on him, a sweet, lemon smell. And for the first time I noticed his shoes. They were two-tones, black with white tops and black laces. They stuck out below his baggy pants and were long and polished and shiny, as if he had been planning on a big occasion. They looked like shoes some country singer would wear, or a salesman. He was handsome, but only like someone you would see beside you in a dime store and not notice again.

"I like it out here," Woody said, his head down, looking at his shoes. "Nothing to bother you. I bet you'd see Chicago if the world was flat. The Great Plains commence here."

"I don't know," I said.

Woody looked up at me, cupping his smoke with one hand. "Do you play football?"

"No," I said. I thought about asking him something about my mother. But I had no idea what it would be.

"I *have* been drinking," Woody said, "but I'm not drunk now."

The wind rose then, and from behind the house I could hear Major bark once from far away, and I could smell the irrigation ditch, hear it hiss in the field. It ran down from Highwood Creek to the Missouri, twenty miles away. It was nothing Woody knew about, nothing he could hear or smell. He knew nothing about anything that was here. I heard my father say the words, "That's a real joke," from inside the house, then the sound of a drawer being opened and shut, and a door closing. Then nothing else.

Woody turned and looked into the dark toward where the glow of Great Falls rose on the horizon, and we both could see the flashing lights of a plane lowering to land there. "I once passed my brother in the Los Angeles airport and didn't even recognize him," Woody said, staring into the night. "He recognized *me*, though. He said, 'Hey, bro, are you mad at me, or what?' I wasn't mad at him. We both had to laugh."

Woody turned and looked at the house. His hands were still in his pockets, his cigarette clenched between his teeth, his arms taut. They were, I saw, bigger, stronger arms than I had thought. A vein went down the front of each of them. I wondered what Woody knew that I didn't. Not about my mother—I didn't know anything about that and didn't want to—but about a lot of things, about the life out in the dark, about coming out here, about airports, even about me. He and I were not so far apart in age, I knew that. But Woody was one thing, and I was another. And I wondered how I would ever get to be like him, since it didn't necessarily seem so bad a thing to be.

"Did you know your mother was married before?" Woody said.

"Yes," I said. "I knew that."

"It happens to all of them, now," he said. "They can't wait to get divorced."

"I guess so," I said.

Woody dropped his cigarette into the gravel and toed it out with his black-and-white shoe. He looked up at me and smiled the way he had inside the house, a smile that said he knew something he wouldn't tell, a smile to make you feel bad because you weren't Woody and never could be.

It was then that my father came out of the house. He still had on his plaid hunting coat and his wool cap, but his face was as white as snow, as white as I have ever seen a human being's face to be. It was odd. I had the feeling that he might've fallen inside, because he looked roughed up, as though he had hurt himself somehow.

My mother came out the door behind him and stood in the floodlight at the top of the steps. She was wearing the powder-blue dress I'd seen through the window, a dress I had never seen her wear before, though she was also wearing a car coat and carrying a suitcase. She looked at me and shook her head in a way that only I was supposed to notice, as if it was not a good idea to talk now.

My father had his hands in his pockets, and he walked right up to Woody. He did not even look at me. "What do you do for a living?" he said, and he was very close to Woody. His coat was close enough to touch Woody's shirt.

"I'm in the Air Force," Woody said. He looked at me and then at my father. He could tell my father was excited.

"Is this your day off, then?" my father said. He moved even closer to Woody, his hands still in his pockets. He pushed Woody with his chest, and Woody seemed willing to let my father push him.

"No," he said, shaking his head.

I looked at my mother. She was just standing, watching. It was as if someone had given her an order, and she was obeying it. She did not smile at me, though I thought she was thinking about me, which made me feel strange.

"What's the matter with you?" my father said into Woody's face, right into his face—his voice tight, as if it had gotten hard for him to talk. "Whatever in the world is the matter with you? Don't you understand something?" My father took a revolver pistol out of his coat and put it up under Woody's chin, into the soft pocket behind the bone, so that Woody's whole face rose, but his arms stayed at his sides, his hands open. "I don't know what to do with you," my father said. "I don't have any idea what to do with you. I just don't." Though I thought that what he wanted to do was hold Woody there just like that until something important took place, or until he could simply forget about all this.

My father pulled the hammer back on the pistol and raised it tighter under Woody's chin, breathing into Woody's face—my mother in the light with her suitcase, watching them, and me watching them. A half a minute must've gone by.

And then my mother said, "Jack, let's stop now. Let's just stop."

My father stared into Woody's face as if he wanted Woody to consider doing something—moving or turning around or anything on his own to stop this—that my father would then put a stop to. My father's eyes grew narrowed, and his teeth were gritted together, his lips snarling up to resemble a smile. "You're crazy, aren't you?" he said. "You're a goddamned crazy man. Are you in love with her, too? Are you, crazy man? Are you? Do you say you love her? Say you love her! Say you love her so I can blow your fucking brains in the sky."

"All right," Woody said. "No. It's all right."

"He doesn't love me, Jack. For God's sake," my mother said. She seemed so calm. She shook her head at me again. I do not think she thought my father would shoot Woody. And I don't think Woody thought so. Nobody did, I think, except my father himself. But I think he did, and was trying to find out how to.

My father turned suddenly and glared at my mother, his eyes shiny and moving, but with the gun still on Woody's skin. I think he was afraid, afraid he was doing this wrong and could mess all of it up and make matters worse without accomplishing anything.

"You're leaving," he yelled at her. "That's why you're packed. Get out. Go on."

"Jackie has to be at school in the morning," my mother said in just her normal voice. And without another word to any one of us, she walked out of the floodlamp light carrying her bag, turned the corner at the front porch steps and disappeared toward the olive trees that ran in rows back into the wheat.

My father looked back at me where I was standing in the gravel, as if he expected to see me go with my mother toward Woody's car. But I hadn't thought about that—though later I would. Later I would think I should have gone with her, and that things between them might've been different. But that isn't how it happened.

"You're sure you're going to get away now, aren't you, mister?" my father said into Woody's face. He was crazy himself, then. Anyone would've been. Everything must have seemed out of hand to him.

"I'd like to," Woody said. "I'd like to get away from here."

"And I'd like to think of some way to hurt you," my father said and blinked his eyes. "I feel helpless about it." We all heard the door to Woody's car close in the dark. "Do you think that I'm a fool?" my father said.

"No," Woody said. "I don't think that."

"Do you think you're important?"

"No," Woody said. "I'm not."

My father blinked again. He seemed to be becoming someone else at that moment, someone I didn't know. "Where are you from?"

And Woody closed his eyes. He breathed in, then out, a long sigh. It was as if this was somehow the hardest part, something he hadn't expected to be asked to say.

"Chicago," Woody said. "A suburb of there."

"Are your parents alive?" my father said, all the time with his blue magnum pistol pushed under Woody's chin.

"Yes," Woody said. "Yessir."

"That's too bad," my father said. "Too bad they have to know what you are. I'm sure you stopped meaning anything to them a long time ago. I'm sure they both wish you were dead. You didn't know that. But I know it. I can't help them out, though. Somebody else'll have to kill you. I don't want to have to think about you anymore. I guess that's it."

My father brought the gun down to his side and stood looking at Woody. He did not back away, just stood, waiting for what I don't know to happen. Woody stood a moment, then he cut his eyes at me uncomfortably. And I know that I looked down. That's all I could do. Though I remember wondering if Woody's heart was broken and what any of this meant to him. Not to me, or my mother, or my father. But to him, since he seemed to be the one left out somehow, the one who would be lonely soon, the one who had done something he would someday wish he hadn't and would have no one to tell him that it was all right, that they forgave him, that these things happen in the world.

Woody took a step back, looked at my father and at me again as if he intended to speak, then stepped aside and walked away toward the front of our house, where the wind chime made a noise in the new cold air.

My father looked at me, his big pistol in his hand. "Does this seem stupid to you?" he said. "All this? Yelling and threatening and going nuts? I wouldn't blame you if it did. You shouldn't even see this. I'm sorry. I don't know what to do now."

"It'll be all right," I said. And I walked out to the road. Woody's car started up behind the olive trees. I stood and watched it back out, its red taillights clouded by exhaust. I could see their two heads inside, with the headlights shining behind them. When they got into the road, Woody touched his brakes, and for a moment I could see that they were talking, their heads turned toward each other, nodding. Woody's head and my mother's. They sat that way for a few seconds, then drove slowly off. And I wondered what they had to say to each other, something important enough that they had to stop right at that moment and say it. Did she say, *I love you?* Did she say, *This is not what I expected to happen?* Did she say, *This is what I've wanted all along?* And did he say, *I'm sorry for all this,* or *I'm glad,* or *None of this matters to me?* These are not the kinds of things you can know if you were not there. And I was not there and did not want to be. It did not seem like I should be there. I heard the door slam when my father went inside, and I turned back from the road where I could still see their taillights disappearing, and went back into the house where I was to be alone with my father.

Things seldom end in one event. In the morning I went to school on the bus as usual, and my father drove in to the air base in his car. We had not said very much about all that had happened. Harsh words, in a sense, are all alike. You can make them up yourself and be right. I think we both believed that we were in a fog we couldn't see through yet, though in a while, maybe not even a long while, we would see lights and know something.

In my third-period class that day a messenger brought a note for me that said I was excused from school at noon, and I should meet my mother at a motel down 10th Avenue South—a place not so far from my school—and we would eat lunch together.

It was a gray day in Great Falls that day. The leaves were off the trees and the mountains to the east of town were obscured by a low sky. The night before had been cold and clear, but today it seemed as if it would rain. It was the beginning of winter in earnest. In a few days there would be snow everywhere.

The motel where my mother was staying was called the Tropicana, and was beside the city golf course. There was a neon parrot on the sign out front, and the cabins made a U shape behind a little white office building. Only a couple of cars were parked in front of cabins, and no car was in front of my mother's cabin. I wondered if Woody would be here, or if he was at the air base. I wondered if my father would see him there, and what they would say.

I walked back to cabin 9. The door was open, though a DO NOT DISTURB sign was hung on the knob outside. I looked through the screen and saw my mother sitting on the bed alone. The television was on, but she was looking at me. She was wearing the powder-blue dress she had had on the night before. She was smiling at me, and I liked the way she looked at that moment, through the screen, in shadows. Her features did not seem as sharp as they had before. She looked comfortable where she was, and I felt like we were going to get along, no matter what had happened, and that I wasn't mad at her—that I had never been mad at her.

She sat forward and turned the television off. "Come in, Jackie," she said, and I opened the screen door and came inside. "It's the height of grandeur in here, isn't it?" My mother looked around the room. Her suitcase was open on the floor by the bathroom door, which I could see through and out the window onto the golf course, where three men were playing under the milky sky. "Privacy can be a burden, sometimes," she said, and reached down and put on her high-heeled shoes. "I didn't sleep very well last night, did you?"

"No," I said, though I had slept all night. I wanted to ask her where Woody was, but it occurred to me at that moment that he was gone now and wouldn't be back, that she wasn't thinking in terms of him and didn't care where he was or ever would be.

"I'd like a nice compliment from you," she said. "Do you have one of those to spend?"

"Yes," I said. "I'm glad to see you."

"That's a nice one," she said and nodded. She had both her shoes on now. "Would you like to go have lunch? We can walk across the street to the cafeteria. You can get hot food."

"No," I said. "I'm not really hungry now."

"That's okay," she said and smiled at me again. And, as I said before, I liked the way she looked. She looked pretty in a way I didn't remember seeing her, as if something that had had a hold on her had let her go, and she could be different about things. Even about me.

"Sometimes, you know," she said, "I'll think about something I did. Just anything. Years ago in Idaho, or last week, even. And it's as if I'd read it. Like a story. Isn't that strange?"

"Yes," I said. And it did seem strange to me because I was certain then what the difference was between what had happened and what hadn't, and knew I always would be.

"Sometimes," she said, and she folded her hands in her lap and stared out the little side window of her cabin at the parking lot and the curving row of other cabins. "Sometimes I even have a moment when I completely forget what life's like. Just altogether." She smiled. "That's not so bad, finally. Maybe it's a disease I have. Do you think I'm just sick and I'll get well?"

"No. I don't know," I said. "Maybe. I hope so." I looked out the bathroom window and saw the three men walking down the golf course fairway carrying golf clubs.

"I'm not very good at sharing things right now," my mother said. "I'm sorry." She cleared her throat, and then she didn't say anything for almost a minute while I stood there. "I *will* answer anything you'd like me to answer, though. Just ask me anything, and I'll answer it the truth, whether I want to or not. Okay? I will. You don't even have to trust me. That's not a big issue with us. We're both grown-ups now."

And I said, "Were you ever married before?"

My mother looked at me strangely. Her eyes got small, and for a moment she looked the way I was used to seeing her—sharp-faced, her mouth set and taut. "No," she said. "Who told you that? That isn't true. I never was. Did Jack say that to you? Did your father say that? That's an awful thing to say. I haven't been that bad."

"He didn't say that," I said.

"Oh, of course he did," my mother said. "He doesn't know just to let things go when they're bad enough."

"I wanted to know that," I said. "I just thought about it. It doesn't matter."

"No, it doesn't," my mother said. "I could've been married eight times. I'm just sorry he said that to you. He's not generous sometimes."

"He didn't say that," I said. But I'd said it enough, and I didn't care if she believed me or didn't. It was true that trust was not a big issue between us then. And in any event, I know now that the whole truth of anything is an idea that stops existing finally.

"Is that all you want to know, then?" my mother said. She seemed mad, but not at me, I didn't think. Just at things in general. And I sympathized with her. "Your life's your own business, Jackie," she said. "Sometimes it scares you to death it's so much your own business. You just want to run."

"I guess so," I said.

"I'd like a less domestic life, is all." She looked at me, but I didn't say anything. I didn't see what she meant by that, though I knew there was nothing I could say to change the way her life would be from then on. And I kept quiet.

In a while we walked across 10th Avenue and ate lunch in the cafeteria. When she paid for the meal I saw that she had my father's silver-dollar money clip in her purse and that there was money in it. And I understood that he had been to see her already that day, and no one cared if I knew it. We were all of us on our own in this.

When we walked out onto the street, it was colder and the wind was blowing. Car exhausts were visible and some drivers had their lights on, though it was only two o'clock in the afternoon. My mother had called a taxi, and we stood and waited for it. I didn't know where she was going, but I wasn't going with her.

"Your father won't let me come back," she said, standing on the curb. It was just a fact to her, not that she hoped I would talk to him or stand up for her or take her part. But I did wish then that I had never let her go the night before. Things can be fixed by staying; but to go out into the night and not come back hazards life, and everything can get out of hand.

My mother's taxi came. She kissed me and hugged me very hard, then got inside the cab in her powder-blue dress and high heels and her car coat. I smelled her perfume on my cheeks as I stood watching her. "I used to be afraid of more things than I am now," she said, looking up at me, and smiled. "I've got a knot in my stomach, of all things." And she closed the cab door, waved at me, and rode away.

I walked back toward my school. I thought I could take the bus home if I got there by three. I walked a long way down 10th Avenue to Second Street, beside the Missouri River, then over to town. I walked by the Great Northern Hotel, where my father had sold ducks and geese and fish of all kinds. There were no passenger trains in the yard and the loading dock looked small. Garbage cans were lined along the edge of it, and the door was closed and locked.

As I walked toward school I thought to myself that my life had turned suddenly, and that I might not know exactly how or which way for possibly a long time. Maybe, in fact, I might never know. It was a thing that happened to you—I knew that—and it had happened to me in this way now. And as I walked on up the cold street that afternoon in Great Falls, the questions I asked myself were these: why wouldn't my father let my mother come back? Why would Woody stand in the cold with me outside my house and risk being killed? Why would he say my mother had been married before, if she hadn't been? And my mother herself—why would she do what she did? In five years my father had gone off to Ely, Nevada, to ride out the oil strike there, and been killed by accident. And in the years since then I have seen my mother from time to time—in one place or another, with one man or other—and I can say, at least, that we know each other. But I have never known the answer to these questions, have never asked anyone their answers. Though possibly it—the answer—is simple: it is just low-life, some coldness in us all, some helplessness that causes us to misunderstand life when it is pure and plain, makes our existence seem like a border between two nothings, and makes us no more or less than animals who meet on the road—watchful, unforgiving, without patience or desire.

1983

RELATED:

—Ford on Bharati Mukherjee's "The Management of Grief," p. 922

# MAVIS GALLANT
*1922–2014*

Mavis Gallant was born in Montreal to an Anglo-Scottish father and an American mother. Her father died when she was ten years old, and her mother remarried shortly thereafter. The family moved so frequently in the next eight years that Gallant attended seventeen different schools before graduating from high school in New York City. Following graduation, Gallant returned to Montreal and became a journalist, working for a number of years at *The Standard*. When she was twenty-eight, Gallant quit her job and departed for Europe to pursue her dream of becoming a full-time fiction writer. She soon settled in France, where she lived until her death in 2014. She published her first short story in *The New Yorker* in 1951. Gallant published a play, two novels—*Green Water, Green Sky* (1959) and *A Fairly Good Time* (1970)—and numerous collections of short stories, among them *The Other Paris* (1956), *My Heart Is Broken* (1964), *Home Truths: Selected Canadian Stories* (1981)—for which she was awarded the Governor General's Award—*In Transit* (1988), and *The Collected Stories of Mavis Gallant* (1996). Gallant was appointed an Officer of the Order of Canada in 1981 (raised to Companion in 1993) and a Foreign Honorary Member of the American Academy of Arts and Letters in 2000. Her awards include the Matt Cohen Award, the Rea Award for the Short Story, and a PEN/Nabokov award.

## The Ice Wagon Going Down the Street

Now that they are out of world affairs and back where they started, Peter Frazier's wife says, "Everybody else did well in the international thing except us."

"You have to be crooked," he tells her.

"Or smart. Pity we weren't."

It is Sunday morning. They sit in the kitchen, drinking their coffee, slowly, remembering the past. They say the names of people as if they were magic. Peter thinks, Agnes Brusen, but there are hundreds of other names. As a private married joke, Peter and Sheilah wear the silk dressing gowns they bought in Hong Kong. Each thinks the other a peacock, rather splendid, but they pretend the dressing gowns are silly and worn in fun.

Peter and Sheilah and their two daughters, Sandra and Jennifer, are visiting Peter's unmarried sister, Lucille. They have been Lucille's guests seventeen weeks, ever since they returned to Toronto from the Far East. Their big old steamer trunk blocks a corner of the kitchen, making a problem of the refrigerator door; but even Lucille says the trunk may as well stay where it is, for the present. The Fraziers' future is so unsettled; everything is still in the air.

Lucille has given her bedroom to her two nieces, and sleeps on a camp cot in the hall. The parents have the living-room divan. They have no privileges here; they sleep after Lucille has seen the last television show that interests her. In the hall closet their clothes are crushed by winter overcoats. They know they are being judged for the first time. Sandra and Jennifer are waiting for Sheilah and Peter to decide. They are waiting to learn where these exotic parents will fly to next. What sort of climate will Sheilah consider? What job will Peter consent to accept? When the parents are ready, the children will make a decision of their own. It is just possible that Sandra and Jennifer will choose to stay with their aunt.

The peacock parents are watched by wrens. Lucille and her nieces are much the same—sandy-colored, proudly plain. Neither of the girls has the father's insouciance or the mother's appearance—her height, her carriage, her thick hair and sky-blue eyes. The children are more cautious than their parents; more Canadian. When they saw their aunt's apartment they had been away from Canada nine years, ever since they were two and four; and Jennifer, the elder, said, "Well, now we're home." Her voice is nasal and flat. Where did she learn that voice? And why should this be home? Peter's answer to anything about his mystifying children is, "It must be in the blood."

On Sunday morning Lucille takes her nieces to church. It seems to be the only condition she imposes on her relations: The children must be decent. The girls go willingly, with their new hats and purses and gloves and coral bracelets and strings of pearls. The parents, ramshackle, sleepy, dim in the brain because it is Sunday, sit down to their coffee and privacy and talk of the past.

"We weren't crooked," says Peter. "We weren't even smart."

Sheilah's head bobs up; she is no drowner. It is wrong to say they have nothing to show for time. Sheilah has the Balenciaga. It is a black afternoon dress, stiff and boned at the waist, long for the fashions of now, but neither Sheilah nor Peter would change a thread. The Balenciaga is their talisman, their treasure; and after they remember it they touch hands and think that the years are not behind them but hazy and marvelous and still to be lived.

The first place they went to was Paris. In the early fifties the pick of the international jobs was there. Peter had inherited the last scrap of money he knew he was ever likely to see, and it was enough to get them over: Sheilah and Peter and the babies and the steamer trunk. To their joy and astonishment they had money in the bank. They said to each other, "It should last a year." Peter was fastidious about the new job; he hadn't come all this distance to accept just anything. In Paris he met Hugh Taylor, who was earning enough smuggling gasoline to keep his wife in Paris and a girl in Rome. That impressed Peter, because he remembered Taylor as a sour scholarship student without the slightest talent for life. Taylor had a job, of course. He hadn't said to himself, I'll go over to Europe and smuggle gasoline. It gave Peter an idea; he saw the shape of things. First you catch your fish. Later, at an international party, he met Johnny Hertzberg, who told him Germany was the place. Hertzberg said that anyone who came out of Germany broke now was too stupid to be here, and deserved to be back home at a desk. Peter nodded, as if he had already thought of that. He began to think about Germany. Paris was fine for a holiday, but it had been picked clean. Yes, Germany. His money was running low. He thought about Germany quite a lot.

That winter was moist and delicate; so fragile that they daren't speak of it now. There seemed to be plenty of everything and plenty of time. They were living the dream of a marriage, the fabric uncut, nothing slashed or spoiled. All winter they spent their money, and went to parties, and talked about Peter's future job. It lasted four months. They spent their money, lived in the future, and were never as happy again.

After four months they were suddenly moved away from Paris, but not to Germany—to Geneva. Peter thinks it was because of the incident at the Trudeau wedding at the Ritz. Paul Trudeau was a French-Canadian Peter had known at school and in the Navy. Trudeau had turned into a snob, proud of his career and his Paris connections. He tried to make the difference felt, but Peter thought the difference was only for strangers. At the wedding reception Peter lay down on the floor and said he was dead. He held a white azalea in a brass pot on his chest, and sang, "Oh, hear us when we cry to Thee for those in peril on the sea." Sheilah bent over him and said, "Peter, darling, get up. Pete, listen, every single person who can do something for you is in this room. If you love me, you'll get up."

"I do love you," he said, ready to engage in a serious conversation. "She's so beautiful," he told a second face. "She's nearly as tall as I am. She was a model in London. I met her over in London in the war. I met her there in the war." He lay on his back with the azalea on his chest, explaining their history. A waiter took the brass pot away, and after Peter had been hauled to his feet he knocked the waiter down. Trudeau's bride, who was freshly out of an Ursuline convent, became hysterical; and even though Paul Trudeau and Peter were old acquaintances, Trudeau never spoke to him again. Peter says now that French-Canadians always have that bit of spite. He says Trudeau asked the embassy to interfere. Luckily, back home there were still a few people to whom the name "Frazier" meant something, and it was to these people that Peter appealed. He wrote letters saying that a French-Canadian combine was preventing his getting a decent job, and could anything be done? No one answered directly, but it was clear that what they settled for was exile to Geneva: a season of meditation and remorse, as he explained to Sheilah, and it was managed tactfully, through Lucille. Lucille wrote that a friend of hers, May Fergus, now a secretary in Geneva, had heard about a job. The job was filing pictures in the information service of an international agency in the Palais des Nations. The pay was so-so, but Lucille thought Peter must be getting fed up doing nothing.

Peter often asks his sister now who put her up to it—what important person told her to write that letter suggesting Peter go to Geneva?

"Nobody," says Lucille. "I mean, nobody in the way *you* mean. I really did have this girl friend working there, and I knew you must be running through your money pretty fast in Paris."

"It must have been somebody pretty high up," Peter says. He looks at his sister admiringly, as he has often looked at his wife.

Peter's wife had loved him in Paris. Whatever she wanted in marriage she found that winter, there. In Geneva, where Peter was a file clerk and they lived in a furnished flat, she pretended they were in Paris and life was still the same. Often, when the children were at supper, she changed as though she and Peter were dining out. She wore the Balenciaga, and put candles on the card table where she and Peter ate their meal. The neckline of the dress was soiled with makeup. Peter remembers her dabbing on the makeup with a wet sponge. He remembers her in the kitchen, in the soiled Balenciaga, patting on the makeup with a filthy sponge. Behind her, at the kitchen table, Sandra and Jennifer, in buttonless pajamas and bunny slippers, ate their supper of marmalade sandwiches and milk. When the children were asleep, the parents dined solemnly, ritually, Sheilah sitting straight as a queen.

It was a mysterious period of exile, and he had to wait for signs, or signals, to know when he was free to leave. He never saw the job any other way. He forgot he had applied for it. He thought he had been sent to Geneva because of a misdemeanor and had to wait to be released. Nobody pressed him at work. His immediate boss had resigned, and he was alone for months in a room with two desks. He read the *Herald Tribune*, and tried to discover how things were here—how the others ran their lives on the pay they were officially getting. But it was a closed conspiracy. He was not dealing with adventurers now but civil servants waiting for pension day. No one ever answered his questions. They pretended to think his questions were a form of wit. His only solace in exile was the few happy weekends he had in the late spring and early summer. He had met another old acquaintance, Mike Burleigh. Mike was a serious liberal who had married a serious heiress. The Burleighs had two guest lists. The first was composed of stuffy people they felt obliged to entertain, while the second was made up of their real friends, the friends they wanted. The real friends strove hard to become stuffy and dull and thus achieve the first guest list, but few succeeded. Peter went on the first list straightaway. Possibly Mike didn't understand, at the beginning, why Peter was pretending to be a file clerk. Peter had such an air—he might have been sent by a universal inspector to see how things in Geneva were being run.

Every Friday in May and June and part of July, the Fraziers rented a sky-blue Fiat and drove forty miles east of Geneva to the Burleighs' summer house. They brought the children, a suitcase, the children's tattered picture books, and a token bottle of gin. This, in memory, is a period of water and water birds; swans, roses, and singing birds. The children were small and still belonged to them. If they remember too much, their mouths water, their stomachs hurt. Peter says, "It was fine while it lasted." Enough. While it lasted Sheilah and Madge Burleigh were close. They abandoned their husbands and spent long summer afternoons comparing their mothers and praising each other's skin and hair. To Madge, and not to Peter, Sheilah opened her Liverpool childhood with the words "rat poor." Peter heard about it later, from Mike. The women's friendship seemed to Peter a bad beginning. He trusted women but not with each other. It lasted ten weeks. One Sunday, Madge said she needed the two bedrooms the Fraziers usually occupied for a party of sociologists from Pakistan, and that was the end. In November, the Fraziers heard that the summer house had been closed, and that the Burleighs were in Geneva, in their winter flat; they gave no sign. There was no help for it, and no appeal.

Now Peter began firing letters to anyone who had ever known his late father. He was living in a mild yellow autumn. Why does he remember the streets of the city dark, and the windows everywhere black with rain? He remembers being with Sheilah and the children as if they clung together while just outside their small shelter it rained and rained. The children slept in the bedroom of the flat because the window gave on the street and they could breathe air. Peter and Sheilah had the living-room couch. Their window was not a real window but a square on a well of cement. The flat seemed damp as a cave. Peter remembers steam in the kitchen, pools under the sink, sweat on the pipes. Water streamed on him from the children's clothes, washed and dripping overhead. The trunk, upended in the children's room, was not quite unpacked. Sheilah had not signed her name to this life; she had not given in. Once Peter heard her drop her aitches. "You kids are lucky," she said to the girls. "I never 'ad so much as a sit-down meal. I ate chips out of a paper or I 'ad a butty out on the stairs." He never asked her what a butty was. He thinks it means bread and cheese.

The day he heard "You kids are lucky" he understood they were becoming in fact something they had only *appeared* to be until now—the shabby civil servant and his brood. If he had been European he would have ridden to work on a bicycle, in the uniform of his class and condition. He would have worn a tight coat, a turned collar, and a dirty tie. He wondered then if coming here had been a mistake, and if he should not, after all, still be in a place where his name meant something. Surely Peter Frazier should live where "Frazier" counts? In Ontario even now when he says "Frazier" an absent look comes over his hearer's face, as if its owner were consulting an interior guide. What is Frazier? What does it mean? Oil? Power? Politics? Wheat? Real estate? The creditors had the house sealed when Peter's father died. His aunt collapsed with a heart attack in somebody's bachelor apartment, leaving three sons and a widower to surmise they had never known her. Her will was a disappointment. None of that generation left enough. One made it: the granite Presbyterian immigrants from Scotland. Their children, a generation of daunted women and maiden men, held still. Peter's father's crowd spent: They were not afraid of their fathers, and their grandfathers were old. Peter and his sister and his cousins lived on the remains. They were left the rinds of income, of notions, and the memories of ideas rather than ideas intact. If Peter can choose his reincarnation, let him be the oppressed son of a Scottish parson. Let Peter grow up on cuffs and iron principles. Let him make the fortune! Let him flee the manse! When he was small his patrimony was squandered under his nose. He remembers people dancing in his father's house. He remembers seeing and nearly understanding adultery in a guest room, among a pile of wraps. He thought he had seen a murder; he never told. He remembers licking glasses wherever he found them—on windowsills, on stairs, in the pantry. In his room he listened while Lucille read Beatrix Potter. The bad rabbit stole the carrot from the good rabbit without saying please, and downstairs was the noise of the party—the roar of the crouched lion. When his father died he saw the chairs upside down and the bailiff's chalk marks. Then the doors were sealed.

He has often tried to tell Sheilah why he cannot be defeated. He remembers his father saying, "Nothing can touch us," and Peter believed it and still does. It has prevented his taking his troubles too seriously. Nothing can be as bad as this, he will tell himself. It is happening to me. Even in Geneva, where his status was file clerk, where he sank and stopped on the level of the men who never emigrated, the men on the bicycles—even there he had a manner of strolling to work as if his office were a pastime, and his real life a secret so splendid he could share it with no one except himself.

In Geneva Peter worked for a woman—a girl. She was a Norwegian from a small town in Saskatchewan. He supposed they had been put together because they were Canadians; but they were as strange to each other as if "Canadian" meant any number of things, or had no real meaning. Soon after Agnes Brusen came to the office she hung her framed university degree on the wall. It was one of the gritty, prideful gestures that stand for push, toil, and family sacrifice. He thought, then, that she must be one of a family of immigrants for whom education is everything. Hugh Taylor had told him that in some families the older children never marry until the youngest have finished school. Sometimes every second child is sacrificed and made to work for the education of the next-born. Those who finish college spend years paying back. They are white-hot Protestants, and they live with a load of work and debt and obligation. Peter placed his new colleague on scraps of information. He had never been in the West.

She came to the office on a Monday morning in October. The office was over-heated and painted cream. It contained two desks, the filing cabinets, a map of the world as it had been in 1945, and the Charter of the United Nations left behind by Agnes Brusen's predecessor. (She took down the Charter without asking Peter if he minded, with the impudence of gesture you find in women who wouldn't say boo to a goose; and then she hung her college degree on the nail where the Charter had been.) Three people brought her in—a whole committee. One of them said, "Agnes, this is Pete Frazier. Pete, Agnes Brusen. Pete's Canadian, too, Agnes. He knows all about the office, so ask him anything."

Of course he knew all about the office: He knew the exact spot where the cord of the venetian blind was frayed, obliging one to give an extra tug to the right.

The girl might have been twenty-three: no more. She wore a brown tweed suit with bone buttons, and a new silk scarf and new shoes. She clutched an unscratched brown purse. She seemed dressed in going-away presents. She said, "Oh, I never smoke," with a convulsive movement of her hand, when Peter offered his case. He was courteous, hiding his disappointment. The people he worked with had told him a Scandinavian girl was arriving, and he had expected a stunner. Agnes was a mole: She was small and brown, and round-shouldered as if she had always carried parcels or younger children in her arms. A mole's profile was turned when she said good-bye to her committee. If she had been foreign, ill-favored though she was, he might have flirted a little, just to show that he was friendly; but their being Canadian, and suddenly left together, was a sexual damper. He sat down and lit his own cigarette. She smiled at him, questionably, he thought, and sat as if she had never seen a chair before. He wondered if his smoking was annoying her. He wondered if she was fidgety about drafts, or allergic to anything, and whether she would want the blind up or down. His social compass was out of order because the others couldn't tell Peter and Agnes apart. There was a world of difference between them, yet it was she who had been brought in to sit at the larger of the two desks.

While he was thinking this she got up and walked around the office, almost on tiptoe, opening the doors of closets and pulling out the filing trays. She looked inside everything except the drawers of Peter's desk. (In any case, Peter's desk was locked. His desk is locked wherever he works. In Geneva he went into Personnel one morning, early, and pinched his application form. He had stated on the form that he had seven years' experience in public relations and could speak French, German, Spanish, and Italian. He has always collected anything important about himself—anything useful. But he can never get on with the final act, which is getting rid of the information. He has kept papers about for years, a constant source of worry.)

"I know this looks funny, Mr. Ferris," said the girl. "I'm not really snooping or anything. I just can't feel easy in a new place unless I know where everything is. In a new place everything seems so hidden."

If she had called him "Ferris" and pretended not to know he was Frazier, it could only be because they had sent her here to spy on him and see if he had repented and was fit for a better place in life. "You'll be all right here," he said. "Nothing's hidden. Most of us haven't got brains enough to have secrets. This is Rainbow Valley." Depressed by the thought that they were having him watched now, he passed his hand over his hair and looked outside to the lawn and the parking lot and the peacocks someone gave the Palais des Nations years ago. The peacocks love no one. They wander about the parked cars looking elderly, bad-tempered, mournful, and lost.

Agnes had settled down again. She folded her silk scarf and placed it just so, with her gloves beside it. She opened her new purse and took out a notebook and a shiny gold pencil. She may have written.

> Duster for desk
> Kleenex
> Glass jar for flowers
> Air-Wick because he smokes
> Paper for lining drawers

because the next day she brought each of these articles to work. She also brought a large black Bible, which she unwrapped lovingly and placed on the left-hand corner of her desk. The flower vase—empty—stood in the middle, and the Kleenex made a counterpoise for the Bible on the right.

When he saw the Bible he knew she had not been sent to spy on his work. The conspiracy was deeper. She might have been dispatched by ghosts. He knew everything about her, all in a moment: He saw the ambition, the terror, the dry pride. She was the true heir of the men from Scotland; she was at the start. She had been sent to tell him, "You can begin, but not begin again." She never opened the Bible, but she dusted it as she dusted her desk, her chair, and any surface the cleaning staff had overlooked. And Peter, the first days, watching her timid movements, her insignificant little face, felt, as you feel the approach of a storm, the charge of moral certainty round her, the belief in work, the faith in undertakings, the bread of the Black Sunday. He recognized and tasted all of it: ashes in the mouth.

After five days their working relations were settled. Of course, there was the Bible and all that went with it, but his tongue had never held the taste of ashes long. She was an inferior girl of poor quality. She had nothing in her favor except the degree on the wall. In the real world, he would not have invited her to his house except to mind the children. That was what he said to Sheilah. He said that Agnes was a mole, and a virgin, and that her tics and mannerisms were sending him round the bend. She had an infuriating habit of covering her mouth when she talked. Even at the telephone she put up her hand as if afraid of losing anything, even a word. Her voice was nasal and flat. She had two working costumes, both dull as the wall. One was the brown suit, the other a navy-blue dress with changeable collars. She dressed for no one; she dressed for her desk, her jar of flowers, her Bible, and her box of Kleenex. One day she crossed the space between the two desks and stood over Peter, who was reading a newspaper. She could have spoken to him from her desk, but she may have felt that being on her feet gave her authority. She had plenty of courage, but authority was something else.

"I thought—I mean, they told me you were the person . . ." She got on with it bravely: "If you don't want to do the filing or any work, all right, Mr. Frazier. I'm not saying anything about that. You might have poor health or your personal reasons. But it's got to be done, so if you'll kindly show me about the filing I'll do it. I've worked in Information before, but it was a different office, and every office is different."

"My dear girl," said Peter. He pushed back his chair and looked at her, astonished. "You've been sitting there fretting, worrying. How insensitive of me. How trying for you. Usually I file on the last Wednesday of the month, so you see, you just haven't been around long enough to see a last Wednesday. Not another word, please. And let us not waste another minute." He emptied the heaped baskets of photographs so swiftly, pushing "Iran—Smallpox Control" into "Irish Red Cross" (close enough), that the girl looked frightened, as if she had raised a whirlwind. She said slowly, "If you'll only show me, Mr. Frazier, instead of doing it so fast, I'll gladly look after it, because you might want to be doing other things, and I feel the filing should be done every day." But Peter was too busy to answer, and so she sat down, holding the edge of her desk.

"There," he said, beaming. "All done." His smile, his sunburst, was wasted, for the girl was staring round the room as if she feared she had not inspected everything the first day after all; some drawer, some cupboard, hid a monster. That evening Peter unlocked one of the drawers of his desk and took away the application form he had stolen from Personnel. The girl had not finished her search.

"How could you *not* know?" wailed Sheilah. "You sit looking at her every day. You must talk about *something*. She must have told you."

"She did tell me," said Peter, "and I've just told you."

It was this: Agnes Brusen was on the Burleighs' guest list. How had the Burleighs met her? What did they see in her? Peter could not reply. He knew that Agnes lived in a bed-sitting room with a Swiss family and had her meals with them. She had been in Geneva three months, but no one had ever seen her outside the office. "You *should* know," said Sheilah. "She must have something, more than you can see. Is she pretty? Is she brilliant? What is it?"

"We don't really talk," Peter said. They talked in a way: Peter teased her and she took no notice. Agnes was not a sulker. She had taken her defeat like a sport. She did her work and a good deal of his. She sat behind her Bible, her flowers, and her Kleenex, and answered when Peter spoke. That was how he learned about the Burleighs—just by teasing and being bored. It was a January afternoon. He said, "*Miss* Brusen. Talk to me. Tell me everything. Pretend we have perfect rapport. Do you like Geneva?"

"It's a nice clean town," she said. He can see to this day the red and blue anemones in the glass jar, and her bent head, and her small untended hands.

"Are you learning beautiful French with your Swiss family?"

"They speak English."

"Why don't you take an apartment of your own?" he said. Peter was not usually impertinent. He was bored. "You'd be independent then."

"I am independent," she said. "I earn my living. I don't think it proves anything if you live by yourself. Mrs. Burleigh wants me to live alone, too. She's looking for something for me. It mustn't be dear. I send money home."

Here was the extraordinary thing about Agnes Brusen: She refused the use of Christian names and never spoke to Peter unless he spoke first, but she would tell anything, as if to say, "Don't waste time fishing. Here it is."

He learned all in one minute that she sent her salary home, and that she was a friend of the Burleighs. The first he had expected; the second knocked him flat.

"She's got to come to dinner," Sheilah said. "We should have had her right from the beginning. If only I'd known! But *you* were the one. You said she looked like—oh, I don't even remember. A Norwegian mole."

She came to dinner one Saturday night in January, in her navy-blue dress, to which she had pinned an organdy gardenia. She sat upright on the edge of the sofa. Sheilah had ordered the meal from a restaurant. There was lobster, good wine, and a *pièce-montée* full of kirsch and cream. Agnes refused the lobster; she had never eaten anything from the sea unless it had been sterilized and tinned, and said so. She was afraid of skin poisoning. Someone in her family had skin poisoning after having eaten oysters. She touched her cheeks and neck to show where the poisoning had erupted. She sniffed her wine and put the glass down without tasting it. She could not eat the cake because of the alcohol it contained. She ate an egg, bread and butter, a sliced tomato, and drank a glass of ginger ale. She seemed unaware she was creating disaster and pain. She did not help clear away the dinner plates. She sat, adequately nourished, decently dressed, and waited to learn why she had been invited here—that was the feeling Peter had. He folded the card table on which they had dined, and opened the window to air the room.

"It's not the same cold as Canada, but you feel it more," he said, for something to say.

"Your blood has gotten thin," said Agnes.

Sheilah returned from the kitchen and let herself fall into an armchair. With her eyes closed she held out her hand for a cigarette. She was performing the haughty-lady act that was a family joke. She flung her head back and looked at Agnes through half-closed lids; then she suddenly brought her head forward, widening her eyes.

"Are you skiing madly?" she said.

"Well, in the first place there hasn't been any snow," said Agnes. "So nobody's doing any skiing so far as I know. All I hear is people complaining because there's no snow. Personally, I don't ski. There isn't much skiing in the part of Canada I come from. Besides, my family never had that kind of leisure."

"Heavens," said Sheilah, as if her family had every kind.

I'll bet they had, thought Peter. On the dole.

Sheilah was wasting her act. He had a suspicion that Agnes knew it was an act but did not know it was also a joke. If so, it made Sheilah seem a fool, and he loved Sheilah too much to enjoy it.

"The Burleighs have been wonderful to me," said Agnes. She seemed to have divined why she was here, and decided to give them all the information they wanted, so that she could put on her coat and go home to bed. "They had me out to their place on the lake every weekend until the weather got cold and they moved back to town. They've rented a chalet for the winter, and they want me to come there, too. But I don't know if I will or not. I don't ski, and, oh, I don't know—I don't drink, either, and I don't always see the point. Their friends are too rich and I'm too Canadian."

She had delivered everything Sheilah wanted and more: Agnes was on the first guest list and didn't care. No, Peter corrected: doesn't know. Doesn't care and doesn't know.

"I thought with you Norwegians it was in the blood, skiing. And drinking," Sheilah murmured.

"Drinking, maybe," said Agnes. She covered her mouth and said behind her spread fingers, "In our family we were religious. We didn't drink or smoke. My brother was in Norway in the war. He saw some cousins. Oh," she said, unexpectedly loud, "Harry said it was just terrible. They were so poor. They had flies in their kitchen. They gave him something to eat a fly had been on. They didn't have a real toilet, and they'd been in the same house about two hundred years. We've only recently built our own home, and we have a bathroom and two toilets. I'm from Saskatchewan," she said. "I'm not from any other place."

Surely one winter here had been punishment enough? In the spring they would remember him and free him. He wrote Lucille, who said he was lucky to have a job at all. The Burleighs had sent the Fraziers a second-guest-list Christmas card. It showed a Moslem refugee child weeping outside a tent. They treasured the card and left it standing long after the others had been given the children to cut up. Peter had discovered by now what had gone wrong in the friendship—Sheilah had charged a skirt at a dressmaker to Madge's account. Madge had told her she might, and then changed her mind. Poor Sheilah! She was new to this part of it—to the changing humors of independent friends. Paris was already a year in the past. At Mardi Gras, the Burleighs gave their annual party. They invited everyone, the damned and the dropped, with the prodigality of a child at prayers. The invitation said "in costume," but the Fraziers were too happy to wear a disguise. They might not be recognized. Like many of the guests they expected to meet at the party, they had been disgraced, forgotten, and rehabilitated. They would be anxious to see one another as they were.

On the night of the party, the Fraziers rented a car they had never seen before and drove through the first snowstorm of the year. Peter had not driven since last summer's blissful trips in the Fiat. He could not find the switch for the windshield wiper in this car. He leaned over the wheel. "Can you see on your side?" he asked. "Can I make a left turn here? Does it look like a one-way?"

"I can't imagine why you took a car with a right-hand drive," said Sheilah.

He had trouble finding a place to park; they crawled up and down unknown streets whose curbs were packed with snow-covered cars. When they stood at last on the pavement, safe and sound, Peter said, "This is the first snow."

"I can see that," said Sheilah. "Hurry, darling. My hair."

"It's the first snow."

"You're repeating yourself," she said. "Please hurry, darling. Think of my poor shoes. My *hair*."

She was born in an ugly city, and so was Peter, but they have this difference: She does not know the importance of the first snow—the first clean thing in a dirty year. He would have told her then that this storm, which was wetting her feet and destroying her hair, was like the first day of the English spring, but she made a frightened gesture, trying to shield her head. The gesture told him he did not understand her beauty.

"Let me," she said. He was fumbling with the key, trying to lock the car. She took the key without impatience and locked the door on the driver's side; and then, to show Peter she treasured him and was not afraid of wasting her life or her beauty, she took his arm and they walked in the snow down a street and around a corner to the apartment house where the Burleighs lived. They were, and are, a united couple. They were afraid of the party, and each of them knew it. When they walk together, holding arms, they give each other whatever each can spare.

Only six people had arrived in costume. Madge Burleigh was disguised as Manet's "Lola de Valence," which everyone mistook for Carmen. Mike was an Impressionist painter, with a straw hat and a glued-on beard. "I am all of them," he said. He would rather have dressed as a dentist, he said, welcoming the Fraziers as if he had parted from them the day before, but Madge wanted him to look as if he had created her. "You know?" he said.

"Perfectly," said Sheilah. Her shoes were stained and the snow had softened her lacquered hair. She was not wasted: She was the most beautiful woman there.

About an hour after their arrival, Peter found himself with no one to talk to. He had told about the Trudeau wedding in Paris and the pot of azaleas, and after he mislaid his audience he began to look round for Sheilah. She was on a window seat, partly concealed by a green velvet curtain. Facing her, so that their profiles were neat and perfect against the night, was a man. Their conversation was private and enclosed, as if they had in minutes covered leagues of time and arrived at the place where everything was implied, understood. Peter began working his way across the room, toward his wife, when he saw Agnes. He was granted the sight of her drowning face. She had dressed with comic intention, obviously with care, and now she was a ragged hobo, half tramp, half clown. Her hair was tucked up under a bowler hat. The six costumed guests who had made the same mistake—the ghost, the gypsy, the Athenian maiden, the geisha, the Martian, and the Apache—were delighted to find a seventh; but Agnes was not amused; she was gasping for life. When a waiter passed with a crowded tray, she took a glass without seeing it; then a wave of the party took her away.

Sheilah's new friend was named Simpson. After Simpson said he thought perhaps he'd better circulate, Peter sat down where he had been. "Now look, Sheilah," he began. Their most intimate conversations have taken place at parties. Once at a party she told him she was leaving him; she didn't, of course. Smiling, blue-eyed, she gazed lovingly at Peter and said rapidly, "Pete, shut up and listen. That man. The man you scared away. He's a big wheel in a company out in India or someplace like that. It's gorgeous out there. Pete, the *servants.* And it's warm. It never never snows. He says there's heaps of jobs. You pick them off the trees like . . . orchids. He says it's even easier now than when we owned all those places, because now the poor pets can't run anything and they'll pay *fortunes.* Pete, he says it's warm, it's heaven, and Pete, they pay."

A few minutes later, Peter was alone again and Sheilah part of a closed, laughing group. Holding her elbow was the man from the place where jobs grew like orchids. Peter edged into the group and laughed at a story he hadn't heard. He heard only the last line, which was "Here comes another tunnel." Looking out from the tight laughing ring, he saw Agnes again, and he thought, I'd be like Agnes if I didn't have Sheilah. Agnes put her glass down on a table and lurched toward the doorway, head forward. Madge Burleigh, who never stopped moving around the room and smiling, was still smiling when she paused and said in Peter's ear, "Go with Agnes, Pete. See that she gets home. People will notice if Mike leaves."

"She probably just wants to walk around the block," said Peter. "She'll be back."

"Oh, stop thinking about yourself, for once, and see that that poor girl gets home," said Madge. "You've still got your Fiat, haven't you?"

He turned away as if he had been pushed. Any command is a release, in a way. He may not want to go in that particular direction, but at least he is going somewhere. And now Sheilah, who had moved inches nearer to hear what Madge and Peter were murmuring, said, "Yes, go, darling," as if he were leaving the gates of Troy.

Peter was to find Agnes and see that she reached home: This he repeated to himself as he stood on the landing, outside the Burleighs' flat, ringing for the elevator. Bored with waiting for it, he ran down the stairs, four flights, and saw that Agnes had stalled the lift by leaving the door open. She was crouched on the floor, propped on her fingertips. Her eyes were closed.

"Agnes," said Peter. "*Miss* Brusen, I mean. That's no way to leave a party. Don't you know you're supposed to curtsy and say thanks? My God, Agnes, anybody going by here just now might have seen you! Come on, be a good girl. Time to go home."

She got up without his help and, moving between invisible crevasses, shut the elevator door. Then she left the building and Peter followed, remembering he was to see that she got home. They walked along the snowy pavement, Peter a few steps behind her. When she turned right for no reason, he turned, too. He had no clear idea where they were going. Perhaps she lived close by. He had forgotten where the hired car was parked, or what it looked like; he could not remember its make or its color. In any case, Sheilah had the key. Agnes walked on steadily, as if she knew their destination, and he thought, Agnes Brusen is drunk in the street in Geneva and dressed like a tramp. He wanted to say, "This is the best thing that ever happened to you, Agnes; it will help you understand how things are for some of the rest of us." But she stopped and turned and, leaning over a low hedge, retched on a frozen lawn. He held her clammy forehead and rested his hand on her arched back, on muscles as tight as a fist. She straightened up and drew a breath but the cold air made her cough. "Don't breathe too deeply," he said. "It's the worst thing you can do. Have you got a handkerchief?" He passed his own handkerchief over her wet weeping face, upturned like the face of one of his little girls. "I'm out without a coat," he said, noticing it. "We're a pair."

"I never drink," said Agnes. "I'm just not used to it." Her voice was sweet and quiet. He had never seen her so peaceful, so composed. He thought she must surely be all right, now, and perhaps he might leave her here. The trust in her tilted face had perplexed him. He wanted to get back to Sheilah and have her explain something. He had forgotten what it was, but Sheilah would know. "Do you live around here?" he said. As he spoke, she let herself fall. He had wiped her face and now she trusted him to pick her up, set her on her feet, take her wherever she ought to be. He pulled her up and she stood, wordless, humble, as he brushed the snow from her tramp's clothes. Snow horizontally crossed the lamplight. The street was silent. Agnes had lost her hat. Snow, which he tasted, melted on her hands. His gesture of licking snow from her hands was formal as a handshake. He tasted snow on her hands and then they walked on.

"I never drink," she said. They stood on the edge of a broad avenue. The wrong turning now could lead them anywhere; it was the changeable avenue at the edge of towns that loses its houses and becomes a highway. She held his arm and spoke in a gentle voice. She said, "In our house we didn't smoke or drink. My mother was ambitious for me, more than for Harry and the others." She said, "I've never been alone before. When I was a kid I would get up in the summer before the others, and I'd see the ice wagon going down the street. I'm alone now. Mrs. Burleigh's found me an apartment. It's only one room. She likes it because it's in the old part of town. I don't like old houses. Old houses are dirty. You don't know who was there before."

"I should have a car somewhere," Peter said. "I'm not sure where we are."

He remembers that on this avenue they climbed into a taxi, but nothing about the drive. Perhaps he fell asleep. He does remember that when he paid the driver Agnes clutched his arm, trying to stop him. She pressed extra coins into the driver's palm. The driver was paid twice.

"I'll tell you one thing about us," said Peter. "We pay everything twice." This was part of a much longer theory concerning North American behavior, and it was not Peter's own. Mike Burleigh had held forth about it on summer afternoons.

Agnes pushed open a door between a stationer's shop and a grocery, and led the way up a narrow inside stair. They climbed one flight, frightening beetles. She had to search every pocket for the latchkey. She was shaking with cold.

Her apartment seemed little warmer than the street. Without speaking to Peter she turned on all the lights. She looked inside the kitchen and the bathroom and then got down on her hands and knees and looked under the sofa. The room was neat and belonged to no one. She left him standing in this unclaimed room—she had forgotten him—and closed a door behind her. He looked for something to do—some useful action he could repeat to Madge. He turned on the electric radiator in the fireplace. Perhaps Agnes wouldn't thank him for it; perhaps she would rather undress in the cold. "I'll be on my way," he called to the bathroom door.

She had taken off the tramp's clothes and put on a dressing gown of orphanage wool. She came out of the bathroom and straight toward him. She pressed her face and rubbed her cheek on his shoulder as if hoping the contact would leave a scar. He saw her back and her profile and his own face in the mirror over the fireplace. He thought, This is how disasters happen. He saw floods of seawater moving with perfect punitive justice over reclaimed land; he saw lava covering vineyards and overtaking dogs and stragglers. A bridge over an abyss snapped in two and the long express train, suddenly V-shaped, floated like snow. He though amiably of every kind of disaster and thought, This is how they occur.

Her eyes were closed. She said, "I shouldn't be over here. In my family we didn't drink or smoke. My mother wanted a lot from me, more than from Harry and the others." But he knew all that; he had known from the day of the Bible, and because once, at the beginning, she had made him afraid. He was not afraid of her now.

She said, "It's no use staying here, is it?"

"If you mean what I think, no."

"It wouldn't be better anywhere."

She let him see full on her blotched face. He was not expected to do anything. He was not required to pick her up when she fell or wipe her tears. She was poor quality, really—he remembered having thought that once. She left him and went quietly into the bathroom and locked the door. He heard taps running and supposed it was a hot bath. He was pretty certain there would be no more tears. He looked at his watch: Sheilah must be home, now, wondering what had become of him. He descended the beetles' staircase and for forty minutes crossed the city under a windless fall of snow.

The neighbor's child who had stayed with Peter's children was asleep on the living-room sofa. Peter woke her and sent her, sleepwalking to her own door. He sat down, wet to the bone, thinking, I'll call the Burleighs. In half an hour I'll call the police. He heard a car stop and the engine running and a confusion of two voices laughing and calling good night. Presently Sheilah let herself in, rosy-faced, smiling. She carried his trench coat over her arm. She said, "How's Agnes?"

"Where were you?" he said. "Whose car was that?"

Sheilah had gone into the children's room. He heard her shutting their window. She returned, undoing her dress, and said, "Was Agnes all right?"

"Agnes is all right. Sheilah, this is about the worst . . ."

She stepped out of the Balenciaga and threw it over a chair. She stopped and looked at him and said, "Poor old Pete, are you in love with Agnes?" And then, as if the answer were of so little importance she hadn't time for it, she locked her arms around him and said, "My love, we're going to Ceylon."

Two days later, when Peter strolled into his office, Agnes was at her desk. She wore the blue dress, with a spotless collar. White and yellow freesias were symmetrically arranged in the glass jar. The room was hot, and the spring snow, glued for a second when it touched the window, blurred the view of parked cars.

"Quite a party," Peter said.

She did not look up. He sighed, sat down, and thought if the snow held he would be skiing at the Burleighs' very soon. Impressed by his kindness to Agnes, Madge had invited the family for the first possible weekend.

Presently Agnes said, "I'll never drink again or go to a house where people are drinking. And I'll never bother anyone the way I bothered you."

"You didn't bother me," he said. "I took you home. You were alone and it was late. It's normal."

"Normal for you, maybe, but I'm used to getting home by myself. Please never tell what happened."

He stared at her. He can still remember the freesias and the Bible and the heat in the room. She looked as if the elements had no power. She felt neither heat nor cold. "Nothing happened," he said.

"I behaved in a silly way. I had no right to. I led you to think I might do something wrong."

"*I* might have tried something," he said gallantly. "But that would be my fault and not yours."

She put her knuckle to her mouth and he could scarcely hear. "It was because of you. I was afraid you might be blamed, or else you'd blame yourself."

"There's no question of any blame," he said. "Nothing happened. We'd both had a lot to drink. Forget about it. Nothing *happened*. You'd remember if it had."

She put down her hand. There was an expression on her face. Now she sees me, he thought. She had never looked at him after the first day. (He has since tried to put a name to the look on her face; but how can he, now, after so many voyages, after Ceylon, and Hong Kong, and Sheilah's nearly leaving him, and all their difficulties—the money owed, the rows with hotel managers, the lost and found steamer trunk, the children throwing up the foreign food?) She sees me now, he thought. What does she see?

She said, "I'm from a big family. I'm not used to being alone. I'm not a suicidal person, but I could have done something after that party, just not to see anymore, or think or listen or expect anything. What can I think when I see these people? All my life I heard, Educated people don't do this, educated people don't do that. And now I'm here, and you're all educated people, and you're nothing but pigs. You're educated and you drink and do everything wrong and you know what you're doing, and that makes you worse than pigs. My family worked to make me an educated person, but they didn't know you. But what if I didn't see and hear and expect anything anymore? It wouldn't change anything. You'd all be still the same. Only *you* might have thought it was your fault. You might have thought you were to blame. It could worry you all your life. It would have been wrong for me to worry you."

He remembered that the rented car was still along a snowy curb somewhere in Geneva. He wondered if Sheilah had the key in her purse and if she remembered where they'd parked.

"I told you about the ice wagon," Agnes said. "I don't remember everything, so you're wrong about remembering. But I remember telling you that. That was the best. It's the best you can hope to have. In a big family, if you want to be alone, you have to get up before the rest of them. You get up early in the morning in the summer and it's you, you, once in your life alone in the universe. You think you know everything that can happen. . . . Nothing is ever like that again."

He looked at the smeared window and wondered if this day could end without disaster. In his mind he saw her falling in the snow wearing a tramp's costume, and he saw her coming to him in the orphanage dressing gown. He saw her drowning face at the party. He was afraid for himself. The story was still unfinished. It had to come to a climax, something threatening to him. But there was no climax. They talked that day, and afterward nothing else was said. They went on in the same office for a short time, until Peter left for Ceylon; until somebody read the right letter, passed it on for the right initials, and the Fraziers began the Oriental tour that should have made their fortune. Agnes and Peter were too tired to speak after that morning. They were like a married couple in danger, taking care.

But what were they talking about that day, so quietly, such old friends? They talked about dying, about being ambitious, about being religious, about different kinds of love. What did she see when she looked at him—taking her knuckle slowly away from her mouth, bringing her hand down to the desk, letting it rest there? They were both Canadians, so they had this much together—the knowledge of the little you dare admit. Death, near death, the best thing, the wrong thing—God knows what they were telling each other. Anyway, nothing happened.

When, on Sunday mornings, Sheilah and Peter talk about those times, they take on the glamour of something still to come. It is then he remembers Agnes Brusen. He never says her name. Sheilah wouldn't remember Agnes. Agnes is the only secret Peter has from his wife, the only puzzle he pieces together without her help. He thinks about families in the West as they were fifteen, twenty years ago—the iron-cold ambition, and every member pushing the next one on. He thinks of his father's parties. When he thinks of his father he imagines him with Sheilah, in a crowd. Actually, Sheilah and Peter's father never met, but they might have liked each other. His father admired good-looking women. Peter wonders what they were doing over there in Geneva—not Sheilah and Peter, *Agnes* and Peter. It is almost as if they had once run away together, silly as children, irresponsible as lovers. Peter and Sheilah are back where they started. While they were out in world affairs picking up microbes and debts, always on the fringe of disaster, the fringe of a fortune, Agnes went on and did—what? They lost each other. He thinks of the ice wagon going down the street. He sees something he has never seen in his life—a Western town that belongs to Agnes. Here is Agnes—small, mole-faced, round-shouldered because she has always carried a younger child. She watches the ice wagon and the trail of ice water in a morning invented for her: hers. He sees the weak prairie trees and the shadows on the sidewalk. Nothing moves except the shadows and the ice wagon and the changing amber of the child's eyes. The child is Peter. He has seen the grain of the cement sidewalk and the grass in the cracks, and the dust, and the dandelions at the edge of the road. He is there. He has taken the morning that belongs to Agnes, he is up before the others, and he knows everything. There is nothing he doesn't know. He could keep the morning, if he wanted to, but what can Peter do with the start of a summer day? Sheilah is here, it is a true Sunday morning, with its dimness and headache and remorse and regrets, and this is life. He says, "We have the Balenciaga." He touches Sheilah's hand. The children have their aunt now, and he and Sheilah have each other. Everything works out, somehow or other. Let Agnes have the start of the day. Let Agnes think it was invented for her. Who wants to be alone in the universe? No, begin at the beginning: Peter lost Agnes. Agnes says to herself somewhere, Peter is lost.

1963

# CHARLOTTE PERKINS GILMAN
## *1860–1935*

Gilman was born in Hartford, Connecticut. Aspiring to be an artist, she briefly attended the Rhode Island School of Design and married the artist Charles Stetson. After the birth of their daughter she went into a deep and long-drawn depression. The medical treatment available not only failed to help her, it angered her. She was told to limit herself to a quiet domestic life and "never to touch pen, brush, or pencil again." From her anger sprang her famous story "The Yellow Wallpaper" and a long career as a lecturer and a writer of tracts and books expounding feminist causes. Her second marriage, when her mental health had improved, was a solid and productive one. Among her writings are the novels *What Diantha Did* (1910), *The Crux* (1911), and *Herland* (1915). She ended her own life in 1935.

## The Yellow Wallpaper

It is very seldom that mere ordinary people like John and myself secure ancestral halls for the summer.

A colonial mansion, a hereditary estate, I would say a haunted house and reach the height of romantic felicity—but that would be asking too much of fate!

Still I will proudly declare that there is something queer about it.

Else, why should it be let so cheaply? And why have stood so long untenanted?

John laughs at me, of course, but one expects that.

John is practical in the extreme. He has no patience with faith, an intense horror of superstition, and he scoffs openly at any talk of things not to be felt and seen and put down in figures.

John is a physician, and *perhaps*—(I would not say it to a living soul, of course, but this is dead paper and a great relief to my mind)—*perhaps* that is one reason I do not get well faster.

You see, he does not believe I am sick! And what can one do?

If a physician of high standing, and one's own husband, assures friends and relatives that there is really nothing the matter with one but temporary nervous depression—a slight hysterical tendency[1]—what is one to do?

---

1. At the time this story was written, *hysteria* was a term used loosely to describe a wide variety of symptoms, thought to be particularly prevalent among women, that indicated emotional disturbance or dysfunction. Depression, anxiety, excitability, and vague somatic complaints were among the conditions treated as "hysteria."

My brother is also a physician, and also of high standing, and he says the same thing.

So I take phosphates or phosphites—whichever it is—and tonics, and air and exercise, and journeys, and am absolutely forbidden to "work" until I am well again.

Personally, I disagree with their ideas.

Personally, I believe that congenial work, with excitement and change, would do me good.

But what is one to do?

I did write for a while in spite of them; but it *does* exhaust me a good deal—having to be so sly about it, or else meet with heavy opposition.

I sometimes fancy that in my condition, if I had less opposition and more society and stimulus—but John says the very worst thing I can do is to think about my condition, and I confess it always makes me feel bad.

So I will let it alone and talk about the house.

The most beautiful place! It is quite alone, standing well back from the road, quite three miles from the village. It makes me think of English places that you read about, for there are hedges and walls and gates that lock, and lots of separate little houses for the gardeners and people.

There is a *delicious* garden! I never saw such a garden—large and shady, full of box-bordered paths, and lined with long grape-covered arbors with seats under them.

There were greenhouses, but they are all broken now.

There was some legal trouble, I believe, something about the heirs and co-heirs; anyhow, the place has been empty for years.

That spoils my ghostliness, I am afraid, but I don't care—there is something strange about the house—I can feel it.

I even said so to John one moonlight evening, but he said what I felt was a draught, and shut the window.

I get unreasonably angry with John sometimes. I'm sure I never used to be so sensitive. I think it is due to this nervous condition.

But John says if I feel so, I shall neglect proper self-control; so I take pains to control myself—before him, at least, and that makes me very tired.

I don't like our room a bit. I wanted one downstairs that opened on the piazza and had roses all over the window, and such pretty old-fashioned chintz hangings! But John would not hear of it.

He said there was only one window and not room for two beds, and no near room for him if he took another.

He is very careful and loving, and hardly lets me stir without special direction.

I have a schedule prescription for each hour in the day; he takes all care from me, and so I feel basely ungrateful not to value it more.

He said we came here solely on my account, that I was to have perfect rest and all the air I could get. "Your exercise depends on your strength, my dear," said he, "and your food somewhat on your appetite; but air you can absorb all the time." So we took the nursery at the top of the house.

It is a big, airy room, the whole floor nearly, with windows that look all ways, and air and sunshine galore. It was nursery first and then playroom and gymnasium, I should judge; for the windows are barred for little children, and there are rings and things in the walls.

The paint and paper look as if a boys' school had used it. It is stripped off—the paper—in great patches all around the head of my bed, about as far as I can reach, and in a great place on the other side of the room low down. I never saw a worse paper in my life. One of those sprawling flamboyant patterns committing every artistic sin.

It is dull enough to confuse the eye in following, pronounced enough to constantly irritate and provoke study, and when you follow the lame uncertain curves for a little distance they suddenly commit suicide—plunge off at outrageous angles, destroy themselves in unheard-of contradictions.

The color is repellant, almost revolting; a smouldering unclean yellow, strangely faded by the slow-turning sunlight. It is a dull yet lurid orange in some places, a sickly sulphur tint in others.

No wonder the children hated it! I should hate it myself if I had to live in this room long.

There comes John, and I must put this away—he hates to have me write a word.

We have been here two weeks, and I haven't felt like writing before, since that first day.

I am sitting by the window now, up in this atrocious nursery, and there is nothing to hinder my writing as much as I please, save lack of strength.

John is away all day, and even some nights when his cases are serious.

I am glad my case is not serious!

But these nervous troubles are dreadfully depressing.

John does not know how much I really suffer. He knows there is no reason to suffer, and that satisfies him.

Of course it is only nervousness. It does weigh on me so not to do my duty in any way!

I mean to be such a help to John, such a real rest and comfort, and here I am a comparative burden already!

Nobody would believe what an effort it is to do what little I am able—to dress and entertain, and order things.

It is fortunate Mary is so good with the baby. Such a dear baby!

And yet I *cannot* be with him, it makes me so nervous.

I suppose John never was nervous in his life. He laughs at me so about this wallpaper!

At first he meant to repaper the room, but afterwards he said that I was letting it get the better of me, and that nothing was worse for a nervous patient than to give way to such fancies.

He said that after the wallpaper was changed it would be the heavy bedstead, and then the barred windows, and then that gate at the head of the stairs, and so on.

"You know the place is doing you good," he said, "and really, dear, I don't care to renovate the house just for a three months' rental."

"Then do let us go downstairs," I said. "There are such pretty rooms there."

Then he took me in his arms and called me a blessed little goose, and said he would go down cellar, if I wished, and have it whitewashed into the bargain.

But he is right enough about the beds and windows and things.

It is as airy and comfortable a room as anyone need wish, and, of course, I would not be so silly as to make him uncomfortable just for a whim.

I'm really getting quite fond of the big room, all but that horrid paper.

Out of one window I can see the garden—those mysterious deep-shaded arbors, the riotous old-fashioned flowers, and bushes and gnarly trees.

Out of another I get a lovely view of the bay and a little private wharf belonging to the estate. There is a beautiful shaded lane that runs down there from the house. I always fancy I see people walking in these numerous paths and arbors, but John has cautioned me not to give way to fancy in the least. He says that with my imaginative power and habit of story-making, a nervous weakness like mine is sure to lead to all manner of excited fancies, and that I ought to use my will and good sense to check the tendency. So I try.

I think sometimes that if I were only well enough to write a little it would relieve the press of ideas and rest me.

But I find I get pretty tired when I try.

It is so discouraging not to have any advice and companionship about my work. When I get really well, John says we will ask Cousin Henry and Julia down for a long visit; but he says he would as soon put fireworks in my pillow-case as to let me have those stimulating people about now.

I wish I could get well faster.

But I must not think about that. This paper looks to me as if it *knew* what a vicious influence it had!

There is a recurrent spot where the pattern lolls like a broken neck and two bulbous eyes stare at you upside down.

I get positively angry with the impertinence of it and the everlastingness. Up and down and sideways they crawl, and those absurd unblinking eyes are everywhere. There is one place where two breadths didn't match, and the eyes go all up and down the line, one a little higher than the other.

I never saw so much expression in an inanimate thing before, and we all know how much expression they have! I used to lie awake as a child and get more entertainment and terror out of blank walls and plain furniture than most children could find in a toy-store.

I remember what a kindly wink the knobs of our big old bureau used to have, and there was one chair that always seemed like a strong friend.

I used to feel that if any of the other things looked too fierce I could always hop into that chair and be safe.

The furniture in this room is no worse than inharmonious, however, for we had to bring it all from downstairs. I suppose when this was used as a play-room they had to take the nursery things out, and no wonder! I never saw such ravages as the children have made here.

The wallpaper, as I said before, is torn off in spots, and it sticketh closer than a brother[2]—they must have had perseverance as well as hatred.

Then the floor is scratched and gouged and splintered, the plaster itself is dug out here and there, and this great heavy bed which is all we found in the room, looks as if it had been through the wars.

But I don't mind it a bit—only the paper.

2. See Proverbs 18:24: "A man that hath friends must show himself friendly; and there is a friend that sticketh closer than a brother."

There comes John's sister. Such a dear girl as she is, and so careful of me! I must not let her find me writing.

She is a perfect and enthusiastic housekeeper, and hopes for no better profession. I verily believe she thinks it is the writing which made me sick!

But I can write when she is out, and see her a long way off from these windows.

There is one that commands the road, a lovely shaded winding road, and one that just looks off over the country. A lovely country, too, full of great elms and velvet meadows.

This wallpaper has a kind of sub-pattern in a different shade, a particularly irritating one, for you can only see it in certain lights, and not clearly then.

But in the places where it isn't faded and where the sun is just so—I can see a strange, provoking, formless sort of figure that seems to skulk about behind that silly and conspicuous front design.

There's sister on the stairs!

Well, the Fourth of July is over! The people are all gone, and I am tired out. John thought it might do me good to see a little company, so we just had Mother and Nellie and the children down for a week.

Of course I didn't do a thing. Jennie sees to everything now.

But it tired me all the same.

John says if I don't pick up faster he shall send me to Weir Mitchell[3] in the fall.

But I don't want to go there at all. I had a friend who was in his hands once, and she says he is just like John and my brother, only more so!

Besides, it is such an undertaking to go so far.

I don't feel as if it was worthwhile to turn my hand over for anything, and I'm getting dreadfully fretful and querulous.

I cry at nothing, and cry most of the time.

Of course I don't when John is here, or anybody else, but when I am alone.

And I am alone a good deal just now. John is kept in town very often by serious cases, and Jennie is good and lets me alone when I want her to.

So I walk a little in the garden or down that lovely lane, sit on the porch under the roses, and lie down up here a good deal.

I'm getting really fond of the room in spite of the wallpaper. Perhaps *because* of the wallpaper.

It dwells in my mind so!

I lie here on this great immovable bed—it is nailed down, I believe—and follow that pattern about by the hour. It is as good as gymnastics, I assure you. I start, we'll say, at the bottom, down in the corner over there where it has not been touched, and I determine for the thousandth time that I *will* follow that pointless pattern to some sort of conclusion.

I know a little of the principle of design, and I know this thing was not arranged on any laws of radiation, or alternation, or repetition, or symmetry, or anything else that I ever heard of.

It is repeated, of course, by the breadths, but not otherwise.

---

**3.** Silas Weir Mitchell (1829–1914), American physician, novelist, and specialist in nerve disorders, popularized the "rest cure" in the management of hysteria, nervous breakdowns, and related disorders.

Looked at in one way, each breadth stands alone; the bloated curves and flourishes—a kind of "debased Romanesque"[4] with delirium tremens—go waddling up and down in isolated columns of fatuity.

But, on the other hand, they connect diagonally, and the sprawling outlines run off in great slanting waves of optic horror, like a lot of wallowing seaweeds in full chase.

The whole thing goes horizontally, too, at least it seems so, and I exhaust myself trying to distinguish the order of its going in that direction.

They have used a horizontal breadth for a frieze,[5] and that adds wonderfully to the confusion.

There is one end of the room where it is almost intact, and there, when the crosslights fade and the low sun shines directly upon it, I can almost fancy radiation after all—the interminable grotesque seems to form around a common center and rush off in headlong plunges of equal distraction.

It makes me tired to follow it. I will take a nap, I guess.

I don't know why I should write this.

I don't want to.

I don't feel able.

And I know John would think it absurd. But I *must* say what I feel and think in some way—it is such a relief!

But the effort is getting to be greater than the relief.

Half the time now I am awfully lazy, and lie down ever so much.

John says I mustn't lose my strength, and has me take cod liver oil and lots of tonics and things, to say nothing of ale and wine and rare meat.

Dear John! He loves me very dearly, and hates to have me sick. I tried to have a real earnest reasonable talk with him the other day, and tell him how I wish he would let me go and make a visit to Cousin Henry and Julia.

But he said I wasn't able to go, nor able to stand it after I got there; and I did not make out a very good case for myself, for I was crying before I had finished.

It is getting to be a great effort for me to think straight. Just this nervous weakness, I suppose.

And dear John gathered me up in his arms, and just carried me upstairs and laid me on the bed, and sat by me and read to me till it tired my head.

He said I was his darling and his comfort and all he had, and that I must take care of myself for his sake, and keep well.

He says no one but myself can help me out of it, that I must use my will and self-control and not let any silly fancies run away with me.

There's one comfort—the baby is well and happy, and does not have to occupy this nursery with the horrid wallpaper.

If we had not used it, that blessed child would have! What a fortunate escape! Why, I wouldn't have a child of mine, an impressionable little thing, live in such a room for worlds.

I never thought of it before, but it is lucky that John kept me here after all, I can stand it so much easier than a baby, you see.

---

4. Romanesque style is here associated with ornamental complexity and repeated motifs and figures.
5. An ornamental band used as a border at the top of the wall.

Of course I never mention it to them any more—I am too wise—but I keep watch for it all the same.

There are things in that paper that nobody knows about but me, or ever will.

Behind that outside pattern the dim shapes get clearer every day.

It is always the same shape, only very numerous.

And it is like a woman stooping down and creeping about behind that pattern. I don't like it a bit. I wonder—I begin to think—I wish John would take me away from here!

It is so hard to talk with John about my case, because he is so wise, and because he loves me so.

But I tried it last night.

It was moonlight. The moon shines in all around just as the sun does.

I hate to see it sometimes, it creeps so slowly, and always comes in by one window or another.

John was asleep and I hated to waken him, so I kept still and watched the moonlight on that undulating wallpaper till I felt creepy.

The faint figure behind seemed to shake the pattern, just as if she wanted to get out.

I got up softly and went to feel and see if the paper *did* move, and when I came back John was awake.

"What is it, little girl?" he said. "Don't go walking about like that—you'll get cold."

I thought it was a good time to talk, so I told him that I really was not gaining here, and that I wished he would take me away.

"Why, darling!" said he. "Our lease will be up in three weeks, and I can't see how to leave before.

"The repairs are not done at home, and I cannot possibly leave town just now. Of course if you were in any danger, I could and would, but you really are better, dear, whether you can see it or not. I am a doctor, dear, and I know. You are gaining flesh and color, your appetite is better, I feel really much easier about you."

"I don't weigh a bit more," said I, "nor as much; and my appetite may be better in the evening when you are here but it is worse in the morning when you are away!"

"Bless her little heart!" said he with a big hug. "She shall be as sick as she pleases! But now let's improve the shining hours by going to sleep, and talk about it in the morning!"

"And you won't go away?" I asked gloomily.

"Why, how can I, dear? It is only three weeks more and then we will take a nice little trip of a few days while Jennie is getting the house ready. Really, dear, you are better!"

"Better in body perhaps—" I began, and stopped short, for he sat up straight and looked at me with such a stern, reproachful look that I could not say another word.

"My darling," said he, "I beg of you, for my sake and for our child's sake, as well as for your own, that you will never for one instant let that idea enter your mind! There is nothing so dangerous, so fascinating, to a temperament like yours. It is a false and foolish fancy. Can you not trust me as a physician when I tell you so?"

So of course I said no more on that score, and we went to sleep before long. He thought I was asleep first, but I wasn't, and lay there for hours trying to decide whether that front pattern and the back pattern really did move together or separately.

On a pattern like this, by daylight, there is a lack of sequence, a defiance of law, that is a constant irritant to a normal mind.

The color is hideous enough, and unreliable enough, and infuriating enough, but the pattern is torturing.

You think you have mastered it, but just as you get well under way in following, it turns a back-somersault and there you are. It slaps you in the face, knocks you down, and tramples upon you. It is like a bad dream.

The outside pattern is a florid arabesque, reminding one of a fungus. If you can imagine a toadstool in joints, an interminable string of toadstools, budding and sprouting in endless convolutions—why, that is something like it.

That is, sometimes!

There is one marked peculiarity about this paper, a thing nobody seems to notice but myself, and that is that it changes as the light changes.

When the sun shoots in through the east window—I always watch for that first long, straight ray—it changes so quickly that I never can quite believe it.

That is why I watch it always.

By moonlight—the moon shines in all night when there is a moon—I wouldn't know it was the same paper.

At night in any kind of light, in twilight, candlelight, lamplight, and worst of all by moonlight, it becomes bars! The outside pattern, I mean, and the woman behind it is as plain as can be.

I didn't realize for a long time what the thing was that showed behind, that dim sub-pattern, but now I am quite sure it is a woman.

By daylight she is subdued, quiet. I fancy it is the pattern that keeps her so still. It is so puzzling. It keeps me quiet by the hour.

I lie down ever so much now. John says it is good for me, and to sleep all I can.

Indeed he started the habit by making me lie down for an hour after each meal.

It is a very bad habit I am convinced, for you see, I don't sleep.

And that cultivates deceit, for I don't tell them I'm awake—O no!

The fact is I am getting a little afraid of John.

He seems very queer sometimes, and even Jennie has an inexplicable look.

It strikes me occasionally, just as a scientific hypothesis, that perhaps it is the paper!

I have watched John when he did not know I was looking, and come into the room suddenly on the most innocent excuses, and I've caught him several times *looking at the paper!* And Jennie too. I caught Jennie with her hand on it once.

She didn't know I was in the room, and when I asked her in a quiet, a very quiet voice, with the most restrained manner possible, what she was doing with the paper—she turned around as if she had been caught stealing, and looked quite angry—asked me why I should frighten her so!

Then she said that the paper stained everything it touched, that she had found yellow smooches on all my clothes and John's, and she wished we would be more careful!

Did not that sound innocent? But I know she was studying that pattern, and I am determined that nobody shall find it out but myself!

Life is very much more exciting now than it used to be. You see I have something more to expect, to look forward to, to watch. I really do eat better, and am more quiet than I was.

John is so pleased to see me improve! He laughed a little the other day, and said I seemed to be flourishing in spite of my wallpaper.

I turned it off with a laugh. I had no intention of telling him it was *because* of the wallpaper—he would make fun of me. He might even want to take me away.

I don't want to leave now until I have found it out. There is a week more, and I think that will be enough.

I'm feeling so much better!

I don't sleep much at night, for it is so interesting to watch developments; but I sleep a good deal during the daytime.

In the daytime it is tiresome and perplexing.

There are always new shoots on the fungus, and new shades of yellow all over it. I cannot keep count of them, though I have tried conscientiously.

It is the strangest yellow, that wallpaper! It makes me think of all the yellow things I ever saw—not beautiful ones like buttercups, but old, foul, bad yellow things.

But there is something else about that paper—the smell! I noticed it the moment we came into the room, but with so much air and sun it was not bad. Now we have had a week of fog and rain, and whether the windows are open or not, the smell is here.

It creeps all over the house.

I find it hovering in the dining-room, skulking in the parlor, hiding in the hall, lying in wait for me on the stairs.

It gets into my hair.

Even when I go to ride, if I turn my head suddenly and surprise it—there is that smell!

Such a peculiar odor, too! I have spent hours in trying to analyze it, to find what it smelled like.

It is not bad—at first—and very gentle, but quite the subtlest, most enduring odor I ever met.

In this damp weather it is awful, I wake up in the night and find it hanging over me.

It used to disturb me at first. I thought seriously of burning the house—to reach the smell.

But now I am used to it. The only thing I can think of that it is like is the *color* of the paper! A yellow smell.

There is a very funny mark on this wall, low down, near the mopboard. A streak that runs round the room. It goes behind every piece of furniture, except the bed, a long, straight, even *smooch,* as if it had been rubbed over and over.

I wonder how it was done and who did it, and what they did it for. Round and round and round—round and round and round—it makes me dizzy!

I really have discovered something at last.

Through watching so much at night, when it changes so, I have finally found out.

The front pattern *does* move—and no wonder! The woman behind shakes it!

Sometimes I think there are a great many women behind, and sometimes only one, and she crawls around fast, and her crawling shakes it all over.

Then in the very bright spots she keeps still, and in the very shady spots she just takes hold of the bars and shakes them hard.

And she is all the time trying to climb through. But nobody could climb through that pattern—it strangles so; I think that is why it has so many heads.

They get through, and then the pattern strangles them off and turns them upside down, and makes their eyes white!

If those heads were covered or taken off it would not be half so bad.

I think that woman gets out in the daytime!

And I'll tell you why—privately—I've seen her!

I can see her out of every one of my windows!

It is the same woman, I know, for she is always creeping, and most women do not creep by daylight.

I see her in that long shaded lane, creeping up and down. I see her in those dark grape arbors, creeping all around the garden.

I see her on that long road under the trees, creeping along, and when a carriage comes she hides under the blackberry vines.

I don't blame her a bit. It must be very humiliating to be caught creeping by daylight!

I always lock the door when I creep by daylight. I can't do it at night, for I know John would suspect something at once.

And John is so queer now that I don't want to irritate him. I wish he would take another room! Besides, I don't want anybody to get that woman out at night but myself.

I often wonder if I could see her out of all the windows at once.

But, turn as fast as I can, I can only see out of one at one time.

And though I always see her, she *may* be able to creep faster than I can turn! I have watched her sometimes away off in the open country, creeping as fast as a cloud shadow in a wind.

If only that top pattern could be gotten off from the under one! I mean to try it, little by little.

I have found out another funny thing, but I shan't tell it this time! It does not do to trust people too much.

There are only two more days to get this paper off, and I believe John is beginning to notice. I don't like the look in his eyes.

And I heard him ask Jennie a lot of professional questions about me. She had a very good report to give.

She said I slept a good deal in the daytime.

John knows I don't sleep very well at night, for all I'm so quiet!

He asked me all sorts of questions, too, and pretended to be very loving and kind.

As if I couldn't see through him!

Still, I don't wonder he acts so, sleeping under this paper for three months.

It only interests me, but I feel sure John and Jennie are affected by it.

Hurrah! This is the last day, but it is enough. John is to stay in town over night, and won't be out until this evening.

Jennie wanted to sleep with me—the sly thing; but I told her I should undoubtedly rest better for a night all alone.

That was clever, for really I wasn't alone a bit! As soon as it was moonlight and that poor thing began to crawl and shake the pattern, I got up and ran to help her.

I pulled and she shook, I shook and she pulled, and before morning we had peeled off yards of that paper.

A strip about as high as my head and half around the room.

And then when the sun came and that awful pattern began to laugh at me, I declared I would finish it today!

We go away tomorrow, and they are moving all my furniture down again to leave things as they were before.

Jennie looked at the wall in amazement, but I told her merrily that I did it out of pure spite at the vicious thing.

She laughed and said she wouldn't mind doing it herself, but I must not get tired.

How she betrayed herself that time!

But I am here, and no person touches this paper but Me—not *alive!*

She tried to get me out of the room—it was too patent! But I said it was so quiet and empty and clean now that I believed I would lie down again and sleep all I could; and not to wake me even for dinner—I would call when I woke.

So now she is gone, and the servants are gone, and the things are gone, and there is nothing left but that great bedstead nailed down, with the canvas mattress we found on it.

We shall sleep downstairs tonight, and take the boat home tomorrow.

I quite enjoy the room, now it is bare again.

How those children did tear about here!

This bedstead is fairly gnawed!

But I must get to work.

I have locked the door and thrown the key down into the front path.

I don't want to go out, and I don't want to have anybody come in, till John comes.

I want to astonish him.

I've got a rope up here that even Jennie did not find. If that woman does get out, and tries to get away, I can tie her!

But I forgot I could not reach far without anything to stand on!

This bed will *not* move!

I tried to lift and push it until I was lame, and then I got so angry I bit off a little piece at one corner—but it hurt my teeth.

Then I peeled off all the paper I could reach standing on the floor. It sticks horribly and the pattern just enjoys it! All those strangled heads and bulbous eyes and waddling fungus growths just shriek with derision!

I am getting angry enough to do something desperate. To jump out of the window would be admirable exercise, but the bars are too strong even to try.

Besides I wouldn't do it. Of course not. I know well enough that a step like that is improper and might be misconstrued.

I don't like to *look* out of the windows even—there are so many of those creeping women, and they creep so fast.

I wonder if they all come out of that wallpaper as I did?

But I am securely fastened now by my well-hidden rope—you don't get *me* out in the road there!

I suppose I shall have to get back behind the pattern when it comes night, and that is hard!

It is so pleasant to be out in this great room and creep around as I please!

I don't want to go outside. I won't, even if Jennie asks me to.

For outside you have to creep on the ground, and everything is green instead of yellow.

But here I can creep smoothly on the floor, and my shoulder just fits in that long smooch around the wall, so I cannot lose my way.

Why there's John at the door!

It is no use, young man, you can't open it!

How he does call and pound!

Now he's crying to Jennie for an axe.

It would be a shame to break down that beautiful door!

"John dear!" said I in the gentlest voice. "The key is down by the front steps, under a plantain leaf!"

That silenced him for a few moments.

Then he said—very quietly indeed, "Open the door, my darling!"

"I can't," said I. "The key is down by the front door under a plantain leaf!"

And then I said it again, several times, very gently and slowly, and said it so often that he had to go and see, and he got it of course, and came in. He stopped short by the door.

"What is the matter?" he cried. "For God's sake, what are you doing!"

I kept on creeping just the same, but I looked at him over my shoulder.

"I've got out at last," said I, "in spite of you and Jane! And I've pulled off most of the paper, so you can't put me back!"

Now why should that man have fainted? But he did, and right across my path by the wall, so that I had to creep over him every time!

1892

# NATHANIEL HAWTHORNE
## *1804–1864*

Hawthorne was born in Salem, Massachusetts, where he lived in quiet seclusion before and after his four years of attendance at Bowdoin College. Seldom leaving his room by daylight, he read, meditated, and wrote the stories and sketches that first appeared in two volumes of *Twice-Told Tales* (1837 and 1842). They brought him neither renown nor money, so in 1839 he took a job in the Boston Custom House and, when he lost it, spent some time at Brook Farm, an experiment in communal living, which would later provide him with background for his novel *The Blithedale Romance* (1852). At the time of his marriage in 1842 he took his wife to live in a historic house called the Old Manse in Concord, publishing more short pieces in 1846 in a volume called *Mosses from an Old Manse. The Scarlet Letter*, his greatest novel, published in 1850, finally brought him recognition as a major literary figure. In 1853 he was appointed consul to Liverpool by his college friend Franklin Pierce, who had become president of the United States. After four years of service in his post, Hawthorne traveled in England and Italy until his return to America in 1860. Much of his work is colored by romanticism, while the weight of his Puritan heritage, with its ethical biases and emphasis on sin, radically shaped his themes. (One of Hawthorne's ancestors had been a judge in the notorious Salem witchcraft trials.) The allegorical strain in much of his imaginative work is compensated by the clear and realistic picture of daily experience in his notebooks and in many travel sketches. His novels include *The House of Seven Gables* (1851) and *The Marble Faun* (1860).

## Young Goodman Brown

Young Goodman[1] Brown came forth at sunset into the street of Salem village; but put his head back, after crossing the threshold, to exchange a parting kiss with his young wife. And Faith, as the wife was aptly named, thrust her own pretty head into the street, letting the wind play with the pink ribbons of her cap while she called to Goodman Brown.

"Dearest heart," whispered she, softly and rather sadly, when her lips were close to his ear, "prithee put off your journey until sunrise and sleep in your own bed to-night. A lone woman is troubled with such dreams and such thoughts that she's afeard of herself sometimes. Pray tarry with me this night, dear husband, of all nights in the year!"

---

**1.** Title of respect for those below the rank of gentleman in colonial New England.

"My love and my Faith," replied young Goodman Brown, "of all nights in the year, this one night must I tarry away from thee. My journey, as thou callest it, forth and back again, must needs be done 'twixt now and sunrise. What, my sweet, pretty wife, dost thou doubt me already, and we but three months married?"

"Then God bless you!" said Faith, with the pink ribbons; "and may you find all well when you come back."

"Amen!" cried Goodman Brown. "Say thy prayers, dear Faith, and go to bed at dusk, and no harm will come to thee."

So they parted; and the young man pursued his way until, being about to turn the corner by the meeting-house, he looked back and saw the head of Faith still peeping after him with a melancholy air, in spite of her pink ribbons.

"Poor little Faith!" thought he, for his heart smote him. "What a wretch am I to leave her on such an errand! She talks of dreams, too. Methought as she spoke there was trouble in her face, as if a dream had warned her what work is to be done to-night. But no, no; 't would kill her to think it. Well, she's a blessed angel on earth; and after this one night I'll cling to her skirts and follow her to heaven."

With this excellent resolve for the future, Goodman Brown felt himself justified in making more haste on his present evil purpose. He had taken a dreary road, darkened by all the gloomiest trees of the forest, which barely stood aside to let the narrow path creep through, and closed immediately behind. It was all as lonely as could be; and there is this peculiarity in such a solitude, that the traveler knows not who may be concealed by the innumerable trunks and the thick boughs overhead; so that with lonely footsteps he may yet be passing through an unseen multitude.

"There may be a devilish Indian behind every tree," said Goodman Brown to himself; and he glanced fearfully behind him as he added, "What if the devil himself should be at my very elbow!"

His head being turned back, he passed a crook of the road, and, looking forward again, beheld the figure of a man, in grave and decent attire, seated at the foot of an old tree. He arose at Goodman Brown's approach and walked onward side by side with him.

"You are late, Goodman Brown," said he. "The clock of the Old South was striking as I came through Boston,[2] and that is full fifteen minutes agone."

"Faith kept me back a while," replied the young man, with a tremor in his voice, caused by the sudden appearance of his companion, though not wholly unexpected.

It was now deep dusk in the forest, and deepest in that part of it where these two were journeying. As nearly as could be discerned, the second traveller was about fifty years old, apparently in the same rank of life as Goodman Brown, and bearing a considerable resemblance to him, though perhaps more in expression than features. Still they might have been taken for father and son. And yet, though the elder person was as simply clad as the younger, and as simple in manner too, he had an indescribable air of one who knew the

---

2. Boston is some fifteen miles from Salem—perhaps an indication of the supernatural speed of the speaker's travel. *Old South:* Boston's Old South Church, established by the Puritans in 1669.

world, and would not have felt abashed at the governor's dinner table or in King William's[3] court, were it possible that his affairs should call him thither. But the only thing about him that could be fixed upon as remarkable was his staff, which bore the likeness of a great black snake, so curiously wrought that it might almost be seen to twist and wriggle itself like a living serpent. This, of course, must have been an ocular deception, assisted by the uncertain light.

"Come, Goodman Brown!" cried his fellow-traveller, "this is a dull pace for the beginning of a journey. Take my staff, if you are so soon weary."

"Friend," said the other, exchanging his slow pace for a full stop, "having kept covenant by meeting thee here, it is my purpose now to return whence I came. I have scruples touching the matter thou wot'st[4] of."

"Sayest thou so?" replied he of the serpent, smiling apart. "Let us walk on, nevertheless, reasoning as we go; and if I convince thee not thou shalt turn back. We are but a little way in the forest yet."

"Too far, too far!" exclaimed the goodman, unconsciously resuming his walk. "My father never went into the woods on such an errand, nor his father before him. We have been a race of honest men and good Christians since the days of the martyrs; and shall I be the first of the name of Brown that ever took this path and kept—"

"Such company, thou wouldst say," observed the elder person, interpreting his pause. "Well said, Goodman Brown! I have been as well acquainted with your family as with ever a one among the Puritans; and that's no trifle to say. I helped your grandfather, the constable, when he lashed the Quaker woman so smartly through the streets of Salem; and it was I that brought your father a pitch-pine knot, kindled at my own hearth, to set fire to an Indian village, in King Philip's war.[5] They were my good friends, both; and many a pleasant walk have we had along this path, and returned merrily after midnight. I would fain be friends with you for their sake."

"If it be as thou sayest," replied Goodman Brown, "I marvel they never spoke of these matters; or, verily, I marvel not, seeing that the least rumor of the sort would have driven them from New England. We are a people of prayer, and good works to boot, and abide no such wickedness."

"Wickedness or not," said the traveler with the twisted staff, "I have a very general acquaintance here in New England. The deacons of many a church have drunk the communion wine with me; the selectmen of divers towns make me their chairman; and a majority of the Great and General Court are firm supporters of my interest. The governor and I, too—But these are state secrets."

"Can this be so?" cried Goodman Brown, with a stare of amazement at his undisturbed companion. "Howbeit, I have nothing to do with the governor and council; they have their own ways, and are no rule for a simple husbandman like me. But, were I to go on with thee, how should I meet the eye of that good old man, our minister, at Salem village? Oh, his voice would make me tremble both Sabbath day and lecture day."

---

**3.** King William III of England (ruled 1689–1702).  **4.** Know (archaic).  **5.** Rebellion by Wampanoag Indians against white settlers (1675–76).

Thus far the elder traveller had listened with due gravity; but now burst into a fit of irrepressible mirth, shaking himself so violently that his snake-like staff actually seemed to wriggle in sympathy.

"Ha! ha! ha!" shouted he again and again; then composing himself, "Well, go on, Goodman Brown, go on; but, prithee, don't kill me with laughing."

"Well, then, to end the matter at once," said Goodman Brown, considerably nettled, "there is my wife, Faith. It would break her dear little heart; and I'd rather break my own."

"Nay, if that be the case," answered the other, "e'en go thy ways, Goodman Brown. I would not for twenty old women like the one hobbling before us that Faith should come to any harm."

As he spoke he pointed his staff at a female figure on the path, in whom Goodman Brown recognized a very pious and exemplary dame, who had taught him his catechism in youth, and was still his moral and spiritual adviser, jointly with the minister and Deacon Gookin.

"A marvel, truly, that Goody[6] Cloyse should be so far in the wilderness at nightfall," said he. "But with your leave, friend, I shall take a cut through the woods until we have left this Christian woman behind. Being a stranger to you, she might ask whom I was consorting with and whither I was going."

"Be it so," said his fellow-traveller. "Betake you to the woods, and let me keep the path."

Accordingly the young man turned aside, but took care to watch his companion, who advanced softly along the road until he had come within a staff's length of the old dame. She, meanwhile, was making the best of her way, with singular speed for so aged a woman, and mumbling some indistinct words—a prayer, doubtless—as she went. The traveller put forth his staff and touched her withered neck with what seemed the serpent's tail.

"The devil!" screamed the pious old lady.

"Then Goody Cloyse knows her old friend?" observed the traveller, confronting her and leaning on his writhing stick.

"Ah, forsooth, and is it your worship indeed?" cried the good dame. "Yea, truly is it, and in the very image of my old gossip,[7] Goodman Brown, the grandfather of the silly fellow that now is. But—would your worship believe it?—my broomstick hath strangely disappeared, stolen, as I suspect, by that unhanged witch, Goody Cory, and that, too, when I was all anointed with the juice of smallage, and cinquefoil, and wolf's-bane—"[8]

"Mingled with fine wheat and the fat of a new-born babe," said the shape of old Goodman Brown.

"Ah, your worship knows the recipe," cried the old lady, cackling aloud. "So, as I was saying, being all ready for the meeting, and no horse to ride on, I made up my mind to foot it; for they tell me there is a nice young man to be taken into communion to-night. But now your good worship will lend me your arm, and we shall be there in a twinkling."

"That can hardly be," answered her friend. "I may not spare you my arm, Goody Cloyse; but here is my staff, if you will."

---

**6.** "Goodwife," title of respect for a married woman.  **7.** Friend.  **8.** Herbs used in witchcraft.

So saying, he threw it down at her feet, where, perhaps, it assumed life, being one of the rods which its owner had formerly lent to the Egyptian magi.[9] Of this fact, however, Goodman Brown could not take cognizance. He had cast up his eyes in astonishment, and, looking down again, beheld neither Goody Cloyse nor the serpentine staff, but this fellow-traveller alone, who waited for him as calmly as if nothing had happened.

"That old woman taught me my catechism," said the young man; and there was a world of meaning in this simple comment.

They continued to walk onward, while the elder traveller exhorted his companion to make good speed and persevere in the path, discoursing so aptly that his arguments seemed rather to spring up in the bosom of his auditor than to be suggested by himself. As they went, he plucked a branch of maple, to serve for a walking stick, and began to strip it of the twigs and little boughs, which were wet with evening dew. The moment his fingers touched them they became strangely withered and dried up as with a week's sunshine. Thus the pair proceeded, at a good free pace, until suddenly, in a gloomy hollow of the road, Goodman Brown sat himself down on the stump of a tree and refused to go any farther.

"Friend," said he, stubbornly, "my mind is made up. Not another step will I budge on this errand. What if a wretched old woman do choose to go to the devil when I thought she was going to heaven: is that any reason why I should quit my dear Faith and go after her?"

"You will think better of this by and by," said his acquaintance, composedly. "Sit here and rest yourself a while; and when you feel like moving again, there is my staff to help you along."

Without more words, he threw his companion the maple stick, and was as speedily out of sight as if he had vanished into the deepening gloom. The young man sat a few moments by the roadside, applauding himself greatly, and thinking with how clear a conscience he should meet the minister in his morning walk, nor shrink from the eye of good old Deacon Gookin. And what calm sleep would be his that very night, which was to have been spent so wickedly, but so purely and sweetly now, in the arms of Faith! Amidst these pleasant and praiseworthy meditations, Goodman Brown heard the tramp of horses along the road, and deemed it advisable to conceal himself within the verge of the forest, conscious of the guilty purpose that had brought him thither, though now so happily turned from it.

On came the hoof tramps and the voices of the riders, two grave old voices, conversing soberly as they drew near. These mingled sounds appeared to pass along the road, within a few yards of the young man's hiding-place; but, owing doubtless to the depth of the gloom at that particular spot, neither the travellers nor their steeds were visible. Though their figures brushed the small boughs by the wayside, it could not be seen that they intercepted, even for a moment, the faint gleam from the strip of bright sky athwart which they must have passed. Goodman Brown alternately crouched and stood on tiptoe, pulling aside the branches and thrusting forth his head as far as he durst without discerning so much as a shadow. It vexed him the more, because he

---

**9.** In Exodus 7:8–12, Moses' brother Aaron throws down his staff before the pharaoh, whereupon it turns into a serpent. The pharaoh has his magicians (magi) do the same, "but Aaron's rod swallowed up their rods."

could have sworn, were such a thing possible, that he recognized the voices of the minister and Deacon Gookin, jogging along quietly, as they were wont to do, when bound to some ordination or ecclesiastical council. While yet within hearing, one of the riders stopped to pluck a switch.

"Of the two, reverend sir," said the voice like the deacon's, "I had rather miss an ordination dinner than to-night's meeting. They tell me that some of our community are to be here from Falmouth[1] and beyond, and others from Connecticut and Rhode Island, besides several of the Indian powwows, who, after their fashion, know almost as much deviltry as the best of us. Moreover, there is a goodly young woman to be taken into communion."

"Mighty well, Deacon Gookin!" replied the solemn old tones of the minister. "Spur up, or we shall be late. Nothing can be done, you know, until I get on the ground."

The hoofs clattered again; and the voices, talking so strangely in the empty air, passed on through the forest, where no church had ever been gathered or solitary Christian prayed. Whither, then, could these holy men be journeying so deep into the heathen wilderness? Young Goodman Brown caught hold of a tree for support, being ready to sink down on the ground, faint and over-burdened with the heavy sickness of his heart. He looked up to the sky, doubting whether there really was a heaven above him. Yet there was the blue arch, and the stars brightening in it.

"With heaven above and Faith below, I will yet stand firm against the devil!" cried Goodman Brown.

While he still gazed upward into the deep arch of the firmament and had lifted his hands to pray, a cloud, though no wind was stirring, hurried across the zenith and hid the brightening stars. The blue sky was still visible, except directly overhead, where this black mass of cloud was sweeping swiftly northward. Aloft in the air, as if from the depths of the cloud, came a confused and doubtful sound of voices. Once the listener fancied that he could distinguish the accents of towns-people of his own, men and women, both pious and ungodly, many of whom he had met at the communion table, and had seen others rioting at the tavern. The next moment, so indistinct were the sounds, he doubted whether he had heard aught but the murmur of the old forest, whispering without a wind. Then came a stronger swell of those familiar tones, heard daily in the sunshine at Salem village, but never until now from a cloud of night. There was one voice, of a young woman, uttering lamentations, yet with an uncertain sorrow, and entreating for some favor, which, perhaps, it would grieve her to obtain; and all the unseen multitude, both saints and sinners, seemed to encourage her onward.

"Faith!" shouted Goodman Brown, in a voice of agony and desperation; and the echoes of the forest mocked him, crying, "Faith! Faith!" as if bewildered wretches were seeking her all through the wilderness.

The cry of grief, rage, and terror was yet piercing the night, when the unhappy husband held his breath for a response. There was a scream, drowned immediately in a louder murmur of voices, fading into far-off laughter, as the dark cloud swept away, leaving the clear and silent sky above Goodman Brown. But

---

1. Port in southern Massachusetts: Salem is in northern Massachusetts.

something fluttered lightly down through the air and caught on the branch of a tree. The young man seized it, and beheld a pink ribbon.

"My Faith is gone!" cried he, after one stupefied moment. "There is no good on earth; and sin is but a name. Come, devil; for to thee is this world given."

And, maddened with despair, so that he laughed loud and long, did Goodman Brown grasp his staff and set forth again, at such a rate that he seemed to fly along the forest path rather than to walk or run. The road grew wilder and drearier and more faintly traced, and vanished at length, leaving him in the heart of the dark wilderness, still rushing onward with the instinct that guides mortal man to evil. The whole forest was peopled with frightful sounds—the creaking of the trees, the howling of wild beasts, and the yell of Indians; while sometimes the wind tolled like a distant church bell, and sometimes gave a broad roar around the traveller, as if all Nature were laughing him to scorn. But he was himself the chief horror of the scene, and shrank not from its other horrors.

"Ha! ha! ha!" roared Goodman Brown when the wind laughed at him. "Let us hear which will laugh loudest. Think not to frighten me with your deviltry. Come witch, come wizard, come Indian powwow, come devil himself, and here comes Goodman Brown. You may as well fear him as he fear you."

In truth, all through the haunted forest, there could be nothing more frightful than the figure of Goodman Brown. On he flew among the black pines, brandishing his staff with frenzied gestures, now giving vent to an inspiration of horrid blasphemy, and now shouting forth such laughter as set all the echoes of the forest laughing like demons around him. The fiend in his own shape is less hideous than when he rages in the breast of man. Thus sped the demoniac on his course, until, quivering among the trees, he saw a red light before him, as when the felled trunks and branches of a clearing have been set on fire, and throw up their lurid blaze against the sky, at the hour of midnight. He paused, in a lull of the tempest that had driven him onward, and heard the swell of what seemed a hymn, rolling solemnly from a distance with the weight of many voices. He knew the tune; it was a familiar one in the choir of the village meeting-house. The verse died heavily away, and was lengthened by a chorus, not of human voices, but of all the sounds of the benighted wilderness pealing in awful harmony together. Goodman Brown cried out, and his cry was lost to his own ear, by its unison with the cry of the desert.

In the interval of silence he stole forward until the light glared full upon his eyes. At one extremity of an open space, hemmed in by the dark wall of the forest, arose a rock, bearing some rude, natural resemblance either to an altar or a pulpit, and surrounded by four blazing pines, their tops aflame, their stems untouched, like candles at an evening meeting. The mass of foliage that had overgrown the summit of the rock was all on fire, blazing high into the night and fitfully illuminating the whole field. Each pendent twig and leafy festoon was in a blaze. As the red light arose and fell, a numerous congregation alternately shone forth, then disappeared in shadow, and again grew, as it were, out of the darkness, peopling the heart of the solitary woods at once.

"A grave and dark-clad company," quoth Goodman Brown.

In truth they were such. Among them, quivering to and fro between gloom and splendor, appeared faces that would be seen next day at the council board of the province, and others which, Sabbath after Sabbath, looked devoutly heavenward, and benignantly over the crowded pews, from the holiest pulpits in the land. Some affirm that the lady of the governor was there. At least there were high dames well known to her, and wives of honored husbands, and widows, a great multitude, and ancient maidens, all of excellent repute, and fair young girls, who trembled lest their mothers should espy them. Either the sudden gleams of light flashing over the obscure field bedazzled Goodman Brown, or he recognized a score of the church members of Salem village famous for their especial sanctity. Good old Deacon Gookin had arrived, and waited at the skirts of that venerable saint, his revered pastor. But, irreverently consorting with these grave, reputable, and pious people, these elders of the church, these chaste dames and dewy virgins, there were men of dissolute lives and women of spotted fame, wretches given over to all mean and filthy vice, and suspected even of horrid crimes. It was strange to see that the good shrank not from the wicked, nor were the sinners abashed by the saints. Scattered also among their pale-faced enemies were the Indian priests, or powwows, who had often scared their native forest with more hideous incantations than any known to English witchcraft.

"But where is Faith?" thought Goodman Brown; and, as hope came into his heart, he trembled.

Another verse of the hymn arose, a slow and mournful strain, such as the pious love, but joined to words which expressed all that our nature can conceive of sin, and darkly hinted at far more. Unfathomable to mere mortals is the lore of fiends. Verse after verse was sung, and still the chorus of the desert swelled between like the deepest tone of a mighty organ; and with the final peal of that dreadful anthem there came a sound, as if the roaring wind, the rushing streams, the howling beasts, and every other voice of the unconverted wilderness were mingling and according with the voice of guilty man in homage to the prince of all. The four blazing pines threw up a loftier flame, and obscurely discovered shapes and visages of horror on the smoke wreaths above the impious assembly. At the same moment the fire on the rock shot redly forth and formed a glowing arch above its base, where now appeared a figure. With reverence be it spoken, the apparition bore no slight similitude, both in garb and manner, to some grave divine[2] of the New England churches.

"Bring forth the converts!" cried a voice that echoed through the field and rolled into the forest.

At the word, Goodman Brown stepped forth from the shadow of the trees and approached the congregation, with whom he felt a loathful brotherhood by the sympathy of all that was wicked in his heart. He could have well-nigh sworn that the shape of his own dead father beckoned him to advance, looking downward from a smoke wreath, while a woman, with dim features of despair, threw out her hand to warn him back. Was it his mother? But he had no power to retreat one step, nor to resist, even in thought, when the minister and good old Deacon Gookin seized his arms and led him to the blazing rock. Thither came also the slender form of a veiled female, led between Goody Cloyse, that pious teacher of the catechism, and Martha Carrier, who had received the devil's promise to be queen of hell. A rampant hag was she. And there stood the proselytes beneath the canopy of fire.

2. Clergyman or theologian.

"Welcome, my children," said the dark figure, "to the communion of your race. Ye have found thus young your nature and your destiny. My children, look behind you!"

They turned; and flashing forth, as it were, in a sheet of flame, the fiend worshippers were seen; the smile of welcome gleamed darkly on every visage.

"There," resumed the sable form, "are all whom ye have reverenced from youth. Ye deemed them holier than yourselves, and shrank from your own sin, contrasting it with their lives of righteousness and prayerful aspirations heavenward. Yet here are they all in my worshipping assembly. This night it shall be granted you to know their secret deeds: how hoary-bearded elders of the church have whispered wanton words to the young maids of their households; how many a woman, eager for widows' weeds, has given her husband a drink at bedtime and let him sleep his last sleep in her bosom; how beardless youths have made haste to inherit their fathers' wealth; and how fair damsels—blush not, sweet ones—have dug little graves in the garden, and bidden me, the sole guest, to an infant's funeral. By the sympathy of your human hearts for sin ye shall scent out all the places—whether in church, bed-chamber, street, field, or forest—where crime has been committed, and shall exult to behold the whole earth one stain of guilt, one mighty blood spot. Far more than this. It shall be yours to penetrate, in every bosom, the deep mystery of sin, the fountain of all wicked arts, and which inexhaustibly supplies more evil impulses than human power—than my power at its utmost—can make manifest in deeds. And now, my children, look upon each other."

They did so; and, by the blaze of the hell-kindled torches, the wretched man beheld his Faith, and the wife her husband, trembling before that unhallowed altar.

"Lo, there ye stand, my children," said the figure, in a deep and solemn tone, almost sad with its despairing awfulness, as if his once angelic nature could yet mourn for our miserable race. "Depending upon one another's hearts, ye had still hoped that virtue were not all a dream. Now are ye undeceived. Evil is the nature of mankind. Evil must be your only happiness. Welcome again, my children, to the communion of your race."

"Welcome," repeated the fiend worshippers, in one cry of despair and triumph.

And there they stood, the only pair, as it seemed, who were yet hesitating on the verge of wickedness in this dark world. A basin was hollowed, naturally, in the rock. Did it contain water, reddened by the lurid light? or was it blood? or, perchance, a liquid flame? Herein did the shape of evil dip his hand and prepare to lay the mark of baptism upon their foreheads, that they might be partakers of the mystery of sin, more conscious of the secret guilt of others, both in deed and thought, than they could now be of their own. The husband cast one look at his pale wife, and Faith at him. What polluted wretches would the next glance show them to each other, shuddering alike at what they disclosed and what they saw!

"Faith! Faith!" cried the husband, "look up to Heaven, and resist the wicked one."

Whether Faith obeyed he knew not. Hardly had he spoken when he found himself amid calm night and solitude, listening to a roar of the wind which died heavily away through the forest. He staggered against the rock and felt it chill and damp, while a hanging twig, that had been all on fire, besprinkled his cheek with the coldest dew.

The next morning young Goodman Brown came slowly into the street of Salem village, staring around him like a bewildered man. The good old minister was taking a walk along the graveyard, to get an appetite for breakfast and meditate his sermon, and bestowed a blessing, as he passed, on Goodman Brown. He shrank from the venerable saint as if to avoid an anathema. Old Deacon Gookin was at domestic worship, and the holy words of his prayer were heard through the open window. "What God doth the wizard pray to?" quoth Goodman Brown. Goody Cloyse, that excellent old Christian, stood in the early sunshine, at her own lattice, catechizing a little girl who had brought her a pint of morning's milk. Goodman Brown snatched away the child as from the grasp of the fiend himself. Turning the corner by the meeting-house, he spied the head of Faith, with the pink ribbons, gazing anxiously forth, and bursting into such joy at sight of him that she skipped along the street and almost kissed her husband before the whole village. But Goodman Brown looked sternly and sadly into her face, and passed on without a greeting.

Had Goodman Brown fallen asleep in the forest, and only dreamed a wild dream of a witch-meeting?

Be it so if you will; but, alas! it was a dream of evil omen for young Goodman Brown. A stern, a sad, a darkly meditative, a distrustful, if not a desperate man did he become from the night of that fearful dream. On the Sabbath day, when the congregation were singing a holy psalm, he could not listen because an anthem of sin rushed loudly upon his ear and drowned all the blessed strain. When the minister spoke from the pulpit with power and fervid eloquence, and, with his hand on the open Bible, of the sacred truths of our religion, and of saint-like lives and triumphant deaths, and of future bliss or misery unutterable, then did Goodman Brown turn pale, dreading lest the roof should thunder down upon the gray blasphemer and his hearers. Often, awaking suddenly at midnight, he shrank from the bosom of Faith; and at morning or eventide, when the family knelt down at prayer, he scowled and muttered to himself, and gazed sternly at his wife, and turned away. And when he had lived long, and was borne to his grave a hoary corpse, followed by Faith, an aged woman, and children and grandchildren, a goodly procession, besides neighbors not a few, they carved no hopeful verse upon his tombstone, for his dying hour was gloom.

1835

RELATED:

—Edgar Allan Poe on Hawthorne's *Twice-Told Tales*, p. 934

# ERNEST HEMINGWAY
## 1899–1961

Hemingway was born in Oak Park, Illinois, the son of a doctor, who gave him an enduring enthusiasm for the outdoor life. As a boy Hemingway spent summer vacations in the woods of northern Michigan, which became the setting for some of his best-known stories. He volunteered for service as an ambulance driver with the Italian Army and was seriously wounded in the fighting on the Austrian front toward the end of World War I. Recovering from his wounds, he went to Paris as a correspondent for the *Toronto Star* and there met, among other writers, Ezra Pound and Gertrude Stein. They encouraged him in the invention of his own style, and by twenty-five he was well on his way to mastery of the craft of fiction. From the publication of his first books he was acclaimed as a spokesman for the "Lost Generation"—the young who had been disillusioned and cast adrift by the murderous blunders of those who had plunged the world into war. The Hemingway hero and his code of conduct—living with "grace under pressure"—were as widely emulated and admired as the style of his short stories and novels. He was an enthusiastic and discriminating bullfight fan, big-game hunter, and fisherman, whose personal exploits kept him often in the limelight. During the Spanish Civil War he went to Spain as a war correspondent and wrote one of his best novels, *For Whom the Bell Tolls* (1940), about that conflict. Later he followed the U.S. Army in Europe as a correspondent before returning to peacetime life at his home in Cuba. He was awarded the Nobel Prize in 1954. At a time when he seemed to be falling out of fashion and his old vigor was waning, he killed himself with a shotgun. His novels include *The Sun Also Rises* (1926), *A Farewell to Arms* (1929), *To Have and Have Not* (1937), and *The Old Man and the Sea* (1952). In *A Moveable Feast*; published posthumously in 1964, he re-creates the Paris of his earlier years. His story collections include *In Our Time* (1925), *Men without Women* (1927), and *Winner Take Nothing* (1933).

## Hills Like White Elephants

The hills across the valley of the Ebro[1] were long and white. On this side there was no shade and no trees and the station was between two lines of rails in the sun. Close against the side of the station there was the warm shadow of the building and a curtain, made of strings of bamboo beads, hung across

1. River in northern Spain.

the open door into the bar, to keep out flies. The American and the girl with him sat at a table in the shade, outside the building. It was very hot and the express from Barcelona would come in forty minutes. It stopped at this junction for two minutes and went on to Madrid.

"What should we drink?" the girl asked. She had taken off her hat and put it on the table.

"It's pretty hot," the man said.

"Let's drink beer."

"Dos cervezas," the man said into the curtain.

"Big ones?" a woman asked from the doorway.

"Yes. Two big ones."

The woman brought two glasses of beer and two felt pads. She put the felt pads and the beer glasses on the table and looked at the man and the girl. The girl was looking off at the line of hills. They were white in the sun and the country was brown and dry.

"They look like white elephants," she said.

"I've never seen one," the man drank his beer.

"No, you wouldn't have."

"I might have," the man said. "Just because you say I wouldn't have doesn't prove anything."

The girl looked at the bead curtain. "They've painted something on it," she said. "What does it say?"

"Anis del Toro. It's a drink."

"Could we try it?"

The man called "Listen" through the curtain. The woman came out from the bar.

"Four reales."[2]

"We want two Anis del Toro."

"With water?"

"Do you want it with water?"

"I don't know," the girl said. "Is it good with water?"

"It's all right."

"You want them with water?" asked the woman.

"Yes, with water."

"It tastes like licorice," the girl said and put the glass down.

"That's the way with everything."

"Yes," said the girl. "Everything tastes of licorice. Especially all the things you've waited so long for, like absinthe."

"Oh, cut it out."

"You started it," the girl said. "I was being amused. I was having a fine time."

"Well, let's try and have a fine time."

"All right. I was trying. I said the mountains looked like white elephants. Wasn't that bright?"

"That was bright."

"I wanted to try this new drink. That's all we do, isn't it—look at things and try new drinks?"

2. Spanish coins.

"I guess so."

The girl looked across at the hills.

"They're lovely hills," she said. "They don't really look like white elephants. I just meant the coloring of their skin through the trees."

"Should we have another drink?"

"All right."

The warm wind blew the bead curtain against the table.

"The beer's nice and cool," the man said.

"It's lovely," the girl said.

"It's really an awfully simple operation, Jig," the man said. "It's not really an operation at all."

The girl looked at the ground the table legs rested on.

"I know you wouldn't mind it, Jig. It's really not anything. It's just to let the air in."

The girl did not say anything.

"I'll go with you and I'll stay with you all the time. They just let the air in and then it's all perfectly natural."

"Then what will we do afterward?"

"We'll be fine afterward. Just like we were before."

"What makes you think so?"

"That's the only thing that bothers us. It's the only thing that's made us unhappy."

The girl looked at the bead curtain, put her hand out and took hold of two of the strings of beads.

"And you think then we'll be all right and be happy."

"I know we will. You don't have to be afraid. I've known lots of people that have done it."

"So have I," said the girl. "And afterward they were all so happy."

"Well," the man said, "if you don't want to you don't have to. I wouldn't have you do it if you didn't want to. But I know it's perfectly simple."

"And you really want to?"

"I think it's the best thing to do. But I don't want you to do it if you don't really want to."

"And if I do it you'll be happy and things will be like they were and you'll love me?"

"I love you now. You know I love you."

"I know. But if I do it, then it will be nice again if I say things are like white elephants, and you'll like it?"

"I'll love it. I love it now but I just can't think about it. You know how I get when I worry."

"If I do it you won't ever worry?"

"I won't worry about that because it's perfectly simple."

"Then I'll do it. Because I don't care about me."

"What do you mean?"

"I don't care about me."

"Well, I care about you."

"Oh, yes. But I don't care about me. And I'll do it and then everything will be fine."

"I don't want you to do it if you feel that way."

The girl stood up and walked to the end of the station. Across, on the other side, were fields of grain and trees along the banks of the Ebro. Far away, beyond the river, were mountains. The shadow of a cloud moved across the field of grain and she saw the river through the trees.

"And we could have all this," she said. "And we could have everything and every day we make it more impossible."

"What did you say?"

"I said we could have everything."

"We can have everything."

"No, we can't."

"We can have the whole world."

"No, we can't."

"We can go everywhere."

"No, we can't. It isn't ours anymore."

"It's ours."

"No, it isn't. And once they take it away, you never get it back."

"But they haven't taken it away."

"We'll wait and see."

"Come on back in the shade," he said. "You mustn't feel that way."

"I don't feel any way," the girl said. "I just know things."

"I don't want you to do anything that you don't want to do—"

"Nor that isn't good for me," she said. "I know. Could we have another beer?"

"All right. But you've got to realize—"

"I realize," the girl said. "Can't we maybe stop talking?"

They sat down at the table and the girl looked across at the hills on the dry side of the valley and the man looked at her and at the table.

"You've got to realize," he said, "that I don't want you to do it if you don't want to. I'm perfectly willing to go through with it if it means anything to you."

"Doesn't it mean anything to you? We could get along."

"Of course it does. But I don't want anybody but you. I don't want anyone else. And I know it's perfectly simple."

"Yes, you know it's perfectly simple."

"It's all right for you to say that, but I do know it."

"Would you do something for me now?"

"I'd do anything for you."

"Would you please please please please please please please stop talking?"

He did not say anything but looked at the bags against the wall of the station. There were labels on them from all the hotels where they had spent nights.

"But I don't want you to," he said, "I don't care anything about it."

"I'll scream," the girl said.

The woman came out through the curtains with two glasses of beer and put them down on the damp felt pads. "The train comes in five minutes," she said.

"What did she say?" asked the girl.

"That the train is coming in five minutes."

The girl smiled brightly at the woman, to thank her.

"I'd better take the bags over to the other side of the station," the man said. She smiled at him.

"All right. Then come back and we'll finish the beer."

He picked up the two heavy bags and carried them around the station to the other tracks. He looked up the tracks but could not see the train. Coming back, he walked through the barroom, where people waiting for the train were drinking. He drank an Anis at the bar and looked at the people. They were all waiting reasonably for the train. He went out through the bead curtain. She was sitting at the table and smiled at him.

"Do you feel better?" he asked.

"I feel fine," she said. "There's nothing wrong with me. I feel fine."

1927

---

RELATED:

—Hemingway, An Interview, p. 883
—Frederick Busch on "Hills Like White Elephants," p. 919

# ZORA NEALE HURSTON
## 1901–1960

Hurston was born in Eatonville, Florida. She became a vigorous activist in the cultural, social, and literary awakening that converged in the Harlem Renaissance of the 1920s and 1930s. She was a trained anthropologist whose personal insights enlarged that discipline, giving it depth and liveliness. Her gifts as a writer helped her absorb the rich diversities of black folklore in Haiti, Jamaica, and Bermuda, as well as in rural and urban areas of the United States. At various times she was a journalist and librarian, and wherever she could make herself heard she bore witness against the stereotyping that denied the multifarious heritage of blacks. Her appreciation of the subtleties and ambiguities of the vernacular influenced the generation of writers who followed her. The thematic core of her work is the love blacks bear for one another rather than the hostilities they feel against their oppressors. Her stories and articles appeared in several distinguished magazines, and she published four novels: *Jonah's Gourd Vine* (1934), *Their Eyes Were Watching God* (1937), *Moses, Man of the Mountain* (1939), and *Seraph on the Suwanee* (1948). Much of her short fiction can be found in *Spunk: The Selected Stories of Zora Neale Hurston* (1985).

## The Conscience of the Court

The clerk of the court took a good look at the tall brown-skinned woman with the head rag on. She sat on the third bench back with a husky officer beside her.

"The People versus Laura Lee Kimble!"

The policeman nudged the woman to get to her feet and led her up to the broad rail. She stood there, looking straight ahead. The hostility in the room reached her without her seeking to find it.

Unpleasant things were ahead of Laura Lee Kimble, but she was ready for this moment. It might be the electric chair or the rest of her life in some big lonesome jail house, or even torn to pieces by a mob, but she had passed three long weeks in jail. She had come to the place where she could turn her face to the wall and feel neither fear nor anguish. So this here so-called trial was nothing to her but a form and a fashion and an outside show to the world. She could stand apart and look on calmly. She stood erect and looked up at the judge.

"Charged with felonious and aggravated assault. Mayhem. Premeditated attempted murder on the person of one Clement Beasley. Obscene and abusive language. Laura Lee Kimble, how do you plead?"

Laura Lee was so fascinated by the long-named things that they were accusing her of that she stood there tasting over the words. *Lawdy me!* she mused inside herself. *Look like I done every crime excepting habeas corpus and stealing a mule.*

"Answer the clerk!" The officer nudged Laura Lee. "Tell him how you plead."

"Plead? Don't reckon I make out just what you all mean by that." She looked from face to face and at last up at the judge, with bewilderment in her eyes. She found him looking her over studiously.

The judge understood the look in her face, but he did not interfere so promptly as he ordinarily would have. This was the man-killing bear cat of a woman that he had heard so much about. Though spare of fat, she was built strongly enough, all right. An odd Negro type. Gray-green eyes, large and striking, looking out of a chestnut-brown face. A great abundance of almost straight hair only partially hidden by the high-knotted colored kerchief about her head. Somehow this woman did not look fierce to him at all. Yet she had beaten a man within an inch of his life. Here was a riddle to solve. With the proud, erect way she held herself, she might be some savage queen. The shabby housedress she had on detracted nothing from this impression. She was a challenge to him somehow or other.

"Perhaps you don't understand what the clerk means, Laura," the judge found himself saying to her in a gentle voice. "He wants you to say whether you are guilty of the charges or not."

"Oh, I didn't know. Didn't even know if he was talking to me or not. Much obliged to you, sir." Laura Lee sent His Honor a shy smile. "'Deed I don't know if I'm guilty or not. I hit the man after he hit me, to be sure, Mister Judge, but if I'm guilty I don't know for sure. All them big words and all."

The clerk shook his head in exasperation and quickly wrote something down. Laura Lee turned her head and saw the man on the hospital cot swaddled all up in bandage rags. Yes, that was the very man who caused her to be here where she was.

"All right, Laura Lee," the judge said. "You can take your seat now until you are called on."

The prosecutor looked a question at the judge and said, "We can proceed." The judge nodded, then halted things as he looked down at Laura Lee.

"The defendant seems to have no lawyer to represent her." Now he leaned forward and spoke to Laura Lee directly. "If you have no money to hire yourself a lawyer to look out for your interests, the court will appoint one for you."

There was a pause, during which Laura Lee covered a lot of ground. Then she smiled faintly at the judge and answered him. "Naw sir, I thank you, Mister Judge. Not to turn you no short answer, but I don't reckon it would do me a bit of good. I'm mighty much obliged to you just the same."

The implications penetrated instantly and the judge flushed. This unlettered woman had called up something that he had not thought about for quite some time. The campus of the University of Virginia and himself as a very young man there, filled with a reverence for his profession amounting to an almost holy dedication. His fascination and awe as a professor traced the more than two thousand years of growth of the concepts of human rights and justice. That brought him to his greatest hero, John Marshall, and his inner resolve to follow in the great man's steps, and even add to interpretations of human rights if his abilities allowed. No, he had not thought about all this for quite some time. The judge flushed slowly and deeply.

Below him there, the prosecutor was moving swiftly, but somehow his brisk cynicism offended the judge. He heard twelve names called, and just like that the jury box was filled and sworn in.

Rapidly now, witnesses took the stand, and their testimony was all damaging to Laura Lee. The doctor who told how terribly Clement Beasley had been hurt. Left arm broken above the elbow, compound fracture of the forearm, two ribs cracked, concussion of the brain and various internal injuries. Two neighbors who had heard the commotion and arrived before the house in time to see Laura Lee fling the plaintiff over the gate into the street. The six arresting officers all got up and had their say, and it was very bad for Laura Lee. A two-legged she-devil no less.

Clement Beasley was borne from his cot to the witness stand, and he made things look a hundred times blacker. His very appearance aroused a bumble of pity, and anger against the defendant. The judge had to demand quiet repeatedly. Beasley's testimony blew strongly on the hot coals.

His story was that he had come in conflict with this defendant by loaning a sizable sum of money to her employer. The money was to be repaid at his office. When the date was long past due, he had gone to the house near the river, just off Riverside Drive, to inquire why Mrs. Clairborne had not paid him, nor even come to see him and explain. Imagine his shock when he wormed it out of the defendant that Mrs. Clairborne had left Jacksonville. Further, he detected evidence that the defendant was picking up the things in the house. The loan had been made, six hundred dollars, on the furnishings of the entire house. He had doubted that the furnishings were worth enough for the amount loaned, but he had wanted to be generous to a widow lady. Seeing the defendant packing away the silver, he was naturally alarmed, and the next morning went to the house with a moving van to seize the furniture and protect the loan. The defendant, surprised, attacked him as soon as he appeared at the front door, injured him as he was, and would have killed him if help had not arrived in time.

Laura Lee was no longer a spectator at her own trial. Now she was in a flaming rage. She would have leaped to her feet as the man pictured Miz' Celestine as a cheat and a crook, and again as he sat up there and calmly lied about the worth of the furniture. All of those wonderful antiques, this man making out that they did not equal his minching six hundred dollars! That lie was a sin and a shame! The People was a meddlesome and unfriendly passel and had no use for the truth. It brought back to her in a taunting way what her husband, Tom, had told her over and over again. This world had no use for the love and friending that she was ever trying to give.

It looked now that Tom could be right. Even Miz' Celestine had turnt her back on her. She was here in this place, the house of The People, all by herself. She had ever disbelieved Tom and had to get to be forty-nine before she found out the truth. Well, just as the old folks said, "It's never too long for a bull frog to wear a stiff-bosom shirt. He's bound to get it dirtied some time or other."

"You have testified," Laura Lee heard the judge talking, "that you came in contact with the defendant through a loan to Mrs. J. Stuart Clairborne, her employer, did you not?"

"Yes, Your Honor," Beasley answered promptly and glibly.

"That being true, the court cannot understand why that note was not offered in evidence."

Beasley glanced quickly at the prosecutor and lowered his eyes. "I—I just didn't see why it was necessary, Your Honor. I have it, but—"

"It is not only pertinent, it is of the utmost importance to this case. I order it sent for immediately and placed in evidence."

The tall, lean, black-haired prosecutor hurled a surprised and betrayed look at the bench, then, after a pause, said in a flat voice, "The State rests."

What was in the atmosphere crawled all over Laura Lee like reptiles. The silence shouted that her goose was cooked. But even if the sentence was death, she didn't mind. Celestine Beaufort Clairborne had failed her. Her husband and all her folks had gone on before. What was there to be so happy to live for anymore? She had writ that letter to Miz' Celestine the very first day that she had been placed in jail. Three weeks had gone by on their rusty ankles, and never one word from her Celestine. Laura Lee choked back a sob and gritted her teeth. You had to bear what was placed on your back for you to tote.

"Laura Lee Kimble," the judge was saying, "you are charged with serious felonies, and the law must take its course according to the evidence. You refused the lawyer that the court offered to provide for you, and that was a mistake on your part. However, you have a right to be sworn and tell the jury your side of the story. Tell them anything that might help you, so long as you tell the truth."

Laura Lee made no move to get to her feet and nearly a minute passed. Then the judge leaned forward.

"Believe it or not, Laura Lee, this is a court of law. It is needful to hear both sides of every question before the court can reach a conclusion and know what to do. Now, you don't strike me as a person that is unobliging at all. I believe if you knew you would be helping me out a great deal by telling your side of the story, you would do it."

Involuntarily Laura Lee smiled. She stood up. "Yes, sir, Mister Judge. If I can be of some help to you, I sure will. And I thank you for asking me."

Being duly sworn, Laura Lee sat in the chair to face the jury as she had been told to do.

"You jury-gentlemens, they asked me if I was guilty or no, and I still don't know whether I is or not. I am a unlearnt woman and common-clad.[1] It don't surprise me to find out I'm ignorant about a whole heap of things. I ain't never rubbed the hair off of my head against no college walls and schooled out nowhere at all. All I'm able to do is to tell you gentlemens how it was and then you can tell me if I'm guilty or no.

"I would not wish to set up here and lie and make out that I never hit this plaintive back. Gentlemens, I ain't had no malice in my heart against the plaintive. I seen him only one time before he come there and commenced that fracas with me. That was three months ago, the day after Tom, my husband, died. Miz' Celestine called up the funeral home and they come and got Tom to fix him up so we could take him back to Georgia to lay him to rest. That's where us all come from, Chatham County—Savannah, that is.

1. Working class, ordinary.

"Then now, Miz' Celestine done something I have never knowed her to do be-fore. She put on her things and went off from home without letting me know where she was bound for. She come back afterwhile with this plaintive, which I had never seen before in all my borned days. I glimpsed him good from the kitchen where I was at, walking all over the dining room and the living room with Miz' Celestine and looking at things, but they was talking sort of low like, and I couldn't make out a word what they was talking about. I figgered that Miz' Celestine must of been kind of beside herself, showing somebody look like this plaintive all her fine things like that. Her things is fine and very scarce old antiques, and I know that she have been offered vast sums of money for 'em, but she would never agree to part with none. Things that been handed down in both the Beaufort and the Clairborne families from way back. That little old minching six hundred dollars that the plaintive mentioned wouldn't even be worth one piece of her things, not to mention her silver. After a while they went off and when Miz' Celestine come back, she told me that everything had been taken care of and she had the tickets to Savannah in her purse.

"Bright and soon next morning we boarded the train for Savannah to bury Tom. Miz' Celestine done even more than she had promised Tom. She took him back like she had promised, so that he could be buried in our family lot, and he was covered with flowers, and his church and his lodges turned out with him, and he was put away like some big mogul of a king. Miz' Celestine was there sitting right along by my side all the time. Then me and Miz' Celestine come on back down here to Jacksonville by ourselves.

"And Mrs. Clairborne didn't run off to keep from paying nobody. She's a Clairborne, and before that, she was born a Beaufort. They don't owe nobody, and they don't run away. That ain't the kind of raising they gets. Miz' Clairborne's got money of her own, and lives off of the interest which she receives regular every six months. She went off down there to Miami Beach to sort of refresh herself and rest up her nerves. What with being off down here in Florida, away from all the folks she used to know, for three whole years, and cooped up there in her house, and remembering her dear husband being dead, and now Tom gone, and nobody left of the old family around excepting her and me, she was nervous and peaked like. It wasn't her, it was me that put her up to going off down there for a couple of months so maybe she would come back to herself. She never cheeped to me about borrowing no money from nobody, and I sure wasn't packing nothing up to move off when this plaintive come to the door. I was just gleaming up the silver to kill time whilst I was there by myself.

"And gentlemens, I never tackled the plaintive just as soon as he mounted the porch like he said. The day before that, he had come there and asked-ed me if Miz' Clairborne was at home. I told him no, and then he asked-ed me just when I expected her back. I told him she was down at Miami Beach, and got the letter that she had sent me so he could get her right address. He thanked me and went off. Then the next morning, here he was back with a great big moving wagon, rapped on the door and didn't use a bit of manners and politeness this time. Without even a 'Good morning' he says for me to git out of his way because he come to haul off all the furniture and things in the house and he is short for time.

"You jury-gentlemens, I told him in the nicest way that I knowed how that he must of been crazy. Miz' Celestine was off from home and she had left me there as a kind of guardeen to look after her house and things, and I sure couldn't so handy leave nobody touch a thing in Mrs. Clairborne's house unlessen she was there and said so.

"He just looked at me like I was something that the buzzards laid and the sun hatched out, and told me to move out of his way so he could come on in and get his property. I propped myself and braced one arm across the doorway to bar him out, reckoning he would have manners enough to go on off. But, no! He flew just as hot as Tucker when the mule kicked his mammy and begun to cuss and double-cuss me, and call me all out of my name, something nobody had never done be-fore in all my borned days. I took it to keep from tearing up peace and agreement. Then he balled up his fists and demanded me to move 'cause he was coming in.

"'Aw, naw you ain't,' I told him. 'You might think that you's going to grow horns, but I'm here to tell you you'll die butt-headed.'

"His mouth slewed one-sided and he hauled off and hit me in my chest with his fist two times. Hollered that nothing in the drugstore would kill me no quicker than he would if I didn't git out of his way. I didn't, and then he upped and kicked me.

"I jumped as salty as the 'gator when the pond went dry. I stretched out my arm and he hit the floor on a prone. Then, that truck with the two men on it took off from there in a big hurry. All I did next was to grab him by his heels and frail[2] the pillar of the porch with him a few times. I let him go, but he just laid there like a log.

"'Don't you lay there, making out you's dead, sir!' I told him. 'Git up from there, even if you is dead, and git on off this place!'

"The contrary scamp laid right there, so I reached down and muscled him up on across my shoulder and toted him to the gate, and heaved him over the fence out into the street. None of my business what become of him and his dirty mouth after that.

"I figgered I done right not to leave him come in there and haul off Miz' Celestine's things which she had left there under my trust and care. But Tom, my husband, would have said I was wrong for taking too much on myself. Tom claimed that he ever loved me harder than the thunder could bump a stump, but I had one habit that he ever wished he could break me of. Claimed that I always placed other folks's cares in front of my own, and more expe-cially Miz' Celestine. Said that I made out of myself a wishbone shining in the sun. Just something for folks to come along and pick up and rub and pull and get their wishes and good luck on. Never looked out for nothing for my ownself.

"I never took a bit of stock in what Tom said like that until I come to be in this trouble. I felt right and good, looking out for Miz' Celestine's interest and standing true and strong, till they took me off to jail and I writ Miz' Celestine a letter to please come see 'bout me and help me out, and give it to the folks there at the jail to mail off for me."

2. Hit.

A sob wrestled inside Laura Lee and she struck silence for a full minute before she could go on.

"Maybe it reached her, and then maybe again it didn't. Anyhow, I ain't had a single scratch from Miz' Celestine, and here I is. But I love her so hard, and I reckon I can't help myself. Look, gentlemens, Celestine was give to me when I was going on five—"

The prosecutor shot up like a striking trout and waved his long arm. "If the court please, this is not a street corner. This is a court of law. The witness cannot be allowed to ramble—"

The judge started as if he had been shaken out of a dream. He looked at the prosecutor and shook his head. "The object of a trial, I need not remind you, is to get at the whole truth of a case. The defendant is unlearned, as she has said. She has no counsel to guide her along the lines of procedure. It is important to find out why an act was committed, as you well know. Please humor the court by allowing the witness to tell her story in her own way." The judge looked at Laura Lee and told her to go ahead. A murmur of approval followed this from all over the room.

"I don't mean that her mama and papa throwed her away. You know how it used to be the style when a baby was born to place it under the special care of a older brother or sister, or somebody that had worked on the place for a long time and was apt to stay. That's what I mean by Celestine was give to me.

"Just going on five, I wasn't yet old enough to have no baby give to me, but that I didn't understand. All I did know that some way I loved babies. I had me a old rag doll-baby that my mama had made for me, and I loved it better'n anything I can mention.

"Never will forget the morning mama said she was going to take me upstairs to Miz' Beaufort's bedroom to lemme see the new baby. Mama was borned on the Beaufort place just like I was. She was the cook, and everything around the place was sort of under her care. Papa was the houseman and drove for the family when they went out anywhere.

"Well, I seen that tee-ninchy baby laying there in a pink crib all trimmed with a lot of ribbons. Gentlemens, it was the prettiest thing I had ever laid my eyes on. I thought that it was a big-size doll-baby laying there, and right away I wanted it. I carried on so till afterwhile Miz' Beaufort said that I could have it for mine if I wanted it. I was so took with it that I went plumb crazy with joy. I asked her again, and she still said that she was giving it to me. My mama said so too. So, for fear they might change they minds, I said right off that I better take my baby home with me so that I could feed it my ownself and make it something to put on and do for it in general.

"I cried and carried on something terrible when they wouldn't leave me take it on out to the little house where we lived on the place. They pacified me by telling me I better leave it with Miz' Beaufort until it was weaned.

"That couldn't keep me from being around Celestine every chance I got. Later on I found out how they all took my carrying-on for jokes. Made out they was serious to my face, but laughing fit to kill behind my back. They wouldn't of done it if they had knowed how I felt inside. I lived just to see and touch Celestine—my baby, I thought. And she took to me right away.

"When Celestine was two, going on three, I found out that they had been funning with me, and that Celestine was not my child at all. I was too little to have a baby, and then again, how could a colored child be the mother of a white child? Celestine belonged to her papa and mama. It was all right for me to play with her all I wanted to, but forget the notion that she was mine.

"Jury-gentlemens, it was mighty hard, but as I growed on and understood more things I knowed what they was talking about. But Celestine wouldn't allow me to quit loving her. She ever leaned on me, and cried after me, and run to me first for every little thing.

"When I was going on sixteen, papa died and Tom Kimble, a young man, got the job that papa used to have. Right off he put in to court me, even though he was twelve years older than me. But lots of fellows around Savannah was pulling after me too. One wanted to marry me that I liked extra fine, but he was settling in Birmingham, and mama was aginst me marrying and settling way off somewhere. She ruthered for me to marry Tom. When Celestine begin to hang on me and beg and beg me not to leave her, I give in and said that I would have Tom, but for the sake of my feelings, I put the marriage off for a whole year. That was my first good chance to break off from Celestine, but I couldn't.

"General Beaufort, the old gentleman, was so proud for me to stay and pacify Celestine, that he built us a nice house on the place and made it over to us for life. Miz' Beaufort give me the finest wedding that any colored folks had ever seen around Savannah. We stood on the floor in the Beaufort parlor with all the trimmings.

"Celestine, the baby, was a young lady by then, and real pretty with reddish-gold hair and blue eyes. The young bloods was hanging after her in swarms. It was me that propped her up when she wanted to marry young J. Stuart Clairborne, a lawyer just out of school, with a heap of good looks, a smiling disposition, a fine family name and no money to mention. He did have some noble old family furniture and silver. So Celestine had her heart's desire, but little money. They was so happy together that it was like a play.

"Then things begin to change. Mama and Miz' Beaufort passed on in a year of each other. The old gentleman lingered around kind of lonesome, then one night he passed away in his sleep, leaving all he had to Celestine and her husband. Things went on fine for five years like that. He was building up a fine practice and things went lovely.

"Then, it seemed all of a sudden, he took to coughing, and soon he was too tired all the time to go to his office and do around like he used to. Celestine spent her money like water, sending her husband and taking him to different places from one end of the nation to the other, and keeping him under every kind of a doctor's care.

"Four years of trying and doing like that, and then even Celestine had to acknowledge that it never did a bit of good. Come a night when Clairborne laid his dark curly head in her lap like a trusting child and breathed his last.

"Inside our own house of nights, Tom would rear and pitch like a mule in a tin stable, trying to get me to consent to pull out with him and find us better-paying jobs elsewhere. I wouldn't hear to that kind of a talk at all. We had been there when times was extra good, and I didn't aim to tear out and leave Miz' Celestine by herself at low water. This was another time I passed up my chance to cut aloose.

"The third chance wasn't too long a-coming. A year after her husband died, Miz' Celestine come to me and told me that the big Beaufort place was too much for her to keep up with the money she had on hand now. She had been seeking around, and she had found a lovely smaller house down at Jacksonville, Florida. No big grounds to keep up and all. She choosed that instead of a smaller place around Savannah because she could not bear to sing small where she had always led off. An' now she had got hold of a family who was willing to buy the Beaufort estate at a very good price.

"Then she told me that she wanted me to move to Florida with her. She realized that she had no right to ask me no such a thing, but she just could not bear to go off down there with none of her family with her. Would I please consent to go? If I would not go with her, she would give Tom and me the worth of our property in cash money and we could do as we pleased. She had no call to ask us to go with her at all, excepting for old-time love and affection.

"Right then, jury-gentlemens, I knowed that I was going. But Tom had ever been a good husband to me, and I wanted him to feel that he was considered, so I told her that I must consult my pillow. Give her my word one way or another the next day.

"Tom pitched a acre of fits the moment that it was mentioned in his hearing. Hollered that we ought to grab the cash and, with what we had put away, buy us a nice home of our own. What was wrong with me nohow? Did I aim to be a wishbone all my days? Didn't I see that he was getting old? He craved to end his days among his old friends, his lodges and his churches. We had a fine cemetery lot, and there was where he aimed to rest.

"Miz' Celestine cried when he told her. Then she put in to meet all of Tom's complaints. Sure, we was all getting on in years, but that was the very reason why we ought not to part now. Cling together and share and lean and depend on one another. Then when Tom still held out, she made a oath. If Tom died before she did, she would fetch him back and put him away right at her own expense. And if she died before either of us, we was to do the same for her. Anything she left was willed to me to do with as I saw fit.

"So we put in to pack up all the finest pieces, enough and plenty to furnish up our new home in Florida, and moved on down here to live. We passed three peaceful years like that, then Tom died."

Laura Lee paused, shifted so that she faced the jury more directly, then summed up.

"Maybe I is guilty sure enough. I could be wrong for staying all them years and making Miz' Celestine's cares my own. You gentlemens is got more book-learning than me, so you would know more than I do. So far as this fracas is concerned, yeah, I hurted this plaintive, but with him acting the way he was, it just couldn't be helped. And 'tain't nary one of you gentlemens but what wouldn't of done the same."

There was a minute of dead silence. Then the judge sent the prosecutor a cut-eye look and asked, "Care to cross-examine?"

"That's all!" the prosecutor mumbled, and waved Laura Lee to her seat.

"I have here," the judge began with great deliberation, "the note made by Mrs. J. Stuart Clairborne with the plaintiff. It specifies that the purpose of the loan was to finance the burial of Thomas Kimble." The judge paused and looked directly at Laura Lee to call her attention to this point. "The importance to this trial, however, is the due date, which is still more than three months away."

The court officers silenced the gasps and mumbles that followed this announcement.

"It is therefore obvious why the plaintiff has suppressed this valuable piece of evidence. It is equally clear to the court that the plaintiff knew that he had no justification whatsoever for being upon the premises of Mrs. Clairborne."

His Honor folded the paper and put it aside, and regarded the plaintiff with cold gray eyes.

"This is the most insulting instance in the memory of the court of an attempt to prostitute the very machinery of justice for an individual's own nefarious ends. The plaintiff first attempts burglary with forceful entry and violence and, when thoroughly beaten for his pains, brazenly calls upon the law to punish the faithful watch-dog who bit him while he was attempting his trespass. Further, it seems apparent that he has taken steps to prevent any word from the defendant reaching Mrs. Clairborne, who certainly would have moved heaven and earth in the defendant's behalf, and rightfully so."

The judge laced the fingers of his hands and rested them on the polished wood before him and went on.

The protection of women and children, he said, was inherent, implicit in Anglo-Saxon civilization, and here in these United States it had become a sacred trust. He reviewed the long, slow climb of humanity from the rule of the club and the stone hatchet to the Constitution of the United States. The English-speaking people had given the world its highest concepts of the rights of the individual, and they were not going to be made a mock of, and nullified by this court.

"The defendant did no more than resist the plaintiff's attempted burglary. Valuable assets of her employer were trusted in her care, and she placed her very life in jeopardy in defending that trust, setting an example which no decent citizen need blush to follow. The jury is directed to find for the defendant."

Laura Lee made her way diffidently to the judge and thanked him over and over again.

"That will do, Laura Lee. I am the one who should be thanking you."

Laura Lee could see no reason why, and wandered off, bewildered. She was instantly surrounded by smiling, congratulating strangers, many of whom made her ever so welcome if ever she needed a home. She was rubbed and polished to a high glow.

Back at the house, Laura Lee did not enter at once. Like a pilgrim before a shrine, she stood and bowed her head. "I ain't fitten to enter. For a time, I allowed myself to doubt my Celestine. But maybe nobody ain't as pure in heart as they aim to be. The cock crowed on Apostle Peter.[3] Old Maker, please take my guilt away and cast it into the sea of forgetfulness where it won't never rise to accuse me in this world, nor condemn me in the next."

Laura Lee entered and opened all the windows with a ceremonial air. She was hungry, but before she would eat, she made a ritual of atonement by serving. She took a finely wrought silver platter from the massive old sideboard and gleamed it to perfection. So the platter, so she wanted her love to shine.

1950

---

**3.** Peter denied Christ three times before the cock crowed (cf. Matthew 26:69–75).

# JAMES JOYCE
## *1882–1941*

Joyce was born in Dublin; and though he fled the narrowness of Catholic Ireland for the broader cultural horizons of Europe, the Dublin of his experience and imagination was the setting for all his major work. In 1904 he went to live permanently on the Continent, supporting himself and his family—barely—by teaching English in language schools in Trieste and Zurich. The fear of censorship, coupled with the timidity of his publisher, delayed until 1914 the publication of his short stories in *Dubliners*. Soon after this, however, Joyce came to the attention of the energetic American poet Ezra Pound, who arranged for the first publication of *A Portrait of the Artist as a Young Man* (1916), Joyce's semiautobiographical novel. Pound's support continued through the following years while Joyce was writing what is generally acknowledged as his masterpiece, the novel *Ulysses* (1922). When parts of it began to appear in a literary magazine, it touched off a storm of controversy that brought him both notoriety and lasting fame. On the one hand, this work experimented more boldly with language and narration, including use of the stream of consciousness, than any work in English that preceded it. On the other, some of the sexual passages were so candid that until 1933 censors banned it from the United States. Joyce continued to explore the resources of language in his years of fame, these experiments reaching their height in the monumentally complex novel *Finnegans Wake* (1939).

## Araby

North Richmond Street, being blind, was a quiet street except at the hour when the Christian Brothers' School set the boys free. An uninhabited house of two storeys stood at the blind end, detached from its neighbours in a square ground. The other houses of the street, conscious of decent lives within them, gazed at one another with brown imperturbable faces.

The former tenant of our house, a priest, had died in the back drawing-room. Air, musty from having been long enclosed, hung in all the rooms, and the waste room behind the kitchen was littered with old useless papers. Among these I found a few paper-covered books, the pages of which were curled and damp: *The Abbot*, by Walter Scott, *The Devout Communicant* and

*The Memoirs of Vidocq*.[1] I liked the last best because its leaves were yellow. The wild garden behind the house contained a central apple-tree and a few straggling bushes under one of which I found the late tenant's rusty bicycle-pump. He had been a very charitable priest; in his will he had left all his money to institutions and the furniture of his house to his sister.

When the short days of winter came dusk fell before we had well eaten our dinners. When we met in the street the houses had grown sombre. The space of sky above us was the colour of ever-changing violet and towards it the lamps of the street lifted their feeble lanterns. The cold air stung us and we played till our bodies glowed. Our shouts echoed in the silent street. The career of our play brought us through the dark muddy lanes behind the houses where we ran the gantlet of the rough tribes from the cottages,[2] to the back doors of the dark dripping gardens where odours arose from the ashpits, to the dark odorous stables where a coachman smoothed and combed the horse or shook music from the buckled harness. When we returned to the street light from the kitchen windows had filled the areas. If my uncle was seen turning the corner we hid in the shadow until we had seen him safely housed. Or if Mangan's sister came out on the doorstep to call her brother in to his tea we watched her from our shadow peer up and down the street. We waited to see whether she would remain or go in and, if she remained, we left our shadow and walked up to Mangan's steps resignedly. She was waiting for us, her figure defined by the light from the half-opened door. Her brother always teased her before he obeyed and I stood by the railings looking at her. Her dress swung as she moved her body and the soft rope of her hair tossed from side to side.

Every morning I lay on the floor in the front parlour watching her door. The blind was pulled down to within an inch of the sash so that I could not be seen. When she came out on the doorstep my heart leaped. I ran to the hall, seized my books and followed her. I kept her brown figure always in my eye and, when we came near the point at which our ways diverged, I quickened my pace and passed her. This happened morning after morning. I had never spoken to her, except for a few casual words, and yet her name was like a summons to all my foolish blood.

Her image accompanied me even in places the most hostile to romance. On Saturday evenings when my aunt went marketing I had to go to carry some of the parcels. We walked through the flaring streets, jostled by drunken men and bargaining women, amid the curses of labourers, the shrill litanies of shop-boys who stood on guard by the barrels of pigs' cheeks, the nasal chanting of street-singers, who sang a *come-all-you* about O'Donovan Rossa,[3] or a ballad about the troubles in our native land. These noises converged in a single sensation of life for me: I imagined that I bore my chalice safely through a throng of foes. Her name sprang to my lips at moments in strange prayers and praises which I myself did not understand. My eyes were often full of tears (I could not tell why) and at times a flood from my heart seemed to pour

---

**1.** Eugène François Vidocq (1775–1857), French detective. *The Devout Communicant:* Roman Catholic devotional manual. *The Abbot:* a novel published in 1820 by Sir Walter Scott (1771–1832), Scottish, novelist and poet. **2.** That is, from a Dublin slum district. **3.** Jeremiah O'Donovan ("O'Dynamite") Rossa (1831–1915), an Irish nationalist banished to the United States in 1870 for revolutionary activities. *Come-all-you*: any popular song beginning "Come all you Irishmen."

itself out into my bosom. I thought little of the future. I did not know whether I would ever speak to her or not or, if I spoke to her, how I could tell her of my confused adoration. But my body was like a harp and her words and gestures were like fingers running upon the wires.

One evening I went into the back drawing-room in which the priest had died. It was a dark rainy evening and there was no sound in the house. Through one of the broken panes I heard the rain impinge upon the earth, the fine incessant needles of water playing in the sodden beds. Some distant lamp or lighted window gleamed below me. I was thankful that I could see so little. All my senses seemed to desire to veil themselves and, feeling that I was about to slip from them, I pressed the palms of my hands together until they trembled, murmuring: *O love! O love!* many times.

At last she spoke to me. When she addressed the first words to me I was so confused that I did not know what to answer. She asked me was I going to *Araby.*[4] I forget whether I answered yes or no. It would be a splendid bazaar, she said; she would love to go.

—And why can't you? I asked.

While she spoke she turned a silver bracelet round and round her wrist. She could not go, she said, because there would be a retreat[5] that week in her convent. Her brother and two other boys were fighting for their caps and I was alone at the railings. She held one of the spikes, bowing her head towards me. The light from the lamp opposite our door caught the white curve of her neck, lit up her hair that rested there and, falling, lit up the hand upon the railing. It fell over one side of her dress and caught the white border of a petticoat, just visible as she stood at ease.

—It's well for you, she said.

—If I go, I said, I will bring you something.

What innumerable follies laid waste my waking and sleeping thoughts after that evening! I wished to annihilate the tedious intervening days. I chafed against the work of school. At night in my bedroom and by day in the classroom her image came between me and the page I strove to read. The syllables of the word *Araby* were called to me through the silence in which my soul luxuriated and cast an Eastern enchantment over me. I asked for leave to go to the bazaar on Saturday night. My aunt was surprised and hoped it was not some Freemason[6] affair. I answered few questions in class. I watched my master's face pass from amiability to sternness; he hoped I was not beginning to idle. I could not call my wandering thoughts together. I had hardly any patience with the serious work of life which, now that it stood between me and my desire, seemed to me child's play, ugly monotonous child's play.

On Saturday morning I reminded my uncle that I wished to go to the bazaar in the evening. He was fussing at the hallstand, looking for the hatbrush, and answered me curtly:

—Yes, boy, I know.

---

4. A billboard sign of the time actually reads: "ARABY in DUBLIN Official Catalogue GRAND ORIENTAL FÊTE May 14th to 19th in aid of Jervis St. Hospital. Admission one shilling." A British shilling, 1/20 of a pound sterling, would be worth about $5 in 2000s U.S. currency.  **5.** A gathering for prayer and meditation in her convent school.  **6.** The Masonic Order was felt by Catholics to be an enemy of the Church.

As he was in the hall I could not go into the front parlour and lie at the window. I left the house in bad humour and walked slowly towards the school. The air was pitilessly raw and already my heart misgave me.

When I came home to dinner my uncle had not yet been home. Still it was early. I sat staring at the clock for some time and, when its ticking began to irritate me, I left the room. I mounted the staircase and gained the upper part of the house. The high cold empty gloomy rooms liberated me and I went from room to room singing. From the front window I saw my companions playing below in the street. Their cries reached me weakened and indistinct and, leaning my forehead against the cool glass, I looked over at the dark house where she lived. I may have stood there for an hour, seeing nothing but the brown-clad figure cast by my imagination, touched discreetly by the lamplight at the curved neck, at the hand upon the railings and at the border below the dress.

When I came downstairs again I found Mrs. Mercer sitting at the fire. She was an old garrulous woman, a pawnbroker's widow, who collected used stamps for some pious purpose. I had to endure the gossip of the tea-table. The meal was prolonged beyond an hour and still my uncle did not come. Mrs. Mercer stood up to go: she was sorry she couldn't wait any longer, but it was after eight o'clock and she did not like to be out late, as the night air was bad for her. When she had gone I began to walk up and down the room, clenching my fists. My aunt said:

—I'm afraid you may put off your bazaar for this night of Our Lord.

At nine o'clock I heard my uncle's latchkey in the halldoor. I heard him talking to himself and heard the hallstand rocking when it had received the weight of his overcoat. I could interpret these signs. When he was midway through his dinner I asked him to give me the money to go to the bazaar. He had forgotten.

—The people are in bed and after their first sleep now, he said.

I did not smile. My aunt said to him energetically:

—Can't you give him the money and let him go? You've kept him late enough as it is.

My uncle said he was very sorry he had forgotten. He said he believed in the old saying: *All work and no play makes Jack a dull boy.* He asked me where I was going and, when I had told him a second time he asked me did I know *The Arab's Farewell to His Steed.*[7] When I left the kitchen he was about to recite the opening lines of the piece to my aunt.

I held a florin[8] tightly in my hand as I strode down Buckingham Street towards the station. The sight of the streets thronged with buyers and glaring with gas recalled to me the purpose of my journey. I took my seat in a third-class carriage of a deserted train. After an intolerable delay the train moved out of the station slowly. It crept onward among ruinous houses and over the twinkling river. At Westland Row Station a crowd of people pressed to the carriage doors; but the porters moved them back, saying that it was a special train for the bazaar. I remained alone in the bare carriage. In a few minutes the train drew up beside an improvised wooden platform. I passed out on to

---

**7.** Sentimental poem by Caroline Norton (1808–1877). The Arab imagines his heartbreak after selling his favorite horse.   **8.** A two-shilling piece, worth four times the "sixpenny entrance" fee.

the road and saw by the lighted dial of a clock that it was ten minutes to ten. In front of me was a large building which displayed the magical name.

I could not find any sixpenny entrance and, fearing that the bazaar would be closed, I passed in quickly through a turnstile, handing a shilling to a weary-looking man. I found myself in a big hall girdled at half its height by a gallery. Nearly all the stalls were closed and the greater part of the hall was in darkness. I recognised a silence like that which pervades a church after a service. I walked into the centre of the bazaar timidly. A few people were gathered about the stalls which were still open. Before a curtain, over which the words *Café Chantant*[9] were written in coloured lamps, two men were counting money on a salver. I listened to the fall of the coins.

Remembering with difficulty why I had come I went over to one of the stalls and examined porcelain vases and flowered tea-sets. At the door of the stall a young lady was talking and laughing with two young gentlemen. I remarked their English accents and listened vaguely to their conversation.

—O, I never said such a thing!

—O, but you did!

—O, but I didn't!

—Didn't she say that?

—Yes. I heard her.

—O, there's a . . . fib!

Observing me the young lady came over and asked me did I wish to buy anything. The tone of her voice was not encouraging; she seemed to have spoken to me out of a sense of duty. I looked humbly at the great jars that stood like eastern guards at either side of the dark entrance to the stall and murmured:

—No, thank you.

The young lady changed the position of one of the vases and went back to the two young men. They began to talk of the same subject. Once or twice the young lady glanced at me over her shoulder.

I lingered before her stall, though I knew my stay was useless, to make my interest in her wares seem the more real. Then I turned away slowly and walked down the middle of the bazaar. I allowed the two pennies to fall against the sixpence in my pocket. I heard a voice call from one end of the gallery that the light was out. The upper part of the hall was now completely dark.

Gazing up into the darkness I saw myself as a creature driven and derided by vanity; and my eyes burned with anguish and anger.

1914

# The Dead

Lily, the caretaker's daughter, was literally run off her feet. Hardly had she brought one gentleman into the little pantry behind the office on the ground floor and helped him off with his overcoat than the wheezy hall-door bell

9. Café offering musical entertainment.

clanged again and she had to scamper along the bare hallway to let in another guest. It was well for her she had not to attend to the ladies also. But Miss Kate and Miss Julia had thought of that and had converted the bathroom upstairs into a ladies' dressing-room. Miss Kate and Miss Julia were there, gossiping and laughing and fussing, walking after each other to the head of the stairs, peering down over the banisters and calling down to Lily to ask her who had come.

It was always a great affair, the Misses Morkan's annual dance. Everybody who knew them came to it, members of the family, old friends of the family, the members of Julia's choir, any of Kate's pupils that were grown up enough and even some of Mary Jane's pupils too. Never once had it fallen flat. For years and years it had gone off in splendid style as long as anyone could remember; ever since Kate and Julia, after the death of their brother Pat, had left the house in Stoney Batter and taken Mary Jane, their only niece, to live with them in the dark gaunt house on Usher's Island,[1] the upper part of which they had rented from Mr. Fulham, the cornfactor[2] on the ground floor. That was a good thirty years ago if it was a day. Mary Jane, who was then a little girl in short clothes, was now the main prop of the household for she had the organ in Haddington Road. She had been through the Academy and gave a pupils' concert every year in the upper room of the Antient Concert Rooms.[3] Many of her pupils belonged to better-class families on the Kingstown and Dalkey line. Old as they were, her aunts also did their share. Julia, though she was quite grey, was still the leading soprano in Adam and Eve's,[4] and Kate, being too feeble to go about much, gave music lessons to beginners on the old square piano in the back room. Lily, the caretaker's daughter, did housemaid's work for them. Though their life was modest they believed in eating well; the best of everything: diamond-bone sirloins, three-shilling tea and the best bottled stout. But Lily seldom made a mistake in the orders so that she got on well with her three mistresses. They were fussy, that was all. But the only thing they would not stand was back answers.

Of course they had good reason to be fussy on such a night. And then it was long after ten o'clock and yet there was no sign of Gabriel and his wife. Besides they were dreadfully afraid that Freddy Malins might turn up screwed.[5] They would not wish for worlds that any of Mary Jane's pupils should see him under the influence; and when he was like that it was sometimes very hard to manage him. Freddy Malins always came late but they wondered what could be keeping Gabriel: and that was what brought them every two minutes to the banisters to ask Lily had Gabriel or Freddy come.

—O, Mr. Conroy, said Lily to Gabriel when she opened the door for him, Miss Kate and Miss Julia thought you were never coming. Good-night, Mrs. Conroy.

—I'll engage they did, said Gabriel, but they forget that my wife here takes three mortal hours to dress herself.

**1.** Dublin street on the south bank of the river Liffey. *Stoney Batter*: Dublin neighborhood. **2.** Agent or broker dealing in grain. **3.** A building in which rooms could be rented for musical or dramatic productions. *The Academy*: the Royal Academy of Music. **4.** A Dublin church. **5.** Drunk.

He stood on the mat, scraping the snow from his goloshes, while Lily led his wife to the foot of the stairs and called out:

—Miss Kate, here's Mrs. Conroy.

Kate and Julia came toddling down the dark stairs at once. Both of them kissed Gabriel's wife, said she must be perished alive and asked was Gabriel with her.

—Here I am as right as the mail, Aunt Kate! Go on up. I'll follow, called out Gabriel from the dark.

He continued scraping his feet vigorously while the three women went upstairs, laughing, to the ladies' dressing-room. A light fringe of snow lay like a cape on the shoulders of his overcoat and like toecaps on the toes of his goloshes; and, as the buttons of his overcoat slipped with a squeaking noise through the snow-stiffened frieze, a cold fragrant air from out-of-doors escaped from crevices and folds.

—Is it snowing again, Mr. Conroy? asked Lily.

She had preceded him into the pantry to help him off with his overcoat. Gabriel smiled at the three syllables she had given his surname and glanced at her. She was a slim, growing girl, pale in complexion and with hay-coloured hair. The gas in the pantry made her look still paler. Gabriel had known her when she was a child and used to sit on the lowest step nursing a rag doll.

—Yes, Lily, he answered, and I think we're in for a night of it.

He looked up at the pantry ceiling, which was shaking with the stamping and shuffling of feet on the floor above, listened for a moment to the piano and then glanced at the girl, who was folding his overcoat carefully at the end of a shelf.

—Tell me, Lily, he said in a friendly tone, do you still go to school?

—O no, sir, she answered. I'm done schooling this year and more.

—O, then, said Gabriel gaily, I suppose we'll be going to your wedding one of these fine days with your young man, eh?

The girl glanced back at him over her shoulder and said with great bitterness:

—The men that is now is only all palaver and what they can get out of you.

Gabriel coloured as if he felt he had made a mistake and, without looking at her, kicked off his goloshes and flicked actively with his muffler at his patent-leather shoes.

He was a stout tallish young man. The high colour of his cheeks pushed upwards even to his forehead where it scattered itself in a few formless patches of pale red; and on his hairless face there scintillated restlessly the polished lenses and the bright gilt rims of the glasses which screened his delicate and restless eyes. His glossy black hair was parted in the middle and brushed in a long curve behind his ears where it curled slightly beneath the groove left by his hat.

When he had flicked lustre into his shoes he stood up and pulled his waist-coat down more tightly on his plump body. Then he took a coin rapidly from his pocket.

—O Lily, he said, thrusting it into her hands, it's Christmas-time, isn't it? Just . . . here's a little. . . .

He walked rapidly towards the door.

—O no, sir! cried the girl, following him. Really, sir, I wouldn't take it.

—Christmas-time! Christmas-time! said Gabriel, almost trotting to the stairs and waving his hand to her in deprecation.

The girl, seeing that he had gained the stairs, called out after him:

—Well, thank you, sir.

He waited outside the drawing-room door until the waltz should finish, listening to the skirts that swept against it and to the shuffling of feet. He was still discomposed by the girl's bitter and sudden retort. It had cast a gloom over him which he tried to dispel by arranging his cuffs and the bows of his tie. Then he took from his waistcoat pocket a little paper and glanced at the headings he had made for his speech. He was undecided about the lines from Robert Browning[6] for he feared they would be above the heads of his hearers. Some quotation that they could recognise from Shakespeare or from the Melodies[7] would be better. The indelicate clacking of the men's heels and the shuffling of their soles reminded him that their grade of culture differed from his. He would only make himself ridiculous by quoting poetry to them which they could not understand. They would think that he was airing his superior education. He would fail with them just as he had failed with the girl in the pantry. He had taken up a wrong tone. His whole speech was a mistake from first to last, an utter failure.

Just then his aunts and his wife came out of the ladies' dressing-room. His aunts were two small plainly dressed old women. Aunt Julia was an inch or so the taller. Her hair, drawn low over the tops of her ears, was grey; and grey also, with darker shadows, was her large flaccid face. Though she was stout in build and stood erect her slow eyes and parted lips gave her the appearance of a woman who did not know where she was or where she was going. Aunt Kate was more vivacious. Her face, healthier than her sister's, was all puckers and creases, like a shrivelled red apple, and her hair, braided in the same old-fashioned way, had not lost its ripe nut colour.

They both kissed Gabriel frankly. He was their favourite nephew, the son of their dead elder sister, Ellen, who had married T. J. Conroy of the Port and Docks.[8]

—Gretta tells me you're not going to take a cab back to Monkstown[9] tonight, Gabriel, said Aunt Kate.

—No, said Gabriel, turning to his wife, we had quite enough of that last year, hadn't we? Don't you remember, Aunt Kate, what a cold Gretta got out of it? Cab windows rattling all the way, and the east wind blowing in after we passed Merrion. Very jolly it was. Gretta caught a dreadful cold.

Aunt Kate frowned severely and nodded her head at every word.

—Quite right, Gabriel, quite right, she said. You can't be too careful.

—But as for Gretta there, said Gabriel, she'd walk home in the snow if she were let.

Mrs. Conroy laughed.

—Don't mind him, Aunt Kate, she said. He's really an awful bother, what with green shades for Tom's eyes at night and making him do the dumb-bells,

---

**6.** English poet (1812–1889).　**7.** The *Irish Melodies* by Thomas Moore (1779–1852), Irish poet.
**8.** Government bureau.　**9.** Seaside district of southeast Dublin.

and forcing Eva to eat the stirabout.[1] The poor child! And she simply hates the sight of it! . . . O, but you'll never guess what he makes me wear now!

She broke out into a peal of laughter and glanced at her husband, whose admiring and happy eyes had been wandering from her dress to her face and hair. The two aunts laughed heartily too, for Gabriel's solicitude was a standing joke with them.

—Goloshes! said Mrs. Conroy. That's the latest. Whenever it's wet underfoot I must put on my goloshes. To-night even he wanted me to put them on, but I wouldn't. The next thing he'll buy me will be a diving suit.

Gabriel laughed nervously and patted his tie reassuringly while Aunt Kate nearly doubled herself, so heartily did she enjoy the joke. The smile soon faded from Aunt Julia's face and her mirthless eyes were directed towards her nephew's face. After a pause she asked:

—And what are goloshes, Gabriel?

—Goloshes, Julia! exclaimed her sister. Goodness me, don't you know what goloshes are? You wear them over your . . . over your boots, Gretta, isn't it?

—Yes, said Mrs. Conroy. Guttapercha[2] things. We both have a pair now. Gabriel says everyone wears them on the continent.

—O, on the continent, murmured Aunt Julia, nodding her head slowly.

Gabriel knitted his brows and said, as if he were slightly angered:

—It's nothing very wonderful but Gretta thinks it very funny because she says the word reminds her of Christy Minstrels.[3]

—But tell me, Gabriel, said Aunt Kate, with brisk tact. Of course, you've seen about the room. Gretta was saying . . .

—O, the room is all right, replied Gabriel. I've taken one in the Gresham.[4]

—To be sure, said Aunt Kate, by far the best thing to do. And the children, Gretta, you're not anxious about them?

—O, for one night, said Mrs. Conroy. Besides, Bessie will look after them.

—To be sure, said Aunt Kate again. What a comfort it is to have a girl like that, one you can depend on! There's that Lily, I'm sure I don't know what has come over her lately. She's not the girl she was at all.

Gabriel was about to ask his aunt some questions on this point but she broke off suddenly to gaze after her sister who had wandered down the stairs and was craning her neck over the banisters.

—Now, I ask you, she said, almost testily, where is Julia going? Julia! Julia! Where are you going?

Julia, who had gone halfway down one flight, came back and announced blandly:

—Here's Freddy.

At the same moment a clapping of hands and a final flourish of the pianist told that the waltz had ended. The drawing-room door was opened from within and some couples came out. Aunt Kate drew Gabriel aside hurriedly and whispered into his ear:

—Slip down, Gabriel, like a good fellow and see if he's all right, and don't let him up if he's screwed. I'm sure he's screwed. I'm sure he is.

---

**1.** Porridge.  **2.** Material similar to rubber.  **3.** Well-known 19th-century minstrel show organized by Edwin P. Christy (1815–1862), American showman.  **4.** Historic hotel in downtown Dublin.

Gabriel went to the stairs and listened over the banisters. He could hear two persons talking in the pantry. Then he recognised Freddy Malins' laugh. He went down the stairs noisily.

—It's such a relief, said Aunt Kate to Mrs. Conroy, that Gabriel is here. I always feel easier in my mind when he's here. . . . Julia, there's Miss Daly and Miss Power will take some refreshment. Thanks for your beautiful waltz, Miss Daly. It made lovely time.

A tall wizen-faced man, with a stiff grizzled moustache and swarthy skin, who was passing out with his partner said:

—And may we have some refreshment, too, Miss Morkan?

—Julia, said Aunt Kate summarily, and here's Mr. Browne and Miss Furlong. Take them in, Julia, with Miss Daly and Miss Power.

—I'm the man for the ladies, said Mr. Browne, pursing his lips until his moustache bristled and smiling in all his wrinkles. You know, Miss Morkan, the reason they are so fond of me is—

He did not finish his sentence, but, seeing that Aunt Kate was out of earshot, at once led the three young ladies into the back room. The middle of the room was occupied by two square tables placed end to end, and on these Aunt Julia and the caretaker were straightening and smoothing a large cloth. On the sideboard were arrayed dishes and plates, and glasses and bundles of knives and forks and spoons. The top of the closed square piano served also as a sideboard for viands and sweets. At a smaller sideboard in one corner two young men were standing, drinking hop-bitters.[5]

Mr. Browne led his charges thither and invited them all, in jest, to some ladies' punch, hot, strong and sweet. As they said they never took anything strong he opened three bottles of lemonade for them. Then he asked one of the young men to move aside, and, taking hold of the decanter, filled out for himself a goodly measure of whisky. The young men eyed him respectfully while he took a trial sip.

—God help me, he said, smiling, it's the doctor's orders.

His wizened face broke into a broader smile, and the three young ladies laughed in musical echo to his pleasantry, swaying their bodies to and fro, with nervous jerks of their shoulders. The boldest said:

—O, now, Mr. Browne, I'm sure the doctor never ordered anything of the kind.

Mr. Browne took another sip of his whisky and said, with sidling mimicry:

—Well, you see, I'm like the famous Mrs. Cassidy, who is reported to have said: *Now, Mary Grimes, if I don't take it, make me take it, for I feel I want it.*

His hot face had leaned forward a little too confidentially and he had assumed a very low Dublin accent so that the young ladies, with one instinct, received his speech in silence. Miss Furlong, who was one of Mary Jane's pupils, asked Miss Daly what was the name of the pretty waltz she had played; and Mr. Browne, seeing that he was ignored, turned promptly to the two young men who were more appreciative.

A red-faced young woman, dressed in pansy, came into the room, excitedly clapping her hands and crying:

—Quadrilles![6] Quadrilles!

**5.** Kind of ale.   **6.** Square dances.

Close on her heels came Aunt Kate, crying:

—Two gentlemen and three ladies, Mary Jane!

—O, here's Mr. Bergin and Mr. Kerrigan, said Mary Jane. Mr. Kerrigan, will you take Miss Power? Miss Furlong, may I get you a partner, Mr. Bergin. O, that'll just do now.

—Three ladies, Mary Jane, said Aunt Kate.

The two young gentlemen asked the ladies if they might have the pleasure, and Mary Jane turned to Miss Daly.

—O, Miss Daly, you're really awfully good, after playing for the last two dances, but really we're so short of ladies to-night.

—I don't mind in the least, Miss Morkan.

—But I've a nice partner for you, Mr. Bartell D'Arcy, the tenor. I'll get him to sing later on. All Dublin is raving about him.

—Lovely voice, lovely voice! said Aunt Kate.

As the piano had twice begun the prelude to the first figure Mary Jane led her recruits quickly from the room. They had hardly gone when Aunt Julia wandered slowly into the room, looking behind her at something.

—What is the matter, Julia? asked Aunt Kate anxiously. Who is it?

Julia, who was carrying in a column of table-napkins, turned to her sister and said, simply, as if the question had surprised her:

—It's only Freddy, Kate, and Gabriel with him.

In fact right behind her Gabriel could be seen piloting Freddy Malins across the landing. The latter, a young man of about forty, was of Gabriel's size and build, with very round shoulders. His face was fleshy and pallid, touched with colour only at the thick hanging lobes of his ears and at the wide wings of his nose. He had coarse features, a blunt nose, a convex and receding brow, tumid and protruded lips. His heavy-lidded eyes and the disorder of his scanty hair made him look sleepy. He was laughing heartily in a high key at a story which he had been telling Gabriel on the stairs and at the same time rubbing the knuckles of his left fist backwards and forwards into his left eye.

—Good-evening, Freddy, said Aunt Julia.

Freddy Malins bade the Misses Morkan good-evening in what seemed an offhand fashion by reason of the habitual catch in his voice and then, seeing that Mr. Browne was grinning at him from the sideboard, crossed the room on rather shaky legs and began to repeat in an undertone the story he had just told to Gabriel.

—He's not so bad, is he? said Aunt Kate to Gabriel.

Gabriel's brows were dark but he raised them quickly and answered:

—O no, hardly noticeable.

—Now, isn't he a terrible fellow! she said. And his poor mother made him take the pledge[7] on New Year's Eve. But come on, Gabriel, into the drawing-room.

Before leaving the room with Gabriel she signalled to Mr. Browne by frowning and shaking her forefinger in warning to and fro. Mr. Browne nodded in answer and, when she had gone, said to Freddy Malins:

—Now, then, Teddy, I'm going to fill you out a good glass of lemonade just to buck you up.

---

7. A formal pledge not to drink.

Freddy Malins, who was nearing the climax of his story, waved the offer aside impatiently but Mr. Browne, having first called Freddy Malins' attention to a disarray in his dress, filled out and handed him a full glass of lemonade. Freddy Malins' left hand accepted the glass mechanically, his right hand being engaged in the mechanical readjustment of his dress. Mr. Browne, whose face was once more wrinkling with mirth, poured out for himself a glass of whisky while Freddy Malins exploded, before he had well reached the climax of his story, in a kink of high-pitched bronchitic laughter and, setting down his untasted and overflowing glass, began to rub the knuckles of his left fist backwards and forwards into his left eye, repeating words of his last phrase as well as his fit of laughter would allow him.

Gabriel could not listen while Mary Jane was playing her Academy piece, full of runs and difficult passages, to the hushed drawing-room. He liked music but the piece she was playing had no melody for him and he doubted whether it had any melody for the other listeners, though they had begged Mary Jane to play something. Four young men, who had come from the refreshment-room to stand in the doorway at the sound of the piano, had gone away quietly in couples after a few minutes. The only persons who seemed to follow the music were Mary Jane herself, her hands racing along the key-board or lifted from it at the pauses like those of a priestess in momentary imprecation, and Aunt Kate standing at her elbow to turn the page.

Gabriel's eyes, irritated by the floor, which glittered with beeswax under the heavy chandelier, wandered to the wall above the piano. A picture of the balcony scene in *Romeo and Juliet* hung there and beside it was a picture of the two murdered princes[8] in the Tower which Aunt Julia had worked in red, blue and brown wools when she was a girl. Probably in the school they had gone to as girls that kind of work had been taught, for one year his mother had worked for him as a birthday present a waistcoat of purple tabinet, with little foxes' heads upon it, lined with brown satin and having round mulberry buttons. It was strange that his mother had had no musical talent though Aunt Kate used to call her the brains carrier of the Morkan family. Both she and Julia had always seemed a little proud of their serious and matronly sister. Her photograph stood before the pierglass.[9] She held an open book on her knees and was pointing out something in it to Constantine who, dressed in a mano'-war suit,[1] lay at her feet. It was she who had chosen the names for her sons for she was very sensible of the dignity of family life. Thanks to her, Constantine was now senior curate in Balbriggan and, thanks to her, Gabriel himself had taken his degree in the Royal University. A shadow passed over his face as he remembered her sullen opposition to his marriage. Some slighting phrases she had used still rankled in his memory; she had once spoken of Gretta as being country cute and that was not true of Gretta at all. It was Gretta who had nursed her during all her last long illness in their house at Monkstown.

He knew that Mary Jane must be near the end of her piece for she was playing again the opening melody with runs of scales after every bar and while he

8. Edward and Richard, sons of King Edward IV of England. The two princes were reputedly murdered by order of King Richard III. 9. A tall mirror. 1. Sailor suit.

waited for the end the resentment died down in his heart. The piece ended with a trill of octaves in the treble and a final deep octave in the bass. Great applause greeted Mary Jane as, blushing and rolling up her music nervously, she escaped from the room. The most vigorous clapping came from the four young men in the doorway who had gone away to the refreshment-room at the beginning of the piece but had come back when the piano had stopped.

Lancers[2] were arranged. Gabriel found himself partnered with Miss Ivors. She was a frank-mannered talkative young lady, with a freckled face and prominent brown eyes. She did not wear a low-cut bodice and the large brooch which was fixed in the front of her collar bore on it an Irish device.

When they had taken their places she said abruptly:

—I have a crow to pluck with you.[3]

—With me? said Gabriel.

She nodded her head gravely.

—What is it? asked Gabriel, smiling at her solemn manner.

—Who is G. C.? answered Miss Ivors, turning her eyes upon him.

Gabriel coloured and was about to knit his brows, as if he did not understand, when she said bluntly:

—O, innocent Amy! I have found out that you write for *The Daily Express*.[4] Now, aren't you ashamed of yourself?

—Why should I be ashamed of myself? asked Gabriel, blinking his eyes and trying to smile.

—Well, I'm ashamed of you, said Miss Ivors frankly. To say you'd write for a rag like that. I didn't think you were a West Briton.[5]

A look of perplexity appeared on Gabriel's face. It was true that he wrote a literary column every Wednesday in *The Daily Express*, for which he was paid fifteen shillings. But that did not make him a West Briton surely. The books he received for review were almost more welcome than the paltry cheque. He loved to feel the covers and turn over the pages of newly printed books. Nearly every day when his teaching in the college[6] was ended he used to wander down the quays to the second-hand booksellers, to Hickey's on Bachelor's Walk, to Webb's or Massey's on Aston's Quay, or to O'Clohissey's in the by-street. He did not know how to meet her charge. He wanted to say that literature was above politics. But they were friends of many years' standing and their careers had been parallel, first at the University and then as teachers: he could not risk a grandiose phrase with her. He continued blinking his eyes and trying to smile and murmured lamely that he saw nothing political in writing reviews of books.

When their turn to cross had come he was still perplexed and inattentive. Miss Ivors promptly took his hand in a warm grasp and said in a soft friendly tone:

—Of course, I was only joking. Come, we cross now.

When they were together again she spoke of the University question[7] and Gabriel felt more at ease. A friend of hers had shown her his review of

---

**2.** A set of quadrilles, danced in sequence. **3.** That is, "I have a bone to pick." **4.** A newspaper opposed to Irish liberation from Great Britain. **5.** In context this means he considers himself British rather than Irish. **6.** In Britain and Ireland, a secondary-level school, not university-level. **7.** The issue was whether to provide equal educational opportunities for Roman Catholic students at the overwhelmingly Protestant Trinity College in Dublin.

Browning's poems. That was how she had found out the secret: but she liked the review immensely. Then she said suddenly:

—O, Mr. Conroy, will you come for an excursion to the Aran Isles[8] this summer? We're going to stay there a whole month. It will be splendid out in the Atlantic. You ought to come. Mr. Clancy is coming, and Mr. Kilkelly and Kathleen Kearney. It would be splendid for Gretta too if she'd come. She's from Connacht,[9] isn't she?

—Her people are, said Gabriel shortly.

—But you will come, won't you? said Miss Ivors, laying her warm hand eagerly on his arm.

—The fact is, said Gabriel, I have already arranged to go—

—Go where? asked Miss Ivors.

—Well, you know every year I go for a cycling tour with some fellows and so—

—But where? asked Miss Ivors.

—Well, we usually go to France or Belgium or perhaps Germany, said Gabriel awkwardly.

—And why do you go to France and Belgium, said Miss Ivors, instead of visiting your own land?

—Well, said Gabriel, it's partly to keep in touch with the languages and partly for a change.

—And haven't you your own language to keep in touch with—Irish?[1] asked Miss Ivors.

—Well, said Gabriel, if it comes to that, you know, Irish is not my language.

Their neighbours had turned to listen to the cross-examination. Gabriel glanced right and left nervously and tried to keep his good humour under the ordeal which was making a blush invade his forehead.

—And haven't you your own land to visit, continued Miss Ivors, that you know nothing of, your own people, and your own country?

—O, to tell you the truth, retorted Gabriel suddenly, I'm sick of my own country, sick of it!

—Why? asked Miss Ivors.

Gabriel did not answer for his retort had heated him.

—Why? repeated Miss Ivors.

They had to go visiting together and, as he had not answered her, Miss Ivors said warmly:

—Of course, you've no answer.

Gabriel tried to cover his agitation by taking part in the dance with great energy. He avoided her eyes for he had seen a sour expression on her face. But when they met in the long chain he was surprised to feel his hand firmly pressed. She looked at him from under her brows for a moment quizzically until he smiled. Then, just as the chain was about to start again, she stood on tiptoe and whispered into his ear:

—West Briton!

---

**8.** Off the west coast of Ireland. Irish traditions were preserved by their Gaelic-speaking natives.   **9.** Province in northwest Ireland. Probably considered rustic and unsophisticated by Dubliners.   **1.** That is, Irish Gaelic, which by Joyce's day had been relegated to the western fringes of Ireland by 800 years of domination by the British.

When the lancers were over Gabriel went away to a remote corner of the room where Freddy Malins' mother was sitting. She was a stout feeble old woman with white hair. Her voice had a catch in it like her son's and she stuttered slightly. She had been told that Freddy had come and that he was nearly all right. Gabriel asked her whether she had had a good crossing. She lived with her married daughter in Glasgow and came to Dublin on a visit once a year. She answered placidly that she had had a beautiful crossing[2] and that the captain had been most attentive to her. She spoke also of the beautiful house her daughter kept in Glasgow, and of all the nice friends they had there. While her tongue rambled on Gabriel tried to banish from his mind all memory of the unpleasant incident with Miss Ivors. Of course the girl or woman, or whatever she was, was an enthusiast but there was a time for all things. Perhaps he ought not to have answered her like that. But she had no right to call him a West Briton before people, even in joke. She had tried to make him ridiculous before people, heckling him and staring at him with her rabbit's eyes.

He saw his wife making her way towards him through the waltzing couples. When she reached him she said into his ear:

—Gabriel, Aunt Kate wants to know won't you carve the goose as usual. Miss Daly will carve the ham and I'll do the pudding.[3]

—All right, said Gabriel.

—She's sending in the younger ones first as soon as this waltz is over so that we'll have the table to ourselves.

—Were you dancing? asked Gabriel.

—Of course I was. Didn't you see me? What words had you with Molly Ivors?

—No words. Why? Did she say so?

—Something like that. I'm trying to get that Mr. D'Arcy to sing. He's full of conceit, I think.

—There were no words, said Gabriel moodily, only she wanted me to go for a trip to the west of Ireland and I said I wouldn't.

His wife clasped her hands excitedly and gave a little jump.

—O, do go, Gabriel, she cried. I'd love to see Galway[4] again.

—You can go if you like, said Gabriel coldly.

She looked at him for a moment, then turned to Mrs. Malins and said:

—There's a nice husband for you, Mrs. Malins.

While she was threading her way back across the room Mrs. Malins, without adverting to the interruption, went on to tell Gabriel what beautiful places there were in Scotland and beautiful scenery. Her son-in-law brought them every year to the lakes and they used to go fishing. Her son-in-law was a splendid fisher. One day he caught a fish, a beautiful big big fish, and the man in the hotel boiled it for their dinner.

Gabriel hardly heard what she said. Now that supper was coming near he began to think again about his speech and about the quotation. When he saw Freddy Malins coming across the room to visit his mother Gabriel left the chair free for him and retired into the embrasure of the window. The room

2. Passage by ferry over the Irish Sea from Glasgow, Scotland. 3. In British usage, any cooked dessert. 4. Capital of Connacht.

had already cleared and from the back room came the clatter of plates and knives. Those who still remained in the drawing-room seemed tired of dancing and were conversing quietly in little groups. Gabriel's warm trembling fingers tapped the cold pane of the window. How cool it must be outside! How pleasant it would be to walk out alone, first along by the river and then through the park! The snow would be lying on the branches of the trees and forming a bright cap on the top of the Wellington Monument.[5] How much more pleasant it would be there than at the supper-table!

He ran over the headings of his speech: Irish hospitality, sad memories, the Three Graces, Paris,[6] the quotation from Browning. He repeated to himself a phrase he had written in his review: *One feels that one is listening to a thought-tormented music.* Miss Ivors had praised the review. Was she sincere? Had she really any life of her own behind all her propagandism? There had never been any ill-feeling between them until that night. It unnerved him to think that she would be at the supper-table, looking up at him while he spoke with her critical quizzing eyes. Perhaps she would not be sorry to see him fail in his speech. An idea came into his mind and gave him courage. He would say, alluding to Aunt Kate and Aunt Julia: *Ladies and Gentlemen, the generation which is now on the wane among us may have had its faults but for my part I think it had certain qualities of hospitality, of humour, of humanity, which the new and very serious and hypereducated generation that is growing up around us seems to me to lack.* Very good: that was one for Miss Ivors. What did he care that his aunts were only two ignorant old women?

A murmur in the room attracted his attention. Mr. Browne was advancing from the door, gallantly escorting Aunt Julia, who leaned upon his arm, smiling and hanging her head. An irregular musketry of applause escorted her also as far as the piano and then, as Mary Jane seated herself on the stool, and Aunt Julia, no longer smiling, half turned so as to pitch her voice fairly into the room, gradually ceased. Gabriel recognised the prelude. It was that of an old song of Aunt Julia's—*Arrayed for the Bridal.*[7] Her voice, strong and clear in tone, attacked with great spirit the runs which embellish the air and though she sang very rapidly she did not miss even the smallest of the grace notes. To follow the voice, without looking at the singer's face, was to feel and share the excitement of swift and secure flight. Gabriel applauded loudly with all the others at the close of the song and loud applause was borne in from the invisible supper-table. It sounded so genuine that a little colour struggled into Aunt Julia's face as she bent to replace in the music-stand the old leather-bound song-book that had her initials on the cover. Freddy Malins, who had listened with his head perched sideways to hear her better, was still applauding when everyone else had ceased and talking animatedly to his mother who nodded her head gravely and slowly in acquiescence. At last, when he could clap no more, he stood up suddenly and hurried across the room to Aunt Julia whose hand he seized and held in both his hands,

---

5. Dublin monument to the Duke of Wellington (1769–1852), Irish-born hero of the Napoleonic Wars.   6. The Trojan prince who was obliged to choose among the goddesses Hera, Athena, and Aphrodite. He awarded the prize (the apple of discord) to Aphrodite, who then helped him carry off Helen. "Three Graces": goddesses representing aspects of beauty—Aglaia (Brilliance), Euphrosyne (Joy), and Thalia (Bloom).   7. Song from Vincenzo Bellini's opera *I Puritani di Scozia* (The Puritans of Scotland, 1835).

shaking it when words failed him or the catch in his voice proved too much for him.

—I was just telling my mother, he said, I never heard you sing so well, never. No, I never heard your voice so good as it is to-night. Now! Would you believe that now? That's the truth. Upon my word and honour that's the truth. I never heard your voice sound so fresh and so . . . so clear and fresh, never.

Aunt Julia smiled broadly and murmured something about compliments as she released her hand from his grasp. Mr. Browne extended his open hand towards her and said to those who were near him in the manner of a showman introducing a prodigy to an audience:

—Miss Julia Morkan, my latest discovery!

He was laughing very heartily at this himself when Freddy Malins turned to him and said:

—Well, Browne, if you're serious you might make a worse discovery. All I can say is I never heard her sing half so well as long as I am coming here. And that's the honest truth.

—Neither did I, said Mr. Browne. I think her voice has greatly improved.

Aunt Julia shrugged her shoulders and said with meek pride:

—Thirty years ago I hadn't a bad voice as voices go.

—I often told Julia, said Aunt Kate emphatically, that she was simply thrown away in that choir. But she never would be said by me.

She turned as if to appeal to the good sense of the others against a refractory child while Aunt Julia gazed in front of her, a vague smile of reminiscence playing on her face.

—No, continued Aunt Kate, she wouldn't be said or led by anyone, slaving there in that choir night and day, night and day. Six o'clock on Christmas morning! And all for what?

—Well, isn't it for the honour of God, Aunt Kate? asked Mary Jane, twisting round on the piano-stool and smiling.

Aunt Kate turned fiercely on her niece and said:

—I know all about the honour of God, Mary Jane, but I think it's not at all honourable for the pope to turn out the women out of the choirs that have slaved there all their lives and put little whipper-snappers of boys over their heads.[8] I suppose it is for the good of the Church if the pope does it. But it's not just, Mary Jane, and it's not right.

She had worked herself into a passion and would have continued in defence of her sister for it was a sore subject with her but Mary Jane, seeing that all the dancers had come back, intervened pacifically:

—Now, Aunt Kate, you're giving scandal to Mr. Browne who is of the other persuasion.[9]

Aunt Kate turned to Mr. Browne, who was grinning at this allusion to his religion, and said hastily:

—O, I don't question the pope's being right. I'm only a stupid old woman and I wouldn't presume to do such a thing. But there's such a thing as common everyday politeness and gratitude. And if I were in Julia's place I'd tell that Father Healy straight up to his face . . .

---

8. In 1903, Pope Pius X decreed that, in Roman Catholic choirs, soprano and alto parts should be sung by boys, not women.  9. That is, Mr. Browne is Protestant, not Roman Catholic.

—And besides, Aunt Kate, said Mary Jane, we really are all hungry and when we are hungry we are all very quarrelsome.

—And when we are thirsty we are also quarrelsome, added Mr. Browne.

—So that we had better go to supper, said Mary Jane, and finish the discussion afterwards.

On the landing outside the drawing-room Gabriel found his wife and Mary Jane trying to persuade Miss Ivors to stay for supper. But Miss Ivors, who had put on her hat and was buttoning her cloak, would not stay. She did not feel in the least hungry and she had already overstayed her time.

—But only for ten minutes, Molly, said Mrs. Conroy. That won't delay you.

—To take a pick itself, said Mary Jane, after all your dancing.

—I really couldn't, said Miss Ivors.

—I am afraid you didn't enjoy yourself at all, said Mary Jane hopelessly.

—Ever so much, I assure you, said Miss Ivors, but you really must let me run off now.

—But how can you get home? asked Mrs. Conroy.

—O, it's only two steps up the quay.

Gabriel hesitated a moment and said:

—If you will allow me, Miss Ivors, I'll see you home if you really are obliged to go.

But Miss Ivors broke away from them.

—I won't hear of it, she cried. For goodness sake go in to your suppers and don't mind me. I'm quite well able to take care of myself.

—Well, you're the comical girl, Molly, said Mrs. Conroy frankly.

—*Beannacht libh*,[1] cried Miss Ivors, with a laugh, as she ran down the staircase.

Mary Jane gazed after her, a moody puzzled expression on her face, while Mrs. Conroy leaned over the banisters to listen for the hall-door. Gabriel asked himself was he the cause of her abrupt departure. But she did not seem to be in ill humour: she had gone away laughing. He stared blankly down the staircase.

At that moment Aunt Kate came toddling out of the supper-room, almost wringing her hands in despair.

—Where is Gabriel? she cried. Where on earth is Gabriel? There's everyone waiting in there, stage to let,[2] and nobody to carve the goose!

—Here I am, Aunt Kate! cried Gabriel, with sudden animation, ready to carve a flock of geese, if necessary.

A fat brown goose lay at one end of the table and at the other end, on a bed of creased paper strewn with sprigs of parsley, lay a great ham, stripped of its outer skin and peppered over with crust crumbs, a neat paper frill round its shin and beside this was a round of spiced beef. Between these rival ends ran parallel lines of side-dishes: two little minsters of jelly, red and yellow; a shallow dish full of blocks of blancmange and red jam, a large green leaf-shaped dish with a stalk-shaped handle, on which lay bunches of purple raisins and peeled almonds, a companion dish on which lay a solid rectangle of Smyrna figs, a dish of custard topped with grated nutmeg, a small bowl full of chocolates and sweets wrapped in gold and silver papers and a glass vase in which

---

1. Blessings on you (Gaelic).   2. That is, ready for a performance.

stood some tall celery stalks. In the centre of the table there stood, as sentries to a fruit-stand which upheld a pyramid of oranges and American apples, two squat old-fashioned decanters of cut glass, one containing port and the other dark sherry. On the closed square piano a pudding in a huge yellow dish lay in waiting and behind it were three squads of bottles of stout and ale and minerals, drawn up according to the colours of their uniforms, the first two black, with brown and red labels, the third and smallest squad white, with transverse green sashes.

Gabriel took his seat boldly at the head of the table and, having looked to the edge of the carver, plunged his fork firmly into the goose. He felt quite at ease now for he was an expert carver and liked nothing better than to find himself at the head of a well-laden table.

—Miss Furlong, what shall I send you? he asked. A wing or a slice of the breast?

—Just a small slice of the breast.

—Miss Higgins, what for you?

—O, anything at all, Mr. Conroy.

While Gabriel and Miss Daly exchanged plates of goose and plates of ham and spiced beef Lily went from guest to guest with a dish of hot floury potatoes wrapped in a white napkin. This was Mary Jane's idea and she had also suggested apple sauce for the goose but Aunt Kate had said that plain roast goose without apple sauce had always been good enough for her and she hoped she might never eat worse. Mary Jane waited on her pupils and saw that they got the best slices and Aunt Kate and Aunt Julia opened and carried across from the piano bottles of stout and ale for the gentlemen and bottles of minerals for the ladies. There was a great deal of confusion and laughter and noise, the noise of orders and counter-orders, of knives and forks, of corks and glass-stoppers. Gabriel began to carve second helpings as soon as he had finished the first round without serving himself. Everyone protested loudly so that he compromised by taking a long draught of stout for he had found the carving hot work. Mary Jane settled down quietly to her supper but Aunt Kate and Aunt Julia were still toddling round the table, walking on each other's heels, getting in each other's way and giving each other unheeded orders. Mr. Browne begged of them to sit down and eat their suppers and so did Gabriel but they said there was time enough so that, at last, Freddy Malins stood up and, capturing Aunt Kate, plumped her down on her chair amid general laughter.

When everyone had been well served Gabriel said, smiling:

—Now, if anyone wants a little more of what vulgar people call stuffing let him or her speak.

A chorus of voices invited him to begin his own supper and Lily came forward with three potatoes which she had reserved for him.

—Very well, said Gabriel amiably, as he took another preparatory draught, kindly forget my existence, ladies and gentlemen, for a few minutes.

He set to his supper and took no part in the conversation with which the table covered Lily's removal of the plates. The subject of talk was the opera company which was then at the Theatre Royal. Mr. Bartell D'Arcy, the tenor, a dark-complexioned young man with a smart moustache, praised very highly the leading contralto of the company but Miss Furlong thought she had a rather vulgar style of production. Freddy Malins said there was a negro chieftain singing in the second part of the Gaiety pantomime who had one of the finest tenor voices he had ever heard.

—Have you heard him? he asked Mr. Bartell D'Arcy across the table.

—No, answered Mr. Bartell D'Arcy carelessly.

—Because, Freddy Malins explained, now I'd be curious to hear your opinion of him. I think he has a grand voice.

—It takes Teddy to find out the really good things, said Mr. Browne familiarly to the table.

—And why couldn't he have a voice too? asked Freddy Malins sharply. Is it because he's only a black?

Nobody answered this question and Mary Jane led the table back to the legitimate opera. One of her pupils had given her a pass for *Mignon*.[3] Of course it was very fine, she said, but it made her think of poor Georgina Burns.[4] Mr. Browne could go back farther still, to the old Italian companies that used to come to Dublin—Tietjens, Ilma de Murzka, Campanini, the great Trebelli, Giuglini, Ravelli, Aramburo.[5] Those were the days, he said, when there was something like singing to be heard in Dublin. He told too of how the top gallery of the old Royal used to be packed night after night, of how one night an Italian tenor had sung five encores to *Let Me Like a Soldier Fall*,[6] introducing a high C every time, and of how the gallery boys would sometimes in their enthusiasm unyoke the horses from the carriage of some great *prima donna* and pull her themselves through the streets to her hotel. Why did they never play the grand old operas now, he asked, *Dinorah, Lucrezia Borgia?*[7] Because they could not get the voices to sing them: that was why.

—O, well, said Mr. Bartell D'Arcy, I presume there are as good singers today as there were then.

—Where are they? asked Mr. Browne defiantly.

—In London, Paris, Milan, said Mr. Bartell D'Arcy warmly. I suppose Caruso,[8] for example, is quite as good, if not better than any of the men you have mentioned.

—Maybe so, said Mr. Browne. But I may tell you I doubt it strongly.

—O, I'd give anything to hear Caruso sing, said Mary Jane.

—For me, said Aunt Kate, who had been picking a bone, there was only one tenor. To please me, I mean. But I suppose none of you ever heard of him.

—Who was he, Miss Morkan? asked Mr. Bartell D'Arcy politely.

—His name, said Aunt Kate, was Parkinson.[9] I heard him when he was in his prime and I think he had then the purest tenor voice that was ever put into a man's throat.

—Strange, said Mr. Bartell D'Arcy. I never even heard of him.

—Yes, yes, Miss Morkan is right, said Mr. Browne. I remember hearing of old Parkinson but he's too far back for me.

**3.** Opera by Ambroise Thomas (1811–1896), French composer. **4.** Late-19th-century Irish soprano. **5.** Some 19th-century singing stars: Therese Tietjens (1831–1877), Ilma di Murzka (1836–1889), Italo Campanini (1845–1896), Zelia Trebelli (1838–1892), Antonio Giuglini (1827–1865), and Antonio Aramburo (1838–1912). Others not identified. **6.** From *Maritana* by Brunn, Fitzball, and Wallace (1845). **7.** Operas by Giacomo Meyerbeer (1791–1864), German composer, and by Gaetano Donizetti (1797–1848), Italian composer. **8.** Enrico Caruso (1873–1921), Italian operatic tenor. **9.** Not identified; perhaps fictional.

—A beautiful pure sweet mellow English tenor, said Aunt Kate with enthusiasm.

Gabriel having finished, the huge pudding was transferred to the table. The clatter of forks and spoons began again. Gabriel's wife served out spoonfuls of the pudding and passed the plates down the table. Midway down they were held up by Mary Jane, who replenished them with raspberry or orange jelly or with blancmange and jam. The pudding was of Aunt Julia's making and she received praises for it from all quarters. She herself said that it was not quite brown enough.

—Well, I hope, Miss Morkan, said Mr. Browne, that I'm brown enough for you because, you know, I'm all brown.

All the gentlemen, except Gabriel, ate some of the pudding out of compliment to Aunt Julia. As Gabriel never ate sweets the celery had been left for him. Freddy Malins also took a stalk of celery and ate it with his pudding. He had been told that celery was a capital thing for the blood and he was just then under doctor's care. Mrs. Malins, who had been silent all through the supper, said that her son was going down to Mount Melleray,[1] in a week or so. The table then spoke of Mount Melleray, how bracing the air was down there, how hospitable the monks were and how they never asked for a penny-piece from their guests.

—And do you mean to say, asked Mr. Browne incredulously, that a chap can go down there and put up there as if it were a hotel and live on the fat of the land and then come away without paying a farthing?

—O, most people give some donation to the monastery when they leave, said Mary Jane.

—I wish we had an institution like that in our Church, said Mr. Browne candidly.

He was astonished to hear that the monks never spoke, got up at two in the morning and slept in their coffins. He asked what they did it for.

—That's the rule of the order, said Aunt Kate firmly.

—Yes, but why? asked Mr. Browne.

Aunt Kate repeated that it was the rule, that was all. Mr. Browne still seemed not to understand. Freddy Malins explained to him, as best he could, that the monks were trying to make up for the sins committed by all the sinners in the outside world. The explanation was not very clear for Mr. Browne grinned and said:

—I like that idea very much but wouldn't a comfortable spring bed do them as well as a coffin?

—The coffin, said Mary Jane, is to remind them of their last end.

As the subject had grown lugubrious it was buried in a silence of the table during which Mrs. Malins could be heard saying to her neighbour in an indistinct undertone:

—They are very good men, the monks, very pious men.

The raisins and almonds and figs and apples and oranges and chocolates and sweets were now passed about the table and Aunt Julia invited all the guests to have either port or sherry. At first Mr. Bartell D'Arcy refused to take either but one of his neighbours nudged him and whispered something to

---

1. Trappist monastery in the south of Ireland.

him upon which he allowed his glass to be filled. Gradually as the last glasses were being filled the conversation ceased. A pause followed, broken only by the noise of the wine and by unsettlings of chairs. The Misses Morkan, all three, looked down at the tablecloth. Someone coughed once or twice and then a few gentlemen patted the table gently as a signal for silence. The silence came and Gabriel pushed back his chair and stood up.

The patting at once grew louder in encouragement and then ceased altogether. Gabriel leaned his ten trembling fingers on the tablecloth and smiled nervously at the company. Meeting a row of upturned faces he raised his eyes to the chandelier. The piano was playing a waltz tune and he could hear the skirts sweeping against the drawing-room door. People, perhaps, were standing in the snow on the quay outside, gazing up at the lighted windows and listening to the waltz music. The air was pure there. In the distance lay the park where the trees were weighted with snow. The Wellington Monument wore a gleaming cap of snow that flashed westward over the white field of Fifteen Acres.[2]

He began:

—Ladies and Gentlemen.

—It has fallen to my lot this evening, as in years past, to perform a very pleasing task but a task for which I am afraid my poor powers as a speaker are all too inadequate.

—No, no! said Mr. Browne.

—But, however that may be, I can only ask you to-night to take the will for the deed and to lend me your attention for a few moments while I endeavour to express to you in words what my feelings are on this occasion.

—Ladies and Gentlemen. It is not the first time that we have gathered together under this hospitable roof, around this hospitable board. It is not the first time that we have been the recipients—or perhaps, I had better say, the victims—of the hospitality of certain good ladies.

He made a circle in the air with his arm and paused. Everyone laughed or smiled at Aunt Kate and Aunt Julia and Mary Jane who all turned crimson with pleasure. Gabriel went on more boldly:

—I feel more strongly with every recurring year that our country has no tradition which does it so much honour and which it should guard so jealously as that of its hospitality. It is a tradition that is unique as far as my experience goes (and I have visited not a few places abroad) among the modern nations. Some would say, perhaps, that with us it is rather a failing than anything to be boasted of. But granted even that, it is, to my mind, a princely failing, and one that I trust will long be cultivated among us. Of one thing, at least, I am sure. As long as this one roof shelters the good ladies aforesaid—and I wish from my heart it may do so for many and many a long year to come—the tradition of genuine warm-hearted courteous Irish hospitality, which our forefathers have handed down to us and which we in turn must hand down to our descendants, is still alive among us.

A hearty murmur of assent ran round the table. It shot through Gabriel's mind that Miss Ivors was not there and that she had gone away discourteously: and he said with confidence in himself:

2. Section of Phoenix Park in which the Wellington Monument stands.

—Ladies and Gentlemen.

—A new generation is growing up in our midst, a generation actuated by new ideas and new principles. It is serious and enthusiastic for these new ideas and its enthusiasm, even when it is misdirected, is, I believe, in the main sincere. But we are living in a sceptical and, if I may use the phrase, a thought-tormented age: and sometimes I fear that this new generation, educated or hypereducated as it is, will lack those qualities of humanity, of hospitality, of kindly humour which belonged to an older day. Listening to-night to the names of all those great singers of the past it seemed to me, I must confess, that we were living in a less spacious age. Those days might, without exaggeration, be called spacious days: and if they are gone beyond recall let us hope, at least, that in gatherings such as this we shall still speak of them with pride and affection, still cherish in our hearts the memory of those dead and gone great ones whose fame the world will not willingly let die.

—Hear, hear! said Mr. Browne loudly.

—But yet, continued Gabriel, his voice falling into a softer inflection, there are always in gatherings such as this sadder thoughts that will recur to our minds: thoughts of the past, of youth, of changes, of absent faces that we miss here to-night. Our path through life is strewn with many such sad memories: and were we to brood upon them always we could not find the heart to go on bravely with our work among the living. We have all of us living duties and living affections which claim, and rightly claim, our strenuous endeavours.

—Therefore, I will not linger on the past. I will not let any gloomy moralising intrude upon us here to-night. Here we are gathered together for a brief moment from the bustle and rush of our everyday routine. We are met here as friends, in the spirit of good-fellowship, as colleagues, also to a certain extent, in the true spirit of *camaraderie*, and as the guests of—what shall I call them?— the Three Graces of the Dublin musical world.

The table burst into applause and laughter at this sally. Aunt Julia vainly asked each of her neighbours in turn to tell her what Gabriel had said.

—He says we are the Three Graces, Aunt Julia, said Mary Jane.

Aunt Julia did not understand but she looked up, smiling, at Gabriel, who continued in the same vein:

—Ladies and Gentlemen.

—I will not attempt to play to-night the part that Paris played on another occasion. I will not attempt to choose between them. The task would be an invidious one and one beyond my poor powers. For when I view them in turn, whether it be our chief hostess herself, whose good heart, whose too good heart, has become a byword with all who know her, or her sister, who seems to be gifted with perennial youth and whose singing must have been a surprise and a revelation to us all to-night, or, last but not least, when I consider our youngest hostess, talented, cheerful, hard-working and the best of nieces, I confess, Ladies and Gentlemen, that I do not know to which of them I should award the prize.

Gabriel glanced down at his aunts and, seeing the large smile on Aunt Julia's face and the tears which had risen to Aunt Kate's eyes, hastened to his close. He raised his glass of port gallantly, while every member of the company fingered a glass expectantly, and said loudly:

—Let us toast them all three together. Let us drink to their health, wealth, long life, happiness and prosperity and may they long continue to hold the proud and self-won position which they hold in their profession and the position of honour and affection which they hold in our hearts.

All the guests stood up, glass in hand, and, turning towards the three seated ladies, sang in unison, with Mr. Browne as leader:

> *For they are jolly gay fellows,*
> *For they are jolly gay fellows,*
> *For they are jolly gay fellows,*
> *Which nobody can deny.*

Aunt Kate was making frank use of her handkerchief and even Aunt Julia seemed moved. Freddy Malins beat time with his pudding-fork and the singers turned towards one another, as if in melodious conference, while they sang, with emphasis:

> *Unless he tells a lie,*
> *Unless he tells a lie.*

Then, turning once more towards their hostesses, they sang:

> *For they are jolly gay fellows,*
> *For they are jolly gay fellows,*
> *For they are jolly gay fellows,*
> *Which nobody can deny.*

The acclamation which followed was taken up beyond the door of the supper-room by many of the other guests and renewed time after time, Freddy Malins acting as officer with his fork on high.

The piercing morning air came into the hall where they were standing so that Aunt Kate said:

—Close the door, somebody. Mrs. Malins will get her death of cold.

—Browne is out there, Aunt Kate, said Mary Jane.

—Browne is everywhere, said Aunt Kate, lowering her voice.

Mary Jane laughed at her tone.

—Really, she said archly, he is very attentive.

—He has been laid on[3] here like the gas, said Aunt Kate in the same tone, all during the Christmas.

She laughed herself this time good-humouredly and then added quickly:

—But tell him to come in, Mary Jane, and close the door. I hope to goodness he didn't hear me.

3. Supplied by plan.

At that moment the hall-door was opened and Mr. Browne came in from the doorstep, laughing as if his heart would break. He was dressed in a long green overcoat with mock astrakhan cuffs and collar and wore on his head an oval fur cap. He pointed down the snow-covered quay from where the sound of shrill prolonged whistling was borne in.

—Teddy will have all the cabs in Dublin out, he said.

Gabriel advanced from the little pantry behind the office, struggling into his overcoat and, looking round the hall, said:

—Gretta not down yet?

—She's getting on her things, Gabriel, said Aunt Kate.

—Who's playing up there? asked Gabriel.

—Nobody. They're all gone.

—O no, Aunt Kate, said Mary Jane. Bartell D'Arcy and Miss O'Callaghan aren't gone yet.

—Someone is strumming at the piano, anyhow, said Gabriel.

Mary Jane glanced at Gabriel and Mr. Browne and said with a shiver:

—It makes me feel cold to look at you two gentlemen muffled up like that. I wouldn't like to face your journey home at this hour.

—I'd like nothing better this minute, said Mr. Browne stoutly, than a rattling fine walk in the country or a fast drive with a good spanking goer[4] between the shafts.

—We used to have a very good horse and trap[5] at home, said Aunt Julia sadly.

—The never-to-be-forgotten Johnny, said Mary Jane, laughing.

Aunt Kate and Gabriel laughed too.

—Why, what was wonderful about Johnny? asked Mr. Browne.

—The late lamented Patrick Morkan, our grandfather, that is, explained Gabriel, commonly known in his later years as the old gentleman, was a glue-boiler.

—O, now, Gabriel, said Aunt Kate, laughing, he had a starch mill.

—Well, glue or starch, said Gabriel, the old gentleman had a horse by the name of Johnny. And Johnny used to work in the old gentleman's mill, walking round and round in order to drive the mill. That was all very well; but now comes the tragic part about Johnny. One fine day the old gentleman thought he'd like to drive out with the quality[6] to a military review in the park.

—The Lord have mercy on his soul, said Aunt Kate compassionately.

—Amen, said Gabriel. So the old gentleman, as I said, harnessed Johnny and put on his very best tall hat and his very best stock collar and drove out in grand style from his ancestral mansion somewhere near Back Lane, I think.

Everyone laughed, even Mrs. Malins, at Gabriel's manner and Aunt Kate said:

—O now, Gabriel, he didn't live in Back Lane, really. Only the mill was there.

—Out from the mansion of his forefathers, continued Gabriel, he drove with Johnny. And everything went on beautifully until Johnny came in sight of King Billy's statue:[7] and whether he fell in love with the horse King Billy

---

4. That is, a fine horse. **5.** One-horse carriage. **6.** Upper classes. **7.** Equestrian statue of King William III of England (William of Orange), last military conquerer of Ireland, at the Battle of the Boyne in 1690.

sits on or whether he thought he was back again in the mill, anyhow he began to walk round the statue.

Gabriel paced in a circle round the hall in his goloshes amid the laughter of the others.

—Round and round he went, said Gabriel, and the old gentleman, who was a very pompous old gentleman, was highly indignant. *Go on, sir! What do you mean, sir? Johnny! Johnny! Most extraordinary conduct! Can't understand the horse!*

The peals of laughter which followed Gabriel's imitation of the incident were interrupted by a resounding knock at the hall-door. Mary Jane ran to open it and let in Freddy Malins. Freddy Malins, with his hat well back on his head and his shoulders humped with cold, was puffing and steaming after his exertions.

—I could only get one cab, he said.

—O, we'll find another along the quay, said Gabriel.

—Yes, said Aunt Kate. Better not keep Mrs. Malins standing in the draught.

Mrs. Malins was helped down the front steps by her son and Mr. Browne and, after many manoeuvres, hoisted into the cab. Freddy Malins clambered in after her and spent a long time settling her on the seat, Mr. Browne helping him with advice. At last she was settled comfortably and Freddy Malins invited Mr. Browne into the cab. There was a good deal of confused talk, and then Mr. Browne got into the cab. The cabman settled his rug over his knees, and bent down for the address. The confusion grew greater and the cabman was directed differently by Freddy Malins and Mr. Browne, each of whom had his head out through a window of the cab. The difficulty was to know where to drop Mr. Browne along the route and Aunt Kate, Aunt Julia and Mary Jane helped the discussion from the doorstep with cross-directions and contradictions and abundance of laughter. As for Freddy Malins he was speechless with laughter. He popped his head in and out of the window every moment, to the great danger of his hat, and told his mother how the discussion was progressing till at last Mr. Browne shouted to the bewildered cabman above the din of everybody's laughter:

—Do you know Trinity College?

—Yes, sir, said the cabman.

—Well, drive bang up against Trinity College gates, said Mr. Browne, and then we'll tell you where to go. You understand now?

—Yes, sir, said the cabman.

—Make like a bird for Trinity College.

—Right, sir, cried the cabman.

The horse was whipped up and the cab rattled off along the quay amid a chorus of laughter and adieus.

Gabriel had not gone to the door with the others. He was in a dark part of the hall gazing up the staircase. A woman was standing near the top of the first flight, in the shadow also. He could not see her face but he could see the terracotta and salmonpink panels of her skirt which the shadow made appear black and white. It was his wife. She was leaning on the banisters, listening to something. Gabriel was surprised at her stillness and strained his ear to listen also. But he could hear little save the noise of laughter and dispute on the front steps, a few chords struck on the piano and a few notes of a man's voice singing.

He stood still in the gloom of the hall, trying to catch the air that the voice was singing and gazing up at his wife. There was grace and mystery in her attitude as if she were a symbol of something. He asked himself what is a woman standing on the stairs in the shadow, listening to distant music, a symbol of. If he were a painter he would paint her in that attitude. Her blue felt hat would show off the bronze of her hair against the darkness and the dark panels of her skirt would show off the light ones. *Distant Music* he would call the picture if he were a painter.

The hall-door was closed; and Aunt Kate, Aunt Julia and Mary Jane came down the hall, still laughing.

—Well, isn't Freddy terrible? said Mary Jane. He's really terrible.

Gabriel said nothing but pointed up the stairs towards where his wife was standing. Now that the hall-door was closed the voice and the piano could be heard more clearly. Gabriel held up his hand for them to be silent. The song seemed to be in the old Irish tonality and the singer seemed uncertain both of his words and of his voice. The voice, made plaintive by distance and by the singer's hoarseness, faintly illuminated the cadence of the air with words expressing grief:

> *O, the rain falls on my heavy locks*
> *And the dew wets my skin,*
> *My babe lies cold . . .*

—O, exclaimed Mary Jane. It's Bartell D'Arcy singing and he wouldn't sing all the night. O, I'll get him to sing a song before he goes.

—O do, Mary Jane, said Aunt Kate.

Mary Jane brushed past the others and ran to the staircase but before she reached it the singing stopped and the piano was closed abruptly.

—O, what a pity! she cried. Is he coming down, Gretta?

Gabriel heard his wife answer yes and saw her come down towards them. A few steps behind her were Mr. Bartell D'Arcy and Miss O'Callaghan.

—O, Mr. D'Arcy, cried Mary Jane, it's downright mean of you to break off like that when we were all in raptures listening to you.

—I have been at him all the evening, said Miss O'Callaghan, and Mrs. Conroy too and he told us he had a dreadful cold and couldn't sing.

—O, Mr. D'Arcy, said Aunt Kate, now that was a great fib to tell.

—Can't you see that I'm as hoarse as a crow? said Mr. D'Arcy roughly.

He went into the pantry hastily and put on his overcoat. The others, taken aback by his rude speech, could find nothing to say. Aunt Kate wrinkled her brows and made signs to the others to drop the subject. Mr. D'Arcy stood swathing his neck carefully and frowning.

—It's the weather, said Aunt Julia, after a pause.

—Yes, everybody has colds, said Aunt Kate readily, everybody.

—They say, said Mary Jane, we haven't had snow like it for thirty years; and I read this morning in the newspapers that the snow is general all over Ireland.

—I love the look of snow, said Aunt Julia sadly.

—So do I, said Miss O'Callaghan. I think Christmas is never really Christmas unless we have the snow on the ground.

—But poor Mr. D'Arcy doesn't like the snow, said Aunt Kate, smiling.

Mr. D'Arcy came from the pantry, fully swathed and buttoned, and in a repentant tone told them the history of his cold. Everyone gave him advice and said it was a great pity and urged him to be very careful of his throat in the night air. Gabriel watched his wife who did not join in the conversation. She was standing right under the dusty fanlight and the flame of the gas lit up the rich bronze of her hair which he had seen her drying at the fire a few days before. She was in the same attitude and seemed unaware of the talk about her. At last she turned towards them and Gabriel saw that there was colour on her cheeks and that her eyes were shining. A sudden tide of joy went leaping out of his heart.

—Mr. D'Arcy, she said, what is the name of that song you were singing?

—It's called *The Lass of Aughrim*,[8] said Mr. D'Arcy, but I couldn't remember it properly. Why? Do you know it?

—*The Lass of Aughrim,* she repeated. I couldn't think of the name.

—It's a very nice air, said Mary Jane. I'm sorry you were not in voice to-night.

—Now, Mary Jane, said Aunt Kate, don't annoy Mr. D'Arcy. I won't have him annoyed.

Seeing that all were ready to start she shepherded them to the door where good-night was said:

—Well, good-night, Aunt Kate, and thanks for the pleasant evening.

—Good-night, Gabriel. Good-night, Gretta!

—Good-night, Aunt Kate, and thanks ever so much. Good-night, Aunt Julia.

—O, good-night, Gretta, I didn't see you.

—Good-night, Mr. D'Arcy. Good-night, Miss O'Callaghan.

—Good-night, Miss Morkan.

—Good-night, again.

—Good-night, all. Safe home.

—Good-night. Good-night.

The morning was still dark. A dull yellow light brooded over the houses and the river; and the sky seemed to be descending. It was slushy underfoot; and only streaks and patches of snow lay on the roofs, on the parapets of the quay and on the area railings. The lamps were still burning redly in the murky air and, across the river, the palace of the Four Courts[9] stood out menacingly against the heavy sky.

She was walking on before him with Mr. Bartell D'Arcy, her shoes in a brown parcel tucked under one arm and her hands holding her skirt up from the slush. She had no longer any grace of attitude but Gabriel's eyes were still bright with happiness. The blood went bounding along his veins; and the thoughts went rioting through his brain, proud, joyful, tender, valorous.

She was walking on before him so lightly and so erect that he longed to run after her noiselessly, catch her by the shoulders and say something foolish and affectionate into her ear. She seemed to him so frail that he longed to defend her against something and then to be alone with her. Moments of

---

**8.** Variant of "The Lass of Loch Royal," Child's ballad No. 76. It tells of a girl seduced and abandoned. She stands in the rain outside the house of her seducer with her baby in her arms; rejected, she puts to sea in a boat and drowns herself and the child.  **9.** Building housing the courts of Ireland.

their secret life together burst like stars upon his memory. A heliotrope envelope was lying beside his breakfast-cup and he was caressing it with his hand. Birds were twittering in the ivy and the sunny web of the curtain was shimmering along the floor: he could not eat for happiness. They were standing on the crowded platform and he was placing a ticket inside the warm palm of her glove. He was standing with her in the cold, looking in through a grated window at a man making bottles in a roaring furnace. It was very cold. Her face, fragrant in the cold air, was quite close to his; and suddenly she called out to the man at the furnace:

—Is the fire hot, sir?

But the man could not hear her with the noise of the furnace. It was just as well. He might have answered rudely.

A wave of yet more tender joy escaped from his heart and went coursing in warm flood along his arteries. Like the tender fires of stars moments of their life together, that no one knew of or would ever know of, broke upon and illumined his memory. He longed to recall to her those moments, to make her forget the years of their dull existence together and remember only their moments of ecstasy. For the years, he felt, had not quenched his soul or hers. Their children, his writing, her household cares had not quenched all their souls' tender fire. In one letter that he had written to her then he had said: *Why is it that words like these seem to me so dull and cold? Is it because there is no word tender enough to be your name?*

Like distant music these words that he had written years before were borne towards him from the past. He longed to be alone with her. When the others had gone away, when he and she were in their room in the hotel, then they would be alone together. He would call her softly:

—Gretta!

Perhaps she would not hear at once: she would be undressing. Then something in his voice would strike her. She would turn and look at him. . . .

At the corner of Winetavern Street they met a cab. He was glad of its rattling noise as it saved him from conversation. She was looking out of the window and seemed tired. The others spoke only a few words, pointing out some building or street. The horse galloped along wearily under the murky morning sky, dragging his old rattling box after his heels, and Gabriel was again in a cab with her, galloping to catch the boat, galloping to their honeymoon.

As the cab drove across O'Connell Bridge Miss O'Callaghan said:

—They say you never cross O'Connell Bridge without seeing a white horse.

—I see a white man this time, said Gabriel.

Where? asked Mr. Bartell D'Arcy.

Gabriel pointed to the statue, on which lay patches of snow. Then he nodded familiarly to it and waved his hand.

—Good-night, Dan,[1] he said gaily.

When the cab drew up before the hotel Gabriel jumped out and, in spite of Mr. Bartell D'Arcy's protest, paid the driver. He gave the man a shilling over his fare. The man saluted and said:

—A prosperous New Year to you, sir.

---

1. The statue is of Daniel O'Connell (1775–1847), Irish patriot, known as "The Liberator," for whom the bridge is named.

—The same to you, said Gabriel cordially.

She leaned for a moment on his arm in getting out of the cab and while standing at the curbstone, bidding the others good-night. She leaned lightly on his arm, as lightly as when she had danced with him a few hours before. He had felt proud and happy then, happy that she was his, proud of her grace and wifely carriage. But now, after the kindling again of so many memories, the first touch of her body, musical and strange and perfumed, sent through him a keen pang of lust. Under cover of her silence he pressed her arm closely to his side; and, as they stood at the hotel door, he felt that they had escaped from their lives and duties, escaped from home and friends and run away together with wild and radiant hearts to a new adventure.

An old man was dozing in a great hooded chair in the hall. He lit a candle in the office and went before them to the stairs. They followed him in silence, their feet falling in soft thuds on the thickly carpeted stairs. She mounted the stairs behind the porter, her head bowed in the ascent, her frail shoulders curved as with a burden, her skirt girt tightly about her. He could have flung his arms about her hips and held her still for his arms were trembling with desire to seize her and only the stress of his nails against the palms of his hands held the wild impulse of his body in check. The porter halted on the stairs to settle his guttering candle. They halted too on the steps below him. In the silence Gabriel could hear the falling of the molten wax into the tray and the thumping of his own heart against his ribs.

The porter led them along a corridor and opened a door. Then he set his unstable candle down on a toilet-table and asked at what hour they were to be called in the morning.

—Eight, said Gabriel.

The porter pointed to the tap of the electric-light and began a muttered apology but Gabriel cut him short.

—We don't want any light. We have light enough from the street. And I say, he added, pointing to the candle, you might remove that handsome article, like a good man.

The porter took up his candle again, but slowly for he was surprised by such a novel idea. Then he mumbled good-night and went out. Gabriel shot the lock to.[2]

A ghostly light from the street lamp lay in a long shaft from one window to the door. Gabriel threw his overcoat and hat on a couch and crossed the room towards the window. He looked down into the street in order that his emotion might calm a little. Then he turned and leaned against a chest of drawers with his back to the light. She had taken off her hat and cloak and was standing before a large swinging mirror, unhooking her waist. Gabriel paused for a few moments, watching her, and then said:

—Gretta!

She turned away from the mirror slowly and walked along the shaft of light towards him. Her face looked so serious and weary that the words would not pass Gabriel's lips. No, it was not the moment yet.

—You looked tired, he said.

—I am a little, she answered.

---

2. That is, locked the deadbolt.

—You don't feel ill or weak?

—No, tired: that's all.

She went on to the window and stood there, looking out. Gabriel waited again and then, fearing that diffidence was about to conquer him, he said abruptly:

—By the way, Gretta!

—What is it?

—You know that poor fellow Malins? he said quickly.

—Yes. What about him?

—Well, poor fellow, he's a decent sort of chap after all, continued Gabriel in a false voice. He gave me back that sovereign[3] I lent him and I didn't expect it really. It's a pity he wouldn't keep away from that Browne, because he's not a bad fellow at heart.

He was trembling now with annoyance. Why did she seem so abstracted? He did not know how he could begin. Was she annoyed, too, about something? If she would only turn to him or come to him of her own accord! To take her as she was would be brutal. No, he must see some ardour in her eyes first. He longed to be master of her strange mood.

—When did you lend him the pound? she asked, after a pause.

Gabriel strove to restrain himself from breaking out into brutal language about the sottish Malins and his pound. He longed to cry to her from his soul, to crush her body against his, to overmaster her. But he said:

—O, at Christmas, when he opened that little Christmas-card shop in Henry Street.

He was in such a fever of rage and desire that he did not hear her come from the window. She stood before him for an instant, looking at him strangely. Then, suddenly raising herself on tiptoe and resting her hands lightly on his shoulders, she kissed him.

—You are a very generous person, Gabriel, she said.

Gabriel, trembling with delight at her sudden kiss and at the quaintness of her phrase, put his hands on her hair and began smoothing it back, scarcely touching it with his fingers. The washing had made it fine and brilliant. His heart was brimming over with happiness. Just when he was wishing for it she had come to him of her own accord. Perhaps her thoughts had been running with his. Perhaps she had felt the impetuous desire that was in him and then the yielding mood had come upon her. Now that she had fallen to him so easily he wondered why he had been so diffident.

He stood, holding her head between his hands. Then, slipping one arm swiftly about her body and drawing her towards him, he said softly:

—Gretta dear, what are you thinking about?

She did not answer nor yield wholly to his arm. He said again, softly:

—Tell me what it is, Gretta. I think I know what is the matter. Do I know?

She did not answer at once. Then she said in an outburst of tears:

—O, I am thinking about that song, *The Lass of Aughrim.*

She broke loose from him and ran to the bed and, throwing her arms across the bed-rail, hid her face. Gabriel stood stock-still for a moment in astonishment and then followed her. As he passed in the way of the cheval-glass he

---

**3.** Gold coin worth one pound.

caught sight of himself in full length, his broad, well-filled shirt-front, the face whose expression always puzzled him when he saw it in a mirror and his glimmering gilt-rimmed eyeglasses. He halted a few paces from her and said:

—What about the song? Why does that make you cry?

She raised her head from her arms and dried her eyes with the back of her hand like a child. A kinder note than he had intended went into his voice.

—Why, Gretta? he asked.

—I am thinking about a person long ago who used to sing that song.

—And who was the person long ago? asked Gabriel, smiling.

—It was a person I used to know in Galway when I was living with my grand-mother, she said.

The smile passed away from Gabriel's face. A dull anger began to gather again at the back of his mind and the dull fires of his lust began to glow angrily in his veins.

—Someone you were in love with? he asked ironically.

—It was a young boy I used to know, she answered, named Michael Furey. He used to sing that song, *The Lass of Aughrim*. He was very delicate.

Gabriel was silent. He did not wish her to think that he was interested in this delicate boy.

—I can see him so plainly, she said after a moment. Such eyes as he had: big dark eyes! And such an expression in them—an expression!

—O then, you were in love with him? said Gabriel.

—I used to go out walking with him, she said, when I was in Galway.

A thought flew across Gabriel's mind.

—Perhaps that was why you wanted to go to Galway with that Ivors girl? he said coldly.

She looked at him and asked in surprise:

—What for?

Her eyes made Gabriel feel awkward. He shrugged his shoulders and said:

—How do I know? To see him perhaps.

She looked away from him along the shaft of light towards the window in silence.

—He is dead, she said at length. He died when he was only seventeen. Isn't it a terrible thing to die so young as that?

—What was he? asked Gabriel, still ironically.

—He was in the gasworks, she said.

Gabriel felt humiliated by the failure of his irony and by the evocation of this figure from the dead, a boy in the gasworks. While he had been full of memories of their secret life together, full of tenderness and joy and desire, she had been comparing him in her mind with another. A shameful consciousness of his own person assailed him. He saw himself as a ludicrous figure, acting as a pennyboy[4] for his aunts, a nervous well-meaning sentimen-talist, orating to vulgarians and idealising his own clownish lusts, the piti-able fatuous fellow he had caught a glimpse of in the mirror. Instinctively he turned his back more to the light lest she might see the shame that burned upon his forehead.

---

**4.** Errand boy.

He tried to keep up his tone of cold interrogation but his voice when he spoke was humble and indifferent.

—I suppose you were in love with this Michael Furey, Gretta, he said.

—I was great[5] with him at that time, she said.

Her voice was veiled and sad. Gabriel, feeling now how vain it would be to try to lead her whither he had purposed, caressed one of her hands and said, also sadly:

—And what did he die of so young, Gretta? Consumption, was it?

—I think he died for me, she answered.

A vague terror seized Gabriel at this answer as if, at that hour when he had hoped to triumph, some impalpable and vindictive being was coming against him, gathering forces against him in its vague world. But he shook himself free of it with an effort of reason and continued to caress her hand. He did not question her again for he felt that she would tell him of herself. Her hand was warm and moist: it did not respond to his touch but he continued to caress it just as he had caressed her first letter to him that spring morning.

—It was in the winter, she said, about the beginning of the winter when I was going to leave my grandmother's and come up here to the convent. And he was ill at the time in his lodgings in Galway and wouldn't be let out and his people in Oughterard[6] were written to. He was in decline, they said, or something like that. I never knew rightly.

She paused for a moment and sighed.

—Poor fellow, she said. He was very fond of me and he was such a gentle boy. We used to go out together, walking, you know, Gabriel, like the way they do in the country. He was going to study singing only for his health. He had a very good voice, poor Michael Furey.

—Well; and then? asked Gabriel.

—And then when it came to the time for me to leave Galway and come up to the convent he was much worse and I wouldn't be let see him so I wrote a letter saying I was going up to Dublin and would be back in the summer and hoping he would be better then.

She paused for a moment to get her voice under control and then went on:

—Then the night before I left I was in my grandmother's house in Nuns' Island, packing up, and I heard gravel thrown up against the window. The window was so wet I couldn't see so I ran downstairs as I was and slipped out the back into the garden and there was the poor fellow at the end of the garden, shivering.

—And did you not tell him to go back? asked Gabriel.

—I implored of him to go home at once and told him he would get his death in the rain. But he said he did not want to live. I can see his eyes as well as well! He was standing at the end of the wall where there was a tree.

—And did he go home? asked Gabriel.

—Yes, he went home. And when I was only a week in the convent he died and he was buried in Oughterard where his people came from. O, the day I heard that, that he was dead!

She stopped, choking with sobs, and, overcome by emotion, flung herself face downward on the bed, sobbing in the quilt. Gabriel held her hand for a

5. Intimate, closely acquainted.   6. Town in Connacht, 20 miles north of Galway.

moment longer, irresolutely, and then, shy of intruding on her grief, let it fall gently and walked quietly to the window.

She was fast asleep.

Gabriel, leaning on his elbow, looked for a few moments unresentfully on her tangled hair and half-open mouth, listening to her deep-drawn breath. So she had had that romance in her life: a man had died for her sake. It hardly pained him now to think how poor a part he, her husband, had played in her life. He watched her while she slept as though he and she had never lived together as man and wife. His curious eyes rested long upon her face and on her hair: and, as he thought of what she must have been then, in that time of her first girlish beauty, a strange friendly pity for her entered his soul. He did not like to say even to himself that her face was no longer beautiful but he knew that it was no longer the face for which Michael Furey had braved death.

Perhaps she had not told him all the story. His eyes moved to the chair over which she had thrown some of her clothes. A petticoat string dangled to the floor. One boot stood upright, its limp upper fallen down: the fellow of it lay upon its side. He wondered at his riot of emotions of an hour before. From what had it proceeded? From his aunt's supper, from his own foolish speech, from the wine and dancing, the merry-making when saying good-night in the hall, the pleasure of the walk along the river in the snow. Poor Aunt Julia! She, too, would soon be a shade with the shade of Patrick Morkan and his horse. He had caught that haggard look upon her face for a moment when she was singing *Arrayed for the Bridal*. Soon, perhaps, he would be sitting in that same drawing-room, dressed in black, his silk hat on his knees. The blinds would be drawn down and Aunt Kate would be sitting beside him, crying and blowing her nose and telling him how Julia had died. He would cast about in his mind for some words that might console her, and would find only lame and useless ones. Yes, yes: that would happen very soon.

The air of the room chilled his shoulders. He stretched himself cautiously along under the sheets and lay down beside his wife. One by one they were all becoming shades. Better pass boldly into that other world, in the full glory of some passion, than fade and wither dismally with age. He thought of how she who lay beside him had locked in her heart for so many years that image of her lover's eyes when he had told her that he did not wish to live.

Generous tears filled Gabriel's eyes. He had never felt like that himself towards any woman but he knew that such a feeling must be love. The tears gathered more thickly in his eyes and in the partial darkness he imagined he saw the form of a young man standing under a dripping tree. Other forms were near. His soul had approached that region where dwell the vast hosts of the dead. He was conscious of, but could not apprehend, their wayward and flickering existence. His own identity was fading out into a grey impalpable world: the solid world itself which these dead had one time reared and lived in was dissolving and dwindling.

A few light taps upon the pane made him turn to the window. It had begun to snow again. He watched sleepily the flakes, silver and dark, falling obliquely against the lamplight. The time had come for him to set out on his journey westward. Yes, the newspapers were right: snow was general all over Ireland. It was falling on every part of the dark central plain, on the treeless hills, falling softly upon the Bog of Allen and, farther westward, softly falling into the dark mutinous Shannon[7] waves. It was falling, too, upon every part of the lonely churchyard on the hill where Michael Furey lay buried. It lay thickly drifted on the crooked crosses and headstones, on the spears of the little gate, on the barren thorns. His soul swooned slowly as he heard the snow falling faintly through the universe and faintly falling, like the descent of their last end, upon all the living and the dead.

1914

RELATED:

—C. C. Loomis Jr., "Structure and Sympathy in Joyce's 'The Dead,'" p. 928

---

7. River flowing westward through Ireland. The Bog of Allen is southwest of Dublin.

# FRANZ KAFKA
## 1883–1924

Kafka was born in Prague, the son of a middle-class Jewish family. After obtaining a law degree at the German University in Prague, he held an inconspicuous position in the civil service for many years. His few intimates remembered him as a warmly humorous man; however, his deep sense of inferiority to his father, the frailty of his health, his indecisive and prolonged engagement that never led to marriage, his preoccupation with suicide, and his last years of struggle against the tuberculosis that killed him suggest some origins of the great anxiety that pervades his literary production. He was not altogether a pessimist but was tormented by the conviction that goodness is very remote and nearly impossible to attain. Though he considered his writing the major task of his life, he had completed very few of his projects at the time of his death and published even fewer. He directed his friend Max Brod to burn his remaining manuscripts when he died. Brod ignored the command and saw that many of them were published. Three unfinished novels—*The Trial* (1925), *The Castle* (1926), and *Amerika* (1927)—brought Kafka his first posthumous fame, but the fairly large body of stories published under Brod's sponsorship shows the complexity of the author's imagination and metaphysical irony perhaps more comprehensively than the novels that earned him his place as a major spokesman for the Age of Anxiety. Indeed, the term "Kafkaesque" is now widely used to describe the most darkly irrational, even nightmarish, aspects of modern life. His stories in English translation can be found in *The Great Wall of China* (1933), *The Penal Colony* (1948), and *The Complete Stories* (1976).

## The Metamorphosis[1]

### I

When Gregor Samsa woke one morning from troubled dreams, he found himself transformed right there in his bed into some sort of monstrous insect. He was lying on his back—which was hard, like a carapace—and when he raised his head a little he saw his curved brown belly segmented by rigid arches atop which the blanket, already slipping, was just barely managing to cling. His many legs, pitifully thin compared to the rest of him, waved helplessly before his eyes.

1. Translated by Susan Bernofsky.

"What in the world has happened to me?" he thought. It was no dream. His room, a proper human room, if admittedly rather too small, lay peacefully between the four familiar walls. Above the table, where an unpacked collection of cloth samples was arranged (Samsa was a traveling salesman), hung the picture he had recently clipped from a glossy magazine and placed in an attractive gilt frame. This picture showed a lady in a fur hat and fur boa who sat erect, holding out to the viewer a heavy fur muff in which her entire forearm had vanished.

Gregor's gaze then shifted to the window, where the bleak weather—raindrops could be heard striking the metal sill—made him feel quite melancholy. "What if I just go back to sleep for a little while and forget all this foolishness," he thought, but this proved utterly impossible, for it was his habit to sleep on his right side, and in his present state he was unable to assume this position. No matter how forcefully he thrust himself onto his side, he kept rolling back. Perhaps a hundred times he attempted it, closing his eyes so as not to have to see those struggling legs, and relented only when he began to feel a faint dull ache in his side, unlike anything he'd ever felt before.

"Good Lord," he thought, "what an exhausting profession I've chosen. Day in and day out on the road. Work like this is far more unsettling than business conducted at home, and then I have the agony of traveling itself to contend with: worrying about train connections, the irregular, unpalatable meals, and human intercourse that is constantly changing, never developing the least constancy or warmth. Devil take it all!" He felt a faint itch high up on his belly; still on his back, he laboriously edged himself over to the bedpost so he could raise his head more easily; identified the site of the itch: a cluster of tiny white dots he was unable to judge; and wanted to probe the spot with a leg, but drew it back again at once, for the touch sent cold shivers rippling through him.

He slid back into his earlier position. "All this early rising," he thought, "it's enough to make one soft in the head. Human beings need their sleep. Other traveling salesmen live like harem girls. When I go back to the boardinghouse, for example, to copy out the morning's commissions: why, these gentlemen may still be sitting at breakfast. I'd like to see my boss's face if I tried that some time; he'd can me on the spot. Although who knows, maybe that would be the best thing for me. If I didn't have to hold back for my parents' sake, I'd have given notice long ago—I'd have marched right up to him and given him a piece of my mind. He'd have fallen right off his desk! And what an odd custom that is: perching high up atop one's elevated desk and from this considerable height addressing one's employee down below, especially as the latter is obliged to stand quite close because his boss is hard of hearing. Well, all hope is not yet lost; as soon as I've saved up enough money to pay back what my parents owe him—another five or six years ought to be enough—I'll most definitely do just that. This will be the great parting of ways. For the time being, though, I've got to get up, my train leaves at five."

And he glanced over at the alarm clock ticking away atop the wardrobe. "Heavenly Father!" he thought. It was half past six, and the clock's hands kept shifting calmly forward, in fact the half-hour had already passed, it was getting on toward six forty-five. Could the alarm have failed to ring? Even from the bed one could see it was properly set for four o'clock; it must have rung. Yes, but was it possible to sleep tranquilly through this furniture-shaking racket? Well, his sleep hadn't been exactly tranquil, but no doubt that's why it had been so sound. But what should he do now? The next train was at seven o'clock; to catch it, he would have to rush like a madman, and his sample case wasn't even packed yet, and he himself felt far from agile or alert. And even if he managed to catch this train, his boss was certain to unleash a thunderstorm of invective upon his head, for the clerk who met the five o'clock train had no doubt long since reported Gregor's absence. This clerk was the boss's underling, a creature devoid of backbone and wit. What if he called in sick? But that would be mortifying and also suspicious, since Gregor had never once been ill in all his five years of service. No doubt his boss would come calling with the company doctor, would reproach Gregor's parents for their son's laziness, silencing all objections by referring them to this doctor, in whose opinion there existed only healthy individuals unwilling to work. And would the doctor be so terribly wrong in this instance? Aside from a mild drowsiness that was certainly superfluous after so many hours of sleep, Gregor felt perfectly fine; in fact, he was ravenous.

While he was considering these matters with the greatest possible speed, yet still without managing to make up his mind to leave the bed (the clock was just striking a quarter to seven), a timid knock came at the door at the head of his bed. "Gregor," the voice called—it was his mother—"it's a quarter to seven. Didn't you want to catch your train?" That gentle voice! Gregor flinched when he heard his own in response: it was unmistakably his old voice, but now it had been infiltrated as if from below by a tortured peeping sound that was impossible to suppress—leaving each word intact, comprehensible, but only for an instant before so completely annihilating it as it continued to reverberate that a person could not tell for sure whether his ears were deceiving him. Gregor had meant to give a proper response explaining everything, but under the circumstances he limited himself to saying, "Yes, thank you, Mother, I'm just getting up." Because of the wooden door, the change in Gregor's voice appeared not to be noticeable from the other side, for his mother was reassured by his response and shuffled off. But their brief conversation had alerted the other family members that Gregor was unexpectedly still at home, and already his father was knocking at one of the room's side doors, softly, but with his fist: "Gregor, Gregor," he called. "What's the problem?" And after a short while he repeated his question in a deeper register: "Gregor! Gregor!" Meanwhile, at the other side door came his sister's faint lament: "Gregor? Are you unwell? Do you need anything?" "Just a second," Gregor answered in both directions at once, making an effort, by enunciating as clearly as possible and inserting long pauses between the individual words, to remove anything conspicuous from his voice. And in fact his father returned to his breakfast, but his sister whispered: "Gregor, open the door, I implore you." But Gregor had no intention of opening the door; he praised the cautious habit he had acquired while traveling of locking all his doors at night, even at home.

First he would get up calmly and undisturbed, he would get dressed and above all have breakfast, and only then would he consider his next steps, for all these supine contemplations, he suddenly realized, would yield no useful results. He recalled often having felt mild aches and pains in bed, caused perhaps by lying in an awkward position, and this pain had then proven to be a figment of his imagination the moment he got up; he was curious to see how this morning's imaginings would gradually fade. The change in his voice was nothing more than the harbinger of a proper head cold, an occupational hazard among traveling salesmen; this he doubted not in the least.

It was simple enough to rid himself of the blanket; he needed only puff himself up a bit, and it fell right off. But the rest proved difficult, not least because he was so exceedingly wide. He would have needed arms and hands to prop himself up; but instead all he had were these many little legs, variously in motion, that he was unable to control. If he tried to bend one leg, it would be the first to straighten; and when he finally succeeded in getting one leg to do his bidding, all the others went flailing about in an unnerving frenzy. "Enough of this lying about uselessly in bed," Gregor said to himself.

At first he tried to maneuver the lower part of his body out of the bed, but this lower part—which, by the way, he had not yet seen and couldn't properly imagine—proved too unwieldy; it all went so slowly; and when at last, half-mad with impatience, he thrust himself recklessly forward with all his strength, it was in the wrong direction, and he slammed against the lower bedpost; the throbbing pain he felt instructed him that for now at least the lower part of his body was perhaps the most sensitive.

So he decided to try leading instead with his upper body and carefully twisted his head toward the edge of the bed. This was easily accomplished, and in the end, despite his width and weight, the mass of his body slowly followed the turning of his head. But once his head was dangling in midair outside the bed, he was afraid to keep shifting forward like this, since if eventually he had to let himself fall in this position, it would be practically a miracle if his head escaped injury. And right now he had to keep his wits about him at all costs, even if it meant staying where he was.

But when, sighing after redoubled efforts, he found himself lying there as before, watching his little legs engaged in their struggles, perhaps more flailingly now, and seeing no possible way to bring calm or order to this chaos, he told himself once more that he could not possibly remain lying here any longer and that the most sensible thing would be to sacrifice anything and everything as long as there remained even the slightest hope of liberating himself from the bed. Simultaneously, though, he continued to remind himself that calm consideration—indeed, the calmest consideration—was far preferable to resolutions seized on in despair. At such moments he fixed his eyes as sharply as possible on the window, but regrettably the view of the morning fog, which veiled even the far side of the narrow street, offered little by way of optimism and good spirits. "Seven o'clock already," he said to himself as the clock struck once more, "already seven and still such dense fog." And for a little while he lay there quietly, his breathing shallow, in the expectation, perhaps, that this perfect silence might possibly restore the real and ordinary state of things.

Then he said to himself: "Before it strikes a quarter past seven, I must absolutely have gotten myself completely out of bed. Besides, by then someone will have come from the office to inquire after me, as the office opens before seven." And he now set himself to rocking his body out of the bed as evenly as possible along his entire length. If he allowed himself to fall from the bed like this, his head—which he intended to lift up cleanly as he fell—would in all likelihood remain unharmed. His back seemed to be hard; surely it would sustain no damage as he fell to the rug. His greatest concern was what to do about the loud crash that would clearly result, no doubt calling forth not terror perhaps but certainly alarm behind each door. Nonetheless it would have to be ventured.

By the time Gregor was already protruding half-way out of bed—this new method was more a game than a struggle, all he had to do was keep rocking sideways a little at a time—it occurred to him how simple things would be if only someone came to his aid. Two strong individuals—he was thinking of his father and the maidservant—would suffice; all they'd have to do was slip their arms beneath his curved back to scoop him out of bed, then crouch down with their burden and wait patiently for him to flip himself over onto the floor, where he hoped those tiny legs of his would take on some meaning. But even aside from the fact that the doors were locked, should he really call for help? Despite his distress, he couldn't help smiling at the thought.

Already he'd reached the point where the vigorous rocking motion was making it almost impossible for him to keep his balance, and soon he would have to make up his mind and take the plunge, for a quarter after seven was only five minutes away—when the front doorbell rang. "It's someone from the office," he said to himself and nearly froze while his little legs went on scrabbling all the more frenetically. For a moment all was still. "They won't answer," Gregor said to himself, caught up in some deluded hope. But then of course, as always, the maid strode resolutely to the door and opened it.

Gregor needed only hear the visitor's first words of greeting to know who it was: the general manager himself. Why oh why was Gregor condemned to serve in a firm where even the most negligible falling short was enough to arouse the greatest possible suspicion? Was every last one of the firm's employees a scoundrel, was there not a single loyal, devoted soul among them who would be driven mad by pangs of conscience should he fail to make the best possible use of even just a few morning hours for his employer's benefit, such that his guilt would render him virtually incapable of rising from his bed? Would it really not have sufficed to send an apprentice to inquire—if indeed such inquiries were necessary at all—did the general manager have to come in person, and was it necessary to demonstrate to the entire innocent family that the investigation of this suspicious matter could be entrusted only to the general manager's sharp intellect? And more because of the agitation aroused in Gregor by this train of thought than because of some proper resolution on his part, he swung himself out of bed with all his might. There was a loud thud, you couldn't really call it a crash. The rug cushioned the impact a little, and since his back was more elastic than he'd thought, the resulting sound was muffled and not so obvious. But he hadn't managed to hold his head up carefully enough and had bumped it; he turned it this way and that, pressing it against the rug in his vexation and pain.

"Something just fell in there," the general manager now said in the room on the left. Gregor tried to imagine whether anything like what he was now experiencing could ever befall the general manager; the possibility must certainly be admitted. But as if brusquely dismissing the question, the manager now took a few purposeful steps in the next room, making his patent leather boots creak. From the room on the right came the whisper of Gregor's sister informing him: "Gregor, the general manager is here." "I know," Gregor murmured; but he didn't dare raise his voice high enough for his sister to hear.

"Gregor," his father now said from the room on the left, "the general manager has come to inquire why you failed to depart by the early train. We don't know what to tell him. Besides, he'd like to have a word with you in person. So please open the door. I'm sure he'll be kind enough not to take offense at the untidiness of your room." "Good morning, Herr[2] Samsa," the general manager now cried out in a friendly tone. "He isn't well," Gregor's mother said to the general manager while his father was still having his say beside the door, "not well at all, take my word for it, sir. Why else would Gregor miss his train! The office is the only thing that boy ever thinks of. It really bothers me that he never goes out in the evening; he's been back in the city an entire week now, but he's spent every last evening at home. He just sits at the table with us, quietly reading the newspaper, or else studies the timetables. Even just doing woodworking projects seems to entertain him. He carved a little picture frame, for example, did it in two or three evenings with his fretsaw; you'll be amazed how pretty it is; it's hanging there in his room; you'll see it in a minute when Gregor opens the door. Oh, and I'm so glad you paid us a visit, sir; on our own we'd never have managed to persuade Gregor to open up; he's so stubborn; and surely he isn't well, even though he denied it this morning." "Be . . . right . . . there," Gregor said, not moving, so as not to miss a single word of their conversation. "No other explanation, madam, is conceivable to me," the general manager said. "Let us hope it is nothing grave. Though on the other hand I would note that, as businessmen—fortunately or unfortunately, as one will—we are very often obliged to suppress indispositions out of consideration for the firm." "So are you ready to let the general manager in?" Gregor's impatient father asked, knocking again at the door. "No," Gregor responded. In the left-hand room horrified silence, while in the room on the right Gregor's sister began to sob.

Why didn't his sister go to join the others? She must have just gotten out of bed and not yet begun to dress. And why was she crying? Because he wasn't getting up and opening his door to the general manager, because he was in danger of losing his position, and because his boss would then start hounding his parents once more over their ancient debt? For the time being, all such worries were assuredly unnecessary. Gregor was still here, and abandoning his family was the farthest thing from his thoughts. At the moment, to be sure, he was lying on the rug, and no one familiar with his current state would seriously expect him to let the general manager in. But surely he wouldn't be sent packing just like that because of so trivial an act of discourtesy, for which it would be simple enough to find an appropriate excuse later on. And it seemed to Gregor it would be far more sensible to just leave him in peace rather than disturbing him with all this weeping and cajoling. But the others were distressed by the uncertainty of it all; their behavior was understandable.

"Herr Samsa," the general manager now called out, raising his voice. "What has come over you? You barricade yourself in your room, you reply to queries

2. Mr. (German).

only with yes and no, you cause your parents onerous, unnecessary worries, and you are neglecting—let me permit myself to note—your professional responsibilities in a truly unprecedented manner. I speak here in the name of your parents as well as your employer and in all seriousness must ask you for a clear and immediate explanation. I am astonished, utterly astonished. I have always known you as a calm, sensible person, and now it seems you've begun to permit yourself the most whimsical extravagances. To be sure, the boss did suggest one possible explanation for your absence this morning—it concerns the cash payments recently entrusted to your care—and truthfully, I all but gave him my word of honor that this explanation could not be correct. But confronted here with your incomprehensible obstinacy, I find myself losing any desire I might have had to come to your defense. And your position is anything but secure. It was originally my intention to discuss all this with you in a private conversation, but since you compel me to waste my time here, I do not know why your esteemed parents should not hear of it as well. In short: your productivity of late has been highly unsatisfactory; admittedly this is not the best season for drumming up business, we do acknowledge this; but a season in which no business at all is drummed up is something that does not, and indeed may not exist, Herr Samsa."

"But sir," Gregor cried out, beside himself and forgetting all else in his agitation, "I shall open the door at once, this very instant. A slight indisposition, a fit of dizziness kept me from getting up. Even now I'm still in bed. But already I am feeling very much refreshed. Here, I'm getting up. Just a moment's patience! It's a bit more difficult than I thought. But already I'm feeling quite fine. How odd, the way such a thing can suddenly come over one. Yesterday evening I felt perfectly all right, my parents can attest to this, or rather: I did in fact feel a mild foreboding yesterday evening already. Surely it was noticeable to anyone looking at me. Why didn't I send word to the office? But we always just assume we'll be able to overcome these illnesses without staying home. Sir! Do be gentle with my parents. The allegations you make are unfounded, and no one has ever mentioned anything of the sort to me. Perhaps you haven't yet looked over the most recent commissions I sent in. In any case, I'll be back on the road in time for the eight o'clock train; these additional hours of rest have fortified me. Please do not allow me to detain you any longer, sir; I shall be at the office myself in no time; do be so good as to say I'm on my way and give my regards to the boss."

And while Gregor was hastily blurting out all of this, scarcely knowing what he said, he edged closer to the wardrobe with minimal effort, no doubt thanks to the practice he had already acquired while still in bed, and now he did his best to haul himself upright. Indeed, he really did want to open the door, to show himself and speak with the general manager; he was eager to learn what the others, who were so anxious to see him, would say when they finally laid eyes on him. If they recoiled in horror, Gregor could surrender all responsibility and rest easy. But if they accepted it all calmly, that meant he too had no reason to get himself worked up, and if he hurried, he could still make it to the station by eight. At first he couldn't get a grip on the wardrobe's smooth surface, but finally he gave a great heave and found himself standing upright; he no longer paid any heed to the pain in his lower body, ache as it might. Now he let himself drop against the back of a nearby chair, clinging to its edges with his little legs. And having thus attained control over himself, he fell silent, for now he could listen to the general manager.

"Did you understand a single word?" the manager was asking Gregor's parents. "Surely he isn't trying to make fools of us?" "For heaven's sake," Gregor's mother cried, already weeping, "he might be gravely ill, and here we are tormenting him. Grete! Grete!" she cried out. "Mother?" Gregor's sister called from the other side. They were communicating through Gregor's room. "You must go for the doctor at once. Gregor is ill. Quick, fetch the doctor. Did you hear him speaking just now?" "That was an animal's voice," the general manager said, speaking in noticeably subdued tones compared to the cries of Gregor's mother. "Anna! Anna!" the father shouted into the kitchen through the vestibule, clapping his hands. "Run and fetch a locksmith, hurry!" And already the two girls were racing through the vestibule, their skirts rustling (how had Gregor's sister possibly gotten dressed so quickly?), and flung open the front door. There was no sound of the door closing again; no doubt they had left it standing open, as one sees with apartments in which a great calamity has occurred.

But Gregor was far less troubled now. Even though the others were no longer able to understand his words—though they had seemed to him clear enough, clearer than in the past, perhaps because his ear had grown accustomed to their sound—they were now convinced that things were not right with him and were prepared to offer help. The confidence and conviction with which these first arrangements had been made comforted him. He felt drawn once more into the circle of humankind and was expecting both the doctor and the locksmith—without properly differentiating between the two—to perform magnificent, astounding feats. So as to have as intelligible a voice as possible for the crucial discussions that lay ahead, he cleared his throat a little, making an effort to do this as discreetly as possible, since even this sound might differ from human throat-clearing, which he no longer trusted himself to judge. In the next room, meanwhile, all was quiet. Perhaps his parents sat whispering at the table with the general manager, or perhaps all of them were leaning against the door, listening.

Gregor slowly pushed himself over to the door using the armchair, then let go and allowed himself to fall against the door, propping himself upright— the pads of his little legs turned out to be slightly sticky—and there he rested briefly from his exertions. Then he set about turning the key in the lock using his mouth. Unfortunately it seemed he had no real teeth—so how was he supposed to grasp the key?—but his jaws turned out to be surprisingly strong; and with their help he actually succeeded in causing the key to move, paying no heed to the fact that he was no doubt injuring himself in the process, for a brown fluid ran out of his mouth and down the key, dripping onto the floor. "Listen to that," the general manager said in the next room, "he's turning the key in the lock." Gregor found these words most encouraging; but all of them should have been cheering him on, including his father and mother: "Come on, Gregor!" they should have shouted, "just keep at it, keep working on that lock!" And now, imagining all of them following his efforts with great suspense, he bit down on the key uncomprehendingly, with all the force he could muster. With each revolution of the key, he danced about the lock, holding himself upright using only his mouth and, as needed, either clinging to the key or using the entire weight of his body to press it down. The brighter sound of the lock finally springing open positively revived him. Sighing in relief, he said to himself: "I guess I didn't need the locksmith after all," and he laid his head upon the handle of the door to press it open.

But he remained hidden from view as the door swung toward him, even after it was wide open. To be seen, he had to work his way slowly around one of the wings of the double door, a delicate operation if he wanted to avoid plopping down awkwardly on his back before he'd even entered the room. He was still occupied with this difficult maneuver and had no leisure to attend to anything else when he heard the general manager utter a loud "Oh!"—it sounded like wind howling—and now he saw him too, saw how the general manager, who was standing closest to the door, pressed his hand to his open mouth, slowly retreating, as though being driven back by an invisible, steady force. Gregor's mother—who despite the general manager's presence stood with her hair still undone from the night, wildly bristling—first looked over at his father, her hands clasped, then took two steps in Gregor's direction before falling down in the midst of all her billowing skirts, her face vanishing completely where it sank to her bosom. Gregor's father clenched his fist with a hostile grimace, as if he intended to thrust Gregor back into his room, then glanced uncertainly about the living room, shaded his eyes with his hands, and wept until his mighty chest shook.

Gregor made no move to enter the room, instead he leaned from the inside against the wing of the door that was bolted fast, so that only half his body and the head inclined sideways above it could be seen as he peered across at the others. Meanwhile it had grown much lighter out; on the far side of the street, a section of the infinitely long, dark gray building opposite—a hospital—came into view with its regular windows punched into the facade; rain was still falling, but only in large drops that were separately visible and seemed to have been hurled one by one to the ground. An inordinate number of breakfast dishes crowded the table, for Gregor's father considered breakfast the most important meal of the day and would drag it out for hours reading various newspapers. Straight ahead, on the opposite wall, hung a photograph of Gregor from his time in the military, showing him as a second lieutenant whose carefree smile as he rested his hand on his dagger commanded respect for his bearing and his uniform. The door to the vestibule was open, and since the front door was open as well, one could see all the way out to the landing and the head of the stairs leading down.

"Well," Gregor said, quite conscious of the fact that he was the only one who had retained his composure, "I shall get dressed at once, pack up my samples and be on my way. As for the rest of you, are you prepared to let me do so? You can see, sir"—he said, addressing the general manager—"I am not obstinate, nor a shirker; traveling is burdensome, but without it I could not live. Where are you going now, sir? To the office? Yes? Will you report all these things truthfully? A person can be incapable of working at the moment, but this is precisely the right time to recall his earlier accomplishments and consider that he will later, once the hindrance has been overcome, work all the more industriously and with greater focus. I am so dreadfully indebted to the boss, surely you're aware of this. On the other hand, I have my parents and sister to think of. Truly I'm in a bind, but I shall work my way out of it. Don't make things more difficult for me than they already are. Take my side at the office! No one loves us drummers, I know. Everyone thinks the salesmen rake in a king's ransom while enjoying life's pleasures. And there's never any particular cause to reconsider this prejudice. But you, sir, have a far better grasp of the general circumstances than the rest of the staff, better even—if I may speak confidentially—than the boss himself, who in his role as businessman can easily err in his opinion to an employee's disadvantage. And you no doubt know quite well that a drummer, who spends almost the entire year away from the office, can easily become the victim of gossip, happenstance and groundless complaints against which he cannot possibly defend himself, as he usually never even learns of them, or only when he has completed one of his journeys, exhausted, and then back at home is forced to observe the dire physical effects of causes that can no longer be identified. Please, sir, do not leave without saying something to show you agree with me at least to some small extent!"

But the general manager had already turned away as soon as Gregor began to speak, and merely glanced back at him over a hunched shoulder, his mouth contorted. And during Gregor's speech he did not stand still for a moment but instead continued to retreat—not letting Gregor out of his sight—in the direction of the door, but only gradually, as though it were secretly prohibited to exit this room. Already he was in the vestibule, and to judge by the abrupt motion with which he withdrew his foot from the living room for the last time, one might have supposed he'd just burned it. Having reached the vestibule, however, he stretched out his right hand, gesturing broadly in the direction of the stairs, as if some all but supernatural salvation awaited him there.

Gregor realized he could not possibly allow the general manager to depart in his present frame of mind if his own position at the firm was not to be put in the gravest jeopardy. His parents didn't fully comprehend his situation: over these long years they had formed the conviction that Gregor was provided for in this office for life, and besides they were so preoccupied with their present worries that they were bereft of all foresight. But Gregor had this foresight. The general manager would have to be detained, reasoned with, convinced and finally won over; after all, Gregor's future and that of his family depended on it. If only his sister were here! She was clever; she had already begun to weep while Gregor was still lying quietly on his back. And surely the general manager, ever the ladies' man, would have let himself be assuaged by her; she would have closed the front door of the apartment and talked him out of his fear in the vestibule. But his sister was not there, so Gregor himself would have to act. And without stopping to consider that he was not yet familiar with his current abilities with respect to locomotion, nor even taking into account the fact that this last speech of his had quite possibly—indeed probably—eluded comprehension, he let go of the door; forced his way through the opening; meant to walk over to where the general manager, already out on the landing, was foolishly clutching at the banister with both hands; but right away, groping in vain for something to catch hold of, he fell with a faint shriek upon his many little legs. No sooner had this occurred than he felt—for the first time all morning—a sense of physical well-being; his legs had solid ground beneath them; they obeyed his will perfectly, as he noted to his delight; they even strove to bear him wherever he wished; and already it seemed to him he would soon be delivered from all his sufferings. But as he lay there on the floor directly in front of his mother and not far from her, swaying with mobility held in check, she suddenly leapt up—rapt as she had appeared within her own contemplations—leapt high up into the air, her arms thrust wide, fingers spread, crying out: "Help me, for God's sake, help!" her head cocked at an angle, as if to see Gregor better, but then, contradicting this, she senselessly retreated; but she had forgotten the table set for breakfast just behind her; sat down hurriedly upon it as soon as she reached it, as if absentmindedly; and didn't seem to notice that the big overturned coffeepot beside her was pouring a thick stream of coffee on the rug.

"Mother, Mother," Gregor said softly, gazing up at her. For a moment he had forgotten all about the general manager; on the other hand, he could not restrain himself, when he beheld this flowing coffee, from snapping his jaws several times. At this, the mother gave another shriek and fled from the table into the arms of Gregor's father as he rushed to her aid. But Gregor had no time for his parents now; the general manager was already on the stairs; his chin propped on the banister, he looked back on the scene one last time. Gregor was just preparing to dash after him to be sure of catching up with him; but the manager must have sensed something, for he leapt down several steps at once and vanished; and the cry of horror he gave as he fled resounded through the stairwell. Unfortunately the manager's flight now appeared to utterly discombobulate Gregor's father, who up till then had been relatively composed, for instead of running after the manager himself or at least not hindering Gregor in his own pursuit, he seized the manager's walking stick in one hand—it had been left lying on an armchair along with his overcoat and hat—with the other took up a large newspaper from the table, and set about driving Gregor back into his room with a great stamping of feet, brandishing both newspaper and stick. All Gregor's entreaties were in vain, nor were they even understood, for as submissively as he might swivel his head, his father only stamped his feet all the more ferociously. Across the room, his mother had flung open a window despite the chilly weather, and, leaning out, she pressed her face into her hands far outside the window frame. Between street and stairwell, a powerful draft arose, the window curtains flew into the air, the newspapers on the table rustled, and a few pages scudded across the floor. Inexorably Gregor's father drove him backward, uttering hissing sounds like a wild man. But Gregor had no practice at all in reverse locomotion, and his progress was very slow. If only he'd been permitted to turn around, he'd have been back in his room at once, but he was afraid of provoking his father's fury with this time-consuming maneuver, and at any moment a fatal blow from the stick in his father's hand might come crashing down on his back or head. In the end, though, he had no alternative: horrified, he realized he was incapable of controlling his direction; and so he began, with constant anxious glances back at his father, to turn around as quickly as he could, which in fact was rather slowly. Perhaps his father discerned his good intentions, for he did not hinder him in this operation but instead even guided his rotation here and there from a distance, using the tip of his stick. If only his father were not making that unbearable hissing noise! It made Gregor lose his head completely. He had already turned almost all the way around when—still with this hissing in his ear—he became confused and started turning back in the wrong direction. But when finally he succeeded in positioning his head in front of the doorway, it turned out that his body was too wide to fit through the opening. And of course in his father's current state it could not possibly have occurred to him to open the door's other wing to create an adequate passage. He was fixated on the notion that Gregor must disappear into his room as quickly as possible. Never would he have tolerated the complicated preparations necessary for Gregor to prop himself up so as possibly to pass through the door in an upright position. Instead, as though there were no obstacle at all, he now drove Gregor before him, raising a great din: what Gregor heard at his back no longer resembled the voice of merely a single father; it was do or die, and Gregor thrust himself—come what would—into the doorway. One side of his body tilted up, rising at an angle as he pressed forward, scraping his one flank raw and leaving ugly stains behind on the white door, and soon he was wedged tight, unable to move on his own; on one side, his little legs dangled trembling in midair, while on the other they were crushed painfully beneath him—then his father administered a powerful shove from behind, a genuinely liberating thrust that sent him flying, bleeding profusely, into the far reaches of his room. The door was banged shut with the stick, and then at last all was still.

## II

Only as dusk was falling did Gregor wake from his heavy, faintlike sleep. He probably wouldn't have slept much longer even without a disturbance, for he felt sufficiently rested and restored, but it seemed to him he had been woken by a fleeting step and the careful shutting of the door to the vestibule. The pallid gleam of the electric streetlamps touched the ceiling here and there and the upper edges of the furniture, but down where Gregor lay, all was dark. Slowly, groping awkwardly with his feelers, which he was only now learning to appreciate, he dragged himself toward the door, wanting to see what had happened. His left side felt like one long unpleasantly contracting scar, and he was forced to limp outright on his two rows of legs. One of these diminutive legs, incidentally, had suffered grievous injuries in the course of the morning's events—it was almost miraculous only one had been injured— and now trailed lifelessly behind him.

Not until he reached the door did he realize what in fact had lured him there: it was the smell of something edible. There stood a bowl filled with sweet milk in which little pieces of white bread were floating. He almost laughed with delight, for his hunger was now even more powerful than in the morning, and right away he dunked his head in the milk almost up to his eyes. But he quickly drew it out again in disappointment; it wasn't just that eating was difficult thanks to his tender left side—and he couldn't eat at all without his entire body becoming gaspingly involved—but beyond that: even though milk had always been his favorite drink, which is no doubt why his sister had brought him some, now it didn't taste good to him at all, indeed it was almost with revulsion that he turned away from the bowl and crept back to the center of the room.

In the living room, as Gregor saw through the crack, the gas had been lit, but while usually at this hour his father liked to read aloud from the afternoon paper to Gregor's mother and sometimes his sister as well in a dramatic voice, now there was not a sound to be heard. Well, perhaps this customary reading aloud that his sister had often told and written him about had recently fallen out of practice. But even in the other rooms everything was so still, even though the apartment was surely not empty. "What a quiet life my family has been leading," Gregor said to himself, and as he gazed fixedly into the darkness before him, he felt great pride at having been able to give his parents and sister a life like this in such a beautiful apartment. But what if all this tranquility, all this prosperity and contentment were now coming to a horrific end? So as not to get lost in such contemplations, Gregor set himself in motion, crawling back and forth across the room.

Once in the course of this long evening one of the side doors was opened a tiny crack and then quickly shut again, and once the other one; someone must have felt an urge to enter and then been overcome by misgivings. Gregor now stationed himself just in front of the living room door, determined to somehow coax the hesitant visitor inside or at least find out who it was; but the door did not open again, and Gregor waited in vain. Before, when all the doors were locked, everyone kept trying to come in, and now that he had opened the one door and the others had apparently been opened during the day, no one came, and the keys were sticking in their locks from the outside.

It was late at night by the time the light in the living room went out, and now it was easy to ascertain that Gregor's parents and sister had remained awake all this time, for all three of them could clearly be heard departing on tiptoe. Now it was unlikely anyone would come into Gregor's room before morning; so he had plenty of time to ponder how best to reorder his life. But this high open room in which he was forced to lie flat on the floor distressed him, without his being able to determine the cause—after all, it was his room, which he had been living in for five years now—and with a half-unconscious motion, and not without a twinge of shame, he scurried beneath the settee, where even though his back was a bit cramped and he could no longer raise his head, he at once felt right at home, his only regret being that his body was too wide across to be accommodated entirely beneath this piece of furniture.

Here he remained the entire night, which he spent by turns dozing—though he was woken again and again by his hunger—and mulling over his worries and indistinct hopes, which however all led to the conclusion that, for the time being, he should behave calmly and, by employing patience and the utmost consideration, assist his family in enduring the inconveniences his current state inevitably forced him to impose on them.

Early the next morning already, so early it was almost still night, Gregor had the opportunity to test the strength of these resolutions he had made, for from the vestibule his sister, almost completely clothed, opened his door and cast an anxious glance into the room. She didn't immediately spot him, but when she noticed him beneath the settee—well, goodness, he had to be somewhere, it's not as if he might have flown away—the sight so alarmed her that, unable to control herself, she slammed the door from the outside. But as if regretting this conduct, she opened it again at once and came in, walking on tiptoe as though she were entering the room of a gravely ill patient or even a stranger. Gregor, having slid his head to just beneath the edge of the settee, observed her. Would she see that he had left the milk standing, and not because of a lack of hunger, and would she bring him some other food more to his liking? If she failed to do so of her own accord, he would sooner starve than call this to her attention, though in fact he felt a nearly monstrous urge to scoot out from beneath the settee, throw himself at his sister's feet, and beg her for something good to eat. But his sister immediately remarked with surprise that the bowl was still full, with just a little of its milk spilled on the floor around it, and she picked it up right away—not with her bare hands, to be sure, but with a rag—and carried it out of the room. Gregor was exceptionally curious to see what she would bring in its stead and mulled over various possibilities. But never would he have been able to predict what his sister in her kindness proceeded to do. To gauge his tastes, she brought him an entire assortment of foodstuffs, all spread out on an old newspaper. There were old, half-rotten vegetables; bones from the family supper the night before caked in a congealed white sauce; a few raisins and almonds; a piece of cheese Gregor had declared inedible two days before; a dry piece of bread; a slice of buttered bread; and a slice of bread with butter and salt. In addition, she placed beside this feast the bowl that apparently had been reserved for Gregor once and for all; it was now filled with water. And out of delicacy, since she knew Gregor would not eat in front of her, she quickly withdrew and even turned the key in the lock so that Gregor would understand he could make himself at home. Gregor's little legs whirred as he now went to take his meal. His wounds, incidentally, seemed to have healed entirely in the meantime, for he no longer felt the least impairment; this was astonishing, for more than a month ago he had cut his finger just a tiny bit with a knife, and this wound had still been painful enough just the day before yesterday. "Might I be less fastidious than before?" he thought, already sucking greedily at the cheese, to which he'd found himself immediately, inexorably drawn, more than to any of the other items. Quickly, his eyes shedding tears of gratification, he devoured in swift succession: the cheese, the vegetables, and the sauce; the fresh food, by contrast, did not taste good to him, in fact he could not even stand the smell of it and so dragged the things he wished to eat a little to one side. He had long since finished everything and was just lying indolently where he was when his sister slowly turned the key in the lock as a signal for him to withdraw. At once he gave a start, though he'd been on the point of nodding off, and he hurried back under the settee. But it cost him a great deal of willpower to remain there even for the short period of time his sister spent in the room, for the hearty meal he'd enjoyed had caused his abdomen to swell, and he could scarcely breathe in his confinement. In between little attacks of suffocation, he peered out with slightly bulging eyes as his sister, oblivious, used a broom to sweep up not only the remains of his meal but also the food he hadn't even touched, as if these items too were no longer fit for consumption, then she hastily dumped everything in a bucket that she covered with a wooden lid before carrying it all out of the room again. She had scarcely turned her back when Gregor hauled himself out from under the settee, stretching and puffing up his body.

This was how Gregor now received his food each day, once in the morning, when his parents and the maid were still asleep, and the second time after everyone had eaten lunch, for his parents would always nap a little afterward, and his sister would send the maid out on some errand or other. Surely they didn't want Gregor to starve either, but perhaps it would have been too much for them to experience his meals through more than hearsay, or perhaps his sister wanted to spare them even this modest sorrow, for Lord knows they were suffering enough.

Gregor never learned on what pretext the doctor and locksmith had been sent away that first morning, for since he himself could not be understood, it occurred to no one, not even his sister, that he could understand the others, so when his sister came to his room, he had to be content merely with hearing the sighs she heaved now and then and her words of supplication addressed to the saints. Only later, when she had started to grow accustomed to all of this—though of course it was impossible to become fully accustomed to cir-cumstances like these—would Gregor sometimes catch a remark that was meant in a friendly way or could be interpreted as such. "He tucked right in today," she would say when Gregor had found the food she left him particu-larly tasty, while in the opposite case, which gradually began to occur more and more often, she was in the habit of saying almost mournfully: "This time he didn't touch a thing."

But while no news reached Gregor directly, he sometimes was able to over-hear this and that from the rooms to either side of his, and whenever he heard voices, he would immediately run over to the door in question and press his entire body against it. Especially in the early days there was rarely a conversation that did not somehow, if only indirectly, refer to him. For two days, every mealtime was spent deliberating how the family should now comport itself; but even between meals this same discussion continued, for at least two members of the household were present at all times, since appar-ently no one wanted to remain at home alone, and of course leaving the apart-ment unattended was out of the question. What's more, the maid had fallen on her knees before Gregor's mother that very first day—it was not entirely clear what and how much she knew of what had occurred—begging to be released from the family's service, and when she took her leave a quarter of an hour later, she tearfully thanked them for dismissing her, as though this were the greatest benefaction she had experienced at their hands, and without any-one asking this of her, she swore a solemn oath never to reveal anything at all to anyone.

Now Gregor's sister was forced to do the cooking in concert with his mother; to be sure, not much effort was involved, as no one did much eating. Again and again Gregor would hear one of them pressing the others to eat—always in vain, and never with any other response than "Thank you, I've had all I want," or similar words. Perhaps they didn't drink anything either. Often Gregor's sister would ask her father if he wouldn't like a beer, affectionately offering to fetch it herself, and when he did not respond, she would say, wishing to relieve him of all scruples, that she could send the porter's wife for it as well, but then the father would utter a great "No," and no one spoke of it any longer.

Already in the course of the first day, Gregor's father explained the family's finances and prospects not only to Gregor's mother but to his sister as well.

Now and then he would get up from the table and, from his small Wertheim safe, which he had salvaged when his business collapsed five years before, extract some receipt or memorandum book. One could hear him opening the complicated lock and then bolting it shut again after removing the desired item. These explanations on his father's part included the first bits of heartening news Gregor had heard since his captivity began. He had been under the impression that his father had retained nothing at all of his former firm's holdings, or at least his father had never said anything to the contrary, and admittedly Gregor himself had never asked him about this. At the time, his only concern had been to do everything in his power to let the family forget, as quickly as possible, the mercantile catastrophe that had plunged all of them into a state of utter hopelessness. And so he had set to work with particular zeal and risen almost overnight from petty clerk to salesman, in which capacity of course he had a quite different earning potential, and his professional accomplishments, in the form of commissions, were immediately transformed into cash that could be plunked down on the table at home, before the eyes of his astonished, delighted family. Those had been lovely times, and never since had they been repeated, at least not with such glory, although Gregor later earned so much money that he was in a position to cover the expenses for the entire family, which he then did. All had grown accustomed to this arrangement, not just the family but Gregor as well: they gratefully accepted the money, and he was happy to provide it, but the exchange no longer felt particularly warm. Only Gregor's sister had remained close to him all this time, and it was his secret plan to send her off to study at the Conservatory next year (unlike Gregor, she dearly loved music and could play the violin quite movingly), despite the considerable costs this would no doubt entail, money that could surely be brought in by other means. Often during the brief periods of time Gregor spent in town, the Conservatory would come up in his conversations with his sister, but only ever as a lovely dream whose realization was unthinkable, and their parents did not like to hear it mentioned even in this innocuous way; but Gregor was thinking the matter over with great determination and intended to make a formal announcement on Christmas Eve.

Thoughts like these, utterly futile in his current state, passed through his head as he stood pressed against the door, eavesdropping. Sometimes general exhaustion made it impossible for him to go on listening, and he would carelessly let his head bump against the door, but then he would immediately hold his head still again, for even the faint sound this produced had been heard in the next room, causing everyone to fall silent. "I wonder what he's getting up to now," his father would say after a while, apparently facing the door, and only then would the interrupted conversation resume.

Gregor now learned, and learned quite well (his father tended to repeat himself in his explanations, in part because it had been so long since he'd last concerned himself with such matters, in part because Gregor's mother did not always understand everything the first time), that despite all their misfortunes, a small nest egg—really only a tiny one—still remained to them from before, and had even grown a little thanks to the untouched interest that had accumulated meanwhile. In addition, the money Gregor had brought home each month—he only ever kept a few gulden for himself—had not yet been entirely used up and had grown into a small capital. Behind his door, Gregor nodded eagerly, delighted at this unexpected prudence and thrift. To be sure, he might have used this surplus to pay off more of his father's debts with his boss, and the day on which he would have been able to divest himself of his post would no longer have been nearly so far off, but as things stood, his father's arrangements were no doubt for the best.

Now this money was by no means sufficient to allow the family to live off the interest or anything of that sort; it might possibly have been enough to sustain the family for a year, two at most, but that's all there was. So in fact it was the the kind of sum one really shouldn't touch, one to be set aside in case of emergency; the money to live on would have to be earned. Gregor's father was admittedly in good health, but he was old and hadn't worked in a full five years, and in any case he was supposed to avoid overtaxing himself; in those five years—the first holiday in his strenuous and yet unsuccessful life—he had put on a lot of weight and now lumbered as he walked. And was Gregor's old mother now supposed to hold down a job, despite her asthma and the fact that it was already an exertion for her to cross from one end of the apartment to the other, for which reason she spent every second day gasping for breath on the sofa beside the open window? And was his sister to go out working, this child of seventeen whose lifestyle no one would begrudge her: dressing nicely, sleeping late, helping out around the house, taking part in a few modest entertainments, and above all, playing the violin? Whenever the family came to speak of the necessity of someone earning money, Gregor would let go of the door and throw himself down upon the cool leather sofa beside it, burning with shame and sorrow.

Often he would lie there the entire long night, not sleeping for a moment, just scrabbling for hours against the leather. Or, not shunning the great effort it cost him to push an armchair over to the window, he would climb up the sill and, propped in the armchair, lean against the window, apparently lost in some sort of reverie of how liberating he'd always found it to gaze outside. For in truth he saw even the objects that were quite near at hand less and less clearly as the days progressed; the hospital across the way whose all too constant sight he had earlier reviled was now no longer even visible to him, and if he had not known perfectly well that he was a resident of Charlottenstrasse, a quiet but perfectly urban street, he might have imagined he was gazing out his window onto a desert in which the gray sky and the gray earth were indistinguishably conjoined. His attentive sister only had to see the armchair standing beside the window twice before she started pushing it back to its place there each time she tidied his room; indeed she even began leaving the window's inner sash open.

If only Gregor had been able to speak to his sister and thank her for all she was compelled to do for him, he would have found her ministrations easier to bear; as it was, he suffered beneath them. His sister, to be sure, did all she could to obscure the awkwardness of the situation, and the more time passed, the better she succeeded, of course, but Gregor came to see it all more and more clearly. Even the way she made her entrance jangled his nerves. The moment she came in, without even pausing to shut the door—although she always took such pains to shield the others from the sight of Gregor's room—she would race straightaway to the window and fling it open with hasty hands as though she were on the point of suffocating, then remain standing there, however cold it might be, gulping in the air. All this racing and racket was inflicted on Gregor twice a day; he would be trembling beneath the settee, painfully aware that she would no doubt have willingly spared him this disruption if it were possible for her to endure being in the same room as Gregor with the window closed.

Once—it must have been a month since Gregor's metamorphosis, so there was no particular call for his sister to be startled by his appearance—she came into his room a little earlier than usual and discovered him, motionless and propped upright as if for horrific effect, gazing out the window. Gregor would not have found it surprising if she had chosen not to enter, since his position prevented her from opening the window right away, but she didn't just not enter: she started in alarm and shut the door; a stranger might have thought Gregor had been lying in wait, meaning to bite her. Gregor naturally went and hid himself away beneath the settee, but he had to wait there until noon before his sister returned, and she seemed far more agitated than usual. From this he understood that his appearance was still unbearable to her and would remain so, and that she no doubt had to struggle to force herself not to run away at the sight of even the small part of his body that protruded from beneath the settee. In order to spare her even this sight, one day he carried the bedsheet over to the settee on his back—this labor cost him four hours—and arranged it in such a way that he was now completely covered, so that his sister would not be able to see him even if she bent down. If she considered the sheet unnecessary, she could have removed it, since it was clear enough that it could not possibly be considered a pleasure for Gregor to shut himself off so completely, but she left the sheet where it was, and Gregor even thought he glimpsed a grateful look when at one point he carefully lifted the sheet just a little with his head to see how his sister liked the new arrangement.

During the first fortnight, Gregor's parents could not bring themselves to enter his room, and often he heard them expressing their heartfelt appreciation of his sister's labors, whereas earlier they had often been annoyed with her, since she had seemed to them a rather useless girl. But now both of them, father and mother alike, would often be waiting just outside Gregor's door while his sister tidied up his room, and as soon as she emerged, she had to give a full report on what things looked like in the room, what Gregor had eaten, how he had behaved this time, and whether perhaps any modest improvement could be seen. His mother, incidentally, had wanted to visit him relatively soon, but his father and sister held her back, appealing at first to her sense of reason as Gregor listened attentively, wholeheartedly approving. Later, though, she had to be held back by force, and when she then cried out: "Let me go to Gregor, he is my unhappy son! Can't you understand that I must go to him?" then Gregor thought it would perhaps be good for his mother to visit him, not every day of course, but perhaps once a week; after all, she had a far better grasp of things than his sister, who despite her courage was still a child and, when it came right down to it, had perhaps only taken on this difficult task out of childish frivolity.

Gregor's wish to see his mother was soon fulfilled. During the day, Gregor avoided showing himself at the window, if only out of consideration for his parents, but there wasn't much crawling he could do in the few square meters of space the floor provided, lying still was already difficult for him to endure during the night, eating had soon ceased to give him even the slightest pleasure, and so to divert himself he took up the habit of crawling back and forth across the walls and ceiling. He particularly liked hanging from the ceiling high above the room; it was completely different from lying on the floor; one could breathe more freely there; a gentle swaying motion rocked the body; and in the almost happy absentmindedness Gregor experienced, it might happen, to his own astonishment, that he would let go and crash to the floor. But now, of course, he had his body far better under control than before, and even as great a fall as this did him no harm. His sister immediately noticed the new entertainment Gregor had devised for himself—his peregrinations left behind sticky trails here and there—and she got it into her head to make it possible for Gregor to range as widely as possible by removing the furniture that impeded his movement, above all the wardrobe and desk. But she wasn't able to do so on her own; she didn't dare ask her father for help; the maid most certainly would not have helped her, for this girl of sixteen or so, though she had courageously remained in the household after the departure of the former cook, had at the same time requested the privilege of keeping the kitchen locked at all times and only opening the door upon particular request; and so the sister had no choice but to summon her mother one day when her father was out. The mother arrived with exclamations of feverish joy but fell silent at the door to Gregor's room. At first, of course, Gregor's sister checked to confirm that all in the room was as it should be; only then did she allow her mother to enter. With the utmost haste, Gregor had tugged the sheet down lower and in looser folds so that it really did look as if a bedsheet just happened to have been tossed over the settee. He also refrained from peering out from beneath the sheet this time; for the moment, he would resign himself to not seeing his mother and just be glad she had come. "It's all right, come in, you won't see him," Gregor's sister said, apparently leading her mother by the hand. Gregor now heard the sounds of these two weak women grappling with this in fact quite heavy old wardrobe, with his sister laying claim to the bulk of the work, not listening to the admonitions of her mother, who was afraid she would overtax herself. It took a very long time. After perhaps a quarter of an hour's labor, Gregor's mother said they should leave the wardrobe where it was after all; in the first place, it was too heavy—they would not finish before Gregor's father came home, and by leaving the wardrobe in the middle of the room, they would prevent Gregor from moving around at all—and secondly, it wasn't even clear they were doing him a favor by taking away the furniture. To her, it seemed the opposite was true: the sight of the empty wall positively oppressed her heart; and why should Gregor not experience this same sentiment, since after all he was long accustomed to having this furniture around him—wouldn't he feel abandoned in an emptied-out room? "And is it not as if," his mother concluded in a low voice—in fact, she had been whispering all along, as though she wished to avoid letting Gregor, whose exact whereabouts she did not know, hear so much as the sound of her voice, for she was convinced he could not understand her words—"and is it not as if by removing the furniture we would be showing that we are giving up all hope of a cure and are ruthlessly abandoning him to his own devices? I think it would be best if we try to keep the room in precisely the same state it was in before, so that when Gregor returns to us he will find everything unchanged, which will make it that much easier for him to forget all that has happened in the meantime."

Hearing his mother's words, Gregor realized that the absence of all direct human address, combined with the monotony of life in his family's midst, must have muddled his understanding over the course of these two months, for he could not otherwise explain to himself how he could seriously have wished to have his room emptied out. Did he really want to have this warm room, comfortably furnished with family heirlooms, transformed into a cave or den—in which, to be sure, he would be able to crawl about unhindered in every direction, but at the price of simultaneously swiftly and completely forgetting his human past? He was already on the verge of forgetting, and only his mother's voice, which he had gone so long now without hearing, had shaken him awake. Nothing should be removed; everything must remain; he was unwilling to forego the good influence this furniture had on his condition; and if the furniture got in the way of his practicing this mindless crawling about, this was by no means to his detriment, in fact, it was a great advantage.

Unfortunately his sister was of a different opinion; she had developed the habit—not entirely without cause, to be sure—of presenting herself as the holder of particular expertise when discussing Gregor with her parents, and so now too her mother's counsel was reason enough for her to insist on the removal not only of the wardrobe and desk, as she had originally been intending, but of every last bit of the room's furnishings, with the exception of the indispensable settee. Naturally, it was not simply childish defiance and the hard-won self-assurance she had so unexpectedly acquired in recent weeks that dictated this demand; she had, in fact, observed that Gregor needed a great deal of space to crawl around in, while as far as anyone could see, he made no use whatever of the furniture. But perhaps the fanciful imagination of a girl of her age played a role as well, a sensibility always seeking its own gratification, and one which Grete now allowed to persuade her to render Gregor's situation even more horrific than before, so as to be able to do even more for him than she had hitherto. For a room in which Gregor held sole dominion over empty walls was a place where no one other than Grete would ever dare to set foot.

And so she held fast to her resolve despite the protests of her mother, who appeared troubled to the point of indecision even by the room in its present state; she soon fell silent and helped Gregor's sister remove the wardrobe as best she could. Well, the wardrobe was something Gregor could do without if need be, but the desk would certainly have to stay. And no sooner had the women left the room with the cabinet, groaning as they pressed against its weight, than Gregor poked out his head from beneath the settee to see how he might, cautiously and as considerately as possible, intervene. But unfortunately his mother was the first to return while Grete was still in the next room, clasping the wardrobe in her arms and tipping it back and forth on her own—without, of course, moving it from the spot. But Gregor's mother was unaccustomed to his appearance, it might have made her ill to catch a glimpse of him, and so Gregor in alarm withdrew as fast as he could to the far end of the settee, but it was too late to prevent the front edge of the bedsheet from stirring a little. This was enough to attract his mother's notice. Startled, she froze for a moment, then went back to where Grete was.

Although Gregor kept telling himself that nothing extraordinary was happening, just a few sticks of furniture being shifted about, he was soon forced to admit that all this coming and going on the part of the women, their little exclamations, the furniture scraping against the floor, had the combined effect of a tumultuous hubbub intensifying all around him, and no matter how tightly he drew his head and legs in and pressed his body against the floor, he soon was forced to consider that he would not be able to endure this much longer. They were clearing out his room; taking from him all that was dear to him; they had already borne away the cabinet in which lay his fretsaw and other tools; and now they were prying loose the desk that had dug itself firmly into the floorboards, this desk at which he had written his homework assignments as a student at the commercial academy, and as a secondary and even primary school pupil—truly there was no time left to explore the good intentions of these two women, whose existence, by the way, he had almost forgotten, for their exhaustion was now making them labor in silence, and one heard only their heavy footsteps.

And so he burst out of hiding—the women in the next room were just leaning on the desk to catch their breath—changing direction four times as he raced about, for he really didn't know what to save first, but then his eyes lit on the picture of the lady clad all in furs, conspicuous now on the otherwise empty wall, and quickly he made his way up to it and pressed himself against the glass, which adhered to him, pleasantly cool against his hot belly. At least this picture, which Gregor's body now covered up completely, was absolutely certain not to be taken away from him. He swiveled his head toward the living room door to observe the women as they returned.

They hadn't permitted themselves much rest at all and were already on their way back; Grete had slung one arm about her mother and was nearly carrying her. "So what should we take next?" Grete said, looking around. Then her eyes met those of Gregor where he clung to the wall. It was no doubt only because of her mother's presence that she kept her composure; bowing her face toward her mother to prevent her from glancing about, she said—hastily and trembling, to be sure—"Let's go back to the living room for a moment, shall we?" Grete's intentions were perfectly clear to Gregor: she meant to bring their mother to safety and then chase him from the wall. Well, let her try! He sat there on his picture and would not give it up. He'd sooner leap right in her face.

But Grete's words succeeded in unsettling her mother even more: taking one step to the side, she saw the huge brown blotch on the flowered wallpaper, and before she was even able to realize that what she saw there was Gregor, she cried out in a hoarse, shrieking voice, "Oh God, oh God!" and fell back upon the settee, her arms spread wide as though she were giving up everything, and lay there without moving. "Gregor!" his sister shouted, raising her fist with a threatening glower. It was the first time she had addressed him directly since his metamorphosis. She ran into the next room to fetch some sort of essence that could be used to awaken her mother from her faint; Gregor wanted to help as well—there would be time enough to save the picture later—but he stuck fast to the glass and had to tear himself away by force;

he too then ran into the next room as if he might offer his sister advice of some sort, like in the old days; but then could only stand idly behind her as she rummaged among various little bottles, and scared her out of her wits when she turned around; one bottle flew to the floor and shattered; a shard of glass scratched Gregor's face, and some sort of corrosive medicine engulfed him; without further delay, Grete took up as many bottles as she could hold and ran with them to her mother, slamming the door behind her with her foot. Gregor was now cut off from his mother, who was possibly on the brink of death, for which he himself was to blame; he could not open the door if he didn't want to drive away his sister, who had to stay there with his mother; there was nothing for him to do but wait; and tormented by his worries and self-reproach, he began to crawl about, crawling over everything, walls, furniture, the ceiling, and finally in his despair, as the entire room began to spin around him, he fell smack in the middle of the big table.

A short while passed. Gregor lay there, spent, and around him all was still, possibly a good sign. Then the bell rang. The maid was naturally locked up in her kitchen and so Grete had to open the door. Their father was back. "What happened?" were his first words; the look on Grete's face had no doubt revealed all. Grete's voice as she responded was muffled, apparently she was pressing her face against his chest: "Mother fainted, but she's better already. Gregor has broken out." "That's just what I expected," the father said. "I kept telling you, but you women refused to listen." To Gregor it was clear his father had misinterpreted Grete's all too brief pronouncement to assume him guilty of some act of violence. So it behooved Gregor to try to pacify his father, as he was lacking both the time and means to enlighten him. With this in mind, he fled to the door of his room and pressed himself against it, so that the moment his father came into the living room from the vestibule he would see that Gregor had every intention of returning at once to his room, that it was unnecessary to drive him back inside, and that one had merely to open the door, and he would disappear at once.

But his father was in no mood to take note of subtleties. "Ah!" he exclaimed upon entering, in a tone of voice suggesting he was at once furious and glad. Gregor pulled his head back from the door and turned it toward his father. He had truly not expected to see his father looking as he looked now standing before him; though to be sure the novelty of crawling about had distracted him recently from paying as much attention as before to the goings-on in the rest of the apartment, and really he ought to have been prepared to find a changed set of circumstances. Even so, even so: was this still his father? The same man who used to lie wearily entombed in his bed when Gregor set off on a business trip; who would greet him on the evening of his return sitting in an armchair in his nightshirt; who, incapable of rising, would merely raise his arms to signify his delight, and on the rare walks they still shared, a few Sundays each year and on major holidays, would trudge between Gregor and his mother, who themselves were already walking rather slowly, moving even a bit slower than they, bundled up in his old overcoat, always with his gingerly advancing cane and almost invariably coming to a halt and collecting his companions around him whenever he had something to say? Now he was standing properly erect; dressed in a smart blue uniform with gold buttons of the sort worn by porters in banking establishments; above the jacket's tall, stiff collar his powerful double chin unfurled; beneath bushy eyebrows, his black eyes peered out acutely and attentively; his once disheveled white hair had been painstakingly combed and parted until it gleamed. He tossed his cap, to which a gold monogram was affixed, probably that of a bank, across the entire room in a wide arc to land on the settee, then advanced grim-faced upon Gregor with the tips of his long uniform jacket flung back and his hands in his trouser pockets. He himself probably had no idea what he intended to do; at any rate, he raised up each foot unusually high, and Gregor marveled at the gigantic dimensions of his boot-soles. But he did not lose any time over them, having learned on the very first day of his new life that his father considered only the utmost severity appropriate for him. And so he fled from his father, hesitating whenever his father stopped short, and then rushing forward again as soon as he stirred. They circled the room several times in this manner without anything decisive occurring, and indeed, given the slow speed at which this interaction was taking place, without its even having the appearance of a chase. For this reason Gregor remained at floor level for the time being, especially as he feared his father might consider it particular wickedness on his part if he were to take refuge on the walls or ceiling. To be sure, he was forced to realize he would not be able to keep up even this pace for long, since each time his father took a step, he himself had to execute any number of motions. A shortness of breath began to set in— even in his earlier life his lungs had been none too reliable. As he now lurched along, reserving all his strength for this continued flight, his eyes barely open (and not thinking, in his stupefaction, that there might be other ways of saving himself than running across the floor, indeed he had almost forgotten he also had the walls at his disposal, though here, to be sure, they were obstructed by delicately carved furniture full of jagged, pointy edges), all at once something flew to the rug beside him, casually flung, and rolled across his path. It was an apple; and already a second one came flying after it; in horror, Gregor stopped in his tracks; there was no point continuing to run now that his father had decided to bombard him. He had filled his pockets from the fruit bowl on the sideboard and now was tossing apple after apple in Gregor's direction, for the moment not even bothering to take particular aim. The petite red apples rolled around the floor as if electrified, knocking into each other. One lightly lobbed apple grazed Gregor's back and slid off again harmlessly. But it was immediately followed by another that embedded itself in his back. Gregor tried to drag himself forward, as if this sudden shocking pain might vanish with a change of place; but he felt nailed to the spot and collapsed there, his legs splaying out, all his senses in a state of utter bewilderment. He caught only a last glimpse of the door to his room flying open, his shrieking sister, and his mother running out of the room before her wearing only a chemise, for his sister had undressed the unconscious woman to let her breathe more freely, then he saw his mother rush to his father's side, her unfastened skirts slipping one by one from about her waist as she ran, saw her stumble across these skirts as she threw herself at his father and, embracing him, in perfect union with him—but now Gregor's vision began to fail him— she clasped her hands at the back of his father's head and pleaded with him to spare Gregor's life.

# III

The grievous wound Gregor had received, which plagued him for over a month—the apple remained lodged there in his flesh, a visible memento, since no one dared to remove it—seemed to have reminded even his father that Gregor, despite his current lamentable, repulsive form, was a member of the family who should not be treated like an enemy, for family duty dictated that the others swallow down the disgust he aroused in them and show him tolerance, only tolerance.

And even though this wound cost Gregor some of his mobility, probably for good, and for the time being he required many, many minutes to hobble across his room like an old invalid—crawling up the walls was out of the question now—he was compensated for this worsening of his condition by what seemed to him a perfectly adequate substitute: as evening approached, the door to the living room, on which he would start keeping a sharp eye an hour or two beforehand, would always be opened so as to permit him, lying in his own dark room and invisible from the living room, to watch the entire family sitting at the brightly lit table and listen to their conversations now, as it were, in an officially sanctioned capacity and thus quite differently than before.

To be sure, these were no longer the animated conversations of earlier times that Gregor used to think back on with a certain longing from various cramped hotel rooms when it was time to throw himself, exhausted, into the damp bedding. Now everything was fairly quiet. Gregor's father would fall asleep in his armchair soon after supper; his mother and sister would admonish one another to silence; his mother, bent far over beneath the light, would be sewing ladies' underthings for a dress shop; his sister, who had taken a job as a salesgirl, was studying stenography and French in the evenings so as possibly to move to a better position later on. Sometimes Gregor's father would wake up and, as if unaware he had been sleeping, would say to Gregor's mother: "How long you've been sewing again today!" and then go right back to sleep, which would prompt Gregor's mother and sister to exchange weary smiles.

In a peculiar form of stubbornness, Gregor's father refused to take off his porter's uniform even at home; and while his nightshirt hung uselessly on its hook, he would slumber where he sat, fully clothed, as though he remained ready for service at all times and even here was awaiting his supervisor's call. As a result, his uniform, which had not been new to start with, soon forfeited much of its cleanliness, despite the care lavished on it by mother and sister, and Gregor would sometimes gaze for an entire evening at this stain-covered jacket resplendent with gold buttons, always highly polished, in which the old man slept in considerable discomfort but nonetheless soundly.

The moment the clock struck ten, Gregor's mother would attempt to rouse his father with a few hushed words and then persuade him to go to bed, for he would get no proper sleep sitting here, and sleep was something Gregor's father— who had to report for duty at six in the morning—desperately needed. But in keeping with the stubbornness that had taken hold of him when he started working as a porter, he always insisted on continuing to sit there at the table, even though he kept falling asleep, and then it was only with the greatest effort that he could be persuaded to exchange armchair for bed. Gregor's mother and sister could persist in their little admonishments as doggedly as they liked; for a quarter of an hour, he would just shake his head slowly, his eyes closed, without getting up. Gregor's mother would pluck at his sleeve, whispering cajoling words in his ear, and his sister would set aside her studies to come to her mother's aid, but to no avail. Gregor's father only settled deeper into his armchair. Only when the women gripped him beneath the arms would he open his eyes, looking by turns at mother and sister and saying: "What sort of life is this? Is this the peace and quiet of my old age?" Then, supported by the two women, he would rise, laboriously, as though he himself were receiving the brunt of this burden, and allow the women to escort him to the doorway, where he would shoo them away and continue on his own, while Gregor's mother hastily threw down her sewing and his sister her pen so they could run after him to offer further assistance. The household was ever further reduced; the maid was now let go after all; a bony giant of a charwoman with white hair flapping about her head came by in the morning and evening to perform the heaviest labors; everything else was handled by Gregor's mother along with all her sewing. It even came to pass that several pieces of jewelry that had been in the family—jewels Gregor's mother and sister had delighted in wearing at entertainments and festivities—were sold, as Gregor would learn in the evening when the price each piece had brought would be discussed. But their greatest lament was always that they were unable to leave this apartment, which was far too large for their current circumstances, since no one could imagine how Gregor might be moved. But Gregor understood that it was not only out of consideration for him that a move was being ruled out, since he could easily enough have been transported in a crate of appropriate size with a few air holes; the main thing keeping the family from moving to a new apartment was their complete sense of hopelessness and the thought that they had been struck with a misfortune such as no one else in their entire circle of relations and friends had ever experienced. They were fulfilling to the utmost the demands the world makes on the poor: Gregor's father fetched breakfast for the petty employees at the bank, his mother sacrificed herself for the underclothes of strangers, his sister ran back and forth behind the shop counter at her customers' behest, but this was all the strength they had. And the wound in Gregor's back would begin to ache anew when mother and sister, having brought his father to bed, would now return and, leaving their work where it lay, huddle close beside one another pressing their cheeks together; when Gregor's mother, gesturing toward his room, would say: "Shut the door now, Grete"; and when Gregor was left in the dark again while next door the two women intermingled their tears or else sat there tearless, staring down at the table.

Gregor spent his nights and days almost entirely without sleeping. Sometimes he thought about taking the family's affairs in hand again, just as he used to, the next time his door was opened; once more his boss and the general manager would appear before his mind's eye after all this time, the clerks and apprentices, the dull-witted hired man, two or three friends from other firms, a chambermaid from a provincial hotel (a sweet, fleeting specter), the shopgirl from a haberdashery whom he had courted earnestly but too slowly—all of these now appeared to him, interspersed with strangers or people already forgotten, but instead of coming to his aid and that of his family, every last one of them was unapproachable, and he was glad when they disappeared. At other times he would be not at all in a frame of mind to look after his family; instead he was filled with rage at how poorly he was attended to, and although he could not imagine anything he would have liked to eat, he plotted how he might gain access to the pantry so as to help himself to what—despite his total absence of hunger—was his due. Without bothering to consider how she might give Gregor particular pleasure, his sister would quickly thrust some randomly chosen foodstuff into his room with her foot on her way to work in the morning or at midday, only to sweep it out again at night with a quick swipe of the broom, paying no heed if the food had been only barely nibbled at or—as was most often the case now—not touched at all. Setting Gregor's room to rights, a task she now saved for the evenings, could not possibly have been done any more perfunctorily. Great streaks of dirt extended across the walls, with balls of dust and rubbish lying scattered about. At first when Gregor's sister came into his room he would position himself in corners particularly indicative of this problem—to reproach her, as it were, by his presence there. But he could just as well have spent entire weeks sitting there without any improvement on his sister's part; after all, she saw the dirt as plainly as he did, but had made up her mind to leave it be. At the same time, with a sensitivity that was new in her, one that had now taken hold of the family as a whole, she was on her guard to make sure the task of tidying Gregor's room was reserved for her. Once Gregor's mother had subjected his room to a thorough scrubbing, which she accomplished only after using up several buckets of water—admittedly, all this moisture was itself an affront to Gregor, who lay stretched out, bitter and immobile, upon the settee—but his mother did not escape punishment. For no sooner had his sister remarked the change in Gregor's room that evening than she ran into the living room, grievously insulted, and ignoring her mother's imploringly raised hands, set to weeping so violently that her parents—naturally her father was startled out of his chair—at first stood by helpless and astonished; until they too began to stir; on the right, Gregor's father reproached his mother for not having left the cleaning of Gregor's room to his sister; while on the left he shouted at Gregor's sister, threatening that she would never again be permitted to clean Gregor's room; while his mother attempted to drag his father, now so agitated he hardly recognized himself, into the bedroom; Gregor's sister, shaking with sobs, pummeled the table with her tiny fists; and Gregor hissed loudly in fury because it had occurred to no one to shut the door of his room to spare him this sight and commotion.

But even if Gregor's sister, who was exhausted by her professional work, had wearied of caring for Gregor as she'd previously done, there was absolutely no need for his mother to fill her shoes, and Gregor needn't have suffered neglect. For now the charwoman was here. This old widow—who had seen and survived the worst in her long life with the help of her sturdy bones—felt no particular repugnance toward Gregor. Without being at all inquisitive, she had once chanced to open the door to his room and, seeing Gregor, who had begun to run back and forth although no one was chasing him, she stood there staring in astonishment, her hands clasped across her lap. Ever since, she never failed to open the door a crack for a moment every morning and evening to look in on him. At the beginning she would call him over to her, saying things that were probably intended to sound friendly, like "Hey, over here, you old dung beetle!" or "Just look at the old dung beetle!" Thus addressed, Gregor gave no reply but instead remained where he was, immobile, as if the door had never been opened. If only this charwoman, instead of being allowed to disturb him uselessly at whim, had been given instructions to clean his room daily! Once, early in the morning—a heavy rain, perhaps already a portent of the coming spring, was beating against the windowpanes—Gregor became so infuriated when the charwoman started up again with her quips that he turned on her as if to attack, if admittedly slowly and decrepitly. But instead of being frightened, the charwoman just picked up a chair that was standing beside the door and held it high in the air; and as she stood there, her mouth gaping wide, her intention was clear: not to close her mouth again until the chair in her hand had come crashing down upon Gregor's back. "Aha, so that's as far as it goes?" she asked as Gregor turned around again, and she placed the chair calmly back in its corner.

Gregor now ate almost nothing at all. Only if he happened by chance to wander past the food that had been prepared for him might he playfully take a bite of something into his mouth, where he would hold it for hours and then usually spit it out again later. At first he thought it was his sorrow at the state of his room that prevented him from eating, but in fact he had resigned himself very quickly to the changes there. Everyone had gotten into the habit of using his room to store things there was no space for in other parts of the apartment, and now there were many such things, since one room of the apartment had been rented out to three lodgers. These solemn gentlemen—all three of them were bearded, as Gregor once noted, peering through the crack of the door—were scrupulously intent on having everything tidy, not just in their room but also, since they were now paying rent here, in the entire household, particularly the kitchen. They could not bear the presence of unnecessary, much less dirty items. Moreover, they had brought most of their own furnishings with them. For this reason, many things had become superfluous, things that could not be sold but were still too valuable to throw out. All of this found its way into Gregor's room. As did the ash box and the garbage pail from the kitchen. The charwoman, always in a great hurry, would simply fling any unserviceable item into Gregor's room; mercifully, Gregor generally saw only the object in question and the hand that held it. The charwoman may have intended at some point, when she had occasion or a free minute, to come collect these things, or else throw all of them out at once, but as it was they remained wherever they first landed, except when Gregor made his way through the refuse, stirring it around—at first out of necessity, since there was no room left for him to crawl about, but later with ever-increasing pleasure, though after these wanderings, which left him mortally exhausted and sad, he would spend hours without moving.

Since the lodgers sometimes also took their supper at home in the shared living room, the living room door remained shut on some evenings, but Gregor was happy to forgo having the door open; in fact, even when it was open, he sometimes failed to take advantage of it and instead, unbeknownst to his family, would remain lying in the darkest corner of his room. Once, however, the charwoman had left the door to the living room slightly ajar, and ajar it remained even when the lodgers came in that evening and struck a light. They sat down at the head of the table where in earlier times Gregor had sat with his father and mother, unfolded the napkins and took up their knives and forks. At once Gregor's mother appeared in the doorway with a serving dish filled with meat, and right behind her came his sister bearing a plate piled high with potatoes. A heavy vapor rose from the steaming food. The lodgers bent over the dishes that had been placed before them, as though wishing to inspect them before beginning their meal, and in fact the one who sat in the middle and appeared to be an authority figure to the other two cut off a piece of meat right there on the platter to check whether it was tender enough and didn't have to be sent back to the kitchen. He was satisfied, and Gregor's mother and sister, who had been watching nervously, now smiled with relief.

The family members themselves ate in the kitchen. Nonetheless Gregor's father visited the living room on his way to the kitchen and with a single bow, cap in hand, took a tour around the table. The lodgers all rose from their seats and mumbled into their beards. Left alone again, they ate in almost perfect silence. It struck Gregor as peculiar that amid all the various sounds of this meal, one could also make out their champing teeth, as if to demonstrate to Gregor that a person needs teeth to eat and that even the most splendid jaws, if toothless, can accomplish nothing at all. "I'm hungry," Gregor said sorrowfully to himself, "but not for these things. Just look how these lodgers take their nourishment while I am wasting away!"

On this very evening—Gregor couldn't remember having heard the violin once in all this time—the sound of it was heard coming from the kitchen. The lodgers had already finished their evening meal, the one in the middle had pulled out a newspaper, giving each of the others a page, and now the three of them were reading, leaning back in their chairs and smoking. When the violin began to play, their interest was piqued, they got up from their chairs and tiptoed over to the doorway leading to the vestibule, where they stood in a tight cluster. The sounds of this activity must have traveled to the kitchen, for Gregor's father now called out: "Are the gentlemen disturbed by this playing? It can be silenced at once." "On the contrary," said the one in the middle, "would the young lady care to join us and play here in the living room, where it is much more comfortable and pleasant?" "Why, of course," Gregor's father exclaimed, as though he were the violinist. The gentlemen went back into the room and waited. Soon Gregor's father arrived with the music stand, his mother with the sheet music and his sister with the violin. His sister calmly prepared to play; his parents, who never rented out rooms in earlier days and therefore were treating these lodgers with exaggerated deference, did not even dare to sit in their own armchairs; his father leaned against the door, his right hand tucked between two buttons of his closed livery jacket; his mother, meanwhile, was offered an armchair by one of the lodgers, and since she left the chair where he had happened to place it, she sat off to one side in a corner.

Gregor's sister began to play; on either side, his father and mother attentively followed each movement of her hands. Attracted by her playing, Gregor had ventured a bit further than usual and was already sticking his head into the living room. It scarcely surprised him that he had become so inconsiderate of the others; earlier on, his considerateness had been a source of pride. And he had all the more reason to keep himself hidden away now: thanks to the dust that lay everywhere in his room and would swirl up at the slightest motion, he too was covered in dust; he dragged around threads, hair and food scraps clinging to his back and sides; his general indifference was far too great now for him to keep up with a habit he'd once practiced several times a day: flipping over so as to scrub his back against the rug. And despite his condition, he did not hesitate now to continue his advance a little way out onto the immaculate floor of the living room.

To be sure, no one paid him the slightest heed. The family was completely absorbed in the violin playing; the lodgers, on the other hand, having at first positioned themselves, hands in their trouser pockets, much too close behind his sister's music stand, so that they could all look at the sheet music, which surely must have distracted her, soon withdrew to the window, conversing in an undertone, and remained there, anxiously observed by Gregor's father. It appeared more than clear they had been disappointed in their expectation of hearing beautiful or entertaining violin music and now, tired of the whole performance, were continuing to tolerate this disturbance of their peace only out of politeness. Particularly the way in which all of them were blowing the smoke of their cigars high into the air from their noses and mouths suggested extreme agitation. And yet his sister's playing was so lovely. Her face was tilted to one side; searchingly, sadly, her eyes followed the lines of notes. Gregor crept a bit farther forward and ducked his head down close to the floor so as perhaps to catch her eye. Was he a beast, that music so moved him? He felt as if he were being shown the way to that unknown nourishment he craved. He was determined to creep all the way up to his sister, to pluck at her skirt and in this way indicate to her that she should come to his room with her violin, for no one here was rewarding her playing as he meant to reward her. He would not allow her to leave his room ever again, at least as long as he was alive; his horrific figure would, for the first time ever, be useful to him; he would be at all the doors of his room at once, growling at his attackers; but his sister should remain with him not by force but of her own free will; she should sit beside him on the settee, bend down, the better to hear, and he would confess to her that he'd had the firm intention of sending her to the Conservatory and that if the disaster had not disrupted his plans, he would have made a general announcement last Christmas— Christmas had passed now, hadn't it?—without letting himself be swayed by objections of any sort. After this declaration, his sister would be moved to the point of tears, and Gregor would raise himself to the height of her armpit and kiss her throat, which, now that she went to the office every day, she wore free of ribbon or collar.

"Herr Samsa!" the gentleman in the middle shouted at Gregor's father, and without wasting a single word, pointed his finger at Gregor, who was slowly advancing. The violin fell silent, the middle lodger at first just smiled and shook his head, turning toward his friends, then looked again at Gregor. Gregor's father apparently found the task of driving Gregor back into his room less urgent than that of calming the lodgers, despite the fact that they did not appear particularly worked up and seemed to be finding Gregor more entertaining than the music. He hurried over to them and tried with outspread arms to herd them back into their room, at the same time using his body to shield Gregor from their view. And now they did in fact become a little angry, though it was no longer clear whether this was on account of Gregor's father's behavior or the realization dawning on them that without their knowledge they had been sharing their home with a roommate of this sort. They demanded explanations of Gregor's father; now it was their turn to throw their arms into the air; they plucked uneasily at their beards and only slowly withdrew in the direction of their room. Meanwhile Gregor's sister, who had been standing there at a loss since her playing had been so unexpectedly interrupted—she still held violin and bow in her carelessly dangling hands, looking over at the notes as though she were continuing to play—all at once pulled herself together, laid her instrument in the lap of her mother, who still sat there in her armchair, her lungs heaving as she fought for breath, and ran into the next room, toward which the lodgers were now moving somewhat more quickly as Gregor's father urged them on. One saw how, beneath his sister's practiced hands, the beds' blankets and pillows flew into the air and into orderliness. Even before the lodgers reached the room, she had finished making up the beds and slipped out. Gregor's father appeared to be once more so firmly in the grip of his own stubbornness that he forgot the basic respect that, after all, he owed his tenants. He kept up his pressing and urging until, already standing in the doorway, the middle lodger thunderously stamped his foot, causing Gregor's father to stop short. "I hereby declare," he said, raising his hand and seeking out Gregor's mother and sister too as he glanced about, "that in consideration of the reprehensible circumstances prevailing in this apartment and family"—and here he spat on the floor without forethought—"I give notice on my room effective immediately. It goes without saying that I will not pay a penny for the days I have spent here; on the contrary, I shall consider whether or not to pursue you with—please believe me—easily justifiable claims." He fell silent and went on looking straight before him expectantly. And indeed his two friends at once chimed in with the words, "We too give notice effective immediately." Hereupon he seized the door handle and with a great crash slammed the door.

Gregor's father staggered to his armchair with groping hands and let himself fall into it; it looked as though he was stretching out for his customary evening nap, but the violent nodding of his anchorless head showed that he was absolutely not sleeping. Gregor had gone on lying quietly on the spot where the lodgers had espied him. His disappointment at the failure of his plan and perhaps also the weakness caused by starvation rendered him incapable of moving. With a certain definitiveness he sensed, terrified, that everything was about to collapse all around him, and so he waited. Not even the violin startled him when it fell from his mother's lap beneath her trembling fingers, giving off a note that echoed in the air.

"Dear parents," his sister said, striking the table by way of preamble, "things cannot go on like this. Even if you two perhaps do not realize it, I most certainly do. I am unwilling to utter my brother's name before this creature, and therefore will say only: we have to try to get rid of it. We have done everything humanly possible to care for it and show it tolerance, I don't think anyone would reproach us on this account."

"She is right a thousand times over," Gregor's father murmured under his breath. His mother, still incapable of breathing freely, began to cough dully into her lifted hand, a lunatic expression in her eyes.

Gregor's sister hurried over to her mother and held her forehead. Her words seemed to have given her father an idea, for he now sat up straight, playing with his uniform cap between the plates left behind on the table from the lodgers' supper and glancing over from time to time at a quiet Gregor.

"We have to try to get rid of it," his sister said, addressing her words exclusively to Gregor's father this time, for his mother was coughing too hard to hear anything. "It'll be the death of you two, I can see it now. When people have to work as hard as all of us have been doing, it just isn't possible to endure these endless torments at home. I cannot bear it anymore either." And she burst into sobs, weeping so forcefully that her tears flowed down upon her mother's face, from which the girl wiped them with a mechanical gesture.

"Child," her father said sympathetically and with noticeable compassion, "but what can we do?"

Gregor's sister just shrugged her shoulders as a sign of the helplessness that had come over her while she was weeping, in contrast to the confidence she'd displayed a moment before.

"If he understood us," Gregor's father said, half-questioning; his sister, still caught up in her weeping, shook one hand vehemently as a sign of how unthinkable she found this.

"If he understood us," his father repeated, closing his eyes to absorb her conviction that this was utterly out of the question, "then it might be possible to come to an agreement with him. But as things stand—"

"It has to go," Gregor's sister cried out, "that's the only way, Father. You just have to try to let go of the notion that this thing is Gregor. The real disaster is that we believed this for so long. But how could it be Gregor? If it were Gregor, it would have realized a long time ago that it just isn't possible for human beings to live beside such a creature, and it would have gone away on its own. We still would have been lacking a brother but we would have been able to go on living and honoring his memory. But now we have this beast tormenting us; it drives away our lodgers and apparently intends to take over the entire apartment and have us sleep in the gutter. Just look, Father," she suddenly shrieked, "he's starting again!" And in a fright that Gregor found bewildering, she now went so far as to leave her mother behind, launching herself from her chair as if she would rather sacrifice her mother than remain in Gregor's proximity, and ran to take cover behind her father who, agitated by the way she was carrying on, rose from his own chair and half-raised his arms as if to shield her.

But Gregor was far from wanting to frighten anyone, above all his sister. All he'd done was start to turn around to make his way back to his room, and admittedly this operation would have been hard not to notice, since in his current injured state he was obliged to use his head to help with this difficult maneuver; he kept raising it up and then thumping it against the floor. Pausing, he glanced around. His good intentions seemed to have been recognized; it had been only a momentary fright. Now all of them gazed at him sadly and in silence. His mother lay in her armchair, her extended legs pressed together, barely able to keep her eyes open in her exhaustion; his father and sister sat side by side, and his sister had draped one hand across her father's neck.

"Perhaps I'll be allowed to turn around now," Gregor thought and resumed his labors. He could not entirely suppress the wheezing this exertion produced, and now and then he had to rest. Otherwise no one was harassing him, he had been left to attend to matters on his own. When he had completed this rotation, he immediately made straight for the door to his room. He was astonished at how great a distance separated him from his destination, and he didn't understand how, weak as he was, he had been able to traverse the same distance just a little while before almost without noticing. Steadfastly concentrating only on crawling as quickly as possible, he scarcely paid any heed to the fact that not a word, not a cry came from his family to disturb him. Only when he was already in the doorway did he turn his head—not all the way around, as he felt his neck growing stiff, but even so he was able to see that all was unchanged behind him, except that his sister had risen to her feet. The last thing he saw was a glimpse of his mother, who had now fallen entirely asleep.

No sooner was he in his room again than the door was hastily pressed shut, locked and bolted. The sudden commotion at his back gave him such a frightful start that his little legs gave way beneath him. It was his sister who had hurried thus. She had already been standing there upright and waiting, then pounced so lightfootedly Gregor didn't hear her approach, and she cried out, "Finally!" to her parents as she turned the key in the lock.

"And now?" Gregor wondered, looking around in the dark. He soon made the discovery that he was no longer capable of moving at all. He wasn't surprised at this; on the contrary, it struck him as unnatural that he had actually until now been able to support himself on those thin little legs. As for the rest, he felt relatively at ease. Admittedly his entire body was racked with pain, but it seemed to him as if it was gradually becoming weaker and weaker and in the end would fade away altogether. Already he could scarcely feel the rotting apple in his back, nor the inflamed area surrounding it, both now enveloped in soft dust. He thought back on his family with tenderness and love. His opinion that he must by all means disappear was possibly even more emphatic than that of his sister. He remained in this state of empty, peaceful reflection until the clock-tower struck the third hour of morning. He watched as everything began to lighten outside his window. Then his head sank all the way to the floor without volition and from his nostrils his last breath faintly streamed.

When the charwoman arrived early the next morning, slamming the doors so loudly in her strength and haste—often as she'd been asked to avoid this—that sleep was out of the question anywhere in the apartment after her arrival, her usual cursory visit to Gregor's room revealed at first nothing out of the ordinary. She thought he was lying there so motionless on purpose, feigning indignation; she considered him perfectly capable of rational thought. Since she happened to be holding the long broom in her hand, she tried tickling Gregor with it from the doorway. When even this had no effect, she grew vexed and began to poke Gregor a little, and only when she had actually shifted him from the spot where he lay with no resistance at all were her suspicions roused. When soon thereafter the facts of the matter became clear to her, she gawked in surprise, gave a low whistle, then without further delay flung open the door of the bedroom and in a loud voice shouted into the darkness: "Come have a look, it's gone and croaked—just lying there, dead as a doornail!"

The Samsa couple shot upright in their marital bed and first had to struggle to recover from their shock at the charwoman's conduct before they were able to grasp her words. But then Herr and Frau[3] Samsa hurriedly got out of bed, one on either side, Herr Samsa threw the blanket about his shoulders while Frau Samsa emerged wearing only her nightdress; in this state, they entered Gregor's room. Meanwhile the door to the living room, where Gregor had been sleeping since the lodgers' arrival, had opened as well; she was fully dressed, as though she had not slept at all, as even the pallor of her cheeks seemed to prove. "Dead?" Frau Samsa asked, looking questioningly up at the charwoman, although she herself was free to investigate and, indeed, could see how things stood even without investigation. "I should say so," the charwoman said, and by way of proof, pushed Gregor's corpse quite some way to the side with her broom. Frau Samsa made a gesture as though she wanted to hold back the broom but didn't. "Well," Herr Samsa said, "now we can thank God." He crossed himself, and the three women followed his example. Grete, who did not take her eyes off the corpse for a moment, said: "Just look how skinny he was. He went such a long time without eating anything at all. All the food that went into his room would come out again just as before." And indeed Gregor's body was completely flat and dry, which hadn't really been noticeable until now when he was no longer raised up on those little legs and nothing else remained to distract the gaze.

"Grete, come sit with us for a bit," Frau Samsa said with a melancholy smile, and Grete, glancing back at the corpse, followed her parents into their bedroom. The charwoman shut the door and opened the window wide. Despite the early morning, the crisp air was already tempered by a certain mildness: after all, it was already the end of March.

The three lodgers now emerged from their room and looked about in astonishment for their breakfast; they had been forgotten. "Where's breakfast?" the one in the middle asked the charwoman peevishly. But she just put a finger to her lips and then quickly, without a word, beckoned the lodgers into Gregor's room. They did as she bade them and with their hands in the pockets of their slightly threadbare little jackets, they surrounded Gregor's corpse in the room that had meanwhile become quite bright.

Then the bedroom door opened, and Herr Samsa appeared wearing his livery, with his wife on one arm, his daughter on the other. All three looked as if they'd been weeping; Grete kept pressing her face against her father's arm.

"Leave my home at once!" Herr Samsa said, pointing at the door without letting go of the womenfolk. "What do you mean?" the gentleman in the middle inquired, dumbfounded, and gave a saccharine smile. The two others held their hands at their backs and kept rubbing them together uninterruptedly, as if in gleeful expectation of a fight that was certain to be decided in their favor. "I mean exactly what I say," Herr Samsa replied, now advancing on the lodger flanked by his two companions. The lodger just stood there at first, looking at the ground, as if things were just rearranging themselves in his head into a new order. "So we'll be leaving," he said then, looking up at Herr Samsa as if this new humility that had suddenly come over him required him to petition for the approval of even this decision. Herr Samsa merely nodded

---

**3.** Mrs. (German).

curtly in his direction a few times, goggle-eyed. At this, the gentleman did, in fact, make haste to stride back out to the vestibule, where his two friends had been listening attentively for some moments, their hands at rest, and now they practically hopped and skipped in their hurry to follow, as if worried Herr Samsa might somehow precede them into the vestibule, cutting off their line of communication with their leader.

In the vestibule, all three of them took their hats from the coat rack, withdrew their walking sticks from the cane stand, made a silent bow and left the apartment. Displaying what soon proved to be an utterly unfounded mistrustfulness, Herr Samsa stepped out onto the landing with the two women; leaning against the banister, they watched as the three gentlemen descended the long staircase, moving slowly but at a steady pace and disappearing on each floor at a certain bend of the stairwell only to appear again a few moments later; the farther down they went, the more the Samsa family's interest in them faded, and when a butcher's apprentice came toward and then passed them on his way up, proudly bearing his tray upon his head, Herr Samsa and the women abandoned the banister, and all of them returned, seemingly relieved, to their apartment.

They decided to spend the day resting and to go out for a stroll; they had not only earned this respite from their work, but were desperately in need of it. And so they all sat down at the table and wrote three letters of excuse: Herr Samsa to his supervisor, Frau Samsa to her employer, and Grete to her superior. While they were writing, the charwoman came in to say she was leaving, as her morning's work was completed. The three scribes at first merely nodded without looking up, and only when the charwoman failed to go on her way did they glance up in annoyance. "Well?" Herr Samsa asked. The charwoman stood smiling in the doorway as if she had some splendid good fortune to announce to the family but would not do so until she was properly questioned. The nearly vertical little ostrich feathers on her hat, which had annoyed Herr Samsa for as long as she had been in the family's service, bobbed gently in all directions. "So what is it you want?" she was asked now by Frau Samsa, the member of the family for whom the charwoman still had the most respect. "Well," the charwoman replied, her own good-natured laughter making it impossible at first for her to go on speaking, "there's no need for you to go worrying about how to get rid of that mess in there. It's already taken care of." Frau Samsa and Grete bent down over their letters as if they meant to go on writing; Herr Samsa, who saw that the charwoman was about to start describing everything in detail, summarily silenced her with an outstretched hand. And since she was not permitted to say what she wished, she suddenly remembered the great hurry she was in, and so with an insulted air she cried, "So long, everyone," turned wildly on her heel, and with the most excruciating slamming of doors left the apartment.

"Tonight she'll be let go," Herr Samsa said, but received an answer neither from his wife nor his daughter, for the charwoman seemed to have disturbed the equanimity they had only just attained. They rose from their seats, went to the window, and remained there with their arms about each other. Herr Samsa turned in his chair to look at them and observed them quietly for a little while. Then he cried out: "So come here already. Let these old matters rest. And show a little consideration for me as well." At once the women obeyed, hurried over to him, caressed him and quickly finished their letters.

Then all three of them left the apartment together, something they had not done for months, and took the electric tram all the way to the open country-side at the edge of town. The car in which they sat all alone was entirely suf-fused with warm sunlight. Cozily leaning back in their seats, they discussed their future prospects, and on closer investigation it appeared that these prospects were not bad at all, for all three of their positions—something they had never before properly discussed—were in fact quite advantageous and above all offered promising opportunities for advancement. The greatest immedi-ate improvement in their situation, of course, would be easily achieved by moving to a new apartment; they now wished to take a smaller and cheaper but more convenient and above all more practical flat than their current one, which had been picked out for them by Gregor. As they were conversing in this way, Herr and Frau Samsa were struck almost as one while observing their daughter, who was growing ever more vivacious, by the thought that despite all the torments that had made her cheeks grow pale, she had recently blossomed into a beautiful, voluptuous girl. Growing quieter now and com-municating with one another almost unconsciously by an exchange of glances, they thought about how it would soon be time to find her a good hus-band. And when they arrived at their destination, it seemed to them almost a confirmation of their new dreams and good intentions when their daughter swiftly sprang to her feet and stretched her young body.

1915

---

RELATED:

—Kafka, Letter to Max Brod, p. 885
—Stanley Corngold, "Kafka's *The Metamorphosis*: Metamorphosis of the Meta-phor," p. 920

# YASUNARI KAWABATA
## 1899–1972

Kawabata was the first Japanese writer to win the Nobel Prize for literature, in 1968. He was born in Osaka and raised in circumstances haunted by loss—he was orphaned at the age of three; his grandmother died when he was seven. Two years later, his only sister died as well. Kawabata's work is a uniquely personal combination of classic Japanese literature and twentieth-century modernism. Perhaps his most famous work is *Snow Country* (1937), which was singled out in his Nobel Prize citation, but Kawabata himself regarded *The Master of Go* (1951) as his finest achievement. His so-called "Palm-of-the-Hand Stories"—never more than two or three pages—show him to be a great writer of short fiction, able to make startling leaps of imagination in a small, highly concentrated space. In his Nobel Prize speech, Kawabata condemned the culture of suicide. Yet two years after his friend and fellow writer Yukio Mishima committed suicide, he too took his own life.

# The White Horse[1]

In the leaves of the oak tree, there was a silver sun.

Raising his face, Noguchi was dazzled by the light. He blinked and looked again. The light was not directly striking his eyes; it was caught amid the dense foliage.

For a Japanese oak, the tree had much too thick a trunk and stood much too tall. A number of other oaks clustered around it. Their lower branches unpruned, they screened the western sun. Beyond the stand of oaks, the summer sun went on sinking.

Because of the thickly intermeshed foliage, the sun itself could not be seen. Instead, the sun was the light that spread itself among the leaves. Noguchi was used to seeing it that way. On the highlands, the green of the leaves was as vivid as that of a Western oak. Absorbing the light, the leaves of the oak turned to a pale, translucent green and made sparkling wavelets of light as they swayed in the breeze.

This evening, the leaves of the tree were quiet. The light on the foliage was still.

"What?" Noguchi said the word out loud. He had just noticed the dusky color of the sky. It was not the color of a sky in which the sun was still halfway up in the high stand of oaks. It was the color of a sky in which the sun had

1. Translation by Martin Holman.

just set. The silvery light on the oak leaves came from a small white cloud beyond the grove that reflected the light of the setting sun. To the left of the grove, the faraway waves of mountains were darkening to a deep, faded blue.

The silvery light, which had been caught by the grove, suddenly went out. The green of the thick foliage slowly blackened. From the summit of the trees, a white horse leapt upward and galloped across the gray sky.

"Ahh . . ." But Noguchi was not that surprised. It was not an unusual dream for him.

"She's riding it again, in a black robe again."

The black robe of the woman astride the horse streamed out behind her. No—the folds of long black cloth that flowed over the stallion's arched tail were attached to the robe but seemed separate from it.

"What is it?" As Noguchi was thinking this, the vision faded away. But the rhythm of the horse's legs remained in his heart. Although the horse seemed to gallop headlong like a racehorse, there was a leisurely rhythm in the gallop. And the legs were the only part of the horse in motion. The hooves were sharply pointed.

"That long black cloth in back of her—what was it? Or was it a cloth?" Noguchi asked himself uneasily.

When Noguchi had been in the upper grades of elementary school, he had played with Taeko in the garden where the sweet oleander hedge was in bloom. They had drawn pictures together. They drew pictures of horses; when Taeko drew a horse galloping across the sky, Noguchi drew one, too.

"That's the horse that stamped on the mountain and made the sacred spring gush up," Taeko said.

"Shouldn't he have wings?" Noguchi asked. The horse he'd drawn was winged.

"He doesn't need any," Taeko answered, "Because he has sharp hooves."

"Who is riding him?"

"Taeko. Taeko is riding him. She's riding the white horse and wearing pink clothes."

"Oh, so Taeko's riding the horse that stamped on the mountain and made the sacred spring gush up."

"That's right. Your horse has wings, but nobody's riding him."

"Here, then." Noguchi hurriedly drew a boy atop the horse. Taeko looked on from the side.

That was all there had been. Noguchi had married another girl, had fathered children, had aged, had forgotten about that kind of thing.

He'd remembered it suddenly, late one sleepless night. His son, having failed his university entrance tests, was studying every night until two or three o'clock. Noguchi, worried about him, could not get to sleep. As the sleepless nights continued, Noguchi came up against the loneliness of life. The son had next year, had hope, did not even go to bed at night. But the father merely lay awake in his bed. It was not for his son's sake. He was experiencing his own loneliness. Once he had been caught by this loneliness, it did not let him go. It put down its roots in the deepest part of him.

Noguchi tried various ways to fall asleep. He tried thinking of quiet fantasies and memories. And, one night, unexpectedly, he remembered Taeko's picture of the white horse. He did not clearly recall the picture. It was no child's picture, but the vision of a white horse galloping through heaven that floated up behind Noguchi's closed eyelids in the dark.

"Is it Taeko riding him? In pink clothes?"

The figure of the white horse, galloping across the sky, was clear. But neither the form nor the color of the rider astride him was clear. It did not seem to be a girl.

As the speed with which the visionary steed galloped through the empty sky slackened and the vision faded away, Noguchi would be drawn down into sleep.

From that night on, Noguchi had used the vision of the white horse as an invitation to sleep. His sleeplessness became a frequent occurrence, a customary thing whenever he suffered or was anxious.

For several years now, Noguchi had been saved from his insomnia by the vision of the white horse. The imaginary white horse was vivid and lively, but the figure riding him seemed to be a woman in black. It was not a girl in pink. The figure of that black-robed woman, aged and weakened, grew mysterious as time went by.

Today was the first time that the dream of the white horse had come to Noguchi, not as he lay in bed with his eyes closed, but as he sat open-eyed in a chair. It was the first time, also, that something like a long black cloth had streamed out behind the woman. Although it flowed in the wind, the drapery was thick and heavy.

"What is it?"

Noguchi gazed at the darkening gray sky from which the vision of the white horse had faded.

He had not seen Taeko in forty years. There was no news of her.

1963

# JAMAICA KINCAID
## b. 1949

Elaine Potter Richardson was born in St. John's, Antigua, West Indies, but at age seventeen she moved to New York City, took the name Jamaica Kincaid, and became a naturalized U.S. citizen. From the time of her first publication of stories about life on Antigua she was acclaimed not only for the vividness of her portrayal of that milieu but also for her mixture of fantasy and reality and the acuity of her style. Her first book, *At the Bottom of the River* (1983), was a collection of short stories, and her second, *Annie John* (1985), was a group of interrelated stories that some critics saw as a novel. Her book-length essay about Antigua, *A Small Place*, won her further praise in 1988. Kincaid's novels include *Lucy* (1990), *The Autobiography of My Mother* (1996), *My Brother* (1997), *Mr. Potter* (2002), and *See Now Then* (2013). Kincaid teaches literature at Claremont McKenna College.

## Girl

Wash the white clothes on Monday and put them on the stone heap; wash the color clothes on Tuesday and put them on the clothesline to dry; don't walk barehead in the hot sun; cook pumpkin fritters in very hot sweet oil; soak your little cloths right after you take them off; when buying cotton to make yourself a nice blouse, be sure that it doesn't have gum on it, because that way it won't hold up well after a wash; soak salt fish overnight before you cook it; is it true that you sing benna[1] in Sunday school?; always eat your food in such a way that it won't turn someone else's stomach; on Sundays try to walk like a lady and not like the slut you are so bent on becoming; don't sing benna in Sunday school; you mustn't speak to wharf-rat boys, not even to give directions; don't eat fruits on the street—flies will follow you; *but I don't sing benna on Sundays at all and never in Sunday school*; this is how to sew on a button; this is how to make a buttonhole for the button you have just sewed on; this is how to hem a dress when you see the hem coming down and so to prevent yourself from looking like the slut I know you are so bent on becoming; this is how you iron your father's khaki shirt so that it doesn't have a crease; this is how you iron your father's khaki pants so that they don't have a crease; this is how you grow okra—far from the house, because okra tree harbors red ants; when you are growing dasheen, make sure it gets plenty of water or else it makes your throat itch when you are eating it; this is how you sweep a corner;

1. A Caribbean folk-music style.

this is how you sweep a whole house; this is how you sweep a yard; this is how you smile to someone you don't like very much; this is how you smile to someone you don't like at all; this is how you smile to someone you like completely; this is how you set a table for tea; this is how you set a table for dinner; this is how you set a table for dinner with an important guest; this is how you set a table for lunch; this is how you set a table for breakfast; this is how to behave in the presence of men who don't know you very well, and this way they won't recognize immediately the slut I have warned you against becoming; be sure to wash every day, even if it is with your own spit; don't squat down to play marbles—you are not a boy, you know; don't pick people's flowers—you might catch something; don't throw stones at blackbirds, because it might not be a blackbird at all; this is how to make a bread pudding; this is how to make doukona;[2] this is how to make pepper pot; this is how to make a good medicine for a cold; this is how to make a good medicine to throw away a child before it even becomes a child; this is how to catch a fish; this is how to throw back a fish you don't like, and that way something bad won't fall on you; this is how to bully a man; this is how a man bullies you; this is how to love a man, and if this doesn't work there are other ways, and if they don't work don't feel too bad about giving up; this is how to spit up in the air if you feel like it, and this is how to move quick so that it doesn't fall on you; this is how to make ends meet; always squeeze bread to make sure it's fresh; *but what if the baker won't let me feel the bread?*; you mean to say that after all you are really going to be the kind of woman who the baker won't let near the bread?

1978

---

2. A spiced pudding, often made from plantains.

# JHUMPA LAHIRI
*b. 1967*

Jhumpa Lahiri was born Nilanjana Sudeshna in London to Indian immigrant parents from West Bengal. When she was two years old, her family moved to the United States, settling in Kingston, Rhode Island. Lahiri earned her B.A. in English literature from Barnard College and went on to receive various degrees from Boston University, including an M.F.A. in creative writing and a Ph.D. in Renaissance studies. The primary characters in Lahiri's often autobiographical fiction are first- and second-generation Indian-American immigrants. For years Lahiri's short stories were rejected for publication, but her first collection, *Interpreter of Maladies*, was awarded the Pulitzer Prize in 1999. This internationally bestselling debut also earned her the PEN/Hemingway Award, the Addison Metcalf Award from the American Academy of Arts and Letters, and the New Yorker Debut of the Year award. In 2003, she published her first novel, *The Namesake*, which was later adapted for the screen. Lahiri has also published a second collection of short fiction, *Unaccustomed Earth* (2008), a number one *New York Times* bestseller, and a second novel, *The Lowland* (2013), which was short-listed for the Man Booker Prize. She has taught at Boston University and the Rhode Island School of Design, and is currently vice president of the PEN American Center.

# Hell-Heaven

Pranab Chakraborty wasn't technically my father's younger brother. He was a fellow-Bengali from Calcutta who had washed up on the barren shores of my parents' social life in the early seventies, when they lived in a rented apartment in Central Square and could number their acquaintances on one hand. But I had no real uncles in America, and so I was taught to call him Pranab Kaku. Accordingly, he called my father Shyamal Da, always addressing him in the polite form, and he called my mother Boudi, which is how Bengalis are supposed to address an older brother's wife, instead of using her first name, Aparna. After Pranab Kaku was befriended by my parents, he confessed that on the day we first met him he had followed my mother and me for the better part of an afternoon around the streets of Cambridge, where she and I tended to roam after I got out of school. He had trailed behind us along Massachusetts Avenue, and in and out of the Harvard Coop, where my mother liked to look at discounted housewares. He wandered with us into Harvard Yard, where my mother often sat on the grass on pleasant days and watched the stream of students and professors filing busily along the paths, until, finally, as we were climbing the steps to Widener Library so that I could use the bathroom, he tapped my mother on the shoulder and inquired, in English, if she might be a Bengali. The answer to his question was clear, given that my mother was wearing the red and white bangles unique to Bengali married women, and a common Tangail sari, and had a thick stem of vermillion powder in the center parting of her hair, and the full round face and large dark eyes that are so typical of Bengali women. He noticed the two or three safety pins she wore fastened to the thin gold bangles that were behind the red and white ones, which she would use to replace a missing hook on a blouse or to draw a string through a petticoat at a moment's notice, a practice he associated strictly with his mother and sisters and aunts in Calcutta. Moreover, Pranab Kaku had overheard my mother speaking to me in Bengali, telling me that I couldn't buy an issue of *Archie* at the Coop. But back then, he also confessed, he was so new to America that he took nothing for granted, and doubted even the obvious.

My parents and I had lived in Central Square for three years prior to that day; before that, we had lived in Berlin, where I was born and where my father had finished his training in microbiology before accepting a position as a researcher at Mass General, and before Berlin my mother and father had lived in India, where they had been strangers to each other, and where their marriage had been arranged. Central Square is the first place I can recall living, and in my memories of our apartment, in a dark-brown shingled house on Ashburton Place, Pranab Kaku is always there. According to the story he liked to recall often, my mother invited him to accompany us back to our apartment that very afternoon, and prepared tea for the two of them; then, after learning that he had not had a proper Bengali meal in more than three months, she served him the leftover curried mackerel and rice that we had eaten for dinner the night before. He remained into the evening, for a second dinner, after my father got home, and after that he showed up for dinner almost every night, occupying the fourth chair at our square Formica kitchen table, and becoming a part of our family in practice as well as in name.

He was from a wealthy family in Calcutta and had never had to do so much as pour himself a glass of water before moving to America, to study engineering at M.I.T. Life as a graduate student in Boston was a cruel shock, and in his first month he lost nearly twenty pounds. He had arrived in January, in the middle of a snowstorm, and at the end of a week he had packed his bags and gone to Logan, prepared to abandon the opportunity he'd worked toward all his life, only to change his mind at the last minute. He was living on Trowbridge Street in the home of a divorced woman with two young children who were always screaming and crying. He rented a room in the attic and was permitted to use the kitchen only at specified times of the day, and instructed always to wipe down the stove with Windex and a sponge. My parents agreed that it was a terrible situation, and if they'd had a bedroom to spare they would have offered it to him. Instead, they welcomed him to our meals, and opened up our apartment to him at any time, and soon it was there he went between classes and on his days off, always leaving behind some vestige of himself: a nearly finished pack of cigarettes, a newspaper, a piece of mail he had not bothered to open, a sweater he had taken off and forgotten in the course of his stay.

I remember vividly the sound of his exuberant laughter and the sight of his lanky body slouched or sprawled on the dull, mismatched furniture that had come with our apartment. He had a striking face, with a high forehead and a thick mustache, and overgrown, untamed hair that my mother said made him look like the American hippies who were everywhere in those days. His long legs jiggled rapidly up and down wherever he sat, and his elegant hands trembled when he held a cigarette between his fingers, tapping the ashes into a teacup that my mother began to set aside for this exclusive purpose. Though he was a scientist by training, there was nothing rigid or predictable or orderly about him. He always seemed to be starving, walking through the door and announcing that he hadn't had lunch, and then he would eat ravenously, reaching behind my mother to steal cutlets as she was frying them, before she had a chance to set them properly on a plate with red-onion salad. In private, my parents remarked that he was a brilliant student, a star at Jadavpur[1] who had come to M.I.T. with an impressive assistantship, but Pranab Kaku was cavalier about his classes, skipping them with frequency. "These Americans are learning equations I knew at Usha's age," he would complain. He was stunned that my second-grade teacher didn't assign any homework, and that at the age of seven I hadn't yet been taught square roots or the concept of pi.

He appeared without warning, never phoning beforehand but simply knocking on the door the way people did in Calcutta and calling out "Boudi!" as he waited for my mother to let him in. Before we met him, I would return from school and find my mother with her purse in her lap and her trenchcoat on, desperate to escape the apartment where she had spent the day alone. But now I would find her in the kitchen, rolling out dough for *luchis*, which she normally made only on Sundays for my father and me, or putting up new curtains she'd bought at Woolworth's. I did not know, back then, that Pranab Kaku's visits were what my mother looked forward to all day, that she changed into a new sari and combed her hair in anticipation of his arrival, and that she planned, days in advance, the snacks she would serve him with such nonchalance. That she lived for the moment she heard him call out "Boudi!" from the porch, and that she was in a foul humor on the days he didn't materialize.

It must have pleased her that I looked forward to his visits as well. He showed me card tricks and an optical illusion in which he appeared to be severing his own thumb with enormous struggle and strength, and taught me to memorize multiplication tables well before I had to learn them in school. His hobby was photography. He owned an expensive camera that required thought before you pressed the shutter, and I quickly became his favorite subject, round-faced, missing teeth, my thick bangs in need of a trim. They are still the pictures of myself I like best, for they convey that confidence of youth I no longer possess, especially in front of a camera. I remember having to run back and forth in Harvard Yard as he stood with the camera, trying to capture me in motion, or posing on the steps of university buildings and on the street and against the trunks of trees. There is only one photograph in which

---

1. Jadavpur University, an elite public university in Kolkata (formerly called Calcutta), the capital of the Indian state of West Bengal.

my mother appears; she is holding me as I sit straddling her lap, her head tilted toward me, her hands pressed to my ears as if to prevent me from hearing something. In that picture, Pranab Kaku's shadow, his two arms raised at angles to hold the camera to his face, hovers in the corner of the frame, his darkened, featureless shape superimposed on one side of my mother's body. It was always the three of us. I was always there when he visited. It would have been inappropriate for my mother to receive him in the apartment alone; this was something that went without saying.

They had in common all the things she and my father did not: a love of music, film, leftist politics, poetry. They were from the same neighborhood in North Calcutta, their family homes within walking distance, the façades familiar to them once the exact locations were described. They knew the same shops, the same bus and tram routes, the same holes-in-the-wall for the best *jelabis* and *moghlai parathas*.[2] My father, on the other hand, came from a suburb twenty miles outside Calcutta, an area that my mother considered the wilderness, and even in her bleakest hours of homesickness she was grateful that my father had at least spared her a life in the stern house of her in-laws, where she would have had to keep her head covered with the end of her sari at all times and use an outhouse that was nothing but a raised platform with a hole, and where, in the rooms, there was not a single painting hanging on the walls. Within a few weeks, Pranab Kaku had brought his reel-to-reel over to our apartment, and he played for my mother medley after medley of songs from the Hindi films of their youth. They were cheerful songs of courtship, which transformed the quiet life in our apartment and transported my mother back to the world she'd left behind in order to marry my father. She and Pranab Kaku would try to recall which scene in which movie the songs were from, who the actors were and what they were wearing. My mother would describe Raj Kapoor and Nargis singing under umbrellas in the rain, or Dev Anand strumming a guitar on the beach in Goa. She and Pranab Kaku would argue passionately about these matters, raising their voices in playful combat, confronting each other in a way she and my father never did.

Because he played the part of a younger brother, she felt free to call him Pranab, whereas she never called my father by his first name. My father was thirty-seven then, nine years older than my mother. Pranab Kaku was twenty-five. My father was monkish by nature, a lover of silence and solitude. He had married my mother to placate his parents; they were willing to accept his desertion as long as he had a wife. He was wedded to his work, his research, and he existed in a shell that neither my mother nor I could penetrate. Conversation was a chore for him; it required an effort he preferred to expend at the lab. He disliked excess in anything, voiced no cravings or needs apart from the frugal elements of his daily routine: cereal and tea in the mornings, a cup of tea after he got home, and two different vegetable dishes every night with dinner. He did not eat with the reckless appetite of Pranab Kaku. My father had a survivor's mentality. From time to time, he liked to remark, in mixed company and often with no relevant provocation, that starving Russians under Stalin had resorted to eating the glue off the back of their wall-

---

2. A type of sweet pretzel and a kind of stuffed bread, respectively.

paper. One might think that he would have felt slightly jealous, or at the very least suspicious, about the regularity of Pranab Kaku's visits and the effect they had on my mother's behavior and mood. But my guess is that my father was grateful to Pranab Kaku for the companionship he provided, freed from the sense of responsibility he must have felt for forcing her to leave India, and relieved, perhaps, to see her happy for a change.

In the summer, Pranab Kaku bought a navy-blue Volkswagen Beetle, and began to take my mother and me for drives through Boston and Cambridge, and soon outside the city, flying down the highway. He would take us to India Tea and Spices in Watertown, and one time he drove us all the way to New Hampshire to look at the mountains. As the weather grew hotter, we started going, once or twice a week, to Walden Pond. My mother always prepared a picnic of hard-boiled eggs and cucumber sandwiches, and talked fondly about the winter picnics of her youth, grand expeditions with fifty of her relatives, all taking the train into the West Bengal countryside. Pranab Kaku listened to these stories with interest, absorbing the vanishing details of her past. He did not turn a deaf ear to her nostalgia, like my father, or listen uncomprehending, like me. At Walden Pond, Pranab Kaku would coax my mother through the woods, and lead her down the steep slope to the water's edge. She would unpack the picnic things and sit and watch us as we swam. His chest was matted with thick dark hair, all the way to his waist. He was an odd sight, with his pole-thin legs and a small, flaccid belly, like an otherwise svelte woman who has had a baby and not bothered to tone her abdomen. "You're making me fat, Boudi," he would complain after gorging himself on my mother's cooking. He swam noisily, clumsily, his head always above the water; he didn't know how to blow bubbles or hold his breath, as I had learned in swimming class. Wherever we went, any stranger would have naturally assumed that Pranab Kaku was my father, that my mother was his wife.

It is clear to me now that my mother was in love with him. He wooed her as no other man had, with the innocent affection of a brother-in-law. In my mind, he was just a family member, a cross between an uncle and a much older brother, for in certain respects my parents sheltered and cared for him in much the same way they cared for me. He was respectful of my father, always seeking his advice about making a life in the West, about setting up a bank account and getting a job, and deferring to his opinions about Kissinger and Watergate. Occasionally, my mother would tease him about women, asking about female Indian students at M.I.T., or showing him pictures of her younger cousins in India. "What do you think of her?" she would ask. "Isn't she pretty?" She knew that she could never have Pranab Kaku for herself, and I suppose it was her attempt to keep him in the family. But, most important, in the beginning he was totally dependent on her, needing her for those months in a way my father never did in the whole history of their marriage. He brought to my mother the first and, I suspect, the only pure happiness she ever felt. I don't think even my birth made her as happy. I was evidence of her marriage to my father, an assumed consequence of the life she had been raised to lead. But Pranab Kaku was different. He was the one totally unanticipated pleasure in her life.

In the fall of 1974, Pranab Kaku met a student at Radcliffe named Deborah, an American, and she began to accompany him to our house. I called

Deborah by her first name, as my parents did, but Pranab Kaku taught her to call my father Shyamal Da and my mother Boudi, something with which Deborah gladly complied. Before they came to dinner for the first time, I asked my mother, as she was straightening up the living room, if I ought to address her as Deborah Kakima, turning her into an aunt as I had turned Pranab into an uncle. "What's the point?" my mother said, looking back at me sharply. "In a few weeks, the fun will be over and she'll leave him." And yet Deborah remained by his side, attending the weekend parties that Pranab Kaku and my parents were becoming more involved with, gatherings that were exclusively Bengali with the exception of her. Deborah was very tall, taller than both my parents and nearly as tall as Pranab Kaku. She wore her long brass-colored hair center-parted, as my mother did, but it was gathered into a low ponytail instead of a braid, or it spilled messily over her shoulders and down her back in a way that my mother considered indecent. She wore small silver spectacles and not a trace of makeup, and she studied philosophy. I found her utterly beautiful, but according to my mother she had spots on her face, and her hips were too small.

For a while, Pranab Kaku still showed up once a week for dinner on his own, mostly asking my mother what she thought of Deborah. He sought her approval, telling her that Deborah was the daughter of professors at Boston College, that her father published poetry, and that both her parents had Ph.D.s. When he wasn't around, my mother complained about Deborah's visits, about having to make the food less spicy even though Deborah said she liked spicy food, and feeling embarrassed to put a fried fish head in the dal. Pranab Kaku taught Deborah to say *khub bhalo* and *aacha*[3] and to pick up certain foods with her fingers instead of with a fork. Sometimes they ended up feeding each other, allowing their fingers to linger in each other's mouth, causing my parents to look down at their plates and wait for the moment to pass. At larger gatherings, they kissed and held hands in front of everyone, and when they were out of earshot my mother would talk to the other Bengali women. "He used to be so different. I don't understand how a person can change so suddenly. It's just hell-heaven, the difference," she would say, always using the English words for her self-concocted, backward metaphor.

The more my mother began to resent Deborah's visits, the more I began to anticipate them. I fell in love with Deborah, the way young girls often fall in love with women who are not their mothers. I loved her serene gray eyes, the ponchos and denim wrap skirts and sandals she wore, her straight hair that she let me manipulate into all sorts of silly styles. I longed for her casual appearance; my mother insisted whenever there was a gathering that I wear one of my ankle-length, faintly Victorian dresses, which she referred to as maxis, and have party hair, which meant taking a strand from either side of my head and joining them with a barrette at the back. At parties, Deborah would, eventually, politely slip away, much to the relief of the Bengali women with whom she was expected to carry on a conversation, and she would play with me. I was older than all my parents' friends' children, but with Deborah I had a companion. She knew all about the books I read, about Pippi Longstocking and Anne of Green Gables. She gave me the sorts of gifts my parents

3. Bengali for "very good" and "oh, really."

had neither the money nor the inspiration to buy: a large book of Grimms' fairy tales with watercolor illustrations on thick, silken pages, wooden puppets with hair fashioned from yarn. She told me about her family, three older sisters and two brothers, the youngest of whom was closer to my age than to hers. Once, after visiting her parents, she brought back three Nancy Drews, her name written in a girlish hand at the top of the first page, and an old toy she'd had, a small paper theatre set with interchangeable backdrops, the exterior of a castle and a ballroom and an open field. Deborah and I spoke freely in English, a language in which, by that age, I expressed myself more easily than Bengali, which I was required to speak at home. Sometimes she asked me how to say this or that in Bengali; once, she asked me what *asobbho* meant. I hesitated, then told her it was what my mother called me if I had done something extremely naughty, and Deborah's face clouded. I felt protective of her, aware that she was unwanted, that she was resented, aware of the nasty things people said.

Outings in the Volkswagen now involved the four of us, Deborah in the front, her hand over Pranab Kaku's while it rested on the gearshift, my mother and I in the back. Soon, my mother began coming up with reasons to excuse herself, headaches and incipient colds, and so I became part of a new triangle. To my surprise, my mother allowed me to go with them, to the Museum of Fine Arts and the Public Garden and the aquarium. She was waiting for the affair to end, for Deborah to break Pranab Kaku's heart and for him to return to us, scarred and penitent. I saw no sign of their relationship foundering. Their open affection for each other, their easily expressed happiness, was a new and romantic thing to me. Having me in the back seat allowed Pranab Kaku and Deborah to practice for the future, to try on the idea of a family of their own. Countless photographs were taken of me and Deborah, of me sitting on Deborah's lap, holding her hand, kissing her on the cheek. We exchanged what I believed were secret smiles, and in those moments I felt that she understood me better than anyone else in the world. Anyone would have said that Deborah would make an excellent mother one day. But my mother refused to acknowledge such a thing. I did not know at the time that my mother allowed me to go off with Pranab Kaku and Deborah because she was pregnant for the fifth time since my birth, and was so sick and exhausted and fearful of losing another baby that she slept most of the day. After ten weeks, she miscarried once again, and was advised by her doctor to stop trying.

By summer, there was a diamond on Deborah's left hand, something my mother had never been given. Because his own family lived so far away, Pranab Kaku came to the house alone one day, to ask for my parents' blessing before giving her the ring. He showed us the box, opening it and taking out the diamond nestled inside. "I want to see how it looks on someone," he said, urging my mother to try it on, but she refused. I was the one who stuck out my hand, feeling the weight of the ring suspended at the base of my finger. Then he asked for a second thing: he wanted my parents to write to his parents, saying that they had met Deborah and that they thought highly of her. He was nervous, naturally, about telling his family that he intended to marry an American girl. He had told his parents all about us, and at one point my parents had received a letter from them, expressing appreciation for taking such good care of their son and for giving him a proper home in America. "It needn't be long," Pranab Kaku said. "Just a few lines. They'll accept it more easily if it comes from you." My father thought neither ill nor well of Deborah, never commenting or criticizing as my mother did, but he assured Pranab Kaku that a letter of endorsement would be on its way to Calcutta by the end of the week. My mother nodded her assent, but the following day I saw the teacup Pranab Kaku had used all this time as an ashtray in the kitchen garbage can, in pieces, and three Band-Aids taped to my mother's hand.

Pranab Kaku's parents were horrified by the thought of their only son marrying an American woman, and a few weeks later our telephone rang in the middle of the night: it was Mr. Chakraborty telling my father that they could not possibly bless such a marriage, that it was out of the question, that if Pranab Kaku dared to marry Deborah he would no longer acknowledge him as a son. Then his wife got on the phone, asking to speak to my mother, and attacked her as if they were intimate, blaming my mother for allowing the affair to develop. She said that they had already chosen a wife for him in Calcutta, that he'd left for America with the understanding that he'd go back after he had finished his studies, and marry this girl. They had bought the neighboring flat in their building for Pranab and his betrothed, and it was sitting empty, waiting for his return. "We thought we could trust you, and yet you have betrayed us so deeply," his mother said, taking out her anger on a stranger in a way she could not with her son. "Is this what happens to people in America?" For Pranab Kaku's sake, my mother defended the engagement, telling his mother that Deborah was a polite girl from a decent family. Pranab Kaku's parents pleaded with mine to talk him out of the engagement, but my father refused, deciding that it was not their place to get embroiled in a situation that had nothing to do with them. "We are not his parents," he told my mother. "We can tell him they don't approve but nothing more." And so my parents told Pranab Kaku nothing about how his parents had berated them, and blamed them, and threatened to disown Pranab Kaku, only that they had refused to give him their blessing. In the face of this refusal, Pranab Kaku shrugged. "I don't care. Not everyone can be as open-minded as you," he told my parents. "Your blessing is blessing enough."

After the engagement, Pranab Kaku and Deborah began drifting out of our lives. They moved in together, to an apartment in Boston, in the South End, a part of the city my parents considered unsafe. We moved as well, to a house in Natick. Though my parents had bought the house, they occupied it as if they were still tenants, touching up scuff marks with leftover paint and reluctant to put holes in the walls, and every afternoon when the sun shone through the living-room window my mother closed the blinds so that our new furniture would not fade. A few weeks before the wedding, my parents invited Pranab Kaku to the house alone, and my mother prepared a special meal to mark the end of his bachelorhood. It would be the only Bengali aspect of the wedding; the rest of it would be strictly American, with a cake and a minister and Deborah in a long white dress and veil. There is a photograph of the dinner, taken by my father, the only picture, to my knowledge, in which my mother and Pranab Kaku appear together. The picture is slightly blurry; I remember Pranab Kaku explaining to my father how to work the camera, and so he is captured looking up from the kitchen table and the elaborate array of food my mother had prepared in his honor, his mouth open, his long arm outstretched and his finger pointing, instructing my father how to read the light meter or some such thing. My mother stands beside him, one hand placed on top of his head in a gesture of blessing, the first and last time she was to touch him in her life. "She will leave him," my mother told her friends afterward. "He is throwing his life away."

The wedding was at a church in Ipswich, with a reception at a country club. It was going to be a small ceremony, which my parents took to mean one or two hundred people as opposed to three or four hundred. My mother was shocked that fewer than thirty people had been invited, and she was more perplexed than honored that, of all the Bengalis Pranab Kaku knew by then, we were the only ones on the list. At the wedding, we sat, like the other guests, first on the hard wooden pews of the church and then at a long table that had been set up for lunch. Though we were the closest thing Pranab Kaku had to a family that day, we were not included in the group photographs that were taken on the grounds of the country club, with Deborah's parents and grandparents and her many siblings, and neither my mother nor my father got up to make a toast. My mother did not appreciate the fact that Deborah had made sure that my parents, who did not eat beef, were given fish instead of filet mignon like everyone else. She kept speaking in Bengali, complaining about the formality of the proceedings, and the fact that Pranab Kaku, wearing a tuxedo, barely said a word to us because he was too busy leaning over the shoulders of his new American in-laws as he circled the table. As usual, my father said nothing in response to my mother's commentary, quietly and methodically working though his meal, his fork and knife occasionally squeaking against the surface of the china, because he was accustomed to eating with his hands. He cleared his plate and then my mother's, for she had pronounced the food inedible, and then he announced that he had overeaten and had a stomach ache. The only time my mother forced a smile was when Deborah appeared behind her chair, kissing her on the cheek and asking if we were enjoying ourselves. When the dancing started, my parents remained at the table, drinking tea, and after two or three songs they decided that it was time for us to go home, my mother shooting me looks to that effect across the room, where I was dancing in a circle with Pranab Kaku and Deborah and the other children at the wedding. I wanted to stay, and when, reluctantly, I walked over to where my parents sat Deborah followed me. "Boudi, let Usha stay. She's having such a good time," she said to my mother. "Lots of people will be heading back your way, someone can drop her off in a little while." But my mother said no, I had had plenty of fun already, and forced me to put on my coat over my long puff-sleeved dress. As we drove home from the wedding I told my mother, for the first but not the last time in my life, that I hated her.

The following year, we received a birth announcement from the Chakrabortys, a picture of twin girls, which my mother did not paste into an album or display on the refrigerator door. The girls were named Srabani and Sabitri, but were called Bonny and Sara. Apart from a thank-you card for our wedding gift, it was their only communication; we were not invited to the new house in Marblehead, bought after Pranab Kaku got a high-paying job at Stone & Webster. For a while, my parents and their friends continued to invite the Chakrabortys to gatherings, but because they never came, or left after staying only an hour, the invitations stopped. Their absences were attributed, by my parents and their circle, to Deborah, and it was universally agreed that she had stripped Pranab Kaku not only of his origins but of his independence. She was the enemy, he was her prey, and their example was invoked as a warning, and as vindication, that mixed marriages were a doomed enterprise. Occasionally, they surprised everyone, appearing at a *pujo*[4] for a few hours with their two identical little girls who barely looked Bengali and spoke only English and were being raised so differently from me and most of the other children. They were not taken to Calcutta every summer, they did not have parents who were clinging to another way of life and exhorting their children to do the same. Because of Deborah, they were exempt from all that, and for this reason I envied them. "Usha, look at you, all grown up and so pretty," Deborah would say whenever she saw me, rekindling, if only for a minute, our bond of years before. She had cut off her beautiful long hair by then, and had a bob. "I bet you'll be old enough to babysit soon," she would say. "I'll call you—the girls would love that." But she never did.

I began to grow out of my girlhood, entering middle school and developing crushes on the American boys in my class. The crushes amounted to nothing; in spite of Deborah's compliments, I was always overlooked at that age. But my mother must have picked up on something, for she forbade me to attend the dances that were held the last Friday of every month in the school cafeteria, and it was an unspoken law that I was not allowed to date. "Don't think you'll get away with marrying an American, the way Pranab Kaku did," she would say from time to time. I was thirteen, the thought of marriage irrelevant to my life. Still, her words upset me, and I felt her grip on me tighten. She would fly into a rage when I told her I wanted to start wearing a bra, or if I wanted to go to Harvard Square with a friend. In the middle of our arguments, she often conjured Deborah as her antithesis, the sort of woman she refused to be. "If *she* were your mother, she would let you do whatever you wanted, because she wouldn't care. Is that what you want, Usha, a mother who doesn't care?" When I began menstruating, the summer before I started ninth grade, my mother gave me a speech, telling me that I was to let no boy touch me, and then she asked if I knew how a woman became pregnant. I told her what I had been taught in science, about the sperm fertilizing the egg, and then she asked if I knew how, exactly, that happened. I saw the terror in her eyes and so, though I knew that aspect of procreation as well, I lied, and told her it hadn't been explained to us.

I began keeping other secrets from her, evading her with the aid of my friends. I told her I was sleeping over at a friend's when really I went to parties, drinking beer and allowing boys to kiss me and fondle my breasts and press their erections against my hip as we lay groping on a sofa or the back seat of a car. I began to pity my mother; the older I got, the more I saw what a desolate life she led. She had never worked, and during the day she watched soap operas to pass the time. Her only job, every day, was to clean and cook for my

4. Religious festival.

father and me. We rarely went to restaurants, my father always pointing out, even in cheap ones, how expensive they were compared with eating at home. When my mother complained to him about how much she hated life in the suburbs and how lonely she felt, he said nothing to placate her. "If you are so unhappy, go back to Calcutta," he would offer, making it clear that their separation would not affect him one way or the other. I began to take my cues from my father in dealing with her, isolating her doubly. When she screamed at me for talking too long on the telephone, or for staying too long in my room, I learned to scream back, telling her that she was pathetic, that she knew nothing about me, and it was clear to us both that I had stopped needing her, definitely and abruptly, just as Pranab Kaku had.

Then, the year before I went off to college, my parents and I were invited to the Chakrabortys' home for Thanksgiving. We were not the only guests from my parents' old Cambridge crowd; it turned out that Pranab Kaku and Deborah wanted to have a sort of reunion of all the people they had been friendly with back then. Normally, my parents did not celebrate Thanksgiving; the ritual of a large sit-down dinner and the foods that one was supposed to eat was lost on them. They treated it as if it were Memorial Day or Veterans Day—just another holiday in the American year. But we drove out to Marblehead, to an impressive stone-faced house with a semicircular gravel driveway clogged with cars. The house was a short walk from the ocean; on our way, we had driven by the harbor overlooking the cold, glittering Atlantic, and when we stepped out of the car we were greeted by the sound of gulls and waves. Most of the living-room furniture had been moved to the basement, and extra tables joined to the main one to form a giant U. They were covered with tablecloths, set with white plates and silverware, and had centerpieces of gourds. I was struck by the toys and dolls that were everywhere, dogs that shed long yellow hairs on everything, all the photographs of Bonny and Sara and Deborah decorating the walls, still more plastering the refrigerator door. Food was being prepared when we arrived, something my mother always frowned upon, the kitchen a chaos of people and smells and enormous dirtied bowls.

Deborah's family, whom we remembered dimly from the wedding, was there, her parents and her brothers and sisters and their husbands and wives and boyfriends and babies. Her sisters were in their thirties, but, like Deborah, they could have been mistaken for college students, wearing jeans and clogs and fisherman sweaters, and her brother Matty, with whom I had danced in a circle at the wedding, was now a freshman at Amherst, with wide-set green eyes and wispy brown hair and a complexion that reddened easily. As soon as I saw Deborah's siblings, joking with one another as they chopped and stirred things in the kitchen, I was furious with my mother for making a scene before we left the house and forcing me to wear a shalwar kameez. I knew they assumed, from my clothing, that I had more in common with the other Bengalis than with them. But Deborah insisted on including me, setting me to work peeling apples with Matty, and out of my parents' sight I was given beer to drink. When the meal was ready, we were told where to sit, in an alternating boy-girl formation that made the Bengalis uncomfortable. Bottles of wine were lined up on the table. Two turkeys were brought out, one stuffed with sausage and one without. My mouth watered at the food, but I knew that afterward, on our way home, my mother would complain that it was all tasteless and bland. "Impossible," my mother said, shaking her hand over the top of her glass when someone tried to pour her a little wine.

Deborah's father, Gene, got up to say grace, and asked everyone at the table to join hands. He bowed his head and closed his eyes. "Dear Lord, we thank you today for the food we are about to receive," he began. My parents were seated next to each other, and I was stunned to see that they complied, that my father's brown fingers lightly clasped my mother's pale ones. I noticed Matty seated on the other side of the room, and saw him glancing at me as his father spoke. After the chorus of amens, Gene raised his glass and said, "Forgive me, but I never thought I'd have the opportunity to say this: Here's to Thanksgiving with the Indians." Only a few people laughed at the joke.

Then Pranab Kaku stood up and thanked everyone for coming. He was relaxed from alcohol, his once wiry body beginning to thicken. He started to talk sentimentally about his early days in Cambridge, and then suddenly he recounted the story of meeting me and my mother for the first time, telling the guests about how he had followed us that afternoon. The people who did not know us laughed, amused by the description of the encounter, and by Pranab Kaku's desperation. He walked around the room to where my mother was sitting and draped a lanky arm around her shoulder, forcing her, for a brief moment, to stand up. "This woman," he declared, pulling her close to his side, "this woman hosted my first real Thanksgiving in America. It might have been an afternoon in May, but that first meal at Boudi's table was Thanksgiving to me. If it weren't for that meal, I would have gone back to Calcutta." My mother looked away, embarrassed. She was thirty-eight, already going gray, and she looked closer to my father's age than to Pranab Kaku's; regardless of his waistline, he retained his handsome, carefree looks. Pranab Kaku went back to his place at the head of the table, next to Deborah, and concluded, "And if that had been the case I'd have never met you, my darling," and he kissed her on the mouth in front of everyone, to much applause, as if it were their wedding day all over again.

After the turkey, smaller forks were distributed and orders were taken for three different kinds of pie, written on small pads by Deborah's sisters, as if they were waitresses. After dessert, the dogs needed to go out, and Pranab Kaku volunteered to take them. "How about a walk on the beach?" he suggested, and Deborah's side of the family agreed that that was an excellent idea. None of the Bengalis wanted to go, preferring to sit with their tea and cluster together, at last, at one end of the room, speaking freely after the forced chitchat with the Americans during the meal. Matty came over and sat in the chair beside me that was now empty, encouraging me to join the walk. When I hesitated, pointing to my inappropriate clothes and shoes but also aware of my mother's silent fury at the sight of us together, he said, "I'm sure Deb can lend you something." So I went upstairs, where Deborah gave me a pair of her jeans and a thick sweater and some sneakers, so that I looked like her and her sisters.

She sat on the edge of her bed, watching me change, as if we were girlfriends, and she asked if I had a boyfriend. When I told her no, she said, "Matty thinks you're cute."

"He told you?"

"No, but I can tell."

As I walked back downstairs, emboldened by this information, in the jeans I'd had to roll up and in which I felt finally like myself, I noticed my mother lift her eyes from her teacup and stare at me, but she said nothing, and off I went, with Pranab Kaku and his dogs and his in-laws, along a road and then down some steep wooden steps to the water. Deborah and one of her sisters stayed behind, to begin the cleanup and see to the needs of those who remained. Initially, we all walked together, in a single row across the sand, but then I noticed Matty hanging back, and so the two of us trailed behind, the distance between us and the others increasing. We began flirting, talking of things I no longer remember, and eventually we wandered into a rocky inlet and Matty fished a joint out of his pocket. We turned our backs to the wind and smoked it, our cold fingers touching in the process, our lips pressed to the same damp section of the rolling paper. At first I didn't feel any effect, but then, listening to him talk about the band he was in, I was aware that his voice sounded miles away, and that I had the urge to laugh, even though what he was saying was not terribly funny. It felt as if we were apart from the group for hours, but when we wandered back to the sand we could still see them, walking out onto a rocky promontory to watch the sun set. It was dark by the time we all headed back to the house, and I dreaded seeing my parents while I was still high. But when we got there Deborah told me that my parents, feeling tired, had left, agreeing to let someone drive me home later. A fire had been lit and I was told to relax and have more pie as the leftovers were put away and the living room slowly put back in order. Of course, it was Matty who drove me home, and sitting in my parents' driveway I kissed him, at once thrilled and terrified that my mother might walk onto the lawn in her nightgown and discover us. I gave Matty my phone number, and for a few weeks I thought of him constantly, and hoped foolishly that he would call.

In the end, my mother was right, and fourteen years after that Thanksgiving, after twenty-three years of marriage, Pranab Kaku and Deborah got divorced. It was he who had strayed, falling in love with a married Bengali woman, destroying two families in the process. The other woman was someone my parents knew, though not very well. Deborah was in her forties by then, Bonny and Sara away at college. In her shock and grief, it was my mother whom Deborah turned to, calling and weeping into the phone. Somehow, through all the years, she had continued to regard us as quasi in-laws, sending flowers when my grandparents died, and giving me a compact edition of the O.E.D.[5] as a college-graduation present. "You knew him so well. How could he do something like this?" Deborah asked my mother. And then, "Did you know anything about it?" My mother answered truthfully that she did not. Their hearts had been broken by the same man, only my mother's had long ago mended, and in an odd way, as my parents approached their old age, she and my father had grown fond of each other, out of habit if nothing else. I believe my absence from the house, once I left for college, had something to do with this, because over the years, when I visited, I noticed a warmth between my parents that had not been there before, a quiet teasing,

5. Oxford English Dictionary.

a solidarity, a concern when one of them fell ill. My mother and I had also made peace; she had accepted the fact that I was not only her daughter but a child of America as well. Slowly, she accepted that I dated one American man, and then another, and then yet another, that I slept with them, and even that I lived with one though we were not married. She welcomed my boyfriends into our home and when things didn't work out she told me I would find someone better. After years of being idle, she decided, when she turned fifty, to get a degree in library science at a nearby university.

On the phone, Deborah admitted something that surprised my mother: that all these years she had felt hopelessly shut out of a part of Pranab Kaku's life. "I was so horribly jealous of you back then, for knowing him, understanding him in a way I never could. He turned his back on his family, on all of you, really, but I still felt threatened. I could never get over that." She told my mother that she had tried, for years, to get Pranab Kaku to reconcile with his parents, and that she had also encouraged him to maintain ties with other Bengalis, but he had resisted. It had been Deborah's idea to invite us to their Thanksgiving; ironically, the other woman had been there, too. "I hope you don't blame me for taking him away from your lives, Boudi. I always worried that you did."

My mother assured Deborah that she blamed her for nothing. She confessed nothing to Deborah about her own jealousy of decades before, only that she was sorry for what had happened, that it was a sad and terrible thing for their family. She did not tell Deborah that a few weeks after Pranab Kaku's wedding, while I was at a Girl Scout meeting and my father was at work, she had gone through the house, gathering up all the safety pins that lurked in drawers and tins, and adding them to the few fastened to her bracelets. When she'd found enough, she pinned them to her sari one by one, attaching the front piece to the layer of material underneath, so that no one would be able to pull the garment off her body. Then she took a can of lighter fluid and a box of kitchen matches and stepped outside, into our chilly back yard, which was full of leaves needing to be raked. Over her sari she was wearing a knee-length lilac trenchcoat, and to any neighbor she must have looked as though she'd simply stepped out for some fresh air. She opened up the coat and removed the tip from the can of lighter fluid and doused herself, then buttoned and belted the coat. She walked over to the garbage barrel behind our house and disposed of the fluid, then returned to the middle of the yard with the box of matches in her coat pocket. For nearly an hour she stood there, looking at our house, trying to work up the courage to strike a match. It was not I who saved her, or my father, but our next-door neighbor, Mrs. Holcomb, with whom my mother had never been particularly friendly. She came out to rake the leaves in her yard, calling out to my mother and remarking how beautiful the sunset was. "I see you've been admiring it for a while now," she said. My mother agreed, and then she went back into the house. By the time my father and I came home in the early evening, she was in the kitchen boiling rice for our dinner, as if it were any other day.

My mother told Deborah none of this. It was to me that she confessed, after my own heart was broken by a man I'd hoped to marry.

2004

# D. H. LAWRENCE
## *1885–1930*

 Lawrence was born in Eastwood, Nottingham-shire, England. His father was a coal miner, his mother a former schoolteacher whose thwarted life and fierce ambition for her son pushed him to struggle up into the world of culture. The anguish of this effort amid family tensions is the subject of the novel *Sons and Lovers* (1913), which established him as a major literary figure. Before World War I he eloped to the Continent with the wife of a Nottingham professor, but spent the war years miserably in England, suspected of dis-loyalty because his wife was of German origin, and oppressed by disgust at what was happening to his country. His distaste for the industrializa-tion and commercialism of English life in his time sent him wandering to Italy, Australia, Mexico, and the mountains of New Mexico in search of an alternative. As he continued to outrage the guardians of public morals—and to reply to them in many of his works with polemic attacks and warnings of the disasters they were brewing—he attracted both passionate disciples and the constant harassment of efforts to censor his books and paintings. His stature as prophet and critic of modern culture has always been a matter of controversy; his explorations of the dark strata of the unconscious, his shrewdly intuitive revisions of conventional notions of human motivation, and the vital energy of his style place him inarguably among the great poets and novelists of his age. Lawrence's life has inspired a flood of biographies; his remarkable marriage and his death by tuberculosis in the south of France seem hardly distinguishable from his creations in prose and verse. Some of his best-known novels are *The Rainbow* (1915), *Women in Love* (1920), and *Lady Chatterley's Lover* (1928). His shorter works and poems are most eas-ily found in *The Complete Stories* (1961), *Four Short Novels* (1965), and *Complete Poems* (1964).

## The Horse Dealer's Daughter

Well, Mabel, and what are you going to do with yourself?" asked Joe, with foolish flippancy. He felt quite safe himself. Without listening for an answer, he turned aside, worked a grain of tobacco to the tip of his tongue, and spat it out. He did not care about anything, since he felt safe himself.

The three brothers and the sister sat round the desolate breakfast-table, attempting some sort of desultory consultation. The morning's post had given the final tap to the family fortunes, and all was over. The dreary dining-room itself, with its heavy mahogany furniture, looked as if it were waiting to be done away with.

But the consultation amounted to nothing. There was a strange air of ineffectuality about the three men, as they sprawled at table, smoking and reflecting vaguely on their own condition. The girl was alone, a rather short, sullen-looking young woman of twenty-seven. She did not share the same life as her brothers. She would have been good-looking, save for the impressive fixity of her face, "bull-dog," as her brothers called it.

There was a confused tramping of horses' feet outside. The three men all sprawled round in their chairs to watch. Beyond the dark holly bushes that separated the strip of lawn from the high-road,[1] they could see a cavalcade of shire horses swinging out of their own yard, being taken for exercise. This was the last time. These were the last horses that would go through their hands. The young men watched with critical, callous look. They were all frightened at the collapse of their lives, and the sense of disaster in which they were involved left them no inner freedom.

Yet they were three fine, well-set fellows enough. Joe, the eldest, was a man of thirty-three, broad and handsome in a hot, flushed way. His face was red, he twisted his black moustache over a thick finger, his eyes were shallow and restless. He had a sensual way of uncovering his teeth when he laughed, and his bearing was stupid. Now he watched the horses with a glazed look of helplessness in his eyes, a certain stupor of downfall.

The great draught-horses swung past. They were tied head to tail, four of them, and they heaved along to where a lane branched off from the highroad, planting their great hoofs floutingly in the fine black mud, swinging their great rounded haunches sumptuously, and trotting a few sudden steps as they were led into the lane, round the corner. Every movement showed a massive, slumbrous strength, and a stupidity which held them in subjection. The groom at the head looked back, jerking the leading rope. And the cavalcade moved out of sight up the lane, the tail of the last horse, bobbed up tight and stiff, held out taut from the swinging great haunches as they rocked behind the hedges in a motion-like sleep.

Joe watched with glazed hopeless eyes. The horses were almost like his own body to him. He felt he was done for now. Luckily he was engaged to a woman as old as himself, and therefore her father, who was steward of a neighbouring estate, would provide him with a job. He would marry and go into harness. His life was over, he would be a subject animal now.

He turned uneasily aside, the retreating steps of the horses echoing in his ears. Then, with foolish restlessness, he reached for the scraps of bacon-rind from the plates, and making a faint whistling sound, flung them to the terrier that lay against the fender. He watched the dog swallow them, and waited till the creature looked into his eyes. Then a faint grin came on his face, and in a high, foolish voice he said:

"You won't get much more bacon, shall you, you little b——?"

The dog faintly and dismally wagged its tail, then lowered its haunches, circled round, and lay down again.

---

1. Highway.

There was another helpless silence at the table. Joe sprawled uneasily in his seat, not willing to go till the family conclave was dissolved. Fred Henry, the second brother, was erect, clean-limbed, alert. He had watched the passing of the horses with more *sang-froid*.[2] If he was an animal, like Joe, he was an animal which controls, not one which is controlled. He was master of any horse, and he carried himself with a well-tempered air of mastery. But he was not master of the situations of life. He pushed his coarse brown moustache upwards, off his lip, and glanced irritably at his sister, who sat impassive and inscrutable.

"You'll go and stop with Lucy for a bit, shan't you?" he asked. The girl did not answer.

"I don't see what else you can do," persisted Fred Henry.

"Go as a skivvy,"[3] Joe interpolated laconically.

The girl did not move a muscle.

"If I was her, I should go in for training for a nurse," said Malcolm, the youngest of them all. He was the baby of the family, a young man of twenty-two, with a fresh, jaunty *museau*.[4]

But Mabel did not take any notice of him. They had talked at her and round her for so many years, that she hardly heard them at all.

The marble clock on the mantelpiece softly chimed the half-hour, the dog rose uneasily from the hearth-rug and looked at the party at the breakfast-table. But still they sat in an ineffectual conclave.

"Oh, all right," said Joe suddenly, apropos of nothing. "I'll get a move on."

He pushed back his chair, straddled his knees with a downward jerk, to get them free, in horsey fashion, and went to the fire. Still he did not go out of the room; he was curious to know what the others would do or say. He began to charge his pipe, looking down at the dog and saying in a high, affected voice:

"Going wi' me? Going wi' me are ter? Tha'rt goin' further than tha counts on just now, dost hear?"[5]

The dog faintly wagged his tail, the man stuck out his jaw and covered his pipe with his hands, and puffed intently, losing himself in the tobacco, looking down all the while at the dog with an absent brown eye. The dog looked up at him in mournful distrust. Joe stood with his knees stuck out, in real horsey fashion.

"Have you had a letter from Lucy?" Fred Henry asked of his sister.

"Last week," came the neutral reply.

"And what does she say?"

There was no answer.

"Does she *ask* you to go and stop there?" persisted Fred Henry.

"She says I can if I like."

"Well, then, you'd better. Tell her you'll come on Monday."

This was received in silence.

"That's what you'll do then, is it?" said Fred Henry, in some exasperation.

But she made no answer. There was a silence of futility and irritation in the room. Malcolm grinned fatuously.

---

**2.** Literally, "cold blood," i.e., imperturbability (French).   **3.** Maid, scullion.   **4.** Face, mug (French).   **5.** That is, "Going with me? Going with me, are you? You are going further than you count on just now, do you hear?" The familiar form *thou* was used in provincial regions of England well into the 20th century.

"You'll have to make up your mind between now and next Wednesday," said Joe loudly, "or else find yourself lodgings on the kerbstone."

The face of the young woman darkened, but she sat on immutable.

"Here's Jack Ferguson!" exclaimed Malcolm, who was looking aimlessly out of the window.

"Where?" exclaimed Joe loudly.

"Just gone past."

"Coming in?"

Malcolm craned his neck to see the gate.

"Yes," he said.

There was a silence. Mabel sat on like one condemned, at the head of the table. Then a whistle was heard from the kitchen. The dog got up and barked sharply. Joe opened the door and shouted:

"Come on."

After a moment a young man entered. He was muffled up in overcoat and a purple woollen scarf, and his tweed cap, which he did not remove, was pulled down on his head. He was of medium height, his face was rather long and pale, his eyes looked tired.

"Hello, Jack! Well, Jack!" exclaimed Malcolm and Joe. Fred Henry merely said: "Jack."

"What's doing?" asked the newcomer, evidently addressing Fred Henry.

"Same. We've got to be out by Wednesday. Got a cold?"

"I have—got it bad, too."

"Why don't you stop in?"

"*Me* stop in? When I can't stand on my legs, perhaps I shall have a chance." The young man spoke huskily. He had a slight Scotch accent.

"It's a knock-out, isn't it," said Joe, boisterously, "if a doctor goes round croaking with a cold. Looks bad for the patients, doesn't it?"

The young doctor looked at him slowly.

"Anything the matter with *you*, then?" he asked sarcastically.

"Not as I know of. Damn your eyes, I hope not. Why?"

"I thought you were very concerned about the patients, wondered if you might be one yourself."

"Damn it, no, I've never been patient to no flaming doctor, and hope I never shall be," returned Joe.

At this point Mabel rose from the table, and they all seemed to become aware of her existence. She began putting the dishes together. The young doctor looked at her, but did not address her. He had not greeted her. She went out of the room with the tray, her face impassive and unchanged.

"When are you off then, all of you?" asked the doctor.

"I'm catching the eleven-forty," replied Malcolm. "Are you goin' down wi' th' trap, Joe?"

"Yes, I've told you I'm going down wi' th' trap,[6] haven't I?"

"We'd better be getting her in then. So long Jack, if I don't see you before I go," said Malcolm, shaking hands.

He went out, followed by Joe, who seemed to have his tail between his legs.

---

6. Light carriage.

"Well, this is the devil's own," exclaimed the doctor, when he was left alone with Fred Henry. "Going before Wednesday, are you?"

"That's the orders," replied the other.

"Where, to Northampton?"[7]

"That's it."

"The devil!" exclaimed Ferguson, with quiet chagrin.

And there was silence between the two.

"All settled up, are you?" asked Ferguson.

"About."

There was another pause.

"Well, I shall miss yer, Freddy, boy," said the young doctor.

"And I shall miss thee, Jack," returned the other.

"Miss you like hell," mused the doctor.

Fred Henry turned aside. There was nothing to say. Mabel came in again, to finish clearing the table.

"What are *you* going to do, then, Miss Pervin?" asked Ferguson. "Going to your sister's, are you?"

Mabel looked at him with her steady, dangerous eyes, that always made him uncomfortable, unsettling his superficial ease.

"No," she said.

"Well, what in the name of fortune *are* you going to do? Say what you mean to do," cried Fred Henry, with futile intensity.

But she only averted her head, and continued her work. She folded the white table-cloth, and put on the chenille cloth.

"The sulkiest bitch that ever trod!" muttered her brother.

But she finished her task with perfectly impassive face, the young doctor watching her interestedly all the while. Then she went out.

Fred Henry stared after her, clenching his lips, his blue eyes fixing in sharp antagonism, as he made a grimace of sour exasperation.

"You could bray her into bits, and that's all you'd get out of her," he said, in a small, narrowed tone.

The doctor smiled faintly.

"What's she *going* to do, then?" he asked.

"Strike me if *I* know!" returned the other.

There was a pause. Then the doctor stirred.

"I'll be seeing you tonight, shall I?" he said to his friend.

"Ay—where's it to be? Are we going over to Jessdale?"

"I don't know. I've got such a cold on me. I'll come round to the 'Moon and Stars', anyway."

"Let Lizzie and May miss their night for once, eh?"

"That's it—if I feel as I do now."

"All's one——"

The two young men went through the passage and down to the back door together. The house was large, but it was servantless now, and desolate. At the back was a small brick house-yard and beyond that a big square, graveled fine and red, and having stables on two sides. Sloping, dank, winter-dark fields stretched away on the open sides.

7. Capital of Nottinghamshire, county in the coal-producing north of England.

But the stables were empty. Joseph Pervin, the father of the family, had been a man of no education, who had become a fairly large horse dealer. The stables had been full of horses, there was a great turmoil and come-and-go of horses and of dealers and grooms. Then the kitchen was full of servants. But of late things had declined. The old man had married a second time, to retrieve his fortunes. Now he was dead and everything was gone to the dogs, there was nothing but debt and threatening.

For months, Mabel had been servantless in the big house, keeping the home together in penury for her ineffectual brothers. She had kept house for ten years. But previously it was with unstinted means. Then, however brutal and coarse everything was, the sense of money had kept her proud, confident. The men might be foul-mouthed, the women in the kitchen might have bad reputations, her brothers might have illegitimate children. But so long as there was money, the girl felt herself established, and brutally proud, reserved.

No company came to the house, save dealers and coarse men. Mabel had no associates of her own sex, after her sister went away. But she did not mind. She went regularly to church, she attended to her father. And she lived in the memory of her mother, who had died when she was fourteen, and whom she had loved. She had loved her father, too, in a different way, depending upon him, and feeling secure in him, until at the age of fifty-four he married again. And then she had set hard against him. Now he had died and left them all hopelessly in debt.

She had suffered badly during the period of poverty. Nothing, however, could shake the curious, sullen, animal pride that dominated each member of the family. Now, for Mabel, the end had come. Still she would not cast about her. She would follow her own way just the same. She would always hold the keys of her own situation. Mindless and persistent, she endured from day to day. Why should she think? Why should she answer anybody? It was enough that this was the end, and there was no way out. She need not pass any more darkly along the main street of the small town, avoiding every eye. She need not demean herself any more, going into the shops and buying the cheapest food. This was at an end. She thought of nobody, not even of herself. Mindless and persistent, she seemed in a sort of ecstasy to be coming nearer to her fulfilment, her own glorification, approaching her dead mother, who was glorified.

In the afternoon, she took a little bag, with shears and sponge and a small scrubbing-brush, and went out. It was a grey, wintry day, with saddened, dark green fields and an atmosphere blackened by the smoke of foundries not far off. She went quickly, darkly along the causeway, heeding nobody, through the town to the churchyard.

There she always felt secure, as if no one could see her, although as a matter of fact she was exposed to the stare of everyone who passed along under the churchyard wall. Nevertheless, once under the shadow of the great looming church, among the graves, she felt immune from the world, reserved within the thick churchyard wall as in another country.

Carefully she clipped the grass from the grave, and arranged the pinky white, small chrysanthemums in the tin cross. When this was done, she took an empty jar from a neighbouring grave, brought water, and carefully, most scrupulously sponged the marble headstone and the coping-stone.

It gave her sincere satisfaction to do this. She felt in immediate contact with the world of her mother. She took minute pains, went through the park in a state bordering on pure happiness, as if in performing this task she came into a subtle, intimate connection with her mother. For the life she followed here in the world was far less real than the world of death she inherited from her mother.

The doctor's house was just by the church. Ferguson, being a mere hired assistant, was slave to the country-side. As he hurried now to attend to the outpatients in the surgery, glancing across the graveyard with his quick eye, he saw the girl at her task at the grave. She seemed so intent and remote, it was like looking into another world. Some mystical element was touched in him. He slowed down as he walked, watching her as if spellbound.

She lifted her eyes, feeling him looking. Their eyes met. And each looked away again at once, each feeling, in some way, found out by the other. He lifted his cap and passed on down the road. There remained distinct in his consciousness, like a vision, the memory of her face, lifted from the tombstone in the churchyard, and looking at him with slow, large, portentous eyes. It *was* portentous, her face. It seemed to mesmerize him. There was a heavy power in her eyes which laid hold of his whole being, as if he had drunk some powerful drug. He had been feeling weak and done before. Now the life came back into him, he felt delivered from his own fretted, daily self.

He finished his duties at the surgery as quickly as might be, hastily filling up the bottles of the waiting people with cheap drugs. Then, in perpetual haste, he set off again to visit several cases in another part of his round, before tea-time. At all times he preferred to walk if he could, but particularly when he was not well. He fancied the motion restored him.

The afternoon was falling. It was grey, deadened, and wintry, with a slow, moist, heavy coldness sinking in and deadening all the faculties. But why should he think or notice? He hastily climbed the hill and turned across the dark green fields, following the black cinder-track. In the distance, across a shallow dip in the country, the small town was clustered like smouldering ash, a tower, a spire, a heap of low, raw, extinct houses. And on the nearest fringe of the town, sloping into the dip, was Oldmeadow, the Pervins' house. He could see the stables and the outbuildings distinctly, as they lay towards him on the slope. Well, he would not go there many more times! Another resource would be lost to him, another place gone: the only company he cared for in the alien, ugly little town he was losing. Nothing but work, drudgery, constant hastening from dwelling to dwelling among the colliers and the iron-workers. It wore him out, but at the same time he had a craving for it. It was a stimulant to him to be in the homes of the working people, moving, as it were, through the innermost body of their life. His nerves were excited and gratified. He could come so near, into the very lives of the rough, inarticulate, powerfully emotional men and women. He grumbled, he said he hated the hellish hole. But as a matter of fact it excited him, the contact with the rough, strongly-feeling people was a stimulant applied direct to his nerves.

Below Oldmeadow, in the green, shallow, soddened hollow of fields, lay a square, deep pond. Roving across the landscape, the doctor's quick eye detected a figure in black passing through the gate of the field, down towards the pond. He looked again. It would be Mabel Pervin. His mind suddenly became alive and attentive.

Why was she going down there? He pulled up on the path on the slope above, and stood staring. He could just make sure of the small black figure moving in the hollow of the failing day. He seemed to see her in the midst of such obscurity, that he was like a clairvoyant, seeing rather with the mind's eye than with ordinary sight. Yet he could see her positively enough, whilst he kept his eye attentive. He felt, if he looked away from her, in the thick, ugly falling dusk, he would lose her altogether.

He followed her minutely as she moved, direct and intent, like something transmitted rather than stirring in voluntary activity, straight down the field towards the pond. There she stood on the bank for a moment. She never raised her head. Then she waded slowly into the water.

He stood motionless as the small black figure walked slowly and deliberately towards the center of the pond, very slowly, gradually moving deeper into the motionless water, and still moving forward as the water got up to her breast. Then he could see her no more in the dusk of the dead afternoon.

"There!" he exclaimed. "Would you believe it?"

And he hastened straight down, running over the wet, soddened fields, pushing through the hedges, down into the depression of callous wintry obscurity. It took him several minutes to come to the pond. He stood on the bank, breathing heavily. He could see nothing. His eyes seemed to penetrate the dead water. Yes, perhaps that was the dark shadow of her black clothing beneath the surface of the water.

He slowly ventured into the pond. The bottom was deep, soft clay, he sank in, and the water clasped dead cold round his legs. As he stirred he could smell the cold, rotten clay that fouled up into the water. It was objectionable in his lungs. Still, repelled and yet not heeding, he moved deeper into the pond. The cold water rose over his thighs, over his loins, upon his abdomen. The lower part of his body was all sunk in the hideous cold element. And the bottom was so deeply soft and uncertain, he was afraid of pitching with his mouth underneath. He could not swim, and was afraid.

He crouched a little, spreading his hands under the water and moving them round, trying to feel for her. The dead cold pond swayed upon his chest. He moved again, a little deeper, and again, with his hands underneath, he felt all around under the water. And he touched her clothing. But it evaded his fingers. He made a desperate effort to grasp it.

And so doing he lost his balance and went under, horribly, suffocating in the foul earthy water, struggling madly for a few moments. At last, after what seemed an eternity, he got his footing, rose again into the air and looked around. He gasped, and knew he was in the world. Then he looked at the water. She had risen near him. He grasped her clothing, and drawing her nearer, turned to take his way to land again.

He went very slowly, carefully, absorbed in the slow progress. He rose higher, climbing out of the pond. The water was now only about his legs; he was thankful, full of relief to be out of the clutches of the pond. He lifted her and staggered onto the bank, out of the horror of wet, grey clay.

He laid her down on the bank. She was quite unconscious and running with water. He made the water come from her mouth, he worked to restore her. He did not have to work very long before he could feel the breathing begin again in her; she was breathing naturally. He worked a little longer. He could feel her live beneath his hands; she was coming back. He wiped her face, wrapped her in his overcoat, looked round into the dim, dark grey world, then lifted her and staggered down the bank and across the fields.

It seemed an unthinkably long way, and his burden so heavy he felt he would never get to the house. But at last he was in the stable-yard, and then in the house-yard. He opened the door and went into the house. In the kitchen he laid her down on the hearth-rug and called. The house was empty. But the fire was burning in the grate.

Then again he kneeled to attend to her. She was breathing regularly, her eyes were wide open and as if conscious, but there seemed something missing in her look. She was conscious in herself, but unconscious of her surroundings.

He ran upstairs, took blankets from a bed, and put them before the fire to warm. Then he removed her saturated, earthy-smelling clothing, rubbed her dry with a towel, and wrapped her naked in the blankets. Then he went into the dining-room, to look for spirits. There was a little whisky. He drank a gulp himself, and put some into her mouth.

The effect was instantaneous. She looked full into his face, as if she had been seeing him for some time, and yet had only just become conscious of him.

"Dr. Ferguson?" she said.

"What?" he answered.

He was divesting himself of his coat, intending to find some dry clothing upstairs. He could not bear the smell of the dead, clayey water, and he was mortally afraid for his own health.

"What did I do?" she asked.

"Walked into the pond," he replied. He had begun to shudder like one sick, and could hardly attend to her. Her eyes remained full on him, he seemed to be going dark in his mind, looking back at her helplessly. The shuddering became quieter in him, his life came back to him, dark and unknowing, but strong again.

"Was I out of my mind?" she asked, while her eyes were fixed on him all the time.

"Maybe, for the moment," he replied. He felt quiet, because his strength had come back. The strange fretful strain had left him.

"Am I out of my mind now?" she asked.

"Are you?" he reflected a moment. "No," he answered truthfully. "I don't see that you are." He turned his face aside. He was afraid now, because he felt dazed, and felt dimly that her power was stronger than his, in this issue. And she continued to look at him fixedly all the time. "Can you tell me where I shall find some dry things to put on?" he asked.

"Did you dive into the pond for me?" she asked.

"No," he answered. "I walked in. But I went in over head as well."

There was silence for a moment. He hesitated. He very much wanted to go upstairs to get into dry clothing. But there was another desire in him. And she seemed to hold him. His will seemed to have gone to sleep, and left him, standing there slack before her. But he felt warm inside himself. He did not shudder at all, though his clothes were sodden on him.

"Why did you?" she asked.

"Because I didn't want you to do such a foolish thing," he said.

"It wasn't foolish," she said, still gazing at him as she lay on the floor, with a sofa cushion under her head. "It was the right thing to do. *I* knew best, then."

"I'll go and shift these wet things," he said. But still he had not the power to move out of her presence, until she sent him. It was as if she had the life of his body in her hands, and he could not extricate himself. Or perhaps he did not want to.

Suddenly she sat up. Then she became aware of her own immediate condition. She felt the blankets about her, she knew her own limbs. For a moment it seemed as if her reason were going. She looked round, with wild eye, as if seeking something. He stood still with fear. She saw her clothing lying scattered.

"Who undressed me?" she asked, her eyes resting full and inevitable on his face.

"I did," he replied, "to bring you round."

For some moments she sat and gazed at him awfully, her lips parted.

"Do you love me, then?" she asked.

He only stood and stared at her, fascinated. His soul seemed to melt.

She shuffled forward on her knees, and put her arms round him, round his legs, as he stood there, pressing her breasts against his knees and thighs, clutching him with strange, convulsive certainty, pressing his thighs against her, drawing him to her face, her throat, as she looked up at him with flaring, humble eyes of transfiguration, triumphant in first possession.

"You love me," she murmured, in strange transport, yearning and triumphant and confident. "You love me. I know you love me, I know."

And she was passionately kissing his knees, through the wet clothing, passionately and indiscriminately kissing his knees, his legs, as if unaware of everything.

He looked down at the tangled wet hair, the wild, bare, animal shoulders. He was amazed, bewildered, and afraid. He had never thought of loving her. He had never wanted to love her. When he rescued her and restored her, he was a doctor, and she was a patient. He had had no single personal thought of her. Nay, this introduction of the personal element was very distasteful to him, a violation of his professional honour. It was horrible to have her there embracing his knees. It was horrible. He revolted from it, violently. And yet—and yet—he had not the power to break away.

She looked at him again, with the same supplication of powerful love, and that same transcendent, frightening light of triumph. In view of the delicate flame which seemed to come from her face like a light, he was powerless. And yet he had never intended to love her. He had never intended. And something stubborn in him could not give way.

"You love me," she repeated, in a murmur of deep, rhapsodic assurance. "You love me."

Her hands were drawing him, drawing him down to her. He was afraid, even a little horrified. For he had, really, no intention of loving her. Yet her hands were drawing him towards her. He put out his hand quickly to steady himself, and grasped her bare shoulder. A flame seemed to burn the hand that grasped her soft shoulder. He had no intention of loving her: his whole will was against his yielding. It was horrible. And yet wonderful was the touch of her shoulders, beautiful the shining of her face. Was she perhaps mad? He had a horror of yielding to her. Yet something in him ached also.

He had been staring away at the door, away from her. But his hand remained on her shoulder. She had gone suddenly very still. He looked down at her. Her eyes were now wide with fear, with doubt, the light was dying from her face, a shadow of terrible greyness was returning. He could not bear the touch of her eyes' question upon him, and the look of death behind the question.

With an inward groan he gave way, and let his heart yield towards her. A sudden gentle smile came on his face. And her eyes, which never left his face, slowly, slowly filled with tears. He watched the strange water rise in her eyes, like some slow fountain coming up. And his heart seemed to burn and melt away in his breast.

He could not bear to look at her any more. He dropped on his knees and caught her head with his arms and pressed her face against his throat. She was very still. His heart, which seemed to have broken, was burning with a kind of agony in his breast. And he felt her slow, hot tears wetting his throat. But he could not move.

He felt the hot tears wet his neck and the hollows of his neck, and he remained motionless, suspended through one of man's eternities. Only now it had become indispensable to him to have her face pressed close to him; he could never let her go again. He could never let her head go away from the close clutch of his arm. He wanted to remain like that for ever, with his heart hurting him in a pain that was also life to him. Without knowing, he was looking down on her damp, soft brown hair.

Then, as it were suddenly, he smelt the horrid stagnant smell of that water. And at the same moment she drew away from him and looked at him. Her eyes were wistful and unfathomable. He was afraid of them, and he fell to kissing her, not knowing what he was doing. He wanted her eyes not to have that terrible, wistful, unfathomable look.

When she turned her face to him again, a faint delicate flush was glowing, and there was again dawning that terrible shining of joy in her eyes, which really terrified him, and yet which he now wanted to see, because he feared the look of doubt still more.

"You love me?" she said, rather faltering.

"Yes." The word cost him a painful effort. Not because it wasn't true. But because it was too newly true, the *saying* seemed to tear open again his newly-torn heart. And he hardly wanted it to be true, even now.

She lifted her face to him, and he bent forward and kissed her on the mouth, gently, with the one kiss that is an eternal pledge. And as he kissed her his heart strained again in his breast. He never intended to love her. But now it was over. He had crossed over the gulf to her, and all that he had left behind had shrivelled and become void.

After the kiss, her eyes again slowly filled with tears. She sat still, away from him, with her face drooped aside, and her hands folded in her lap. The tears fell very slowly. There was complete silence. He too sat there motionless and silent on the hearth-rug. The strange pain of his heart that was broken seemed to consume him. That he should love her? That this was love! That he should be ripped open in this way! Him, a doctor! How they would all jeer if they knew! It was agony to him to think they might know.

In the curious naked pain of the thought he looked again to her. She was sitting there drooped into a muse. He saw a tear fall, and his heart flared hot. He saw for the first time that one of her shoulders was quite uncovered, one arm bare, he could see one of her small breasts; dimly, because it had become almost dark in the room.

"Why are you crying?" he asked, in an altered voice.

She looked up at him, and behind her tears the consciousness of her situation for the first time brought a dark look of shame to her eyes.

"I'm not crying, really," she said, watching him, half frightened.

He reached his hand, and softly closed it on her bare arm.

"I love you! I love you!" he said in a soft, low vibrating voice, unlike himself.

She shrank, and dropped her head. The soft, penetrating grip of his hand on her arm distressed her. She looked up at him.

"I want to go," she said. "I want to go and get you some dry things."

"Why?" he said. "I'm all right."

"But I want to go," she said. "And I want you to change your things."

He released her arm, and she wrapped herself in the blanket, looking at him rather frightened. And still she did not rise.

"Kiss me," she said wistfully.

He kissed her, but briefly, half in anger.

Then, after a second, she rose nervously, all mixed up in the blanket. He watched her in her confusion as she tried to extricate herself and wrap herself up so that she could walk. He watched her relentlessly, as she knew. And as she went, the blanket trailing, and as he saw a glimpse of her feet and her white leg, he tried to remember her as she was when he had wrapped her in the blanket. But then he didn't want to remember, because she had been nothing to him then, and his nature revolted from remembering her as she was when she was nothing to him.

A tumbling, muffled noise from within the dark house startled him. Then he heard her voice: "There are clothes." He rose and went to the foot of the stairs, and gathered up the garments she had thrown down. Then he came back to the fire, to rub himself down and dress. He grinned at his own appearance when he had finished.

The fire was sinking, so he put on coal. The house was now quite dark, save for the light of a street-lamp that shone in faintly from beyond the holly trees. He lit the gas with matches he found on the mantelpiece. Then he emptied the pockets of his own clothes, and threw all his wet things in a heap into the scullery. After which he gathered up her sodden clothes, gently, and put them in a separate heap on the copper-top in the scullery.

It was six o'clock on the clock. His own watch had stopped. He ought to go back to the surgery. He waited, and still she did not come down. So he went to the foot of the stairs and called:

"I shall have to go."

Almost immediately he heard her coming down. She had on her best dress of black voile, and her hair was tidy, but still damp. She looked at him—and in spite of herself, smiled.

"I don't like you in those clothes," she said.

"Do I look a sight?" he answered.

They were shy of one another.

"I'll make you some tea," she said.

"No, I must go."

"Must you?" And she looked at him again with the wide, strained, doubtful eyes. And again, from the pain of his breast, he knew how he loved her. He went and bent to kiss her, gently, passionately, with his heart's painful kiss.

"And my hair smells so horrible," she murmured in distraction. "And I'm so awful, I'm so awful! Oh no, I'm too awful." And she broke into bitter, heartbroken sobbing. "You can't want to love me, I'm horrible."

"Don't be silly, don't be silly," he said, trying to comfort her, kissing her, holding her in his arms. "I want you, I want to marry you, we're going to be married, quickly, quickly—to-morrow if I can."

But she only sobbed terribly, and cried:

"I feel awful. I feel awful. I feel I'm horrible to you."

"No, I want you, I want you," was all he answered, blindly, with that terrible intonation which frightened her almost more than her horror lest he should *not* want her.

1922

# URSULA K. LE GUIN
## b. 1929

Le Guin was born in Berkeley, California, to a writer/folklorist mother and an anthropologist father. She was educated at Radcliffe College and Columbia University and spent a year as a Fulbright student in Paris, where she married the historian Charles Le Guin. A fantastically prolific author, she has won an extraordinary number of science fiction prizes, and her thematically charged use of the medium and her detailed depictions of complex fictional societies caught the mood of readers of the 1970s and 1980s. Some of her novels are *A Wizard of Earthsea* (1968), *The Tombs of Atuan* (1971), *The Farthest Shore* (1972) (which comprise the Earthsea Trilogy), *The Left Hand of Darkness* (1969), *The Dispossessed* (1974), *Always Coming Home* (1985), *The Telling* (2000), *Gifts* (2004), *Powers* (2007), and *Lavinia* (2008). Some of her shorter works have been collected in *The Wind's Twelve Quarters* (1975), *Orsinian Tales* (1976), *The Birthday of the World* (2002), *Changing Planes* (2003), and *The Wild Girls* (2011).

# The Ones Who Walk Away from Omelas

### *(Variations on a Theme by William James)*[1]

With a clamor of bells that set the swallows soaring, the Festival of Summer came to the city Omelas, bright-towered by the sea. The rigging of the boats in harbor sparkled with flags. In the streets between houses with red roofs and painted walls, between old moss-grown gardens and under avenues of trees, past great parks and public buildings, processions moved. Some were decorous: old people in long stiff robes of mauve and grey, grave master workmen, quiet, merry women carrying their babies and chatting as they walked. In other streets the music beat faster, a shimmering of gong and tambourine, and the people went dancing, the procession was a dance. Children dodged in and out, their high calls rising like the swallows' crossing flights over the music and the singing. All the processions wound towards the north side of the city, where on the great water-meadow called the Green Fields boys and girls, naked in the bright air, with mud-stained feet and ankles and long, lithe arms, exercised their restive horses before the race. The horses wore no gear at all but a halter without bit. Their manes were braided with streamers of silver, gold, and green. They flared their nostrils and pranced and boasted

---

1. American philosopher and experimental psychologist (1842–1910).

to one another; they were vastly excited, the horse being the only animal who has adopted our ceremonies as his own. Far off to the north and west the mountains stood up half encircling Omelas on her bay. The air of morning was so clear that the snow still crowning the Eighteen Peaks burned with white-gold fire across the miles of sunlit air, under the dark blue of the sky. There was just enough wind to make the banners that marked the racecourse snap and flutter now and then. In the silence of the broad green meadows one could hear the music winding through the city streets, farther and nearer and ever approaching, a cheerful faint sweetness of the air that from time to time trembled and gathered together and broke out into the great joyous clanging of the bells.

Joyous! How is one to tell about joy? How describe the citizens of Omelas?

They were not simple folk, you see, though they were happy. But we do not say the words of cheer much any more. All smiles have become archaic. Given a description such as this one tends to make certain assumptions. Given a description such as this one tends to look next for the King, mounted on a splendid stallion and surrounded by his noble knights, or perhaps in a golden litter borne by great-muscled slaves. But there was no king. They did not use swords, or keep slaves. They were not barbarians. I do not know the rules and laws of their society, but I suspect that they were singularly few. As they did without monarchy and slavery, so they also got on without the stock exchange, the advertisement, the secret police, and the bomb. Yet I repeat that these were not simple folk, not dulcet shepherds, noble savages, bland utopians. They were not less complex than us. The trouble is that we have a bad habit, encouraged by pedants and sophisticates, of considering happiness as something rather stupid. Only pain is intellectual, only evil interesting. This is the treason of the artist: a refusal to admit the banality of evil and the terrible boredom of pain. If you can't lick 'em, join 'em. If it hurts, repeat it. But to praise despair is to condemn delight, to embrace violence is to lose hold of everything else. We have almost lost hold, we can no longer describe a happy man, nor make any celebration of joy. How can I tell you about the people of Omelas? They were not naïve and happy children—though their children were, in fact, happy. They were mature, intelligent, passionate adults whose lives were not wretched. O miracle! but I wish I could describe it better. I wish I could convince you. Omelas sounds in my words like a city in a fairy tale, long ago and far away, once upon a time. Perhaps it would be best if you imagined it as your own fancy bids, assuming it will rise to the occasion, for certainly I cannot suit you all. For instance, how about technology? I think that there would be no cars or helicopters in and above the streets; this follows from the fact that the people of Omelas are happy people. Happiness is based on a just discrimination of what is necessary, what is neither necessary nor destructive, and what is destructive. In the middle category, however—that of the unnecessary but undestructive, that of comfort, luxury, exuberance, etc.—they could perfectly well have central heating, subway trains, washing machines, and all kinds of marvelous devices not yet invented here, floating light-sources, fuelless power, a cure for the common cold. Or they could have none of that: it doesn't matter. As you like it. I incline to think that people from towns up and down the coast have been coming in to Omelas during the last days before the Festival on very fast little trains and double-decked trams, and that the train station of Omelas is actually the handsomest building in town, though plainer than the magnificent Farmers' Market. But even granted trains, I fear that Omelas so far strikes some of you as goody-goody. Smiles, bells, parades, horses, bleh. If so, please add an orgy. If an orgy would help, don't hesitate. Let us not, however, have temples from which issue beautiful nude priests and priestesses already half in ecstasy and ready to copulate with any man or woman, lover or stranger, who desires union with the deep godhead of the blood, although that was my first idea. But really it would be better not to have any temples in Omelas—at least, not manned temples. Religion yes, clergy no. Surely the beautiful nudes can just wander about, offering themselves like divine soufflés to the hunger of the needy and the rapture of the flesh. Let them join the processions. Let tambourines be struck above the copulations, and the glory of desire be proclaimed upon the gongs, and (a not unimportant point) let the offspring of these delightful rituals be beloved and looked after by all. One thing I know there is none of in Omelas is guilt. But what else should there be? I thought at first there were no drugs, but that is puritanical. For those who like it, the faint insistent sweetness of *drooz* may perfume the ways of the city, *drooz* which first brings a great lightness and brilliance to the mind and limbs, and then after some hours a dreamy languor, and wonderful visions at last of the very arcana and inmost secrets of the Universe, as well as exciting the pleasure of sex beyond all belief; and it is not habit-forming. For more modest tastes I think there ought to be beer. What else, what else belongs in the joyous city? The sense of victory, surely, the celebration of courage. But as we did without clergy, let us do without soldiers. The joy built upon successful slaughter is not the right kind of joy; it will not do; it is fearful and it is trivial. A boundless and generous contentment, a magnanimous triumph felt not against some outer enemy but in communion with the finest and fairest in the souls of all men everywhere and the splendor of the world's summer: this is what swells the hearts of the people of Omelas, and the victory they celebrate is that of life. I really don't think many of them need to take *drooz*.

Most of the processions have reached the Green Fields by now. A marvelous smell of cooking goes forth from the red and blue tents of the provisioners. The faces of small children are amiably sticky; in the benign grey beard of a man a couple of crumbs of rich pastry are entangled. The youths and girls have mounted their horses and are beginning to group around the starting line of the course. An old woman, small, fat, and laughing, is passing out flowers from a basket, and tall young men wear her flowers in their shining hair. A child of nine or ten sits at the edge of the crowd, alone, playing on a wooden flute. People pause to listen, and they smile, but they do not speak to him, for he never ceases playing and never sees them, his dark eyes wholly rapt in the sweet, thin magic of the tune.

He finishes, and slowly lowers his hands holding the wooden flute.

As if that little private silence were the signal, all at once a trumpet sounds from the pavilion near the starting line: imperious, melancholy, piercing. The horses rear on their slender legs, and some of them neigh in answer. Sober-faced, the young riders stroke the horses' necks and soothe them, whispering, "Quiet, quiet, there my beauty, my hope...." They begin to form in rank along the starting line. The crowds along the racecourse are like a field of grass and flowers in the wind. The Festival of Summer has begun.

Do you believe? Do you accept the festival, the city, the joy? No? Then let me describe one more thing.

In a basement under one of the beautiful public buildings of Omelas, or perhaps in the cellar of one of its more spacious private homes, there is a room. It has one locked door, and no window. A little light seeps in dustily between cracks in the boards, secondhand from a cobwebbed window somewhere across the cellar. In one corner of the little room a couple of mops, with stiff, clotted, foul-smelling heads, stand near a rusty bucket. The floor is dirt, a little damp to the touch, as cellar dirt usually is. The room is about three paces long and two wide: a mere broom closet or disused tool room. In the room a child is sitting. It could be a boy or a girl. It looks about six, but actually is nearly ten. It is feeble-minded. Perhaps it was born defective, or perhaps it has become imbecile through fear, malnutrition, and neglect. It picks its nose and occasionally fumbles vaguely with its toes or genitals, as it sits hunched in the corner farthest from the bucket and the two mops. It is afraid of the mops. It finds them horrible. It shuts its eyes, but it knows the mops are still standing there; and the door is locked; and nobody will come. The door is always locked; and nobody ever comes, except that sometimes—the child has no understanding of time or interval—sometimes the door rattles terribly and opens, and a person, or several people, are there. One of them may come in and kick the child to make it stand up. The others never come close, but peer in at it with frightened, disgusted eyes. The food bowl and the water jug are hastily filled, the door is locked, the eyes disappear. The people at the door never say anything, but the child, who has not always lived in the tool room, and can remember sunlight and its mother's voice, sometimes speaks. "I will be good," it says. "Please let me out. I will be good!" They never answer. The child used to scream for help at night, and cry a good deal, but now it only makes a kind of whining, "eh-haa, eh-haa," and it speaks less and less often. It is so thin there are no calves to its legs; its belly protrudes; it lives on a half-bowl of corn meal and grease a day. It is naked. Its buttocks and thighs are a mass of festered sores, as it sits in its own excrement continually.

They all know it is there, all the people of Omelas. Some of them have come to see it, others are content merely to know it is there. They all know that it has to be there. Some of them understand why, and some do not, but they all understand that their happiness, the beauty of their city, the tenderness of their friendships, the health of their children, the wisdom of their scholars, the skill of their makers, even the abundance of their harvest and the kindly weathers of their skies, depend wholly on this child's abominable misery.

This is usually explained to children when they are between eight and twelve, whenever they seem capable of understanding; and most of those who come to see the child are young people, though often enough an adult comes, or comes back, to see the child. No matter how well the matter has been explained to them, these young spectators are always shocked and sickened at the sight. They feel disgust, which they had thought themselves superior to. They feel anger, outrage, impotence, despite all the explanations. They would like to do something for the child. But there is nothing they can do. If the child were brought up into the sunlight out of the vile place, if it were cleaned and fed and comforted, that would be a good thing, indeed; but if it were done, in that day and hour all the prosperity and beauty and delight of Omelas would wither and be destroyed. Those are the terms. To exchange all the goodness and grace of every life in Omelas for that single, small improvement: to throw away the happiness of thousands for the chance of the happiness of one: that would be to let guilt within the walls indeed.

The terms are strict and absolute; there may not even be a kind word spoken to the child.

Often the young people go home in tears, or in a tearless rage, when they have seen the child and faced this terrible paradox. They may brood over it for weeks or years. But as time goes on they begin to realize that even if the child could be released, it would not get much good of its freedom: a little vague pleasure of warmth and food, no doubt, but little more. It is too degraded and imbecile to know any real joy. It has been afraid too long ever to be free of fear. Its habits are too uncouth for it to respond to humane treatment. Indeed, after so long it would probably be wretched without walls about it to protect it, and darkness for its eyes, and its own excrement to sit in. Their tears at the bitter injustice dry when they begin to perceive the terrible justice of reality, and to accept it. Yet it is their tears and anger, the trying of their generosity and the acceptance of their helplessness, which are perhaps the true source of the splendor of their lives. Theirs is no vapid, irresponsible happiness. They know that they, like the child, are not free. They know compassion. It is the existence of the child, and their knowledge of its existence, that makes possible the nobility of their architecture, the poignancy of their music, the profundity of their science. It is because of the child that they are so gentle with children. They know that if the wretched one were not there snivelling in the dark, the other one, the flute-player, could make no joyful music as the young riders line up in their beauty for the race in the sunlight of the first morning of summer.

Now do you believe in them? Are they not more credible? But there is one more thing to tell, and this is quite incredible.

At times one of the adolescent girls or boys who go to see the child does not go home to weep or rage, does not, in fact, go home at all. Sometimes also a man or woman much older falls silent for a day or two, and then leaves home. These people go out into the street, and walk down the street alone. They keep walking, and walk straight out of the city of Omelas, through the beautiful gates. They keep walking across the farmlands of Omelas. Each one goes alone, youth or girl, man or woman. Night falls; the traveler must pass down village streets, between the houses with yellow-lit windows, and on out into the darkness of the fields. Each alone, they go west or north, towards the mountains. They go on. They leave Omelas, they walk ahead into the darkness, and they do not come back. The place they go towards is a place even less imaginable to most of us than the city of happiness. I cannot describe it at all. It is possible that it does not exist. But they seem to know where they are going, the ones who walk away from Omelas.

1975

# KATHERINE MANSFIELD
## 1888–1923

Mansfield was born in Wellington, New Zealand. Though her intention in going to England at the end of her teens was to study music, there she made the acquaintance of literary people—among them D. H. Lawrence, who was for a while a close friend, and John Middleton Murry, whom she later married. Under their influence she began to write, first as a journalist and then as an innovative artist in the short story. Her first collection, *In a German Pension,* appeared in 1911. The impressionism of many of her stories has led to some comparisons with Chekhov, who was, in any case, an example on whom she meant to model her working life. Her persistent ill health and the death of a beloved brother in World War I were among the circumstances that darkened her personal life more than they influenced the temper of her fiction, which remained eager and venturesome. Her keen satire was often directed at the self-righteousness of the upper classes and the intelligentsia, at the complacencies insulating them from the realities of existence as experienced by ordinary people. *The Short Stories of Katherine Mansfield* was published in 1937 and her critical essays, *Novels and Novelists,* in 1930.

## The Garden Party

And after all the weather was ideal. They could not have had a more perfect day for a garden party if they had ordered it. Windless, warm, the sky without a cloud. Only the blue was veiled with a haze of light gold, as it is sometimes in early summer. The gardener had been up since dawn, mowing the lawns and sweeping them, until the grass and the dark flat rosettes where the daisy plants had been seemed to shine. As for the roses, you could not help feeling they understood that roses are the only flowers that impress people at garden parties; the only flowers that everybody is certain of knowing. Hundreds, yes, literally hundreds, had come out in a single night; the green bushes bowed down as though they had been visited by archangels.

Breakfast was not yet over before the men came to put up the marquee.

'Where do you want the marquee put, mother?'

'My dear child, it's no use asking me. I'm determined to leave everything to you children this year. Forget I am your mother. Treat me as an honoured guest.'

But Meg could not possibly go and supervise the men. She had washed her hair before breakfast, and she sat drinking her coffee in a green turban, with a dark wet curl stamped on each cheek. Jose, the butterfly, always came down in a silk petticoat and a kimono jacket.

'You'll have to go, Laura, you're the artistic one.'

Away Laura flew, still holding her piece of bread-and-butter. It's so delicious to have an excuse for eating out of doors, and besides, she loved having to arrange things; she always felt she could do it so much better than anybody else.

Four men in their shirt-sleeves stood grouped together on the garden path. They carried staves covered with rolls of canvas, and they had big tool-bags slung on their backs. They looked impressive. Laura wished now that she was not holding that piece of bread-and-butter, but there was nowhere to put it, and she couldn't possibly throw it away. She blushed and tried to look severe and even a little bit short-sighted as she came up to them.

'Good morning,' she said, copying her mother's voice. But that sounded so fearfully affected that she was ashamed, and stammered like a little girl, 'Oh—er—have you come—is it about the marquee?'

'That's right, miss,' said the tallest of the men, a lanky, freckled fellow, and he shifted his tool-bag, knocked back his straw hat and smiled down at her. 'That's about it.'

His smile was so easy, so friendly, that Laura recovered. What nice eyes he had, small, but such a dark blue! And now she looked at the others, they were smiling too. 'Cheer up, we won't bite,' their smile seemed to say. How very nice workmen were! And what a beautiful morning! She mustn't mention the morning; she must be business-like. The marquee.

'Well, what about the lily-lawn? Would that do?'

And she pointed to the lily-lawn with the hand that didn't hold the bread-and-butter. They turned, they stared in the direction. A little fat chap thrust out his under-lip, and the tall fellow frowned.

'I don't fancy it,' said he. 'Not conspicuous enough. You see, with a thing like a marquee,' and he turned to Laura in his easy way, 'you want to put it somewhere where it'll give you a bang slap in the eye, if you follow me.'

Laura's upbringing made her wonder for a moment whether it was quite respectful of a workman to talk to her of bangs slap in the eye. But she did quite follow him.

'A corner of the tennis-court,' she suggested. 'But the band's going to be in one corner.'

'H'm, going to have a band, are you?' said another of the workmen. He was pale. He had a haggard look as his dark eyes scanned the tennis-court. What was he thinking?

'Only a very small band,' said Laura gently. Perhaps he wouldn't mind so much if the band was quite small. But the tall fellow interrupted.

'Look here, miss, that's the place. Against those trees. Over there. That'll do fine.'

Against the karakas.[1] Then the karaka-trees would be hidden. And they were so lovely, with their broad, gleaming leaves, and their clusters of yellow fruit. They were like trees you imagined growing on a desert island, proud, solitary, lifting their leaves and fruits to the sun in a kind of silent splendour. Must they be hidden by a marquee?

---

1. A tree native to New Zealand.

They must. Already the men had shouldered their staves and were making for the place. Only the tall fellow was left. He bent down, pinched a sprig of lavender, put his thumb and forefinger to his nose and snuffed up the smell. When Laura saw the gesture she forgot all about the karakas in her wonder at him caring for things like that—caring for the smell of lavender. How many men that she knew would have done such a thing. Oh, how extraordinarily nice workmen were, she thought. Why couldn't she have workmen for friends rather than the silly boys she danced with and who came to Sunday night supper? She would get on much better with men like these.

It's all the fault, she decided, as the tall fellow drew something on the back of an envelope, something that was to be looped up or left to hang, of these absurd class distinctions. Well, for her part, she didn't feel them. Not a bit, not an atom. . . . And now there came the chock-chock of wooden hammers. Some one whistled, some one sang out, 'Are you right there, matey?' 'Matey!' The friendliness of it, the—the—Just to prove how happy she was, just to show the tall fellow how at home she felt, and how she despised stupid conventions, Laura took a big bite of her bread-and-butter as she stared at the little drawing. She felt just like a work-girl.

'Laura, Laura, where are you? Telephone, Laura!' a voice cried from the house.

'Coming!' Away she skimmed, over the lawn, up the path, up the steps, across the veranda, and into the porch. In the hall her father and Laurie were brushing their hats ready to go to the office.

'I say, Laura,' said Laurie very fast, 'you might just give a squiz at my coat before this afternoon. See if it wants pressing.'

'I will,' said she. Suddenly she couldn't stop herself. She ran at Laurie and gave him a small, quick squeeze. 'Oh, I do love parties, don't you?' gasped Laura.

'Ra-ther,' said Laurie's warm, boyish voice, and he squeezed his sister too, and gave her a gentle push. 'Dash off to the telephone, old girl.'

The telephone. 'Yes, yes; oh yes. Kitty? Good morning, dear. Come to lunch? Do, dear. Delighted of course. It will only be a very scratch meal—just the sandwich crusts and broken meringue-shells and what's left over. Yes, isn't it a perfect morning? Your white? Oh, I certainly should. One moment—hold the line. Mother's calling.' And Laura sat back. 'What, mother? Can't hear.'

Mrs Sheridan's voice floated down the stairs. 'Tell her to wear that sweet hat she had on last Sunday.'

'Mother says you're to wear that *sweet* hat you had on last Sunday. Good. One o'clock. Bye-bye.'

Laura put back the receiver, flung her arms over her head, took a deep breath, stretched and let them fall. 'Huh,' she sighed, and the moment after the sigh she sat up quickly. She was still, listening. All the doors in the house seemed to be open. The house was alive with soft, quick steps and running voices. The green baize door that led to the kitchen regions swung open and shut with a muffled thud. And now there came a long, chuckling absurd sound. It was the heavy piano being moved on its stiff castors. But the air! If you stopped to notice, was the air always like this? Little faint winds were playing chase in at the tops of the windows, out at the doors. And there were two tiny spots of sun, one on the inkpot, one on a silver photograph frame, playing too. Darling little spots. Especially the one on the inkpot lid. It was quite warm. A warm little silver star. She could have kissed it.

The front door bell pealed, and there sounded the rustle of Sadie's print skirt on the stairs. A man's voice murmured. Sadie answered, careless, 'I'm sure I don't know. Wait. I'll ask Mrs Sheridan.'

'What is it, Sadie?' Laura came into the hall.

'It's the florist, Miss Laura.'

It was, indeed. There, just inside the door, stood a wide, shallow tray full of pots of pink lilies. No other kind. Nothing but lilies—canna lilies, big pink flowers, wide open, radiant, almost frighteningly alive on bright crimson stems.

'O-oh, Sadie!' said Laura, and the sound was like a little moan. She crouched down as if to warm herself at that blaze of lilies; she felt they were in her fingers, on her lips, growing in her breast.

'It's some mistake,' she said faintly. 'Nobody ever ordered so many. Sadie, go and find mother.'

But at that moment Mrs Sheridan joined them.

'It's quite right,' she said calmly. 'Yes, I ordered them. Aren't they lovely?' She pressed Laura's arm. 'I was passing the shop yesterday, and I saw them in the window. And I suddenly thought for once in my life I shall have enough canna lilies. The garden party will be a good excuse.'

'But I thought you said you didn't mean to interfere,' said Laura. Sadie had gone. The florist's man was still outside at his van. She put her arm round her mother's neck and gently, very gently, she bit her mother's ear.

'My darling child, you wouldn't like a logical mother, would you? Don't do that. Here's the man.'

He carried more lilies still, another whole tray.

'Bank them up, just inside the door, on both sides of the porch, please,' said Mrs Sheridan. 'Don't you agree, Laura?'

'Oh, I *do*, mother.'

In the drawing-room Meg, Jose and good little Hans had at last succeeded in moving the piano.

'Now, if we put this chesterfield against the wall and move everything out of the room except the chairs, don't you think?'

'Quite.'

'Hans, move these tables into the smoking-room, and bring a sweeper to take these marks off the carpet and—one moment, Hans—' Jose loved giving orders to the servants, and they loved obeying her. She always made them feel they were taking part in some drama. 'Tell mother and Miss Laura to come here at once.'

'Very good, Miss Jose.'

She turned to Meg. 'I want to hear what the piano sounds like, just in case I'm asked to sing this afternoon. Let's try over "This Life is Weary".'

*Pom!* Ta-ta-ta *Tee*-ta! The piano burst out so passionately that Jose's face changed. She clasped her hands. She looked mournfully and enigmatically at her mother and Laura as they came in.

> This Life is *Wee*-ary,
> A Tear—a Sigh.
> A Love that *Chan*-ges,
> This Life is *Wee*-ary,
> A Tear—a Sigh.

> A Love that *Chan*-ges,
> And then . . . Good-bye!

But at the word 'Good-bye', and although the piano sounded more desperate than ever, her face broke into a brilliant, dreadfully unsympathetic smile. 'Aren't I in good voice, mummy?' she beamed.

> This Life is *Wee*-ary,
> Hope comes to Die.
> A Dream—a *Wa*-kening.

But now Sadie interrupted them. 'What is it, Sadie?'

'If you please, m'm, cook says have you got the flags for the sandwiches?'

'The flags for the sandwiches, Sadie?' echoed Mrs Sheridan dreamily. And the children knew by her face that she hadn't got them. 'Let me see.' And she said to Sadie firmly, 'Tell cook I'll let her have them in ten minutes.'

Sadie went.

'Now, Laura,' said her mother quickly, 'come with me into the smoking-room. I've got the names somewhere on the back of an envelope. You'll have to write them out for me. Meg, go upstairs this minute and take that wet thing off your head. Jose, run and finish dressing this instant. Do you hear me, children, or shall I have to tell your father when he comes home to-night? And—and, Jose, pacify cook if you do go into the kitchen, will you? I'm terrified of her this morning.'

The envelope was found at last behind the dining-room clock, though how it had got there Mrs Sheridan could not imagine.

'One of you children must have stolen it out of my bag, because I remember vividly—cream-cheese and lemon-curd. Have you done that?'

'Yes.'

'Egg and—' Mrs Sheridan held the envelope away from her. 'It looks like mice. It can't be mice, can it?'

'Olive, pet,' said Laura, looking over her shoulder.

'Yes, of course, olive. What a horrible combination it sounds. Egg and olive.'

They were finished at last, and Laura took them off to the kitchen. She found Jose there pacifying the cook, who did not look at all terrifying.

'I have never seen such exquisite sandwiches,' said Jose's rapturous voice. 'How many kinds did you say there were, cook? Fifteen?'

'Fifteen, Miss Jose.'

'Well, cook, I congratulate you.'

Cook swept up crusts with the long sandwich knife, and smiled broadly.

'Godber's has come,' announced Sadie, issuing out of the pantry. She had seen the man pass the window.

That meant the cream puffs had come. Godber's were famous for their cream puffs. Nobody ever thought of making them at home.

'Bring them in and put them on the table, my girl,' ordered cook.

Sadie brought them in and went back to the door. Of course Laura and Jose were far too grown-up to really care about such things. All the same, they couldn't help agreeing that the puffs looked very attractive. Very. Cook began arranging them, shaking off the extra icing sugar.

'Don't they carry one back to all one's parties?' said Laura.

'I suppose they do,' said practical Jose, who never liked to be carried back. 'They look beautifully light and feathery, I must say.'

'Have one each, my dears,' said cook in her comfortable voice. 'Yer ma won't know.'

Oh, impossible. Fancy cream puffs so soon after breakfast. The very idea made one shudder. All the same, two minutes later Jose and Laura were licking their fingers with that absorbed inward look that only comes from whipped cream.

'Let's go into the garden, out by the back way,' suggested Laura. 'I want to see how the men are getting on with the marquee. They're such awfully nice men.'

But the back door was blocked by cook, Sadie, Godber's man and Hans. Something had happened.

'Tuk-tuk-tuk,' clucked cook like an agitated hen. Sadie had her hand clapped to her cheek as though she had toothache. Hans's face was screwed up in the effort to understand. Only Godber's man seemed to be enjoying himself; it was his story.

'What's the matter? What's happened?'

'There's been a horrible accident,' said cook. 'A man killed.'

'A man killed! Where? How? When?'

But Godber's man wasn't going to have his story snatched from under his very nose.

'Know those little cottages just below here, miss?' Know them? Of course, she knew them. 'Well, there's a young chap living there, name of Scott, a carter. His horse shied at a traction-engine, corner of Hawke Street this morning, and he was thrown out on the back of his head. Killed.'

'Dead!' Laura stared at Godber's man.

'Dead when they picked him up,' said Godber's man with relish. 'They were taking the body home as I come up here.' And he said to the cook, 'He's left a wife and five little ones.'

'Jose, come here.' Laura caught hold of her sister's sleeve and dragged her through the kitchen to the other side of the green baize door. There she paused and leaned against it. 'Jose!' she said, horrified, 'however are we going to stop everything?'

'Stop everything, Laura!' cried Jose in astonishment. 'What do you mean?'

'Stop the garden party, of course.' Why did Jose pretend?

But Jose was still more amazed. 'Stop the garden party? My dear Laura, don't be so absurd. Of course we can't do anything of the kind. Nobody expects us to. Don't be so extravagant.'

'But we can't possibly have a garden party with a man dead just outside the front gate.'

That really was extravagant, for the little cottages were in a lane to themselves at the very bottom of a steep rise that led up to the house. A broad road ran between. True, they were far too near. They were the greatest possible eyesore, and they had no right to be in that neighbourhood at all. They were little mean dwellings painted a chocolate brown. In the garden patches there was nothing but cabbage stalks, sick hens and tomato cans. The very smoke coming out of their chimneys was poverty-stricken. Little rags and shreds of smoke, so unlike the great silvery plumes that uncurled from the Sheridans' chimneys. Washerwomen lived in the lane and sweeps and a cobbler, and a man whose house-front was studded all over with minute bird-cages. Children swarmed. When the Sheridans were little they were forbidden to set foot there because of the revolting language and of what they might catch. But since they were grown up, Laura and Laurie on their prowls sometimes walked through. It was disgusting and sordid. They came out with a shudder. But still one must go everywhere; one must see everything. So through they went.

'And just think of what the band would sound like to that poor woman,' said Laura.

'Oh, Laura!' Jose began to be seriously annoyed. 'If you're going to stop a band playing every time some one has an accident, you'll lead a very strenuous life. I'm every bit as sorry about it as you. I feel just as sympathetic.' Her eyes hardened. She looked at her sister just as she used to when they were little and fighting together. 'You won't bring a drunken workman back to life by being sentimental,' she said softly.

'Drunk! Who said he was drunk?' Laura turned furiously on Jose. She said just as they had used to say on those occasions, 'I'm going straight up to tell mother.'

'Do, dear,' cooed Jose.

'Mother, can I come into your room?' Laura turned the big glass door-knob.

'Of course, child. Why, what's the matter? What's given you such a colour?' And Mrs Sheridan turned round from her dressing-table. She was trying on a new hat.

'Mother, a man's been killed,' began Laura.

'Not in the garden?' interrupted her mother.

'No, no!'

'Oh, what a fright you gave me!' Mrs Sheridan sighed with relief, and took off the big hat and held it on her knees.

'But listen, mother,' said Laura. Breathless, half-choking, she told the dreadful story. 'Of course, we can't have our party, can we?' she pleaded. 'The band and everybody arriving. They'd hear us, mother; they're nearly neighbours!'

To Laura's astonishment her mother behaved just like Jose; it was harder to bear because she seemed amused. She refused to take Laura seriously.

'But, my dear child, use your common sense. It's only by accident we've heard of it. If some one had died there normally—and I can't understand how they keep alive in those poky little holes—we should still be having our party, shouldn't we?'

Laura had to say 'yes' to that, but she felt it was all wrong. She sat down on her mother's sofa and pinched the cushion frill.

'Mother, isn't it really terribly heartless of us?' she asked.

'Darling!' Mrs Sheridan got up and came over to her, carrying the hat. Before Laura could stop her she had popped it on. 'My child!' said her mother, 'the hat is yours. It's made for you. It's much too young for me. I have never seen you look such a picture. Look at yourself!' And she held up her hand-mirror.

'But, mother,' Laura began again. She couldn't look at herself; she turned aside.

This time Mrs Sheridan lost patience just as Jose had done.

'You are being very absurd, Laura,' she said coldly. 'People like that don't expect sacrifices from us. And it's not very sympathetic to spoil everybody's enjoyment as you're doing now.'

'I don't understand,' said Laura, and she walked quickly out of the room into her own bedroom. There, quite by chance, the first thing she saw was this charming girl in the mirror, in her black hat trimmed with gold daisies, and a long black velvet ribbon. Never had she imagined she could look like that. Is mother right? she thought. And now she hoped her mother was right. Am I being extravagant? Perhaps it was extravagant. Just for a moment she had another glimpse of that poor woman and those little children, and the body being carried into the house. But it all seemed blurred, unreal, like a picture in the newspaper. I'll remember it again after the party's over, she decided. And somehow that seemed quite the best plan. . . .

Lunch was over by half-past one. By half-past two they were all ready for the fray. The green-coated band had arrived and was established in a corner of the tennis-court.

'My dear!' trilled Kitty Maitland, 'aren't they too like frogs for words? You ought to have arranged them round the pond with the conductor in the middle on a leaf.'

Laurie arrived and hailed them on his way to dress. At the sight of him Laura remembered the accident again. She wanted to tell him. If Laurie agreed with the others, then it was bound to be all right. And she followed him into the hall.

'Laurie!'

'Hallo!' He was half-way upstairs, but when he turned round and saw Laura he suddenly puffed out his cheeks and goggled his eyes at her. 'My word, Laura! You do look stunning,' said Laurie. 'What an absolutely topping hat!'

Laura said faintly 'Is it?' and smiled up at Laurie, and didn't tell him after all.

Soon after that people began coming in streams. The band struck up; the hired waiters ran from the house to the marquee. Wherever you looked there were couples strolling, bending to the flowers, greeting, moving on over the lawn. They were like bright birds that had alighted in the Sheridans' garden for this one afternoon, on their way to—where? Ah, what happiness it is to be with people who all are happy, to press hands, press cheeks, smile into eyes.

'Darling Laura, how well you look!'

'What a becoming hat, child!'

'Laura, you look quite Spanish. I've never seen you look so striking.'

And Laura, glowing, answered softly, 'Have you had tea? Won't you have an ice? The passion-fruit ices really are rather special.' She ran to her father and begged him. 'Daddy darling, can't the band have something to drink?'

And the perfect afternoon slowly ripened, slowly faded, slowly its petals closed.

'Never a more delightful garden party. . . .' 'The greatest success. . . .' 'Quite the most. . . .'

Laura helped her mother with the good-byes. They stood side by side in the porch till it was all over.

'All over, all over, thank heaven,' said Mrs Sheridan. 'Round up the others, Laura. Let's go and have some fresh coffee. I'm exhausted. Yes, it's been very successful. But oh, these parties, these parties! Why will you children insist on giving parties!' And they all of them sat down in the deserted marquee.

'Have a sandwich, daddy dear. I wrote the flag.'

'Thanks.' Mr Sheridan took a bite and the sandwich was gone. He took another. 'I suppose you didn't hear of a beastly accident that happened to-day?' he said.

'My dear,' said Mrs Sheridan, holding up her hand, 'we did. It nearly ruined the party. Laura insisted we should put it off.'

'Oh, mother!' Laura didn't want to be teased about it.

'It was a horrible affair all the same,' said Mr Sheridan. 'The chap was married too. Lived just below in the lane, and leaves a wife and half a dozen kiddies, so they say.'

An awkward little silence fell. Mrs Sheridan fidgeted with her cup. Really, it was very tactless of father. . . .

Suddenly she looked up. There on the table were all those sandwiches, cakes, puffs, all un-eaten, all going to be wasted. She had one of her brilliant ideas.

'I know,' she said. 'Let's make up a basket. Let's send that poor creature some of this perfectly good food. At any rate, it will be the greatest treat for the children. Don't you agree? And she's sure to have neighbours calling in and so on. What a point to have it all ready prepared. Laura!' She jumped up. 'Get me the big basket out of the stairs cupboard.'

'But, mother, do you really think it's a good idea?' said Laura.

Again, how curious, she seemed to be different from them all. To take scraps from their party. Would the poor woman really like that?

'Of course! What's the matter with you to-day? An hour or two ago you were insisting on us being sympathetic, and now—'

Oh well! Laura ran for the basket. It was filled, it was heaped by her mother.

'Take it yourself, darling,' said she. 'Run down just as you are. No, wait, take the arum lilies too. People of that class are so impressed by arum lilies.'

'The stems will ruin her lace frock,' said practical Jose.

So they would. Just in time. 'Only the basket, then. And, Laura!'—her mother followed her out of the marquee—'don't on any account—'

'What mother?'

No, better not put such ideas into the child's head! 'Nothing! Run along.'

It was just growing dusky as Laura shut their garden gates. A big dog ran by like a shadow. The road gleamed white, and down below in the hollow the little cottages were in deep shade. How quiet it seemed after the afternoon. Here she was going down the hill to somewhere where a man lay dead, and she couldn't realize it. Why couldn't she? She stopped a minute. And it seemed to her that kisses, voices, tinkling spoons, laughter, the smell of crushed grass were somehow inside her. She had no room for anything else. How strange! She looked up at the pale sky, and all she thought was, 'Yes, it was the most successful party.'

Now the broad road was crossed. The lane began, smoky and dark. Women in shawls and men's tweed caps hurried by. Men hung over the palings; the children played in the doorways. A low hum came from the mean little cottages. In some of them there was a flicker of light, and a shadow, crab-like, moved across the window. Laura bent her head and hurried on. She wished now she had put on a coat. How her frock shone! And the big hat with the velvet streamer—if only it was another hat! Were the people looking at her? They must be. It was a mistake to have come; she knew all along it was a mistake. Should she go back even now?

No, too late. This was the house. It must be. A dark knot of people stood outside. Beside the gate an old, old woman with a crutch sat in a chair, watching. She had her feet on a newspaper. The voices stopped as Laura drew near. The group parted. It was as though she was expected, as though they had known she was coming here.

Laura was terribly nervous. Tossing the velvet ribbon over her shoulder, she said to a woman standing by, 'Is this Mrs Scott's house?' and the woman, smiling queerly, said, 'It is, my lass.'

Oh, to be away from this! She actually said, 'Help me, God,' as she walked up the tiny path and knocked. To be away from those staring eyes, or to be covered up in anything, one of those women's shawls even. I'll just leave the basket and go, she decided. I shan't even wait for it to be emptied.

Then the door opened. A little woman in black showed in the gloom.

Laura said, 'Are you Mrs Scott?' But to her horror the woman answered, 'Walk in, please, miss,' and she was shut in the passage.

'No,' said Laura, 'I don't want to come in. I only want to leave this basket. Mother sent—'

The little woman in the gloomy passage seemed not to have heard her. 'Step this way, please, miss,' she said in an oily voice, and Laura followed her.

She found herself in a wretched little low kitchen, lighted by a smoky lamp. There was a woman sitting before the fire.

'Em,' said the little creature who had let her in. 'Em! It's a young lady.' She turned to Laura. She said meaningly, 'I'm 'er sister, miss. You'll excuse 'er, won't you?'

'Oh, but of course!' said Laura. 'Please, please don't disturb her. I—I only want to leave—'

But at that moment the woman at the fire turned round. Her face, puffed up, red, with swollen eyes and swollen lips, looked terrible. She seemed as though she couldn't understand why Laura was there. What did it mean? Why was this stranger standing in the kitchen with a basket? What was it all about? And the poor face puckered up again.

'All right, my dear,' said the other. 'I'll thenk the young lady.'

And again she began. 'You'll excuse her, miss. I'm sure,' and her face, swollen too, tried an oily smile.

Laura only wanted to get out, to get away. She was back in the passage. The door opened. She walked straight through into the bedroom where the dead man was lying.

'You'd like a look at 'im, wouldn't you?' said Em's sister, and she brushed past Laura over to the bed. 'Don't be afraid, my lass,'—and now her voice sounded fond and sly, and fondly she drew down the sheet—' 'e looks a picture. There's nothing to show. Come along, my dear.'

Laura came.

There lay a young man, fast asleep—sleeping so soundly, so deeply, that he was far, far away from them both. Oh, so remote, so peaceful. He was dreaming. Never wake him up again. His head was sunk in the pillow, his eyes were closed; they were blind under the closed eyelids. He was given up to his dream. What did garden parties and baskets and lace frocks matter to him? He was far from all those things. He was wonderful, beautiful. While they were laughing and while the band was playing, this marvel had come to the lane. Happy ... happy. ... All is well, said that sleeping face. This is just as it should be. I am content.

But all the same you had to cry, and she couldn't go out of the room without saying something to him. Laura gave a loud childish sob.

'Forgive my hat,' she said.

And this time she didn't wait for Em's sister. She found her way out of the door, down the path, past all those dark people. At the corner of the lane she met Laurie.

He stepped out of the shadow. 'Is that you, Laura?'

'Yes.'

'Mother was getting anxious. Was it all right?'

'Yes, quite. Oh, Laurie!' She took his arm, she pressed up against him.

'I say, you're not crying, are you?' asked her brother.

Laura shook her head. She was.

Laurie put his arm round her shoulder. 'Don't cry,' he said in his warm, loving voice. 'Was it awful?'

'No,' sobbed Laura. 'It was simply marvellous. But, Laurie—' She stopped, she looked at her brother. 'Isn't life,' she stammered, 'isn't life—' But what life was she couldn't explain. No matter. He quite understood.

'*Isn't* it, darling?' said Laurie.

1921

# BOBBIE ANN MASON
*b. 1940*

Mason was born and grew up on her family's dairy farm near Mayfield, Kentucky. After studying journalism at the University of Kentucky, she moved to New York and wrote for *Movie Stars, Movie Life,* and *T.V. Star Parade.* She then earned a doctorate at the University of Connecticut and began teaching English. She has been awarded National Endowment for the Arts fellowships, has had stories in *Best American Short Stories* in 1981 and 1983, and won the Pushcart Prize for fiction in 1983. *Shiloh and Other Stories* (1982), her first collection, won the Ernest Hemingway Foundation Award. She has also written four novels, *In Country* (1985), *Feather Crowns* (1993), *An Atomic Romance* (2005), and *The Girl in the Blue Beret* (2011); a short novel, *Spence and Lila* (1988); and four more collections of short stories, *Love Life* (1989), *Midnight Magic* (1998), *Zigzagging Down a Wild Trail* (2001), and *Nancy Culpepper* (2006). Her memoir, *Clear Springs* (1999), was a finalist for the Pulitzer Prize.

# Shiloh

Leroy Moffitt's wife, Norma Jean, is working on her pectorals. She lifts three-pound dumbbells to warm up, then progresses to a twenty-pound barbell. Standing with her legs apart, she reminds Leroy of Wonder Woman.

"I'd give anything if I could just get these muscles to where they're real hard," says Norma Jean. "Feel this arm. It's not as hard as the other one."

"That's cause you're right-handed," says Leroy, dodging as she swings the barbell in an arc.

"Do you think so?"

"Sure."

Leroy is a truckdriver. He injured his leg in a highway accident four months ago, and his physical therapy, which involves weights and a pulley, prompted Norma Jean to try building herself up. Now she is attending a body-building class. Leroy has been collecting temporary disability since his tractor-trailer jackknifed in Missouri, badly twisting his left leg in its socket. He has a steel pin in his hip. He will probably not be able to drive his rig again. It sits in the backyard, like a gigantic bird that has flown home to roost. Leroy has been home in Kentucky for three months, and his leg is almost healed, but the accident frightened him and he does not want to drive any more long hauls. He is not sure what to do next. In the meantime, he makes things from craft kits. He started by building a miniature log cabin from notched Popsicle sticks. He varnished it and placed it on the TV set, where it remains. It reminds him of a rustic Nativity scene. Then he tried string art (sailing ships on black velvet), a macramé owl kit, a snap-together B-17 Flying Fortress,[1] and a lamp made out of a model truck, with a light fixture screwed in the top of the cab. At first the kits were diversions, something to kill time, but now he is thinking about building a full-scale log house from a kit. It would be considerably cheaper than building a regular house, and besides, Leroy has grown to appreciate how things are put together. He has begun to realize that in all the years he was on the road he never took time to examine anything. He was always flying past scenery.

"They won't let you build a log cabin in any of the new subdivisions," Norma Jean tells him.

"They will if I tell them it's for you," he says, teasing her. Ever since they were married, he has promised Norma Jean he would build her a new home one day. They have always rented, and the house they live in is small and nondescript. It does not even feel like a home, Leroy realizes now.

Norma Jean works at the Rexall drugstore, and she has acquired an amazing amount of information about cosmetics. When she explains to Leroy the three stages of complexion care, involving creams, toners, and moisturizers, he thinks happily of other petroleum products—axle grease, diesel fuel. This is a connection between him and Norma Jean. Since he has been home, he has felt unusually tender about his wife and guilty over his long absences. But he can't tell what she feels about him. Norma Jean has never complained about his traveling; she has never made hurt remarks, like calling his truck a "widow-maker." He is reasonably certain she has been faithful to him, but he wishes she would celebrate his permanent homecoming more happily. Norma Jean is often startled to find Leroy at home, and he thinks she seems a little disappointed about it. Perhaps he reminds her too much of the early days of their marriage, before he went on the road. They had a child who died as an infant, years ago. They never speak about their memories of Randy, which have almost faded, but now that Leroy is home all the time, they sometimes feel awkward around each other, and Leroy wonders if one of them should mention the child. He has the feeling that they are waking up out of a dream together—that they must create a new marriage, start afresh. They are lucky they are still married. Leroy has read that for most people losing a child destroys the marriage—or else he heard this on *Donahue*. He can't always remember where he learns things anymore.

At Christmas, Leroy bought an electric organ for Norma Jean. She used to play the piano when she was in high school. "It don't leave you," she told him once. "It's like riding a bicycle."

The new instrument had so many keys and buttons that she was bewildered by it at first. She touched the keys tentatively, pushed some buttons, then pecked out "Chopsticks." It came out in an amplified fox-trot rhythm, with marimba sounds.

"It's an orchestra!" she cried.

The organ had a pecan-look finish and eighteen preset chords, with optional flute, violin, trumpet, clarinet, and banjo accompaniments. Norma Jean

---

1. American World War II bomber.

mastered the organ almost immediately. At first she played Christmas songs. Then she bought *The Sixties Songbook* and learned every tune in it, adding variations to each with the rows of brightly colored buttons.

"I didn't like these old songs back then," she said. "But I have this crazy feeling I missed something."

"You didn't miss a thing," said Leroy.

Leroy likes to lie on the couch and smoke a joint and listen to Norma Jean play "Can't Take My Eyes Off You" and "I'll Be Back." He is back again. After fifteen years on the road, he is finally settling down with the woman he loves. She is still pretty. Her skin is flawless. Her frosted curls resemble pencil trimmings.

Now that Leroy has come home to stay, he notices how much the town has changed. Subdivisions are spreading across western Kentucky like an oil slick. The sign at the edge of town says "Pop: 11,500"—only seven hundred more than it said twenty years before. Leroy can't figure out who is living in all the new houses. The farmers who used to gather around the courthouse square on Saturday afternoons to play checkers and spit tobacco juice have gone. It has been years since Leroy has thought about the farmers, and they have disappeared without his noticing.

Leroy meets a kid named Stevie Hamilton in the parking lot at the new shopping center. While they pretend to be strangers meeting over a stalled car, Stevie tosses an ounce of marijuana under the front seat of Leroy's car. Stevie is wearing orange jogging shoes and a T-shirt that says CHATTAHOOCHEE SUPER-RAT. His father is a prominent doctor who lives in one of the expensive subdivisons in a new white-columned brick house that looks like a funeral parlor. In the phone book under his name there is a separate number, with the listing "Teenagers."

"Where do you get this stuff?" asks Leroy. "From your pappy!"

"That's for me to know and you to find out," Stevie says. He is slit-eyed and skinny.

"What else you got?"

"What you interested in?'

"Nothing special. Just wondered."

Leroy used to take speed on the road. Now he has to go slowly. He needs to be mellow. He leans back against the car and says, "I'm aiming to build me a log house, soon as I get time. My wife, though, I don't think she likes the idea."

"Well, let me know when you want me again," Stevie says. He has a cigarette in his cupped palm, as though sheltering it from the wind. He takes a long drag, then stomps it on the asphalt and slouches away.

Stevie's father was two years ahead of Leroy in high school. Leroy is thirty-four. He married Norma Jean when they were both eighteen, and their child Randy was born a few months later, but he died at the age of four months and three days. He would be about Stevie's age now. Norma Jean and Leroy were at the drive-in, watching a double feature (*Dr. Strangelove* and *Lover Come Back*),[2] and the baby was sleeping in the back seat. When the first movie ended, the baby was dead. It was the sudden infant death syndrome. Leroy remembers

---

2. Respectively, Stanley Kubrick's 1963 satire on nuclear war and a 1961 Rock Hudson–Doris Day romantic comedy.

handing Randy to a nurse at the emergency room, as though he were offering her a large doll as a present. A dead baby feels like a sack of flour. "It just happens sometimes," said the doctor, in what Leroy always recalls as a nonchalant tone. Leroy can hardly remember the child anymore, but he still sees vividly a scene from *Dr. Strangelove* in which the President of the United States was talking in a folksy voice on the hot line to the Soviet premier about the bomber accidentally headed toward Russia. He was in the War Room, and the world map was lit up. Leroy remembers Norma Jean catatonically beside him in the hospital and himself thinking: Who is this strange girl? He had forgotten who she was. Now scientists are saying that crib death is caused by a virus. Nobody knows anything, Leroy thinks. The answers are always changing.

When Leroy gets home from the shopping center, Norma Jean's mother, Mabel Beasley, is there. Until this year, Leroy has not realized how much time she spends with Norma Jean. When she visits, she inspects the closets and then the plants, informing Norma Jean when a plant is droopy or yellow. Mabel calls the plants "flowers," although there are never any blooms. She always notices if Norma Jean's laundry is piling up. Mabel is a short, overweight woman whose tight, brown-dyed curls look more like a wig than the actual wig she sometimes wears. Today she has brought Norma Jean an off-white dust ruffle she made for the bed; Mabel works in a custom-upholstery shop.

"This is the tenth one I made this year," Mabel says. "I got started and couldn't stop."

"It's real pretty," says Norma Jean.

"Now we can hide things under the bed," says Leroy, who gets along with his mother-in-law primarily by joking with her. Mabel has never really forgiven him for disgracing her by getting Norma Jean pregnant. When the baby died, she said that fate was mocking her.

"What's that thing?" Mabel says to Leroy in a loud voice, pointing to a tangle of yarn on a piece of canvas.

Leroy holds it up for Mabel to see. "It's my needlepoint," he explains. "This is a *Star Trek* pillow cover."

"That's what a woman would do," says Mabel. "Great day in the morning!"

"All the big football players on TV do it," he says.

"Why, Leroy, you're always trying to fool me. I don't believe you for one minute. You don't know what to do with yourself—that's the whole trouble. Sewing!"

"I'm aiming to build us a log house," says Leroy. "Soon as my plans come."

"Like *heck* you are," says Norma Jean. She takes Leroy's needlepoint and shoves it into a drawer. "You have to find a job first. Nobody can afford to build now anyway."

Mabel straightens her girdle and says, "I still think before you get tied down y'all ought to take a little run to Shiloh."

"One of these days, Mama," Norma Jean says impatiently.

Mabel is talking about Shiloh, Tennessee. For the past few years, she has been urging Leroy and Norma Jean to visit the Civil War battleground there.[3]

---

3. Site of an April 1862 Civil War battle between more than 100,000 Union and Confederate troops, a quarter of whom were killed. Shiloh put an end to the hopes of those, North and South, who had believed that the war would be brief and relatively bloodless.

Mabel went there on her honeymoon—the only real trip she ever took. Her husband died of a perforated ulcer when Norma Jean was ten, but Mabel, who was accepted into the United Daughters of the Confederacy in 1975, is still preoccupied with going back to Shiloh.

"I've been to kingdom come and back in that truck out yonder," Leroy says to Mabel, "but we never yet set foot in that battleground. Ain't that something? How did I miss it?"

"It's not even that far," Mabel says.

After Mabel leaves, Norma Jean reads to Leroy from a list she has made. "Things you could do," she announces. "You could get a job as a guard at Union Carbide, where they'd let you set on a stool. You could get on at the lumberyard. You could do a little carpenter work, if you want to build so bad. You could—"

"I can't do something where I'd have to stand up all day."

"You ought to try standing up all day behind a cosmetics counter. It's amazing that I have strong feet, coming from two parents that never had strong feet at all." At the moment Norma Jean is holding on to the kitchen counter, raising her knees one at a time as she talks. She is wearing two-pound ankle weights.

"Don't worry," says Leroy. "I'll do something."

"You could truck calves to slaughter for somebody. You wouldn't have to drive any big old truck for that."

"I'm going to build you this house," says Leroy. "I want to make you a real home."

"I don't want to live in any log cabin."

"It's not a cabin. It's a house."

"I don't care. It looks like a cabin."

"You and me together could lift those logs. It's just like lifting weights."

Norma Jean doesn't answer. Under her breath, she is counting. Now she is marching through the kitchen. She is doing goose steps.

Before his accident, when Leroy came home he used to stay in the house with Norma Jean, watching TV in bed and playing cards. She would cook fried chicken, picnic ham, chocolate pie—all his favorites. Now he is home alone much of the time. In the mornings, Norma Jean disappears, leaving a cooling place in the bed. She eats a cereal called Body Buddies, and she leaves the bowl on the table, with soggy tan balls floating in a milk puddle. He sees things about Norma Jean that he never realized before. When she chops onions, she stares off into a corner, as if she can't bear to look. She puts on her house slippers almost precisely at nine o'clock every evening and nudges her jogging shoes under the couch. She saves bread heels for the birds. Leroy watches the birds at the feeder. He notices the peculiar way goldfinches fly past the window. They close their wings, then fall, then spread their wings to catch and lift themselves. He wonders if they close their eyes when they fall. Norma Jean closes her eyes when they are in bed. She wants the lights turned out. Even then, he is sure she closes her eyes.

He goes for long drives around town. He tends to drive a car rather carelessly. Power steering and an automatic shift make a car feel so small and inconsequential that his body is hardly involved in the driving process. His injured leg stretches out comfortably. Once or twice he has almost hit something, but even the prospect of an accident seems minor in a car. He cruises the new subdivisions, feeling like a criminal rehearsing for a robbery. Norma Jean is probably right about a log house being inappropriate here in the new subdivisions. All the houses look grand and complicated. They depress him.

One day when Leroy comes home from a drive he finds Norma Jean in tears. She is in the kitchen making a potato and mushroom-soup casserole, with grated-cheese topping. She is crying because her mother caught her smoking.

"I didn't hear her coming. I was standing here puffing away pretty as you please," Norma Jean says, wiping her eyes.

"I knew it would happen sooner or later," says Leroy, putting his arm around her.

"She don't know the meaning of the word 'knock,'" says Norma Jean. "It's a wonder she hadn't caught me years ago."

"Think of it this way," Leroy says. "What if she caught me with a joint?"

"You better not let her!" Norma Jean shrieks. "I'm warning you, Leroy Moffitt!"

"I'm just kidding. Here, play me a tune. That'll help you relax."

Norma Jean puts the casserole in the oven and sets the timer. Then she plays a ragtime tune, with horns and banjo, as Leroy lights up a joint and lies on the couch, laughing to himself about Mabel's catching him at it. He thinks of Stevie Hamilton—a doctor's son pushing grass. Everything is funny. The whole town seems crazy and small. He is reminded of Virgil Mathis, a boastful policeman Leroy used to shoot pool with. Virgil recently led a drug bust in a back room at a bowling alley, where he seized ten thousand dollars' worth of marijuana. The newspaper had a picture of him holding up the bags of grass and grinning widely. Right now, Leroy can imagine Virgil breaking down the door and arresting him with a lungful of smoke. Virgil would probably have been alerted to the scene because of all the racket Norma Jean is making. Now she sounds like a hard-rock band. Norma Jean is terrific. When she switches to a latin-rhythm version of "Sunshine Superman," Leroy hums along. Norma Jean's foot goes up and down, up and down.

"Well, what do you think?" Leroy says, when Norma Jean pauses to search through her music.

"What do I think about what?"

His mind has gone blank. Then he says, "I'll sell my rig and build us a house." That wasn't what he wanted to say. He wanted to know what she thought—what she *really* thought—about them.

"Don't start in on that again," says Norma Jean. She begins playing "Who'll Be the Next in Line?"

Leroy used to tell hitchhikers his whole life story—about his travels, his hometown, the baby. He would end with a question: "Well, what do you think?" It was just a rhetorical question. In time, he had the feeling that he'd been telling the same story over and over to the same hitchhikers. He quit talking to hitchhikers when he realized how his voice sounded—whining and self-pitying, like some teenage-tragedy song. Now Leroy has the sudden impulse to tell Norma Jean about himself, as if he had just met her. They have known each other so long they have forgotten a lot about each other. They could become reacquainted. But when the oven timer goes off and she runs to the kitchen, he forgets why he wants to do this.

The next day, Mabel drops by. It is Saturday and Norma Jean is cleaning. Leroy is studying the plans of his log house, which have finally come in the mail. He has them spread out on the table—big sheets of stiff blue paper, with diagrams and numbers printed in white. While Norma Jean runs the vacuum, Mabel drinks coffee. She sets her coffee cup on a blueprint.

"I'm just waiting for time to pass," she says to Leroy, drumming her fingers on the table.

As soon as Norma Jean switches off the vacuum, Mabel says in a loud voice, "Did you hear about the datsun dog that killed the baby?"

Norma Jean says, "The word is 'dachshund.'"

"They put the dog on trial. It chewed the baby's legs off. The mother was in the next room all the time." She raises her voice. "They thought it was neglect."

Norma Jean is holding her ears. Leroy manages to open the refrigerator and get some Diet Pepsi to offer Mabel. Mabel still has some coffee and she waves away the Pepsi.

"Datsuns are like that," Mabel says. "They're jealous dogs. They'll tear a place to pieces if you don't keep an eye on them."

"You better watch out what you're saying, Mabel," says Leroy.

"Well, facts is facts."

Leroy looks out the window at his rig. It is like a huge piece of furniture gathering dust in the backyard. Pretty soon it will be an antique. He hears the vacuum cleaner. Norma Jean seems to be cleaning the living room rug again.

Later, she says to Leroy, "She just said that about the baby because she caught me smoking. She's trying to pay me back."

"What are you talking about?" Leroy says, nervously shuffling blueprints.

"You know good and well," Norma Jean says. She is sitting in a kitchen chair with her feet up and her arms wrapped around her knees. She looks small and helpless. She says, "The very idea, her bringing up a subject like that! Saying it was neglect."

"She didn't mean that," Leroy says.

"She might not have *thought* she meant it. She always says things like that. You don't know how she goes on."

"But she didn't really mean it. She was just talking."

Leroy opens a king-sized bottle of beer and pours it into two glasses, dividing it carefully. He hands a glass to Norma Jean and she takes it from him mechanically. For a long time, they sit by the kitchen window watching the birds at the feeder.

Something is happening. Norma Jean is going to night school. She has graduated from her six-week body-building course and now she is taking an adult-education course in composition at Paducah Community College. She spends her evenings outlining paragraphs.

"First you have a topic sentence," she explains to Leroy. "Then you divide it up. Your secondary topic has to be connected to your primary topic."

To Leroy, this sounds intimidating. "I never was any good in English," he says.

"It makes a lot of sense."

"What are you doing this for, anyhow?"

She shrugs. "It's something to do." She stands up and lifts her dumbbells a few times.

"Driving a rig, nobody cared about my English."

"I'm not criticizing your English."

Norma Jean used to say, "If I lose ten minutes' sleep, I just drag all day." Now she stays up late, writing compositions. She got a B on her first paper—a how-to theme on soup-based casseroles. Recently Norma Jean has been cooking unusual foods—tacos, lasagna, Bombay chicken. She doesn't play the organ anymore, though her second paper was called "Why Music Is Important to Me." She sits at the kitchen table, concentrating on her outlines, while Leroy plays with his log house plans, practicing with a set of Lincoln Logs. The thought of getting a truckload of notched, numbered logs scares him, and he wants to be prepared. As he and Norma Jean work together at the kitchen table, Leroy has the hopeful thought that they are sharing something, but he knows he is a fool to think this. Norma Jean is miles away. He knows he is going to lose her. Like Mabel, he is just waiting for time to pass.

One day, Mabel is there before Norma Jean gets home from work, and Leroy finds himself confiding in her. Mabel, he realizes, must know Norma Jean better than he does.

"I don't know what's got into that girl," Mabel says. "She used to go to bed with the chickens. Now you say she's up all hours. Plus her a-smoking. I like to died."

"I want to make her this beautiful home," Leroy says, indicating the Lincoln Logs. "I don't think she even wants it. Maybe she was happier with me gone."

"She don't know what to make of you, coming home like this."

"Is that it?"

Mabel takes the roof off his Lincoln Log cabin. "You couldn't get *me* in a log cabin," she says. "I was raised in one. It's no picnic, let me tell you."

"They're different now," says Leroy.

"I tell you what," Mabel says, smiling oddly at Leroy.

"What?"

"Take her on down to Shiloh. Y'all need to get out together, stir a little. Her brain's all balled up over them books."

Leroy can see traces of Norma Jean's features in her mother's face. Mabel's face has the texture of crinkled cotton, but suddenly she looks pretty. It occurs to Leroy that Mabel has been hinting all along that she wants them to take her with them to Shiloh.

"Let's all go to Shiloh," he says. "You and me and her. Come Sunday."

Mabel throws up her hands in protest. "Oh, no, not me. Young folks want to be by theirselves."

When Norma Jean comes in with groceries, Leroy says excitedly, "Your mama here's been dying to go to Shiloh for thirty-five years. It's about time we went, don't you think?"

"I'm not going to butt in on anybody's second honeymoon," Mabel says.

"Who's going on a honeymoon, for Christ's sake?" Norma Jean says loudly.

"I never raised no daughter of mine to talk that-a-way," Mabel says.

"You ain't seen nothing yet," says Norma Jean. She starts putting away boxes and cans, slamming cabinet doors.

"There's a log cabin at Shiloh." Mabel says, "It was there during the battle. There's bullet holes in it."

"When are you going to *shut up* about Shiloh, Mama?" asks Norma Jean.

"I always thought Shiloh was the prettiest place, so full of history," Mabel goes on. "I just hoped y'all could see it once before I die, so you could tell me about it." Later, she whispers to Leroy, "You do what I said. A little change is what she needs."

"Your name means 'the king,'" Norma Jean says to Leroy that evening. He is trying to get her to go to Shiloh, and she is reading a book about another century.

"Well, I reckon I ought to be right proud."

"I guess so."

"Am I still king around here?"

Norma Jean flexes her biceps and feels them for hardness. "I'm not fooling around with anybody, if that's what you mean," she says.

"Would you tell me if you were?"

"I don't know."

"What does *your* name mean?"

"It was Marilyn Monroe's real name."

"No kidding!"

"Norma comes from the Normans. They were invaders," she says. She closes her book and looks hard at Leroy. "I'll go to Shiloh with you if you'll stop staring at me."

On Sunday, Norma Jean packs a picnic and they go to Shiloh. To Leroy's relief, Mabel says she does not want to come with them. Norma Jean drives, and Leroy, sitting beside her, feels like some boring hitchhiker she has picked up. He tries some conversation, but she answers him in monosyllables. At Shiloh, she drives aimlessly through the park, past bluffs and trails and steep ravines. Shiloh is an immense place, and Leroy cannot see it as a battleground. It is not what he expected. He thought it would look like a golf course. Monuments are everywhere, showing through the thick clusters of trees. Norma Jean passes the log cabin Mabel mentioned. It is surrounded by tourists looking for bullet holes.

"That's not the kind of log house I've got in mind," says Leroy apologetically.

"I know *that*."

"This is a pretty place. Your mama was right."

"It's O.K.," says Norma Jean. "Well, we've seen it. I hope she's satisfied."

They burst out laughing together.

At the park museum, a movie on Shiloh is shown every half hour, but they decide that they don't want to see it. They buy a souvenir Confederate flag for Mabel, and then they find a picnic spot near the cemetery. Norma Jean has brought a picnic cooler, with pimiento sandwiches, soft drinks, and Yodels. Leroy eats a sandwich and then smokes a joint, hiding it behind the picnic cooler. Norma Jean has quit smoking altogether. She is picking cake crumbs from the cellophane wrapper, like a fussy bird.

Leroy says, "So the boys in gray ended up in Corinth. The Union soldiers zapped 'em finally. April 7, 1862."

They both know that he doesn't know any history. He is just talking about some of the historical plaques they have read. He feels awkward, like a boy on a date with an older girl. They are still just making conversation.

"Corinth is where Mama eloped to," says Norma Jean.

They sit in silence and stare at the cemetery for the Union dead and, beyond, at a tall cluster of trees. Campers are parked nearby, bumper to bumper, and small children in bright clothing are cavorting and squealing. Norma Jean wads up the cake wrapper and squeezes it tightly in her hand. Without looking at Leroy, she says, "I want to leave you."

Leroy takes a bottle of Coke out of the cooler and flips off the cap. He holds the bottle poised near his mouth but cannot remember to take a drink. Finally he says, "No, you don't."

"Yes, I do."

"I won't let you."

"You can't stop me."

"Don't do me that way."

Leroy knows Norma Jean will have her own way. "Didn't I promise to be home from now on?" he says.

"In some ways, a woman prefers a man who wanders," says Norma Jean. "That sounds crazy, I know."

"You're not crazy."

Leroy remembers to drink from his Coke. Then he says, "Yes, you *are* crazy. You and me could start all over again. Right back at the beginning."

"We *have* started all over again," says Norma Jean. "And this is how it turned out."

"What did I do wrong?"

"Nothing."

"Is this one of those women's lib things?" Leroy asks.

"Don't be funny."

The cemetery, a green slope dotted with white markers, looks like a subdivision site. Leroy is trying to comprehend that his marriage is breaking up, but for some reason he is wondering about white slabs in a graveyard.

"Everything was fine till Mama caught me smoking," says Norma Jean, standing up. "That set something off."

"What are you talking about?"

"She won't leave me alone—*you* won't leave me alone." Norma Jean seems to be crying, but she is looking away from him. "I feel eighteen again. I can't face that all over again." She starts walking away. "No, it *wasn't* fine. I don't know what I'm saying. Forget it."

Leroy takes a lungful of smoke and closes his eyes as Norma Jean's words sink in. He tries to focus on the fact that thirty-five hundred soldiers died on the grounds around him. He can only think of that war as a board game with plastic soldiers. Leroy almost smiles, as he compares the Confederates' daring attack on the Union camps and Virgil Mathis's raid on the bowling alley. General Grant, drunk and furious, shoved the Southerners back to Corinth, where Mabel and Jet Beasley were married years later, when Mabel was still thin and good-looking. The next day, Mabel and Jet visited the battleground, and then Norma Jean was born, and then she married Leroy and they had a baby, which they lost, and now Leroy and Norma Jean are here at the same battleground. Leroy knows he is leaving out a lot. He is leaving out the insides of history. History was always just names and dates to him. It occurs to him that building a house out of logs is similarly empty—too simple. And the real inner workings of a marriage, like most of history, have escaped him. Now he sees that building a log house is the dumbest idea he could have had. It was clumsy of him to think Norma Jean would want a log house. It was a crazy idea. He'll have to think of something else, quickly. He will wad the blueprints into tight balls and fling them into the lake. Then he'll get moving again. He opens his eyes. Norma Jean has moved away and is walking through the cemetery, following a serpentine brick path.

Leroy gets up to follow his wife, but his good leg is asleep and his bad leg still hurts him. Norma Jean is far away, walking rapidly toward the bluff by the river, and he tries to hobble toward her. Some children run past him, screaming noisily. Norma Jean has reached the bluff, and she is looking out over the Tennessee River. Now she turns toward Leroy and waves her arms. Is she beckoning to him? She seems to be doing an exercise for her chest muscles. The sky is unusually pale—the color of the dust ruffle Mabel made for their bed.

1982

# GUY DE MAUPASSANT
## 1850–1893

Maupassant was born near Dieppe, France. His parents were friends of the novelist Gustave Flaubert, whose views on literature and the artistic life influenced Maupassant even in his early years. Rebellious in school, he accepted army discipline during the Franco-Prussian War of 1870–71, and then for nearly ten years apprenticed himself to Flaubert to learn the craft of fiction, discarding most of what he wrote. In 1880 he became famous with the publication of a single story, *Boule de Suif,* which contrasts the patriotism of a young prostitute with the amorality of middle-class citizens. Maupassant published, during the next ten years, nearly three hundred short stories, half a dozen novels, some plays, verse, and travel books. The short stories, which appeared regularly in popular periodicals, sampled military and peasant life, the decadent world of politics and journalism, prostitution, perversion, the supernatural, and the hypocrisies of solid citizens. Maupassant's income from his prodigious literary output permitted him to indulge the appetites for women and luxury that had always been part of his character, but in his last years syphilis, which he apparently contracted before he was twenty, began to unravel his capacity for concentrated work. He sought relief in drugs and travels on his yacht but became completely insane before he died of paresis. His novels include *Une Vie (A Life,* 1883), *Bel Ami (Handsome Friend,* 1885), and *Pierre et Jean* (1888). His short stories are most readily available in his collected works.

## An Adventure in Paris

Is there any feeling in a woman stronger than curiosity? Fancy seeing, knowing, touching what one has dreamed about! What would a woman not do for that? Once a woman's eager curiosity is aroused, she will be guilty of any folly, commit any imprudence, venture upon anything, and recoil from nothing. I speak of women who are really women, who are endowed with that triple-bottomed disposition, which appears to be reasonable and cool on the surface, but whose three secret compartments are filled as follows: The first, with female uneasiness, which is always in a state of fluttering; the next, with sly dodges always brought into play under color of complete sincerity; the sophistical and formidable wiles of seemingly straightforward women; and the last, with all those charming, improper acts, that delightful deceit, exquisite perfidy, and all those wayward qualities that drive stupidly credulous lovers to suicide, but delight other men.

The woman whose adventure I am about to relate was a little person from the provinces, who had been insipidly respectable till the moment when my story begins. Her life, which was on the surface so calm, was spent at home, with a busy husband and two children, whom she brought up in the fashion of an irreproachable mother. But her heart beat with unsatisfied curiosity and with longing for the unknown. She was continually thinking of Paris, and read the fashionable papers eagerly. The accounts of parties, of dresses, and various entertainments, excited her longing; but, above all, she was strangely agitated by those paragraphs which were full of double meaning, by those veils half raised by clever phrases which gave her a glimpse of culpable and ravishing delights. From her home in the provinces she saw in Paris an apotheosis of magnificent and corrupt luxury.

During the long nights, when she dreamed, lulled by the rhythmical snores of a husband who lay sleeping on his back by her side with a silk handkerchief tied round his head, she saw in her sleep those well-known men whose names appeared regularly on the front page of the newspapers like stars in the dark sky. She pictured to herself their lives—continual excitement, constant debauchery, orgies such as were practiced in ancient Rome, horribly voluptuous and with refinements of sensuality so complicated that she could not even imagine them.

The boulevards seemed to her a kind of abyss of human passions, and she did not doubt that the houses that lined them concealed mysteries of prodigious love. But she felt that she was growing old without having known life, except in those recurrent repellently monotonous, everyday occupations which constitute the happiness of the home. She was still pretty, for she was well preserved by a tranquil existence, like winter fruit in a cool cupboard; but she was consumed, agitated, and upset by her secret longings. She used to ask herself if she was meant to die without having experienced any of those damning, intoxicating joys, without having plunged once, just once, into that flood of Parisian voluptuousness.

By dint of much perseverance, she paved the way for a journey to Paris, found a pretext, got some relatives to invite her, and as her husband could not go with her, she went alone. As soon as she arrived, she invented a reason for remaining for some days, or rather for some nights, if necessary. She told him that she had met some friends who lived a little way out of town.

And then she set out on a voyage of discovery. She went up and down the boulevards, without seeing anything except roving and licensed vice. She looked into the large cafés, and read the Agony Column of the *Figaro*,[1] which every morning seemed to her like a tocsin, a summons to love. But nothing put her on the track of those orgies of actors and actresses; nothing revealed to her those temples of debauchery which opened, she imagined, at some magic word, like the cave of Ali Baba or the catacombs of Rome, where the mysteries of a persecuted religion were secretly celebrated.

Her relatives, who were quite middle-class people, could not introduce her to any of those well-known men of whose names her head was full; and in despair she was thinking of returning, when chance came to her aid. One day, as she

---

1. *Le Figaro*, leading French newspaper, published in Paris.

was going along the Rue de la Chaussée d'Antin,[2] she stopped to look into a shop full of those colored Japanese knickknacks which attract the eye by their color. She was gazing at the grotesque little ivories, the tall vases of flaming enamel, and the curious bronzes, when she heard the shopkeeper inside dilating, with many bows, on the value of an enormous, pot-bellied, comical figure—which was unique, he said—to a little, bald-headed, gray-bearded man.

At every moment, the shopkeeper repeated his customer's name, which was a celebrated one, in a voice like a trumpet. The other customers, young women and well-dressed gentlemen, gave a swift and furtive but respectful glance at the celebrated writer, who was looking admiringly at the china figure. Man and figure were equally ugly, as ugly as two brothers who had sprung from the same ugly mother.

"To you the price will be a thousand francs, Monsieur Varin, and that is exactly what it cost me. I should ask anybody else fifteen hundred, but I think a great deal of my literary and artistic customers, and have special prices for them. They all come to me, Monsieur Varin. Yesterday, Monsieur Busnach bought a large, antique goblet from me, and the other day I sold two candelabra like this (aren't they beautiful?) to Monsieur Alexandre Dumas. If Monsieur Zola were to see that Japanese figure he would buy it immediately, Monsieur Varin."[3]

The author hesitated in perplexity. He wanted the figure, but the price was above him, and he thought no more about being stared at than if he had been alone in the desert. She came in trembling, her eyes fixed shamelessly upon him, and she did not even ask herself whether he was good-looking, elegant, or young. It was Jean Varin himself, Jean Varin! After a long struggle and painful hesitation, he put the figure down onto the table.

"No, it is too expensive," he said.

The shopkeeper's eloquence redoubled. "Oh! Monsieur Varin, too expensive? It is worth two thousand francs, if it is worth a sou."

But the man of letters replied sadly, still looking at the figure with the enameled eyes, "I do not say it is not: but it is too expensive for me."

And thereupon, she, seized by a kind of mad audacity, came forward and said, "What will you charge me for the figure?"

The shopkeeper, in surprise, replied, "Fifteen hundred francs, Madame."

"I will take it."

The writer, who had not even noticed her till that moment, turned round suddenly. He looked her over from head to foot, with half-closed eyes, observantly, taking in the details like a connoisseur. She was charming, suddenly animated by the flame which had hitherto been dormant in her. And then, a woman who gives fifteen hundred francs for a knickknack is not to be met with every day.

She was overcome by a feeling of delightful delicacy, and turning to him, she said in a trembling voice:

"Excuse me, Sir; no doubt I have been rather hasty. You have probably not made up your mind."

He, however, bowed and said, "Indeed I had, Madame."

---

**2.** Street in Parisian shopping district.   **3.** "Jean Varin" is fictitious, but the other names in this paragraph are actual French authors, contemporaries of Maupassant. William Busnach (1832–1907), playwright. Alexandre Dumas (1824–1895), playwright and novelist. Émile Zola (1840–1902), novelist.

And she, filled with emotion, continued, "Well, if either today, or at any other time, you change your mind, you may have this Japanese figure. I bought it only because you seemed to like it."

He was visibly flattered, and smiled. "I should like to find out how you know who I am?" he said.

Then she told him how she admired him, and became quite eloquent as she quoted his works, and while they were talking, he rested his arms on a table and fixed his bright eyes upon her, trying to make out who and what she really was. But the shopkeeper, who was pleased to have that living puff of his goods, called out, from the other end of the shop, "Just look at this, Monsieur Varin; is it not beautiful?"

And then everyone looked round, and she almost trembled with pleasure at being seen talking so intimately with such a well-known man.

At last, however, intoxicated, as it were, by her feelings, she grew bold, like a general who is about to order an assault.

"Sir," she said, "will you do me a great, a very great pleasure? Will you allow me to offer you this comic Japanese figure, as a souvenir from a woman who admires you passionately, and whom you have seen for ten minutes."

He refused. She persisted. Still he resisted her offer, very much amused, and laughing heartily. But that only made her more obstinate, and she said, "Very well, then, I shall take it to your house immediately; where do you live?"

He refused to give her his address, but she got it from the shopkeeper, and when she had paid for her purchase, she ran out to take a cab. The writer went after her, not wishing to accept a present from a person he did not know. He reached her just as she was getting into the cab. Getting in after her, he almost fell on top of her, as the cab gave a jolt. Then he sat down by her side, feeling very much annoyed.

It was no good for him to argue and to beg; she showed herself intractable, and when they got to the door, she stated her conditions, "I will undertake not to leave this with you," she said, "if you will promise to do all I want today." And the whole affair seemed so amusing to him that he agreed.

"What do you generally do at this time?" she asked him; and after hesitating for a few moments, he replied, "I generally go for a walk."

"Very well, then, we will go to the Bois de Boulogne!" she said, in a resolute voice, and they started.

He was obliged to tell her the names of all the well-known women they crossed, pure or impure, with every detail about them—their mode of life, their habits, their homes, and their vices; and when it was getting dusk, she said to him, "What do you do every day at this time?"

"I have some absinthe," he replied with a laugh.

"Very well, then," she went on seriously; "let us go and have some absinthe."

They went into a large café on the boulevard which he frequented, and where he met some of his colleagues, whom he introduced to her. She was half beside herself with pleasure, and kept saying to herself, "At last! At last!"

But time went on, and she asked, "Is it your dinner time?" To which he replied, "Yes."

"Then, let us go and have dinner."

When they left Bignon's[4] after dinner, she wanted to know what he did in the evening, and looking at her fixedly, he replied, "That depends; sometimes I go to the theater."

"Very well, then, let us go to the theater."

They went to the Vaudeville[5] with a pass, thanks to him, and, to her great pride, the whole house saw her sitting by his side in the stalls.

When the play was over, he gallantly kissed her hand, and said, "It only remains for me to thank you for this delightful day."

But she interrupted him, "What do you do at this time, every night?"

"Why—why—I go home."

She began to laugh, a little tremulous laugh: "Very well, let us go to your rooms."

They did not say anything more. She shivered occasionally from head to foot, feeling inclined to stay, and inclined to run away, but with a fixed determination, after all, to see it out to the end. She was so excited that she had to hold on to the banister as she went upstairs, and he went on ahead of her, with a lighted match in his hand.

As soon as they were in the flat, she undressed quickly and retired without saying a word. Then she waited for him, cowering against the wall. But she was as simple as it was possible for a provincial lawyer's wife to be, and he was more exacting than a pasha with thirty wives, so that they did not really get on at all.

At last, however, he went to sleep. The night passed, its silence disturbed only by the tic-toc of the clock, while she, lying motionless, thought of her conjugal nights. By the light of a Chinese lantern, she lay nearly heartbroken and stared at the little fat man lying on his back, his round stomach puffing out the bedclothes like a balloon filled with gas. He snored with the noise of a wheezy organ pipe, with prolonged snorts and comic chokings. His few hairs profited by his sleep to stand up in a very strange way, as if they were tired of having been glued for so long to that pate whose bareness they were trying to cover. And a thin stream of saliva trickled from the corner of his half-opened mouth.

At last daylight appeared through the drawn blinds. She got up and dressed without making any noise. Opening the door, she made the lock creak, and he woke up and rubbed his eyes. He was some moments coming to himself, and then, when he remembered what had happened, he said:

"What! Going already?"

She remained standing, in some confusion, and then said, in a hesitant voice: "Yes, of course; it is morning."

Then he sat up, and said, "Look here, I have something to ask you, in my turn." And as she did not reply, he went on, "You have astonished me most confoundedly since yesterday. Be frank, and tell me why you did it all, for upon my word I cannot understand it in the least."

She went over to him, blushing as if she had been a virgin, and said, "I wanted to know—what—what vice—really was, and—well—well, it is not at all funny."

And she ran out of the room and down the stairs into the street.

---

**4.** Parisian restaurant   **5.** Music hall.

The street-cleaners were already at work, sweeping the road, sending their brushes along the gutters, bringing together the rubbish in neat little heaps. With movements as regular as the motion of mowers in a meadow, they swept the refuse before them in broad semi-circular strokes. She met them in every street, like dancing puppets, walking automatically with a swaying motion, and it seemed to her as if something had been swept out of her; as if her over-excited dreams had been brushed into the gutter, or down into the sewers. So she went home, out of breath and very cold, and all that she could remember was the sensation of the motion of those brooms sweeping the streets of Paris in the early morning.

When she got to her room, she threw herself onto her bed and cried.

1881

RELATED:

—Maupassant, "The Novel," p. 887

# JAMES ALAN McPHERSON
## b. 1943

A native of Savannah, Georgia, McPherson earned a degree from Atlanta's Morris Brown College and studied at the Harvard and Yale law schools as well as the University of Iowa's Writers' Workshop. Not surprisingly, then, his remarkable career has proceeded on very different tracks. On the one hand, McPherson is a distinguished essayist, historian, and editor; his publications include contributions to *A World Unsuspected* (1987), *The Prevailing South* (1988), and *Confronting Racial Difference* (1990); the memoir *Crabcakes* (1997), the essay collection *A Region Not Home: Reflections from Exile* (1999), and a number of American history textbooks. At the same time, McPherson has flourished as a fiction writer, beginning when his story "Gold Coast," from his first collection, *Hue and Cry* (1968), won a contest in the *Atlantic Monthly* magazine. With his second collection, *Elbow Room* (1977), he became the first African American to win the Pulitzer Prize for fiction. In 1981 he was awarded a MacArthur Fellowship. A writer who takes enormous pains and works very slowly, McPherson manages to produce stories remarkable for their fluidity and their music. He has taught at the University of Virginia and, since 1981, at the University of Iowa.

## Why I Like Country Music

No one will believe that I like country music. Even my wife scoffs when told such a possibility exists. "Go on!" Gloria tells me. "I can see blues, bebop, maybe even a little buckdancing. But not bluegrass." Gloria says, "Hillbilly stuff is not just music. It's like the New York Stock Exchange. The minute you see a sharp rise in it, you better watch out."

I tend to argue the point, but quietly, and mostly to myself. Gloria was born and raised in New York; she has come to believe in the stock exchange as the only index of economic health. My perceptions were shaped in South Carolina; and long ago I learned there, as a waiter in private clubs, to gauge economic flux by the tips people gave. We tend to disagree on other matters too, but the thing that gives me most frustration is trying to make her understand why I like country music. Perhaps it is because she hates the South and has capitulated emotionally to the horror stories told by refugees from down home. Perhaps it is because Gloria is third generation Northern-born. I do not know. What I do know is that, while the two of us are black, the distance between us is sometimes as great as that between Ibo and Yoruba.[1] And I do know that, despite her protestations, I like country music.

"You are crazy," Gloria tells me.

I tend to argue the point, but quietly, and mostly to myself.

Of course I do not like all country stuff; just pieces that make the right connections. I like banjo because sometimes I hear ancestors in the strumming. I like the fiddle-like refrain in "Dixie" for the very same reason. But most of all I like square dancing—the interplay between fiddle and caller, the stomping, the swishing of dresses, the strutting, the proud turnings, the laughter. Most of all I like the laughter. In recent months I have wondered why I like this music and this dance. I have drawn no general conclusions, but from time to time I suspect it is because the square dance is the only dance form I ever mastered.

"I wouldn't say that in public," Gloria warns me.

I agree with her, but still affirm the truth of it, although quietly, and mostly to myself.

Dear Gloria: This is the truth of how it was:

In my youth in that distant country, while others learned to strut, I grew stiff as a winter cornstalk. When my playmates harmonized their rhythms, I stood on the sidelines in atonic detachment. While they shimmied, I merely jerked in lackluster imitation. I relate these facts here, not in remorse or self-castigation, but as a true confession of my circumstances. In those days, down in our small corner of South Carolina, proficiency in dance was a form of storytelling. A boy could say, "I traveled here and there, saw this and fought that, conquered him and made love to her, lied to them, told a few others the truth, just so I could come back here and let you know what things out there are really like." He could communicate all this with smooth, graceful jiggles of his round bottom, synchronized with intricately coordinated sweeps of his arms and small, unexcited movements of his legs. Little girls could communicate much more.

But sadly, I could do none of it. Development of these skills depended on the ministrations of family and neighbors. My family did not dance; our closest neighbor was a true-believing Seventh Day Adventist.[2] Moreover, most new dances came from up North, brought to town usually by people returning to riff on the good life said to exist in those far Northern places. They prowled our dirt streets in rented Cadillacs; paraded our brick sidewalks exhibiting styles abstracted from the fullness of life in Harlem, South Philadelphia, Roxbury, Baltimore and the South Side of Chicago. They confronted our provincial clothes merchants with the arrogant reminder, "But people ain't wearin' this in New Yokkk!" Each of their movements, as well as their world-weary smoothness, told us locals meaningful tales of what was missing in our lives. Unfortunately, those of us under strict parental supervision, or those of us without Northern connections, could only stand at a distance and worship these envoys of culture. We stood on the sidelines—styleless, gestureless, danceless, doing nothing more than an improvised one-butt shuffle—hoping

---

1. Long-time rival ethnic groups of West Africa.    2. Christian denomination known for its strictures against secular pastimes.

for one of them to touch our lives. It was my good fortune, during my tenth year on the sidelines, to have one of these Northerners introduce me to the square dance.

My dear, dear Gloria, her name was Gweneth Lawson:

She was a pretty, chocolate brown little girl with dark brown eyes and two long black braids. After all these years, the image of these two braids evokes in me all there is to remember about Gweneth Lawson. They were plaited across the top of her head and hung to a point just above the back of her Peter Pan collar. Sometimes she wore two bows, one red and one blue, and these tended to sway lazily near the place on her neck where the smooth brown of her skin and the white of her collar met the ink-bottle black of her hair. Even when I cannot remember her face, I remember the rainbow of deep, rich colors in which she lived. This is so because I watched them, every weekday, from my desk directly behind hers in our fourth-grade class. And she wore the most magical perfume, or lotion, smelling just slightly of fresh-cut lemons, that wafted back to me whenever she made the slightest movement at her desk. Now I must tell you this much more, dear Gloria: whenever I smell fresh lemons, whether in the market or at home, I look around me—not for Gweneth Lawson, but for some quiet corner where I can revive in private certain memories of her. And in pursuing these memories across such lemony bridges, I rediscover that I loved her.

Gweneth was from the South Carolina section of Brooklyn. Her parents had sent her south to live with her uncle, Mr. Richard Lawson, the brick mason, for an unspecified period of time. Just why they did this I do not know, unless it was their plan to have her absorb more of South Carolina folkways than conditions in Brooklyn would allow. She was a gentle, soft-spoken girl; I recall no condescension in her manner. This was all the more admirable because our unrestrained awe of a Northern-born black person usually induced in him some grand sense of his own importance. You must know that in those days older folks would point to someone and say, "He's from the North," and the statement would be sufficient in itself. Mothers made their children behave by advising that, if they led exemplary lives and attended church regularly, when they died they would go to New York. Only someone who understands what London meant to Dick Whittington, or how California and the suburbs function in the national mind, could appreciate the mythical dimensions of this Northlore.

But Gweneth Lawson was above regional idealization. Though I might have loved her partly because she was a Northerner, I loved her more because of the world of colors that seemed to be suspended above her head. I loved her glowing forehead and I loved her bright, dark brown eyes; I loved the black braids, the red and blue and sometimes yellow and pink ribbons; I loved the way the deep, rich brown of her neck melted into the pink or white cloth of her Peter Pan collar; I loved the lemony vapor on which she floated and from which, on occasion, she seemed to be inviting me to be buoyed up, up, up into her happy world; I loved the way she caused my heart to tumble whenever, during a restless moment, she seemed about to turn her head in my direction; I loved her more, though torturously, on the many occasions when she did not turn. Because I was a shy boy, I loved the way I could love her silently, at least six hours a day, without ever having to disclose my love.

My platonic state of mind might have stretched onward into a blissful infinity had not Mrs. Esther Clay Boswell, our teacher, made it her business to pry into the affair. Although she prided herself on being a strict disciplinarian, Mrs. Boswell was not without a sense of humor. A round, full-breasted woman in her early forties, she liked to amuse herself, and sometimes the class as well, by calling the attention of all eyes to whomever of us violated the structure she imposed on classroom activities. She was particularly hard on people like me who could not contain an impulse to daydream, or those who allowed their eyes to wander too far away from lessons printed on the blackboard. A black and white sign posted under the electric clock next to the door summed up her attitude toward this kind of truancy: NOTICE TO ALL CLOCKWATCHERS, it read, TIME PASSES, WILL YOU? Nor did she abide timidity in her students. Her voice booming, "Speak up, boy!" was more than enough to cause the more emotional among us, including me, to break into convenient flows of warm tears. But by doing this we violated yet another rule, one on which depended our very survival in Mrs. Esther Clay Boswell's class. She would spell out this rule for us as she paced before her desk, slapping a thick, homemade ruler against the flat of her brown palm. "There ain't no *babies* in here," she would recite. *Thaap!* "Anybody thinks he's still a *baby* . . ." *Thaap!* ". . . should crawl back home to his mama's *titty.*" *Thaap!* "You little bunnies shed your *last water* . . ." *Thaap!* ". . . the minute you left home to come in here." *Thaap!* "From now on, you g'on do all your *cryin'* . . ." *Thaap!* ". . . in *church!*" *Thaap!* Whenever one of us compelled her to make this speech it would seem to me that her eyes paused overlong on my face. She would seem to be daring me, as if suspicious that, in addition to my secret passion for Gweneth Lawson, which she might excuse, I was also in the habit of throwing fits of temper.

She had read me right. I was the product of too much attention from my father. He favored me, paraded me around on his shoulder, inflated my ego constantly with what, among us at least, was a high compliment: "You my nigger if you don't get no bigger." This statement, along with my father's generous attentions, made me selfish and used to having my own way. I *expected* to have my own way in most things, and when I could not, I tended to throw tantrums calculated to break through any barrier raised against me.

Mrs. Boswell was also perceptive in assessing the extent of my infatuation with Gweneth Lawson. Despite my stealth in telegraphing emissions of affection into the back part of Gweneth's brain, I could not help but observe, occasionally, Mrs. Boswell's cool glance pausing on the two of us. But she never said a word. Instead, she would settle her eyes momentarily on Gweneth's face and then pass quickly to mine. But in that instant she seemed to be saying, "Don't look back now, girl, but I *know* that bald-headed boy behind you has you on his mind." She seemed to watch me daily, with a combination of amusement and absolute detachment in her brown eyes. And when she stared, it was not at me but at the normal focus of my attention: the end of Gweneth Lawson's black braids. Whenever I sensed Mrs. Boswell watching I would look away quickly, either down at my brown desk top or across the room to the blackboard. But her eyes could not be eluded this easily. Without looking at anyone in particular, she could make a specific point to one person in a manner so general that only long afterward did the real object of her attention realize it had been intended for him.

"Now you little brown bunnies," she might say, "and you black buck rabbits and you few cottontails mixed in, some of you starting to smell yourselves under the arms without knowing what it's all about." And here, it sometimes seemed to me, she allowed her eyes to pause casually on me before resuming their sweep of the entire room. "Now I know your mamas already made you think life is a bed of roses, but in *my* classroom you got to know the footpaths through the *sticky* parts of the rose-bed." It was her custom during this ritual to prod and goad those of us who were developing reputations for meekness and indecision; yet her method was Socratic in that she compelled us, indirectly, to supply our own answers by exploiting one person as the walking symbol of the error she intended to correct. Clarence Buford, for example, an oversized but good-natured boy from a very poor family, served often as the helpmeet in this exercise.

"Buford," she might begin, slapping the ruler against her palm, "how does a tongue-tied country boy like you expect to get a wife?"

"I don't want no wife," Buford might grumble softly.

Of course the class would laugh.

"Oh yes you do," Mrs. Boswell would respond. "All you buck rabbits want wives." *Thaap!* "So how do you let a girl know you not just a bump on a log?"

"I know! I know!" a high voice might call from a seat across from mine. This, of course, would be Leon Pugh. A peanut-brown boy with curly hair, he seemed to know everything. Moreover, he seemed to take pride in being the only one who knew answers to life questions and would wave his arms excitedly whenever our attentions were focused on such matters. It seemed to me his voice would be extra loud and his arms waved more strenuously whenever he was certain that Gweneth Lawson, seated across from him, was interested in an answer to Mrs. Esther Clay Boswell's question. His eager arms, it seemed to me, would be reaching out to grasp Gweneth instead of the question asked.

"Buford, you twisted-tongue, bunion-toed country boy," Mrs. Boswell might say, ignoring Leon Pugh's hysterical armwaving, "you gonna let a cottontail like Leon get a girlfriend before you?"

"I don't want no girlfriend," Clarence Buford would almost sob. "I don't like no girls."

The class would laugh again while Leon Pugh manipulated his arms like a flight navigator under battle conditions. "I know! I know! I swear to *God* I know!"

When at last Mrs. Boswell would turn in his direction, I might sense that she was tempted momentarily to ask me for an answer. But as in most such exercises, it was the worldly-wise Leon Pugh who supplied this. "What do *you* think, Leon?" she would ask inevitably, but with a rather lifeless slap of the ruler against her palm.

"My daddy told me . . ." Leon would shout, turning slyly to beam at Gweneth, ". . . my daddy and my big brother from the Bronx New York told me that to git *anythin'* in this world you gotta learn how to blow your own horn."

"Why, Leon?" Mrs. Boswell might ask in a bored voice.

"Because," the little boy would recite, puffing out his chest, "because if you don't blow your own horn ain't nobody else g'on blow it for you. That's what my daddy said."

"What do you think about that, Buford?" Mrs. Boswell would ask.

"I don't want no girlfriend anyhow," the puzzled Clarence Buford might say. And then the cryptic lesson would suddenly be dropped.

This was Mrs. Esther Clay Boswell's method of teaching. More than anything written on the blackboard, her questions were calculated to make us turn around in our chairs and inquire in guarded whispers of each other, and especially of the wise and confident Leon Pugh, "What does she mean?" But none of us, besides Pugh, seemed able to comprehend what it was we ought to know but did not know. And Mrs. Boswell, plump brown fox that she was, never volunteered any more in the way of confirmation than was necessary to keep us interested. Instead, she paraded around us, methodically slapping the homemade ruler against her palm, suggesting by her silence more depth to her question, indeed, more implications in Leon's answer, than we were then able to perceive. And during such moments, whether inspired by selfishness or by the peculiar way Mrs. Boswell looked at me, I felt that finding answers to such questions was a task she had set for me, of all the members of the class.

Of course Leon Pugh, among other lesser lights, was my chief rival for the affections of Gweneth Lawson. All during the school year, from September through the winter rains, he bested me in my attempts to look directly into her eyes and say a simple, heartfelt, "hey." This was my ambition, but I never seemed able to get close enough to her attention. At Thanksgiving I helped draw a bounteous yellow cornucopia on the blackboard, with fruits and flowers matching the colors that floated around Gweneth's head; Leon Pugh made one by himself, a masterwork of silver paper and multicolored crepe, which he hung on the door. Its silver tail curled upward to a point just below the face of Mrs. Boswell's clock. At Christmas, when we drew names out of a hat for the exchange of gifts, I drew the name of Queen Rose Phipps, a fairly unattractive squash-yellow girl of absolutely no interest to me. Pugh, whether through collusion with the boy who handled the lottery or through pure luck, pulled forth from the hat the magic name of Gweneth Lawson. He gave her a set of deep purple bows for her braids and a basket of pecans from his father's tree. Uninterested now in the spirit of the occasion, I delivered to Queen Rose Phipps a pair of white socks. Each time Gweneth wore the purple bows she would glance over at Leon and smile. Each time Queen Rose wore my white socks I would turn away in embarrassment, lest I should see them pulling down into her shoes and exposing her skinny ankles.

After class, on wet winter days, I would trail along behind Gweneth to the bus stop, pause near the steps while she entered, and follow her down the aisle until she chose a seat. Usually, however, in clear violation of the code of conduct to which all gentlemen were expected to adhere, Leon Pugh would already be on the bus and shouting to passersby, "Move off! Get away! This here seat by me is reserved for the girl from Brooklyn New York." Discouraged but not defeated, I would swing into the seat next nearest her and cast calf-eyed glances of wounded affection at the back of her head or at the brown, rainbow profile of her face. And at her stop, some eight or nine blocks from mine, I would disembark behind her along with a crowd of other love-struck boys. There would then follow a well-rehearsed scene in which all of us, save Leon Pugh, pretended to have gotten off the bus either too late or too soon to wend our proper paths homeward. And at slight cost to ourselves we enjoyed the advantage of being able to walk close by her as she glided toward her uncle's green-frame house.

There, after pausing on the wooden steps and smiling radiantly around the crowd like a spring sun in that cold winter rain, she would sing, "Bye, y'all," and disappear into the structure with the mystery of a goddess. Afterward I would walk away, but slowly, much slower than the other boys, warmed by the music and light in her voice against the sharp, wet winds of the February afternoon.

I loved her, dear Gloria, and I danced with her and smelled the lemony youth of her and told her that I loved her, all this in a way you would never believe:

You would not know or remember, as I do, that in those days, in our area of the country, we enjoyed a pleasingly ironic mixture of Yankee and Confederate folkways. Our meals and manners, our speech, our attitudes toward certain ambiguous areas of history, even our acceptance of tragedy as the normal course of life—these things and more defined us as Southern. Yet the stern morality of our parents, their toughness and penny-pinching and attitudes toward work, their covert allegiance toward certain ideals, even the directions toward which they turned our faces, made us more Yankee than Cavalier. Moreover, some of our schools were named for Confederate men of distinction, but others were named for the stern-faced believers who had swept down from the North to save a people back, back long ago, in those long forgotten days of once upon a time. Still, our schoolbooks, our required classroom songs, our flags, our very relation to the statues and monuments in public parks, negated the story that these dreamers from the North had ever come. We sang the state song, memorized the verses of homegrown poets, honored in our books the names and dates of historical events both before and after that Historical Event which, in our region, supplanted even the division of the millennia introduced by the followers of Jesus Christ. Given the silent circumstances of our cultural environment, it was ironic, and perhaps just, that we maintained a synthesis of two traditions no longer supportive of each other. Thus it became traditional at our school to celebrate the arrival of spring on May first by both the ritual plaiting of the Maypole and square dancing.

On that day, as on a few others, the Superintendent of Schools and several officials were likely to visit our schoolyard and stand next to the rusty metal swings, watching the fourth, fifth, and sixth graders bob up and down and behind and before each other, around the gaily painted Maypoles. These happy children would pull and twist long runs of billowy crepe paper into wondrous, multicolored plaits. Afterward, on the edges of thunderous applause from teachers, parents and visiting dignitaries, a wave of elaborately costumed children would rush out onto the grounds in groups of eight and proceed with the square dance. "Dog*gone!*" the Superintendent of Schools was heard to exclaim on one occasion. "Y'all do it so good it just makes your *bones* set up and take notice."

Such was the schedule two weeks prior to May first, when Mrs. Boswell announced to our class that as fourth graders we were now eligible to participate in the festivities. The class was divided into two general sections of sixteen each, one group preparing to plait the pole and a second group, containing an equal number of boys and girls, practicing turns for our part in the square dance. I was chosen to square dance; so was Leon Pugh. Gweneth Lawson was placed with the pole plaiters. I was depressed until I remembered, happily, that I could not dance a lick. I reported this fact to Mrs. Boswell just after drawing, during recess, saying that my lack of skill would only result in our class making a poor showing. I asked to be reassigned to the group of Maypole plaiters. Mrs. B. looked me over with considerable amusement tugging at the corners of her mouth. "Oh, you don't have to *dance* to do the square dance," she said. "That's a dance that was made up to mock folks that couldn't dance." She paused a second before adding thoughtfully: "The worse you are at dancing, the better you can square dance. It's just about the best dance in the world for a stiff little bunny like you."

"I want to plait the Maypole," I said.

"You'll square dance or I'll grease your little butt," Mrs. Esther Clay Boswell said.

"I ain't gonna do *nothin'!*" I muttered. But I said this quietly, and mostly to myself, while walking away from her desk. For the rest of the day she watched me closely, as if she knew what I was thinking.

The next morning I brought a note from my father. "Dear Mrs. Boswell:" I had watched him write earlier that morning, "My boy does not square dance. Please excuse him as I am afraid he will break down and cry and mess up the show. Yours truly . . ."

Mrs. Boswell said nothing after she had read the note. She merely waved me to my seat. But in the early afternoon, when she read aloud the lists of those assigned to dancing and Maypole plaiting, she paused as my name rolled off her tongue. "You don't have to stay on the square dance team," she called to me. "You go on out in the yard with the Maypole team."

I was ecstatic. I hurried to my place in line some three warm bodies behind Gweneth Lawson. We prepared to march out.

"Wait a minute," Mrs. Boswell called. "Now it looks like we got seventeen bunnies on the Maypole team and fifteen on the square dance. We have to even things up." She made a thorough examination of both lists, scratching her head. Then she looked carefully up and down the line of stomping Maypoleites. "Miss Gweneth Lawson, you cute little cottontail you, it looks like you gonna have to go over to the square dance team. That'll give us eight sets of partners for the square dance . . . but now we have another problem." She made a great display of counting the members of the two squads of square dancers. "Now there's sixteen square dancers all right, but when we pair them off we got a problem of higher mathematics. With nine girls and only seven *boys*, looks like we gotta switch a girl from square dancing to Maypole and a boy from Maypole to square dancing."

I waited hopefully for Gweneth Lawson to volunteer. But just at that moment the clever Leon Pugh grabbed her hand and began jitterbugging as though he could hardly wait for the record player to be turned on and the dancing to begin.

"What a cute couple," Mrs. Boswell observed absently. "Now which one of you other girls wants to join up with the Maypole team?"

Following Pugh's example, the seven remaining boys grabbed the girls they wanted as partners. Only skinny Queen Rose Phipps and shy Beverly Hankins remained unclaimed. Queen Rose giggled nervously.

"Queen Rose," Mrs. B. called, "I know you don't mind plaiting the Maypole." She waved her ruler in a gesture of casual dismissal. Queen Rose raced across the room and squeezed into line.

"*Now,*" Mrs. Boswell said, "I need a boy to come across to the square dancers."

I was not unmindful of the free interchange of partners involved in square dancing, even though Leon Pugh had beat me in claiming the partner of my choice. All I really wanted was one moment swinging Gweneth Lawson in my arms. I raised my hand slowly.

"Oh, not *you,* little bunny," Mrs. Boswell said. "You and your daddy claim you don't like to square dance." She slapped her ruler against her palm. *Thaap! Thaap!* Then she said, "Clarence Buford, I *know* a big-footed country boy like you can square dance better than anybody. Come on over here and kiss cute little Miss Beverly Hankins."

"I don't like no girls *noway,*" Buford mumbled. But he went over and stood next to the giggling Beverly Hankins.

"Now!" said Mrs. B. "March on out in that yard and give that pole a good plaiting!"

We started to march out. Over my shoulder, as I reached the door, I glimpsed the overjoyed Leon Pugh whirling lightly on his toes. He sang in a confident tone:

> "*I saw the Lord give Moses a pocketful of roses.*
> *I skid Ezekiel's wheel on a ripe banana peel.*
> *I rowed the Nile, flew over a stile,*
> *Saw Jack Johnson pick his teeth*
> *With toenails from Jim Jeffries' feets . . .*"

"Grab your partners!" Mrs. Esther Clay Boswell was saying as the oak door slammed behind us.

I had been undone. For almost two weeks I was obliged to stand on the sidelines and watch Leon Pugh allemande left and do-si-do[3] my beloved Gweneth. Worse, she seemed to be enjoying it. But I must give Leon proper credit: he was a dancing fool. In a matter of days he had mastered, and then improved on, the various turns and bows and gestures of the square dance. He leaped while the others plodded, whirled each girl through his arms with lightness and finesse, chattered playfully at the other boys when they tumbled over their own feet. Mrs. Boswell stood by the record player calling, "Put some *strut* in it, Buford, you big potato sack. Watch Leon and see how *he* does it." I leaned against the classroom wall and watched the dancers, my own group having already exhausted the limited variations possible in matters of Maypole plaiting.

At home each night I begged my father to send another note to Mrs. Boswell, this time stating that I had no interest in the Maypole. But he resisted my entreaties and even threatened me with a whipping if I did not participate and make him proud of me. The real cause of his irritation was the considerable investment he had already made in purchasing an outfit for me. Mrs. Boswell had required all her students, square dancers and Maypole plaiters alike, to report on May first in outfits suitable for square dancing. My father had bought a new pair of dungarees, a blue shirt, a red and white polka-dot

3. Literally, "German" left and "back to back" (French), both figures used in square dancing.

bandanna and a cowboy hat. He was in no mood to bend under the emotional weight of my new demands. As a matter of fact, early in the morning of May first he stood beside my bed with the bandanna in his left hand and his leather belt in his right hand, just in case I developed a sudden fever.

I dragged myself heavily through the warm, blue spring morning toward school, dressed like a carnival cowboy. When I entered the classroom I sulked against the wall, being content to watch the other children. And what happy buzzings and jumping and excitement they made as they compared costumes. Clarence Buford wore a Tom Mix hat and a brown vest over a green shirt with red six-shooter patterns embossed on its collar. Another boy, Paul Carter, was dressed entirely in black, with a fluffy white handkerchief puffing from his neck. But Leon Pugh caught the attention of all our eyes. He wore a red and white checkered shirt, a loose green bandanna clasped at his throat by a shining silver buffalo head, brown chaps sewed onto his dungarees, and shiny brown cowboy boots with silver spurs that clanked each time he moved. In his hand he carried a carefully creased brown cowboy hat. He announced his fear that it would lose its shape and planned to put it on only when the dancing started. He would allow no one to touch it. Instead, he stood around clanking his feet and smoothing the crease in his fabulous hat and saying loudly, "My daddy says it pays to look good no matter what you put on."

The girls seemed prettier and much older than their ages. Even Queen Rose Phipps wore rouge on her cheeks that complemented her pale color. Shy Beverly Hankins had come dressed in a blue and white checkered bonnet and a crisp blue apron; she looked like a frontier mother. But Gweneth Lawson, my Gweneth Lawson, dominated the group of girls. She wore a long red dress with sheaves and sheaves of sparkling white crinoline belling it outward so it seemed she was floating. On her honey-brown wrists golden bracelets sparkled. A deep blue bandanna enclosed her head with the wonder of a summer sky. Black patent leather shoes glistened like half-hidden stars beneath the red and white of her hemline. She stood smiling before us and we marveled. At that moment I would have given the world to have been able to lead her about on my arm.

Mrs. Boswell watched us approvingly from behind her desk. Finally, at noon, she called, "Let's go on out!" Thirty-two living rainbows cascaded toward the door. Pole plaiters formed one line. Square dancers formed another. Mrs. Boswell strolled officiously past us in review. It seemed to me she almost paused while passing the spot where I stood on line. But she brushed past me, straightening an apron here, applying spittle and a rub to a rouged cheek there, waving a wary finger at an over-anxious boy. Then she whacked her ruler against her palm and led us out into the yard. The fifth and sixth graders had already assembled. On one end of the playground were a dozen or so tall painted poles with long, thin wisps of green and blue and yellow and rust-brown crepe floating lazily on the sweet spring breezes.

"Maypole teams *up!*" called Mr. Henry Lucas, our principal, from his platform by the swings. Beside him stood the white Superintendent of Schools (who said later of the square dance, it was reported to all the classes, "Lord y'all square dance so *good* it makes me plumb *ashamed* us white folks ain't takin' better care of our art stuff"). "Maypole teams up!" Mr. Henry Lucas shouted again. Some fifty of us, screaming shrilly, rushed to grasp our favorite color crepe. Then, to the music of "Sing Praise for All the Brightness and the Joy of

Spring," we pulled and plaited in teams of six or seven until every pole was twisted as tight and as colorfully as the braids on Gweneth Lawson's head. Then, to the applause of proud teachers and parents and the whistles of the Superintendent of Schools, we scattered happily back under the wings of our respective teachers. I stood next to Mrs. Boswell, winded and trembling but confident I had done my best. She glanced down at me and said in a quiet voice, "I do believe you are learning the rhythm of the thing."

I did not respond.

"Let's *go!*" Leon Pugh shouted to the other kids, grabbing Gweneth Lawson's arm and taking a few clanking steps forward.

"Wait a minute, Leon," Mrs. Boswell hissed. "Mr. Lucas has to change the record."

Leon sighed. "But if we don't git out there first, all them other teams will take the best spots."

"Wait!" Mrs. Boswell ordered.

Leon sulked. He inched closer to Gweneth. I watched him swing her hand impatiently. He stamped his feet and his silver spurs jangled.

Mrs. Boswell looked down at his feet. "Why, Leon," she said, "you can't go out there with razors on your shoes."

"These ain't razors," Leon muttered. "These here are spurs my brother in Bronx New York sent me just for this here dance."

"You have to take them off," Mrs. Boswell said.

Leon growled. But he reached down quickly and attempted to jerk the silver spurs from the heels of his boots. They did not come off. "No time!" he called, standing suddenly. "Mr. Lucas done put the record on."

"Leon, you might *cut* somebody with those things," Mrs. Boswell said. "Miss Gweneth Lawson's pretty red dress could get caught in those things and then she'll fall as surely as I'm standin' here."

"I'll just go out with my boots off," Leon replied.

But Mrs. Boswell shook her head firmly. "You just run on to the lunchroom and ask cook for some butter or mayo. That'll help 'em slip off." She paused, looking out over the black dirt playground. "And if you miss the first dance, why there'll be a second and maybe even a third. We'll get a Maypole plaiter to sub for you."

My heart leaped. Leon sensed it and stared at me. His hand tightened on Gweneth's as she stood radiant and smiling in the loving spring sunlight. Leon let her hand drop and bent quickly, pulling at the spurs with the fury of a Samson.

"Square dancers *up!*" Mr. Henry Lucas called.

"Sonofa*bitch!*" Leon grunted.

"Square dancers *up!*" called Mr. Lucas.

The fifth and sixth graders were screaming and rushing toward the center of the yard. Already the record was scratching out the high, slick voice of the caller. *"Sonofabitch!"* Leon moaned.

Mrs. Boswell looked directly at Gweneth, standing alone and abandoned next to Leon. "Miss Gweneth Lawson," Mrs. Boswell said in a cool voice, "it's a cryin' shame there ain't no prince to take you to that ball out there."

I do not remember moving, but I know I stood with Gweneth at the center of the yard. What I did there I do not know, but I remember watching the movements of others and doing what they did just after they had done it. Still, I cannot remember just when I looked into my partner's face or what I saw there. The scratchy voice of the caller bellowed directions and I obeyed:

> *"Allemande left with your left hand*
> *Right to your partner with a right and left grand . . ."*

Although I was told later that I made an allemande right instead of left, I have no memory of the mistake.

> *"When you get to your partner pass her by*
> *And pick up the next girl on the sly . . ."*

Nor can I remember picking up any other girl. I only remember that during many turns and do-si-dos I found myself looking into the warm brown eyes of Gweneth Lawson. I recall that she smiled at me. I recall that she laughed on another turn. I recall that I laughed with her an eternity later.

> *". . . promenade that dear old thing*
> *Throw your head right back and sing* be-*cause, just*
> be-*cause . . ."*

I do remember quite well that during the final promenade before the record ended, Gweneth stood beside me and I said to her in a voice much louder than that of the caller, "When I get up to Brooklyn I hope I see you." But I do not remember what she said in response. I want to remember that she smiled.

I know I smiled, dear Gloria. I smiled with the lemonness of her and the loving of her pressed deep into those saving places of my private self. It was my plan to savor these, and I did savor them. But when I reached New York, many years later, I did not think of Brooklyn. I followed the old, beaten, steady paths into uptown Manhattan.[4] By then I had learned to dance to many other kinds of music. And I had forgotten the savory smell of lemon. But I think sometimes of Gweneth now when I hear country music. And although it is difficult to explain to you, I still maintain that I am no mere arithmetician in the art of the square dance. I am into the calculus of it.

"Go on!" you will tell me, backing into your Northern mythology. "I can see the hustle, the hump, maybe even the Ibo highlife. But no hillbilly."

These days I am firm about arguing the point, but, as always, quietly, and mostly to myself.

1977

---

4. That is, into Harlem.

# HERMAN MELVILLE
## 1819–1891

Melville was born in New York City, the son of a New England merchant who died when Melville was still young. He took on jobs as clerk, farmhand, and schoolteacher before shipping to the South Seas on the whaler *Acushnet*. In a helter-skelter period of adventure he deserted his ship, lived among cannibals, took part in a mutiny aboard an Australian vessel, and then spent almost two years on an American man-of-war. At last home in America, he began successfully to romanticize these adventures in fiction. In six years he published seven novels, the first of which, *Typee* (1846), was a literary sensation. By the time Melville wrote *Moby-Dick* (1851), now universally regarded as one of the masterworks of American fiction, his popularity was already waning. The short stories in *Piazza Tales* (1856) did little to refurbish his reputation. Neither the fine poems he wrote about the Civil War, *Battle-Pieces* (1866), nor his long narrative poem *Clarel* (1876) received much notice. As his writing activities declined, Melville made another sea voyage around Cape Horn to San Francisco on a clipper ship commanded by his brother, and for nineteen quiet years he was a customs inspector in New York. By the time he died, Melville was virtually forgotten. It was not until the 1920s when his last fictional masterpiece, *Billy Budd* (1924), was finally published, that critical interest in his work revived. Since then it has increased in fervor and scope, discovering the richly ambiguous thought structured into his most ambitious work. His novels include *Omoo* (1847), *Mardi* (1849), *Pierre* (1852), and *The Confidence-Man* (1856).

# Bartleby, the Scrivener

### A Story of Wall Street

I am a rather elderly man. The nature of my avocations for the last thirty years has brought me into more than ordinary contact with what would seem an interesting and somewhat singular set of men, of whom as yet nothing that I know of has ever been written:—I mean the law-copyists or scriveners. I have known very many of them, professionally and privately, and if I pleased, could relate divers histories, at which good-natured gentlemen might smile, and sentimental souls might weep. But I waive the biographies of all other scriveners for a few passages in the life of Bartleby, who was a scrivener the strangest I ever saw or heard of. While of other law-copyists I might write the complete life, of Bartleby nothing of that sort can be done. I believe that no materials exist for a full and satisfactory biography of this man. It is an irreparable loss to literature. Bartleby was one of those beings of whom nothing is ascertainable, except from the original sources, and in his case those are very small. What my own astonished eyes saw of Bartleby, *that* is all I know of him, except, indeed, one vague report which will appear in the sequel.[1]

Ere introducing the scrivener, as he first appeared to me, it is fit I make some mention of myself, my *employés,* my business, my chambers, and general surroundings; because some such description is indispensable to an adequate understanding of the chief character about to be presented.

*Imprimis:*[2] I am a man who, from his youth upward, has been filled with a profound conviction that the easiest way of life is the best. Hence, though I belong to a profession proverbially energetic and nervous, even to turbulence, at times, yet nothing of that sort have I ever suffered to invade my peace. I am one of those unambitious lawyers who never addresses a jury, or in any way draws down public applause; but in the cool tranquillity of a snug retreat, do a snug business among rich men's bonds and mortgages and title-deeds. All who know me, consider me an eminently *safe* man. The late John Jacob Astor,[3] a personage little given to poetic enthusiasm, had no hesitation in pronouncing my first grand point to be prudence; my next, method. I do not speak it in vanity, but simply record the fact, that I was not unemployed in my profession by the late John Jacob Astor; a name which, I admit, I love to repeat, for it hath a rounded and orbicular sound to it, and rings like unto bullion. I will freely add, that I was not insensible to the late John Jacob Astor's good opinion.

Some time prior to the period at which this little history begins, my avocations had been largely increased. The good old office, now extinct in the State of New-York, of a Master in Chancery,[4] had been conferred upon me. It was not a very arduous office, but very pleasantly remunerative. I seldom lose my temper; much more seldom indulge in dangerous indignation at wrongs and outrages; but I must be permitted to be rash here and declare, that I consider the sudden and violent abrogation of the office of Master in Chancery, by the new Constitution, as a—premature act; inasmuch as I had counted upon a life-lease of the profits, whereas I only received those of a few short years. But this is by the way.

My chambers were upstairs at No.___Wall Street. At one end they looked upon the white wall of the interior of a spacious skylight shaft, penetrating the building from top to bottom. This view might have been considered rather tame than otherwise, deficient in what landscape painters call "life." But if so, the view from the other end of my chambers offered, at least, a contrast, if nothing more. In that direction my windows commanded an unobstructed view of a lofty brick wall, black by age and everlasting shade; which wall required no spy-glass to bring out its lurking beauties, but for the benefit of all near-sighted spectators, was pushed up to within ten feet of my window panes. Owing to the great height of the surrounding buildings, and my

---

1. That is, in the following story.   2. In the first place (Latin).   3. American landowner (1763–1848), capitalist, and fur merchant who died the richest man in the United States.   4. The duty of this office was to temper the rigidity of the law with "dictates of conscience"; the office was abolished in 1847.

chambers being on the second floor, the interval between this wall and mine not a little resembled a huge square cistern.

At the period just preceding the advent of Bartleby, I had two persons as copyists in my employment, and a promising lad as an office-boy. First, Turkey; second, Nippers; third, Ginger Nut. These may seem names, the like of which are not usually found in the Directory.[5] In truth they were nicknames, mutually conferred upon each other by my three clerks, and were deemed expressive of their respective persons or characters. Turkey was a short, pursy Englishman of about my own age, that is, somewhere not far from sixty. In the morning, one might say, his face was of a fine florid hue, but after twelve o'clock, meridian—his dinner hour—it blazed like a grate full of Christmas coals; and continued blazing—but, as it were, with a gradual wane—till 6 o'clock P.M. or thereabouts, after which I saw no more of the proprietor of the face, which, gaining its meridian with the sun, seemed to set with it, to rise, culminate, and decline the following day, with the like regularity and undiminished glory. There are many singular coincidences I have known in the course of my life, not the least among which was the fact, that exactly when Turkey displayed his fullest beams from his red and radiant countenance, just then, too, at that critical moment, began the daily period when I considered his business capacities as seriously disturbed for the remainder of the twenty-four hours. Not that he was absolutely idle, or averse to business then; far from it. The difficulty was, he was apt to be altogether too energetic. There was a strange, inflamed, flurried, flighty recklessness of activity about him. He would be incautious in dipping his pen into his inkstand. All his blots upon my documents were dropped there after twelve o'clock, meridian. Indeed, not only would he be reckless and sadly given to making blots in the afternoon, but some days he went further, and was rather noisy. At such times, too, his face flamed with augmented blazonry, as if cannel coal had been heaped on anthracite.[6] He made an unpleasant racket with his chair; spilled his sand-box;[7] in mending his pens, impatiently split them all to pieces, and threw them on the floor in a sudden passion; stood up and leaned over his table, boxing his papers about in a most indecorous manner, very sad to behold in an elderly man like him. Nevertheless, as he was in many ways a most valuable person to me, and all the time before twelve o'clock, meridian, was the quickest, steadiest creature too, accomplishing a great deal of work in a style not easy to be matched—for these reasons, I was willing to overlook his eccentricities, though indeed, occasionally, I remonstrated with him. I did this very gently, however, because, though the civilest, nay, the blandest and most reverential of men in the morning, yet in the afternoon he was disposed, upon provocation, to be slightly rash with his tongue, in fact, insolent. Now, valuing his morning services as I did, and resolved not to lose them—yet, at the same time made uncomfortable by his inflamed ways after twelve o'clock; and being a man of peace, unwilling by my admonitions to call forth unseemly retorts from him—I took upon me, one Saturday noon (he was always worse on Saturdays), to hint to him, very kindly, that perhaps now that he was growing old, it might be well to abridge his labors; in short, he

---

**5.** Post Office Directory.  **6.** Oily, quick-burning coal heaped on a hard, slow-burning kind.  **7.** That is, sand used to dry ink.

need not come to my chambers after twelve o'clock, but, dinner over, had best go home to his lodgings and rest himself till tea-time. But no; he insisted upon his afternoon devotions. His countenance became intolerably fervid, as he oratorically assured me—gesticulating with a long ruler at the other end of the room—that if his services in the morning were useful, how indispensable, then, in the afternoon?

"With submission, sir," said Turkey on this occasion, "I consider myself your right-hand man. In the morning I but marshal and deploy my columns; but in the afternoon I put myself at their head, and gallantly charge the foe, thus!"—and he made a violent thrust with the ruler.

"But the blots, Turkey," intimated I.

"True,—but, with submission, sir, behold these hairs! I am getting old. Surely, sir, a blot or two of a warm afternoon is not to be severely urged against gray hairs. Old age—even if it blot the page—is honorable. With submission, sir, we *both* are getting old."

This appeal to my fellow-feeling was hardly to be resisted. At all events, I saw that go he would not. So I made up my mind to let him stay, resolving, nevertheless, to see to it, that during the afternoon he had to do with my less important papers.

Nippers, the second on my list, was a whiskered, sallow, and, upon the whole, rather piratical-looking young man of about five and twenty. I always deemed him the victim of two evil powers—ambition and indigestion. The ambition was evinced by a certain impatience of the duties of a mere copyist—an unwarrantable usurpation of strictly professional affairs, such as the original drawing up of legal documents. The indigestion seemed betokened in an occasional nervous testiness and grinning irritability, causing the teeth to audibly grind together over mistakes committed in copying; unnecessary maledictions, hissed, rather than spoken, in the heat of business; and especially by a continual discontent with the height of the table where he worked. Though of a very ingenious mechanical turn, Nippers could never get this table to suit him. He put chips under it, blocks of various sorts, bits of pasteboard, and at last went so far as to attempt an exquisite adjustment by final pieces of folded blotting-paper. But no invention would answer. If, for the sake of easing his back, he brought the table lid at a sharp angle well up towards his chin, and wrote there like a man using the steep roof of a Dutch house for his desk—then he declared that it stopped the circulation in his arms. If now he lowered the table to his waistbands, and stooped over it in writing, then there was a sore aching in his back. In short, the truth of the matter was, Nippers knew not what he wanted. Or, if he wanted anything, it was to be rid of a scrivener's table altogether. Among the manifestations of his diseased ambition was a fondness he had for receiving visits from certain ambiguous-looking fellows in seedy coats, whom he called his clients. Indeed I was aware that not only was he, at times, considerable of a ward-politician, but he occasionally did a little business at the Justices' courts, and was not unknown on the steps of the Tombs.[8] I have good reason to believe, however, that one individual who called upon him at my chambers, and who, with a

---

8. The Manhattan House of Detention is often called "the Tombs" because of its distinctive Egyptian architecture. As "ward-politician" Nippers was a fixer who seems to have made extralegal arrangements for constituents of his district of the city when they had legal problems.

grand air, he insisted was his client, was no other than a dun,[9] and the alleged title-deed, a bill. But with all his failings, and the annoyances he caused me, Nippers, like his compatriot Turkey, was a very useful man to me; wrote a neat, swift hand; and, when he chose, was not deficient in a gentlemanly sort of deportment. Added to this, he always dressed in a gentlemanly sort of way; and so, incidentally, reflected credit upon my chambers. Whereas with respect to Turkey, I had much ado to keep him from being a reproach to me. His clothes were apt to look oily and smell of eating-houses. He wore his pantaloons very loose and baggy in summer. His coats were execrable; his hat not to be handled. But while the hat was a thing of indifference to me, inasmuch as his natural civility and deference, as a dependent Englishman, always led him to doff it the moment he entered the room, yet his coat was another matter. Concerning his coats, I reasoned with him; but with no effect. The truth was, I suppose, that a man with so small an income, could not afford to sport such a lustrous face and a lustrous coat at one and the same time. As Nippers once observed, Turkey's money went chiefly for red ink. One winter day I presented Turkey with a highly-respectable looking coat of my own, a padded gray coat, of a most comfortable warmth, and which buttoned straight up from the knee to the neck. I thought Turkey would appreciate the favour, and abate his rashness and obstreperousness of afternoons. But no. I verily believe that buttoning himself up in so downy and blanket-like a coat had a pernicious effect upon him; upon the same principle that too much oats are bad for horses. In fact, precisely as a rash, restive horse is said to feel his oats, so Turkey felt his coat. It made him insolent. He was a man whom prosperity harmed.

Though concerning the self-indulgent habits of Turkey I had my own private surmises, yet touching Nippers I was well persuaded that whatever might be his faults in other respects, he was, at least, a temperate young man. But, indeed, nature herself seemed to have been his vintner, and at his birth charged him so thoroughly with an irritable, brandy-like disposition, that all subsequent potations were needless. When I consider how, amid the stillness of my chambers, Nippers would sometimes impatiently rise from his seat, and stooping over his table, spread his arms wide apart, seize the whole desk, and move it, and jerk it, with a grim, grinding motion on the floor, as if the table were a perverse voluntary agent, intent on thwarting and vexing him; I plainly perceive that for Nippers, brandy and water were altogether superfluous.

It was fortunate for me that, owing to its peculiar cause—indigestion—the irritability and consequent nervousness of Nippers, were mainly observable in the morning, while in the afternoon he was comparatively mild. So that Turkey's paroxysms only coming on about twelve o'clock, I never had to do with their eccentricities at one time. Their fits relieved each other like guards. When Nippers' was on, Turkey's was off; and *vice versa*. This was a good natural arrangement under the circumstances.

Ginger Nut, the third on my list, was a lad some twelve years old. His father was a carman,[1] ambitious of seeing his son on the bench instead of a cart, before he died. So he sent him to my office as student at law, errand boy, and cleaner and sweeper, at the rate of one dollar a week. He had a little desk to himself, but he did not use it much. Upon inspection, the drawer exhibited a

---

**9.** Bill-collector.   **1.** Driver of a cart used for hauling goods.

great array of the shells of various sorts of nuts. Indeed, to this quick-witted youth the whole noble science of the law was contained in a nut-shell. Not the least among the employments of Ginger Nut, as well as one which he discharged with the most alacrity, was his duty as cake and apple purveyor for Turkey and Nippers. Copying law papers being proverbially a dry, husky sort of business, my two scriveners were fain to moisten their mouths very often with Spitzenbergs[2] to be had at the numerous stalls nigh the Custom House and Post Office. Also, they sent Ginger Nut very frequently for that peculiar cake—small, flat, round, and very spicy—after which he had been named by them. Of a cold morning when business was but dull, Turkey would gobble up scores of these cakes, as if they were mere wafers—indeed they sell them at the rate of six or eight for a penny—the scrape of his pen blending with the crunching of the crisp particles in his mouth. Of all the fiery after-noon blunders and flurried rashnesses of Turkey, was his once moistening a ginger-cake between his lips, and clapping it on to a mortgage for a seal. I came within an ace of dismissing him then. But he mollified me by making an oriental bow, and saying—"With submission, sir, it was generous of me to find you in[3] stationery on my own account."

Now my original business—that of a conveyancer and title hunter,[4] and drawer-up of recondite documents of all sorts—was considerably increased by receiving the master's office. There was now great work for scriveners. Not only must I push the clerks already with me, but I must have additional help. In answer to my advertisement, a motionless young man one morning stood upon my office threshold, the door being open, for it was summer. I can see that figure now—pallidly neat, pitiably respectable, incurably forlorn! It was Bartleby.

After a few words touching his qualifications, I engaged him, glad to have among my corps of copyists a man of so singularly sedate an aspect, which I thought might operate beneficially upon the flighty temper of Turkey, and the fiery one of Nippers.

I should have stated before that ground glass folding-doors divided my premises into two parts, one of which was occupied by my scriveners, the other by myself. According to my humour I threw open these doors, or closed them. I resolved to assign Bartleby a corner by the folding-doors, but on my side of them, so as to have this quiet man within easy call, in case any trifling thing was to be done. I placed his desk close up to a small side-window in that part of the room, a window which originally had afforded a lateral view of certain grimy back-yards and bricks, but which, owing to subsequent erections, com-manded at present no view at all, though it gave some light. Within three feet of the panes was a wall, and the light came down from far above, between two lofty buildings, as from a very small opening in a dome. Still further to a sat-isfactory arrangement, I procured a high green folding screen, which might entirely isolate Bartleby from my sight, though not remove him from my voice. And thus, in a manner, privacy and society were conjoined.

At first Bartleby did an extraordinary quantity of writing. As if long fam-ishing for something to copy, he seemed to gorge himself on my documents.

---

2. Apples.   3. "To provide you with."   4. That is, examining the abstract of property deeds. A convey-ance is a legal paper for transferring property.

There was no pause for digestion. He ran a day and night line, copying by sunlight and by candle-light. I should have been quite delighted with his application, had he been cheerfully industrious. But he wrote on silently, palely, mechanically.

It is, of course, an indispensable part of a scrivener's business to verify the accuracy of his copy, word by word. Where there are two or more scriveners in an office, they assist each other in this examination, one reading from the copy, the other holding the original. It is a very dull, wearisome, and lethargic affair. I can readily imagine that to some sanguine temperaments it would be altogether intolerable. For example, I cannot credit that the mettlesome poet Byron would have contentedly sat down with Bartleby to examine a law document of, say five hundred pages, closely written in a crimpy hand.

Now and then, in the haste of business, it had been my habit to assist in comparing some brief document myself, calling Turkey or Nippers for this purpose. One object I had in placing Bartleby so handy to me behind the screen, was to avail myself of his services on such trivial occasions. It was on the third day, I think, of his being with me, and before any necessity had arisen for having his own writing examined, that, being much hurried to complete a small affair I had in hand, I abruptly called to Bartleby. In my haste and natural expectancy of instant compliance, I sat with my head bent over the original on my desk, and my right hand sideways, and somewhat nervously extended with the copy, so that immediately upon emerging from his retreat, Bartleby might snatch it and proceed to business without the least delay.

In this very attitude did I sit when I called to him, rapidly stating what it was I wanted him to do—namely, to examine a small paper with me. Imagine my surprise, nay, my consternation, when without moving from his privacy, Bartleby in a singularly mild, firm voice, replied, "I would prefer not to."

I sat awhile in perfect silence, rallying my stunned faculties. Immediately it occurred to me that my ears had deceived me, or Bartleby had entirely misunderstood my meaning. I repeated my request in the clearest tone I could assume. But in quite as clear a one came the previous reply, "I would prefer not to."

"Prefer not to," echoed I, rising in high excitement, and crossing the room with a stride. "What do you mean? Are you moon-struck?[5] I want you to help me compare this sheet here—take it," and I thrust it toward him.

"I would prefer not to," said he.

I looked at him steadfastly. His face was leanly composed; his gray eye dimly calm. Not a wrinkle of agitation rippled him. Had there been the least uneasiness, anger, impatience or impertinence in his manner; in other words, had there been anything ordinarily human about him, doubtless I should have violently dismissed him from the premises. But as it was, I should have as soon thought of turning my pale plaster-of-paris bust of Cicero[6] out of doors. I stood gazing at him awhile, as he went on with his own writing, and then reseated myself at my desk. This is very strange, thought I. What had one best do? But my business hurried me. I concluded to forget the matter for

---

5. This popular synonym for *crazy* incorporates the old belief that the lunatic was affected by phases of the moon (Latin: *luna*).   **6.** Marcus Tullius Cicero (106–43 B.C.E.), pro-republic Roman statesman, barrister, writer, and orator.

the present, reserving it for my future leisure. So calling Nippers from the other room, the paper was speedily examined.

A few days after this, Bartleby concluded four lengthy documents, being quadruplicates of a week's testimony taken before me in my High Court of Chancery. It became necessary to examine them. It was an important suit, and great accuracy was imperative. Having all things arranged, I called Turkey, Nippers and Ginger Nut from the next room, meaning to place the four copies in the hands of my four clerks, while I should read from the original. Accordingly Turkey, Nippers and Ginger Nut had taken their seats in a row, each with his document in hand, when I called to Bartleby to join this interesting group.

"Bartleby! quick, I am waiting."

I heard a slow scrape of his chair legs on the uncarpeted floor, and soon he appeared standing at the entrance of his hermitage.

"What is wanted?" said he mildly.

"The copies, the copies," said I hurriedly. "We are going to examine them. There"—and I held towards him the fourth quadruplicate.

"I would prefer not to," he said, and gently disappeared behind the screen.

For a few moments I was turned into a pillar of salt,[7] standing at the head of my seated column of clerks. Recovering myself, I advanced toward the screen, and demanded the reason for such extraordinary conduct.

"*Why* do you refuse?"

"I would prefer not to."

With any other man I should have flown outright into a dreadful passion, scorned all further words, and thrust him ignominiously from my presence. But there was something about Bartleby that not only strangely disarmed me, but in a wonderful manner touched and disconcerted me. I began to reason with him.

"These are your own copies we are about to examine. It is labour saving to you, because one examination will answer for your four papers. It is common usage. Every copyist is bound to help examine his copy. Is it not so? Will you not speak? Answer!"

"I prefer not to," he replied in a flute-like tone. It seemed to me that while I had been addressing him, he carefully revolved every statement that I made; fully comprehended the meaning; could not gainsay the irresistible conclusion; but, at the same time, some paramount consideration prevailed with him to reply as he did.

"You are decided, then, not to comply with my request—a request made according to common usage and common sense?"

He briefly gave me to understand that on that point my judgment was sound. Yes: his decision was irreversible.

It is not seldom the case that when a man is browbeaten in some unprecedented and violently unreasonable way, he begins to stagger in his own plainest faith. He begins, as it were, vaguely to surmise that, wonderful as it may be, all the justice and all the reason are on the other side. Accordingly, if any

---

7. That is, was paralyzed. The allusion is to Genesis 19:26; Lot's wife is turned into a pillar of salt when she looks back at the destruction of Sodom.

disinterested persons are present, he turns to them for some reinforcement for his own faltering mind.

"Turkey," said I, "what do you think of this? Am I not right?"

"With submission, sir," said Turkey, with his blandest tone, "I think that you are."

"Nippers," said I, "what do *you* think of it?"

"I think I should kick him out of the office."

(The reader of nice perceptions will here perceive that, it being morning, Turkey's answer is couched in polite and tranquil terms, but Nippers's reply in ill-tempered ones. Or, to repeat a previous sentence, Nippers's ugly mood was on duty, and Turkey's off.)

"Ginger Nut," said I, willing to enlist the smallest suffrage[8] in my behalf, "what do *you* think of it?"

"I think, sir, he's a little *luny*,"[9] replied Ginger Nut, with a grin.

"You hear what they say," said I, turning towards the screen, "come forth and do your duty."

But he vouchsafed no reply. I pondered a moment in sore perplexity. But once more business hurried me. I determined again to postpone the consideration of this dilemma to my future leisure. With a little trouble we made out to examine the papers without Bartleby, though at every page or two, Turkey deferentially dropped his opinion that this proceeding was quite out of the common; while Nippers, twitching in his chair with a dyspeptic nervousness, ground out between his set teeth occasional hissing maledictions against the stubborn oaf behind the screen. And for his (Nippers's) part, this was the first and the last time he would do another man's business without pay.

Meanwhile Bartleby sat in his hermitage, oblivious to everything but his own peculiar business there.

Some days passed, the scrivener being employed upon another lengthy work. His late remarkable conduct led me to regard his ways narrowly. I observed that he never went to dinner; indeed that he never went any where. As yet I had never of my personal knowledge known him to be outside of my office. He was a perpetual sentry in the corner. At about eleven o'clock though, in the morning, I noticed that Ginger Nut would advance toward the opening in Bartleby's screen, as if silently beckoned thither by a gesture invisible to me where I sat. The boy would then leave the office jingling a few pence, and reappear with a handful of ginger-nuts which he delivered in the hermitage, receiving two of the cakes for his trouble.

He lives, then, on ginger-nuts, thought I; never eats a dinner, properly speaking; he must be a vegetarian then; but no; he never eats even vegetables, he eats nothing but ginger-nuts. My mind then ran on in reveries concerning the probable effects upon the human constitution of living entirely on ginger-nuts. Ginger-nuts are so called because they contain ginger as one of their peculiar constituents, and the final flavoring one. Now what was ginger? A hot, spicy thing. Was Bartleby hot and spicy? Not at all. Ginger, then, had no effect upon Bartleby. Probably he preferred it should have none.

Nothing so aggravates an earnest person as a passive resistance. If the individual so resisted be of a not inhumane temper, and the resisting one perfectly

---

**8.** Favorable vote.   **9.** Loony—here Melville's spelling recalls the word *lunatic*.

harmless in his passivity; then, in the better moods of the former, he will endeavor charitably to construe to his imagination what proves impossible to be solved by his judgment. Even so, for the most part, I regarded Bartleby and his ways. Poor fellow! thought I, he means no mischief; it is plain he intends no insolence; his aspect sufficiently evinces that his eccentricities are involuntary. He is useful to me. I can get along with him. If I turn him away, the chances are he will fall in with some less indulgent employer, and then he will be rudely treated, and perhaps driven forth miserably to starve. Yes. Here I can cheaply purchase a delicious self-approval. To befriend Bartleby; to humour him in his strange wilfulness, will cost me little or nothing, while I lay up in my soul what will eventually prove a sweet morsel for my conscience. But this mood was not invariable with me. The passiveness of Bartleby sometimes irritated me. I felt strangely goaded on to encounter him in new opposition, to elicit some angry spark from him answerable to my own. But indeed I might as well have essayed to strike fire with my knuckles against a bit of Windsor soap.[1] But one afternoon the evil impulse in me mastered me, and the following little scene ensued:

"Bartleby," said I, "when those papers are all copied, I will compare them with you."

"I would prefer not to."

"How? Surely you do not mean to persist in that mulish vagary?"

No answer.

I threw open the folding-doors near by, and turning upon Turkey and Nippers, exclaimed in an excited manner:

"He says, a second time, he won't examine his papers. What do you think of it, Turkey?"

It was afternoon, be it remembered. Turkey sat glowing like a brass boiler, his bald head steaming, his hands reeling among his blotted papers.

"Think of it?" roared Turkey; "I think I'll just step behind his screen, and black his eyes for him!"

So saying, Turkey rose to his feet and threw his arms into a pugilistic position. He was hurrying away to make good his promise, when I detained him, alarmed at the effect of incautiously rousing Turkey's combativeness after dinner.

"Sit down, Turkey," said I, "and hear what Nippers has to say. What do you think of it, Nippers? Would I not be justified in immediately dismissing Bartleby?"

"Excuse me, that is for you to decide, sir. I think his conduct quite unusual, and indeed unjust, as regards Turkey and myself. But it may only be a passing whim."

"Ah," exclaimed I, "You have strangely changed your mind then—you speak very gently of him now."

"All beer," cried Turkey; "gentleness is effects of beer—Nippers and I dined together to-day. You see how gentle *I* am, sir. Shall I go and black his eyes?"

"You refer to Bartleby, I suppose. No, not to-day, Turkey," I replied; "pray, put up your fists."

1. Fine, scented soap.

I closed the doors, and again advanced towards Bartleby. I felt additional incentives tempting me to my fate. I burned to be rebelled against again. I remembered that Bartleby never left the office.

"Bartleby," said I, "Ginger Nut is away; just step round to the Post Office, won't you? (it was but a three minutes' walk), and see if there is any thing for me."

"I would prefer not to."

"You *will* not?"

"I *prefer* not."

I staggered to my desk, and sat there in a deep study. My blind inveteracy returned. Was there any other thing in which I could procure myself to be ignominiously repulsed by this lean, penniless wight?—my hired clerk? What added thing is there, perfectly reasonable, that he will be sure to refuse to do?

"Bartleby!"

No answer.

"Bartleby," in a louder tone.

No answer.

"Bartleby," I roared.

Like a very ghost, agreeably to the laws of magical invocation, at the third summons, he appeared at the entrance of his hermitage.

"Go to the next room, and tell Nippers to come to me."

"I prefer not to," he respectfully and slowly said, and mildly disappeared.

"Very good, Bartleby," said I, in a quiet sort of serenely severe self-possessed tone, intimating the unalterable purpose of some terrible retribution very close at hand. At the moment I half intended something of the kind. But upon the whole, as it was drawing towards my dinner-hour, I thought it best to put on my hat and walk home for the day, suffering much from perplexity and distress of mind.

Shall I acknowledge it? The conclusion of this whole business was, that it soon became a fixed fact of my chambers, that a pale young scrivener, by the name of Bartleby, had a desk there; that he copied for me at the usual rate of four cents a folio (one hundred words); but he was permanently exempt from examining the work done by him, that duty being transferred to Turkey and Nippers, out of compliment doubtless to their superior acuteness; moreover, said Bartleby was never on any account to be despatched on the most trivial errand of any sort; and that even if entreated to take upon him such a matter, it was generally understood that he would prefer not to—in other words, that he would refuse point-blank.

As days passed on, I became considerably reconciled to Bartleby. His steadiness, his freedom from all dissipation, his incessant industry (except when he chose to throw himself into a standing revery behind his screen), his great stillness, his unalterableness of demeanor under all circumstances, made him a valuable acquisition. One prime thing was this,—*he was always there;*—first in the morning, continually through the day, and the last at night. I had a singular confidence in his honesty. I felt my most precious papers perfectly safe in his hands. Sometimes to be sure I could not, for the very soul of me, avoid falling into sudden spasmodic passions with him. For it was exceeding difficult to bear in mind all the time those strange peculiarities, privileges, and unheard of exemptions, forming the tacit stipulations on Bartleby's part under which he remained in my office. Now and then, in the eagerness of despatching pressing business, I would inadvertently summon Bartleby, in a short, rapid tone, to put his finger, say, on the incipient tie of a bit of red tape with which I was about compressing some papers. Of course, from behind the screen the usual answer, "I prefer not to," was sure to come; and then, how could a human creature with common infirmities of our nature, refrain from bitterly exclaiming upon such perverseness—such unreasonableness. However, every added repulse of this sort which I received only tended to lessen the probability of my repeating the inadvertence.

Here it must be said, that according to the customs of most legal gentlemen occupying chambers in densely-populated law buildings, there were several keys to my door. One was kept by a woman residing in the attic, which person weekly scrubbed and daily swept and dusted my apartments. Another was kept by Turkey for convenience sake. The third I sometimes carried in my own pocket. The fourth I knew not who had.

Now, one Sunday morning I happened to go to Trinity Church,[2] to hear a celebrated preacher, and finding myself rather early on the ground, I thought I would walk round to my chambers for awhile. Luckily I had my key with me; but upon applying it to the lock, I found it resisted by something inserted from the inside. Quite surprised, I called out; when to my consternation a key was turned from within; and thrusting his lean visage at me, and holding the door ajar, the apparition of Bartleby appeared, in his shirt sleeves, and otherwise in a strangely tattered dishabille, saying quietly that he was sorry, but he was deeply engaged just then, and—preferred not admitting me at present. In a brief word or two, he moreover added, that perhaps I had better walk round the block two or three times, and by that time he would probably have concluded his affairs.

Now, the utterly unsurmised appearance of Bartleby, tenanting my law-chambers of a Sunday morning, with his cadaverously gentlemanly *nonchalance,* yet withal firm and self-possessed, had such a strange effect upon me, that incontinently I slunk away from my own door, and did as desired. But not without sundry twinges of impotent rebellion against the mild effrontery of this unaccountable scrivener. Indeed, it was his wonderful mildness chiefly, which not only disarmed me, but unmanned me, as it were. For I consider that one, for the time, is in a way unmanned when he tranquilly permits his hired clerk to dictate to him, and order him away from his own premises. Furthermore, I was full of uneasiness as to what Bartleby could possibly be doing in my office in his shirt sleeves, and in an otherwise dismantled condition of a Sunday morning. Was any thing amiss going on? Nay, that was out of the question. It was not to be thought of for a moment that Bartleby was an immoral person. But what could he be doing there—copying? Nay again, whatever might be his eccentricities, Bartleby was an eminently decorous person. He would be the last man to sit down to his desk in any state approaching to nudity. Besides, it was Sunday; and there was something about Bartleby that forbade the supposition that he would by any secular occupation violate the proprieties of the day.

2. Venerable church in the Wall Street district.

Nevertheless, my mind was not pacified; and full of a restless curiosity, at last I returned to the door. Without hindrance I inserted my key, opened it, and entered. Bartleby was not to be seen. I looked round anxiously, peeped behind his screen; but it was very plain that he was gone. Upon more closely examining the place, I surmised that for an indefinite period Bartleby must have ate, dressed, and slept in my office, and that too without plate, mirror, or bed. The cushioned seat of a ricketty old sofa in one corner bore the faint impress of a lean, reclining form. Rolled away under his desk, I found a blanket; under the empty grate, a blacking box[3] and brush; on a chair, a tin basin, with soap and a ragged towel; in a newspaper a few crumbs of ginger-nuts and a morsel of cheese. Yes, thought I, it is evident enough that Bartleby has been making his home here, keeping bachelor's hall all by himself. Immediately then the thought came sweeping across me, What miserable friendlessness and loneliness are here revealed! His poverty is great; but his solitude, how horrible! Think of it. Of a Sunday, Wall Street is deserted as Petra;[4] and every night of every day it is an emptiness. This building too, which of week-days hums with industry and life, at nightfall echoes with sheer vacancy, and all through Sunday is forlorn. And here Bartleby makes his home; sole spectator of a solitude which he has seen all populous—a sort of innocent and transformed Marius brooding among the ruins of Carthage![5]

For the first time in my life a feeling of overpowering stinging melancholy seized me. Before, I had never experienced aught but a not-unpleasing sadness. The bond of a common humanity now drew me irresistibly to gloom. A fraternal melancholy! For both I and Bartleby were sons of Adam. I remembered the bright silks and sparkling faces I had seen that day, in gala trim, swan-like sailing down the Mississippi of Broadway; and I contrasted them with the pallid copyist, and thought to myself, Ah, happiness courts the light, so we deem the world is gay; but misery hides aloof, so we deem that misery there is none. These sad fancyings—chimeras, doubtless, of a sick and silly brain—led on to other and more special thoughts, concerning the eccentricities of Bartleby. Presentiments of strange discoveries hovered round me. The scrivener's pale form appeared to me laid out, among uncaring strangers, in its shivering winding sheet.

Suddenly I was attracted by Bartleby's closed desk, the key in open sight left in the lock.

I mean no mischief, seek the gratification of no heartless curiosity, thought I; besides, the desk is mine, and its contents too, so I will make bold to look within. Everything was methodically arranged, the papers smoothly placed. The pigeon holes were deep, and, removing the files of documents, I groped into their recesses. Presently I felt something there, and dragged it out. It was an old bandanna handkerchief, heavy and knotted. I opened it, and saw it was a savings' bank.

I now recalled all the quiet mysteries which I had noted in the man. I remembered that he never spoke but to answer; that though at intervals he had considerable time to himself, yet I had never seen him reading—no, not even a

**3.** Box of shoe polish.  **4.** Long-ruined and deserted Middle Eastern city.  **5.** Caius Marius (157–86 B.C.E.), Roman consul and general expelled from Rome and who sought sanctuary in Carthage, the African city Rome had destroyed; i.e., a ruined man in a ruined city.

newspaper; that for long periods he would stand looking out, at his pale window behind the screen, upon the dead brick wall; I was quite sure he never visited any refectory or eating-house; while his pale face clearly indicated that he never drank beer like Turkey, or tea and coffee even, like other men; that he never went anywhere in particular that I could learn; never went out for a walk, unless indeed that was the case at present; that he had declined telling who he was, or whence he came, or whether he had any relatives in the world; that though so thin and pale, he never complained of ill health. And more than all, I remembered a certain unconscious air of pallid—how shall I call it?—of pallid haughtiness, say, or rather an austere reserve about him, which had positively awed me into my tame compliance with his eccentricities, when I had feared to ask him to do the slightest incidental thing for me, even though I might know, from his long-continued motionlessness, that behind his screen he must be standing in one of those dead-wall reveries of his.

Revolving all these things, and coupling them with the recently discovered fact that he made my office his constant abiding place and home, and not forgetful of his morbid moodiness; revolving all these things, a prudential feeling began to steal over me. My first emotions had been those of pure melancholy and sincerest pity; but just in proportion as the forlornness of Bartleby grew and grew to my imagination, did that same melancholy merge into fear, that pity into repulsion. So true it is, and so terrible too, that up to a certain point the thought or sight of misery enlists our best affections; but, in certain special cases, beyond that point it does not. They err who would assert that invariably this is owing to the inherent selfishness of the human heart. It rather proceeds from a certain hopelessness of remedying excessive and organic ill. To a sensitive being, pity is not seldom pain. And when at last it is perceived that such pity cannot lead to effectual succor, common sense bids the soul be rid of it. What I saw that morning persuaded me that the scrivener was the victim of innate and incurable disorder. I might give alms to his body; but his body did not pain him; it was his soul that suffered, and his soul I could not reach.

I did not accomplish the purpose of going to Trinity Church that morning. Somehow, the things I had seen disqualified me for the time from church-going. I walked homeward, thinking what I would do with Bartleby. Finally, I resolved upon this:—I would put certain calm questions to him the next morning, touching his history, &c., and if he declined to answer them openly and unreservedly (and I supposed he would prefer not), then to give him a twenty dollar bill over and above whatever I might owe him, and tell him his services were no longer required; but that if in any other way I could assist him, I would be happy to do so, especially if he desired to return to his native place, wherever that might be, I would willingly help to defray the expenses. Moreover, if, after reaching home, he found himself at any time in want of aid, a letter from him would be sure of a reply.

The next morning came.

"Bartleby," said I, gently calling to him behind his screen.

No reply.

"Bartleby," said I, in a still gentler tone, "come here; I am not going to ask you to do anything you would prefer not to do—I simply wish to speak to you."

Upon this he noiselessly slid into view.

"Will you tell me, Bartleby, where you were born?"

"I would prefer not to."

"Will you tell me *anything* about yourself?"

"I would prefer not to."

"But what reasonable objection can you have to speak to me? I feel friendly towards you."

He did not look at me while I spoke, but kept his glance fixed upon my bust of Cicero, which, as I then sat, was directly behind me, some six inches above my head.

"What is your answer, Bartleby?" said I, after waiting a considerable time for a reply, during which his countenance remained immovable, only there was the faintest conceivable tremor of the white attenuated mouth.

"At present I prefer to give no answer," he said, and retired into his hermitage.

It was rather weak in me I confess, but his manner on this occasion nettled me. Not only did there seem to lurk in it a certain calm disdain, but his perverseness seemed ungrateful, considering the undeniable good usage and indulgence he had received from me.

Again I sat ruminating what I should do. Mortified as I was at his behavior, and resolved as I had been to dismiss him when I entered my office, nevertheless I strangely felt something superstitious knocking at my heart, and forbidding me carry out my purpose, and denouncing me for a villain if I dared to breathe one bitter word against this forlornest of mankind. At last, familiarly drawing my chair behind his screen, I sat down and said: "Bartleby, never mind then about revealing your history; but let me entreat you, as a friend, to comply as far as may be with the usages of this office. Say now you will help to examine papers to-morrow or next day: in short, say now that in a day or two you will begin to be a little reasonable:—say so, Bartleby."

"At present I would prefer not to be a little reasonable," was his mildly cadaverous reply.

Just then the folding-doors opened, and Nippers approached. He seemed suffering from an unusually bad night's rest, induced by severer indigestion than common. He overheard those final words of Bartleby.

"*Prefer not*, eh?" gritted Nippers—"I'd *prefer* him, if I were you, sir," addressing me—"I'd *prefer* him; I'd give him preferences, the stubborn mule! What is it, sir, pray, that he *prefers* not to do now?"

Bartleby moved not a limb.

"Mr. Nippers," said I, "I'd prefer that you would withdraw for the present."

Somehow, of late I had got into the way of involuntarily using this word "prefer" upon all sorts of not exactly suitable occasions. And I trembled to think that my contact with the scrivener had already and seriously affected me in a mental way. And what further and deeper aberration might it not yet produce? This apprehension had not been without efficacy in determining me to summary means.

As Nippers, looking very sour and sulky, was departing, Turkey blandly and deferentially approached.

"With submission, sir," said he, "yesterday I was thinking about Bartleby here, and I think that if he would but prefer to take a quart of good ale every day, it would do much towards mending him, and enabling him to assist in examining his papers."

"So you have got the word too," said I, slightly excited.

"With submission, what word, sir," asked Turkey, respectfully crowding himself into the contracted space behind the screen, and by so doing, making me jostle the scrivener. "What word, sir?"

"I would prefer to be left alone here," said Bartleby, as if offended at being mobbed in his privacy.

"*That's* the word, Turkey," said I—"*that's* it."

"Oh, *prefer?* oh, yes—queer word. I never use it myself. But, sir, as I was saying, if he would but prefer—"

"Turkey," interrupted I, "you will please withdraw."

"Oh certainly, sir, if you prefer that I should."

As he opened the folding-door to retire, Nippers at his desk caught a glimpse of me, and asked whether I would prefer to have a certain paper copied on blue paper or white. He did not in the least roguishly accent the word *prefer*. It was plain that it involuntarily rolled from his tongue. I thought to myself, surely I must get rid of a demented man, who already has in some degree turned the tongues, if not the heads, of myself and clerks. But I thought it prudent not to break the dismission at once.

The next day I noticed that Bartleby did nothing but stand at his window in his dead-wall revery. Upon asking him why he did not write, he said that he had decided upon doing no more writing.

"Why, how now? what next?" exclaimed I, "do no more writing?"

"No more."

"And what is the reason?"

"Do you not see the reason for yourself," he indifferently replied.

I looked steadfastly at him, and perceived that his eyes looked dull and glazed. Instantly it occurred to me, that his unexampled diligence in copying by his dim window for the first few weeks of his stay with me might have temporarily impaired his vision.

I was touched. I said something in condolence with him. I hinted that of course he did wisely in abstaining from writing for a while, and urged him to embrace that opportunity of taking wholesome exercise in the open air. This, however, he did not do. A few days after this, my other clerks being absent, and being in a great hurry to dispatch certain letters by the mail, I thought that, having nothing else earthly to do, Bartleby would surely be less inflexible than usual, and carry these letters to the Post Office. But he blankly declined. So, much to my inconvenience, I went myself.

Still added days went by. Whether Bartleby's eyes improved or not, I could not say. To all appearance, I thought they did. But when I asked him if they did, he vouchsafed no answer. At all events, he would do no copying. At last, in reply to my urgings, he informed me that he had permanently given up copying.

"What!" exclaimed I; "suppose your eyes should get entirely well—better than ever before—would you not copy then?"

"I have given up copying," he answered and slid aside.

He remained, as ever, a fixture in my chamber. Nay—if that were possible—he became still more of a fixture than before. What was to be done? He would do nothing in the office: why should he stay there? In plain fact, he had now become a millstone[6] to me, not only useless as a necklace, but afflictive to bear. Yet I was sorry for him. I speak less than truth when I say that, on his own account, he occasioned me uneasiness. If he would but have named a single relative or friend, I would instantly have written, and urged their taking the poor fellow away to some convenient retreat. But he seemed alone, absolutely alone in the universe. A bit of wreckage in the mid-Atlantic. At length, necessities connected with my business tyrannized over all other considerations. Decently as I could, I told Bartleby that in six days' time he must unconditionally leave the office. I warned him to take measures, in the interval, for procuring some other abode. I offered to assist him in this endeavor, if he himself would but take the first step towards a removal. "And when you finally quit me, Bartleby," added I, "I shall see that you go away not entirely unprovided. Six days from this hour, remember."

At the expiration of that period, I peeped behind the screen, and lo! Bartleby was there.

I buttoned up my coat, balanced myself; advanced slowly towards him, touched his shoulder, and said, "The time has come; you must quit this place; I am sorry for you; here is money; but you must go."

"I would prefer not," he replied, with his back still towards me.

"You *must*."

He remained silent.

Now I had an unbounded confidence in this man's common honesty. He had frequently restored to me sixpences and shillings carelessly dropped upon the floor, for I am apt to be very reckless in such shirt-button affairs. The proceeding then which followed will not be deemed extraordinary.

"Bartleby," said I, "I owe you twelve dollars on account; here are thirty-two; the odd twenty are yours.—Will you take it?" and I handed the bills towards him.

But he made no motion.

"I will leave them here then," putting them under a weight on the table. Then taking my hat and cane and going to the door, I tranquilly turned and added—"After you have removed your things from these offices, Bartleby, you will of course lock the door—since every one is now gone for the day but you— and if you please, slip your key underneath the mat, so that I may have it in the morning. I shall not see you again; so good-bye to you. If hereafter in your new place of abode I can be of any service to you, do not fail to advise me by letter. Good-bye, Bartleby, and fare you well."

But he answered not a word; like the last column of some ruined temple, he remained standing mute and solitary in the middle of the otherwise deserted room.

As I walked home in a pensive mood, my vanity got the better of my pity. I could not but highly plume myself on my masterly management in getting rid of Bartleby. Masterly I call it, and such it must appear to any dispassionate thinker. The beauty of my procedure seemed to consist in its perfect quietness. There was no vulgar bullying, no bravado of any sort, no choleric hectoring,

---

**6.** Heavy stone for grinding grain, conventional image of a burden hung on someone. Matthew 18:6: "But whoso shall offend one of these little ones which believe in me, it were better for him that a millstone were hanged about his neck, and that he were drowned in the depths of the sea."

no striding to and fro across the apartment, jerking out vehement commands for Bartleby to bundle himself off with his beggarly traps.[7] Nothing of the kind. Without loudly bidding Bartleby depart—as an inferior genius might have done—I *assumed* the ground that depart he must; and upon that assumption built all I had to say. The more I thought over my procedure, the more I was charmed with it. Nevertheless, next morning, upon awakening, I had my doubts,—I had somehow slept off the fumes of vanity. One of the coolest and wisest hours a man has, is just after he awakes in the morning. My procedure seemed as sagacious as ever,—but only in theory. How it would prove in practice—there was the rub. It was truly a beautiful thought to have assumed Bartleby's departure; but, after all, that assumption was simply my own, and none of Bartleby's. The great point was, not whether I had assumed that he would quit me, but whether he would prefer so to do. He was more a man of preferences than assumptions.

After breakfast, I walked down town, arguing the probabilities *pro* and *con*. One moment I thought it would prove a miserable failure, and Bartleby would be found all alive at my office as usual; the next moment it seemed certain that I should see his chair empty. And so I kept veering about. At the corner of Broadway and Canal Street, I saw quite an excited group of people standing in earnest conversation.

"I'll take odds he doesn't," said a voice as I passed.

"Doesn't go?—done!" said I, "put up your money."

I was instinctively putting my hand in my pocket to produce my own, when I remembered that this was an election day. The words I had overheard bore no reference to Bartleby, but to the success or non-success of some candidate for the mayoralty. In my intent frame of mind, I had, as it were, imagined that all Broadway shared in my excitement, and were debating the same question with me. I passed on, very thankful that the uproar of the street screened my momentary absent-mindedness.

As I had intended, I was earlier than usual at my office door. I stood listening for a moment. All was still. He must be gone. I tried the knob. The door was locked. Yes, my procedure had worked to a charm; he indeed must be vanished. Yet a certain melancholy mixed with this: I was almost sorry for my brilliant success. I was fumbling under the door mat for the key, which Bartleby was to have left there for me, when accidentally my knee knocked against a panel, producing a summoning sound, and in response a voice came to me from within—"Not yet; I am occupied."

It was Bartleby.

I was thunderstruck. For an instant I stood like the man who, pipe in mouth, was killed one cloudless afternoon long ago in Virginia, by summer lightning; at his own warm open window he was killed, and remained leaning out there upon the dreamy afternoon, till some one touched him, and he fell.

"Not gone!" I murmured at last. But again obeying that wondrous ascendancy which the inscrutable scrivener had over me—and from which ascendancy, for all my chafing, I could not completely escape—I slowly went down stairs and out into the street, and while walking round the block, considered

7. Personal belongings.

what I should next do in this unheard-of perplexity. Turn the man out by an actual thrusting I could not; to drive him away by calling him hard names would not do; calling in the police was an unpleasant idea; and yet, permit him to enjoy his cadaverous triumph over me,—this too I could not think of. What was to be done? or, if nothing could be done, was there anything further that I could *assume* in the matter? Yes, as before I had prospectively assumed that Bartleby would depart, so now I might retrospectively assume that departed he was. In the legitimate carrying out of this assumption, I might enter my office in a great hurry, and pretending not to see Bartleby at all, walk straight against him as if he were air. Such a proceeding would in a singular degree have the appearance of a home-thrust.[8] It was hardly possible that Bartleby could withstand such an application of the doctrine of assumptions. But, upon second thought, the success of the plan seemed rather dubious. I resolved to argue the matter over with him again.

"Bartleby," said I, entering the office, with a quietly severe expression, "I am seriously displeased. I am pained, Bartleby. I had thought better of you. I had imagined you of such a gentlemanly organization, that in any delicate dilemma a slight hint would suffice—in short, an assumption. But it appears I am deceived. Why," I added, unaffectedly starting, "you have not even touched that money yet," pointing to it, just where I had left it the evening previous.

He answered nothing.

"Will you, or will you not, quit me?" I now demanded in a sudden passion, advancing close to him.

"I would prefer *not* to quit you," he replied, gently emphasizing the *not*.

"What earthly right have you to stay here? Do you pay any rent? Do you pay my taxes? Or is this property yours?"

He answered nothing.

"Are you ready to go on and write now? Are your eyes recovered? Could you copy a small paper for me this morning? or help examine a few lines? or step round to the Post Office? In a word, will you do any thing at all, to give a colouring to your refusal to depart the premises?"

He silently retired into his hermitage.

I was now in such a state of nervous resentment that I thought it but prudent to check myself, at present, from further demonstrations. Bartleby and I were alone. I remembered the tragedy of the unfortunate Adams and the still more unfortunate Colt[9] in the solitary office of the latter; and how poor Colt, being dreadfully incensed by Adams, and imprudently permitting himself to get wildly excited, was at unawares hurried into his fatal act—an act which certainly no man could possibly deplore more than the actor himself. Often it had occurred to me in my ponderings upon the subject, that had that altercation taken place in the public street, or at a private residence, it would not have terminated as it did. It was the circumstance of being alone in a solitary office, upstairs, of a building entirely unhallowed by humanizing domestic associations—an uncarpeted office, doubtless, of a dusty, haggard sort of appearance;—this it must have been, which greatly helped to enhance the irritable desperation of the hapless Colt.

---

**8.** In fencing, a successful thrust to the opponent's body.  **9.** In 1841, John C. Colt, brother of the famous gunmaker, killed Samuel Adams, a printer, when he hit him on the head during a fight.

But when this old Adam[1] of resentment rose in me and tempted me concerning Bartleby, I grappled him and threw him. How? Why, simply by recalling the divine injunction: "A new commandment give I unto you, that ye love one another."[2] Yes, this it was that saved me. Aside from higher considerations, charity often operates as a vastly wise and prudent principle—a great safeguard to its possessor. Men have committed murder for jealousy's sake, and anger's sake, and hatred's sake, and selfishness' sake, and spiritual pride's sake; but no man that ever I heard of, ever committed a diabolical murder for sweet charity's sake. Mere self-interest, then, if no better motive can be enlisted, should, especially with high-tempered men, prompt all beings to charity and philanthropy. At any rate, upon the occasion in question, I strove to drown my exasperated feelings towards the scrivener by benevolently constructing his conduct. Poor fellow, poor fellow! thought I, he doesn't mean anything; and besides, he has seen hard times, and ought to be indulged.

I endeavored also immediately to occupy myself, and at the same time to comfort my despondency. I tried to fancy that in the course of the morning, at such time as might prove agreeable to him, Bartleby, of his own free accord, would emerge from his hermitage, and take up some decided line of march in the direction of the door. But no. Half-past twelve o'clock came; Turkey began to glow in the face, overturn his inkstand, and become generally obstreperous; Nippers abated down into quietude and courtesy; Ginger Nut munched his noon apple; and Bartleby remained standing at his window in one of his profoundest dead-wall reveries. Will it be credited? Ought I to acknowledge it? That afternoon I left the office without saying one further word to him.

Some days now passed, during which, at leisure intervals I looked a little into "Edwards on the Will," and "Priestley on Necessity."[3] Under the circumstances, those books induced a salutary feeling. Gradually I slid into the persuasion that these troubles of mine, touching the scrivener, had been all predestinated from eternity, and Bartleby was billeted upon me for some mysterious purpose of an all-wise Providence, which it was not for a mere mortal like me to fathom. Yes, Bartleby, stay there behind your screen, thought I; I shall persecute you no more; you are harmless and noiseless as any of these old chairs; in short, I never feel so private as when I know you are here. At least I see it, I feel it; I penetrate to the predestinated purpose of my life. I am content. Others may have loftier parts to enact; but my mission in this world, Bartleby, is to furnish you with office-room for such period as you may see fit to remain.

I believe that this wise and blessed frame of mind would have continued with me, had it not been for the unsolicited and uncharitable remarks obtruded upon me by my professional friends who visited the rooms. But thus it often is, that the constant friction of illiberal minds wears out at last the best resolves of the more generous. Though to be sure, when I reflected upon it, it

1. The sinful element in man. Christ is sometimes called the "New Adam." 2. John 13:34 and John 15:17. 3. The reference is obscure because of the form Melville has given the titles, but the books indicated are probably *The Freedom of the Will* by Jonathan Edwards (1703–1758) and *The Doctrine of Philosophical Necessity* by Joseph Priestley (1733–1804). The theses of these two books conform to the "persuasion" Melville here describes.

was not strange that people entering my office should be struck by the peculiar aspect of the unaccountable Bartleby, and so be tempted to throw out some sinister observations concerning him. Sometimes an attorney having business with me, and calling at my office, and finding no one but the scrivener there, would undertake to obtain some sort of precise information from him touching my whereabouts; but without heeding his idle talk, Bartleby would remain standing immovable in the middle of the room. So, after contemplating him in that position for a time, the attorney would depart, no wiser than he came.

Also, when a Reference[4] was going on, and the room full of lawyers and witnesses and business was driving fast, some deeply occupied legal gentleman present, seeing Bartleby wholly unemployed, would request him to run round to his (the legal gentleman's) office and fetch some papers for him. Thereupon, Bartleby would tranquilly decline, and yet remain idle as before. Then the lawyer would give a great stare, and turn to me. And what could I say? At last I was made aware that all through the circle of my professional acquaintance, a whisper of wonder was running round, having reference to the strange creature I kept at my office. This worried me very much. And as the idea came upon me of his possibly turning out a long-lived man, and keep occupying my chambers, and denying my authority; and perplexing my visitors; and scandalizing my professional reputation; and casting a general gloom over the premises; keeping soul and body together to the last upon his savings (for doubtless he spent but half a dime a day), and in the end perhaps outlive me, and claim possession of my office by right of his perpetual occupancy: as all these dark anticipations crowded upon me more and more, and my friends continually intruded their relentless remarks upon the apparition in my room, a great change was wrought in me. I resolved to gather all my faculties together, and for ever rid me of this intolerable incubus.[5]

Ere revolving any complicated project, however, adapted to this end, I first simply suggested to Bartleby the propriety of his permanent departure. In a calm and serious tone, I commended the idea to his careful and mature consideration. But having taken three days to meditate upon it, he apprised me that his original determination remained the same; in short, that he still preferred to abide with me.

What shall I do? I now said to myself, buttoning up my coat to the last button. What shall I do? what ought I to do? what does conscience say I *should* do with this man, or rather ghost? Rid myself of him, I must; go, he shall. But how? You will not thrust him, the poor, pale, passive mortal,—you will not thrust such a helpless creature out of your door? you will not dishonour yourself by such cruelty? No, I will not, I cannot do that. Rather would I let him live and die here, and then mason up his remains in the wall. What then will you do? For all your coaxing, he will not budge. Bribes he leaves under your own paper-weight on your table; in short, it is quite plain that he prefers to cling to you.

Then something severe, something unusual must be done. What! surely you will not have him collared by a constable, and commit his innocent pallor to the common jail? And upon what ground could you procure such a

4. Conference.    5. Imaginary demon supposed to descend on sleepers.

thing to be done?—a vagrant, is he? What! he a vagrant, a wanderer, who refuses to budge? It is because he will *not* be a vagrant, then, that you seek to count him *as* a vagrant. That is too absurd. No visible means of support: there I have him. Wrong again: for indubitably he *does* support himself, and that is the only unanswerable proof that any man can show of his possessing the means so to do. No more then. Since he will not quit me, I must quit him. I will change my offices; I will move elsewhere; and give him fair notice, that if I find him on my new premises I will then proceed against him as a common trespasser.

Acting accordingly, next day I thus addressed him: "I find these chambers too far from the City Hall; the air is unwholesome. In a word, I propose to remove my offices next week, and shall no longer require your services. I tell you this now, in order that you may seek another place."

He made no reply, and nothing more was said.

On the appointed day I engaged carts and men, proceeded to my chambers, and having but little furniture, every thing was removed in a few hours. Throughout all, the scrivener remained standing behind the screen, which I directed to be removed the last thing. It was withdrawn; and being folded up like a huge folio, left him the motionless occupant of a naked room. I stood in the entry watching him a moment, while something from within me upbraided me.

I re-entered, with my hand in my pocket—and—and my heart in my mouth.

"Good-bye, Bartleby; I am going—good-bye, and God some way bless you; and take that," slipping something in his hand. But it dropped upon the floor, and then—strange to say—I tore myself from him whom I had so longed to be rid of.

Established in my new quarters, for a day or two I kept the door locked, and started at every footfall in the passages. When I returned to my rooms after any little absence, I would pause at the threshold for an instant, and attentively listen, ere applying my key. But these fears were needless. Bartleby never came nigh me.

I thought all was going well, when a perturbed looking stranger visited me, inquiring whether I was the person who had recently occupied rooms at No.__ Wall Street.

Full of forebodings, I replied that I was.

"Then sir," said the stranger, who proved a lawyer, "you are responsible for the man you left there. He refuses to do any copying, he refuses to do any thing; he says he prefers not to; and he refuses to quit the premises."

"I am very sorry, sir," said I, with assumed tranquillity, but an inward tremor, "but, really, the man you allude to is nothing to me—he is no relation or apprentice of mine, that you should hold me responsible for him."

"In mercy's name, who is he?"

"I certainly cannot inform you. I know nothing about him. Formerly I employed him as a copyist; but he has done nothing for me now for some time past."

"I shall settle him then,—good morning, sir."

Several days passed, and I heard nothing more; and though I often felt a charitable prompting to call at the place and see poor Bartleby, yet a certain squeamishness of I know not what withheld me.

All is over with him, by this time, thought I at last, when through another week no further intelligence reached me. But coming to my room the day after, I found several persons waiting at my door in a high state of nervous excitement.

"That's the man—here he comes," cried the foremost one, whom I recognized as the lawyer who had previously called upon me alone.

"You must take him away, sir, at once," cried a portly person among them, advancing upon me, and whom I knew to be the landlord of No. ___ Wall Street. "These gentlemen, my tenants, cannot stand it any longer; Mr.B___," pointing to the lawyer, "has turned him out of his room, and he now persists in haunting the building generally, sitting upon the banisters of the stairs by day, and sleeping in the entry by night. Everybody is concerned; clients are leaving the offices; some fears are entertained of a mob; something you must do, and that without delay."

Aghast at this torrent, I fell back before it, and would fain have locked myself in my new quarters. In vain I persisted that Bartleby was nothing to me—no more than to any one else. In vain:—I was the last person known to have anything to do with him, and they held me to the terrible account. Fearful then of being exposed in the papers (as one person present obscurely threatened) I considered the matter, and at length said, that if the lawyer would give me a confidential interview with the scrivener, in his (the lawyer's) own room, I would that afternoon strive my best to rid them of the nuisance they complained of.

Going up stairs to my old haunt, there was Bartleby silently sitting upon the banister at the landing.

"What are you doing here, Bartleby?" said I.

"Sitting upon the banister," he mildly replied.

I motioned him into the lawyer's room, who then left us.

"Bartleby," said I, "are you aware that you are the cause of great tribulation to me, by persisting in occupying the entry after being dismissed from the office?"

No answer.

"Now one of two things must take place. Either you must do something, or something must be done to you. Now what sort of business would you like to engage in? Would you like to re-engage in copying for some one?"

"No; I would prefer not to make any change."

"Would you like a clerkship in a dry-goods store?"

"There is too much confinement about that. No, I would not like a clerkship; but I am not particular."

"Too much confinement," I cried, "why you keep yourself confined all the time!"

"I would prefer not to take a clerkship," he rejoined, as if to settle that little item at once.

"How would a bartender's business suit you? There is no trying of the eyesight in that."

"I would not like it at all; though, as I said before, I am not particular."

His unwonted wordiness inspired me. I returned to the charge.

"Well then, would you like to travel through the country collecting bills for the merchants? That would improve your health."

"No, I would prefer to be doing something else."

"How then would going as a companion to Europe to entertain some young gentleman with your conversation,—how would that suit you?"

"Not at all. It does not strike me that there is anything definite about that. I like to be stationary. But I am not particular."

"Stationary you shall be then," I cried, now losing all patience, and for the first time in all my exasperating connection with him fairly flying into a passion. "If you do not go away from these premises before night, I shall feel bound—indeed I *am* bound—to—to—to quit the premises myself!" I rather absurdly concluded, knowing not with what possible threat to try to frighten his immobility into compliance. Despairing of all further efforts, I was precipitately leaving him, when a final thought occurred to me—one which had not been wholly unindulged before.

"Bartleby," said I, in the kindest tone I could assume under such exciting circumstances, "will you go home with me now—not to my office, but my dwelling— and remain there till we can conclude upon some convenient arrangement for you at our leisure? Come, let us start now, right away."

"No: at present I would prefer not to make any change at all."

I answered nothing; but effectually dodging every one by the suddenness and rapidity of my flight, rushed from the building, ran up Wall Street towards Broadway, and jumping into the first omnibus was soon removed from pursuit. As soon as tranquillity returned I distinctly perceived that I had now done all that I possibly could, both in respect to the demands of the landlord and his tenants, and with regard to my own desire and sense of duty, to benefit Bartleby, and shield him from rude persecution. I now strove to be entirely care-free and quiescent; and my conscience justified me in the attempt; though indeed it was not so successful as I could have wished. So fearful was I of being again hunted out by the incensed landlord and his exasperated tenants, that, surrendering my business to Nippers, for a few days I drove about the upper part of the town and through the suburbs, in my rockaway;[6] crossed over to Jersey City and Hoboken, and paid fugitive visits to Manhattanville and Astoria. In fact I almost lived in my rockaway for the time.

When again I entered my office, lo, a note from the landlord lay upon the desk. I opened it with trembling hands. It informed me that the writer had sent to the police, and had Bartleby removed to the Tombs as a vagrant. Moreover, since I knew more about him than any one else, he wished me to appear at that place, and make a suitable statement of the facts. These tidings had a conflicting effect upon me. At first I was indignant; but at last almost approved. The landlord's energetic, summary disposition had led him to adopt a procedure which I do not think I would have decided upon myself; and yet as a last resort, under such peculiar circumstances, it seemed the only plan.

As I afterwards learned, the poor scrivener, when told that he must be conducted to the Tombs, offered not the slightest obstacle, but in his pale, unmoving way silently acquiesced.

Some of the compassionate and curious bystanders joined the party; and headed by one of the constables, arm in arm with Bartleby the silent procession

<hr />

6. Light, four-wheeled carriage.

filed its way through all the noise, and heat, and joy of the roaring thorough-
fares at noon.

The same day I received the note I went to the Tombs, or, to speak more
properly, the Halls of Justice. Seeking the right officer, I stated the purpose of
my call, and was informed that the individual I described was indeed within.
I then assured the functionary that Bartleby was a perfectly honest man, and
greatly to be a compassionated, (however unaccountable) eccentric. I narrated
all I knew, and closed by suggesting the idea of letting him remain in as indulgent confinement as possible till something less harsh might be done—though
indeed I hardly knew what. At all events, if nothing else could be decided
upon, the alms-house must receive him. I then begged to have an interview.

Being under no disgraceful charge, and quite serene and harmless in all his
ways, they had permitted him freely to wander about the prison, and especially in the inclosed grass-platted yards thereof. And so I found him there,
standing all alone in the quietest of the yards, his face towards a high wall—
while all around, from the narrow slits of the jail windows, I thought I saw
peering out upon him the eyes of murderers and thieves.

"Bartleby!"

"I know you," he said, without looking round,—"and I want nothing to say
to you."

"It was not I that brought you here, Bartleby," said I, keenly pained at his
implied suspicion. "And to you, this should not be so vile a place. Nothing
reproachful attaches to you by being here. And see, it is not so sad a place as
one might think. Look, there is the sky and here is the grass."

"I know where I am," he replied, but would say nothing more, and so I
left him.

As I entered the corridor again, a broad, meat-like man, in an apron, accosted
me, and jerking his thumb over his shoulder said—"Is that your friend?"

"Yes."

"Does he want to starve? If he does, let him live on the prison fare, that's all."

"Who are you?" asked I, not knowing what to make of such an unofficially
speaking person in such a place.

"I am the grub-man. Such gentlemen as have friends here, hire me to provide them with something good to eat."

"Is this so?" said I, turning to the turnkey.

He said it was.

"Well then," said I, slipping some silver into the grub-man's hands (for so
they called him), "I want you to give particular attention to my friend there;
let him have the best dinner you can get. And you must be as polite to him as
possible."

"Introduce me, will you?" said the grub-man, looking at me with an expression which seemed to say he was all impatience for an opportunity to give a
specimen of his breeding.

Thinking it would prove of benefit to the scrivener, I acquiesced; and asking the grub-man his name, went up with him to Bartleby.

"Bartleby, this is Mr. Cutlets; you will find him very useful to you."

"Your sarvant, sir, your sarvant," said the grub-man, making a low salutation behind his apron. "Hope you find it pleasant here, sir;—spacious grounds—
cool apartments, sir—hope you'll stay with us some time—try to make it

agreeable. May Mrs. Cutlets and I have the pleasure of your company to dinner, sir, in Mrs. Cutlets' private room?"

"I prefer not to dine to-day," said Bartleby, turning away. "It would disagree with me; I am unused to dinners." So saying, he slowly moved to the other side of the inclosure and took up a position fronting the dead-wall.

"How's this?" said the grub-man, addressing me with a stare of astonishment. "He's odd, ain't he?"

"I think he is a little deranged," said I, sadly.

"Deranged? deranged is it? Well now, upon my word, I thought that friend of yourn was a gentleman forger; they are always pale and genteel-like, them forgers. I can't help pity 'em—can't help it, sir. Did you know Monroe Edwards?"[7] he added touchingly, and paused. Then, laying his hand pityingly on my shoulder, sighed, "he died of consumption at Sing-Sing. So you weren't acquainted with Monroe?"

"No, I was never socially acquainted with any forgers. But I cannot stop longer. Look to my friend yonder. You will not lose by it. I will see you again."

Some few days after this, I again obtained admission to the Tombs, and went through the corridors in quest of Bartleby; but without finding him.

"I saw him coming from his cell not long ago," said a turnkey, "maybe he's gone to loiter in the yards."

So I went in that direction.

"Are you looking for the silent man?" said another turnkey passing me. "Yonder he lies—sleeping in the yard there. 'Tis not twenty minutes since I saw him lie down."

The yard was entirely quiet. It was not accessible to the common prisoners. The surrounding walls, of amazing thickness, kept off all sounds behind them. The Egyptian character of the masonry weighed upon me with its gloom. But a soft imprisoned turf grew under foot. The heart of the eternal pyramids, it seemed, wherein, by some strange magic, through the clefts grass-seed, dropped by birds, had sprung.

Strangely huddled at the base of the wall—his knees drawn up, and lying on his side, his head touching the cold stones—I saw the wasted Bartleby. But nothing stirred. I paused; then went close up to him; stooped over, and saw that his dim eyes were open; otherwise he seemed profoundly sleeping. Something prompted me to touch him. I felt his hand, when a tingling shiver ran up my arm and down my spine to my feet.

The round face of the grub-man peered upon me now. "His dinner is ready. Won't he dine to-day, either? Or does he live without dining?"

"Lives without dining," said I, and closed the eyes.

"Eh!—He's asleep, ain't he?"

"With kings and counsellors,"[8] murmured I.

There would seem little need for proceeding further in this history. Imagination will readily supply the meagre recital of poor Bartleby's interment. But ere parting with the reader, let me say, that if this little narrative has sufficiently interested him, to awaken curiosity as to who Bartleby was, and what manner of life he led prior to the present narrator's making his acquaintance,

---

7. Famously flamboyant forger and swindler (1808–1847), who died in Sing Sing prison, north of New York City in Ossining, New York. **8.** That is, he is dead. Job 3:13–14: "then had I been at rest, With kings and counsellors of the earth, which built desolate places for themselves."

I can only reply, that in such curiosity I fully share—but am wholly unable to gratify it. Yet here I hardly know whether I should divulge one little item of rumour, which came to my ear a few months after the scrivener's decease. Upon what basis it rested, I could never ascertain; and hence, how true it is I cannot now tell. But inasmuch as this vague report has not been without a certain strange suggestive interest to me, however sad, it may prove the same with some others; and so I will briefly mention it. The report was this: that Bartleby had been a subordinate clerk in the Dead Letter Office[9] at Washington, from which he had been suddenly removed by a change in the administration. When I think over this rumor I cannot adequately express the emotions which seize me. Dead letters! Does it not sound like dead men? Conceive a man by nature and misfortune prone to a pallid hopelessness: can any business seem more fitted to heighten it than that of continually handling these dead letters, and assorting them for the flames? For by the cart-load they are annually burned. Sometimes from out the folded paper the pale clerk takes a ring:—the finger it was meant for, perhaps, moulders in the grave; a bank-note sent in swiftest charity:—he whom it would relieve, nor eats nor hungers any more; pardon for those who died despairing; hope for those who died unhoping; good tidings for those who died stifled by unrelieved calamities. On errands of life, these letters speed to death.

Ah Bartleby! Ah humanity!

1853

---

RELATED:

—Leo Marx, "Melville's Parable of the Walls," p. 931

---

**9.** Place for storage and disposition of undeliverable mail.

# BHARATI MUKHERJEE
## b. 1940

Born to wealthy parents in Kolkata (Calcutta), Mukherjee spent her early years with her family in England but returned to India in her teens to study. She continued her education in the 1960s at the University of Iowa, where she met and married the writer Clark Blaise while earning both an M.F.A. in creative writing and a Ph.D. in English and Comparative Literature. They lived in Canada for the next ten years, where she published her first two novels, *The Tiger's Daughter* (1971) and *Wife* (1975). Later, when the couple traveled in India, they collaborated on *Days and Nights in Calcutta* (1977), a nonfiction book drawn from their observations and impressions of Indian life. Her stories are collected in *Darkness* (1985) and *The Middleman and Other Stories* (1988). Her most recent novels are *Jasmine* (1989), *The Holder of the World* (1993), *Leave It to Me* (1997), *Desirable Daughters* (2002), *The Tree Bride* (2004), and *Miss New India* (2011). She now lives in the United States and teaches at the University of California at Berkeley.

# The Management of Grief

A woman I don't know is boiling tea the Indian way in my kitchen. There are a lot of women I don't know in my kitchen, whispering, and moving tactfully. They open doors, rummage through the pantry, and try not to ask me where things are kept. They remind me of when my sons were small, on Mother's Day or when Vikram and I were tired, and they would make big, sloppy omelettes. I would lie in bed pretending I didn't hear them.

Dr. Sharma, the treasurer of the Indo-Canada Society, pulls me into the hallway. He wants to know if I am worried about money. His wife, who has just come up from the basement with a tray of empty cups and glasses, scolds him. "Don't bother Mrs. Bhave with mundane details." She looks so monstrously pregnant her baby must be days overdue. I tell her she shouldn't be carrying heavy things. "Shaila," she says, smiling, "this is the fifth." Then she grabs a teenager by his shirt-tails. He slips his Walkman off his head. He has to be one of her four children, they have the same domed and dented foreheads. "What's the official word now?" she demands. The boy slips the headphones back on. "They're acting evasive, Ma. They're saying it could be an accident or a terrorist bomb."

All morning, the boys have been muttering, Sikh Bomb, Sikh Bomb. The men, not using the word, bow their heads in agreement. Mrs. Sharma touches her forehead at such a word. At least they've stopped talking about space debris and Russian lasers.

Two radios are going in the dining room. They are tuned to different stations. Someone must have brought the radios down from my boys' bedrooms. I haven't gone into their rooms since Kusum came running across the front lawn in her bathrobe. She looked so funny, I was laughing when I opened the door.

The big TV in the den is being whizzed through American networks and cable channels.

"Damn!" some man swears bitterly. "How can these preachers carry on like nothing's happened?" I want to tell him we're not that important. You look at the audience, and at the preacher in his blue robe with his beautiful white hair, the potted palm trees under a blue sky, and you know they care about nothing.

The phone rings and rings. Dr. Sharma's taken charge. "We're with her," he keeps saying. "Yes, yes, the doctor has given calming pills. Yes, yes, pills are having necessary effect." I wonder if pills alone explain this calm. Not peace, just a deadening quiet. I was always controlled, but never repressed. Sound can reach me, but my body is tensed, ready to scream. I hear their voices all around me. I hear my boys and Vikram cry, "Mommy, Shaila!" and their screams insulate me, like headphones.

The woman boiling water tells her story again and again. "I got the news first. My cousin called from Halifax before six A.M., can you imagine? He'd gotten up for prayers and his son was studying for medical exams and he heard on a rock channel that something had happened to a plane. They said first it had disappeared from the radar, like a giant eraser just reached out. His father called me, so I said to him, what do you mean, 'something bad'? You mean a hijacking? And he said, *behn*,[1] there is no confirmation of anything yet, but check with your neighbors because a lot of them must be on that plane. So I called poor Kusum straightaway. I knew Kusum's husband and daughter were booked to go yesterday."

Kusum lives across the street from me. She and Satish had moved in less than a month ago. They said they needed a bigger place. All these people, the Sharmas and friends from the Indo-Canada Society had been there for the housewarming. Satish and Kusum made homemade tandoori on their big gas grill and even the white neighbors piled their plates high with that luridly red, charred, juicy chicken. Their younger daughter had danced, and even our boys had broken away from the Stanley Cup telecast to put in a reluctant appearance. Everyone took pictures for their albums and for the community newspapers—another of our families had made it big in Toronto—and now I wonder how many of those happy faces are gone. "Why does God give us so much if all along He intends to take it away?" Kusum asks me.

I nod. We sit on carpeted stairs, holding hands like children. "I never once told him that I loved him," I say. I was too much the well brought up woman. I was so well brought up I never felt comfortable calling my husband by his first name.

"It's all right," Kusum says. "He knew. My husband knew. They felt it. Modern young girls have to say it because what they feel is fake."

---

1. No (Hindi).

Kusum's daughter, Pam, runs in with an overnight case. Pam's in her McDonald's uniform. "Mummy! You have to get dressed!" Panic makes her cranky. "A reporter's on his way here."

"Why?"

"You want to talk to him in your bathrobe?" She starts to brush her mother's long hair. She's the daughter who's always in trouble. She dates Canadian boys and hangs out in the mall, shopping for tight sweaters. The younger one, the goody-goody one according to Pam, the one with a voice so sweet that when she sang bhajans[2] for Ethiopian relief even a frugal man like my husband wrote out a hundred dollar check, *she* was on that plane. *She* was going to spend July and August with grandparents because Pam wouldn't go. Pam said she'd rather waitress at McDonald's. "If it's a choice between Bombay and Wonderland, I'm picking Wonderland," she'd said.

"Leave me alone," Kusum yells. "You know what I want to do? If I didn't have to look after you now, I'd hang myself."

Pam's young face goes blotchy with pain. "Thanks," she says, "don't let me stop you."

"Hush," pregnant Mrs. Sharma scolds Pam. "Leave your mother alone. Mr. Sharma will tackle the reporters and fill out the forms. He'll say what has to be said."

Pam stands her ground. "You think I don't know what Mummy's thinking? *Why ever?* that's what. That's sick! Mummy wishes my little sister were alive and I were dead."

Kusum's hand in mine is trembly hot. We continue to sit on the stairs.

She calls before she arrives, wondering if there's anything I need. Her name is Judith Templeton and she's an appointee of the provincial government. "Multiculturalism?" I ask, and she says, "partially," but that her mandate is bigger. "I've been told you knew many of the people on the flight," she says. "Perhaps if you'd agree to help us reach the others . . . ?"

She gives me time at least to put on tea water and pick up the mess in the front room. I have a few samosas[3] from Kusum's housewarming that I could fry up, but then I think, why prolong this visit?

Judith Templeton is much younger than she sounded. She wears a blue suit with a white blouse and a polka dot tie. Her blond hair is cut short, her only jewelry is pearl drop earrings. Her briefcase is new and expensive looking, a gleaming cordovan leather. She sits with it across her lap. When she looks out the front windows onto the street, her contact lenses seem to float in front of her light blue eyes.

"What sort of help do you want from me?" I ask. She has refused the tea, out of politeness, but I insist, along with some slightly stale biscuits.[4]

"I have no experience," she admits. "That is, I have an MSW[5] and I've worked in liaison with accident victims, but I mean I have no experience with a tragedy of this scale—"

"Who could?" I ask.

---

2. Hymns (Hindi). 3. Fried turnovers filled with meat or vegetable mixtures (Hindi). 4. That is, cookies. 5. Master of Social Welfare (or Work) degree.

"—and with the complications of culture, language, and customs. Someone mentioned that Mrs. Bhave is a pillar—because you've taken it more calmly."

At this, perhaps, I frown, for she reaches forward, almost to take my hand. "I hope you understand my meaning, Mrs. Bhave. There are hundreds of people in Metro directly affected, like you, and some of them speak no English. There are some widows who've never handled money or gone on a bus, and there are old parents who still haven't eaten or gone outside their bedrooms. Some houses and apartments have been looted. Some wives are still hysterical. Some husbands are in shock and profound depression. We want to help, but our hands are tied in so many ways. We have to distribute money to some people, and there are legal documents—these things can be done. We have interpreters, but we don't always have the human touch, or maybe the right human touch. We don't want to make mistakes, Mrs. Bhave, and that's why we'd like to ask you to help us."

"More mistakes, you mean," I say.

"Police matters are not in my hands," she answers.

"Nothing I can do will make any difference," I say. "We must all grieve in our own way."

"But you are coping very well. All the people said, Mrs. Bhave is the strongest person of all. Perhaps if the others could see you, talk with you, it would help them."

"By the standards of the people you call hysterical, I am behaving very oddly and very badly, Miss Templeton." I want to say to her, *I wish I could scream, starve, walk into Lake Ontario, jump from a bridge.* "They would not see me as a model. I do not see myself as a model."

I am a freak. No one who has ever known me would think of me reacting this way. This terrible calm will not go away.

She asks me if she may call again, after I get back from a long trip that we all must make. "Of course," I say. "Feel free to call, anytime."

Four days later, I find Kusum squatting on a rock overlooking a bay in Ireland. It isn't a big rock, but it juts sharply out over water. This is as close as we'll ever get to them. June breezes balloon out her sari and unpin her knee-length hair. She has the bewildered look of a sea creature whom the tides have stranded.

It's been one hundred hours since Kusum came stumbling and screaming across my lawn. Waiting around the hospital, we've heard many stories. The police, the diplomats, they tell us things thinking that we're strong, that knowledge is helpful to the grieving, and maybe it is. Some, I know, prefer ignorance, or their own versions. The plane broke into two, they say. Unconsciousness was instantaneous. No one suffered. My boys must have just finished their breakfasts. They loved eating on planes, they loved the smallness of plates, knives, and forks. Last year they saved the airline salt and pepper shakers. Half an hour more and they would have made it to Heathrow.

Kusum says that we can't escape our fate. She says that all those people—our husbands, my boys, her girl with the nightingale voice, all those Hindus, Christians, Sikhs, Muslims, Parsis, and atheists on that plane—were fated to die together off this beautiful bay. She learned this from a swami in Toronto.

I have my Valium.

Six of us "relatives"—two widows and four widowers—choose to spend the day today by the waters instead of sitting in a hospital room and scanning photographs of the dead. That's what they call us now: relatives. I've looked through twenty-seven photos in two days. They're very kind to us, the Irish are very understanding. Sometimes understanding means freeing a tourist bus for this trip to the bay, so we can pretend to spy our loved ones through the glassiness of waves or in sunspeckled cloud shapes.

I could die here, too, and be content.

"What is that, out there?" She's standing and flapping her hands and for a moment I see a head shape bobbing in the waves. She's standing in the water, I, on the boulder. The tide is low, and a round, black, headsized rock has just risen from the waves. She returns, her sari end dripping and ruined and her face is a twisted remnant of hope, the way mine was a hundred hours ago, still laughing but inwardly knowing that nothing but the ultimate tragedy could bring two women together at six o'clock on a Sunday morning. I watch her face sag into blankness.

"That water felt warm, Shaila," she says at length.

"You can't," I say. "We have to wait for our turn to come."

I haven't eaten in four days, haven't brushed my teeth.

"I know," she says. "I tell myself I have no right to grieve. They are in a better place than we are. My swami says I should be thrilled for them. My swami says depression is a sign of our selfishness."

Maybe I'm selfish. Selfishly I break away from Kusum and run, sandals slapping against stones, to the water's edge. What if my boys aren't lying pinned under the debris? What if they aren't stuck a mile below that innocent blue chop? What if, given the strong currents. . . .

Now I've ruined my sari, one of my best. Kusum has joined me, knee-deep in water that feels to me like a swimming pool. I could settle in the water, and my husband would take my hand and the boys would slap water in my face just to see me scream.

"Do you remember what good swimmers my boys were, Kusum?"

"I saw the medals," she says.

One of the widowers, Dr. Ranganathan from Montreal, walks out to us, carrying his shoes in one hand. He's an electrical engineer. Someone at the hotel mentioned his work is famous around the world, something about the place where physics and electricity come together. He has lost a huge family, something indescribable. "With some luck," Dr. Ranganathan suggests to me, "a good swimmer could make it safely to some island. It is quite possible that there may be many, many microscopic islets scattered around."

"You're not just saying that?" I tell Dr. Ranganathan about Vinod, my elder son. Last year he took diving as well.

"It's a parent's duty to hope," he says. "It is foolish to rule out possibilities that have not been tested. I myself have not surrendered hope."

Kusum is sobbing once again. "Dear lady," he says, laying his free hand on her arm, and she calms down.

"Vinod is how old?" he asks me. He's very careful, as we all are. *Is,* not was.

"Fourteen. Yesterday he was fourteen. His father and uncle were going to take him down to the Taj and give him a big birthday party. I couldn't go with them because I couldn't get two weeks off from my stupid job in June." I process bills for a travel agent. June is a big travel month.

Dr. Ranganathan whips the pockets of his suit jacket inside out. Squashed roses, in darkening shades of pink, float on the water. He tore the roses off creepers in somebody's garden. He didn't ask anyone if he could pluck the roses, but now there's been an article about it in the local papers. When you see an Indian person, it says, please give him or her flowers.

"A strong youth of fourteen," he says, "can very likely pull to safety a younger one."

My sons, though four years apart, were very close. Vinod wouldn't let Mithun drown. *Electrical engineering,* I think, foolishly perhaps: this man knows important secrets of the universe, things closed to me. Relief spins me light-headed. No wonder my boys' photographs haven't turned up in the gallery of photos of the recovered dead. "Such pretty roses," I say.

"My wife loved pink roses. Every Friday I had to bring a bunch home. I used to say, why? After twenty odd years of marriage you're still needing proof positive of my love?" He has identified his wife and three of his children. Then others from Montreal, the lucky ones, intact families with no survivors. He chuckles as he wades back to shore. Then he swings around to ask me a question. "Mrs. Bhave, you are wanting to throw in some roses for your loved ones? I have two big ones left."

But I have other things to float: Vinod's pocket calculator; a half-painted model B-52 for my Mithun. They'd want them on their island. And for my husband? For him I let fall into the calm, glassy waters a poem I wrote in the hospital yesterday. Finally he'll know my feelings for him.

"Don't tumble, the rocks are slippery," Dr. Ranganathan cautions. He holds out a hand for me to grab.

Then it's time to get back on the bus, time to rush back to our waiting posts on hospital benches.

Kusum is one of the lucky ones. The lucky ones flew here, identified in multiplicate their loved ones, then will fly to India with the bodies for proper ceremonies. Satish is one of the few males who surfaced. The photos of faces we saw on the walls in an office at Heathrow and here in the hospital are mostly of women. Women have more body fat, a nun said to me matter-of-factly. They float better.

Today I was stopped by a young sailor on the street. He had loaded bodies, he'd gone into the water when—he checks my face for signs of strength—when the sharks were first spotted. I don't blush, and he breaks down. "It's all right," I say. "Thank you." I had heard about the sharks from Dr. Ranganathan. In his orderly mind, science brings understanding, it holds no terror. It is the shark's duty. For every deer there is a hunter, for every fish a fisherman.

The Irish are not shy; they rush to me and give me hugs and some are crying. I cannot imagine reactions like that on the streets of Toronto. Just strangers, and I am touched. Some carry flowers with them and give them to any Indian they see.

After lunch, a policeman I have gotten to know quite well catches hold of me. He says he thinks he has a match for Vinod. I explain what a good swimmer Vinod is.

"You want me with you when you look at photos?" Dr. Ranganathan walks ahead of me into the picture gallery. In these matters, he is a scientist, and I am grateful. It is a new perspective. "They have performed miracles," he says. "We are indebted to them."

The first day or two the policemen showed us relatives only one picture at a time; now they're in a hurry, they're eager to lay out the possibles, and even the probables.

The face on the photo is of a boy much like Vinod; the same intelligent eyes, the same thick brows dipping into a V. But this boy's features, even his cheeks, are puffier, wider, mushier.

"No." My gaze is pulled by other pictures. There are five other boys who look like Vinod.

The nun assigned to console me rubs the first picture with a fingertip. "When they've been in the water for a while, love, they look a little heavier." The bones under the skin are broken, they said on the first day—try to adjust your memories. It's important.

"It's not him. I'm his mother. I'd know."

"I know this one!" Dr. Ranganathan cries out suddenly from the back of the gallery. "And this one!" I think he senses that I don't want to find my boys. "They are the Kutty brothers. They were also from Montreal." I don't mean to be crying. On the contrary, I am ecstatic. My suitcase in the hotel is packed heavy with dry clothes for my boys.

The policeman starts to cry. "I am so sorry, I am so sorry, ma'am. I really thought we had a match."

With the nun ahead of us and the policeman behind, we, the unlucky ones without our children's bodies, file out of the makeshift gallery.

From Ireland most of us go on to India. Kusum and I take the same direct flight to Bombay, so I can help her clear customs quickly. But we have to argue with a man in uniform. He has large boils on his face. The boils swell and glow with sweat as we argue with him. He wants Kusum to wait in line and he refuses to take authority because his boss is on a tea break. But Kusum won't let her coffins out of sight, and I shan't desert her though I know that my parents, elderly and diabetic, must be waiting in a stuffy car in a scorching lot.

"You bastard!" I scream at the man with the popping boils. Other passengers press closer. "You think we're smuggling contraband in those coffins!"

Once upon a time we were well brought up women; we were dutiful wives who kept our heads veiled, our voices shy and sweet.

In India, I become, once again, an only child of rich, ailing parents. Old friends of the family come to pay their respects. Some are Sikh, and inwardly, involuntarily, I cringe. My parents are progressive people; they do not blame communities for a few individuals.

In Canada it is a different story now.

"Stay longer," my mother pleads. "Canada is a cold place. Why would you want to be all by yourself?" I stay.

Three months pass. Then another.

"Vikram wouldn't have wanted you to give up things!" they protest. They call my husband by the name he was born with. In Toronto he'd changed to

Vik so the men he worked with at his office would find his name as easy as
Rod or Chris. "You know, the dead aren't cut off from us!"

My grandmother, the spoiled daughter of a rich *zamindar*,[6] shaved her head
with rusty razor blades when she was widowed at sixteen. My grandfather
died of childhood diabetes when he was nineteen, and she saw herself as the
harbinger of bad luck. My mother grew up without parents, raised indifferently by an uncle, while her true mother slept in a hut behind the main estate
house and took her food with the servants. She grew up a rationalist. My parents abhor mindless mortification.

The zamindar's daughter kept stubborn faith in Vedic rituals; my parents
rebelled. I am trapped between two modes of knowledge. At thirty-six, I am
too old to start over and too young to give up. Like my husband's spirit, I flutter between worlds.

Courting aphasia, we travel. We travel with our phalanx of servants and
poor relatives. To hill stations and to beach resorts. We play contract bridge
in dusty gymkhana clubs. We ride stubby ponies up crumbly mountain trails.
At tea dances, we let ourselves be twirled twice round the ballroom. We hit the
holy spots we hadn't made time for before. In Varanasi, Kalighat, Rishikesh,
Hardwar, astrologers and palmists seek me out and for a fee offer me cosmic
consolations.

Already the widowers among us are being shown new bride candidates.
They cannot resist the call of custom, the authority of their parents and older
brothers. They must marry; it is the duty of a man to look after a wife. The
new wives will be young widows with children, destitute but of good family.
They will make loving wives, but the men will shun them. I've had calls from
the men over crackling Indian telephone lines. "Save me," they say, these sub-
stantial, educated, successful men of forty. "My parents are arranging a marriage for me." In a month they will have buried one family and returned to
Canada with a new bride and partial family.

I am comparatively lucky. No one here thinks of arranging a husband for
an unlucky widow.

Then, on the third day of the sixth month into this odyssey, in an abandoned temple in a tiny Himalayan village, as I make my offering of flowers
and sweetmeats to the god of a tribe of animists, my husband descends to me.
He is squatting next to a scrawny *sadhu*[7] in moth-eaten robes. Vikram wears
the vanilla suit he wore the last time I hugged him. The *sadhu* tosses petals on
a butter-fed flame, reciting Sanskrit mantras and sweeps his face of flies. My
husband takes my hands in his.

*You're beautiful,* he starts. Then, *What are you doing here?*

*Shall I stay?* I ask. He only smiles, but already the image is fading. *You must
finish alone what we started together.* No seaweed wreathes his mouth. He speaks
too fast just as he used to when we were an envied family in our pink split-
level. He is gone.

In the windowless altar room, smoky with joss sticks and clarified butter
lamps, a sweaty hand gropes for my blouse. I do not shriek. The *sadhu* arranges
his robe. The lamps hiss and sputter out.

---

**6.** Landowner (Hindi).   **7.** Hindu holy man.

When we come out of the temple, my mother says, "Did you feel something weird in there?"

My mother has no patience with ghosts, prophetic dreams, holy men, and cults.

"No," I lie. "Nothing."

But she knows that she's lost me. She knows that in days I shall be leaving.

Kusum's put her house up for sale. She wants to live in an ashram in Hardwar. Moving to Hardwar was her swami's idea. Her swami runs two ashrams, the one in Hardwar and another here in Toronto.

"Don't run away," I tell her.

"I'm not running away," she says. "I'm pursuing inner peace. You think you or that Ranganathan fellow are better off?"

Pam's left for California. She wants to do some modelling, she says. She says when she comes into her share of the insurance money she'll open a yoga-cum-aerobics studio in Hollywood. She sends me postcards so naughty I daren't leave them on the coffee table. Her mother has withdrawn from her and the world.

The rest of us don't lose touch, that's the point. Talk is all we have, says Dr. Ranganathan, who has also resisted his relatives and returned to Montreal and to his job, alone. He says, whom better to talk with than other relatives? We've been melted down and recast as a new tribe.

He calls me twice a week from Montreal. Every Wednesday night and every Saturday afternoon. He is changing jobs, going to Ottawa. But Ottawa is over a hundred miles away, and he is forced to drive two hundred and twenty miles a day. He can't bring himself to sell his house. The house is a temple, he says; the king-sized bed in the master bedroom is a shrine. He sleeps on a folding cot. A devotee.

There are still some hysterical relatives. Judith Templeton's list of those needing help and those who've "accepted" is in nearly perfect balance. Acceptance means you speak of your family in the past tense and you make active plans for moving ahead with your life. There are courses at Seneca and Ryerson[8] we could be taking. Her gleaming leather briefcase is full of college catalogues and lists of cultural societies that need our help. She has done impressive work, I tell her.

"In the textbooks on grief management," she replies—I am her confidante, I realize, one of the few whose grief has not sprung bizarre obsessions—"there are stages to pass through: rejection, depression, acceptance, reconstruction." She has compiled a chart and finds that six months after the tragedy, none of us still reject reality, but only a handful are reconstructing. "Depressed Acceptance" is the plateau we've reached. Remarriage is a major step in reconstruction (though she's a little surprised, even shocked, over *how* quickly some of the men have taken on new families). Selling one's house and changing jobs and cities is healthy.

How do I tell Judith Templeton that my family surrounds me, and that like creatures in epics, they've changed shapes? She sees me as calm and accepting

---

8. Ryerson University, Toronto. Seneca College of Applied Arts and Technology, in Willowdale, Toronto.

but worries that I have no job, no career. My closest friends are worse off than I. I cannot tell her my days, even my nights, are thrilling.

She asks me to help with families she can't reach at all. An elderly couple in Agincourt whose sons were killed just weeks after they had brought their parents over from a village in Punjab. From their names, I know they are Sikh. Judith Templeton and a translator have visited them twice with offers of money for air fare to Ireland, with bank forms, power-of-attorney forms, but they have refused to sign, or to leave their tiny apartment. Their sons' money is frozen in the bank. Their sons' investment apartments have been trashed by tenants, the furnishings sold off. The parents fear that anything they sign or any money they receive will end the company's or the country's obligations to them. They fear they are selling their sons for two airline tickets to a place they've never seen.

The high-rise apartment is a tower of Indians and West Indians, with a sprinkling of Orientals. The nearest bus stop kiosk is lined with women in saris. Boys practice cricket in the parking lot. Inside the building, even I wince a bit from the ferocity of onion fumes, the distinctive and immediate Indianness of frying *ghee*,[9] but Judith Templeton maintains a steady flow of information. These poor old people are in imminent danger of losing their place and all their services.

I say to her, "They are Sikh. They will not open up to a Hindu woman." And what I want to add is, as much as I try not to, I stiffen now at the sight of beards and turbans. I remember a time when we all trusted each other in this new country, it was only the new country we worried about.

The two rooms are dark and stuffy. The lights are off, and an oil lamp sputters on the coffee table. The bent old lady has let us in, and her husband is wrapping a white turban over his oiled, hip-length hair. She immediately goes to the kitchen, and I hear the most familiar sound of an Indian home, tap water hitting and filling a teapot.

They have not paid their utility bills, out of fear and the inability to write a check. The telephone is gone; electricity and gas and water are soon to follow. They have told Judith their sons will provide. They are good boys, and they have always earned and looked after their parents.

We converse a bit in Hindi. They do not ask about the crash and I wonder if I should bring it up. If they think I am here merely as a translator, then they may feel insulted. There are thousands of Punjabi-speakers, Sikhs, in Toronto to do a better job. And so I say to the old lady, "I too have lost my sons, and my husband, in the crash."

Her eyes immediately fill with tears. The man mutters a few words which sound like a blessing. "God provides and God takes away," he says.

I want to say, but only men destroy and give back nothing. "My boys and my husband are not coming back," I say. "We have to understand that."

Now the old woman responds. "But who is to say? Man alone does not decide these things." To this her husband adds his agreement.

Judith asks about the bank papers, the release forms. With a stroke of the pen, they will have a provincial trustee to pay their bills, invest their money, send them a monthly pension.

9. Semiliquid clarified butter (Hindi).

"Do you know this woman?" I ask them.

The man raises his hand from the table, turns it over and seems to regard each finger separately before he answers. "This young lady is always coming here, we make tea for her and she leaves papers for us to sign." His eyes scan a pile of papers in the corner of the room. "Soon we will be out of tea, then will she go away?"

The old lady adds, "I have asked my neighbors and no one else gets *angrezi*[1] visitors. What have we done?"

"It's her job," I try to explain. "The government is worried. Soon you will have no place to stay, no lights, no gas, no water."

"Government will get its money. Tell her not to worry, we are honorable people."

I try to explain the government wishes to give money, not take. He raises his hand. "Let them take," he says. "We are accustomed to that. That is no problem."

"We are strong people," says the wife. "Tell her that."

"Who needs all this machinery?" demands the husband. "It is unhealthy, the bright lights, the cold air on a hot day, the cold food, the four gas rings. God will provide, not government."

"When our boys return," the mother says. Her husband sucks his teeth. "Enough talk," he says.

Judith breaks in. "Have you convinced them?" The snaps on her cordovan briefcase go off like firecrackers in that quiet apartment. She lays the sheaf of legal papers on the coffee table. "If they can't write their names, an X will do— I've told them that."

Now the old lady has shuffled to the kitchen and soon emerges with a pot of tea and two cups. "I think my bladder will go first on a job like this," Judith says to me, smiling. "If only there was some way of reaching them. Please thank her for the tea. Tell her she's very kind."

I nod in Judith's direction and tell them in Hindi, "She thanks you for the tea. She thinks you are being very hospitable but she doesn't have the slightest idea what it means."

I want to say, humor her. I want to say, my boys and my husband are with me too, more than ever. I look in the old man's eyes and I can read his stubborn, peasant's message: *I have protected this woman as best I can. She is the only person I have left. Give to me or take from me what you will, but I will not sign for it. I will not pretend that I accept.*

In the car, Judith says, "You see what I'm up against? I'm sure they're lovely people, but their stubbornness and ignorance are driving me crazy. They think signing a paper is signing their sons' death warrants, don't they?"

I am looking out the window. I want to say, *In our culture, it is a parent's duty to hope.*

"Now Shaila, this next woman is a real mess. She cries day and night, and she refuses all medical help. We may have to—"

"—Let me out at the subway," I say.

"I beg your pardon?" I can feel those blue eyes staring at me.

---

1. English, Anglo (Hindi).

It would not be like her to disobey. She merely disapproves, and slows at a corner to let me out. Her voice is plaintive. "Is there anything I said? Anything I did?"

I could answer her suddenly in a dozen ways, but I choose not to. "Shaila? Let's talk about it," I hear, then slam the door.

A wife and mother begins her new life in a new country, and that life is cut short. Yet her husband tells her: Complete what we have started. We, who stayed out of politics and came halfway around the world to avoid religious and political feuding have been the first in the New World to die from it. I no longer know what we started, nor how to complete it. I write letters to the editors of local papers and to members of Parliament. Now at least they admit it was a bomb. One MP answers back, with sympathy, but with a challenge. You want to make a difference? Work on a campaign. Work on mine. Politicize the Indian voter.

My husband's old lawyer helps me set up a trust. Vikram was a saver and a careful investor. He had saved the boys' boarding school and college fees. I sell the pink house at four times what we paid for it and take a small apartment downtown. I am looking for a charity to support.

We are deep in the Toronto winter, gray skies, icy pavements. I stay indoors, watching television. I have tried to assess my situation, how best to live my life, to complete what we began so many years ago. Kusum has written me from Hardwar that her life is now serene. She has seen Satish and has heard her daughter sing again. Kusum was on a pilgrimage, passing through a village when she heard a young girl's voice, singing one of her daughter's favorite *bhajans*. She followed the music through the squalor of a Himalayan village, to a hut where a young girl, an exact replica of her daughter, was fanning coals under the kitchen fire. When she appeared, the girl cried out, "Ma!" and ran away. What did I think of that?

I think I can only envy her.

Pam didn't make it to California, but writes me from Vancouver. She works in a department store, giving make-up hints to Indian and Oriental girls. Dr. Ranganathan has given up his commute, given up his house and job, and accepted an academic position in Texas where no one knows his story and he has vowed not to tell it. He calls me now once a week.

I wait, I listen, and I pray, but Vikram has not returned to me. The voices and the shapes and the nights filled with visions ended abruptly several weeks ago.

I take it as a sign.

One rare, beautiful, sunny day last week, returning from a small errand on Yonge Street, I was walking through the park from the subway to my apartment. I live equidistant from the Ontario Houses of Parliament and the University of Toronto. The day was not cold, but something in the bare trees caught my attention. I looked up from the gravel, into the branches and the clear blue sky beyond. I thought I heard the rustling of larger forms, and I waited a moment for voices. Nothing.

"What?" I asked.

Then as I stood in the path looking north to Queen's Park and west to the university, I heard the voices of my family one last time. *Your time has come,* they said. *Go, be brave.*

I do not know where this voyage I have begun will end. I do not know which direction I will take. I dropped the package on a park bench and started walking.

1988

---

RELATED:

—Mukherjee, "A Four-Hundred-Year-Old Woman," p. 889
—Richard Ford on "The Management of Grief," p. 922

# ALICE MUNRO
*b. 1931*

Widely considered Canada's finest short-story writer, Munro was born on a farm in Wingham, Ontario, and was educated at the University of Western Ontario. Her first collection of stories, *Dance of the Happy Shades* (1968), won the Governor General's Award, and her novel *Lives of Girls and Women* (1971) won the Canadian Booksellers Association Award. Munro is best known for stories that find the humanity in small-town life, and her output has been prodigious. In 1978 and 1986 she twice again received the Governor General's Award for *Who Do You Think You Are?* (published in the United States as *The Beggar Maid*) and *The Progress of Love*. Her more recent books include *Open Secrets* (1994), *Selected Stories* (1996), *The Love of a Good Woman* (1998), *Hateship, Friendship, Courtship, Loveship, Marriage* (2001), *Runaway* (2004), *The View from Castle Rock* (2006), *Too Much Happiness* (2009), and what she says is her final book, *Dear Life* (2013). In recognition of a brilliant and distinguished career, Munro won the Man Booker International Prize in 2009 and the Nobel Prize in Literature in 2013.

## Royal Beatings

R*oyal beating.* That was Flo's promise. You are going to get one Royal Beating.

The word Royal lolled on Flo's tongue, took on trappings. Rose had a need to picture things, to pursue absurdities, that was stronger than the need to stay out of trouble, and instead of taking this threat to heart she pondered: how is a beating royal? She came up with a tree-lined avenue, a crowd of formal spectators, some white horses and black slaves. Someone knelt, and the blood came leaping out like banners. An occasion both savage and splendid. In real life they didn't approach such dignity, and it was only Flo who tried to supply the event with some high air of necessity and regret. Rose and her father soon got beyond anything presentable.

Her father was king of the royal beatings. Those Flo gave never amounted to much; they were quick cuffs and slaps dashed off while her attention remained elsewhere. You get out of my road, she would say. You mind your own business. You take that look off your face.

They lived behind a store in Hanratty, Ontario. There were four of them: Rose, her father, Flo, Rose's young half brother Brian. The store was really a house, bought by Rose's father and mother when they married and set up here in the furniture and upholstery repair business. Her mother could do upholstery. From both parents Rose should have inherited clever hands, a quick sympathy with materials, an eye for the nicest turns of mending, but she hadn't. She was clumsy, and when something broke she couldn't wait to sweep it up and throw it away.

Her mother had died. She said to Rose's father during the afternoon, "I have a feeling that is so hard to describe. It's like a boiled egg in my chest, with the shell left on." She died before night, she had a blood clot on her lung. Rose was a baby in a basket at the time, so of course could not remember any of this. She heard it from Flo, who must have heard it from her father. Flo came along soon afterward, to take over Rose in the basket, marry her father, open up the front room to make a grocery store. Rose, who had known the house only as a store, who had known only Flo for a mother, looked back on the sixteen or so months her parents spent here as an orderly, far gentler and more ceremonious time, with little touches of affluence. She had nothing to go on but some egg cups her mother had bought, with a pattern of vines and birds on them, delicately drawn as if with red ink; the pattern was beginning to wear away. No books or clothes or pictures of her mother remained. Her father must have got rid of them, or else Flo would. Flo's only story about her mother, the one about her death, was oddly grudging. Flo liked the details of a death: the things people said, the way they protested or tried to get out of bed or swore or laughed (some did those things), but when she said that Rose's mother mentioned a hard-boiled egg in her chest she made the comparison sound slightly foolish, as if her mother really was the kind of person who might think you could swallow an egg whole.

Her father had a shed out behind the store, where he worked at his furniture repairing and restoring. He caned chair seats and backs, mended wickerwork, filled cracks, put legs back on, all most admirably and skillfully and cheaply. That was his pride: to startle people with such fine work, such moderate, even ridiculous charges. During the Depression people could not afford to pay more, perhaps, but he continued the practice through the war, through the years of prosperity after the war, until he died. He never discussed with Flo what he charged or what was owing. After he died she had to go out and unlock the shed and take all sorts of scraps of paper and torn envelopes from the big wicked-looking hooks that were his files. Many of these she found were not accounts or receipts at all but records of the weather, bits of information about the garden, things he had been moved to write down.

Ate new potatoes 25th June. Record.
Dark Day, 1880's, nothing supernatural. Clouds of ash from forest fires.
Aug 16, 1938. Giant thunderstorm in evng. Lightning str. Pres. Church,
Turberry Twp. Will of God?
Scald strawberries to remove acid.
All things are alive. Spinoza.[1]

---

1. Benedict de Spinoza (1632–1677), Dutch philosopher who reasoned that all things, material and immaterial, are manifestations of nature and of God.

Flo thought Spinoza must be some new vegetable he planned to grow, like broccoli or eggplant. He would often try some new thing. She showed the scrap of paper to Rose and asked, did she know what Spinoza was? Rose did know, or had an idea—she was in her teens by that time—but she replied that she did not. She had reached an age where she thought she could not stand to know any more, about her father, or about Flo; she pushed any discovery aside with embarrassment and dread.

There was a stove in the shed, and many rough shelves covered with cans of paint and varnish, shellac and turpentine, jars of soaking brushes and also some dark sticky bottles of cough medicine. Why should a man who coughed constantly, whose lungs took in a whiff of gas in the War (called, in Rose's earliest childhood, not the First, but the Last,[2] War), spend all his days breathing fumes of paint and turpentine? At the time, such questions were not asked as often as they are now. On the bench outside Flo's store several old men from the neighborhood sat gossiping, drowsing, in the warm weather, and some of these old men coughed all the time too. The fact is they were dying, slowly and discreetly, of what was called, without any particular sense of grievance, "the foundry disease." They had worked all their lives at the foundry in town, and now they sat still, with their wasted yellow faces, coughing, chuckling, drifting into aimless obscenity on the subject of women walking by, or any young girl on a bicycle.

From the shed came not only coughing, but speech, a continual muttering, reproachful or encouraging, usually just below the level at which separate words could be made out. Slowing down when her father was at a tricky piece of work, taking on a cheerful speed when he was doing something less demanding, sandpapering or painting. Now and then some words would break through and hang clear and nonsensical on the air. When he realized they were out, there would be a quick bit of cover-up coughing, a swallowing, an alert, unusual silence.

"Macaroni, pepperoni, Botticelli,[3] beans—"

What could that mean? Rose used to repeat such things to herself. She could never ask him. The person who spoke these words and the person who spoke to her as her father were not the same, though they seemed to occupy the same space. It would be the worst sort of taste to acknowledge the person who was not supposed to be there; it would not be forgiven. Just the same, she loitered and listened.

The cloud-capped towers, she heard him say once.

"The cloud-capped towers, the gorgeous palaces."[4]

That was like a hand clapped against Rose's chest, not to hurt, but astonish her, to take her breath away. She had to run then, she had to get away. She knew that was enough to hear, and besides, what if he caught her? It would be terrible.

This was something the same as bathroom noises. Flo had saved up, and had a bathroom put in, but there was no place to put it except in a corner of the kitchen. The door did not fit, the walls were only beaver-board. The result

---

**2.** World War I was referred to as "the war to end all wars" by many idealists. **3.** Sandro Botticelli (1444?–1510), Italian painter. **4.** "The cloud-capped towers, the gorgeous palaces, / The solemn temples, the great globe itself. / Yea, all which it inherit, shall dissolve, / And, like this insubstantial pageant faded, / Leave not a wrack behind." Shakespeare's *Tempest* Act IV, scene 1.

was that even the tearing of a piece of toilet paper, the shifting of a haunch, was audible to those working or talking or eating in the kitchen. They were all familiar with each other's nether voices, not only in their more explosive moments but in their intimate sighs and growls and pleas and statements. And they were all most prudish people. So no one ever seemed to hear, or be listening, and no reference was made. The person creating the noises in the bathroom was not connected with the person who walked out.

They lived in a poor part of town. There was Hanratty and West Hanratty, with the river flowing between them. This was West Hanratty. In Hanratty the social structure ran from doctors and dentists and lawyers down to foundry workers and factory workers and draymen[5]; in West Hanratty it ran from factory workers and foundry workers down to large improvident families of casual bootleggers and prostitutes and unsuccessful thieves. Rose thought of her own family as straddling the river, belonging nowhere, but that was not true. West Hanratty was where the store was and they were, on the straggling tail end of the main street. Across the road from them was a blacksmith shop, boarded up about the time the war started, and a house that had been another store at one time. The Salada Tea sign had never been taken out of the front window; it remained as a proud and interesting decoration though there was no Salada Tea for sale inside. There was just a bit of sidewalk, too cracked and tilted for roller-skating, though Rose longed for roller skates and often pictured herself whizzing along in a plaid skirt, agile and fashionable. There was one street light, a tin flower; then the amenities gave up and there were dirt roads and boggy places, front-yard dumps and strange-looking houses. What made the houses strange-looking were the attempts to keep them from going completely to ruin. With some the attempt had never been made. These were gray and rotted and leaning over, falling into a landscape of scrub hollows, frog ponds, cattails and nettles. Most houses, however, had been patched up with tarpaper, a few fresh shingles, sheets of tin, hammered-out stovepipes, even cardboard. This was, of course, in the days before the war, days of what would later be legendary poverty, from which Rose would remember mostly low-down things— serious-looking anthills and wooden steps, and a cloudy, interesting, problematical light on the world.

There was a long truce between Flo and Rose in the beginning. Rose's nature was growing like a prickly pineapple, but slowly, and secretly, hard pride and skepticism overlapping, to make something surprising even to herself. Before she was old enough to go to school, and while Brian was still in the baby carriage, Rose stayed in the store with both of them—Flo sitting on the high stool behind the counter, Brian asleep by the window; Rose knelt or lay on the wide creaky floorboards working with crayons on pieces of brown paper too torn or irregular to be used for wrapping.

People who came to the store were mostly from the houses around. Some country people came too, on their way home from town, and a few people from Hanratty, who walked across the bridge. Some people were always on the main street, in and out of stores, as if it was their duty to be always on display and their right to be welcomed. For instance, Becky Tyde.

5. Men hired to haul heavy loads by dray, a type of strong cart or wagon.

Becky Tyde climbed up on Flo's counter, made room for herself beside an open tin of crumbly jam-filled cookies.

"Are these any good?" she said to Flo, and boldly began to eat one. "When are you going to give us a job, Flo?"

"You could go and work in the butcher shop," said Flo innocently. "You could go and work for your brother."

"Roberta?" said Becky with a stagey sort of contempt. "You think I'd work for him?" Her brother who ran the butcher shop was named Robert but often called Roberta, because of his meek and nervous ways. Becky Tyde laughed. Her laugh was loud and noisy like an engine bearing down on you.

She was a big-headed loud-voiced dwarf, with a mascot's sexless swagger, a red velvet tam, a twisted neck that forced her to hold her head on one side, always looking up and sideways. She wore little polished high-heeled shoes, real lady's shoes. Rose watched her shoes, being scared of the rest of her, of her laugh and her neck. She knew from Flo that Becky Tyde had been sick with polio as a child, that was why her neck was twisted and why she had not grown any taller. It was hard to believe that she had started out differently, that she had ever been normal. Flo said she was not cracked, she had as much brains as anybody, but she knew she could get away with anything.

"You know I used to live out here?" Becky said, noticing Rose. "Hey! What's-your-name! Didn't I used to live out here, Flo?"

"If you did it was before my time," said Flo, as if she didn't know anything.

"That was before the neighborhood got so downhill. Excuse me saying so. My father built his house out here and he built his slaughterhouse and we had half an acre of orchard."

"Is that so?" said Flo, using her humoring voice, full of false geniality, humility even. "Then why did you ever move away?"

"I told you, it got to be such a downhill neighborhood," said Becky. She would put a whole cookie in her mouth if she felt like it, let her cheeks puff out like a frog's. She never told any more.

Flo knew anyway, and who didn't. Everyone knew the house, red brick with the veranda pulled off and the orchard, what was left of it, full of the usual outflow—car seats and washing machines and bedsprings and junk. The house would never look sinister, in spite of what had happened in it, because there was so much wreckage and confusion all around.

Becky's old father was a different kind of butcher from her brother according to Flo. A bad-tempered Englishman. And different from Becky in the matter of mouthiness. His was never open. A skinflint, a family tyrant. After Becky had polio he wouldn't let her go back to school. She was seldom seen outside the house, never outside the yard. He didn't want people gloating. That was what Becky said, at the trial. Her mother was dead by that time and her sisters married. Just Becky and Robert at home. People would stop Robert on the road and ask him, "How about your sister, Robert? Is she altogether better now?"

"Yes."

"Does she do the housework? Does she get your supper?"

"Yes."

"And is your father good to her, Robert?"

The story being that the father beat them, had beaten all his children and beaten his wife as well, beat Becky more now because of her deformity, which some people believed he had caused (they did not understand about polio). The stories persisted and got added to. The reason that Becky was kept out of sight was now supposed to be her pregnancy, and the father of the child was supposed to be her own father. Then people said it had been born, and disposed of.

"What?"

"Disposed of," Flo said. "They used to say go and get your lamb chops at Tyde's, get them nice and tender! It was all lies in all probability," she said regretfully.

Rose could be drawn back—from watching the wind shiver along the old torn awning, catch in the tear—by this tone of regret, caution, in Flo's voice. Flo telling a story—and this was not the only one, or even the most lurid one, she knew—would incline her head and let her face go soft and thoughtful, tantalizing, warning.

"I shouldn't even be telling you this stuff."

More was to follow.

Three useless young men, who hung around the livery stable, got together—or were got together, by more influential and respectable men in town—and prepared to give old man Tyde a horsewhipping, in the interests of public morality. They blacked their faces. They were provided with whips and a quart of whiskey apiece, for courage. They were: Jelly Smith, a horse-racer and a drinker; Bob Temple, a ballplayer and strongman; and Hat Nettleton, who worked on the town dray, and had his nickname from a bowler hat he wore, out of vanity as much as for the comic effect. He still worked on the dray, in fact; he had kept the name if not the hat, and could often be seen in public almost as often as Becky Tyde—delivering sacks of coal, which blackened his face and arms. That should have brought to mind his story, but didn't. Present time and past, the shady melodramatic past of Flo's stories, were quite separate, at least for Rose. Present people could not be fitted into the past. Becky herself, town oddity and public pet, harmless and malicious, could never match the butcher's prisoner, the cripple daughter, a white streak at the window: mute, beaten, impregnated. As with the house, only a formal connection could be made.

The young men primed to do the horsewhipping showed up late, outside Tyde's house, after everybody had gone to bed. They had a gun, but they used up their ammunition firing it off in the yard. They yelled for the butcher and beat on the door; finally they broke it down. Tyde concluded they were after his money, so he put some bills in a handkerchief and sent Becky down with them, maybe thinking those men would be touched or scared by the sight of a little wry-necked girl, a dwarf. But that didn't content them. They came upstairs and dragged the butcher out from under his bed, in his nightgown. They dragged him outside and stood him in the snow. The temperature was four below zero, a fact noted later in court. They meant to hold a mock trial but they could not remember how it was done. So they began to beat him and kept beating him until he fell. They yelled at him, *Butcher's meat!* and continued beating him while his nightgown and the snow he was lying in turned red. His son Robert said in court that he had not watched the beating. Becky said that Robert had watched at first but had run away and hid. She herself had watched all the way through. She watched the men leave at last and her father make his delayed bloody progress through the snow and up the steps of the veranda. She did not go out to help him, or open the door until he got to it. Why not? she was asked in court, and she said she did not go out because she just had her nightgown on, and she did not open the door because she did not want to let the cold into the house.

Old man Tyde then appeared to have recovered his strength. He sent Robert to harness the horse, and made Becky heat water so that he could wash. He dressed and took all the money and with no explanation to his children got into the cutter and drove to Belgrave where he left the horse tied in the cold and took the early morning train to Toronto. On the train he behaved oddly, groaning and cursing as if he was drunk. He was picked up on the streets of Toronto a day later, out of his mind with fever, and was taken to a hospital, where he died. He still had all the money. The cause of death was given as pneumonia.

But the authorities got wind, Flo said. The case came to trial. The three men who did it all received long prison sentences. A farce, said Flo. Within a year they were all free, had all been pardoned, had jobs waiting for them. And why was that? It was because too many higher-ups were in on it. And it seemed as if Becky and Robert had no interest in seeing justice done. They were left well-off. They bought a house in Hanratty. Robert went into the store. Becky after her long seclusion started on a career of public sociability and display.

That was all. Flo put the lid down on the story as if she was sick of it. It reflected no good on anybody.

"Imagine," Flo said.

Flo at this time must have been in her early thirties. A young woman. She wore exactly the same clothes that a woman of fifty, or sixty, or seventy, might wear: print housedresses loose at the neck and sleeves as well as the waist; bib aprons, also of print, which she took off when she came from the kitchen into the store. This was a common costume at the time, for a poor though not absolutely poverty-stricken woman; it was also, in a way, a scornful deliberate choice. Flo scorned slacks, she scorned the outfits of people trying to be in style, she scorned lipstick and permanents. She wore her own black hair cut straight across, just long enough to push behind her ears. She was tall but fine-boned, with narrow wrists and shoulders, a small head, a pale, freckled, mobile, monkeyish face. If she had thought it worthwhile, and had the resources, she might have had a black-and-pale, fragile, nurtured sort of prettiness; Rose realized that later. But she would have to have been a different person altogether; she would have to have learned to resist making faces, at herself and others.

Rose's earliest memories of Flo were of extraordinary softness and hardness. The soft hair, the long, soft, pale cheeks, soft almost invisible fuzz in front of her ears and above her mouth. The sharpness of her knees, hardness of her lap, flatness of her front.

When Flo sang:

Oh the buzzin' of the bees in the cigarette trees
And the soda-*water* fountain . . . [6]

---

6. From the ballad "The Big Rock Candy Mountain."

Rose thought of Flo's old life before she married her father, when she worked as a waitress in the coffee shop in Union Station, and went with her girl friends Mavis and Irene to Centre Island,[7] and was followed by men on dark streets and knew how pay phones and elevators worked. Rose heard in her voice the reckless dangerous life of cities, the gum-chewing sharp answers.

And when she sang:

> Then slowly, slowly, she got up
> And slowly she came nigh him
> And all she said, that she ever did say,
> Was young man I think, you're dyin'![8]

Rose thought of a life Flo seemed to have had beyond that, earlier than that, crowded and legendary, with Barbara Allen and Becky Tyde's father and all kinds of outrages and sorrows jumbled up together in it.

The royal beatings. What got them started?

Suppose a Saturday, in spring. Leaves not out yet but the doors open to the sunlight. Crows. Ditches full of running water. Hopeful weather. Often on Saturdays Flo left Rose in charge of the store—it's a few years now, these are the years when Rose was nine, ten, eleven, twelve—while she herself went across the bridge to Hanratty (going uptown they called it) to shop and see people, and listen to them. Among the people she listened to were Mrs. Lawyer Davies, Mrs. Anglican Rector Henley-Smith, and Mrs. Horse-Doctor McKay. She came home and imitated their flibberty voices. Monsters, she made them seem; of foolishness, and showiness, and self-approbation.

When she finished shopping she went into the coffee shop of the Queen's Hotel and had a sundae. What kind? Rose and Brian wanted to know when she got home, and they would be disappointed if it was only pineapple or butterscotch, pleased if it was a Tin Roof, or Black and White. Then she smoked a cigarette. She had some ready-rolled, that she carried with her, so that she wouldn't have to roll one in public. Smoking was the one thing she did that she would have called showing off in anybody else. It was a habit left over from her working days, from Toronto. She knew it was asking for trouble. Once the Catholic priest came over to her right in the Queen's Hotel, and flashed his lighter at her before she could get her matches out. She thanked him but did not enter into conversation, lest he should try to convert her.

Another time, on the way home, she saw at the town end of the bridge a boy in a blue jacket, apparently looking at the water. Eighteen, nineteen years old. Nobody she knew. Skinny, weakly looking, something the matter with him, she saw at once. Was he thinking of jumping? Just as she came up even with him, what does he do but turn and display himself, holding his jacket open, also his pants. What he must have suffered from the cold, on a day that had Flo holding her coat collar tight around her throat.

When she first saw what he had in his hand, Flo said, all she could think of was, what is he doing out here with a baloney sausage?

---

7. Park in Toronto Harbour. Union Station is the main railroad terminal in Toronto.  8. From the ballad "Barbara Allen."

She could say that. It was offered as truth; no joke. She maintained that she despised dirty talk. She would go out and yell at the old men sitting in front of her store.

"If you want to stay where you are you better clean your mouths out!"

Saturday, then. For some reason Flo is not going uptown, has decided to stay home and scrub the kitchen floor. Perhaps this has put her in a bad mood. Perhaps she was in a bad mood anyway, due to people not paying their bills, or the stirring-up of feelings in spring. The wrangle with Rose has already commenced, has been going on forever, like a dream that goes back and back into other dreams, over hills and through doorways, maddeningly dim and populous and familiar and elusive. They are carting all the chairs out of the kitchen preparatory to the scrubbing, and they have also got to move some extra provisions for the store, some cartons of canned goods, tins of maple syrup, coal-oil cans, jars of vinegar. They take these things out to the wood-shed. Brian who is five or six by this time is helping drag the tins.

"Yes," says Flo, carrying on from our lost starting point. "Yes, and that filth you taught to Brian."

"What filth?"

"And he doesn't know any better."

There is one step down from the kitchen to the woodshed, a bit of carpet on it so worn Rose can't even remember seeing the pattern. Brian loosens it, dragging a tin.

"Two Vancouvers," she says softly.

Flo is back in the kitchen. Brian looks from Flo to Rose and Rose says again in a slightly louder voice, an encouraging singsong, "Two Vancouvers—"

"Fried in snot!" finishes Brian, not able to control himself any longer.

"Two pickled arseholes—"

"—tied in a knot!"

There it is. The filth.

Two Vancouvers fried in snot!
Two pickled arseholes tied in a knot!

Rose has known that for years, learned it when she first went to school. She came home and asked Flo, what is a Vancouver?

"It's a city. It's a long ways away."

"What else besides a city?"

Flo said, what did she mean, what else? How could it be fried, Rose said, approaching the dangerous moment, the delightful moment, when she would have to come out with the whole thing.

"Two Vancouvers fried in snot! / Two pickled arseholes tied in a knot!"

"You're going to get it!" cried Flo in a predictable rage. "Say that again and you'll get a good clout!"

Rose couldn't stop herself. She hummed it tenderly, tried saying the inno-cent words aloud, humming through the others. It was not just the words snot and arsehole that gave her pleasure, though of course they did. It was the pickling and tying and the unimaginable Vancouvers. She saw them in her mind shaped rather like octopuses, twitching in the pan. The tumble of reason; the spark and spit of craziness.

Lately she has remembered it again and taught it to Brian, to see if it has the same effect on him, and of course it has.

"Oh, I heard you!" says Flo. "I heard that! And I'm warning you!"

So she is. Brian takes the warning. He runs away, out the woodshed door, to do as he likes. Being a boy, free to help or not, involve himself or not. Not committed to the household struggle. They don't need him anyway, except to use against each other, they hardly notice his going. They continue, can't help continuing, can't leave each other alone. When they seem to have given up they really are just waiting and building up steam.

Flo gets out the scrub pail and the brush and the rag and the pad for her knees, a dirty red rubber pad. She starts to work on the floor. Rose sits on the kitchen table, the only place left to sit, swinging her legs. She can feel the cool oilcloth, because she is wearing shorts, last summer's tight faded shorts dug out of the summer-clothes bag. They smell a bit moldy from winter storage.

Flo crawls underneath, scrubbing with the brush, wiping with the rag. Her legs are long, white and muscular, marked all over with blue veins as if somebody had been drawing rivers on them with an indelible pencil. An abnormal energy, a violent disgust, is expressed in the chewing of the brush at the linoleum, the swish of the rag.

What do they have to say to each other? It doesn't really matter. Flo speaks of Rose's smart-aleck behavior, rudeness and sloppiness and conceit. Her willingness to make work for others, her lack of gratitude. She mentions Brian's innocence, Rose's corruption. Oh, don't you think you're somebody, says Flo, and a moment later, Who do you think you are? Rose contradicts and objects with such poisonous reasonableness and mildness, displays theatrical unconcern. Flo goes beyond her ordinary scorn and self-possession and becomes amazingly theatrical herself, saying it was for Rose that she sacrificed her life. She saw her father saddled with a baby daughter and she thought, what is that man going to do? So she married him, and here she is, on her knees.

At that moment the bell rings, to announce a customer in the store. Because the fight is on, Rose is not permitted to go into the store and wait on whoever it is. Flo gets up and throws off her apron, groaning—but not communicatively, it is not a groan whose exasperation Rose is allowed to share—and goes in and serves. Rose hears her using her normal voice.

"About time! Sure is!"

She comes back and ties on her apron and is ready to resume.

"You never have a thought for anybody but your ownself! You never have a thought for what I'm doing."

"I never asked you to do anything. I wish you never had. I would have been a lot better off."

Rose says this smiling directly at Flo, who has not yet gone down on her knees. Flo sees the smile, grabs the scrub rag that is hanging on the side of the pail, and throws it at her. It may be meant to hit her in the face but instead it falls against Rose's leg and she raises her foot and catches it, swinging it negligently against her ankle.

"All right," says Flo. "You've done it this time. All right."

Rose watches her go to the woodshed door, hears her tramp through the woodshed, pause in the doorway, where the screen door hasn't yet been hung, and the storm door is standing open, propped with a brick. She calls Rose's father. She calls him in a warning, summoning voice, as if against her will preparing him for bad news. He will know what this is about.

The kitchen floor has five or six different patterns of linoleum on it. Ends, which Flo got for nothing and ingeniously trimmed and fitted together, bordering them with tin strips and tacks. While Rose sits on the table waiting, she looks at the floor, at this satisfying arrangement of rectangles, triangles, some other shape whose name she is trying to remember. She hears Flo coming back through the woodshed, on the creaky plank walk laid over the dirt floor. She is loitering, waiting, too. She and Rose can carry this no further, by themselves.

Rose hears her father come in. She stiffens, a tremor runs through her legs, she feels them shiver on the oilcloth. Called away from some peaceful, absorbing task, away from the words running in his head, called out of himself, her father has to say something. He says, "Well? What's wrong?"

Now comes another voice of Flo's. Enriched, hurt, apologetic, it seems to have been manufactured on the spot. She is sorry to have called him from his work. Would never have done it, if Rose was not driving her to distraction. How to distraction? With her back talk and impudence and her terrible tongue. The things Rose has said to Flo are such that, if Flo had said them to her mother, she knows her father would have thrashed her into the ground.

Rose tries to butt in, to say this isn't true.

What isn't true?

Her father raises a hand, doesn't look at her, says, "Be quiet."

When she says it isn't true, Rose means that she herself didn't start this, only responded, that she was goaded by Flo, who is now, she believes, telling the grossest sort of lies, twisting everything to suit herself. Rose puts aside her other knowledge that whatever Flo has said or done, whatever she herself has said or done, does not really matter at all. It is the struggle itself that counts, and that can't be stopped, can never be stopped, short of where it has got to, now.

Flo's knees are dirty, in spite of the pad. The scrub rag is still hanging over Rose's foot.

Her father wipes his hands, listening to Flo. He takes his time. He is slow at getting into the spirit of things, tired in advance, maybe, on the verge of rejecting the role he has to play. He won't look at Rose, but at any sound or stirring from Rose, he holds up his hand.

"Well we don't need the public in on this, that's for sure," Flo says, and she goes to lock the door of the store, putting in the store window the sign that says BACK SOON, a sign Rose made for her with a great deal of fancy curving and shading of letters in black and red crayon. When she comes back she shuts the door to the store, then the door to the stairs, then the door to the woodshed.

Her shoes have left marks on the clean wet part of the floor.

"Oh, I don't know," she says now, in a voice worn down from its emotional peak. "I don't know what to do about her." She looks down and sees her dirty knees (following Rose's eyes) and rubs at them viciously with her bare hands, smearing the dirt around.

"She humiliates me," she says, straightening up. There it is, the explanation. "She humiliates me," she repeats with satisfaction. "She has no respect."

"I do not!"

"Quiet, you!" says her father.

"If I hadn't called your father you'd still be sitting there with that grin on your face! What other way is there to manage you?"

Rose detects in her father some objections to Flo's rhetoric, some embarrassment and reluctance. She is wrong, and ought to know she is wrong, in thinking that she can count on this. The fact that she knows about it, and he knows she knows, will not make things any better. He is beginning to warm up. He gives her a look. This look is at first cold and challenging. It informs her of his judgment, of the hopelessness of her position. Then it clears, it begins to fill up with something else, the way a spring fills up when you clear the leaves away. It fills with hatred and pleasure. Rose sees that and knows it. Is that just a description of anger, should she see his eyes filling up with anger? No. Hatred is right. Pleasure is right. His face loosens and changes and grows younger, and he holds up his hand this time to silence Flo.

"All right," he says, meaning that's enough, more than enough, this part is over, things can proceed. He starts to loosen his belt.

Flo has stopped anyway. She has the same difficulty Rose does, a difficulty in believing that what you know must happen really will happen, that there comes a time when you can't draw back.

"Oh, I don't know, don't be too hard on her." She is moving around nervously as if she has thoughts of opening some escape route. "Oh, you don't have to use the belt on her. Do you have to use the belt?"

He doesn't answer. The belt is coming off, not hastily. It is being grasped at the necessary point. *All right you.* He is coming over to Rose. He pushes her off the table. His face, like his voice, is quite out of character. He is like a bad actor, who turns a part grotesque. As if he must savor and insist on just what is shameful and terrible about this. That is not to say he is pretending, that he is acting, and does not mean it. He is acting, and he means it. Rose knows that, she knows everything about him.

She has since wondered about murders, and murderers. Does the thing have to be carried through, in the end, partly for the effect, to prove to the audience of one—who won't be able to report, only register, the lesson—that such a thing can happen, that there is nothing that can't happen, that the most dreadful antic is justified, feelings can be found to match it?

She tries again looking at the kitchen floor, that clever and comforting geometrical arrangement, instead of looking at him or his belt. How can this go on in front of such daily witnesses—the linoleum, the calendar with the mill and creek and autumn trees, the old accommodating pots and pans?

*Hold out your hand!*

Those things aren't going to help her, none of them can rescue her. They turn bland and useless, even unfriendly. Pots can show malice, the patterns of linoleum can leer up at you, treachery is the other side of dailiness.

At the first, or maybe the second, crack of pain, she draws back. She will not accept it. She runs around the room, she tries to get to the doors. Her father blocks her off. Not an ounce of courage or of stoicism in her, it would seem. She runs, she screams, she implores. Her father is after her, cracking the belt at her when he can, then abandoning it and using his hands. Bang over the ear, then bang over the other ear. Back and forth, her head ringing. Bang in the face. Up against the wall and bang in the face again. He shakes her and hits her against the wall, he kicks her legs. She is incoherent, insane, shrieking. *Forgive me! Oh please, forgive me!*

Flo is shrieking too. *Stop, stop!*

Not yet. He throws Rose down. Or perhaps she throws herself down. He kicks her legs again. She has given up on words but is letting out a noise, the sort of noise that makes Flo cry, *Oh, what if people can hear her?* The very last-ditch willing sound of humiliation and defeat it is, for it seems Rose must play her part in this with the same grossness, the same exaggeration, that her father displays, playing his. She plays his victim with a self-indulgence that arouses, and maybe hopes to arouse, his final, sickened contempt.

They will give this anything that is necessary, it seems, they will go to any lengths.

Not quite. He has never managed really to injure her, though there are times, of course, when she prays that he will. He hits her with an open hand, there is some restraint in his kicks.

Now he stops, he is out of breath. He allows Flo to move in, he grabs Rose up and gives her a push in Flo's direction, making a sound of disgust. Flo retrieves her, opens the stair door, shoves her up the stairs.

"Go on up to your room now! Hurry!"

Rose goes up the stairs, stumbling, letting herself stumble, letting herself fall against the steps. She doesn't bang her door because a gesture like that could still bring him after her, and anyway, she is weak. She lies on the bed. She can hear through the stovepipe hole Flo snuffling and remonstrating, her father saying angrily that Flo should have kept quiet then, if she did not want Rose punished she should not have recommended it. Flo says she never recommended a hiding like that.

They argue back and forth on this. Flo's frightened voice is growing stronger, getting its confidence back. By stages, by arguing, they are being drawn back into themselves. Soon it's only Flo talking; he will not talk anymore. Rose has had to fight down her noisy sobbing, so as to listen to them, and when she loses interest in listening, and wants to sob some more, she finds she can't work herself up to it. She has passed into a state of calm, in which outrage is perceived as complete and final. In this state events and possibilities take on a lovely simplicity. Choices are mercifully clear. The words that come to mind are not the quibbling, seldom the conditional. Never is a word to which the right is suddenly established. She will never speak to them, she will never look at them with anything but loathing, she will never forgive them. She will punish them; she will finish them. Encased in these finalities, and in her bodily pain, she floats in curious comfort, beyond herself, beyond responsibility.

Suppose she dies now? Suppose she commits suicide? Suppose she runs away? Any of these things would be appropriate. It is only a matter of choosing, of figuring out the way. She floats in her pure superior state as if kindly drugged.

And just as there is a moment, when you are drugged, in which you feel perfectly safe, sure, unreachable, and then without warning and right next to it a moment in which you know the whole protection has fatally cracked, though it is still pretending to hold soundly together, so there is a moment now—the moment, in fact, when Rose hears Flo step on the stairs—that contains for her both present peace and freedom and a sure knowledge of the whole downspiraling course of events from now on.

Flo comes into the room without knocking, but with a hesitation that shows it might have occurred to her. She brings a jar of cold cream. Rose is hanging on to advantage as long as she can, lying face down on the bed, refusing to acknowledge or answer.

"Oh come on," Flo says uneasily. "You aren't so bad off, are you? You put some of this on and you'll feel better."

She is bluffing. She doesn't know for sure what damage has been done. She has the lid off the cold cream. Rose can smell it. The intimate, babyish, humiliating smell. She won't allow it near her. But in order to avoid it, the big ready clot of it in Flo's hand, she has to move. She scuffles, resists, loses dignity, and lets Flo see there is not really much the matter.

"All right," Flo says. "You win. I'll leave it here and you can put it on when you like."

Later still a tray will appear. Flo will put it down without a word and go away. A large glass of chocolate milk on it, made with Vita-Malt from the store. Some rich streaks of Vita-Malt around the bottom of the glass. Little sandwiches, neat and appetizing. Canned salmon of the first quality and reddest color, plenty of mayonnaise. A couple of butter tarts from a bakery package, chocolate biscuits with a peppermint filling. Rose's favorites, in the sandwich, tart and cookie line. She will turn away, refuse to look, but left alone with these eatables will be miserably tempted, roused and troubled and drawn back from thoughts of suicide or flight by the smell of salmon, the anticipation of crisp chocolate, she will reach out a finger, just to run it around the edge of one of the sandwiches (crusts cut off!) to get the overflow, get a taste. Then she will decide to eat one, for strength to refuse the rest. One will not be noticed. Soon, in helpless corruption, she will eat them all. She will drink the chocolate milk, eat the tarts, eat the cookies. She will get the malty syrup out of the bottom of the glass with her finger, though she sniffles with shame. Too late.

Flo will come up and get the tray. She may say, "I see you got your appetite still," or, "Did you like the chocolate milk, was it enough syrup in it?" depending on how chastened she is feeling, herself. At any rate, all advantage will be lost. Rose will understand that life has started up again, that they will all sit around the table eating again, listening to the radio news. Tomorrow morning, maybe even tonight. Unseemly and unlikely as that may be. They will be embarrassed, but rather less than you might expect considering how they have behaved. They will feel a queer lassitude, a convalescent indolence, not far off satisfaction.

One night after a scene like this they were all in the kitchen. It must have been summer, or at least warm weather, because her father spoke of the old men who sat on the bench in front of the store.

"Do you know what they're talking about now?" he said, and nodded his head toward the store to show who he meant, though of course they were not there now, they went home at dark.

"Those old coots," said Flo. "What?"

There was about them both a geniality not exactly false but a bit more emphatic than was normal, without company.

Rose's father told them then that the old men had picked up the idea somewhere that what looked like a star in the western sky, the first star that came out after sunset, the evening star, was in reality an airship hovering over Bay City, Michigan, on the other side of Lake Huron. An American invention, sent up to rival the heavenly bodies. They were all in agreement about this, the idea was congenial to them. They believed it to be lit by ten thousand electric light bulbs. Her father had ruthlessly disagreed with them, pointing out that it was the planet Venus they saw, which had appeared in the sky long before the invention of an electric light bulb. They had never heard of the planet Venus.

"Ignoramuses," said Flo. At which Rose knew, and knew her father knew, that Flo had never heard of the planet Venus either. To distract them from this, or even apologize for it, Flo put down her teacup, stretched out with her head resting on the chair she had been sitting on and her feet on another chair (somehow she managed to tuck her dress modestly between her legs at the same time), and lay stiff as a board, so that Brian cried out in delight, "Do that! Do that!"

Flo was double-jointed and very strong. In moments of celebration or emergency she would do tricks.

They were silent while she turned herself around, not using her arms at all but just her strong legs and feet. Then they all cried out in triumph, though they had seen it before.

Just as Flo turned herself Rose got a picture in her mind of that airship, an elongated transparent bubble, with its strings of diamond lights, floating in the miraculous American sky.

"The planet Venus!" her father said, applauding Flo. "Ten thousand electric lights!"

There was a feeling of permission, relaxation, even a current of happiness, in the room.

Years later, many years later, on a Sunday morning, Rose turned on the radio. This was when she was living by herself in Toronto.

*Well Sir.*

*It was a different kind of place in our day. Yes it was.*

*It was all horses then. Horses and buggies. Buggy races up and down the main street on the Saturday nights.*

"Just like the chariot races," says the announcer's, or interviewer's, smooth encouraging voice.

*I never seen a one of them.*

"No sir, that was the old Roman chariot races I was referring to. That was before your time."

*Musta been before my time. I'm a hunerd and two years old.*

"That's a wonderful age, sir."

*It is so.*

She left it on, as she went around the apartment kitchen, making coffee for herself. It seemed to her that this must be a staged interview, a scene from some play, and she wanted to find out what it was. The old man's voice was so vain and belligerent, the interviewer's quite hopeless and alarmed, under its practiced gentleness and ease. You were surely meant to see him holding the microphone up to some toothless, reckless, preening centenarian, wondering what in God's name he was doing here, and what would he say next?

"They must have been fairly dangerous."

*What was dangerous?*

"Those buggy races."

*They was. Dangerous. Used to be the runaway horses. Used to be a-plenty of accidents. Fellows was dragged along on the gravel and cut their face open. Wouldna matter so much if they was dead. Heh.*

*Some of them horses was the high-steppers. Some, they had to have the mustard under their tail. Some wouldn step out for nothin. That's the thing it is with the horses. Some'll work and pull till they drop down dead and some wouldn pull your cock out of a pail of lard. Hehe.*

It must be a real interview after all. Otherwise they wouldn't have put that in, wouldn't have risked it. It's all right if the old man says it. Local color. Anything rendered harmless and delightful by his hundred years.

*Accidents all the time then. In the mill. Foundry. Wasn't the precautions.*

"You didn't have so many strikes then, I don't suppose? You didn't have so many unions?"

*Everybody taking it easy nowadays. We worked and we was glad to get it. Worked and was glad to get it.*

"You didn't have television."

*Didn't have no TV. Didn't have no radio. No picture show.*

"You made your own entertainment."

*That's the way we did.*

"You had a lot of experiences young men growing up today will never have."

*Experiences.*

"Can you recall any of them for us?"

*I eaten groundhog meat one time. One winter. You wouldna cared for it. Heh.*

There was a pause, of appreciation, it would seem, then the announcer's voice saying that the foregoing had been an interview with Mr. Wilfred Nettleton of Hanratty, Ontario, made on his hundred and second birthday, two weeks before his death, last spring. A living link with our past. Mr. Nettleton had been interviewed in the Wawanash County Home for the aged.

Hat Nettleton.

Horsewhipper into centenarian. Photographed on his birthday, fussed over by nurses, kissed no doubt by a girl reporter. Flash bulbs popping at him. Tape recorder drinking in the sound of his voice. Oldest resident. Oldest horsewhipper. Living link with our past.

Looking out from her kitchen window at the cold lake, Rose was longing to tell somebody. It was Flo who would enjoy hearing. She thought of her saying *Imagine!* in a way that meant she was having her worst suspicions gorgeously confirmed. But Flo was in the same place Hat Nettleton had died in, and there wasn't any way Rose could reach her. She had been there even when that interview was recorded, though she would not have heard it, would not have known about it. After Rose put her in the Home, a couple of years earlier, she had stopped talking. She had removed herself, and spent most of her time sitting in a corner of her crib, looking crafty and disagreeable, not answering anybody, though she occasionally showed her feelings by biting a nurse.

1977

# Miles City, Montana

My father came across the field carrying the body of the boy who had been drowned. There were several men together, returning from the search, but he was the one carrying the body. The men were muddy and exhausted, and walked with their heads down, as if they were ashamed. Even the dogs were dispirited, dripping from the cold river. When they all set out, hours before, the dogs were nervy and yelping, the men tense and determined, and there was a constrained, unspeakable excitement about the whole scene. It was understood that they might find something horrible.

The boy's name was Steve Gauley. He was eight years old. His hair and clothes were mud-colored now and carried some bits of dead leaves, twigs, and grass. He was like a heap of refuse that had been left out all winter. His face was turned in to my father's chest, but I could see a nostril, an ear, plugged up with greenish mud.

I don't think so. I don't think I really saw all this. Perhaps I saw my father carrying him, and the other men following along, and the dogs, but I would not have been allowed to get close enough to see something like mud in his nostril. I must have heard someone talking about that and imagined that I saw it. I see his face unaltered except for the mud—Steve Gauley's familiar, sharp-honed, sneaky-looking face—and it wouldn't have been like that; it would have been bloated and changed and perhaps muddied all over after so many hours in the water.

To have to bring back such news, such evidence, to a waiting family, particularly a mother, would have made searchers move heavily, but what was happening here was worse. It seemed a worse shame (to hear people talk) that there was no mother, no woman at all—no grandmother or aunt, or even a sister—to receive Steve Gauley and give him his due of grief. His father was a hired man, a drinker but not a drunk, an erratic man without being entertaining, not friendly but not exactly a troublemaker. His fatherhood seemed accidental, and the fact that the child had been left with him when the mother went away, and that they continued living together, seemed accidental. They lived in a steep-roofed, gray-shingled hillbilly sort of house that was just a bit better than a shack—the father fixed the roof and put supports under the porch, just enough and just in time—and their life was held together in a similar manner; that is, just well enough to keep the Children's Aid at bay. They didn't eat meals together or cook for each other, but there was food. Sometimes the father would give Steve money to buy food at the store, and Steve was seen to buy quite sensible things, such as pancake mix and macaroni dinner.

I had known Steve Gauley fairly well. I had not liked him more often than I had liked him. He was two years older than I was. He would hang around our place on Saturdays, scornful of whatever I was doing but unable to leave me alone. I couldn't be on the swing without him wanting to try it, and if I wouldn't give it up he came and pushed me so that I went crooked. He teased the dog. He got me into trouble—deliberately and maliciously, it seemed to me afterwards—by daring me to do things I wouldn't have thought of on my own: digging up the potatoes to see how big they were when they were still only the size of marbles, and pushing over the stacked firewood to make a pile we could jump off. At school, we never spoke to each other. He was solitary, though not tormented. But on Saturday mornings, when I saw his thin, self-possessed figure sliding through the cedar hedge, I knew I was in for something and he would decide what. Sometimes it was all right. We pretended we were cowboys who had to tame wild horses. We played in the pasture by the river, not far from the place where Steve drowned. We were horses and riders both, screaming and neighing and bucking and waving whips of tree branches beside a little nameless river that flows into the Saugeen in southern Ontario.

The funeral was held in our house. There was not enough room at Steve's father's place for the large crowd that was expected because of the circumstances. I have a memory of the crowded room but no picture of Steve in his coffin, or of the minister, or of wreaths of flowers. I remember that I was holding one flower, a white narcissus, which must have come from a pot somebody forced indoors, because it was too early for even the forsythia bush or the trilliums and marsh marigolds in the woods. I stood in a row of children, each of us holding a narcissus. We sang a children's hymn, which somebody played on our piano: "When He Cometh, When He Cometh, to Make Up His Jewels." I was wearing white ribbed stockings, which were disgustingly itchy, and wrinkled at the knees and ankles. The feeling of these stockings on my legs is mixed up with another feeling in my memory. It is hard to describe. It had to do with my parents. Adults in general but my parents in particular. My father, who had carried Steve's body from the river, and my mother, who must have done most of the arranging of this funeral. My father in his dark-blue suit and my mother in her brown velvet dress with the creamy satin collar. They stood side by side opening and closing their mouths for the hymn, and I stood removed from them, in the row of children, watching. I felt a furious and sickening disgust. Children sometimes have an access of disgust concerning adults. The size, the lumpy shapes, the bloated power. The breath, the coarseness, the hairiness, the horrid secretions. But this was more. And the accompanying anger had nothing sharp and self-respecting about it. There was no release, as when I would finally bend and pick up a stone and throw it at Steve Gauley. It could not be understood or expressed, though it died down after a while into a heaviness, then just a taste, an occasional taste—a thin, familiar misgiving.

Twenty years or so later, in 1961, my husband, Andrew, and I got a brand-new car, our first—that is, our first brand-new. It was a Morris Oxford, oyster-colored (the dealer had some fancier name for the color)—a big small car, with plenty of room for us and our two children. Cynthia was six and Meg three and a half.

Andrew took a picture of me standing beside the car. I was wearing white pants, a black turtleneck, and sunglasses. I lounged against the car door, canting my hips to make myself look slim.

"Wonderful," Andrew said. "Great. You look like Jackie Kennedy." All over this continent probably, dark-haired, reasonably slender young women were told, when they were stylishly dressed or getting their pictures taken, that they looked like Jackie Kennedy.

Andrew took a lot of pictures of me, and of the children, our house, our garden, our excursions and possessions. He got copies made, labelled them carefully, and sent them back to his mother and his aunt and uncle in Ontario. He got copies for me to send to my father, who also lived in Ontario, and I did so, but less regularly than he sent his. When he saw pictures he thought I had already sent lying around the house, Andrew was perplexed and annoyed. He liked to have this record go forth.

That summer, we were presenting ourselves, not pictures. We were driving back from Vancouver, where we lived, to Ontario, which we still called "home," in our new car. Five days to get there, ten days there, five days back. For the first time, Andrew had three weeks' holiday. He worked in the legal department at B. C. Hydro.[1]

On a Saturday morning, we loaded suitcases, two thermos bottles—one filled with coffee and one with lemonade—some fruit and sandwiches, picture books and coloring books, crayons, drawing pads, insect repellent, sweaters (in case it got cold in the mountains), and our two children into the car. Andrew locked the house, and Cynthia said ceremoniously, "Goodbye, house."

Meg said, "Goodbye, house." Then she said, "Where will we live now?"

"It's not goodbye forever," said Cynthia. "We're coming back. Mother! Meg thought we weren't ever coming back!"

"I did not," said Meg, kicking the back of my seat.

Andrew and I put on our sunglasses, and we drove away, over the Lions Gate Bridge and through the main part of Vancouver. We shed our house, the neighborhood, the city, and—at the crossing point between Washington and British Columbia—our country. We were driving east across the United States, taking the most northerly route, and would cross into Canada again at Sarnia, Ontario. I don't know if we chose this route because the Trans-Canada Highway was not completely finished at the time or if we just wanted the feeling of driving through a foreign, a very slightly foreign, country—that extra bit of interest and adventure.

We were both in high spirits. Andrew congratulated the car several times. He said he felt so much better driving it than our old car, a 1951 Austin that slowed down dismally on the hills and had a fussy-old-lady image. So Andrew said now.

"What kind of image does this one have?" said Cynthia. She listened to us carefully and liked to try out new words such as *image*. Usually she got them right.

"Lively," I said. "Slightly sporty. It's not show-off."

"It's sensible, but it has class," Andrew said. "Like my image."

Cynthia thought that over and said with a cautious pride, "That means like you think you want to be, Daddy?"

As for me, I was happy because of the shedding. I loved taking off. In my own house, I seemed to be often looking for a place to hide—sometimes from the children but more often from the jobs to be done and the phone ringing and the sociability of the neighborhood. I wanted to hide so that I could get busy at my real work, which was a sort of wooing of distant parts of myself. I lived in a state of siege, always losing just what I wanted to hold on to. But on trips there was no difficulty. I could be talking to Andrew, talking to the children and looking at whatever they wanted me to look at—a pig on a sign, a

---

1. British Columbia Hydroelectric, public energy utility.

pony in a field, a Volkswagen on a revolving stand—and pouring lemonade into plastic cups, and all the time those bits and pieces would be flying together inside me. The essential composition would be achieved. This made me hopeful and lighthearted. It was being a watcher that did it. A watcher, not a keeper.

We turned east at Everett and climbed into the Cascades. I showed Cynthia our route on the map. First I showed her the map of the whole United States, which showed also the bottom part of Canada. Then I turned to the separate maps of each of the states we were going to pass through. Washington, Idaho, Montana, North Dakota, Minnesota, Wisconsin. I showed her the dotted line across Lake Michigan, which was the route of the ferry we would take. Then we would drive across Michigan to the bridge that linked the United States and Canada at Sarnia, Ontario. Home.

Meg wanted to see too.

"You won't understand," said Cynthia. But she took the road atlas into the back seat.

"Sit back," she said to Meg. "Sit still. I'll show you."

I could hear her tracing the route for Meg, very accurately, just as I had done it for her. She looked up all the states' maps, knowing how to find them in alphabetical order.

"You know what that line is?" she said. "It's the road. That line is the road we're driving on. We're going right along this line."

Meg did not say anything.

"Mother, show me where we are right this minute," said Cynthia.

I took the atlas and pointed out the road through the mountains, and she took it back and showed it to Meg. "See where the road is all wiggly?" she said. "It's wiggly because there are so many turns in it. The wiggles are the turns." She flipped some pages and waited a moment. "Now," she said, "show me where we are." Then she called to me, "Mother, she understands! She pointed to it! Meg understands maps!"

It seems to me now that we invented characters for our children. We had them firmly set to play their parts. Cynthia was bright and diligent, sensitive, courteous, watchful. Sometimes we teased her for being too conscientious, too eager to be what we in fact depended on her to be. Any reproach or failure, any rebuff, went terribly deep with her. She was fair-haired, fair-skinned, easily showing the effects of the sun, raw winds, pride, or humiliation. Meg was more solidly built, more reticent—not rebellious but stubborn sometimes, mysterious. Her silences seemed to us to show her strength of character, and her negatives were taken as signs of an imperturbable independence. Her hair was brown, and we cut it in straight bangs. Her eyes were a light hazel, clear and dazzling.

We were entirely pleased with these characters, enjoying their contradictions as well as the confirmations of them. We disliked the heavy, the uninventive, approach to being parents. I had a dread of turning into a certain kind of mother—the kind whose body sagged, who moved in a woolly-smelling, milky-smelling fog, solemn with trivial burdens. I believed that all the attention these mothers paid, their need to be burdened, was the cause of colic, bed-wetting, asthma. I favored another approach—the mock desperation, the inflated irony of the professional mothers who wrote for magazines. In those magazine pieces, the children were splendidly self-willed, hard-edged, perverse, indomitable. So were the mothers, through their wit, indomitable. The real-life mothers I warmed to were the sort who would phone up and say, "Is my embryo Hitler by any chance over at your house?" They cackled clear above the milky fog.

We saw a dead deer strapped across the front of a pickup truck.

"Somebody shot it," Cynthia said. "Hunters shoot the deer."

"It's not hunting season yet," Andrew said. "They may have hit it on the road. See the sign for deer crossing?"

"I would cry if we hit one," Cynthia said sternly.

I had made peanut-butter-and-marmalade sandwiches for the children and salmon-and-mayonnaise for us. But I had not put any lettuce in, and Andrew was disappointed.

"I didn't have any," I said.

"Couldn't you have got some?"

"I'd have had to buy a whole head of lettuce just to get enough for sandwiches, and I decided it wasn't worth it."

This was a lie. I had forgotten.

"They're a lot better with lettuce."

"I didn't think it made that much difference." After a silence, I said, "Don't be mad."

"I'm not mad. I like lettuce on sandwiches."

"I just didn't think it mattered that much."

"How would it be if I didn't bother to fill up the gas tank?"

"That's not the same thing."

"Sing a song," said Cynthia. She started to sing:

> *"Five little ducks went out one day,*
> *Over the hills and far away.*
> *Our little duck went*
> *'Quack-quack-quack.'*
> *Four little ducks came swimming back."*

Andrew squeezed my hand and said, "Let's not fight."

"You're right. I should have got lettuce."

"It doesn't matter that much."

I wished that I could get my feelings about Andrew to come together into a serviceable and dependable feeling. I had even tried writing two lists, one of things I liked about him, one of things I disliked—in the cauldron of intimate life, things I loved and things I hated—as if I hoped by this to prove something, to come to a conclusion one way or the other. But I gave it up when I saw that all it proved was what I already knew—that I had violent contradictions. Sometimes the very sound of his footsteps seemed to me tyrannical, the set of his mouth smug and mean, his hard, straight body a barrier interposed—quite consciously, even dutifully, and with a nasty pleasure in its masculine authority—between me and whatever joy or lightness I could get in life. Then, with not much warning, he became my good friend and most essential companion. I felt the sweetness of his light bones and serious ideas, the vulnerability of his love, which I imagined to be much purer and more straightforward than my own. I could be greatly moved by an inflexibility, a harsh propriety, that at other times I scorned. I would think how humble he was, really, taking on such a ready-made role of husband, father, breadwinner, and how I myself in comparison was really a secret monster of egotism. Not so secret, either—not from him.

At the bottom of our fights, we served up what we thought were the ugliest truths. "I know there is something basically selfish and basically untrustworthy about you," Andrew once said. "I've always known it. I also know that that is why I fell in love with you."

"Yes," I said, feeling sorrowful but complacent.

"I know that I'd be better off without you."

"Yes. You would."

"You'd be happier without me."

"Yes."

And finally—finally—wracked and purged, we clasped hands and laughed, laughed at those two benighted people, ourselves. Their grudges, their grievances, their self-justification. We leapfrogged over them. We declared them liars. We would have wine with dinner, or decide to give a party.

I haven't seen Andrew for years, don't know if he is still thin, has gone completely gray, insists on lettuce, tells the truth, or is hearty and disappointed.

We stayed the night in Wenatchee, Washington, where it hadn't rained for weeks. We ate dinner in a restaurant built about a tree—not a sapling in a tub but a tall, sturdy cottonwood. In the early-morning light, we climbed out of the irrigated valley, up dry, rocky, very steep hillsides that would seem to lead to more hills, and there on the top was a wide plateau, cut by the great Spokane and Columbia rivers. Grainland and grassland, mile after mile. There were straight roads here, and little farming towns with grain elevators. In fact, there was a sign announcing that this county we were going through, Douglas County, had the second-highest wheat yield of any county in the United States. The towns had planted shade trees. At least, I thought they had been planted, because there were no such big trees in the countryside.

All this was marvellously welcome to me. "Why do I love it so much?" I said to Andrew. "Is it because it isn't scenery?"

"It reminds you of home," said Andrew. "A bout of severe nostalgia." But he said this kindly.

When we said "home" and meant Ontario, we had very different places in mind. My home was a turkey farm, where my father lived as a widower, and though it was the same house my mother had lived in, had papered, painted, cleaned, furnished, it showed the effects now of neglect and of some wild sociability. A life went on in it that my mother could not have predicted or condoned. There were parties for the turkey crew, the gutters and pluckers, and sometimes one or two of the young men would be living there temporarily, inviting their own friends and having their own impromptu parties. This life, I thought, was better for my father than being lonely, and I did not disapprove, had certainly no right to disapprove. Andrew did not like to go there, naturally enough, because he was not the sort who could sit around the kitchen table with the turkey crew, telling jokes. They were intimidated by him and contemptuous of him, and it seemed to me that my father, when they were around, had to be on their side. And it wasn't only Andrew who had trouble. I could manage those jokes, but it was an effort.

I wished for the days when I was little, before we had the turkeys. We had cows, and sold the milk to the cheese factory. A turkey farm is nothing like as pretty as a dairy farm or a sheep farm. You can see that the turkeys are on a straight path to becoming frozen carcasses and table meat. They don't have the pretense of a life of their own, a browsing idyll, that cattle have, or pigs in the dappled orchard. Turkey barns are long, efficient buildings—tin sheds. No beams or hay or warm stables. Even the smell of guano seems thinner and more offensive than the usual smell of stable manure. No hints there of hay coils and rail fences and songbirds and the flowering hawthorn. The turkeys were all let out into one long field, which they picked clean. They didn't look like great birds there but like fluttering laundry.

Once, shortly after my mother died, and after I was married—in fact, I was packing to join Andrew in Vancouver—I was at home alone for a couple of days with my father. There was a freakishly heavy rain all night. In the early light, we saw that the turkey field was flooded. At least, the low-lying parts of it were flooded—it was like a lake with many islands. The turkeys were huddled on these islands. Turkeys are very stupid. (My father would say, "You know a chicken? You know how stupid a chicken is? Well, a chicken is an Einstein compared with a turkey.") But they had managed to crowd to higher ground and avoid drowning. Now they might push each other off, suffocate each other, get cold and die. We couldn't wait for the water to go down. We went out in an old rowboat we had. I rowed and my father pulled the heavy, wet turkeys into the boat and we took them to the barn. It was still raining a little. The job was difficult and absurd and very uncomfortable. We were laughing. I was happy to be working with my father. I felt close to all hard, repetitive, appalling work, in which the body is finally worn out, the mind sunk (though sometimes the spirit can stay marvellously light), and I was homesick in advance for this life and this place. I thought that if Andrew could see me there in the rain, red-handed, muddy, trying to hold on to turkey legs and row the boat at the same time, he would only want to get me out of there and make me forget about it. This raw life angered him. My attachment to it angered him. I thought that I shouldn't have married him. But who else? One of the turkey crew?

And I didn't want to stay there. I might feel bad about leaving, but I would feel worse if somebody made me stay.

Andrew's mother lived in Toronto, in an apartment building looking out on Muir Park. When Andrew and his sister were both at home, his mother slept in the living room. Her husband, a doctor, had died when the children were still too young to go to school. She took a secretarial course and sold her house at Depression prices, moved to this apartment, managed to raise her children, with some help from relatives—her sister Caroline, her brother-in-law Roger. Andrew and his sister went to private schools and to camp in the summer.

"I suppose that was courtesy of the Fresh Air Fund?" I said once, scornful of his claim that he had been poor. To my mind, Andrew's urban life had been sheltered and fussy. His mother came home with a headache from working all day in the noise, the harsh light of a department-store office, but it did not occur to me that hers was a hard or admirable life. I don't think she herself believed that she was admirable—only unlucky. She worried about her work in the office, her clothes, her cooking, her children. She worried most of all about what Roger and Caroline would think.

Caroline and Roger lived on the east side of the park, in a handsome stone house. Roger was a tall man with a bald, freckled head, a fat, firm stomach. Some operation on his throat had deprived him of his voice—he spoke in a rough whisper. But everybody paid attention. At dinner once in the stone house—where all the dining-room furniture was enormous, darkly glowing, palatial—I asked him a question. I think it had to do with Whittaker Chambers, whose story was then appearing in the *Saturday Evening Post*.[2] The question was mild in tone, but he guessed its subversive intent and took to calling me Mrs. Gromyko,[3] referring to what he alleged to be my "sympathies." Perhaps he really craved an adversary, and could not find one. At that dinner, I saw Andrew's hand tremble as he lit his mother's cigarette. His Uncle Roger had paid for Andrew's education, and was on the board of directors of several companies.

"He is just an opinionated old man," Andrew said to me later. "What is the point of arguing with him?"

Before we left Vancouver, Andrew's mother had written, *Roger seems quite intrigued by the idea of your buying a small car!* Her exclamation mark showed apprehension. At that time, particularly in Ontario, the choice of a small European car over a large American car could be seen as some sort of declaration—a declaration of tendencies Roger had been sniffing after all along.

"It isn't that small a car," said Andrew huffily.

"That's not the point," I said. "The point is, it isn't any of his business!"

We spent the second night in Missoula. We had been told in Spokane, at a gas station, that there was a lot of repair work going on along Highway 2, and that we were in for a very hot, dusty drive, with long waits, so we turned onto the interstate and drove through Coeur d'Alene and Kellogg into Montana. After Missoula, we turned south toward Butte, but detoured to see Helena, the state capital. In the car, we played Who Am I?

Cynthia was somebody dead, and an American, and a girl. Possibly a lady. She was not in a story. She had not been seen on television. Cynthia had not read about her in a book. She was not anybody who had come to the kindergarten, or a relative of any of Cynthia's friends.

"Is she human?" said Andrew, with a sudden shrewdness.

"No! That's what you forgot to ask!"

"An animal," I said reflectively.

"Is that a question? Sixteen questions!"

"No, it is not a question. I'm thinking. A dead animal."

"It's the deer," said Meg, who hadn't been playing.

---

**2.** Illustrated news magazine published weekly from 1821 until 1969. Whittaker Chambers: American journalist and spy (1901–1961), notorious for his 1948 testimony before the House Committee on Un-American Activities, in which he admitted engaging in espionage for the Soviet Union in the 1930s. **3.** That is, the wife of Andrei Gromyko (1909–1989), longtime Soviet foreign minister.

"That's not fair!" said Cynthia. "She's not playing!"

"What deer?" said Andrew.

I said, "Yesterday."

"The day before," said Cynthia. "Meg wasn't playing. Nobody got it."

"The deer on the truck," said Andrew.

"It was a lady deer, because it didn't have antlers, and it was an American and it was dead," Cynthia said.

Andrew said, "I think it's kind of morbid, being a dead deer."

"I got it," said Meg.

Cynthia said, "I think I know what morbid is. It's depressing."

Helena, an old silver-mining town, looked forlorn to us even in the morning sunlight. Then Bozeman and Billings, not forlorn in the slightest—energetic, strung-out towns, with miles of blinding tinsel fluttering over used-car lots. We got too tired and hot even to play Who Am I? These busy, prosaic cities reminded me of similar places in Ontario, and I thought about what was really waiting there—the great tombstone furniture of Roger and Caroline's dining room, the dinners for which I must iron the children's dresses and warn them about forks, and then the other table a hundred miles away, the jokes of my father's crew. The pleasures I had been thinking of—looking at the country-side or drinking a Coke in an old-fashioned drugstore with fans and a high, pressed-tin ceiling—would have to be snatched in between.

"Meg's asleep," Cynthia said. "She's so hot. She makes me hot in the same seat with her."

"I hope she isn't feverish," I said, not turning around.

What are we doing this for, I thought, and the answer came—to show off. To give Andrew's mother and my father the pleasure of seeing their grand-children. That was our duty. But beyond that we wanted to show them some-thing. What strenuous children we were, Andrew and I, what relentless seekers of approbation. It was as if at some point we had received an unforgettable, indigestible message—that we were far from satisfactory, and that the most commonplace success in life was probably beyond us. Roger dealt out such messages, of course—that was his style—but Andrew's mother, my own mother and father couldn't have meant to do so. All they meant to tell us was "Watch out. Get along." My father, when I was in high school, teased me that I was getting to think I was so smart I would never find a boyfriend. He would have forgotten that in a week. I never forgot it. Andrew and I didn't forget things. We took umbrage.

"I wish there was a beach," said Cynthia.

"There probably is one," Andrew said. "Right around the next curve."

"There isn't any curve," she said, sounding insulted.

"That's what I mean."

"I wish there was some more lemonade."

"I will just wave my magic wand and produce some," I said. "Okay, Cyn-thia? Would you rather have grape juice? Will I do a beach while I'm at it?"

She was silent, and soon I felt repentant. "Maybe in the next town there might be a pool," I said. I looked at the map. "In Miles City. Anyway, there'll be something cool to drink."

"How far is it?" Andrew said.

"Not so far," I said. "Thirty miles, about."

"In Miles City," said Cynthia, in the tones of an incantation, "there is a beautiful blue swimming pool for children, and a park with lovely trees."

Andrew said to me, "You could have started something."

But there was a pool. There was a park too, though not quite the oasis of Cynthia's fantasy. Prairie trees with thin leaves—cottonwoods and poplars—worn grass, and a high wire fence around the pool. Within this fence, a wall, not yet completed, of cement blocks. There were no shouts or splashes; over the entrance I saw a sign that said the pool was closed every day from noon until two o'clock. It was then twenty-five after twelve.

Nevertheless I called out, "Is anybody there?" I thought somebody must be around, because there was a small truck parked near the entrance. On the side of the truck were these words: *We have Brains, to fix your Drains. (We have Roto-Rooter too.)*

A girl came out, wearing a red lifeguard's shirt over her bathing suit. "Sorry, we're closed."

"We were just driving through," I said.

"We close every day from twelve until two. It's on the sign." She was eating a sandwich.

"I saw the sign," I said. "But this is the first water we've seen for so long, and the children are awfully hot, and I wondered if they could just dip in and out—just five minutes. We'd watch them."

A boy came into sight behind her. He was wearing jeans and a T-shirt with the words *Roto-Rooter* on it.

I was going to say that we were driving from British Columbia to Ontario, but I remembered that Canadian place names usually meant nothing to Americans. "We're driving right across the country," I said. "We haven't time to wait for the pool to open. We were just hoping the children could get cooled off."

Cynthia came running up barefoot behind me. "Mother. Mother, where is my bathing suit?" Then she stopped, sensing the serious adult negotiations. Meg was climbing out of the car—just wakened, with her top pulled up and her shorts pulled down, showing her pink stomach.

"Is it just those two?" the girl said.

"Just the two. We'll watch them."

"I can't let any adults in. If it's just the two, I guess I could watch them. I'm having my lunch." She said to Cynthia, "Do you want to come in the pool?"

"Yes, please," said Cynthia firmly.

Meg looked at the ground.

"Just a short time, because the pool is really closed," I said. "We appreciate this very much," I said to the girl.

"Well, I can eat my lunch out there, if it's just the two of them." She looked toward the car as if she thought I might try to spring some more children on her.

When I found Cynthia's bathing suit, she took it into the changing room. She would not permit anybody, even Meg, to see her naked. I changed Meg, who stood on the front seat of the car. She had a pink cotton bathing suit with straps that crossed and buttoned. There were ruffles across the bottom.

"She *is* hot," I said. "But I don't think she's feverish."

I loved helping Meg to dress or undress, because her body still had the solid unself-consciousness, the sweet indifference, something of the milky smell, of a baby's body. Cynthia's body had long ago been pared down, shaped and altered, into Cynthia. We all liked to hug Meg, press and nuzzle her. Sometimes she would scowl and beat us off, and this forthright independence, this ferocious bashfulness, simply made her more appealing, more apt to be tormented and tickled in the way of family love.

Andrew and I sat in the car with the windows open. I could hear a radio playing, and thought it must belong to the girl or her boyfriend. I was thirsty, and got out of the car to look for a concession stand, or perhaps a soft-drink machine, somewhere in the park. I was wearing shorts, and the backs of my legs were slick with sweat. I saw a drinking fountain at the other side of the park and was walking toward it in a roundabout way, keeping to the shade of the trees. No place became real till you got out of the car. Dazed with the heat, with the sun on the blistered houses, the pavement, the burnt grass, I walked slowly. I paid attention to a squashed leaf, ground a Popsicle stick under the heel of my sandal, squinted at a trash can strapped to a tree. This is the way you look at the poorest details of the world resurfaced, after you've been driving for a long time—you feel their singleness and precise location and the forlorn coincidence of your being there to see them.

*Where are the children?*

I turned around and moved quickly, not quite running, to a part of the fence beyond which the cement wall was not completed. I could see some of the pool. I saw Cynthia, standing about waist-deep in the water, fluttering her hands on the surface and discreetly watching something at the end of the pool, which I could not see. I thought by her pose, her discretion, the look on her face, that she must be watching some byplay between the lifeguard and her boyfriend. I couldn't see Meg. But I thought she must be playing in the shallow water—both the shallow and deep ends of the pool were out of my sight.

"Cynthia!" I had to call twice before she knew where my voice was coming from. "Cynthia! Where's Meg?"

It always seems to me, when I recall this scene, that Cynthia turns very gracefully toward me, then turns all around in the water—making me think of a ballerina on pointe—and spreads her arms in a gesture of the stage. "Dis-ap-peared!"

Cynthia was naturally graceful, and she did take dancing lessons, so these movements may have been as I have described. She did say "Disappeared" after looking all around the pool, but the strangely artificial style of speech and gesture, the lack of urgency, is more likely my invention. The fear I felt instantly when I couldn't see Meg—even while I was telling myself she must be in the shallower water—must have made Cynthia's movements seem unbearably slow and inappropriate to me, and the tone in which she could say "Disappeared" before the implications struck her (or was she covering, at once, some ever-ready guilt?) was heard by me as quite exquisitely, monstrously self-possessed.

I cried out for Andrew, and the lifeguard came into view. She was pointing toward the deep end of the pool, saying, "What's that?"

There, just within my view, a cluster of pink ruffles appeared, a bouquet, beneath the surface of the water. Why would a lifeguard stop and point, why would she ask what that was, why didn't she just dive into the water and swim to it? She didn't swim; she ran all the way around the edge of the pool. But by that time Andrew was over the fence. So many things seemed not quite plausible—Cynthia's behavior, then the lifeguard's—and now I had the impression that Andrew jumped with one bound over this fence, which seemed about seven feet high. He must have climbed it very quickly, getting a grip on the wire.

I could not jump or climb it, so I ran to the entrance, where there was a sort of lattice gate, locked. It was not very high, and I did pull myself over it. I ran through the cement corridors, through the disinfectant pool for your feet, and came out on the edge of the pool.

The drama was over.

Andrew had got to Meg first, and had pulled her out of the water. He just had to reach over and grab her, because she was swimming somehow, with her head underwater—she was moving toward the edge of the pool. He was carrying her now, and the lifeguard was trotting along behind. Cynthia had climbed out of the water and was running to meet them. The only person aloof from the situation was the boyfriend, who had stayed on the bench at the shallow end, drinking a milkshake. He smiled at me, and I thought that unfeeling of him, even though the danger was past. He may have meant it kindly. I noticed that he had not turned the radio off, just down.

Meg had not swallowed any water. She hadn't even scared herself. Her hair was plastered to her head and her eyes were wide open, golden with amazement.

"I was getting the comb," she said. "I didn't know it was deep."

Andrew said, "She was swimming! She was swimming by herself. I saw her bathing suit in the water and then I saw her swimming."

"She nearly drowned," Cynthia said. "Didn't she? Meg nearly drowned."

"I don't know how it could have happened," said the lifeguard. "One moment she was there, and the next she wasn't."

What had happened was that Meg had climbed out of the water at the shallow end and run along the edge of the pool toward the deep end. She saw a comb that somebody had dropped lying on the bottom. She crouched down and reached in to pick it up, quite deceived about the depth of the water. She went over the edge and slipped into the pool, making such a light splash that nobody heard—not the lifeguard, who was kissing her boyfriend, or Cynthia, who was watching them. That must have been the moment under the trees when I thought, Where are the children? It must have been the same moment. At that moment, Meg was slipping, surprised, into the treacherously clear blue water.

"It's okay," I said to the lifeguard, who was nearly crying. "She can move pretty fast." (Though that wasn't what we usually said about Meg at all. We said she thought everything over and took her time.)

"You swam, Meg," said Cynthia, in a congratulatory way. (She told us about the kissing later.)

"I didn't know it was deep," Meg said. "I didn't drown."

We had lunch at a takeout place, eating hamburgers and fries at a picnic table not far from the highway. In my excitement, I forgot to get Meg a plain hamburger, and had to scrape off the relish and mustard with plastic spoons, then wipe the meat with a paper napkin, before she would eat it. I took advantage of the trash can there to clean out the car. Then we resumed driving east, with the car windows open in front. Cynthia and Meg fell asleep in the back seat.

Andrew and I talked quietly about what had happened. Suppose I hadn't had the impulse just at that moment to check on the children? Suppose we had gone uptown to get drinks, as we had thought of doing? How had Andrew got over the fence? Did he jump or climb? (He couldn't remember.) How had he reached Meg so quickly? And think of the lifeguard not watching. And Cynthia, taken up with the kissing. Not seeing anything else. Not seeing Meg drop over the edge.

Disappeared.

But she swam. She held her breath and came up swimming.

What a chain of lucky links.

That was all we spoke about—luck. But I was compelled to picture the opposite. At this moment, we could have been filling out forms. Meg removed from us, Meg's body being prepared for shipment. To Vancouver—where we had never noticed such a thing as a graveyard—or to Ontario? The scribbled drawings she had made this morning would still be in the back seat of the car. How could this be borne all at once, how did people bear it? The plump, sweet shoulders and hands and feet, the fine brown hair, the rather satisfied, secretive expression—all exactly the same as when she had been alive. The most ordinary tragedy. A child drowned in a swimming pool at noon on a sunny day. Things tidied up quickly. The pool opens as usual at two o'clock. The lifeguard is a bit shaken up and gets the afternoon off. She drives away with her boyfriend in the Roto-Rooter truck. The body sealed away in some kind of shipping coffin. Sedatives, phone calls, arrangements. Such a sudden vacancy, a blind sinking and shifting. Waking up groggy from the pills, thinking for a moment it wasn't true. Thinking if only we hadn't stopped, if only we hadn't taken this route, if only they hadn't let us use the pool. Probably no one would ever have known about the comb.

There's something trashy about this kind of imagining, isn't there? Something shameful. Laying your finger on the wire to get the safe shock, feeling a bit of what it's like, then pulling back. I believed that Andrew was more scrupulous than I about such things, and that at this moment he was really trying to think about something else.

When I stood apart from my parents at Steve Gauley's funeral and watched them, and had this new, unpleasant feeling about them, I thought that I was understanding something about them for the first time. It was a deadly serious thing. I was understanding that they were implicated. Their big, stiff, dressed-up bodies did not stand between me and sudden death, or any kind of death. They gave consent. So it seemed. They gave consent to the death of children and to my death not by anything they said or thought but by the very fact that they had made children—they had made me. They had made me, and for that reason my death—however grieved they were, however they carried on—would seem to them anything but impossible or unnatural. This was a fact, and even then I knew they were not to blame.

But I did blame them. I charged them with effrontery, hypocrisy. On Steve Gauley's behalf, and on behalf of all children, who knew that by rights they should have sprung up free, to live a new, superior kind of life, not to be caught in the snares of vanquished grownups, with their sex and funerals.

Steve Gauley drowned, people said, because he was next thing to an orphan and was let run free. If he had been warned enough and given chores to do and kept in check, he wouldn't have fallen from an untrustworthy tree branch into a spring pond, a full gravel pit near the river—he wouldn't have drowned. He was neglected, he was free, so he drowned. And his father took it as an accident, such as might happen to a dog. He didn't have a good suit for the funeral, and he didn't bow his head for the prayers. But he was the only grownup that I let off the hook. He was the only one I didn't see giving consent. He couldn't prevent anything, but he wasn't implicated in anything, either—not like the others, saying the Lord's Prayer in their unnaturally weighted voices, oozing religion and dishonor.

At Glendive, not far from the North Dakota border, we had a choice—either to continue on the interstate or head northeast, toward Williston, taking Route 16, then some secondary roads that would get us back to Highway 2.

We agreed that the interstate would be faster, and that it was important for us not to spend too much time—that is, money—on the road. Nevertheless we decided to cut back to Highway 2.

"I just like the idea of it better," I said.

Andrew said, "That's because it's what we planned to do in the beginning."

"We missed seeing Kalispell and Havre. And Wolf Point. I like the name."

"We'll see them on the way back."

Andrew's saying "on the way back" was a surprising pleasure to me. Of course, I had believed that we would be coming back, with our car and our lives and our family intact, having covered all that distance, having dealt somehow with those loyalties and problems, held ourselves up for inspection in such a foolhardy way. But it was a relief to hear him say it.

"What I can't get over," said Andrew, "is how you got the signal. It's got to be some kind of extra sense that mothers have."

Partly I wanted to believe that, to bask in my extra sense. Partly I wanted to warn him—to warn everybody—never to count on it.

"What I can't understand," I said, "is how you got over the fence."

"Neither can I."

So we went on, with the two in the back seat trusting us, because of no choice, and we ourselves trusting to be forgiven, in time, for everything that had first to be seen and condemned by those children: whatever was flippant, arbitrary, careless, callous—all our natural, and particular, mistakes.

1985

---

RELATED:

—Author in Depth: Alice Munro, p. 956

# VLADIMIR NABOKOV
## 1899–1977

Nabokov was born in St. Petersburg, Russia, to rich and cultured parents who spoke Russian, French, and English—"a typical trilingual upbringing," as he would later recall. At the time of the Communist revolution, he fled with his family into Western Europe. He attended Cambridge University in England and took a degree in modern languages there in 1923. Thereafter, he spent years in Berlin and Paris, supporting himself by coaching tennis and making up chess problems, all the while writing novels in Russian and English. Living in France when it was overrun by the Nazis, he escaped with his family to the United States, where he became a citizen and—by a remarkable imaginative transformation—an American writer, beginning with *The Real Life of Sebastian Knight* (1941). He taught Russian and comparative literature at Cornell University until *Lolita* (a best seller in 1955) and subsequent novels gave him enough money to allow him a full-time commitment to writing and his other eminent career: Nabokov was also a world-renowned lepidopterist, a scientist of moths and butterflies. He lived the last twenty years of his life in Montreux, Switzerland. His complete works in all languages would run to thirty or forty volumes, exemplifying the complexity of his life and his interests in language and experience. In most of his fiction, memories of a dissolving past mingle with an ironic sense of a precarious present. Among his many novels are *Laughter in the Dark* (self-translated in 1938), *Lolita* (1955), *Pnin* (1957), *Pale Fire* (1962), and *Ada* (1969). His collected poems and chess problems were published in 1971; *The Stories of Vladimir Nabokov* was published in 1995.

# Signs and Symbols

## I

For the fourth time in as many years they were confronted with the problem of what birthday present to bring a young man who was incurably deranged in his mind. He had no desires. Man-made objects were to him either hives of evil, vibrant with a malignant activity that he alone could perceive, or gross comforts for which no use could be found in his abstract world. After eliminating a number of articles that might offend him or frighten him (anything in the gadget line for instance was taboo), his parents chose a dainty and innocent trifle: a basket with ten different fruit jellies in ten little jars.

At the time of his birth they had been married already for a long time; a score of years had elapsed, and now they were quite old. Her drab gray hair was done anyhow. She wore cheap black dresses. Unlike other women of her age (such as Mrs. Sol, their next-door neighbor, whose face was all pink and mauve with paint and whose hat was a cluster of brookside flowers), she presented a naked white countenance to the fault-finding light of spring days. Her husband, who in the old country had been a fairly successful businessman, was now wholly dependent on his brother Isaac, a real American of almost forty years standing. They seldom saw him and had nicknamed him "the Prince."

That Friday everything went wrong. The underground train lost its life current between two stations, and for a quarter of an hour one could hear nothing but the dutiful beating of one's heart and the rustling of newspapers. The bus they had to take next kept them waiting for ages; and when it did come, it was crammed with garrulous high-school children. It was raining hard as they walked up the brown path leading to the sanitarium. There they waited again; and instead of their boy shuffling into the room as he usually did (his poor face blotched with acne, ill-shaven, sullen, and confused), a nurse they knew, and did not care for, appeared at last and brightly explained that he had again attempted to take his life. He was all right, she said, but a visit might disturb him. The place was so miserably understaffed, and things got mislaid or mixed up so easily, that they decided not to leave their present in the office but to bring it to him next time they came.

She waited for her husband to open his umbrella and then took his arm. He kept clearing his throat in a special resonant way he had when he was upset. They reached the bus-stop shelter on the other side of the street and he closed his umbrella. A few feet away, under a swaying and dripping tree, a tiny half-dead unfledged bird was helplessly twitching in a puddle.

During the long ride to the subway station, she and her husband did not exchange a word; and every time she glanced at his old hands (swollen veins, brown-spotted skin), clasped and twitching upon the handle of his umbrella, she felt the mounting pressure of tears. As she looked around trying to hook her mind onto something, it gave her a kind of soft shock, a mixture of compassion and wonder, to notice that one of the passengers, a girl with dark hair and grubby red toenails, was weeping on the shoulder of an older woman. Whom did that woman resemble? She resembled Rebecca Borisovna, whose daughter had married one of the Soloveichiks—in Minsk,[1] years ago.

The last time he had tried to do it, his method had been, in the doctor's words, a masterpiece of inventiveness; he would have succeeded, had not an envious fellow patient thought he was learning to fly—and stopped him. What he really wanted to do was to tear a hole in his world and escape.

The system of his delusions had been the subject of an elaborate paper in a scientific monthly, but long before that she and her husband had puzzled it out for themselves. "Referential mania," Herman Brink had called it. In these very rare cases the patient imagines that everything happening around him is a veiled reference to his personality and existence. He excludes real people from the conspiracy—because he considers himself to be so much more intelligent than other men. Phenomenal nature shadows him wherever he goes. Clouds in the staring sky transmit to one another, by means of slow signs,

1. A city in western Russia.

incredibly detailed information regarding him. His inmost thoughts are discussed at nightfall, in manual alphabet,[2] by darkly gesticulating trees. Pebbles or stains or sun flecks form patterns representing in some awful way messages which he must intercept. Everything is a cipher and of everything he is the theme. Some of the spies are detached observers, such as glass surfaces and still pools; others, such as coats in store windows, are prejudiced witnesses, lynchers at heart; others again (running water, storms) are hysterical to the point of insanity, have a distorted opinion of him and grotesquely misinterpret his actions. He must be always on his guard and devote every minute and module of life to the decoding of the undulation of things. The very air he exhales is indexed and filed away. If only the interest he provokes were limited to his immediate surroundings—but alas it is not! With distance the torrents of wild scandal increase in volume and volubility. The silhouettes of his blood corpuscles, magnified a million times, flit over vast plains; and still farther, great mountains of unbearable solidity and height sum up in terms of granite and groaning firs the ultimate truth of his being.

## I I

When they emerged from the thunder and foul air of the subway, the last dregs of the day were mixed with the street lights. She wanted to buy some fish for supper, so she handed him the basket of jelly jars, telling him to go home. He walked up to the third landing and then remembered he had given her his keys earlier in the day.

In silence he sat down on the steps and in silence rose when some ten minutes later she came, heavily trudging upstairs, wanly smiling, shaking her head in deprecation of her silliness. They entered their two-room flat and he at once went to the mirror. Straining the corners of his mouth apart by means of his thumbs, with a horrible masklike grimace, he removed his new hopelessly uncomfortable dental plate and severed the long tusks of saliva connecting him to it. He read his Russian-language newspaper while she laid the table. Still reading, he ate the pale victuals that needed no teeth. She knew his moods and was also silent.

When he had gone to bed, she remained in the living room with her pack of soiled cards and her old albums. Across the narrow yard where the rain tinkled in the dark against some battered ash cans, windows were blandly alight and in one of them a black-trousered man with his bare elbows raised could be seen lying supine on an untidy bed. She pulled the blind down and examined the photographs. As a baby he looked more surprised than most babies. From a fold in the album, a German maid they had had in Leipzig and her fat-faced fiancé fell out. Minsk, the Revolution, Leipzig,[3] Berlin, Leipzig, a slanting house front badly out of focus. Four years old, in a park: moodily, shyly, with puckered forehead, looking away from an eager squirrel as he would from any other stranger. Aunt Rose, a fussy, angular, wild-eyed old lady, who had lived in a tremulous world of bad news, bankruptcies, train accidents, cancerous growths—until the Germans put her to death, together with all the

---

**2.** Sign language used by the deaf.  **3.** Leipzig is a city in Germany. The Revolution is the Russian Revolution of 1917–20.

people she had worried about. Age six—that was when he drew wonderful birds with human hands and feet, and suffered from insomnia like a grown-up man. His cousin, now a famous chess player. He again, aged about eight, already difficult to understand, afraid of the wallpaper in the passage, afraid of a certain picture in a book which merely showed an idyllic landscape with rocks on a hillside and an old cart wheel hanging from the branch of a leaf-less tree. Aged ten: the year they left Europe. The shame, the pity, the humili-ating difficulties, the ugly, vicious, backward children he was with in that special school. And then came a time in his life, coinciding with a long conva-lescence after pneumonia, when those little phobias of his which his parents had stubbornly regarded as the eccentricities of a prodigiously gifted child hardened as it were into a dense tangle of logically interacting illusions, mak-ing him totally inaccessible to normal minds.

This, and much more, she accepted—for after all living did mean accepting the loss of one joy after another, not even joys in her case—mere possibilities of improvement. She thought of the endless waves of pain that for some rea-son or other she and her husband had to endure; of the invisible giants hurt-ing her boy in some unimaginable fashion; of the incalculable amount of tenderness contained in the world; of the fate of this tenderness, which is either crushed, or wasted, or transformed into madness; of neglected children hum-ming to themselves in unswept corners; of beautiful weeds that cannot hide from the farmer and helplessly have to watch the shadow of his simian stoop leave mangled flowers in its wake, as the monstrous darkness approaches.

### III

It was past midnight when from the living room she heard her husband moan; and presently he staggered in, wearing over his nightgown the old overcoat with astrakhan[4] collar which he much preferred to the nice blue bathrobe he had.

"I can't sleep," he cried.

"Why," she asked, "why can't you sleep? You were so tired."

"I can't sleep because I am dying," he said and lay down on the couch.

"Is it your stomach? Do you want me to call Dr. Solov?"

"No doctors, no doctors," he moaned. "To the devil with doctors! We must get him out of there quick. Otherwise we'll be responsible. Responsible!" he repeated and hurled himself into a sitting position, both feet on the floor, thumping his forehead with his clenched fist.

"All right," she said quietly, "we shall bring him home tomorrow morning."

"I would like some tea," said her husband and retired to the bathroom.

Bending with difficulty, she retrieved some playing cards and a photograph or two that had slipped from the couch to the floor: knave of hearts, nine of spades, ace of spades, Elsa and her bestial beau.

He returned in high spirits, saying in a loud voice:

"I have it all figured out. We will give him the bedroom. Each of us will spend part of the night near him and the other part on this couch. By turns. We will have the doctor see him at least twice a week. It does not matter what the Prince says. He won't have to say much anyway because it will come out cheaper."

---

4. Lustrous, tight-curled wool (from Astrakhan, a city in southeast Russia).

The telephone rang. It was an unusual hour for their telephone to ring. His left slipper had come off and he groped for it with his heel and toe as he stood in the middle of the room, and childishly, toothlessly, gaped at his wife. Having more English than he did, it was she who attended to calls.

"Can I speak to Charlie," said a girl's dull little voice.

"What number you want? No. That is not the right number."

The receiver was gently cradled. Her hand went to her old tired heart.

"It frightened me," she said.

He smiled a quick smile and immediately resumed his excited monologue. They would fetch him as soon as it was day. Knives would have to be kept in a locked drawer. Even at his worst he presented no danger to other people.

The telephone rang a second time. The same toneless anxious young voice asked for Charlie.

"You have the incorrect number. I will tell you what you are doing: you are turning the letter O instead of zero."

They sat down to their unexpected festive midnight tea. The birthday present stood on the table. He sipped noisily; his face was flushed; every now and then he imparted a circular motion to his raised glass so as to make the sugar dissolve more thoroughly. The vein on the side of his bald head where there was a large birthmark stood out conspicuously and, although he had shaved that morning, a silvery bristle showed on his chin. While she poured him another glass of tea, he put on his spectacles and re-examined with pleasure the luminous yellow, green, red little jars. His clumsy moist lips spelled out their eloquent labels: apricot, grape, beech plum, quince. He had got to crab apple, when the telephone rang again.

1958

# JOYCE CAROL OATES
## b. 1938

Oates grew up in the country near Lockport, New York. She received degrees from Syracuse University and the University of Wisconsin before launching one of the more spectacularly prolific—and honored—careers among contemporary writers. Poet and critic as well as fiction writer, she continues to astonish readers with the ingenuity of her formal innovations as with the sheer volume of her production. Violence, madness, and social disorder are frequently her subject matter. The mysteries of psychological and sociological motivation fascinate her; she constructs ingenious theories to explain them and to focus their moral significance. Her more than forty novels include *them* (1969), *Bellefleur* (1980), *You Must Remember This* (1987), *We Were the Mulvaneys* (1996), *The Falls* (2004), *Little Bird of Heaven* (2009), and *The Accursed* (2013). Her short stories number more than 700; her many collections include *Marriages and Infidelities* (1972), *Where Are You Going, Where Have You Been?* (1993), *I Am No One You Know* (2004), *and Evil Eye* (2013). She has published thrillers under pseudonyms as well as a memoir, *A Widow's Story* (2011).

# How I Contemplated the World from the Detroit House of Correction and Began My Life Over Again

Notes for an Essay for an English Class at Baldwin Country Day School; Poking Around in Debris; Disgust and Curiosity; A Revelation of the Meaning of Life; A Happy Ending . . .

### I. Events

1. The girl (myself) is walking through Branden's, that excellent store. Suburb of a large famous city that is a symbol for large famous American cities. The event sneaks up on the girl, who believes she is herding it along with a small fixed smile, a girl of fifteen, innocently experienced. She dawdles in a certain style by a counter of costume jewelry. Rings, earrings, necklaces. Prices from $5 to $50, all within reach. All ugly. She eases over to the glove counter, where everything is ugly too. In her close-fitted coat with its black fur collar she contemplates the luxury of Branden's, which she has known for many

years: its many mild pale lights, easy on the eye and the soul, its elaborate tinkly decorations, its women shoppers with their excellent shoes and coats and hairdos, all dawdling gracefully, in no hurry.

Who was ever in a hurry here?

2. The girl seated at home. A small library, paneled walls of oak. Some one is talking to me. An earnest, husky, female voice drives itself against my ears, nervous, frightened, groping around my heart, saying, "If you wanted gloves, why didn't you say so? Why didn't you ask for them?" That store, Branden's, is owned by Raymond Forrest who lives on Du Maurier Drive. We live on Sioux Drive. Raymond Forrest. A handsome man? An ugly man? A man of fifty or sixty, with gray hair, or a man of forty with earnest, courteous eyes, a good golf game; who is Raymond Forrest, this man who is my salvation? Father has been talking to him. Father is not his physician; Dr. Berg is his physician. Father and Dr. Berg refer patients to each other. There is a connection. Mother plays bridge with . . . On Mondays and Wednesdays our maid Billie works at . . . The strings draw together in a cat's cradle, making a net to save you when you fall. . . .

3. *Harriet Arnold's.* A small shop, better than Branden's. Mother in her black coat, I in my close-fitted blue coat. Shopping. Now look at this, isn't this cute, do you want this, why don't you want this, try this on, take this with you to the fitting room, take this also, what's wrong with you, what can I do for you, why are you so strange . . . ? "I wanted to steal but not to buy," I don't tell her. The girl droops along in her coat and gloves and leather boots, her eyes scan the horizon, which is pastel pink and decorated like Branden's, tasteful walls and modern ceilings with graceful glimmering lights.

4. Weeks later, the girl at a bus stop. Two o'clock in the afternoon, a Tuesday; obviously she has walked out of school.

5. The girl stepping down from a bus. Afternoon, weather changing to colder. Detroit. Pavement and closed-up stores; grillwork over the windows of a pawnshop. What is a pawnshop, exactly?

## II. Characters

1. The girl stands five feet five inches tall. An ordinary height. Baldwin Country Day School draws them up to that height. She dreams along the corridors and presses her face against the Thermoplex glass. No frost or steam can ever form on that glass. A smudge of grease from her forehead . . . could she be boiled down to grease? She wears her hair loose and long and straight in suburban teen-age style, 1968. Eyes smudged with pencil, dark brown. Brown hair. Vague green eyes. A pretty girl? An ugly girl? She sings to herself under her breath, idling in the corridor, thinking of her many secrets (the thirty dollars she once took from the purse of a friend's mother, just for fun, the basement window she smashed in her own house just for fun) and thinking of her brother who is at Susquehanna Boys' Academy, an excellent preparatory school

in Maine, remembering him unclearly...he has long manic hair and a squeaking voice and he looks like one of the popular teen-age singers of 1968, one of those in a group, *The Certain Forces, The Way Out, The Maniacs Responsible.* The girl in her turn looks like one of those fieldsful of girls who listen to the boys' singing, dreaming and mooning restlessly, breaking into high sullen laughter, innocently experienced.

2. The mother. A Midwestern woman of Detroit and suburbs. Belongs to the Detroit Athletic Club. Also the Detroit Golf Club. Also the Bloomfield Hills Country Club. The Village Women's Club at which lectures are given each winter on Genet and Sartre and James Baldwin,[1] by the Director of the Adult Education Program at Wayne State University....The Bloomfield Art Association. Also the Founders Society of the Detroit Institute of Arts. Also...Oh, she is in perpetual motion, this lady, hair like blown-up gold and finer than gold, hair and fingers and body of inestimable grace. Heavy weighs the gold on the back of her hairbrush and hand mirror. Heavy heavy the candlesticks in the dining room. Very heavy is the big car, a Lincoln, long and black, that on one cool autumn day split a squirrel's body in two unequal parts.

3. The father. Dr. _____. He belongs to the same clubs as #2. A player of squash and golf; he has a golfer's umbrella of stripes. Candy stripes. In his mouth nothing turns to sugar, however; saliva works no miracles here. His doctoring is of the slightly sick. The sick are sent elsewhere (to Dr. Berg?), the deathly sick are sent back for more tests and their bills are sent to their homes, the unsick are sent to Dr. Coronet (Isabel, a lady), an excellent psychiatrist for unsick people who angrily believe they are sick and want to do something about it. If they demand a male psychiatrist, the unsick are sent by Dr. _____ (my father) to Dr. Lowenstein, a male psychiatrist, excellent and expensive, with a limited practice.

4. Clarita. She is twenty, twenty-five, she is thirty or more? Pretty, ugly, what? She is a woman lounging by the side of a road, in jeans and a sweater, hitchhiking, or she is slouched on a stool at a counter in some roadside diner. A hard line of jaw. Curious eyes. Amused eyes. Behind her eyes processions move, funeral pageants, cartoons. She says, "I never can figure out why girls like you bum around down here. What are you looking for anyway?" An odor of tobacco about her. Unwashed underclothes, or no underclothes, unwashed skin, gritty toes, hair long and falling into strands, not recently washed.

5. Simon. In this city the weather changes abruptly, so Simon's weather changes abruptly. He sleeps through the afternoon. He sleeps through the morning. Rising, he gropes around for something to get him going, for a cigarette or a pill to drive him out to the street, where the temperature is hovering around 35°. Why doesn't it drop? Why, why doesn't the cold clean air come down from Canada; will he have to go up into Canada to get it? will he have

---

1. American novelist and essayist (1924–1987). Jean Genet (1910–1986), French playwright and memoirist. Jean-Paul Sartre (1905–1980), French novelist, dramatist, and philosopher.

to leave the Country of his Birth and sink into Canada's frosty fields . . . ? Will the F.B.I. (which he dreams about constantly) chase him over the Canadian border on foot, hounded out in a blizzard of broken glass and horns . . . ?

"Once I was Huckleberry Finn," Simon says, "but now I am Roderick Usher."[2] Beset by frenzies and fears, this man who makes my spine go cold, he takes green pills, yellow pills, pills of white and capsules of dark blue and green . . . he takes other things I may not mention, for what if Simon seeks me out and climbs into my girl's bedroom here in Bloomfield Hills and strangles me, what then . . . ? (As I write this I begin to shiver. Why do I shiver? I am now sixteen and sixteen is not an age for shivering.) It comes from Simon, who is always cold.

### III. World Events

Nothing.

### IV. People and Circumstances Contributing to This Delinquency

Nothing.

### V. Sioux Drive

George, Clyde G. 240 Sioux. A manufacturer's representative; children, a dog, a wife. Georgian with the usual columns. You think of the White House, then of Thomas Jefferson, then your mind goes blank on the white pillars and you think of nothing. Norris, Ralph W. 246 Sioux. Public relations. Colonial. Bay window, brick, stone, concrete, wood, green shutters, sidewalk, lantern, grass, trees, blacktop drive, two children, one of them my classmate Esther (Esther Norris) at Baldwin. Wife, cars. Ramsey, Michael D. 250 Sioux. Colonial. Big living room, thirty by twenty-five, fireplaces in living room, library, recreation room, paneled walls wet bar five bathrooms five bedrooms two lavatories central air conditioning automatic sprinkler automatic garage door three children one wife two cars a breakfast room a patio a large fenced lot fourteen trees a front door with a brass knocker never knocked. Next is our house. Classic contemporary. Traditional modern. Attached garage, attached Florida room, attached patio, attached pool and cabana, attached roof. A front door mail slot through which pour *Time Magazine, Fortune, Life, Business Week,* the *Wall Street Journal,* the *New York Times,* the *New Yorker,* the *Saturday Review, M.D., Modern Medicine, Disease of the Month* . . . and also. . . . And in addition to all this, a quiet sealed letter from Baldwin saying: *Your daughter is not doing work compatible with her performance on the Stanford-Binet[3]. . . .* And your son is not doing well, not well at all, very sad. Where is your son anyway? Once he stole trick-and-treat candy from some six-year-old kids, he himself being a robust ten. The beginning. Now your daughter steals. In the Village Pharmacy she made off with, yes she did, don't deny it, she made off with a copy of *Pageant Magazine* for no reason, she swiped a roll of Life Savers

---

**2.** That is, he has changed from a wholesome American boy into a morbid neurotic. Huck Finn is the young hero of Mark Twain's novel *Adventures of Huckleberry Finn.* Usher is the chief character in Edgar Allan Poe's *Fall of the House of Usher.*  **3.** An intelligence test.

in a green wrapper and was in no need of saving her life or even in need of sucking candy; when she was no more than eight years old she stole, don't blush, she stole a package of Tums only because it was out on the counter and available, and the nice lady behind the counter (now dead) said nothing. . . . Sioux Drive. Maples, oaks, elms. Diseased elms cut down. Sioux Drive runs into Roosevelt Drive. Slow, turning lanes, not streets, all drives and lanes and ways and passes. A private police force. Quiet private police, in unmarked cars. Cruising on Saturday evenings with paternal smiles for the residents who are streaming in and out of houses, going to and from parties, a thousand parties, slightly staggering, the women in their furs alighting from automobiles bought of Ford and General Motors and Chrysler, very heavy automobiles. No foreign cars. Detroit. In 275 Sioux, down the block in that magnificent French-Normandy mansion, lives _____ himself, who has the C_____ account itself, imagine that! Look at where he lives and look at the enormous trees and chimneys, imagine his many fireplaces, imagine his wife and children, imagine his wife's hair, imagine her fingernails, imagine her bathtub of smooth clean glowing pink, imagine their embraces, his trouser pockets filled with odd coins and keys and dust and peanuts, imagine their ecstasy on Sioux Drive, imagine their income tax returns, imagine their little boy's pride in his experimental car, a scaled down C_____, as he roars round the neighborhood on the sidewalks frightening dogs and Negro maids, oh imagine all these things, imagine everything, let your mind roar out all over Sioux Drive and Du Maurier Drive and Roosevelt Drive and Ticonderoga Pass and Burning Bush Way and Lincolnshire Pass and Lois Lane.

When spring comes, its winds blow nothing to Sioux Drive, no odors of hollyhocks or forsythia, nothing Sioux Drive doesn't already possess, everything is planted and performing. The weather vanes, had they weather vanes, don't have to turn with the wind, don't have to contend with the weather. There is no weather.

## VI. Detroit

There is always weather in Detroit. Detroit's temperature is always 32°. Fast-falling temperatures. Slow-rising temperatures. Wind from the north-northeast four to forty miles an hour, small-craft warnings, partly cloudy today and Wednesday changing to partly sunny through Thursday . . . small warnings of frost, soot warnings, traffic warnings, hazardous lake conditions for small craft and swimmers, restless Negro gangs, restless cloud formations, restless temperatures aching to fall out the very bottom of the thermometer or shoot up over the top and boil everything over in red mercury.

Detroit's temperature is 32°. Fast-falling temperatures. Slow-rising temperatures. Wind from the north-northeast four to forty miles an hour. . . .

## VII. Events

1. The girl's heart is pounding. In her pocket is a pair of gloves! In a plastic bag! Airproof breathproof plastic bag, gloves selling for twenty-five dollars on Branden's counter! In her pocket! Shoplifted! . . . In her purse is a blue

comb, not very clean. In her purse is a leather billfold (a birthday present from her grandmother in Philadelphia) with snapshots of the family in clean plastic windows, in the billfold are bills, she doesn't know how many bills. . . . In her purse is an ominous note from her friend Tykie *What's this about Joe H. and the kids hanging around at Louise's Sat. night? You heard anything?* . . . passed in French class. In her purse is a lot of dirty yellow Kleenex, her mother's heart would break to see such very dirty Kleenex, and at the bottom of her purse are brown hairpins and safety pins and a broken pencil and a ballpoint pen (blue) stolen from somewhere forgotten and a purse-size compact of Cover Girl Make-Up, Ivory Rose. . . . Her lipstick is Broken Heart, a corrupt pink; her fingers are trembling like crazy; her teeth are beginning to chatter; her insides are alive; her eyes glow in her head; she is saying to her mother's astonished face *I want to steal but not to buy.*

2. At Clarita's. Day or night? What room is this? A bed, a regular bed, and a mattress on the floor nearby. Wallpaper hanging in strips. Clarita says she tore it like that with her teeth. She was fighting a barbaric tribe that night, high from some pills; she was battling for her life with men wearing helmets of heavy iron and their faces no more than Christian crosses to breathe through, every one of those bastards looking like her lover Simon, who seems to breathe with great difficulty through the slits of mouth and nostrils in his face. Clarita has never heard of Sioux Drive. Raymond Forrest cuts no ice with her, nor does the C＿＿＿＿ account and its millions; Harvard Business School could be at the corner of Vernor and 12th Street for all she cares, and Vietnam might have sunk by now into the Dead Sea under its tons of debris, for all the amazement she could show . . . her face is overworked, overwrought, at the age of twenty (thirty?) it is already exhausted but fanciful and ready for a laugh. Clarita says mournfully to me *Honey somebody is going to turn you out let me give you warning.* In a movie shown on late television Clarita is not a mess like this but a nurse, with short neat hair and a dedicated look, in love with her doctor and her doctor's patients and their diseases, enamored of needles and sponges and rubbing alcohol. . . . Or no: she is a private secretary. Robert Cummings is her boss. She helps him with fantastic plots, the canned audience laughs, no, the audience doesn't laugh because nothing is funny, instead her boss is Robert Taylor and they are not boss and secretary but husband and wife, she is threatened by a young starlet, she is grim, handsome, wifely, a good companion for a good man. . . . She is Claudette Colbert. Her sister too is Claudette Colbert. They are twins, identical. Her husband Charles Boyer[4] is a very rich handsome man and her sister, Claudette Colbert, is plotting her death in order to take her place as the rich man's wife, no one will know because they are *twins*. . . . All these marvelous lives Clarita might have lived, but she fell out the bottom at the age of thirteen. At the age when I was packing my overnight case for a slumber party at Toni Deshield's she was tearing filthy sheets off a bed and scratching up a rash on her arms. . . . Thirteen is uncommonly young for a white girl in Detroit, Miss Brock of the Detroit House of Correction said in a sad newspaper interview for the *Detroit News;* fifteen and sixteen are more likely. Eleven, twelve, thirteen are not surprising

---

4. Cummings, Taylor, Colbert, and Boyer are romantic film stars of the 1930s to 1950s.

in colored . . . they are more precocious. What can we do? Taxes are rising and the tax base is falling. The temperature rises slowly but falls rapidly. Everything is falling out the bottom, Woodward Avenue is filthy, Livernois Avenue is filthy! Scraps of paper flutter in the air like pigeons, dirt flies up and hits you right in the eye, oh Detroit is breaking up into dangerous bits of newspaper and dirt, watch out. . . .

Clarita's apartment is over a restaurant. Simon her lover emerges from the cracks at dark. Mrs. Olesko, a neighbor of Clarita's, an aged white wisp of a woman, doesn't complain but sniffs with contentment at Clarita's noisy life and doesn't tell the cops, hating cops, when the cops arrive. I should give more fake names, more blanks, instead of telling all these secrets. I myself am a secret; I am a minor.

3. My father reads a paper at a medical convention in Los Angeles. There he is, on the edge of the North American continent, when the unmarked detective put his hand so gently on my arm in the aisle of Branden's and said, "Miss, would you like to step over here for a minute?"

And where was he when Clarita put her hand on my arm, that wintry dark sulphurous aching day in Detroit, in the company of closed-down barber shops, closed-down diners, closed-down movie houses, homes, windows, basements, faces . . . she put her hand on my arm and said, "Honey, are you looking for somebody down here?"

And was he home worrying about me, gone for two weeks solid, when they carried me off . . . ? It took three of them to get me in the police cruiser, so they said, and they put more than their hands on my arm.

4. I work on this lesson. My English teacher is Mr. Forest, who is from Michigan State. Not handsome, Mr. Forest, and his name is plain, unlike Raymond Forrest's, but he is sweet and rodentlike, he has conferred with the principal and my parents, and everything is fixed . . . treat her as if nothing has happened, a new start, begin again, only sixteen years old, what a shame, how did it happen?—nothing happened, nothing could have happened, a slight physiological modification known only to a gynecologist or to Dr. Coronet. I work on my lesson. I sit in my pink room. I look around the room with my sad pink eyes. I sigh, I dawdle, I pause. I eat up time. I am limp and happy to be home, I am sixteen years old suddenly, my head hangs heavy as a pumpkin on my shoulders, and my hair has just been cut by Mr. Faye at the Crystal Salon and is said to be very becoming.

(Simon too put his hand on my arm and said, "Honey, you have got to come with me," and in his six-by-six room we got to know each other. Would I go back to Simon again? Would I lie down with him in all that filth and craziness? Over and over again.

a Clarita is being betrayed as in front of a Cunningham Drug Store she is nervously eyeing a colored man who may or may not have money, or a nervous white boy of twenty with sideburns and an Appalachian look, who may or may not have a knife hidden in his jacket pocket, or a husky red-faced man of friendly countenance who may or may not be a member of the Vice Squad out for an early twilight walk.)

I work on my lesson for Mr. Forest. I have filled up eleven pages. Words pour out of me and won't stop. I want to tell everything . . . what was the song Simon was always humming, and who was Simon's friend in a very new trench coat with an old high school graduation ring on his finger . . . ? Simon's bearded friend? When I was down too low for him, Simon kicked me out and gave me to him for three days, I think, on Fourteenth Street in Detroit, an airy room of cold cruel drafts with newspapers on the floor. . . . Do I really remember that or am I piecing it together from what they told me? Did they tell the truth? Did they know much of the truth?

## VIII. Characters

1. Wednesdays after school, at four; Saturday mornings at ten. Mother drives me to Dr. Coronet. Ferns in the office, plastic or real, they look the same. Dr. Coronet is queenly, an elegant nicotine-stained lady who would have studied with Freud had circumstances not prevented it, a bit of a Catholic, ready to offer you some mystery if your teeth will ache too much without it. Highly recommended by Father! Forty dollars an hour, Father's forty dollars! Progress! Looking up! Looking better! That new haircut is so becoming, says Dr. Coronet herself, showing how normal she is for a woman with an I.Q. of 180 and many advanced degrees.

2. Mother. A lady in a brown suede coat. Boots of shiny black material, black gloves, a black fur hat. She would be humiliated could she know that of all the people in the world it is my ex-lover Simon who walks most like her . . . self-conscious and unreal, listening to distant music, a little bowlegged with craftiness. . . .

3. Father. Tying a necktie. In a hurry. On my first evening home he put his hand on my arm and said, "Honey, we're going to forget all about this."

4. Simon. Outside, a plane is crossing the sky, in here we're in a hurry. Morning. It must be morning. The girl is half out of her mind, whimpering and vague; Simon her dear friend is wretched this morning . . . he is wretched with morning itself . . . he forces her to give him an injection with that needle she knows is filthy, she had a dread of needles and surgical instruments and the odor of things that are to be sent into the blood, thinking somehow of her father. . . . This is a bad morning, Simon says that his mind is being twisted out of shape, and so he submits to the needle that he usually scorns and bites his lip with his yellowish teeth, his face going very pale. *Ah baby!* he says in his soft mocking voice, which with all women is a mockery of love, *do it like this— Slowly—*And the girl, terrified, almost drops the precious needle but manages to turn it up to the light from the window . . . is it an extension of herself then? She can give him this gift then? *I wish you wouldn't do this to me,* she says, wise in her terror, because it seems to her that Simon's danger—in a few minutes he may be dead—is a way of pressing her against him that is more powerful than

any other embrace. She has to work over his arm, the knotted corded veins of his arm, her forehead wet with perspiration as she pushes and releases the needle, staring at that mixture of liquid now stained with Simon's bright blood. . . . When the drug hits him she can feel it herself, she feels that magic that is more than any woman can give him, striking the back of his head and making his face stretch as if with the impact of a terrible sun. . . . She tries to embrace him but he pushes her aside and stumbles to his feet. *Jesus Christ,* he says. . . .

5. Princess, a Negro girl of eighteen. What is her charge? She is closed-mouthed about it, shrewd and silent, you know that no one had to wrestle her to the sidewalk to get her in here; she came with dignity. In the recreation room she sits reading *Nancy Drew and the Jewel Box Mystery,*[5] which inspires in her face tiny wrinkles of alarm and interest: what a face! Light brown skin, heavy shaded eyes, heavy eyelashes, a serious sinister dark brow, graceful fingers, graceful wristbones, graceful legs, lips, tongue, a sugar-sweet voice, a leggy stride more masculine than Simon's and my mother's, decked out in a dirty white blouse and dirty white slacks; vaguely nautical is Princess' style. . . . At breakfast she is in charge of clearing the table and leans over me, saying, *Honey you sure you ate enough?*

6. The girl lies sleepless, wondering. Why here, why not there? Why Bloomfield Hills and not jail? Why jail and not her pink room? Why downtown Detroit and not Sioux Drive? What is the difference? Is Simon all the difference? The girl's head is a parade of wonders. She is nearly sixteen, her breath is marvelous with wonders, not long ago she was coloring with crayons and now she is smearing the landscape with paints that won't come off and won't come off her fingers either. She says to the matron *I am not talking about anything,* not because everyone has warned her not to talk but because, because she will not talk; because she won't say anything about Simon, who is her secret. And she says to the matron, *I won't go home,* up until that night in the lavatory when everything was changed. . . . "No, I won't go home I want to stay here," she says, listening to her own words with amazement, thinking that weeds might climb everywhere over that marvelous $180,000 house and dinosaurs might return to muddy the beige carpeting, but never never will she reconcile four o'clock in the morning in Detroit with eight o'clock breakfasts in Bloomfield Hills. . . . oh, she aches still for Simon's hands and his caressing breath, though he gave her little pleasure, he took everything from her (five-dollar bills, ten-dollar bills, passed into her numb hands by men and taken out of her hands by Simon) until she herself was passed into the hands of other men, police, when Simon evidently got tired of her and her hysteria. . . . *No, I won't go home, I don't want to be bailed out.* The girl thinks as a *Stubborn* and *Wayward Child* (one of several charges lodged against her), and the matron understands her crazy white-rimmed eyes that are seeking out some new violence that will keep her in jail, should someone threaten to let her out. Such children try to strangle the matrons, the attendants, or one another . . .

5. Mystery story for juveniles.

they want the locks locked forever, the doors nailed shut . . . and this girl is no different up until that night her mind is changed for her. . . .

## IX. That Night

Princess and Dolly, a little white girl of maybe fifteen, hardy however as a sergeant and in the House of Correction for armed robbery, corner her in the lavatory at the farthest sink and the other girls look away and file out to bed, leaving her. God, how she is beaten up! Why is she beaten up? Why do they pound her, why such hatred? Princess vents all the hatred of a thousand silent Detroit winters on her body, this girl whose body belongs to me, fiercely she rides across the Midwestern plains on this girl's tender bruised body . . . revenge on the oppressed minorities of America! revenge on the slaughtered Indians! revenge on the female sex, on the male sex, revenge on Bloomfield Hills, revenge revenge. . . .

## X. Detroit

In Detroit, weather weighs heavily upon everyone. The sky looms large. The horizon shimmers in smoke. Downtown the buildings are imprecise in the haze. Perpetual haze. Perpetual motion inside the haze. Across the choppy river is the city of Windsor, in Canada. Part of the continent has bunched up here and is bulging outward, at the tip of Detroit; a cold hard rain is forever falling on the expressways. . . . Shoppers shop grimly, their cars are not parked in safe places, their windshields may be smashed and graceful ebony hands may drag them out through their shatterproof smashed windshields, crying, *Revenge of the Indians!* Ah, they all fear leaving Hudson's and being dragged to the very tip of the city and thrown off the parking roof of Cobo Hall, that expensive tomb, into the river. . . .

## XI. Characters We Are Forever Entwined With

1. Simon drew me into his tender rotting arms and breathed gravity into me. Then I came to earth, weighed down. He said, *You are such a little girl,* and he weighed me down with his delight. In the palms of his hands were teeth marks from his previous life experiences. He was thirty-five, they said. Imagine Simon in this room, in my pink room: he is about six feet tall and stoops slightly, in a feline cautious way, always thinking, always on guard, with his scuffed light suede shoes and his clothes that are anyone's clothes, slightly rumpled ordinary clothes that ordinary men might wear to not-bad jobs. Simon has fair long hair, curly hair, spent languid curls that are like . . . exactly like the curls of wood shavings to the touch, I am trying to be exact . . . and he smells of unheated mornings and coffee and too many pills coating his tongue with a faint green-white scum. . . . Dear Simon, who would be panicked in this room and in this house (right now Billie is vacuuming next door in my parents' room; a vacuum cleaner's roar is a sign of all good things), Simon who is said to have come from a home not much different from this, years ago, fleeing all the carpeting and the polished banisters . . . Simon has a deathly face, only desperate people fall in love

with it. His face is bony and cautious, the bones of his cheeks prominent as if with the rigidity of his ceaseless thinking, plotting, for he has to make money out of girls to whom money means nothing, they're so far gone they can hardly count it, and in a sense money means nothing to him either except as a way of keeping on with his life. *Each Day's Proud Struggle,* the title of a novel we could read at jail. . . . Each day he needs a certain amount of money. He devours it. It wasn't love he uncoiled in me with his hollowed-out eyes and his courteous smile, that remnant of a prosperous past, but a dark terror that needed to press itself flat against him, or against another man . . . but he was the first, he came over to me and took my arm, a claim. We struggled on the stairs and I said, *Let me loose, you're hurting my neck, my face,* it was such a surprise that my skin hurt where he rubbed it, and afterward we lay face to face and he breathed everything into me. In the end I think he turned me in.

2.  Raymond Forrest. I just read this morning that Raymond Forrest's father, the chairman of the board at _____, died of a heart attack on a plane bound for London. I would like to write Raymond Forrest a note of sympathy. I would like to thank him for not pressing charges against me one hundred years ago, saving me, being so generous . . . well, men like Raymond Forrest are generous men, not like Simon. I would like to write him a letter telling of my love, or of some other emotion that is positive and healthy. Not like Simon and his poetry, which he scrawled down when he was high and never changed a word . . . but when I try to think of something to say, it is Simon's language that comes back to me, caught in my head like a bad song, it is always Simon's language:

> There is no reality only dreams
> Your neck may get snapped when you wake
> My love is drawn to some violent end
> She keeps wanting to get away
> My love is heading downward
> And I am heading upward
> She is going to crash on the sidewalk
> And I am going to dissolve into the clouds

## XII. Events

1.  Out of the hospital, bruised and saddened and converted, with Princess' grunts still tangled in my hair . . . and Father in his overcoat, looking like a prince himself, come to carry me off. Up the expressway and out north to home. Jesus Christ, but the air is thinner and cleaner here. Monumental houses. Heartbreaking sidewalks, so clean.

2.  Weeping in the living room. The ceiling is two stories high and two chandeliers hang from it. Weeping, weeping, though Billie the maid is *probably listening.* I will never leave home again. Never. Never leave home. Never leave this home again, never.

3.  Sugar doughnuts for breakfast. The toaster is very shiny and my face is distorted in it. Is that my face?

4.  The car is turning in the driveway. Father brings me home. Mother embraces me. Sunlight breaks in movieland patches on the roof of our traditional-contemporary home, which was designed for the famous automotive stylist whose identity, if I told you the name of the famous car he designed, you would all know, so I can't tell you because my teeth chatter at the thought of being sued . . . or having someone climb into my bedroom window with a rope to strangle me. . . . The car turns up the blacktop drive. The house opens to me like a doll's house, so lovely in the sunlight, the big living room beckons to me with its walls falling away in a delirium of joy at my return, Billie the maid is *no doubt* listening from the kitchen as I burst into tears and the hysteria Simon got so sick of. Convulsed in Father's arms, I say I will never leave again, never, why did I leave, where did I go, what happened, my mind is gone wrong, my body is one big bruise, my backbone was sucked dry, it wasn't the men who hurt me and Simon never hurt me but only those girls . . . my God, how they hurt me . . . I will never leave home again. . . . The car is perpetually turning up the drive and I am perpetually breaking down in the living room and we are perpetually taking the right exit from the expressway (Lahser Road) and the wall of the rest room is perpetually banging against my head and perpetually are Simon's hands moving across my body and adding everything up and so too are Father's hands on my shaking bruised back, far from the surface of my skin on the surface of my good blue cashmere coat (dry-cleaned for my release). . . . I weep for all the money here, for God in gold and beige carpeting, for the beauty of chandeliers and the miracle of a clean polished gleaming toaster and faucets that run both hot and cold water, and I tell them, *I will never leave home, this is my home, I love everything here, I am in love with everything here.* . . .
    I am home.

1970

# TIM O'BRIEN

### b. 1946

O'Brien was born in Austin, Minnesota, and educated at Macalester College. Upon graduating he was drafted into the U.S. Army and sent to fight in Vietnam, after which he emerged as one of the most brilliant chroniclers of that carnage. Though there is a solid vein of realism in his work, it also has something in common with the "magical realism" of contemporary South American novelists; fantasy is entwined with his reliable reportage. He is the author of *If I Die in a Combat Zone, Box Me Up and Ship Me Home* (1973); *Northern Lights* (1974); the National Book Award–winning *Going after Cacciato* (1978); *The Nuclear Age* (1985); *The Things They Carried* (1990), a collection of his stories that was a Pulitzer Prize finalist; *In the Lake of the Woods* (1994); *Tomcat in Love* (1998); and *July, July* (2002). In 2012 O'Brien was awarded a Lifetime Achievement award from the Dayton Literary Peace Prize, and in 2013 won the Pritzker Military Library Literature Award.

## The Things They Carried

First Lieutenant Jimmy Cross carried letters from a girl named Martha, a junior at Mount Sebastian College in New Jersey. They were not love letters, but Lieutenant Cross was hoping, so he kept them folded in plastic at the bottom of his rucksack. In the late afternoon, after a day's march, he would dig his foxhole, wash his hands under a canteen, unwrap the letters, hold them with the tips of his fingers, and spend the last hour of light pretending. He would imagine romantic camping trips into the White Mountains in New Hampshire. He would sometimes taste the envelope flaps, knowing her tongue had been there. More than anything, he wanted Martha to love him as he loved her, but the letters were mostly chatty, elusive on the matter of love. She was a virgin, he was almost sure. She was an English major at Mount Sebastian, and she wrote beautifully about her professors and roommates and midterm exams, about her respect for Chaucer and her great affection for Virginia Woolf. She often quoted lines of poetry; she never mentioned the war, except to say, Jimmy, take care of yourself. The letters weighed ten ounces. They were signed "Love, Martha," but Lieutenant Cross understood that "Love" was only a way of signing and did not mean what he sometimes pretended it meant. At dusk, he would carefully return the letters to his rucksack. Slowly, a bit distracted, he would get up and move among his men, checking the perimeter, then at full dark he would return to his hole and watch the night and wonder if Martha was a virgin.

The things they carried were largely determined by necessity. Among the necessities or near necessities were P-38 can openers, pocket knives, heat tabs, wrist watches, dog tags, mosquito repellent, chewing gum, candy, cigarettes, salt tablets, packets of Kool-Aid, lighters, matches, sewing kits, Military Payment Certificates, C rations, and two or three canteens of water. Together, these items weighed between fifteen and twenty pounds, depending upon a man's habits or rate of metabolism. Henry Dobbins, who was a big man, carried extra rations; he was especially fond of canned peaches in heavy syrup over pound cake. Dave Jensen, who practiced field hygiene, carried a toothbrush, dental floss, and several hotel-size bars of soap he'd stolen on R&R[1] in Sydney, Australia. Ted Lavender, who was scared, carried tranquilizers until he was shot in the head outside the village of Than Khe in mid-April. By necessity, and because it was SOP,[2] they all carried steel helmets that weighed five pounds including the liner and camouflage cover. They carried the standard fatigue jackets and trousers. Very few carried underwear. On their feet they carried jungle boots—2.1 pounds—and Dave Jensen carried three pairs of socks and a can of Dr. Scholl's foot powder as a precaution against trench foot. Until he was shot, Ted Lavender carried six or seven ounces of premium dope, which for him was a necessity. Mitchell Sanders, the RTO,[3] carried condoms. Norman Bowker carried a diary. Rat Kiley carried comic books. Kiowa, a devout Baptist, carried an illustrated New Testament that had been presented to him by his father, who taught Sunday school in Oklahoma City, Oklahoma. As a hedge against bad times, however, Kiowa also carried his grandmother's distrust of the white man, his grandfather's old hunting hatchet. Necessity dictated. Because the land was mined and booby-trapped, it was SOP for each man to carry a steel-centered, nylon-covered flak jacket, which weighed 6.7 pounds, but which on hot days seemed much heavier. Because you could die so quickly, each man carried at least one large compress bandage, usually in the helmet band for easy access. Because the nights were cold, and because the monsoons were wet, each carried a green plastic poncho that could be used as a raincoat or ground sheet or makeshift tent. With its quilted liner, the poncho weighed almost two pounds, but it was worth every ounce. In April, for instance, when Ted Lavender was shot, they used his poncho to wrap him up, then to carry him across the paddy, then to lift him into the chopper that took him away.

They were called legs or grunts.

To carry something was to "hump" it, as when Lieutenant Jimmy Cross humped his love for Martha up the hills and through the swamps. In its intransitive form, "to hump" meant "to walk," or "to march," but it implied burdens far beyond the intransitive.

Almost everyone humped photographs. In his wallet, Lieutenant Cross carried two photographs of Martha. The first was a Kodachrome snapshot signed "Love," though he knew better. She stood against a brick wall. Her eyes were gray and neutral, her lips slightly open as she stared straight-on at the camera. At night, sometimes, Lieutenant Cross wondered who had taken the picture, because he knew she had boyfriends, because he loved her so much,

---

1. Rest and recreation leave.   2. Standard operating procedure.   3. Radio and telephone operator.

and because he could see the shadow of the picture taker spreading out against the brick wall. The second photograph had been clipped from the 1968 Mount Sebastian yearbook. It was an action shot—women's volleyball—and Martha was bent horizontal to the floor, reaching, the palms of her hands in sharp focus, the tongue taut, the expression frank and competitive. There was no visible sweat. She wore white gym shorts. Her legs, he thought, were almost certainly the legs of a virgin, dry and without hair, the left knee cocked and carrying her entire weight, which was just over one hundred pounds. Lieutenant Cross remembered touching that left knee. A dark theater, he remembered, and the movie was *Bonnie and Clyde,*[4] and Martha wore a tweed skirt, and during the final scene, when he touched her knee, she turned and looked at him in a sad, sober way that made him pull his hand back, but he would always remember the feel of the tweed skirt and the knee beneath it and the sound of the gunfire that killed Bonnie and Clyde, how embarrassing it was, how slow and oppressive. He remembered kissing her good night at the dorm door. Right then, he thought, he should've done something brave. He should've carried her up the stairs to her room and tied her to the bed and touched that left knee all night long. He should've risked it. Whenever he looked at the photographs, he thought of new things he should've done.

What they carried was partly a function of rank, partly of field specialty.

As a first lieutenant and platoon leader, Jimmy Cross carried a compass, maps, code books, binoculars, and a .45-caliber pistol that weighed 2.9 pounds fully loaded. He carried a strobe light and the responsibility for the lives of his men.

As an RTO, Mitchell Sanders carried the PRC-25 radio, a killer, twenty-six pounds with its battery.

As a medic, Rat Kiley carried a canvas satchel filled with morphine and plasma and malaria tablets and surgical tape and comic books and all the things a medic must carry, including M&M's[5] for especially bad wounds, for a total weight of nearly twenty pounds.

As a big man, therefore a machine gunner, Henry Dobbins carried the M-60, which weighed twenty-three pounds unloaded, but which was almost always loaded. In addition, Dobbins carried between ten and fifteen pounds of ammunition draped in belts across his chest and shoulders.

As PFCs or Spec 4s, most of them were common grunts and carried the standard M-16 gas-operated assault rifle. The weapon weighed 7.5 pounds unloaded, 8.2 pounds with its full twenty-round magazine. Depending on numerous factors, such as topography and psychology, the riflemen carried anywhere from twelve to twenty magazines, usually in cloth bandoliers, adding on another 8.4 pounds at minimum, fourteen pounds at maximum. When it was available, they also carried M-16 maintenance gear—rods and steel brushes and swabs and tubes of LSA oil—all of which weighed about a pound. Among the grunts, some carried the M-79 grenade launcher, 5.9 pounds unloaded, a reasonably light weapon except for the ammunition, which was heavy. A single round weighed ten ounces. The typical load was twenty-five

4. 1967 film starring Faye Dunaway and Warren Beatty.  5. Apparently this candy was used as a placebo since it would have no other medicinal value.

rounds. But Ted Lavender, who was scared, carried thirty-four rounds when he was shot and killed outside Than Khe, and he went down under an exceptional burden, more than twenty pounds of ammunition, plus the flak jacket and helmet and rations and water and toilet paper and tranquilizers and all the rest, plus the unweighed fear. He was dead weight. There was no twitching or flopping. Kiowa, who saw it happen, said it was like watching a rock fall, or a big sandbag or something—just boom, then down—not like the movies where the dead guy rolls around and does fancy spins and goes ass over teakettle—not like that, Kiowa said, the poor bastard just flat-fuck fell. Boom. Down. Nothing else. It was a bright morning in mid-April. Lieutenant Cross felt the pain. He blamed himself. They stripped off Lavender's canteens and ammo, all the heavy things, and Rat Kiley said the obvious, the guy's dead, and Mitchell Sanders used his radio to report one U.S. KIA[6] and to request a chopper. Then they wrapped Lavender in his poncho. They carried him out to a dry paddy, established security, and sat smoking the dead man's dope until the chopper came. Lieutenant Cross kept to himself. He pictured Martha's smooth young face, thinking he loved her more than anything, more than his men, and now Ted Lavender was dead because he loved her so much and could not stop thinking about her. When the dust-off[7] arrived, they carried Lavender aboard. Afterward they burned Than Khe. They marched until dusk, then dug their holes, and that night Kiowa kept explaining how you had to be there, how fast it was, how the poor guy just dropped like so much concrete. Boom-down, he said. Like cement.

In addition to the three standard weapons—the M-60, M-16, and M-79—they carried whatever presented itself, or whatever seemed appropriate as a means of killing or staying alive. They carried catch-as-catch-can. At various times, in various situations, they carried M-14s and CAR-15s and Swedish Ks and grease guns and captured AK-47s and Chi-Coms and RPGs and Simonov carbines and black-market Uzis and .38-caliber Smith & Wesson handguns and 66mm LAWs and shotguns and silencers and blackjacks and bayonets and C-4 plastic explosives. Lee Strunk carried a slingshot; a weapon of last resort, he called it. Mitchell Sanders carried brass knuckles. Kiowa carried his grandfather's feathered hatchet. Every third or fourth man carried a Claymore antipersonnel mine—3.5 pounds with its firing device. They all carried fragmentation grenades—fourteen ounces each. They all carried at least one M-18 colored smoke grenade—twenty-four ounces. Some carried CS or tear-gas grenades. Some carried white-phosphorus grenades. They carried all they could bear, and then some, including a silent awe for the terrible power of the things they carried.

In the first week of April, before Lavender died, Lieutenant Jimmy Cross received a good-luck charm from Martha. It was a simple pebble, an ounce at most. Smooth to the touch, it was a milky-white color with flecks of orange and violet, oval-shaped, like a miniature egg. In the accompanying letter, Martha wrote that she had found the pebble on the Jersey shoreline, precisely where the land touched water at high tide, where things came together but also separated. It was this separate-but-together quality, she wrote, that had

---

**6.** Killed in action.   **7.** Helicopter.

inspired her to pick up the pebble and to carry it in her breast pocket for several days, where it seemed weightless, and then to send it through the mail, by air, as a token of her truest feelings for him. Lieutenant Cross found this romantic. But he wondered what her truest feelings were, exactly, and what she meant by separate-but-together. He wondered how the tides and waves had come into play on that afternoon along the Jersey shoreline when Martha saw the pebble and bent down to rescue it from geology. He imagined bare feet. Martha was a poet, with the poet's sensibilities, and her feet would be brown and bare, the toenails unpainted, the eyes chilly and somber like the ocean in March, and though it was painful, he wondered who had been with her that afternoon. He imagined a pair of shadows moving along the strip of sand where things came together but also separated. It was phantom jealousy, he knew, but he couldn't help himself. He loved her so much. On the march, through the hot days of early April, he carried the pebble in his mouth, turning it with his tongue, tasting sea salts and moisture. His mind wandered. He had difficulty keeping his attention on the war. On occasion he would yell at his men to spread out the column, to keep their eyes open, but then he would slip away into daydreams, just pretending, walking barefoot along the Jersey shore, with Martha, carrying nothing. He would feel himself rising. Sun and waves and gentle winds, all love and lightness.

What they carried varied by mission.

When a mission took them to the mountains, they carried mosquito netting, machetes, canvas tarps, and extra bug juice.

If a mission seemed especially hazardous, or if it involved a place they knew to be bad, they carried everything they could. In certain heavily mined AOs,[8] where the land was dense with Toe Poppers and Bouncing Betties, they took turns humping a twenty-eight-pound mine detector. With its headphones and big sensing plate, the equipment was a stress on the lower back and shoulders, awkward to handle, often useless because of the shrapnel in the earth, but they carried it anyway, partly for safety, partly for the illusion of safety.

On ambush, or other night missions, they carried peculiar little odds and ends. Kiowa always took along his New Testament and a pair of moccasins for silence. Dave Jensen carried night-sight vitamins high in carotin. Lee Strunk carried his slingshot; ammo, he claimed, would never be a problem. Rat Kiley carried brandy and M&M's. Until he was shot, Ted Lavender carried the starlight scope, which weighed 6.3 pounds with its aluminum carrying case. Henry Dobbins carried his girlfriend's pantyhose wrapped around his neck as a comforter. They all carried ghosts. When dark came, they would move out single file across the meadows and paddies to their ambush coordinates, where they would quietly set up the Claymores and lie down and spend the night waiting.

Other missions were more complicated and required special equipment. In mid-April, it was their mission to search out and destroy the elaborate tunnel complexes in the Than Khe area south of Chu Lai. To blow the tunnels, they carried one-pound blocks of pentrite high explosives, four blocks to a man, sixty-eight pounds in all. They carried wiring, detonators, and battery-powered

---

8. Areas of operations.

clackers. Dave Jensen carried earplugs. Most often, before blowing the tunnels, they were ordered by higher command to search them, which was considered bad news, but by and large they just shrugged and carried out orders. Because he was a big man, Henry Dobbins was excused from tunnel duty. The others would draw numbers. Before Lavender died there were seventeen men in the platoon, and whoever drew the number seventeen would strip off his gear and crawl in head first with a flashlight and Lieutenant Cross's .45-caliber pistol. The rest of them would fan out as security. They would sit down or kneel, not facing the hole, listening to the ground beneath them, imagining cobwebs and ghosts, whatever was down there—the tunnel walls squeezing in—how the flashlight seemed impossibly heavy in the hand and how it was tunnel vision in the very strictest sense, compression in all ways, even time, and how you had to wiggle in—ass and elbows—a swallowed-up feeling—and how you found yourself worrying about odd things—will your flashlight go dead? Do rats carry rabies? If you screamed, how far would the sound carry? Would your buddies hear it? Would they have the courage to drag you out? In some respects, though not many, the waiting was worse than the tunnel itself. Imagination was a killer.

On April 16, when Lee Strunk drew the number seventeen, he laughed and muttered something and went down quickly. The morning was hot and very still. Not good, Kiowa said. He looked at the tunnel opening, then out across a dry paddy toward the village of Than Khe. Nothing moved. No clouds or birds or people. As they waited, the men smoked and drank Kool-Aid, not talking much, feeling sympathy for Lee Strunk but also feeling the luck of the draw. You win some, you lose some, said Mitchell Sanders, and sometimes you settle for a rain check. It was a tired line and no one laughed.

Henry Dobbins ate a tropical chocolate bar. Ted Lavender popped a tranquilizer and went off to pee.

After five minutes, Lieutenant Jimmy Cross moved to the tunnel, leaned down, and examined the darkness. Trouble, he thought—a cave-in maybe. And then suddenly, without willing it, he was thinking about Martha. The stresses and fractures, the quick collapse, the two of them buried alive under all that weight. Dense, crushing love. Kneeling, watching the hole, he tried to concentrate on Lee Strunk and the war, all the dangers, but his love was too much for him, he felt paralyzed, he wanted to sleep inside her lungs and breathe her blood and be smothered. He wanted her to be a virgin and not a virgin, all at once. He wanted to know her. Intimate secrets—why poetry? Why so sad? Why that grayness in her eyes? Why so alone? Not lonely, just alone—riding her bike across campus or sitting off by herself in the cafeteria. Even dancing, she danced alone—and it was the aloneness that filled him with love. He remembered telling her that one evening. How she nodded and looked away. And how, later, when he kissed her, she received the kiss without returning it, her eyes wide open, not afraid, not a virgin's eyes, just flat and uninvolved.

Lieutenant Cross gazed at the tunnel. But he was not there. He was buried with Martha under the white sand at the Jersey shore. They were pressed together, and the pebble in his mouth was her tongue. He was smiling. Vaguely, he was aware of how quiet the day was, the sullen paddies, yet he could not bring himself to worry about matters of security. He was beyond that. He was just a kid at war, in love. He was twenty-two years old. He couldn't help it.

A few moments later Lee Strunk crawled out of the tunnel. He came up grinning, filthy but alive. Lieutenant Cross nodded and closed his eyes while the others clapped Strunk on the back and made jokes about rising from the dead.

Worms, Rat Kiley said. Right out of the grave. Fuckin' zombie.

The men laughed. They all felt great relief.

Spook City, said Mitchell Sanders.

Lee Strunk made a funny ghost sound, a kind of moaning, yet very happy, and right then, when Strunk made that high happy moaning sound, when he went *Ahhooooo*, right then Ted Lavender was shot in the head on his way back from peeing. He lay with his mouth open. The teeth were broken. There was a swollen black bruise under his left eye. The cheekbone was gone. Oh shit, Rat Kiley said, the guy's dead. The guy's dead, he kept saying, which seemed profound—the guy's dead. I mean really.

The things they carried were determined to some extent by superstition. Lieutenant Cross carried his good-luck pebble. Dave Jensen carried a rabbit's foot. Norman Bowker, otherwise a very gentle person, carried a thumb that had been presented to him as a gift by Mitchell Sanders. The thumb was dark brown, rubbery to the touch, and weighed four ounces at most. It had been cut from a VC corpse, a boy of fifteen or sixteen. They'd found him at the bottom of an irrigation ditch, badly burned, flies in his mouth and eyes. The boy wore black shorts and sandals. At the time of his death he had been carrying a pouch of rice, rifle, and three magazines of ammunition.

You want my opinion, Mitchell Sanders said, there's a definite moral here.

He put his hand on the dead boy's wrist. He was quiet for a time, as if counting a pulse, then he patted the stomach, almost affectionately, and used Kiowa's hunting hatchet to remove the thumb.

Henry Dobbins asked what the moral was.

Moral?

You know. *Moral.*

Sanders wrapped the thumb in toilet paper and handed it across to Norman Bowker. There was no blood. Smiling, he kicked the boy's head, watched the flies scatter, and said, It's like with that old TV show—Paladin. Have gun, will travel.

Henry Dobbins thought about it.

Yeah, well, he finally said. I don't see no moral.

There it *is*, man.

Fuck off.

They carried USO stationery and pencils and pens. They carried Sterno, safety pins, trip flares, signal flares, spools of wire, razor blades, chewing tobacco, liberated joss sticks and statuettes of the smiling Buddha, candles, grease pencils, *The Stars and Stripes*, fingernail clippers, Psy Ops[9] leaflets, bush hats, bolos, and much more. Twice a week, when the resupply choppers came in, they carried hot chow in green Mermite cans and large canvas bags filled with iced beer and soda pop. They carried plastic water containers, each with

---

**9.** Psychological Operations.

a two-gallon capacity. Mitchell Sanders carried a set of starched tiger fatigues for special occasions. Henry Dobbins carried Black Flag insecticide. Dave Jensen carried empty sandbags that could be filled at night for added protection. Lee Strunk carried tanning lotion. Some things they carried in common. Taking turns, they carried the big PRC-77 scrambler radio, which weighed thirty pounds with its battery. They shared the weight of memory. They took up what others could no longer bear. Often, they carried each other, the wounded or weak. They carried infections. They carried chess sets, basketballs, Vietnamese-English dictionaries, insignia of rank, Bronze Stars and Purple Hearts, plastic cards imprinted with the Code of Conduct. They carried diseases, among them malaria and dysentery. They carried lice and ringworm and leeches and paddy algae and various rots and molds. They carried the land itself—Vietnam, the place, the soil—a powdery orange-red dust that covered their boots and fatigues and faces. They carried the sky. The whole atmosphere, they carried it, the humidity, the monsoons, the stink of fungus and decay, all of it, they carried gravity. They moved like mules. By daylight they took sniper fire, at night they were mortared, but it was not battle, it was just the endless march, village to village, without purpose, nothing won or lost. They marched for the sake of the march. They plodded along slowly, dumbly, leaning forward against the heat, unthinking, all blood and bone, simple grunts, soldiering with their legs, toiling up the hills and down into the paddies and across the rivers and up again and down, just humping, one step and then the next and then another, but no volition, no will, because it was automatic, it was anatomy, and the war was entirely a matter of posture and carriage, the hump was everything, a kind of inertia, a kind of emptiness, a dullness of desire and intellect and conscience and hope and human sensibility. Their principles were in their feet. Their calculations were biological. They had no sense of strategy or mission. They searched the villages without knowing what to look for, not caring, kicking over jars of rice, frisking children and old men, blowing tunnels, sometimes setting fires and sometimes not, then forming up and moving on to the next village, then other villages, where it would always be the same. They carried their own lives. The pressures were enormous. In the heat of early afternoon, they would remove their helmets and flak jackets, walking bare, which was dangerous but which helped ease the strain. They would often discard things along the route of march. Purely for comfort, they would throw away rations, blow their Claymores and grenades, no matter, because by nightfall the resupply choppers would arrive with more of the same, then a day or two later still more, fresh watermelons and crates of ammunition and sunglasses and woolen sweaters—the resources were stunning—sparklers for the Fourth of July, colored eggs for Easter. It was the great American war chest—the fruits of science, the smokestacks, the canneries, the arsenals at Hartford, the Minnesota forests, the machine shops, the vast fields of corn and wheat—they carried like freight trains; they carried it on their backs and shoulders—and for all the ambiguities of Vietnam, all the mysteries and unknowns, there was at least the single abiding certainty that they would never be at a loss for things to carry.

After the chopper took Lavender away, Lieutenant Jimmy Cross led his men into the village of Than Khe. They burned everything. They shot chickens and dogs, they trashed the village well, they called in artillery and watched the wreckage, then they marched for several hours through the hot afternoon, and then at dusk, while Kiowa explained how Lavender died, Lieutenant Cross found himself trembling.

He tried not to cry. With his entrenching tool, which weighed five pounds, he began digging a hole in the earth.

He felt shame. He hated himself. He had loved Martha more than his men, and as a consequence Lavender was now dead, and this was something he would have to carry like a stone in his stomach for the rest of the war.

All he could do was dig. He used his entrenching tool like an ax, slashing, feeling both love and hate, and then later, when it was full dark, he sat at the bottom of his foxhole and wept. It went on for a long while. In part, he was grieving for Ted Lavender, but mostly it was for Martha, and for himself, because she belonged to another world, which was not quite real, and because she was a junior at Mount Sebastian College in New Jersey, a poet and a virgin and uninvolved, and because he realized she did not love him and never would.

Like cement, Kiowa whispered in the dark. I swear to God—boom-down. Not a word.

I've heard this, said Norman Bowker.

A pisser, you know? Still zipping himself up. Zapped while zipping.

All right, fine. That's enough.

Yeah, but you had to see it, the guy just—

I *heard*, man. Cement. So why not shut the fuck *up*?

Kiowa shook his head sadly and glanced over at the hole where Lieutenant Jimmy Cross sat watching the night. The air was thick and wet. A warm, dense fog had settled over the paddies and there was the stillness that precedes rain.

After a time Kiowa sighed.

One thing for sure, he said. The Lieutenant's in some deep hurt. I mean that crying jag—the way he was carrying on—it wasn't fake or anything, it was real heavy-duty hurt. The man cares.

Sure, Norman Bowker said.

Say what you want, the man does care.

We all got problems.

Not Lavender.

No, I guess not, Bowker said. Do me a favor, though.

Shut up?

That's a smart Indian. Shut up.

Shrugging, Kiowa pulled off his boots. He wanted to say more, just to lighten up his sleep, but instead he opened his New Testament and arranged it beneath his head as a pillow. The fog made things seem hollow and unattached. He tried not to think about Ted Lavender, but then he was thinking how fast it was, no drama, down and dead, and how it was hard to feel anything except surprise. It seemed un-Christian. He wished he could find some great sadness, or even anger, but the emotion wasn't there and he couldn't make it happen. Mostly he felt pleased to be alive. He liked the smell of the New Testament under his cheek, the leather and ink and paper and glue, whatever the chemicals were. He liked hearing the sounds of night. Even his fatigue, it felt fine, the stiff muscles and the prickly awareness of his own body, a float-ing feeling. He enjoyed not being dead. Lying there, Kiowa admired Lieuten-ant Jimmy Cross's capacity for grief. He wanted to share the man's pain, he wanted to care as Jimmy Cross cared. And yet when he closed his eyes, all he could think was Boom-down, and all he could feel was the pleasure of having his boots off and the fog curling in around him and the damp soil and the Bible smells and the plush comfort of night.

After a moment Norman Bowker sat up in the dark.

What the hell, he said. You want to talk, *talk*. Tell it to me.

Forget it.

No, man, go on. One thing I hate, it's a silent Indian.

For the most part they carried themselves with poise, a kind of dignity. Now and then, however, there were times of panic, when they squealed or wanted to squeal but couldn't, when they twitched and made moaning sounds and covered their heads and said Dear Jesus and flopped around on the earth and fired their weapons blindly and cringed and sobbed and begged for the noise to stop and went wild and made stupid promises to themselves and to God and to their mothers and fathers, hoping not to die. In different ways, it happened to all of them. Afterward, when the firing ended, they would blink and peek up. They would touch their bodies, feeling shame, then quickly hiding it. They would force themselves to stand. As if in slow motion, frame by frame, the world would take on the old logic—absolute silence, then the wind, then sunlight, then voices. It was the burden of being alive. Awkwardly, the men would reassemble themselves, first in private, then in groups, becom-ing soldiers again. They would repair the leaks in their eyes. They would check for casualties, call in dust-offs, light cigarettes, try to smile, clear their throats and spit and begin cleaning their weapons. After a time someone would shake his head and say, No lie, I almost shit my pants, and someone else would laugh, which meant it was bad, yes, but the guy had obviously not shit his pants, it wasn't that bad, and in any case nobody would ever do such a thing and then go ahead and talk about it. They would squint into the dense, oppressive sunlight. For a few moments, perhaps, they would fall silent, light-ing a joint and tracking its passage from man to man, inhaling, holding in the humiliation. Scary stuff, one of them might say. But then someone else would grin or flick his eyebrows and say, Roger-dodger, almost cut me a new asshole, *almost*.

There were numerous such poses. Some carried themselves with a sort of wistful resignation, others with pride or stiff soldierly discipline or good humor or macho zeal. They were afraid of dying but they were even more afraid to show it.

They found jokes to tell.

They used a hard vocabulary to contain the terrible softness. *Greased*, they'd say. *Offed, lit up, zapped while zipping*. It wasn't cruelty, just stage presence. They were actors and the war came at them in 3-D. When someone died, it wasn't quite dying, because in a curious way it seemed scripted, and because they had their lines mostly memorized, irony mixed with tragedy, and because they called it by other names, as if to encyst and destroy the reality of death itself. They kicked corpses. They cut off thumbs. They talked grunt lingo. They told stories about Ted Lavender's supply of tranquilizers, how the poor guy didn't feel a thing, how incredibly tranquil he was.

There's a moral here, said Mitchell Sanders.

They were waiting for Lavender's chopper, smoking the dead man's dope.

The moral's pretty obvious, Sanders said, and winked. Stay away from drugs. No joke, they'll ruin your day every time.

Cute, said Henry Dobbins.

Mind-blower, get it? Talk about wiggy—nothing left, just blood and brains.

They made themselves laugh.

There it is, they'd say, over and over, as if the repetition itself were an act of poise, a balance between crazy and almost crazy, knowing without going. There it is, which meant be cool, let it ride, because oh yeah, man, you can't change what can't be changed, there it is, there it absolutely and positively and fucking well *is*.

They were tough.

They carried all the emotional baggage of men who might die. Grief, terror, love, longing—these were intangibles, but the intangibles had their own mass and specific gravity, they had tangible weight. They carried shameful memories. They carried the common secret of cowardice barely restrained, the instinct to run or freeze or hide, and in many respects this was the heaviest burden of all, for it could never be put down, it required perfect balance and perfect posture. They carried their reputations. They carried the soldier's greatest fear, which was the fear of blushing. Men killed, and died, because they were embarrassed not to. It was what had brought them to the war in the first place, nothing positive, no dreams of glory or honor, just to avoid the blush of dishonor. They died so as not to die of embarrassment. They crawled into tunnels and walked point and advanced under fire. Each morning, despite the unknowns, they made their legs move. They endured. They kept humping. They did not submit to the obvious alternative, which was simply to close the eyes and fall. So easy, really. Go limp and tumble to the ground and let the muscles unwind and not speak and not budge until your buddies picked you up and lifted you into the chopper that would roar and dip its nose and carry you off to the world. A mere matter of falling, yet no one ever fell. It was not courage, exactly; the object was not valor. Rather, they were too frightened to be cowards.

By and large they carried these things inside, maintaining the masks of composure. They sneered at sick call. They spoke bitterly about guys who had found release by shooting off their own toes or fingers. Pussies, they'd say. Candyasses. It was fierce, mocking talk, with only a trace of envy or awe, but even so, the image played itself out behind their eyes.

They imagined the muzzle against flesh. They imagined the quick, sweet pain, then the evacuation to Japan, then a hospital with warm beds and cute geisha nurses.

They dreamed of freedom birds.

At night, on guard, staring into the dark, they were carried away by jumbo jets. They felt the rush of takeoff. *Gone!* they yelled. And then velocity, wings and engines, a smiling stewardess—but it was more than a plane, it was a real bird, a big sleek silver bird with feathers and talons and high screeching. They were flying. The weights fell off, there was nothing to bear. They laughed and held on tight, feeling the cold slap of wind and altitude, soaring, thinking *It's over, I'm gone!*—they were naked, they were light and free—it was all lightness, bright and fast and buoyant, light as light, a helium buzz in the brain, a giddy bubbling in the lungs as they were taken up over the clouds and the war, beyond duty, beyond gravity and mortification and global entanglements— *Sin loi!*[1] they yelled, *I'm sorry, motherfuckers, but I'm out of it, I'm goofed, I'm on a space cruise, I'm gone!*—and it was a restful, disencumbered sensation, just riding the light waves, sailing that big silver freedom bird over the mountains and oceans, over America, over the farms and great sleeping cities and cemeteries and highways and the golden arches of McDonald's. It was flight, a kind of fleeing, a kind of falling, falling higher and higher, spinning off the edge of the earth and beyond the sun and through the vast, silent vacuum where there were no burdens and where everything weighed exactly nothing. *Gone!* they screamed, *I'm sorry but I'm gone!* And so at night, not quite dreaming, they gave themselves over to lightness, they were carried, they were purely borne.

On the morning after Ted Lavender died, First Lieutenant Jimmy Cross crouched at the bottom of his foxhole and burned Martha's letters. Then he burned the two photographs. There was a steady rain falling, which made it difficult, but he used heat tabs and Sterno to build a small fire, screening it with his body, holding the photographs over the tight blue flame with the tips of his fingers.

He realized it was only a gesture. Stupid, he thought. Sentimental, too, but mostly just stupid.

Lavender was dead. You couldn't burn the blame.

Besides, the letters were in his head. And even now, without photographs, Lieutenant Cross could see Martha playing volleyball in her white gym shorts and yellow T-shirt. He could see her moving in the rain.

When the fire died out, Lieutenant Cross pulled his poncho over his shoulders and ate breakfast from a can.

There was no great mystery, he decided.

In those burned letters Martha had never mentioned the war, except to say, Jimmy, take care of yourself. She wasn't involved. She signed the letters "Love," but it wasn't love, and all the fine lines and technicalities did not matter.

The morning came up wet and blurry. Everything seemed part of everything else, the fog and Martha and the deepening rain.

It was a war, after all.

Half smiling, Lieutenant Jimmy Cross took out his maps. He shook his head hard, as if to clear it, then bent forward and began planning the day's march. In ten minutes, or maybe twenty, he would rouse the men and they would pack up and head west, where the maps showed the country to be green and inviting. They would do what they had always done. The rain might add some weight, but otherwise it would be one more day layered upon all the other days.

He was realistic about it. There was that new hardness in his stomach.

No more fantasies, he told himself.

---

1. Sorry about that (Vietnamese).

Henceforth, when he thought about Martha, it would be only to think that she belonged elsewhere. He would shut down the daydreams. This was not Mount Sebastian, it was another world, where there were no pretty poems or midterm exams, a place where men died because of carelessness and gross stupidity. Kiowa was right. Boom-down, and you were dead, never partly dead.

Briefly, in the rain, Lieutenant Cross saw Martha's gray eyes gazing back at him.

He understood.

It was very sad, he thought. The things men carried inside. The things men did or felt they had to do.

He almost nodded at her, but didn't.

Instead he went back to his maps. He was now determined to perform his duties firmly and without negligence. It wouldn't help Lavender, he knew that, but from this point on he would comport himself as a soldier. He would dispose of his good-luck pebble. Swallow it, maybe, or use Lee Strunk's slingshot, or just drop it along the trail. On the march he would impose strict field discipline. He would be careful to send out flank security, to prevent straggling or bunching up, to keep his troops moving at the proper pace and at the proper interval. He would insist on clean weapons. He would confiscate the remainder of Lavender's dope. Later in the day, perhaps, he would call the men together and speak to them plainly. He would accept the blame for what had happened to Ted Lavender. He would be a man about it. He would look them in the eyes, keeping his chin level, and he would issue the new SOPs in a calm, impersonal tone of voice, an officer's voice, leaving no room for argument or discussion. Commencing immediately, he'd tell them, they would no longer abandon equipment along the route of march. They would police up their acts. They would get their shit together, and keep it together, and maintain it neatly and in good working order.

He would not tolerate laxity. He would show strength, distancing himself.

Among the men there would be grumbling, of course, and maybe worse, because their days would seem longer and their loads heavier, but Lieutenant Cross reminded himself that his obligation was not to be loved but to lead. He would dispense with love; it was not now a factor. And if anyone quarreled or complained, he would simply tighten his lips and arrange his shoulders in the correct command posture. He might give a curt little nod. Or he might not. He might just shrug and say Carry on, then they would saddle up and form into a column and move out toward the villages of Than Khe.

1986

# FLANNERY O'CONNOR
## 1925–1964

O'Connor was born in Savannah, Georgia. Her undergraduate writing at the Georgia State College for Women won her a fellowship to the Writers' Workshop of the University of Iowa, where she earned an M.F.A. degree. She began her professional career with two years in New York, but a diagnosis of lupus, a painful autoimmune disorder, forced her to return to Georgia, where she lived with her mother on a farm near Milledgeville, raising peafowls, writing, and painting. For the rest of her life illness restricted her activities, though she traveled occasionally to give lectures and read from her work. She was a devout and uncompromising Roman Catholic; the extraordinary violence of her fiction is designed to expose the precarious condition of the spirit in a temporal world, as the startling comedy disintegrates the pretenses of a facile civilization. Her work won many honors, including three O. Henry first prizes and a posthumous National Book Award for *The Complete Stories* (1971). Her novels are *Wise Blood* (1952) and *The Violent Bear It Away* (1960). Her other books of short stories are *A Good Man Is Hard to Find* (1955) and *Everything That Rises Must Converge* (1965). A selection of her letters was edited by Sally Fitzgerald and published in 1979 under the title *The Habit of Being.*

## A Good Man Is Hard to Find

The grandmother didn't want to go to Florida. She wanted to visit some of her connections in east Tennessee and she was seizing every chance to change Bailey's mind. Bailey was the son she lived with, her only boy. He was sitting on the edge of his chair at the table, bent over the orange sports section of the *Journal.* "Now look here, Bailey," she said, "see here, read this," and she stood with one hand on her thin hip and the other rattling the newspaper at his bald head. "Here this fellow that calls himself The Misfit is aloose from the Federal Pen and headed toward Florida and you read here what it says he did to these people. Just you read it. I wouldn't take my children in any direction with a criminal like that aloose in it. I couldn't answer to my conscience if I did."

Bailey didn't look up from his reading so she wheeled around then and faced the children's mother; a young woman in slacks, whose face was as broad and innocent as a cabbage and was tied around with a green headkerchief that had two points on the top like rabbit's ears. She was sitting on the sofa, feeding the baby his apricots out of a jar. "The children have been to

Florida before," the old lady said. "You all ought to take them somewhere else for a change so they would see different parts of the world and be broad. They never have been to east Tennessee."

The children's mother didn't seem to hear her, but the eight-year-old boy, John Wesley, a stocky child with glasses, said, "If you don't want to go to Florida, why dontcha stay at home?" He and the little girl, June Star, were reading the funny papers on the floor.

"She wouldn't stay at home to be queen for a day," June Star said without raising her yellow head.

"Yes, and what would you do if this fellow, The Misfit, caught you?" the grandmother asked.

"I'd smack his face," John Wesley said.

"She wouldn't stay at home for a million bucks," June Star said. "Afraid she'd miss something. She has to go everywhere we go."

"All right, Miss," the grandmother said. "Just remember that the next time you want me to curl your hair."

June Star said her hair was naturally curly.

The next morning the grandmother was the first one in the car, ready to go. She had her big black valise that looked like the head of a hippopotamus in one corner, and underneath it she was hiding a basket with Pitty Sing,[1] the cat, in it. She didn't intend for the cat to be left alone in the house for three days because he would miss her too much and she was afraid he might brush against one of the gas burners and accidentally asphyxiate himself. Her son, Bailey, didn't like to arrive at a motel with a cat.

She sat in the middle of the back seat with John Wesley and June Star on either side of her. Bailey and the children's mother and the baby sat in the front and they left Atlanta at eight forty-five with the mileage on the car at 55890. The grandmother wrote this down because she thought it would be interesting to say how many miles they had been when they got back. It took them twenty minutes to reach the outskirts of the city.

The old lady settled herself comfortably, removing her white cotton gloves and putting them up with her purse on the shelf in front of the back window. The children's mother still had on slacks and still had her head tied up in a green kerchief, but the grandmother had on a navy blue straw sailor hat with a bunch of white violets on the brim and a navy blue dress with a small white dot in the print. Her collar and cuffs were white organdy trimmed with lace and at her neckline she had pinned a purple spray of cloth violets containing a sachet. In case of an accident, anyone seeing her dead on the highway would know at once that she was a lady.

She said she thought it was going to be a good day for driving, neither too hot nor too cold, and she cautioned Bailey that the speed limit was fifty-five miles an hour and that the patrolmen hid themselves behind billboards and small clumps of trees and sped out after you before you had a chance to slow down. She pointed out interesting details of the scenery: Stone Mountain; the blue granite that in some places came up to both sides of the highway; the brilliant red clay banks slightly streaked with purple; and the various crops

---

1. Named for Pitti-Sing, one of the "three little maids from school" in *The Mikado*, an 1885 operetta by Gilbert and Sullivan.

that made rows of green lace-work on the ground. The trees were full of silver-white sunlights and the meanest of them sparkled. The children were reading comic magazines and their mother had gone back to sleep.

"Let's go through Georgia fast so we won't have to look at it much," John Wesley said.

"If I were a little boy," said the grandmother, "I wouldn't talk about my native state that way. Tennessee has the mountains and Georgia has the hills."

"Tennessee is just a hillbilly dumping ground," John Wesley said, "and Georgia is a lousy state too."

"You said it," June Star said.

"In my time," said the grandmother, folding her thin veined fingers, "children were more respectful of their native states and their parents and everything else. People did right then. Oh look at the cute little pickaninny!" she said and pointed to a Negro child standing in the door of a shack. "Wouldn't that make a picture, now?" she asked and they all turned and looked at the little Negro out of the back window. He waved.

"He didn't have any britches on," June Star said.

"He probably didn't have any," the grandmother explained. "Little niggers in the country don't have things like we do. If I could paint, I'd paint that picture," she said.

The children exchanged comic books.

The grandmother offered to hold the baby and the children's mother passed him over the front seat to her. She set him on her knee and bounced him and told him about the things they were passing. She rolled her eyes and screwed up her mouth and stuck her leathery thin face into his smooth bland one. Occasionally he gave her a faraway smile. They passed a large cotton field with five or six graves fenced in the middle of it, like a small island. "Look at the graveyard!" the grandmother said, pointing it out. "That was the old family burying ground. That belonged to the plantation."

"Where's the plantation?" John Wesley asked.

"Gone with the Wind,"[2] said the grandmother. "Ha. Ha."

When the children finished all the comic books they had brought, they opened the lunch and ate it. The grandmother ate a peanut butter sandwich and an olive and would not let the children throw the box and the paper napkins out the window. When there was nothing else to do they played a game by choosing a cloud and making the other two guess what shape it suggested. John Wesley took one the shape of a cow and June Star guessed a cow and John Wesley said, no, an automobile, and June Star said he didn't play fair, and they began to slap each other over the grandmother.

The grandmother said she would tell them a story if they would keep quiet. When she told a story, she rolled her eyes and waved her head and was very dramatic. She said once when she was a maiden lady she had been courted by a Mr. Edgar Atkins Teagarden from Jasper, Georgia. She said he was a very good-looking man and a gentleman and that he brought her a watermelon every Saturday afternoon with his initials cut in it, E.A.T. Well, one Saturday,

---

**2.** Title of the best-selling 1936 novel by Margaret Mitchell (as well as an immensely popular 1939 movie); in Mitchell's story a large Southern plantation, Tara, is destroyed by Union troops during the Civil War.

she said, Mr. Teagarden brought the watermelon and there was nobody at home and he left it on the front porch and returned in his buggy to Jasper, but she never got the watermelon, she said, because a nigger boy ate it when he saw the initials, E.A.T.! This story tickled John Wesley's funny bone and he giggled and giggled but June Star didn't think it was any good. She said she wouldn't marry a man that just brought her a watermelon on Saturday. The grandmother said she would have done well to marry Mr. Teagarden because he was a gentleman and had bought Coca-Cola stock when it first came out and that he had died only a few years ago, a very wealthy man.

They stopped at The Tower for barbecued sandwiches. The Tower was a part-stucco and part-wood filling station and dance hall set in a clearing outside of Timothy. A fat man named Red Sammy Butts ran it and there were signs stuck here and there on the building and for miles up and down the highway saying, TRY RED SAMMY'S FAMOUS BARBECUE. NONE LIKE FAMOUS RED SAMMY'S! RED SAM! THE FAT BOY WITH THE HAPPY LAUGH. A VETERAN! RED SAMMY'S YOUR MAN!

Red Sammy was lying on the bare ground outside The Tower with his head under a truck while a gray monkey about a foot high, chained to a small chinaberry tree, chattered nearby. The monkey sprang back into the tree and got on the highest limb as soon as he saw the children jump out of the car and run toward him.

Inside, The Tower was a long dark room with a counter at one end and tables at the other and dancing space in the middle. They all sat down at a broad table next to the nickelodeon and Red Sam's wife, a tall burnt-brown woman with hair and eyes lighter than her skin, came and took their order. The children's mother put a dime in the machine and played "The Tennessee Waltz," and the grandmother said that tune always made her want to dance. She asked Bailey if he would like to dance but he only glared at her. He didn't have a naturally sunny disposition like she did and trips made him nervous. The grandmother's brown eyes were very bright. She swayed her head from side to side and pretended she was dancing in her chair. June Star said play something she could tap to so the children's mother put in another dime and played a fast number and June Star stepped out onto the dance floor and did her tap routine.

"Ain't she cute?" Red Sam's wife said, leaning over the counter. "Would you like to come be my little girl?"

"No, I certainly wouldn't," June Star said. "I wouldn't live in a broken-down place like this for a million bucks!" and she ran back to the table.

"Ain't she cute?" the woman repeated, stretching her mouth politely.

"Aren't you ashamed?" hissed the grandmother.

Red Sam came in and told his wife to quit lounging on the counter and hurry up with these people's order. His khaki trousers reached just to his hip bones and his stomach hung over them like a sack of meal swaying under his shirt. He came over and sat down at a table nearby and let out a combination sigh and yodel. "You can't win," he said. "You can't win," and he wiped his sweating red face off with a gray handkerchief. "These days you don't know who to trust," he said. "Ain't that the truth?"

"People are certainly not nice like they used to be," said the grandmother.

"Two fellers come in here last week," Red Sammy said, "driving a Chrysler. It was an old beat-up car but it was a good one and these boys looked all right to me. Said they worked at the mill and you know I let them fellers charge the gas they bought? Now why did I do that?"

"Because you're a good man!" the grandmother said at once.

"Yes'm, I suppose so," Red Sam said as if he were struck with this answer.

His wife brought the orders, carrying the five plates all at once without a tray, two in each hand and one balanced on her arm. "It isn't a soul in this green world of God's that you can trust," she said. "And I don't count nobody out of that, not nobody," she repeated, looking at Red Sammy.

"Did you read about that criminal, The Misfit, that's escaped?" asked the grandmother.

"I wouldn't be a bit surprised if he didn't attack this place right here," said the woman. "If he hears about it being here, I wouldn't be none surprised to see him. If he hears it's two cent in the cash register, I wouldn't be a tall surprised if he . . ."

"That'll do," Red Sam said. "Go bring these people their Co'-Colas," and the woman went off to get the rest of the order.

"A good man is hard to find," Red Sammy said. "Everything is getting terrible. I remember the day you could go off and leave your screen door unlatched. Not no more."

He and the grandmother discussed better times. The old lady said that in her opinion Europe was entirely to blame for the way things were now. She said the way Europe acted you would think we were made of money and Red Sam said it was no use talking about it, she was exactly right. The children ran outside into the white sunlight and looked at the monkey in the lacy chinaberry tree. He was busy catching fleas on himself and biting each one carefully between his teeth as if it were a delicacy.

They drove off again into the hot afternoon. The grandmother took cat naps and woke up every few minutes with her own snoring. Outside of Toombsboro she woke up and recalled an old plantation that she had visited in this neighborhood once when she was a young lady. She said the house had six white columns across the front and that there was an avenue of oaks leading up to it and two little wooden trellis arbors on either side in front where you sat down with your suitor after a stroll in the garden. She recalled exactly which road to turn off to get to it. She knew that Bailey would not be willing to lose any time looking at an old house, but the more she talked about it, the more she wanted to see it once again and find out if the little twin arbors were still standing. "There was a secret panel in this house," she said craftily, not telling the truth but wishing that she were, "and the story went that all the family silver was hidden in it when Sherman[3] came through but it was never found . . ."

"Hey!" John Wesley said. "Let's go see it! We'll find it! We'll poke all the woodwork and find it! Who lives there? Where do you turn off at? Hey Pop, can't we turn off there?"

"We never have seen a house with a secret panel!" June Star shrieked. "Let's go to the house with the secret panel! Hey, Pop, can't we go see the house with the secret panel!"

---

**3.** In November and December 1864 the Union general William Tecumseh Sherman marched his army through Georgia from Atlanta to the Atlantic coast, plundering and burning as they went.

"It's not far from here, I know," the grandmother said. "It wouldn't take over twenty minutes."

Bailey was looking straight ahead. His jaw was as rigid as a horseshoe. "No," he said.

The children began to yell and scream that they wanted to see the house with the secret panel. John Wesley kicked the back of the front seat and June Star hung over her mother's shoulder and whined desperately into her ear that they never had any fun even on their vacation, that they could never do what THEY wanted to do. The baby began to scream and John Wesley kicked the back of the seat so hard that his father could feel the blows in his kidney.

"All right!" he shouted and drew the car to a stop at the side of the road. "Will you all shut up? Will you all just shut up for one second? If you don't shut up, we won't go anywhere."

"It would be very educational for them," the grandmother murmured.

"All right," Bailey said, "but get this. This is the only time we're going to stop for anything like this. This is the one and only time."

"The dirt road that you have to turn down is about a mile back," the grandmother directed. "I marked it when we passed."

"A dirt road," Bailey groaned.

After they had turned around and were headed toward the dirt road, the grandmother recalled other points about the house, the beautiful glass over the front doorway and the candle lamp in the hall. John Wesley said that the secret panel was probably in the fireplace.

"You can't go inside this house," Bailey said. "You don't know who lives there."

"While you all talk to the people in front, I'll run around behind and get in a window," John Wesley suggested.

"We'll all stay in the car," his mother said.

They turned onto the dirt road and the car raced roughly along in a swirl of pink dust. The grandmother recalled the times when there were no paved roads and thirty miles was a day's journey. The dirt road was hilly and there were sudden washes in it and sharp curves on dangerous embankments. All at once they would be on a hill, looking down over the blue tops of trees for miles around, then the next minute, they would be in a red depression with the dust-coated trees looking down on them.

"This place had better turn up in a minute," Bailey said, "or I'm going to turn around."

The road looked as if no one had traveled on it in months.

"It's not much farther," the grandmother said and just as she said it, a horrible thought came to her. The thought was so embarrassing that she turned red in the face and her eyes dilated and her feet jumped up, upsetting her valise in the corner. The instant the valise moved, the newspaper top she had over the basket under it rose with a snarl and Pitty Sing, the cat, sprang onto Bailey's shoulder.

The children were thrown to the floor and their mother, clutching the baby, was thrown out the door onto the ground; the old lady was thrown into the front seat. The car turned over once and landed right-side-up in a gulch on the side of the road. Bailey remained in the driver's seat with the cat—gray-striped with a broad white face and an orange nose—clinging to his neck like a caterpillar.

As soon as the children saw they could move their arms and legs, they scrambled out of the car, shouting, "We've had an ACCIDENT!" The grandmother was curled up under the dashboard, hoping she was injured so that Bailey's wrath would not come down on her all at once. The horrible thought she had had before the accident was that the house she had remembered so vividly was not in Georgia but in Tennessee.

Bailey removed the cat from his neck with both hands and flung it out the window against the side of a pine tree. Then he got out of the car and started looking for the children's mother. She was sitting against the side of the red gutted ditch, holding the screaming baby, but she only had a cut down her face and a broken shoulder. "We've had an ACCIDENT!" the children screamed in a frenzy of delight.

"But nobody's killed," June Star said with disappointment as the grandmother limped out of the car, her hat still pinned to her head but the broken front brim standing up at a jaunty angle and the violet spray hanging off the side. They all sat down in the ditch, except the children, to recover from the shock. They were all shaking.

"Maybe a car will come along," said the children's mother hoarsely.

"I believe I have injured an organ," said the grandmother, pressing her side, but no one answered her. Bailey's teeth were clattering. He had on a yellow sport shirt with bright blue parrots designed in it and his face was as yellow as the shirt. The grandmother decided that she would not mention that the house was in Tennessee.

The road was about ten feet above and they could see only the tops of the trees on the other side of it. Behind the ditch they were sitting in there were more woods, tall and dark and deep. In a few minutes they saw a car some distance away on top of a hill, coming slowly as if the occupants were watching them. The grandmother stood up and waved both arms dramatically to attract their attention. The car continued to come on slowly, disappeared around a bend and appeared again, moving even slower, on top of the hill they had gone over. It was a big black battered hearselike automobile. There were three men in it.

It came to a stop over them and for some minutes, the driver looked down with a steady expressionless gaze to where they were sitting, and didn't speak. Then he turned his head and muttered something to the other two and they got out. One was a fat boy in black trousers and a red sweat shirt with a silver stallion embossed on the front of it. He moved around on the right side of them and stood staring, his mouth partly open in a kind of loose grin. The other had on khaki pants and a blue striped coat and a gray hat pulled down very low, hiding most of his face. He came around slowly on the left side. Neither spoke.

The driver got out of the car and stood by the side of it, looking down at them. He was an older man than the other two. His hair was just beginning to gray and he wore silver-rimmed spectacles that gave him a scholarly look. He had a long creased face and didn't have on any shirt or undershirt. He had on blue jeans that were too tight for him and was holding a black hat and a gun. The two boys also had guns.

"We've had an ACCIDENT!" the children screamed.

The grandmother had the peculiar feeling that the bespectacled man was someone she knew. His face was as familiar to her as if she had known him all her life but she could not recall who he was. He moved away from the car and began to come down the embankment, placing his feet carefully so that he wouldn't slip. He had on tan and white shoes and no socks, and his ankles were red and thin. "Good afternoon," he said. "I see you all had you a little spill."

"We turned over twice!" said the grandmother.

"Oncet," he corrected. "We seen it happen. Try their car and see will it run, Hiram," he said quietly to the boy with the gray hat.

"What you got that gun for?" John Wesley asked. "Whatcha gonna do with that gun?"

"Lady," the man said to the children's mother, "would you mind calling them children to sit down by you? Children make me nervous. I want all you all to sit down right together there where you're at."

"What are you telling us what to do for?" June Star asked.

Behind them the line of woods gaped like a dark open mouth. "Come here," said their mother.

"Look here now," Bailey began suddenly, "we're in a predicament! We're in . . ."

The grandmother shrieked. She scrambled to her feet and stood staring. "You're The Misfit!" she said. "I recognized you at once!"

"Yes'm," the man said, smiling slightly as if he were pleased in spite of himself to be known, "but it would have been better for all of you, lady, if you hadn't of reckernized me."

Bailey turned his head sharply and said something to his mother that shocked even the children. The old lady began to cry and The Misfit reddened.

"Lady," he said, "don't you get upset. Sometimes a man says things he don't mean. I don't reckon he meant to talk to you thataway."

"You wouldn't shoot a lady, would you?" the grandmother said and removed a clean handkerchief from her cuff and began to slap at her eyes with it.

The Misfit pointed the toe of his shoe into the ground and made a little hole and then covered it up again. "I would hate to have to," he said.

"Listen," the grandmother almost screamed, "I know you're a good man. You don't look a bit like you have common blood. I know you must come from nice people!"

"Yes mam," he said, "finest people in the world." When he smiled he showed a row of strong white teeth. "God never made a finer woman than my mother and my daddy's heart was pure gold," he said. The boy with the red sweat shirt had come around behind them and was standing with his gun at his hip. The Misfit squatted down on the ground. "Watch them children, Bobby Lee," he said. "You know they make me nervous." He looked at the six of them huddled together in front of him and he seemed to be embarrassed as if he couldn't think of anything to say. "Ain't a cloud in the sky," he remarked, looking up at it. "Don't see no sun but don't see no cloud neither."

"Yes, it's a beautiful day," said the grandmother. "Listen," she said, "you shouldn't call yourself The Misfit because I know you're a good man at heart. I can just look at you and tell."

"Hush!" Bailey yelled. "Hush! Everybody shut up and let me handle this!" He was squatting in the position of a runner about to spring forward but he didn't move.

"I pre-chate that, lady," The Misfit said and drew a little circle in the ground with the butt of his gun.

"It'll take a half a hour to fix this here car," Hiram called, looking over the raised hood of it.

"Well, first you and Bobby Lee get him and that little boy to step over yonder with you," The Misfit said, pointing to Bailey and John Wesley. "The boys want to ask you something," he said to Bailey. "Would you mind stepping back in them woods there with them?"

"Listen," Bailey began, "we're in a terrible predicament! Nobody realizes what this is," and his voice cracked. His eyes were as blue and intense as the parrots in his shirt and he remained perfectly still.

The grandmother reached up to adjust her hat brim as if she were going to the woods with him but it came off in her hand. She stood staring at it and after a second she let it fall on the ground. Hiram pulled Bailey up by the arm as if he were assisting an old man. John Wesley caught hold of his father's hand and Bobby Lee followed. They went off toward the woods and just as they reached the dark edge, Bailey turned and supporting himself against a gray naked pine trunk, he shouted, "I'll be back in a minute, Mamma, wait on me!"

"Come back this instant!" his mother shrilled but they all disappeared into the woods.

"Bailey Boy!" the grandmother called in a tragic voice but she found she was looking at The Misfit squatting on the ground in front of her. "I just know you're a good man," she said desperately. "You're not a bit common!"

"Nome, I ain't a good man," The Misfit said after a second as if he had considered her statement carefully, "but I ain't the worst in the world neither. My daddy said I was a different breed of dog from my brothers and sisters. 'You know,' Daddy said, 'it's some that can live their whole life out without asking about it and it's others has to know why it is, and this boy is one of the latters. He's going to be into everything!'" He put on his black hat and looked up suddenly and then away deep into the woods as if he were embarrassed again. "I'm sorry I don't have on a shirt before you ladies," he said, hunching his shoulders slightly. "We buried our clothes that we had on when we escaped and we're just making do until we can get better. We borrowed these from some folks we met," he explained.

"That's perfectly all right," the grandmother said. "Maybe Bailey has an extra shirt in his suitcase."

"I'll look and see terrectly," The Misfit said.

"Where are they taking him?" the children's mother screamed.

"Daddy was a card himself," The Misfit said. "You couldn't put anything over on him. He never got in trouble with the Authorities though. Just had the knack of handling them."

"You could be honest too if you'd only try," said the grandmother. "Think how wonderful it would be to settle down and live a comfortable life and not have to think about somebody chasing you all the time."

The Misfit kept scratching in the ground with the butt of his gun as if he were thinking about it. "Yes'm, somebody is always after you," he murmured.

The grandmother noticed how thin his shoulder blades were just behind his hat because she was standing up looking down on him. "Do you ever pray?" she asked.

He shook his head. All she saw was the black hat wiggle between his shoulder blades. "Nome," he said.

There was a pistol shot from the woods, followed closely by another. Then silence. The old lady's head jerked around. She could hear the wind move through the tree tops like a long satisfied insuck of breath. "Bailey Boy!" she called.

"I was a gospel singer for a while," The Misfit said. "I been most everything. Been in the arm service, both land and sea, at home and abroad, been twict married, been an undertaker, been with the railroads, plowed Mother Earth, been in a tornado, seen a man burnt alive oncet," and he looked up at the children's mother and the little girl who were sitting close together, their faces white and their eyes glassy; "I even seen a woman flogged," he said.

"Pray, pray," the grandmother began, "pray, pray . . ."

"I never was a bad boy that I remember of," The Misfit said in an almost dreamy voice, "but somewheres along the line I done something wrong and got sent to the penitentiary. I was buried alive," and he looked up and held her attention to him by a steady stare.

"That's when you should have started to pray," she said. "What did you do to get sent to the penitentiary that first time?"

"Turn to the right, it was a wall," The Misfit said, looking up again at the cloudless sky. "Turn to the left, it was a wall. Look up it was a ceiling, look down it was a floor. I forget what I done, lady. I set there and set there, trying to remember what it was I done and I ain't recalled it to this day. Oncet in a while, I would think it was coming to me, but it never come."

"Maybe they put you in by mistake," the old lady said vaguely.

"Nome," he said. "It wasn't no mistake. They had the papers on me."

"You must have stolen something," she said.

The Misfit sneered slightly. "Nobody had nothing I wanted," he said. "It was a head-doctor at the penitentiary said what I had done was kill my daddy but I known that for a lie. My daddy died in nineteen ought nineteen of the epidemic flu[4] and I never had a thing to do with it. He was buried in the Mount Hopewell Baptist churchyard and you can go there and see for yourself."

"If you would pray," the old lady said, "Jesus would help you."

"That's right," The Misfit said.

"Well then, why don't you pray?" she asked trembling with delight suddenly.

"I don't want no hep," he said. "I'm doing all right by myself."

Bobby Lee and Hiram came ambling back from the woods. Bobby Lee was dragging a yellow shirt with bright blue parrots in it.

"Throw me that shirt, Bobby Lee," The Misfit said. The shirt came flying at him and landed on his shoulder and he put it on. The grandmother couldn't name what the shirt reminded her of. "No, lady," The Misfit said while he was buttoning up, "I found out the crime don't matter. You can do one thing or you can do another, kill a man or take a tire off his car, because sooner or later you're going to forget what it was you done and just be punished for it."

The children's mother had begun to make heaving noises as if she couldn't get her breath. "Lady," he asked, "would you and that little girl like to step off yonder with Bobby Lee and Hiram and join your husband?"

"Yes, thank you," the mother said faintly. Her left arm dangled helplessly and she was holding the baby, who had gone to sleep, in the other. "Hep that

---

4. A devastating, worldwide epidemic of influenza in 1918–19 followed the end of World War I.

lady up, Hiram," The Misfit said as she struggled to climb out of the ditch, "and Bobby Lee, you hold onto that little girl's hand."

"I don't want to hold hands with him," June Star said. "He reminds me of a pig."

The fat boy blushed and laughed and caught her by the arm and pulled her off into the woods after Hiram and her mother.

Alone with The Misfit, the grandmother found that she had lost her voice. There was not a cloud in the sky nor any sun. There was nothing around her but woods. She wanted to tell him that he must pray. She opened and closed her mouth several times before anything came out. Finally she found herself saying, "Jesus, Jesus," meaning, Jesus will help you, but the way she was saying it, it sounded as if she might be cursing.

"Yes'm," The Misfit said as if he agreed. "Jesus thrown everything off balance. It was the same case with Him as with me except He hadn't committed any crime and they could prove I had committed one because they had the papers on me. Of course," he said, "they never shown me my papers. That's why I sign myself now. I said long ago, you get you a signature and sign everything you do and keep a copy of it. Then you'll know what you done and you can hold up the crime to the punishment and see do they match and in the end you'll have something to prove you ain't been treated right. I call myself The Misfit," he said, "because I can't make what all I done wrong fit what all I gone through in punishment."

There was a piercing scream from the woods, followed closely by a pistol report. "Does it seem right to you, lady, that one is punished a heap and another ain't punished at all?"

"Jesus!" the old lady cried. "You've got good blood! I know you wouldn't shoot a lady! I know you come from nice people! Pray! Jesus, you ought not to shoot a lady. I'll give you all the money I've got!"

"Lady," The Misfit said, looking beyond her far into the woods, "there never was a body that give the undertaker a tip."

There were two more pistol reports and the grandmother raised her head like a parched old turkey hen crying for water and called, "Bailey Boy, Bailey Boy!" as if her heart would break.

"Jesus was the only One that ever raised the dead," The Misfit continued, "and He shouldn't have done it. He thown everything off balance. If He did what He said, then it's nothing for you to do but thow away everything and follow Him, and if He didn't then it's nothing for you to do but enjoy the few minutes you got left the best way you can—by killing somebody or burning down his house or doing some other meanness to him. No pleasure but meanness," he said and his voice had become almost a snarl.

"Maybe He didn't raise the dead," the old lady mumbled, not knowing what she was saying and feeling so dizzy that she sank down in the ditch with her legs twisted under her.

"I wasn't there so I can't say He didn't," The Misfit said. "I wisht I had of been there," he said, hitting the ground with his fist. "It ain't right I wasn't there because if I had of been there I would of known. Listen lady," he said in a high voice, "if I had of been there I would of known and I wouldn't be like I am now." His voice seemed about to crack and the grandmother's head cleared for an instant. She saw the man's face twisted close to her own as if he were going to cry and she murmured, "Why, you're one of my babies. You're one of my own children!" She reached out and touched him on the shoulder. The Misfit sprang back as if a snake had bitten him and shot her three times through the chest. Then he put his gun down on the ground and took off his glasses and began to clean them.

Hiram and Bobby Lee returned from the woods and stood over the ditch, looking down at the grandmother who half sat and half lay in a puddle of blood with her legs crossed under her like a child's and her face smiling up at the cloudless sky.

Without his glasses, The Misfit's eyes were red-rimmed and pale and defenseless-looking. "Take her off and thow her where you thown the others," he said, picking up the cat that was rubbing itself against his leg.

"She was a talker, wasn't she?" Bobby Lee said, sliding down the ditch with a yodel.

"She would of been a good woman," The Misfit said, "if it had been somebody there to shoot her every minute of her life."

"Some fun!" Bobby Lee said.

"Shut up, Bobby Lee," The Misfit said. "It's no real pleasure in life."

1953

# Good Country People

Besides the neutral expression that she wore when she was alone, Mrs. Freeman had two others, forward and reverse, that she used for all her human dealings. Her forward expression was steady and driving like the advance of a heavy truck. Her eyes never swerved to left or right but turned as the story turned as if they followed a yellow line down the center of it. She seldom used the other expression because it was not often necessary for her to retract a statement, but when she did, her face came to a complete stop, there was an almost imperceptible movement of her black eyes, during which they seemed to be receding, and then the observer would see that Mrs. Freeman, though she might stand there as real as several grain sacks thrown on top of each other, was no longer there in spirit. As for getting anything across to her when this was the case, Mrs. Hopewell had given it up. She might talk her head off. Mrs. Freeman could never be brought to admit herself wrong on any point. She would stand there and if she could be brought to say anything, it was something like, "Well, I wouldn't of said it was and I wouldn't of said it wasn't," or letting her gaze range over the top kitchen shelf where there was an assortment of dusty bottles, she might remark, "I see you ain't ate many of them figs you put up last summer."

They carried on their most important business in the kitchen at breakfast. Every morning Mrs. Hopewell got up at seven o'clock and lit her gas heater and Joy's. Joy was her daughter, a large blonde girl who had an artificial leg. Mrs. Hopewell thought of her as a child though she was thirty-two years old and highly educated. Joy would get up while her mother was eating and lumber into the bathroom and slam the door, and before long, Mrs. Freeman would arrive at the back door. Joy would hear her mother call, "Come on in," and then they would talk for a while in low voices that were indistinguishable in the bathroom. By the time Joy came in, they had usually finished the weather report and were on one or the other of Mrs. Freeman's daughters, Glynese or Carramae, Joy called them Glycerin and Caramel. Glynese, a redhead, was eighteen and had many admirers; Carramae, a blonde, was only fifteen but already married and pregnant. She could not keep anything on her stomach. Every morning Mrs. Freeman told Mrs. Hopewell how many times she had vomited since the last report.

Mrs. Hopewell liked to tell people that Glynese and Carramae were two of the finest girls she knew and that Mrs. Freeman was a *lady* and that she was never ashamed to take her anywhere or introduce her to anybody they might meet. Then she would tell how she had happened to hire the Freemans in the first place and how they were a godsend to her and how she had had them four years. The reason for her keeping them so long was that they were not trash. They were good country people. She had telephoned the man whose name they had given as a reference and he had told her that Mr. Freeman was a good farmer but that his wife was the nosiest woman ever to walk the earth. "She's got to be into everything," the man said. "If she don't get there before the dust settles, you can bet she's dead, that's all. She'll want to know all your business. I can stand him real good," he had said, "but me nor my wife neither could have stood that woman one more minute on this place." That had put Mrs. Hopewell off for a few days.

She had hired them in the end because there were no other applicants but she had made up her mind beforehand exactly how she would handle the woman. Since she was the type who had to be into everything, then, Mrs. Hopewell had decided, she would not only let her be into everything, she would *see to it* that she was into everything—she would give her the responsibility of everything, she would put her in charge. Mrs. Hopewell had no bad qualities of her own but she was able to use other people's in such a constructive way that she never felt the lack. She had hired the Freemans and she had kept them four years.

Nothing is perfect. This was one of Mrs. Hopewell's favorite sayings. Another was: that is life! And still another, the most important, was: well, other people have their opinions too. She would make these statements, usually at the table, in a tone of gentle insistence as if no one held them but her, and the large hulking Joy, whose constant outrage had obliterated every expression from her face, would stare just a little to the side of her, her eyes icy blue, with the look of someone who has achieved blindness by an act of will and means to keep it.

When Mrs. Hopewell said to Mrs. Freeman that life was like that, Mrs. Freeman would say, "I always said so myself." Nothing had been arrived at by anyone that had not first been arrived at by her. She was quicker than Mr. Freeman. When Mrs. Hopewell said to her after they had been on the place a while, "You know, you're the wheel behind the wheel," and winked, Mrs. Freeman had said, "I know it. I've always been quick. It's some that are quicker than others."

"Everybody is different," Mrs. Hopewell said.

"Yes, most people is," Mrs. Freeman said.

"It takes all kinds to make the world."

"I always said it did myself."

The girl was used to this kind of dialogue for breakfast and more of it for dinner; sometimes they had it for supper too. When they had no guest they ate in the kitchen because that was easier. Mrs. Freeman always managed to arrive at some point during the meal and to watch them finish it. She would stand in the doorway if it were summer but in the winter she would stand with one elbow on top of the refrigerator and look down on them, or she would stand by the gas heater, lifting the back of her skirt slightly. Occasionally she would stand against the wall and roll her head from side to side. At no time was she in any hurry to leave. All this was very trying on Mrs. Hopewell but she was a woman of great patience. She realized that nothing is perfect and that in the Freemans she had good country people and that if, in this day and age, you get good country people, you had better hang onto them.

She had had plenty of experience with trash. Before the Freemans she had averaged one tenant family a year. The wives of these farmers were not the kind you would want to be around you for very long. Mrs. Hopewell, who had divorced her husband long ago, needed someone to walk over the fields with her; and when Joy had to be impressed for these services, her remarks were usually so ugly and her face so glum that Mrs. Hopewell would say, "If you can't come pleasantly, I don't want you at all," to which the girl, standing square and rigid-shouldered with her neck thrust slightly forward, would reply, "If you want me, here I am—LIKE I AM."

Mrs. Hopewell excused this attitude because of the leg (which had been shot off in a hunting accident when Joy was ten). It was hard for Mrs. Hopewell to realize that her child was thirty-two now and that for more than twenty years she had had only one leg. She thought of her still as a child because it tore her heart to think instead of the poor stout girl in her thirties who had never danced a step or had any *normal* good times. Her name was really Joy but as soon as she was twenty-one and away from home, she had had it legally changed. Mrs. Hopewell was certain that she had thought and thought until she had hit upon the ugliest name in any language. Then she had gone and had the beautiful name, Joy, changed without telling her mother until after she had done it. Her legal name was Hulga.

When Mrs. Hopewell thought the name, Hulga, she thought of the broad blank hull of a battleship. She would not use it. She continued to call her Joy to which the girl responded but in a purely mechanical way.

Hulga had learned to tolerate Mrs. Freeman who saved her from taking walks with her mother. Even Glynese and Carramae were useful when they occupied attention that might otherwise have been directed at her. At first she had thought she could not stand Mrs. Freeman for she had found that it was not possible to be rude to her. Mrs. Freeman would take on strange resentments and for days together she would be sullen but the source of her displeasure was always obscure; a direct attack, a positive leer, blatant ugliness to her face—these never touched her. And without warning one day, she began calling her Hulga.

She did not call her that in front of Mrs. Hopewell who would have been incensed but when she and the girl happened to be out of the house together, she would say something and add the name Hulga to the end of it, and the big spectacled Joy-Hulga would scowl and redden as if her privacy had been intruded upon. She considered the name her personal affair. She had arrived at it first purely on the basis of its ugly sound and then the full genius of its fitness had struck her. She had a vision of the name working like the ugly sweating Vulcan[1] who stayed in the furnace and to whom, presumably, the goddess had to come when called. She saw it as the name of her highest creative act. One of her major triumphs was that her mother had not been able to turn her dust into Joy, but the greater one was that she had been able to turn it herself into Hulga. However, Mrs. Freeman's relish for using the name only irritated her. It was as if Mrs. Freeman's beady steel-pointed eyes had penetrated far enough behind her face to reach some secret fact. Something about her seemed to fascinate Mrs. Freeman and then one day Hulga realized that it was the artificial leg. Mrs. Freeman had a special fondness for the details of secret infections, hidden deformities, assaults upon children. Of diseases, she preferred the lingering or incurable. Hulga had heard Mrs. Hopewell give her the details of the hunting accident, how the leg had been literally blasted off, how she had never lost consciousness. Mrs. Freeman could listen to it anytime as if it had happened an hour ago.

When Hulga stumped into the kitchen in the morning (she could walk without making the awful noise but she made it—Mrs. Hopewell was certain—because it was ugly-sounding), she glanced at them and did not speak. Mrs. Hopewell would be in her red kimono with her hair tied around her head in rags. She would be sitting at the table, finishing her breakfast and Mrs. Freeman would be hanging by her elbow outward from the refrigerator, looking down at the table. Hulga always put her eggs on the stove to boil and then stood over them with her arms folded, and Mrs. Hopewell would look at her—a kind of indirect gaze divided between her and Mrs. Freeman—and would think that if she would only keep herself up a little, she wouldn't be so bad looking. There was nothing wrong with her face that a pleasant expression wouldn't help. Mrs. Hopewell said that people who looked on the bright side of things would be beautiful even if they were not.

Whenever she looked at Joy this way, she could not help but feel that it would have been better if the child had not taken the Ph.D. It had certainly not brought her out any and now that she had it, there was no more excuse for her to go to school again. Mrs. Hopewell thought it was nice for girls to go to school to have a good time but Joy had "gone through." Anyhow, she would not have been strong enough to go again. The doctors had told Mrs. Hopewell that with the best of care, Joy might see forty-five. She had a weak heart. Joy had made it plain that if it had not been for this condition, she would be far from these red hills and good country people. She would be in a university lecturing to people who knew what she was talking about. And Mrs. Hopewell could very well picture her there, looking like a scarecrow and lecturing to more of the same. Here she went about all day in a six-year-old skirt and a yellow sweat shirt with a faded cowboy on a horse embossed on it. She thought this was funny; Mrs. Hopewell thought it was idiotic and showed simply that she was still a child. She was brilliant but she didn't have a grain of sense. It

1. Roman god of fire and the forge; husband of Venus, goddess of love.

seemed to Mrs. Hopewell that every year she grew less like other people and more like herself—bloated, rude, and squint-eyed. And she said such strange things! To her own mother she had said—without warning, without excuse, standing up in the middle of a meal with her face purple and her mouth half full—"Woman! do you ever look inside? Do you ever look inside and see what you are *not*? God!" she had cried sinking down again and staring at her plate, "Malebranche was right: we are not our own light. We are not our own light!" Mrs. Hopewell had no idea to this day what brought that on. She had only made the remark, hoping Joy would take it in, that a smile never hurt anyone.

The girl had taken the Ph.D. in philosophy and this left Mrs. Hopewell at a complete loss. You could say, "My daughter is a nurse," or "My daughter is a schoolteacher," or even, "My daughter is a chemical engineer." You could not say, "My daughter is a philosopher." That was something that had ended with the Greeks and Romans. All day Joy sat on her neck in a deep chair, reading. Sometimes she went for walks but she didn't like dogs or cats or birds or flowers or nature or nice young men. She looked at nice young men as if she could smell their stupidity.

One day Mrs. Hopewell had picked up one of the books the girl had just put down and opening it at random, she read, "Science, on the other hand, has to assert its soberness and seriousness afresh and declare that it is concerned solely with what-is. Nothing—how can it be for science anything but a horror and a phantasm? If science is right, then one thing stands firm: science wishes to know nothing of nothing. Such is after all the strictly scientific approach to Nothing. We know it by wishing to know nothing of Nothing." These words had been underlined with a blue pencil and they worked on Mrs. Hopewell like some evil incantation in gibberish. She shut the book quickly and went out of the room as if she were having a chill.

This morning when the girl came in, Mrs. Freeman was on Carramae. "She thrown up four times after supper," she said, "and was up twict in the night after three o'clock. Yesterday she didn't do nothing but ramble in the bureau drawer. All she did. Stand up there and see what she could run up on."

"She's got to eat," Mrs. Hopewell muttered, sipping her coffee, while she watched Joy's back at the stove. She was wondering what the child had said to the Bible salesman. She could not imagine what kind of a conversation she could possibly have had with him.

He was a tall gaunt hatless youth who had called yesterday to sell them a Bible. He had appeared at the door, carrying a large black suitcase that weighted him so heavily on one side that he had to brace himself against the door facing. He seemed on the point of collapse but he said in a cheerful voice. "Good morning, Mrs. Cedars!" and set the suitcase down on the mat. He was not a bad-looking young man though he had on a bright blue suit and yellow socks that were not pulled up far enough. He had prominent face bones and a streak of sticky-looking brown hair falling across his forehead.

"I'm Mrs. Hopewell," she said.

"Oh!" he said, pretending to look puzzled but with his eyes sparkling, "I saw it said 'The Cedars' on the mailbox so I thought you was Mrs. Cedars!" and he burst out in a pleasant laugh. He picked up the satchel and under cover of a pant, he fell forward into her hall. It was rather as if the suitcase had moved first, jerking him after it. "Mrs. Hopewell!" he said and grabbed her hand. "I hope you are well!" and he laughed again and then all at once his face sobered completely. He paused and gave her a straight earnest look and said, "Lady, I've come to speak of serious things."

"Well, come in," she muttered, none too pleased because her dinner was almost ready. He came into the parlor and sat down on the edge of a straight chair and put the suitcase between his feet and glanced around the room as if he were sizing her up by it. Her silver gleamed on the two sideboards; she decided he had never been in a room as elegant as this.

"Mrs. Hopewell," he began, using her name in a way that sounded almost intimate, "I know you believe in Chrustian service."

"Well yes," she murmured.

"I know," he said and paused, looking very wise with his head cocked on one side, "that you're a good woman. Friends have told me."

Mrs. Hopewell never liked to be taken for a fool. "What are you selling?" she asked.

"Bibles," the young man said and his eye raced around the room before he added, "I see you have no family Bible in your parlor, I see that is the one lack you got!"

Mrs. Hopewell could not say, "My daughter is an atheist and won't let me keep the Bible in the parlor." She said, stiffening slightly, "I keep my Bible by my bedside." This was not the truth. It was in the attic somewhere.

"Lady," he said, "the word of God ought to be in the parlor."

"Well, I think that's a matter of taste," she began. "I think . . ."

"Lady," he said, "for a Chrustian, the word of God ought to be in every room in the house besides in his heart. I know you're a Chrustian because I can see it in every line of your face."

She stood up and said, "Well, young man, I don't want to buy a Bible and I smell my dinner burning."

He didn't get up. He began to twist his hands and looking down at them, he said softly, "Well lady, I'll tell you the truth—not many people want to buy one nowadays and besides, I know I'm real simple. I don't know how to say a thing but to say it. I'm just a country boy." He glanced up into her unfriendly face. "People like you don't like to fool with country people like me!"

"Why!" she cried, "good country people are the salt of the earth! Besides, we all have different ways of doing, it takes all kinds to make the world go 'round. That's life!"

"You said a mouthful," he said.

"Why, I think there aren't enough good country people in the world!" she said, stirred. "I think that's what's wrong with it!"

His face had brightened. "I didn't inraduce myself," he said. "I'm Manley Pointer from out in the country around Willohobie, not even from a place, just from near a place."

"You wait a minute," she said. "I have to see about my dinner." She went out to the kitchen and found Joy standing near the door where she had been listening.

"Get rid of the salt of the earth," she said, "and let's eat."

Mrs. Hopewell gave her a pained look and turned the heat down under the vegetables. "I can't be rude to anybody," she murmured and went back into the parlor.

He had opened the suitcase and was sitting with a Bible on each knee. "You might as well put those up," she told him. "I don't want one."

"I appreciate your honesty," he said. "You don't see any more real honest people unless you go away out in the country."

"I know," she said, "real genuine folks!" Through the crack in the door she heard a groan.

"I guess a lot of boys come telling you they're working their way through college," he said, "but I'm not going to tell you that. Somehow," he said, "I don't want to go to college. I want to devote my life to Christian service. See," he said, lowering his voice, "I got this heart condition. I may not live long. When you know it's something wrong with you and you may not live long, well then, lady . . ." He paused, with his mouth open, and stared at her.

He and Joy had the same condition! She knew that her eyes were filling with tears but she collected herself quickly and murmured, "Won't you stay for dinner? We'd love to have you!" and was sorry the instant she heard herself say it.

"Yes mam," he said in an abashed voice, "I would sher love to do that!"

Joy had given him one look on being introduced to him and then throughout the meal had not glanced at him again. He had addressed several remarks to her, which she had pretended not to hear. Mrs. Hopewell could not understand deliberate rudeness, although she lived with it, and she felt she had always to overflow with hospitality to make up for Joy's lack of courtesy. She urged him to talk about himself and he did. He said he was the seventh child of twelve and that his father had been crushed under a tree when he himself was eight year old. He had been crushed very badly, in fact, almost cut in two and was practically not recognizable. His mother had got along the best she could by hard working and she had always seen that her children went to Sunday School and that they read the Bible every evening. He was now nineteen year old and he had been selling Bibles for four months. In that time he had sold seventy-seven Bibles and had the promise of two more sales. He wanted to become a missionary because he thought that was the way you could do most for people. "He who losest his life shall find it," he said simply and he was so sincere, so genuine and earnest that Mrs. Hopewell would not for the world have smiled. He prevented his peas from sliding onto the table by blocking them with a piece of bread which he later cleaned his plate with. She could see Joy observing sidewise how he handled his knife and fork and she saw too that every few minutes, the boy would dart a keen appraising glance at the girl as if he were trying to attract her attention.

After dinner Joy cleared the dishes off the table and disappeared and Mrs. Hopewell was left to talk with him. He told her again about his childhood and his father's accident and about various things that had happened to him. Every five minutes or so she would stifle a yawn. He sat for two hours until finally she told him she must go because she had an appointment in town. He packed his Bibles and thanked her and prepared to leave, but in the doorway he stopped and wrung her hand and said that not on any of his trips had he met a lady as nice as her and he asked if he could come again. She had said she would always be happy to see him.

Joy had been standing in the road, apparently looking at something in the distance, when he came down the steps toward her, bent to the side with his heavy valise. He stopped where she was standing and confronted her directly. Mrs. Hopewell could not hear what he said but she trembled to think what Joy would say to him. She could see that after a minute Joy said something and that then the boy began to speak again, making an excited gesture with his free hand. After a minute Joy said something else at which the boy began to speak once more. Then to her amazement, Mrs. Hopewell saw the two of them walk off together, toward the gate. Joy had walked all the way to the gate with him and Mrs. Hopewell could not imagine what they had said to each other, and she had not yet dared to ask.

Mrs. Freeman was insisting upon her attention. She had moved from the refrigerator to the heater so that Mrs. Hopewell had to turn and face her in order to seem to be listening. "Glynese gone out with Harvey Hill again last night," she said. "She had this sty."

"Hill," Mrs. Hopewell said absently, "is that the one who works in the garage?"

"Nome, he's the one that goes to chiropracter school," Mrs. Freeman said. "She had this sty. Been had it two days. So she says when he brought her in the other night he says, 'Lemme get rid of that sty for you,' and she says, 'How?' and he says, 'You just lay yourself down acrost the seat of that car and I'll show you.' So she done it and he popped her neck. Kept on a-popping it several times until she made him quit. This morning," Mrs. Freeman said, "she ain't got no sty. She ain't got no traces of a sty."

"I never heard of that before," Mrs. Hopewell said.

"He ast her to marry him before the Ordinary,"[2] Mrs. Freeman went on, "and she told him she wasn't going to be married in no *office*."

"Well, Glynese is a fine girl," Mrs. Hopewell said. "Glynese and Carramae are both fine girls."

"Carramae said when her and Lyman was married Lyman said it sure felt sacred to him. She said he said he wouldn't take five hundred dollars for being married by a preacher."

"How much would he take?" the girl asked from the stove.

"He said he wouldn't take five hundred dollars," Mrs. Freeman repeated.

"Well we all have work to do," Mrs. Hopewell said.

"Lyman said it just felt more sacred to him," Mrs. Freeman said. "The doctor wants Carramae to eat prunes. Says instead of medicine. Says them cramps is coming from pressure. You know where I think it is?"

"She'll be better in a few weeks," Mrs. Hopewell said.

"In the tube," Mrs. Freeman said. "Else she wouldn't be as sick as she is."

Hulga had cracked her two eggs into a saucer and was bringing them to the table along with a cup of coffee that she had filled too full. She sat down carefully and began to eat, meaning to keep Mrs. Freeman there by questions if for any reason she showed an inclination to leave. She could perceive her mother's eye on her. The first round-about question would be about the Bible salesman and she did not wish to bring it on. "How did he pop her neck?" she asked.

Mrs. Freeman went into a description of how he had popped her neck. She said he owned a '55 Mercury but that Glynese said she would rather marry a man with only a '36 Plymouth who would be married by a preacher. The girl

2. Local clergyman.

asked what if he had a '32 Plymouth and Mrs. Freeman said what Glynese had said was a '36 Plymouth.

Mrs. Hopewell said there were not many girls with Glynese's common sense. She said what she admired in those girls was their common sense. She said that reminded her that they had had a nice visitor yesterday, a young man selling Bibles. "Lord," she said, "he bored me to death but he was so sincere and genuine I couldn't be rude to him. He was just good country people, you know," she said, "—just the salt of the earth."

"I seen him walk up," Mrs. Freeman said, "and then later—I seen him walk off," and Hulga could feel the slight shift in her voice, the slight insinuation, that he had not walked off alone, had he? Her face remained expressionless but the color rose into her neck and she seemed to swallow it down with the next spoonful of egg. Mrs. Freeman was looking at her as if they had a secret together.

"Well, it takes all kinds of people to make the world go 'round," Mrs. Hopewell said. "It's very good we aren't all alike."

"Some people are more alike than others," Mrs. Freeman said.

Hulga got up and stumped, with about twice the noise that was necessary, into her room and locked the door. She was to meet the Bible salesman at ten o'clock at the gate. She had thought about it half the night. She had started thinking of it as a great joke and then she had begun to see profound implications in it. She had lain in bed imagining dialogues for them that were insane on the surface but that reached below to depths that no Bible salesman would be aware of. Their conversation yesterday had been of this kind.

He had stopped in front of her and had simply stood there. His face was bony and sweaty and bright, with a little pointed nose in the center of it, and his look was different from what it had been at the dinner table. He was gazing at her with open curiosity, with fascination, like a child watching a new fantastic animal at the zoo, and he was breathing as if he had run a great distance to reach her. His gaze seemed somehow familiar but she could not think where she had been regarded with it before. For almost a minute he didn't say anything. Then on what seemed an insuck of breath, he whispered, "You ever ate a chicken that was two days old?"

The girl looked at him stonily. He might have just put this question up for consideration at the meeting of a philosophical association. "Yes," she presently replied as if she had considered it from all angles.

"It must have been mighty small!" he said triumphantly and shook all over with little nervous giggles, getting very red in the face, and subsiding finally into his gaze of complete admiration, while the girl's expression remained exactly the same.

"How old are you?" he asked softly.

She waited some time before she answered. Then in a flat voice she said, "Seventeen."

His smiles came in succession like waves breaking on the surface of a little lake. "I see you got a wooden leg," he said. "I think you're brave. I think you're real sweet."

The girl stood blank and solid and silent.

"Walk to the gate with me," he said. "You're a brave sweet little thing and I liked you the minute I seen you walk in the door."

Hulga began to move forward.

"What's your name?" he asked, smiling down on the top of her head.

"Hulga," she said.

"Hulga," he murmured, "Hulga. Hulga. I never heard of anybody name Hulga before. You're shy, aren't you, Hulga?" he asked.

She nodded, watching his large red hand on the handle of the giant valise.

"I like girls that wear glasses," he said. "I think a lot. I'm not like these people that a serious thought don't ever enter their heads. It's because I may die."

"I may die too," she said suddenly and looked up at him. His eyes were very small and brown, glittering feverishly.

"Listen," he said, "don't you think some people was meant to meet on account of what all they got in common and all? Like they both think serious thoughts and all?" He shifted the valise to his other hand so that the hand nearest her was free. He caught hold of her elbow and shook it a little. "I don't work on Saturday," he said. "I like to walk in the woods and see what Mother Nature is wearing. O'er the hills and far away. Pic-nics and things. Couldn't we go on a pic-nic tomorrow? Say yes, Hulga," he said and gave her a dying look as if he felt his insides about to drop out of him. He had even seemed to sway slightly toward her.

During the night she had imagined that she seduced him. She imagined that the two of them walked on the place until they came to the storage barn beyond the two back fields and there, she imagined, that things came to such a pass that she very easily seduced him and that then, of course, she had to reckon with his remorse. True genius can get an idea across even to an inferior mind. She imagined that she took his remorse in hand and changed it into a deeper understanding of life. She took all his shame away and turned it into something useful.

She set off for the gate at exactly ten o'clock, escaping without drawing Mrs. Hopewell's attention. She didn't take anything to eat, forgetting that food is usually taken on a picnic. She wore a pair of slacks and a dirty white shirt, and as an afterthought, she had put some Vapex on the collar of it since she did not own any perfume. When she reached the gate no one was there.

She looked up and down the empty highway and had the furious feeling that she had been tricked, that he had only meant to make her walk to the gate after the idea of him. Then suddenly he stood up, very tall, from behind a bush on the opposite embankment. Smiling, he lifted his hat which was new and wide-brimmed. He had not worn it yesterday and she wondered if he had bought it for the occasion. It was toast-colored with a red and white band around it and was slightly too large for him. He stepped from behind the bush still carrying the black valise. He had on the same suit and the same yellow socks sucked down in his shoes from walking. He crossed the highway and said, "I knew you'd come!"

The girl wondered acidly how he had known this. She pointed to the valise and asked, "Why did you bring your Bibles?"

He took her elbow, smiling down on her as if he could not stop. "You can never tell when you'll need the word of God, Hulga," he said. She had a moment in which she doubted that this was actually happening and then they began to climb the embankment. They went down into the pasture toward the woods.

The boy walked lightly by her side, bouncing on his toes. The valise did not seem to be heavy today; he even swung it. They crossed half the pasture without saying anything and then, putting his hand easily on the small of her back, he asked softly, "Where does your wooden leg join on?"

She turned an ugly red and glared at him and for an instant the boy looked abashed. "I didn't mean you no harm," he said. "I only meant you're so brave and all. I guess God takes care of you."

"No," she said, looking forward and walking fast, "I don't even believe in God."

At this he stopped and whistled. "No!" he exclaimed as if he were too astonished to say anything else.

She walked on and in a second he was bouncing at her side, fanning with his hat. "That's very unusual for a girl," he remarked, watching her out of the corner of his eye. When they reached the edge of the wood, he put his hand on her back again and drew her against him without a word and kissed her heavily.

The kiss, which had more pressure than feeling behind it, produced that extra surge of adrenalin in the girl that enables one to carry a packed trunk out of a burning house, but in her, the power went at once to the brain. Even before he released her, her mind, clear and detached and ironic anyway, was regarding him from a great distance, with amusement but with pity. She had never been kissed before and she was pleased to discover that it was an unexceptional experience and all a matter of the mind's control. Some people might enjoy drain water if they were told it was vodka. When the boy, looking expectant but uncertain, pushed her gently away, she turned and walked on, saying nothing as if such business, for her, were common enough.

He came along panting at her side, trying to help her when he saw a root that she might trip over. He caught and held back the long swaying blades of thorn vine until she had passed beyond them. She led the way and he came breathing heavily behind her. Then they came out on a sunlit hillside, sloping softly into another one a little smaller. Beyond, they could see the rusted top of the old barn where the extra hay was stored.

The hill was sprinkled with small pink weeds. "Then you ain't saved?" he asked suddenly, stopping.

The girl smiled. It was the first time she had smiled at him at all. "In my economy," she said, "I'm saved and you are damned but I told you I didn't believe in God."

Nothing seemed to destroy the boy's look of admiration. He gazed at her now as if the fantastic animal at the zoo had put its paw through the bars and given him a loving poke. She thought he looked as if he wanted to kiss her again and she walked on before he had the chance.

"Ain't there somewheres we can sit down sometime?" he murmured, his voice softening toward the end of the sentence.

"In that barn," she said.

They made for it rapidly as if it might slide away like a train. It was a large two-story barn, cool and dark inside. The boy pointed up the ladder that led into the loft and said, "It's too bad we can't go up there."

"Why can't we?" she asked.

"Yer leg," he said reverently.

The girl gave him a contemptuous look and putting both hands on the ladder, she climbed it while he stood below, apparently awestruck. She pulled herself expertly through the opening and then looked down at him and said, "Well, come on if you're coming," and he began to climb the ladder, awkwardly bringing the suitcase with him.

"We won't need the Bible," she observed.

"You never can tell," he said, panting. After he had got into the loft, he was a few seconds catching his breath. She had sat down in a pile of straw. A wide sheath of sunlight, filled with dust particles, slanted over her. She lay back against a bale, her face turned away, looking out the front opening of the barn where hay was thrown from a wagon into the loft. The two pink-speckled hillsides lay back against a dark ridge of woods. The sky was cloudless and cold blue. The boy dropped down by her side and put one arm under her and the other over her and began methodically kissing her face, making little noises like a fish. He did not remove his hat but it was pushed far enough back not to interfere. When her glasses got in his way, he took them off of her and slipped them into his pocket.

The girl at first did not return any of the kisses but presently she began to and after she had put several on his cheek, she reached his lips and remained there, kissing him again and again as if she were trying to draw all the breath out of him. His breath was clear and sweet like a child's and the kisses were sticky like a child's. He mumbled about loving her and about knowing when he first seen her that he loved her, but the mumbling was like the sleepy fretting of a child being put to sleep by his mother. Her mind, throughout this, never stopped or lost itself for a second to her feelings. "You ain't said you loved me none," he whispered finally, pulling back from her. "You got to say that."

She looked away from him off into the hollow sky and then down at a black ridge and then down farther into what appeared to be two green swelling lakes. She didn't realize he had taken her glasses but this landscape could not seem exceptional to her for she seldom paid any close attention to her surroundings.

"You got to say it," he repeated. "You got to say you love me."

She was always careful how she committed herself. "In a sense," she began, "if you use the word loosely, you might say that. But it's not a word I use. I don't have illusions. I'm one of those people who see *through* to nothing."

The boy was frowning. "You got to say it. I said it and you got to say it," he said.

The girl looked at him almost tenderly. "You poor baby," she murmured. "It's just as well you don't understand," and she pulled him by the neck, face-down, against her. "We are all damned," she said, "but some of us have taken off our blindfolds and see that there's nothing to see. It's a kind of salvation."

The boy's astonished eyes looked blankly through the ends of her hair. "Okay," he almost whined, "but do you love me or don'tcher?"

"Yes," she said and added, "in a sense. But I must tell you something. There mustn't be anything dishonest between us." She lifted his head and looked him in the eye. "I am thirty years old," she said. "I have a number of degrees."

The boy's look was irritated but dogged. "I don't care," he said. "I don't care a thing about what all you done. I just want to know if you love me or don'tcher?" and he caught her to him and wildly planted her face with kisses until she said, "Yes, yes."

"Okay then," he said, letting her go. "Prove it."

She smiled, looking dreamily out on the shifty landscape. She had seduced him without even making up her mind to try. "How?" she asked, feeling that he should be delayed a little.

He leaned over and put his lips to her ear. "Show me where your wooden leg joins on," he whispered.

The girl uttered a sharp little cry and her face instantly drained of color. The obscenity of the suggestion was not what shocked her. As a child she had sometimes been subject to feelings of shame but education had removed the last traces of that as a good surgeon scrapes for cancer; she would no more have felt it over what he was asking than she would have believed in his Bible. But she was as sensitive about the artificial leg as a peacock about his tail. No one ever touched it but her. She took care of it as someone else would his soul, in private and almost with her own eyes turned away. "No," she said.

"I known it," he muttered, sitting up. "You're just playing me for a sucker."

"Oh no no!" she cried. "It joins on at the knee. Only at the knee. Why do you want to see it?"

The boy gave her a long penetrating look. "Because," he said, "it's what makes you different. You ain't like anybody else."

She sat staring at him. There was nothing about her face or her round freezing-blue eyes to indicate that this had moved her; but she felt as if her heart had stopped and left her mind to pump her blood. She decided that for the first time in her life she was face to face with real innocence. This boy, with an instinct that came from beyond wisdom, had touched the truth about her. When after a minute, she said in a hoarse high voice, "All right," it was like surrendering to him completely. It was like losing her own life and finding it again, miraculously, in his.

Very gently he began to roll the slack leg up. The artificial limb, in a white sock and brown flat shoe, was bound in a heavy material like canvas and ended in an ugly jointure where it was attached to the stump. The boy's face and his voice were entirely reverent as he uncovered it and said, "Now show me how to take it off and on."

She took it off for him and put it back on again and then he took it off himself, handling it as tenderly as if it were a real one. "See!" he said with a delighted child's face. "Now I can do it myself!"

"Put it back on," she said. She was thinking that she would run away with him and that every night he would take the leg off and every morning put it back on again. "Put it back on," she said.

"Not yet," he murmured, setting it on its foot out of her reach. "Leave it off for a while. You got me instead."

She gave a little cry of alarm but he pushed her down and began to kiss her again. Without the leg she felt entirely dependent on him. Her brain seemed to have stopped thinking altogether and to be about some other function that it was not very good at. Different expressions raced back and forth over her face. Every now and then the boy, his eyes like two steel spikes, would glance behind him where the leg stood. Finally she pushed him off and said, "Put it back on me now."

"Wait," he said. He leaned the other way and pulled the valise toward him and opened it. It had a pale blue spotted lining and there were only two Bibles in it. He took one of these out and opened the cover of it. It was hollow and contained a pocket flask of whiskey, a pack of cards, and a small blue box with printing on it. He laid these out in front of her one at a time in an evenly-spaced row, like one presenting offerings at the shrine of a goddess. He put the blue box in her hand. THIS PRODUCT TO BE USED ONLY FOR THE PREVENTION OF DISEASE, she read, and dropped it. The boy was unscrewing the top of the flask. He stopped and pointed, with a smile, to the deck of cards. It was not an ordinary deck but one with an obscene picture on the back of each card. "Take a swig," he said, offering her the bottle first. He held it in front of her, but like one mesmerized, she did not move.

Her voice when she spoke had an almost pleading sound. "Aren't you," she murmured, "aren't you just good country people?"

The boy cocked his head. He looked as if he were just beginning to understand that she might be trying to insult him. "Yeah," he said, curling his lip slightly, "but it ain't held me back none. I'm as good as you any day in the week."

"Give me my leg," she said.

He pushed it farther away with his foot. "Come on now, let's begin to have us a good time," he said coaxingly. "We ain't got to know one another good yet."

"Give me my leg!" she screamed and tried to lunge for it but he pushed her down easily.

"What's the matter with you all of a sudden?" he asked, frowning as he screwed the top on the flask and put it quickly back inside the Bible. "You just a while ago said you didn't believe in nothing. I thought you was some girl!"

Her face was almost purple. "You're a Christian!" she hissed. "You're a fine Christian! You're just like them all—say one thing and do another. You're a perfect Christian, you're . . ."

The boy's mouth was set angrily. "I hope you don't think," he said in a lofty indignant tone, "that I believe in that crap! I may sell Bibles but I know which end is up and I wasn't born yesterday and I know where I'm going!"

"Give me my leg!" she screeched. He jumped up so quickly that she barely saw him sweep the cards and the blue box into the Bible and throw the Bible into the valise. She saw him grab the leg and then she saw it for an instant slanted forlornly across the inside of the suitcase with a Bible at either side of its opposite ends. He slammed the lid shut and snatched up the valise and swung it down the hole and then stepped through himself.

When all of him had passed but his head, he turned and regarded her with a look that no longer had any admiration in it. "I've gotten a lot of interesting things," he said. "One time I got a woman's glass eye this way. And you needn't to think you'll catch me because Pointer ain't really my name. I use a different name at every house I call at and don't stay nowhere long. And I'll tell you another thing, Hulga," he said, using the name as if he didn't think much of it, "you ain't so smart. I been believing in nothing ever since I was born!" and then the toast-colored hat disappeared down the hole and the girl was left, sitting on the straw in the dusty sunlight. When she turned her churning face toward the opening, she saw his blue figure struggling successfully over the green speckled lake.

Mrs. Hopewell and Mrs. Freeman, who were in the back pasture, digging up onions, saw him emerge a little later from the woods and head across the meadow toward the highway. "Why, that looks like that nice dull young man that tried to sell me a Bible yesterday," Mrs. Hopewell said, squinting. "He must have been selling them to the Negroes back in there. He was so simple," she said, "but I guess the world would be better off if we were all that simple."

Mrs. Freeman's gaze drove forward and just touched him before he disappeared under the hill. Then she returned her attention to the evil-smelling onion shoot she was lifting from the ground. "Some can't be that simple," she said. "I know I never could."

1955

RELATED:

—Author in Depth: Flannery O'Connor, p. 968

# FRANK O'CONNOR
## *1903–1966*

O'Connor is the pen name of Michael O'Donovan, who was born in Cork, Ireland, of a family too poor to give him a university education. During Ireland's struggle for independence he was briefly a member of the Irish Republican Army. Then he worked as a librarian in Cork and Dublin and for a time was director of the Abbey Theatre before he became established as a writer of short stories. From 1931 on he published regularly in American magazines, and he taught for some years at Harvard, Northwestern, and Stanford Universities. His declared objective in shaping his material was to find the natural rhythms and stresses of the storyteller's voice. He rewrote many of his stories—often after first publication—ten, twenty, or thirty times. The subsequent publication of these revisions makes it hard to pin down the exact scale of his life's work, but he is credited with more than 150 works. He was in any event a prolific historian of Irish manners and the Irish character. His titles include *Guests of the Nation* (1931), *Crab Apple Jelly* (1944), *An Only Child* (O'Connor's autobiography, 1961), *A Set of Variations* (1971), and *Collected Stories* (1981).

## Guests of the Nation

### I

At dusk the big Englishman, Belcher, would shift his long legs out of the ashes and say "Well, chums, what about it?" and Noble or me would say "All right, chum" (for we had picked up some of their curious expressions), and the little Englishman, Hawkins, would light the lamp and bring out the cards. Sometimes Jeremiah Donovan would come up and supervise the game and get excited over Hawkins's cards, which he always played badly, and shout at him as if he was one of our own, "Ah, you divil, you, why didn't you play the tray?"

But ordinarily Jeremiah was a sober and contented poor devil like the big Englishman, Belcher, and was looked up to only because he was a fair hand at documents, though he was slow enough even with them. He wore a small cloth hat and big gaiters over his long pants, and you seldom saw him with his hands out of his pockets. He reddened when you talked to him, tilting from toe to heel and back, and looking down all the time at his big farmer's feet. Noble and me used to make fun of his broad accent, because we were from the town.

I couldn't at the time see the point of me and Noble guarding Belcher and Hawkins at all, for it was my belief that you could have planted that pair down anywhere from this to Claregalway and they'd have taken root there like a native weed. I never in my short experience seen two men to take to the country as they did.

They were handed on to us by the Second Battalion when the search[1] for them became too hot, and Noble and myself, being young, took over with a natural feeling of responsibility, but Hawkins made us look like fools when he showed that he knew the country better than we did.

"You're the bloke they calls Bonaparte," he says to me. "Mary Brigid O'Connell told me to ask you what you done with the pair of her brother's socks you borrowed."

For it seemed, as they explained it, that the Second used to have little evenings, and some of the girls of the neighbourhood turned in, and, seeing they were such decent chaps, our fellows couldn't leave the two Englishmen out of them. Hawkins learned to dance "The Walls of Limerick," "The Siege of Ennis," and "The Waves of Tory"[2] as well as any of them, though naturally, he couldn't return the compliment, because our lads at that time did not dance foreign dances on principle.

So whatever privileges Belcher and Hawkins had with the Second they just naturally took with us, and after the first day or two we gave up all pretence of keeping a close eye on them. Not that they could have got far, for they had accents you could cut with a knife and wore khaki tunics and overcoats with civilian pants and boots. But it's my belief that they never had any idea of escaping and were quite content to be where they were.

It was a treat to see how Belcher got off with the old woman of the house where we were staying. She was a great warrant to scold, and cranky even with us, but before ever she had a chance to giving our guests, as I may call them, a lick of her tongue, Belcher had made her his friend for life. She was breaking sticks, and Belcher, who hadn't been more than ten minutes in the house, jumped up from his seat and went over to her.

"Allow me, madam," he says, smiling his queer little smile, "please allow me"; and he takes the bloody hatchet. She was struck too paralytic to speak, and after that, Belcher would be at her heels, carrying a bucket, a basket, or a load of turf, as the case might be. As Noble said, he got into looking before she leapt, and hot water, or any little thing she wanted, Belcher would have it ready for her. For such a huge man (and though I am five foot ten myself I had to look up at him) he had an uncommon shortness—or should I say lack?—of speech. It took us some time to get used to him, walking in and out, like a ghost, without a word. Especially because Hawkins talked enough for a platoon, it was strange to hear big Belcher with his toes in the ashes come out with a solitary "Excuse me, chum," or "That's right, chum." His one and only passion was cards, and I will say for him that he was a good card-player. He could have fleeced myself and Noble, but whatever we lost to him Hawkins lost to us, and Hawkins played with the money Belcher gave him.

Hawkins lost to us because he had too much old gab, and we probably lost to Belcher for the same reason. Hawkins and Noble would spit at one another

---

1. Belcher and Hawkins are English soldiers, captured during the Irish battle for independence of 1922. The British Army and its collaborators are searching for them. 2. Native Irish dances.

about religion into the early hours of the morning, and Hawkins worried the soul out of Noble, whose brother was a priest, with a string of questions that would puzzle a cardinal. To make it worse even in treating of holy subjects, Hawkins had a deplorable tongue. I never in all my career met a man who could mix such a variety of cursing and bad language into an argument. He was a terrible man, and a fright to argue. He never did a stroke of work, and when he had no one else to talk to, he got stuck in the old woman.

He met his match in her, for one day when he tried to get her to complain profanely of the drought, she gave him a great comedown by blaming it entirely on Jupiter Pluvius (a deity neither Hawkins nor I had ever heard of, though Noble said that among the pagans it was believed that he had something to do with the rain).[3] Another day he was swearing at the capitalists for starting the German war[4] when the old lady laid down her iron, puckered up her little crab's mouth, and said: "Mr. Hawkins, you can say what you like about the war, and think you'll deceive me because I'm only a simple poor countrywoman, but I know what started the war. It was the Italian Count that stole the heathen divinity out of the temple in Japan. Believe me, Mr. Hawkins, nothing but sorrow and want can follow the people that disturb the hidden powers."

A queer old girl, all right.

## II

We had our tea one evening, and Hawkins lit the lamp and we all sat into cards. Jeremiah Donovan came in too, and sat down and watched us for a while, and it suddenly struck me that he had no great love for the two Englishmen. It came as a great surprise to me, because I hadn't noticed anything about him before.

Late in the evening a really terrible argument blew up between Hawkins and Noble, about capitalists and priests and love of your country.

"The capitalists," says Hawkins with an angry gulp, "pays the priests to tell you about the next world so as you won't notice what the bastards are up to in this."

"Nonsense, man!" says Noble, losing his temper. "Before ever a capitalist was thought of, people believed in the next world."

Hawkins stood up as though he was preaching a sermon.

"Oh, they did, did they?" he says with a sneer. "They believed all the things you believe, isn't that what you mean? And you believe that God created Adam, and Adam created Shem, and Shem created Jehoshophat.[5] You believe all that silly old fairytale about Eve and Eden and the apple. Well, listen to me, chum. If you're entitled to hold a silly belief like that, I'm entitled to hold my silly belief—which is that the first thing your God created was a bleeding capitalist, with morality and Rolls-Royce complete. Am I right, chum?" he says to Belcher.

"You're right, chum," says Belcher with his amused smile, and got up from the table to stretch his long legs into the fire and stroke his moustache. So, seeing that Jeremiah Donovan was going, and that there was no knowing

---

**3.** The chief Roman god, Jupiter, had many functions, among them bringing rain for the crops, hence "Pluvius" (rainy). **4.** World War I, in which England was at war with Germany. **5.** Hawkins's scrambled version of Old Testament lore.

when the argument about religion would be over, I went out with him. We strolled down to the village together, and then he stopped and started blushing and mumbling and saying I ought to be behind, keeping guard on the prisoners. I didn't like the tone he took with me, and anyway I was bored with life in the cottage, so I replied by asking him what the hell we wanted guarding them at all for. I told him I'd talked it over with Noble, and that we'd both rather be out with a fighting column.

"What use are those fellows to us?" says I.

He looked at me in surprise and said: "I thought you knew we were keeping them as hostages."

"Hostages?" I said.

"The enemy have prisoners belonging to us," he says, "and now they're talking of shooting them. If they shoot our prisoners, we'll shoot theirs."

"Shoot them?" I said.

"What else did you think we were keeping them for?" he says.

"Wasn't it very unforeseen of you not to warn Noble and myself of that in the beginning?" I said.

"How was it?" says he. "You might have known it."

"We couldn't know it, Jeremiah Donovan," says I. "How could we when they were on our hands so long?"

"The enemy have our prisoners as long and longer," says he.

"That's not the same thing at all," says I.

"What difference is there?" says he.

I couldn't tell him, because I knew he wouldn't understand. If it was only an old dog that was going to the vet's, you'd try and not get too fond of him, but Jeremiah Donovan wasn't a man that would ever be in danger of that.

"And when is this thing going to be decided?" says I.

"We might hear tonight," he says. "Or tomorrow or the next day at latest. So if it's only hanging round here that's a trouble to you, you'll be free soon enough."

It wasn't the hanging round that was a trouble to me at all by this time. I had worse things to worry about. When I got back to the cottage the argument was still on. Hawkins was holding forth in his best style, maintaining that there was no next world, and Noble was maintaining that there was; but I could see that Hawkins had had the best of it.

"Do you know what, chum?" he was saying with a saucy smile. "I think you're just as big a bleeding unbeliever as I am. You say you believe in the next world, and you know just as much about the next world as I do, which is sweet damn-all. What's heaven? You don't know. Where's heaven? You don't know. You know sweet damn-all! I ask you again, do they wear wings?"

"Very well, then," says Noble, "they do. Is that enough for you? They do wear wings."

"Where do they get them, then? Who makes them? Have they a factory for wings? Have they a sort of store where you hands in your chit and takes your bleeding wings?"

"You're an impossible man to argue with," says Noble. "Now, listen to me—" And they were off again.

It was long after midnight when we locked up and went to bed. As I blew out the candle I told Noble what Jeremiah Donovan was after telling me.

Noble took it very quietly. When we'd been in bed about an hour he asked me did I think we ought to tell the Englishmen. I didn't think we should, because it was more than likely that the English wouldn't shoot our men, and even if they did, the brigade officers, who were always up and down with the Second Battalion and knew the Englishmen well, wouldn't be likely to want them plugged. "I think so too," says Noble. "It would be great cruelty to put the wind to them now."

"It was very unforeseen of Jeremiah Donovan anyhow," says I.

It was next morning that we found it so hard to face Belcher and Hawkins. We went about the house all day scarcely saying a word. Belcher didn't seem to notice; he was stretched into the ashes as usual, with his look unusual of waiting in quietness for something unforeseen to happen, but Hawkins noticed and put it down to Noble's being beaten in the argument of the night before.

"Why can't you take a discussion in the proper spirit?" he says severely. "You and your Adam and Eve! I'm a Communist, that's what I am. Communist or anarchist, it all comes to much the same thing." And for hours he went round the house, muttering when the fit took him. "Adam and Eve! Adam and Eve! Nothing better to do with their time than picking bleeding apples!"

## III

I don't know how we got through that day, but I was very glad when it was over, the tea things were cleared away, and Belcher said in his peaceable way: "Well, chums, what about it?" We sat round the table and Hawkins took out the cards, and just then I heard Jeremiah Donovan's footstep on the path and a dark presentiment crossed my mind. I rose from the table and caught him before he reached the door.

"What do you want?" I asked.

"I want those two soldier friends of yours," he says, getting red.

"Is that the way, Jeremiah Donovan?" I asked.

"That's the way. There were four of our lads shot this morning, one of them a boy of sixteen."

"That's bad," I said.

At that moment Noble followed me out, and the three of us walked down the path together, talking in whispers. Feeney, the local intelligence officer, was standing by the gate.

"What are you going to do about it?" I asked Jeremiah Donovan.

"I want you and Noble to get them out; tell them they're being shifted again; that'll be the quietest way."

"Leave me out of that," says Noble under his breath.

Jeremiah Donovan looks at him hard.

"All right," he says. "You and Feeney get a few tools from the shed and dig a hole by the far end of the bog. Bonaparte and myself will be after you. Don't let anyone see you with the tools. I wouldn't like it to go beyond ourselves."

We saw Feeney and Noble go round to the shed and went in ourselves. I left Jeremiah Donovan to do the explanations. He told them that he had orders to send them back to the Second Battalion. Hawkins let out a mouthful of curses, and you could see that though Belcher didn't say anything, he was a bit upset too. The old woman was for having them stay in spite of us, and she didn't stop advising them until Jeremiah Donovan lost his temper and turned on her. He had a nasty temper, I noticed. It was pitch-dark in the cottage by this time, but no one thought of lighting the lamp, and in the darkness the two Englishmen fetched their topcoats and said good-bye to the old woman.

"Just as a man makes a home of a bleeding place, some bastard at head-quarters thinks you're too cushy and shunts you off," says Hawkins, shaking her hand.

"A thousand thanks, madam," says Belcher. "A thousand thanks for everything"—as though he'd made it up.

We went round to the back of the house and down towards the bog. It was only then that Jeremiah Donovan told them. He was shaking with excitement.

"There were four of our fellows shot in Cork this morning and now you're to be shot as a reprisal."

"What are you talking about?" snaps Hawkins. "It's bad enough being mucked about as we are without having to put up with your funny jokes."

"It isn't a joke," says Donovan. "I'm sorry, Hawkins, but it's true," and begins on the usual rigmarole about duty and how unpleasant it is.

I never noticed that people who talk a lot about duty find it much of a trouble to them.

"Oh, cut it out!" says Hawkins.

"Ask Bonaparte," says Donovan, seeing that Hawkins isn't taking him seriously. "Isn't it true, Bonaparte?"

"It is," I say, and Hawkins stops.

"Ah, for Christ's sake, chum!"

"I mean it, chum," I say.

"You don't sound as if you meant it."

"If he doesn't mean it, I do," says Donovan, working himself up.

"What have you against me, Jeremiah Donovan?"

"I never said I had anything against you. But why did your people take out four of our prisoners and shoot them in cold blood?"

He took Hawkins by the arm and dragged him on, but it was impossible to make him understand that we were in earnest. I had the Smith and Wesson[6] in my pocket and I kept fingering it and wondering what I'd do if they put up a fight for it or ran, and wishing to God they'd do one or the other. I knew if they did run for it, that I'd never fire on them. Hawkins wanted to know was Noble in it, and when we said yes, he asked us why Noble wanted to plug him. Why did any of us want to plug him? What had he done to us? Weren't we all chums? Didn't we understand him and didn't he understand us? Did we imagine for an instant that he'd shoot us for all the so-and-so officers in the so-and-so British Army?

By this time we'd reached the bog, and I was so sick I couldn't even answer him. We walked along the edge of it in the darkness, and every now and then Hawkins would call a halt and begin all over again, as if he was wound up, about our being chums, and I knew that nothing but the sight of the grave would convince him that we had to do it. And all the time I was hoping that something would happen; that they'd run for it or that Noble would take

---

6. Revolver, as is the Webley, below.

over the responsibility from me. I had the feeling that it was worse on Noble than on me.

## IV

At last we saw the lantern in the distance and made towards it. Noble was carrying it, and Feeney was standing somewhere in the darkness behind him, and the picture of them so still and silent in the bogland brought it home to me that we were in earnest, and banished the last bit of hope I had.

Belcher, on recognizing Noble, said: "Hallo, chum," in his quiet way, but Hawkins flew at him at once, and the argument began all over again, only this time Noble had nothing to say for himself and stood with his head down, holding the lantern between his legs.

It was Jeremiah Donovan who did the answering. For the twentieth time, as though it was haunting his mind, Hawkins asked if anybody thought he'd shoot Noble.

"Yes, you would," says Jeremiah Donovan.

"No, I wouldn't, damn you!"

"You would, because you'd know you'd be shot for not doing it."

"I wouldn't, not if I was to be shot twenty times over. I wouldn't shoot a pal. And Belcher wouldn't—isn't that right, Belcher?"

"That's right, chum," Belcher said, but more by way of answering the question than of joining in the argument. Belcher sounded as though whatever unforeseen thing he'd always been waiting for had come at last.

"Anyway, who says Noble would be shot if I wasn't? What do you think I'd do if I was in his place, out in the middle of a blasted bog?"

"What would you do?" asks Donovan.

"I'd go with him wherever he was going, of course. Share my last bob with him and stick by him through thick and thin. No one can ever say of me that I let down a pal."

"We had enough of this," says Jeremiah Donovan, cocking his revolver. "Is there any message you want to send?"

"No, there isn't."

"Do you want to say your prayers?"

Hawkins came out with a cold-blooded remark that even shocked me and turned on Noble again.

"Listen to me, Noble," he says. "You and me are chums. You can't come over to my side, so I'll come over to your side. That show you I mean what I say? Give me a rifle and I'll go along with you and the other lads."

Nobody answered him. We knew that was no way out.

"Hear what I'm saying?" he says. "I'm through with it. I'm a deserter or anything else you like. I don't believe in your stuff, but it's no worse than mine. That satisfy you?"

Noble raised his head, but Donovan began to speak and he lowered it again without replying.

"For the last time, have you any messages to send?" says Donovan in a cold excited sort of voice.

"Shut up, Donovan! You don't understand me, but these lads do. They're not the sort to make a pal and kill a pal. They're not the tools of any capitalist."

I alone of the crowd saw Donovan raise his Webley to the back of Hawkins's neck, and as he did so I shut my eyes and tried to pray. Hawkins had begun to say something else when Donovan fired, and as I opened my eyes at the bang, I saw Hawkins stagger at the knees and lie out flat at Noble's feet, slowly and as quiet as a kid falling asleep, with the lantern-light on his lean legs and bright farmer's boots. We all stood very still, watching him settle out in the last agony.

Then Belcher took out a handkerchief and began to tie it about his own eyes (in our excitement we'd forgotten to do the same for Hawkins), and, seeing it wasn't big enough, turned and asked for the loan of mine. I gave it to him and he knotted the two together and pointed with his foot at Hawkins.

"He's not quite dead," he says. "Better give him another."

Sure enough, Hawkins's left knee is beginning to rise. I bend down and put my gun to his head; then, recollecting myself, I get up again. Belcher understands what's in my mind.

"Give him his first," he says. "I don't mind. Poor bastard, we don't know what's happening to him now."

I knelt and fired. By this time I didn't seem to know what I was doing. Belcher, who was fumbling a bit awkwardly with the handkerchiefs, came out with a laugh as he heard the shot. It was the first time I heard him laugh and it sent a shudder down my back; it sounded so unnatural.

"Poor bugger!" he said quietly. "And last night he was so curious about it all. It's very queer, chums, I always think. Now he knows as much about it as they'll ever let him know, and last night he was all in the dark."

Donovan helped him to tie the handkerchiefs about his eyes. "Thanks, chum," he said. Donovan asked if there were any messages he wanted sent.

"No, chum," he says. "Not for me. If any of you would like to write to Hawkins's mother, you'll find a letter from her in his pocket. He and his mother were great chums. But my missus left me eight years ago. Went away with another fellow and took the kid with her. I like the feeling of a home, as you may have noticed, but I couldn't start again after that."

It was an extraordinary thing, but in those few minutes Belcher said more than in all the weeks before. It was just as if the sound of the shot had started a flood of talk in him and he could go on the whole night like that, quite happily, talking about himself. We stood round like fools now that he couldn't see us any longer. Donovan looked at Noble, and Noble shook his head. Then Donovan raised his Webley, and at that moment Belcher gives his queer laugh again. He may have thought we were talking about him, or perhaps he noticed the same thing I'd noticed and couldn't understand it.

"Excuse me, chums," he says. "I feel I'm talking the hell of a lot, and so silly, about my being so handy about a house and things like that. But this thing came on me suddenly. You'll forgive me, I'm sure."

"You don't want to say a prayer?" asks Donovan.

"No, chum," he says. "I don't think it would help. I'm ready, and you boys want to get it over."

"You understand that we're only doing our duty?" says Donovan.

Belcher's head was raised like a blind man's so that you could only see his chin and the tip of his nose in the lantern-light.

"I never could make out what duty was myself," he said. "I think you're all good lads, if that's what you mean. I'm not complaining."

Noble, just as if he couldn't bear any more of it, raised his fist at Donovan, and in a flash Donovan raised his gun and fired. The big man went over like a sack of meal, and this time there was no need for a second shot.

I don't remember much about the burying, but that it was worse than all the rest because we had to carry them to the grave. It was all mad lonely with nothing but a patch of lantern-light between ourselves and the dark, and birds hooting and screeching all round, disturbed by the guns. Noble went through Hawkins's belongings to find the letter from his mother, and then joined his hands together. He did the same with Belcher. Then, when we'd filled in the grave, we separated from Jeremiah Donovan and Feeney and took our tools back to the shed. All the way we didn't speak a word. The kitchen was dark and cold as we'd left it, and the old woman was sitting over the hearth, saying her beads. We walked past her into the room, and Noble struck a match to light the lamp. She rose quietly and came to the doorway with all her cantankerousness gone.

"What did ye do with them?" she asked in a whisper, and Noble started so that the match went out in his hand.

"What's that?" he asked without turning round.

"I heard ye," she said.

"What did you hear?" asked Noble.

"I heard ye. Do ye think I didn't hear ye, putting the spade back in the houseen?"[7]

Noble struck another match and this time the lamp lit for him.

"Was that what ye did to them?" she asked.

Then, by God, in the very doorway, she fell on her knees and began praying, and after looking at her for a minute or two Noble did the same by the fireplace. I pushed my way out past her and left them at it. I stood at the door, watching the stars and listening to the shrieking of the birds dying out over the bogs. It is so strange what you feel at times like that that you can't describe it. Noble says he saw everything ten times the size, as though there were nothing in the whole world but that little patch of bog with the two Englishmen stiffening into it, but with me it was as if the patch of bog where the Englishmen were was a million miles away, and even Noble and the old woman, mumbling behind me, and the birds and the bloody stars were all far away, and I was somehow very small and very lost and lonely like a child astray in the snow. And anything that happened to me afterwards, I never felt the same about again.

1931

---

RELATED:

—Edward P. Jones on "Guests of the Nation," p. 927

---

7. Shed.

# TILLIE OLSEN
## *1912–2007*

Olsen was born in Omaha, Nebraska, the daughter of Russian political exiles. She began to write in the 1930s, but most of her life was committed to working in industry and raising her four children. It wasn't until after they were grown that she studied writing at San Francisco State College, won a fellowship at Stanford University, and began to publish in earnest. When the four stories collected in *Tell Me a Riddle* (1961) appeared in the 1950s, she attracted a small group of enthusiastic readers who touted her talents until she gained a wider reputation. Although her body of work is quite small, she established a reputation as an ardent feminist known for her devotion to social and political causes. She taught or was a writer-in-residence at such colleges and universities as Amherst College, Stanford University, MIT, and Kenyon College. She was the recipient of five honorary degrees, a National Endowment for the Arts Fellowship, a Guggenheim Fellowship, and the O. Henry Award for best short story. *Silences* (1978) is a collection of essays and meditations. Her novel, *Yonnondio,* was published in 1974. *Mothers and Daughters* (1987), a collection of photographs, features Olsen's introductory essays. Her work has appeared in over one hundred anthologies.

# O Yes

## I

They are the only white people there, sitting in the dimness of the Negro church that had once been a corner store, and all through the bubbling, swelling, seething of before the services, twelve-year-old Carol clenches tight her mother's hand, the other resting lightly on her friend, Parialee Phillips, for whose baptism she has come.

The white-gloved ushers hurry up and down the aisle, beckoning people to their seats. A jostle of people. To the chairs angled to the left for the youth choir, to the chairs angled to the right for the ladies' choir, even up to the platform, where behind the place for the dignitaries and the mixed choir, the new baptismal tank gleams—and as if pouring into it from the ceiling, the blue-painted River of Jordan, God standing in the waters, embracing a brown man in a leopard skin and pointing to the letters of gold:

REJOICE

D        L

O   IS   O

          V

G         E

I AM THE WAY     THE TRUTH     THE LIFE

At the clear window, the crucified Christ embroidered on the starched white curtain leaps in the wind of the sudden singing. And the choirs march in. Robes of wine, of blue, of red.

"We stands and sings too," says Parialee's mother, Alva, to Helen; though already Parialee has pulled Carol up. Singing, little Lucinda Phillips fluffs out her many petticoats; singing, little Bubbie bounces up and down on his heels.

> *Any day now I'll reach that land of freedom,*
> > *Yes, o yes*
> *Any day now, know that promised land*

The youth choir claps and taps to accent the swing of it. Beginning to tap, Carol stiffens. "Parry, look. Somebody from school."

"Once more once," says Parialee, in the new way she likes to talk now.

"Eddie Garlin's up there. He's in my math."

"Couple cats from Franklin Jr. chirps in the choir. No harm or alarm."

Anxiously Carol scans the faces to see who else she might know, who else might know her, but looks quickly down to Lucinda's wide skirts, for it seems Eddie looks back at her, sullen or troubled, though it is hard to tell, faced as she is into the window of curtained sunblaze.

> *I know my robe will fit me well*
> *I tried it on at the gates of hell*

If it were a record she would play it over and over, Carol thought, to untwine the intertwined voices, to search how the many rhythms rock apart and yet are one glad rhythm.

> *When I get to heaven gonna sing and shout*
> *Nobody be able to turn me out*

"That's Mr. Chairback Evans going to invocate," Lucinda leans across Parry to explain. "He don't invoke good like Momma."

"Shhhh."

"Momma's the only lady in the church that invocates. She made the prayer last week. (Last month, Lucy.) I made the children's 'nouncement last time. (That was way back Thanksgiving.) And Bubbie's 'nounced too. Lots of times."

"Lucy-inda. SIT!"

Bible study announcements and mixed-choir practice announcements and Teen Age Hearts meeting announcements.

If Eddie said something to her about being there, worried Carol, if he talked to her right in front of somebody at school.

Messengers of Faith announcements and Mamboettes announcement and Committee for the Musical Tea.

Parry's arm so warm. Not realizing, starting up the old game from grade school, drumming a rhythm on the other's arm to see if the song could be guessed. "Parry, guess."

But Parry is pondering the platform.

The baptismal tank? "Parry, are you scared . . . the baptizing?"

"This cat? No." Shaking her head so slow and scornful, the barrette in her hair, sun fired, strikes a long rail of light. And still ponders the platform.

New Strangers Baptist Church invites you and Canaan Fair Singers announcements and Battle of Song and Cosmopolites meet. "O Lord, I couldn't find no ease," a solo. The ladies' choir:

> *O what you say seekers, o what you say seekers,*
> *Will you never turn back no more?*

The mixed choir sings:

> *Ezekiel saw that wheel of time*
> *Every spoke was of humankind . . .*

And the slim worn man in the pin-stripe suit starts his sermon On the Nature of God. How God is long-suffering. Oh, how long he has suffered. Calling the roll of the mighty nations, that rose and fell and now are dust for grinding the face of Man.

O voice of drowsiness and dream to which Carol does not need to listen. As long ago. Parry warm beside her too, as it used to be, there in the classroom at Mann Elementary, and the feel of drenched in sun and dimness and dream. Smell and sound of the chalk wearing itself away to nothing, rustle of books, drumming tattoo of Parry's fingers on her arm: *Guess.*

And as the preacher's voice spins happy and free, it is the used-to-be play-yard. Tag. Thump of the volley ball. Ecstasy of the jump rope. Parry, do pepper. Carol, do pepper. Parry's bettern Carol, Carol's bettern Parry. . . .

*Did someone scream?*

It seemed someone screamed—but all were sitting as before, though the sun no longer blared through the windows. She tried to see up where Eddie was, but the ushers were standing at the head of the aisle now, the ladies in white dresses like nurses or waitresses wear, the men holding their white-gloved hands up so one could see their palms.

"And God is Powerful," the preacher was chanting. "Nothing for him to scoop out the oceans and pat up the mountains. Nothing for him to scoop up the miry clay and create man. Man, I said, create Man."

The lady in front of her moaned *"O yes"* and others were moaning *"O yes."*

"And when the earth mourned the Lord said, Weep not, for all will be returned to you, every dust, every atom. And the tired dust settles back, goes back. Until that Judgment Day. That great day."

*"O yes."*

The ushers were giving out fans. Carol reached for one and Parry said: "What *you* need one for?" but she took it anyway.

"You think Satchmo can blow; you think Muggsy can blow; you think Dizzy[1] can blow?" He was straining to an imaginary trumpet now, his head far back and his voice coming out like a trumpet.

"Oh Parry, he's so good."

"Well. Jelly jelly."

"Nothing to Gabriel on that great getting-up morning. And the horn wakes up Adam, and Adam runs to wake up Eve, and Eve moans; Just one more minute, let me sleep, and Adam yells, Great Day, woman, don't you know it's the Great Day?"

"*Great Day, Great Day,*" the mixed choir behind the preacher rejoices:

> *When our cares are past*
> *when we're home at last . . .*

"And Eve runs to wake up Cain." Running round the platform, stooping and shaking imaginary sleepers, "and Cain runs to wake up Abel." Looping, scalloping his voice—"Grea-aaa-aat Daaaay." All the choirs thundering:

> *Great Day*
> *When the battle's fought*
> *And the victory's won*

Exultant spirals of sound. And Carol caught into it (Eddie forgotten, the game forgotten) chanting with Lucy and Bubbie: "*Great Day.*"

"Ohhhhhhhhhh," his voice like a trumpet again, "the re-unioning. Ohhh-hhhhhh, the rejoicing. After the ages immemorial of longing."

Someone *was* screaming. And an awful thrumming sound with it, like feet and hands thrashing around, like a giant jumping of a rope.

"*Great Day.*" And no one stirred or stared as the ushers brought a little woman out into the aisle, screaming and shaking, just a little shrunk-up woman not much taller than Carol, the biggest thing about her her swollen hands and the cascades of tears wearing her face.

The shaking inside Carol too. Turning and trembling to ask: "What . . . that lady?" But Parry still ponders the platform; little Lucy loops the chain of her bracelet round and round; and Bubbie sits placidly, dreamily. Alva Phillips is up fanning a lady in front of her; two lady ushers are fanning other people Carol cannot see. And her mother, her mother looks in a sleep.

Yes. He raised up the dead from the grave. He made old death behave.

*Yes. Yes.* From all over, hushed. *O Yes*

He was your mother's rock. Your father's mighty tower. And he gave us a little baby. A little baby to love.

*I am so glad*

Yes, your friend, when you're friendless. Your father when you're fatherless. Way maker. Door opener.

---

**1.** John Birks "Dizzy" Gillespie (1917-1993), American jazz trumpeter and composer. Muggsy: Francis "Muggsy" Spanier (1906-1967), American jazz cornetist. Satchmo: Louis "Satchmo" Armstrong (1900-1971), American jazz trumpet virtuoso and bandleader.

*Yes*

When it seems you can't go on any longer, he's there. You can, he says, you can.

*Yes*

And that burden you been carrying—ohhhhh that burden—not for always will it be. No, not for always.

*Stay with me, Lord*

I will put my Word in you and it is power. I will put my Truth in you and it is power.

*O Yes*

Out of your suffering I will make you to stand as a stone. A tried stone. Hewn out of the mountains of ages eternal.

Ohhhhhhhhhhh. Out of the mire I will lift your feet. Your tired feet from so much wandering. From so much work and wear and hard times.

*Yes*

From so much journeying—and never the promised land. And I'll wash them in the well your tears made. And I'll shod them in the gospel of peace, and of feeling good. Ohhhhhhhhh.

*O Yes.*

Behind Carol, a trembling wavering scream. Then the thrashing. Up above, the singing:

> *They taken my blessed Jesus and flogged him to*
> *    the woods*
> *And they made him hew out his cross and they*
> *    dragged him to Calvary*
> *Shout brother, Shout shout shout. He never cried*
> *a word.*

Powerful throbbing voices. Calling and answering to each other.

> *They taken my blessed Jesus and whipped him up*
> *    the hill*
> *With a knotty whip and a raggedy thorn he never*
> *    cried a word*
> *Shout, sister. Shout shout shout. He never cried*
> *a word.*

> *Go tell the people the Saviour has risen*
> *Has risen from the dead and will live forevermore*
> *        And won't have to die no more.*
> *Halleloo.*

> *    Shout, brother, shout*
> *    We won't have to die no more!*

A single exultant lunge of shriek. Then the thrashing. All around a clapping. Shouts with it. The piano whipping, whipping air to a froth. Singing now.

> *I once was lost who now am found*
> *Was blind who now can see*

On Carol's fan, a little Jesus walked on wondrously blue waters to where bearded disciples spread nets out of a fishing boat. If she studied the fan— became it—it might make a wall around her. If she could make what was happening (*what* was happening?) into a record small and round to listen to far and far as if into a seashell—the stamp and rills and spirals all tiny (but never any screaming).

*wade wade in the water*

*Jordan's water is chilly and wild*
*I've got to get home to the other side*
*God's going to trouble the waters*

The music leaps and prowls. Ladders of screamings. Drumming feet of ushers running. And still little Lucy fluffs her skirts, loops the chain on her bracelet; still Bubbie sits and rocks dreamily; and only eyes turn for an instant to the aisle as if nothing were happening. "Mother, let's go home," Carol begs, but her mother holds her so tight. Alva Phillips, strong Alva, rocking too and chanting. *O Yes.* No, do not look.

*Wade,*
*Sea of trouble all mingled with fire*
*Come on my brethren it's time to go higher*
*Wade wade*

The voices in great humming waves, slow, slow (when did it become the humming?), everyone swaying with it too, moving like in slow waves and singing, and up where Eddie is, a new cry, wild and open, "O help me, Jesus," and when Carol opens her eyes she closes them again, quick, but still can see the new known face from school (not Eddie), the thrashing, writhing body struggling against the ushers with the look of grave and loving support on their faces, and hear the torn, tearing cry: "Don't take me away, life everlasting don't take me away."

And now the rhinestones in Parry's hair glitter wicked; the white hands of the ushers, fanning, foam in the air; the blue-painted waters of Jordan swell and thunder; Christ spirals on his cross in the window—and she is drowned under the sluice of the slow singing and the sway.

So high up and forgotten the waves and the world, so stirless the deep cool green and the wrecks of what had been. Here now Hostess Foods, where Alva Phillips works her nights—but different from that time Alva had taken them through before work, for it is all sunken under water, the creaking loading platform where they had left the night behind; the closet room where Alva's swaddles of sweaters, boots, and cap hung, the long hall lined with pickle barrels, the sharp freezer door swinging open.

Bubbles of breath that swell. A gulp of numbing air. She swims into the chill room where the huge wheels of cheese stand, and Alva swims too, deftly oiling each machine: slicers and wedgers and the convey, that at her touch start to roll and grind. The light of day blazes up and Alva is holding a cup, saying: Drink this, baby.

"DRINK IT." Her mother's voice and the numbing air demanding her to pay attention. Up through the waters and into the car.

"That's right, lambie, now lie back." Her mother's lap.

"Mother."

"Shhhhh. You almost fainted, lambie."

Alva's voice. "You gonna be all right, Carol . . . Lucy, I'm telling you for the last time, you and Buford get back into that church. Carol is *fine*."

"Lucyinda, if I had all your petticoats I could float." Crying. "Why didn't you let me wear my full skirt with the petticoats, Mother."

"Shhhhh, lamb." Smoothing her cheek. "Just breathe, take long deep breaths."

". . . How you doing now, you little ol' consolation prize?" It is Parry, but she does not come in the car or reach to Carol through the open window: "No need to cuss and fuss. You going to be sharp as a tack, Jack."

Answering automatically: "And cool as a fool."

Quick, they look at each other.

"Parry, we have to go home now, don't we, Mother? I almost fainted, didn't I, Mother? . . . Parry, I'm sorry I got sick and have to miss your baptism."

"Don't feel sorry. I'll feel better you not there to watch. It was our mommas wanted you to be there, not me."

"Parry!" Three voices.

"Maybe I'll come over to play kickball after. If you feeling better. Maybe. Or bring the pogo." Old shared joys in her voice. "Or any little thing."

In just a whisper: "Or any little thing. Parry. Good-bye, Parry."

And why does Alva have to talk now?

"You all right? You breathin' deep like your momma said? Was it too close 'n hot in there? Did something scare you, Carrie?"

Shaking her head to lie, "No."

"I blames myself for not paying attention. You not used to people letting go that way. Lucy and Bubbie, Parialee, they used to it. They been coming since they lap babies."

"Alva, that's all right. Alva. Mrs. Phillips."

"You *was* scared. Carol, it's something to study about. You'll feel better if you understand."

Trying not to listen.

"You not used to hearing what people keeps inside, Carol. You know how music can make you feel things? Glad or sad or like you can't sit still? That was religion music, Carol."

"I have to breathe deep, Mother said."

"Not everybody feels religion the same way. Some it's in their mouth, but some it's like a hope in their blood, their bones. And they singing songs every word that's real to them, Carol, every word out of they own life. And the preaching finding lodgment in their hearts."

The screaming was tuning up in her ears again, high above Alva's patient voice and the waves lapping and fretting.

"Maybe somebody's had a hard week, Carol, and they locked up with it. Maybe a lot of hard weeks bearing down."

"Mother, my head hurts."

"And they're home, Carol, church is home. Maybe the only place they can feel how they feel and maybe let it come out. So they can go on. And it's all right."

"Please, Alva. Mother, tell Alva my head hurts."

"Get Happy, we call it, and most it's a good feeling, Carol. When you got all that locked up inside you."

"Tell her we have to go home. It's all right, Alva. Please, Mother. Say good-bye. Good-bye."

*When I was carrying Parry and her father left me, and I fifteen years old, one thousand miles away from home, sin-sick and never really believing, as still I don't believe all, scorning, for what have it done to help, waiting there in the clinic and maybe sleeping, a voice called: Alva, Alva. So mournful and so sweet: Alva. Fear not, I have loved you from the foundation of the universe. And a little small child tugged on my dress. He was carrying a parade stick, on the end of it a star that outshined the sun. Follow me, he said. And the real sun went down and he hidden his stick. How dark it was, how dark. I could feel the darkness with my hands. And when I could see, I screamed. Dump trucks run, dumping bodies in hell, and a convey line run, never ceasing with souls, weary ones having to stamp and shove them along, and the air like fire. Oh I never want to hear such screaming. Then the little child jumped on a motorbike making a path no bigger than my little finger. But first he greased my feet with the hands of my momma when I was a knee baby. They shined like the sun was on them. Eyes he placed all around my head, and as I journeyed upward after him, it seemed I heard a mourning: "Mama Mama you must help carry the world." The rise and fall of nations I saw. And the voice called again Alva Alva, and I flew into a world of light, multitudes singing, Free, free, I am so glad.*

## II

Helen began to cry, telling her husband about it.

"You and Alva ought to have your heads examined, taking her there cold like that," Len said. "All right, wreck my best handkerchief. Anyway, now that she's had a bath, her Sunday dinner. . . ."

"And been fussed over," seventeen-year-old Jeannie put in.

"She seems good as new. Now *you* forget it, Helen."

"I can't. Something . . . deep happened. If only I or Alva had told her what it would be like. . . . But I didn't realize."

You don't realize a lot of things, Mother, Jeannie said, but not aloud.

"So Alva talked about it after instead of before. Maybe it meant more that way."

"Oh Len, she didn't listen."

"You don't know if she did or not. Or what there was in the experience for her. . . ."

Enough to pull that kid apart two ways even more, Jeannie said, but still not aloud.

"I was so glad she and Parry were going someplace together again. Now that'll be between them too. Len, they really need, miss each other. What happened in a few months? When I think of how close they were, the hours of makebelieve and dressup and playing ball and collecting. . . ."

"Grow up, Mother." Jeannie's voice was harsh. "Parialee's collecting something else now. Like her own crowd. Like jivetalk and rhythmandblues. Like teachers who treat her like a dummy and white kids who treat her like dirt; boys who think she's really something and chicks who. . . ."

"Jeannie, I know. It hurts."

"Well, maybe it hurts Parry too. Maybe. At least she's got a crowd. Just don't let it hurt Carol though, 'cause there's nothing she can do about it. That's all through, her and Parialee Phillips, put away with their paper dolls."

"No, Jeannie, no."

"It's like Ginger and me. Remember Ginger, my best friend in Horace Mann? But you hardly noticed when it happened to us, did you . . . because she was white? Yes, Ginger, who's got two kids now, who quit school year before last. Parry's never going to finish either. What's she got to do with Carrie any more? They're going different places. Different places, different crowds. And they're sorting. . . ."

"Now wait, Jeannie. Parry's just as bright, just as capable."

"They're in junior high, Mother. Don't you know about junior high? How they sort? And it's all where you're going. Yes and Parry's colored and Carrie's white. And you have to watch everything, what you wear and how you wear it and who you eat lunch with and how much homework you do and how you act to the teacher and what you laugh at. . . . And run with your crowd."

"It's that final?" asked Len. "Don't you think kids like Carol and Parry can show it doesn't *have* to be that way."

"They can't. They can't. They don't let you."

"No need to shout," he said mildly. "And who do you mean by 'they' and what do you mean by 'sorting'?"

*How they sort.* A foreboding of comprehension whirled within Helen. What was it Carol had told her of the Welcome Assembly the first day in junior high? The models showing How to Dress and How Not to Dress and half the girls in their loved new clothes watching their counterparts up on the stage—*their* straight skirt, their sweater, their earrings, lipstick, hairdo—"How Not to Dress," "a bad reputation for your school." It was nowhere in Carol's description, yet picturing it now, it seemed to Helen that a mute cry of violated dignity hung in the air. Later there had been a story of going to another Low 7 homeroom on an errand and seeing a teacher trying to wipe the forbidden lipstick off a girl who was fighting back and cursing. Helen could hear Carol's frightened, self-righteous tones: ". . . and I hope they expel her; she's the kind that gives Franklin Jr. a bad rep; she doesn't care about anything and always gets into fights." Yet there was nothing in these incidents to touch the heavy comprehension that waited. . . . Homework, the wonderings those times Jeannie and Carol needed help: "What if there's no one at home to give the help, and the teachers with their two hundred and forty kids a day can't or don't or the kids don't ask and they fall hopelessly behind, what then?"—but this too was unrelated. And what had it been that time about Parry? "Mother, Melanie and Sharon won't go if they know Parry's coming." Then of course you'll go with Parry, she's been your friend longer, she had answered, but where was it they were going and what had finally happened? Len, my head hurts, she felt like saying, in Carol's voice in the car, but Len's eyes were grave on Jeannie who was saying passionately:

"If you think it's so goddam important why do we have to live here where it's for real; why don't we move to Ivy like Betsy (yes, I know, money), where it's the deal to be buddies, in school anyway, three coloured kids and their father's a doctor or judge or something big wheel and one always gets elected President or head song girl or something to prove oh how we're democratic. . . . What do you want of that poor kid anyway? Make up your mind. Stay friends with Parry—but be one of the kids. Sure. Be a brain—but not a square. Rise on up, college prep, but don't get separated. Yes, stay one of the kids but. . . ."

"Jeannie. You're not talking about Carol at all, are you, Jeannie? Say it again. I wasn't listening. I was trying to think."

"She will not say it again," Len said firmly, "you look about ready to pull a Carol. One a day's our quota. And you, Jeannie, we'd better cool it. Too much to talk about for one session. . . . Here, come to the window and watch the Carol and Parry you're both all worked up about."

In the wind and the shimmering sunset light, half the children of the block are playing down the street. Leaping, bouncing, hallooing, tugging the kites of spring. In the old synchronized understanding, Carol and Parry kick, catch, kick, catch. And now Parry jumps on her pogo stick (the last time), Carol shadowing her, and Bubbie, arching his body in a semicircle of joy, bounding after them, high, higher, higher.

And the months go by and supposedly it is forgotten, except for the now and then when, self-important, Carol will say: I really truly did nearly faint, didn't I, Mother, that time I went to church with Parry?

And now seldom Parry and Carol walk the hill together. Melanie's mother drives by to pick up Carol, and the several times Helen has suggested Parry, too, Carol is quick to explain: "She's already left" or "She isn't ready; she'll make us late."

And after school? Carol is off to club or skating or library or someone's house, and Parry can stay for kickball only on the rare afternoons when she does not have to hurry home where Lucy, Bubbie, and the cousins wait to be cared for, now Alva works the four to twelve-thirty shift.

No more the bending together over the homework. All semester the teachers have been different, and rarely Parry brings her books home, for where is there space or time and what is the sense? And the phone never rings with: what you going to wear tomorrow, are you bringing your lunch, or come on over, let's design some clothes for the Katy Keane comic-book contest. And Parry never drops by with Alva for Saturday snack to or from grocery shopping.

And the months go by and the sorting goes on and seemingly it is over until that morning when Helen must stay home from work, so swollen and feverish is Carol with mumps.

The afternoon before, Parry had come by, skimming up the stairs, spilling books and binders on the bed: Hey frail, lookahere and wail, your momma askin for homework, what she got against YOU? . . . looking quickly once then not looking again and talking fast. . . . Hey, you bloomed. You gonna be your own pumpkin, hallowe'en? Your momma know yet it's mu-umps? And lumps. Momma says: no distress, she'll be by tomorrow morning see do you need anything while your momma's to work. . . . (Singing: *whole latta shakin goin on.*) All your 'signments is inside; Miss Rockface says the teachers to write 'em cause I mightn't get it right all right.

*But did not tell:* Does your mother work for Carol's mother? Oh, you're neighbors! Very well, I'll send along a monitor to open Carol's locker but you're only to take these things I'm writing down, nothing else. Now say after me: Miss Campbell is trusting me to be a good responsible girl. And go right to Carol's house. After school. Not stop anywhere on the way. Not lose anything. And only take. What's written on the list. You really gonna mess with that book stuff? Sign on *mine* says do-not-open-until-eX-mas. . . . That Mrs. Fernandez doll she didn't send nothin, she was the only, says feel better and read a book to report if you feel like and I'm the most for takin care for you; she's my most, wish I could get her but she only teaches 'celerated. . . . Flicking the old read books on the shelf but not opening to mock-declaim as once she used to . . . Vicky, Eddie's g.f. in Rockface office, she's on suspended for sure, yellin to Rockface: you bitchkitty don't you give me no more bad shit. That Vicky she can sure sling-ating-ring it. Staring out the window as if the tree not there in which they had hid out and rocked so often. . . . For sure. (*Keep mo-o-vin.*) Got me a new pink top and lilac skirt. Look sharp with this purple? Cinching in the wide belt as if delighted with what newly swelled above and swelled below. Wear it Saturday night to Sweet's, Modernaires Sounds of Joy, Leroy and Ginny and me goin if Momma'll stay home. IF. (*Shake my baby shake*). How come old folks still likes to party? Huh? Asking of Rembrandt's weary old face looking from the wall. How come (softly) you long-gone you. Touching her face to his quickly, lightly. NEXT mumps is your buddybud Melanie's turn to tote your stuff. *I'm* gettin the hoovus goovus. Hey you so unneat, don't care what you bed with. Removing the books and binders, ranging them on the dresser one by one, marking lipstick faces—bemused or mocking or amazed—on each paper jacket. Better. Fluffing out smoothing the quilt with exaggerated energy. Any little thing I can get, cause I gotta blow. Tossing up and catching their year-ago, arm-in-arm graduation picture, replacing it deftly, upside down, into its mirror crevice. Joe. Bring you joy juice or fizz water or kickapoo? Adding a frown line to one bookface. Twanging the paper fishkite, the Japanese windbell overhead, setting the mobile they had once made of painted eggshells and decorated straws to twirling and rocking. And is gone.

She talked to the lipstick faces after, in her fever, tried to stand on her head to match the picture, twirled and twanged with the violent overhead.

Sleeping at last after the disordered night. Having surrounded herself with the furnishings of that world of childhood she no sooner learned to live in comfortably, then had to leave.

The dollhouse stands there to arrange and rearrange; the shell and picture card collections to re-sort and remember; the population of dolls given away to little sister, borrowed back, propped all around to dress and undress and caress.

She has thrown off her nightgown because of the fever, and her just budding breast is exposed where she reaches to hold the floppy plush dog that had been her childhood pillow.

Not for anything would Helen have disturbed her. Except that in the unaccustomedness of a morning at home, in the bruised restlessness after the sleepless night, she clicks on the radio—and the storm of singing whirls into the room:

> . . . *sea of trouble all mingled with fire*
> *Come on my brethern we've got to go higher*
> *Wade, wade. . . .*

And Carol runs down the stairs, shrieking and shrieking. "Turn it off, Mother, turn it off." Hurling herself at the dial and wrenching it so it comes off in her hand.

"Ohhhhh," choked and convulsive, while Helen tries to hold her, to quiet.

"Mother, why did they sing and scream like that?"

"At Parry's church?"

"Yes." Rocking and strangling the cries. "I hear it all the time." Clinging and beseeching. ". . . What was it, Mother? Why?"

*Emotion,* Helen thought of explaining, *a characteristic of the religion of all oppressed peoples, yes your very own great-grandparents*—thought of saying. And discarded.

*Aren't you now, haven't you had feelings in yourself so strong they had to come out some way?* ("what howls restrained by decorum")—thought of saying. And discarded.

Repeat Alva: *hope . . . every word out of their own life. A place to let go. And church is home.* And discarded.

*The special history of the Negro people—history?—just you try living what must be lived every day*—thought of saying. And discarded.

And said nothing.

And said nothing.

And soothed and held.

"Mother, a lot of the teachers and kids don't like Parry when they don't even know what she's like. Just because . . ." Rocking again, convulsive and shamed. "And I'm not really her friend any more."

No news. Betrayal and shame. Who betrayed? Whose shame? Brought herself to say aloud: "But may be friends again. As Alva and I are."

The sobbing a whisper. "That girl Vicky who got that way when I fainted, she's in school. She's the one keeps wearing the lipstick and they wipe it off and she's always in trouble and now maybe she's expelled. Mother."

"Yes, lambie."

"She acts so awful outside but I remember how she was in church and whenever I see her now I have to wonder. And hear . . . like I'm her, Mother, like I'm her." Clinging and trembling. "Oh why do I have to feel it's happening to me too?"

"Mother, I want to forget about it all, and not care like Melanie. Why can't I forget? Oh why is it like it is and why do I have to care?"

Caressing, quieting.

Thinking: *caring asks doing. It is a long baptism into the seas of humankind, my daughter. Better immersion than to live untouched. . . . Yet how will you sustain?*

*Why is it like it is?*

Sheltering her daughter close, mourning the illusion of the embrace.

*And why do I have to care?*

While in her, her own need leapt and plunged for the place of strength that was not—where one could scream or sorrow while all knew and accepted, and gloved and loving hands waited to support and understand.

*For Margaret Heaton, who always taught*

1956

# GRACE PALEY
## *1922–2007*

Grace Paley was born Grace Goodside in New York City to Russian Jewish immigrants. Paley studied for one year at Hunter College and then at the New School with W.H. Auden, but never earned a degree. She left school and married her first husband, cinematographer Jess Paley, at age nineteen, with whom she had two children. Paley knew at an early age that she wanted to be a poet and wrote only verse until the 1950s. She is now best known for her lyrical short stories, whose characters are mostly working-class New York women. Though plot is minimal in a typical Paley story, as *The New York Times* describes it, "the language is so immediate, the characters so authentic, that the text is propelled by an innate urgency." Paley's first collection of short fiction, *The Little Disturbances of Man* (1959), though well received, earned her only moderate success. Gradually her recognition grew, and *The Little Disturbances of Man* was reissued by Viking Press nine years later, in 1968. Paley then published two more collections of short fiction, *Enormous Changes at the Last Minute* (1974) and *Later the Same Day* (1985), as well as three collections of poetry. Among her awards are a 1961 Guggenheim Fellowship, the Rea Award for the Short Story and the Vermont Governor's Award for Excellence in the Arts in 1993, and the PEN/Malamud Award for Excellence in Short Fiction in 1994. Her *Collected Stories* (1994) was a finalist for the National Book Award. Paley was a political activist all her life, as well as a teacher at Columbia University, Syracuse University, and Sarah Lawrence College.

## The Used-Boy Raisers

There were two husbands disappointed by eggs.

I don't like them that way either, I said. Make your own eggs. They sighed in unison. One man was livid; one was pallid.

There isn't a drink around here, is there? asked Livid.

Never find one here, said Pallid. Don't look; driest damn house. Pallid pushed the eggs away, pain and disgust his escutcheon.

Livid said, Now really, isn't there a drink? Beer? he hoped.

Nothing, said Pallid, who'd been through the pantries, closets, and refrigerators looking for a white shirt.

You're damn right, I said. I buttoned the high button of my powder-blue duster. I reached under the kitchen table for a brown paper bag full of an embroidery which asked God to Bless Our Home.

I was completing this motto for the protection of my sons, who were also Livid's. It is true that some months earlier, from a far place—the British plains in Africa—he had written hospitably to Pallid: I do think they're fine boys, you understand. I love them too, but Faith is their mother and now Faith is your wife. I'm so much away. If you want to think of them as yours, old man, go ahead.

Why, thank you, Pallid had replied, airmail, overwhelmed. Then he implored the boys, when not in use, to play in their own room. He made all efforts to be kind.

Now as we talked of time past and upon us, I pierced the ranch house that nestles in the shade of a cloud and a Norway maple, just under the golden script.

Ha-ha, said Livid, dripping coffee on his pajama pants, you'll never guess whom I met up with, Faith.

Who? I asked.

Saw your old boy friend Clifford at the Green Coq. He looks well. One thing must be said, he addressed Pallid, she takes good care of her men.

True, said Pallid.

How is he? I asked coolly. What's he doing? I haven't seen him in two years.

Oh, you'll never guess. He's marrying. A darling girl. She was with him. Little tootsies, little round bottom, little tummy—she must be twenty-two, but she looks seventeen. One long yellow braid down her back. A darling girl. Stubby nose, fat little underlip. Her eyes put on in pencil. Shoulders down like a dancer . . . slender neck. Oh, darling, darling.

You certainly observed her, said Pallid.

I have a functioning retina, said Livid. Then he went on. Better watch out, Faith. You'd be surprised, the dear little chicks are hatching out all over the place. All the sunny schoolgirls rolling their big black eyes. I hope you're really settled this time. To me, whatever is under the dam is in another county; however, in my life you remain an important person historically, he said. And that's why I feel justified in warning you. I must warn you. Watch out, sweetheart! he said, leaning forward to whisper harshly and give me a terrible bellyache.

What's all this about? asked Pallid innocently. In the first place, she's settled . . . and then she's still an attractive woman. Look at her.

Oh yes, said Livid, looking. An attractive woman. Magnificent, sometimes.

We were silent for several seconds in honor of that generous remark.

Then Livid said, Yes, magnificent, but I just wanted to warn you, Faith.

He pushed his eggs aside finally and remembered Clifford. A mystery wrapped in an enigma . . . I wonder why he wants to marry.

I don't know, it just ties a man down, I said.

And yet, said Pallid seriously, what would I be without marriage? In luminous recollection—a gay dog, he replied.

At this moment, the boys entered: Richard the horse thief and Tonto the crack shot.

Daddy! they shouted. They touched Livid, tickled him, unbuttoned his pajama top, whistled at the several gray hairs coloring his chest. They tweaked his ear and rubbed his beard the wrong way.

Well, well, he cautioned. How are you boys, have you been well? You look fine. Sturdy. How are your grades? he inquired. He dreamed that they were just up from Eton for the holidays.

I don't go to school, said Tonto. I go to the park.

I'd like to hear the child read, said Livid.

Me. I can read, Daddy, said Richard. I have a book with a hundred pages.

Well, well, said Livid. Get it.

I kindled a fresh pot of coffee. I scrubbed cups and harassed Pallid into opening a sticky jar of damson-plum jam. Very shortly, what could be read, had been, and Livid, knotting the tie strings of his pants vigorously, approached me at the stove. Faith, he admonished, that boy can't read a tinker's damn. Seven years old.

Eight years old, I said.

Yes, said Pallid, who had just remembered the soap cabinet and was rummaging in it for a pint. If they were my sons in actuality as they are in everyday life, I would send them to one of the good parochial schools in the neighborhood where reading is taught. Reading. St. Bartholomew's, St. Bernard's, St. Joseph's.

Livid became deep purple and gasped. Over my dead body. *Merde*,[1] he said in deference to the children. I've said, yes, you may think of the boys as your own, but if I ever hear they've come within an inch of that church, I'll run you through, you bastard. I was fourteen years old when in my own good sense I walked out of that grotto of deception, head up. You sonofabitch, I don't give a damn how *au courant*[2] it is these days, how gracious to be seen under a dome on Sunday. . . . Shit! Hypocrisy. Corruption. Cave dwellers. Idiots. Morons.

Recalling childhood and home, poor Livid writhed in his seat. Pallid listened, head to one side, his brows gathering the onsets of grief.

You know, he said slowly, we iconoclasts . . . we freethinkers . . . we latter-day masons . . . we idealists . . . we dreamers . . . we are never far from our nervous old mother, the Church. She is never far from us.

Wherever we are, we can hear, no matter how faint, her hourly bells, tolling the countryside, reverberating in the cities, bringing to our civilized minds the passionate deed of Mary. Every hour on the hour we are startled with remembrance of what was done for us. FOR US.

Livid muttered in great pain, Those bastards, oh oh oh, those contemptible, goddamnable bastards. Do we have to do the nineteenth century all over again? All right, he bellowed, facing us all, I'm ready. That Newman! He turned to me for approval.

You know, I said, this subject has never especially interested me. It's your little dish of lava.

Pallid spoke softly, staring past the arched purple windows of his soul. I myself, although I lost God a long time ago, have never lost faith.

What the hell are you talking about, you moron? roared Livid.

I have never lost my love for the wisdom of the Church of the World. When I go to sleep at night, I inadvertently pray. I also do so when I rise. It is not to God, it is to that unifying memory out of childhood. The first words I ever

---

1. Shit (French).  2. Fashionable (French).

wrote were: What are the sacraments? Faith, can you ever forget your old grandfather intoning Kaddish?[3] It will sound in your ears forever.

Are you kidding? I was furious to be drawn into their conflict. Kaddish? What do I know about Kaddish. Who's dead? You know my opinions perfectly well. I believe in the Diaspora,[4] not only as a fact but a tenet. I'm against Israel on technical grounds. I'm very disappointed that they decided to become a nation in my lifetime. I believe in the Diaspora. After all, they *are* the chosen people. Don't laugh. They really are. But once they're huddled in one little corner of a desert, they're like anyone else: Frenchies, Italians, temporal nationalities. Jews have one hope only—to remain a remnant in the basement of world affairs—no, I mean something else—a splinter in the toe of civilizations, a victim to aggravate the conscience.

Livid and Pallid were astonished at my outburst, since I rarely express my opinion on any serious matter but only live out my destiny, which is to be, until my expiration date, laughingly the servant of man.

I continued. I hear they don't even look like Jews any more. A bunch of dirt farmers with no time to read.

They're your own people, Pallid accused, dilating in the nostril, clenching his jaw. And they're under the severest attack. This is not the time to revile them.

I had resumed my embroidery. I sighed. My needle was now deep in the clouds which were pearl gray and late afternoon. I am only trying to say that they aren't meant for geographies but for history. They are not supposed to take up space but to continue in time.

They looked at me with such grief that I decided to consider all sides of the matter. I said, Christ probably had all that trouble—now that you mention it—because he knew he was going to gain the whole world but he forgot Jerusalem.

When you married us, said Pallid, and accused me, didn't you forget Jerusalem?

I never forget a thing, I said. Anyway, guess what. I just read somewhere that England is bankrupt. The country is wadded with installment paper.

Livid's hand trembled as he offered Pallid a light. Nonsense, he said. That's not true. Nonsense. The great British Island is the tight little fist of the punching arm of the Commonwealth.

What's true is true, I said, smiling.

Well, I said, since no one stirred, do you think you'll ever get to work today? Either of you?

Oh, my dear, I haven't even seen you and the boys in over a year. It's quite pleasant and cozy here this morning, said Livid.

Yes, isn't it? said Pallid, the surprised host. Besides, it's Saturday.

How do you find the boys? I asked Livid, the progenitor.

American, American, rowdy, uncontrolled. But you look well, Faith. Plumper, but womanly and well.

Very well, said Pallid, pleased.

But the boys, Faith. Shouldn't they be started on something? Just lining up little plastic cowboys. It's silly, really.

---

**3.** Hymns of praise to God in Judaism, here specifically part of the mourning ritual in prayer.   **4.** Literally, scattering. Here refers to the worldwide community of Jews dispersed (with a sense of exile) outside of Israel.

They're so young, apologized Pallid, the used-boy raiser.

You'd both better go to work, I suggested, knotting the pearl-gray late-afternoon thread. Please put the dishes in the sink first. Please. I'm sorry about the eggs.

Livid yawned, stretched, peeked at the clock, sighed. Saturday or no, alas, my time is not my own. I've got an appointment downtown in about forty-five minutes, he said.

I do too, said Pallid. I'll join you on the subway.

I'm taking a cab, said Livid.

I'll split it with you, said Pallid.

They left for the bathroom, where they shared things nicely—shaving equipment, washstand, shower, and so forth.

I made the beds and put the aluminum cot away. Livid would find a hotel room by nightfall. I did the dishes and organized the greedy day; dinosaurs in the morning, park in the afternoon, peanut butter in between, and at the end of it all, to reward us for a week of beans endured, a noble rib roast with little onions, dumplings, and pink applesauce.

Faith, I'm going now, Livid called from the hall. I put my shopping list aside and went to collect the boys, who were wandering among the rooms looking for Robin Hood. Go say goodbye to your father, I whispered.

Which one? they asked.

The real father, I said. Richard ran to Livid. They shook hands manfully. Pallid embraced Tonto and was kissed eleven times for his affection.

Goodbye now, Faith, said Livid. Call me if you want anything at all. Anything at all, my dear. Warmly with sweet propriety he kissed my cheek. Ascendant, Pallid kissed me with considerable business behind the ear.

Goodbye, I said to them.

I must admit that they were at last clean and neat, rather attractive, shiny men in their thirties, with the grand affairs of the day ahead of them. Dark night, the search for pleasure and oblivion were well ahead. Goodbye, I said, have a nice day. Goodbye, they said once more, and set off in pride on paths which are not my concern.

1959

# JAYNE ANNE PHILLIPS
*b. 1952*

Jayne Anne Phillips was born and raised in West Virginia and earned her B.A. from West Virginia University in 1974. Phillips felt "intricately bound" to her home, but she also knew she "wanted to leave." Following her graduation, she embarked on a wandering journey to California, and her various work and social experiences as she crossed America had a significant influence on her fiction. Phillips went on to earn an M.F.A. from the prestigious Iowa Writers' Workshop and published her award-winning first collection, *Sweethearts* (1976), consisting of 24 one-page stories, before she graduated. Her first major short story collection, *Black Tickets* (1979), earned her national commercial success and the Sue Kaufman Prize for First Fiction. Phillips' lyric prose, known for its unsentimental focus on love, loss, and lone survivors, is not restricted to short stories. Five years after *Black Tickets* came her first and bestselling novel, *Machine Dreams* (1984), nominated for the National Book Critics Circle Award and named one of the twelve best books of the year by the *New York Times Book Review*. For her second novel, *Shelter* (1995), Phillips won an Academy Award in Literature from the American Academy of Arts and Letters. Her other works include another short fiction collection, *Fast Lanes* (1987), and the novels *MotherKind* (2000), *Lark & Termite* (2009)—nominated for the National Book Award and the National Book Critics Circle Award—and, most recently, *Quiet Dell* (2013). Phillips is the recipient of a Guggenheim Fellowship and two National Endowment for the Arts fellowships. She has taught at numerous colleges and universities including Harvard University and Williams College, and she currently teaches in the creative writing program at Rutgers University.

# El Paso

### Dude

See I'd met this old dirt farmer in a bar the night before. Said he was selling his truck cheap and I could come down to La Rosa and pick it up. Said three hundred dollars and it didn't run too bad but I'd better buy it now. So I hitched down Sunday morning, mud churches on all three dirt streets ringing their black bells. I found him wringing a chicken's neck in the yard, did it quick and finished before he looked at me. Dark seamed face under a broad hat and the chicken head a little dangling thing hanging out his fist. I told him, said

I'd come about the truck, did he still want—thinking we were both pretty drunk and he might have dreamed he had a truck, since it didn't look like he had anything but a shanty house that leaned right into dirt. He spat and turned for me to follow him, holding the chicken now by a splayed leg that was bright orange in the rising heat. The nails on his hands were colored that same dull shine as hen's claws.

Us walking in the dust yard past old tires and a rotten bedspring, mule tied to a pump by the chicken shed, and he stands finally by this thing that's a red fifties Chevy with a built-on bed shelved with chicken cages. Crosses and a blackened corn husk doll hanging from the mirror, keys strung on a hair ribbon. I got in and drove around the yard fast, chickens squawking and the old cur dogs snapping at the wheels. The old man squatted where he was, plucked the hen. Feathers flew and dropped as I pulled up. I said the truck ran good and if he had the title I'd pay him now and take it.

He motioned me inside a house somehow dark even in all that light. Smell of wool shawls and vinegar. I stumble blind into a table and voices, Spanish curses, stop and start. I look up and Rita, she's standing there not three feet away, having ripped the curtains off one window; she's screaming in her voice that goes throaty and harsh, and the light pours in all over her. Hot yellow gravy of light, her black eyes, and the red skirt tight; blouse loose old lace ripped at the shoulder. I wanted to roll my hand in her; I could feel her wet against my legs. The old woman stands by the stove, side of her face shining, and when she turns I see she's not crying but one eye weeps. Rita walks past me steaming from her hands, the cheap plastic curtains clutched and dragging.

I watch the old man rummage in a drawer but feel her at the end of the long room. Rita moving, bending over a small chair. Old man counts the money and I turn to watch her. The light rolling now, leaked into the dark, ripples the skin of the dark and flies fly up in loose knots; low slow buzz in corners yellowed and pulled out by the light that rolls across the surfaces of things in yellow blocks. Dust in the light; and her body moving down the long room pulls a white path like an animal leaving water. She bends from the waist; under the cloth her thighs are muscles, long curves. In the chair sits a baby whose head is too big. His legs don't reach the floor; his skin is stretched tight and pale like the light is under it. His hair is white and fine, swirled on his man-sized head, and I know he is a child only by the way he cradles a shoe to his face. Rocks the shoe slow in short arms. Rita has her hands in his hair, her shoulders tensed and curved to him. A sound catches in her throat and comes out low, folding into the yellow room. Thick juice of light circling, curling us in. Child wheezing and rocking, rocking the shoe slow; his mouth on it. It is her shoe and Rita croons, rocking with him, pulling the shoe away.

## Rita

I bought my mother those glasses so she wouldn't have to live in the dark, spent a hundred dollars on an El Paso doctor so she could see in the light without the eye burning. And she wouldn't wear them. Would hide them and move like a bat in the dark, the windows covered. The child in his chair with his sounds, she singing her songs low in the dark, he weaving in his chair. Me youngest of six, and at near fifty she gave birth to him, his white skin and his head hanging like a heavy bloom on the neck that couldn't move it. His eyes rolling back to see in that head that must have been a field of snow inside. No father, she said, he is what was in me. And the eye in her too, still pouring from her slow. Bringing grain from the store on the mule, she crossed against the light and a truck knocked her down, the mule kicking her face. And so the eye weeps and hurts in the daylight. Pounding meal on the wood table she sings in the dark like she sang then, my five brothers building ears in the yard, and me they called *brujita*, little witch.

At dusk the townspeople came to be healed. Paid her in corn and cloth. Then the corn stacked by the door and tomatoes hung to dry and sides of bacon, their white fat thick as my waist. She in her white shawls and her almost black skin put her hands in powders ground from roots. The villagers knelt, her sound wheeling over them. Their eyes fluttered and their hands unclenched, jerking as sounds came. *Muerte dios muerte muerte.* They got up and bowed to the witch their children won't touch. Castanets' slow dull clack followed them, their feet going away in the dark yard. From the time I was a baby she gave me a sharp stick and told me to draw them in the dirt to keep their spirits from returning. She made her witching dolls from husks; when I was older she gave me paints to draw their faces. I made them: farmers' heads and goitered women already old.

My father was gone long weeks to Las Vegas, Reno. Sometimes when he came back we moved to hotels in El Paso and bought clothes in stores. Remember, she'd say, cracked voice clacking on her teeth, you ain't no Spanish brats— You got Gypsy blood and your daddy's Apache cheeks. I remember her long fingers on my face. He didn't come back. The house was her power and she wouldn't leave. The town still creeps to her at dusk, women with shawls low over faces. The priest says it's sacrilege, they heaping ashes by the door.

Already I was with men and she was big, her belly strained, and the labor went two days. Women from the town wouldn't help. She cut herself to let the child's head pass and the women, hearing she had a devil, burned candles by their beds. Later the old man came with his shriveled dolls, his silence, and no name I ever heard her say. He built a chair on rollers when the child could sit and kept lanterns lit all night to make the sounds soft.

Now the child's sounds are muffled and low except when I dance. He knows me, holds out his hands for my shoes. My mother takes dried cactus from a wood box and grinds it, sprinkles a powder on his hair. I make the signs and the castanets warm in my fingers; we put the child's chair in the center of the room and my feet on brushed boards start slow thud. The drum, her low voice quavering, my arms high, the clack silver clack and the child's eyes focus, hold me fast, faster, me spinning around him. He holds up his head, and under his skin, I see the pale blue veins. Faster, my feet pound floor, her voice louder, and he whines a high clean whine that holds me spinning. Ceiling twists, floor circles smaller, small. My hands over him stop. Suddenly he sleeps, he sleeps and we lie, all of us, in the hot dark house. Listen to him breathe.

The old man sells his truck, won't take my money. He sees girls grind in city bars, knows how the money comes: my rooms, hotels, the avenue. The child's sounds are whispers, now; he sleeps too long. At the white hospital, us black against walls, they say the shunt in his head won't drain. He won't eat anymore, drinks from bottles, watches me; why do I come here. She hacks at the naked chicken on a board. Her face, the eye drawn; I moving away through the yard. This dust on my legs yellow as meal is burning, burning.

## Dude

She walks out through dirt yard to the road. I run, touch her arm. Her skin bare, dark walnut skin stained milky, and I stand, my hand drenched in her skin, ask her, is she going back to El Paso. In the truck the land goes by us glaring as a lidless eye, sun a high glittering ring. Seeming to whirl in itself like hornets, it throws its heat on land laid out flat to the burning. We glide horizontal on a strip of road. In the tiny room of the truck I feel heavy in the rivery heat. Between us on the cracked seat a space gets small. Her satin skirt is faded in circles I could crush to my thumb. Under her heavy hair, her damp temples, I want to feel the shape of her skull. My hands are deaf. Eyes stony with light she watches me try to see the road, her opaled eyes seeming to come out at me yet falling back in their deep oil that scalds the side of my face.

I pull over, stop the truck, get out, lean against it. Up the road a café, all night lights still on, runs a lit band of letters around its roof: hamburgers, thick shakes, onion rings fried gold. I walk up there and a woman with her hair dyed brass swabs the counter with a rag. Her wide grin red, her front tooth gold, she lets me talk and counting change she fingers my palm.

Ice cream packed hard melts slow on my hands as I'm walking back. I see Rita hitching by the side of the road. I hand her a cone, get in the truck and start the engine. She climbs in. Motor idling, sweet cold in our mouths, I pull her across the seat and press my fingers hard at the base of her neck. My breath comes out a ragged curve against her eyes.

## Watching

He so in love with her it was something to see. Dude so caught up and dedicated like a single eye to his own loving. How she touched it off. I suppose he was about to pack it in before he saw her and thought there was still something to do. Walking up the hill, touching him with her hip and walking, she moved her hip was delicate and blue beside his thigh.

This was El Paso, 1965. She danced in topless bars, said really she was a painter but she needed supplies. Supplies she said are always hard to get, sometimes you just have to put out and get them and go off with them. It was plain he wanted to go off with her but in the summer in El Paso it's hard to move anywhere except down the street to the bars. I remember there was always dog puke on the sidewalks in El Paso. All those strays get the sweats around noon and bring up the garbage they ate in the back alleys of beanerys at dawn. Think about Texas and there's those skinny fanned ribs heaving.

Dude used to go down to Bimpy's nights and watch her dance. Bimpy was a greasy-kneed old faggot who liked him plenty and gave us free bourbon. She'd come over between songs and do a number with us, wringing with sweat so she'd wet the paper and we'd have to keep lighting it. She danced on this three-foot-square red stage, under two old ceiling fans that looked like little airplane propellers. She moved under their sleepy drone; always there was something about to break out. From our table in the corner I could smell the old roses smell of her. She was dark-haired and black-eyed though she swore she wasn't Spanish, medium-sized but small-boned with green apple breasts; then suddenly her twisted child-bearing hips that were somehow off-center and rolled gentle to the left when she walked, rolling slow up the hill past the plate glass liquor stores. Dancing, she'd throw her dusty scent past the two old spots Bimpy had and the cowboys threw bills on the stage. Dude hated the dancing; said she was frigid as hell afterward, like loving a wind-up doll except for her mouth and the curves it took on in the dark. She wouldn't even move with the lights on, he said.

After the show she'd stay and help Bimp sweep up and then we'd walk out the door into the oily night. Everything wide awake and the fat yam-skinned women talking Spanish to their boyfriends, walking with their stemmed words and twined fingers past the blank-eyed 5 & 10's. We'd walk up the hill, they in front and me trailing behind. She talked in her Texas voice about nothing usually, it just being important there in the lit-up black to have her voice with its honeyed drawl and bitter edge; she walking slope slide up the hill, whisper of her nylons brushing and the Mexican boys shooting craps on the sidewalk. They ain't but thirteen, she'd say when they looked up at her heels clicking, Old enough. My daddy made a small fortune at craps. He used to call it dealin with the demon. She'd say that and slap Dude on the ass.

She'd boil those stark black Colombian beans on a stove in their flat and it'd heat up the kitchen so we'd have to sit out the window on the roof. By this time the town was near silent and steaming slow like a wet iron. Always drink hot coffee on hot nights, she'd say, Brings the sweat to the outside and lets you sleep. Dude dozed with his head in her lap and she'd turn to me, ask me, oils are on sale and could she borrow a few bucks till next week. You know, she'd say, twisting his hair in her fingers, Them stars are just holes in the sky after all. And while I'm sleeping in that hot bed everything I ever thought of having falls into em.

Finally I'd go to bed and hear them in the hall going back and forth to the bathroom, him usually drunk by then and tripping at the door. People up and down the hall behind doors yelled at him to shut up. Her arms reaching in the yellow blouse to grab the light string, her hips moving in their funny bumbling slow walk past my door, not quite touching his legs, and the mosquitoes louder than her quiet laughter: this was 4 A.M. in El Paso.

I saw him a couple of years later in Toledo, said he was into racing junk cars, said it was some kick. Said you're tearing around and around under the lights in these things that are all going to fly apart and pile up. Said he heard she was living down in Austin with some dyke. Said cracking up those cars was great, said he was making money and cracking them up was some kick, it was really something.

## Bimp

When I opened the place in '46 I didn't think no one could pull nothin over on me again. I was in the war just like anyone else, ain't no one gonna tell me I got any debt. I had enough tin food and muddy boots and hair lice to last me. One goddamn big lie is what it was, I figured that out. There ain't no losing or winning anywhere is what I figured out, ain't nobody gonna pitch me into no fake contest again. I sailed into San Fran with a knee like a corkscrew and the salt air made it ache like a bitch. I came back home and opened the place and I figured I was standing ground. Back then the Mexicans used to skunk around at the alley door till I told em to beat it. I can see em now, slinking off in their red shirts under that one streetlamp between the trash cans. My own grandmother was a Mex. She smelled like a rotten cantaloupe and raved in Spanish about the goddamn Church that did nothin but bury her endless brats and the man that beat her. There ain't no losing or winning. These black-eyed thieves and yellow Mex boys think I got something they want, let em swagger in the front door so what. I could tell em if they ask—no matter what they got they got more to get and the thing don't end. Gaining like a squirrel on a wheel, sure. When I saw them three kids I knew what the game was. Her saying what I needed was a dancer, the dude pretty as a rodeo star, and his sidekick one of them hunched-up watchers. I said Listen, I got me a dancer, and she said Try me out. The dude stood there grinding a butt into the floor in his high-heeled boots. I said Well I don't allow no dancers in here without escorts, gets plenty rough in here ya know, this ain't Philadelphia. She said she was from La Rosa, one of them dirt-eating border towns, and I laughed, said You didn't get far didja. She smiled, her mouth dark pink and those flashy Spanish teeth strong as an animal's. The cowboy finally looked at me, said, rolling the filter of his cigarette, We'll be here at nine. The watcher stood there looking from face to face like he was judge of the whole damn game and I said Suit yourselves.

## Dude

Back then I was a carpenter like everyone. I quit school and went down to Texas, air so thick and slow it's like swimming. That flat-out heat comes after you and drinks you up; she'd been there all her life. The steam in her; I lost what I was thinking in rooms thick, full of us; her black hair in the sheets a wound thread, thick black lines of drawings she kept hidden, her charcoaled fingertips. She worked on the avenue, turned tricks in a hotel room with a blue ceiling and one light bulb in a fringed shade. I told her she had to stop it and she said well, she'd dance but she wasn't carrying no slop to farmers in a beanery. The difference is, she said, I say how I'm used.

By noon those days I was a walking fever, my hands cut and sore from tar-ring feed store roofs, and since I first saw her I come into the heat the place the heat like a bitch dog and lived with it. When I got home it was late evening and she lay almost naked on the roof. Past crooked streets the tracks ran off white, cutting their light and crossing. Sluggish trains changed cars in the hard-baked yard. Beside her on the shingled heat, I smelled her salt skin and she laughed, pulled my face to her throat. We rolled, hot shingles pressed to my back, and later the shower was cold. We drank iced whiskey in jelly glasses and she danced up the hall dripping, throwing water off her hair. In the sti-fled space, window at the end painted over and light through the cracked paint patterned on the floor, her back was beaded and swaying. Water backed up past the drain spilled cold past my feet onto the floor and in our rooms we wet the sheets, slept in their damp. Her hair looped in my hands dried slow: past us the trains whistled their open howls.

It was too hot to cook and we ate avocados, jalapeños, white cheese. City lights came on, blue and pink neon stood out cool and she leaning into the mirror painted her face for the bar. I forget all of it but her lacquered eyes. And she stepping off the curb in those high-heeled shoes, kids in Chevys grinning.

Sometimes she came back from Bimp's so late the light was coming up. Been with a john: she only did it she said when the money was too good to pass up. She'd come home with a bottle of brandy, get into bed with a pack of cards and we'd play poker to win till the sun was flat on the floor. Cards buckled finally and thrown against the wall, shades drawn, we lay there see, until we could talk. Her face in the white bed, her face by the window; light behind the shade as she stood there colored her face blurred and fading like a photograph. It's all right just come here.

## Bimp

Like I said, I had another dancer. She was blond, from the East, up North I think. She had the look of someone didn't sweat much, just burned a coal inside. Ran off finally with some slick Mex to Panama. Could tell easy she was one to leave home over and over till her feet wore down to a root that just planted where she ran out of steam. The men liked that white hair and light eyes and those rhinestone shoes she wore. She had that hard crumpled look of a dame that's been around but don't know why. I knew she was thirty-five but I hired her anyway. Them white blonds is scarce down here.

I put em onstage together the first night and they set up a wheel the whole place was turning on, what with the smaller one and her seventeen-year-old's tits and them hips moving so you knew she'd been used since she was old enough to wiggle. Them border girls start with big brother in the alley, them towns full of female things dropping litters in the street. She moved with that clinched dark face, all of it a fist in her hips, and beside her the tall blond looked like a movie magazine none of em could touch. There was some kind of confusion, smelled like burning rubber. Spilt drinks and a goddamn brawl in the back at the card table. I got em offstage and turned up the lights and ordered everyone out of the place. Was just me picking up broken glass and the girls leaning by the bar and the two men dealing a hand at the corner table like nothing happened. The girls were dressed, the blond fooling with her necklace, talking low. Her blue eyes drinking that Spanish mouth she say soft, Hey Honey, how long you figure on dancing with that swayback of yours and that funny hip—dawn, can you get this thing fastened—no, here—Lemme put it on and you can maybe pinch it with your teeth—She leans over the Spanish, her red lips apart like she's still talking, beer tipped in her hand and dripping all over their stockings. And the smaller one, black hair to her waist hands midway in the air, stands there like a stone saying over and over, I can't fix it, I can't fix it.

After that I had em alternate nights and a week later the blond split. The cowboy and his sidekick was in here nights with the Spanish the two of em diddling with cards and race forms in the corner. Figure it's been ten years ago. Gave me a few good tips and then same as now—when I hit at the track I blow it all same night, ain't nobody gonna tell me I won nothin.

## The Blond

Rita. She left the avenue, the hotel, smell of urine and spent sex in the halls. We traded johns and other things; me by her door in blue light, cognac in my hand and my robe open. I asked her low, A toast to the hungry jokers? mouth on my raised glass and she let me in . . .

She let on like we never knew each other, but them hot nights I told her stories. Like how it was when I was seventeen like her. Ginette Hatcher was my name then, in Maine all the gray years. She born and died in Maine, she dying there still I guess. I took the name the first truck driver gave me, called me Babe and I answered to it ever since. I left my husband that I only saw in the dark after the boats came in or before they went out, that man always cold and fish slime on his hands. I left soon as the baby was born, thinking the best anyone could tell the kid was that Mama took off. There something out there besides that gray wet, that heavy roll. My cousins and uncles was all lobstermen ever since I can remember. My dad too, but he died when I was so young all he is to me is a furred chest and smell of oiled rope. He died of lobster is what Mom said, and she killed hundreds of them. Scratch-clink of those claws against the boiling pot was a woman sound, a metallic scratch round as rings.

Wind and rock and weeds on the beach a gray stink, no color cold; I kept fish eyes in bottles and sold them all summer to the tourists, to the queers and dandies and the painted old things with poodles. Once an old woman with money asked me to come to her hotel and read the Bible to her. She opened it and I started in. After a while I looked up and she was staring out the window like a sleepwalker, her old hat in her lap. She said what a blessed child I was to come to womanhood here by the sea, so far from heat and corruption. I said Yes Ma'am. The fire comes from the feet, she said, from the walkers and the black hair. She didn't see me anymore. I grabbed my sweater and ran home across the hotel beach, the big umbrellas blind and rolling on their sides. I found twenty dollars folded in my pocket and I bought me some red patent leather spike heels. I hid them in my room and only put them on at night and I was the walker walking and the dancer dancing in my fiery feet, and holes in the floor where I burned through.

Tires on the big trucks burn. You smell them in the cab, smell the motor boiling; my suitcase wedged between my knees and the truckers touching my dress. I lived everywhere and been to Mexico. I danced mostly, waited tables, worked in a library once and couldn't feel my feet for the shiny floor. Down in Texas any man on the street would buy me supper. By the time I got to Bimp's those nights I was already loaded. Blur, dark oiled skins past the lights, ice in glasses. Cold melts in a circle, hot whiskey, hot Texas. And Rita shows up, so smooth and so hot; eyes like black glass, sunk in, burned young. Onstage she scared me, made that cold ocean roll in my head . . . then the lights were on, jeers from the floor, and that little pimp pushing us stumbling into the dressing room. Where I lean against the wall and watch her shaking by the sink, cold water on her wrists, and we look at each other. They say the world ends in fire and ice; I say it's already over. That hot pavement burns you straight through: that's why I did it, kept moving—no slow cooking and my claws raking walls. These streets, raunchy brass, my feet on fire burns up that dead ice.

I split way south with a rich dude. Red birds and black-eyed men. Been some since then. I'm doing OK, I got it made, and the cold don't come so much now.

## *Rita*

I lived with Dude those months in two rooms, rickety bed on blocks and past the windows the roof steamed between shingles. Long afternoons I cut the thin tar bubbles with my nails, oils warm on the paper, and the tubes heated till their lettering came off in my hands. I drew the trains: red gashes and the tracks black rips underneath. His hands felt furred with dust. When he was roofing, tar smudged the lines and crosses in his palms, left the whorls of his fingers and their black smell on my hips. Some days we stayed in bed, kept the fans turning, buzzing; we had cold wine and coarse brown bread. At night the bars were crowded with drunks, some of them sick in the heat. Dancing, I didn't watch them; I saw the flat brushed land outside the house in La Rosa, looking tawny-colored from the shaded rooms, but out there, walking, you felt hard hot sand and the color spreads into a wasted brown.

I think of what happened and it happens each time the same way. When I go back they are padding the cart with skins. Inside in his bed the child's face is drawn and blue. He breathes faint strangled bleats and my mother waits, sewing pelts to wrap him. At dark she feels his throat and says there's no breath; we leave with the cart. In the skins his face is white and his light hair long as a girl's. The hitched mule swings its head, flares nostrils at the fresh smell and moves skittish toward the hills. The old man bends in brimmed hat, shuffles to low chant, and she walks behind, scatters fine powder on the ground. Cart rocking slow and the child's face in my lap is sunken, lids on rolled eyes tight closed. All night we keep moving on the sloped land. Sand rolls its barren striped bars; the sky is inked and slashed in the foothills where we stop, take bundled wood from the cart, tie it with cords. She knots leather in the dark and the old man's voice is hoarse. At dawn she piles brush and the corded wood; we lift the child, straining, jangling the bracelets on his arms. She lights dried skins wrapped on a stick, touches him, and he starts to burn. The wood catches and through the fire I think I see his face move. It moves again and I throw her back, digging, clawing at the hot wood under him. They watch me try to reach him, now he is all fire. Running around the stench I fall and their old faces over me say I only dreamed it. I smell the skins and his flesh, the incense burning under him.

Mule leading then down the ravine to where the light stretches out on land like a smooth film of egg. I stumble and touch the animal's hide, feel ribs under stiff mousy hair. The old man walks ahead, his back a leathered board under cloth. She stays there by the smell until it is finished; quiet, she waits to take the bones.

Hours walking, sun high and the road a sudden empty strip. The old man waits for me, then turns in the glare and tells me again that I dreamed it. I see his knife and serape on his waist, know he's not going back for her. I won't go back to her either. Smoke in my mouth, I smell the wheeling birds and the tight white face behind the bristled fire. Old man walking away on the road with his mule and there are trucks, horns, voices, Baby wanna ride?

## Dude

I remember the rains had started, blown in off the Gulf. She'd been to La Rosa. Always when she came back she was this hunted dog, stringy and gutted and ready to gnaw its own foot. I came in and she was walking circles in the room, rubbing her hands. I saw her fingers were torn; bruised purple under the nails. The rolled drawings were torn and smoldering on the floor. I moved to stomp them out and heard her moan, turned saw matches in her hands; she striking and tossing them in the air where they'd flare and fall smoking. I grabbed her arms and everything was breaking, chairs cracking on the floor and the light bulb splintering. I saw her hair on fire under my hand and I rolled her onto the bed. All the time she moaned long and low like I wasn't there except that this thing was on top of her. Her eyes were calm and her burned hair broke in my hand. I pulled her down and heard my breath coming high and watered like a woman's; she fell and lay there, her lips moving. She drooled and the spit flecked red where her teeth had cut. I stood over her and yelled for her to see me. Her eyes rolling past me pulled my hands to her clothes and the cloth ripped. I slapped her, kept slapping her and my hands were fists. I looked up and he's watching us—always goddamn watching us—then he is talking quietly and pulling her from under me.

## Watching

He was ramming his fists into the floor beside her head but he thought he was hitting her and asked me later had he killed her. The floor was splintered, fine wood in his hands, and she under him stared glazed at the ceiling. Her mumbled Spanish mixed in the room with the sulfur smell of something burned. When I pulled her from under him I saw her hair was burned ragged and her shirt seared in the back. I took it off and wrapped her in blankets; she was shivering. There was broken glass and her fingers were bloodied somehow. She kept talking to nothing, tossing her head from side to side, hands clinched in my hair so tight that when I lay her down I can't move from her. Have to bend over her, my face close though she doesn't see me; I touch her lips, the cuts scabbing and her teeth flecked with the dull dried blood. I smell her breath coming shallow and fast, say her name over and over until she hears me. Almost focusing she slides her hands slow from my hair down my face to her breasts, holding them.

Late that night, Dude sits by the window. Rain spills in; he watches the smoky trains jerk in the yard, moisture on warm soot a fine dust in the air. He blinks like he's slapped when he hears her clutch her throat and turn in her sleep. I talk, Dude smells her on his split knuckles, and the streaked curtains move all night.

Toward morning he paced the room, circling from door to window. Hands held delicate, he looked at me. His eyes I think were gray and heavy-lashed;

the lid of the right one drooped and softened that side of his face. Finally he turned and left; his pointed boots tapped a faint click on the stairs each step down.

She woke up in twisted blankets and raised her fingers to her face. We ate the bread slow, her mouth bleeding a little. I'm seeing her in summer by the stove in their room, sweat clouding her hair and her lips pursed with cheap wine; she smoothing her cotton skirt and throwing back her hair to bend over the burner with a cigarette, frowning as the blue flame jets up fast. On the street under my window she is walking early in the day, tight black skirt ripped in the slit that moves on her leg. Looking back she sees me watching and buys carnations from the blind man on the corner, walks back, tosses them up to me. She laughs and the flowers falling all around her are pale; their long stems tangling. The street is shaded in buildings and her face turned up to me is lost in black hair. She is small and she is washed in grilled shadow.

Fingers too swollen to button her shirt, she asked me would I get her something to soak them in. At the drugstore buying antiseptic and gauze I felt her standing shakily by the couch, touching her mouth with her purple fingers. Walking back fast I knew she was gone, took almost nothing. The ashed drawings were swept up and thrown probably from the window. He left for good soon after, thirty pounds of Mexican grass stashed in the truck for a connection in Detroit. I went far north as I could get, snow that winter in Ottawa a constant slow sift that cooled and cleaned a dirt heat I kept feeling for months; having nothing of her but a sketch I'd taken from where she hid them: a picture of trains dark slashed on tracks, and behind them the sky opens up like a hole.

1979

# EDGAR ALLAN POE
## *1809–1849*

Poe was born in Boston, the son of itinerant actors who died before he was three years old. He was adopted by a Virginia couple, the Allans, whose name he added to his own. His student days at the University of Virginia were brought to a quick end by his drinking and gambling; but then, enlisting in the army, he served soberly and well from 1827 to 1829. Accepted into West Point in 1830, he quickly ruined his prospects for a military career by more carousing, and that established a pattern he never again escaped. In 1836 he married his cousin Virginia Clemm, then a girl of thirteen, and tried to support her by writing and editing. He was an editor of the Richmond *Southern Literary Messenger,* among other publications, and for a time had his own magazine, *The Stylus.* He won a number of literary prizes early in his writing career, but his earnings remained meager, and alcoholic excesses repeatedly cost him his jobs in journalism. After his wife died in 1847, he became engaged to a wealthy widow; there was hope of relief from his long run of misfortune and poverty. Traveling to meet her in 1849, he met some acquaintances and with them set out to celebrate the change in his luck. After this binge he was found nearly unconscious in a Baltimore street and died a few days later. His short fiction, with its effects of terror and its supernatural trappings, made him a household name for American readers, though in fact there are few traces of American experience in his work. Gothic devices and the mood of German romanticism were his specialty. He has been called the inventor of the detective story. His critical writings—including, for example, his insistence on unity of effect in the short story—have deeply influenced literary taste and practice. His poetry has been admired more greatly and persistently abroad, particularly in France, than at home. He is remembered, as well, for the precariousness of his career, for his striking personal appearance, his fine manners, his debauchery, and his poverty—the stuff of romantic legend. His work is readily available in numerous anthologies and collected editions.

## The Fall of the House of Usher

*Son cœur est un luth suspendu;*
*Sitôt qu'on le touche il résonne.*
—De Béranger[1]

---

**1.** His heart is a ready lute/As soon as it is touched it resounds; from *Le Refus* (lines 41–42), by Pierre-Jean de Béranger (1780–1857), French poet.

During the whole of a dull, dark, and soundless day in the autumn of the year, when the clouds hung oppressively low in the heavens, I had been passing alone, on horseback, through a singularly dreary tract of country; and at length found myself, as the shades of the evening drew on, within view of the melancholy House of Usher. I know not how it was—but, with the first glimpse of the building, a sense of insufferable gloom pervaded my spirit. I say insufferable; for the feeling was unrelieved by any of that half-pleasurable, because poetic, sentiment, with which the mind usually receives even the sternest natural images of the desolate or terrible. I looked upon the scene before me—upon the mere house, and the simple landscape features of the domain, upon the bleak walls, upon the vacant eye-like windows, upon a few rank sedges, and upon a few white trunks of decayed trees—with an utter depression of soul which I can compare to no earthly sensation more properly than to the after-dream of the reveller upon opium: the bitter lapse into everyday life, the hideous dropping off of the veil. There was an iciness, a sinking, a sickening of the heart, an unredeemed dreariness of thought which no goading of the imagination could torture into aught of the sublime. What was it—I paused to think—what was it that so unnerved me in the contemplation of the House of Usher? It was a mystery all insoluble; nor could I grapple with the shadowy fancies that crowded upon me as I pondered. I was forced to fall back upon the unsatisfactory conclusion, that while, beyond doubt, there *are* combinations of very simple natural objects which have the power of thus affecting us, still the analysis of this power lies among considerations beyond our depth. It was possible, I reflected, that a mere different arrangement of the particulars of the scene, of the details of the picture, would be sufficient to modify, or perhaps to annihilate its capacity for sorrowful impression; and, acting upon this idea, I reined my horse to the precipitous brink of a black and lurid tarn that lay in unruffled lustre by the dwelling, and gazed down—but with a shudder even more thrilling than before—upon the remodelled and inverted images of the gray sedge, and the ghastly tree-stems, and the vacant and eye-like windows.

Nevertheless, in this mansion of gloom I now proposed to myself a sojourn of some weeks. Its proprietor, Roderick Usher, had been one of my boon companions in boyhood; but many years had elapsed since our last meeting. A letter, however, had lately reached me in a distant part of the country—a letter from him—which, in its wildly importunate nature, had admitted of no other than a personal reply. The MS.[2] gave evidence of nervous agitation. The writer spoke of acute bodily illness, of a mental disorder, which oppressed him, and of an earnest desire to see me, as his best, and indeed his only personal friend, with a view of attempting, by the cheerfulness of my society, some alleviation of his malady. It was the manner in which all this, and much more, was said—it was the apparent *heart* that went with his request—which allowed me no room for hesitation; and I accordingly obeyed forthwith what I still considered a very singular summons.

Although, as boys, we had been even intimate associates, yet I really knew little of my friend. His reserve had been always excessive and habitual. I was aware, however, that his very ancient family had been noted, time out of

2. Manuscript.

mind, for a peculiar sensibility of temperament, displaying itself, through long ages, in many works of exalted art, and manifested, of late, in repeated deeds of munificent yet unobtrusive charity, as well as in a passionate devotion to the intricacies, perhaps even more than to the orthodox and easily recognizable beauties, of musical science. I had learned, too, the very remarkable fact, that the stem of the Usher race, all time-honored as it was, had put forth, at no period, any enduring branch; in other words, that the entire family lay in the direct line of descent, and had always, with very trifling and very temporary variation, so lain. It was this deficiency, I considered, while running over in thought the perfect keeping of the character of the premises with the accredited character of the people, and while speculating upon the possible influence which the one, in the long lapse of centuries, might have exercised upon the other—it was this deficiency, perhaps, of collateral issue, and the consequent undeviating transmission, from sire to son, of the patrimony with the name, which had, at length, so identified the two as to merge the original title of the estate in the quaint and equivocal appellation of the "House of Usher"—an appellation which seemed to include, in the minds of the peasantry who used it, both the family and the family mansion.

I have said that the sole effect of my somewhat childish experiment, that of looking down within the tarn, had been to deepen the first singular impression. There can be no doubt that the consciousness of the rapid increase of my superstition—for why should I not so term it?—served mainly to accelerate the increase itself. Such, I have long known, is the paradoxical law of all sentiments having terror as a basis. And it might have been for this reason only, that, when I again uplifted my eyes to the house itself, from its image in the pool, there grew in my mind a strange fancy—a fancy so ridiculous, indeed, that I but mention it to show the vivid force of the sensations which oppressed me. I had so worked upon my imagination as really to believe that about the whole mansion and domain there hung an atmosphere peculiar to themselves and their immediate vicinity: an atmosphere which had no affinity with the air of heaven, but which had reeked up from the decayed trees, and the gray wall, and the silent tarn: a pestilent and mystic vapor, dull, sluggish, faintly discernible, and leaden-hued.

Shaking off from my spirit what *must* have been a dream, I scanned more narrowly the real aspect of the building. Its principal feature seemed to be that of an excessive antiquity. The discoloration of ages had been great. Minute fungi overspread the whole exterior, hanging in a fine tangled web-work from the eaves. Yet all this was apart from any extraordinary dilapidation. No portion of the masonry had fallen; and there appeared to be a wild inconsistency between its still perfect adaptation of parts, and the crumbling condition of the individual stones. In this there was much that reminded me of the specious totality of old woodwork which has rotted for long years in some neglected vault, with no disturbance from the breath of the external air. Beyond this indication of extensive decay, however, the fabric gave little token of instability. Perhaps the eye of a scrutinizing observer might have discovered a barely perceptible fissure, which, extending from the roof of the building in front, made its way down the wall in a zigzag direction, until it became lost in the sullen waters of the tarn.

Noticing these things, I rode over a short causeway to the house. A servant in waiting took my horse, and I entered the Gothic archway of the hall. A valet, of stealthy step, thence conducted me, in silence, through many dark and intricate passages in my progress to the *studio* of his master. Much that I encountered on the way contributed, I know not how, to heighten the vague sentiments of which I have already spoken. While the objects around me— while the carvings of the ceilings, the sombre tapestries of the walls, the ebon blackness of the floors, and the phantasmagoric armorial trophies which rattled as I strode, were but matters to which, or to such as which, I had been accustomed from my infancy—while I hesitated not to acknowledge how familiar was all this—I still wondered to find how unfamiliar were the fancies which ordinary images were stirring up. On one of the staircases, I met the physician of the family. His countenance, I thought, wore a mingled expression of low cunning and perplexity. He accosted me with trepidation and passed on. The valet now threw open a door and ushered me into the presence of his master.

The room in which I found myself was very large and lofty. The windows were long, narrow, and pointed, and at so vast a distance from the black oaken floor as to be altogether inaccessible from within. Feeble gleams of encrimsoned light made their way through the trellised panes, and served to render sufficiently distinct the more prominent objects around; the eye, however, struggled in vain to reach the remoter angles of the chamber, or the recesses of the vaulted and fretted ceiling. Dark draperies hung upon the walls. The general furniture was profuse, comfortless, antique, and tattered. Many books and musical instruments lay scattered about, but failed to give any vitality to the scene. I felt that I breathed an atmosphere of sorrow. An air of stern, deep, and irredeemable gloom hung over and pervaded all.

Upon my entrance, Usher arose from a sofa upon which he had been lying at full length, and greeted me with a vivacious warmth which had much in it, I at first thought of an overdone cordiality—of the constrained effort of the *ennuyé*[3] man of the world. A glance, however, at his countenance convinced me of his perfect sincerity. We sat down; and for some moments, while he spoke not, I gazed upon him with a feeling half of pity, half of awe. Surely, man had never before so terribly altered, in so brief a period, as had Roderick Usher! It was with difficulty that I could bring myself to admit the identity of the wan being before me with the companion of my early boyhood. Yet the character of his face had been at all times remarkable. A cadaverousness of complexion; an eye large, liquid, and luminous beyond comparison, lips somewhat thin and very pallid, but of a surpassingly beautiful curve; a nose of a delicate Hebrew model, but with a breadth of nostril unusual in similar formations; a finely moulded chin, speaking, in its want of prominence, of a want of moral energy; hair of a more than web-like softness and tenuity; these features, with an inordinate expansion above the regions of the temple, made up altogether a countenance not easily to be forgotten. And now in the mere exaggeration of the prevailing character of these features, and of the expression they were wont to convey, lay so much of change that I doubted to whom I spoke. The now ghastly pallor of the skin, and the now miraculous

---

**3.** Bored, jaded (French).

lustre of the eye, above all things startled and even awed me. The silken hair, too, had been suffered to grow all unheeded, and as, in its wild gossamer texture, it floated rather than fell about the face, I could not, even with effort, connect its Arabesque[4] expression with any idea of simple humanity.

In the manner of my friend I was at once struck with an incoherence—an inconsistency; and I soon found this to arise from a series of feeble and futile struggles to overcome an habitual trepidancy, an excessive nervous agitation. For something of this nature I had indeed been prepared, no less by his letter, than by reminiscences of certain boyish traits, and by conclusions deduced from his peculiar physical conformation and temperament. His action was alternately vivacious and sullen. His voice varied rapidly from a tremulous indecision (when the animal spirits seemed utterly in abeyance) to that species of energetic concision—that abrupt, weighty, unhurried, and hollow-sounding enunciation—that leaden, self-balanced and perfectly modulated gutteral utterance, which may be observed in the lost drunkard, or the irreclaimable eater of opium, during the periods of his most intense excitement.

It was thus that he spoke of the object of my visit, of his earnest desire to see me, and of the solace he expected me to afford him. He entered, at some length, into what he conceived to be the nature of his malady. It was, he said, a constitutional and a family evil, and one for which he despaired to find a remedy—a mere nervous affection, he immediately added, which would undoubtedly soon pass off. It displayed itself in a host of unnatural sensations. Some of these, as he detailed them, interested and bewildered me; although, perhaps, the terms, and the general manner of the narration had their weight. He suffered much from a morbid acuteness of the senses; the most insipid food was alone endurable; he could wear only garments of certain texture; the odors of all flowers were oppressive; his eyes were tortured by even a faint light; and there were but peculiar sounds, and these from stringed instruments, which did not inspire him with horror.

To an anomalous species of terror I found him a bounden slave. "I shall perish," said he, "I *must* perish in this deplorable folly. Thus, thus, and not otherwise, shall I be lost. I dread the events of the future, not in themselves, but in their results. I shudder at the thought of any, even the most trivial, incident, which may operate upon this intolerable agitation of soul. I have, indeed, no abhorrence of danger, except in its absolute effect—in terror. In this unnerved—in this pitiable condition, I feel that I must inevitably abandon life and reason together, in some struggle with the grim phantasm, FEAR."

I learned, moreover, at intervals, and through broken and equivocal hints, another singular feature of his mental condition. He was enchained by certain superstitious impressions in regard to the dwelling which he tenanted, and from whence, for many years, he had never ventured forth—in regard to an influence whose suppositious force was conveyed in terms too shadowy here to be re-stated—an influence which some peculiarities in the mere form and substance of his family mansion, had, by dint of long sufferance, he said, obtained over his spirit—an effect which the *physique* of the gray walls and turrets, and of the dim tarn into which they all looked down, had, at length, brought about upon the *morale* of his existence.

---

4. Elaborately ornamental, in the manner of Arab decoration.

He admitted, however, although with hesitation, that much of the peculiar gloom which thus afflicted him could be traced to a more natural and far more palpable origin—to the severe and long-continued illness, indeed to the evidently approaching dissolution, of a tenderly beloved sister—his sole companion for long years, his last and only relative on earth. "Her decease," he said, with a bitterness which I can never forget, "would leave him (him the hopeless and the frail) the last of the ancient race of the Ushers." While he spoke, the lady Madeline (for so was she called) passed slowly through a remote portion of the apartment, and, without having noticed my presence, disappeared. I regarded her with an utter astonishment not unmingled with dread, and yet I found it impossible to account for such feelings. A sensation of stupor oppressed me, as my eyes followed her retreating steps. When a door, at length, closed upon her, my glance sought instinctively and eagerly the countenance of the brother; but he had buried his face in his hands, and I could only perceive that a far more than ordinary wanness had overspread the emaciated fingers through which trickled many passionate tears.

The disease of the lady Madeline had long baffled the skill of her physicians. A settled apathy, a gradual wasting away of the person, and frequent although transient affections of a partially cataleptical[5] character, were the unusual diagnosis. Hitherto she had steadily borne up against the pressure of her malady, and had not betaken herself finally to bed; but, on the closing in of the evening of my arrival at the house, she succumbed (as her brother told me at night with inexpressible agitation) to the prostrating power of the destroyer; and I learned that the glimpse I had obtained of her person would thus probably be the last I should obtain—that the lady, at least while living, would be seen by me no more.

For several days ensuing, her name was unmentioned by either Usher or myself: and, during this period, I was busied in earnest endeavors to alleviate the melancholy of my friend. We painted and read together; or I listened, as if in a dream, to the wild improvisations of his speaking guitar. And thus, as a closer and still closer intimacy admitted me more unreservedly into the recesses of his spirit, the more bitterly did I perceive the futility of all attempt at cheering a mind from which darkness, as if an inherent positive quality, poured forth upon all objects of the moral and physical universe, in one unceasing radiation of gloom.

I shall ever bear about me a memory of the many solemn hours I thus spent alone with the master of the House of Usher. Yet I should fail in any attempt to convey an idea of the exact character of the studies, or of the occupations, in which he involved me, or led me the way. An excited and highly distempered ideality threw a sulphureous lustre over all. His long improvised dirges will ring for ever in my ears. Among other things, I hold painfully in mind a certain singular perversion and amplification of the wild air of the last waltz of Von Weber.[6] From the paintings over which his elaborate fancy brooded, and which grew, touch by touch, into vaguenesses at which I shuddered the more thrillingly, because I shuddered knowing not why;—from these paintings (vivid

---

**5.** Psychologically paralyzed.   **6.** Carl Maria von Weber (1786–1826), German composer. Karl Gottlieb Reissiger succeeded Weber as conductor of the German Opera at Dresden. A nondramatic work by Reissiger contains a piece misleadingly known as *Weber's Last Waltz* or, literally, *Weber's Last Thought*.

as their images now are before me) I would in vain endeavor to educe more than a small portion which should lie within the compass of merely written words. By the utter simplicity, by the nakedness of his designs, he arrested and overawed attention. If ever mortal painted an idea, that mortal was Roderick Usher. For me at least—in the circumstances then surrounding me, there arose out of the pure abstractions which the hypochondriac contrived to throw upon his canvas, an intensity of intolerable awe, no shadow of which felt I ever yet in the contemplation of the certainly glowing yet too concrete reveries of Fuseli.[7]

One of the phantasmagoric conceptions of my friend, partaking not so rigidly of the spirit of abstraction, may be shadowed forth, although feebly, in words. A small picture presented the interior of an immensely long and rectangular vault or tunnel, with low walls, smooth, white, and without interruption or device.[8] Certain accessory points of the design served well to convey the idea that this excavation lay at an exceeding depth below the surface of the earth. No outlet was observed in any portion of its vast extent, and no torch, or other artificial source of light was discernible; yet a flood of intense rays rolled throughout, and bathed the whole in a ghastly and inappropriate splendor.

I have just spoken of that morbid condition of the auditory nerve which rendered all music intolerable to the sufferer, with the exception of certain effects of stringed instruments. It was, perhaps, the narrow limits to which he thus confined himself upon the guitar, which gave birth, in great measure, to the fantastic character of his performances. But the fervid *facility* of his impromptus could not be so accounted for. They must have been, and were, in the notes, as well as in the words of his wild fantasias (for he not unfrequently accompanied himself with rhymed verbal improvisations), the result of that intense mental collectedness and concentration to which I have previously alluded as observable only in particular moments of the highest artificial excitement. The words of one of these rhapsodies I have easily remembered. I was, perhaps, the more forcibly impressed with it, as he gave it, because, in the under or mystic current of its meaning, I fancied that I perceived, and for the first time, a full consciousness on the part of Usher, of the tottering of his lofty reason upon her throne. The verses, which were entitled "The Haunted Palace," ran very nearly, if not accurately, thus:

> In the greenest of our valleys,
>   By good angels tenanted,
> Once a fair and stately palace—
>   Radiant palace—reared its head.
> In the monarch Thought's dominion,
>   It stood there!
> Never seraph spread a pinion
>   Over fabric half so fair.
>
> Banners yellow, glorious, golden,
>   On its roof did float and flow,

7. Henry Fuseli (Johann Heinrich Füssli; 1741–1825), Anglo-Swiss painter.  8. Design, ornament.

(This—all this—was in the olden
      Time long ago)
And every gentle air that dallied,
      In that sweet day,
Along the ramparts plumed and pallid,
      A winged odor went away.

Wanderers in that happy valley
      Through two luminous windows, saw
Spirits moving musically
      To a lute's well-tunèd law,
Round about a throne where, sitting
      Porphyrogene![9]
In state his glory well befitting,
      The ruler of the realm was seen.

And all with pearl and ruby glowing
      Was the fair palace door,
Through which came flowing, flowing, flowing,
      And sparkling evermore,
A troop of Echoes, whose sweet duty
      Was but to sing,
In voices of surpassing beauty,
      The wit and wisdom of their king.

But evil things, in robes of sorrow,
      Assailed the monarch's high estate;
(Ah, let us mourn!—for never morrow
      Shall dawn upon him, desolate!)
And, round about his home, the glory
      That blushed and bloomed
Is but a dim-remembered story
      Of the old time entombed.

And travellers now, within that valley,
      Through the red-litten[1] windows see
Vast forms that move fantastically
      To a discordant melody;
While, like a ghastly rapid river,
      Through the pale door
A hideous throng rush out forever,
      And laugh—but smile no more.

 I well remember that suggestions arising from this ballad led us into a train of thought wherein there became manifest an opinion of Usher's which I mention not so much on account of its novelty, (for other men have thought thus), as on account of the pertinacity with which he maintained it. This opinion, in its general form, was that of the sentience of all vegetable things. But, in his disordered fancy, the idea had assumed a more daring character,

---

**9.** One born to the purple—i.e., of royal blood.  **1.** Lit with red.

and trespassed, under certain conditions, upon the kingdom of inorganiza-
tion. I lack words to express the full extent, or the earnest *abandon* of his persuasion. The belief, however, was connected (as I have previously hinted) with
the gray stones of the home of his forefathers. The condition of the sentience
had been here, he imagined, fulfilled in the method of collocation of these
stones—in the order of their arrangement, as well as in that of the many *fungi*
which overspread them, and of the decayed trees which stood around—above
all, in the long undisturbed endurance of this arrangement, and in its redu-
plication in the still waters of the tarn. Its evidence—the evidence of the
sentience—was to be seen, he said, (and I here started as he spoke), in the gradual yet certain condensation of an atmosphere of their own about the waters
and the walls. The result was discoverable, he added, in that silent, yet importunate and terrible influence which for centuries had moulded the destinies
of his family, and which made *him* what I now saw him—what he was. Such
opinions need no comment, and I will make none.

Our books—the books which, for years, had formed no small portion of the
mental existence of the invalid—were, as might be supposed, in strict keeping
with this character of phantasm. We pored together over such works as the
*Ververt et Chartreuse* of Gresset; the *Belphegor* of Machiavelli; the *Heaven and
Hell* of Swedenborg; the *Subterranean Voyage of Nicholas Klimm* by Holberg; the
*Chiromancy* of Robert Flud, of Jean d'Indaginé, and of De la Chambre; the
*Journey into the Blue Distance* of Tieck; and the *City of the Sun* of Campanella.
One favorite volume was a small octavo edition of the *Directorium Inquisitorium*, by the Dominican Eymeric de Gironne; and there were passages in Pom-
ponius Mela, about the old African Satyrs and Aegipans, over which Usher
would sit dreaming for hours.[2] His chief delight, however, was found in the
perusal of an exceedingly rare and curious book in quarto Gothic—the manual of a forgotten church—the *Vigilae Mortuorum Secundum Chorum Ecclesiæ
Maguntinæn*.[3]

I could not help thinking of the wild ritual of this work, and of its probable
influence upon the hypochondriac, when, one evening, having informed me
abruptly that the lady Madeline was no more, he stated his intention of preserving her corpse for a fortnight, (previously to its final interment), in one of
the numerous vaults within the main walls of the building. The wordly reason, however, assigned for this singular proceeding, was one which I did not
feel at liberty to dispute. The brother had been led to his resolution (so he told
me) by considerations of the unusual character of the malady of the deceased,

---

2. Exotic and romantic literary works. *Ververt* and *Chartreuse* are anticlerical satires by French poet
and dramatist Jean Baptiste Louis Gresset (1709–1777). The novel of Niccolò Machiavelli (1469–1527)
concerns a demon come to earth to prove that the damnation of man is woman. Emmanuel Swedenborg (1688–1772), a Swedish scientist and theologian, offers in *Heaven and Hell* (1758) an argument
concerning the continuity of spiritual identity. The book of Ludwig Holberg (1684–1754), a German
dramatist, concerns a round-trip voyage to the world of the dead. Chiromancy, the art of palm reading, is the concern of Robert Flud (1574–1637), British alchemist, of Jean D'Indaginé (*Chiromantia*,
1522), and of Marin Cureau de la Chambre (*Principes de la Chiromancie*, 1653). The next two titles by the
German novelist Johann Ludwig Tieck (1773–1853) and the Italian scientist and philosopher Tom-
maso Campanella (1568–1639), respectively, are concerned with voyages to other worlds. The Spanish
historian Nicolas Eymeric de Girone (1320–1399) in *Inquisitorium Directorium* gives an outline of tortures
and appropriate procedures. Satyrs were goatmen of Greek mythology. Pomponius Mela, a Roman of
the first century C.E., gives an account of "Aegipans," supposedly goatmen of Africa, in his work *Geography*. 3. Vigil for the Dead, Second Chorus, Church of the Maguntinae (Latin).

of certain obtrusive and eager inquiries on the part of her medical men,[4] and of the remote and exposed situation of the burial-ground of the family, I will not deny that when I called to mind the sinister countenance of the person whom I met upon the staircase, on the day of my arrival at the house, I had no desire to oppose what I regarded as at best but a harmless, and by no means an unnatural, precaution.

At the request of Usher, I personally aided him in the arrangements for the temporary entombment. The body having been encoffined, we two alone bore it to its rest. The vault in which we placed it (and which had been so long unopened that our torches, half smothered in its oppressive atmosphere, gave us little opportunity for investigation) was small, damp, and entirely without means of admission for light; lying, at great depth, immediately beneath that portion of the building in which was my own sleeping apartment. It had been used, apparently, in remote feudal times, for the worst purposes of a donjon-keep,[5] and, in later days, as a place of deposit for powder, or other highly combustible substance, as a portion of its floor, and the whole interior of a long archway through which we reached it, were carefully sheathed with copper. The door, of massive iron, had been, also, similarly protected. Its immense weight caused an unusually sharp grating sound, as it moved upon its hinges.

Having deposited our mournful burden upon tressels within this region of horror, we partially turned aside the yet unscrewed lid of the coffin, and looked upon the face of the tenant. The exact similitude between the brother and sister now first arrested my attention; and Usher, divining, perhaps, my thoughts, murmured out some few words from which I learned that the deceased and himself had been twins, and that sympathies of a scarcely intelligible nature had always existed between them. Our glances, however, rested not long upon the dead—for we could not regard her unawed. The disease which had thus entombed the lady in the maturity of youth, had left, as usual in all maladies of a strictly cataleptical character, the mockery of a faint blush upon the bosom and the face, and that suspiciously lingering smile upon the lip which is so terrible in death. We replaced and screwed down the lid, and, having secured the door of iron, made our way, with toil, into the scarcely less gloomy apartments of the upper portion of the house.

And now, some days of bitter grief having elapsed, an observable change came over the features of the mental disorder of my friend. His ordinary manner had vanished. His ordinary occupations were neglected or forgotten. He roamed from chamber to chamber with hurried, unequal, and objectless step. The pallor of his countenance had assumed, if possible, a more ghastly hue—but the luminousness of his eye had utterly gone out. The once occasional huskiness of his tone was heard no more; and a tremulous quaver, as if of extreme terror, habitually characterized his utterance. There were times, indeed, when I thought his unceasingly agitated mind was laboring with an oppressive secret, to divulge which he struggled for the necessary courage. At times, again, I was obliged to resolve all into the mere inexplicable vagaries of madness, as I beheld him gazing upon vacancy for long hours, in an attitude of the profoundest attention, as if listening to some imaginary sound. It was no

---

4. Usher appears to be afraid the doctors will exhume her corpse to satisfy their professional curiosity about her ailment.   5. Dungeon, prison.

wonder that his condition terrified—that it infected me. I felt creeping upon me, by slow yet certain degrees, the wild influences of his own fantastic yet impressive superstitions.

It was, especially, upon retiring to bed late in the night of the seventh or eighth day after the placing of the lady Madeline within the donjon, that I experienced the full power of such feelings. Sleep came not near my couch—while the hours waned and waned away. I struggled to reason off the nervousness which had dominion over me. I endeavored to believe that much, if not all of what I felt, was due to the bewildering influence of the gloomy furniture of the room—of the dark and tattered draperies, which, tortured into motion by the breath of a rising tempest, swayed fitfully to and fro upon the walls, and rustled uneasily about the decorations of the bed. But my efforts were fruitless. An irrepressible tremor gradually pervaded my frame; and, at length, there sat upon my very heart an incubus of utterly causeless alarm. Shaking this off with a gasp and a struggle, I uplifted myself upon the pillows, and, peering earnestly within the intense darkness of the chamber, harkened—I know not why, except that an instinctive spirit prompted me—to certain low and indefinite sounds which came, through the pauses of the storm, at long intervals I knew not whence. Overpowered by an intense sentiment of horror, unaccountable yet unendurable, I threw on my clothes with haste (for I felt that I should sleep no more during the night), and endeavored to arouse myself from the pitiable condition into which I had fallen, by pacing rapidly to and fro through the apartment.

I had taken but few turns in this manner, when a light step on an adjoining staircase arrested my attention. I presently recognized it as that of Usher. In an instant afterward he rapped, with a gentle touch, at my door, and entered, bearing a lamp. His countenance was, as usually, cadaverously wan—but there was a species of mad hilarity in his eyes—an evidently restrained *hysteria* in his whole demeanor. His air appalled me—but anything was preferable to the solitude which I had so long endured, and I even welcomed his presence as a relief.

"And you have not seen it?" he said abruptly, after having stared about him for some moments in silence—"you have not then seen it?—but, stay! you shall." Thus speaking, and having carefully shaded his lamp, he hurried to one of the casements, and threw it freely open to the storm.

The impetuous fury of the entering gust nearly lifted us from our feet. It was, indeed, a tempestuous yet sternly beautiful night, and one wildly singular in its terror and its beauty. A whirlwind had apparently collected its force in our vicinity; for there were frequent and violent alterations in the direction of the wind; and the exceeding density of the clouds (which hung so low as to press upon the turrets of the house) did not prevent our perceiving the life-like velocity with which they flew careering from all points against each other, without passing away into the distance. I say that even their exceeding density did not prevent our perceiving this; yet we had no glimpse of the moon or stars, nor was there any flashing forth of the lightning. But the under surfaces of the huge masses of agitated vapor, as well as all terrestrial objects immediately around us, were glowing in the unnatural light of a faintly luminous and distinctly visible gaseous exhalation which hung about and enshrouded the mansion.

"You must not—you shall not behold this!" said I, shudderingly, to Usher, as I led him, with a gentle violence, from the window to a seat. "These appearances, which bewilder you, are merely electrical phenomena not uncommon—or it may be that they have their ghastly origin in the rank miasma of the tarn. Let us close this casement; the air is chilling and dangerous to your frame. Here is one of your favorite romances. I will read, and you shall listen; and so we will pass away this terrible night together."

The antique volume which I had taken up was the *Mad Trist* of Sir Launcelot Canning;[6] but I had called it a favorite of Usher's more in sad jest than in earnest; for, in truth, there is little in its uncouth and unimaginative prolixity which could have had interest for the lofty and spiritual ideality of my friend. It was, however, the only book immediately at hand; and I indulged a vague hope that the excitement which now agitated the hypochondriac might find relief (for the history of mental disorder is full of similar anomalies) even in the extremeness of the folly which I should read. Could I have judged, indeed, by the wild, overstrained air of vivacity with which he hearkened, or apparently hearkened, to the words of the tale, I might have well congratulated myself upon the success of my design.

I had arrived at that well-known portion of the story where Ethelred, the hero of the *Trist*, having sought in vain for peaceable admission into the dwelling of the hermit, proceeds to make good an entrance by force. Here, it will be remembered, the words of the narrative run thus:

> And Ethelred, who was by nature of a doughty heart, and who was now mighty withal, on account of the powerfulness of the wine which he had drunken, waited no longer to hold parley with the hermit, who, in sooth, was of an obstinate and maliceful turn, but, feeling the rain upon his shoulders, and fearing the rising of the tempest, uplifted his mace outright, and, with blows, made quickly room in the plankings of the door for his gauntleted hand; and now pulling therewith sturdily, he so cracked, and ripped, and tore all asunder, that the noise of the dry and hollow-sounding wood alarumed and reverberated throughout the forest.

At the termination of this sentence I started, and, for a moment, paused; for it appeared to me (although I at once concluded that my excited fancy had deceived me)—it appeared to me that, from some very remote portion of the mansion, there came, indistinctly, to my ears, what might have been, in its exact similarity of character, the echo (but a stifled and dull one certainly) of the very cracking and ripping sound which Sir Launcelot had so particularly described. It was, beyond doubt, the coincidence alone which had arrested my attention; for, amid the rattling of the sashes of the casements, and the ordinary commingled noises of the still increasing storm, the sound, in itself, had nothing, surely, which should have interested or disturbed me. I continued the story:

> But the good champion Ethelred, now entering within the door, was sore enraged and amazed to perceive no signal of the maliceful hermit; but, in the stead thereof, a dragon of scaly and prodigious demeanor, and of a fiery tongue, which sate in guard before a palace of gold, with a floor of silver; and upon the wall there hung a shield of shining brass with this legend enwritten—

6. Poe's invention.

*Who entereth herein, a conqueror hath bin,*
*Who slayeth the dragon, the shield he shall win.*

And Ethelred uplifted his mace, and struck upon the head of the dragon, which fell before him, and gave up his pesty breath, with a shriek so horrid and harsh, and withal so piercing, that Ethelred had fain to close his ears with his hands against the dreadful noise of it, the like whereof was never before heard.

Here again I paused abruptly, and now with a feeling of wild amazement—for there could be no doubt whatever that, in this instance, I did actually hear (although from what direction it proceeded I found it impossible to say) a low and apparently distant, but harsh, protracted, and most unusual screaming or grating sound—the exact counterpart of what my fancy had already conjured up as the sound of the dragon's unnatural shriek as described by the romancer.

Oppressed, as I certainly was, upon the occurrence of this second and most extraordinary coincidence, by a thousand conflicting sensations, in which wonder and extreme terror were predominant, I still retained sufficient presence of mind to avoid exciting, by any observation, the sensitive nervousness of my companion. I was by no means certain that he had noticed the sounds in question; although, assuredly, a strange alteration had, during the last few minutes, taken place in his demeanor. From a position fronting my own, he had gradually brought round his chair, so as to sit with his face to the door of the chamber; and thus I could but partially perceive his features, although I saw that his lips trembled as if he were murmuring inaudibly. His head had dropped upon his breast—yet I knew that he was not asleep, from the wide and rigid opening of the eye, as I caught a glance of it in profile. The motion of his body, too, was at variance with this idea—for he rocked from side to side with a gentle yet constant and uniform sway. Having rapidly taken notice of all this, I resumed the narrative of Sir Launcelot, which thus proceeded:

And now, the champion, having escaped from the terrible fury of the dragon, bethinking himself of the brazen shield, and of the breaking up of the enchantment which was upon it, removed the carcass from out of the way before him, and approached valorously over the silver pavement of the castle to where the shield was upon the wall; which in sooth tarried not for his full coming, but fell down at his feet upon the silver floor, with a mighty great and terrible ringing sound.

No sooner had these syllables passed my lips, than—as if a shield of brass had indeed, at the moment, fallen heavily upon a floor of silver—I became aware of a distinct, hollow, metallic and clangorous yet apparently muffled reverberation. Completely unnerved, I leaped to my feet; but the measured rocking movement of Usher was undisturbed. I rushed to the chair in which he sat. His eyes were bent fixedly before him, and throughout his whole countenance there reigned a more than stony rigidity. But as I laid my hand upon his shoulder, there came a strong shudder over his whole person; a sickly smile quivered about his lips; and I saw that he spoke in a low, hurried, and gibbering murmur, as if unconscious of my presence. Bending closely over him, I at length drank in the hideous import of his words.

"Not hear it?—yes, I hear it, and *have* heard it. Long—long—long—many minutes, many hours, many days, have I heard it—yet I dared not—oh, pity me; miserable wretch that I am!—I dared not—I *dared* not speak! *We have put her living in the tomb!* Said I not that my senses were acute?—I *now* tell you that I heard her first feeble movements in the hollow coffin. I heard them—many, many days ago—yet I dared not—*I dared not speak!* And now—to-night—Ethelred—ha! ha!—the breaking of the hermit's door, and the death-cry of the dragon, and the clangor of the shield!—say, rather, the rending of her coffin, and the grating of the iron hinges of her prison, and her struggles within the coppered archway of the vault! Oh whither shall I fly? Will she not be here anon? Is she not hurrying to upbraid me for my haste? Have I not heard her footstep on the stair? Do I not distinguish that heavy and horrible beating of her heart? MADMAN!" here he sprang violently to his feet, and shrieked out his syllables, as if in the effort he were giving up his soul—"*Madman! I tell you that she now stands without the door!*"

As if in the superhuman energy of his utterance there had been found the potency of a spell, the huge antique panels to which the speaker pointed, threw slowly back, upon the instant, their ponderous and ebony jaws. It was the work of the rushing gust—but then without those doors there DID stand the lofty and enshrouded figure of the lady Madeline of Usher. There was blood upon her white robes, and the evidence of some bitter struggle upon every portion of her emaciated frame. For a moment she remained trembling and reeling to and fro upon the threshold—then, with a low moaning cry, fell heavily inward upon the person of her brother, and in her violent and now final death-agonies, bore him to the floor a corpse, and a victim to the terrors he had anticipated.

From that chamber, and from that mansion, I fled aghast. The storm was still abroad in all its wrath as I found myself crossing the old causeway. Suddenly there shot along the path a wild light, and I turned to see whence a gleam so unusual could have issued; for the vast house and its shadows were alone behind me. The radiance was that of the full, setting, and blood-red moon, which now shone vividly through that once barely-discernible fissure of which I have before spoken as extending from the roof of the building, in a zigzag direction, to the base. While I gazed, this fissure rapidly widened—there came a fierce breath of the whirlwind—the entire orb of the satellite burst at once upon my sight—my brain reeled as I saw the mighty walls rushing asunder—there was a long tumultuous shouting sound like the voice of a thousand waters—and the deep and dank tarn at my feet closed sullenly and silently over the fragments of the HOUSE OF USHER.

1840

---

RELATED:

—Poe, "The Philosophy of Composition," p. 891
—Poe, Review of Hawthorne's *Twice-Told Tales*, p. 934
—Richard Wilbur, "The House of Poe," p. 941

# KATHERINE ANNE PORTER
## *1890–1980*

Porter was born in Indian Creek, Texas, and brought up in Texas and Louisiana. She was educated at home, in private schools, and in an Ursuline convent. Though she began to write stories as soon as she could form letters on paper, she made no attempt to publish until she was past thirty, and she associated with no literary people until she had become something of a celebrity with the publication of her first book of stories, *Flowering Judas* (1930). Before and after that date she earned a meager living by journalism, traveling from city to city with little baggage except her manuscripts—trunkfuls of which were destroyed, bit by bit, as she found them inadequate to meet her exacting standards. She lived for a time in Mexico, which provided material for some of her most famous stories, and in Europe, where she continued to publish her stories. Her novel *Ship of Fools* was begun during the 1930s but not finished for more than two decades. It was at last published in 1962. Her many shorter works may be found in *The Collected Stories of Katherine Anne Porter*, which appeared in 1965, winning both the Pulitzer Prize and the National Book Award.

## The Jilting of Granny Weatherall

She flicked her wrist neatly out of Doctor Harry's pudgy careful fingers and pulled the sheet up to her chin. The brat ought to be in knee breeches. Doctoring around the country with spectacles on his nose! "Get along now, take your schoolbooks and go. There's nothing wrong with me."

Doctor Harry spread a warm paw like a cushion on her forehead where the forked green vein danced and made her eyelids twitch. "Now, now, be a good girl, and we'll have you up in no time."

"That's no way to speak to a woman nearly eighty years old just because she's down. I'd have you respect your elders, young man."

"Well, Missy, excuse me." Doctor Harry patted her cheek. "But I've got to warn you, haven't I? You're a marvel, but you must be careful or you're going to be good and sorry."

"Don't tell me what I'm going to be. I'm on my feet now, morally speaking. It's Cornelia. I had to go to bed to get rid of her."

Her bones felt loose, and floated around in her skin, and Doctor Harry floated like a balloon around the foot of the bed. He floated and pulled down his waistcoat and swung his glasses on a cord. "Well, stay where you are, it certainly can't hurt you."

"Get along and doctor your sick," said Granny Weatherall. "Leave a well woman alone. I'll call for you when I want you. . . . Where were you forty years ago when I pulled through milk-leg and double pneumonia? You weren't even born. Don't let Cornelia lead you on," she shouted, because Doctor Harry appeared to float up to the ceiling and out. "I pay my own bills, and I don't throw my money away on nonsense!"

She meant to wave good-by, but it was too much trouble. Her eyes closed of themselves, it was like a dark curtain drawn around the bed. The pillow rose and floated under her, pleasant as a hammock in a light wind. She listened to the leaves rustling outside the window. No, somebody was swishing newspapers: no, Cornelia and Doctor Harry were whispering together. She leaped broad awake, thinking they whispered in her ear.

"She was never like this, *never* like this!" "Well, what can we expect?" "Yes, eighty years old. . . ."

Well, and what if she was? She still had ears. It was like Cornelia to whisper around doors. She always kept things secret in such a public way. She was always being tactful and kind. Cornelia was dutiful; that was the trouble with her. Dutiful and good; "So good and dutiful," said Granny, "that I'd like to spank her." She saw herself spanking Cornelia and making a fine job of it.

"What'd you say, Mother?"

Granny felt her face tying up in hard knots.

"Can't a body think, I'd like to know?"

"I thought you might want something."

"I do. I want a lot of things. First off, go away and don't whisper."

She lay and drowsed, hoping in her sleep that the children would keep out and let her rest a minute. It had been a long day. Not that she was tired. It was always pleasant to snatch a minute now and then. There was always so much to be done, let me see: tomorrow.

Tomorrow was far away and there was nothing to trouble about. Things were finished somehow when the time came; thank God there was always a little margin over for peace: then a person could spread out the plan of life and tuck in the edges orderly. It was good to have everything clean and folded away, with the hair brushes and tonic bottles sitting straight on the white embroidered linen: the day started without fuss and the pantry shelves laid out with rows of jelly glasses and brown jugs and white stone-china jars with blue whirligigs and words painted on them: coffee, tea, sugar, ginger, cinnamon, allspice: and the bronze clock with the lion on top nicely dusted off. The dust that lion could collect in twenty-four hours! The box in the attic with all those letters tied up, well, she'd have to go through that tomorrow. All those letters—George's letters and John's letters and her letters to them both—lying around for the children to find afterwards made her uneasy. Yes, that would be tomorrow's business. No use to let them know how silly she had been once.

While she was rummaging around she found death in her mind and it felt clammy and unfamiliar. She had spent so much time preparing for death there was no need for bringing it up again. Let it take care of itself now. When she was sixty she had felt very old, finished, and went around making farewell trips to see her children and grandchildren, with a secret in her mind: This is the very last of your mother, children! Then she made her will and came down with a long fever. That was all just a notion like a lot of other things, but it was lucky too, for she had once for all got over the idea of dying for a long time. Now she couldn't be worried. She hoped she had better sense now. Her father had lived to be one hundred and two years old and had drunk a noggin of strong hot toddy on his last birthday. He told the reporters it was his daily habit, and he owed his long life to that. He had made quite a scandal and was very pleased about it. She believed she'd just plague Cornelia a little.

"Cornelia! Cornelia!" No footsteps, but a sudden hand on her cheek. "Bless you, where have you been?"

"Here, Mother."

"Well, Cornelia, I want a noggin of hot toddy."

"Are you cold, darling?"

"I'm chilly, Cornelia. Lying in bed stops the circulation. I must have told you that a thousand times."

Well, she could just hear Cornelia telling her husband that Mother was getting a little childish and they'd have to humor her. The thing that most annoyed her was that Cornelia thought she was deaf, dumb, and blind. Little hasty glances and tiny gestures tossed around her and over her head saying, "Don't cross her, let her have her way, she's eighty years old," and she sitting there as if she lived in a thin glass cage. Sometimes Granny almost made up her mind to pack up and move back to her own house where nobody could remind her every minute that she was old. Wait, wait, Cornelia, till your own children whisper behind your back!

In her day she had kept a better house and had got more work done. She wasn't too old yet for Lydia to be driving eighty miles for advice when one of the children jumped the track, and Jimmy still dropped in and talked things over: "Now, Mammy, you've a good business head, I want to know what you think of this? . . ." Old. Cornelia couldn't change the furniture around without asking. Little things, little things! They had been so sweet when they were little. Granny wished the old days were back again with the children young and everything to be done over. It had been a hard pull, but not too much for her. When she thought of all the food she had cooked, and all the clothes she had cut and sewed, and all the gardens she had made—well, the children showed it. There they were, made out of her, and they couldn't get away from that. Sometimes she wanted to see John again and point to them and say, Well, I didn't do so badly, did I? But that would have to wait. That was for tomorrow. She used to think of him as a man, but now all the children were older than their father, and he would be a child beside her if she saw him now. It seemed strange and there was something wrong in the idea. Why, he couldn't possibly recognize her. She had fenced in a hundred acres once, digging the post holes herself and clamping the wires with just a negro boy to help. That changed a woman. John would be looking for a young woman with the peaked Spanish comb in her hair and the painted fan. Digging post holes changed a woman. Riding country roads in the winter when women had their babies was another thing: sitting up nights with sick horses and sick negroes and sick children and hardly ever losing one. John, I hardly ever lost one of them! John would see that in a minute, that would be something he could understand, she wouldn't have to explain anything!

It made her feel like rolling up her sleeves and putting the whole place to rights again. No matter if Cornelia was determined to be everywhere at once, there were a great many things left undone on this place. She would start tomorrow and do them. It was good to be strong enough for everything, even if all you made melted and changed and slipped under your hands, so that by the time you finished you almost forgot what you were working for. What was it I set out to do? she asked herself intently, but she could not remember. A fog rose over the valley, she saw it marching across the creek swallowing the trees and moving up the hill like an army of ghosts. Soon it would be at the near edge of the orchard, and then it was time to go in and light the lamps. Come in, children, don't stay out in the night air.

Lighting the lamps had been beautiful. The children huddled up to her and breathed like little calves waiting at the bars in the twilight. Their eyes followed the match and watched the flame rise and settle in a blue curve, then they moved away from her. The lamp was lit, they didn't have to be scared and hang on to mother anymore. Never, never, never more. God, for all my life I thank Thee. Without Thee, my God, I could never have done it. Hail, Mary, full of grace.

I want you to pick all the fruit this year and see that nothing is wasted. There's always someone who can use it. Don't let good things rot for want of using. You waste life when you waste good food. Don't let things get lost. It's bitter to lose things. Now, don't let me get to thinking, not when I am tired and taking a little nap before supper. . . .

The pillow rose about her shoulders and pressed against her heart and the memory was being squeezed out of it: oh, push down the pillow, somebody: it would smother her if she tried to hold it. Such a fresh breeze blowing and such a green day with no threats in it. But he had not come, just the same. What does a woman do when she has put on the white veil and set out the white cake for a man and he doesn't come? She tried to remember. No, I swear he never harmed me but in that. He never harmed me but in that . . . and what if he did? There was the day, the day, but a whirl of dark smoke rose and covered it, crept up and over into the bright field where everything was planted so carefully in orderly rows. That was hell, she knew hell when she saw it. For sixty years she had prayed against remembering him and against losing her soul in the deep pit of hell, and now the two things were mingled in one and the thought of him was a smoky cloud from hell that moved and crept in her head when she had just got rid of Doctor Harry and was trying to rest a minute. Wounded vanity, Ellen, said a sharp voice in the top of her mind. Don't let your wounded vanity get the upper hand of you. Plenty of girls get jilted. You were jilted, weren't you? Then stand up to it. Her eyelids wavered and let in streamers of blue-gray light like tissue paper over her eyes. She must get up and pull the shades down or she'd never sleep. She was in bed again and the shades were not down. How could that happen? Better turn over, hide from the light, sleeping in the light gave you nightmares. "Mother, how do you feel now?" and a stinging wetness on her forehead. But I don't like having my face washed in cold water!

Hapsy? George? Lydia? Jimmy? No, Cornelia, and her features were swollen and full of little puddles. "They're coming, darling, they'll all be here soon." Go wash your face, child, you look funny.

Instead of obeying, Cornelia knelt down and put her head on the pillow. She seemed to be talking but there was no sound. "Well, are you tongue-tied? Whose birthday is it? Are you going to give a party?"

Cornelia's mouth moved urgently in strange shapes. "Don't do that, you bother me, daughter."

"Oh, no, Mother. Oh, no. . . ."

Nonsense. It was strange about children. They disputed your every word. "No what, Cornelia?"

"Here's Doctor Harry."

"I won't see that boy again. He just left five minutes ago."

"That was this morning, Mother. It's night now. Here's the nurse."

"This is Doctor Harry, Mrs. Weatherall. I never saw you look so young and happy!"

"Ah, I'll never be young again—but I'd be happy if they'd let me lie in peace and get rested."

She thought she spoke up loudly, but no one answered. A warm weight on her forehead, a warm bracelet on her wrist, and a breeze went on whispering, trying to tell her something. A shuffle of leaves in the everlasting hand of God, He blew on them and they danced and rattled. "Mother, don't mind, we're going to give you a little hypodermic." "Look here, daughter, how do ants get in this bed? I saw sugar ants yesterday." Did you send for Hapsy too?

It was Hapsy she really wanted. She had to go a long way back through a great many rooms to find Hapsy standing with a baby on her arm. She seemed to herself to be Hapsy also, and the baby on Hapsy's arm was Hapsy and himself and herself, all at once, and there was no surprise in the meeting. Then Hapsy melted from within and turned flimsy as gray gauze and the baby was a gauzy shadow, and Hapsy came up close and said, "I thought you'd never come," and looked at her very searchingly and said, "You haven't changed a bit!" They leaned forward to kiss, when Cornelia began whispering from a long way off, "Oh, is there anything you want to tell me? Is there anything I can do for you?"

Yes, she had changed her mind after sixty years and she would like to see George. I want you to find George. Find him and be sure to tell him I forgot him. I want him to know I had my husband just the same and my children and my house like any other woman. A good house too and a good husband that I loved and fine children out of him. Better than I hoped for even. Tell him I was given back everything he took away and more. Oh, no, oh, God, no, there was something else besides the house and the man and the children. Oh, surely they were not all? What was it? Something not given back. . . . Her breath crowded down under her ribs and grew into a monstrous frightening shape with cutting edges; it bored up into her head, and the agony was unbelievable: Yes, John, get the Doctor now, no more talk, my time has come.

When this one was born it should be the last. The last. It should have been born first, for it was the one she had truly wanted. Everything came in good time. Nothing left out, left over. She was strong, in three days she would be as well as ever. Better. A woman needed milk in her to have her full health.

"Mother, do you hear me?"

"I've been telling you—"

"Mother, Father Connolly's here."

"I went to Holy Communion only last week. Tell him I'm not so sinful as all that."

"Father just wants to speak to you."

He could speak as much as he pleased. It was like him to drop in and inquire about her soul as if it were a teething baby, and then stay on for a cup of tea and a round of cards and gossip. He always had a funny story of some sort, usually about an Irishman who made his little mistakes and confessed them, and the point lay in some absurd thing he would blurt out in the confessional showing his struggles between native piety and original sin. Granny felt easy about her soul. Cornelia, where are your manners? Give Father Connolly a chair. She had her secret comfortable understanding with a few favorite saints who cleared a straight road to God for her. All as surely signed and sealed as the papers for the new Forty Acres. Forever . . . heirs and assigns forever. Since the day the wedding cake was not cut, but thrown out and wasted. The whole bottom dropped out of the world, and there she was blind and sweating with nothing under her feet and the walls falling away. His hand had caught her under the breast, she had not fallen, there was the freshly polished floor with the green rug on it, just as before. He had cursed like a sailor's parrot and said, "I'll kill him for you." Don't lay a hand on him, for my sake leave something to God. "Now, Ellen, you must believe what I tell you. . . ."

So there was nothing, nothing to worry about anymore, except sometimes in the night one of the children screamed in a nightmare, and they both hustled out shaking and hunting for the matches and calling, "There, wait a minute, here we are!" John, get the doctor now, Hapsy's time has come. But there was Hapsy standing by the bed in a white cap. "Cornelia, tell Hapsy to take off her cap. I can't see her plain."

Her eyes opened very wide and the room stood out like a picture she had seen somewhere. Dark colors with the shadows rising towards the ceiling in long angles. The tall black dresser gleamed with nothing on it but John's picture, enlarged from a little one, with John's eyes very black when they should have been blue. You never saw him, so how do you know how he looked? But the man insisted the copy was perfect, it was very rich and handsome. For a picture, yes, but it's not my husband. The table by the bed had a linen cover and a candle and a crucifix. The light was blue from Cornelia's silk lampshades. No sort of light at all, just frippery. You had to live forty years with kerosene lamps to appreciate honest electricity. She felt very strong and she saw Doctor Harry with a rosy nimbus around him.

"You look like a saint, Doctor Harry, and I vow that's as near as you'll ever come to it."

"She's saying something."

"I heard you, Cornelia. What's all this carrying-on?"

"Father Connolly's saying—"

Cornelia's voice staggered and bumped like a cart in a bad road. It rounded corners and turned back again and arrived nowhere. Granny stepped up in the cart very lightly and reached for the reins, but a man sat beside her and she knew him by his hands, driving the cart. She did not look in his face, for she knew without seeing, but looked instead down the road where the trees leaned over and bowed to each other and a thousand birds were singing a Mass. She felt like singing too, but she put her hand in the bosom of her dress and pulled out a rosary, and Father Connolly murmured Latin in a very solemn voice and tickled her feet. My God, will you stop that nonsense? I'm a married woman. What if he did run away and leave me to face the priest by myself?

I found another a whole world better. I wouldn't have exchanged my husband for anybody except St. Michael himself, and you may tell him that for me with a thank you in the bargain.

Light flashed on her closed eyelids, and a deep roaring shook her. Cornelia, is that lightning? I hear thunder. There's going to be a storm. Close all the windows. Call the children in. . . . "Mother, here we are, all of us." "Is that you, Hapsy?" "Oh, no, I'm Lydia. We drove as fast as we could." Their faces drifted above her, drifted away. The rosary fell out of her hands and Lydia put it back. Jimmy tried to help, their hands fumbled together, and Granny closed two fingers around Jimmy's thumb. Beads wouldn't do, it must be something alive. She was so amazed her thoughts ran round and round. So, my dear Lord, this is my death and I wasn't even thinking about it. My children have come to see me die. But I can't, it's not time. Oh, I always hated surprises. I wanted to give Cornelia the amethyst set—Cornelia, you're to have the amethyst set, but Hapsy's to wear it when she wants, and, Doctor Harry, do shut up. Nobody sent for you. Oh, my dear Lord, do wait a minute. I meant to do something about the Forty Acres, Jimmy doesn't need it and Lydia will later on, with that worthless husband of hers. I meant to finish the altar cloth and send six bottles of wine to Sister Borgia for her dyspepsia. I want to send six bottles of wine to Sister Borgia, Father Connolly, now don't let me forget.

Cornelia's voice made short turns and tilted over and crashed. "Oh, Mother, oh, Mother, oh, Mother. . . ."

"I'm not going, Cornelia. I'm taken by surprise. I can't go."

You'll see Hapsy again. What about her? "I thought you'd never come." Granny made a long journey outward, looking for Hapsy. What if I don't find her? What then? Her heart sank down and down, there was no bottom to death, she couldn't come to the end of it. The blue light from Cornelia's lampshade drew into a tiny point in the center of her brain, it flickered and winked like an eye, quietly it fluttered and dwindled. Granny lay curled down within herself, amazed and watchful, staring at the point of light that was herself; her body was now only a deeper mass of shadow in an endless darkness and this darkness would curl around the light and swallow it up. God, give a sign!

For the second time there was no sign. Again no bridegroom and the priest in the house. She could not remember any other sorrow because this grief wiped them all away. Oh, no, there's nothing more cruel than this—I'll never forgive it. She stretched herself with a deep breath and blew out the light.

1929

RELATED:

—Porter, An Interview, p. 892

# E. ANNIE PROULX
### *b. 1935*

Edna Ann Proulx, commonly known as Annie Proulx, was born and spent the early years of her childhood in Norwich, Connecticut. After graduating from high school in Portland, Maine, she attended Colby College for a brief period in the 1950s, leaving to marry her first husband. Proulx ended up earning a bachelor's degree in history from the University of Vermont in 1969 and, shortly after, an M.A. from Sir George Williams University (now Concordia) in Quebec. Despite affirming that for most of her adult life she did not think of herself as a writer, Proulx began writing full time upon leaving Concordia, beginning as a journalist but soon turning to short fiction. Several of her short stories appeared in *The Best American Short Stories* prior to the publication of her first collection, *Heart Songs and Other Stories* (1988). For her first novel, *Postcards* (1992), Proulx won the PEN/Faulkner Award, following which she was awarded NEA and Guggenheim fellowships. Two years later, her second novel, *The Shipping News* (1993), earned Proulx the Pulitzer Prize and the National Book Award for Fiction. Two of her short stories have received the O. Henry Award, one of which, *Brokeback Mountain*, was made into an Academy Award–winning major motion picture.

## What Kind of Furniture Would Jesus Pick?

Budgel Wolfscale, a telegraph clerk from Missouri on his way to Montana to search for the yellow metal, stopped at a Wyoming road ranch one day in 1898 for a supper of fried venison and coffee, heard there was good range. For the next week he rode around the country, finally staked a homestead claim on a spread east of the Big Horns that had been cut from the holdings of a Scots outfit that pulled out the year before.

A year-round stream, Bull Jump Creek, cut the property, fringed by cottonwoods and willows, the shining maroon branches of water birch. It was still open country, though barbwire was coming in with the nesters. He built a shotgun cabin of hauled-out lodgepole, married one of the girls from a whorehouse in Ham's Fork, and, naming the ranch after the harp his mother had played, thought himself a Wyoming rancher. He wasn't that, but his sons and grandsons were.

The Harp skidded down the generations to Gilbert Wolfscale, born on the ranch in 1945, and in middle age still living a son's life with his mother in the old house, which had been gradually enlarged with telescoped additions until the structure resembled a giant spyglass built of logs. He ran a cow-calf operation, usually worked the place alone, for even inept help was hard to find. He was a tall man with heavy bones. His coarse skin seemed made of old leather upholstery, and, instead of lips, a small seam opened and disclosed his cement-colored teeth. There were no horses that could match his stamina. Despite his muscle mass he moved with fluid quickness. He surrounded himself with an atmosphere of affronted hostility, but balanced it with a wild and boister-ous laugh that erupted at inappropriate times.

The old world was gone, he knew that. For some reason a day in the nineteen-fifties when all the ranchers and their hands had worked on the road rose often in his mind and with such vividness that he could smell the mud, the mineral odor of wet rock. He had been eight years old. It was the last rainy spring before that decade's drought sucked the marrow out of the state. The county road that ran between Kingring and Sheridan passed through seven ranches over a fifty-mile stretch. Under heavy melt from the mountains, it became an impass-able sump of greasy mud and standing water. The county had no money. If the ranchers wanted to get to town they would have to fix the road themselves or wait until it dried. On a drizzling morning in April his father drank his coffee standing up.

"What say, Gib? Want to come along?"

They rode together on Butch, his father's roan saddle mount. The rain had stopped but heavy clouds moved with the bumping wind. Gilbert clutched the lard pail that held their lunch. They came to a place where men with shov-els were strung out along the road. There was a section of an old corral still standing near the road and here men had leaned their tools, lunchpails, and bottles. A few had thrown their jackets on the ground. His father tethered Butch to a post.

While the men cleaned the borrow ditches and culverts, cut new drainage channels, built water bars, and hauled gravel, Gilbert hacked manfully at the mud with a broken hoe, but when Old Man Bunner told him to get out of his way or he'd chop off his legs he went to the weathered corral to play with sticks and rocks. He built a play corral of mud and broken miner's candle stems, and placed inside the rocks that were his horses. The wind cleared out the weather and by noon there was broken blue sky.

"Warmin up," called one of the men, stretching his back. The sun shone behind his ears, which turned the color of chokecherry jelly.

The lunch of cold pork and boiled eggs seemed the best thing Gilbert had ever eaten. There were two squares of his mother's coarse white cake with peanut-butter icing at the bottom of the pail. His father said Gilbert could have both pieces. He fell asleep on the way home, rocked by Butch's easy walk. His mother groaned with rage when she saw the mud on his clothes. The next morning his father went to work on the road without him and he cried until his mother slapped him. The work went on for a week, and when it ended a truck could get over the road. The first time they drove past the place he looked for his play corral. He could see one miner's candle stem. The rest had blown away. The rock horses were still there. Fifty years later the road was gravelled and graded by the county but he still looked when he drove past the place, the old corral now nothing but a single post. The prairie had swallowed his horse rocks.

After Gilbert Wolfscale inherited the ranch, he enlarged the two irrigated alfalfa fields, which made it possible, in bad years, to feed the cattle through the winter and, in good years, to sell hay to less fortunate outfits. These two fields kept the ledger ink black. He came up with other ideas to increase income. He thought of butchering and packing the beef himself to bypass the middlemen who took the money while the rancher did the work, but the local stores preferred to stay with the chain suppliers. So he put an ad in the paper looking for customers and found half a dozen, but they didn't eat enough beef to make the venture pay and a woman from town complained that there were bone splinters in the ground beef. He raised turkeys, thinking surefire Thanksgiving and Christmas markets, but never sold very many, even when he put strings of cranberries around their necks. His mother spent days making the cranberry necklaces, but people wanted the plastic-wrapped, pre-basted Safeway turkeys with breasts like Las Vegas strippers. He and his mother ate the turkeys themselves, his mother canning most of the meat. By spring, they were sick of the smell of turkey soup.

Some of the original chock-and-log fence—built not of split rails nor slender poles but big logs—stood in the high pastures nearest the forest, but much had been replaced with five-strand barbwire. He could almost see the ground compressing under the heavy log weight. How many men had helped his grandfather build that fence of tree trunks? Gilbert put in his time working on the barb fences, which no longer had the tensile strength of fresh wire but were patched and mended with short lengths of various gauge. In an earlier decade, struggling to finish the job on a hot afternoon, he had cast about for a stick or something to twist tight a diagonal cross-brace wire, but the only thing at hand was a cow's bleached leg bone with its trochlea head, which seemed made to jam fence wire tight. It worked so well that he collected and used cow bones in dozens of places. These bony fences and the coyote skulls nailed to the corner posts gave the Harp a murderous air.

He was a model of rancher stubbornness, savagely possessive of his property. He did everything in an odd, deliberate way, Gilbert Wolfscale's way, and never retreated once he had taken a position. Neighbors said he was self-reliant, but there was a way they said it that meant something else.

Seven miles north of the Harp on the Stump Hole Road lived May and Jim Codenhead. Gilbert had gone to grade school with May—she was then May Alwen. May's brother, Sedley Alwen, a big, good-natured kid with stringy arms, had been Gilbert's best friend. Gilbert had courted May for a year, taken it for granted that Sedley would be his brother-in-law, but she'd strung him along and then, in a sudden move on Christmas Day in 1966, married Jim Codenhead. Jim then was nothing more than an illiterate Montana hand working on the Alwen place.

May taught him to read until he could fumble through the newspaper.

"That's the shits, man," said Sedley sympathetically and took Gilbert on a two-day drunk, as much a salute to his draft notice as balm for Gilbert's disappointment.

The marriage wasn't unprecedented. For those who took the long view and had patience it was the classic route for a lowly cowhand to own his own spread—marry the rancher's daughter. In retaliation Gilbert went to a New Year's dance in Sheridan, found Suzzy New, and in ten days pressured her into a fast marriage.

Suzzy New was slender and small-boned, with something French about her child-size wrists, a contrast to Gilbert, six foot four, bullnecked with heavy shoulders. She was nimble-fingered and a talented embroiderer. In the flush of their first months together Gilbert bragged that she was so handy she could make a pair of chaps for a hummingbird. She was quiet, disliked arguments and shouting, the only child of elderly parents. She held herself tensely and had a way of retreating into her thoughts. She believed herself to be a very private person. She slept badly, sensitive to the slightest abnormal sound—the creak of a house timber, the rising wind, a raccoon forcing its way through the skirting of the house and under the kitchen floorboards. She had let herself be bullied into marrying Gilbert, and within days of the ruinous act she bitterly regretted it.

All her life she had heard and felt the Wyoming wind and took it for granted. There had even been a day when she was a young girl standing by the road waiting for the school bus when a spring wind, fresh and warm and perfumed with pine resin, had caused a bolt of wild happiness to surge through her, its liveliness promising glinting chances. But out at the ranch it was different. The house lay directly in line with a gap in the encircling hills to the north-west, and through this notch the prevailing wind poured, falling on the house with ferocity. The house shuddered as the wind punched it and slid along its sides like a released torrent from a broken dam. Week after week in winter it sank and rose, attacked and feinted. When she put her head down and went out to the truck it yanked at her clothing, shot up her sleeves, whisked her hair into a ravelled fright wig. Gilbert seemed not to notice, but then, she thought, he probably regarded it as *his* wind, and no doubt took pleasure in such a powerful possession.

Sedley went to Vietnam. Gilbert, who had a growth inside his nose, was 4-F[1] despite his strength and muscle. Sedley was captured by the Vietcong[2] and spent several years in a bamboo cage. He came back a different person, criss-crossed with sudden rages brought on by inconsequential events such as the rattle of dishes or a truck crossing the bridge. He was thought to be unstable and in need of watchful care. He moved in with May and Jim. May could calm Sedley down when he was having one of his fits. She had always been close to him, had, from the time she was a small child with nightmares, padded down the hall to his moonless north room, climbed into his bed for warmth and protection. The infant she bore six months after she married Jim Codenhead might have been her brother's child or, for that matter, Gilbert Wolfscale's, or even Jim Codenhead's. For years, whenever Gilbert was at their house, he studied the child, Patty, trying to work out whom she resembled. He could come to no conclusion.

1. Unfit for military service.  2. North Vietnamese army.

Vietnam nightmares tortured Sedley Alwen. Sometimes, to give May a break, Gilbert made the long drive to Cheyenne, taking Sedley to the Veterans Administration hospital, where he saw the shrink and got his prescriptions renewed. It was a two-day trip and they stayed at a motel overnight, sharing a room. After the session Sedley would be talkative. Gilbert listened attentively to his stories of torture and comrades' deaths. It was at these times Sedley resembled the friend of his childhood, excited and eager. But he could not have whiskey. They tried it once and found out. Whiskey made him act up, smashing the motel furniture and howling at the light fixture in the ceiling.

By 1999 Gilbert was fifty-four and caught in the downward ranching spiral of too much work, not enough money, drought. It got drier and drier, grasshoppers appearing as early as April and promising a plague in August. The grass crackled like eggshells under his feet. There was no color in the landscape, the alkali dust muting sage, stones, the earth itself. When a vehicle passed along the road a fine cloud spread out and slowly settled. The air was baked of scent except for the chalky dust. He was conscious of how many things could go wrong, of how poorly he'd reckoned the ranch's problems.

To the new-moneyed suitcase ranchers who had moved in all around him—ex-California real-estate agents, fabulous doctors, and retired cola executives—the Harp looked a skanky run-down outfit. They noticed the yard littered with stacks of rusted sheet metal held down by railroad ties, a pile of crooked fence posts inhabited by chipmunks, the long string of log additions to the old house. Some of these rich people, heated with land fever and the thought of a bargain, came to Gilbert and offered to buy his ranch. He could see in their eyes how they planned to bulldoze the house and build mansions with guest cottages.

"Them rich pricks are lower than a snake's ass in a wagon track," he said to his mother. "I told him my granddad homesteaded this place and if I ever seen his California butt on my property again I'd shoot it off. I looked him right in the eye and he got the message. He turned color so fast he farted."

His mother produced her hard little laugh.

It had always been dry country and no one born there expected more than a foot of rainfall in a good year. The drought halved that and he could see the metamorphosis of grazing land into desert. The country wanted to turn to sand dunes and rattlesnakes, wanted to scrape off its human ticks. Gilbert didn't have enough hay to feed his own stock. Everything told him that the day of the rancher was fading, but he dodged admitting it. He blamed the government, he blamed Salt Lake City. The damn Mormons, he said, had seeded the clouds for the Olympics,[3] sucking out all the snow moisture before it reached Wyoming. The ranch-house well was eleven hundred feet deep and the water brackish. In the drought years of the nineteen-thirties and again in the fifties his father had put in earthen dams and stock ponds, and in wet years they had held water but were now silted up and dried and stood as unsightly pits filled with weeds. In the center of one dry hole he piled an immense stack of brush, adding more every year, intending to burn it with the first good snow.

**3.** The 2002 Winter Olympics were held in Salt Lake City, Utah.

He was pestered. Some newcomer wanted a shortcut easement through the ranch to his million-dollar luxury house on the other side. A long-nosed Game and Fish biologist nagged him about fences that blocked the passage of prong-horn. Hunters wanted to shoot his deer. A busybody woman straight out of agricultural school came from the Extension Service one day and lectured him about protecting stream banks from cow-hoof erosion, about pasture rota-tion to prevent overgrazing.

"I heard all that shit. But I'll tell you what. I let the cows graze where they want and drink where they will. Been doin this for a while. Guess I know somethin about it." He stood in a truculent posture, legs apart, chin thrust forward. The woman shrugged and left.

His wife, Suzzy, had left him to live in Sheridan, sixty miles distant, in the spring of 1977, when the two boys, Monty and Rod, were still young. Those boys were doomed, said Gilbert, smacking his hand on the table for emphasis, to grow up without a father's guidance and example, injured because they were denied a boy's life on the ranch.

"If he wants a see the kids why can't he just come into town?" Suzzy said to her mother on the phone after the split. Her complaining voice rose, dipped. "You know I put in years on that ranch, and nothin really worked right. Half the time there wasn't water and when there was water it was nasty. We couldn't get in or out in the winter. No telephone, no electricity, no neighbors, his mother always naggin, and the *work!* He wore me down. 'Do this, do that,' bullyin ways. Keep that old house clean? Couldn't be done. He could a sold the place fifty times over and lived decent if he got a job like a normal human bein, but would he? No. I wouldn't relive those years for nothin." Once she had made up her mind to leave, her own stubbornness emerged. But Gilbert refused to agree to a divorce and the separation and enmity dragged on.

In town she got a cash-register job at the Big Billy supermarket and as soon as the two boys were old enough to run errands and deliver papers she made them get after-school and weekend jobs as well. She wanted to show them there were better things than cows and debt.

The Big Billy job was no good. Not only was the pay low but she disliked having to repeat "Have a nice day" to people who deserved to be ridden bare-back by the Devil wearing can openers for spurs, and one day she quit to take a job as a filing clerk in the county treasurer's office. It gravelled Gilbert that she handled his property-tax and vehicle-registration papers.

She wore him down on the divorce and he gave up after a fight in town in her new house. She had bought an old brick mansion with big trees in the yard and an ornamental iron fence around it. In the eighteen-eighties the house had belonged to a Chicago merchant who used it two or three times a year to oversee his ranch investments. Gilbert did not understand how she could afford this house. They had argued, then screamed. Gilbert stood with his legs apart and his arms hanging loose. Another man would have recognized this as a bad sign but she could not stop blaming him, and he, goaded to vio-lence, slapped her a good one and she came at him and yanked out a clump of his hair in the front where it would show, ran to the back of the house, and called the sheriff. When the law came she accused Gilbert of assault, showing the red mark on her cheek as proof.

"What about *this?*" shouted Gilbert, pointing to his bleeding scalp, but Sheriff Brant Smich, his second cousin, ignored him. When the divorce finally came through it was settled that if he wanted the boys to help out on the ranch for a weekend he would have to drive in and fetch them and he would have to pay them for their labor. He had paid practically nothing for child support during the long separation, she said, it was the least he could do. He protested, said he had cancelled checks to prove he had certainly paid adequate if not luxurious support.

"Take it to court," she said, "you think you been treated so bad."

Neither of the boys came willingly to the ranch. They appeared only in times of crisis after Gilbert telephoned Suzzy, demanding their help—spring branding, fence work. They let themselves be dragged out for a weekend then, sulky and grudging. They sassed their grandmother and whispered and snickered when they saw cows bulling. A day's work was not in them. They wanted only to ride the horses. It was clear to Gilbert that at his death they would sell the place as fast as they could. One day someone would find his stiff corpse out in the pasture, the wire cutters in his hand, or they would find him fallen in the muddy irrigation ditch, as he had found his own father. He would never be able to pass on to them how he felt about the land.

His allegiance to the place was not much of a secret, for even outsiders perceived his scalding passion for the ranch. His possessive gaze fell on the pale teeth of distant mountains, on the gullies and washes, the long draw shedding Indian scrapers and arrowheads. His feeling for the ranch was the strongest emotion that had ever moved him, a strangling love tattooed on his heart. It was his. It was as if he had drunk from some magic goblet full of the elixir of ownership. And although the margins of Bull Jump Creek had been trampled bare and muddy by generations of cows, although there were only one or two places along it still flushed with green willow, the destruction had happened so gradually that he had not noticed, for he thought of the ranch as timeless and unchanging in its beauty. It needed only young men to put it right. So his thoughts turned again and again on ways to get his sons to see and love the ranch.

In 1982, Monty was fourteen and Rod two years younger. Gilbert, waiting in the truck in front of Suzzy's house, heard Monty inside bellowing at his mother in his cracking voice, "I don't want a go. It stinks out there, there's nothin a do," and he could not dodge the fact that his sons hated the ranch. In a desperate attempt to make the place more attractive to them he had the power company run out poles and wires, a terrible expense and useless, too, as the boys came no more often. The only benefit, if benefit it was, was the small television set he bought and put in the living room, where he would lie on the sofa under one of his mother's quilts and watch men wrestling anacondas, riding motorcycles inside enormous wooden barrels. His mother liked the television, but claimed to be shocked by much of what she saw.

"It is company, I'll say that, but where they find them fool people to cut up so I don't know."

He wasn't lonely. There was his mother, he was a church deacon, a member of the Cattlemen's Association, he went to his neighbors' potluck suppers and barbecues, and about once a month drove to town and got half drunk, bought a woman, and made it back to the ranch before the old haymaker cleared the horizon. He was not a veteran but he knew all the local veterans and often went to the V.F.W.[4] with them to drink and listen to Vietnam stories.

He had always taken an interest in Vietnam. He wondered what it was about combat that so changed men, for all of those who had been in school with him, the ones who came back, were marked by what they had seen and endured. He knew them and he didn't know them. Sedley came back angry and crazy, Russ Fleshman returned as a windbag, Pete Kitchen was reclusive and lived in a horse trailer at the back of the old Kitchen ranch. Something had gone wrong for Willis McNitt, leaving him dead-voiced and troubled. They all referred emotionally to the war, now so many years past, and Fleshman sometimes put his face in his hands and cried. And there were the ones who didn't come back: Todd Likwartz, Howard Marr, and several he hadn't known. When Gilbert thought of them a phrase came into his mind—"Now they know what Rhamses knows." His mother belonged to the generation that had memorized poems in school, and one, "Little Mattie," on the death of a thirteen-year-old girl, had fastened itself relentlessly in her recall with the tolling line "Now she knows what Rhamses knows." She quoted from it throughout her life and still sometimes treated her son to a recitation of the entire piece with the stilted emphasis learned so long ago in a little Wyoming schoolhouse.

Gilbert Wolfscale listened to the veterans. He wanted to understand what he had missed. It had been the great experience of the time of his young manhood and he had been absent. It was as though the veterans had learned a different language, he thought, listening to Fleshman's scattershot of *didi mau,* Agent Orange, *beaucoup,* Jodies, 105s, Willy-Petes, and K-Bars.[5] He caught at the names—Phu Bai, Khe Sanh, Quang Tri—wondering if these were the Vietnamese equivalents of Rawlins or Thermopolis. The veterans did not seem so much tragic victims as eccentric members of a select club. He felt himself an outsider. They had got the edge on him.

One year, Willis McNitt sat behind him at the August rodeo. It was the hottest summer he had ever known. The horses were blowing and their coats white with salty sweat, the bulls stood in the chutes with their heads down and bucked feebly. There had been a freak accident at the stock pens. The rodeo grounds were old, put up in the nineteen-thirties, all wood fence and posts, and somehow a kid watering the roping calves had fallen or been knocked down and mashed his face against a splintery post. A long sliver had run into the flesh below his eyebrow and he had stumbled away from the pens, blood coursing down the back of his hand, which he had put instinctively to the wound. He had not cried out, just stumbled into sight with blood seeping between his fingers, making the crowd gasp. As the ambulance bore him away Gilbert said to no one in particular, "They ought a tear out them damn old wood posts and get good metal."

"I seen somethin like that in Nam," said Willis behind him in his flat, heavy voice. Willis had a son at the university, studying anthropology. The

4. Veterans of Foreign Wars, an organization for American Veterans.  5. *Didi mau,* go quickly (Vietnamese); Agent Orange, a defoliating chemical weapon; *beaucoup,* many (French); Jodies, civilian men, often romantic rivals of soldiers; 105s, Republic F-105 Thunderchief, an Air Force fighter-bomber deployed in the early years of the Vietnam War; Willy-Petes, white phosphorus, an incendiary munition; K-Bars, combat knives.

kid—Coot McNitt—had a half-baked theory that rice cultivation had developed to replace a shortage of maggots in early man's diet. If you listened to him long enough he'd make you believe it. "We was in a free-fire zone and the kid next a me got shot in the eye. He said, 'I been shot in the eye,' said it five or six times, real quiet, like he couldn't quite take it in. Couldn't believe it. Then he laid down beside me and commenced a kick and thrash and ever time he kicked the blood pumped up through his eye like a school water fountain."

"God," said Gilbert. "Did he—?"

"Died. A kid, eighteen years old, younger'n Coot. Couldn't believe he'd been shot. I was nineteen but after that I felt like a old man."

"You ain't old, Willis. Hell, you're my age."

"Yeah."

The word dropped like a stone.

One day, Gilbert Wolfscale's mother opened an official-looking letter from the California State Allocation Department. She read that she had inherited a sum of money from someone in that state. All she had to do was fill out the enclosed form, mail it back, and in six or eight weeks she would receive the inheritance. She spent two hours filling out the form, with its demands for address, Social Security number, date of birth, bank-account numbers, and other tedious details. She sat so long at the table with this form that her left leg went to sleep and when she got up to go to the kitchen and make a cup of tea it buckled. She fell and broke her hip.

She recuperated very slowly. Even after the break had healed, Gilbert had to drive her in to Sheridan for weekly therapy. He sometimes wondered why she didn't get one of her friends to drive her. She was always on the phone gabbing with her cronies and most of them still drove. He heard her talking with them about football, which she watched avidly on the television.

"I'm for them Bears. I couldn't never be for them Packers."

When he asked her why she did not arrange a trip to town with Luce or Florence or Helen she said, "They're not family. Suppose the doctor was to give me bad news. I'd want a be with blood kin, not some other person."

While she was in with the therapist Gilbert walked around the windy town streets rather than sit in a plastic chair in the stuffy waiting room. In a music store he looked at CDs, wondering at the proliferation of bands with trendy, foolish names. Behind a stiff plastic divider labelled "MISCELLANEOUS" he found birdcalls, tap dancing, the whistles of steam locomotives from around the world. The last CD was "Remembering Vietnam." The cover showed a grimy infantryman staring up at a helicopter. The back copy listed "Firefight," "Shrapnel," "ARVN," "Jungle Patrol," "Rain," "APC Convoy." He bought it.

In the truck driving home his mother said, "I don't have to go back there but a few more times, looks like, and thanks to heaven. Some a the strangest people settin in that waitin room. These two women got talkin about their Bible class. Sounded pretty modern, you know, tryin a link the Bible to nowadays. But this Bible class *they* went to was tryin a guess how it would be if Jesus showed up in Sheridan. That got them all excited and there they set, what would he do for work. They both said he could easy find a job workin construction. Would he have his own house and would it be like a trailer or a regular house or a apartment? Then they got at the furniture, what kind a furniture would Jesus pick for his place. And you know how you get thinkin about things you overhear? Wasn't none a my business but there I set, crazy as they was, wonderin if he'd pick out a maple rockin chair or a sofa with that Scotchgard fabric or what."

A month before her fall his mother had bought some bright-colored kitchen sponges. One of them was purple and she had developed an affection for it, never using it on greasy pots or to wipe up nasty spills. He dribbled coffee on the counter one morning and began to mop at the spill with the distinguished sponge.

"What are you doin! Don't use that—take the pink one. You dunderhead, I'm savin that one."

"For what, Ma?"

"For the good glasses." She meant the crystal wineglasses with the gold rims that had been passed down from Granny Webb and had stood inverted in the china cupboard for as long as he could remember. He had never known them to be used. Inside the china cupboard next to the glasses was a photograph of his father's mother in a black silk twill dress, looking freeze-dried and mournful.

"Where is that stupid mailman?" his mother said, pulling back the curtain and looking for the plume of dust along the road.

It was days before he had a chance to listen to the CD. He was on his way to the bank. The soul of leaf susurration, cicadas, crickets, mortars, a calling bird with a voice like a kid hooting down a cardboard tube, snatches of talk, incoming fire, deafening helicopter fibrillation filled the truck.

Saturday was grocery day, but his mother said, "I don't feel up to it. You just get what we need, bread and eggs. Coffee. Whatever else you see that looks good. I don't have much appetite these days anyhow. And I want a wait for the mail. I'm expectin mail."

He bought the groceries and on the way out of town passed the library. Two miles beyond it he thought of books—books on Vietnam—and he turned around. He came away with three, all they had, read them in bed that night, and fell asleep with a book on his face. He awoke frightened and shouting, thinking something was smothering him. The exhaled moisture from his mouth had formed a round dimple in the page.

It was not long after this that his mother began to give way. She would look at him and say, "Where's Gilbert? Out playin, I bet. I want him to fill up that wood box." And later she would tell him, "You'll have to fend for yourself for supper. I can't cook without no wood." He felt a pang of guilt, for there had been many times when he was a boy that he had dodged the wood box. But she kept asking if the mail had come until Gilbert, exasperated, said, "You expectin a letter from the President or what?" She shook her head and said nothing.

In 1999, Gilbert's son Monty turned thirty-two, a big dark-haired fellow, still single, who worked as a roofer in Colorado. Gilbert hadn't seen him in years. Rod, the younger one, lived in Sheridan, a block away from his mother, worked in Buffalo in a video-rental store. He was married and had two children, twin girls, whom Gilbert had seen only once and had never touched nor held. The little girls had never been to the ranch. The boy's wife, Debra, worked, too, answering the telephone at Equality Cowboy Travel. Gilbert sometimes dreamed that they would have more children—boys—and that these little grandsons would love the ranch, would grow up knowing what a beautiful place the Wolfscales owned. They would love it as he did and take it on when he went.

Gilbert's mother turned eighty-one. The purple sponge, though somewhat faded, was largely unchanged, not to be used. She took to rummaging through the desk looking for pencil and paper, settled on a little notebook, spiral-bound at the top and with lined paper. She spent hours at the kitchen table bent over this notebook, thinking, occasionally scrawling something down or erasing everything, tearing out the spoiled sheet and crumpling it.

"What are you writin, Ma? Your biography? Cowgirl poetry?"

"No," she said and put her arm around the notebook so he couldn't see it, like a child protecting a test paper from a cheating neighbor.

On a very cold March day he went into town to the ranch-equipment center; the used aircraft tires he'd ordered for the bush hog were in. If the weather warmed up later in the week he'd work on pulling old sagebrush out of the three-mile pasture. In town the bank thermometer read minus two and a harsh wind made it seem like the freezing pits of Hell. He ordered a pizza. Clouds were moving in as he drove back, eating the cheesy slices, and as he turned in to the ranch the first fine flakes fell through the air.

The house was silent. He thought his mother might be napping and went out to the shop, where he changed the bush hog's tires. The days were growing longer and he worked until twilight. Back in the house he was disturbed by the deep silence. Usually his mother watched crime programs on television at this hour. He went to her room and knocked on the door.

"Ma! Ma, you O.K.? I'm goin a start supper now." There was no answer. He opened the door and saw his mother would not again want any supper.

It was a shock to learn that her bank account was at flat zero. He couldn't understand what she had spent the money on. He remembered her telling him when she broke her hip that she had over six thousand dollars set aside for "—*you* know." And he did know. For her funeral costs. He had to scratch to come up with the money for a decent coffin.

Cleaning out her room, he came across the spiral-bound notebook. It was filled with plaintive letters to the California State Allocation Department, asking when her inheritance would come. Folded in the front of the notebook was the original letter. He telephoned the number at the bottom of the page but got a message that the number had been disconnected. Gilbert began to guess there was some sort of scam. He called Sheriff Brant Smich, asked him if he knew anything about California State Allocation.

"Hell, yes. You get a letter from them sayin about you inherited some money and askin for your bank-account numbers? Don't believe none of it. Don't answer them. Bring the letter to the post office. They're after that outfit for mail fraud."

With his mother gone, civilization began to fall away from him like feathers from a molting hen. In a matter of weeks he was eating straight from the frying pan.

As is usual in the ranch world, things went from bad to worse. The drought settled deeper, like a lamprey eel sucking at the region's vitals. He had half-seen the scores of trucks emblazoned CPC—Consolidated Petroleum Company—speeding along the dusty road for the past year, and knew that they were drilling for coal-bed methane on public land adjacent to his ranch. They pumped the saline wastewater laden with mineral toxins into huge containment pits. The water was no good, he knew that, and it seemed a terrible irony that in such arid country water could be worthless. He had always voted Republican and supported energy development as the best way to make jobs in the hinterland. But when the poison wastewater seeped from the containment pits into the groundwater, into Bull Jump Creek, into his alfalfa irrigation ditches, even into the household well water, he saw it was killing the ranch.

He fought back. Like other ranchers who once again felt betrayed by state and federal government, he wrote letters and went to meetings protesting coal-bed methane drilling and the hundreds of service roads and drill rigs and heavy trucks that were tearing up the country. The meetings were strange, for ecological conservationists and crusty ranchers came together in the same room, in agreement for once. He noted with satisfaction that the schoolteacher, Dan Moorhen, a bleeding-heart liberal ecology-minded freak, admitted that ranchers were the best defense against developers chopping up the land, that ranches and ranchers kept the Old West alive. When the gas-company reps or politicians came, the meetings were rancorous and loud and at the end people signed petitions with such force their pens ripped the paper, but it all meant nothing. The drilling continued, the poison water seeped, the grass and sage and alfalfa died. All he could do was hang on to the place.

He was unprepared for the telephone call from a neighbor, Fran Bangharmer. It was the morning of the Fourth of July.

"Too bad about Suzzy, all that right on the front page, too."

"What do you mean?" he said. "What was on the front page?"

"Arrested for embezzlin. Monday's paper."

"What!" Fran's voice was subtly triumphant, tinged with Schadenfreude, but Gilbert barely listened, hung up as soon as he could and drove into town to find a three-day-old paper and read for himself that his ex-wife had, for years, been siphoning tax money into a private bank account by a complex series of computer sleights of hand he could not understand.

He went to the county jail and tried to see her but was turned away.

"She don't want to see you, Gib, and she's got that right."

Half of the stores in town were closed for the holiday. Already there were clusters of people along the sidewalk, although the parade didn't start until one o'clock. In despair he drove down to Buffalo to the video store where Rod worked. It was open, the windows draped with red-white-and-blue ribbons. A huge poster read: "RODEO DAYS! JULY 4 TO 10!"

He found his younger son stocking the shelves with gaudy boxes. As he stood behind him he noticed the son's thinning hair and felt the hot breath of passing time.

"Rod?" he said, and the young man turned around.

"Dad." They looked at each other and the son dropped his eyes. Gilbert could smell his son's aftershave lotion. He himself had never used the stuff in his life.

"I came to . . . I want to . . . Well. Your mother?"

"Yeah. Do you want a have lunch?"

"You mean dinner?"

The son flushed at the old-fashioned word. "Yeah. 'Dinner.' Go down the KFC and eat in the car."

"I come in the truck. Come on, let's go."

"I got a tell somebody I'm goin."

That's what it was like, thought Gilbert, working for somebody else. You had to tell them what you did or were going to do and they could say no.

He drove to the fast-food strip at the north end of town, shouted into the drive-through intercom. Sitting in the truck, the windows down and the hot sun burning their arms, they gnawed at the salty, overspiced chicken, huge crumbs falling. They both sucked on straws stuck into vanilla milkshakes.

"I tried a see her," said Gilbert. "She wouldn't see me."

"She's still pretty bitter, you know. Feels like her life was wasted, or at least some years of it. She's that way. She takes a position and that's it. You can't argue her out of nothin. She's stubborn."

"I know that pretty well. How's it affectin you that your mother is a crook and a jailbird?" He glanced sideways at Rod, seeing the pale, indoor complexion, the clerk's shirt with creases ironed into the sleeves. The boy had the heavy Wolfscale jaw and beaky nose.

"Hell, I don't know. I don't think of it that way. People look at me kind a funny but they don't say nothin. Except Deb. She is gettin a lot a snide comment down at the travel agency. It's no fun for her. It's my girls I worry about, if some kid at school this fall is goin a taunt them."

"Kids got short memories. By the time school starts they won't recall it. What do you think they'll do to her?"

"Probly go pretty light. She's got a good lawyer. You know, she made restitution of about twelve grand. That'll count for a lot. They already got a lien on the house, repossessed her car. That's what she used the most a the money for, buy the house and fix it up. That house was everthing to her. She put in a swimmin pool two years ago."

"I used a wonder how she could afford it. And I heard a couple years ago that she went out to Las Vegas?" He couldn't believe he'd found a packet of salt beneath the flabby biscuit. Did anyone ever think their chicken not salty enough?

"It was a whole bunch a them that work at the county offices. They all went. She won four thousand bucks."

For some reason this remark incensed Gilbert. Rod said it with a tone of pride that his lying, cheating, stealing, double-dealing mother had won some money gambling. He changed the subject abruptly. "What do you hear from your brother?"

"Aw, he calls up now and then. We get together with him when we take Arlene down to Denver for her treatment. You know she's had that cancer. It's in remission now and you'd never know she'd been sick a day."

Gilbert did not know his granddaughter had been sick a day. He shuddered. In the distance he could hear a school marching band. Buffalo's parade was starting, or maybe just warming up.

"Is he still workin for that roofin contractor?"

"Well, no. He's workin in a restaurant. He's workin in a Jap restaurant. But he's healthy, thank God, considerin his—life style."

"What does that mean, his 'life style'?" Gilbert wiped his hands of the chicken, wadded the napkin, and thrust it into the grease-stained box.

"Well, he's—you know."

"I know what?"

"Dad, it's not up to me to say nothin about Monty." Rod was folding and crushing the box. He wiped his right hand on his pants leg.

"I ain't heard or seen him for quite a few years. Not likely to. Now what the hell is this about his 'life style'?"

"For Christ sake, Dad. It's nothin. Just he's sort a—more—sophisticated. He likes a different kind a stuff than most people come from Wyomin."

"I hear you talkin but I don't know what you're sayin."

But he did. As a child Monty had hung around the kitchen and his mother constantly, and to get him to help with chores had been more labor than doing the jobs himself. That is, until Myrl Otter came to work on the ranch on weekends. Myrl was a big blond Scandinavian type, muscular and good-looking. The man's wife had her work cut out for her keeping an eye on him, as girls flirted with Myrl and he reciprocated willingly. After he came to work on the ranch Monty began to tag after the fellow like a yellowjacket after pears. Gilbert noticed, but as the boy was only seven or eight it seemed just a little kid's fancy, nothing much. Kids got attached to dogs and blankets and maybe even hired men. He thought nothing of it and after a few months Myrl Otter, in the way of so many ranch hands, stopped showing up for work and Gilbert had forgotten him until now. The marching music, carried by the light wind, seemed nearer.

"I better get goin. Don't want a get tied up in that damn parade." He got out, threw his chicken box at the trash can. Rod, too, tossed his crumpled box, but it hit the side of the can and sprayed chicken bones.

"Forget it," said Gilbert. "They get paid a pick up."

He dropped Rod back at the video store and headed north, thinking to beat the parade by taking a side street, but he was too late. He stopped for a red light that wouldn't change and the parade came surging around a corner, passing in front of him, and he had to wait. A section of the high-school band strag-gled past, sweaty kids, many of them obese, their white marching trousers bunched at the crotch. He remembered schoolmates in his own childhood, skinny, quick ranch kids, no one fat and sweaty, Pete Kitchen looking like he was made of kindling wood and insulation wire, Willis McNitt small enough to shit behind a sagebrush and never be noticed.

Behind the band came two teen-age boys dressed as Indians, breechclouts over swim trunks, a load of beads around their necks, black wigs with braids and feathers. One carried a bongo drum, striking it irregularly with his hand. Their skin had been darkened with some streaky substance. Then two men whom he recognized as Sheridan car mechanics slouched along in buckskin suits and fur hats, carrying antique flintlocks. One had a demijohn that he lifted to his lips every thirty seconds, crying "Yee-haw!" The other had a few shiny No. 2 traps over his shoulder. Gilbert could see the hardware-store price tags on them. He knew he was going to get the whole hokey Wild West treatment before he could move.

Now came two horses, both bearing kids dressed as cowboys, in heavy woolly chaps, pearl-button Western shirts, limp bandannas, big hats, and boots. Both twirled guns on their fingers, aiming at friends in the crowd. They were followed by a stock outlaw and a sheriff's posse, and behind them half the town's women and small children in pioneer regalia—long calico dresses, aprons and sunbonnets, big Nikes flashing incongruously with every step. One of these women was Patty Codenhead and for a moment he was startled at how much she looked like the photograph of his father's mother in the china cupboard. It was the costume, he thought. The parade came down to a few trick riders in neon satin, and Sedley Alwen, who, crazy or not, was in every public procession showing off his roping skills, stepping in and out of his fluid loops and somehow avoiding the horse manure that marked the path. The last of all was a CPC pickup, three hard-hatted methane-gas workers sitting in back smoking cigarettes and joking with each other. Now he could go.

He could go but he found it difficult to step on the accelerator. The light turned green, red, then green again, yet he couldn't move until drivers behind him began to sound their horns. There had been something wrong with the parade, something seriously wrong, but he couldn't think what.

Driving through the open country on the way back, he forgot the parade and thought about Monty and what form his "sophistication" might take, about his embezzling wife, the other son who had not bothered to tell him that his grandchild had cancer. He couldn't tell the size of things. He was very thirsty and blamed the salty chicken.

The buildings and traffic fell away and he was on the empty road, the dusty sage flying past, the white ground. The sky was a hard cheerful blue, empty but for a few torn contrails. Plastic bags impaled on the barb fences flapped in the hot wind. A small herd of pronghorn in the distance had their heads down. He saw his neighbor's cattle spread out on the parched land and it came to him that there had been no ranchers in the parade—it was all pioneers, outlaws, Indians, and gas.

He knew what kind of furniture Jesus would pick for his place in Wyoming. He would choose a few small pines in the National Forest, go there at night, fell and limb them, debark the sappy rind with a spud, exposing the pale, worm-tunnelled wood, and from the timbers he would make the simplest round-legged furniture, everything pegged, no nails or screws.

He wished his mother were still alive. He'd say to her, "One thing sure. He wouldn't get hisself tangled up with no ranch." It didn't come close to saying what he meant but it was all he could do.

2003

# GEORGE SAUNDERS
## b. 1958

George Saunders was born in Amarillo, Texas, and raised on Chicago's south side. After graduating from the Colorado School of Mines with a degree in exploration geophysics, he worked as a geophysical engineer, a store clerk, a doorman, a roofer, a guitarist, and a slaughterhouse laborer before receiving his M.F.A. from Syracuse University, where he is now a professor of creative writing. Best known for his satirical short fiction, Saunders has published four short story collections: *CivilWarLand in Bad Decline* (1996), *Pastoralia* (2001), *In Persuasion Nation* (2006), and *Tenth of December* (2013), named one of the ten best books of the year by *The New York Times Book Review*. He has also written an illustrated fable, a bestselling children's book, a book of essays, and two screenplays. In 2002, Saunders was selected by *The New Yorker* as one of the 20 best writers under 40. Since then he has been awarded a Guggenheim Fellowship, a MacArthur Fellowship, and an Academy Award from the American Academy of Arts and Letters.

## Victory Lap

Three days shy of her fifteenth birthday, Alison Pope paused at the top of the stairs.

Say the staircase was marble. Say she descended and all heads turned. Where was {special one}? Approaching now, bowing slightly, he exclaimed, How can so much grace be contained in one small package? Oops. Had he said *small package*? And just stood there? Broad princelike face totally bland of expression? Poor thing! Sorry, no way, down he went, he was definitely not {special one}.

What about this guy, behind Mr. Small Package, standing near the home entertainment center? With a thick neck of farmer integrity yet tender ample lips, who, placing one hand on the small of her back, whispered, Dreadfully sorry you had to endure that bit about the small package just now. Let us go stand on the moon. Or, uh, in the moon. In the moonlight.

Had he said, *Let us go stand on the moon*? If so, she would have to be like, {eyebrows up}. And if no wry acknowledgment was forthcoming, be like, Uh, I am not exactly dressed for standing on the moon, which, as I understand it, is super-cold?

Come on, guys, she couldn't keep treading gracefully on this marble stairwell in her mind forever! That dear old white-hair in the tiara was getting all like, *Why are those supposed princes making that darling girl march in place ad nausea?* Plus she had a recital tonight and had to go fetch her tights from the dryer.

Egads! One found oneself still standing at the top of the stairs.

Do the thing where, facing upstairs, hand on railing, you hop down the stairs one at a time, which was getting a lot harder lately, due to, someone's feet were getting longer every day, seemed like.

*Pas de chat, pas de chat.*

*Changement, changement.*[1]

Hop over thin metal thingie separating hallway tile from living-room rug.

Curtsy to self in entryway mirror.

Come on, Mom, get here. We do not wish to be castigated by Ms. Callow again in the wings.

Although actually she loved Ms. C. So strict! Also loved the other girls in class. And the girls from school. *Loved* them. Everyone was so nice. Plus the boys at her school. Plus the teachers at her school. All of them were doing their best. Actually, she loved her whole town. That adorable grocer, spraying his lettuce! Pastor Carol, with her large comfortable butt! The chubby postman, gesticulating with his padded envelopes! It had once been a mill town. Wasn't that crazy? What did that even mean?

Also she loved her house. Across the creek was the Russian church. So ethnic! That onion dome had loomed in her window since her Pooh footie days. Also loved Gladsong Drive. Every house on Gladsong was a Corona del Mar. That was amazing! If you had a friend on Gladsong, you already knew where everything was in his or her home.

*Jeté, jeté, rond de jambe.*

*Pas de bourrée.*[2]

On a happy whim, do front roll, hop to your feet, kiss the picture of Mom and Dad taken at Penney's back in the Stone Ages, when you were that little cutie right there {kiss} with a hair bow bigger than all outdoors.

Sometimes, feeling happy like this, she imagined a baby deer trembling in the woods.

Where's your mama, little guy?

I don't know, the deer said in the voice of Heather's little sister Becca.

Are you afraid? she asked it. Are you hungry? Do you want me to hold you?

Okay, the baby deer said.

Here came the hunter now, dragging the deer's mother by the antlers. Her guts were completely splayed. Jeez, that was nice! She covered the baby's eyes and was like, Don't you have anything better to do, dank hunter, than kill this baby's mom? You seem like a nice enough guy.

Is my mom killed? the baby said in Becca's voice.

No, no, she said. This gentleman was just leaving.

The hunter, captivated by her beauty, toffed or doffed his cap, and, going down on one knee, said, If I could will life back into this fawn. I would do so, in hopes you might defer one tender kiss upon our elderly forehead.

---

**1.** "Step of the cat" and "changing" (French). Dance steps in ballet.   **2.** "Jump" and "stuffing step" (French). More ballet steps.

Go, she said. Only, for your task of penance, do not eat her. Lay her out in a field of clover, with roses strewn about her. And bestow a choir, to softly sing of her foul end.

Lay who out? the baby deer said.

No one, she said. Never mind. Stop asking so many questions.

*Pas de chat, pas de chat.*

*Changement, changement.*

She felt hopeful that {special one} would hail from far away. The local boys possessed a certain *je ne sais quoi*, which, tell the truth, she was not *très* crazy about, such as: actually named their own nuts. She had overheard that! And aspired to work for CountyPower because the work shirts were awesome and you got them free.

So ixnay on the local boys. A special ixnay on Matt Drey, owner of the largest mouth in the land. Kissing him last night at the pep rally had been like kissing an underpass. Scary! Kissing Matt was like suddenly this cow in a sweater is bearing down on you, who will not take no for an answer, and his huge cow head is being flooded by chemicals that are drowning out what little powers of reason Matt actually did have.

What she liked was being in charge of her. Her body, her mind. Her thoughts, her career, her future.

That was what she liked.

So be it.

We might have a slight snack.

*Un petit repas.*[3]

Was she special? Did she consider herself special? Oh, gosh, she didn't know. In the history of the world, many had been more special than her. Helen Keller had been awesome; Mother Teresa was amazing; Mrs. Roosevelt was quite chipper in spite of her husband, who was handicapped, which, in addition, she had been gay, with those big old teeth, long before such time as being gay and First Lady was even conceptual. She, Alison, could not hope to compete in the category of those ladies. Not yet, anyway!

There was so much she didn't know! Like how to change the oil. Or even check the oil. How to open the hood. How to bake brownies. That was embarrassing, actually, being a girl and all. And what was a mortgage? Did it come with the house? When you breast-fed, did you have to like push the milk out?

Egads. Who was this wan figure, visible through the living-room window, trotting up Gladsong Drive? Kyle Boot, palest kid in all the land? Still dressed in his weird cross-country toggles?

Poor thing. He looked like a skeleton with a mullet. Were those cross-country shorts from the like *Charlie's Angels* days or *quoi*? How could he run so well when he seemed to have literally no muscles? Every day he ran home like this, shirtless with his backpack on, then hit the remote from down by the Fungs' and scooted into his garage without breaking stride.

You almost had to admire the poor goof.

They'd grown up together, been little beaners in that mutual sandbox down by the creek. Hadn't they bathed together when wee or some such crud? She hoped that never got out. Because in terms of friends, Kyle was basically

---

3. A little meal (French).

down to Feddy Slavko, who walked leaning way backward and was always retrieving things from between his teeth, announcing the name of the retrieved thing in Greek, then re-eating it. Kyle's mom and dad didn't let him do squat. He had to call home if the movie in World Culture might show bare boobs. Each of the items in his lunch box was clearly labeled.

*Pas de bourrée.*

And curtsy.

Pour quantity of Cheez Doodles into compartmentalized old-school Tupperware dealie.

Thanks, Mom, thanks, Dad. Your kitchen *rocks.*

Shake Tupperware dealie back and forth like panning for gold, then offer to some imaginary poor gathered round.

Please enjoy. Is there anything else I can do for you folks?

You have already done enough, Alison, by even deigning to speak to us.

That is so not true! Don't you understand, all people deserve respect? Each of us is a rainbow.

Uh, really? Look at this big open sore on my poor shriveled flank.

Allow me to fetch you some Vaseline.

That would be much appreciated. This thing kills.

But as far as that rainbow idea? She believed that. People were amazing. Mom was awesome, Dad was awesome, her teachers worked so hard and had kids of their own, and some were even getting divorced, such as Mrs. Dees, but still always took time for their students. What she found especially inspiring about Mrs. Dees was that, even though Mr. Dees was cheating on Mrs. Dees with the lady who ran the bowling alley, Mrs. Dees was still teaching the best course ever in Ethics, posing such questions as: Can goodness win? Or do good people always get shafted, evil being more reckless? That last bit seemed to be Mrs. Dees taking a shot at the bowling-alley gal. But seriously! Is life fun or scary? Are people good or bad? On the one hand, that clip of those gauntish pale bodies being steamrolled while fat German ladies looked on chomping gum. On the other hand, sometimes rural folks, even if their particular farms were on hills, stayed up late filling sandbags.

In their straw poll she had voted for people being good and life being fun, with Mrs. Dees giving her a pitying glance as she stated her views: To do good, you just have to decide to do good. You have to be brave. You have to stand up for what's right. At that last, Mrs. Dees had made this kind of groan. Which was fine. Mrs. Dees had a lot of pain in her life, yet, interestingly? Still obviously found something fun about life and good about people, because otherwise why sometimes stay up so late grading you come in next day all exhausted, blouse on backward, having messed it up in the early-morning dark, you dear discombobulated thing?

Here came a knock on the door. Back door. In-ter-est-ing. Who could it be? Father Dmitri from across the way? UPS? FedEx? With *un petit* check *pour Papa*?

*Jeté, jeté, rond de jambe.*

*Pas de bourrée.*

Open door, and—

Here was a man she did not know. Quite huge fellow, in one of those meter-reader vests.

Something told her to step back in, slam the door. But that seemed rude. Instead she froze, smiled, did {eyebrow raise} to indicate: May I help you?

Kyle Boot dashed through the garage, into the living area, where the big clocklike wooden indicator was set at All Out. Other choices included: Mom & Dad Out; Mom Out; Dad Out; Kyle Out; Mom & Kyle Out; Dad & Kyle Out; and All In.

Why did they even need All In? Wouldn't they know it when they were All In? Would he like to ask Dad that? Who, in his excellent totally silent downstairs woodshop, had designed and built the Family Status Indicator?

Ha.

Ha ha.

On the kitchen island was a Work Notice.

> *Scout: New geode on deck. Place in yard per included drawing. No goofing. Rake areas first, put down plastic as I have shown you. Then lay in white rock. THIS GEODE EXPENSIVE. Pls take seriously. No reason this should not be done by time I get home. This = five (5) Work Points.*

Gar, Dad, do you honestly feel it fair that I should have to slave in the yard until dark after a rigorous cross-country practice that included sixteen 440s, eight 880s, a mile-for-time, a kajillion Drake sprints, and a five-mile Indian relay?

Shoes off, mister.

Yoinks, too late. He was already at the TV. And had left an incriminating trail of microclods. Way verboten.[4] Could the microclods be hand-plucked? Although, problem: if he went back to hand-pluck the microclods, he'd leave an incriminating new trail of microclods.

He took off his shoes and stood mentally rehearsing a little show he liked to call WHAT IF . . . RIGHT NOW?

WHAT IF they came home RIGHT NOW?

It's a funny story, Dad! I came in thoughtlessly! Then realized what I'd done! I guess, when I think about it, what I'm happy about? Is how quickly I self-corrected! The reason I came in so thoughtlessly was, I wanted to get right to work, Dad, per your note!

He raced in his socks to the garage, threw his shoes into the garage, ran for the vacuum, vacuumed up the microclods, then realized, holy golly, he had thrown his shoes into the garage rather than placing them on the Shoe Sheet as required, toes facing away from the door for ease of donnage later.

He stepped into the garage, placed his shoes on the Shoe Sheet, stepped back inside.

Scout, Dad said in his head, has anyone ever told you that even the most neatly maintained garage is going to have some oil on its floor, which is now on your socks, being tracked all over the tan Berber?

Oh gar, his ass was grass.

But no—*celebrate good times, come on*—no oil stain on rug.

He tore off his socks. It was absolutely verboten for him to be in the main living area barefoot. Mom and Dad coming home to find him Tarzaning around like some sort of white trasher would not be the least fucking bit—

---

4. Forbidden (German).

Swearing in your head? Dad said in his head. Step up, Scout, be a man. If you want to swear, swear aloud.

I don't want to swear aloud.

Then don't swear in your head.

Mom and Dad would be heartsick if they could hear the swearing he sometimes did in his head, such as crap-cunt shit-turd dick-in-the-ear butt-creamery. Why couldn't he stop doing that? They thought so highly of him, sending weekly braggy emails to both sets of grandparents, such as: Kyle's been superbusy keeping up his grades while running varsity cross-country though still a sophomore, while setting aside a little time each day to manufacture such humdingers as cunt-swoggle rear-fuck—

What was wrong with him? Why couldn't he be grateful for all that Mom and Dad did for him, instead of—

Cornhole the ear-cunt.

Flake-fuck the pale vestige with a proddering dick-knee.

You could always clear the mind with a hard pinch on your own minimal love handle.

Ouch.

Hey, today was Tuesday, a Major Treat day. The five (5) new Work Points for placing the geode, plus his existing two (2) Work Points, totaled seven (7) Work Points, which, added to his eight (8) accrued Usual Chore Points, made fifteen (15) Total Treat Points, which could garner him a Major Treat (for example, two handfuls of yogurt-covered raisins) plus twenty free-choice TV minutes, although the particular show would have to be negotiated with Dad at time of cash-in.

One thing you will not be watching, Scout, is *America's Most Outspoken Dirt Bikers*.

Whatever.

Whatever, Dad.

Really, Scout? "Whatever"? Will it be "whatever" when I take away all your Treat Points and force you to quit cross-country, as I have several times threatened to do if a little more cheerful obedience wasn't forthcoming?

No, no, no. I don't want to quit, Dad. Please. I'm good at it. You'll see, first meet. Even Matt Drey said—

Who is Matt Drey? Some ape on the football team?

Yes.

Is his word law?

No.

What did he say?

*Little shit can run.*

Nice talk, Scout. Ape talk. Anyway, you may not make it to the first meet. Your ego seems to be overflowing its banks. And why? Because you can jog? Anyone can jog. Beasts of the field can jog.

I'm not quitting! Anal-cock shit-bird rectum-fritz! Please, I'm begging you, it's the only thing I'm decent at! Mom, if he makes me quit I swear to God I'll—

Drama doesn't suit you, Beloved Only.

If you want the privilege of competing in a team sport, Scout, show us that you can live within our perfectly reasonable system of directives designed to benefit you.

Hello.

A van had just pulled up in the St. Mikhail's parking lot.

Kyle walked in a controlled, gentlemanly manner to the kitchen counter. On the counter was Kyle's Traffic Log, which served the dual purpose of (1) buttressing Dad's argument that Father Dmitri should build a soundproof retaining wall and (2) constituting a data set for a possible Science Fair project for him, Kyle, entitled, by Dad, "Correlation of Church Parking Lot Volume vs. Day of Week, with Ancillary Investigation of Sunday Volume Throughout Year."

Smiling agreeably as if he enjoyed filling out the Log, Kyle very legibly filled out the Log:

Vehicle: VAN.
Color: GRAY.
Make: CHEVY.
Year: UNKNOWN.

A guy got out of the van. One of the usual Rooskies. "Rooskie" was an allowed slang. Also "dang it." Also "holy golly." Also "crapper." The Rooskie was wearing a jean jacket over a hoodie, which, in Kyle's experience, was not unusual church-wear for the Rooskies, who sometimes came directly over from Jiffy Lube still wearing coveralls.

Under "Vehicle Driver" he wrote, PROBABLE PARISHIONER.

That sucked. Stank, rather. The guy being a stranger, he, Kyle, now had to stay inside until the stranger left the neighborhood. Which totally futzed up his geode placing. He'd be out there until midnight. What a detriment!

The guy put on a Day Glo-vest. Ah, dude was a meter reader.

The meter reader looked left, then right, leaped across the creek, entered the Pope backyard, passed between the soccer-ball rebounder and the in-ground pool, then knocked on the Pope door.

Good leap there, Boris.

The door swung open.

Alison.

Kyle's heart was singing. He'd always thought that was just a phrase. Alison was like a national treasure. In the dictionary under "beauty" there should be a picture of her in that jean skort. Although lately she didn't seem to like him all that much.

Now she stepped across her deck so the meter reader could show her something. Something electrical wrong on the roof? The guy seemed eager to show her. Actually, he had her by the wrist. And was like tugging.

That was weird. Wasn't it? Something had never been weird around here before. So probably it was fine. Probably the guy was just a really new meter reader?

Somehow Kyle felt like stepping out onto the deck. He stepped out. The guy froze. Alison's eyes were scared-horse eyes. The guy cleared his throat, turned slightly to let Kyle see something.

A knife.

The meter reader had a knife.

Here's what you're doing, the guy said. Standing right there until we leave. Move a muscle, I knife her in the heart. Swear to God. Got it?

Kyle's mouth was so spitless all he could do was make his mouth do the shape it normally did when saying Yes.

Now they were crossing the yard. Alison threw herself to the ground. The guy hauled her up. She threw herself down. He hauled her up. It was odd seeing Alison tossed like a rag doll in the sanctuary of the perfect yard her dad had made for her. She threw herself down.

The guy hissed something and she rose, suddenly docile.

In his chest Kyle felt the many directives, Major and Minor, he was right now violating. He was on the deck shoeless, on the deck shirtless, was outside when a stranger was near, had engaged with that stranger.

Last week Sean Ball had brought a wig to school to more effectively mimic the way Bev Mirren chewed her hair when nervous. Kyle had briefly considered intervening. At Evening Meeting, Mom had said that she considered Kyle's decision not to intervene judicious. Dad had said, That was none of your business. You could have been badly hurt. Mom had said, Think of all the resources we've invested in you, Beloved Only. Dad had said, I know we sometimes strike you as strict but you are literally all we have.

They were at the soccer-ball rebounder now, Alison's arm up behind her back. She was making a low repetitive sound of denial, like she was trying to invent a noise that would adequately communicate her feelings about what she'd just this instant realized was going to happen to her.

He was just a kid. There was nothing he could do. In his chest he felt the lush release of pressure that always resulted when he submitted to a directive. There at his feet was the geode. He should just look at that until they left. It was a great one. Maybe the greatest one ever. The crystals at the cutaway glistened in the sun. It would look nice in the yard. Once he placed it. He'd place it once they were gone. Dad would be impressed that even after what had occurred he'd remembered to place the geode.

That's the ticket, Scout.

We are well pleased, Beloved Only.

Super job, Scout.

Holy crap. It was happening. She was marching along all meek like the trouper he'd known she'd be. He'd had her in mind since the baptism of what's-his-name. Sergei's kid. At the Russian church. She'd been standing in her yard, her dad or some such taking her picture.

He'd been like, Hello, Betty.

Kenny had been like, Little young, bro.

He'd been like, For you, grandpa.

When you studied history, the history of cultures, you saw your own individual time as hidebound. There were various theories of acquiescence. In Bible days a king might ride through a field and go: That one. And she would be brought unto him. And they would duly be betrothed and if she gave birth unto a son, super, bring out the streamers, she was a keeper. Was she, that first night, digging it? Probably not. Was she shaking like a leaf? Didn't matter. What mattered was offspring and the furtherance of the lineage. Plus the exaltation of the king, which resulted in righteous kingly power.

Here was the creek.

He marched her through.

The following bullet points remained in the decision matrix: take to side van door, shove in, follow in, tape wrists/mouth, hook to chain, make speech. He had the speech down cold. Had practiced it both in his head and on the recorder: *Calm your heart, darling, I know you're scared because you don't know me yet and didn't expect this today but give me a chance and you will see we will fly high. See I am putting the knife right over here and I don't expect I'll have to use it, right?*

If she wouldn't get in the van, punch hard in gut. Then pick up, carry to side van door, throw in, tape wrists/mouth, hook to chain, make speech, etc., etc.

Stop, pause, he said.

Gal stopped.

Fucksake. Side door of the van was locked. How undisciplined was that. Ensuring that the door was unlocked was clearly indicated on the pre-mission matrix. Melvin appeared in his mind. On Melvin's face was the look of hot disappointment that had always preceded an ass whooping, which had always preceded the other thing. Put up your hands, Melvin said, defend yourself.

True, true. Little error there. Should have double-checked the pre-mission matrix.

No biggie.

Joy not fear.

Melvin was dead fifteen years. Mom dead twelve.

Little bitch was turned around now, looking back at the house. That will-fulness wouldn't stand. That was going to get nipped in the bud. He'd have to remember to hurt her early, establish a baseline.

Turn the fuck around, he said.

She turned around.

He unlocked the door, swung it open. Moment of truth. If she got in, let him use the tape, they were home free. He'd picked out a place in Sackett, big-ass cornfield, dirt road leading in. If fuckwise it went good they'd pick up the freeway from there. Basically steal the van. It was Kenny's van. He'd borrowed it for the day. Screw Kenny. Kenny had once called him stupid. Too bad, Kenny, that remark just cost you one van. If fuckwise it went bad, she didn't properly arouse him, he'd abort the activity, truncate the subject, heave the thing out, clean van as necessary, go buy corn, return van to Kenny, say, Hey, bro, here's a shitload of corn, thanks for the van, I never could've bought a suitable quantity of corn in my car. Then lay low, watch the papers like he'd done with the nonarousing redhead out in—

Gal gave him an imploring look, like, Please don't.

Was this a good time? To give her one in the gut, knock the wind out of her sails?

It was.

He did.

The geode was beautiful. What a beautiful geode. What made it beautiful? What were the principal characteristics of a beautiful geode? Come on, think. Come on, concentrate.

She'll recover in time, Beloved Only.

None of our affair, Scout.

We're amazed by your good judgment, Beloved Only.

Dimly he noted that Alison had been punched. Eyes on the geode, he heard the little *oof.*

His heart dropped at the thought of what he was letting happen. They'd used goldfish snacks as coins. They'd made bridges out of rocks. Down by the creek. Back in the day. Oh God. He should've never stepped outside. Once they were gone he'd just go back inside, pretend he'd never stepped out, make the model-railroad town, still be making it when Mom and Dad got home. When eventually someone told him about it? He'd make a certain face. Already on his face he could feel the face he would make, like, What? Alison? Raped? Killed? Oh God. Raped and killed while I innocently made my railroad town, sitting cross-legged and unaware on the floor like a tiny little—

No. No, no, no. They'd be gone soon. Then he could go inside. Call 911. Although then everyone would know he'd done nothing. All his future life would be bad. Forever he'd be the guy who'd done nothing. Besides, calling wouldn't do any good. They'd be long gone. The parkway was just across Featherstone, with like a million arteries and cloverleafs or whatever spouting out of it. So that was that. In he'd go. As soon as they left. Leave, leave, leave, he thought, so I can go inside, forget this ever—

Then he was running. Across the lawn. Oh God! What was he doing, what was he doing? Jesus, shit, the directives he was violating! Running in the yard (bad for the sod); transporting a geode without its protective wrapping; hopping the fence, which stressed the fence, which had cost a pretty penny; leaving the yard; leaving the yard barefoot; entering the Secondary Area without permission; entering the creek barefoot (broken glass, dangerous microorganisms), and, not only that, oh God, suddenly he saw what this giddy part of himself intended, which was to violate a directive so Major and absolute that it wasn't even a directive, since you didn't need a directive to know how totally verboten it was to—

He burst out of the creek, the guy still not turning, and let the geode fly into his head, which seemed to emit a weird edge-seep of blood even before the skull visibly indented and the guy sat right on his ass.

Yes! Score! It was fun! Fun dominating a grown-up! Fun using the most dazzling gazelle-like leg speed ever seen in the history of mankind to dash soundlessly across space and master this huge galoot, who otherwise, right now, would be—

What if he hadn't?

God, what if he hadn't?

He imagined the guy bending Alison in two like a pale garment bag while pulling her hair and thrusting bluntly, as he, Kyle, sat cowed and obedient, tiny railroad viaduct grasped in his pathetic babyish—

Jesus! He skipped over and hurled the geode through the windshield of the van, which imploded, producing an inward rain of glass shards that made the sound of thousands of tiny bamboo wind chimes.

He scrambled up the hood of the van, retrieved the geode.

Really? Really? You were going to ruin her life, ruin my life, you cunt-probe dick-munch ass-gashing Animal? Who's bossing who now? Gash-ass, jizz-lips, turd-munch—

He'd never felt so strong/angry/wild. Who's the man? Who's your daddy? What else must he do? To ensure that Animal did no further harm? You still moving, freak? Got a plan, stroke-dick? Want a skull gash on top of your existing skull gash, big man? You think I won't? You think I—

Easy, Scout, you're out of control.

Slow your motor down, Beloved Only.

Quiet. I'm the boss of me.

FUCK!

What the hell? What was he doing on the ground? Had he tripped? Did someone wonk him? Did a branch fall? God damn. He touched his head. His hand came away bloody.

The beanpole kid was bending. To pick something up. A rock. Why was that kid off the porch? Where was the knife?

Where was the gal?

Crab-crawling toward the creek.

Flying across her yard.

Going into her house.

Fuck it, everything was fucked. Better hit the road. With what, his good looks? He had like eight bucks total.

Ah Christ! The kid had smashed the windshield! With the rock! Kenny was not going to like that one bit.

He tried to stand but couldn't. The blood was just pouring out. He was not going to jail again. No way. He'd slit his wrists. Where was the knife? He'd stab himself in the chest. That had nobility. Then the people would know his name. Which of them had the balls to samurai themselves with a knife in the chest?

None.

Nobody.

Go ahead, pussy. Do it.

No. The king does not take his own life. The superior man silently accepts the mindless rebuke of the rabble. Waits to rise and fight anew. Plus he had no idea where the knife was. Well, he didn't need it. He'd crawl into the woods, kill something with his bare hands. Or make a trap from some grass. Ugh. Was he going to barf? There, he had. Right on his lap.

Figures you'd blow the simplest thing, Melvin said.

Melvin, God, can't you see my head is bleeding so bad?

A kid did it to you. You're a joke. You got fucked by a kid.

Oh, sirens, perfect.

Well, it was a sad day for the cops. He'd fight them hand to hand. He'd sit until the last moment, watching them draw near, doing a silent death mantra that would centralize all his life power in his fists.

He sat thinking about his fists. They were huge granite boulders. They were a pit bull each. He tried to get up. Somehow his legs weren't working. He hoped the cops would get here soon. His head really hurt. When he touched up there, things moved. It was like he was wearing a gore cap. He was going to need a bunch of stitches. He hoped it wouldn't hurt too much. Probably it would, though.

Where was that beanpole kid?

Oh, here he was.

Looming over him, blocking out the sun, rock held high, yelling something, but he couldn't tell what, because of the ringing in his ears.

Then he saw that the kid was going to bring the rock down. He closed his eyes and waited and was not at peace at all but instead felt the beginnings of a terrible dread welling up inside him, and if that dread kept growing at the current rate, he realized in a flash of insight, there was a name for the place he would be then, and it was Hell.

Alison stood at the kitchen window. She'd peed herself. Which was fine. People did that. When super-scared. She'd noticed it while making the call. Her hands had been shaking so bad. They still were. One leg was doing that Thumper thing. God, the stuff he'd said to her. He'd punched her. He'd pinched her. There was a big blue mark on her arm. How could Kyle still be out there? But there he was, in those comical shorts, so confident he was goofing around, hands clenched over his head like a boxer from some cute alt universe where a kid that skinny could actually win a fight against a guy with a knife.

Wait.

His hands weren't clenched. He was holding the rock, shouting something down at the guy, who was on his knees, like the blindfolded prisoner in that video they'd seen in History, about to get sword-killed by a formal dude in a helmet.

Kyle, don't, she whispered.

For months afterward she had nightmares in which Kyle brought the rock down. She was on the deck trying to scream his name but nothing was coming out. Down came the rock. Then the guy had no head. The blow just literally dissolved his head. Then his body tumped over and Kyle turned to her with this heartbroken look of, My life is over. I killed a guy.

Why was it, she sometimes wondered, that in dreams we can't do the simplest things? Like a crying puppy is standing on some broken glass and you want to pick it up and brush the shards off its pads but you can't because you're balancing a ball on your head. Or you're driving and there's this old guy on crutches, and you go, to Mr. Feder, your Driver's Ed teacher, Should I swerve? And he's like, Uh, probably. But then you hear this big clunk and Feder makes a negative mark in his book.

Sometimes she'd wake up crying from the dream about Kyle. The last time, Mom and Dad were already there, going, That's not how it was. Remember, Allie? How did it happen? Say it. Say it out loud. Allie, can you tell Mommy and Daddy how it really happened?

I ran outside, she said. I shouted.

That's right, Dad said. You shouted. Shouted like a champ.

And what did Kyle do? Mom said.

Put down the rock, she said.

A bad thing happened to you kids, Dad said. But it could have been worse.

So much worse, Mom said.

But because of you kids, Dad said, it wasn't.

You did so good, Mom said.

Did beautiful, Dad said.

2009

# DANZY SENNA

### b. 1970

Danzy Senna was born in Boston to an Irish-American mother and an Afro-Mexican father, both writers and civil rights activists. She earned her B.A. at Stanford University and an M.F.A. in creative writing from the University of California, Irvine. Senna's writing often examines the complex issues of race and class within modern America. Her two novels, *Caucasia* (1998), a national bestseller and winner of the Book of the Month Club's Stephen Crane Award for First Fiction, and *Symptomatic* (2004), are told from the perspectives of biracial young women. In her 2009 memoir *Where Did You Sleep Last Night?*—written during her fellowship at the New York Public Library's Cullman Center for Scholars and Writers—Senna explores her own identity by delving into her parents' divergent pasts and their defiant (and ultimately failed) marriage. In 2011, she published her first collection of short stories, *You Are Free*, to great critical acclaim. She lives in Los Angeles with her husband, novelist and story writer Percival Everett, and their two sons.

## Admission

The letter was unexpected. Cassie stared at it for a long time as she sipped her coffee, trying to decipher a hidden clue, though the language was crisp, the message to the point. They had been invited for an interview.

You recently completed the first stage of the application process when you attended a tour of the Institute for Early Childhood Development. You have been selected for the second step—an interview. This is for parents only. Please arrange appropriate childcare. Your interview time and date are:

TUESDAY, FEB. 18, 2:00 p.m.

Please call to confirm your attendance.

Cassie headed across the wet grass to Duncan's studio, letter in hand. She peered in the window to see if he was working. He was sitting in front of his television eating a mango with a knife. She opened the door and stepped inside. He was watching a basketball game and lurched back in his seat. "Fucking foul! That was so over the line."

"Duncan."

He turned and looked at her. "I didn't hear you come in."

"We got an interview."

He stared blankly.

"At the Institute."

He squinted. "The Institute?"

They'd toured the place two weeks ago and already he'd forgotten. "The fancy school."

"Oh yeah, that." He turned back to the game: "Speaking of children, where is ours?"

"Brittany took him to the park."

"Well, then, you should be working. This is our window. Time's a-wastin'."

"I know," she said. "But this letter. What should we do about the interview? They've offered us a time and a date."

"How kind of them."

"Duncan. I'm serious."

He turned around slowly, his mouth glistening from the mango. "We aren't interested, remember? So an interview would be a waste of time. Cody is already all set to go to Wee Things." He swiveled back to the television.

Cassie bit her lip and stared at the back of Duncan's head. It looked egg-shaped and vulnerable from the back.

It was true that they'd only gone on the tour because she'd said she needed to research the play she was writing. She still had no more than the barest sketches of the characters and situation: a wealthy Los Angeles family, a disconsolate bulimic wife, an eight-year-old girl's suicide attempt. She had not yet decided whether the attempt would be successful.

She'd half believed the research excuse herself. But as she'd driven them over to the Institute that morning in the old Subaru—Duncan grumpy that he'd had to put on clothes—she had to admit that she was weirdly, secretly excited.

Several of the mothers in her playgroup had briefed her on the application process, which was famously mysterious and daunting.

"You have to be a Spielberg or something to even get an interview."

"I heard Will and Jada got wait-listed."

The Institute for Early Childhood Development. She and Duncan had moved out west only recently from Providence, Rhode Island; he'd gotten a teaching job, she'd gotten an NEA[1] grant for her next play. They were subletting a house—a friend of a friend's—in Larchmont Village, a precious neighborhood with a quaint, Mayberry feel to it, though it was on the edge of West Hollywood and the residents were all film industry people. Cassie had already found a school for Cody in walking distance, but she'd applied to the Institute anyway, for research. She needed to know the rituals and mores of the city's elite. Anyway, the application wasn't hard, just a square white card with blanks for her and Duncan's names, their occupations, and their child's name, address, date of birth, and race. Hillary, a playgroup mother who had applied and been rejected twice, observed with some bitterness that the application was so barebones because the Institute got the rest of your information off the Internet.

---

**1.** National Endowment for the Arts.

"You have to be Google-worthy," she said.

The school was located in the middle of the city. It was across the street from a public school, an old brick building with brightly colored Spanish and English signs posted on the chain-link fence. The Institute looked more like a museum than a school—a sleek modernist building surrounded by a high cement wall lined with brightly colored turrets that stabbed the sky at odd angles.

"This better not take too long," Duncan grumbled as they approached the building. "I've got work to do."

She'd expected a small group of select applicants, but nearly every seat in the auditorium was filled, and the tension in the air was palpable. The crowd, on the surface at least, was diverse—black and brown and yellow and white, gay and straight. Duncan went for the muffins and coffee while she got on line for their name tags and a folder with information about the school. They found seats in the middle of the room. Nearby she noticed a familiar face. For a moment she thought it was someone she knew, but no, it was a famous actress. She nudged Duncan. "Look who's sitting two rows down."

Duncan was leafing through the information packet. He snorted. "Check out the second question here." He was pointing to a green sheet labeled "Frequently Asked Questions."

QUESTION #1: "Is it true that all the children at the Institute are the children of celebrities?"
ANSWER: "No. Only a modest percentage of our parents are celebrities. We pride ourselves on our diverse community—which includes plenty of people you've never heard of."

The chatter in the room began to quiet as a small, zaftig white woman in an elegant blue pantsuit and clicking heels walked across the floor to the microphone and tapped it twice. Obedient silence fell over the crowd.

The woman smiled and spoke into the microphone. She had a vaguely European accent. "Welcome, parents. I'm Esther Vale, director of the Institute. I'm so pleased to see all of you here today."

She went on to give a speech about the school's pedagogy while the giant screen behind her showed images of the Institute children in action: an Asian girl frozen in hysterical laughter on the playground; a white boy with a mop of blond curls wearing safety goggles and staring at fluid in a beaker; a black girl onstage in a ladybug costume, her face alight with a gap-toothed smile.

The crowd around Cassie seemed to thrum, silently, with excitement and desire. She eyed their rapt faces as they listened to Esther Vale speak.

"Now I'm going to tell you who should not apply to the Institute," Esther was saying, a small, bemused smile on her face. "And I'm going to be honest with you. Can I be honest? You should not apply to the Institute if you don't see the value of our generous financial aid program that allows families of all income levels to attend. You should not apply to the Institute if you aren't interested in being an active member of our school community. You should not apply to the Institute if you are uncomfortable with nontraditional families—gay parents, single parents. You should not apply to the Institute if you are uncomfortable with your child making friends of different racial and ethnic backgrounds. You should not apply to the Institute if you don't want your child to have as much art—drama, painting, poetry, sculpture—in their curriculum as they have reading, writing, and arithmetic. If these aren't the qualities you want in a school, then this isn't the school for you, and there are plenty of private schools in Los Angeles that will suit your needs."

The crowd burst into applause as Esther strode off the stage. They had been given instructions to meet their tour guides at the front of the auditorium, based on the color of the sticker on their folder. Cassie and Duncan's sticker was blue and they joined the cluster around their group leader, a petite blond woman.

For the next forty-five minutes, she led them through the school—peering into classrooms, telling them about the amazing programs the school had to offer and her own children's experiences there. Duncan jiggled his keys in his pocket and kept checking his watch. Every so often they would pass another group of parents, and Cassie would recognize a face or a name on a name tag. She felt like she was in a dream. *There was Julia Roberts, and there was Donald Sutherland, and there was President Nixon . . .*

The last stop on the tour was the preschool area. Their guide explained that the window in the door was actually a two-way mirror, the kind used in police lineups. It allowed parents to come and watch their children as they worked and played. The parents in their group took turns stepping up to the window and peering through it at the class of toddlers.

"They're having snack time," the tour guide explained.

Cassie looked and saw a cluster of children sitting at a table eating what looked like edamame.

"I'm not impressed," Duncan said when they were safely outside the gates, heading toward their car. "The digs are fancy, sure, but there isn't anything special about the teaching. Sure ain't worth the insane tuition. Did you see the figures?"

"Esther said they have a generous financial aid program," Cassie said.

"Whatever. That's for poor people, their 'socioeconomic tokens'—not for our upper-middle-class Negroid asses. Or did you forget, we made it, sweetheart. We on da East Side now." He pulled a muffin from his pocket, loosely wrapped in a napkin. He ate as he talked. "I'd rather send Cody to the school across the street. Did you get a peek at that? I wonder how Esther explains that little eyesore to all the Institute kids."

Cassie was silent as she pulled out of the parking space. She felt a burning of longing in her chest she couldn't admit to Duncan just now. She'd been impressed by the Institute—by the aggressively multicultural creed Esther professed, but also by the cheerful yet cloistered feeling of the hallways and classrooms. It seemed so civilized compared to the rough-and-tumble public schools she had attended growing up in Philadelphia. She wanted her child to grow up around *these* people, not *those* people, but she couldn't admit that to Duncan.

"So did you get all the details you need for your parody?" he asked.

She cleared her throat the way she always did when she was about to lie. "Yes," she said. "I think so."

And now here she was, holding this letter that invited them to go one step further. The Institute wanted to meet them. They were good enough to meet.

She didn't mention it again until later that night, after they'd had rugged sex. He was lying beside her in a postcoital coma when she said, "Duncan, baby, I'd like to do that interview at the Institute."

"I thought you finished your research."

"Not quite. I need the interview. It's the best part."

He sighed. "Okay. I guess we can go."

Brittany was the only white nanny in the neighborhood. Duncan, who was originally from the South, had insisted on racial subversion—and he'd ended up with a "real live cracker," as he put it, an Alabama native who had been in Los Angeles ten years, fruitlessly pursuing a singing career while she cared for other people's children. Brittany was in her thirties and vaguely pretty, though Duncan said, "The dew is off the rose." He liked the irony of the situation: a black couple with a Southern white mammy caring for their brown child. Of course, they truly liked Brittany as well. More important, Cody adored her. He was even picking up her twangy accent.

"So, Brit," Cassie said, "we should be back from the interview in an hour. Can you give Cody lunch?"

Brittany sat still while Cody drove his Hot Wheels up her blue-jeaned leg, making a *vrooming* sound.

"Sure thing, darlin'. Take your time. And break a leg!"

Brittany didn't know it was just research.

The reception area was empty and Duncan sat playing a video game on his cell phone while they waited to be called inside.

"Can you put that away?"

"No, I'm winning."

She squirmed beside him, irritated. Moments later, a couple—a black couple, slightly ragged-looking, definitely "socioeconomic tokens," as Duncan would say—came out wearing bashful smiles. They nodded at Cassie and Duncan but their smiles were tight and their eyes frightened.

A moment later, a middle-aged white woman came out to greet them, smiling with big teeth, her hand extended. "Hello, I'm Penny Washburn, director of admissions. Come on in."

She was rather sexless in the way of New England WASPs, with a long, thin face, graying blond hair, and bright blue eyes. She wore belted khakis, comfortable shoes, a pink oxford shirt tucked in.

They followed her down a plush-carpeted hallway to her office.

Inside, Cassie and Duncan took their seats. Cassie looked around. On Penny's desk sat a photo of two children—preteens with braces—who might be hers. Beside it was a framed picture of a smiling Barack Obama, which, silly as it was, made her feel more comfortable.

The interview lasted about twenty minutes. Cassie wasn't sure what she'd been expecting, but Penny's questions surprised her in their blunt specificity: When had Cody crawled? When had he walked? How long had he been breast-fed? How many words—approximately—did he have in his vocabulary? How did they choose to discipline him, if at all? What was his typical diet?

Cody was advanced in all areas, so Cassie felt a surge of pride as she answered. *Six months, ten months, thirteen months,* and *at least one hundred.* They disciplined him with time-outs and he ate a healthy diet, though a little heavier on cheese than Cassie would have liked.

"He's very precocious," Cassie said. "He already knows all his numbers and letters. Duncan thinks he might even be sight-reading."

"He's two, though," Duncan countered. "And an only child. Spoiled. Which means there are plenty of days when we'd like to send him back to the factory."

Cassie shot Duncan a dirty look. He didn't notice.

Penny, giving nothing away, nodded and scribbled in her notebook.

Then she wanted to know about their backgrounds, their work. Duncan told her about his paintings, the collage technique he used. Cassie was vague about her plays. Penny made interested sounds in her throat and nodded and scribbled more notes.

Then the interview was over and Penny was leading them to the door, wearing a placid, completely unreadable smile on her face.

Cassie breathed a sigh of relief when they were on the sidewalk. Though they'd only gone in the spirit of research, she had felt nervous, as if she were really trying to get her kid into the school.

"Penny seemed nice enough," she said when she'd started the engine.

"Whatever."

"It was cool she had a picture of Obama on her desk."

"Yeah, so what. He's the new Mickey Mouse." Duncan buckled his seat belt. "Anyway, are you finished?"

"Finished what?"

"With your fieldwork."

"I guess so," she said, and stared out the windshield at two women, one white and blond, the other Asian, mothers presumably, who were chatting on the sidewalk outside the school. The Asian one was familiar, from some television show maybe, though Cassie couldn't place her. They were both glamorous in high heels, with identical sheathlike hairstyles that fell across their faces. They made her think of Malibu Barbie and the ethnic Barbie, "Kira." She'd owned both in her youth. The women's matching silver SUVs were parked in the loading zone beside them. Two girls, their children, came striding out the gate of the school in matching Ugg boots, and waved goodbye to each other as their mothers led them to their respective vehicles.

Cody was napping when they got home and Brittany was wearing her iPod and singing along to country music in a husky voice as she folded their laundry. Cassie told Duncan she was going out for a walk to think about her play. But once outside, she didn't think about it at all. Instead she went over and over every detail of the interview, trying to imagine what Penny had thought of them, how they'd come across. That slight and inscrutable smile—was it just what Penny's face did, or did it mean something?

She thought about the school—the vast splendor of it—and the schools she'd attended at that age, the children she'd known. Each child was tagged in her memory with a tragedy or a defect. Tasha in third grade—one of a handful of foster kids in the class—had worn a wig that all the kids teased her about. When Cassie's mother learned about the teasing, she scolded Cassie harshly, explaining that the girl's hair had been burned off by her very own mother. A tall white boy named Dougie had a big head and lived with his aunt and uncle in a trailer because his family had burned to death in a fire. Why had there been so many fire-related tragedies? Some of the kids she'd known had been mean and some had been nice, some had been funny and some had been cruel. Some had been quick as whips and others had been slow. They'd been good little fighters, all of them, when the situation called for it. The school had been diverse in a way—there had been white kids, black kids, Puerto Rican kids, a few Vietnamese kids—but they were all so dingy in her memory, a gang right out of *Oliver Twist*. Had they really been that dingy? And what had happened to them all?

She found herself on the street of the other school. Wee Things Nursery. She headed up the block toward it. Apparently it was one of the oldest nursery schools in Los Angeles, and it was beloved. When they'd toured it months ago, Cassie had been charmed by it. She and Duncan had watched a group of toddlers sitting at their child-size table eating their bag lunches and drinking their juice, and Cassie had felt an unbearable tenderness and sadness at the thought of Cody joining them, joining the world beyond their home. They had been delighted when the director called to say there was a spot for Cody. It meant they could walk him to school every morning, and he would be only blocks away, in case he needed or wanted to come home early.

Now she stood in the shadows of a sycamore tree watching as parents picked up their children. They were not so different-looking from the parents at the other school—your basic upper-middle-class industry types. Their cars were mostly high-end luxury models. But now that she had a chance, a sliver of a possibility, of getting into the Institute, Wee Things had lost its luster. It looked run-down, slightly too hippie to be hygienic.

At home, Brittany had gone and Duncan was seated on the nursery floor with Cody on his lap. Cody stared up at him with huge black eyes as Duncan read from Dr. Seuss. It was Cody's favorite, *The Sneetches*. Cassie stood listening to the doggerel about the two factions, the Star-Belly Sneetches and the Plain-Belly Sneetches, the creatures identical to each other in every way except for this belly marking.

Neither father nor son saw her where she stood in the shadows.

Then the preschool interview, along with her own work, faded into white noise in the back of her mind, because Brittany's mother went into a diabetic coma. Brittany had to go home to Alabama for a few weeks to tend to her, and Cassie learned what it was to be a full-time mother. From morning to night, she was manically caring for Cody—feeding him breakfast, brushing his tiny teeth, changing his diaper, wiping his butt, rushing him to the toilet to see if he'd poop there, and driving all over Los Angeles. Duncan helped when he could, but he was teaching two classes that semester. So Cassie hauled Cody from one mommy-and-me class to another, because sitting with a group of other mothers and children beat the tedium of sitting alone with him on the floor at home.

She found herself immersed in a world of mothers—women who'd had careers once, as actresses and scriptwriters, lawyers and businesswomen, women who'd gone to grad school, but were taking time off to be mothers. They were an unusual lot in that they could afford nannies but weren't relying on them full-time. Cassie, hanging on until Brittany came back, felt like a fraud in their midst.

Among the mothers, the question of schools almost always came up. It was an anxiety that every woman seemed to feel: Where would her child land? Inevitably, the Institute came up too. Every one of the mothers wanted their child to go there. When Cassie pressed them as to why, they said vaguely, "It's just the best," or, "It's supposed to be amazing." They said it was a "feeder school" for the best grammar schools, which were feeder schools for the best high schools, which were feeder schools for the Ivy League. In other words, the Institute was a "feeder" for a life of success.

Mostly, though, they talked about how hard it was to get in, and every one of them had an anecdote they'd heard about somebody famous or powerful who had not gotten their child in, even when they'd offered the school some vast sum of money. The Institute, they said, never changed its mind. "If they don't want you, they don't want you." Then they would all sigh and move on to less depressing topics, like C-section scars or vaginal reconstruction.

One afternoon she slogged home through traffic with Cody after a tumbling class in Beverly Hills. He was tired and hungry and shrieking about some toy tractor he'd dropped in the parking lot, which Cassie had been unable to find. She was relieved to see Duncan's car in the driveway. She found him sprawled on the sofa watching television. She dropped Cody's hand, said, "He's all yours," and kept walking toward the kitchen.

She had the beginnings of a migraine. She gulped a long glass of water. She put it down and picked up the stack of mail on the counter. She flipped through some bills and then she saw it: a large white envelope from the Institute.

Her skin prickled. She picked up the envelope and tore it open. Her eyes flashed over the words:

> Congratulations. Your son Cody has been accepted into our Toddler Program.

From the other room, she heard Duncan making monster noises, Cody squealing.

She went and stood in the doorway, watching them, the envelope in hand.

Duncan held Cody upside down. Cody was laughing hysterically. Duncan glanced over and caught her eye.

"You didn't tell me," she said.

"Tell you what?" he said, out of breath, letting Cody down onto the floor.

"We heard from the Institute." She didn't know what to do with her face, what expression to wear. She tried to smirk, but her mouth was not moving right. "We've been accepted."

"Oh yeah, I saw that. Well, la-di-da-da, ain't we special," Duncan said.

There were cartoons on the television; Cody went and stood directly in front of them, so that he became just a black silhouette against the manic flashing colors of the screen.

"I knew we'd get in," Duncan said, leaning down to pick the throw pillows off the floor and set them back on the couch. "That school is rich on money and poor on class. See, baby, we's culcha'd. We is some certified, authentified intellectuals, baby. We stood out in a sea of celebrities and millionaires. You gotta love it."

She swallowed. "I wasn't sure we would. I mean, do you know the odds? Six hundred parents applied for twelve spots. At least admit to feeling a little, I don't know, surprised."

"I'm shocked, shocked," he said, deadpan, then brushed past her on his way to the kitchen. He picked up a bottle of wine and set to opening it. "It's gotta be five-thirty somewhere in the world." He said this same line every day at four-thirty. He poured himself a glass, leaned against the counter, and took a sip, watching her. "What's wrong with your face?"

"What do you mean?"

"Your mouth is all twisted funny. And your left eye is twitching."

She felt the pulsing now that he said it. She touched it gingerly. She tried to sound casual, nonchalant. "Listen, I know this isn't what we'd planned, but do you think we should consider accepting? I mean, it's supposed to be an amazing school." She realized as she spoke that she had been rehearsing this speech for the past two weeks. Somewhere in the back of her mind she'd been preparing these words. "I mean, once you're in, you're in through grade school. We wouldn't have to worry about schools again in two years the way we will at Wee Things."

He sighed. "Cass, we already have a school for Cody. A perfectly good pre-school for a fraction of the cost. A sandbox is a sandbox. I refuse to pay out the ass for preschool. And did you read the fine print on the brochure we got on that tour? I did. Each year the price goes up. And we have to buy insurance on our tuition because if something happens, if we decide to pull Cody out, they will not return our money. Yeah, because you have to pay the whole fucking year's tuition in one lump sum—because it's a school for people who have fifteen, twenty grand lying around in their checking account. Honey, they will sap us of every penny we have. No more trips to France in the summer. Shit, no more lattes with a side of biscotti. We will have to scale back—seriously—just so the kid can get to sit in a classroom with future Rich Fucks of America." He took another gulp of wine, a big one. He'd been preparing his speech too, she realized. Secretly, he'd been storing this up, preparing for this day, because secretly, they'd both known that they were going to get accepted.

"I know," she said. "I know all that. It's just—well, we got in. It's kind of a big deal."

"No it's not," he said. "We only went on the tour as a joke—remember? You were gonna write this acerbic parody about the stupidity and vapidity of American culture in the age of late capitalism. I line-edited your fucking NEA grant."

"But the thing is, I don't want Cody to rot away in a public school. I mean, we send him to public school and maybe he'll survive, maybe he won't. It's a wild card what will happen to him, what he'll become."

"It's a wild card everywhere, my dear. I'm sorry to inform you."

"No, not in the same way. This is where the world begins to divide. This is where the tone is set for the rest of his life."

"You sound like a *New Yorker* cartoon," he said with a chortle.

She felt the blood slamming against the inside of her head. She wanted to say, *Don't you dare take this from me, I'm almost there, I've almost made it to the other side, don't fuck this up for me.* But instead she said, "Not everything has to be a political statement, Duncan."

"This isn't about politics." He stepped to the window and looked out at the street, his back to her. "Have you ever noticed how boring and stupid kids from the fancy private schools are? Have you ever met one of those saps? They're like overbred puppies. They have no grit. Their limbs are all rubbery. Public school kids are scrappy, like pound mutts."

"Are you drunk?"

"No. Not yet." He sounded sober and calm. "I just don't want my kids going to the Institute—"

"What's the Institute?" It was Cody. He stood at the door, honey-colored, with a mop of shiny black curls.

"It's a school," Cassie said, squatting down to look at him eye to eye. "You're going to go to school soon, like a big boy, and your papa and I are trying to decide which one would be best for you." She paused, then said, "The big one or the little one."

"Which one has swings?" Cody asked.

"Both," Duncan said behind her. "They both have swings."

The girl, Tasha, the one with the burned scalp and the crooked pageboy wig, ate her lunch alone every day. She was tall and big-boned and wore a strange assortment of clothes—sequined disco shirts during the day, sweatshirts with snowflakes on them in the spring, huge white no-name sneakers that the other kids called "bobos." They were clothes that Cassie learned at some point, she didn't know how, had come from charity. The other kids said Tasha smelled bad. Cassie got to test this theory once, when she was paired up with Tasha in English class. They were supposed to write a story together, using adjectives and adverbs, as part of a new program that paired advanced students with remedial students, rather than splitting them into separate classes. Cassie's friends laughed and pointed at her when they saw who she had been paired with. Up close, Tasha didn't smell bad, but when she bent over the desk to write a sentence, Cassie saw a patch of burned skin at the nape of her neck, pale and glossy and webbed, leading up to and underneath her wig.

Duncan sat at the kitchen table across from her, watching as she made the call.

She jiggled her leg under the table. She felt nervous, angry, forced into it.

"Penny Washburn," answered a peppy voice.

"Hi, this is Cassie Rogers. My husband and I—"

"Cassie! Of course. I remember you and Duncan. Congratulations, you made it." She laughed. "I guess you know how difficult it is to get in. A lot of people would give their eyeteeth to be in your position."

"Yes, I know. We're so honored to have been accepted." Cassie looked at Duncan, winced, unsure all over again. This morning it had seemed clear, she'd woken and seen the light, remembered the play she was supposed to be writing—but now she was having second thoughts.

Duncan nodded his head and gestured for her to carry on as planned.

"So what's up?" Penny said.

"I'm really sorry, but we've decided Cody won't be able to accept your offer. It's, well, it's just that the schedule of the toddler program doesn't work for our, our lifestyle."

Duncan whispered, "Thank you and good-bye."

Penny was silent on the other end for a beat. "Oh. Well." She sounded surprised. "Are you sure?"

Cassie swallowed. No, she wasn't sure. But she felt Duncan's eyes boring into her and carried on. "Yes, we're sure. I'm so sorry. Perhaps we can reapply in a future year."

"Would financial aid help out? Would that change things for you? We have quite a generous financial aid program, as you know."

"I don't think so," Cassie said. "I don't think we'd be eligible."

"You'd be surprised," Penny said. "You'd be surprised at the range of income levels that are considered eligible here."

Cassie had not expected the conversation to go on so long. The school had a wait list a mile long. She had expected an icy thanks and good-bye.

"Thanks, Penny, but there are a number of factors influencing our decision. We're so sorry to have to pass on the offer this year. But I hope we can keep in touch."

There was silence. Cassie frowned at Duncan, who was sitting across from her, drumming his fingers. "Hang up," he whispered.

She raised a hand to shush him. "Hello? Penny?"

"Yes, I'm here." Penny's voice sounded strange—taut, as if she were holding in a cough. "So you're sure about this."

"Yes," Cassie said. "I'm sure."

"Okay," came a small voice. "Okay."

Cassie waited for Penny to say good-bye first, but when she said nothing, Cassie said, "Well, thanks, Penny. Bye."

Again, nothing. She hung up the phone.

"Jesus, that took ages," Duncan said. "What the hell were you discussing?"

"She was just making sure I meant it, I guess. I felt like she really was disappointed Cody wasn't coming."

"Oh, come on," Duncan said. "You saw the auditorium. Packed. She is calling her next set of parents right now and offering them his spot."

At two in the morning she lay beside Duncan, listening to his breathing. The light coming through the window was gray, half lit by streetlamps. She could hear crickets humming. She had a pain in her stomach, a gnawing of regret.

Duncan Dickie was a black sheep; he was the only artist in a family of doctors. When she'd married him she'd been attracted to his strong opinions. She'd liked how he'd chafed at groups, anything smacking of mob mentality. He was what her mother called an iconoclast. But he had grown up in the bastion of the black middle class. As far as she could tell, the most traumatic thing that had happened to him as a child was being teased about his name. A bully named Eddie used to lead a playground chant. *When the weather's hot and sticky, that's no time for dunkin' Dickie. But when the frost is on the pumpkin, now that's the time for Dickie dunkin!*

He'd told her the story once, in the dark. He said she was the only person he'd ever told, as if the humiliation was still fresh.

Cassie had grown up poor, the daughter of a struggling single mother and a deadbeat father who showed up at some birthdays, drunk. Once in fifth grade, at recess, she'd been surrounded by a group of retarded boys, escapees from the special education class, who'd groped her. All her life she'd wanted to belong, to *have*, to possess what the other side possessed.

She sat up and stared down at Duncan's sleeping face. He was the problem. He was the barrier to her getting what she wanted—the perfect life. His face, even in sleep, had a kind of arrogance.

His eyes blinked open and he jerked, startled. "What are you doing?"

"Thinking."

He glanced at the clock radio. "About what?"

"About the school. The Institute. Did we just make a huge mistake?"

"Oh Jesus. Not this again. No, we made the right decision. Now can we drop it and get some sleep?"

"But it's the school everybody wants."

"Who the hell is 'everybody'? The ladies of Larchmont Village?"

"Nobody will believe it if I tell them we turned it down."

"So don't tell anybody."

She turned to her side and hugged her pillow, her cheeks warm with rage.

Duncan got out of bed. "Now I can't get back to sleep," he muttered. "I'm going to work in my studio." He left, sighing dramatically, and she lay there in the dark.

The problem with modern marriage was that everything had to be a consensus. Each choice had to be something they both wanted. For a moment, fear gripped her, a physical sensation—cold wetness under her arms, a dry mouth, a quickening of her heartbeat. *They had turned down the Institute.* She struggled to breathe. She felt as if she were falling into a long dark hole. She felt as if something large and warm and malevolent was pressing down on her, crushing her under its weight.

The next night while Cassie was sautéing garlic, the phone rang.

"Cassie," the voice on the other end of the line said when she answered. "It's me, Penny."

For a moment, she was confused.

"Penny Washburn," the woman clarified. "At the Institute."

"Oh, hi."

"Are you sure?"

"Excuse me?"

"Are you sure there's not something we can do to, well, make the offer more attractive?"

Cassie felt a momentary thrill. She turned off the heat under the saucepan. Duncan was out on the lawn reading a book to Cody. *The Sneetches* again. She remembered the arguments, the money. Duncan's position.

"It's so nice of you to call," she said, flushed, flattered. "Thanks for, well, for double-checking." She stared out at Duncan, her jaw clenched. "But yes, I'm afraid we've made up our minds. For this year anyway."

Penny went on. "It's just that I was about to offer your spot to somebody else, and I thought, let me just double-check. One more time. I'd hate for Cody to miss out on the opportunity, and I can't guarantee a spot next year."

Cassie felt a surge of doubt again. Was she sure? She saw Duncan rising and walking toward the house. "Yes, we're sure," she said. "But it's so nice of you to call. I realize how coveted these spots are."

This time the silence went on for so long that she thought Penny had hung up.

"Penny?"

"Yes, I'm just thinking. Listen. How about this: I'm not going to give your slot away tonight. It's too late. I'm going home. But let me give you my home number. If you change your mind, just give me a ring. I won't do a thing until tomorrow, say, after lunch."

She rattled off her home number before Cassie could find a pen. But she knew she'd committed it to memory.

Duncan came in the door just as she was hanging up.

"Who was that?"

She paused. "Nobody. I mean, just a prank call. Kids."

She told the lie automatically, without knowing exactly why.

"Kids still make those?"

"Apparently," she said, turning her face so he couldn't see her expression.

Duncan picked up a wine bottle and pulled the cork out. "It's gotta be five-thirty somewhere in the world, right?"

The next morning Cassie brought Cody to his music class. She went through the motions of singing along to the folksinger with him on her lap, then chatting with the other mothers afterward, but her mind was elsewhere. She looked up at the clock ticking on the wall and thought of her chance ticking away with it. When she got home it was already noon, and she felt a wave of sadness, as if something precious and irretrievable had been washed out to sea. She imagined Cody twenty years from now, in prison for grand auto theft, imagined herself leaving the jail after visiting hours. She thought about how she would look back to this decision as the cause of all his troubles. She imagined Penny Washburn picking up the phone to call the lucky parents of the child who would go to the Institute instead. Her mouth tasting of metal, she imagined how they would celebrate.

The phone broke into her thoughts. She picked up, expecting Duncan.

"It's me, Penny."

"Oh. Hello."

"It's past noon," Penny said.

"I know."

"I was waiting for you to call."

"I thought I was only going to call if we changed our minds."

"And did you change it?"

Cassie felt a bug crawling on her arm and slapped at it, but nothing was there.

"I'm so sorry, but no." She felt strange, suddenly, unsettled by the woman's phone call. "We didn't change our minds. That's why I didn't call."

Penny sighed. "You know, a lot of families would give their eyeteeth to go here."

"Yes, I—I know that."

"So what's the hitch? The diversity issue? We're almost forty percent nonwhite."

"That's—that's great. That wasn't the problem."

"Then what was it?"

Cassie shifted uncomfortably, looked over the counter at Cody playing with his cars in the living room. She tried to remember Penny's eyes, her face, from their one meeting, but all she could remember was the picture of smiling Barack Obama on her desk. "I can't explain it."

She heard Duncan's car pulling into the driveway.

"Thank you," she said quickly, "for calling. I'm sorry it didn't work out."

She hung up without waiting for Penny to say good-bye.

She went onto the porch to greet Duncan, but once again—for some reason she couldn't articulate—she didn't tell him about Penny's call.

The phone rang early the next morning, a shrill screech that cut through her morning haze as she set a bowl of cereal in front of Cody. Duncan was still asleep.

She looked at the caller ID. It was Penny's home number. She remembered it.

She didn't answer. She sat at the table, Cody slurping his cereal beside her, and watched the phone until it stopped ringing. She breathed out relief.

But a moment later it began ringing again. She went to it and stared down at it, as if it were alive.

Later that morning, Duncan took Cody to swim class. It was a rare moment of aloneness. But just as Cassie sat down at her desk, the phone rang. She picked it up without checking the caller ID.

"The spot is still open," Penny's voice said. "We've been holding it for you."

Her voice sounded strange, muffled, and behind it Cassie could hear traffic, a car horn, distant mariachi music.

Cassie was frightened now, and didn't speak.

Penny said, "You're just the kind of family we've been looking for."

Cassie closed her eyes. She felt a pain like a mallet to her chest.

"Was it your husband?" Penny said. "Duncan Dickie?"

Cassie opened her eyes, breathed in sharply, and hung up the phone.

The week went by without any more calls from Penny Washburn. She thought of telling Duncan about them, Penny's odd, desperate tone, but every time she opened her mouth, she stopped. It would seem strange to him that she hadn't said anything earlier, and she would have to explain that too, which she couldn't. She decided to put the whole episode behind her, just like Duncan was doing. It was a problem she had—she always regretted a decision after it was made, no matter what. She never could leave things be. She decided not to mention the Institute or Penny Washburn again as long as she lived.

She began work on her play. It was going slowly, but a character was emerging, the wife of a neurosurgeon. Nedra. Her name was Nedra. Pretty but woefully insecure Nedra. She was the type of woman who applied lipstick each night before getting into bed with her husband of fifteen years. Nedra was obsessed with her nose, convinced that it was the wrong shape and size. She would have several surgeries in the course of the play to "correct" it.

In bed, Cassie chattered to Duncan about her work. "She's going to be a sort of vehicle for me to discuss so much—race, sex, body dysmorphia. I see her as a kind of symbol of our times. Nedra. What do you think of that name?"

Duncan didn't answer. She looked up and saw he was fast asleep, his reading glasses still on his face.

She read *The Sneetches* aloud to Cody one evening, snuggled beside him in his toddler bed. Outside was a rare heavy rain. The sound of it reminded her of her childhood, Philadelphia, real weather. She remembered her mother snuggled beside her on such nights, reading to her—the standard of happiness to which all other moments would be compared. Cody rested his head against her chest and brushed his fingers against her collarbone. She'd read the story to him so many times that she barely had to look at the page. The Star-Belly Sneetches were having a beach party, gorging themselves on hotdogs and marshmallows, while the sad Plain-Belly Sneetches stood watching, cold and bereft in the sandy gloom.

She realized that she too was comforted by the story, perhaps because it was so very familiar.

When she went to turn the page, she realized that Cody had fallen asleep. She could have slid him off her chest and turned out the light and left him there, but she was enjoying the feeling of his warm body pressed against her. Duncan was out back in his studio, working. Dinner was warming in the oven. She had only the salad to make. She closed her eyes. For some reason she thought about that girl, Tasha, the one with the burned scalp. Cassie's mother had made her promise to be nice to the girl. In fact, she had made Cassie promise to sit with her at lunch. But in the cafeteria the next day, seeing Tasha sitting all alone, Cassie had balked. She had hovered beside Tasha for a moment, holding her tray, but then had moved on to her table of friends. Later she told her mother about sitting with the burned girl. It was her first lie, or the first she'd been conscious of telling, anyway.

Distantly, she was aware of the sound of knocking. Somebody was knocking at the front door.

She slid Cody to the mattress and rose carefully, switching off the light.

Out in the front room, the knocking was hard and persistent. She went to the door and looked through the peephole.

A figure stood on the doorstep, tiny and warped, head turned toward the street.

Cassie opened the door.

Penny Washburn stood on the steps. The rain had flattened her hair, making her look gaunt and ravaged. There was a puddle around her sodden loafers and she was hugging herself, shivering. The air outside was cold and rain blew in on Cassie.

"Can I come in?" Penny's voice was plaintive, beseeching.

Cassie stared at her, unable, momentarily, to speak. She finally managed: "I'm sorry, but we were just about to sit down to dinner."

"Just for a few minutes," Penny said, hacking into her hand. "See, we've kept the spot open, there's still a place for you. I can give you a few more days to reconsider."

"We're not interested," Cassie said, sure of it now.

"Why not?" Penny emitted a sound—half sob, half laugh. "Just give me a reason. I don't understand. None of us understand."

From the back of the house, Cassie could hear the glass door sliding open, Duncan coming inside, whistling. She couldn't let him find her here, couldn't let him see how far it had gone.

"We don't want you," she whispered into the night. "The answer is no." She hesitated, then hissed into the lashing rain: *"Go away."*

She could hear Penny's bewildered shout, "Lots of people would give their eyeteeth—" before it was cut short by the sound of the closing door.

2011

# ISAAC BASHEVIS SINGER
## 1902–1991

Singer was born in Leoncin, Poland. His father, a rabbi, was an author, as was his brother, the novelist I. J. Singer. Before he emigrated to the United States in 1935, Singer worked as a journalist in Warsaw, and in New York he resumed similar work with the *Jewish Daily Forward,* continuing to write in his masterful Yiddish. His fiction is characteristically in the tradition of the spoken tale, mingling forthright literalness about the visible world with an equally literal rendition of fantastic and supernatural worlds beyond. Flavored with the colorful residue of folk tales, his explorations of Jewish life, past and present, are haunting allegories of the irrationality of history. Among his many children's books and 18 novels are *The Family Moskat* (1950), *The Slave* (1962), *The Manor* (1967), *The Estate* (1970), *Enemies: A Love Story* (1972), *Shosha* (1978), and *Meshugah,* published posthumously in 1994. His stories are most easily found in *The Collected Stories of Isaac Bashevis Singer* (1982). He was awarded the Nobel Prize in 1978.

# Gimpel the Fool[1]

## I

I am Gimpel the fool. I don't think myself a fool. On the contrary. But that's what folks call me. They gave me the name while I was still in school. I had seven names in all: imbecile, donkey, flax-head, dope, glump, ninny, and fool. The last name stuck. What did my foolishness consist of? I was easy to take in. They said, "Gimpel, you know the rabbi's wife has been brought to childbed?" So I skipped school. Well, it turned out to be a lie. How was I supposed to know? She hadn't had a big belly. But I never looked at her belly. Was that really so foolish? The gang laughed and hee-hawed, stomped and danced and chanted a good-night prayer. And instead of the raisins they give when a woman's lying in, they stuffed my hand full of goat turds. I was no weakling. If I slapped someone he'd see all the way to Cracow.[2] But I'm really not a slugger by nature. I think to myself: Let it pass. So they take advantage of me.

I was coming home from school and heard a dog barking. I'm not afraid of dogs, but of course I never want to start up with them. One of them may be mad, and if he bites there's not a Tartar[3] in the world who can help you. So I

1. Translated by Saul Bellow.   2. Krakow, city in southern Poland.   3. Supposedly fierce people of central Asia.

made tracks. Then I looked around and saw the whole market place wild with laughter. It was no dog at all but Wolf-Leib the thief. How was I supposed to know it was he? It sounded like a howling bitch.

When the pranksters and leg-pullers found that I was easy to fool, every one of them tried his luck with me. "Gimpel, the czar is coming to Frampol; Gimpel, the moon fell down in Turbeen; Gimpel, little Hodel Furpiece found a treasure behind the bathhouse." And I like a golem believed everyone. In the first place, everything is possible, as it is written in *The Wisdom of the Fathers*.[4] I've forgotten just how. Second, I had to believe when the whole town came down on me! If I ever dared to say, "Ah, you're kidding!" there was trouble. People got angry. "What do you mean! You want to call everyone a liar?" What was I to do? I believed them, and I hope at least that did them some good.

I was an orphan. My grandfather who brought me up was already bent toward the grave. So they turned me over to a baker, and what a time they gave me there! Every woman or girl who came to bake a batch of noodles had to fool me at least once. "Gimpel, there's a fair in Heaven; Gimpel, the rabbi gave birth to a calf in the seventh month; Gimpel, a cow flew over the roof and laid brass eggs." A student from the yeshiva came once to buy a roll, and he said, "You, Gimpel, while you stand here scraping with your baker's shovel the Messiah has come. The dead have risen." "What do you mean?" I said. "I heard no one blowing the ram's horn!" He said, "Are you deaf?" And all began to cry, "We heard it, we heard!" Then in came Rietze the candle-dipper and called out in her hoarse voice, "Gimpel, your father and mother have stood up from the grave. They're looking for you."

To tell the truth, I knew very well that nothing of the sort had happened, but all the same, as folks were talking, I threw on my wool vest and went out. Maybe something had happened. What did I stand to lose by looking? Well, what a cat music went up! And then I took a vow to believe nothing more. But that was no go either. They confused me so that I didn't know the big end from the small.

I went to the rabbi to get some advice. He said, "It is written, better to be a fool all your days than for one hour to be evil. You are not a fool. They are the fools. For he who causes his neighbor to feel shame loses Paradise himself." Nevertheless, the rabbi's daughter took me in. As I left the rabbinical court she said, "Have you kissed the wall yet?" I said, "No; what for?" She answered, "It's the law; you've got to do it after every visit." Well, there didn't seem to be any harm in it. And she burst out laughing. It was a fine trick. She put one over on me, all right.

I wanted to go off to another town, but then everyone got busy matchmaking, and they were after me so they nearly tore my coat tails off. They talked at me and talked until I got water on the ear. She was no chaste maiden, but they told me she was virgin pure. She had a limp, and they said it was deliberate, from coyness. She had a bastard, and they told me the child was her little brother. I cried, "You're wasting your time. I'll never marry that whore." But they said indignantly, "What a way to talk! Aren't you ashamed of yourself? We can take you to the rabbi and have you fined for giving her a bad name."

---

**4.** Spiritual sayings of Ben Zoma, a 2nd-century C.E. Jewish sage. *Golem:* an artificial human being (Hebrew).

I saw then that I wouldn't escape them so easily and I thought: They're set on making me their butt. But when you're married the husband's the master, and if that's all right with her it's agreeable to me too. Besides, you can't pass through life unscathed, nor expect to.

I went to her clay house, which was built on the sand, and the whole gang, hollering and chorusing, came after me. They acted like bearbaiters. When we came to the well they stopped all the same. They were afraid to start anything with Elka. Her mouth would open as if it were on a hinge, and she had a fierce tongue. I entered the house. Lines were strung from wall to wall and clothes were drying. Barefoot she stood by the tub, doing the wash. She was dressed in a worn hand-me-down gown of plush. She had her hair put up in braids and pinned across her head. It took my breath away, almost, the reek of it all.

Evidently she knew who I was. She took a look at me and said, "Look who's here! He's come, the drip. Grab a seat."

I told her all; I denied nothing. "Tell me the truth," I said, "are you really a virgin, and is that mischievous Yechiel actually your little brother? Don't be deceitful with me, for I'm an orphan."

"I'm an orphan myself," she answered, "and whoever tries to twist you up, may the end of his nose take a twist. But don't let them think they can take advantage of me. I want a dowry of fifty guilders, and let them take up a collection besides. Otherwise they can kiss my you-know-what." She was very plain-spoken. I said, "It's the bride and not the groom who gives a dowry." Then she said, "Don't bargain with me. Either a flat yes or a flat no. Go back where you came from."

I thought: No bread will ever be baked from *this* dough. But ours is not a poor town. They consented to everything and proceeded with the wedding. It so happened that there was a dysentery epidemic at the time. The ceremony was held at the cemetery gates, near the little corpse-washing hut. The fellows got drunk. While the marriage contract was being drawn up I heard the most pious high rabbi ask, "Is the bride a widow or a divorced woman?" And the sexton's wife answered for her, "Both a widow and divorced." It was a black moment for me. But what was I to do, run away from under the marriage canopy?

There was singing and dancing. An old granny danced opposite me, hugging a braided white hallah.[5] The master of revels made a "God 'a mercy" in memory of the bride's parents. The schoolboys threw burrs, as on Tishe b'Av[6] fast day. There were a lot of gifts after the sermon: a noodle board, a kneading trough, a bucket, brooms, ladles, household articles galore. Then I took a look and saw two strapping young men carrying a crib. "What do we need this for?" I asked. So they said, "Don't rack your brains about it. It's all right, it'll come in handy." I realized I was going to be rooked. Take it another way though, what did I stand to lose? I reflected: I'll see what comes of it. A whole town can't go altogether crazy.

## II

At night I came where my wife lay, but she wouldn't let me in. "Say, look here, is this what they married us for?" I said. And she said, "My monthly has

---

5. Or "challah," a kind of bread made of braided dough (Hebrew).  6. A Jewish day of mourning.

come." "But yesterday they took you to the ritual bath, and that's afterwards, isn't it supposed to be?" "Today isn't yesterday," said she, "and yesterday's not today. You can beat it if you don't like it." In short, I waited.

Not four months later, she was in childbed. The townsfolk hid their laughter with their knuckles. But what could I do? She suffered intolerable pains and clawed at the walls. "Gimpel," she cried, "I'm going. Forgive me!" The house filled with women. They were boiling pans of water. The screams rose to the welkin.

The thing to do was to go to the house of prayer to repeat psalms, and that was what I did.

The townsfolk liked that, all right. I stood in a corner saying psalms and prayers, and they shook their heads at me. "Pray, pray!" they told me. "Prayer never made any woman pregnant." One of the congregation put a straw to my mouth and said, "Hay for the cows." There was something to that too, by God!

She gave birth to a boy. Friday at the synagogue the sexton stood up before the Ark, pounded on the reading table, and announced, "The wealthy Reb[7] Gimpel invites the congregation to a feast in honor of the birth of a son." The whole house of prayer rang with laughter. My face was flaming. But there was nothing I could do. After all, I *was* the one responsible for the circumcision honors and rituals.

Half the town came running. You couldn't wedge another soul in. Women brought peppered chick-peas, and there was a keg of beer from the tavern. I ate and drank as much as anyone, and they all congratulated me. Then there was a circumcision, and I named the boy after my father, may he rest in peace. When all were gone and I was left with my wife alone, she thrust her head through the bed-curtain and called me to her.

"Gimpel," said she, "why are you silent? Has your ship gone and sunk?"

"What shall I say?" I answered. "A fine thing you've done to me! If my mother had known of it she'd have died a second time."

She said, "Are you crazy, or what?"

"How can you make such a fool," I said, "of one who should be the lord and master?"

"What's the matter with you?" she said. "What have you taken it into your head to imagine?"

I saw that I must speak bluntly and openly. "Do you think this is the way to use an orphan?" I said. "You have borne a bastard."

She answered, "Drive this foolishness out of your head. The child is yours."

"How can he be mine?" I argued. "He was born seventeen weeks after the wedding."

She told me then that he was premature. I said, "Isn't he a little too premature?" She said, she had had a grandmother who carried just as short a time and she resembled this grandmother of hers as one drop of water does another. She swore to it with such oaths that you would have believed a peasant at the fair if he had used them. To tell the plain truth, I didn't believe her; but when I talked it over the next day with the schoolmaster, he told me that the very same thing had happened to Adam and Eve. Two they went up to bed, and four they descended.

7. Rabbi, here used derisively.

"There isn't a woman in the world who is not the granddaughter of Eve," he said.

That was how it was; they argued me dumb. But then, who really knows how such things are?

I began to forget my sorrow. I loved the child madly, and he loved me too. As soon as he saw me he'd wave his little hands and want me to pick him up, and when he was colicky I was the only one who could pacify him. I bought him a little bone teething ring and a little gilded cap. He was forever catching the evil eye from someone, and then I had to run to get one of those abracadabras for him that would get him out of it. I worked like an ox. You know how expenses go up when there's an infant in the house. I don't want to lie about it; I didn't dislike Elka either, for that matter. She swore at me and cursed, and I couldn't get enough of her. What strength she had! One of her looks could rob you of the power of speech. And her orations! Pitch and sulphur, that's what they were full of, and yet somehow also full of charm. I adored her every word. She gave me bloody wounds though.

In the evening I brought her a white loaf as well as a dark one, and also poppyseed rolls I baked myself. I thieved because of her and swiped everything I could lay hands on: macaroons, raisins, almonds, cakes. I hoped I may be forgiven for stealing from the Saturday pots the women left to warm in the baker's oven. I would take out scraps of meat, a chunk of pudding, a chicken leg or head, a piece of tripe, whatever I could nip quickly. She ate and became fat and handsome.

I had to sleep away from home all during the week, at the bakery. On Friday nights when I got home she always made an excuse of some sort. Either she had heartburn, or a stitch in the side, or hiccups, or headaches. You know what women's excuses are. I had a bitter time of it. It was rough. To add to it, this little brother of hers, the bastard, was growing bigger. He'd put lumps on me, and when I wanted to hit back she'd open her mouth and curse so powerfully I saw a green haze floating before my eyes. Ten times a day she threatened to divorce me. Another man in my place would have taken French leave[8] and disappeared. But I'm the type that bears it and says nothing. What's one to do? Shoulders are from God, and burdens too.

One night there was a calamity at the bakery; the oven burst, and we almost had a fire. There was nothing to do but go home, so I went home. Let me, I thought, also taste the joy of sleeping in bed in midweek. I didn't want to wake the sleeping mite and tiptoed into the house. Coming in, it seemed to me that I heard not the snoring of one but, as it were, a double snore, one a thin enough snore and the other like the snoring of a slaughtered ox. Oh, I didn't like that! I didn't like it at all. I went up to the bed, and things suddenly turned black. Next to Elka lay a man's form. Another in my place would have made an uproar, and enough noise to rouse the whole town, but the thought occurred to me that I might wake the child. A little thing like that—why frighten a little swallow, I thought. All right then, I went back to the bakery and stretched out on a sack of flour and till morning I never shut an eye. I shivered as if I had had malaria. "Enough of being a donkey," I said to myself.

---

8. That is, a hasty or secret departure.

"Gimpel isn't going to be a sucker all his life. There's a limit even to the foolishness of a fool like Gimpel."

In the morning I went to the rabbi to get advice, and it made a great commotion in the town. They sent the beadle for Elka right away. She came, carrying the child. And what do you think she did? She denied it, denied everything, bone and stone! "He's out of his head," she said. "I know nothing of dreams of divinations." They yelled at her, warned her, hammered on the table, but she stuck to her guns: it was a false accusation, she said.

The butchers and the horse-traders took her part. One of the lads from the slaughterhouse came by and said to me, "We've got our eye on you, you're a marked man." Meanwhile, the child started to bear down and soiled itself. In the rabbinical court there was an Ark of the Covenant, and they couldn't allow that, so they sent Elka away.

I said to the rabbi, "What shall I do?"

"You must divorce her at once," said he.

"And what if she refuses?" I asked.

He said, "You must serve the divorce. That's all you'll have to do."

I said, "Well, all right, Rabbi. Let me think about it."

"There's nothing to think about," said he. "You mustn't remain under the same roof with her."

"And if I want to see the child?" I asked.

"Let her go, the harlot," said he, "and her brood of bastards with her."

The verdict he gave was that I mustn't even cross her threshold—never again, as long as I should live.

During the day it didn't bother me so much. I thought: It was bound to happen, the abscess had to burst. But at night when I stretched out upon the sacks I felt it all very bitterly. A longing took me, for her and for the child. I wanted to be angry, but that's my misfortune exactly, I don't have it in me to be really angry. In the first place—this was how my thoughts went—there's bound to be a slip sometimes. You can't live without errors. Probably that lad who was with her led her on and gave her presents and what not, and women are often long on hair and short on sense, and so he got around her. And then since she denies it so, maybe I was only seeing things? Hallucinations do happen. You see a figure or a mannikin or something, but when you come up closer it's nothing, there's not a thing there. And if that's so, I'm doing her an injustice. And when I got so far in my thoughts I started to weep. I sobbed so that I wet the flour where I lay. In the morning I went to the rabbi and told him that I had made a mistake. The rabbi wrote on with his quill, and he said that if that were so he would have to reconsider the whole case. Until he had finished I wasn't to go near my wife, but I might send her bread and money by messenger.

### III

Nine months passed before all the rabbis could come to an agreement. Letters went back and forth. I hadn't realized that there could be so much erudition about a matter like this.

Meanwhile, Elka gave birth to still another child, a girl this time. On the Sabbath I went to the synagogue and invoked a blessing on her. They called me up to the Torah, and I named the child for my mother-in-law—may she rest in peace. The louts and loudmouths of the town who came into the bakery gave me a going over. All Frampol refreshed its spirits because of my trouble and grief. However, I resolved that I would always believe what I was told. What's the good of *not* believing? Today it's your wife you don't believe; tomorrow it's God Himself you won't take stock in.

By an apprentice who was her neighbor I sent her daily a corn or a wheat loaf, or a piece of pastry, rolls or bagels, or, when I got the chance, a slab of pudding, a slice of honeycake, or wedding strudel—whatever came my way. The apprentice was a goodhearted lad, and more than once he added something on his own. He had formerly annoyed me a lot, plucking my nose and digging me in the ribs, but when he started to be a visitor to my house he became kind and friendly. "Hey, you, Gimpel," he said to me, "you have a very decent little wife and two fine kids. You don't deserve them."

"But the things people say about her," I said.

"Well, they have long tongues," he said, "and nothing to do with them but babble. Ignore it as you ignore the cold of last winter."

One day the rabbi sent for me and said, "Are you certain, Gimpel, that you were wrong about your wife?"

I said, "I'm certain."

"Why, but look here! You yourself saw it."

"It must have been a shadow," I said.

"The shadow of what?"

"Just of one of the beams, I think."

"You can go home then. You owe thanks to the Yanover rabbi. He found an obscure reference in Maimonides[9] that favored you."

I seized the rabbi's hand and kissed it.

I wanted to run home immediately. It's no small thing to be separated for so long a time from wife and child. Then I reflected: I'd better go back to work now, and go home in the evening. I said nothing to anyone, although as far as my heart was concerned it was like one of the Holy Days. The women teased and twitted me as they did every day, but my thought was: Go on, with your loose talk. The truth is out, like the oil upon the water. Maimonides says it's right, and therefore it is right!

At night, when I had covered the dough to let it rise, I took my share of bread and a little sack of flour and started homeward. The moon was full and the stars were glistening, something to terrify the soul. I hurried onward, and before me darted a long shadow. It was winter, and a fresh snow had fallen. I had a mind to sing, but it was growing late and I didn't want to wake the householders. Then I felt like whistling, but I remembered that you don't whistle at night because it brings the demons out. So I was silent and walked as fast as I could.

Dogs in the Christian yards barked at me when I passed, but I thought: Bark your teeth out! What are you but mere dogs? Whereas I am a man, the husband of a fine wife, the father of promising children.

As I approached the house my heart started to pound as though it were the heart of a criminal. I felt no fear, but my heart went thump! thump! Well, no

9. Jewish scholastic philosopher (1135–1204).

drawing back. I quietly lifted the latch and went in. Elka was asleep. I looked at the infant's cradle. The shutter was closed, but the moon forced its way through the cracks. I saw the newborn child's face and loved it as soon as I saw it—immediately—each tiny bone.

Then I came near to the bed. And what did I see but the apprentice lying there beside Elka. The moon went out all at once. It was utterly black, and I trembled. My teeth chattered. The bread fell from my hands, and my wife waked and said, "Who is that, ah?"

I muttered, "It's me."

"Gimpel?" she asked. "How come you're here? I thought it was forbidden."

"The rabbi said," I answered and shook as with a fever.

"Listen to me, Gimpel," she said, "go out to the shed and see if the goat's all right. It seems she's been sick." I have forgotten to say that we had a goat. When I heard she was unwell I went into the yard. The nannygoat was a good little creature. I had nearly human feeling for her.

With hesitant steps I went up to the shed and opened the door. The goat stood there on her four feet. I felt her everywhere, drew her by the horns, examined her udders, and found nothing wrong. She had probably eaten too much bark. "Good night, little goat," I said. "Keep well." And the little beast answered with a "Maa" as though to thank me for the good will.

I went back. The apprentice had vanished.

"Where," I asked, "is the lad?"

"What lad?" my wife answered.

"What do you mean?" I said. "The apprentice. You were sleeping with him."

"The things I have dreamed this night and the night before," she said, "may they come true and lay you low, body and soul! An evil spirit has taken root in you and dazzles your sight." She screamed out, "You hateful creature! You moon calf! You spook! You uncouth man! Get out, or I'll scream all Frampol out of bed!"

Before I could move, her brother sprang out from behind the oven and struck me a blow on the back of the head. I thought he had broken my neck. I felt that something about me was deeply wrong, and I said, "Don't make a scandal. All that's needed now is that people should accuse me of raising spooks and dybbuks."[1] For that was what she had meant. "No one will touch bread of my baking."

In short, I somehow calmed her.

"Well," she said, "that's enough. Lie down, and be shattered by wheels."

Next morning I called the apprentice aside. "Listen here, brother!" I said. And so on and so forth. "What do you say?" He stared at me as though I had dropped from the roof or something.

"I swear," he said, "you'd better go to an herb doctor or some healer. I'm afraid you have a screw loose, but I'll hush it up for you." And that's how the thing stood.

To make a long story short, I lived twenty years with my wife. She bore me six children, four daughters and two sons. All kinds of things happened, but I neither saw nor heard. I believed, and that's all. The rabbi recently said to me, "Belief in itself is beneficial. It is written that a good man lives by his faith."

---

1. Ghosts and wandering souls (Hebrew).

Suddenly my wife took sick. It began with a trifle, a little growth upon the breast. But she evidently was not destined to live long; she had no years. I spent a fortune on her. I have forgotten to say that by this time I had a bakery of my own and in Frampol was considered to be something of a rich man. Daily the healer came, and every witch doctor in the neighborhood was brought. They decided to use leeches, and after that to try cupping. They even called a doctor from Lublin, but it was too late. Before she died she called me to her bed and said, "Forgive me, Gimpel."

I said, "What is there to forgive? You have been a good and faithful wife."

"Woe, Gimpel!" she said. "It was ugly how I deceived you all these years. I want to go clean to my Maker, and so I have to tell you that the children are not yours."

If I had been clouted on the head with a piece of wood it couldn't have bewildered me more.

"Whose are they?" I asked.

"I don't know," she said. "There were a lot . . . but they're not yours." And as she spoke she tossed her head to the side, her eyes turned glassy, and it was all up to Elka. On her whitened lips there remained a smile.

I imagined that, dead as she was, she was saying, "I deceived Gimpel. That was the meaning of my brief life."

## IV

One night, when the period of mourning was done, as I lay dreaming on the flour sacks, there came the Spirit of Evil himself and said to me, "Gimpel, why do you sleep?"

I said, "What should I be doing? Eating kreplech?"[2]

"The whole world deceives you," he said, "and you ought to deceive the world in your turn."

"How can I deceive all the world?" I asked him.

He answered, "You might accumulate a bucket of urine every day and at night pour it into the dough. Let the sages of Frampol eat filth."

"What about the judgment in the world to come?" I said.

"There is no world to come," he said. "They've sold you a bill of goods and talked you into believing you carried a cat in your belly. What nonsense!"

"Well then," I said, "and is there a God?"

He answered, "There is no God either."

"What," I said, "is there, then?"

"A thick mire."

He stood before my eyes with a goatish beard and horn, long-toothed, and with a tail. Hearing such words, I wanted to snatch him by the tail, but I tumbled from the flour sacks and nearly broke a rib. Then it happened that I had to answer the call of nature, and, passing, I saw the risen dough, which seemed to say to me, "Do it!" In brief, I let myself be persuaded.

At dawn the apprentice came. We kneaded the bread, scattered caraway seeds on it, and set it to bake. Then the apprentice went away, and I was left sitting in the little trench by the oven, on a pile of rags. Well, Gimpel, I thought, you've

2. Stuffed dumplings, usually served in soup.

revenged yourself on them for all the shame they've put on you. Outside the frost glittered, but it was warm beside the oven. The flames heated my face. I bent my head and fell into a doze.

I saw in a dream, at once, Elka in her shroud. She called to me, "What have you done, Gimpel?"

I said to her, "It's all your fault," and started to cry.

"You fool!" she said. "You fool! Because I was false is everything false too? I never deceived anyone but myself. I'm paying for it all, Gimpel. They spare you nothing here."

I looked at her face. It was black; I was startled and waked, and remained sitting dumb. I sensed that everything hung in the balance. I seized the long shovel and took out the loaves, carried them into the yard, and started to dig a hole in the frozen earth.

My apprentice came back as I was doing it. "What are you doing, boss?" he said, and grew pale as a corpse.

"I know what I'm doing," I said, and I buried it all before his very eyes.

Then I went home, took my hoard from its hiding place, and divided it among the children. "I saw your mother tonight," I said. "She's turning black, poor thing."

They were so astounded they couldn't speak a word.

"Be well," I said, "and forget that such a one as Gimpel ever existed." I put on my short coat, a pair of boots, took the bag that held my prayer shawl in one hand, my stock in the other, and kissed the mezuzah.[3] When people saw me in the street they were greatly surprised.

"Where are you going?" they said.

I answered, "Into the world." And so I departed from Frampol.

I wandered over the land, and good people did not neglect me. After many years I became old and white; I heard a great deal, many lies and falsehoods, but the longer I lived the more I understood that there were really no lies. Whatever doesn't really happen is dreamed at night. It happens to one if it doesn't happen to another, tomorrow if not today, or a century hence if not next year. What difference can it make? Often I heard tales of which I said, "Now this is a thing that cannot happen." But before a year had elapsed I heard that it actually had come to pass somewhere.

Going from place to place, eating at strange tables, it often happens that I spin yarns—improbable things that could never have happened—about devils, magicians, windmills, and the like. The children run after me, calling, "Grandfather, tell us a story." Sometimes they ask for particular stories, and I try to please them. A fat young boy once said to me, "Grandfather, it's the same story you told us before." The little rogue, he was right.

So it is with dreams too. It is many years since I left Frampol, but as soon as I shut my eyes I am there again. And whom do you think I see? Elka. She is standing by the washtub, as at our first encounter, but her face is shining and her eyes are as radiant as the eyes of a saint, and she speaks outlandish words to me, strange things. When I wake I have forgotten it all. But while the dream lasts I am comforted. She answers all my queries, and what comes out is that

---

**3.** A case containing parchment inscribed with verses from the Torah, attached to the door frame of a faithful Jewish household (Hebrew).

all is right. I weep and implore, "Let me be with you." And she consoles me and tells me to be patient. The time is nearer than it is far. Sometimes she strokes and kisses me and weeps upon my face. When I awaken I feel her lips and taste the salt of her tears.

No doubt the world is entirely an imaginary world, but it is only once removed from the true world. At the door of the hovel where I lie, there stands the plank on which the dead are taken away. The grave-digger Jew has his spade ready. The grave waits and the worms are hungry; the shrouds are prepared—I carry them in my beggar's sack. Another *shnorrer*[4] is waiting to inherit my bed of straw. When the time comes I will go joyfully. Whatever may be there, it will be real, without complication, without ridicule, without deception. God be praised: there even Gimpel cannot be deceived.

1953

4. Beggar, sponger (Yiddish).

# JOHN STEINBECK
## *1902–1968*

Steinbeck was born in Salinas, California. His mother was a former schoolteacher, who encouraged him to read widely as a child, but his formal schooling made little impression on him. He attended Stanford University intermittently, leaving in 1926 to drift through an array of odd jobs that educated him in the life of working people. His first, rather romantic novel, *Cup of Gold*, appeared in 1929. By 1936 his involvement with the struggles of migrant workers resulted in his militantly political novel *In Dubious Battle*. In 1937 his short novel *Of Mice and Men* proved immensely popular and provided the basis for an equally popular film, as did *The Grapes of Wrath* in 1939. He served as a war correspondent during World War II. His postwar novels include *East of Eden* (1952) and *The Winter of Our Discontent* (1961). In 1962 he was awarded the Nobel Prize. Much of Steinbeck's finest short work can be found in the collection *Steinbeck: Novels and Stories 1932–1937* (1978).

## The Chrysanthemums

The high grey-flannel fog of winter closed off the Salinas Valley from the sky and from all the rest of the world. On every side it sat like a lid on the mountains and made of the great valley a closed pot. On the broad, level land floor the gang ploughs bit deep and left the black earth shining like metal where the shares had cut. On the foot-hill ranches across the Salinas River, the yellow stubble fields seemed to be bathed in pale cold sunshine, but there was no sunshine in the valley now in December. The thick willow scrub along the river flamed with sharp and positive yellow leaves.

It was a time of quiet and of waiting. The air was cold and tender. A light wind blew up from the southwest so that the farmers were mildly hopeful of a good rain before long; but fog and rain do not go together.

Across the river, on Henry Allen's foot-hill ranch there was little work to be done, for the hay was cut and stored and the orchards were ploughed up to receive the rain deeply when it should come. The cattle on the higher slopes were becoming shaggy and rough-coated.

Elisa Allen, working in her flower garden, looked down across the yard and saw Henry, her husband, talking to two men in business suits. The three of them stood by the tractor-shed, each man with one foot on the side of the little Fordson. They smoked cigarettes and studied the machine as they talked.

Elisa watched them for a moment and then went back to her work. She was thirty-five. Her face was lean and strong and her eyes were as clear as water. Her figure looked blocked and heavy in her gardening costume, a man's black hat pulled low down over her eyes, clod-hopper shoes, a figured print dress almost completely covered by a big corduroy apron with four big pockets to hold the snips, the trowel and scratcher, the seeds and the knife she worked with. She wore heavy leather gloves to protect her hands while she worked.

She was cutting down the old year's chrysanthemum stalks with a pair of short and powerful scissors. She looked down toward the men by the tractor-shed now and then. Her face was eager and mature and handsome; even her work with the scissors was overeager, over-powerful. The chrysanthemum stems seemed too small and easy for her energy.

She brushed a cloud of hair out of her eyes with the back of her glove, and left a smudge of earth on her cheek in doing it. Behind her stood the neat white farmhouse with red geraniums close-banked around it as high as the windows. It was a hard-swept-looking little house, with hard-polished windows, and a clean mud-mat on the front steps.

Elisa cast another glance toward the tractor-shed. The strangers were getting into their Ford coupé. She took off a glove and put her strong fingers down into the forest of new green chrysanthemum sprouts that were growing around the old roots. She spread the leaves and looked down among the close-growing stems. No aphids were there, no sow bugs or snails or cut-worms. Her terrier fingers destroyed such pests before they could get started.

Elisa started at the sound of her husband's voice. He had come near quietly, and he leaned over the wire fence that protected her flower garden from cattle and dogs and chickens.

"At it again," he said. "You've got a strong new crop coming."

Elisa straightened her back and pulled on the gardening glove again. "Yes. They'll be strong this coming year." In her tone and on her face there was a little smugness.

"You've got a gift with things," Henry observed. "Some of those yellow chrysanthemums you had this year were ten inches across. I wish you'd work out in the orchard and raise some apples that big."

Her eyes sharpened. "Maybe I could do it, too. I've a gift with things, all right. My mother had it. She could stick anything in the ground and make it grow. She said it was having planters' hands that knew how to do it."

"Well, it sure works with flowers," he said.

"Henry, who were those men you were talking to?"

"Why, sure, that's what I came to tell you. They were from the Western Meat Company. I sold those thirty head of three-year-old steers. Got nearly my own price, too."

"Good," she said. "Good for you."

"And I thought," he continued, "I thought how it's Saturday afternoon, and we might go into Salinas for dinner at a restaurant, and then to a picture show—to celebrate, you see."

"Good," she repeated. "Oh, yes. That will be good."

Henry put on his joking tone. "There's fights tonight. How'd you like to go to the fights?"

"Oh, no," she said breathlessly. "No, I wouldn't like fights."

"Just fooling, Elisa. We'll go to a movie. Let's see. It's two now. I'm going to take Scotty and bring down those steers from the hill. It'll take us maybe two hours. We'll go in town about five and have dinner at the Cominos Hotel. Like that?"

"Of course I'll like it. It's good to eat away from home."

"All right, then. I'll go get up a couple of horses."

She said: "I'll have plenty of time to transplant some of these sets, I guess."

She heard her husband calling Scotty down by the barn. And a little later she saw the two men ride up the pale yellow hillside in search of the steers.

There was a little square sandy bed kept for rooting the chrysanthemums. With her trowel she turned the soil over and over, and smoothed it and patted it firm. Then she dug ten parallel trenches to receive the sets. Back at the chrysanthemum bed she pulled out the little crisp shoots, trimmed off the leaves of each one with her scissors and laid it on a small orderly pile.

A squeak of wheels and plod of hoofs came from the road. Elisa looked up. The country road ran along the dense bank of willows and cottonwoods that bordered the river, and up this road came a curious vehicle, curiously drawn. It was an old spring-wagon, with a round canvas top on it like the cover of a prairie schooner. It was drawn by an old bay horse and a little grey-and-white burro. A big stubble-bearded man sat between the cover flaps and drove the crawling team. Underneath the wagon, between the hind wheels, a lean and rangy mongrel dog walked sedately. Words were painted on the canvas, in clumsy, crooked letters. "Pots, pans, knives, sisors, lawn mores, Fixed." Two rows of articles, and the triumphantly definitive "Fixed" below. The black paint had run down in little sharp points beneath each letter.

Elisa, squatting on the ground, watched to see the crazy, loose-jointed wagon pass by. But it didn't pass. It turned into the farm road in front of her house, crooked old wheels skirling and squeaking. The rangy dog darted from between the wheels and ran ahead. Instantly the two ranch shepherds flew out at him. Then all three stopped, and with stiff and quivering tails, with taut straight legs, with ambassadorial dignity, they slowly circled, sniffing daintily. The caravan pulled up to Elisa's wire fence and stopped. Now the newcomer dog, feeling out-numbered, lowered his tail and retired under the wagon with raised hackles and bared teeth.

The man on the wagon seat called out: "That's a bad dog in a fight when he gets started."

Elisa laughed. "I see he is. How soon does he generally get started?"

The man caught up her laughter and echoed it heartily. "Sometimes not for weeks and weeks," he said. He climbed stiffly down, over the wheel. The horse and the donkey drooped like unwatered flowers.

Elisa saw that he was a very big man. Although his hair and beard were greying, he did not look old. His worn black suit was wrinkled and spotted with grease. The laughter had disappeared from his face and eyes the moment his laughing voice ceased. His eyes were dark, and they were full of the brooding that gets in the eyes of teamsters and of sailors. The calloused hands he rested on the wire fence were cracked, and every crack was a black line. He took off his battered hat.

"I'm off my general road, ma'am," he said. "Does this dirt road cut over across the river to the Los Angeles highway?"

Elisa stood up and shoved the thick scissors in her apron pocket. "Well, yes, it does, but it winds around and then fords the river. I don't think your team could pull through the sand."

He replied with some asperity: "It might surprise you what them beasts can pull through."

"When they get started?" she asked.

He smiled for a second. "Yes. When they get started."

"Well," said Elisa, "I think you'll save time if you go back to the Salinas road and pick up the highway there."

He drew a big finger down the chicken wire and made it sing. "I ain't in any hurry, ma'am. I go from Seattle to San Diego and back every year. Takes all my time. About six months each way. I aim to follow nice weather."

Elisa took off her gloves and stuffed them in the apron pocket with the scissors. She touched the under edge of her man's hat, searching for fugitive hairs. "That sounds like a nice kind of way to live," she said.

He leaned confidentially over the fence. "Maybe you noticed the writing on my wagon. I mend pots and sharpen knives and scissors. You got any of them things to do?"

"Oh, no," she said quickly. "Nothing like that." Her eyes hardened with resistance.

"Scissors is the worst thing," he explained. "Most people just ruin scissors trying to sharpen 'em, but I know how. I got a special tool. It's a little bobbit kind of thing, and patented. But it sure does the trick."

"No. My scissors are all sharp."

"All right, then. Take a pot," he continued earnestly, "a bent pot, or a pot with a hole. I can make it like new so you don't have to buy no new ones. That's a saving for you."

"No," she said shortly. "I tell you I have nothing like that for you to do."

His face fell to an exaggerated sadness. His voice took on a whining undertone. "I ain't had a thing to do today. Maybe I won't have no supper tonight. You see I'm off my regular road. I know folks on the highway clear from Seattle to San Diego. They save their things for me to sharpen up because they know I do it so good and save them money."

"I'm sorry," Elisa said irritably. "I haven't anything for you to do."

His eyes left her face and fell to searching the ground. They roamed about until they came to the chrysanthemum bed where she had been working. "What's them plants, ma'am?"

The irritation and resistance melted from Elisa's face. "Oh, those are chrysanthemums, giant whites and yellows. I raise them every year, bigger than anybody around here."

"Kind of a long-stemmed flower? Looks like a quick puff of colored smoke?" he asked.

"That's it. What a nice way to describe them."

"They smell kind of nasty till you get used to them," he said.

"It's a good bitter smell," she retorted, "not nasty at all."

He changed his tone quickly. "I like the smell myself."

"I had ten-inch blooms this year," she said.

The man leaned farther over the fence. "Look. I know a lady down the road a piece, has got the nicest garden you ever seen. Got nearly every kind of flower but no chrysanthemums. Last time I was mending a copper-bottom washtub for her (that's a hard job but I do it good), she said to me: 'If you ever run acrost some nice chrysanthemums I wish you'd try to get me a few seeds.' That's what she told me."

Elisa's eyes grew alert and eager. "She couldn't have known much about chrysanthemums. You *can* raise them from seed, but it's much easier to root the little sprouts you see here."

"Oh," he said. "I s'pose I can't take none to her, then."

"Why yes you can," Elisa cried. "I can put some in damp sand, and you can carry them right along with you. They'll take root in the pot if you keep them damp. And then she can transplant them."

"She'd sure like to have some, ma'am. You say they're nice ones?"

"Beautiful," she said. "Oh, beautiful." Her eyes shone. She tore off the battered hat and shook out her dark pretty hair. "I'll put them in a flowerpot, and you can take them right with you. Come into the yard."

While the man came through the picket gate Elisa ran excitedly along the geranium-bordered path to the back of the house. And she returned carrying a big red flower-pot. The gloves were forgotten now. She kneeled on the ground by the starting bed and dug up the sandy soil with her fingers and scooped it into the bright new flower-pot. Then she picked up the little pile of shoots she had prepared. With her strong fingers she pressed them into the sand and tamped around them with her knuckles. The man stood over her. "I'll tell you what to do," she said. "You remember so you can tell the lady."

"Yes, I'll try to remember."

"Well, look. These will take root in about a month. Then she must set them out, about a foot apart in good rich earth like this, see?" She lifted a handful of dark soil for him to look at. "They'll grow fast and tall. Now remember this: In July tell her to cut them down, about eight inches from the ground."

"Before they bloom?" he asked.

"Yes, before they bloom." Her face was tight with eagerness. "They'll grow right up again. About the last of September the buds will start."

She stopped and seemed perplexed. "It's the budding that takes the most care," she said hesitantly. "I don't know how to tell you." She looked deep into his eyes, searchingly. Her mouth opened a little, and she seemed to be listening. "I'll try to tell you," she said. "Did you ever hear of planting hands?"

"Can't say I have, ma'am."

"Well, I can only tell you what it feels like. It's when you're picking off the buds you don't want. Everything goes right down into your fingertips. You watch your fingers work. They do it themselves. You can feel how it is. They pick and pick the buds. They never make a mistake. They're with the plant. Do you see? Your fingers and the plant. You can feel that, right up your arm. They know. They never make a mistake. You can feel it. When you're like that you can't do anything wrong. Do you see that? Can you understand that?"

She was kneeling on the ground looking up at him. Her breast swelled passionately.

The man's eyes narrowed. He looked away self-consciously.

"Maybe I know," he said. "Sometimes in the night in the wagon there——"

Elisa's voice grew husky. She broke in on him: "I've never lived as you do, but I know what you mean. When the night is dark—why, the stars are sharp-pointed, and there's quiet. Why, you rise up and up! Every pointed star gets driven into your body. It's like that. Hot and sharp and—lovely."

Kneeling there, her hand went out toward his legs in the greasy black trousers. Her hesitant fingers almost touched the cloth. Then her hand dropped to the ground. She crouched low like a fawning dog.

He said: "It's nice, just like you say. Only when you don't have no dinner, it ain't."

She stood up then, very straight, and her face was ashamed. She held the flower-pot out to him and placed it gently in his arms. "Here. Put it in your wagon, on the seat, where you can watch it. Maybe I can find something for you to do."

At the back of the house she dug in the can pile and found two old and battered aluminum saucepans. She carried them back and gave them to him. "Here, maybe you can fix these."

His manner changed. He became professional. "Good as new I can fix them." At the back of his wagon he set a little anvil, and out of an oily toolbox dug a small machine hammer. Elisa came through the gate to watch him while he pounded out the dents in the kettles. His mouth grew sure and knowing. At a difficult part of the work he sucked his underlip.

"You sleep right in the wagon?" Elisa asked.

"Right in the wagon, ma'am. Rain or shine I'm dry as a cow in there."

"It must be nice," she said. "It must be very nice. I wish women could do such things."

"It ain't the right kind of a life for a woman."

Her upper lip raised a little, showing her teeth. "How do you know? How can you tell?" she said.

"I don't know, ma'am," he protested. "Of course I don't know. Now here's your kettles, done. You don't have to buy no new ones."

"How much?"

"Oh, fifty cents'll do. I keep my prices down and my work good. That's why I have all them satisfied customers up and down the highway."

Elisa brought him a fifty-cent piece from the house and dropped it in his hand. "You might be surprised to have a rival some time. I can sharpen scissors, too. And I can beat the dents out of little pots. I could show you what a woman might do."

He put his hammer back in the oily box and shoved the little anvil out of sight. "It would be a lonely life for a woman, ma'am, and a scarey life, too, with animals creeping under the wagon all night." He climbed over the singletree, steadying himself with a hand on the burro's white rump. He settled himself in the seat, picked up the lines. "Thank you kindly ma'am," he said. "I'll do like you told me; I'll go back and catch the Salinas road."

"Mind," she called, "if you're long in getting there, keep the sand damp."

"Sand, ma'am? . . . Sand? Oh, sure. You mean around the chrysanthemums. Sure I will." He clucked his tongue. The beasts leaned luxuriously into their collars. The mongrel dog took his place between the back wheels. The wagon turned and crawled out the entrance road and back the way it had come, along the river.

Elisa stood in front of her wire fence watching the slow progress of the caravan. Her shoulders were straight, her head thrown back, her eyes half-closed, so that the scene came vaguely into them. Her lips moved silently, forming the words "Good-bye—good-bye." Then she whispered: "That's a bright direction. There's a glowing there." The sound of her whisper startled her. She shook herself free and looked about to see whether anyone had been listening. Only the dogs had heard. They lifted their heads toward her from their sleeping in the dust, and then stretched out their chins and settled asleep again. Elisa turned and ran hurriedly into the house.

In the kitchen she reached behind the stove and felt the water tank. It was full of hot water from the noonday cooking. In the bathroom she tore off her soiled clothes and flung them into the corner. And then she scrubbed herself with a little block of pumice, legs and thighs, loins and chest and arms, until her skin was scratched and red. When she had dried herself she stood in front of a mirror in her bedroom and looked at her body. She tightened her stomach and threw out her chest. She turned and looked over her shoulders at her back.

After a while she began to dress, slowly. She put on her newest underclothing and her nicest stockings and the dress which was the symbol of her prettiness. She worked carefully on her hair, pencilled her eyebrows and rouged her lips.

Before she was finished she heard the little thunder of hoofs and the shouts of Henry and his helper as they drove the red steers into the corral. She heard the gate bang shut and set herself for Henry's arrival.

His step sounded on the porch. He entered the house calling: "Elisa, where are you?"

"In my room, dressing. I'm not ready. There's hot water for your bath. Hurry up. It's getting late."

When she heard him splashing in the tub, Elisa laid his dark suit on the bed, and shirt and socks and tie beside it. She stood his polished shoes on the floor beside the bed. Then she went to the porch and sat primly and stiffly down. She looked toward the river road where the willow-line was still yellow with frosted leaves so that under the high grey fog they seemed a thin band of sunshine. This was the only color in the grey afternoon. She sat unmoving for a long time. Her eyes blinked rarely.

Henry came banging out of the door, shoving his tie inside his vest as he came. Elisa stiffened and her face grew tight. Henry stopped short and looked at her. "Why—why, Elisa. You look so nice!"

"Nice? You think I look nice? What do you mean by 'nice'?"

Henry blundered on. "I don't know. I mean you look different, strong and happy."

"I am strong? Yes, strong. What do you mean 'strong'?"

He looked bewildered. "You're playing some kind of a game," he said helplessly. "It's a kind of a play. You look strong enough to break a calf over your knee, happy enough to eat it like a watermelon."

For a second she lost her rigidity. "Henry! Don't talk like that. You didn't know what you said." She grew complete again. "I'm strong," she boasted. "I never knew before how strong."

Henry looked down toward the tractor-shed, and when he brought his eyes back to her, they were his own again. "I'll get out the car. You can put on your coat while I'm starting."

Elisa went into the house. She heard him drive to the gate and idle down his motor, and then she took a long time to put on her hat. She pulled it here and pressed it there. When Henry turned the motor off she slipped into her coat and went out.

The little roadster bounced along on the dirt road by the river, raising the birds and driving the rabbits into the brush. Two cranes flapped heavily over the willow-line and dropped into the river-bed.

Far ahead on the road Elisa saw a dark speck. She knew.

She tried not to look as they passed it, but her eyes would not obey. She whispered to herself sadly: "He might have thrown them off the road. That wouldn't have been much trouble, not very much. But he kept the pot," she explained. "He had to keep the pot. That's why he couldn't get them off the road."

The roadster turned a bend and she saw the caravan ahead. She swung full around toward her husband so she could not see the little covered wagon and the mis-matched team as the car passed them.

In a moment it was over. The thing was done. She did not look back.

She said loudly, to be heard above the motor: "It will be good, tonight, a good dinner."

"Now you've changed again," Henry complained. He took one hand from the wheel and patted her knee. "I ought to take you in to dinner oftener. It would be good for both of us. We get so heavy out on the ranch."

"Henry," she asked, "could we have wine at dinner?"

"Sure we could. Say! That will be fine."

She was silent for a while; then she said: "Henry, at those prize-fights, do the men hurt each other very much?"

"Sometimes a little, not often. Why?"

"Well, I've read how they break noses, and blood runs down their chests. I've read how the fighting gloves get heavy and soggy with blood."

He looked around at her. "What's the matter, Elisa? I didn't know you read things like that." He brought the car to a stop, then turned to the right over the Salinas River bridge.

"Do any women ever go to the fights?" she asked.

"Oh, sure, some. What's the matter, Elisa? Do you want to go? I don't think you'd like it, but I'll take you if you really want to go."

She relaxed limply in the seat. "Oh, no. No. I don't want to go. I'm sure I don't." Her face was turned away from him. "It will be enough if we can have wine. It will be plenty." She turned up her coat collar so he could not see that she was crying weakly—like an old woman.

1938

# AMY TAN
## *b. 1952*

Tan was born in Oakland, California, and educated at San Jose State University and the University of California at Berkeley. She has worked on
programs for disabled children and as a reporter
and businesswoman. Material for her widely
popular fiction comes from the lives of Chinese-
American women and the cultural ambivalence
of their circumstances in the United States. Her
novels are *The Joy Luck Club* (1989), *The Kitchen
God's Wife* (1991), *The Hundred Secret Senses* (1995),
*The Bonesetter's Daughter* (2001), *Saving Fish from
Drowning* (2005) *Rules for Virgins* (2011), and *The
Valley of Amazement* (2013). She has also published
two books for children, *The Moon Lady* (1992) and
*The Chinese Siamese Cat* (1994), and an essay collection, *The Opposite of Fate:
A Book of Musings* (2003).

# Rules of the Game

I was six when my mother taught me the art of invisible strength. It was a
strategy for winning arguments, respect from others, and eventually, though
neither of us knew it at the time, chess games.

"Bite back your tongue," scolded my mother when I cried loudly, yanking
her hand toward the store that sold bags of salted plums. At home, she said,
"Wise guy, he not go against wind. In Chinese we say, Come from South, blow
with wind—poom!—North will follow. Strongest wind cannot be seen."

The next week I bit back my tongue as we entered the store with the forbidden candies. When my mother finished her shopping, she quietly plucked a
small bag of plums from the rack and put it on the counter with the rest of
the items.

My mother imparted her daily truths so she could help my older brothers
and me rise above our circumstances. We lived in San Francisco's Chinatown.
Like most of the other Chinese children who played in the back alleys of restaurants and curio shops, I didn't think we were poor. My bowl was always
full, three five-course meals every day, beginning with a soup of mysterious
things I didn't want to know the names of.

We lived on Waverly Place, in a warm, clean, two-bedroom flat that sat
above a small Chinese bakery specializing in steamed pastries and dim sum.[1]

---

1. Variety of traditional Chinese foods served in small portions.

In the early morning, when the alley was still quiet, I could smell fragrant red beans as they were cooked down to a pasty sweetness. By daybreak, our flat was heavy with the odor of fried sesame balls and sweet curried chicken crescents. From my bed, I would listen as my father got ready for work, then locked the door behind him, one-two-three clicks.

At the end of our two-block alley was a small sandlot playground with swings and slides well-shined down the middle with use. The play area was bordered by wood-slat benches where old-country people sat cracking roasted watermelon seeds with their golden teeth and scattering the husks to an impatient gathering of gurgling pigeons. The best playground, however, was the dark alley itself. It was crammed with daily mysteries and adventures. My brothers and I would peer into the medicinal herb shop, watching old Li dole out onto a stiff sheet of white paper the right amount of insect shells, saffron-colored seeds, and pungent leaves for his ailing customers. It was said that he once cured a woman dying of an ancestral curse that had eluded the best of American doctors. Next to the pharmacy was a printer who specialized in gold-embossed wedding invitations and festive red banners.

Farther down the street was Ping Yuen Fish Market. The front window displayed a tank crowded with doomed fish and turtles struggling to gain footing on the slimy green-tiled sides. A hand-written sign informed tourists, "Within this store, is all for food, not for pet." Inside, the butchers with their bloodstained white smocks deftly gutted the fish while customers cried out their orders and shouted, "Give me your freshest," to which the butchers always protested, "All are freshest." On less crowded market days, we would inspect the crates of live frogs and crabs which we were warned not to poke, boxes of dried cuttlefish, and row upon row of iced prawns, squid, and slippery fish. The sanddabs made me shiver each time; their eyes lay on one flattened side and reminded me of my mother's story of a careless girl who ran into a crowded street and was crushed by a cab. "Was smash flat," reported my mother.

At the corner of the alley was Hong Sing's, a four-table café with a recessed stairwell in front that led to a door marked "Tradesmen." My brothers and I believed the bad people emerged from this door at night. Tourists never went to Hong Sing's, since the menu was printed only in Chinese. A Caucasian man with a big camera once posed me and my playmates in front of the restaurant. He had us move to the side of the picture window so the photo would capture the roasted duck with its head dangling from a juice-covered rope. After he took the picture, I told him he should go into Hong Sing's and eat dinner. When he smiled and asked me what they served, I shouted, "Guts and duck's feet and octopus gizzards!" Then I ran off with my friends, shrieking with laughter as we scampered across the alley and hid in the entryway grotto of the China Gem Company, my heart pounding with hope that he would chase us.

My mother named me after the street that we lived on: Waverly Place Jong, my official name for important American documents. But my family called me Meimei, "Little Sister." I was the youngest, the only daughter. Each morning before school, my mother would twist and yank on my thick black hair until she had formed two tightly wound pigtails. One day, as she struggled to weave a hard-toothed comb through my disobedient hair, I had a sly thought.

I asked her, "Ma, what is Chinese torture?" My mother shook her head. A bobby pin was wedged between her lips. She wetted her palm and smoothed the hair above my ear, then pushed the pin in so that it nicked sharply against my scalp.

"Who say this word?" she asked without a trace of knowing how wicked I was being. I shrugged my shoulders and said, "Some boy in my class said Chinese people do Chinese torture."

"Chinese people do many things," she said simply. "Chinese people do business, do medicine, do painting. Not lazy like American people. We do torture. Best torture."

My older brother Vincent was the one who actually got the chess set. We had gone to the annual Christmas party held at the First Chinese Baptist Church at the end of the alley. The missionary ladies had put together a Santa bag of gifts donated by members of another church. None of the gifts had names on them. There were separate sacks for boys and girls of different ages.

One of the Chinese parishioners had donned a Santa Claus costume and a stiff paper beard with cotton balls glued to it. I think the only children who thought he was the real thing were too young to know that Santa Claus was not Chinese. When my turn came up, the Santa man asked me how old I was. I thought it was a trick question; I was seven according to the American formula and eight by the Chinese calendar. I said I was born on March 17, 1951. That seemed to satisfy him. He then solemnly asked if I had been a very, very good girl this year and did I believe in Jesus Christ and obey my parents. I knew the only answer to that. I nodded back with equal solemnity.

Having watched the older children opening their gifts, I already knew that the big gifts were not necessarily the nicest ones. One girl my age got a large coloring book of biblical characters, while a less greedy girl who selected a smaller box received a glass vial of lavender toilet water. The sound of the box was also important. A ten-year-old boy had chosen a box that jangled when he shook it. It was a tin globe of the world with a slit for inserting money. He must have thought it was full of dimes and nickels, because when he saw that it had just ten pennies, his face fell with such undisguised disappointment that his mother slapped the side of his head and led him out of the church hall, apologizing to the crowd for her son who had such bad manners he couldn't appreciate such a fine gift.

As I peered into the sack, I quickly fingered the remaining presents, testing their weight, imagining what they contained. I chose a heavy, compact one that was wrapped in shiny silver foil and a red satin ribbon. It was a twelve-pack of Life Savers and I spent the rest of the party arranging and rearranging the candy tubes in the order of my favorites. My brother Winston chose wisely as well. His present turned out to be a box of intricate plastic parts; the instructions on the box proclaimed that when they were properly assembled he would have an authentic miniature replica of a World War II submarine.

Vincent got the chess set, which would have been a very decent present to get at a church Christmas party, except it was obviously used and, as we discovered later, it was missing a black pawn and a white knight. My mother graciously thanked the unknown benefactor, saying, "Too good. Cost too much." At which point, an old lady with fine white, wispy hair nodded toward our family and said with a whistling whisper, "Merry, merry Christmas."

When we got home, my mother told Vincent to throw the chess set away. "She not want it. We not want it." she said, tossing her head stiffly to the side with a tight, proud smile. My brothers had deaf ears. They were already lining up the chess pieces and reading from the dog-eared instruction book.

I watched Vincent and Winston play during Christmas week. The chessboard seemed to hold elaborate secrets waiting to be untangled. The chessmen were more powerful than old Li's magic herbs that cured ancestral curses. And my brothers wore such serious faces that I was sure something was at stake that was greater than avoiding the tradesmen's door to Hong Sing's.

"Let me! Let me!" I begged between games when one brother or the other would sit back with a deep sigh of relief and victory, the other annoyed, unable to let go of the outcome. Vincent at first refused to let me play, but when I offered my Life Savers as replacements for the buttons that filled in for the missing pieces, he relented. He chose the flavors: wild cherry for the black pawn and peppermint for the white knight. Winner could eat both.

As our mother sprinkled flour and rolled out small doughy circles for the steamed dumplings that would be our dinner that night, Vincent explained the rules, pointing to each piece. "You have sixteen pieces and so do I. One king and queen, two bishops, two knights, two castles, and eight pawns. The pawns can only move forward one step, except on the first move. Then they can move two. But they can only take men by moving crossways like this, except in the beginning, when you can move ahead and take another pawn."

"Why?" I asked as I moved my pawn. "Why can't they move more steps?"

"Because they're pawns," he said.

"But why do they go crossways to take other men? Why aren't there any women and children?"

"Why is the sky blue? Why must you always ask stupid questions?" asked Vincent. "This is a game. These are the rules. I didn't make them up. See. Here in the book." He jabbed a page with a pawn in his hand. "Pawn. P-A-W-N. Pawn. Read it yourself."

My mother patted the flour off her hands. "Let me see book," she said quietly. She scanned the pages quickly, not reading the foreign English symbols, seeming to search deliberately for nothing in particular.

"This American rules," she concluded at last. "Every time people come out from foreign country, must know rules. You not know, judge say, Too bad, go back. They not telling you why so you can use their way go forward. They say, Don't know why, you find out yourself. But they knowing all the time. Better you take it, find out why yourself." She tossed her head back with a satisfied smile.

I found out about all the whys later. I read the rules and looked up all the big words in a dictionary. I borrowed books from the Chinatown library. I studied each chess piece, trying to absorb the power each contained.

I learned about opening moves and why it's important to control the center early on; the shortest distance between two points is straight down the middle. I learned about the middle game and why tactics between two adversaries are like clashing ideas; the one who plays better has the clearest plans for both attacking and getting out of traps. I learned why it is essential in the endgame to have foresight, a mathematical understanding of all possible moves, and patience; all weaknesses and advantages become evident to a strong adversary and are obscured to a tiring opponent. I discovered that for the whole game one must gather invisible strengths and see the endgame before the game begins.

I also found out why I should never reveal "why" to others. A little knowledge withheld is a great advantage one should store for future use. That is the power of chess. It is a game of secrets in which one must show and never tell.

I loved the secrets I found within the sixty-four black and white squares. I carefully drew a handmade chessboard and pinned it to the wall next to my bed, where I would stare for hours at imaginary battles. Soon I no longer lost any games or Life Savers, but I lost my adversaries. Winston and Vincent decided they were more interested in roaming the streets after school in their Hopalong Cassidy cowboy hats.

On a cold spring afternoon, while walking home from school, I detoured through the playground at the end of our alley. I saw a group of old men, two seated across a folding table playing a game of chess, others smoking pipes, eating peanuts, and watching. I ran home and grabbed Vincent's chess set, which was bound in a cardboard box with rubber bands. I also carefully selected two prized rolls of Life Savers. I came back to the park and approached a man who was observing the game.

"Want to play?" I asked him. His face widened with surprise and he grinned as he looked at the box under my arm.

"Little sister, been a long time since I play with dolls," he said, smiling benevolently. I quickly put the box down next to him on the bench and displayed my retort.

Lau Po, as he allowed me to call him, turned out to be a much better player than my brothers. I lost many games and many Life Savers. But over the weeks, with each diminishing roll of candies, I added new secrets. Lau Po gave me the names. The Double Attack from the East and West Shores. Throwing Stones on the Drowning Man. The Sudden Meeting of the Clan. The Surprise from the Sleeping Guard. The Humble Servant Who Kills the King. Sand in the Eyes of Advancing Forces. A Double Killing Without Blood.

There were also the fine points of chess etiquette. Keep captured men in neat rows, as well-tended prisoners. Never announce "Check" with vanity, lest someone with an unseen sword slit your throat. Never hurl pieces into the sandbox after you have lost a game, because then you must find them again, by yourself, after apologizing to all around you. By the end of the summer, Lau Po had taught me all he knew, and I had become a better chess player.

A small weekend crowd of Chinese people and tourists would gather as I played and defeated my opponents one by one. My mother would join the crowds during these outdoor exhibition games. She sat proudly on the bench, telling my admirers with proper Chinese humility, "Is luck."

A man who watched me play in the park suggested that my mother allow me to play in local chess tournaments. My mother smiled graciously, an answer that meant nothing. I desperately wanted to go, but I bit back my tongue. I knew she would not let me play among strangers. So as we walked home I said in a small voice that I didn't want to play in the local tournament. They would have American rules. If I lost, I would bring shame on my family.

"Is shame you fall down nobody push you," said my mother.

During my first tournament, my mother sat with me in the front row as I waited for my turn. I frequently bounced my legs to unstick them from the cold metal seat of the folding chair. When my name was called, I leapt up. My mother unwrapped something in her lap. It was her *chang*, a small tablet of red jade which held the sun's fire. "Is luck," she whispered, and tucked it into my dress pocket. I turned to my opponent, a fifteen-year-old boy from Oakland. He looked at me, wrinkling his nose.

As I began to play, the boy disappeared, the color ran out of the room, and I saw only my white pieces and his black ones waiting on the other side. A light wind began blowing past my ears. It whispered secrets only I could hear.

"Blow from the South," it murmured. "The wind leaves no trail." I saw a clear path, the traps to avoid. The crowd rustled. "Shhh! Shhh!" said the corners of the room. The wind blew stronger. "Throw sand from the East to distract him." The knight came forward ready for the sacrifice. The wind hissed, louder and louder. "Blow, blow, blow. He cannot see. He is blind now. Make him lean away from the wind so he is easier to knock down."

"Check," I said, as the wind roared with laughter. The wind died down to little puffs, my own breath.

My mother placed my first trophy next to a new plastic chess set that the neighborhood Tao society had given to me. As she wiped each piece with a soft cloth, she said, "Next time win more, lose less."

"Ma, it's not how many pieces you lose," I said. "Sometimes you need to lose pieces to get ahead."

"Better to lose less, see if you really need."

At the next tournament, I won again, but it was my mother who wore the triumphant grin.

"Lost eight piece this time. Last time was eleven. What I tell you? Better off lose less!" I was annoyed, but I couldn't say anything.

I attended more tournaments, each one farther away from home. I won all games, in all divisions. The Chinese bakery downstairs from our flat displayed my growing collection of trophies in its window, amidst the dust-covered cakes that were never picked up. The day after I won an important regional tournament, the window encased a fresh sheet cake with whipped-cream frosting and red script saying "Congratulations, Waverly Jong, Chinatown Chess Champion." Soon after that, a flower shop, headstone engraver, and funeral parlor offered to sponsor me in national tournaments. That's when my mother decided I no longer had to do the dishes. Winston and Vincent had to do my chores.

"Why does she get to play and we do all the work," complained Vincent.

"Is new American rules," said my mother. "Meimei play, squeeze all her brains out for win chess. You play, worth squeeze towel."

By my ninth birthday, I was a national chess champion. I was still some 429 points away from grand-master status, but I was touted as the Great American Hope, a child prodigy and a girl to boot. They ran a photo of me in *Life* magazine next to a quote in which Bobby Fischer said, "There will never be a woman grand master." "Your move, Bobby," said the caption.

The day they took the magazine picture I wore neatly plaited braids clipped with plastic barrettes trimmed with rhinestones. I was playing in a large high school auditorium that echoed with phlegmy coughs and the squeaky rubber knobs of chair legs sliding across freshly waxed wooden floors. Seated across from me was an American man, about the same age as Lau Po, maybe fifty. I remember that his sweaty brow seemed to weep at my every move. He wore a dark, malodorous suit. One of his pockets was stuffed with a great white kerchief on which he wiped his palm before sweeping his hand over the chosen chess piece with great flourish.

In my crisp pink-and-white dress with scratchy lace at the neck, one of two my mother had sewn for these special occasions, I would clasp my hands under my chin, the delicate points of my elbows poised lightly on the table in the manner my mother had shown me for posing for the press. I would swing my patent leather shoes back and forth like an impatient child riding on a school bus. Then I would pause, suck in my lips, twirl my chosen piece in midair as if undecided, and then firmly plant it in its new threatening place, with a triumphant smile thrown back at my opponent for good measure.

I no longer played in the alley of Waverly Place. I never visited the playground where the pigeons and old men gathered. I went to school, then directly home to learn new chess secrets, cleverly concealed advantages, more escape routes.

But I found it difficult to concentrate at home. My mother had a habit of standing over me while I plotted out my games. I think she thought of herself as my protective ally. Her lips would be sealed tight, and after each move I made, a soft "Hmmmmph" would escape from her nose.

"Ma, I can't practice when you stand there like that," I said one day. She retreated to the kitchen and made loud noises with the pots and pans. When the crashing stopped, I could see out of the corner of my eye that she was standing in the doorway. "Hmmmmph!" Only this one came out of her tight throat.

My parents made many concessions to allow me to practice. One time I complained that the bedroom I shared was so noisy that I couldn't think. Thereafter, my brothers slept in a bed in the living room facing the street. I said I couldn't finish my rice; my head didn't work right when my stomach was too full. I left the table with half-finished bowls and nobody complained. But there was one duty I couldn't avoid. I had to accompany my mother on Saturday market days when I had no tournament to play. My mother would proudly walk with me, visiting many shops, buying very little. "This my daughter Wave-ly Jong," she said to whoever looked her way.

One day after we left a shop I said under my breath, "I wish you wouldn't do that, telling everybody I'm your daughter." My mother stopped walking. Crowds of people with heavy bags pushed past us on the sidewalk, bumping into first one shoulder, than another.

"Aiii-ya. So shame be with mother?" She grasped my hand even tighter as she glared at me.

I looked down. "It's not that, it's just so obvious. It's just so embarrassing."

"Embarrass you be my daughter?" Her voice was cracking with anger.

"That's not what I meant. That's not what I said."

"What you say?"

I knew it was a mistake to say anything more, but I heard my voice speaking, "Why do you have to use me to show off? If you want to show off, then why don't you learn to play chess?"

My mother's eyes turned into dangerous black slits. She had no words for me, just sharp silence.

I felt the wind rushing around my hot ears. I jerked my hand out of my mother's tight grasp and spun around, knocking into an old woman. Her bag of groceries spilled to the ground.

"Aii-ya! Stupid girl!" my mother and the woman cried. Oranges and tin cans careened down the sidewalk. As my mother stooped to help the old woman pick up the escaping food, I took off.

I raced down the street, dashing between people, not looking back as my mother screamed shrilly, "Meimei! Meimei!" I fled down an alley, past dark, curtained shops and merchants washing the grime off their windows. I sped into the sunlight, into a large street crowded with tourists examining trinkets and souvenirs. I ducked into another dark alley, down another street, up another alley. I ran until it hurt and I realized I had nowhere to go, that I was not running from anything. The alleys contained no escape routes.

My breath came out like angry smoke. It was cold. I sat down on an upturned plastic pail next to a stack of empty boxes, cupping my chin with my hands, thinking hard. I imagined my mother, first walking briskly down one street or another looking for me, then giving up and returning home to await my arrival. After two hours, I stood up on creaking legs and slowly walked home.

The alley was quiet and I could see the yellow lights shining from our flat like two tiger's eyes in the night. I climbed the sixteen steps to the door, advancing quietly up each so as not to make any warning sounds. I turned the knob; the door was locked. I heard a chair moving, quick steps, the locks turning—click! click! click!—and then the door opened.

"About time you got home," said Vincent. "Boy, are you in trouble."

He slid back to the dinner table. On a platter were the remains of a large fish, its fleshy head still connected to bones swimming upstream in vain escape. Standing there waiting for my punishment, I heard my mother speak in a dry voice.

"We not concerning this girl. This girl not have concerning for us."

Nobody looked at me. Bone chopsticks clinked against the inside of bowls being emptied into hungry mouths.

I walked into my room, closed the door, and lay down on my bed. The room was dark, the ceiling filled with shadows from the dinnertime lights of neighboring flats.

In my head, I saw a chessboard with sixty-four black and white squares. Opposite me was my opponent, two angry black slits. She wore a triumphant smile. "Strongest wind cannot be seen," she said.

Her black men advanced across the plane, slowly marching to each successive level as a single unit. My white pieces screamed as they scurried and fell off the board one by one. As her men drew closer to my edge, I felt myself growing light. I rose up into the air and flew out the window. Higher and higher, above the alley, over the tops of tiled roofs, where I was gathered up by the wind and pushed up toward the night sky until everything below me disappeared and I was alone.

I closed my eyes and pondered my next move.

1989

# LEO TOLSTOY
## *1828–1910*

Tolstoy—generally considered the greatest of nineteenth-century novelists—was born at his family estate, Yasnaya Polyana, Russia, into the Russian nobility. His youth was restless and without direction. He was vain, dissolute, and immoderate, a poor student and a reckless gambler. It was only after he entered military service that he became interested in writing—autobiographical stories first, then sketches of military life as he knew it during the Crimean War. Leaving the army in 1857, he traveled in western Europe, but his disdain for the vanities of cultured life was merely deepened by what he saw in Paris. On his return to Russia he started an experimental school for children, structuring it on generally anarchic principles. At the same time he was producing the novels that ensure his place in world literature: *War and Peace* (1869), an account of Russia in the years of Napoleon's conquests and his attempt to consolidate his empire by the conquest of Russia; and *Anna Karenina* (1877), the story of a woman caught in the immemorial conflict of personal, biological, and social demands, finally destroyed by her inability to reconcile them. In spite of his triumph with these novels, Tolstoy was painfully dissatisfied with them as he grew older, considering them flawed by the earthly preoccupations he was trying to escape. To appease his self-doubt he adopted a primitive version of Christianity that often put him at odds with the established Orthodox church. For nearly twenty years he wrote chiefly on moral and spiritual matters, and these later moralistic writings, including the novel *Resurrection* (1899), gave him enormous moral influence throughout the world; his home at Yasnaya Polyana became a mecca for pilgrims who sought his advice on the right way to live. His Russian followers were persecuted by the government, though he himself remained immune from political pressure. But he never found the spiritual peace for which he struggled; the turbulence of his inner conflicts drove him several times to leave his home and his wife, and on one of these tormented flights he died in a provincial railway station.

# The Death of Ivan Ilyich[1]

## I

During a break in the hearing of the Melvinsky case, the members of the court and the prosecutor met in Ivan Yegorovich Shebek's room in the big

1. Translated by Peter Carson and Mary Beard.

law courts building and began talking about the famous Krasovsky case. Fyodor Vasilyevich became heated, contending that it didn't come under their jurisdiction; Ivan Yegorovich held his ground; while Pyotr Ivanovich, not having joined in the argument at the beginning, took no part in it and was looking through the *Gazette*, which had just been delivered.

"Gentlemen!" he said. "Ivan Ilyich has died."

"He hasn't!"

"Look, read this," he said to Fyodor Vasilyevich, handing him a fresh copy which still smelled of ink.

Within a black border was printed: "Praskovya Fyodorovna Golovina with deep sorrow informs family and friends of the passing of her beloved spouse Ivan Ilyich Golovin, member of the Court of Justice, which took place on the 4th of February of this year 1882. The funeral will be on Friday at 1 P.M."

Ivan Ilyich was a colleague of the gentlemen meeting there and they all liked him. He had been ill for several weeks; people were saying his illness was incurable. His position had been kept for him, but there had been conjectures that, in the event of his death, Alekseyev might be appointed to his position, and either Vinnikov or Shtabel to Alekseyev's. So on hearing of Ivan Ilyich's death the first thought of each of the gentlemen meeting in the room was of the significance the death might have for the transfer or promotion of the members themselves or their friends.

*Now I will probably get Shtabel's or Vinnikov's position,* thought Fyodor Vasilyevich. *It was promised to me long ago and this promotion means a raise of eight hundred rubles, plus a private office.*

*Now I must ask about the transfer of my brother-in-law from Kaluga,* thought Pyotr Ivanovich. *My wife will be very pleased. Now she won't be able to say that I've never done anything for her family.*

"I thought he wouldn't leave his bed," Pyotr Ivanovich said aloud. "Such a pity."

"What was actually wrong with him?"

"The doctors couldn't make a diagnosis. That is, they did, but different ones. When I saw him the last time, I thought he would recover."

"And I didn't go and see him after the holidays. I kept meaning to."

"Did he have any money?"

"I think his wife had a very small income. But next to nothing."

"Yes, we'll have to go and see her. They lived a terribly long way off."

"That is, a long way from you. Everything's a long way from you."

"He just can't forgive me for living on the other side of the river," said Pyotr Ivanovich, smiling at Shebek. And they started talking about distances in the city, and went back into the courtroom.

Apart from the thoughts the death brought each of them about the possible moves and changes at work that might follow, the actual fact of the death of a close acquaintance evoked, as always, in all who learned of it a complacent feeling that it was "he who had died, not I."

*So—he's dead; but here I am still,* each thought or felt. At this point his closer acquaintances, the so-called friends of Ivan Ilyich, involuntarily thought that they now needed to carry out the very tedious requirements of etiquette and go to the requiem service and pay a visit of condolence to the widow.

Closest of all were Fyodor Vasilyevich and Pyotr Ivanovich.

Pyotr Ivanovich was a friend from law school and considered himself under an obligation to Ivan Ilyich.

Having given his wife over dinner the news of Ivan Ilyich's death and his thoughts about the possibility of his brother-in-law's transfer to their district, Pyotr Ivanovich didn't lie down to have a rest but put on a formal tailcoat and drove to Ivan Ilyich's.

At the entrance to Ivan Ilyich's apartment stood a carriage and two cabs. Downstairs in the hall by the coatrack, leaning against the wall, was the brocade-covered lid of the coffin with tassels and a gold braid that had been cleaned with powder. Two ladies in black were taking off their fur coats. One of them, Ivan Ilyich's sister, he knew; the other was an unknown lady. Pyotr Ivanovich's colleague Schwarz was coming downstairs and, seeing from the top step who had come in, he winked at him as if to say, "Ivan Ilyich has made a silly mess of things; you and I have done things differently."

Schwarz's face with his English side-whiskers and his whole thin figure in a tailcoat as usual had an elegant solemnity, and this solemnity, which was always at odds with Schwarz's playful character, was especially piquant here. So Pyotr Ivanovich thought.

Pyotr Ivanovich let the ladies go in front of him and slowly followed them up the stairs. Schwarz didn't come down but stayed at the top. Pyotr Ivanovich understood why: he obviously wanted to arrange where they should play *vint*[2] today. The ladies went up the stairs to the widow but Schwarz, with a serious set to his strong lips and a playful look, indicated by a twitch of his eyebrows that Pyotr Ivanovich should go to the right, into the room where the corpse lay.

Pyotr Ivanovich went in, feeling, as is always the case, at a loss as to what he should do there. One thing he did know was that in these circumstances it never does any harm to cross oneself. He wasn't altogether sure whether one should also bow and so he chose a middle course: entering the room, he started to cross himself and made a kind of slight bow. Insofar as the movements of his head and hands would allow, he looked round the room at the same time. Two young men, probably nephews, one of them a gymnasium pupil, were crossing themselves as they left the room. An old woman stood motionless, and a lady with oddly arched eyebrows was saying something to her in a whisper. A church lector in a frock coat with a vigorous and decisive way to him was reading something out loudly with an expression that permitted no contradiction; the peasant manservant Gerasim, stepping lightly in front of Pyotr Ivanovich, scattered something on the ground. Seeing that, Pyotr Ivanovich at once sensed the faint smell of a decomposing body. On his last visit to Ivan Ilyich he had seen this peasant in the study; he carried out the duties of a sick-nurse, and Ivan Ilyich was especially fond of him. Pyotr Ivanovich kept crossing himself and bowing slightly in an intermediate direction between the coffin, the lector, and the icons on a table in the corner. Then, when he thought the movement of crossing himself with his hand had gone on for too long, he stopped and started to examine the dead man.

The dead man lay, as dead men always do, especially heavily, his stiffened limbs sunk in the padded lining of the coffin with his head bent back forever

---

2. A card game, similar to bridge.

on the pillow, and, as always with dead men, his yellow waxen forehead sticking out, showing bald patches on his hollow temples, his nose protruding as if it pressed on his upper lip. He had greatly changed, had become even thinner since Pyotr Ivanovich had seen him, but like all dead men, his face was handsomer, above all more imposing than when he was alive. On his face was an expression that said what had to be done had been done, and done properly. This expression also held a reproach or reminder to the living. Pyotr Ivanovich found this reminder inappropriate—or at the least one not applying to himself. This gave Pyotr Ivanovich an unpleasant feeling, and so he hurriedly crossed himself once more and turned, too hurriedly he thought, and not in accordance with propriety, and went to the door. Schwarz was waiting for him in the next room, his legs wide apart and both hands playing behind his back with his top hat. One look at Schwarz's playful, neat, and elegant figure refreshed Pyotr Ivanovich. Pyotr Ivanovich felt that Schwarz stood above all this and didn't allow himself to give in to depressing thoughts. The very way he looked stated the following: the fact of Ivan Ilyich's requiem cannot serve as a sufficient reason to consider the order of the courts disrupted; in other words, nothing can stop us unsealing and shuffling a pack of cards this evening while the manservant puts out four fresh candles; in general there are no grounds for assuming that this fact can prevent us from spending a pleasant evening, even today. He said this in a whisper to Pyotr Ivanovich as he came in, proposing they meet for a game at Fyodor Vasilyevich's. But apparently Pyotr Ivanovich was not fated to play *vint* this evening. Praskovya Fyodorovna, a short, plump woman who broadened from the shoulders down in spite of all her efforts to achieve the opposite, was dressed all in black with her head covered in lace and with oddly arched eyebrows like the lady standing by the coffin. She came out of her rooms with the other ladies, and taking them to the door where the dead man lay, said:

"Now there'll be the requiem; do go in."

Schwarz stopped, making a vague bow—clearly neither accepting nor rejecting this proposal. Praskovya Fyodorovna, recognizing Pyotr Ivanovich, sighed, went right up to him, took him by the hand, and said:

"I know that you were a true friend of Ivan Ilyich . . ." and looked at him, waiting for an action on his part that corresponded to these words.

Pyotr Ivanovich knew that just as in that room one had had to cross oneself, so here one must press the hand, sigh, and say, "Believe me!" And that's what he did. And having done it he felt that the desired result had been obtained: he was moved and she was moved.

"Come while they haven't started in there; I need to talk to you," said the widow. "Give me your hand."

Pyotr Ivanovich gave his hand and they went off into the inner rooms, past Schwarz who winked sadly at Pyotr Ivanovich. "There's your *vint* gone! Don't take it out on us; we'll find another partner. Maybe you can cut in once you've gotten free," said his playful look.

Pyotr Ivanovich sighed even more deeply and sadly, and Praskovya Fyodorovna gratefully pressed his hand. They went into her dimly lit drawing room hung with pink cretonne and sat down by a table, she on a sofa and Pyotr Ivanovich on a low pouf built on springs that awkwardly gave way as he sat down. (Praskovya Fyodorovna was going to warn him to sit on another chair but found such a warning inappropriate for the situation and changed her mind.) As he sat down on the pouf, Pyotr Ivanovich remembered how Ivan Ilyich had arranged this drawing room and consulted him about this very pink cretonne with green leaves. On her way to sit down on the sofa, as she passed the table (the whole drawing room was full of furniture and knick-knacks), the widow caught the lace of her black mantilla on the carving of the table. Pyotr Ivanovich got up to unhook her, and the sprung pouf now released below began to sway and push at him. The widow started to unhook the lace herself and Pyotr Ivanovich sat down again, quelling the rebellious pouf underneath him. But the widow hadn't unhooked it all, and Pyotr Iva-novich again got up and the pouf again rebelled and even made a noise. When all this was over she took out a clean cambric handkerchief and began to cry. Pyotr Ivanovich felt chilled by the episode of the lace and the battle with the pouf and sat frowning. This awkward situation was interrupted by Sokolov, Ivan Ilyich's butler, reporting that the place in the cemetery Praskovya Fyodor-ovna had selected would cost two hundred rubles. She stopped crying and, looking at Pyotr Ivanovich with the air of a victim, said in French that she was suffering greatly. Pyotr Ivanovich made a silent sign expressing a firm conviction that it couldn't be otherwise.

"Do smoke, please," she said in a gracious and, at the same time, broken voice and talked to Sokolov about the matter of the price of the place in the cemetery. Pyotr Ivanovich smoked and heard her asking very detailed ques-tions about the different prices of plots and deciding on the one that should be bought. When that was done, she went on to give instructions about the singers. Sokolov went out.

"I do everything myself," she said to Pyotr Ivanovich, moving some albums lying on the table to one side. Noticing that his ash was posing a threat to the table, she speedily pushed an ashtray towards Pyotr Ivanovich and said, "I find it a pretence to state that because of grief I can't deal with practical mat-ters. On the contrary, if there is something that can ... not console ... but distract me, then it's bothering about him." She again took out her handker-chief as if she were going to cry, and suddenly, as if pulling herself together, she shook herself and began to speak quietly:

"However, I have to talk to you about something."

Pyotr Ivanovich bowed, not letting the pouf release its springs, which had at once started to move underneath him.

"He suffered terribly in the last days."

"Did he suffer very much?" Pyotr Ivanovich asked.

"Oh. Terribly! At the end he never stopped screaming, not for minutes, for hours. For three whole days he screamed without drawing breath. It was unbearable. I can't understand how I bore it; one could hear it from three doors away. Oh, what I've been through!"

"And was he really conscious?" Pyotr Ivanovich asked.

"Yes," she whispered, "till the final moment. He said goodbye to us a quar-ter of an hour before he died and asked as well for Volodya to be taken out."

The thought of the sufferings of a man he had known so well, first as a cheerful lad, a schoolboy, then as an adult colleague, suddenly horrified Pyotr Ivanovich in spite of his unpleasant consciousness of his own and this woman's pretense. He saw again that forehead, the nose pressing on the lip, and he became fearful for himself.

*Three days of terrible suffering and death. That can happen to me too, now, any minute,* he thought, and for a moment he became frightened. But right away, he didn't know how, there came to his aid the ordinary thought that this had happened to Ivan Ilyich and not to him, and this ought not and could not happen to him; that in thinking like this he was giving in to gloomy thoughts, which one shouldn't, as had been clear from Schwarz's face. And having reached this conclusion, Pyotr Ivanovich was reassured and started to ask with interest about the details of Ivan Ilyich's end, as if death were an adventure peculiar to Ivan Ilyich but absolutely not to himself.

After some talk about the details of the truly terrible physical sufferings which Ivan Ilyich had undergone (details that Pyotr Ivanovich learned only by way of the effect that Ivan Ilyich's torment had had on Praskovya Fyodorovna's nerves), the widow apparently found it necessary to move on to business.

"Ah, Pyotr Ivanovich, it's so hard, so terribly hard." And she again started to cry.

Pyotr Ivanovich sighed and waited for to her to blow her nose. When she had blown her nose, he said:

"Believe me . . ." and again she talked away and unburdened herself of what was clearly her main business with him—how on her husband's death she could get money from the treasury. She gave the appearance of asking Pyotr Ivanovich for advice about the pension, but he saw that she already knew down to the smallest details even what he didn't know—everything that one could extract from the public purse on this death—but that she wanted to learn if one couldn't somehow extract a bit more money. Pyotr Ivanovich tried to think of a way, but, having thought a little and out of politeness abusing the government for its meanness, he said that he thought one couldn't get more. Then she sighed and clearly began to think of a way to get rid of her visitor. He understood this, put out his cigarette, got up, shook her hand, and went into the hall.

In the dining room with the clock that Ivan Ilyich had been so pleased to buy in a junk shop, Pyotr Ivanovich met the priest and also a few acquaintances who had come to the requiem, and he saw a beautiful young lady he knew, Ivan Ilyich's daughter. She was all in black. That made her very slender waist seem even more so. She had a somber, decisive, almost angry expression. She bowed to Pyotr Ivanovich as if he had done something wrong. Behind the daughter, with a similarly offended expression, stood a rich young man whom Pyotr Ivanovich knew, an examining magistrate who he'd heard was her fiancé. He glumly bowed to them and was about to go on into the room where the dead man lay when from under the stairs there appeared the figure of the son, a gymnasium student, who looked terribly like Ivan Ilyich. He was a little Ivan Ilyich just as Pyotr Ivanovich remembered him at law school. His eyes were tearstained and had the look that the eyes of boys with impure thoughts have at the age of thirteen or fourteen. When he recognized Pyotr Ivanovich the boy began to scowl sullenly and shamefacedly. Pyotr Ivanovich nodded to him and went into the dead man's room. The requiem began—candles, groans, incense, tears, sobs. Pyotr Ivanovich stood frowning, looking at the feet in front of him. He didn't look once at the dead man and right until the end didn't give in to any depressing influences. He was one of the first to leave. There was no one in the hall. Gerasim, the peasant manservant, darted out of the dead man's study, rummaged with his strong hands among all the fur coats to find Pyotr Ivanovich's, and gave it to him.

"So, Gerasim my friend," said Pyotr Ivanovich in order to say something. "It's sad, isn't it?"

"It's God's will. We'll all be there," said Gerasim, showing his white, regular, peasant's teeth, and like a man in the full swing of intensive work, briskly opened the door, called the coachman, helped Pyotr Ivanovich in, and jumped back to the steps as if trying to think what else he might do.

It was particularly pleasant for Pyotr Ivanovich to breathe the fresh air after the smells of incense, the dead body, and the carbolic acid.[3]

"Where to, sir?" asked the coachman.

"It's not late. So I'll still drop in at Fyodor Vasilyevich's."

And off Pyotr Ivanovich went. And indeed he found his friends finishing the first rubber;[4] it was easy for him to cut in as a fifth.

## I I

Ivan Ilyich's past life had been very simple and ordinary and very awful.

Ivan Ilyich had died at the age of forty-five, a member of the Court of Justice. He was the son of a St. Petersburg civil servant who had in various ministries and departments the kind of career that brings people to a position in which, although it is quite clear that they are incapable of performing any meaningful job, they still by reason of their long past service and seniority cannot be dismissed; so they receive invented, fictitious positions and thousands of rubles, from six to ten thousand, which are not fictitious, with which they live on to a ripe old age.

Such was Privy Councillor Ilya Yefimovich Golovin, the superfluous member of various superfluous institutions.

He had three sons, Ivan Ilyich being the second. The eldest had the same kind of career as his father, only in a different ministry, and he was already approaching the age at which salary starts increasing automatically. The third son was a failure. Wherever he had been in various positions he had made a mess of things and he was now working in the railways. Both his father and his brothers, and especially their wives, not only didn't like to see him but didn't even mention his existence unless absolutely compelled to do so. Their sister was married to Baron Gref, the same kind of St. Petersburg civil servant as his father-in-law. Ivan Ilyich was *le phénix de la famille*,[5] as they said. He wasn't as cold and precise as the eldest or as hopeless as the youngest. He was somewhere between them—a clever, lively, pleasant, and decent man. He had been educated with his younger brother in the law school. The younger one didn't finish and was expelled from the fifth class. Ivan Ilyich completed the course with good marks. In law school he was already what he would later be during his entire life: a capable, cheerful, good-natured, and sociable man, but one who strictly did what he considered his duty, and he considered his

---

**3.** A disinfectant.   **4.** Round of hands in bridge.   **5.** The paragon of the family (French).

duty to be everything that it was considered to be by his superiors. Neither as a boy nor afterward as a grown man did he seek to ingratiate himself, but there was in him from a young age the characteristic of being drawn to people of high station like a fly toward the light; he adopted their habits and their views on life and established friendly relations with them. All the passions of childhood and youth went by without leaving much of a trace in him; he gave in both to sensuality and to vanity, and—toward the end, in the senior classes—to liberalism, but always within the defined limits that his sense accurately indicated to him as correct.

At law school he had done things that previously had seemed to him quite vile and had filled him with self-disgust while he did them; but later, seeing these things were done by people in high positions and were not thought by them to be bad, he didn't quite think of them as good but completely forgot them and wasn't at all troubled by memories of them.

Having left law school in the tenth class and received money from his father for fitting himself out, Ivan Ilyich ordered clothes at Sharmer's,[6] hung on his watch chain a medallion with the inscription *respice finem*,[7] took his leave of the princely patron of the school and his tutor, dined with his schoolmates at Donon's,[8] and, equipped with a new and fashionable trunk, linen, clothes, shaving and toilet things, and traveling rug ordered and bought from the very best shops, he went off to a provincial city to the post of assistant to the governor for special projects, which his father had procured for him.

In the provincial city Ivan Ilyich at once established for himself the kind of easy and pleasant position he had had at law school. He worked, made his career, and at the same time amused himself in a pleasant and seemly way; from time to time he went around the district towns on a mission from his chief. He behaved to both superiors and inferiors with dignity and he carried out the responsibilities he had been given, mainly for the affairs of religious dissenters, with an exactness and incorruptible honesty of which he could not but be proud.

In his work, despite his youth and liking for frivolous amusement, he was exceptionally reserved, formal, and even severe; but in society he was often playful and witty and always good-humored, well-behaved and a *bon enfant*,[9] as his chief and his chief's wife, with whom he was one of the family, used to say of him.

There was also in the provincial city an affair with one of the ladies who attached herself to the smart lawyer; there was a little dressmaker; there were drinking sessions with visiting aides-de-camp and trips to a remote street after supper; there was also some fawning deference to his chief and even to his chief's wife, but all this wore such a high tone of probity that it couldn't be described in bad words; all this could only go under the rubric of the French expression *il faut que jeunesse se passe*.[1] Everything took place with clean hands, in clean shirts, with French words, and, most importantly, in the highest society, consequently with the approval of people in high position.

Ivan Ilyich worked in this way for five years, and then there came changes in his official life. New legal bodies were founded; new men were needed.

---

6. A fashionable tailor in St. Petersburg.  7. That is, look before you leap (Latin).  8. A first-class restaurant in St. Petersburg.  9. Good boy (French).  1. Youth must have its fling (French).

And Ivan Ilyich was this new man.

Ivan Ilyich was offered the position of examining magistrate and he accepted it, despite the fact that this position was in another province and he had to abandon the relationships he had established and establish new ones. His friends saw Ivan Ilyich off: they took a group photograph, they presented him with a silver cigarette case, and off he went to his new position.

As an examining magistrate Ivan Ilyich was just as *comme il faut*,[2] well-behaved, capable of separating his official duties from his private life and of inspiring general respect as he had been as a special projects officer. The actual work of a magistrate had much more interest and attraction for him than his previous work. In his previous position it had been pleasant to walk with a light step in his Sharmer uniform past trembling petitioners and envious officials waiting to be seen, straight into his chief's room to sit down with him over a cup of tea with a cigarette. But there were few people who depended directly on his say-so—only district police officers and religious schismatics when he was sent on missions—and he liked to treat such people dependent on him politely, almost as comrades; he liked to let them feel that here he was, someone who could crush them, treating them in a simple and friendly way. There were only a few such people then. Now, as an examining magistrate, Ivan Ilyich felt that all of them, all without exception, even the most important, self-satisfied people, were in his hands, and that he only had to write certain words on headed paper and this or that important, self-satisfied man would be brought to him as a defendant or a witness, and if he wouldn't let him sit down, would have to stand before him and answer his questions. Ivan Ilyich never abused this power of his—on the contrary he tried to use it lightly—but the consciousness of this power and the possibility of using it lightly constituted for him the chief interest and attraction of his new job. In the work itself, in the actual investigations, Ivan Ilyich very quickly mastered a way of setting aside all circumstances that didn't relate to the investigation and expressing the most complicated case in a terminology in which the case only appeared on paper in its externals and his personal view was completely excluded, and most importantly all requisite formality was observed. This work was something new. And he was one of the first people who worked out the practical application of the statutes of 1864.[3]

Moving to a new city to the post of examining magistrate, Ivan Ilyich made new acquaintances and connections, positioned himself afresh, and adopted a slightly different tone. He positioned himself at a certain respectable distance from the governing authorities, but chose the best circle of the lawyers and nobles who lived in the city and adopted a tone of slight dissatisfaction with government, moderate liberalism, and enlightened civic-mindedness. Moreover, without changing the elegance of his dress, in his new job Ivan Ilyich stopped shaving his chin and let his beard grow freely.

Ivan Ilyich's life turned out very pleasantly in the new city as well: the society that took a critical view of the governor was good and friendly; his salary was larger; and a not inconsiderable pleasure was added to his life by *vint*,

---

**2.** Proper, decorous (French).   **3.** A thorough reform of judicial proceedings in Russia, which followed the freeing of the serfs in 1861.

which Ivan Ilyich started to play, having an ability to play cards cheerfully, quick-wittedly, and very shrewdly so that generally he won.

After two years working in the new city Ivan Ilyich met his future wife. Praskovya Fyodorovna Mikhel was the most attractive, cleverest, most brilliant girl of the group in which Ivan Ilyich moved. Among the other amusements and relaxations from the labors of a magistrate Ivan Ilyich developed a playful, easy relationship with Praskovya Fyodorovna.

While he had been a special assignments official Ivan Ilyich used to dance as a matter of course; as an examining magistrate he now danced only on special occasions. He danced now in the sense that although he was a part of the new institutions and in the fifth grade,[4] when it came to dancing, then he could show that in this field he could do things better than others. So from time to time at the end of an evening he used to dance with Praskovya Fyodorovna, and it was during these dances in particular that he conquered her. She fell in love with him. Ivan Ilyich didn't have a clear, defined intention of marrying, but when the girl fell in love with him, he asked himself a question. "Actually, why not get married?" he said to himself.

Miss Praskovya Fyodorovna was from a good noble family, was not bad-looking, and had a bit of money. Ivan Ilyich could aspire to a more brilliant match, but this too was a good match. Ivan Ilyich had his salary; she, he hoped, would have as much again. The family connection was good; she was a sweet, pretty, and absolutely decent woman. To say that Ivan Ilyich married because he fell in love with his bride and found in her sympathy for his views on life would have been as unjust as to say that he married because people in his social circle approved of the match. Ivan Ilyich married because of both considerations: he was doing something pleasant for himself in acquiring such a wife, and at the same time he was doing something his superiors thought a right thing to do.

And so Ivan Ilyich married.

The actual process of marriage and the first period of married life, with its conjugal caresses, new furniture, new china, and new linen, went very well until his wife's pregnancy, so that Ivan Ilyich was beginning to think that marriage not only would not destroy the character of an easy, pleasant, cheerful life, one wholly decorous and approved of by society, which Ivan Ilyich thought the true quality of life, but would enhance it further. But then from the first months of his wife's pregnancy something new appeared, something unexpected, unpleasant, oppressive, and indecorous that one couldn't expect and from which one couldn't escape.

His wife for no reason, so Ivan Ilyich thought, as he said to himself, began *de gaieté de coeur*[5] to destroy the pleasant tenor and decorum of life. She was jealous of him without any cause, demanded attentions to herself from him, found fault with everything, and made crude and unpleasant scenes.

At first Ivan Ilyich had hoped to be freed from the unpleasantness of this situation by the same easy and decorous attitude to life which had rescued him before—he tried to ignore his wife's state of mind and continued to live pleasantly and decorously as before: he invited friends home for a game of

---

**4.** Fifth highest level of official rank, out of fourteen; the lowest level of the higher eschelons of Civil Service.    **5.** From sheer impulsiveness (French).

cards; he tried to go out to his club or see his friends. But on one occasion his wife started to abuse him rudely with such energy and continued to abuse him so persistently every time he didn't fulfill her demands, clearly having made a firm decision not to stop until he would submit—that is, sit at home and be miserable like her—that Ivan Ilyich was horrified. He understood that married life—at any rate with his wife—does not always make for the pleasures and decorum of life but on the contrary often destroys them, and therefore it was essential to protect himself from this destruction. And Ivan Ilyich began to seek the means for this. His official work was one thing that impressed Praskovya Fyodorovna, and Ivan Ilyich through his official work and the duties that arose out of it began to fight his wife, securing his own independent world.

A child was born. There were attempts at feeding and various failures in this, along with the real and imaginary illnesses of child and mother. Sympathy for all this was demanded from Ivan Ilyich but he could understand nothing of it. So the requirement of Ivan Ilyich to fence in a world for himself outside of the family became all the more pressing.

As his wife became more irritable and demanding, so Ivan Ilyich moved the center of gravity of his life more and more into his official work. He came to like his work more and became more ambitious than he had been before.

Very soon, not more than a year after their marriage, Ivan Ilyich understood that married life, which offers certain conveniences, in reality is a very complicated and difficult business with which, in order to do one's duty—that is, to lead a decorous life that is approved of by society—one has to develop a defined relationship as one does with one's work.

And Ivan Ilyich did develop for himself such a relationship with married life. He required of family life only those conveniences it could give him, of dinner at home, a mistress of the house, a bed, and most importantly, that decorum of external appearances which were defined by public opinion. For the rest he looked for cheerfulness and pleasure, and if he found them was very grateful; if he met rejection and querulousness, he at once went off into the separate world of official work that he had fenced in for himself and found pleasure there.

Ivan Ilyich was valued as a good official and in three years he was made assistant prosecutor. His new responsibilities, their importance, the ability to bring anyone to trial and send him to prison, the public nature of his speeches, the success Ivan Ilyich had in this work—all of this tied him even more closely to his official work.

More children came. His wife became more and more querulous and angry, but the relationship Ivan Ilyich had developed with domestic life had made him almost impervious to her querulousness.

After seven years of working in one city Ivan Ilyich was promoted to the position of prosecutor in a different province. They moved; they now had little money and his wife didn't like the place to which they had moved. Though his salary was more than it had been, life cost more; also two children died, and so family life became even more unpleasant for Ivan Ilyich.

Praskovya Fyodorovna blamed her husband for all the misfortunes that befell them in their new home. Most subjects of conversation between husband

and wife, particularly the education of the children, led to questions that recalled past disputes, and quarrels were ready to break out at every minute. There remained only rare periods of tenderness that came to the married couple but did not last long. These were islands on which they landed for a while but then again sailed off into the sea of hidden animosity which expressed itself in their alienation from each other. This alienation might have distressed Ivan Ilyich if he had thought that it should not be like this, but he now recognized this situation not just as normal but as the actual goal of his family life. His object was to free himself more and more from these unpleasant things and to give them a character of innocuous decorum; he achieved it by spending less and less time with his family and when he was forced to do it, he tried to protect his situation by the presence of outsiders. The important thing was that Ivan Ilyich had his official work. For him all the interest of life was concentrated in that official world, and this interest absorbed him. The consciousness of his power, of his ability to bring down anyone he chose to, his importance, even in externals when he entered the court and at meetings with subordinates, his mastery of conducting the work—all this made him feel glad, and together with talking to his friends, with dinners and *vint*, it filled up his life. So overall Ivan Ilyich's life continued to go on as he thought that it should: pleasantly and with decorum.

So he lived for another seven years. His elder daughter was now sixteen, another child had died, and there only remained a boy at the gymnasium, a subject of dissension. Ivan Ilyich had wanted to send him to law school but to spite him Praskovya Fyodorovna had sent the boy to the gymnasium. The daughter was taught at home and had grown into a good-looking girl; the boy too wasn't bad at his studies.

### III

That was Ivan Ilyich's life for seventeen years after his marriage. He was now a senior prosecutor, having refused various promotions in the expectation of a more desirable position, when something very unpleasant happened which completely destroyed the tranquility of his life. Ivan Ilyich was expecting the position of president of the tribunal in a university town, but somehow Hoppe overtook him and got the place. Ivan Ilyich was angry, started to make accusations, and quarreled with him and his closest superiors; they cooled towards him and passed him over for the next appointment.

That was in 1880. That year was the hardest in Ivan Ilyich's life. In that year his salary wasn't sufficient for living; everyone forgot him, and what appeared to him to be the greatest, the cruellest injustice toward him was found by others to be something completely ordinary. Even his father didn't see it as his duty to help him. He felt everyone had abandoned him, considering his situation on a 3,500-ruble salary quite normal and even fortunate. He alone knew that with his consciousness of the injustices done to him, his wife's constant nagging, and the debts he was beginning to run, living above his means—he alone knew that his situation was far from normal.

In the summer of that year, to ease his finances he took some leave and went with his wife to spend the summer at Praskovya Fyodorovna's brother's home.

In the country, without his work, Ivan Ilyich for the first time felt not just boredom but unbearable depression, felt that he could not live like that and that he absolutely had to take some decisive action.

Having spent a sleepless night pacing the terrace, Ivan Ilyich decided to go to Petersburg to make a petition and, in order to punish *them*, those who could not appreciate him, to transfer to another ministry.

The next day, in spite of all the attempts of his wife and brother-in-law to dissuade him, he traveled to Petersburg.

He went for one thing: to obtain a five-thousand-ruble salary. He was no longer holding out for any particular ministry or direction or type of work. He just needed a position, a position on five thousand rubles, in government, in banking, in the railways, in the Empress Maria's Foundations,[6] even in customs, but he absolutely had to have five thousand rubles and he absolutely had to leave the ministry where they couldn't appreciate him.

And now this trip of Ivan Ilyich's was crowned with amazing, unexpected success. In Kursk he was joined in a first-class carriage by F. S. Ilyin, someone he knew, who told him about a telegram the governor of Kursk had just received that announced a reorganization to take place in the ministry: Pyotr Ivanovich's position was going to be taken by Ivan Semyonovich.

The planned upheaval, apart from its significance for Russia, had a particular significance for Ivan Ilyich: by promoting a new face, Pyotr Petrovich, and of course Zakhar Ivanovich, his classmate and friend, it was highly propitious for him.

In Moscow the news was confirmed. And when he reached Petersburg, Ivan Ilyich found Zakhar Ivanovich and got the promise of a sure place in his old ministry of justice.

After a week he telegraphed his wife: *Zakhar has Miller's place stop I receive position at next report.*

Thanks to this change of personnel Ivan Ilyich got this position in his old ministry, which placed him two ranks above his old colleagues as well as a salary of 5,000 rubles and 3,500 for removal expenses. All his anger against his former enemies and the entire ministry was forgotten, and Ivan Ilyich was altogether happy.

Ivan Ilyich returned to the country more cheerful and content than he had ever been. Praskovya Fyodorovna cheered up too and a truce was established between them. Ivan Ilyich told her how in Petersburg everyone had feted him, how all his old enemies had been shamed and were now crawling before him, how he was envied for his position, and especially how highly he was regarded by everyone in Petersburg.

Praskovya Fyodorovna listened to all this and appeared to believe it, and she didn't contradict him in anything but just made plans for their new life in the city to which they were moving. And Ivan Ilyich joyfully saw that these plans were his plans, that the plans were tallying, and that his life which had faltered was again taking on its true and natural character of cheerful pleasantness and decorum.

Ivan Ilyich had come just for a short time. On September 10 he had to take up the new job and furthermore he needed time to settle in their new home,

---

6. Charitable organizations founded by the wife of Tsar Paul I (1754–1801).

to move everything from the provincial city, and to buy and order many more things; in a word, to settle as had been decided in his own mind and almost exactly as had been decided in that of Praskovya Fyodorovna.

And now, when everything had worked out so well and he and his wife were agreed about their goals (and furthermore weren't living much together), they got on harmoniously as they hadn't done since the first years of married life. Ivan Ilyich thought of taking his family away with him immediately but the insistence of his brother-in-law and his wife, who had suddenly become particularly friendly and familial towards Ivan Ilyich and his family, resulted in Ivan Ilyich going away alone.

Ivan Ilyich left, and the cheerful state of mind brought about by his success and the harmony with his wife, one reinforcing the other, stayed with him the whole time. A delightful apartment was found, the very one husband and wife had been dreaming of. High, spacious, old-fashioned reception rooms; a comfortable, imposing study; rooms for his wife and daughter; a schoolroom for his son—everything as if devised purposely for them. Ivan Ilyich set about arranging it himself: he chose wallpaper, he bought more furniture (antiques in particular whose style he found particularly *comme il faut*), he had things upholstered, and it all grew and grew and approached the ideal he had composed for himself. Even when he had half arranged things, his arrangements exceeded his expectation. He understood the *comme il faut* look, elegant without vulgarity, which everything would take on once it was ready. As he went to sleep he imagined to himself how the reception room would be. Looking at the drawing room, which wasn't yet finished, he could already see the fireplace, the screen, the whatnot and the little chairs disposed about the room, the plates and saucers on the walls, and the bronzes all standing in their places. He was pleased by the thought that he would surprise Pasha and Lizanka, his wife and daughter, who also had a taste for this. They were certainly not expecting this. He was particularly successful in finding old things and buying them cheaply; they gave everything a particularly aristocratic air. In his letters he deliberately described everything in less attractive terms than the reality to surprise them. All this absorbed him so much that even his new job absorbed him less than he had expected—though he loved his work. During sittings of the court he had moments of absent mindedness; he started thinking about whether the curtain pelmets should be straight or curved. He was so absorbed by this that he often did things himself; he even moved the furniture about and rehung the curtains himself. Once he got up on a ladder to show a slow-witted decorator how he wanted the drapes hung; he missed his footing and fell, but being a strong and agile man he held his balance and only knocked his side on the handle of the window frame. The bruise was painful but soon disappeared. During all this time Ivan Ilyich felt particularly well and cheerful. He wrote, "I feel I'm fifteen years younger." He thought the work would be finished in September but it dragged on till mid-October. But the apartment was delightful—it wasn't just he who said this but everyone who saw it said so to him.

In actual fact it was the same as the houses of all people who are not so rich but want to be like the rich and so are only like one another: brocade, ebony, flowers, carpets, and bronzes, everything dark and shiny—everything that all people of a certain type do to be like all people of a certain type. And what he had was so like that that one couldn't even notice it, but to him it all looked somehow special. When he met his family at the railway station and took them to his apartment, all finished and lit up, and a manservant in a white tie opened the door into the flower-decked hall, and they went into the drawing room and study, he was very happy, he took them everywhere, drank in their praise, and beamed with pleasure. That evening, when over tea Praskovya Fyodorovna asked him among other things how he had fallen, he laughed and in front of them showed how he had gone flying and frightened the decorator.

"It's lucky I am a gymnast. Someone else might have been killed but I only knocked myself a bit here; when you touch it—it hurts, but it'll pass; it's just a bruise."

And they started to live in the new home which, as always, once they had settled in properly, turned out to have one room too few, with the new income which, as always, turned out to be too little (only not by very much—five hundred rubles). And life was very good. Especially good at first when all was not yet done and more still had to be done: things to be bought, ordered, moved, adjusted. Although there were some disagreements between husband and wife, they were both so pleased and there was so much to do that everything was finished without serious quarrels. When there was nothing left to do, it became a bit more boring and something seemed lacking, but now friend-ships were made and habits established and life filled up.

After spending the morning in court Ivan Ilyich returned for dinner, and at first his mood was good, although it suffered a little, specifically because of their home. (Every stain on a tablecloth or brocade or broken curtain cord irritated him; he had put in so much work into the arrangement that every disruption of it was painful to him.) But in general Ivan Ilyich's life went on just as in his view life should flow: easily, pleasantly, and decorously. He rose at nine, drank his coffee, read the newspapers, then put on his uniform and drove to the court. There the harness in which he worked was already molded for him and he slipped into it right away: petitioners, chancery inquiries, the chancery itself, public and executive sittings of the court. In all of these one had to know how to exclude anything raw and vital, which always destroys the even flow of official work: one couldn't admit any human relationships except official ones; the occasion for a relationship had to be solely official and so had the relationship itself. For example, a man would come in and want to find out something. Outside his official role Ivan Ilyich could not have any relationship with him; but if this man had a relationship with him as a member of the court, one that could be expressed on headed paper—then within the bounds of this relationship Ivan Ilyich would do everything, abso-lutely everything he could, and in doing this would observe the semblance of friendly relations, that is, courtesy. As soon as the official relationship was ended, so was any other. This ability to separate out the official side without combining it with his real life Ivan Ilyich possessed in the highest degree, and by his talents and long practice he had developed it to such a point that he even sometimes, like a virtuoso, would allow himself as if in jest to combine personal and official relationships. He would allow himself this because he always felt in himself the power to split off the official again when necessary and to reject the personal. Ivan Ilyich handled this work of his not just easily, agreeably, and decorously but even with the mastery of a virtuoso. Between cases he would smoke, drink tea, chat a bit about politics, a bit about generalities, a bit about cards, and most of all about official appointments. And he would return home tired but with the feeling of a virtuoso who had given a lucid performance of his part, one of the first violins in the orchestra. At home mother and daughter would go out somewhere or someone came to see them; his son was at the gymnasium, preparing his lessons with tutors and diligently studying the things they teach in a gymnasium. Everything was good. After dinner, if there were no guests, Ivan Ilyich would sometimes read a book about which people were talking a lot, and in the evenings he would sit down to his work, that is, read his papers, consult the law, examine testimony, and check it against the law. All this he found neither boring nor amusing. It was boring if he could be playing *vint*; but if there was no *vint*—then all the same this was better than sitting by himself or with his wife. Ivan Ilyich's pleasures were little dinners to which he would invite ladies and gentlemen who were important in terms of worldly position and spending his time with them: that was just like the usual way such people spend their time, just as his drawing room was like all drawing rooms.

Once they even had an evening party, with dancing. And Ivan Ilyich felt cheerful and everything was good, except he had a big quarrel with his wife over the cakes and sweets: Praskovya Fyodorovna had her own plan, but Ivan Ilyich insisted on getting everything from an expensive confectioner and the quarrel was because there were cakes left over and the confectioner's bill came to forty-five rubles. The quarrel was a big and unpleasant one to such a point that Praskovya Fyodorovna called him "an idiot and a misery," and he took his head in his hands and in a fit of temper said something about divorce. But the actual party was enjoyable. The very best society was there and Ivan Ilyich danced with Princess Trufonova, sister of the famous founder of the Goodbye Sorrow Society. His official pleasures were pleasures of pride; his social pleasures were pleasures of vanity; but Ivan Ilyich's real pleasures were the pleasures of playing *vint*. He admitted that after all the various unhappy events in his life the pleasure that burnt like a candle above all others was to sit down at *vint* with good players and partners who didn't shout, definitely in a four (when you're five it's really annoying to have to stand out, although you pretend you very much like it), and to have an intelligent, serious game (when the cards are right), and then to have supper and drink a glass of wine. After *vint*, especially after a little win (a big win was unpleasant), Ivan Ilyich went to bed in an especially good mood.

That's how they lived. They formed around them a group of the best society, important people went to them and young people, too.

Husband, wife, and daughter were agreed in their views of their circle of acquaintances, and without any formal understanding they dropped and were rid of all sorts of shabby little friends and relatives who used to drop in to see them, spouting endearments into the drawing room with Japanese plates hanging on the wall. Soon these shabby little friends stopped dropping in and the Golovins were left with just the very best society. Young men paid court to Lizanka and Petrishchev, an examining magistrate, the son of Dmitry Ivanovich Petrishchev and sole heir to his property, began to pay so much attention to her that Ivan Ilyich even talked about it to Praskovya Fyodorovna.

Shouldn't they bring them together in a troika ride or organize some theatricals? That's how they lived. And everything went on like that, without any change, and everything was very good.

## IV

They were all in good health. One couldn't call poor health the fact that Ivan Ilyich sometimes said he had an odd taste in his mouth and something felt uncomfortable on the left side of his stomach.

But it happened that this discomfort started to grow and to become not quite pain but the consciousness of a constant heaviness in his side accompanied by a bad mood. This bad mood, which got worse and worse, began to spoil the pleasant course of the easy and decorous life that had been established in the Golovin house. Husband and wife began to quarrel more and more often, and soon the ease and pleasantness disappeared and only decorum was preserved, with difficulty. Again scenes became more frequent. Again there remained just some islands of calm, and only a few of those, on which husband and wife could meet without an outburst.

And Praskovya Fyodorovna now said, not without cause, that her husband had a difficult character. With her natural habit of exaggeration she said he had always had this dreadful character, and that one needed her good nature to stand it for twenty years. It was true that the quarrels now started with him. His fault-finding always began just before dinner and often when he was starting to eat, over the soup. He would remark that one of the dishes was damaged, or the food wasn't right, or his son had his elbow on the table, or it was his daughter's hairstyle. And he blamed Praskovya Fyodorovna for everything. At first Praskovya Fyodorovna answered back and was rude to him, but a couple of times at the beginning of dinner he flew into such a rage that she understood this was a morbid condition brought on by the intake of food, so she controlled herself and didn't answer back but ate her dinner quickly. Praskovya Fyodorovna regarded her self-control as greatly to her own credit. Having decided that her husband had a dreadful character and that he had created the unhappiness of her life, she started to feel sorry for herself. And the more she felt sorry for herself, the more she hated her husband. She began to wish that he would die, but she couldn't wish for that because then there would be no salary. And that irritated her even more. She considered herself terribly unhappy precisely because even his death could not rescue her and she became irritated; she concealed it and her concealed irritation increased his own irritation.

After one scene, in which Ivan Ilyich was particularly unfair, and after which in explaining himself he said he was indeed prone to irritability but that it came from his illness, she said to him that if he was ill then he must get treatment, and demanded from him that he see a famous doctor.

He went. Everything was as he had expected; everything happened as it always does. The waiting and the doctor's assumed pompousness, something familiar to him that he knew from himself in court, and the tapping and the auscultation and the questions requiring predetermined and clearly unnecessary answers, and the meaningful air suggesting that you just submit to us, we'll fix everything—we know, we have no doubts about how to fix everything, in the very same way for any man you choose. Everything was precisely as in court. Just as he in court put on an air towards the accused, so in precisely the same way the famous doctor put on an air towards him.

The doctor said: such and such shows that you have such and such inside; but if that isn't confirmed by examining such and such, then one must assume you have such and such. If one does assume such and such, then . . . and so forth. Only one question was important to Ivan Ilyich: was his condition dangerous or not? But the doctor ignored this inappropriate question. From the doctor's point of view the question was pointless and wasn't the one under discussion; it was only a question of assessing various possibilities—a floating kidney, chronic catarrh, or an infection of the appendix. It wasn't a question of Ivan Ilyich's life but an argument between a floating kidney and the appendix. And before Ivan Ilyich's eyes the doctor resolved the argument brilliantly in favor of the floating kidney, with the reservation that an examination of his urine could provide new evidence and then the case would be looked at again. All this was very precisely what Ivan Ilyich himself had done a thousand times with defendants and as brilliantly. The doctor did his summing-up just as brilliantly, triumphantly, even cheerfully, looking at the defendant over his glasses. From the doctor's summing-up Ivan Ilyich drew the conclusion that things were bad, that it didn't matter much to the doctor or probably to anyone else, but that for him things were bad. And Ivan Ilyich was painfully struck by this conclusion that aroused in him a feeling of great self-pity and of great anger toward this doctor who was indifferent to such an important question.

But he didn't say anything and got up, put the money on the desk, and said with a sigh:

"Probably we patients often put inappropriate questions to you. In general terms, is this a dangerous illness or not?"

The doctor gave him one stern look through his glasses as if to say: Accused, if you will not stay within the boundaries of the questions that are put to you, then I will be compelled to give instructions for your removal from the courtroom.

"I have already told you what I consider necessary and proper," said the doctor. "An examination will show the rest." And the doctor bowed.

Ivan Ilyich slowly went out, despondently got into the sleigh, and went home. For the whole journey he ceaselessly went over everything the doctor had said, trying to turn those confused, unclear, scientific words into simple language and to read in them an answer to the question: Am I in a bad way, or a very bad way, or aren't things yet so bad? And he thought that the sense of everything the doctor had said was that he was in a very bad way. Everything in the streets looked sad to Ivan Ilyich. The cab drivers were sad, the houses were sad, the passersby, the shops. This pain, this dull nagging pain that didn't stop for a single second, combined with the doctor's unclear pronouncements acquired another more serious meaning. Ivan Ilyich listened to his pain with a new heavy feeling.

He arrived home and started to tell his wife. His wife listened but in the middle of his account his daughter came in wearing a hat: she and her mother were going out. She sat down for a moment to listen to this boring stuff but she couldn't stand it for long, and her mother didn't listen to the end.

"Now I'm very pleased," his wife said. "So mind you take your medicine properly. Give me the prescription, I'll send Gerasim to the chemist's." And she went to dress.

While she was in the room he was barely able to breathe and he sighed heavily when she went out.

"Well then," he said. "Perhaps it's not so bad."

He began to take the medicines and to follow the doctor's directions, which changed after the urine examination. But it was the case now that there had been some kind of confusion in the examination and in what followed from it. It was impossible to get through to the doctor himself, but it turned out that what was happening was not what the doctor had told him. Either he had forgotten or he had lied or he had concealed something from Ivan Ilyich.

But Ivan Ilyich still started to follow the directions precisely and in doing so at first found some comfort.

From the time he visited the doctor Ivan Ilyich's chief occupations became the precise following of the doctor's directions about hygiene and the monitoring of his pain and all his bodily functions. Ivan Ilyich's chief interests became human illness and human health. When others talked in front of him about people who were ill or had died or had gotten better, and in particular about any illness that resembled his own, he would listen, trying to conceal his agitation, ask questions, and apply what was said to his own illness.

The pain got no less but Ivan Ilyich made an effort to force himself to think he was better. And he could deceive himself as long as nothing disturbed him. But as soon as there was some unpleasantness with his wife or something went wrong at work or he had bad cards at *vint*, he at once felt the full force of his illness. In the past he had endured things going wrong in the expectation that *I'll soon put things right, I'll overcome, I'll be successful, I'll get a grand slam.* Now anything that went wrong brought him down and cast him into despair. He would say to himself, "I was just starting to get better and the medicine was already beginning to work, and along comes this cursed accident or unpleasantness. . . ." And he was angry with the accident or with the people who were causing him unpleasantnesses and killing him, and he felt that this anger was killing him but he couldn't restrain himself. One might have thought it would have been clear to him that this anger against circumstances and people made his illness worse, and that therefore he shouldn't pay any attention to unpleasant incidents, but his reasoning was quite the reverse: He said he needed calm; he watched out for anything that might breach that calm and at the smallest breach he got angry. His condition was made worse by the fact that he consulted medical books and doctors. His deterioration progressed so evenly that comparing one day with another he could deceive himself—there was little difference. But when he consulted doctors, he thought he was getting worse and that very quickly. And in spite of that he constantly consulted doctors.

That month he went to see another celebrity doctor; this other celebrity doctor said almost the same as the first but put the questions differently. And consulting this celebrity doctor only deepened Ivan Ilyich's doubt and terror. A friend of a friend—a very good doctor—diagnosed his illness quite differently, and in spite of promising recovery, his questions and assumptions confused Ivan Ilyich even more and increased his doubts. A homeopath diagnosed his illness again quite differently and gave him some medicine, and Ivan Ilyich took it in secret from everyone for about a week. But after a week, feeling no relief and having lost confidence both in the previous treatments and in this one, he fell into greater despair. On one occasion a lady he knew was talking about the healing powers of icons. Ivan Ilyich found himself listening carefully and believing the reality of this. This incident frightened him. "Have I really become so feeble-minded?" he said to himself. "What rubbish! It's all nonsense. I mustn't give in to hypochondria, but having chosen one doctor I must firmly stick to his treatment. That's what I'll do. Now it's settled. I'm not going to think and I'm going to follow the treatment strictly till the summer. Then there'll be something to show. Let's now have an end to all this wavering!" It was easy to say that but impossible to put it into action. The pain in his side wore him down; it seemed to keep getting worse; it became constant; the taste in his mouth became stronger; he thought a disgusting smell was coming from his mouth; and his appetite and strength were going. He couldn't deceive himself: something terrible, new, and important was happening in him, something more important than anything that had happened to Ivan Ilyich in his life. And only he knew about this; all those around him either didn't understand or didn't want to understand and thought that everything in the world was going on as before. That was what tormented Ivan Ilyich most of all. He could see that his household—chiefly his wife and daughter who were in the full swing of visits and parties—understood nothing, and they were vexed that he was so gloomy and demanding, as if he were guilty in that. Although they tried to conceal it, he saw that he was a burden to them, but that his wife had evolved a particular attitude to his illness and adhered to that irrespective of what he said and did. Her attitude was like this:

"You know," she would say to friends, "Ivan Ilyich can't strictly follow a prescribed treatment, as most good people can. Today he'll take his drops and eat what he's been told to and go to bed in good time, but tomorrow if I don't look properly, he'll suddenly forget to take them and eat oysters (which are forbidden him) and sit down to *vint* till one in the morning."

"When did I do that?" Ivan Ilyich would say crossly. "Once at Pyotr Ivanovich's."

"Yesterday with Shebek."

"I just couldn't sleep from the pain . . ."

"Well, whatever it was from, like that you won't get better and you make us miserable."

Praskovya Fyodorovna's public attitude to her husband's illness, which she expressed to others and to him, was that this illness was Ivan Ilyich's own fault and that the whole illness was a new unpleasantness he was bringing down on his wife. Ivan Ilyich felt that this came out in her involuntarily, but that didn't make it any easier for him.

In court Ivan Ilyich noticed or thought he noticed the same strange attitude to him: now he would think that people were scrutinizing him like a man whose position was soon going to be vacant; now all of a sudden his friends would start to joke in an amicable way about his hypochondria, as if this thing, this awful, terrible, unheard-of thing that had grown in him and was ceaselessly gnawing at him and irrepressibly dragging him somewhere, were the most pleasant subject for a joke. He was especially irritated by Schwarz with his playfulness and energy and *comme il faut* ways, all of which reminded Ivan Ilyich of himself ten years back.

Friends came to make up a game; they sat down. They dealt, bending the new cards; he put diamonds next to diamonds, seven of them. His partner bid no trumps—and held two diamonds. What could be better? Things were cheerful and bright—they had a grand slam. And suddenly Ivan Ilyich felt that gnawing pain, that taste in the mouth, and there seemed to him to be something absurd in the fact that he could rejoice in a grand slam.

He looked at Mikhail Mikhaylovich, his partner, rapping his powerful hand on the table and politely and condescendingly refraining from scooping up the tricks but pushing the cards toward Ivan Ilyich to give him the pleasure of picking them up without straining himself and stretching out his arm. "Does he think I'm so weak I can't stretch out my arm?" Ivan Ilyich thought. He forgot about trumps and trumped his partner, losing the grand slam by three tricks—and what was really dreadful was that he saw how Mikhail Mikhaylovich was suffering, but he didn't care. And it was dreadful to think just why he didn't care.

They all saw he was feeling bad and said to him, "We can stop if you are tired. You must rest." Rest? No, he wasn't tired at all, and they finished the rubber. They were all gloomy and silent. Ivan Ilyich felt he had brought down this gloom upon them and he couldn't dispel it. They had supper and went their ways, and Ivan Ilyich was left alone with the knowledge that his life had been poisoned for him, that it was poisoning the lives of others, and that this poison wasn't losing its power but was penetrating his whole being more and more.

And with this knowledge, with the physical pain, and with the terror, he had to get into bed and often be unable to sleep from the pain the greater part of the night. And the next morning he had to get up again, dress, go to court, talk, write, or if he didn't go to court he had to stay at home with those twenty-four hours of the day, each one of which was a torment. And he had to live like that on the brink of the abyss, all alone, without a single person who could understand and take pity on him.

## V

A month went by like that and then another. Before the new year his brother-in-law came to the city and stayed with them. Ivan Ilyich was in court. Praskovya Fyodorovna had gone out shopping. When Ivan Ilyich went into his study he found his brother-in-law, a healthy, full-blooded fellow, unpacking his suitcase himself. He raised his head when he heard Ivan Ilyich's footsteps and looked at him for a second in silence. That look revealed everything to Ivan Ilyich. His brother-in-law opened his mouth to say "oh" and stopped himself. That movement confirmed everything.

"So, I've changed, haven't I?"

"Yes . . . there is a change."

And however much afterwards Ivan Ilyich turned the conversation with his brother-in-law to his appearance, his brother-in-law said nothing. Praskovya

Fyodorovna arrived, his brother-in-law went out to her. Ivan Ilyich locked his door and started to examine himself in the mirror—face-on, then from the side. He took up a photograph of himself with his wife and compared the image with the one he saw in the mirror. The change was huge. Then he bared his arms to the elbow, looked, rolled his sleeves down again, and sat on an ottoman, and his mood became darker than night.

"You mustn't, you mustn't," he said to himself; he jumped up, went to the desk, opened a case file, and began to read it, but he couldn't. He unlocked the door and went into the salon. The drawing-room door was shut. He tiptoed to it and began to listen.

"No, you're exaggerating," said Praskovya Fyodorovna.

"Exaggerating? You don't see—he's a dead man, look at his eyes. There's no light in them. What's the matter with him?"

"Nobody knows. Nikolayev [that was the second doctor] said something, but I don't know what. Leshchetitsky [that was the celebrated doctor] said the opposite . . ."

Ivan Ilyich moved away, went to his room, lay down, and started to think: *A kidney, a floating kidney.* He remembered everything the doctor had told him—how it had become detached and was floating. And with an effort of the imagination he tried to understand his kidney and to halt it and strengthen it; so little was needed for that, he thought. *No, I'll go again to Pyotr Ivanovich.* (That was the friend who had a friend who was a doctor.) He rang, gave orders for the horse to be harnessed, and got ready to leave.

"Where are you off to, *Jean?*"[7] his wife said, using a particularly sad and unusually kind expression.

This unusual kindness angered him. He looked at her morosely.

"I have to go to Pyotr Ivanovich."

He went to his friend who had a friend who was a doctor. He found him at home and had a long conversation with him.

When he considered both the anatomical and physiological details of what, in the doctor's opinion, had been happening inside him, he understood everything.

There was something, a little something in the appendix. All that might be put right. Stimulate the activity of one organ, weaken the activity of another; the something would be absorbed and everything would be put right. He got back a little late for dinner, talked cheerfully for a bit, but for a long time he couldn't go to his room to work. Finally he went into his study and at once sat down to work. He read his cases and worked, but the consciousness that he had set something aside—an important and intimate matter which he would take up once his work was over—did not leave him. When he had finished his cases, he remembered that this intimate matter was his thinking about his appendix. But he didn't indulge it; he went to the drawing room for tea. There were guests, including the examining magistrate, his daughter's intended; they talked and played the piano and sang. Ivan Ilyich spent the evening, as Praskovya Fyodorovna noticed, more cheerfully than he had spent others, but he didn't forget for one minute that he had set aside some important

---

7. The French equivalent for Ivan. In the 19th century, Russians of the upper classes frequently spoke French to each other.

thinking about his appendix. At eleven o'clock he said goodnight and went to his room. Since he had become ill he slept in a little room next to his study. He went in, undressed, and picked up a novel of Zola's,[8] which he didn't read. He began thinking instead. The desired cure of the appendix took place in his imagination. Matter was absorbed, matter was expelled, and normal activity was restored. "Yes, that's how it all is," he said to himself. "Only nature needs a little help." He remembered his medicine, sat up, took it, watching for the beneficial effects of the medicine and the removal of the pain. "Just take it regularly and avoid unhealthy influences; I already feel a bit better, much better." He started to feel his side—it wasn't painful to the touch. "Yes, I can't feel it; I'm really much better now." He put out the candle and lay on his side. "The appendix is getting better; things are being absorbed." Suddenly he felt the familiar old dull nagging pain, the persistent, quiet, serious pain. The familiar nastiness in his mouth. His heart began to pump, his head turned. "My God, my God!" he said. "It's here again, it's here again and it's never going to stop." And suddenly his case presented itself to him from a different perspective. "Appendix! Kidney!" he said to himself. "It's not a case of the appendix or of the kidney, but of life . . . and death. Yes, I had life and now it's passing, passing, and I can't hold it back. That's it. Why deceive oneself? Isn't it obvious to everyone but myself that I am dying, and it's only a question of the number of weeks, days—maybe now. There was light and now there's darkness. I was here but now I'm going there! Where?" A chill came over him, his breathing stopped. He could only hear the beating of his heart.

"I won't exist, so what will exist? Nothing will exist. So where will I be when I don't exist? Is this really death? No, I don't want it." He got up quickly, tried to light a candle, groped with shaking hands, dropped the candle and candlestick on the floor, and slumped back again onto the pillow. "Why? Nothing matters," he said to himself, looking into the darkness with open eyes. "Death. Yes, death. And none of them knows and they don't want to know and they have no pity for me. They're enjoying themselves." Outside the door he could hear the distant noise of music and singing. "They don't care but they too will die. Fools. It'll come to me first, to them later; they too will have the same. But they're having fun, the beasts!" Anger choked him. And he felt painful, unbearable misery. "It cannot be that we're all doomed to this terrible fear." He raised himself.

"Something's not right; I must calm down, I must think over everything from the outset." And he began to think. "Yes, the start of my illness. I knocked my side, and I stayed just the same that day and the next; it ached a bit, then more, then the doctors, then depression, despair, the doctors again; and I kept getting nearer and nearer to the abyss. Less strength. Nearer and nearer. And now I've wasted away, there's no light in my eyes. And death, and I think about my appendix. I think of how to mend my appendix, but this is death. Is it really death?" Again horror came over him; he bent down, tried to find the matches, and banged his elbow on the nighttable. It got in his way and hurt him; he got angry with it; in his irritation he banged his elbow harder and

---

**8.** Émile Zola (1840–1902), French novelist.

knocked the nighttable over. And in his despair he fell back, gasping for breath, expecting death to come now.

Now the guests were leaving. Praskovya Fyodorovna was seeing them out. She heard something fall and came in.

"What's the matter with you?"

"Nothing. I knocked it over by mistake."

She went out and brought back a candle. He lay breathing heavily and very fast, like a man who has run a mile, looking at her with motionless eyes.

"What's the matter with you, *Jean*?"

"Nothing. I... knocked... it... over." (*What should I say? She won't under- stand*, he thought.)

Indeed she didn't. She picked the table up, lit a candle for him, and quickly went out; she had to see a guest out.

When she returned, he was lying in the same position, on his back, look- ing up.

"How are you feeling? Is it worse?"

"Yes, it is."

She shook her head and sat down.

"You know, *Jean*, I am wondering whether we shouldn't ask Leshchetitsky to the house."

That meant asking the celebrated doctor regardless of cost. He smiled ven- omously and said, "No." She sat for a while, then went over to him and kissed him on the forehead.

When she kissed him he hated her with all his might and made an effort not to push her away.

"Good night. With God's help you'll go to sleep."

"Yes."

## V I

Ivan Ilyich saw that he was dying and was in constant despair.

Ivan Ilyich knew in the very depths of his soul that he was dying but not only could he not get accustomed to this, he simply didn't understand it; he just couldn't understand it.

All his life the example of a syllogism he had studied in Kiesewetter's[9] logic— "Caius is a man, men are mortal, therefore Caius is mortal"—had seemed to him to be true only in relation to Caius but in no way to himself. There was Caius the man, man in general, and it was quite justified, but he wasn't Caius and he wasn't man in general, and he had always been something quite, quite special apart from all other beings; he was Vanya,[1] with Mama, with Papa, with Mitya and Volodya, with his toys and the coachman, with Nyanya, then with Katenka, with all the joys, sorrows, passions of childhood, boyhood, youth. Did Caius know the smell of the striped leather ball Vanya loved so much? Did Caius kiss his mother's hand like that and did the silken folds of Caius's mother's dress rustle like that for him? Was Caius in love like that? Could Caius chair a session like that?

---

9. The *Outline of Logic according to Kantian Principles* by Kiesewetter (1766–1819) was widely used as a Rus- sian text book. 1. The diminutive of Ivan, what he would have been called as a child.

*And Caius is indeed mortal and it's right that he should die, but for me, Vanya, Ivan Ilyich, with all my feelings and thoughts—for me it's quite different. And it cannot be that I should die. It would be too horrible.*

That's what he felt.

"If I had to die like Caius, then I would know it, an inner voice would be telling me, but nothing like that happened in me, and I and all my friends—we understood that things weren't at all like with Caius. But now there's this!" he said to himself. "It can't be. It can't be, but it is. How has this happened? How can one understand it?"

And he couldn't understand it and tried to banish this thought as false, inaccurate, morbid, and to replace it with other true and healthy thoughts. But this thought, and not just the thought but reality as it were came and stopped in front of him.

And in the place of this thought he called up others in turn in the hope of finding support in them. He tried to return to his previous ways of thought, which had concealed the thought of death from him. But—strangely—everything which previously had concealed and covered up and obliterated the awareness of death now could no longer produce this result. Ivan Ilyich now spent most of his time attempting to restore his previous ways of feeling that had concealed death. Now he would say to himself, "I'll take up some work, that's what I live by." And he went to court, banishing all his doubts; he talked to friends and sat down, absentmindedly looking over the crowd of people with a pensive look as he used to and supporting both wasted hands on the arms of his oak chair; leaning over toward a friend as usual, moving the papers of a case, whispering together, and then suddenly raising his eyes and sitting up straight, he would pronounce the particular words and open the case. But suddenly in the middle of it, the pain in his side, ignoring the stages of the case's development, began its own gnawing work. Ivan Ilyich listened and tried not to think about it, but it kept on. It came and stood right in front of him and looked at him, and he became petrified; the fire in his eyes died down, and he again began to ask himself, "Is it alone the truth?" And his friends and staff saw with surprise and dismay that he, such a brilliant, subtle judge, was getting confused and making mistakes. He would give himself a shake, make an effort to recover himself, and somehow or other bring the session to an end, and he would return home with the depressing awareness that his work as a judge couldn't hide from him as it used to what he wanted it to hide; that with his work as a judge he couldn't be rid of It. And what was worst of all was that It was distracting him not to make him do anything but only for him to look at It, right in the eye, look at it and without doing anything endure inexpressible sufferings.

And to rescue himself from this condition, Ivan Ilyich looked for relief—for new screens—and new screens appeared and for a short time seemed to offer him salvation, but very soon they again not so much collapsed as let the light through, as if It penetrated everything and nothing could hide it.

Latterly he would go into the drawing room he had arranged—the drawing room where he had fallen—how venomously comic it was to think of it—for the arrangement of which he had sacrificed his life, for he knew that his illness had started with that injury; he would go in and see that something had made a scratch on a polished table. He would look for the cause and find it in the bronze ornament of an album that had become bent at the edge. He would pick up the album, an expensive one he had lovingly compiled, and be cross at the carelessness of his daughter and her friends—things were torn and the photographs bent. He would carefully set things to rights and bend the decoration back again.

He then would have the thought of moving this whole *établissement*[2] of albums over into another corner by the flowers. He would call the manservant; either his daughter or his wife would come to his help; they would disagree, contradict him; he would argue, get angry, but everything would be all right because he didn't remember It, couldn't see It.

And then his wife would say when he himself was moving something, "Let the servants do it, you'll hurt yourself again," and suddenly It would flash through the screens; he would see It flash just for a moment, and he still would hope It would disappear, but without wanting to he would pay attention to his side—the same thing would still be sitting there, still aching, and he couldn't forget it, and It would be looking at him quite openly from behind the flowers. Why?

*It's true, it was here on these curtains that I lost my life as if in an assault. Did I really? How terrible and how stupid! It can't be so! It can't be, but it is.*

He would go into his study, lie down, and be left alone with It. Face-to-face with It, but nothing to be done with It. Just look at It and turn cold.

## VII

How it happened in the third month of Ivan Ilyich's illness is impossible to say because it happened step by step, imperceptibly, but it did happen that his wife and his daughter and his son and the servants and his friends and the doctors and, above all, he himself knew that all interest others had in him lay solely in whether he would soon, at last, vacate his place, free the living from the constraint brought about by his presence, and be liberated himself from his sufferings.

He slept less and less; they gave him opium and started to inject morphine. But that gave him no relief. The dull pangs he felt in his half-somnolent state at first gave him relief as being something new, but then they became as agonizing as outright pain or even more so.

They prepared special food to the doctors' prescriptions, but this food he found more and more tasteless, more and more disgusting.

Special contrivances had to be made for excretion, and every time this was a torment for him. A torment because of the uncleanliness, the loss of decorum, and the odor, from the consciousness that another person had to take part in this.

But some comfort for Ivan Ilyich did come out of this unpleasant business. Gerasim, the manservant, always came to take things out for him.

Gerasim was a clean, fresh young peasant who had filled out on city food. He was always cheerful and sunny. At first Ivan Ilyich was embarrassed by seeing this man, always dressed in his clean, traditional clothes, having to do this repulsive job.

---

2. Arrangement (French).

Once getting up from the pan and lacking the strength to pull up his trousers, he collapsed into an easy chair and looked with horror at his feeble bare thighs with their sharply defined muscles.

Gerasim came in with firm, light steps in his heavy boots, giving off a pleasant smell of tar from the boots and of fresh winter air; he had on a clean hessian apron and a clean cotton shirt, the sleeves rolled up over his strong, young, bare arms; without looking at Ivan Ilyich, he went to the vessel, obviously masking the joy in living shining out from his face so as not to hurt the sick man.

"Gerasim," Ivan Ilyich said weakly.

Gerasim started, obviously scared he had made some mistake, and with a quick movement turned toward the sick man his fresh, kind, simple, young face, which was just beginning to grow a beard.

"Do you need something, sir?"

"I think this must be unpleasant for you. You must forgive me. I can't manage."

"No, sir." Gerasim's eyes were shining and he showed his young white teeth. "What's a little trouble? You've got an illness."

And with strong, dexterous hands he did his usual job and went out, treading lightly. And in five minutes, treading just as lightly, he came back.

Ivan Ilyich was still sitting there like that in the armchair.

"Gerasim," he said when Gerasim had put down the clean, rinsed vessel, "please, come here and help me." Gerasim came. "Lift me up. It's difficult by myself and I've sent Dmitry away."

Gerasim came over to him; he put his strong arms around him and, gently and deftly, the same way he walked, lifted and supported him; he pulled up his trousers with one hand and was going to sit him down. But Ivan Ilyich asked Gerasim to take him to the sofa. Effortlessly and with next to no pressure, Gerasim led him, almost carrying him, to the sofa and sat him down.

"Thank you. How easily, how well . . . you do everything."

Gerasim again smiled and was about to go out. But Ivan Ilyich felt so good with him around that he didn't want to let him go.

"Now. Please move this chair over to me. No, that one, underneath my legs. I feel better when my legs are higher."

Gerasim brought the chair, placed it without making any noise, lowering it in one movement to the floor, and lifted Ivan Ilyich's legs onto the chair; Ivan Ilyich thought he felt better the moment Gerasim raised up his legs.

"I feel better when my legs are higher," Ivan Ilyich said. "Put that cushion under me."

Gerasim did that. Again he lifted his legs up and put the cushion into position. Again Ivan Ilyich felt better when Gerasim held his legs up. When he lowered them, he thought he felt worse.

"Gerasim," he said to him, "are you busy now?"

"No sir, not at all," said Gerasim, who had learned from the townsfolk how to talk to the gentry.

"What do you still have to do?"

"What is there to do? I've done everything; I've just got to chop the wood for tomorrow."

"So hold my legs up a bit higher, can you do that?"

"Of course I can." Gerasim lifted up his legs and Ivan Ilyich thought that in this position he felt absolutely no pain.

"But what about the wood?"

"Don't worry, sir. We'll manage."

Ivan Ilyich told Gerasim to sit down and hold up his legs, and he talked to him. And—strange to say—he thought he felt better while Gerasim held up his legs.

From that day Ivan Ilyich started sometimes to call Gerasim in to him and made him hold up his legs on his shoulders, and he liked to talk to him. Gerasim did this easily, willingly, simply, and with a goodness of heart that touched Ivan Ilyich. In all other people Ivan Ilyich was offended by health, strength, high spirits; only Gerasim's strength and high spirits didn't depress but calmed Ivan Ilyich.

Ivan Ilyich's chief torment was the lie—that lie, for some reason recognized by everyone, that he was only ill but not dying, and that he only needed rest and treatment and then there would be some very good outcome. But he knew that whatever they did, there would be no outcome except even more painful suffering and death. And he was tormented by this lie; he was tormented by their unwillingness to acknowledge what everyone knew and he knew, by their wanting to lie to him about his terrible situation, by their wanting him to and making him take part in that lie himself. The lie, this lie being perpetrated above him on the eve of his death, the lie which could only bring down this terrible solemn act of his death to the level of all their visits and curtains and sturgeon for dinner . . . was horribly painful for Ivan Ilyich. And, strangely, many times when they were performing their tricks above him, he was within a hair's breadth of crying out to them, "Stop lying; you know and I know that I am dying; so at least stop lying." But he never had the strength to do it. The terrible, horrific act of his dying, he saw, had been brought down by all those surrounding him to the level of a casual unpleasantness, some breach of decorum (as one treats a man who, entering a drawing room, emits a bad smell); brought down by that very "decorum" he had served his whole life, he saw that no one had pity for him because no one even wanted to understand his situation. Only Gerasim understood his situation and felt pity for him. And so Ivan Ilyich only felt comfortable with Gerasim. He felt comfortable when Gerasim held up his legs, sometimes for whole nights without a break, and wouldn't go off to bed, saying, "Please, sir, don't worry, Ivan Ilyich, I'll still get plenty of sleep"; or when he would suddenly add, going over to the familiar "thou," "You're sick, so why shouldn't I do something for you?" Gerasim was the only one not to lie; everything showed he was the only one who understood what the matter was and didn't think it necessary to hide it, and simply felt pity for his wasted, feeble master. He even once said directly when Ivan Ilyich was dismissing him:

"We'll all die. So why not take a little trouble?" He said this, conveying by it that he wasn't bothered by the work precisely because he was doing it for a dying man and hoped that in his time someone would do this work for him.

Apart from this lie, or as a consequence of it, what was most painful for Ivan Ilyich was that no one had pity on him as he wanted them to have pity;

at some moments after prolonged sufferings Ivan Ilyich wanted most of all, however much he felt ashamed to admit it, for someone to have pity on him like a sick child. He wanted them to caress him, to kiss him, to cry over him as one caresses and comforts children. He knew he was an important legal official, that he had a graying beard and that therefore this was impossible, but he still wanted it. And in his relations with Gerasim there was something close to that, and therefore his relations with Gerasim comforted him. Ivan Ilyich would want to cry, would want them to caress him and cry over him; then in would come his friend, the lawyer Shebek, and instead of crying and caresses Ivan Ilyich would assume a serious, stern, pensive expression and out of inertia would give his opinion on the meaning of a verdict of the court of appeal and stubbornly insist on it. This lie all around him and inside him more than anything poisoned the last days of Ivan Ilyich's life.

## VIII

It was morning. It was morning only because Gerasim had gone out and Pyotr the manservant came in, put out the candles, opened one curtain, and started quietly to tidy up. Whether it was morning or evening, Friday or Sunday, was immaterial, it was all one and the same: the gnawing, agonizing pain that didn't abate for a moment; the consciousness of life departing without hope but still not yet departed; the same terrible, hateful death advancing, which was the only reality, and always the same lie. What did days, weeks, and times of day matter here?

"Would you like some tea?"

*He has to have order; masters should drink tea in the mornings,* he thought and only said:

"No."

"Would you like to move to the sofa?"

*He has to tidy the chamber, and I'm in the way; I am dirt, disorder,* he thought and only said:

"No, leave me be."

The manservant did some more things. Ivan Ilyich stretched out his hand. Pyotr came up to serve.

"What do you want?"

"My watch."

Pyotr got the watch, which was lying right there, and handed it to him.

"Half past eight. Have they got up?"

"No, sir. Vasily Ivanovich"—that was his son—"has gone to the gymnasium, but Praskovya Fyodorovna gave orders to wake her if you asked for her. Shall I?"

"No, don't." *Shall I try some tea?* he thought. "Yes, tea . . . bring it."

Pyotr went to the door. Ivan Ilyich felt terrified of being left alone. *How can I detain him? Yes, my medicine.* "Pyotr, give me my medicine." *Why not, maybe the medicine will still help.* He took the spoon and drank. *No, it won't help. It's all nonsense and a sham,* he decided as soon as he sensed the familiar sickly, hopeless taste. *No, I can't believe in it any more. But the pain, why the pain, if it would just go down even for a minute.* And he groaned. Pyotr turned round again. "No, go away. Bring me some tea."

Pyotr went out. Left alone, Ivan Ilyich groaned not so much from the pain, however frightful it was, as from anguish. "Always the same, always these endless days and nights. If only it could be soon. What could be soon? Death, darkness. No, no. Anything is better than death!"

When Pyotr came in with the tea on a tray, Ivan Ilyich looked distractedly at him for a long time, not taking in who and what he was. Pyotr was embarrassed by this stare. And when Pyotr was embarrassed, Ivan Ilyich came to himself.

"Yes," he said, "tea . . . good, put it down. Only help me wash and give me a clean shirt."

And Ivan Ilyich began to wash. Stopping to rest, he washed his hands, his face, cleaned his teeth, began to brush his hair, and looked in the mirror. He felt frightened, especially frightened by the way his hair stuck flat to his forehead.

When his shirt was being changed, he knew that he would be even more frightened if he looked at his body, and so he didn't look at himself. But now it was all done. He put on a dressing gown, covered himself with a blanket, and sat in an armchair to have his tea. For one minute he felt refreshed, but as soon as he began to drink the tea, again the same taste, the same pain. With an effort he finished the tea and lay down, stretching out his legs. He lay down and sent Pyotr away.

Always the same. There'd be a small flash of hope, then a sea of despair would surge, and always pain, always pain, always despair, and always the same. It was horribly depressing being alone; he wanted to ask for someone but he knew in advance that with others there it would be even worse. "If only I could have morphine again—and lose consciousness. I'll tell him, the doctor, to think of something else. Like this it's impossible, impossible."

An hour, a couple of hours would go by like that. But now there's a bell in the hall. Maybe it's the doctor. It is; it's the doctor, fresh, bright, plump, cheerful, his expression saying, "You've gotten frightened of something there but now we'll fix all that for you." The doctor knows that this expression isn't appropriate here, but he has assumed it once and for all and he can't take it off, like a man who has put on a tailcoat in the morning and is paying visits.

The doctor rubs his hands briskly and reassuringly.

"I'm cold. There's a cracking frost. Let me warm myself up," he says, his expression being as if one just had to wait a little for him to warm himself, and when he had, then he would set everything to rights.

"So, how are we?"

Ivan Ilyich feels the doctor wants to say, "How are things?" but feels one can't talk like that, and he says, "How did you spend the night?"

Ivan Ilyich looks at the doctor, his expression asking, "Will you really never be ashamed of telling lies?" But the doctor doesn't want to understand the question.

And Ivan Ilyich says:

"Just as dreadfully. The pain isn't going, it isn't going away. If I could just have something!"

"Yes, you patients are always like that. Well, sir, now I've warmed up, even our very particular Praskovya Fyodorovna wouldn't have anything to say against my temperature. So, sir, good morning." And the doctor shakes his hand.

And, dropping all his earlier playfulness, the doctor begins to examine the patient with a serious expression, takes pulse and temperature, and then begin the tappings and auscultations.[3]

Ivan Ilyich knows firmly and without any doubt that all this is nonsense, an empty fraud, but when the doctor on his knees stretches over him, applying his ear first higher, then lower, and performs over him various gymnastic exercises, Ivan Ilyich succumbs to all this as he used to succumb to lawyers' speeches when he knew very well that they were lying and why they were lying.

The doctor, kneeling on the sofa, was still tapping something when there was a rustling at the door of Praskovya Fyodorovna's silk dress, and they could hear her scolding Pyotr for not informing her of the doctor's arrival.

She comes in, kisses her husband, and at once starts to make it clear that she has got up long ago and that it's because of a misunderstanding that she wasn't there when the doctor came.

Ivan Ilyich looks at her, examines her closely, and holds against her the whiteness and plumpness and cleanliness of her arms and neck, the gloss of her hair and the shine of her eyes that are so full of life. He hates her with his whole soul. And her touch makes him suffer from a surge of hatred towards her.

Her attitude to him and to his illness is always the same. Just as the doctor has developed for himself an attitude toward his patients which he hasn't been able to put aside, so has she developed a simple attitude towards him—he isn't doing something he should be doing, and it's his fault, and she lovingly scolds him for this—and she hasn't yet managed to put this attitude toward him aside.

"He just doesn't listen. He doesn't take his medicine when he should. And above all—he lies in a position that has to be bad for him—with his legs up." She described how he makes Gerasim hold his legs.

The doctor smiled a smile of amiable scorn, as if saying, "What can one do? Sometimes these patients dream up such silly things; but one can forgive them."

When the examination was over the doctor looked at his watch, and then Praskovya Fyodorovna announced to Ivan Ilyich that whatever he might want, today she had asked in a famous doctor and he and Mikhail Danilovich (that was the usual doctor's name) would examine him together and discuss the case.

"So please don't go against this. I'm doing this for myself," she said ironically, letting him understand that she did everything for him and just by her saying this he was given no right to refuse her. He said nothing and frowned. He felt that the lies surrounding him had become so tangled that it was difficult now to see anything clearly.

Everything she did for him she did only for herself, and she told him so, as if that was something so unlikely that he had to understand it in the opposite sense.

Indeed the famous doctor did arrive at half past eleven. Again there started the auscultations and serious conversations, both in front of Ivan Ilyich and

---

**3.** Listening to the internal sounds of the body, such as heart beats or inhalations, usually performed with a stethoscope.

in another room, about his kidney and appendix, and questions and answers delivered with such a serious air that again, instead of the real question about life and death which now was the only one that confronted him, there came a question about his kidney and appendix, which were doing something not quite as they should be and which Mikhail Danilovich and the celebrity doctor would get to grips with right away and make them correct themselves.

The famous doctor said his goodbyes with a serious expression, but one that hadn't given up hope. And to the timid question Ivan Ilyich put to him, raising eyes that were shining with fear and hope—is there any possibility of recovery?—he answered that though one couldn't guarantee it, there was a possibility. The look of hope with which Ivan Ilyich said goodbye to the doctor was so pitiful that, when she saw it, Praskovya Fyodorovna burst into tears as she went through the study doors to give the famous doctor his fee.

The rise in his spirits brought about by the doctor's encouragement didn't last long. Again it was the same room, the same pictures, curtains, wallpaper, medicine bottles, and his same hurting, suffering body. And Ivan Ilyich started to groan; they gave him an injection and he lost consciousness.

When he came to, it was beginning to get dark; they brought in his dinner. With some effort he took some broth; and again all those same things and again night was coming on.

After dinner at seven o'clock Praskovya Fyodorovna came into his room dressed for an evening out, her breasts large and lifted and traces of powder on her face. That morning she had reminded him that they were going to the theater. Sarah Bernhardt[4] was visiting and they had a box which Ivan Ilyich had insisted they take. Now he had forgotten that, and her clothes outraged him. But he concealed his outrage when he remembered that he himself had insisted they get a box and go because it was a cultural treat for their children.

Praskovya Fyodorovna came in pleased with herself but also with a kind of guilty feeling. She sat down, asked about his health—as he could see, just for the sake of asking rather than to learn, knowing that there was nothing to learn—and began to say what she needed to: that she wouldn't have gone out for anything but the box was taken and Hélène was going and their daughter and Petrishchev (the examining magistrate, their daughter's fiancé), and it was impossible to let them go alone. But it would be so much more agreeable for her to sit with him. He must just do what the doctor had ordered without her.

"Yes, and Fyodor Petrovich—the fiancé—wanted to come in. Can he? Liza, too."

"Let them come in."

His daughter came in all dressed up with her young body bared, that body which made him suffer so. But she was flaunting it. Strong, healthy, clearly in love and angry at the illness, suffering, and death that stood in the way of her happiness.

Fyodor Petrovich came too, in a tailcoat, his hair curled à la Capoul,[5] his long sinewy neck encased in a white collar, with a huge white shirtfront and

---

4. French actress (1844–1923) who had a great popular following. 5. An ornate and elaborate form of men's hairstyling (French).

with powerful thighs squeezed into narrow black trousers, with one white glove pulled onto his hand and an opera hat.

After him the schoolboy crept in inconspicuously in a new school uniform, poor fellow, wearing white gloves and with terrible dark patches under his eyes, the meaning of which Ivan Ilyich knew.

His son always made him feel sorry for him. And the look he gave him was terrible, full of sympathy and fear. Apart from Gerasim, only Vasya understood him and felt pity for him, so Ivan Ilyich thought.

They all sat down, asked again about his health. A silence fell. Liza asked her mother about the opera glasses. There ensued an argument between mother and daughter about who had put them where. It felt unpleasant.

Fyodor Petrovich asked Ivan Ilyich if he had seen Sarah Bernhardt. At first Ivan Ilyich didn't understand what he was being asked and then said:

"No, but have you?"

"Yes, in *Adrienne Lecouvreur.*"[6]

Praskovya Fyodorovna said that she was particularly good in something or other. Their daughter disagreed. There began a conversation about the elegance and realism of her acting—that conversation which is always exactly the same.

In the middle of the conversation Fyodor Petrovich looked at Ivan Ilyich and fell silent. The others looked and fell silent. Ivan Ilyich looked straight ahead with shining eyes, clearly becoming angry with them. This had to be put right, but it was quite impossible to put right. Somehow this silence had to be broken. No one had the resolve, and they all became frightened that somehow the decorous lie would collapse and the true state of things would become obvious to all. Liza was the first to take the resolve. She broke the silence. She wanted to hide what they were all feeling, but she said it wrong.

"So, *if we are going to go*, it's time," she said, looking at her watch, a present from her father, and she gave a barely perceptible smile to the young man, which meant something known to them alone, and got up, her dress rustling.

They all got up, said goodbye, and went off.

When they had gone out, Ivan Ilyich thought he felt better: the lie wasn't there—it had gone out with them—but the pain remained. The same constant pain, the same constant fear made nothing more difficult, nothing easier. Everything was worse.

Again minute followed minute, hour followed hour; it was always the same and there was still no end and the inevitable end became more terrifying.

"Yes, send me Gerasim," he said in reply to a question Pyotr asked.

# IX

His wife came back late at night. She walked on tiptoe but he heard her; he opened his eyes and quickly shut them again. She wanted to send Gerasim away and sit with him herself. He opened his eyes and said:

"No. Go away."

"Are you in a lot of pain?"

"It doesn't matter."

**6.** A French tragedy by Eugène Scribe (1791–1861) and Ernest Legouvé (1807–1903), written in 1849.

"Take some opium."

He agreed and drank. She went out.

Till three o'clock he was in a tormented stupor. He thought that in some way they were pushing him and his pain into a narrow, deep, black sack; they kept pushing further but they couldn't push them right in. And this terrible business for him was crowned by his suffering. And he was both struggling and wanting to drop right down, both fighting against it and assisting. And suddenly he was free and fell and came to. The same Gerasim was still sitting on the bed at his feet, dozing quietly, patiently. And Ivan Ilyich was lying there, having lifted his emaciated legs in their socks onto Gerasim's shoulders; there was the same candle with its shade and the same unceasing pain.

"Go, Gerasim," he whispered.

"It doesn't matter, sir, I'll sit a bit longer."

"No, go."

He removed his legs and lay on his side on top of his arm, and he began to feel sorry for himself. He waited for Gerasim to go out into the next room and he couldn't control himself anymore, and he burst into tears like a child. He wept for his helplessness, for his horrible loneliness, for people's cruelty, for God's cruelty, for God's absence.

"Why have you done all this? Why have you brought me here? Why, why do you torment me so horribly?"

He didn't expect an answer, but he also wept because there wasn't and couldn't be an answer. The pain increased again but he didn't move or call anyone. He said to himself, "More, go on, beat me! But why? What have I done to you, why?"

Then he calmed down; he not only stopped weeping, he stopped breathing and became all attention, as if he were listening not to a voice speaking in sounds but to the voice of his soul, to the train of thoughts rising within him.

"What do you want?" was the first clear idea capable of being expressed in words that he heard. "What do you want? What do you want?" he repeated to himself. "What? Not to suffer. To live," he answered.

And again he became absorbed with such intense attention that even the pain did not distract him.

"To live? To live how?" asked the voice of his soul.

"Yes, to live, as I lived before: well and pleasantly."

"As you lived before, well, pleasantly?" asked the voice. And he began to go over in his imagination the best moments of his pleasant life. But—strange to relate—all these best moments of a pleasant life now seemed quite different from what they had seemed then. All of them—except for his first memories of childhood. There in childhood was something so truly pleasant with which he could live, if it returned. But the person who had experienced those pleasant things no longer existed: it was like a memory of something else.

As soon as the process began which had resulted in Ivan Ilyich, the man of today, all the things which had seemed joys melted away before his eyes and were changed into something worthless and often vile.

And the further from childhood, the nearer to the present, the more worthless and dubious were the joys. That began with law school. There was still something there truly good: there was gaiety, there was friendship, there were hopes. But in the senior classes these good moments were already less frequent. After that, at the time of his first period of service with the governor, again good moments appeared: there were memories of love for a woman. After that all this became confused and there was even less of what was good. Further on there was still less good, and the further he went the less there was.

Marriage . . . so casually entered, and disillusionment, and the smell that came from his wife's mouth, and sensuality, hypocrisy! And that deadly work of his and those worries about money, and on for a year, and two, and ten, and twenty—and always the same. And the further he went, the more deadly it became. "As if I were walking downhill at a regular pace, imagining I was walking uphill. That's how it was. In the eyes of the world I was walking uphill, and to just that extent life was slipping away from under me . . . And now it's time, to die!

"So what is this? Why? It can't be. It can't be that life was so meaningless and vile. But if it was indeed so meaningless and vile, then why die and die suffering? Something is wrong.

"Maybe I have lived not as I should have"—the thought suddenly came into his head. "But how so when I did everything in the proper way?" he said to himself, and immediately rejected this solution of the whole riddle of life as something wholly impossible.

"What do you want now? To live? To live how? To live as you lived in court when the court officer pronounces, 'The court is opening!' The court is opening, opening, the court," he repeated to himself. "Here's the court! But I'm not guilty!" he shouted angrily. "For what?" And he stopped weeping and, turning his face to the wall, he began to think of just the one thing: why all this horror, for what?

But however much he thought, he found no answer. And when there came to him the thought, as it often did, that all this was happening because he had lived wrongly, he at once remembered all the correctness of his life and rejected this strange thought.

## X

Two more weeks went by. Ivan Ilyich didn't get up from the sofa anymore. He didn't want to lie in bed and instead lay on the sofa. And, lying almost all the time with his face to the wall, he suffered in his loneliness all those same insoluble sufferings and in his loneliness thought the same insoluble thoughts. What is this? Is it really true that this is death? And a voice within answered: Yes, it's true. Why these torments? And the voice answered: That's the way it is; there is no why. Apart from that there was nothing more.

From the very start of his illness, when Ivan Ilyich went to the doctor for the first time, his life was divided into two diametrically opposed moods, which alternated with each other: on the one hand despair and the expectation of an incomprehensible and horrible death, on the other hope and the absorbed observation of the activity of his body. Now he had before his eyes just a kidney or appendix which for a time had deviated from the performance of its duties; now there was just incomprehensible, horrible death from which it was impossible to escape in any way.

From the very beginning of his illness these two moods alternated with each other; but the more the illness progressed, the more fantastic and questionable became thoughts about his kidney and the more real the consciousness of approaching death.

He only had to remember what he had been three months previously and what he was now—to remember how he had been walking downhill at a regular pace—for all possibility of hope to crumble.

In the recent loneliness in which he found himself, lying with his face to the back of the sofa, loneliness in the midst of a crowded city and his numerous acquaintances and family—loneliness that could not be more absolute anywhere, either at the bottom of the sea or underneath the earth—in his recent terrible loneliness Ivan Ilyich lived only by his imagination in the past. One after another pictures of his past presented themselves to him. It always began with the closest in time and went back to the most remote, to his childhood, and rested there. If Ivan Ilyich thought of the stewed prunes he was offered to eat now, he remembered the moist, wrinkled French prunes of his childhood, their particular taste and the flow of saliva when he got to the stone, and alongside this memory of taste there arose a whole row of memories of that time: his *nyanya*,[7] his brother, his toys. "You mustn't think of that. . . . It's too painful," Ivan Ilyich said to himself, and was again transported into the present. A button on the back of the sofa and the creases in its morocco leather. "Morocco is expensive and wears badly; there was a quarrel because of it. But it was different leather and a different row when we ripped our father's briefcase and were punished, but Mama brought us some pies." And again he stopped in his childhood and again it was painful for Ivan Ilyich, and he tried to push it away and think of something else.

And here again, together with this train of memories, another train of memories went through his mind—of how his illness had intensified and grown. It was the same; the further back he went, the more life there was. There was more good in life and more of life itself. And the two merged together. *As my torments kept getting worse and worse, so the whole of life became worse and worse,* he thought. One bright spot, there, at the start of his life, and after that everything blacker and blacker, and everything quicker and quicker. *In inverse ratio to the square of the distance from death,* thought Ivan Ilyich. And an image of a stone flying downward with increasing speed became fixed in his mind. Life, a sequence of increasing sufferings, flies quicker and quicker to the end, to the most terrible suffering of all. *I am flying . . .* He shivered, moved, tried to resist, but he now knew that resistance was impossible, and again, with eyes that were tired of looking but which couldn't help looking at what was in front of him, he gazed at the back of the sofa and waited—waited for that terrible fall, the crash, and annihilation. "I can't resist," he said to himself. "But if I could just understand why. That too I can't. I might be able to explain it if I said I had lived not as I should have. But it's impossible to admit that," he said to himself, remembering all the lawfulness, the correctness, and the decorum of his life. "It's impossible to admit that now," he said to himself, grimacing with his lips, as if anyone could see this smile of his and be deceived by it. "There's no explanation! Torment, death. . . . Why?"

---

7. Nanny (Russian).

## XI

Two weeks went by like that. In those weeks an event took place that had been desired by Ivan Ilyich and his wife: Petrishchev made a formal proposal. It happened in the evening. The next day Praskovya Fyodorovna went in to her husband, wondering how to announce Fyodor Petrovich's proposal to him, but that very night Ivan Ilyich had taken a turn for the worse. Praskovya Fyodorovna found him on the same sofa, but in a new position. He was lying on his back, groaning and looking ahead with a fixed gaze.

She started talking about medicines. He turned his eyes to her. She didn't finish what she had begun to say; there was so much anger expressed in those eyes, aimed directly at her.

"For Christ's sake, let me die in peace," he said.

She was about to go, but at that moment his daughter came in and went up to say good morning. He looked at his daughter as he had at his wife and to her questions about his health he drily said to her that he would soon liberate them all from himself. They both said nothing, sat briefly, and went out.

"What can we be blamed for?" Liza said to her mother. "As if we'd done this! I'm sorry for Papa, but why must he torment us?"

The doctor came at the usual time. Ivan Ilyich answered him "yes, no," not taking his angry eyes from him, and finally said:

"You know that you won't be of any help, so leave me."

"We can relieve the suffering," the doctor said.

"You can't do that either; leave me."

The doctor went out into the drawing room and informed Praskovya Fyodorovna that things were very bad and that there was only one resource—opium, to relieve the suffering, which must be terrible.

The doctor said that Ivan Ilyich's physical sufferings were terrible, and that was true; but even more terrible than his physical sufferings were his mental sufferings, and there was his chief torment.

His mental sufferings lay in the fact that that night, as he looked at Gerasim's sleepy, good-natured face with its high cheekbones, there suddenly had entered his head the thought: *But what if in actual fact all my life, my conscious life, has been "wrong"?*

It occurred to him that the notion that had previously seemed to him a complete impossibility—that he had not lived his life as he should have done—could be the truth. It occurred to him that his barely noticeable attempts at struggling against what was considered good by those in high positions above him, those barely noticeable attempts which he had immediately rejected, could be genuine, and everything else wrong. His work and the structure of his life and his family and his social and professional interests—all that could be wrong. He tried to defend all that to himself. And suddenly he felt the fragility of what he was defending. And there was nothing to defend.

"But if this is so," he said to himself, "and I am leaving life with the realization that I have lost everything I was given and that it's impossible to put right, then what?" He lay on his back and started to go over his whole life afresh. When in the morning he saw the manservant, then his wife, then his daughter, then the doctor—every one of their movements, every one of their words confirmed for him the terrible truth that had been disclosed to him in the night. He saw in them himself, everything by which he had lived, and saw clearly that all this was wrong, all this was a terrible, huge fraud concealing both life and death. This realization increased, increased tenfold his physical sufferings. He groaned and tossed about and pulled at the clothes on him. He felt suffocated and crushed. And he hated them for that.

They gave him a big dose of opium; he lost consciousness, but at dinnertime the same began again. He drove them all away from him and tossed about from side to side.

His wife came to him and said:

"*Jean*, my dear, do this for me. It can't do any harm, but it often helps. So, it's nothing. And people in good health often . . ."

He opened his eyes wide.

"What? Take communion? Why? There's no need to! But then . . ."

She started crying.

"Yes, my dear? I'll call for our man, he's so sweet."

"Fine, very well," he said.

When the priest came and took his confession, he was calmed; he felt a kind of relief from his doubts and, as a consequence of that, from his sufferings, and a moment of hope came to him. He again began to think of his appendix and the possibility of curing it. He received communion with tears in his eyes.

When, after communion, he was put to bed, for a moment he felt comfortable and hope for life appeared again. He began to think of the operation being suggested to him. "To live, I want to live," he said to himself. His wife came to congratulate him on taking communion; she said the usual words and added:

"You feel better, don't you?"

Without looking at her he said, "Yes."

Her clothes, her body, the expression of her face, the sound of her voice—everything said to him one thing: "Wrong. Everything by which you have lived and are living is a lie, a fraud, concealing life and death from you." And as soon as he thought that, hatred rose up in him, and together with hatred agonizing physical suffering, and with those sufferings an awareness of the end, nearby and unavoidable. Something new happened: his breath started to strain and come in spurts and be squeezed out.

His expression when he said "yes" was terrible. Having said that yes, he looked her straight in the eye and with unusual strength for his weakness turned himself facedown and cried:

"Go away, go away, leave me!"

## XII

From that minute began three days of unceasing screams that were so horrible one couldn't hear them from two doors away without feeling horror. The minute he answered his wife, he understood that he was lost, that there was no return, that the end had come, the very end, but the doubt still wasn't resolved; it still remained doubt.

"Oh! Oh! Oh!" he cried out in various tones. He began to cry out, "I don't want to, no!" and went on like that crying out the letter *O*.

For the whole three days, during which time did not exist for him, he tossed about in the black sack into which he was being pushed by an invisible, insurmountable force. He struggled as a man condemned to death struggles in the arms of the executioner, knowing he cannot save himself; and with every minute he felt that for all his efforts at struggling he was coming nearer and nearer to what filled him with horror. He felt that his agony lay both in being pushed into that black hole and even more in being unable to get into it. He was prevented from climbing in by his declaration that his life had been good. This justification of his life caught on something and stopped him from going forward, and that distressed him most of all.

Suddenly some kind of force struck him in the chest and on the side; his breath was constricted even more; he collapsed into the hole and there at the bottom of the hole some light was showing. There happened to him what he used to experience in a railway carriage when you think you are going forward but are going backward and suddenly realize your true direction.

"Yes, everything was wrong," he said to himself, "but it doesn't matter. I can, I can do what is right. But what is right?" he asked himself, and at once fell silent.

It was the end of the third day, an hour before his death. At that very moment the gymnasium schoolboy quietly slipped into his father's room and approached his bed. The dying man was still crying out despairingly and waving his arms about. One of his hands hit the schoolboy's head. The schoolboy took it, pressed it to his lips, and wept.

At that very moment Ivan Ilyich fell through and saw a light, and it was revealed to him that his life had been wrong but that it was still possible to mend things. He asked himself, "What is right?" and fell silent, listening. Now he felt someone was kissing his hand. He opened his eyes and looked at his son. He felt sorry for him. His wife came to him. He looked at her. She looked at him, mouth open and tears on her nose and cheeks that she hadn't wiped away. He felt sorry for her.

"Yes, I make them unhappy," he thought. "They are sorry for me, but it'll be better for them when I die." He wanted to say that but didn't have the strength to utter it. "However, why say things? One must act," he thought. With a look to his wife he pointed to his son and said:

"Take him away... sorry for him... and for you..." He wanted to add "forgive" but said "give," and not having the strength to correct himself, waved his hand, knowing that He who needed to understand would understand.

And suddenly it became clear to him that what had been oppressing him and not coming to an end—now everything was coming to an end at once, on two sides, on ten sides, on every side. He was sorry for them, he must make it so they had no pain. Free them and free himself from these sufferings. "So good and so simple," he thought. "And the pain?" he asked himself. "Where's it gone? Well, where are you, pain?"

He began to listen.

"There it is. So—let the pain be. And death? Where is it?"

He searched for his old habitual fear of death and didn't find it. Where was death? What death? There was no fear, because there was no death.

Instead of death there was light.

"So that's it!" he suddenly said aloud. "Such joy!"

For him all this took place in a moment, and the significance of this moment didn't change. For those there his death agony lasted two hours more. Something bubbled in his chest; his emaciated body shivered. Then the gurgling and wheezing became less and less frequent.

"It is finished!" someone said above him.

He heard these words and repeated them in his heart. "Death is finished," he said to himself. "It is no more."

He breathed in, stopped halfway, stretched himself, and died.

1886

RELATED:

—Tolstoy, "What Is Art?" p. 895
—Gary Saul Morson, "The Reader as Voyeur: Tolstoi and the Poetics of Didactic Fiction," p. 933

# JOHN UPDIKE
*b. 1932–2009*

Updike was born in Shillington, Pennsylvania, an only child. His mother—a writer—gave him the idea that art would lead him to a happy life, so he launched himself as a cartoonist for the *Harvard Lampoon* during his college years, and for a year after graduation studied drawing in England. Soon after this he joined the staff of the *New Yorker* and served the magazine in a number of capacities until 1957; he contributed verse, reviews, and fiction to its pages. Astonishingly prolific, Updike published, on average, a book a year throughout his adult life. His fiction is often topical—people trapped in American fads and prejudices figure often in his most characteristic writing. His many novels have won two Pulitzer Prizes and the National Book Award, among other honors. Best-known titles include *Rabbit, Run* (1960), *The Centaur* (1963), *Couples* (1968), *Rabbit Redux* (1971), *Rabbit Is Rich* (1982), *The Witches of Eastwick* (1984), *Roger's Version* (1986), *Rabbit at Rest* (1990), *Toward the End of Time* (1997), *Terrorist* (2006), and his last novel, *The Widows of Eastwick* (2008). A winner of the Rea Award for the Short Story (2006), his stories have been collected in *Problems* (1979), *The Afterlife* (1994), *Early Stories, 1953–1975* (2003), *Three Trips* (2003), *My Father's Tears* (2009), and *The Maples Stories* (2009). The two volumes of his *Collected Stories* appeared in 2013.

# A&P

In walks these three girls in nothing but bathing suits. I'm in the third checkout slot, with my back to the door, so I don't see them until they're over by the bread. The one that caught my eye first was the one in the plaid green two-piece. She was a chunky kid, with a good tan and a sweet broad soft-looking can with those two crescents of white just under it, where the sun never seems to hit, at the top of the backs of her legs. I stood there with my hand on a box of HiHo crackers trying to remember if I rang it up or not. I ring it up again and the customer starts giving me hell. She's one of these cash-register-watchers, a witch about fifty with rouge on her cheekbones and no eyebrows, and I know it made her day to trip me up. She'd been watching cash registers for fifty years and probably never seen a mistake before.

By the time I got her feathers smoothed and her goodies into a bag—she gives me a little snort in passing, if she'd been born at the right time they would have burned her over in Salem[1]—by the time I get her on her way the girls had circled around the bread and were coming back, without a pushcart, back my way along the counters, in the aisle between the checkouts and the Special bins. They didn't even have shoes on. There was this chunky one, with the two-piece—it was bright green and the seams on the bra were still sharp and her belly was still pretty pale so I guessed she just got it (the suit)—there was this one, with one of those chubby berry-faces, the lips all bunched together under her nose, this one, and a tall one, with black hair that hadn't quite frizzed right, and one of these sunburns right across under the eyes, and a chin that was too long—you know, the kind of girl other girls think is very "striking" and "attractive" but never quite makes it, as they very well know, which is why they like her so much—and then the third one, that wasn't quite so tall. She was the queen. She kind of led them, the other two peeking around and making their shoulders round. She didn't look around, not this queen, she just walked straight on slowly, on these long white primadonna legs. She came down a little hard on her heels, as if she didn't walk in bare feet that much, putting down her heels and then letting the weight move along to her toes as if she was testing the floor with every step, putting a little deliberate extra action into it. You never know for sure how girls' minds work (do you really think it's a mind in there or just a little buzz like a bee in a glass jar?) but you got the idea she had talked the other two into coming here with her, and now she was showing them how to do it, walk slow and hold yourself straight.

She had on a kind of dirty-pink—beige maybe, I don't know—bathing suit with a little nubble all over it and, what got me, the straps were down. They were off her shoulders looped loose around the cool tops of her arms, and I guess as a result the suit had slipped a little on her, so all around the top of the cloth there was this shining rim. If it hadn't been there you wouldn't have known there could have been anything whiter than those shoulders. With the straps pushed off, there was nothing between the top of the suit and the top of her head except just *her*, this clean bare plane of the top of her chest down from the shoulder bones like a dented sheet of metal tilted in the light. I mean, it was more than pretty.

She had a sort of oaky hair that the sun and salt had bleached, done up in a bun that was unravelling, and a kind of prim face. Walking into the A&P with your straps down, I suppose it's the only kind of face you *can* have. She held her head so high her neck, coming up out of those white shoulders, looked kind of stretched, but I didn't mind. The longer her neck was, the more of her there was.

She must have felt in the corner of her eye me and over my shoulder Stokesie in the second slot watching, but she didn't tip. Not this queen. She kept her eyes moving across the racks, and stopped, and turned so slow it made my stomach rub the inside of my apron, and buzzed to the other two, who kind of huddled against her for relief, and then they all three of them went up the cat-and-dog-food-breakfast-cereal-macaroni-rice-raisins-seasonings-spreads-spaghetti-soft-drinks-crackers-and-cookies aisle. From the third slot I look straight up this aisle to the meat counter, and I watched them all the

---

1. Massachusetts seaport famous for the execution of "witches" in 1692.

way. The fat one with the tan sort of fumbled with the cookies, but on second thought she put the package back. The sheep pushing their carts down the aisle—the girls were walking against the usual traffic (not that we have one-way signs or anything)—were pretty hilarious. You could see them, when Queenie's white shoulders dawned on them, kind of jerk, or hop, or hiccup, but their eyes snapped back to their own baskets and on they pushed. I bet you could set off dynamite in an A&P and the people would by and large keep reaching and checking oatmeal off their lists and muttering "Let me see, there was a third thing, began with A, asparagus, no, ah, yes, applesauce!" or whatever it is they do mutter. But there was no doubt, this jiggled them. A few houseslaves in pin curlers even looked around after pushing their carts past to make sure what they had seen was correct.

You know, it's one thing to have a girl in a bathing suit down on the beach, where what with the glare nobody can look at each other much anyway, and another thing in the cool of the A&P, under the fluorescent lights, against all those stacked packages, with her feet paddling along naked over our checker-board green-and-cream rubber-tile floor.

"Oh Daddy," Stokesie said beside me. "I feel so faint."

"Darling," I said. "Hold me tight." Stokesie's married, with two babies chalked up on his fuselage already, but as far as I can tell that's the only difference. He's twenty-two, and I was nineteen this April.

"Is it done?" he asks, the responsible married man finding his voice. I forgot to say he thinks he's going to be manager some sunny day, maybe in 1990 when it's called the Great Alexandrov and Petrooshki Tea Company[2] or something.

What he meant was, our town is five miles from a beach, with a big summer colony out on the Point, but we're right in the middle of town, and the women generally put on a shirt or shorts or something before they get out of the car into the street. And anyway these are usually women with six children and varicose veins mapping their legs and nobody, including them, could care less. As I say, we're right in the middle of town, and if you stand at our front doors you can see two banks and the Congregational church and the newspaper store and three real-estate offices and about twenty-seven old freeloaders tearing up Central Street because the sewer broke again. It's not as if we're on the Cape;[3] we're north of Boston and there's people in this town haven't seen the ocean for twenty years.

The girls had reached the meat counter and were asking McMahon something. He pointed, they pointed, and they shuffled out of sight behind a pyramid of Diet Delight peaches. All that was left for us to see was old McMahon patting his mouth and looking after them sizing up their joints. Poor kids, I began to feel sorry for them, they couldn't help it.

Now here comes the sad part of the story, at least my family says it's sad, but I don't think it's so sad myself. The store's pretty empty, it being Thursday afternoon, so there was nothing much to do except lean on the register and wait for the girls to show up again. The whole store was like a pinball machine

---

2. The actual name of the A&P supermarket chain is The Great Atlantic and Pacific Tea Company.
3. Cape Cod, Massachusetts, a resort area where fashions of dress are usually informal.

and I didn't know which tunnel they'd come out of. After a while they come around out of the far aisle, around the light bulbs, records at discount of the Caribbean Six or Tony Martin Sings or some such gunk you wonder they waste the wax on, six-packs of candy bars, and plastic toys done up in cellophane that fall apart when a kid looks at them anyway. Around they come, Queenie still leading the way, and holding a little gray jar in her hand. Slots Three through Seven are unmanned and I could see her wondering between Stokes and me, but Stokesie with his usual luck draws an old party in baggy gray pants who stumbles up with four giant cans of pineapple juice (what do these bums *do* with all that pineapple juice? I've often asked myself) so the girls come to me. Queenie puts down the jar and I take it into my fingers icy cold. Kingfish Fancy Herring Snacks in Pure Sour Cream: 49¢. Now her hands are empty, not a ring or a bracelet, bare as God made them, and I wonder where the money's coming from. Still with that prim look she lifts a folded dollar bill out of the hollow at the center of her nubbled pink top. The jar went heavy in my hand. Really, I thought that was so cute.

Then everybody's luck begins to run out. Lengel comes in from haggling with a truck full of cabbages on the lot and is about to scuttle into that door marked MANAGER behind which he hides all day when the girls touch his eye. Lengel's pretty dreary, teaches Sunday school and the rest, but he doesn't miss that much. He comes over and says, "Girls, this isn't the beach."

Queenie blushes, though maybe it's just a brush of sunburn I was noticing for the first time, now that she was so close. "My mother asked me to pick up a jar of herring snacks." Her voice kind of startled me, the way voices do when you see the people first, coming out so flat and dumb yet kind of tony, too, the way it ticked over "pick up" and "snacks." All of a sudden I slid right down her voice into her living room. Her father and the other men were standing around in ice-cream coats and bow ties and the women were in sandals picking up herring snacks on toothpicks off a big glass plate and they were all holding drinks the color of water with olives and sprigs of mint in them. When my parents have somebody over they get lemonade and if it's a real racy affair Schlitz in tall glasses with "They'll Do It Every Time"[4] cartoons stencilled on.

"That's all right," Lengel said. "But this isn't the beach." His repeating this struck me as funny, as if it had just occurred to him, and he had been thinking all these years the A&P was a great big dune and he was the head lifeguard. He didn't like my smiling—as I say he doesn't miss much—but he concentrates on giving the girls that sad Sunday-school-superintendent stare.

Queenie's blush is no sunburn now, and the plump one in plaid, that I liked better from the back—a really sweet can—pipes up, "We weren't doing any shopping. We just came in for the one thing."

"That makes no difference," Lengel tells her, and I could see from the way his eyes went that he hadn't noticed she was wearing a two-piece before. "We want you decently dressed when you come in here."

"We *are* decent," Queenie says suddenly, her lower lip pushing, getting sore now that she remembers her place, a place from which the crowd that runs the A&P must look pretty crummy. Fancy Herring Snacks flashed in her very blue eyes.

---

4. Popular newspaper comic, created by Jimmy Hatlo, that first appeared in 1929.

"Girls, I don't want to argue with you. After this come in here with your shoulders covered. It's our policy." He turns his back. That's policy for you. Policy is what the kingpins want. What the others want is juvenile delinquency.

All this while, the customers had been showing up with their carts but, you know, sheep, seeing a scene, they had all bunched up on Stokesie, who shook open a paper bag as gently as peeling a peach, not wanting to miss a word. I could feel in the silence everybody getting nervous, most of all Lengel, who asks me, "Sammy, have you rung up their purchase?"

I thought and said "No" but it wasn't about that I was thinking. I go through the punches, 4, 9, GROC, TOT—it's more complicated than you think, and after you do it often enough, it begins to make a little song, that you hear words to, in my case "Hello (*bing*) there, you (*gung*) hap-py *pee*-pul (*splat*)!"—the *splat* being the drawer flying out. I uncrease the bill, tenderly as you may imagine, it just having come from between the two smoothest scoops of vanilla I had ever known there were, and pass a half and a penny into her narrow pink palm, and nestle the herrings in a bag and twist its neck and hand it over, all the time thinking.

The girls, and who'd blame them, are in a hurry to get out, so I say "I quit" to Lengel quick enough for them to hear, hoping they'll stop and watch me, their unsuspected hero. They keep right on going, into the electric eye; the door flies open and they flicker across the lot to their car, Queenie and Plaid and Big Tall Goony-Goony (not that as raw material she was so bad), leaving me with Lengel and a kink in his eyebrow.

"Did you say something, Sammy?"

"I said I quit."

"I thought you did."

"You didn't have to embarrass them."

"It was they who were embarrassing us."

I started to say something that came out "Fiddle-de-do." It's a saying of my grandmother's, and I know she would have been pleased.

"I don't think you know what you're saying," Lengel said.

"I know you don't," I said. "But I do." I pull the bow at the back of my apron and start shrugging it off my shoulders. A couple of customers that had been heading for my slot begin to knock against each other, liked scared pigs in a chute.

Lengel sighs and begins to look very patient and old and gray. He's been a friend of my parents for years. "Sammy, you don't want to do this to your Mom and Dad," he tells me. It's true, I don't. But it seems to me that once you begin a gesture it's fatal not to go through with it. I fold the apron, "Sammy" stitched in red on the pocket, and put it on the counter, and drop the bow tie on top of it. The bow tie is theirs, if you've ever wondered. "You'll feel this for the rest of your life," Lengel says, and I know that's true, too, but remembering how he made that pretty girl blush makes me so scrunchy inside I punch the No Sale tab and the machine whirs "pee-pul" and the drawer splats out. One advantage to this scene taking place in summer, I can follow this up with a clean exit, there's no fumbling around getting your coat and galoshes, I just saunter into the electric eye in my white shirt that my mother ironed the night before, and the door heaves itself open, and outside the sunshine is skating around on the asphalt.

I look around for my girls, but they're gone, of course. There wasn't anybody but some young married screaming with her children about some candy they didn't get by the door of a powder-blue Falcon station wagon. Looking back in the big windows, over the bags of peat moss and aluminum lawn furniture stacked on the pavement, I could see Lengel in my place in the slot, checking the sheep through. His face was dark gray and his back stiff, as if he's just had an injection of iron, and my stomach kind of fell as I felt how hard the world was going to be to me hereafter.

1962

RELATED:

—Updike, "Accepting the Howells Medal," p. 897

# HELENA MARÍA VIRAMONTES
## b. 1954

Viramontes was born in East Los Angeles. She earned her B.A. from Immaculate Heart College, where she began writing, first poetry and then fiction. Her stories were soon published and recognized. In 1979 she was awarded the fiction prize in the Chicano Literary Contest at the University of California at Irvine; she went on to earn her M.F.A. there. Her books include *The Moths* (1985); *Under the Feet of Jesus* (1995); and *Their Dogs Came with Them* (2007). A professor at Cornell University, she was named a Ford Fellow in Literature in 2007 by United States Artists and received the Dos Passos Award for Literature and an NEA Fellowship.

## The Moths

I was fourteen years old when Abuelita[1] requested my help. And it seemed only fair. Abuelita had pulled me through the rages of scarlet fever by placing, removing, and replacing potato slices on the temples of my forehead; she had seen me through several whippings, an arm broken by a dare-jump off Tío[2] Enrique's toolshed, puberty, and my first lie. Really, I told Amá,[3] it was only fair.

Not that I was her favorite granddaughter or anything special. I wasn't even pretty or nice like my older sisters and I just couldn't do the girl things they could do. My hands were too big to handle the fineries of crocheting or embroidery and I always pricked my fingers or knotted my colored threads time and time again while my sisters laughed and called me bull hands with their cute waterlike voices. So I began keeping a piece of jagged brick in my sock to bash my sisters or anyone who called me bull hands. Once, while we all sat in the bedroom, I hit Teresa on the forehead, right above her eyebrow, and she ran to Amá with her mouth open, her hand over her eye while blood seeped between her fingers. I was used to the whippings by then.

I wasn't respectful either. I even went so far as to doubt the power of Abuelita's slices, the slices she said absorbed my fever. "You're still alive, aren't you?" Abuelita snapped back, her pasty gray eye beaming at me and burning holes in my suspicions. Regretful that I had let secret questions drop out of my mouth, I couldn't look into her eyes. My hands began to fan out, grow like a liar's nose until they hung by my side like low weights. Abuelita made a balm out of dried moth wings and Vicks and rubbed my hands, shaping them back to size. It was the strangest feeling. Like bones melting. Like sun shining

---

1. "Little Grandma" (Spanish).   2. Uncle (Spanish).   3. Child's name for "Mother" (Spanish).

through the darkness of your eyelids. I didn't mind helping Abuelita after that, so Amá would always send me over to her.

In the early afternoon Amá would push her hair back, hand me my sweater and shoes, and tell me to go to Mama Luna's. This was to avoid another fight and another whipping, I knew. I would deliver one last direct shot on Marisela's arm and jump out of our house, the slam of the screen door burying her cries of anger, and I'd gladly go help Abuelita plant her wild lilies or jasmine or heliotrope or cilantro or hierbabuena[4] in red Hills Brothers coffee cans. Abuelita would wait for me at the top step of her porch holding a hammer and nail and empty coffee cans. And although we hardly spoke, hardly looked at each other as we worked over root transplants, I always felt her gray eye on me. It made me feel, in a strange sort of way, safe and guarded and not alone. Like God was supposed to make you feel.

On Abuelita's porch, I would puncture holes in the bottom of the coffee cans with a nail and a precise hit of a hammer. This completed, my job was to fill them with red clay mud from beneath her rose bushes, packing it softly, then making a perfect hole, four fingers round, to nest a sprouting avocado pit, or the spidery sweet potatoes that Abuelita rooted in mayonnaise jars with toothpicks and daily water, or prickly chayotes[5] that produced vines that twisted and wound all over her porch pillars, crawling to the roof, up and over the roof, and down the other side, making her small brick house look like it was cradled within the vines that grew pear-shaped squashes ready for the pick, ready to be steamed with onions and cheese and butter. The roots would burst out of the rusted coffee cans and search for a place to connect. I would then feed the seedlings with water.

But this was a different kind of help, Amá said, because Abuelita was dying. Looking into her gray eye, then into her brown one, the doctor said it was just a matter of days. And so it seemed only fair that these hands she had melted and formed found use in rubbing her caving body with alcohol and marihuana, rubbing her arms and legs, turning her face to the window so that she could watch the Bird of Paradise blooming or smell the scent of clove in the air. I toweled her face frequently and held her hand for hours. Her gray wiry hair hung over the mattress. Since I could remember, she'd kept her long hair in braids. Her mouth was vacant and when she slept, her eyelids never closed all the way. Up close, you could see her gray eye beaming out the window, staring hard as if to remember everything. I never kissed her. I left the window open when I went to the market.

Across the street from Jay's Market there was a chapel. I never knew its denomination, but I went in just the same to search for candles. I sat down on one of the pews because there were none. After I cleaned my fingernails, I looked up at the high ceiling. I had forgotten the vastness of these places, the coolness of the marble pillars and the frozen statues with blank eyes. I was alone. I knew why I had never returned.

That was one of Apá's[6] biggest complaints. He would pound his hands on the table, rocking the sugar dish or spilling a cup of coffee and scream that if I didn't go to Mass every Sunday to save my goddamn sinning soul, then I

---

4. Yerba buena, an evergreen herb (Spanish).   5. Small vegetable in the gourd family.   6. Child's name for "Father" (Spanish).

had no reason to go out of the house, period. Punto final.[7] He would grab my arm and dig his nails into me to make sure I understood the importance of catechism. Did he make himself clear? Then he strategically directed his anger at Amá for her lousy ways of bringing up daughters, being disrespectful and unbelieving, and my older sisters would pull me aside and tell me if I didn't get to Mass right this minute, they were all going to kick the holy shit out of me. Why am I so selfish? Can't you see what it's doing to Amá, you idiot? So I would wash my feet and stuff them in my black Easter shoes that shone with Vaseline, grab a missal and veil, and wave good-bye to Amá.

I would walk slowly down Lorena to First to Evergreen, counting the cracks on the cement. On Evergreen I would turn left and walk to Abuelita's. I liked her porch because it was shielded by the vines of the chayotes and I could get a good look at the people and car traffic on Evergreen without them knowing. I would jump up the porch steps, knock on the screen door as I wiped my feet and call Abuelita, mi Abuelita? As I opened the door and stuck my head in, I would catch the gagging scent of toasting chile on the placa.[8] When I entered the sala[9] she would greet me from the kitchen, wringing her hands in her apron. I'd sit at the corner of the table to keep from being in her way. The chiles made my eyes water. Am I crying? No, Mama Luna, I'm sure not crying. I don't like going to Mass, but my eyes watered anyway, the tears dropping on the tablecloth like candle wax. Abuelita lifted the burnt chiles from the fire and sprinkled water on them until the skins began to separate. Placing them in front of me, she turned to check the menudo.[1] I peeled the skins off and put the flimsy, limp-looking green and yellow chiles in the molcajete[2] and began to crush and crush and twist and crush the heart out of the tomato, the clove of garlic, the stupid chiles that made me cry, crushed them until they turned into liquid under my bull hand. With a wooden spoon, I scraped hard to destroy the guilt, and my tears were gone. I put the bowl of chile next to a vase filled with freshly cut roses. Abuelita touched my hand and pointed to the bowl of menudo that steamed in front of me. I spooned some chile into the menudo and rolled a corn tortilla thin with the palms of my hands. As I ate, a fine Sunday breeze entered the kitchen and a rose petal calmly feathered down to the table.

I left the chapel without blessing myself and walked to Jay's. Most of the time Jay didn't have much of anything. The tomatoes were always soft and the cans of Campbell soups had rusted spots on them. There was dust on the tops of cereal boxes. I picked up what I needed: rubbing alcohol, five cans of chicken broth, a big bottle of Pine Sol. At first Jay got mad because I thought I had forgotten the money. But it was there all the time, in my back pocket.

When I returned from the market, I heard Amá crying in Abuelita's kitchen. She looked up at me with puffy eyes. I placed the bags of groceries on the table and began putting the cans of soup away. Amá sobbed quietly. I never kissed her. After a while, I patted her on the back for comfort. Finally: "¿Y mi Amá?"[3] she asked in a whisper, then choked again and cried into her apron.

Abuelita fell off the bed twice yesterday, I said, knowing that I shouldn't have said it and wondering why I wanted to say it because it only made Amá

---

7. Period (Spanish); the end, case closed.  8. Hot plate (Spanish).  9. Living room (Spanish).  1. Tripe soup (Spanish).  2. Mortar (Mexican Spanish).  3. And my Mama? (Spanish).

cry harder. I guess I became angry and just so tired of the quarrels and beatings and unanswered prayers and my hands just there hanging helplessly by my side. Amá looked at me again, confused, angry, and her eyes were filled with sorrow. I went outside and sat on the porch swing and watched the people pass. I sat there until she left. I dozed off repeating the words to myself like rosary prayers: when do you stop giving when do you start giving when do you . . . and when my hands fell from my lap, I awoke to catch them. The sun was setting, an orange glow, and I knew Abuelita was hungry.

There comes a time when the sun is defiant. Just about the time when moods change, inevitable seasons of a day, transitions from one color to another, that hour or minute or second when the sun is finally defeated, finally sinks into the realization that it cannot with all its power to heal or burn, exist forever, there comes an illumination where the sun and earth meet, a final burst of burning red orange fury reminding us that although endings are inevitable, they are necessary for rebirths, and when that time came, just when I switched on the light in the kitchen to open Abuelita's can of soup, it was probably then that she died.

The room smelled of Pine Sol and vomit, and Abuelita had defecated the remains of her cancerous stomach. She had turned to the window and tried to speak, but her mouth remained open and speechless. I heard you, Abuelita, I said, stroking her cheek, I heard you. I opened the windows of the house and let the soup simmer and overboil on the stove. I turned the stove off and poured the soup down the sink. From the cabinet I got a tin basin, filled it with lukewarm water and carried it carefully to the room. I went to the linen closet and took out some modest bleached white towels. With the sacredness of a priest preparing his vestments, I unfolded the towels one by one on my shoulders. I removed the sheets and blankets from her bed and peeled off her thick flannel night-gown. I toweled her puzzled face, stretching out the wrinkles, removing the coils of her neck, toweled her shoulders and breasts. Then I changed the water. I returned to towel the creases of her stretch-marked stomach, her sporadic vaginal hairs, and her sagging thighs. I removed the lint from between her toes and noticed a mapped birthmark on the fold of her buttock. The scars on her back, which were as thin as the life lines on the palms of her hands, made me realize how little I really knew of Abuelita. I covered her with a thin blanket and went into the bathroom. I washed my hands, turned on the tub faucets and watched the water pour into the tub with vitality and steam. When it was full, I turned off the water and undressed. Then I went to get Abuelita.

She was not as heavy as I thought and when I carried her in my arms, her body fell into a V. And yet my legs were tired, shaky, and I felt as if the distance between the bedroom and bathroom was miles and years away. Amá, where are you?

I stepped into the bathtub one leg first, then the other. I bent my knees slowly to descend into the water slowly so I wouldn't scald her skin. There, there, Abuelita, I said, cradling her, smoothing her as we descended, I heard you. Her hair fell back and spread across the water like eagles' wings. The water in the tub overflowed and poured onto the tile of the floor. Then the moths came. Small gray ones that came from her soul and out through her mouth fluttering to light, circling the single dull light bulb of the bathroom.

Dying is lonely and I wanted to go to where the moths were, stay with her and plant chayotes whose vines would crawl up her fingers and into the clouds; I wanted to rest my head on her chest with her stroking my hair, telling me about the moths that lay within the soul and slowly eat the spirit up; I wanted to return to the waters of the womb with her so that we would never be alone again. I wanted. I wanted my Amá. I removed a few strands of hair from Abuelita's face and held her small light head within the hollow of my neck. The bathroom was filled with moths, and for the first time in a long time I cried, rocking us, crying for her, for me, for Amá, the sobs emerging from the depths of anguish, the misery of feeling half-born, sobbing until finally the sobs rippled into circles and circles of sadness and relief. There, there, I said to Abuelita, rocking us gently, there, there.

1995

# ALICE WALKER
## *b. 1944*

Walker was born in Eatonton, Georgia, and graduated from Sarah Lawrence College, where she
wrote her first book of poems. After experience in
the civil rights movement and employment as a
caseworker for the New York City welfare department, she worked as an editor for *Ms.* magazine.
An article she published there in 1975 revived
interest in the work of Zora Neale Hurston. Since
then she has been a teacher of creative writing
and black literature at Jackson State College,
Tougaloo College, Wellesley, and Yale. Her short
stories are collected in *In Love and Trouble: Stories
of Black Women* (1973) and *You Can't Keep a Good
Woman Down* (1982). Her novels include *The Third
Life of Grange Copeland* (1970); *Meridian* (1976); *The Color Purple* (1982), which
won both the Pulitzer Prize and the American Book Award; *The Temple of My
Familiar* (1989); *Possessing the Secret of Joy* (1992), *By the Light of My Father's Smile*
(1998), and most recently, *Now Is the Time to Open Your Heart* (2004). She has
published two memoirs, *The Same River Twice: Honoring the Difficult* (1996), and
*Chicken Chronicles* (2011). Her book of essays on political and social activism,
*Anything We Love Can Be Saved*, was published in 1997. Walker's *Collected Poems*
appeared in 2005.

# Everyday Use

*for your grandmamma*

I will wait for her in the yard that Maggie and I made so clean and wavy yesterday afternoon. A yard like this is more comfortable than most people
know. It is not just a yard. It is like an extended living room. When the hard
clay is swept clean as a floor and the fine sand around the edges lined with
tiny, irregular grooves, anyone can come and sit and look up into the elm tree
and wait for the breezes that never come inside the house.

Maggie will be nervous until after her sister goes: she will stand hopelessly
in corners, homely and ashamed of the burn scars down her arms and legs,
eying her sister with a mixture of envy and awe. She thinks her sister has held
life always in the palm of one hand, that "no" is a word the world never learned
to say to her.

You've no doubt seen those TV shows where the child who has "made it" is
confronted, as a surprise, by her own mother and father, tottering in weakly
from backstage. (A pleasant surprise, of course: What would they do if parent

and child came on the show only to curse out and insult each other?) On TV mother and child embrace and smile into each other's faces. Sometimes the mother and father weep, the child wraps them in her arms and leans across the table to tell how she would not have made it without their help. I have seen these programs.

Sometimes I dream a dream in which Dee and I are suddenly brought together on a TV program of this sort. Out of a dark and soft-seated limousine I am ushered into a bright room filled with many people. There I meet a smiling, gray, sporty man like Johnny Carson who shakes my hand and tells me what a fine girl I have. Then we are on the stage and Dee is embracing me with tears in her eyes. She pins on my dress a large orchid, even though she has told me once that she thinks orchids are tacky flowers.

In real life I am a large, big-boned woman with rough, man-working hands. In the winter I wear flannel nightgowns to bed and overalls during the day. I can kill and clean a hog as mercilessly as a man. My fat keeps me hot in zero weather. I can work outside all day, breaking ice to get water for washing; I can eat pork liver cooked over the open fire minutes after it comes steaming from the hog. One winter I knocked a bull calf straight in the brain between the eyes with a sledge hammer and had the meat hung up to chill before nightfall. But of course all this does not show on television. I am the way my daughter would want me to be: a hundred pounds lighter, my skin like an uncooked barley pancake. My hair glistens in the hot bright lights. Johnny Carson has much to do to keep up with my quick and witty tongue.

But that is a mistake. I know even before I wake up. Who ever knew a Johnson with a quick tongue? Who can even imagine me looking a strange white man in the eye? It seems to me I have talked to them always with one foot raised in flight, with my head turned in whichever way is farthest from them. Dee, though. She would always look anyone in the eye. Hesitation was no part of her nature.

"How do I look, Mama?" Maggie says, showing just enough of her thin body enveloped in pink skirt and red blouse for me to know she's there, almost hidden by the door.

"Come out into the yard," I say.

Have you ever seen a lame animal, perhaps a dog run over by some careless person rich enough to own a car, sidle up to someone who is ignorant enough to be kind to them? That is the way my Maggie walks. She has been like this, chin on chest, eyes on ground, feet in shuffle, ever since the fire that burned the other house to the ground.

Dee is lighter than Maggie, with nicer hair and a fuller figure. She's a woman now, though sometimes I forget. How long ago was it that the other house burned? Ten, twelve years? Sometimes I can still hear the flames and feel Maggie's arms sticking to me, her hair smoking and her dress falling off her in little black papery flakes. Her eyes seemed stretched open, blazed open by the flames reflected in them. And Dee. I see her standing off under the sweet gum tree she used to dig gum out of; a look of concentration on her face as she watched the last dingy gray board of the house fall in toward the red-hot brick chimney. Why don't you do a dance around the ashes? I'd wanted to ask her. She had hated the house that much.

I used to think she hated Maggie, too. But that was before we raised the money, the church and me, to send her to Augusta to school. She used to read to us without pity; forcing words, lies, other folks' habits, whole lives upon us two, sitting trapped and ignorant underneath her voice. She washed us in a river of make-believe, burned us with a lot of knowledge we didn't necessarily need to know. Pressed us to her with the serious way she read, to shove us away at just the moment, like dimwits, we seemed about to understand.

Dee wanted nice things. A yellow organdy dress to wear to her graduation from high school; black pumps to match a green suit she'd made from an old suit somebody gave me. She was determined to stare down any disaster in her efforts. Her eyelids would not flicker for minutes at a time. Often I fought off the temptation to shake her. At sixteen she had a style of her own: and knew what style was.

I never had an education myself. After second grade the school was closed down. Don't ask me why: in 1927 colored asked fewer questions than they do now. Sometimes Maggie reads to me. She stumbles along good naturedly but can't see well. She knows she is not bright. Like good looks and money, quickness passed her by. She will marry John Thomas (who has mossy teeth in an earnest face) and then I'll be free to sit here and I guess just sing church songs to myself. Although I never was a good singer. Never could carry a tune. I was always better at a man's job. I used to love to milk till I was hooked[1] in the side in '49. Cows are soothing and slow and don't bother you, unless you try to milk them the wrong way.

I have deliberately turned my back on the house. It is three rooms, just like the one that burned, except the roof is tin; they don't make shingle roofs anymore. There are no real windows, just some holes cut in the sides, like the portholes in a ship, but not round and not square, with rawhide holding the shutters up on the outside. This house is in a pasture, too, like the other one. No doubt when Dee sees it she will want to tear it down. She wrote me once that no matter where we "choose" to live, she will manage to come see us. But she will never bring her friends. Maggie and I thought about this and Maggie asked me, "Mama, when did Dee ever *have* any friends?"

She had a few. Furtive boys in pink shirts hanging about on washday after school. Nervous girls who never laughed. Impressed with her they worshiped the well-turned phrase, the cute shape, the scalding humor that erupted like bubbles in lye. She read to them.

When she was courting Jimmy T she didn't have much time to pay to us, but turned all her faultfinding power on him. He *flew* to marry a cheap city girl from a family of ignorant flashy people. She hardly had time to recompose herself.

When she comes I will meet—but there they are!

Maggie attempts to make a dash for the house, in her shuffling way, but I stay her with my hand. "Come back here," I say. And she stops and tries to dig a well in the sand with her toe.

---

1. That is, by the horn of the cow being milked.

It is hard to see them clearly through the strong sun. But even the first glimpse of leg out of the car tells me it is Dee. Her feet were always neat-looking, as if God himself had shaped them with a certain style. From the other side of the car comes a short, stocky man. Hair is all over his head a foot long and hanging from his chin like a kinky mule tail. I hear Maggie suck in her breath. "Uhnnnh," is what it sounds like. Like when you see the wriggling end of a snake just in front of your foot on the road. "Uhnnnh."

Dee next. A dress down to the ground, in this hot weather. A dress so loud it hurts my eyes. There are yellows and oranges enough to throw back the light of the sun. I feel my whole face warming from the heat waves it throws out. Earrings gold, too, and hanging down to her shoulders. Bracelets dangling and making noises when she moves her arm up to shake the folds of the dress out of her armpits. The dress is loose and flows, and as she walks closer, I like it. I hear Maggie go "Uhnnnh" again. It is her sister's hair. It stands straight up like the wool on a sheep. It is black as night and around the edges are two long pigtails that rope about like small lizards disappearing behind her ears.

"Wa-su-zo-Tean-o!" she says, coming on in that gliding way the dress makes her move. The short stocky fellow with the hair to his navel is all grinning and he follows up with "Asalamalakim,[2] my mother and sister!" He moves to hug Maggie but she falls back, right up against the back of my chair. I feel her trembling there and when I look up I see the perspiration falling off her chin.

"Don't get up," says Dee. Since I am stout it takes something of a push. You can see me trying to move a second or two before I make it. She turns, showing white heels through her sandals, and goes back to the car. Out she peeks next with a Polaroid. She stoops down quickly and lines up picture after picture of me sitting there in front of the house with Maggie cowering behind me. She never takes a shot without making sure the house is included. When a cow comes nibbling around the edge of the yard she snaps it and me and Maggie *and* the house. Then she puts the Polaroid in the back seat of the car, and comes up and kisses me on the forehead.

Meanwhile Asalamalakim is going through motions with Maggie's hand. Maggie's hand is as limp as a fish, and probably as cold, despite the sweat, and she keeps trying to pull it back. It looks like Asalamalakim wants to shake hands but wants to do it fancy. Or maybe he don't know how people shake hands. Anyhow, he soon gives up on Maggie.

"Well," I say. "Dee."

"No, Mama," she says. "Not 'Dee,' Wangero Leewanika Kemanjo!"

"What happened to 'Dee'?" I wanted to know.

"She's dead," Wangero said. "I couldn't bear it any longer, being named after the people who oppress me."

"You know as well as me you was named after your aunt Dicie," I said. Dicie is my sister. She named Dee. We called her "Big Dee" after Dee was born.

"But who was *she* named after?" asked Wangero.

"I guess after Grandma Dee," I said.

"And who was she named after?" asked Wangero.

---

2. Phonetic rendering of an Arabic greeting meaning "Peace be upon you." "Wa-su-zo-Tean-o" is a rendering of an African dialect salutation.

"Her mother," I said, and saw Wangero was getting tired. "That's about as far back as I can trace it," I said. Though, in fact, I probably could have carried it back beyond the Civil War through the branches.

"Well," said Asalamalakim, "there you are."

"Uhnnnh," I heard Maggie say.

"There I was not," I said, "before 'Dicie' cropped up in our family, so why should I try to trace it that far back?"

He just stood there grinning, looking down on me like somebody inspecting a Model A car. Every once in a while he and Wangero sent eye signals over my head.

"How do you pronounce this name?" I asked.

"You don't have to call me by it if you don't want to," said Wangero.

"Why shouldn't I?" I asked. "If that's what you want us to call you, we'll call you."

"I know it might sound awkward at first," said Wangero.

"I'll get used to it," I said. "Ream it out again."

Well, soon we got the name out of the way. Asalamalakim had a name twice as long and three times as hard. After I tripped over it two or three times he told me to just call him Hakim-a-barber. I wanted to ask him was he a barber, but I didn't really think he was, so I didn't ask.

"You must belong to those beef-cattle peoples down the road," I said. They said "Asalamalakim" when they met you, too, but they didn't shake hands. Always too busy: feeding the cattle, fixing the fences, putting up salt-lick shelters, throwing down hay. When the white folks poisoned some of the herd the men stayed up all night with rifles in their hands. I walked a mile and a half just to see the sight.

Hakim-a-barber said, "I accept some of their doctrines, but farming and raising cattle is not my style." (They didn't tell me, and I didn't ask, whether Wangero (Dee) had really gone and married him.)

We sat down to eat and right away he said he didn't eat collards and pork was unclean. Wangero, though, went on through the chitlins and corn bread, the greens and everything else. She talked a blue streak over the sweet potatoes. Everything delighted her. Even the fact that we still used the benches her daddy made for the table when we couldn't afford to buy chairs.

"Oh, Mama!" she cried. Then turned to Hakim-a-barber. "I never knew how lovely these benches are. You can feel the rump prints," she said, running her hands underneath her and along the bench. Then she gave a sigh and her hand closed over Grandma Dee's butter dish. "That's it!" she said. "I knew there was something I wanted to ask you if I could have." She jumped up from the table and went over in the corner where the churn stood, the milk in it clabber by now. She looked at the churn and looked at it.

"This churn top is what I need," she said. "Didn't Uncle Buddy whittle it out of a tree you all used to have?"

"Yes," I said.

"Uh huh," she said happily. "And I want the dasher, too."

"Uncle Buddy whittle that, too?" asked the barber.

Dee (Wangero) looked up at me.

"Aunt Dee's first husband whittled the dash," said Maggie so low you almost couldn't hear her. "His name was Henry, but they called him Stash."

"Maggie's brain is like an elephant's," Wangero said, laughing. "I can use the churn top as a centerpiece for the alcove table," she said, sliding a plate over the churn, "and I'll think of something artistic to do with the dasher."

When she finished wrapping the dasher the handle stuck out. I took it for a moment in my hands. You didn't even have to look close to see where hands pushing the dasher up and down to make butter had left a kind of sink in the wood. In fact, there were a lot of small sinks; you could see where thumbs and fingers had sunk into the wood. It was beautiful light yellow wood, from a tree that grew in the yard where Big Dee and Stash had lived.

After dinner Dee (Wangero) went to the trunk at the foot of my bed and started rifling through it. Maggie hung back in the kitchen over the dishpan. Out came Wangero with two quilts. They had been pieced by Grandma Dee and then Big Dee and me had hung them on the quilt frames on the front porch and quilted them. One was in the Lone Star pattern. The other was Walk Around the Mountain. In both of them were scraps of dresses Grandma Dee had worn fifty and more years ago. Bits and pieces of Grandpa Jarrell's Paisley shirts. And one teeny faded blue piece, about the size of a penny matchbox, that was from Great Grandpa Ezra's uniform that he wore in the Civil War.

"Mama," Wangero said sweet as a bird. "Can I have these old quilts?"

I heard something fall in the kitchen, and a minute later the kitchen door slammed.

"Why don't you take one or two of the others?" I asked. "These old things was just done by me and Big Dee from some tops your grandma pieced before she died."

"No," said Wangero. "I don't want those. They are stitched around the borders by machine."

"That'll make them last better," I said.

"That's not the point," said Wangero. "These are all pieces of dresses Grandma used to wear. She did all this stitching by hand. Imagine!" She held the quilts securely in her arms, stroking them.

"Some of the pieces, like those lavender ones, come from old clothes her mother handed down to her," I said, moving up to touch the quilts. Dee (Wangero) moved back just enough so that I couldn't reach the quilts. They already belonged to her.

"Imagine!" she breathed again, clutching them closely to her bosom.

"The truth is," I said, "I promised to give them quilts to Maggie, for when she marries John Thomas."

She gasped like a bee had stung her.

"Maggie can't appreciate these quilts!" she said. "She'd probably be backward enough to put them to everyday use."

"I reckon she would," I said. "God knows I been saving 'em for long enough with nobody using 'em. I hope she will!" I didn't want to bring up how I had offered Dee (Wangero) a quilt when she went away to college. Then she had told me they were old-fashioned, out of style.

"But they're *priceless*!" she was saying now, furiously; for she has a temper. "Maggie would put them on the bed and in five years they'd be in rags. Less than that!"

"She can always make some more," I said. "Maggie knows how to quilt."

Dee (Wangero) looked at me with hatred. "You just will not understand. The point is these quilts, *these* quilts!"

"Well," I said, stumped. "What would *you* do with them?"

"Hang them," she said. As if that was the only thing you *could* do with quilts.

Maggie by now was standing in the door. I could almost hear the sound her feet made as they scraped over each other.

"She can have them, Mama," she said, like somebody used to never winning anything, or having anything reserved for her. "I can 'member Grandma Dee without the quilts."

I looked at her hard. She had filled her bottom lip with checkerberry snuff and it gave her a face a kind of dopey, hangdog look. It was Grandma Dee and Big Dee who taught her how to quilt herself. She stood there with her scarred hands hidden in the folds of her skirt. She looked at her sister with something like fear but she wasn't mad at her. This was Maggie's portion. This was the way she knew God to work.

When I looked at her like that something hit me in the top of my head and ran down to the soles of my feet. Just like when I'm in church and the spirit of God touches me and I get happy and shout. I did something I never had done before: hugged Maggie to me, then dragged her on into the room, snatched the quilts out of Miss Wangero's hands and dumped them into Maggie's lap. Maggie just sat there on my bed with her mouth open.

"Take one or two of the others," I said to Dee.

But she turned without a word and went out to Hakim-a-barber.

"You just don't understand," she said, as Maggie and I came out to the car.

"What don't I understand?" I wanted to know.

"Your heritage," she said. And then she turned to Maggie, kissed her, and said, "You ought to try to make something of yourself, too, Maggie. It's really a new day for us. But from the way you and Mama still live you'd never know it."

She put on some sunglasses that hid everything above the tip of her nose and her chin.

Maggie smiled; maybe at the sunglasses. But a real smile, not scared. After we watched the car dust settle I asked Maggie to bring me a dip of snuff. And then the two of us sat there just enjoying, until it was time to go in the house and go to bed.

1973

# ROBERT PENN WARREN
## 1905–1989

Warren was born in Guthrie, Kentucky. He was educated at Vanderbilt University, the University of California at Berkeley, Yale, and Oxford. One of the original Fugitive Poets, his many publications include *Understanding Fiction* (1943); the novels *At Heaven's Gate* (1943), the Pulitzer Prize–winning *All the King's Men* (1946), *World Enough and Time* (1950), and *A Place to Come To* (1977); a collection of stories, *The Circus in the Attic* (1949); and *New and Selected Poems, 1923–1985* (1985). Along with such luminaries as William Faulkner and Eudora Welty, Warren is one of the giants of Southern literature. He won two more Pulitzer Prizes for his poems and was the first poet laureate of the United States.

## Blackberry Winter

*To Joseph Warren and Dagmar Beach*

It was getting into June and past eight o'clock in the morning, but there was a fire—even if it wasn't a big fire, just a fire of chunks—on the hearth of the big stone fireplace in the living room. I was standing on the hearth, almost into the chimney, hunched over the fire, working my bare toes slowly on the warm stone. I relished the heat which made the skin of my bare legs warp and creep and tingle, even as I called to my mother, who was somewhere back in the dining room or kitchen, and said: "But it's June, I don't have to put them on!"

"You put them on if you are going out," she called.

I tried to assess the degree of authority and conviction in the tone, but at that distance it was hard to decide. I tried to analyze the tone, and then I thought what a fool I had been to start out the back door and let her see that I was barefoot. If I had gone out the front door or the side door, she would never have known, not till dinner time anyway, and by then the day would have been half gone and I would have been all over the farm to see what the storm had done and down to the creek to see the flood. But it had never crossed my mind that they would try to stop you from going barefoot in June, no matter if there had been a gully-washer and a cold spell.

Nobody had ever tried to stop me in June as long as I could remember, and when you are nine years old, what you remember seems forever; for you remember everything and everything is important and stands big and full and fills up Time and is so solid that you can walk around and around it like a tree and look at it. You are aware that time passes, that there is a movement in time, but that is not what Time is. Time is not a movement, a flowing, a wind then, but is, rather, a kind of climate in which things are, and when a thing happens it begins to live and keeps on living and stands solid in Time like the tree that you can walk around. And if there is a movement, the movement is not Time itself, any more than a breeze is climate, and all the breeze does is to shake a little the leaves on the tree which is alive and solid. When you are nine, you know that there are things that you don't know, but you know that when you know something you know it. You know how a thing has been and you know that you can go barefoot in June. You do not understand that voice from back in the kitchen which says that you cannot go barefoot outdoors and run to see what has happened and rub your feet over the wet shivery grass and make the perfect mark of your foot in the smooth, creamy, red mud and then muse upon it as though you had suddenly come upon that single mark on the glistening auroral beach of the world.[1] You have never seen a beach, but you have read the book and how the footprint was there.

The voice had said what it had said, and I looked savagely at the black stockings and the strong, scuffed brown shoes which I had brought from my closet as far as the hearth rug. I called once more, "But it's June," and waited.

"It's June," the voice replied from far away, "but it's blackberry winter."

I had lifted my head to reply to that, to make one more test of what was in that tone, when I happened to see the man.

The fireplace in the living room was at the end; for the stone chimney was built, as in so many of the farmhouses in Tennessee, at the end of a gable, and there was a window on each side of the chimney. Out of the window on the north side of the fireplace I could see the man. When I saw the man I did not call out what I had intended, but, engrossed by the strangeness of the sight, watched him, still far off, come along the path by the edge of the woods.

What was strange was that there should be a man there at all. That path went along the yard fence, between the fence and the woods which came right down to the yard, and then on back past the chicken runs and on by the woods until it was lost to sight where the woods bulged out and cut off the back field. There the path disappeared into the woods. It led on back, I knew, through the woods and to the swamp, skirted the swamp where the big trees gave way to sycamores and water oaks and willows and tangled cane, and then led on to the river. Nobody ever went back there except people who wanted to gig frogs in the swamp or to fish in the river or to hunt in the woods, and those people, if they didn't have a standing permission from my father, always stopped to ask permission to cross the farm. But the man whom I now saw wasn't, I could tell even at that distance, a sportsman. And what would a sportsman have been doing down there after a storm? Besides, he was coming from the river, and nobody had gone down there that morning. I knew that for a fact, because if anybody had passed, certainly if a stranger had passed, the dogs would have made a racket and would have been out on him. But this man was coming up from the river and had come up through the woods. I suddenly had a vision of him moving up the grassy path in the woods, in the green twilight under the big trees, not making any sound on the path, while now and then, like drops off the eaves, a big drop of water would fall from a leaf or bough and strike a stiff oak leaf lower down with a small, hollow sound

1. An allusion to Daniel Defoe's *Robinson Crusoe*.

like a drop of water hitting tin. That sound, in the silence of the woods, would be very significant.

When you are a boy and stand in the stillness of woods, which can be so still that your heart almost stops beating and makes you want to stand there in the green twilight until you feel your very feet sinking into and clutching the earth like roots and your body breathing slow through its pores like the leaves—when you stand there and wait for the next drop to drop with its small, flat sound to a lower leaf, that sound seems to measure out something, to put an end to something, to begin something, and you cannot wait for it to happen and are afraid it will not happen, and then when it has happened, you are waiting again, almost afraid.

But the man whom I saw coming through the woods in my mind's eye did not pause and wait, growing into the ground and breathing with the enormous, soundless breathing of the leaves. Instead, I saw him moving in the green twilight inside my head as he was moving at that very moment along the path by the edge of the woods, coming toward the house. He was moving steadily, but not fast, with his shoulders hunched a little and his head thrust forward, like a man who has come a long way and has a long way to go. I shut my eyes for a couple of seconds, thinking that when I opened them he would not be there at all. There was no place for him to have come from, and there was no reason for him to come where he was coming, toward our house. But I opened my eyes, and there he was, and he was coming steadily along the side of the woods. He was not yet even with the back chicken yard.

"Mama," I called.

"You put them on," the voice said.

"There's a man coming," I called, "out back."

She did not reply to that, and I guessed that she had gone to the kitchen window to look. She would be looking at the man and wondering who he was and what he wanted, the way you always do in the country, and if I went back there now, she would not notice right off whether or not I was barefoot. So I went back to the kitchen.

She was standing by the window. "I don't recognize him," she said, not looking around at me.

"Where could he be coming from?" I asked.

"I don't know," she said.

"What would he be doing down at the river? At night? In the storm?"

She studied the figure out the window, then said, "Oh, I reckon maybe he cut across from the Dunbar place."

That was, I realized, a perfectly rational explanation. He had not been down at the river in the storm, at night. He had come over this morning. You could cut across from the Dunbar place if you didn't mind breaking through a lot of elder and sassafras and blackberry bushes which had about taken over the old cross path, which nobody ever used anymore. That satisfied me for a moment, but only for a moment. "Mama," I asked, "what would he be doing over at the Dunbar place last night?"

Then she looked at me, and I knew I had made a mistake, for she was looking at my bare feet. "You haven't got your shoes on," she said.

But I was saved by the dogs. That instant there was a bark which I recognized as Sam, the collie, and then a heavier, churning kind of bark which was

Bully, and I saw a streak of white as Bully tore round the corner of the back porch and headed out for the man. Bully was a big bone-white bulldog, the kind of dog that they used to call a farm bulldog but that you don't see anymore, heavy-chested and heavy-headed, but with pretty long legs. He could take a fence as light as a hound. He had just cleared the white paling fence toward the woods when my mother ran out to the back porch and began calling, "Here you, Bully! Here you!"

Bully stopped in the path, waiting for the man, but he gave a few more of those deep, gargling, savage barks that reminded you of something down a stone-lined well. The red-clay mud, I saw, was splashed up over his white chest and looked exciting, like blood.

The man, however, had not stopped walking even when Bully took the fence and started at him. He had kept right on coming. All he had done was to switch a little paper parcel which he carried from the right hand to the left, and then reach into his pants pocket to get something. Then I saw the glitter and knew that he had a knife in his hand, probably the kind of mean knife just made for devilment and nothing else, with a blade as long as the blade of a frog-sticker, which will snap out ready when you press a button in the handle. That knife must have had a button in the handle, or else how could he have had the blade out glittering so quick and with just one hand?

Pulling his knife against the dogs was a funny thing to do, for Bully was a big, powerful brute and fast, and Sam was all right. If those dogs had meant business, they might have knocked him down and ripped him before he got a stroke in. He ought to have picked up a heavy stick, something to take a swipe at them with and something which they could see and respect when they came at him. But he apparently did not know much about dogs. He just held the knife blade close against the right leg, low down, and kept on moving down the path.

Then my mother had called, and Bully had stopped. So the man let the blade of the knife snap back into the handle, and dropped it into his pocket, and kept on coming. Many women would have been afraid with the strange man who they knew had that knife in his pocket. That is, if they were alone in the house with nobody but a nine-year-old boy. And my mother was alone, for my father had gone off, and Dellie, the cook, was down at her cabin because she wasn't feeling well. But my mother wasn't afraid. She wasn't a big woman, but she was clear and brisk about everything she did and looked everybody and everything right in the eye from her own blue eyes in her tanned face. She had been the first woman in the country to ride a horse astride (that was back when she was a girl and long before I was born), and I have seen her snatch up a pump gun and go out and knock a chicken hawk out of the air like a busted skeet when he came over her chicken yard. She was a steady and self-reliant woman, and when I think of her now after all the years she has been dead, I think of her brown hands, not big, but somewhat square for a woman's hands, with square-cut nails. They looked, as a matter of fact, more like a young boy's hands than a grown woman's. But back then it never crossed my mind that she would ever be dead.

She stood on the back porch and watched the man enter the back gate, where the dogs (Bully had leaped back into the yard) were dancing and muttering and giving sidelong glances back to my mother to see if she meant what she had said. The man walked right by the dogs, almost brushing them, and didn't pay them any attention. I could see now that he wore old khaki pants, and a dark wool coat with stripes in it, and a gray felt hat. He had on a gray shirt with blue stripes in it, and no tie. But I could see a tie, blue and reddish, sticking in his side coat-pocket. Everything was wrong about what he wore. He ought to have been wearing blue jeans or overalls, and a straw hat or an old black felt hat, and the coat, granting that he might have been wearing a wool coat and not a jumper, ought not to have had those stripes. Those clothes, despite the fact that they were old enough and dirty enough for any tramp, didn't belong there in our back yard, coming down the path, in Middle Tennessee, miles away from any big town, and even a mile off the pike.

When he got almost to the steps, without having said anything, my mother, very matter-of-factly, said, "Good morning."

"Good morning," he said, and stopped and looked her over. He did not take off his hat, and under the brim you could see the perfectly unmemorable face, which wasn't old and wasn't young, or thick or thin. It was grayish and covered with about three days of stubble. The eyes were a kind of nondescript, muddy hazel, or something like that, rather bloodshot. His teeth, when he opened his mouth, showed yellow and uneven. A couple of them had been knocked out. You knew that they had been knocked out, because there was a scar, not very old, there on the lower lip just beneath the gap.

"Are you hunting work?" my mother asked him.

"Yes," he said—not "yes, mam"—and still did not take off his hat.

"I don't know about my husband, for he isn't here," she said, and didn't mind a bit telling the tramp, or whoever he was, with the mean knife in his pocket, that no man was around, "but I can give you a few things to do. The storm has drowned a lot of my chicks. Three coops of them. You can gather them up and bury them. Bury them deep so the dogs won't get at them. In the woods. And fix the coops the wind blew over. And down yonder beyond that pen by the edge of the woods are some drowned poults. They got out and I couldn't get them in. Even after it started to rain hard. Poults haven't got any sense."

"What are them things—poults?" he demanded, and spat on the brick walk. He rubbed his foot over the spot, and I saw that he wore a black pointed-toe low shoe, all cracked and broken. It was a crazy kind of shoe to be wearing in the country.

"Oh, they're young turkeys," my mother was saying. "And they haven't got any sense. I oughtn't to try to raise them around here with so many chickens, anyway. They don't thrive near chickens, even in separate pens. And I won't give up my chickens." Then she stopped herself and resumed briskly on the note of business. "When you finish that, you can fix my flower beds. A lot of trash and mud and gravel has washed down. Maybe you can save some of my flowers if you are careful."

"Flowers," the man said, in a low, impersonal voice which seemed to have a wealth of meaning, but a meaning which I could not fathom. As I think back on it, it probably was not pure contempt. Rather, it was a kind of impersonal and distant marveling that he should be on the verge of grubbing in a flower bed. He said the word, and then looked off across the yard.

"Yes, flowers," my mother replied with some asperity, as though she would have nothing said or implied against flowers. "And they were very fine this year." Then she stopped and looked at the man. "Are you hungry?" she demanded.

"Yeah," he said.

"I'll fix you something," she said, "before you get started." She turned to me. "Show him where he can wash up," she commanded, and went into the house.

I took the man to the end of the porch where a pump was and where a couple of wash pans sat on a low shelf for people to use before they went into the house. I stood there while he laid down his little parcel wrapped in newspaper and took off his hat and looked around for a nail to hang it on. He poured the water and plunged his hands into it. They were big hands, and strong-looking, but they did not have the creases and the earth-color of the hands of men who work outdoors. But they were dirty, with black dirt ground into the skin and under the nails. After he had washed his hands, he poured another basin of water and washed his face. He dried his face, and with the towel still dangling in his grasp, stepped over to the mirror on the house wall. He rubbed one hand over the stubble on his face. Then he carefully inspected his face, turning first one side and then the other, and stepped back and settled his striped coat down on his shoulders. He had the movements of a man who has just dressed up to go to church or a party—the way he settled his coat and smoothed it and scanned himself in the mirror.

Then he caught my glance on him. He glared at me for an instant out of the bloodshot eyes, then demanded in a low, harsh voice, "What you looking at?"

"Nothing," I managed to say, and stepped back a step from him.

He flung the towel down, crumpled, on the shelf, and went toward the kitchen door and entered without knocking.

My mother said something to him which I could not catch. I started to go in again, then thought about my bare feet, and decided to go back of the chicken yard, where the man would have to come to pick up the dead chicks. I hung around behind the chicken house until he came out.

He moved across the chicken yard with a fastidious, not quite finicking motion, looking down at the curdled mud flecked with bits of chicken-droppings. The mud curled up over the soles of his black shoes. I stood back from him some six feet and watched him pick up the first of the drowned chicks. He held it up by one foot and inspected it.

There is nothing deader-looking than a drowned chick. The feet curl in that feeble, empty way which back when I was a boy, even if I was a country boy who did not mind hog-killing or frog-gigging, made me feel hollow in the stomach. Instead of looking plump and fluffy, the body is stringy and limp with the fluff plastered to it, and the neck is long and loose like a little string of rag. And the eyes have that bluish membrane over them which makes you think of a very old man who is sick about to die.

The man stood there and inspected the chick. Then he looked all around as though he didn't know what to do with it.

"There's a great big old basket in the shed," I said, and pointed to the shed attached to the chicken house.

He inspected me as though he had just discovered my presence, and moved toward the shed.

"There's a spade there, too," I added.

He got the basket and began to pick up the other chicks, picking each one up slowly by a foot and then flinging it into the basket with a nasty, snapping motion. Now and then he would look at me out of the bloodshot eyes. Every time he seemed on the verge of saying something, but he did not. Perhaps he was building up to say something to me, but I did not wait that long. His way of looking at me made me so uncomfortable that I left the chicken yard.

Besides, I had just remembered that the creek was in flood, over the bridge, and that people were down there watching it. So I cut across the farm toward the creek. When I got to the big tobacco field I saw that it had not suffered much. The land lay right and not many tobacco plants had washed out of the ground. But I knew that a lot of tobacco round the country had been washed right out. My father had said so at breakfast.

My father was down at the bridge. When I came out of the gap in the osage hedge into the road, I saw him sitting on his mare over the heads of the other men who were standing around, admiring the flood. The creek was big here, even in low water; for only a couple of miles away it ran into the river, and when a real flood came, the red water got over the pike where it dipped down to the bridge, which was an iron bridge, and high over the floor and even the side railings of the bridge. Only the upper iron work would show, with the water boiling and frothing red and white around it. That creek rose so fast and so heavy because a few miles back it came down out of the hills, where the gorges filled up with water in no time when a rain came. The creek ran in a deep bed with limestone bluffs along both sides until it got within three quarters of a mile of the bridge, and when it came out from between those bluffs in flood it was boiling and hissing and steaming like water from a fire hose.

Whenever there was a flood, people from half the county would come down to see the sight. After a gully-washer there would not be any work to do anyway. If it didn't ruin your crop, you couldn't plow and you felt like taking a holiday to celebrate. If it did ruin your crop, there wasn't anything to do except to try to take your mind off the mortgage, if you were rich enough to have a mortgage, and if you couldn't afford a mortgage, you needed something to take your mind off how hungry you would be by Christmas. So people would come down to the bridge and look at the flood. It made something different from the run of days.

There would not be much talking after the first few minutes of trying to guess how high the water was this time. The men and kids just stood around, or sat their horses or mules, as the case might be, or stood up in the wagon beds. They looked at the strangeness of the flood for an hour or two, and then somebody would say that he had better be getting on home to dinner and would start walking down the gray, puddled limestone pike, or would touch heel to his mount and start off. Everybody always knew what it would be like when he got down to the bridge, but people always came. It was like church or a funeral. They always came, that is, if it was summer and the flood unexpected. Nobody ever came down in winter to see high water.

When I came out of the gap in the bodock hedge, I saw the crowd, perhaps fifteen or twenty men and a lot of kids, and saw my father sitting his mare, Nellie Gray. He was a tall, limber man and carried himself well. I was always proud to see him sit a horse, he was so quiet and straight, and when I stepped through the gap of the hedge that morning, the first thing that happened was, I remember, the warm feeling I always had when I saw him up on a horse, just sitting. I did not go toward him, but skirted the crowd on the far side, to get a look at the creek. For one thing, I was not sure what he would say about the fact that I was barefoot. But the first thing I knew, I heard his voice calling, "Seth!"

I went toward him, moving apologetically past the men, who bent their large, red or thin, sallow faces above me. I knew some of the men, and knew their names, but because those I knew were there in a crowd, mixed with the strange faces, they seemed foreign to me, and not friendly. I did not look up at my father until I was almost within touching distance of his heel. Then I looked up and tried to read his face, to see if he was angry about my being bare-foot. Before I could decide anything from that impassive, high-boned face, he had leaned over and reached a hand to me. "Grab on," he commanded.

I grabbed on and gave a little jump, and he said, "Up-see-daisy!" and whisked me, light as a feather, up to the pommel of his McClellan saddle.[2]

"You can see better up here," he said, slid back on the cantle a little to make me more comfortable, and then, looking over my head at the swollen, tumbling water, seemed to forget all about me. But his right hand was laid on my side, just above my thigh, to steady me.

I was sitting there as quiet as I could, feeling the faint stir of my father's chest against my shoulders as it rose and fell with his breath, when I saw the cow. At first, looking up the creek, I thought it was just another big piece of driftwood steaming down the creek in the ruck of water, but all at once a pretty good-size boy who had climbed part way up a telephone pole by the pike so that he could see better yelled out, "Golly-damn, look at that-air cow!"

Everybody looked. It was a cow all right, but it might just as well have been driftwood; for it was dead as a chunk, rolling and roiling down the creek, appearing and disappearing, feet up or head up, it didn't matter which.

The cow started up the talk again. Somebody wondered whether it would hit one of the clear places under the top girder of the bridge and get through or whether it would get tangled in the drift and trash that had piled against the upright girders and braces. Somebody remembered how about ten years before, so much driftwood had piled up on the bridge that it was knocked off its foundations. Then the cow hit. It hit the edge of the drift against one of the girders, and hung there. For a few seconds it seemed as though it might tear loose, but then we saw that it was really caught. It bobbed and heaved on its side there in a slow, grinding, uneasy fashion. It had a yoke around its neck, the kind made out of a forked limb to keep a jumper behind fence.

"She shore jumped one fence," one of the men said.

And another: "Well, she done jumped her last one, fer a fack."

Then they began to wonder about whose cow it might be. They decided it must belong to Milt Alley. They said that he had a cow that was a jumper, and kept her in a fenced-in piece of ground up the creek. I had never seen Milt Alley, but I knew who he was. He was a squatter and lived up the hills a way, on a shirt-tail patch of set-on-edge land, in a cabin. He was pore white trash. He had lots of children. I had seen the children at school, when they came.

2. Military saddle developed in 1859 by George B. McClellan, who went on to command the Union army in the Civil War.

They were thin-faced, with straight, sticky-looking, dough-colored hair, and they smelled something like old sour buttermilk, not because they drank so much buttermilk but because that is the sort of smell which children out of those cabins tend to have. The big Alley boy drew dirty pictures and showed them to the little boys at school.

That was Milt Alley's cow. It looked like the kind of cow he would have, a scrawny, old, sway-backed cow, with a yoke around her neck. I wondered if Milt Alley had another cow.

"Poppa," I said, "do you think Milt Alley has got another cow?"

"You say 'Mr. Alley,'" my father said quietly.

"Do you think he has?"

"No telling," my father said.

Then a big gangly boy, about fifteen, who was sitting on a scraggly little old mule with a piece of croker sack thrown across the sawtooth spine, and who had been staring at the cow, suddenly said to nobody in particular, "Reckin anybody ever et drownt cow?"

He was the kind of boy who might just as well as not have been the son of Milt Alley, with his faded and patched overalls ragged at the bottom of the pants and the mud-stiff brogans hanging off his skinny, bare ankles at the level of the mule's belly. He had said what he did, and then looked embarrassed and sullen when all the eyes swung at him. He hadn't meant to say it, I am pretty sure now. He would have been too proud to say it, just as Milt Alley would have been too proud. He had just been thinking out loud, and the words had popped out.

There was an old man standing there on the pike, an old man with a white beard. "Son," he said to the embarrassed and sullen boy on the mule, "you live long enough and you'll find a man will eat anything when the time comes."

"Time gonna come fer some folks this year," another man said.

"Son," the old man said, "in my time I et things a man don't like to think on. I was a sojer and I rode with Gin'l Forrest,[3] and them things we et when the time come. I tell you. I et meat what got up and run when you taken out yore knife to cut a slice to put on the fire. You had to knock it down with a carbeen butt, it was so active. That-air meat would jump like a bullfrog, it was so full of skippers."

But nobody was listening to the old man. The boy on the mule turned his sullen sharp face from him, dug a heel into the side of the mule, and went off up the pike with a motion which made you think that any second you would hear mule bones clashing inside that lank and scrofulous hide.

"Cy Dundee's boy," a man said, and nodded toward the figure going up the pike on the mule.

"Reckin Cy Dundee's young-uns seen times they'd settle fer drownt cow," another man said.

The old man with the beard peered at them both from his weak, slow eyes, first at one and then at the other. "Live long enough," he said, "and a man will settle fer what he kin git."

Then there was silence again, with the people looking at the red, foam-flecked water.

---

**3.** Nathan Bedford Forrest (1821–1877), Confederate general.

My father lifted the bridle rein in his left hand, and the mare turned and walked around the group and up the pike. We rode on up to our big gate, where my father dismounted to open it and let me myself ride Nellie Gray through. When he got to the lane that led off from the drive about two hundred yards from our house, my father said, "Grab on." I grabbed on, and he let me down to the ground. "I'm going to ride down and look at my corn," he said. "You go on." He took the lane, and I stood there on the drive and watched him ride off. He was wearing cowhide boots and an old hunting coat, and I thought that that made him look very military, like a picture. That and the way he rode.

I did not go to the house. Instead, I went by the vegetable garden and crossed behind the stables, and headed down for Dellie's cabin. I wanted to go down and play with Jebb, who was Dellie's little boy about two years older than I was. Besides, I was cold. I shivered as I walked, and I had gooseflesh. The mud which crawled up between my toes with every step I took was like ice. Dellie would have a fire, but she wouldn't make me put on shoes and stockings.

Dellie's cabin was of logs, with one side, because it was on a slope, set on limestone chunks, with a little porch attached to it, and had a little white-washed fence around it and a gate with plow-points on a wire to clink when somebody came in, and had two big white oaks in the yard and some flowers and a nice privy in the back with some honeysuckle growing over it. Dellie and Old Jebb, who was Jebb's father and who lived with Dellie and had lived with her for twenty-five years even if they never had got married, were careful to keep everything nice around their cabin. They had the name all over the community for being clean and clever Negroes. Dellie and Jebb were what they used to call "white-folks' niggers." There was a big difference between their cabin and the other two cabins farther down where the other tenants lived. My father kept the other cabins weatherproof, but he couldn't undertake to go down and pick up after the litter they strewed. They didn't take the trouble to have a vegetable patch like Dellie and Jebb or to make preserves from wild plum, and jelly from crab apple the way Dellie did. They were shiftless, and my father was always threatening to get shed of them. But he never did. When they finally left, they just up and left on their own, for no reason, to go and be shiftless somewhere else. Then some more came. But meanwhile they lived down there, Matt Rawson and his family, and Sid Turner and his, and I played with their children all over the farm when they weren't working. But when I wasn't around they were mean sometimes to Little Jebb. That was because the other tenants down there were jealous of Dellie and Jebb.

I was so cold that I ran the last fifty yards to Dellie's gate. As soon as I had entered the yard, I saw that the storm had been hard on Dellie's flowers. The yard was, as I have said, on a slight slope, and the water running across had gutted the flower beds and washed out all the good black woods-earth which Dellie had brought in. What little grass there was in the yard was plastered sparsely down on the ground, the way the drainage water had left it. It reminded me of the way the fluff was plastered down on the skin of the drowned chicks that the strange man had been picking up, up in my mother's chicken yard.

I took a few steps up the path to the cabin, and then I saw that the drainage water had washed a lot of trash and filth out from under Dellie's house. Up toward the porch, the ground was not clean any more. Old pieces of rag, two or three rusted cans, pieces of rotten rope, some hunks of old dog dung, broken glass, old paper, and all sorts of things like that had washed out from under Dellie's house to foul her clean yard. It looked just as bad as the yards of the other cabins, or worse. It was worse, as a matter of fact, because it was a surprise. I had never thought of all that filth being under Dellie's house. It was not anything against Dellie that the stuff had been under the cabin. Trash will get under any house. But I did not think of that when I saw the foulness which had washed out on the ground which Dellie sometimes used to sweep with a twig broom to make nice and clean.

I picked my way past the filth, being careful not to get my bare feet on it, and mounted to Dellie's door. When I knocked, I heard her voice telling me to come in.

It was dark inside the cabin, after the daylight, but I could make out Dellie piled up in bed under a quilt, and Little Jebb crouched by the hearth, where a low fire simmered. "Howdy," I said to Dellie, "how you feeling?"

Her big eyes, the whites surprising and glaring in the black face, fixed on me as I stood there, but she did not reply. It did not look like Dellie, or act like Dellie, who would grumble and bustle around our kitchen, talking to herself, scolding me or Little Jebb, clanking pans, making all sorts of unnecessary noises and mutterings like an old-fashioned black steam thrasher engine when it has got up an extra head of steam and keeps popping the governor and rumbling and shaking on its wheels. But now Dellie just lay up there on the bed, under the patchwork quilt, and turned the black face, which I scarcely recognized, and the glaring white eyes to me.

"How you feeling?" I repeated.

"I'se sick," the voice said croakingly out of the strange black face which was not attached to Dellie's big, squat body, but stuck out from under a pile of tangled bedclothes. Then the voice added: "Mighty sick."

"I'm sorry," I managed to say.

The eyes remained fixed on me for a moment, then they left me and the head rolled back on the pillow. "Sorry," the voice said, in a flat way which wasn't question or statement of anything. It was just the empty word put into the air with no meaning or expression, to float off like a feather or a puff of smoke, while the big eyes, with the whites like the peeled white of hard-boiled eggs, stared at the ceiling.

"Dellie," I said after a minute, "there's a tramp up at the house. He's got a knife."

She was not listening. She closed her eyes.

I tiptoed over to the hearth where Jebb was and crouched beside him. We began to talk in low voices. I was asking him to get out his train and play train. Old Jebb had put spool wheels on three cigar boxes and put wire links between the boxes to make a train for Jebb. The box that was the locomotive had the top closed and a length of broom stick for a smoke stack. Jebb didn't want to get the train out, but I told him I would go home if he didn't. So he got out the train, and the colored rocks, and fossils of crinoid stems, and other junk he used for the load, and we began to push it around, talking the way we thought trainmen talked, making a chuck-chucking sound under the breath for the noise of the locomotive and now and then uttering low, cautious toots for the whistle. We got so interested in playing train that the toots got louder. Then, before he thought, Jebb gave a good, loud *toot-toot*, blowing for a crossing.

"Come here," the voice said from the bed.

Jebb got up slow from his hands and knees, giving me a sudden, naked, inimical look.

"Come here!" the voice said.

Jebb went to the bed. Dellie propped herself weakly up on one arm, muttering, "Come closer."

Jebb stood closer.

"Last thing I do, I'm gonna do it," Dellie said. "Done tole you to be quiet."

Then she slapped him. It was an awful slap, more awful for the kind of weakness which it came from and brought to focus. I had seen her slap Jebb before, but the slapping had always been the kind of easy slap you would expect from a good-natured, grumbling Negro woman like Dellie. But this was different. It was awful. It was so awful that Jebb didn't make a sound. The tears just popped out and ran down his face, and his breath came sharp, like gasps.

Dellie fell back. "Cain't even be sick," she said to the ceiling. "Git sick and they won't even let you lay. They tromp all over you. Cain't even be sick." Then she closed her eyes.

I went out of the room. I almost ran getting to the door, and I did run across the porch and down the steps and across the yard, not caring whether or not I stepped on the filth which had washed out from under the cabin. I ran almost all the way home. Then I thought about my mother catching me with the bare feet. So I went down to the stables.

I heard a noise in the crib, and opened the door. There was Big Jebb, sitting on an old nail keg, shelling corn into a bushel basket. I went in, pulling the door shut behind me, and crouched on the floor near him. I crouched there for a couple of minutes before either of us spoke, and watched him shelling the corn.

He had very big hands, knotted and grayish at the joints, with calloused palms which seemed to be streaked with rust, with the rust coming up between the fingers to show from the back. His hands were so strong and tough that he could take a big ear of corn and rip the grains right off the cob with the palm of his hand, all in one motion, like a machine. "Work long as me," he would say, "and the good Lawd'll give you a hand lak cass-ion won't nuthin' hurt." And his hands did look like cast iron, old cast iron streaked with rust.

He was an old man, up in his seventies, thirty years or more older than Dellie, but he was strong as a bull. He was a squat sort of man, heavy in the shoulders, with remarkably long arms, the kind of build they say the river natives have on the Congo from paddling so much in their boats. He had a round bullet-head, set on powerful shoulders. His skin was very black, and the thin hair on his head was now grizzled like tufts of old cotton batting. He had small eyes and a flat nose, not big, and the kindest and wisest old face in the world, the blunt, sad, wise face of an old animal peering tolerantly out on the goings-on of the merely human creatures before him. He was a good man, and I loved him next to my mother and father. I crouched there on the floor of the crib and watched him shell corn with the rusty cast-iron hands, while he looked down at me out of the little eyes set in the blunt face.

"Dellie says she's mighty sick," I said.

"Yeah," he said.

"What's she sick from?"

"Woman-mizry," he said.

"What's woman-mizry?"

"Hit comes on 'em," he said. "Hit jest comes on 'em when the time comes."

"What is it?"

"Hit is the change," he said. "Hit is the change of life and time."

"What changes?"

"You too young to know."

"Tell me."

"Time come and you find out everthing."

I knew that there was no use in asking him any more. When I asked him things and he said that, I always knew that he would not tell me. So I continued to crouch there and watch him. Now that I had sat there a little while, I was cold again.

"What you shiver fer?" he asked me.

"I'm cold. I'm cold because it's blackberry winter," I said.

"Maybe 'tis and maybe 'tain't," he said.

"My mother says it is."

"Ain't sayen Miss Sallie doan know and ain't sayen she do. But folks doan know everthing."

"Why isn't it blackberry winter?"

"Too late fer blackberry winter. Blackberries done bloomed."

"She said it was."

"Blackberry winter jest a leetle cold spell. Hit come and then hit go away, and hit is growed summer of a sudden lak a gunshot. Ain't no tellen hit will go way this time."

"It's June," I said.

"June," he replied with great contempt. "That what folks say. What June mean? Maybe hit is come cold to stay."

"Why?"

"'Cause this-here old yearth is tahrd. Hit is tahrd and ain't gonna perduce. Lawd let hit come rain one time forty days and forty nights, 'cause He was tahrd of sinful folks. Maybe this-here old yearth say to the Lawd, Lawd, I done plum tahrd, Lawd, lemme rest. And Lawd say, Yearth, you done yore best, you give 'em cawn and you give 'em taters, and all they think on is they gut, and, Yearth, you kin take a rest."

"What will happen?"

"Folks will eat up everthing. The yearth won't perduce no more. Folks cut down all the trees and burn 'em 'cause they cold, and the yearth won't grow no more. I been tellen 'em. I been tellen folks. Sayen, maybe this year, hit is the time. But they doan listen to me, how the yearth is tahrd. Maybe this year they find out."

"Will everything die?"

"Everthing and everbody, hit will be so."

"This year?"

"Ain't no tellen. Maybe this year."

"My mother said it is blackberry winter," I said confidently, and got up.

"Ain't sayen nuthin' agin Miss Sallie," he said.

I went to the door of the crib. I was really cold now. Running, I had got up a sweat and now I was worse.

I hung on the door, looking at Jebb, who was shelling corn again.

"There's a tramp came to the house," I said. I had almost forgotten the tramp.

"Yeah."

"He came by the back way. What was he doing down there in the storm?"

"They comes and they goes," he said, "and ain't no teller."

"He had a mean knife."

"The good ones and the bad ones, they comes and they goes. Storm or sun, light or dark. They is folks and they comes and they goes lak folks."

I hung on the door, shivering.

He studied me a moment, then said, "You git on to the house. You ketch yore death. Then what yore mammy say?"

I hesitated.

"You git," he said.

When I came to the back yard, I saw that my father was standing by the back porch and the tramp was walking toward him. They began talking before I reached them, but I got there just as my father was saying, "I'm sorry, but I haven't got any work. I got all the hands on the place I need now. I won't need any extra until wheat thrashing."

The stranger made no reply, just looked at my father.

My father took out his leather coin purse, and got out a half-dollar. He held it toward the man. "This is for half a day," he said.

The man looked at the coin, and then at my father, making no motion to take the money. But that was the right amount. A dollar a day was what you paid them back in 1910. And the man hadn't even worked half a day.

Then the man reached out and took the coin. He dropped it into the right side pocket of his coat. Then he said, very slowly and without feeling, "I didn't want to work on your—farm."

He used the word which they would have frailed me to death for using.

I looked at my father's face and it was streaked white under the sunburn. Then he said, "Get off this place. Get off this place or I won't be responsible."

The man dropped his right hand into his pants pocket. It was the pocket where he kept the knife. I was just about to yell to my father about the knife when the hand came back out with nothing in it. The man gave a kind of twisted grin, showing where the teeth had been knocked out above the new scar. I thought that instant how maybe he had tried before to pull a knife on somebody else and had got his teeth knocked out.

So now he just gave that twisted, sickish grin out of the unmemorable, grayish face, and then spat on the brick path. The glob landed just about six inches from the toe of my father's right boot. My father looked down at it, and so did I. I thought that if the glob had hit my father's boot, something would have happened. I looked down and saw the bright glob, and on one side of it my father's strong cowhide boots, with the brass eyelets and the leather thongs, heavy boots splashed with good red mud and set solid on the bricks, and on the other side the pointed-toe, broken, black shoes, on which the mud looked so sad and out of place. Then I saw one of the black shoes move a little, just a twitch first, then a real step backward.

The man moved in a quarter circle to the end of the porch, with my father's steady gaze upon him all the while. At the end of the porch, the man reached up to the shelf where the wash pans were to get his little newspaper-wrapped parcel. Then he disappeared around the corner of the house and my father mounted the porch and went into the kitchen without a word.

I followed around the house to see what the man would do. I wasn't afraid of him now, no matter if he did have the knife. When I got around in front, I saw him going out the yard gate and starting up the drive toward the pike. So I ran to catch up with him. He was sixty yards or so up the drive before I caught up.

I did not walk right up even with him at first, but trailed him, the way a kid will, about seven or eight feet behind, now and then running two or three steps in order to hold my place against his longer stride. When I first came up behind him, he turned to give me a look, just a meaningless look, and then fixed his eyes up the drive and kept on walking.

When we had got around the bend in the drive which cut the house from sight, and were going along by the edge of the woods, I decided to come up even with him. I ran a few steps, and was by his side, or almost, but some feet off to the right. I walked along in this position for a while, and he never noticed me. I walked along until we got within sight of the big gate that let on the pike.

Then I said, "Where did you come from?"

He looked at me then with a look which seemed almost surprised that I was there. Then he said, "It ain't none of yore business."

We went on another fifty feet.

Then I said, "Where are you going?"

He stopped, studied me dispassionately for a moment, then suddenly took a step toward me and leaned his face down at me. The lips jerked back, but not in any grin, to show where the teeth were knocked out and to make the scar on the lower lip come white with the tension.

He said, "Stop following me. You don't stop following me and I cut yore throat, you little son-of-a-bitch."

Then he went on to the gate, and up the pike.

That was thirty-five years ago. Since that time my father and mother have died. I was still a boy, but a big boy, when my father got cut on the blade of a mowing machine and died of lockjaw. My mother sold the place and went to town to live with her sister. But she never took hold after my father's death, and she died within three years, right in middle life. My aunt always said, "Sallie just died of a broken heart, she was so devoted." Dellie is dead, too, but she died, I heard, quite a long time after we sold the farm.

As for Little Jebb, he grew up to be a mean and ficey[4] Negro. He killed another Negro in a fight and got sent to the penitentiary, where he is yet, the last I heard tell. He probably grew up to be mean and ficey from just being

---

4. Aggressive, confrontational.

picked on so much by the children of the other tenants, who were jealous of Jebb and Dellie for being thrifty and clever and being white-folks' niggers.

Old Jebb lived forever. I saw him ten years ago and he was about a hundred then, and not looking much different. He was living in town then, on relief— that was back in the Depression—when I went to see him. He said to me: "Too strong to die. When I was a young feller just comen on and seen how things wuz, I prayed the Lawd. I said, Oh, Lawd, gimme strength and meke me strong fer to do and to in-dure. The Lawd hearkened to my prayer. He give me strength. I was in-duren proud fer being strong and me much man. The Lawd give me my prayer and my strength. But now He done gone off and fergot me and left me alone with my strength. A man doan know what to pray fer, and him mortal."

Jebb is probably living yet, as far as I know.

That is what has happened since the morning when the tramp leaned his face down at me and showed his teeth and said: "Stop following me. You don't stop following me and I cut yore throat, you little son-of-a-bitch." That was what he said, for me not to follow him. But I did follow him, all the years.

1946

# EUDORA WELTY
## 1909–2001

Welty was born in Jackson, Mississippi, where she lived for most of her productive life as the "First Lady of Southern Literature." She received her formal education at the Mississippi State College for Women and the University of Wisconsin, also studying advertising at Columbia University for a brief period. Her early ambitions to be a painter were subordinated by the success of her first book of stories, *A Curtain of Green* (1941). Readers recognized in this and following works a writer who gave full value to the quality and spectacle of her home region and the people she knew best, while at the same time she displayed a cosmopolitan awareness and technical sophistication. Other books of short stories are *The Wide Net* (1943), *The Golden Apples* (1949), *The Bride of the Innisfallen* (1955), *Thirteen Stories* (1965), and the *Collected Stories of Eudora Welty* (1980). Her novels include *Delta Wedding* (1946), *The Ponder Heart* (1954), and *The Optimist's Daughter* (1972), which won a Pulitzer Prize. *One Writer's Beginnings* (1984), based on three lectures Welty delivered at Harvard, is autobiographical. In 1998 the Library of America published a two-volume edition of her selected works, making her the first living author they had published.

# A Worn Path

It was December—a bright frozen day in the early morning. Far out in the country there was an old Negro woman with her head tied in a red rag, coming along a path through the pinewoods. Her name was Phoenix Jackson. She was very old and small and she walked slowly in the dark pine shadows, moving a little from side to side in her steps, with the balanced heaviness and lightness of a pendulum in a grandfather clock. She carried a thin, small cane made from an umbrella, and with this she kept tapping the frozen earth in front of her. This made a grave and persistent noise in the still air, that seemed meditative like the chirping of a solitary little bird.

She wore a dark striped dress reaching down to her shoe tops, and an equally long apron of bleached sugar sacks, with a full pocket: all neat and tidy, but every time she took a step she might have fallen over her shoelaces, which dragged from her unlaced shoes. She looked straight ahead. Her eyes were blue with age. Her skin had a pattern all its own of numberless branching wrinkles and as though a whole little tree stood in the middle of her forehead, but a golden color ran underneath, and the two knobs of her cheeks were illumined by a yellow burning under the dark. Under the red rag her hair came down on her neck in the frailest of ringlets, still black, and with an odor like copper.

Now and then there was a quivering in the thicket. Old Phoenix said, "Out of my way, all you foxes, owls, beetles, jack rabbits, coons and wild animals! . . . Keep out from under these feet, little bob-whites. . . . Keep the big wild hogs out of my path. Don't let none of those come running my direction. I got a long way." Under her small black-freckled hand her cane, limber as a buggy whip, would switch at the brush as if to rouse up any hiding things.

On she went. The woods were deep and still. The sun made the pine needles almost too bright to look at, up where the wind rocked. The cones dropped as light as feathers. Down in the hollow was the mourning dove—it was not too late for him.

The path ran up a hill. "Seem like there is chains about my feet, time I get this far," she said, in the voice of argument old people keep to use with themselves. "Something always take a hold of me on this hill—pleads I should stay."

After she got to the top she turned and gave a full, severe look behind her where she had come. "Up through pines," she said at length. "Now down through oaks."

Her eyes opened their widest, and she started down gently. But before she got to the bottom of the hill a bush caught her dress.

Her fingers were busy and intent, but her skirts were full and long, so that before she could pull them free in one place they were caught in another. It was not possible to allow the dress to tear. "I in the thorny bush," she said. "Thorns, you doing your appointed work. Never want to let folks pass, no sir. Old eyes thought you was a pretty little *green* bush."

Finally, trembling all over, she stood free, and after a moment dared to stoop for her cane.

"Sun so high!" she cried, leaning back and looking, while the thick tears went over her eyes. "The time getting all gone here."

At the foot of this hill was a place where a log was laid across the creek.

"Now comes the trial," said Phoenix.

Putting her right foot out, she mounted the log and shut her eyes. Lifting her skirt, leveling her cane fiercely before her, like a festival figure in some parade, she began to march across. Then she opened her eyes and she was safe on the other side.

"I wasn't as old as I thought," she said.

But she sat down to rest. She spread her skirts on the bank around her and folded her hands over her knees. Up above her was a tree in a pearly cloud of mistletoe. She did not dare to close her eyes, and when a little boy brought her a plate with a slice of marble-cake on it she spoke to him. "That would be acceptable," she said. But when she went to take it there was just her own hand in the air.

So she left that tree, and had to go through a barbed-wire fence. There she had to creep and crawl, spreading her knees and stretching her fingers like a baby trying to climb the steps. But she talked loudly to herself: she could not let her dress be torn now, so late in the day, and she could not pay for having her arm or her leg sawed off if she got caught fast where she was.

At last she was safe through the fence and risen up out in the clearing. Big dead trees, like black men with one arm, were standing in the purple stalks of the withered cotton field. There sat a buzzard.

"Who you watching?"

In the furrow she made her way along.

"Glad this not the season for bulls," she said, looking sideways, "and the good Lord made his snakes to curl up and sleep in the winter. A pleasure I don't see no two-headed snake coming around that tree, where it come once. It took a while to get by him, back in the summer."

She passed through the old cotton and went into a field of dead corn. It whispered and shook and was taller than her head. "Through the maze now," she said, for there was no path.

Then there was something tall, black, and skinny there, moving before her.

At first she took it for a man. It could have been a man dancing in the field. But she stood still and listened, and it did not make a sound. It was as silent as a ghost.

"Ghost," she said sharply, "who be you the ghost of? For I have heard of nary death close by."

But there was no answer—only the ragged dancing in the wind.

She shut her eyes, reached out her hand, and touched a sleeve. She found a coat and inside that an emptiness, cold as ice.

"You scarecrow," she said. Her face lighted. "I ought to be shut up for good," she said with laughter. "My senses is gone. I too old. I the oldest people I ever know. Dance, old scarecrow," she said, "while I dancing with you."

She kicked her foot over the furrow, and with mouth drawn down, shook her head once or twice in a little strutting way. Some husks blew down and whirled in streamers about her skirts.

Then she went on, parting her way from side to side with the cane, through the whispering field. At last she came to the end, to a wagon track where the silver grass blew between the red ruts. The quail were walking around like pullets, seeming all dainty and unseen.

"Walk pretty," she said. "This the easy place. This the easy going."

She followed the track, swaying through the quiet bare fields, through the little strings of trees silver in their dead leaves, past cabins silver from weather, with the doors and windows boarded shut, all like old women under a spell sitting there. "I walking in their sleep," she said, nodding her head vigorously.

In a ravine she went where a spring was silently flowing through a hollow log. Old Phoenix bent and drank. "Sweet-gum makes the water sweet," she said, and drank more. "Nobody know who made this well, for it was here when I was born."

The track crossed a swampy part where the moss hung as white as lace from every limb. "Sleep on, alligators, and blow your bubbles." Then the track went into the road.

Deep, deep the road went down between the high green-colored banks. Overhead the live-oaks met, and it was as dark as a cave.

A black dog with a lolling tongue came up out of the weeds by the ditch. She was meditating, and not ready, and when he came at her she only hit him a little with her cane. Over she went in the ditch, like a little puff of milkweed.

Down there, her senses drifted away. A dream visited her, and she reached her hand up, but nothing reached down and gave her a pull. So she lay there and presently went to talking. "Old woman," she said to herself, "that black dog come up out of the weeds to stall you off, and now there he sitting on his fine tail, smiling at you."

A white man finally came along and found her—a hunter, a young man, with his dog on a chain.

"Well, Granny!" he laughed. "What are you doing there?"

"Lying on my back like a June-bug waiting to be turned over, mister," she said, reaching up her hand.

He lifted her up, gave her a swing in the air, and set her down. "Anything broken, Granny?"

"No sir, them old dead weeds is springy enough," said Phoenix, when she had got her breath. "I thank you for your trouble."

"Where do you live, Granny?" he asked, while the two dogs were growling at each other.

"Away back yonder, sir, behind the ridge. You can't even see it from here."

"On your way home?"

"No sir, I going to town."

"Why, that's too far! That's as far as I walk when I come out myself, and I get something for my trouble." He patted the stuffed bag he carried, and there hung down a little closed claw. It was one of the bob-whites, with its beak hooked bitterly to show it was dead. "Now you go on home, Granny!"

"I bound to go to town, mister," said Phoenix. "The time come around."

He gave another laugh, filling the whole landscape. "I know you old colored people! Wouldn't miss going to town to see Santa Claus!"

But something held old Phoenix very still. The deep lines in her face went into a fierce and different radiation. Without warning, she had seen with her own eyes a flashing nickel fall out of the man's pocket onto the ground.

"How old are you, Granny?" he was saying.

"There's no telling, mister," she said, "no telling."

Then she gave a little cry and clapped her hands and said, "Git on away from here, dog! Look! Look at that dog!" She laughed as if in admiration. "He ain't scared of nobody. He a big black dog." She whispered, "Sic him!"

"Watch me get rid of that cur," said the man. "Sic him, Pete! Sic him!"

Phoenix heard the dogs fighting, and heard the man running and throwing sticks. She even heard a gunshot. But she was slowly bending forward by that time, further and further forward, the lids stretched down over her eyes, as if she were doing this in her sleep. Her chin was lowered almost to her knees. The yellow palm of her hand came out from the fold of her apron. Her fingers slid down and along the ground under the piece of money with the grace and care they would have in lifting an egg from under a setting hen. Then she slowly straightened up, she stood erect, and the nickel was in her apron pocket. A bird flew by. Her lips moved. "God watching me the whole time. I come to stealing."

The man came back, and his own dog panted about them. "Well, I scared him off that time," he said, and then he laughed and lifted his gun and pointed it at Phoenix.

She stood straight and faced him.

"Doesn't the gun scare you?" he said, still pointing it.

"No, sir, I seen plenty go off closer by, in my day, and for less than what I done," she said, holding utterly still.

He smiled, and shouldered the gun. "Well, Granny," he said, "you must be a hundred years old, and scared of nothing. I'd give you a dime if I had any money with me. But you take my advice and stay home, and nothing will happen to you."

"I bound to go on my way, mister," said Phoenix. She inclined her head in the red rag. Then they went in different directions, but she could hear the gun shooting again and again over the hill.

She walked on. The shadows hung from the oak trees to the road like curtains. Then she smelled wood-smoke, and smelled the river, and she saw a steeple and the cabins on their steep steps. Dozens of little black children whirled around her. There ahead was Natchez shining. Bells were ringing. She walked on.

In the paved city it was Christmas time. There were red and green electric lights strung and crisscrossed everywhere, and all turned on in the daytime. Old Phoenix would have been lost if she had not distrusted her eyesight and depended on her feet to know where to take her.

She paused quietly on the sidewalk where people were passing by. A lady came along in the crowd, carrying an armful of red-, green- and silver-wrapped presents; she gave off perfume like the red roses in hot summer, and Phoenix stopped her.

"Please, missy, will you lace up my shoe?" She held up her foot.

"What do you want, Grandma?"

"See my shoe," said Phoenix. "Do all right for out in the country, but wouldn't look right to go in a big building."

"Stand still then, Grandma," said the lady. She put her packages down on the sidewalk beside her and laced and tied both shoes tightly.

"Can't lace 'em with a cane," said Phoenix. "Thank you, missy. I doesn't mind asking a nice lady to tie up my shoe, when I gets out on the street."

Moving slowly and from side to side, she went into the big building, and into the tower of steps, where she walked up and around and around until her feet knew to stop.

She entered a door, and there she saw nailed up on the wall the document that had been stamped with the gold seal and framed in the gold frame, which matched the dream that was hung up in her head.

"Here I be," she said. There was a fixed and ceremonial stiffness over her body.

"A charity case, I suppose," said an attendant who sat at the desk before her.

But Phoenix only looked above her head. There was sweat on her face, the wrinkles in her skin shone like a bright net.

"Speak up, Grandma," the woman said. "What's your name? We must have your history, you know. Have you been here before? What seems to be the trouble with you?"

Old Phoenix only gave a twitch to her face as if a fly were bothering her.

"Are you deaf?" cried the attendant.

But then the nurse came in.

"Oh, that's just old Aunt Phoenix," she said. "She doesn't come for herself—she has a little grandson. She makes these trips just as regular as clockwork. She lives away back off the Old Natchez Trace."[1] She bent down. "Well, Aunt Phoenix, why don't you just take a seat? We won't keep you standing after your long trip." She pointed.

The old woman sat down, bolt upright in the chair.

"Now, how is the boy?" asked the nurse.

Old Phoenix did not speak.

"I said, how is the boy?"

But Phoenix only waited and stared straight ahead, her face very solemn and withdrawn into rigidity.

"Is his throat any better?" asked the nurse. "Aunt Phoenix, don't you hear me? Is your grandson's throat any better since the last time you came for the medicine?"

With her hands on her knees, the old woman waited, silent, erect and motionless, just as if she were in armor.

"You mustn't take up our time this way, Aunt Phoenix," the nurse said. "Tell us quickly about your grandson, and get it over. He isn't dead, is he?"

At last there came a flicker and then a flame of comprehension across her face, and she spoke.

"My grandson. It was my memory had left me. There I sat and forgot why I made my long trip."

"Forgot?" The nurse frowned. "After you came so far?"

Then Phoenix was like an old woman begging a dignified forgiveness for waking up frightened in the night. "I never did go to school, I was too old at the Surrender,"[2] she said in a soft voice. "I'm an old woman without an education. It was my memory fail me. My little grandson, he is just the same, and I forgot it in the coming."

"Throat never heals, does it?" said the nurse, speaking in a loud, sure voice to old Phoenix. By now she had a card with something written on it, a little list. "Yes. Swallowed lye. When was it?—January—two-three years ago—"

Phoenix spoke unmasked now. "No, missy, he not dead, he just the same. Every little while his throat begin to close up again, and he not able to swallow. He not get his breath. He not able to help himself. So the time come around, and I go on another trip for the soothing medicine."

"All right. The doctor said as long as you came to get it, you could have it," said the nurse. "But it's an obstinate case."

"My little grandson, he sit up there in the house all wrapped up, waiting by himself," Phoenix went on. "We is the only two left in the world. He suffer and it don't seem to put him back at all. He got a sweet look. He going to last. He wear a little patch quilt and peep out holding his mouth open like a little bird. I remembers so plain now. I not going to forget him again, no, the whole enduring time. I could tell him from all the others in creation."

"All right." The nurse was trying to hush her now. She brought her a bottle of medicine. "Charity," she said, making a check mark in a book.

---

1. Historic road from Natchez, Mississippi, to Nashville, Tennessee. 2. The surrender of General Robert E. Lee (1807–1870) of the Confederacy on April 9, 1865, to General Ulysses S. Grant (1822–1885) of the Union, thus ending the Civil War.

Old Phoenix held the bottle close to her eyes, and then carefully put it into her pocket.

"I thank you," she said.

"It's Christmas time, Grandma," said the attendant. "Could I give you a few pennies out of my purse?"

"Five pennies is a nickel," said Phoenix stiffly.

"Here's a nickel," said the attendant.

Phoenix rose carefully and held out her hand. She received the nickel and then fished the other nickel out of her pocket and laid it beside the new one. She stared at her palm closely, with her head on one side.

Then she gave a tap with her cane on the floor.

"This is what come to me to do," she said. "I going to the store and buy my child a little windmill they sells, made out of paper. He going to find it hard to believe there such a thing in the world. I'll march myself back where he waiting, holding it straight up in this hand."

She lifted her free hand, gave a little nod, turned around, and walked out of the doctor's office. Then her slow step began on the stairs, going down.

1941

RELATED:

—Welty, An Interview, p. 898
—Susan Dodd on "A Worn Path," p. 921

# WILLIAM CARLOS WILLIAMS
## *1883–1963*

Williams was born in Rutherford, New Jersey. He took a medical degree at the University of Pennsylvania and practiced as a pediatrician through the long years of his literary career. Leaving behind the European-inspired Imagist movement, he defined himself as utterly American in taste and spirit, becoming the friend, supporter, and colleague of several of the leaders of the avant-garde in American literature. His work as a poet culminated in the massive chronicle *Paterson* (1946–58), and the imagination that shaped his verse informed his speculations on American history and its character in his book of essays *In the American Grain* (1925). Among his many volumes of verse, *Pictures from Brueghel and Other Poems* won the Pulitzer Prize in 1963. In his fiction as in his several plays he achieves an illuminated mirror image of the flat banality of ordinary lives. His novels include *White Mule* (1937) and *In the Money* (1940). *The Collected Stories of William Carlos Williams* appeared in 1996.

## The Use of Force

They were new patients to me, all I had was the name, Olson. Please come down as soon as you can, my daughter is very sick. When I arrived I was met by the mother, a big startled looking woman, very clean and apologetic who merely said, Is this the doctor? and let me in. In the back, she added. You must excuse us, doctor, we have her in the kitchen where it is warm. It is very damp here sometimes.

The child was fully dressed and sitting on her father's lap near the kitchen table. He tried to get up, but I motioned for him not to bother, took off my overcoat and started to look things over. I could see that they were all very nervous, eyeing me up and down distrustfully. As often, in such cases, they weren't telling me more than they had to, it was up to me to tell them; that's why they were spending three dollars on me.

The child was fairly eating me up with her cold, steady eyes, and no expression to her face whatever. She did not move and seemed, inwardly, quiet; an unusually attractive little thing, and as strong as a heifer in appearance. But her face was flushed, she was breathing rapidly, and I realized that she had a high fever. She had magnificent blonde hair, in profusion. One of those picture children often reproduced in advertising leaflets and the photogravure sections of the Sunday papers.

She's had a fever for three days, began the father and we don't know what it comes from. My wife has given her things, you know, like people do, but it don't do no good. And there's been a lot of sickness around. So we tho't you'd better look her over and tell us what is the matter.

As doctors often do I took a trial shot at it as a point of departure. Has she had a sore throat?

Both parents answered me together, No ... No, she says her throat don't hurt her.

Does your throat hurt you? added the mother to the child. But the little girl's expression didn't change nor did she move her eyes from my face.

Have you looked?

I tried to, said the mother, but I couldn't see.

As it happens we had been having a number of cases of diphtheria in the school to which this child went during that month and we were all, quite apparently, thinking of that, though no one had as yet spoken of the thing.

Well, I said, suppose we take a look at the throat first. I smiled in my best professional manner and asking for the child's first name I said, come on, Mathilda, open your mouth and let's take a look at your throat.

Nothing doing.

Aw, come on, I coaxed, just open your mouth wide and let me take a look. Look, I said opening both hands wide, I haven't anything in my hands. Just open up and let me see.

Such a nice man, put in the mother. Look how kind he is to you. Come on, do what he tells you to. He won't hurt you.

At that I ground my teeth in disgust. If only they wouldn't use the word "hurt" I might be able to get somewhere. But I did not allow myself to be hurried or disturbed but speaking quietly and slowly I approached the child again.

As I moved my chair a little nearer suddenly with one catlike movement both her hands clawed instinctively for my eyes and she almost reached them too. In fact she knocked my glasses flying and they fell, though unbroken, several feet away from me on the kitchen floor.

Both the mother and father almost turned themselves inside out in embarrassment and apology. You bad girl, said the mother, taking her and shaking her by one arm. Look what you've done. The nice man ...

For heaven's sake, I broke in. Don't call me a nice man to her. I'm here to look at her throat on the chance that she might have diphtheria[1] and possibly die of it. But that's nothing to her. Look here, I said to the child, we're going to look at your throat. You're old enough to understand what I'm saying. Will you open it now by yourself or shall we have to open it for you?

Not a move. Even her expression hadn't changed. Her breaths however were coming faster and faster. Then the battle began. I had to do it. I had to have a throat culture for her own protection. But first I told the parents that it was entirely up to them. I explained the danger but said that I would not insist on a throat examination so long as they would take the responsibility.

---

**1.** Bacterial disease that killed millions, mostly children, in the era before antibiotic medicines and effective programs of immunization. The most common sign of infection is a thick, bluish-white membrane coating the tonsils and throat.

If you don't do what the doctor says you'll have to go to the hospital, the mother admonished her severely.

Oh yeah? I had to smile to myself. After all, I had already fallen in love with the savage brat, the parents were contemptible to me. In the ensuing struggle they grew more and more abject, crushed, exhausted while she surely rose to magnificent heights of insane fury of effort bred of her terror of me.

The father tried his best, and he was a big man but the fact that she was his daughter, his shame at her behavior and his dread of hurting her made him release her just at the critical times when I had almost achieved success, till I wanted to kill him. But his dread also that she might have diphtheria made him tell me to go on, go on though he himself was almost fainting, while the mother moved back and forth behind us raising and lowering her hands in an agony of apprehension.

Put her in front of you on your lap, I ordered, and hold both her wrists.

But as soon as he did the child let out a scream. Don't, you're hurting me. Let go of my hands. Let them go I tell you. Then she shrieked terrifyingly, hysterically. Stop it! Stop it! You're killing me!

Do you think she can stand it, doctor! said the mother.

You get out, said the husband to his wife. Do you want her to die of diphtheria?

Come on now, hold her, I said.

Then I grasped the child's head with my left hand and tried to get the wooden tongue depressor between her teeth. She fought, with clenched teeth, desperately! But now I also had grown furious—at a child. I tried to hold myself down but I couldn't. I know how to expose a throat for inspection. And I did my best. When finally I got the wooden spatula behind the last teeth and just the point of it into the mouth cavity, she opened up for an instant but before I could see anything she came down again and gripping the wooden blade between her molars, she reduced it to splinters before I could get it out again.

Aren't you ashamed, the mother yelled at her. Aren't you ashamed to act like that in front of the doctor?

Get me a smooth-handled spoon of some sort, I told the mother. We're going through with this. The child's mouth was already bleeding. Her tongue was cut and she was screaming in wild hysterical shrieks. Perhaps I should have desisted and come back in an hour or more. No doubt it would have been better. But I have seen at least two children lying dead in bed of neglect in such cases, and feeling that I must get a diagnosis now or never I went at it again. But the worst of it was that I too had got beyond reason. I could have torn the child apart in my own fury and enjoyed it. It was a pleasure to attack her. My face was burning with it.

The damned little brat must be protected against her own idiocy, one says to one's self at such times. Others must be protected against her. It is a social necessity. And all these things are true. But a blind fury, a feeling of adult shame, bred of a longing for muscular release are the operatives. One goes on to the end.

In the final unreasoning assault I overpowered the child's neck and jaws. I forced the heavy silver spoon back of her teeth and down her throat till she gagged. And there it was—both tonsils covered with membrane. She had fought valiantly to keep me from knowing her secret. She had been hiding that sore throat for three days at least and lying to her parents in order to escape just such an outcome as this.

Now truly she was furious. She had been on the defensive before but now she attacked. Tried to get off her father's lap and fly at me while tears of defeat blinded her eyes.

1950

# TOBIAS WOLFF
## b. 1945

Wolff was born in Alabama and grew up in Washington State. Since his education at Oxford and Stanford Universities he has taught at Syracuse University and Indiana University. His stories are collected in *In the Garden of the North American Martyrs* (1981), *Back in the World* (1985), *The Night in Question* (1996), and *Our Story Begins* (2008); his novels include *Ugly Rumours* (1975) and *The Barracks Thief* (1984), winner of the PEN/Faulkner Award. Wolff is probably best known for his remarkable memoirs: *This Boy's Life* (1989) and *Old School* (2003) recount his boyhood; *In Pharaoh's Army* (1994) depicts his experiences as a soldier in the Vietnam War. He has also edited several anthologies, among them *The Vintage Book of Contemporary American Short Stories* (1993) and *Best American Short Stories* (1994). He currently teaches at Stanford University.

## Bullet in the Brain

Anders couldn't get to the bank until just before it closed, so of course the line was endless and he got stuck behind two women whose loud, stupid conversation put him in a murderous temper. He was never in the best of tempers anyway, Anders—a book critic known for the weary, elegant savagery with which he dispatched almost everything he reviewed.

With the line still doubled around the rope, one of the tellers stuck a "POSITION CLOSED" sign in her window and walked to the back of the bank, where she leaned against a desk and began to pass the time with a man shuffling papers. The women in front of Anders broke off their conversation and watched the teller with hatred. "Oh, that's nice," one of them said. She turned to Anders and added, confident of his accord, "One of those little human touches that keep us coming back for more."

Anders had conceived his own towering hatred of the teller, but he immediately turned it on the presumptuous crybaby in front of him. "Damned unfair," he said. "Tragic, really. If they're not chopping off the wrong leg, or bombing your ancestral village, they're closing their positions."

She stood her ground. "I didn't say it was tragic," she said. "I just think it's a pretty lousy way to treat your customers."

"Unforgivable," Anders said. "Heaven will take note."

She sucked in her cheeks but stared past him and said nothing. Anders saw that the other woman, her friend, was looking in the same direction. And then the tellers stopped what they were doing, and the customers slowly turned, and silence came over the bank. Two men wearing black ski masks and blue business suits were standing to the side of the door. One of them had a pistol pressed against the guard's neck. The guard's eyes were closed, and his lips were moving. The other man had a sawed-off shotgun. "Keep your big mouth shut!" the man with the pistol said, though no one had spoken a word. "One of you tellers hits the alarm, you're all dead meat. Got it?"

The tellers nodded.

"Oh, bravo," Anders said. "*Dead meat.*" He turned to the woman in front of him. "Great script, eh? The stern, brass-knuckled poetry of the dangerous classes."

She looked at him with drowning eyes.

The man with the shotgun pushed the guard to his knees. He handed the shotgun to his partner and yanked the guard's wrists up behind his back and locked them together with a pair of handcuffs. He toppled him onto the floor with a kick between the shoulder blades. Then he took his shotgun back and went over to the security gate at the end of the counter. He was short and heavy and moved with peculiar slowness, even torpor. "Buzz him in," his partner said. The man with the shotgun opened the gate and sauntered along the line of tellers, handing each of them a Hefty bag. When he came to the empty position he looked over at the man with the pistol, who said, "Whose slot is that?"

Anders watched the teller. She put her hand to her throat and turned to the man she'd been talking to. He nodded. "Mine," she said.

"Then get your ugly ass in gear and fill that bag."

"There you go," Anders said to the woman in front of him. "Justice is done."

"Hey! Bright boy! Did I tell you to talk?"

"No," Anders said.

"Then shut your trap."

"Did you hear that?" Anders said. "'Bright boy.' Right out of 'The Killers.'"

"Please be quiet," the woman said.

"Hey, you deaf or what?" The man with the pistol walked over to Anders. He poked the weapon into Anders' gut. "You think I'm playing games?"

"No," Anders said, but the barrel tickled like a stiff finger and he had to fight back the titters. He did this by making himself stare into the man's eyes, which were clearly visible behind the holes in the mask: pale blue and rawly red-rimmed. The man's left eyelid kept twitching. He breathed out a piercing, ammoniac smell that shocked Anders more than anything that had happened, and he was beginning to develop a sense of unease when the man prodded him again with the pistol.

"You like me, bright boy?" he said. "You want to suck my dick?"

"No," Anders said.

"Then stop looking at me."

Anders fixed his gaze on the man's shiny wing-tip shoes.

"Not down there. Up there." He stuck the pistol under Anders' chin and pushed it upward until Anders was looking at the ceiling.

Anders had never paid much attention to that part of the bank, a pompous old building with marble floors and counters and pillars, and gilt scrollwork over the tellers' cages. The domed ceiling had been decorated with mythological figures whose fleshy, toga-draped ugliness Anders had taken in at a glance many years earlier and afterward declined to notice. Now he had no choice but to scrutinize the painter's work. It was even worse than he remembered, and all of it executed with the utmost gravity. The artist had a few tricks up his sleeve and used them again and again—a certain rosy blush on the underside of the clouds, a coy backward glance on the faces of the cupids and fauns. The ceiling was crowded with various dramas, but the one that caught Anders' eye was Zeus and Europa—portrayed, in this rendition, as a bull ogling a cow from behind a haystack. To make the cow sexy, the painter had canted her hips suggestively and given her long, droopy eyelashes through which she gazed back at the bull with sultry welcome. The bull wore a smirk and his eyebrows were arched. If there'd been a bubble coming out of his mouth, it would have said, "Hubba hubba."

"What's so funny, bright boy?"

"Nothing."

"You think I'm comical? You think I'm some kind of clown?"

"No."

"You think you can fuck with me?"

"No."

"Fuck with me again, you're history. *Capiche?*"

Anders burst out laughing. He covered his mouth with both hands and said, "I'm sorry, I'm sorry," then snorted helplessly through his fingers and said, "*Capiche*—oh, God, *capiche*," and at that the man with the pistol raised the pistol and shot Anders right in the head.

The bullet smashed Anders' skull and ploughed through his brain and exited behind his right ear, scattering shards of bone into the cerebral cortex, the corpus callosum, back toward the basal ganglia, and down into the thalamus. But before all this occurred, the first appearance of the bullet in the cerebrum set off a crackling chain of ion transports and neuro-transmissions. Because of their peculiar origin these traced a peculiar pattern, flukishly calling to life a summer afternoon some forty years past, and long since lost to memory. After striking the cranium the bullet was moving at 900 feet per second, a pathetically sluggish, glacial pace compared to the synaptic lightning that flashed around it. Once in the brain, that is, the bullet came under the mediation of brain time, which gave Anders plenty of leisure to contemplate the scene that, in a phrase he would have abhorred, "passed before his eyes."

It is worth noting what Anders did not remember, given what he did remember. He did not remember his first lover, Sherry, or what he had most madly loved about her, before it came to irritate him—her unembarrassed carnality, and especially the cordial way she had with his unit, which she called Mr. Mole, as in, "Uh-oh, looks like Mr. Mole wants to play," and, "Let's hide Mr. Mole!" Anders did not remember his wife, whom he had also loved before she exhausted him with her predictability, or his daughter, now a sullen professor of economics at Dartmouth. He did not remember standing just outside his daughter's door as she lectured her bear about his naughtiness and described the truly appalling punishments Paws would receive unless he changed his ways. He did not remember a single line of the hundreds of poems he had committed to memory in his youth so that he could give himself the shivers at will—not "Silent, upon a peak in Darien," or "My God, I heard this day," or "All my pretty ones? Did you say all? O hell-kite! All?"[1] None of these did he remember; not one. Anders did not remember his dying mother saying of his father, "I should have stabbed him in his sleep."

He did not remember Professor Josephs telling his class how Athenian prisoners in Sicily had been released if they could recite Aeschylus, and then reciting Aeschylus himself, right there, in the Greek. Anders did not remember how his eyes had burned at those sounds. He did not remember the surprise of seeing a college classmate's name on the jacket of a novel not long after they graduated, or the respect he had felt after reading the book. He did not remember the pleasure of giving respect.

Nor did Anders remember seeing a woman leap to her death from the building opposite his own just days after his daughter was born. He did not remember shouting, "Lord have mercy!" He did not remember deliberately crashing his father's car into a tree, or having his ribs kicked in by three policemen at an anti-war rally, or waking himself up with laughter. He did not remember when he began to regard the heap of books on his desk with boredom and dread, or when he grew angry at writers for writing them. He did not remember when everything began to remind him of something else.

This is what he remembered. Heat. A baseball field. Yellow grass, the whirr of insects, himself leaning against a tree as the boys of the neighborhood gather for a pickup game. He looks on as the others argue the relative genius of Mantle and Mays. They have been worrying this subject all summer, and it has become tedious to Anders: an oppression, like the heat.

Then the last two boys arrive, Coyle and a cousin of his from Mississippi. Anders has never met Coyle's cousin before and will never see him again. He says hi with the rest but takes no further notice of him until they've chosen sides and someone asks the cousin what position he wants to play. "Short-stop," the boy says. "Short's the best position they is." Anders turns and looks at him. He wants to hear Coyle's cousin repeat what he's just said, but he knows better than to ask. The others will think he's being a jerk, ragging the kid for his grammar. But that isn't it, not at all—it's that Anders is strangely roused, elated, by those final two words, their pure unexpectedness and their music. He takes the field in a trance, repeating them to himself.

The bullet is already in the brain; it won't be outrun forever, or charmed to a halt. In the end it will do its work and leave the troubled skull behind, dragging its comet's tail of memory and hope and talent and love into the marble hall of commerce. That can't be helped. But for now Anders can still make time. Time for the shadows to lengthen on the grass, time for the tethered dog to bark at the flying ball, time for the boy in right field to smack his sweat-blackened mitt and softly chant, *They is, they is, they is.*

1995

---

1. Lines from Keats' (1795–1821) "On First Looking into Chapman's Homer," George Herbert's (1593–1633) "Man," and William Shakespeare's (1564–1616) *Macbeth* (Act IV, Scene 3, lines 217–218).

# VIRGINIA WOOLF
## 1882–1941

Woolf was born in London, the daughter of a publishing heiress, Julia Jackson Duckworth, and a
distinguished literary critic, Sir Leslie Stephen.
At her father's death in 1904 she moved with her
sister and two brothers to Bloomsbury, a fashion-
ably bohemian section of London, and when she
began to publish she was firmly associated with
the "Bloomsbury Group" of writers and intellectuals. In 1912 she married the journalist and political philosopher Leonard Woolf and with him
established the Hogarth Press, which published
many of her works. By the example of her first
novels and in essays she made a case against the
objective realism of such then-popular practitio-
ners as Arnold Bennett. Her preference was for lyric adaptations of the stream
of consciousness, best exemplified by *To the Lighthouse* (1927) and *The Waves*
(1931). In her popular *Mrs. Dalloway* (1925) she showed the possibilities of her
methods in developing the nondramatic, contrapuntal presentation of a sensitive, unstable war veteran and an unfulfilled woman committed to the maintenance of her social position—perhaps a fictional transformation of two
major aspects of Woolf's own personality. In 1916 she suffered a terrifying
mental breakdown; she killed herself in 1941 in fear of a recurrence. *A Room of
One's Own* (1929) is a feminist work of enduring influence, and the essays on
literature collected in the two volumes of *The Common Reader* (1925, 1933) did
much to shape modern taste with their easy, keen suggestiveness. Her stories
were collected in *A Haunted House* (1944).

# Kew Gardens[1]

From the oval-shaped flower-bed there rose perhaps a hundred stalks
spreading into heart-shaped or tongue-shaped leaves half-way up and unfurl-
ing at the tip red or blue, or yellow petals marked with spots of colour raised
upon the surface; and from the red, blue, or yellow gloom of the throat emerged
a straight bar, rough with gold dust and slightly clubbed at the end. The petals were voluminous enough to be stirred by the summer breeze, and when
they moved, the red, blue, and yellow lights passed one over the other, staining an inch of the brown earth beneath with a spot of the most intricate
colour. The light fell either upon the smooth, grey back of a pebble, or the
shell of a snail with its brown, circular veins, or falling into a raindrop, it

---

1. Established as a state institution in 1841, Kew Gardens is the home of the Royal Botanic Gardens; it is
in the London suburb of Kew, Surrey.

expanded with such intensity of red, blue, and yellow the thin walls of water that one expected them to burst and disappear. Instead, the drop was left in a second silver grey once more, and the light now settled upon the flesh of a leaf, revealing the branching thread of fibre beneath the surface, and again it moved on and spread its illumination in the vast green spaces beneath the dome of the heart-shaped and tongue-shaped leaves. Then the breeze stirred rather more briskly overhead and the colour was flashed into the air above, into the eyes of the men and women who walk in Kew Gardens in July.

The figures of these men and women straggled past the flower-bed with a curiously irregular movement not unlike that of the white and blue butter-flies who crossed the turf in zig-zag flights from bed to bed. The man was about six inches in front of the woman, strolling carelessly, while she bore on with greater purpose, only turning her head now and then to see that the children were not too far behind. The man kept this distance in front of the woman purposely, though perhaps unconsciously, for he wished to go on with his thoughts.

"Fifteen years ago I came here with Lily," he thought. "We sat somewhere over there by a lake and I begged her to marry me all through the hot after-noon. How the dragonfly kept circling round us: how clearly I see the dragon-fly and her shoe with the square silver buckle at the toe. All the time I spoke I saw her shoe and when it moved impatiently I knew without looking up what she was going to say: the whole of her seemed to be in her shoe. And my love, my desire, were in the dragonfly; for some reason I thought that if it settled there, on that leaf, the broad one with the red flower in the middle of it, if the dragonfly settled on the leaf she would say 'Yes' at once. But the dragonfly went round and round: it never settled anywhere—of course not, happily not, or I shouldn't be walking here with Eleanor and the children. Tell me, Eleanor. D'you ever think of the past?"

"Why do you ask, Simon?"

"Because I've been thinking of the past. I've been thinking of Lily, the woman I might have married. . . . Well, why are you silent? Do you mind my thinking of the past?"

"Why should I mind, Simon? Doesn't one always think of the past, in a garden with men and women lying under the trees. Aren't they one's past, all that remains of it, those men and women, those ghosts lying under the trees, . . . one's happiness, one's reality?"

"For me, a square silver shoe buckle and a dragonfly—"

"For me, a kiss. Imagine six little girls sitting before their easels twenty years ago, down by the side of a lake, painting the water-lilies, the first red water-lilies I'd ever seen. And suddenly a kiss, there on the back of my neck. And my hand shook all the afternoon so that I couldn't paint. I took out my watch and marked the hour when I would allow myself to think of the kiss for five minutes only—it was so precious—the kiss of an old grey-haired woman with a wart on her nose, the mother of all my kisses all my life. Come, Caroline, come, Hubert."

They walked on past the flower-bed, now walking four abreast, and soon diminished in size among the trees and looked half transparent as the sun-light and shade swam over their backs in large trembling irregular patches.

In the oval flower-bed the snail, whose shell had been stained red, blue, and yellow for the space of two minutes or so, now appeared to be moving very slightly in its shell, and next began to labour over the crumbs of loose earth which broke away and rolled down as it passed over them. It appeared to have a definite goal in front of it, differing in this respect from the singular high stepping angular green insect who attempted to cross in front of it, and waited for a second with its antennae trembling as if in deliberation, and then stepped off as rapidly and strangely in the opposite direction. Brown cliffs with deep green lakes in the hollows, flat, blade-like trees that waved from root to tip, round boulders of grey stone, vast crumpled surfaces of a thin crackling texture—all these objects lay across the snail's progress between one stalk and another to his goal. Before he had decided whether to circumvent the arched tent of a dead leaf or to breast it there came past the bed the feet of other human beings.

This time they were both men. The younger of the two wore an expression of perhaps unnatural calm; he raised his eyes and fixed them very steadily in front of him while his companion spoke, and directly his companion had done speaking he looked on the ground again and sometimes opened his lips only after a long pause and sometimes did not open them at all. The elder man had a curiously uneven and shaky method of walking, jerking his hand forward and throwing up his head abruptly, rather in the manner of an impatient carriage horse tired of waiting outside a house; but in the man these gestures were irresolute and pointless. He talked almost incessantly; he smiled to himself and again began to talk, as if the smile had been an answer. He was talking about spirits—the spirits of the dead, who, according to him, were even now telling him all sorts of odd things about their experiences in Heaven.

"Heaven was known to the ancients as Thessaly, William, and now, with this war, the spirit matter[2] is rolling between the hills like thunder." He paused, seemed to listen, smiled, jerked his head and continued:

"You have a small electric battery and a piece of rubber to insulate the wire—isolate?—insulate?—well, we'll skip the details, no good going into details that wouldn't be understood—and in short the little machine stands in any convenient position by the head of the bed, we will say, on a neat mahogany stand. All arrangements being properly fixed by workmen under my direction, the widow applies her ear and summons the spirit by sign as agreed. Women! Widows! Women in black—"

Here he seemed to have caught sight of a woman's dress in the distance, which in the shade looked a purple black. He took off his hat, placed his hand upon his heart, and hurried towards her muttering and gesticulating feverishly. But William caught him by the sleeve and touched a flower with the tip of his walking-stick in order to divert the old man's attention. After looking at it for a moment in some confusion the old man bent his ear to it and seemed to answer a voice speaking from it, for he began talking about the forests of Uruguay which he had visited hundreds of years ago in company with the most beautiful young woman in Europe. He could be heard murmuring about forests of Uruguay blanketed with the wax petals of tropical roses, nightingales, sea beaches, mermaids, and women drowned at sea, as he suffered

---

2. That is, spiritualism. Thessaly: a region in Greece. "This war": World War I.

himself to be moved on by William, upon whose face the look of stoical patience grew slowly deeper and deeper.

Following his steps so closely as to be slightly puzzled by his gestures came two elderly women of the lower middle class, one stout and ponderous, the other rosy cheeked and nimble. Like most people of their station they were frankly fascinated by other signs of eccentricity betokening a disordered brain, especially in the well-to-do; but they were too far off to be certain whether the gestures were merely eccentric or genuinely mad. After they had scrutinized the old man's back in silence for a moment and given each other a queer, sly look, they went on energetically piecing together their very complicated dialogue:

"Nell, Bert, Lot, Cess, Phil, Pa, he says, I says, she says, I says, I says—"
"My Bert, Sis, Bill, Grandad, the old man, sugar,

> Sugar, flour, kippers, greens,
> Sugar, sugar, sugar."

The ponderous woman looked through the pattern of falling words at the flowers standing cool, firm, and upright in the earth, with a curious expression. She saw them as a sleeper waking from a heavy sleep sees a brass candlestick reflecting the light in an unfamiliar way, and closes his eyes and opens them, and seeing the brass candlestick again, finally starts broad awake and stares at the candlestick with all his powers. So the heavy woman came to a standstill opposite the oval-shaped flower-bed, and ceased even to pretend to listen to what the other woman was saying. She stood there letting the words fall over her, swaying the top part of her body slowly backwards and forwards, looking at the flowers. Then she suggested that they should find a seat and have their tea.

The snail had now considered every possible method of reaching his goal without going round the dead leaf or climbing over it. Let alone the effort needed for climbing a leaf, he was doubtful whether the thin texture which vibrated with such an alarming crackle when touched even by the tips of his horns would bear his weight; and this determined him finally to creep beneath it, for there was a point where the leaf curved high enough from the ground to admit him. He had just inserted his head in the opening and was taking stock of the high brown roof and was getting used to the cool brown light when two other people came past outside on the turf. This time they were both young, a young man and a young woman. They were both in the prime of youth, the season before the smooth pink folds of the flower have burst their gummy case, when the wings of the butterfly, though fully grown, are motionless in the sun.

"Lucky it isn't Friday," he observed.
"Why? D'you believe in luck?"
"They make you pay sixpence on Friday."
"What's a sixpence anyway? Isn't it worth sixpence?"
"What's 'it'—what do you mean by 'it'?"
"O, anything—I mean—you know what I mean."

Long pauses came between each of these remarks; they were uttered in toneless and monotonous voices. The couple stood still on the edge of the flower-bed, and together pressed the end of her parasol deep down into the soft earth. The action and the fact that his hand rested on the top of hers expressed their feelings in a strange way, as these short insignificant words also expressed something, words with short wings for their heavy body of meaning, inadequate to carry them far and thus alighting awkwardly upon the very common objects that surrounded them, and were to their inexperienced touch so massive; but who knows (so they thought as they pressed the parasol into the earth) what precipices aren't concealed in them, or what slopes of ice don't shine in the sun on the other side? Who knows? Who has ever seen this before? Even when she wondered what sort of tea they gave you at Kew, he felt that something loomed up behind her words, and stood vast and solid behind them; and the mist very slowly rose and uncovered—O, Heavens, what were those shapes?—little white tables, and waitresses who looked first at her and then at him; and there was a bill that he would pay with a real two-shilling piece, and it was real, all real, he assured himself, fingering the coin in his pocket, real to everyone except to him and to her; even to him it began to seem real; and then—but it was too exciting to stand and think any longer, and he pulled the parasol out of the earth with a jerk and was impatient to find the place where one had tea with other people, like other people.

"Come along, Trissie; it's time we had our tea."

"Wherever *does* one have one's tea?" she asked with the oddest thrill of excitement in her voice, looking vaguely round and letting herself be drawn down the grass path, trailing her parasol; turning her head this way and that way forgetting her tea, wishing to go down there and then down there, remembering orchids and cranes among wild flowers, a Chinese pagoda and a crimson crested bird; but he bore her on.

Thus one couple after another with much the same irregular and aimless movement passed the flower-bed and were enveloped in layer after layer of green-blue vapour, in which at first their bodies had substance and a dash of colour, but later both substance and colour dissolved in the green-blue atmosphere. How hot it was! So hot that even the thrush chose to hop, like a mechanical bird, in the shadow of the flowers, with long pauses between one movement and the next; instead of rambling vaguely the white butterflies dance one above another, making with their white shifting flakes the outline of a shattered, marble column above the tallest flowers; the glass roofs of the palm house shone as if a whole market full of shiny green umbrellas had opened in the sun; and in the drone of the aeroplane the voice of the summer sky murmured its fierce soul. Yellow and black, pink and snow white, shapes of all these colours, men, women, and children were spotted for a second upon the horizon, and then, seeing the breadth of yellow that lay upon the grass, they wavered and sought shade beneath the trees, dissolving like drops of water in the yellow and green atmosphere, staining it faintly with red and blue. It seemed as if all gross and heavy bodies had sunk down in the heat motionless and lay huddled upon the ground, but their voices went wavering from them as if they were flames lolling from the thick waxen bodies of candles. Voices. Yes, voices. Wordless voices, breaking the silence suddenly with such depth of contentment, such passion of desire, or, in the voices of children, such freshness of surprise; breaking the silence? But there was no silence; all the time the motor omnibuses were turning their wheels and changing their gear; like a vast nest of Chinese boxes all of wrought steel turning ceaselessly one within another the city murmured; on the top of which the voices cried aloud and the petals of myriads of flowers flashed their colours into the air.

1943

# RICHARD WRIGHT
## 1908–1960

Wright was born on a plantation near Natchez, Mississippi, the grandson of slaves, the son of a mill worker and a schoolteacher. Deserted by his father at an early age, he lived intermittently in orphan asylums or wandered with his mother from city to city in an erratic pattern that continued for him after her death. In 1927 he turned up in Chicago, where he joined the Communist Party and began to write. His growing reputation as a short-story writer was solidified with the publication in 1940 of his first novel, *Native Son,* a pathetic and gory narrative of a young black man hurled blindly into crime. *Black Boy,* a vivid personal narrative, was published in 1945, followed in 1953 by the novel *The Outsider* and in 1954 by *Black Power,* an extensive report on the African Gold Coast countries. Many of his stories are collected in *Uncle Tom's Children* (1938) and *Eight Men* (1961). *American Hunger,* a continuation of *Black Boy,* appeared posthumously in 1977.

## The Man Who Was Almost a Man

Dave struck out across the fields, looking homeward through paling light. Whuts the usa talkin wid em niggers in the field? Anyhow, his mother was putting supper on the table. Them niggers can't understand *nothing.* One of these days he was going to get a gun and practice shooting, then they can't talk to him as though he were a little boy. He slowed, looking at the ground. Shucks, Ah ain scareda them even ef they are biggern me! Aw, Ah know whut Ahma do. ... Ahm going by ol Joe's sto n git that Sears Roebuck catlog n look at them guns. Mabbe Ma will lemme buy one when she gits mah pay from ol man Hawkins. Ahma beg her t gimme some money. Ahm ol ernough to hava gun. Ahm seventeen. Almos a man. He strode, feeling his long, loose-jointed limbs. Shucks, a man oughta hava little gun aftah he done worked hard all day. ...

He came in sight of Joe's store. A yellow lantern glowed on the front porch. He mounted steps and went through the screen door, hearing it bang behind him. There was a strong smell of coal oil and mackerel fish. He felt very confident until he saw fat Joe walk in through the rear door, then his courage began to ooze.

"Howdy, Dave! Whutcha want?"

"How yuh, Mistah Joe? Aw, Ah don wanna buy nothing. Ah jus wanted t see ef yuhd lemme look at tha ol catlog erwhile."

"Sure! You wanna see it here?"

"Nawsuh. Ah wans t take it home wid me. Ahll bring it back termorrow when Ah come in from the fiels."

"You plannin on buying something?"

"Yessuh."

"Your ma lettin you have your own money now?"

"Shucks. Mistah Joe, Ahm gittin t be a man like anybody else!"

Joe laughed and wiped his greasy white face with a red bandanna.

"Whut you plannin on buyin?"

Dave looked at the floor, scratched his head, scratched his thigh, and smiled. Then he looked up shyly.

"Ahll tell yuh, Mistah Joe, ef yuh promise yuh won't tell."

"I promise."

"Waal, Ahma buy a gun."

"A gun? Whut you want with a gun?"

"Ah wanna keep it."

"You ain't nothing but a boy. You don't need a gun."

"Aw, lemme have the catlog, Mistah Joe. Ahll bring it back."

Joe walked through the rear door. Dave was elated. He looked around at barrels of sugar and flour. He heard Joe coming back. He craned his neck to see if he were bringing the book. Yeah, he's got it. Gawddog, he's got it!

"Here, but be sure you bring it back. It's the only one I got."

"Sho, Mistah Joe."

"Say, if you wanna buy a gun, why don't you buy one from me? I gotta gun to sell."

"Will it shoot?"

"Sure it'll shoot."

"Whut kind is it?"

"Oh, it's kinda old. . . . A left-hand Wheeler. A pistol. A big one."

"Is it got bullets in it?"

"It's loaded."

"Kin Ah see it?"

"Where's your money?"

"Whu yuh wan fer it?"

"I'll let you have it for two dollars."

"Just two dollahs? Shucks, Ah could buy tha when Ah git mah pay."

"I'll have it here when you want it."

"Awright, suh. Ah be in fer it."

He went through the door, hearing it slam again behind him. Ahma git some money from Ma n buy me a gun! Only two dollahs! He tucked the thick catalogue under his arm and hurried.

"Where yuh been, boy?" His mother held a steaming dish of black-eyed peas.

"Aw, Ma, Ah jus stopped down the road t talk wid th boys."

"Yuh know bettah than t keep suppah waitin."

He sat down, resting the catalogue on the edge of the table.

"Yuh git up from there and git to the well n wash yosef! Ah ain feedin no hogs in mah house!"

She grabbed his shoulder and pushed him. He stumbled out of the room, then came back to get the catalogue.

"Whut this?"

"Aw, Ma, it's jusa catlog."

"Who yuh git it from?"

"From Joe, down at the sto."

"Waal, thas good. We kin use it around the house."

"Naw, Ma." He grabbed for it. "Gimme mah catlog, Ma."

She held onto it and glared at him.

"Quit hollerin at me! Whut's wrong wid yuh? Yuh crazy?"

"But Ma, please. It ain mine! It's Joe's! He tol me t bring it back t im termorrow."

She gave up the book. He stumbled down the back steps, hugging the thick book under his arm. When he had splashed water on his face and hands, he groped back to the kitchen and fumbled in a corner for the towel. He bumped into a chair; it clattered to the floor. The catalogue sprawled at his feet. When he had dried his eyes he snatched up the book and held it again under his arm. His mother stood watching him.

"Now, ef yuh gonna acka fool over that ol book, Ahll take it n burn it up."

"Naw, Ma, please."

"Waal, set down n be still!"

He sat and drew the oil lamp close. He thumbed page after page, unaware of the food his mother set on the table. His father came in. Then his small brother.

"Whutcha got there, Dave?" his father asked.

"Jusa catlog," he answered, not looking up.

"Yeah, here they is!" His eyes glowed at blue-and-black revolvers. He glanced up, feeling sudden guilt. His father was watching him. He eased the book under the table and rested it on his knees. After the blessing was asked, he ate. He scooped up peas and swallowed fat meat without chewing. Buttermilk helped to wash it down. He did not want to mention money before his father. He would do much better by cornering his mother when she was alone. He looked at his father uneasily out of the edge of his eye.

"Boy, how come yuh don quit foolin wid tha book n eat yo suppah?"

"Yessuh."

"How yuh n ol man Hawkins gittin erlong?"

"Suh?"

"Can't yuh hear? Why don yuh lissen? Ah ast yu how wuz yuh n ol man Hawkins gittin erlong?"

"Oh, swell, Pa. Ah plows mo lan than anybody over there."

"Waal, yuh oughta keep yo min on whut yuh doin."

"Yessuh."

He poured his plate full of molasses and sopped at it slowly with a chunk of cornbread. When his father and brother had left the kitchen, he still sat and looked again at the guns in the catalogue, longing to muster courage enough to present his case to his mother. Lawd, ef Ah only had the pretty one! He could almost feel the slickness of the weapon with his fingers. If he had a gun like that he would polish it and keep it shining so it would never rust. N Ah'd keep it loaded, by Gawd!

"Ma?" His voice was hesitant.

"Hunh?"

"Ol man Hawkins give yuh mah money yit?"

"Yeah, but ain no usa yuh thinkin bout thowin nona it erway. Ahm keepin tha money sos yuh kin have cloes t go to school this winter."

He rose and went to her side with the open catalogue in his palms. She was washing dishes, her head bent low over a pan. Shyly he raised the book. When he spoke, his voice was husky, faint.

"Ma, Gawd knows Ah wans one of these."

"One of whut?" she asked, not raising her eyes.

"One of these," he said again, not daring even to point. She glanced up at the page, then at him with wide eyes.

"Nigger, is yuh gone plum crazy?"

"Aw, Ma——"

"Git outta here! Don yuh talk t me bout no gun! Yuh a fool!"

"Ma, Ah kin buy one fer *two* dollahs."

"Not ef Ah knows it yuh ain!"

"But yuh promised me one——"

"Ah don care whut Ah promised! Yuh ain nothing but a boy yit!"

"Ma, ef yuh lemme buy one Ahll *never* ast yuh fer nothing no mo."

"Ah tol yuh t git outta here! Yuh ain gonna toucha penny of tha money fer no gun! Thas how come Ah has Mistah Hawkins t pay yo wages to me, cause Ah knows yuh ain got no sense."

"But Ma, we needa gun. Pa ain got no gun. We needa gun in the house. Yuh kin never tell whut might happen."

"Now don yuh try to maka fool outta me, boy! Ef we did hava gun yuh wouldn't have it!"

He laid the catalogue down and slipped his arm around her waist.

"Aw, Ma, Ah done worked hard alla summer n ain ast yuh fer nothin, is Ah, now?"

"Thas whut yuh spose to do!"

"But Ma, Ah wans a gun. Yuh kin lemme have two dollahs outta mah money. Please, Ma. I kin give it to Pa . . . Please, Ma! Ah loves yuh, Ma."

When she spoke her voice came soft and low.

"Whut yuh wan wida gun, Dave? Yun don need no gun. Yuhll git in trouble. N ef yo Pa jus *thought* Ah let yuh have money t buy a gun he'd hava fit."

"Ahll hide it, Ma, it ain but two dollahs."

"Lawd, chil, whuts wrong wid yuh?"

"Ain nothing wrong, Ma. Ahm almos a man now. Ah wants a gun."

"Who gonna sell yuh a gun?"

"Ol Joe at the sto."

"N it don cos but two dollahs?"

"Thas all, Ma. Just two dollahs. Please, Ma."

She was stacking the plates away; her hands moved slowly, reflectively. Dave kept an anxious silence. Finally, she turned to him.

"Ahll let yuh git tha gun ef yuh promise me one thing."

"Whuts tha, Ma?"

"Yuh bring it straight back t *me*, yuh hear? It be fer Pa."

"Yessum! Lemme go now, Ma."

She stooped, turned slightly to one side, raised the hem of her dress, rolled down the top of her stocking, and came up with a slender wad of bills.

"Here," she said, "Lawd knows yuh don need no gun. But yer Pa does. Yuh bring it right back to *me*, yuh hear? Ahma put it up. Now ef yuh don, Ahma have yuh Pa lick yuh so hard yuh won ferget it."

"Yessum."

He took the money, ran down the steps, and across the yard.

"Dave! Yuuuuuh Daaaaave!"

He heard, but he was not going to stop now. "Naw, Lawd!"

The first movement he made the following morning was to reach under his pillow for the gun. In the gray light of dawn he held it loosely, feeling a sense of power. Could kill a man with a gun like this. Kill anybody, black or white. And if he were holding his gun in his hand, nobody could run over him; they would have to respect him. It was a big gun, with a long barrel and a heavy handle. He raised and lowered it in his hand, marveling at its weight.

He had not come straight home with it as his mother had asked; instead he had stayed out in the fields, holding the weapon in his hand, aiming it now and then at some imaginary foe. But he had not fired it; he had been afraid that his father might hear. Also he was not sure he knew how to fire it.

To avoid surrendering the pistol he had not come into the house until he knew that all were asleep. When his mother had tiptoed to his bedside late that night and demanded the gun, he had first played 'possum; then he had told her that the gun was hidden outdoors, that he would bring it to her in the morning. Now he lay turning it slowly in his hands. He broke it, took out the cartridges, felt them, and then put them back.

He slid out of bed, got a long strip of old flannel from a trunk, wrapped the gun in it, and tied it to his naked thigh while it was still loaded. He did not go in to breakfast. Even though it was not yet daylight, he started for Jim Hawkins' plantation. Just as the sun was rising he reached the barns where the mules and plows were kept.

"Hey! That you, Dave?"

He turned. Jim Hawkins stood eying him suspiciously.

"What're yuh doing here so early?"

"Ah didn't know Ah wuz gittin up so early, Mistah Hawkins. Ah wuz fixin t hitch up ol Jenny n take her t the fiels."

"Good. Since you're so early, how about plowing that stretch down by the woods?"

"Suits me, Mistah Hawkins."

"O.K. Go to it!"

He hitched Jenny to a plow and started across the fields. Hot dog! This was just what he wanted. If he could get down by the woods, he could shoot his gun and nobody would hear. He walked behind the plow, hearing the traces creaking, feeling the gun tied tight to his thigh.

When he reached the woods, he plowed two whole rows before he decided to take out the gun. Finally, he stopped, looked in all directions, then untied the gun and held it in his hand. He turned to the mule and smiled.

"Know whut this is, Jenny? Naw, yuh wouldn't know! Yuhs jusa ol mule! Anyhow, this is a gun, n it kin shoot, by Gawd!"

He held the gun at arm's length. Whut t hell, Ahma shoot this thing! He looked at Jenny again.

"Lissen here, Jenny! When Ah pull this ol trigger Ah don wan yuh t run n acka fool now."

Jenny stood with head down, her short ears pricked straight. Dave walked off about twenty feet, held the gun far out from him, at arm's length, and turned his head. Hell, he told himself, Ah ain afraid. The gun felt loose in his fingers; he waved it wildly for a moment. Then he shut his eyes and tightened his forefinger. *Blooom!* A report half-deafened him and he thought his right hand was torn from his arm. He heard Jenny whinnying and galloping over the field, and he found himself on his knees, squeezing his fingers hard between his legs. His hand was numb; he jammed it into his mouth, trying to warm it, trying to stop the pain. The gun lay at his feet. He did not quite know what had happened. He stood up and stared at the gun as though it were a live thing. He gritted his teeth and kicked the gun. Yuh almos broke mah arm! He turned to look for Jenny; she was far over the fields, tossing her head and kicking wildly.

"Hol on ther, ol mule!"

When he caught up with her she stood trembling, walling her big white eyes at him. The plow was far away; the traces had broken. Then Dave stopped short, looking, not believing. Jenny was bleeding. Her left side was red and wet with blood. He went closer. Lawd have mercy! Wondah did Ah shoot this mule? He grabbed for Jenny's mane. She flinched, snorted, whirled, tossing her head.

"Hol on now! Hol on."

Then he saw the hole in Jenny's side, right between the ribs. It was round, wet, red. A crimson stream streaked down the front leg, flowing fast. Good Gawd! Ah wuznt shootin at tha mule. He felt panic. He knew he had to stop that blood, or Jenny would bleed to death. He had never seen so much blood in all his life. He ran the mule for half a mile, trying to catch her. Finally, she stopped, breathing hard, stumpy tail half arched. He caught her mane and led her back to where the plow and gun lay. Then he stopped and grabbed handfuls of damp black earth and tried to plug the bullet hole. Jenny shuddered, whinnied, and broke from him.

"Hol on! Hol on now!"

He tried to plug it again, but blood came anyhow. His fingers were hot and sticky. He rubbed dirt hard into his palms, trying to dry them. Then again he attempted to plug the bullet hole, but Jenny shied away, kicking her heels high. He stood helpless. He had to do something. He ran at Jenny; she dodged him. He watched a red stream of blood flow down Jenny's leg and form a bright pool at her feet.

"Jenny . . . Jenny," he called weakly.

His lips trembled. She's bleeding t death! He looked in the direction of home, wanting to go back, wanting to get help. But he saw the pistol lying in the damp black clay. He had a queer feeling that if he only did something, this would not be; Jenny would not be there bleeding to death.

When he went to her this time, she did not move. She stood with sleepy, dreamy eyes; and when he touched her she gave a low-pitched whinny and knelt to the ground, her front knees slopping in blood.

"Jenny . . . Jenny," he whispered.

For a long time she held her neck erect; then her head sank, slowly. Her ribs swelled with a mighty heave and she went over.

Dave's stomach felt empty, very empty. He picked up the gun and held it gingerly between his thumb and forefinger. He buried it at the foot of a tree. He took a stick and tried to cover the pool of blood with dirt—but what was the use? There was Jenny lying with her mouth open and her eyes walled and glassy. He could not tell Jim Hawkins he had shot his mule. But he had to tell something. Yeah, Ah'll tell em Jenny started gittin wil n fell on the joint of the plow. . . . But that would hardly happen to a mule. He walked across the field slowly, head down.

It was sunset. Two of Jim Hawkins' men were over near the edge of the woods digging a hole in which to bury Jenny. Dave was surrounded by a knot of people, all of whom were looking down at the dead mule.

"I don't see how in the world it happened," said Jim Hawkins for the tenth time.

The crowd parted and Dave's mother, father, and small brother pushed into the center.

"Where Dave?" his mother called.

"There he is," said Jim Hawkins.

His mother grabbed him.

"Whut happened, Dave? Whut yuh done?"

"Nothing."

"C'mon, boy, talk," his father said.

Dave took a deep breath and told the story he knew nobody believed.

"Waal," he drawled. "Ah brung ol Jenny down here sos Ah could do mah plowin. Ah plowed bout two rows, just like yuh see." He stopped and pointed at the long rows of upturned earth. "Then something musta been wrong wid ol Jenny. She wouldn't ack right a-tall. She started snortin n kickin her heels. Ah tried to hol her, but she pulled erway, rearin n goin on. Then when the point of the plow was stickin up in the air, she swung erroun n twisted hersef back on it. . . . She stuck hersef n started t bleed. N fo Ah could do anything, she wuz dead."

"Did you ever hear of anything like that in all your life?" asked Jim Hawkins.

There were white and black standing in the crowd. They murmured. Dave's mother came close to him and looked hard into his face. "Tell the truth, Dave," she said.

"Looks like a bullet hole ter me," said one man.

"Dave, whut yuh do wid the gun?" his mother asked.

The crowd surged in, looking at him. He jammed his hands into his pockets, shook his head slowly from left to right, and backed away. His eyes were wide and painful.

"Did he hava gun?" asked Jim Hawkins.

"By Gawd, Ah tol yuh tha wuz a *gun* wound," said a man, slapping his thigh.

His father caught his shoulders and shook him till his teeth rattled.

"Tell whut happened, yuh rascal! Tell whut . . ."

Dave looked at Jenny's stiff legs and began to cry.

"Whut yuh do wid tha gun?" his mother asked.

"Whut wuz he doin wida gun?" his father asked.

"Come on and tell the truth," said Hawkins. "Ain't nobody going to hurt you . . ."

His mother crowded close to him.

"Did yuh shoot that mule, Dave?"

Dave cried, seeing blurred white and black faces.

"Ahh ddinn gggo tt sshoooot hher . . . Ah ssswear ffo Gawd Ahh ddin. . . . Ah wuz a-tryin t sssee ef the ol gggun would sshoot—"

"Where yuh git the gun from?" his father asked.

"Ah got it from Joe, at the sto."

"Where yuh git the money?"

"Ma give it t me."

"He kept worryin me, Bob. Ah had t. Ah tol im t bring the gun right back t me . . . It was fer yuh, the gun."

"But how yuh happen to shoot that mule?" asked Jim Hawkins.

"Ah wuzn shootin at the mule, Mistah Hawkins. The gun jumped when Ah pulled the trigger . . . N fo Ah knowed anything Jenny wuz there a-bleedin."

Somebody in the crowd laughed. Jim Hawkins walked close to Dave and looked into his face.

"Well, looks like you have bought you a mule, Dave."

"Ah swear fo Gawd, Ah didn't go t kill the mule, Mistah Hawkins!"

"But you killed her!"

All the crowd was laughing now. They stood on tiptoe and poked heads over one another's shoulders.

"Well, boy, looks like yuh done bought a dead mule! Hahaha!"

"Ain tha ershame."

"Hohohohoho."

Dave stood, head down, twisting his feet in the dirt.

"Well, you needn't worry about it, Bob," said Jim Hawkins to Dave's father. "Just let the boy keep on working and pay me two dollars a month."

"Whut yuh wan fer yo mule, Mistah Hawkins?"

Jim Hawkins screwed up his eyes.

"Fifty dollars."

"Whut yuh do wid tha gun?" Dave's father demanded.

Dave said nothing.

"Yuh wan me t take a tree lim n beat yuh till yuh talk!"

"Nawsuh!"

"Whut yuh do wid it?"

"Ah thowed it erway."

"Where?"

"Ah . . . Ah thowed it in the creek."

"Waal, c mon home. N firs thing in the mawnin git to tha creek n fin tha gun."

"Yessuh."

"Whut yuh pay fer it?"

"Two dollahs."

"Take tha gun n git yo money back n carry it t Mistah Hawkins, yuh hear? N don fergit Ahma lam yo black bottom good fer this! Now march yosef on home, suh!"

Dave turned and walked slowly. He heard people laughing. Dave glared, his eyes welling with tears. Hot anger bubbled in him. Then he swallowed and stumbled on.

That night Dave did not sleep. He was glad that he had gotten out of killing the mule so easily, but he was hurt. Something hot seemed to turn over inside him each time he remembered how they had laughed. He tossed on his bed, feeling his hard pillow. N Pa says he's gonna beat me. . . . He remembered other beatings, and his back quivered. Naw, naw, Ah sho don wan im t beat me tha way no mo. Dam em all! Nobody ever gave him anything. All he did was work. They treat me lika mule, n then they beat me. He gritted his teeth. N Ma had t tell on me.

Well, if he had to, he would take old man Hawkins that two dollars. But that meant selling the gun. And he wanted to keep that gun. Fifty dollars for a dead mule.

He turned over, thinking of how he had fired the gun. He had an itch to fire it again. Ef other men kin shoota gun, by Gawd, Ah kin! He was still, listening. Mebbe they all sleepin now. . . . The house was still. He heard the soft breathing of his brother. Yes, now! He would go down and get that gun and see if he could fire it! He eased out of bed and slipped into overalls.

The moon was bright. He ran almost all the way to the edge of the woods. He stumbled over the ground, looking for the spot where he had buried the gun. Yeah, here it is. Like a hungry dog scratching for a bone, he pawed it up. He puffed his black cheeks and blew dirt from the trigger and barrel. He broke it and found four cartridges unshot. He looked around; the fields were filled with silence and moonlight. He clutched the gun stiff and hard in his fingers. But, as soon as he wanted to pull the trigger, he shut his eyes and turned his head. Naw, Ah can't shoot wid mah eyes closed n mah head turned. With effort he held his eyes open; then he squeezed. *Blooooom!* He was stiff, not breathing. The gun was still in his hands. Dammit, he'd done it! He fired again. *Blooooom!* He smiled. *Blooooom! Blooooom! Click, click.* There! It was empty. If anybody could shoot a gun, he could. He put the gun into his hip pocket and started across the fields.

When he reached the top of a ridge he stood straight and proud in the moonlight, looking at Jim Hawkins' big white house, feeling the gun sagging in his pocket. Lawd, ef Ah had just one mo bullet Ah'd taka shot at tha house. Ah'd like t scare ol man Hawkins jusa little. . . . Jusa enough t let im know Dave Sanders is a man.

To his left the road curved, running to the tracks of the Illinois Central. He jerked his head, listening. From far off came a faint *hoooof-hoooof; hoooof-hoooof; hoooof-hoooof* . . . Tha's number eight. He took a swift look at Jim Hawkins' white house; he thought of pa, of ma, of his little brother, and the boys. He thought of the dead mule and heard *hoooof-hoooof; hoooof-hoooof; hoooof-hoooof* . . . He stood rigid. Two dollahs a mont. Les see now. . . . Tha means itll take bout two years. Shucks! Ahll be dam!

He started down the road, toward the tracks. Yeah, here she comes! He stood beside the track and held himself stiffly. Here she comes, erroun the ben. . . . C mon, yuh slow poke! C mon! He had his hand on his gun; something quivered in his stomach. Then the train thundered past, the gray and brown box cars rumbling and clinking. He gripped the gun tightly; then he jerked his hand out of his pocket. Ah betcha Bill wouldn't do it! Ah betcha. . . . The cars slid past, steel grinding upon steel. Ahm riding yuh ternight so hep me Gawd! He was hot all over. He hesitated just a moment; then he grabbed, pulled atop of a car, and lay flat. He felt his pocket; the gun was still there. Ahead the long rails were glinting in the moonlight, stretching away, away to somewhere, somewhere where he could be a man. . . .

1961

# Writers on Writing

Any writer, I suppose, feels that the world into which he was born is nothing less than a conspiracy against the cultivation of his talent—which attitude certainly has a great deal to support it. On the other hand, it is only because the world looks on his talent with such a frightening indifference that the artist is compelled to make his talent important.

*James Baldwin*

Most of the basic material a writer works with is acquired before the age of fifteen.

*Willa Cather*

I start with a tingle, a kind of feeling of the story I will write. Then come the characters, and they take over, they make the story.

*Isak Dinesen*

Read, read, read. Read everything—trash, classics, good and bad, and see how they do it. Just like a carpenter who works as an apprentice and studies the master. Read! You'll absorb it. Then write. If it is good, you'll find out. If it's not, throw it out the window.

*William Faulkner*

A book ought to be an icepick to break up the frozen sea within us.

*Franz Kafka*

Looking back, I imagine I was always writing. Twaddle it was, too. But better far write twaddle or anything, anything, than nothing at all.

*Katherine Mansfield*

There is only one school of literature—that of talent.

*Vladimir Nabokov*

Beginning a book is unpleasant. I'm entirely uncertain about the character and the predicament, and a character in his predicament is what I have to begin with. Worse than not knowing your subject is not knowing how to treat it, because that's finally everything. I type out beginnings and they're awful, more of an unconscious parody of my previous book than the breakaway from it that I want. I need something driving down the center of a book, a magnet to draw everything to it—that's what I look for during the first months of writing something new.

*Philip Roth*

We work in our own darkness a great deal with little real knowledge of what we are doing.

*John Steinbeck*

Writing doesn't require drive. It's like saying a chicken has to have drive to lay an egg.

*John Updike*

## MARGARET ATWOOD

### Why Do You Write?[1]

You learn to write by reading and writing, writing and reading. As a craft it's acquired through the apprentice system, but you choose your own teachers. Sometimes they're alive, sometimes dead.

As a vocation, it involves the laying on of hands. You receive your vocation and in your turn you must pass it on. Perhaps you will do this only through your work, perhaps in other ways. Either way, you're part of a community, the community of writers, the community of storytellers that stretches back through time to the beginning of human society.

As for the particular human society to which you yourself belong— sometimes you'll feel you're speaking for it, sometimes—when it's taken an unjust form—against it, or for that other community, the community of the oppressed, the exploited, the voiceless. Either way, the pressures on you will be intense; in other countries, perhaps fatal. But even here—speak "for women," or for any other group which is feeling the boot, and there will be many at hand, both for and against, to tell you to shut up, or to say what they want you to say, or to say it a different way. Or to save them. The billboard awaits you, but if you succumb to its temptations you'll end up two-dimensional.

Tell what is yours to tell. Let others tell what is theirs.

## TONI CADE BAMBARA

### What Is It I Think I'm Doing Anyhow?[2]

When I replay the tapes on file in my head, tapes of speeches I've given at writing conferences over the years, I invariably hear myself saying—"A writer, like any other cultural worker, like any other member of the community, ought to try to put her/his skills in the service of the community." Some years ago when I returned south, my picture in the paper prompted several neighbors to come visit. "You a writer? What all you write?" Before I could begin the catalogue, one old gent interrupted with—"Ya know Miz Mary down the block? She need a writer to help her send off a letter to her grandson overseas." So I began a career as the neighborhood scribe—letters to relatives, snarling letters to the traffic chief about the promised stop sign, nasty letters to the utilities, angry letters to the principal about that confederate flag hanging in front of the school, contracts to transfer a truck from seller to buyer etc. While my efforts have been graciously appreciated in the form of sweet potato dumplings, herb teas, hair braiding, and the like, there is still much room for improvement—"For a writer, honey, you've got a mighty bad hand. Didn't they teach penmanship at that college?" Another example, I guess, of

**1.** From *The Writer on Her Work*, Vol. II, ed. by Janet Sternburg (1991). **2.** From *The Writer on Her Work*, Vol. I, ed. by Janet Sternburg (1980).

words setting things in motion. What goes around, comes around, as the elders say.

It will be a pleasure to get back to the shorts; they allow me to share. I much prefer to haul around story collections to prisons, schools, senior citizen centers, and rallies and then select from the "menu" something that suits the moment and is all of a piece. But the novel's pull is powerful. And since the breakthrough achieved in the sixties by the Neo-Black Arts Movement,[3] the possibilities are stunning. Characters that have been waiting in the wings for generations, characters that did not fit into the roster of stereotypes, can now be brought down center stage. Now that I/we have located our audience, we are free to explore the limits of language. Now that American history, American literature, the American experience is being redefined by so many communities, the genre too will undergo changes. So I came to the novel with a sense that everything is possible. And I'm attempting to blueprint for myself the merger of these two camps: the political and the spiritual. The possibilities of healing that split are exciting. The implications of actually yoking those energies and of fusing that power quite take my breath away.

## RICHARD BAUSCH

### Letter to a Young Writer

While there are of course thousands of reasons why people begin to write— some of them rather shabby ones, too—there usually is only one reason why they continue: and that is that the work has become necessary. We are habit-forming creatures, and this work is very habit-forming if one has any talent at all. Of course, you don't know when you begin if you really *have* any talent. You hope you do; perhaps you even suspect that you do. Sometimes you go back and forth, believing on some days, and disbelieving on others. Mostly you believe the last thing you read or heard concerning the work, and you probably tend to listen to the negative things more; the last negative thing you heard has sunk deeper into you and has lasted a longer time than any positive comment.

Painful as this is, it is also perfectly normal.

My best advice has nothing to do with technique, or aesthetics or the craft itself, really. It is more to do with training oneself to be shrewd. To live intelligently where the work is concerned: as I have said many times in classes, writing is not an indulgence; the indulgences are what you give up to write. You don't go to as many parties, you don't watch as much television, you don't listen to as much music. You make decisions in light of what you have to do in a given day. How much you get done depends in large part not on your talent—which is whatever it is, and is mostly constant—but on your own attitude *about* what you are doing.

So.

---

**3.** Movement of the mid-1960s through the early 1970s led by groups of artists and writers in New York, Chicago, Detroit, and California's Bay Area. The movement promoted African-American political engagement, cultural pride, and empowerment as key parts of its aesthetic.

I have devised a sort of Ten Commandments for you, which are the result of some of my own struggles with this blessed occupation, and of what I have been able to learn from reading or being around writers who are better than I. Here they are.

*1. Read.*

You must try to know everything that has ever been written that is worth remembering, and you must keep up with what your contemporaries are doing. Fitzgerald's advice to his daughter, Scottie, is as good as any there is on this subject: you must try to *absorb* (italics mine) six good authors a year. This means that you do not read books as an English major is trained to read them; you *swallow* them. You *ingest* them, and move on. You do not stop to analyze or think much; you just take them into yourself, and go on to the next one. And you read obsessively, too: if you really like something, you read it over and over through the years. You come to know the world's literature by heart. Every good writer I know or have known began with an insatiable appetite for books, for plundering what is in them, for the nourishment provided by them, which you can't get from any other source.

*2. Imitate.*

While you are doing this reading, you spend time trying to sound like the various authors—just as a painter, learning to paint, sets up his easel in the museum and *copies* the work of the masters. You learn by trying the sound and the stance of other writers. You develop an ear, through your reading and imitating, for how good writing is *supposed* to sound.

*3. "Be regular and ordinary in your habits, like a Petit Bourgeois, so you may be violent and original in your work."*

This comes from Flaubert, and is quite good advice. It has to do with what I was talking about in the first paragraph, and is of course better expressed. The thing that separates the amateur writer from the professional, often enough, is simply the amount of time spent working the craft. Know that if you really want to write, if you hope to produce something that will stand up to the winds of criticism and the scrutiny of strangers, you are going to have to work harder than you ever worked on anything else in your life—hour upon hour upon hour, with nothing in the way of encouragement, no good feeling except the sense that you have been true to the silently admonishing example of the writers who came before you, the ones whose company you would like to be in, and of whose respect you would like to be worthy.

*4. Train yourself to be able to work anywhere.*

Once, when our first child was a baby, my mother came to visit, and after the baby went to sleep I began tiptoeing around trying to make no noise. My mother said, "What the heck are you doing?" I said, "The baby's asleep." She said, "Have some friends over, put some music on, rattle some dishes, make noise. You're training that boy to be a bad sleeper." That wise advice applies to this craft, too. If you set up a certain area of expectation about when and how you'll be able to do the work, you train yourself to be silent. Shostakovich wrote his famous 7th Symphony, the Leningrad Symphony, *during* the siege of Leningrad. Bombs were falling all around him, and he understood perfectly well that there was a very good chance he would die within the next few hours, or days. Teach yourself to write in busy places, under the barrage of noises the world makes—work in rooms where children are playing, with music on, even with the television on. Work in the faith that if something is really good, it will not escape back into oblivion if you get distracted from it. It will turn up again. There is no known excuse for not working. Whole societies have for centuries been based on that reality.

### 5. Be patient.

You are trying to do something that is harder than just about anything there is to do, even when it feels easy. You will write many more failures than successes. Say to yourself, *I accept failure as the condition of this life, this work, I freely accept it as my destiny.* Then go on and do the work. You never ask yourself anything beyond *did I work today?*

### 6. Be willing.

Accepting failure as a part of your destiny, learn to be willing to fail—to take the chances that often lead to failure, in the hope that one of them might lead to something good. Be *open for business* all the time. You must try to be that person on whom nothing is lost. This does not mean that you are taking notes while people around you suffer. You are not that kind of observer. It means that *in the work room* you are willing to follow whatever your dreaming presents you with, openly and without judgment or attitude or even opinions.

### 7. Eschew politics.

If you have opinions, leave them out of the workplace. If you have anything worthwhile to say, let it surprise you. John Gardner once told me, "If one of your characters makes a long speech filled with his deepest-held beliefs, make sure *you* don't believe one word of it." I think that is very sound advice. You are in the business of portraying the personal life, the personal cost of events, so even if history is part of your story, it should only serve as backdrop. The writers who have gotten into trouble with despots over the shameful history of tyranny did so because they insisted on *not paying any attention to the politics* except as it applied to the personal lives of the people they were creating. They told the truth, in other words, and refused to *be* political. The paradoxical truth of the matter is that a writer who pays attention to the personal life is subversive precisely because he refuses to pay attention to anything else. Bad politics hurts people on the personal level and good writers report from there about the damage. And the totalitarians are rightfully afraid of those writers.

### 8. Do not think, dream.

If you believe you are thinking when you write, make yourself *stop* thinking. You are trying to tap a part of yourself that is closest to the dreaming side, the side that is most active when you sleep. You are trying to recover the literal vision of a child. This is what Flannery O'Connor means when she says, "A good story is literal in the same sense that a child's drawing is literal." Dream the story up, make it up, be fanciful, follow what occurs to you to say, and try not to worry about whether or not it's smart, or shows your sensitive nature in the best light, or delivers the matters of living that you think you have learned. Just dream it up and let the thing play itself out as it seems to want to, and then write it again, and still again, dreaming it through, and *then* try to be terribly smart about it. Read it with the cold detachment of a doctor looking at an X-ray. Which is to say that you must learn to re-read your own sentences as a stranger might. And say everything aloud. Listen to how it *sounds*.

*9. Don't compare yourself to anyone, and learn to keep from building expectations.*

People develop at different rates, with different results, and luck is also involved. Your only worry for yourself should be *did I work today?* Be happy for the successes of your friends, because good fortune for one of us is good fortune for all of us. When a friend or acquaintance has good luck, you may feel envy because envy is a natural human reaction; but, as George Garrett once put it, when that stuff rises to your mind, you must train yourself to *contend* with it there. That is what determines everything else about you as an artist. You will never write anything worth keeping if you allow yourself to give in to petty worries over whether you are treated as you think you deserve, or your rewards are commensurate to the work you've done. That will almost never be the case, and the artist who expects great rewards and complete understanding is a fool.

*10. Be wary of all general advice.*

Discard everything that precedes this commandment if, for you, it gets in the way of writing good stories. Because for every last assertion in this letter, there are several notable exceptions.

Finally, try to remember that what you are aiming to do is a beautiful—even a noble—thing, trying to write, or make, the truth as straightly and honestly and artfully as you can; and that it is also, always, an inherently optimistic act, because it stems from the belief that there will be civilized others whose sensibilities you may affect, if you are lucky and good and faithful to the task at hand. No matter how tragic the vision, it is always a hopeful occupation, and therefore you have to cultivate the ability to balance things: to entertain high hopes without allowing those hopes to become expectations. To do your work without worrying too much about what the world will have to say about it or do to it. Mostly, of course, the world will ignore it, and so you will have that in common with many very great writers, good men and women who came before you. By giving it everything you have, and being faithful to the work, you honor their fidelity to it; you *partake* of it, you accept their silent admonition to write like all hell, to be as good as they were.

### JOSEPH CONRAD

*Preface*[4]

A work that aspires, however humbly, to the condition of art should carry its justification in every line. And art itself may be defined as a single-minded attempt to render the highest kind of justice to the visible universe, by bringing to light the truth, manifold and one, underlying its every aspect. It is an attempt to find in its forms, in its colours, in its light, in its shadows, in the aspects of matter and in the facts of life, what of each is fundamental, what is enduring and essential—their one illuminating and convincing quality—the very truth of their existence. The artist, then, like the thinker or the scientist, seeks the truth and makes his appeal. Impressed by the aspect of the world the thinker plunges into ideas, the scientist into facts—whence, presently, emerging they make their appeal to those qualities of our being that fit us best for the hazardous enterprise of living. They speak authoritatively to our common-sense, to our intelligence, to our desire of peace or to our desire of unrest; not seldom to our prejudices, sometimes to our fears, often to our egoism—but always to our credulity. And their words are heard with reverence, for their concern is with weighty matters; with the cultivation of our minds and the proper care of our bodies: with the attainment of our ambitions: with the perfection of the means and the glorification of our precious aims.

It is otherwise with the artist.

Confronted by the same enigmatical spectacle the artist descends within himself, and in that lonely region of stress and strife, if he be deserving and fortunate, he finds the terms of his appeal. His appeal is made to our less obvious capacities: to that part of our nature which, because of the warlike conditions of existence, is necessarily kept out of sight within the more resisting and hard qualities—like the vulnerable body within a steel armour. His appeal is less loud, more profound, less distinct, more stirring—and sooner forgotten. Yet its effect endures forever. The changing wisdom of successive generations discards ideas, questions facts, demolishes theories. But the artist appeals to that part of our being which is not dependent on wisdom; to that in us which is a gift and not an acquisition—and, therefore, more permanently enduring. He speaks to our capacity for delight and wonder, to the sense of mystery surrounding our lives: to our sense of pity, and beauty, and pain: to the latent feeling of fellowship with all creation—and to the subtle but invincible, conviction of solidarity that knits together the loneliness of innumerable hearts: to the solidarity in dreams, in joy, in sorrow, in aspirations, in illusions, in hope, in fear, which binds men to each other, which binds together all humanity—the dead to the living and the living to the unborn.

It is only some such train of thought, or rather of feeling, that can in a measure explain the aim of the attempt, made in the tale which follows,[5] to present an unrestful episode in the obscure lives of a few individuals out of all the disregarded multitude of the bewildered, the simple, and the voiceless. For, if there is any part of truth in the belief confessed above, it becomes evident that there is not a place of splendour or a dark corner of the earth that

---

4. The Preface (1897), *The Nigger of the "Narcissus."*  5. That is, *The Nigger of the "Narcissus."*

does not deserve, if only a passing glance of wonder and pity. The motive, then, may be held to justify the matter of the work; but this preface, which is simply an avowal of endeavour, cannot end here—for the avowal is not yet complete.

Fiction—if it at all aspires to be art—appeals to temperament. And in truth it must be, like painting, like music, like all art, the appeal of one temperament to all the other innumerable temperaments whose subtle and resistless power endows passing events with their true meaning, and creates the moral, the emotional atmosphere of the place and time. Such an appeal to be effective must be an impression conveyed through the senses; and, in fact, it cannot be made in any other way, because temperament, whether individual or collective, is not amenable to persuasion. All art, therefore, appeals primarily to the senses, and the artistic aim when expressing itself in written words must also make its appeal through the senses, if its high desire is to reach the secret spring of responsive emotions. It must strenuously aspire to the plasticity of sculpture, to the colour of painting, and to the magic suggestiveness of music—which is the art of arts. And it is only through complete, unswerving devotion to the perfect blending of form and substance; it is only through an unremitting never-discouraged care for the shape and ring of sentences that an approach can be made to plasticity, to colour; and the light of magic suggestiveness may be brought to play for an evanescent instant over the commonplace surface of words: of the old, old words, worn thin, defaced by ages of careless usage.

The sincere endeavour to accomplish that creative task, to go as far on the road as his strength will carry him, to go undeterred by faltering, weariness, or reproach, is the only valid justification for the worker in prose. And if his conscience is clear, his answer to those who, in the fulness of a wisdom which looks for immediate profit, demand specifically to be edified, consoled, amused; who demand to be promptly improved, or encouraged, or frightened, or shocked, or charmed, must run thus:—My task which I am trying to achieve is, by the power of the written word, to make you hear, to make you feel—it is, before all, to make you *see*. That—and no more, and it is everything. If I succeed, you shall find there according to your deserts: encouragement, consolation, fear, charm—all you demand and, perhaps, also that glimpse of truth for which you have forgotten to ask.

To snatch in a moment of courage, from the remorseless rush of time, a passing phase of life, is only the beginning of the task. The task approached in tenderness and faith is to hold up unquestioningly, without choice and without fear, the rescued fragment before all eyes and in the light of a sincere mood. It is to show its vibration, its colour, its form; and through its movement, its form, and its colour, reveal the substance of its truth—disclose its inspiring secret: the stress and passion within the core of each convincing moment. In a single-minded attempt of that kind, if one be deserving and fortunate, one may perchance attain to such clearness of sincerity that at last the presented vision of regret or pity, of terror or mirth, shall awaken in the hearts of the beholders that feeling of unavoidable solidarity; of the solidarity in mysterious origin, in toil, in joy, in hope, in uncertain fate, which binds men to each other and all mankind to the visible world.

It is evident that he who, rightly or wrongly, holds by the convictions expressed above cannot be faithful to any one of the temporary formulas of his craft. The enduring part of them—the truth which each only imperfectly veils—should abide with him as the most precious of his possessions, but they all: Realism, Romanticism, Naturalism, even the unofficial sentimentalism (which like the poor,[6] is exceedingly difficult to get rid of), all these gods must, after a short period of fellowship, abandon him—even on the very threshold of the temple—to the stammerings of his conscience and to the outspoken consciousness of the difficulties of his work. In that uneasy solitude the supreme cry of Art for Art, itself, loses the exciting ring of its apparent immorality. It sounds far off. It has ceased to be a cry, and is heard only as a whisper, often incomprehensible, but at times and faintly encouraging.

Sometimes, stretched at ease in the shade of a roadside tree, we watch the motions of a labourer in a distant field, and after a time, begin to wonder languidly as to what the fellow may be at. We watch the movements of his body, the waving of his arms, we see him bend down, stand up, hesitate, begin again. It may add to the charm of an idle hour to be told the purpose of his exertions. If we know he is trying to lift a stone, to dig a ditch, to uproot a stump, we look with a more real interest at his efforts; we are disposed to condone the jar of his agitation upon the restfulness of the landscape; and even, if in a brotherly frame of mind, we may bring ourselves to forgive his failure. We understood his object, and, after all, the fellow has tried, and perhaps he had not the strength— and perhaps he had not the knowledge. We forgive, go on our way—and forget.

And so it is with the workman of art. Art is long and life is short,[7] and success is very far off. And thus, doubtful of strength to travel so far, we talk a little about the aim—the aim of art, which, like life itself, is inspiring, difficult— obscured by mists. It is not in the clear logic of a triumphant conclusion; it is not in the unveiling of one of those heartless secrets which are called the Laws of Nature. It is not less great, but only more difficult.

To arrest, for the space of a breath, the hands busy about the work of the earth, and compel men entranced by the sight of distant goals to glance for a moment at the surrounding vision of form and colour, of sunshine and shadows; to make them pause for a look, for a sigh, for a smile—such is the aim, difficult and evanescent, and reserved only for a very few to achieve. But sometimes, by the deserving and the fortunate, even that task is accomplished. And when it is accomplished—behold!—all the truth of life is there: a moment of vision, a sigh, a smile—and the return to an eternal rest.

## JOSEPH CONRAD

### Letter to Barrett H. Clark, May 4, 1918[8]

Some critics have found fault with me for not being constantly myself. But they are wrong. I am always myself. I am a man of formed character. Certain conclusions remain immovably fixed in my mind, but I am no slave to prejudices and formulas, and I shall never be. My attitude to subjects and

**6.** John 12.8.   **7.** Attributed to Hippocrates, 5th century B.C.E.   **8.** From a letter to Barrett H. Clark, May 4, 1918. Clark (1890–1953) was a drama editor, translator, and critic.

expressions, the angles of vision, my methods of composition will, within limits, be always changing—not because I am unstable or unprincipled but because I am free. Or perhaps it may be more exact to say, because I am always trying for freedom—within my limits.

Coming now to the subject of your inquiry, I wish at first to put before you a general proposition: that a work of art is very seldom limited to one exclusive meaning and not necessarily tending to a definite conclusion. And this for the reason that the nearer it approaches art, the more it acquires a symbolic character. This statement may surprise you, who may imagine that I am alluding to the Symbolist School of poets or prose writers. Theirs, however, is only a literary proceeding against which I have nothing to say. I am concerned here with something much larger. But no doubt you have meditated on this and kindred questions yourself.

So I will only call your attention to the fact that the symbolic conception of a work of art has this advantage, that it makes a triple appeal covering the whole field of life. All the great creations of literature have been symbolic, and in that way have gained in complexity, in power, in depth and in beauty.

I don't think you will quarrel with me on the ground of lack of precision; for as to precision of images and analysis my artistic conscience is at rest. I have given there all the truth that is in me; and all that the critics may say can make my honesty neither more nor less. But as to "final effect" my conscience has nothing to do with that. It is the critic's affair to bring to its contemplation his own honesty, his sensibility and intelligence. The matter for his conscience is just his judgment. If his conscience is busy with petty scruples and trammelled by superficial formulas then his judgment will be superficial and petty. But an artist has no right to quarrel with the inspirations, either lofty or base, of another soul.

## STEPHEN CRANE

### Letter to John Northern Hilliard, February 1895[?][9]

As far as myself and my own meagre success are concerned, I began the battle of life with no talent, no equipment, but with an ardent admiration and desire. I did little work at school, but confined my abilities, such as they were, to the diamond. Not that I disliked books, but the cut-and-dried curriculum of the college did not appeal to me. Humanity was a much more interesting study. When I ought to have been at recitations I was studying faces on the streets, and when I ought to have been studying my next day's lessons I was watching the trains roll in and out of the Central Station. So, you see, I had, first of all, to recover from college. I had to build up, so to speak. And my chiefest desire was to write plainly and unmistakably, so that all men (and some women) might read and understand. That to my mind is good writing. There is a great deal of labor connected with literature. I think that is the hardest thing about it. There is nothing to respect in art save one's own opinion of it.

---

9. Crane met Hilliard, journalist, novelist, and dramatist (1872–1935), when they were reporters in New York City during 1892–93.

## RALPH ELLISON

### *An Interview*[1]

ELLISON: Let me say right now that my book is not an autobiographical work.

INTERVIEWERS: You weren't thrown out of school like the boy in your novel?

ELLISON: No. Though, like him, I went from one job to another.

INTERVIEWERS: Why did you give up music and begin writing?

ELLISON: I didn't give up music but I became interested in writing through incessant reading. In 1935 I discovered Eliot's *The Waste Land* which moved and intrigued me but defied my powers of analysis—such as they were—and I wondered why I had never read anything of equal intensity and sensibility by an American Negro writer. Later on, in New York, I read a poem by Richard Wright, who, as luck would have it, came to town the next week. He was editing a magazine called *New Challenge* and asked me to try a book review of E. Waters Turpin's *These Low Grounds*. On the basis of this review Wright suggested that I try a short story, which I did. I tried to use my knowledge of riding freight trains. He liked the story well enough to accept it and it got as far as the galley proofs when it was bumped from the issue because there was too much material. Just after that the magazine failed.

INTERVIEWERS: But you went on writing—

ELLISON: With difficulty, because this was the Recession of 1937. I went to Dayton, Ohio, where my brother and I hunted and sold game to earn a living. At night I practiced writing and studied Joyce, Dostoevski, Stein, and Hemingway. Especially Hemingway; I read him to learn his sentence structure and how to organize a story. I guess many young writers were doing this, but I also used his description of hunting when I went into the fields the next day. I had been hunting since I was eleven, but no one had broken down the process of wing-shooting for me, and it was from reading Hemingway that I learned to lead a bird. When he describes something in print, believe him; believe him even when he describes the process of art in terms of baseball or boxing; he's been there.

INTERVIEWERS: Were you affected by the social realism of the period?

ELLISON: I was seeking to learn and social realism was a highly regarded theory, though I didn't think too much of the so-called proletarian fiction even when I was most impressed by Marxism. I was intrigued by Malraux, who at that time was being claimed by the Communists. I noticed, however, that whenever the heroes of *Man's Fate* regarded their condition during moments of heightened self-consciousness, their thinking was something other than Marxist. Actually they were more profoundly intellectual than their real-life counterparts. Of course, Malraux was more of a humanist than most of the Marxist writers of that period—and also much more of an artist. He was the artist-revolutionary rather than a politician when he wrote *Man's Fate*, and the book lives not because of a political position embraced at the time but because of its larger concern with the tragic struggle of humanity. Most of the social realists

---

1. From *Writers at Work*, The Paris Review *Interviews*, Vol. 2, ed. George Plimpton (1963).

of the period were concerned less with tragedy than with injustice. I wasn't and am not, *primarily* concerned with injustice, but with art.

INTERVIEWERS: Then you consider your novel a purely literary work as opposed to one in the tradition of social protest.

ELLISON: Now, mind, I recognize no dichotomy between art and protest. Dostoevski's *Notes from Underground* is, among other things, a protest against the limitations of nineteenth-century rationalism; *Don Quixote, Man's Fate, Oedipus Rex, The Trial*—all these embody protest, even against the limitation of human life itself. If social protest is antithetical to art, what then shall we make of Goya, Dickens, and Twain? One hears a lot of complaints about the so-called "protest novel," especially when written by Negroes; but it seems to me that the critics could more accurately complain about the lack of crafts-manship and the provincialism which is typical of such works.

INTERVIEWERS: But isn't it going to be difficult for the Negro writer to escape provincialism when his literature is concerned with a minority?

ELLISON: All novels are about certain minorities: the individual is a minor-ity. The universal in the novel—and isn't that what we're all clamoring for these days?—is reached only through the depiction of the specific man in a specific circumstance.

INTERVIEWERS: But still, how is the Negro writer, in terms of what is expected of him by critics and readers, going to escape his particular need for social protest and reach the "universal" you speak of?

ELLISON: If the Negro, or any other writer, is going to do what is expected of him, he's lost the battle before he takes the field. I suspect that all the agony that goes into writing is borne precisely because the writer longs for acceptance—but it must be acceptance on his own terms. Perhaps, though, this thing cuts both ways: the Negro novelist draws his blackness too tightly around him when he sits down to write—that's what the anti-protest critics believe—but perhaps the white reader draws his whiteness around himself when he sits down to read. He doesn't want to identify himself with Negro characters in terms of our immediate racial and social situation, though on the deeper human level identification can become compelling when the situa-tion is revealed artistically. The white reader doesn't want to get too close, not even in an imaginary re-creation of society. Negro writers have felt this, and it has led to much of our failure.

Too many books by Negro writers are addressed to a white audience. By doing this the authors run the risk of limiting themselves to the audience's presumptions of what a Negro is or should be; the tendency is to become involved in polemics, to plead the Negro's humanity. You know, many white people question that humanity, but I don't think that Negroes can afford to indulge in such a false issue. For us the question should be, what are the spe-cific *forms* of that humanity, and what in our background is worth preserving or abandoning. The clue to this can be found in folklore, which offers the first drawings of any group's character. It preserves mainly those situations which have repeated themselves again and again in the history of any given group. It describes those rites, manners, customs, and so forth, which insure the good life, or destroy it; and it describes those boundaries of feeling, thought, and action which that particular group has found to be the limita-tion of the human condition. It projects this wisdom in symbols which express the group's will to survive; it embodies those values by which the group lives and dies. These drawings may be crude but they are nonetheless profound in that they represent the group's attempt to humanize the world. It's no accident that great literature, the product of individual artists, is erected upon this humble base. The hero of Dostoevski's *Notes from Underground* and the hero of Gogol's "The Overcoat" appear in their rudimentary forms far back in Russian folklore. French literature has never ceased exploring the nature of the Frenchman.

## ERNEST HEMINGWAY

### An Interview[2]

INTERVIEWER: Do the titles come to you while you're in the process of doing the story?

HEMINGWAY: No. I make a list of titles *after* I've finished the story or the book—sometimes as many as a hundred. Then I start eliminating them, sometimes all of them.

INTERVIEWER: And you do this even with a story whose title is supplied from the text—"Hills Like White Elephants," for example?

HEMINGWAY: Yes. The title comes afterwards. I met a girl in Prunier where I'd gone to eat oysters before lunch. I knew she'd had an abortion. I went over and we talked, not about that, but on the way home I thought of the story, skipped lunch, and spent that afternoon writing it.

INTERVIEWER: So when you're not writing, you remain constantly the observer, looking for something which can be of use.

HEMINGWAY: Surely. If a writer stops observing he is finished. But he does not have to observe consciously nor think how it will be useful. Perhaps that would be true at the beginning. But later everything he sees goes into the great reserve of things he knows or has seen. If it is any use to know it, I always try to write on the principle of the iceberg. There is seven-eighths of it under-water for every part that shows. Anything you know you can eliminate and it only strengthens your iceberg. It is the part that doesn't show. If a writer omits something because he does not know it then there is a hole in the story.

*The Old Man and the Sea* could have been over a thousand pages long and had every character in the village in it and all the processes of how they made their living, were born, educated, bore children, etc. That is done excellently and well by other writers. In writing you are limited by what has already been done satisfactorily. So I have tried to learn to do something else. First I have tried to eliminate everything unnecessary to conveying experience to the reader so that after he or she has read something it will become a part of his or her experience and seem actually to have happened. This is very hard to do and I've worked at it very hard.

Anyway, to skip how it is done, I had unbelievable luck this time and could convey the experience completely and have it be one that no one had ever conveyed. The luck was that I had a good man and a good boy and lately writers have forgotten there still are such things. Then the ocean is worth writing

---

2. From *Writers at Work*, The Paris Review *Interviews*, Vol. 2, ed. George Plimpton (1963).

about just as man is. So I was lucky there. I've seen the marlin mate and know about that. So I leave that out. I've seen a school (or pod) of more than fifty sperm whales in that same stretch of water and once harpooned one nearly sixty feet in length and lost him. So I left that out. All the stories I know from the fishing village I leave out. But the knowledge is what makes the underwater part of the iceberg.

INTERVIEWER: Archibald MacLeish has spoken of a method of conveying experience to a reader which he said you developed while covering baseball games back in those *Kansas City Star* days. It was simply that experience is communicated by small details, intimately preserved, which have the effect of indicating the whole by making the reader conscious of what he had been aware of only subconsciously. . . .

HEMINGWAY: The anecdote is apocryphal. I never wrote baseball for the *Star.* What Archie was trying to remember was how I was trying to learn in Chicago in around 1920 and was searching for the unnoticed things that made emotions, such as the way an outfielder tossed his glove without looking back to where it fell, the squeak of resin on canvas under a fighter's flat-soled gym shoes, the gray color of Jack Blackburn's skin when he had just come out of stir, and other things I noted as a painter sketches. You saw Blackburn's strange color and the old razor cuts and the way he spun a man before you knew his history. These were the things which moved you before you knew the story.

INTERVIEWER: Have you ever described any type of situation of which you had no personal knowledge?

HEMINGWAY: That is a strange question. By personal knowledge do you mean carnal knowledge? In that case the answer is positive. A writer, if he is any good, does not describe. He invents or *makes* out of knowledge personal and impersonal and sometimes he seems to have unexplained knowledge which could come from forgotten racial or family experience. Who teaches the homing pigeon to fly as he does; where does a fighting bull get his bravery, or a hunting dog his nose? This is an elaboration or a condensation of that stuff we were talking about in Madrid that time when my head was not to be trusted.

INTERVIEWER: How detached must you be from an experience before you can write about it in fictional terms? The African air crashes you were involved in, for instance?

HEMINGWAY: It depends on the experience. One part of you sees it with complete detachment from the start. Another part is very involved. I think there is no rule about how soon one should write about it. It would depend on how well adjusted the individual was and on his or her recuperative powers. Certainly it is valuable to a trained writer to crash in an aircraft which burns. He learns several important things very quickly. Whether they will be of use to him is conditioned by survival. Survival, with honor, that outmoded and all-important word, is as difficult as ever and as all-important to a writer. Those who do not last are always more beloved since no one has to see them in their long, dull, unrelenting, no-quarter-given-no-quarter-received, fights that they make to do something as they believe it should be done before they die. Those who die or quit early and easy and with every good reason are preferred because they are understandable and human. Failure and well-disguised cowardice are more human and more beloved.

INTERVIEWER: Could I ask you to what extent you think the writer should concern himself with the socio-political problems of his times?

HEMINGWAY: Everyone has his own conscience, and there should be no rules about how a conscience should function. All you can be sure about in a political-minded writer is that if his work should last you will have to skip the politics when you read it. Many of the so-called politically enlisted writers change their politics frequently. This is very exciting to them and to their political-literary reviews. Sometimes they even have to rewrite their viewpoints . . . and in a hurry. Perhaps it can be respected as a form of the pursuit of happiness.

INTERVIEWER: Would you say, ever, that there is any didactic intention in your work?

HEMINGWAY: Didactic is a word that has been misused and has spoiled. *Death in the Afternoon* is an instructive book.

INTERVIEWER: It has been said that a writer only deals with one or two ideas throughout his work. Would you say your work reflects one or two ideas?

HEMINGWAY: Who said that? It sounds much too simple. The man who said it possibly *had* only one or two ideas.

INTERVIEWER: Well, perhaps it would be better put this way: Graham Greene said that a ruling passion gives to a shelf of novels the unity of a system. You yourself have said, I believe, that great writing comes out of a sense of injustice. Do you consider it important that a novelist be dominated in this way—by some such compelling sense?

HEMINGWAY: Mr. Greene has a facility for making statements that I do not possess. It would be impossible for me to make generalizations about a shelf of novels or a wisp of snipe or a gaggle of geese. I'll try a generalization though. A writer without a sense of justice and of injustice would be better off editing the Year Book of a school for exceptional children than writing novels. Another generalization. You see; they are not so difficult when they are sufficiently obvious. The most essential gift for a good writer is a built-in, shock-proof, shit detector. This is the writer's radar and all great writers have had it.

INTERVIEWER: Finally, a fundamental question: namely, as a creative writer what do you think is the function of your art? Why a representation of fact, rather than fact itself?

HEMINGWAY: Why be puzzled by that? From things that have happened and from things as they exist and from all things that you know and all those you cannot know, you make something through your invention that is not a representation but a whole new thing truer than anything true and alive, and you make it alive, and if you make it well enough, you give it immortality. That is why you write and for no other reason that you know of. But what about all the reasons that no one knows?

## FRANZ KAFKA

### Letter to Max Brod, July 5, 1922[3]

To put it first of all in general terms, I fear the traveling. . . . But it is not only fear of traveling itself; . . . Rather it is a fear of change, a fear of attracting the attention of the gods by what is a major act for a person of my sort.

3. Translated by Richard and Clara Winston.

Last night as I lay sleepless and let everything continually veer back and forth between my aching temples, what I had almost forgotten during the last relatively quiet time became clear to me: namely, on what frail ground or rather altogether nonexistent ground I live, over a darkness from which the dark power emerges when it wills and, heedless of my stammering, destroys my life. Writing sustains me, but is it not more accurate to say that it sustains this kind of life? By this I don't mean, of course, that my life is better when I don't write. Rather it is much worse then and wholly unbearable and has to end in madness. But that, granted, only follows from the postulate that I am a writer, which is actually true even when I am not writing, and a nonwriting writer is a monster inviting madness. But what about being a writer itself? Writing is a sweet and wonderful reward, but for what? In the night it became clear to me, as clear as a child's lesson book, that it is the reward for serving the devil. This descent to the dark powers, this unshackling of spirits bound by nature, these dubious embraces and whatever else may take place in the nether parts which the higher parts no longer know, when one writes one's stories in the sunshine. Perhaps there are other forms of writing, but I know only this kind; at night, when fear keeps me from sleeping, I know only this kind. And the diabolic element in it seems very clear to me. It is vanity and sensuality which continually buzz about one's own or even another's form—and feast on him. The movement multiplies itself—it is a regular solar system of vanity. Sometimes a naïve person will wish, "I would like to be dead and see how everyone mourns me." Such a writer is continually staging such a scene: He dies (or rather he does not live) and continually mourns himself. From this springs a terrible fear of death, which need not reveal itself as fear of death but may also appear as fear of change. . . . The reasons for this fear of death may be divided into two main categories. First he has a terrible fear of dying because he has not yet lived. By this I do not mean that wife and child, fields and cattle are essential to living. What is essential to life is only to forgo complacency, to move into the house instead of admiring it and hanging garlands around it. In reply to this, one might say that this is a matter of fate and is not given into anyone's hand. But then why this sense of repining, this repining that never ceases? To make oneself finer and more savory? That is a part of it. But why do such nights leave one always with the refrain: I could live and I do not live. The second reason—perhaps it is all really one, the two do not want to stay apart for me now—is the belief: "What I have playacted is really going to happen. I have not bought myself off by my writing. I died my whole life long and now I will really die. My life was sweeter than other peoples' and my death will be more terrible by the same degree. Of course the writer in me will die right away, since such a figure has no base, no substance, is less than dust. He is only barely possible in the broil of earthly life, is only a construct of sensuality. That is your writer for you. But I myself cannot go on living because I have not lived, I have remained clay, I have not blown the spark into fire, but only used it to light up my corpse." It will be a strange burial: the writer, insubstantial as he is, consigning the old corpse, the long-time corpse, to the grave. I am enough of a writer to appreciate the scene with all my senses, or—and it is the same thing—to want to describe it with total self-forgetfulness—not alertness, but self-forgetfulness is the writer's first prerequisite. But there will be no more of such describing. But why am I talking of actual dying? It is just the same in life. I sit here in the comfortable posture of the writer, ready for all sorts of fine things, and must idly look on—for what can I do but write?—as my true ego, this wretched, defenseless ego, is nipped by the devil's pincers, cudgeled, and almost ground to pieces on a random pretext—a little trip.... Since I was not at home, what right have I to be alarmed when the house suddenly collapses. After all, I know what preceded the collapse. Did I not emigrate and leave the house to all the evil powers?

## GUY DE MAUPASSANT

### The Novel[4]

The man who seeks only to amuse the public by already known methods writes with confidence, in the candor of his mediocrity, for the ignorant, the idle. But those on whom all the ages of past literature weigh heavily; those whom nothing satisfies, whom everything disgusts because it does not come up to their dreams; those to whom every flower seems to have been plucked, to whom their work always gives the impression of a useless and common labor— arrive at the opinion that literary art is an intangible, mysterious thing, only partially revealed to us in some of the pages of the greatest masters.

Twenty verses, twenty phrases, may suddenly thrill us to the heart as a sur- prising revelation; but the following verses resemble all verses, and the prose that follows resembles all other prose.

Men of genius, doubtless, do not experience this anguish and torture, because they have in themselves a resistless creative power. They do not sit in judgment on themselves. The rest of us, who are simply conscientious and persistent workers, can only by continued effort fight against overwhelming discouragement.

Two men by their simple and lucid teachings gave me this power of persis- tent effort—Louis Bouilhet and Gustave Flaubert.

If I speak of them and of myself in this place it is because their advice, summed up in a few lines, may be useful, perhaps, to some young writers with less self-esteem than is usually found in literary débutants.

Bouilhet, with whom I formed a rather intimate acquaintance about two years before I gained the friendship of Flaubert, by dint of repeating to me that a hundred verses, or even less, insured the reputation of an artist, provided they were faultless and embodied the essence of the talent and originality of a man, even of second-rate talent, made me understand that.

I also learned that the best-known writers have seldom left more than one volume; and that the first essential is to have the luck to find and discern, amid the multiplicity of subjects that present themselves, that subject that will absorb all our faculties, all our ability, all our artistic power.

Later on Flaubert, whom I sometimes saw, conceived a liking for me. I ven- tured to submit to him some of my attempts. He kindly read them, and replied: "I do not know if you have talent; what you have shown me proves that you possess a certain degree of intelligence. But do not forget this, young man,

4. From the essay "The Novel" (1887).

that talent—to quote the saying of Buffon—is merely 'long patience.' Keep on working."

I did so, and often revisited him, as I perceived that he liked me, for he laughingly called me his disciple.

For seven years I wrote verses, I wrote stories, I wrote novels, I even wrote a detestable play. Of these nothing survives. The master read them all, and on the following Sunday at luncheon he would give me his criticism, and inculcate little by little two or three principles that sum up his long and patient lessons. "If one has any originality, the first thing requisite is to bring it out; if one has none, the first thing to be done is to acquire it."

Talent is long patience. Everything which one desires to express must be considered with sufficient attention, and during a sufficiently long time, to discover in it some aspect which no one has as yet seen or described. In everything there is still some spot unexplored, because we are accustomed to look at things only with the recollection of what others before us have thought of the subject we are contemplating. The smallest object contains something unknown. Let us find it. In order to describe a fire that flames, and a tree on the plain, we must keep looking at that flame and that tree, until to our eyes they no longer resemble any other tree, any other fire.

This is the way to become original.

Having, besides, laid down this truth that there are not in the whole world two grains of sand, two specks, two hands, or two noses exactly alike, he compelled me to describe, in a few phrases, a being or an object in such a manner as to clearly particularize it and distinguish it from all the other beings, or all the other objects of the same race or the same species.

"When you pass," he would say, "a grocer seated at his shop door, a janitor smoking his pipe, a stand of hackney coaches, show me that grocer and that janitor, their attitude, their whole physical appearance, including also by a skillful description their whole moral nature, so that I cannot confound them with any other grocer or any other janitor; make me see, in one word, that a certain cab horse does not resemble the fifty others that follow or precede it."

I have stated elsewhere his ideas on style. They are closely related to the theory of observation which I have just explained.

Whatever be the thing one wishes to say, there is only one noun to express it, only one verb to give it life, only one adjective to qualify it. We must search, then, till that noun, that verb, that adjective, are discovered; never be content with an approximation, never resort to tricks, however happy, or to buffooneries of language, to avoid a difficulty.

We can interpret and describe the most subtle things if we bear in mind the verse of Boileau:

"*D'un mot mis en sa place enseigna le pouvoir.*"

"He taught the force of a word in the right place."

There is no need of the eccentric, complicated, multifarious sort of Chinese vocabulary, which is inflicted on us at the present day under the name of artistic writing, to enable us to describe every shade of thought; but it is necessary to discern, with the utmost lucidity, all the modifications of the value of a word according to the position it occupies. Let us have fewer nouns, verbs and adjectives with almost incomprehensible meanings, and more varied phrases, differently constructed, ingeniously turned, sonorous and full of skillful rhythms. Let us endeavor to be excellent stylists, rather than collectors of rare terms.

It is, in fact, more difficult to turn a phrase to suit one's self, to make it say everything (even that which it does not express), to fill it with hidden meanings, and with secret suggestions which are not formulated, than to invent new expressions, or to seek in the depths of old forgotten books all those that are obsolete and have lost their significance, and for us are only dead words.

## BHARATI MUKHERJEE

### A Four-Hundred-Year-Old Woman[5]

It took me ten painful years, from the early seventies to the early eighties, to overthrow the smothering tyranny of nostalgia. The remaining struggle for me is to make the American readership, meaning the editorial and publishing industries as well, acknowledge the same fact. (As the reception of such films as *Gandhi* and *A Passage to India* as well as *The Far Pavillions* and *The Jewel in the Crown* shows, nostalgia is a two-way street. Americans can feel nostalgic for a world they never knew.) The foreign-born, the exotically raised Third World immigrant with non-Western religions and non-European languages and appearance, can be as American as any steerage passenger from Ireland, Italy, or the Russian Pale. As I have written in another context (a review article in *The Nation* on books by Studs Terkel and Al Santoli), we are probably only a few years away from a Korean *What Makes Choon-li Run?* or a Hmong *Call It Sleep*. In other words, my literary agenda begins by acknowledging that America has transformed *me*. It does not end until I show how I (and the hundreds of thousands like me) have transformed America.

The agenda is simply stated, but in the long run revolutionary. Make the familiar exotic; the exotic familiar.

I have had to create an audience. I cannot rely on shorthand references to my community, my religion, my class, my region, or my old school tie. I've had to sensitize editors as well as readers to the richness of the lives I'm writing about. The most moving form of praise I receive from readers can be summed up in three words: *I never knew*. Meaning, I see these people (call them Indians, Filipinos, Koreans, Chinese) around me all the time and I never knew they had an inner life. I never knew they schemed and cheated, suffered, felt so strongly, cared so passionately. When even the forms of praise are so rudimentary, the writer knows she has an inexhaustible fictional population to enumerate. Perhaps even a mission, to appropriate a good colonial word.

I have been blessed with an enormity of material. I can be Chekhovian and Tolstoyan—with melancholy and philosophical perspectives on the breaking of hearts as well as the fall of civilizations—and I can be a brash and raucous homesteader, Huck Finn and Woman Warrior, on the unclaimed plains of American literature. My material, reduced to jacket-flap copy, is the rapid and

5. From *The Writer on Her Work*, Vol. II, ed. Janet Sternberg (1991).

dramatic transformation of the United States since the early 1970s. Within that perceived perimeter, however, I hope to wring surprises.

Yet (I am a writer much given to "yet") my imaginative home is also in the tales told by my mother and grandmother, the world of the Hindu epics. For all the hope and energy I have placed in the process of immigration and accommodation—I'm a person who couldn't ride a public bus when she first arrived, and now I'm someone who watches tractor pulls on obscure cable channels—there are parts of me that remain Indian, parts that slide against the masks of newer selves. The form that my stories and novels take inevitably reflects the resources of Indian mythology—shape-changing, miracles, godly perspectives. My characters can, I hope, transcend the straitjacket of simple psychologizing. The people I write about are culturally and politically several hundred years old: consider the history they have witnessed (colonialism, technology, education, liberation, civil war, uprooting). They have shed old identities, taken on new ones, and learned to hide the scars. They may sell you newspapers, or clean your offices at night.

Writers (especially American writers, weaned on the luxury of affluence and freedom) often disavow the notion of a "literary duty" or "political consciousness," citing the all-too-frequent examples of writers ruined by their shrill commitments. Glibness abounds on both sides of the argument, but finally I have to side with my "Third World" compatriots: I do have a duty, beyond telling a good story or drawing a convincing character. My duty is to give voice to continents, but also to redefine the nature of *American* and what makes an American. In the process, work like mine and dozens like it will open up the canon of American literature.

• • •

My theme is the making of new Americans. Wherever I travel in the (very) Old World, I find "Americans" in the making, whether or not they ever make it to these shores. I see them as dreamers and conquerors, not afraid of transforming themselves, not afraid of abandoning some of their principles along the way. In *Jasmine*, my "American" is born in a Punjabi village, marries at fourteen, and is widowed at sixteen. Nevertheless, she is an American and will enter the book as an Iowa banker's wife.

Ancestral habits of mind can be constricting; they also confer one's individuality. I know I can appropriate the American language, but I can never be a minimalist. I have too many stories to tell. I am aware of myself as a four-hundred-year-old woman, born in the captivity of a colonial, pre-industrial oral culture and living now as a contemporary New Yorker.

My image of artistic structure and artistic excellence is the Moghul miniature painting with its crazy foreshortening of vanishing point, its insistence that everything happens simultaneously, bound only by shape and color. In the miniature paintings of India, there are a dozen separate foci, the most complicated stories can be rendered on a grain of rice, the corners are as elaborated as the centers. There is a sense of the interpenetration of all things. In the Moghul miniature of my life, there would be women investigating their bodies with mirrors, but they would be doing it on a distant balcony under fans wielded by bored serving girls; there would be a small girl listening to a bent old woman; there would be a white man eating popcorn and watching a baseball game; there would be cocktail parties and cornfields and a village set among rice paddies and skyscrapers. In a sense, I wrote that story, "Courtly Vision," at the end of *Darkness*. And in a dozen other ways I'm writing it today, and I will be writing, in the Moghul style, till I get it right.

## EDGAR ALLAN POE

### The Philosophy of Composition[6]

Charles Dickens, in a note now lying before me, alluding to an examination I once made of the mechanism of "Barnaby Rudge," says—"By the way, are you aware that Godwin[7] wrote his 'Caleb Williams' backwards? He first involved his hero in a web of difficulties, forming the second volume, and then, for the first, cast about him for some mode of accounting for what had been done."

I cannot think this the *precise* mode of procedure on the part of Godwin—and indeed what he himself acknowledges, is not altogether in accordance with Mr. Dickens' idea—but the author of "Caleb Williams" was too good an artist not to perceive the advantage derivable from at least a somewhat similar process. Nothing is more clear than that every plot, worth the name, must be elaborated to its *dénouement* before any thing be attempted with the pen. It is only with the *dénouement* constantly in view that we can give a plot its indispensable air of consequence, or causation, by making the incidents, and especially the tone at all points, tend to the development of the intention.

There is a radical error, I think, in the usual mode of constructing a story. Either history affords a thesis—or one is suggested by an incident of the day—or, at best, the author sets himself to work in the combination of striking events to form merely the basis of his narrative—designing, generally, to fill in with description, dialogue, or autorial comment, whatever crevices of fact, or action, may, from page to page, render themselves apparent.

I prefer commencing with the consideration of an *effect*. Keeping originality *always* in view—for he is false to himself who ventures to dispense with so obvious and so easily attainable a source of interest—I say to myself, in the first place, "Of the innumerable effects, or impressions, of which the heart, the intellect, or (more generally) the soul is susceptible, what one shall I, on the present occasion, select?" Having chosen a novel, first, and secondly a vivid effect, I consider whether it can best be wrought by incident or tone—whether by ordinary incidents and peculiar tone, or the converse, or by peculiarity both of incident and tone—afterward looking about me (or rather within) for such combinations of event, or tone, as shall best aid me in the construction of the effect.

---

**6.** Reprinted from *Graham's* of April 1846.    **7.** William Godwin (1756–1836). British writer and philosopher who wrote *Caleb Williams* (1794) as a mystery novel.

## KATHERINE ANNE PORTER

### *An Interview*[8]

INTERVIEWER: You once said that every story begins with an ending, that until the end is known there is no story.

PORTER: That is where the artist begins to work: With the consequences of acts, not the acts themselves. Or the events. The event is important only as it affects your life and the lives of those around you. The reverberations, you might say, the overtones: that is where the artist works. In that sense it has sometimes taken me ten years to understand even a little of some important event that had happened to me. Oh, I could have given a perfectly factual account of what had happened, but I didn't know what it meant until I knew the consequences. If I didn't know the ending of a story, I wouldn't begin. I always write my last lines, my last paragraph, my last page first, and then I go back and work towards it. I know where I'm going. I know what my goal is. And how I get there is God's grace.

INTERVIEWER: That's a very classical view of the work of art—that it must end in resolution.

PORTER: Any true work of art has got to give you the feeling of reconciliation—what the Greeks would call catharsis, the purification of your mind and imagination—through an ending that is endurable because it is right and true. Oh, not in any pawky individual idea of morality or some parochial idea of right and wrong. Sometimes the end is very tragic, because it needs to be. One of the most perfect and marvelous endings in literature—it raises my hair now—is the little boy at the end of *Wuthering Heights,* crying that he's afraid to go across the moor because there's a man and woman walking there.

And there are three novels that I reread with pleasure and delight—three almost perfect novels, if we're talking about form, you know. One is *A High Wind in Jamaica* by Richard Hughes, one is *A Passage to India* by E. M. Forster, and the other is *To the Lighthouse* by Virginia Woolf. Every one of them begins with an apparently insoluble problem, and every one of them works out of confusion into order. The material is all used so that you are going toward a goal. And that goal is the clearing up of disorder and confusion and wrong, to a logical and human end. I don't mean a happy ending, because after all at the end of *A High Wind in Jamaica* the pirates are all hanged and the children are all marked for life by their experience, but it comes out to an orderly end. The threads are all drawn up. I have had people object to Mr. Thompson's suicide at the end of *Noon Wine,* and I'd say, "All right, where was he going? Given what he was, his own situation, what else could he do?" Every once in a while when I see a character of mine just going towards perdition, I think, "Stop, stop, you can always stop and choose, you know." But no, being what he was, he already *has* chosen, and he can't go back on it now. I suppose the first idea that man had was the idea of fate, of the servile will, of a deity who destroyed as he would, without regard for the creature. But I think the idea of free will was the second idea.

**8.** From *Writers at Work,* The Paris Review *Interviews,* Vol. 2, ed. George Plimpton (1963).

INTERVIEWER: Has a story never surprised you in the writing? A character suddenly taken a different turn?

PORTER: Well, in the vision of death at the end of "Flowering Judas" I knew the real ending—that she was not going to be able to face her life, what she'd done. And I knew that the vengeful spirit was going to come in a dream to tow her away into death, but I didn't know until I'd written it that she was going to wake up saying, "No!" and be afraid to go to sleep again.

INTERVIEWER: That was, in a fairly literal sense, a "true" story, wasn't it?

PORTER: The truth is, I have never written a story in my life that didn't have a very firm foundation in actual human experience—somebody else's experience quite often, but an experience that became my own by hearing the story, by witnessing the thing, by hearing just a word perhaps. It doesn't matter, it just takes a little—a tiny seed. Then it takes root, and it grows. It's an organic thing. That story had been on my mind for years, growing out of this one little thing that happened in Mexico. It was forming and forming in my mind, until one night I was quite desperate. People are always so sociable, and I'm sociable too, and if I live around friends. . . . Well, they were insisting that I come and play bridge. But I was very firm, because I knew the time had come to write that story, and I had to write it.

INTERVIEWER: What was that "little thing" from which the story grew?

PORTER: Something I saw as I passed a window one evening. A girl I knew had asked me to come and sit with her, because a man was coming to see her, and she was afraid of him. And as I went through the courtyard, past the flowering judas tree, I glanced in the window and there she was sitting with an open book on her lap, and there was this great big fat man sitting beside her. Now Mary and I were friends, both American girls living in this revolutionary situation. She was teaching at an Indian school, and I was teaching dancing at a girls' technical school in Mexico City. And we were having a very strange time of it. I was more skeptical, and so I had already begun to look with a skeptical eye on a great many of the revolutionary leaders. Oh, the idea was all right, but a lot of men were misapplying it.

And when I looked through that window that evening, I saw something in Mary's face, something in her pose, something in the whole situation, that set up a commotion in my mind. Because until that moment I hadn't really understood that she was not able to take care of herself, because she was not able to face her own nature and was afraid of everything. I don't know why I saw it. I don't believe in intuition. When you get sudden flashes of perception, it is just the brain working faster than usual. But you've been getting ready to know it for a long time, and when it comes, you feel you've known it always.

INTERVIEWER: You speak of a story "forming" in your mind. Does it begin as a visual impression, growing to a narrative? Or how?

PORTER: All my senses were very keen; things came to me through my eyes, through all my pores. Everything hit me at once, you know. That makes it very difficult to describe just exactly what is happening. And then, I think the mind works in such a variety of ways. Sometimes an idea starts completely inarticulately. You're not thinking in images or words or—well, it's exactly like a dark cloud moving in your head. You keep wondering what will come out of this, and then it will dissolve itself into a set of—well, not images exactly, but really thoughts. You begin to think directly in words. Abstractly. Then the words transform themselves into images. By the time I write the story my people are up and alive and walking around and taking things into their own hands. They exist as independently inside my head as you do before me now. I have been criticized for not enough detail in describing my characters, and not enough furniture in the house. And the odd thing is that I see it all so clearly.

INTERVIEWER: What about the technical problems a story presents—its formal structure? How deliberate are you in matters of technique? For example, the use of the historical present in "Flowering Judas"?

PORTER: The first time someone said to me, "Why did you write 'Flowering Judas' in the historical present?" I thought for a moment and said, "Did I?" I'd never noticed it. Because I didn't *plan* to write it any way. A story forms in my mind and forms and forms, and when it's ready to go, I strike it down—it takes just the time I sit at the typewriter. I never think about form at all. In fact, I would say that I've never been interested in anything about writing after having learned, I hope, to write. That is, I mastered my craft as well as I could. There is a technique, there is a craft, and you have to learn it. Well, I did as well as I could with that, but now all in the world I am interested in is telling a story. I have something to tell you that I, for some reason, think is worth telling, and so I want to tell it as clearly and purely and simply as I can. But I had spent fifteen years at least learning to write. I practiced writing in every possible way that I could. I wrote a pastiche of other people, imitating Dr. Johnson and Laurence Sterne, and Petrarch and Shakespeare's sonnets, and then I tried writing my own way. I spent fifteen years learning to trust myself: that's what it comes to. Just as a pianist runs his scales for ten years before he gives his concert: because when he gives that concert, he can't be thinking of his fingering or of his hands; he has to be thinking of his interpretation, of the music he's playing. He's thinking of what he's trying to communicate. And if he hasn't got his technique perfected by then, he needn't give the concert at all.

• • •

INTERVIEWER: You are frequently spoken of as a stylist. Do you think a style can be cultivated, or at least refined?

PORTER: I've been called a stylist until I really could tear my hair out. And I simply don't believe in style. The style is you. Oh, you can cultivate a style, I suppose, if you like. But I should say it remains a cultivated style. It remains artificial and imposed, and I don't think it deceives anyone. A cultivated style would be like a mask. Everybody knows it's a mask, and sooner or later you must show yourself—or at least, you show yourself as someone who could not afford to show himself, and so created something to hide behind. Style is the man. Aristotle said it first, as far as I know, and everybody has said it since, because it is one of those unarguable truths. You do not create a style. You work, and develop yourself; your style is an emanation from your own being. Symbolism is the same way. I never consciously took or adopted a symbol in my life. I certainly did not say, "This blooming tree upon which Judas is supposed to have hanged himself is going to be the center of my story." I named "Flowering Judas" after it was written, because when reading back over it I suddenly saw the whole symbolic plan and pattern of which I was totally unconscious while I was writing. There's a pox of symbolist theory going the rounds these days in American colleges in the writing courses. Miss Mary McCarthy, who is one of the wittiest and most acute and in some ways the worst-tempered woman in American letters, tells about a little girl who came to her with a story. Now Miss McCarthy is an extremely good critic, and she found this to be a good story, and she told the girl that it was— that she considered it a finished work, and that she could with a clear conscience go on to something else. And the little girl said, "But Miss McCarthy, my writing teacher said, 'Yes, it's a good piece of work, but now we must go back and put in the symbols!'" I think that's an amusing story, and it makes my blood run cold.

## LEO TOLSTOY

### *What Is Art?*[9]

*The art of the future is not the possession of a select minority but a means towards perfection and unity.*

People talk of the art of the future, meaning by art of the future some especially refined new art which they imagine will be developed out of that exclusive art of one class which is now considered the highest art. But no such new art of the future can or will be found. Our exclusive art, that of the upper classes of Christendom, has found its way into a blind alley. The direction in which it has been going leads nowhere. Having once lost hold of that which is most essential to art (namely, the guidance given by religious perception), this art has become ever more and more exclusive and therefore ever more and more perverted, until finally it has come to nothing. The art of the future, that which is really coming, will not be a development of present-day art, but will arise on quite other and new foundations having nothing in common with those by which our present art of the upper classes is guided.

Art of the future, that is to say, such part of art as will be chosen from among all the art diffused among mankind, will consist not in transmitting feelings accessible only to members of the rich classes, as is the case to-day, but in transmitting feelings embodying the highest religious perception of our times. Only those productions will be esteemed art which transmit feelings drawing men together in brotherly union, or such universal feelings as can unite all men. Only such art will be chosen, tolerated, approved, and diffused. But art transmitting feelings flowing from antiquated, outworn, religious teaching; ecclesiastical art, patriotic art, voluptuous art; transmitting feelings of superstitious fear, of pride, of vanity, of ecstatic admiration of national heroes; art exciting exclusive love of one's own people, or sensuality, will be considered bad, harmful art, and will be censured and despised by public opinion. All the rest of art, transmitting feelings accessible only to a section of people, will be considered unimportant, and will be neither blamed nor praised. And the appraisement of art in general will devolve not as is now the case on a separate class of rich people, but on the whole people; so that for

---

**9.** From *What Is Art? and Essays on Art* (1960).

a work to be thought good and to be approved and diffused, it will have to satisfy the demands not of a few people living under similar and often unnatural conditions, but of all those great masses of people who undergo the natural conditions of laborious life.

Nor will the artists producing the art be as now merely a few people selected from a small section of the nation, members of the upper classes or their hangers-on, but they will consist of all those gifted members of the whole people who prove capable of, and have an inclination towards, artistic activity.

Artistic activity will then be accessible to all men. It will become accessible to the whole people because (in the first place) in the art of the future not only will that complex technique which deforms the productions of the art of to-day, and requires so great an effort and expenditure of time, not be demanded, but on the contrary the demand will be for clearness, simplicity, and brevity— conditions brought about not by mechanical methods but through the education of taste. And secondly, artistic activity will become accessible to all men of the people because, instead of the present professional schools which only some can enter, all will learn music and graphic art (singing and drawing) equally with letters, in the elementary schools, in such a way that every man, having received the first principles of drawing and music and feeling a capacity for and a call to one or other of the arts, will be able to perfect himself in it.

People think that if there are no special art-schools the technique of art will deteriorate. Undoubtedly it will deteriorate if by technique we understand those *complexities* of art which are now considered an excellence; but if by technique is understood clearness, beauty, simplicity, and compression, in works of art, then even if the elements of drawing and music were not to be taught in the national schools, not only will the technique not deteriorate but, as shown by all peasant art, it will be a hundred times better. It will be improved because all the artists of genius now hidden among the masses will become producers of art and supply models of excellence which (as has always been the case) will be the best schools of technique for their successors. For even now every true artist chiefly learns his technique not in the schools but in life, from the examples of the great masters, and then—when art is produced by the best artists of the whole nation and there are more such examples and they are more accessible—such part of school training as the future artist may lose will be a hundredfold compensated for by the training he will receive from the numerous examples of good art diffused in society.

Such will be one difference between present and future art. Another difference will be that art will not be produced by professional artists receiving payment for their work and engaged on nothing else besides their art. The art of the future will be produced by all the members of the community who feel need of such activity, but they will occupy themselves with art only when they feel such need.

In our society people think that an artist will work better and produce more if he has a secured maintenance; and this opinion once more would prove quite clearly, were such proof still needed, that what among us is considered to be art is not art but only a counterfeit. It is quite true that for the production of boots or loaves division of labour is very advantageous, and that the bootmaker or baker who need not prepare his own dinner or fetch his own fuel will make more boots or loaves than if he had to busy himself with those matters. But art is not a handicraft, it is the transmission of feeling the artist has experienced. And sound feeling can only be engendered in a man when he is living a life in all respects natural and proper to man. Therefore security of maintenance is a condition most harmful to an artist's true productiveness, since it removes him from the condition natural to all men—that of struggle with nature for the maintenance both of his own life and the lives of others—and thus deprives him of the opportunity and possibility of experiencing the most important and most natural feelings of man. There is no position more injurious to an artist's productiveness than the position of complete security and luxury in which in our society artists usually live.

The artist of the future will live the common life of man, earning his subsistence by some kind of labour. The fruits of the highest spiritual strength that passes through him he will try to share with the greatest possible number of people, for in such transmission to others of the feelings that have arisen in him he will find his happiness and reward. The artist of the future will be unable to understand how an artist, whose chief delight is in the wide diffusion of his works, could give them only in exchange for a certain payment.

Until the dealers are driven out, the temple of art will not be a temple. But the art of the future will drive them out.

## JOHN UPDIKE

### Accepting the Howells Medal[1]

William Dean Howells, in whose name this medal is given, was a considerable theorist of fiction, and of American fiction. As a practitioner and critic he sought to hold himself and other writers to a standard of realism that rose above the romantic exaggerations and implausible adventures that characterized popular fiction in his day and, indeed, in ours. He thought progress was being made, and in 1891 wrote, "Fiction is now a finer art than it has ever been hitherto. . . . I have hopes of real usefulness in it . . . but I am by no means certain that it will be the ultimate literary form. . . . On the contrary, it is quite imaginable that when the great mass of readers, now sunk in the foolish joys of mere fable, shall be lifted to an interest in the meaning of things through the faithful portrayal of life in fiction, then fiction the most faithful may be superseded by a still more faithful form of contemporaneous history."

The situation now is more drastic, I think, than Howells conceived it, for what looms is not a mere change of literary fashion or shift of genres but a loss of literature itself, rendered passé by the bright flickering tongues of the electronic modes of entertainment and instruction. Young students, it is reported from academia, are less and less willing and able to read, and the language of even as limpid a nineteenth-century style as that of Hawthorne is reportedly impenetrable to them. Those of us who grew up on a diet of the modernist masterpieces, and have tried to write works that would enchant and challenge readers such as we were, may be like those Renaissance poets who mastered the art of Latin verse, in quixotic or elitist defiance of a widespread linguistic

1. From *More Matter: Essays and Criticism*, John Updike, 1999. pp. 815–816.

death. We are writing for an audience that less and less exists, and a posterity that will not exist.

And yet, when this most dire of scenarios has been sketched, how empowering the practice of fiction remains! Faced with the gradually filling emptiness of a novel in progress, the writer feels he is at the controls of a device whose potential is infinite, a tool that outrivals even a computer in its plasticity and nimbleness, in its inexhaustible capacity for the imitation of life in its real shadings and farraginous details, and for the generation of a narrative music and a weave of symbols and a poetry both of expression and of circumstance. Writing fiction, as those of us who do it know, is, beneath the anxious travail of it, a bliss, a healing, an elicitation of order from disorder, a praise of what is, a salvaging of otherwise overlookable truths from the ruthless sweep of generalization, a beating of daily dross into something shimmering and absolute.

For somewhat these reasons, I imagine, are medals and prizes for the novel awarded—not so much to the lucky individual prizewinner as to this permissive, hybrid, democratic, curious art form itself, in thanks for the validation it bestows upon our common humanity and for the persistence of its faith (once the prerogative of philosophy and religion) that what Howells called "the meaning of things" can be laid bare.

## EUDORA WELTY

### An Interview[2]

INTERVIEWER: Your interest is in psychology also, so that a story such as "Why I Live at the P.O." is a comedy of hysteria. The humor comes out of a pathological behavior.

WELTY: No, I tell you I don't think of them at all as being pathological stories. I know Katherine Anne Porter refers to the girl as a case of dementia praecox in the introduction [of *A Curtain of Green*]. She believed I thought so, but it's far from what I was doing in that story. I was trying to show how, in these tiny little places such as where they come from, the only entertainment people have is dramatizing the family situation, which they do fully knowing what they are doing. They're having a good time. They're not caught up, it's not pathological. There is certainly the undertone, you're right, which is one of wishing things would change. Even though Sister goes and lives in the post office, she'll probably be home by the weekend, and it could happen all over again. They just go through it. I've heard people talk, and they just dramatize everything—"I'll never speak to you again!" It's a Southern kind of exaggeration. There is something underlying it, needless to say. That's what gives it its reason for being.

INTERVIEWER: But the current beneath the humor is despair, isn't it?

WELTY: I know in those early stories I have a number of characters where something visibly is wrong, they're deaf and dumb. Although I didn't think about it, it was a beginning writer's effort to show how alone some of these people felt. I made it a visible reason which is, of course, inside everybody. I must have chosen that as a direct, perhaps oversimplified way. I was not aware

**2.** From *Conversations with American Authors*, ed. Carl Ruas.

at the time that that was what I was doing—for instance, the story about the feeble-minded girl, Lily Daw. Nearly every little town had somebody like that in that part of the world, and the whole town made it their business to take care of her. They wouldn't usually send her away to the Institute for the Feeble-Minded unless they really reached an emergency, which they felt this was. Everybody takes care of everybody to the point where it's not taking care at all. You could see the futility of what they were doing. It was something I observed, just as I observed how people talk in exaggeration. All these things are rooted in a reality which I can use for the story, but I didn't invent it.

INTERVIEWER: "The Wide Net" is a comedy of misunderstanding between newlyweds. The young wife threatens to kill herself, and the husband calls the community together to drag the river for her body. Your description of the forest in autumn is elegiac, knowing that all things must come to an end, and yet inevitably return.

WELTY: That's exactly how I felt when I was writing. They were going on an excursion. Old Doc says, "The excursion is the same when you go looking for your sorrow as when you go looking for your joy." Young love is a mysterious thing, and anything might have happened. Things could have been very terrible. William Wallace, who was so inarticulate, could fish and dive down to the bottom of this water. That's part of it, because they wanted the presence of mystery and the possibility to be there. That's about the season of the year, the fall and the changing times.

INTERVIEWER: Young lovers acting out the drama in the fall reminded me of Chekhov, and I wondered if he influenced your concept of the short story.

WELTY: He certainly was my ideal. I didn't consciously try to base things, although that is an acknowledged method of teaching yourself. I guess I never thought I could base anything on a master like that.

INTERVIEWER: Did your reading determine your direction?

WELTY: I'm sure it must have done it indirectly, but not directly. I feel that when I'm really working on something, I'm not aware of anything but the story. I'm not thinking of myself, or of another writer. I'm just trying to get the story the way I want it. Those things can certainly help and bear down on me, but it's done at other times. Then they are worked out in the story without my conscious knowledge.

INTERVIEWER: When you began writing, did you identify with the Southern tradition?

WELTY: I'm self-taught, so I really didn't. I just wrote stories. I was befriended by Robert Penn Warren and Cleanth Brooks, who published me in *The Southern Review;* I met Katherine Anne Porter fairly early; and they were already long-established writers, but we had no group. We're all such individuals, I hardly see how we could. I'm thinking of Walker Percy and Peter Taylor and many more. We all met in the course of things without seeking one another out, just meeting as life opened and enjoyed each other.

INTERVIEWER: Katherine Anne Porter was a lifelong friend, and I wondered if she was involved with the direction of your writing.

WELTY: I don't know that I would have known how to take any kind of direction. What she did for me that was so great was to believe in my work. This was like a bolt of lightning from the sky, that people whose work I loved thought well of mine. It made me feel that I was really in the world, that I had understanding and some readers. That's the greatest thing you can do for somebody.

INTERVIEWER: You have this independence in your work. Does it carry over also to publishers, because they are at such a geographical distance?

WELTY: I don't think about that end of it when I write. All I want to do is write that story, and I had such a long wait before stories appeared. I began writing six years before a story appeared in *The Atlantic Monthly*, which was my first national magazine, but from the beginning they were welcomed by university and college magazines. I was published, which gave me a sense of reaching somebody. I don't know what would have happened to me if I'd waited to be published to write the next story. One blessing about living at home—although I imagine I would do it anywhere—is that I write just the way I want to, and when I want to, until I get it nearly as I can to what I want. Then its fate is up to the other end. I've always been blessed with wonderful editors and agents. I didn't even realize how extremely lucky I was.

# Writing Fiction

One of the very good ways to learn more about the art of fiction is to practice it—to take the plunge and write stories of your own. It is also a very natural outgrowth of the emotional and intellectual excitement that reading the top-flight work collected here has generated. Whether or not you have written any fiction before, like most people you have been *telling* stories for most of your life. The next step is to make the more complex effort of giving them a written form of the sort your reading has taught you to respect. Often teachers offer the option of writing a story as an alternative to preparing at least one of the papers required in a course where the main emphasis is on improving skills in reading critically. The relation between reading and writing is so important—and so intimate—that undertaking more than one form of written work can help you read with keener enthusiasm and a much better understanding of what can be communicated in fiction.

Courses specifically devoted to fiction writing are enhanced by the guidance offered in masterful variety by the authors whose finest efforts are assembled in this text. In years to come great work will be done by some of you in writing classes who are now beginning a serious apprenticeship, learning your craft by a devoted scrutiny of what has been accomplished by both remote and recent generations of fiction writers.

Thus whatever the nature of the class—and whatever your long- or short-range expectations may be when you set out to write your first, or fifth, or twentieth short story—it must be obvious as a general principle that good models of short fiction can discipline and accelerate your progress. To be sure, everything will depend eventually on the quality of your personal and unique imagination, your judgment, your dexterity with language that suits your subject, and the excellence of your observation of life. The happy truth is that drawing on models will not impede your personal talents—it will release them by sparing you the waste and frustration of striking blind.

Surely the writer you hope to become must be an observer and a listener, sharp-eyed and attentive to experience, and with the ability to retain or recall things seen and heard: the shape of a child's mouth when his birthday balloon pops in his hands; the words your sister used to describe a new boyfriend to your parents; the atmosphere in a forest clearing on a summer day. And if you are already very good at such observation, the chances are that your reading of stories has been an essential part of your preparation as an observer.

The genius of fiction is to train readers in what it is *important* to take note of among the incredible profusion of details and events crowding everyday existence—to train us to select what counts, what signifies, what fits with other details of observation to give a sum of meaning to patterns emerging from the apparent chaos of life. In a word, readers of fiction are continuously modeling their habits of observation on those of writers who, in their turn, no doubt, modeled theirs on a continuous narrative tradition still evolving.

But when we have conceded the inevitable role of models in the formation of skill and craft in writing fiction, we may still became bogged down in a widespread prejudice that causes us to resist the very idea of following models. To do so smacks of imitation, and the cardinal motive for creative writing is to be *original*, is it not? You want to write stories to free yourself from the formulas and limitations that inhibit your other kinds of writing.

You want to—and should—turn out something original when you are ready to do so. But you haven't a very good chance of doing so until you have learned more ways of observing and shaping your material as the masters of the art have done. When students in creative-writing classes don't or won't accept good models for their development, all too often they begin half-consciously to model their stories on each other's. The blind follow the blind, and standards are much lower than they should be for all the investment of labor and good intention.

Assuming you are willing to use what is freely offered by the excellent models of fiction in this text, we had better come down to specifics about the ways you can effectively go about it. Actually using these stories as models, in all the ways they can be used, requires more than devout appreciation. It requires putting words on paper, whether as exercises, as notes, or as part of a story of your own.

## Imitation and Comparison

To begin with a bedrock, basic form of exercise, some writers have found it useful to copy passages word for word from an admired example. Such "slavish" copying may have the merit of training you in habits of syntax and verbal rhythm that worked well for writers from whom you intend to learn. Word for word copying might be good for a daily—or occasional—warm-up exercise to get the juices of your imagination flowing. As an icebreaker it can coordinate the sheer mechanics of writing with a flow of idea and emotion into words on paper.

Better than this, a bit of literal copying may be a specially rigorous way of *reading*, which forces you to pay some attention to each word without skimming. And if you have the devotion to make it so, it may be the occasion for pondering the function of each word and each syntactical element as these build into sentences and paragraphs.

Please don't just nod over this suggestion and pass on. Grab your laptop, or a pen and paper, and copy the first paragraph of Frank O'Connor's "Guests of the Nation." Had you noticed before how this first-person narration is identified as such by the three pronouns *me, we,* and *our*? How the time of day (dusk) is made more concrete by the lighting of the lamp? How the crucial word *chum* (a synonym for "friend") is emphasized by repetition and set in opposition to the word *divil* (a synonym for "enemy" or "hated adversary")? Yes, of course you can understand the meaning of the paragraph without dwelling on such trivial indicators of the situation and the conflict to come. But *by* dwelling on them—as you are privileged and perhaps enticed to do in the exercise of copying—you may learn something precious about getting a story started. Your task will be slavish only if you let it be so. And as much can be said for any other assignment, even if self-assigned.

Yet, your verbal imagination will no doubt be more constructively engaged if you base another sort of exercise on O'Connor's paragraph (or a passage from some other story you admire): following his sentence pattern closely, substitute language and subject matter of your own. Your subject might be the relation of two antagonistic groups in your school or community. As you know, the narrator need not be yourself, but can be an imagined character. Whichever way your imagination veers, the result might be something like this:

> At lunchtime the pockmarked Nicaraguan boy Manuel would jingle his change and ask, "Amigos, you up for it today?" and Scott would say, "Why not, amigo?" (since we pretended we also spoke Spanish) and the smaller Nicaraguan Greniero would brush off a table and roll out his own set of dice. As often as not Martin Stark would join us to watch and get angry at Greniero's style, which was pretty gaudy, and read him out the way he did us "Come on you clown, why are you wobbling the table?"

As you see, we have made a transition from outright copying to parody. And though this example of parody (or the one you will now write) may be only a warmup for truly original composition, pause to reflect that parody *can* be pushed to the level of the highest art, as readers of Joyce's *Ulysses* know so well.

Most of the time when we are developing our own material with the guidance of models, we aren't so committed to a single text or author as in the case of parodistic exercises. Although we continue to learn by a process of imitation and constant comparison, our comparisons usually range freely over three distinct items: (1) our own manuscript, in whatever state of development it may have reached; (2) the segment of reality we mean to represent; and (3) the storytelling tactics and styles of several writers who have dealt similarly with similar subjects.

Particularly in matters of diction and dialogue we continue this simultaneous three-layered scrutiny as a natural part of the writing process. We go on observing and listening to tangible things around us—in fact, observation is now intensified because we have given it focus by beginning to write about some segment of observable behavior, and we listen more intently to test whether people like our fictional characters really do speak as we are saying in our story that they do. We want to add more beads to the string, so we listen for characterizing utterances we have not been able to imagine or remember. And—while we are verifying our writing in progress by what might be called fieldwork—we are turning back to the text of this book to see how Mansfield or Woolf, Hemingway or Faulkner, Oates or Munro has handled confrontations like those we are writing about. We reassess Hemingway's exploitation of understatement, Faulkner's probing with highly charged rhetoric—and are encouraged to remember that either tactic is available to us if we can fit it to the material we are now developing. We turn to the pages of our predecessors for promptings, and when we are lucky we bring away something which sharpens what we have begun.

What we are searching for in such repeated comparative surveys is probably not something we can directly parody, but a principle or an approach suitable to many fine stories. Thus if we turn to Williams's "The Use of Force" while we are at work on a story in which the voice of the first-person narrator is a necessary component, it is not at all with the aim of imitating the particular voice Williams has created, but to see as sharply as we can how small modifications of flat and rather impersonal language can further individualize the character beginning to emerge on our own pages, and to see how this author has fused the idiosyncrasies of speech with the flavor of the situation being recounted. It is very important to remember that Williams's effects are not and could not be achieved merely by inventive manipulation on his part. Clearly he has listened—in actuality and over and over again in memory—to a voice that is finally remorseful. One of the most valuable things you can learn from choosing his story as a model is that you must go into the corners of your world and back in to the dark labyrinth of your own memory listening for the timbre of such a voice.

Dialogue passages in such stories as "Hills Like White Elephants," "Great Falls," and the climactic last scene from "The Dead" can teach you, first of all, what to listen for in actual conversation and, second, how to structure the patterns of ordinary speech into revealing and dramatic sequences. As you become a keener listener, you will note that dialogue is not usually a matter of question and answer or direct responses to purely rational propositions.

The man in Hemingway's story says: "'. . . But you've got to realize—.'" Without waiting for him to finish the sentence the young woman responds, "'I realize. Can't we maybe stop talking?'" Her impatient breaking in reveals better than any explanation that could be provided by the author how weary she is of the persistent argument. Yet, just a moment later her despair of reaching agreement is modulated when she catches at something he says and echoes it back: "'. . . if it means anything to you,'" he says, and she answers, "'Doesn't it mean anything to you? We could get along.'" Even in despair she is still fighting to make him really hear something besides his own voice, his own wish. If you read such a passage aloud—instead of copying it silently—you will see and *hear* how skillfully the author has implied the tones of voice of the two speakers. In some comparable scene in one of your own stories you can use the same effect.

In "The Dead," Gabriel Conroy asks his wife, "'And what did he die of so young, Gretta? Consumption, was it?' 'I think he died for me,' she answered." At first glance this may appear to be a direct response on the wife's part. But look again at the context of the question and answer. The powerful shock in her reply comes from the fact that the two are speaking in quite distinct levels of discourse—his mundane, hers mystic and profound. It is from this revelation of incompatible modes of adjusting to reality that the resolution of the story emerges.

These examples illustrate the principle that what we call dialogue is often, in truth, two or more monologues rather loosely fitted together by the circumstances of the scene.

Even when you are not intentionally searching for model fragments of written dialogue, you will come across one sort or another of striking examples that you will want to collect for later reference. It is a fairly simple matter to photocopy such passages and keep them handy in a notebook or file—a very good practice for the writer commencing a serious career.

## Story-Generating Models

As Chaucer's Canterbury pilgrims go on their way, a story told by one of them prompts a story from another. So it goes with all of us. When we hear or read a story, we are reminded of something we have to tell. Like the spreading wake of a boat, waves of memory veer out, stirring flotsam that has lain dormant on the beach, activating inert material we have not yet quite imagined might be the stuff for a story of our own. It will be like—and yet fascinatingly different from—the example that stirred the waves of imagination.

Consider Sherwood Anderson's "I Want to Know Why," which deals with a boy's disillusionment following a moment of triumph. Surely very many of its readers will be reminded of similar shocks in their own lives. It would not be surprising if a lot of them toyed with the possibility of writing about how such a common disappointment seemed very particular and very personal to them—or that most of them felt balked by uncertainty about how to approach their material, which is plentiful enough but unmanageably formless in the rag bag of memory.

Well, a story not only stimulates a reader's memory, its form gives bold hints about the way you might shape what you are moved to write about. Anderson opens his story with the *arrival* of the narrator and some other boys, at Saratoga, where the climactic race will be run. Then, in an apparently rambling fashion, the boy's feelings about horses and racing are spilled out. In fact these clumsy declarations are put forth as a preparation before the horse Sunstreak is named—before they are all summed up and focused on the actual drama of the race and the disillusioning aftermath when Jerry Tillford brags in the company of prostitutes.

A decision to follow Anderson's example would, first of all, oblige you to concentrate on the end, the dramatic resolution of your fictional situation, and then to measure out the necessary preparation of material, feelings, and circumstances required to give full force to this resolution. In a word, the model shows you how to construct your story backward, starting to work from the end and adding the material required for the opening. What feelings and what qualities will your central character have? The more you review your material and cull the possibilities, something approaching certainty will be established, for memory works that way once we guide it by fictional craft. Of course in your reminiscence you will be directed by the need to choose a character who has the potential for jolting the protagonist as Jerry Tillford jolts the narrator. That is, you may have to invent, or change, the personages when those you remember do not quite fit the requirements of the story.

Almost as universal as Anderson's basic story of the loss of innocence is the situation in Walker's "Everyday Use." Much of the tension in the American experience generally is the conflict between those who have clung to the places where they have their roots and those who have "gone to the city"—migrated in search of a broader or more fulfilling life. Most students returning home during their college years find themselves caught in a cross fire between old values and new ones. Walker built her story around a number of physical details of setting—the grassless yard, the churn, and the quilts—which have different values and potentials for the stay-at-homes and for the daughter who has briefly returned.

In preparing to write a story about the return of an offspring to the original home you might well begin by (1) listing a number of such specific things in the setting you know or imagine, (2) by noting after each some of the potentially different values they might have for those with conflicting life-styles, and (3) imagining or simply remembering the characters who would be most likely to clash in their perception of the values in such possessions.

Making lists of this sort is not at all the cut-and-dried matter you might suppose before you try it. Selection of sights and sounds, names and voices, thunderstorms and carnivals, the furniture in church basements, things stored in attics or garages—picking over such things, mentally following streams of association, and then building complete sentences around the things named in your list is creative work of the richest kind. It is a preliminary shaping of the substance that will give life to your finished story. There is no rule for choosing which of the concrete details you assemble will function most effectively in the development of plot, characterization, or theme. But, rather than trying to select details to fit some predetermined idea or outline, you ought to be always eager to follow the significance suggested by the details themselves. Thus an imitation of Walker's approach can be transformed into something uniquely and unpredictably original.

Many of the same suggestions can be made if Joyce's "Araby" is chosen as a model. Again the basic experience is close to being universal—humiliation in an encounter between romantic expectation and banal actuality. (Who among us hasn't pushed some childish desire until it burst in a shattering embarrassment?) "Araby," like "I Want to Know Why" and "Everyday Use," is told in the first person. We may concede there were ample reasons why this mode was chosen by the three authors. Yet, just because you may be modeling your work on theirs, this does not mean your story will or should be told in the first person, however close to your actual experience it may be. The decision whether to use first- or third-person narration ought to be based on some trials and some sketch work in both methods. You might learn something useful by recasting the final scene of "Araby" as a third person account with a somewhat altered point of view (probably one more detached from the consciousness of the main character). You will find that much more is required than a simple change of pronouns from first to third person if either the emotion of the story or the significance of its resolution is to be retained.

Suppose you were to rewrite "Everyday Use" from the point of view of the daughter Dee, in either first or third person. What modifications would have to be made to reveal the same significance in the circumstances? Some useful answers to such a question will occur to you from purely passive analysis. Better answers—and ones much more useful to you as a committed student of the craft of fiction—can come only from your putting on paper at least a partial rewrite of your model. However much you respect that model in its published form, you must realize it came to that form through a series of authorial choices of the kind you are forced to make in your reconstruction.

## Models for Revision

When the personal computer first appeared in the 1980s, some believed that it would take the curse off revision—the implication being that revision is always unpleasant, though necessary, and that use of a labor-saving device is the best way to have done with it.

Most writers believe, however, that revision is simply a continuation of the imaginative act of writing; for most, it has been the most pleasant part. It is in revision that the nice touches can be laid on, the tones and colors harmonized, and clarifications made to show the precise meaning of what was often cloudy or indistinct in some phases of the compositional process.

To go even further, let us admit that revision is not merely the final phase of the process. It has been going on since the concept first began to take shape. Very few of us write as much as a sentence on paper without some juggling and readjustment of an idea and the words that seem fit to express it. We change the nouns and verbs that first entered our minds; we add or drop some adjectives or move them around in the process of inscribing a sentence on a page. As the sentences follow each other, we keep shifting our thoughts by reviewing what has already been put down and what is now required to keep the story flowing and to prepare for what is still to come. At the end of a page or the end of a draft of the whole story, our minds are still teeming with reasons for the choice of wording we have made and the possibilities that have been rejected. Or, if this still-bubbling mental activity *isn't* continuing, then no word processor is going to be of any help.

The only absolute requirement for revision is that there must be something to revise. This means that in your initial surge you have got something on paper. Something that won't shift and fade and drift away as a purely mental construct often does. Something that can be examined and reconsidered on the morning after, marked for change, or cut apart and repasted. A writer is not a daydreamer, but is a worker with paper, and the joy of the craft can only be experienced by the trials and revisions made on paper. You have finished a story only when nothing remains to be done to improve it.

Just because you have written a story through from beginning to end, this does not mean you have finished it. If it is good in the form you have first given it—even if it is published or publishable—it may be bettered by revisions. When you have a "finished" draft of a story in hand, you have come to a point where it is natural to pause, take a long hard look, and weigh the possibilities still to be wrung from material you have successfully coaxed this far along. Such points offer a natural occasion for comparing what you have done with examples from the text that may prod your imagination with suggestions for improvement.

Suppose that, for reasons that then seemed sufficient, you began your story with a striking line of dialogue and moved directly into a scene beginning the central action. Now you will reflect that the risk of such a brisk leap into the action is that the characters are more shallowly drawn than they must be to bring out the significance of what they are doing or saying to each other. While it is certainly not necessary to explain characters before you let them move, background information, histories, and individual idiosyncrasies must be incorporated somewhere and somehow without impeding the movements of events.

When your work is fresh and hot—and unfinished—on the desk in front of you, the time is favorable for comparing your opening presentation with those of Lawrence in "The Horse Dealer's Daughter," and Hemingway's "Hills Like White Elephants." Lawrence begins with dialogue that is part of an ongoing present scene (though this is stretched to permit the author to weave in some of the background of the family now in a moment of crisis). Hemingway begins with a scene that is almost purely objective and pictorial. He strikingly avoids giving any information about the characters or where they have come from. Before the story is done we will know what is essential to be known about them, but this emerges entirely from their dialogue.

A careful study of just these two stories in comparison with your own material may suggest to you what you can cut and what you might need to build up in terms of background information for the reader. The value of analytic comparison can be enhanced by actually cutting and pasting your own work to make it conform to your models. (It should go without saying that you cannot move paragraphs and scenes around this way without some rewriting to make the pieces fit together in a coherent whole.)

Before undertaking a second draft of your story, it is worth reconsidering and making comparisons of all the elements of fiction you have learned by reading and discussion to identify. Consult examples of descriptive passages, narrative passages in which long stretches of time are compressed, and scenes. Note that the lush and detailed description that opens "Kew Gardens" functions in a certain way to serve the peculiar demands of that story, while the descriptions of Parisian street scenes accomplish something distinctly different in "Babylon Revisited." In "The Open Boat" an insistent series of sensory descriptions of the ocean and the shoreline runs as an accompaniment to the adventure of the shipwrecked men, vivifying their experience and contributing much to the reader's inferences about what it all means. "The horizon narrowed and widened, and dipped and rose, and at all times its edge was jagged with waves that seemed thrust up in points like rocks." "The color of the sea changed from slate to emerald green streaked with amber lights, and the foam was like tumbling snow." "On the distant dunes were set many little black cottages, and a tall white windmill reared above them. No man, nor dog, nor bicycle appeared on the beach." Surely such a series of pictorial renditions is worth imitating if your story requires its characters to be immersed in conflict with their environment—just as surely it would be inappropriate if the conflict were more confined to personal oppositions.

In "The Veldt" Bradbury plays a very nifty trick in his description of the images projected on the nursery walls. That is, instead of describing them as if they were, indeed, *pictures,* he slants the descriptions forcibly to make them seem as if he were talking about direct encounters with the dangerous African habitat itself—as in the twist of his fantasy, they turn out to be. Descriptions of the barbecue stand in "A Good Man Is Hard to Find" intensify the atmosphere of grotesque contemporary reality. The coming of dawn at the end of "Barn Burning" serves as an indirect revelation of the emotional state of the boy who has—for good reasons—betrayed his own father. You can and should continue your list of examples, make a collection for convenient reference, *and* remember that no one descriptive device is suitable for all kinds of story objectives.

How long a period of time is covered by the action of your story? If it is several years, months, days, or even hours, the chances are that you will need to account for the longer stretches with narrative passages in which the language is specifically adapted to show persisting as distinct from immediate action. Time is compressed by statements on the order of "during July he exercised daily in the college gym." There is a tendency for such passages to become thin, flat, and lacking in concrete detail. In the example just given, no picture is drawn of the person at his exercise, the weather or the mood of the summer, or the sounds, sights, and smells of a gym during this season. In a fully finished story this may not be the case.

Part of "Everyday Use" compresses time effectively—without losing richness of concrete detail—in the reminiscence of the narrator: "I used to think she hated Maggie, too. But that was before we raised the money, the church and me, to send her to Augusta to school. She used to read to us without pity. . . . She washed us in a river of make-believe, burned us with a lot of knowledge we didn't necessarily need to know. . . . Often I fought off the temptation to shake her. At sixteen she had a style of her own; and knew what style was."

As you accumulate examples from other stories that reach over too much time to be presented in continuous scenes, pay particular attention to the time modifiers that indicate the action is an extended one—"she would often," "by the time he graduated he had," etc. These mechanical connectives can, and should, be given the function of keeping your story vivid and convincing, just as the detail and dialogue of a scene will do.

Perhaps for the beginning writer scenes are the easiest part of writing fiction. At least, the most fun. In such writing you are more likely to have ready-made models from life as you observe it. A conversation begins, and the exchange back and forth between characters builds naturally, because the response of the second speaker is roughly governed by what the first one has said. You follow the example of movies, in which essentially everything is revealed by a succession of related scenes, requiring no authorial account of what has ripened or changed in the interim between them. But the more demanding an artisan you become—coming up hard against the difficulties of fitting one item with another to make a fictional pattern—the more you'll perceive the need for specific models.

A number of stories in this text consist of a single scene, and we turn naturally to something like Updike's "A&P" for a precise examination of the way in which the characters are brought into the reader's view, how their encounter is progressively complicated, and how the concluding action gives point and meaning to the dramatized spectacle. The mere presence of the three girls in the store and the narrator's appraisal of them would have made a fictional scene, in the bare technical meaning of the word, but it is the intervention of the store manager in the midst of the scene that makes it, all by itself, a story in which no follow-up material is needed to round it out.

Compare "A&P" with "Everyday Use"—another story that contains only a single scene. In the latter the design is significantly different. The author sets up her characters and their traits with an extended expository passage before the main action starts. What is then required of the scene is that it dramatize the traits already enumerated and show what they amount to when brought to the test. The correspondence between the mother's analysis and what Dee (Wangero) reveals by her spoken lines should be closely analyzed as a model for what can be intensified in a scene you have written that may have been perfect in its verisimilitude but lacking in point.

With material requiring a number of scenes for its full development not only does one need the aptitude for getting the most out of each scene but there must be a suitable design for the sequence in which the scenes will be laid out, and a series of connectives to move economically from one scene to another. There is also an ever-present question of proportion—which of the scenes can be treated summarily and briefly, which must be given some amplitude. Fitzgerald's example in "Babylon Revisited" can be useful for a start in learning such management. Mark the beginnings and ends of all the scenes in this story, and then ask of each one: What is accomplished to advance the story by this scene? How have we been brought into it from the preceding one?

The first, between Charlie and Alix in the bar, is what may be called an "establishing" scene. It presents the main character on his return to a once-familiar environment and ticks off some changes in him, in the places he is taking another look at, and in his judgment and perception.

The next full scene takes place in the home of Charlie's in-laws. But how has he come there from scene one? He has taxied across Paris (a bit of drab and routine transportation that *should* have been omitted—except that the author uses it to give another glimpse of the Parisian setting and to record Charlie's regret at having "spoiled" this good place for himself). The second scene serves to demonstrate the bond of affection between father and daughter—and to signal the potential for opposition, hostility, and dislike between Charlie and the woman who will be his chief antagonist in the principal conflict of the story.

The third scene gives us Charlie alone in the city that once proved an irresistible temptation for his dissipations. It is a test intended to demonstrate (to the reader as well as to the character himself) how far he has recovered from the previous crackup. It climaxes in his rejection of the woman who encourages him to plunge into vice once more. He has not failed the test. As the section ends, his hopes are bright for showing that he is now fit to reclaim his daughter.

What occurs in the first scene of section II is crucial preparation for the outcome of the story. Not only does Charlie have a pleasant, promising lunch with Honoria, he seems to have once again side-stepped formerly destructive temptations by his coolness to Duncan and Lorraine. But what Fitzgerald has, in fact, accomplished here is to plant a superficially successful evasion as the time bomb that will presently blast Charlie's prospects and hopes.

By mapping out for yourself the design of this story, you may discover the best design for your own story—the best progression of scenes; what to hold back and what to put forward. And of course this is true of the study of any story if you study it as a craftsman would; that is, if you look at it not so much in a scholarly way, but in the nuts-and-bolts way of one writer examining the gestures and the technique of another. No work of fiction is ever created in a vacuum.

# A Local Habitation and A Name: Meditations on Writing

*Selections from Richard Bausch's Facebook Posts, 2008–2014*

> The poet's eye, in fine frenzy rolling,
> Doth glance from heaven to earth, from earth to heaven;
> And as imagination bodies forth
> The forms of things unknown, the poet's pen
> Turns them to shapes and gives to airy nothing
> A local habitation and a name . . .
> —WILLIAM SHAKESPEARE

One of the most endearing things about all the writers I know—and of course I know a lot of them—is that not one of them has any material ambitions. They want money, yes, because like all of us they need it, but when they get it they use it mostly to buy one thing: Time. That's all any of them want. To be able to purchase a little Time from the world's daily demands, and they want that time, all of them that I know, for one reason. To work. No material matter comes close to that for them. I think that's a wonderful thing. And when the various kinds of wrangling and petty quarrels and vanities arise that come from being human and trying to do something very hard in a world that is mostly indifferent—well, I try to remember that. It's something very beautiful about us that we all share: that sweet almost child-like quality of wanting from the world only a little time to keep doing this thing we love so much that even when it tortures us we long to be there in it and with it.

•　•　•

To write seriously and get it right is to remove the walls between people, to break down the notion of others as monoliths of cultural difference, and so it is terribly important to do it with everything you have, even knowing that the world may ignore it. The world ignores many very great writers every day. But even remembering all this, also remember that if a work of narrative art or of poetry, or non-fiction does not engage and entertain, then it is a failure, no matter how serious its intent. So spend the time to make the reading of the sentences and the lines pleasurable. That must be the first thing. Let the other stuff surprise you. If you are striving to be truthful, and faithful to the thing for itself, the chances are very good that it will shine as it should with those matters that can indeed bring about something like salvation itself for a time.

•　•　•

The word *talent* used to denote a monetary unit. The parable of the ten talents is that the father gave ten talents to each of his three sons. The first one squandered them: the second hoarded them; the third one *used* them. And of course he was the one who was blessed. Talent connotes responsibility. If you have any talent at all you are *supposed* to be using it. It is your moral obligation to use it with everything you've got—you have the words. There are so many people out there who do not have the words, and a big part of our work is simply, by our own struggles with this art form, to let them see they are not alone. It is what Conrad was talking about when he spoke of 'The solidarity of the human family.'

•  •  •

Remember that even when it seems most difficult and most unyielding, it is always 'going well' if you are doing it, struggling with it, even struggling to dream up the next line, because it is in that state of becoming, and so what if some of the stages of its becoming are painful or confusing. Seems to me something is lacking if that is NOT the case. If you are lucky enough to have a place and time to be pained and confused while you give it what it needs to bring it into being, then everything is as it should be. Nothing is wasted. Go on and do the work, which can also mean sitting and staring at it for a time.

•  •  •

You don't have to be so terribly smart, or fast. You only have to be willing. You get smart going through it and through it after being open to what it is tending toward. Don't worry about what you will finally say; it will tell you.

•  •  •

You have to change something—change it. You're not moving stones, not carving in granite. Change it. It's like you're at the edge of a beautiful stream and the fish are jumping into your hands and you can make any arrangement of them that pleases you. Change it and see where that takes you. The truth you are seeking to deliver is the truth of experience, felt life. Not philosophy.

•  •  •

We are all struggling with the obstacle of ourselves.

•  •  •

Don't let anyone tell you it's all one thing or all the other. It isn't entirely 'show don't tell.' As I've been saying for years, it's show AND tell, and you have to let it teach you when to do the one and when to do the other.

•  •  •

Say anything to begin. Anything at all. What you say then predicates something else. And that in turn predicates its own something else. It is always at least partly a matter of setting into motion. Putting the words down and seeing where they take you.

•  •  •

You touch one part of it, and the whole thing shivers, from one end to the other. It's such a delicate thing, revision, and revision is where the artistry is; and so you have to be ruthless, and put away anything—even parts you like the sound of, even the matters that speak from your secret self to who you hope you are—put away anything that does not contribute to the whole thing.

•  •  •

The doubt you feel *is* your talent: the whole feeling stems from having the ear in the first place to be able to tell when it isn't singing as you want it to; it comes from hearing how far it is from the way you hope to make it sound. You can hear the difference because you have the talent, the ear. And, because the piece takes its slow sweet hard time getting right, you feel that fact as evidence that you can't do it or won't be able to do it; you look at the work of others, who also did it seventy-five times to get it right, and you can't escape the sense that their smooth elegant lines are how it arrived the first time for them—whole cloth, as printed. So you turn that on yourself and start feeling it won't ever be good enough, and the doubt sweeps in. Just do the day's work. A little at a time. And then take yourself elsewhere in your life until the next day's work.

•  •  •

Too many times you think of this work as something you have to haul up out of yourself—you're writing then more *about* your experience, than you are writing *with* it. Forget hauling anything up out of the self. Think of it as a path. You're just going to go for a morning stroll through experience as the outside weather of the world. You make the path by walking it, and you can walk anywhere, right? Let it lead you, put down what comes to you to say even if it sounds wrong to you, or off the subject; and when at last you reach somewhere, it will probably have elements of surprise in it. That's good. No surprises for the writer, Frost tells us, no surprises for the reader. Now you go back, knowing finally where it was always leading; and you strive to be terribly smart about the whole thing. Now, instead of using the dream side of your being, you're using the side that figures how to get a door open when your hands are full. So you use all of yourself, before it's over: the day-dreamer and the one with the ingenuity. It's so hard not because you're not up to it; it's so hard because it's so important to do it right, to get it down right. And it's hard for everybody.

• • •

I used to pace, near sick with fear, before I'd sit down to try it, try putting something down, anything. I don't know why I was afraid, since *nothing* in one day's work comes remotely near to defining *anything* about what you are doing. It isn't even an indication of anything. It is hard. It confuses. One feels uninspired and flat. One looks at a line and it starts to dissolve into all the other possibilities. And you get scared. What if it's like this tomorrow? And what if it's *always* like this. And? And? And? *This* is what frightens you? The territory? The very deepest nature of the thing itself? Of course it always is terribly hard because it is coming into being and that is always difficult. Welcome to the territory. The province of creation. The cave of making, as James Dickey used to call it. Who ever said it would be easy? It only looks as if it was easy after you've done it and re-done it and re-done it again and again, as many times as it takes. But it is, after all, *work*. And you are lucky to have it to do. You should try to cultivate a healthy sense of respect for it, of course, while also learning to see the plain silliness of being afraid of one little step on the way to wherever it will take you. The whole thing is a lovely adventure.

• • •

I've been thinking lately about the word *hackneyed* as it is sometimes applied to prose or poetry. I think it is destructively reductive and usually wrong, especially when it is used by a writer about his/her own work. Everything we ever write needs our attention and it needs work and it will usually need many revisions and efforts to sharpen it and make it clearer. To say anything is hackneyed is a little like using an ethnic slur about a person—it doesn't really say anything. It reduces everything to a stone cold abstraction; it strips away the dignity of something one is spending one's self to do well. So strike it from your vocabulary about this work. It has no place there. Just keep going and striving to be splendid and clear. And stop cutting your own legs out from under you with that kind of language.

• • •

I would write all morning and then put it in a side drawer of the desk. I didn't want to look at it because I believed that lurking in all that work was the one killing indication that I was not a writer, that it was all a pipe dream of a lazy kid who was afraid of nine to five. I was twenty-two, and twenty-three, and I still had that awful sense that I might discover some fatal sign that I was not a writer; I would find it in the pages. It was waiting for me there. The something *unfixably* wrong. So I'd sit and stare into the sound hole of the guitar and play songs, and sing and tell myself I had done something creative with the day, that it was all part of the same thing. And this didn't really change until I got to where there wasn't anything *else* to do but stay on it, and keep going with something, and I wrote three full manuscripts in a kind of hectic, obsessed, all-hours, frantic, drowning, shivering, controlled desperation. This whole blessed occupation, as William Maxwell called it once in a letter to me, is made out of our doubts, and the continuing sense of inadequacy to the task. The territory is what I call it for myself, which is neither original with me, nor particularly new; but it keeps me focused and accepting of the struggle. Welcome to the wilderness.

• • •

Say anything. What you say predicates the next thing. Say one sentence, no matter what it is, and the thing is set in motion. You say, "I was being chased by a gigantic angry giraffe." And then you have to say something after that. And what you say next is determined by what you just said. If you can get the heavy critic who stands at your shoulder saying no, no, no, who's going to want to read that, that's not good, that can't lead anywhere, that doesn't look as good as (insert whoever you're reading)—if you can make that petty stuffy overly conscious hidebound censor shut up, and just dream it on through and play it out as it seems to want to go, you'll get a lot more done. Stop thinking so much, and dream it up. There's plenty of time to think about it later and use your smarts on it. You'll use all your various selves on it—but at the beginning, you must try to be that infant with speech.

• • •

It is no accident that for *centuries* writers believed in a muse that spoke through them. Because the experience, when it is going well, is very much as if someone is murmuring in your ear, giving you the words, the musical notes in the prose, and the meaning, too. That, too. Visit it, each day, let it know you're there, and then as you come to the end of the day's visit, try to make it so you know what the next scene is going to be or begin with (best advice Hemingway ever gave) and then occupy yourself with *anything* else until time for the next visit.

• • •

The confusions often have less to do with the work, than with your own expectations toward it. Let go of thinking *about* it and its possible place in the world, including the world of your own work, and think inside it, imagining your way into the physical and mental *being* of your people—deed them the right to be other than mouthpieces for what you think you think. I believe that's how they become alive, when they leave you behind and stop waiting for you to decide what they should do, and start doing things that surprise—and may even horrify you, with all your dignity and compassion.

• • •

You never really learn to write, as it is usually conceived; there is no template you are trying to decipher. What you learn, eventually, is how to write this one thing you're working on. It's no accident that we feel as if we have to learn everything all over again each time we try to do it. Because that is indeed the situation. You have to learn how to write each one, and each one contains secrets and mysteries that you have to solve, and those secrets and mysteries change as the story changes, and so you have to learn it all over. The thing you *can* treat like a template is *habit*, the habits of work that you develop, that you can strive consciously to develop. The habit of being shrewd about it all: making up your mind that you will start trying to work without demanding too much in the way of specific conditions (silence, certain light, certain time of day, certain place); teaching yourself to write in changing conditions and with the noises and distractions of being alive on this very hectic and un-peaceful planet all around you. Just visiting it each day, letting it know you're there. So I am really seldom teaching writing: I'm teaching habits, and revision, and practice, and stubbornness, the life, and understanding that confusion is quite normal and even healthy because it leads you into what you don't know about what you thought you knew.

• • •

History, even in a historical novel, is always backdrop. Because the novel is always about the personal life, and the personal cost of things. We care more about Natasha and Sonja and Pierre and Prince Andrei, and old Bolkonsky and Maria, than we do about Russia's war with Napoleon. And the scene that shows this best is when Natasha is sitting in the window and she believes she'll never see Andrei again, and also believes she has failed him, and her best friend Sonja, with whom she was raised, comes to her and says, "Natasha, look. Moscow is burning." And Natasha, still a teenager, a young woman with a broken heart, turns and looks over her shoulder and says, "Oh, yes. Moscow." Your characters not only have a right to their personal problems, the novel you're writing requires that those problems take center stage.

• • •

When you come upon some difficulty or trouble regarding the motions or reactions of your characters—when something starts to look cheesy to you, or forced, or silly or managed—try to remember that the whole enterprise is a *cooperation* between you and the reader, and that therefore your deepest responsibility is to *keep* the reader's trust, the reader's belief in what you're telling him/her. So, just try to be straight about it all. Remember that you are the docent in your own museum—the gallery, as it were, where your story unfolds. That museum. Face into whatever the problems are *with* the reader. Let him/her know that you are aware of the depth of whatever problem arises from your imagining and from the history out of which you are imagining (and work to remember that if what you are describing is "roughly" contemporary, even if that is so about it—it is also true that if it is more than fifteen minutes past, you are in history)—give the reader the license to partake in the creation of your story by letting him/her in on the problems of its creation, without announcing them as such. At the very least, try to acknowledge, with every gesture, that the enterprise you are offering involves them as privileged partners in the journey, which is always a journey to Truth. All this adds up to an honesty that daily social life never requires of us. Fiction demands it from the first tentative lines to the last touches of revision.

• • •

If you don't know what's next with one scene, work on another part of it. Everything you do to any part of it affects the whole of it, and working on another part might supply you with unexpected answers to the part that is troubling you. The thing to remember is that while they may read sequentially, with events held in suspension over the story's aboutness like a cable car over a river, they are quite often not written in sequence; it's all expression. Let it come as it wants to, and trust it to let you find your winding way to its secrets.

•  •  •

It is all *seeming*. It is all a *magic show*. Sleight of hand. It is contrivance, too. You conceal the artificialness of it, but remember that the first three letters of the word artificial are *a-r-l*. When you look at statue by Bernini or Michelangelo, you can not make your mind believe fully that you are looking at stone and not flesh, the artifice is so successful. So, as a writer, your job is to learn how to make the words produce a made human thing that convinces the reader in the same way the sculpture convinces the onlooker: by involving the reader's senses, and maintaining the living dream on the inside of his head. About your vision, or your grand theme—forget all that. Write about what matters deeply to you, what moves you, what frightens you to death, even what makes you angry or sorry, but do it with the viscera, the nerve-endings, get into it beyond your opinions about it and beyond what you think you think—beyond what you thought you knew—about it, and be *clear*, make it count in the reader's nerve-endings. And everything else will take care of itself.

•  •  •

Participate with Richard Bausch in an ongoing conversation about writing. Visit www.facebook.com/RichardBauschWriter.

Remember that in the essay called "Writing About Fiction" there was mention of criticism as an ongoing polite "conversation" about various aspects or examples of the form. Here are some examples of that great conversation, several from practicing short-story writers whose work is included in this anthology. These commentaries and reviews range from simple remarks about a story or a writer, to more detailed discussion concerning elements of criticism about a given story. Any of these pieces might serve as a departure point for both writing about fiction and simply discussing it.

## ANDREA BARRETT

### Willa Cather's "Paul's Case"

"His eyes were remarkable for a certain hysterical brilliancy"—there is Willa Cather's Paul, defiantly himself, easy enough not to like. Lonely, motherless, sporting his hopeless red carnation, he's cursed with a vivid imagination and a febrile sensibility, no apparent talent, and no one to show him the way. He's vain and shallow and oversensitive, sentimental and provincial despite his hatred for things provincial; he can't distinguish true art from false, and he confuses the aristocracy of money with that of the spirit.

Yet he speaks to me, as he does to many writers. Perhaps he is who we most dread being. He sees what we all see—that horrifying vision of the world as "Cordelia Street"—but he can do nothing with that knowledge. Through his eyes, that "highly respectable street, where all the houses were exactly alike, and where business men of moderate means begot and reared large families of children" becomes an increasingly potent symbol for the aspects of bourgeois life that an adolescent, or an artist, might despise. Those respectable beds and kitchen odors and smug, pot-bellied householders; the endless chatter of getting and spending and the swarms of children doomed to reproduce their parents' lives exactly—those are what Paul fights, and flees. When his attempt to build another life fails, what he feels is "the old depression exaggerated; all the world had become Cordelia Street."

Another character might have made something from that disgust and despair. Paul makes what he can, within his limitations, with the materials he has at hand. If he can't make art, and can only buy what he desires for a few days, with stolen money: still he can make of his life an artful (if wasteful and violent) shape. And so he does.

I love Cather's astonishing, painful, truthful rendition of Paul's flawed being; I love the story's economy, its swift deep descriptions, and its concentration on Paul's powerful longing for Paradise. If it's a flawed Paradise, misconceived from tawdry elements, misunderstood in its very nature—still it is Paradise to him. That drive toward transformation, that falling into fate, is what makes the story so moving: along with our simultaneous understanding that the narrowness of Paul's surroundings and upbringing has caused him to hurl himself away.

### RICHARD BAUSCH

#### Anton Chekhov's "Gusev"

The unusual thing about this story—even as a story of Chekhov's—is its point of view: the radical way it shifts in the last paragraphs, from the limited omniscience of Gusev's consciousness, to a kind of omniscience that includes even the sea and the sky. The way it leaves the province of human thought and action, as Gusev is dropped into the ocean, and enters the animal kingdom. The pilot fish are "in ecstasy," and the shark "languidly opens its jaws with two rows of teeth." The sailcloth that contains Gusev is torn open, the gridiron that was to carry him to the bottom of the sea falls out, and "frightens" the pilot fish. All of this after we have been privy to Gusev's dreams of home, his frustrations with his fellow passengers, his delirium.

Those dreams, his present life as a sick man returning with other sick men to the motherland, a passenger among other passengers, who argue and contend with each other and express strong opinions and speculations about the fate of all of them—this is all delivered with such acute specificity, such fidelity to objects and shapes, personalities and appearances, that we are drawn into it completely: real things in a real world, the palpable world, Gusev's personal life as he sees it in memory and fever:

> Gusev...pictures an immense pond covered with drifts. On one side of the pond is the brick-colored building of the pottery with a tall chimney and clouds of black smoke; on the other side is a village. His brother Alexey drives out of the fifth yard from the end in a sleigh; behind him sits his little son Vanka in big felt boots, and his little girl Akulka also wearing felt boots. Alexey has had a drop, Vanka is laughing, Akulka can't be seen, she is muffled up.... Gusev's thoughts abruptly break off and suddenly without rhyme or reason the pond is replaced by a huge bull's head without eyes, and the horse and sleigh are no longer going straight ahead but are whirling round and round, wrapped in black smoke.

We are deceived into thinking the story is about Gusev, because most of the world's good stories—indeed, most of its great ones, too—when they make such gestures, follow them out. Chekhov is using the particulars of this character to lead us into a perception we do not want: the enormity of the world and the universe, and our puny place in it. Yet the seeds of what he is about are in the very first line of the story: "It is already dark, it will soon be night." And there are things the men say to each other that carry the story toward its fantastic shift from the reasonable world of men in the hold of a ship to the unreasonable world itself, the unhuman world of matter:

> "One minute a vessel bumps into a fish, the next the wind breaks loose from its chain . . . Is the wind a beast that it breaks loose from its chain? . . . One must have one's head on one's shoulders and reason it out. You have no sense."

When Gusev dies, Chekhov doesn't even mention it. We are told that he sleeps for two days and that at noon on the third day two sailors come and carry him up on deck, where he is wrapped in sailcloth, with two gridirons for weight; they pray over him, and he is dropped over-board, "plop!" into the sea. And the point of view continues to move from him, like a movie camera backing away to an enormous distance. As he performs this feat, Chekhov ends up using an antique literary device, *personification*, which modern writers discarded long ago, and which one of the characters in this very story has questioned ("Is the wind a beast that breaks loose from its chain?") in that astonishing last paragraph, the ocean *looks* at the sky, it actually *frowns*. "But soon it, too, takes on tender, joyous, passionate colors for which it is hard to find a name in the language of man." A modern reader, coming upon this last line, might feel as if an amateur had written it, were it not for the power and richness of detail that precedes it and the turn it makes on what has been, after all, the story of one humble man's death.

There is no more audacious or shocking short story in the world, and it is very great writing indeed, for although it does express, with what is the equivalent of a jolt to the nervous system, the frailty of human life and hope, it also lends this one man's death a strange dignity, even a majesty, in the middle of the tremendous indignity of dying in the hold of a steamer, at sea, among strangers.

## FREDERICK BUSCH

### Ernest Hemingway's "Hills Like White Elephants"

It's the story to which I send students who want to learn how to write dialogue, and it's the story to which I return when I want to read about selfishness, disputation, and the fragility of the imagination. In this story, the imagination—the ability to see in metaphors, as opposed to the strength that crushes them, that insists on seeing, say, a hill as a hill and as nothing else—is linked, in its pregnancy, to the body of a pregnant woman. Her lover or husband wants the fetus aborted, and she wants to keep him. He will win.

We have just seen the Spanish countryside: the hills "were white in the sun and the country was brown and dry." But she sees the landscape this way: "They look like white elephants." He replies, with the bullying facticity of a country-club Babbit, that he's never seen one, and they proceed to squabble. Eventually, she dismantles her vision in an effort to win his approval. "They don't really look like white elephants," she explains, "I just meant the coloring of their skin through the trees."

But the hills, and her analogy, bear the weight of their real subject—her will, and her body, which Hemingway sets in opposition to her lover's plans for her body in spite of her will. When he stands in the bar, he notices the waiting passengers: "They are all waiting reasonably for the train." She, then, is not waiting "reasonably"; she wants them to live with regard for one another and in such a way that "if I say things are like white elephants . . . you'll like it." He swears that he does, that he will; but you know that he won't, for his notion of behaving "reasonably" has to do with pleasure, with self-aggrandizement, but not with birth of any sort.

He becomes a force for death as she, now wooing him, buries her way of seeing as she will bury her child. He asks if she feels "better," as if the way one
viewed the world were an illness, or a misbehavior, from which one recovers.
And she cooperates, betraying herself, to reply in the terms he has dictated:
"There's nothing wrong with me," she says. Imagination and the pulse of life
are "wrong," or are an illness, a deviation from his definition of health. "I feel
fine," she lies.

We can feel the energy of coercion and the weight of despair in the awful
white spaces that separate the lines, the paragraphs, the words.

### STANLEY CORNGOLD

*Kafka's* The Metamorphosis: *Metamorphosis of the Metaphor*[1]

> What is literature? Where does it come from? What use is
> it? What questionable things! Add to this questionableness
> the further questionableness of what you say, and what you
> get is a monstrosity.
>
> FRANZ KAFKA, *Dearest Father*

To judge from its critical reception, Franz Kafka's *The Metamorphosis* (*Die Ver-
wandlung*) is the most haunting and universal of all his stories, and yet Kafka
never claimed for it any special distinction. He never, for example, accorded it
the importance he reserved for "The Judgment," a work it resembles but which
it surpasses in depth and scope.[2] On the morning of September 23, 1912, after
the night he spent composing "The Judgment," Kafka, with a fine elation,
wrote in his diary: "Only *in this way* can writing be done, only with such coherence, with such a complete opening out of the body and the soul." But throughout the period of the composition of *The Metamorphosis*—from November 17 to
December 7, 1912—and until the beginning of the new year, his diary does
not show an entry of any kind; and when it resumes on February 11, 1913, it is
with an interpretation not of *The Metamorphosis* but of "The Judgment." The
diary does finally acknowledge the new story, almost a year after its composition, with this remark: "I have been reading *The Metamorphosis* at home, and
I find it bad."

Kafka was especially disappointed with the conclusion of the story. On
January 19, 1914, he wrote, "Great antipathy to *The Metamorphosis*. Unreadable
ending," and he blamed the botched conclusion on a business trip he was
obliged to make just as he was well advanced into the piece. His annoyance
and remorse at having to interrupt his work is vivid in the letters written at
the time to his fiancée, Felice Bauer. These letters reveal Kafka's moods all
during the composition of the story—moods almost entirely negative. The
story originates "during my misery in bed and oppresses me with inmost

---

**1.** Adapted from *Franz Kafka: The Necessity of Form* (Ithaca: Cornell, 1988) 47–80 (1970, rev. 1986).
**2.** Elias Canetti wrote: "In *The Metamorphosis* Kafka reached the height of his mastery: he wrote something which he could never surpass, because there is nothing which *The Metamorphosis* could be surpassed
by—one of the few great, perfect poetic works of this century" (*Der andere Prozeß: Kafkas Briefe an Felice*
[Munich: Hanser, 1969], pp. 22–23).

intensity" [*innerlichst bedrängt*]." The tonality of the piece appears again as "despair" and "monotony." On November 23 the story is said to be "a little horrible [*fürchterlich*]"; a day later, "exceptionally repulsive." A trace of liking and concern for *The Metamorphosis* appears in a later letter: "It's a pity that in many passages of the story my states of exhaustion and other interruptions and extraneous worries are clearly inscribed [*eingezeichnet*]; it could certainly have been done more purely [*reiner*]; this can be seen precisely from the charming [*süße*] pages." But by this time Kafka has begun to consider *The Metamorphosis* more and more an interruption of the writing of the uncompleted novel that was to become *Amerika*. Finally, on the morning of December 7, he states the complaint that will recur: "My little story is finished, but today's ending does not make me happy at all; it really could have been better, no doubt about that."

Kafka's own sense of *The Metamorphosis* compels us to consider the work essentially unfinished. The interruptions that set in so frequently past the midpoint of the story tend to shift the weight of its significance back toward its beginning. This view draws support from other evidence establishing what might be termed the general and fundamental priority of the beginning in Kafka's works. One thinks of the innumerable openings to stories scattered throughout the diaries and notebooks, suddenly appearing and as swiftly vanishing, leaving undeveloped the endless dialectical structures they contain. On October 16, 1921, Kafka explicitly invoked "the misery of having perpetually to begin, the lack of the illusion that anything is more than, or even as much as, a beginning." For Dieter Hasselblatt, Kafka's prose "is in flight from the beginning, it does not strive toward the end: *initiofugal*, not final. And since it takes the impulse of its progression from what is set forth or what is just present at the outset, it cannot be completed. The end, the conclusion, is unimportant compared to the opening situation."[3]

One is directed, it would seem, by these empirical and theoretical considerations to formulate the overwhelming question of *The Metamorphosis* as the question of the meaning of its beginning. What fundamental intention inspires the opening sentence: "When Gregor Samsa woke up one morning from unsettling dreams, he found himself changed in his bed into a monstrous vermin [*ungeheueres Ungeziefer*]"? We shall do well to keep in mind, in the words of Edward Said, "the identity [of the beginning] as *radical* starting point; the intransitive and conceptual aspect, that which has no object but its own constant clarification."[4] Much of the action of *The Metamorphosis* consists of Kafka's attempt to come to terms with its beginning.

SUSAN DODD

*Eudora Welty's "A Worn Path"*

*But who is she when she's at home?* an Irish friend asks when I identify someone by name and occupation. Miss Eudora, no just-the-facts-ma'am kind of writer, has made it her serious lifelong business to let us in on just who her characters

3. Dieter Hasselblatt, *Zauber und Logik: Eine Kafka Studie* (Cologne: Verlag Wissenschaft und Politik), p. 61. 4. Edward Said, "Beginnings," *Salmagundi*, Fall 1968, p. 49.

are when they're at home. Has she ever done so more clearly, more beautifully, more *deeply* than with Phoenix Jackson?

"A Worn Path" is, on the face of it, a simple, straightforward story. If it were a picture hanging in a museum, the canvas would be of modest dimension, would stand for no ornate gilt frame making a spectacle of it. No call for a viewer's eye to dart about, sorting out the picture's "busyness." No, "A Worn Path" would simply pull you inside it, keep you there, and when you came back out you'd sense you'd been long gone and far.

Miss Eudora doesn't *tell* us, of course, who Phoenix Jackson is when she's at home. Instead, she sends us packing on a rough and gloried hike in the company of a woman at home in her own skin. Alone though she is, Phoenix goes utterly *accompanied:* the sounds and smells and sights, the very air, are her sidekicks. This old woman and her surroundings fit together in a natural and familiar embrace. We take measure of Phoenix Jackson not by how the world receives her (though that comes eventually), but by the very span of her as she throws herself open to the world. Her gaze is dead ahead, her risky traverse of the creek a parade march. Every obstacle comes in for back talk. Not even hallucination can scramble her sense of direction.

To read "A Worn Path" is to have the seams of one's soul let out. The story's compassion enlarges our own; that is its greatness. Its *writing* is what brings that about, though, word by single word. Words are what paint Phoenix alive for the eye: the red head rag and striped dress and the cane fashioned from an umbrella. Dwell on the plain and perfect accuracy of the verbs (she *switches at* the brush to *rouse up* any hiding things . . . something in the hill *pleads* she should stay). Study the scrupulous choice of adjectives: the *grave* and *persistent* noise of her cane tapping the frozen earth . . . and oh, those *frailest* ringlets of her still-black hair. Listen to the perfect pitch of the dialogue, how the sounds of the words linger, ever deepening, after the simple saying: *Now comes the trial.* And: *The time come around.* And: *This is what come to me to do.*

And sometime, maybe some morning when you can't think how to begin, trace the canny route of similes running through "A Worn Path." No sore thumbs sticking out here, only the ordinary landscape of a woman's life. But tucked in among the domestic details (shadows hanging like curtains, babies and clocks and laying hens) and the expected particulars of the natural world (birds and milkweed and mistletoe) come glimpses of a life lived on intimate terms with the whip's lash, the chain's drag, imagination's (or is it memory's?) all-too-ready reference to black bodies dismembered and maimed.

Long before we learn of the singular sorrow that awaits her at home, by such suggestive images are we given to know who Phoenix Jackson is there, to know *precisely.*

RICHARD FORD

*Bharati Mukherjee's "The Management of Grief"*

Bharati Mukherjee's "The Management of Grief" is a story of great intelligence, poignant surprise, and elegant simplicity. A jetliner has exploded over the seas off Ireland. All passengers are seemingly lost, including families of those characters who, as grieving survivors, populate the story—most prominently Mrs. Bhave, its narrator, who has lost her husband and two young sons. Dramatizing how these characters and Mrs. Bhave herself feel, express, and indeed manage their awful grief becomes the story's subject and its strategy for revealing those nuances of grief that ordinary experience does not alert us to (that it can be thrilling as well as defeating, for instance). And this also becomes the story's means of assuring us that grief can be withstood.

As in any story—great or otherwise—what provokes and surprises us, and what provides the reader's experience of its primary intellectual *ground*, is the writer's decision about which segment or segments of life to tell us and which to leave untold. Obviously this decision determines what is emphasized, and thus what our notice and curiosity will be sharpened to. Often in great stories, such as Mukherjee's, what is emphasized by being told is different from what conventional understanding has prepared us to believe is important. We admire writers who show us the world in this fresh way—show us what we did not expect to be important. And as we're shown the world newly, our awareness and appreciation of it are redeemed.

Indeed, in Mukherjee's story, human survivorship, the facing of grief, and the obligation to narrate one's stricken life in order to save it are depicted almost entirely separate from the terrible physical devastation—the plane crash—which might seem the indispensable dramatic element if we were to learn of the events in a news story or on TV. But grief, in Mukherjee's story, is experienced in its own vivid, intense, but nearly sealed realm. True, it is a force born of disaster, but in Mukherjee's fine vision, grief is best understood and complexly felt—and most hopefully accommodated—almost entirely by itself.

## ALLAN GURGANUS

### Stephen Crane's "The Open Boat"

Few people are inconvenienced by shipwrecks. And fiction faces problems even tougher than your average sailing accident: how to elevate an ordinary landlocked day—its carpooling, its comparison shopping—into drama as life-and-death urgent as all those sharks aimed openmouthed toward your little lifeboat.

Great fiction requires more skill and spirit than simply "writing up" some endured disaster. If that alone made for major works of art, *Titanic* survivors and the bombardiers over Hiroshima would be modern letters' ruling geniuses. Happily for us surburbanites and mall-rats, they are not.

(In a double-parked station wagon, one mom slumps, waiting till her daughter, fourteen, completes the hundredth lesson on a clarinet this same girl will, by age eighteen, have cleanly forgotten: now that takes heroism.)

Stephen Crane, a Methodist preacher's hell-raising youngest son, would die of tuberculosis before age twenty-nine. Weaned on the Bible he resisted, Crane still dragged that book's undertow—its ethics and solemn sweetness—into baseball parks, pool halls, battle zones, Manhattan's darkest slums. The boy compacted into his fraction of a life many an ancient mariner's reckless quest.

The first day of 1897, a young newspaper reporter, seeking stories from the Spanish-American War, boarded *The Commodore*, a Cuba-bound ship. Loaded with rifles, rebels, and ammo, the vessel ran aground, then set to sea anyway.

Mistake. A fast leak soon flooded the engine room. On deck, hysteria. One sailor fell to his knees before the captain, begging to be thrown overboard. Of our handsome correspondent, the captain would later say, "That man Crane is the spunkiest fellow out. . . . Many got sick but Crane was like an old sailor. . . . He was the first to volunteer to help. In the dinghy, he suggested putting up his overcoat for a sail. . . . He took his turn at the oars . . . he's a thoroughbred."

We now know that our narrative guide behaved well; we know he survived events not unlike those he shaped (that first week ashore) into "The Open Boat." But, how did young Stephen Crane transform this anecdotal mishap into a shape so fully mythic? Genius always helps. Crane bypasses the usual glamorous spectacle of a sinking ship; he understands which guys to include, and where to start his tale (40 percent of the way in). He riddles the raw experience with all five senses' awe.

"None of them knew the color of the sky." So our story begins, sensually, in living color, but with the horizon's usual twenty-twenty orientation suspended, withheld. We already feel adrift, hungry for news, eager for some fable's shoreline of hard-earned wisdom. Crane presents his voyage in prose as brisk and water-clear as superb journalism. And yet, the language of this preacher's kid (all those Sundays, he was listening to Dad) grows rhythmically fulfilling and stained-glass pure as the King James Bible. Crane renders his waterlogged survivors as Everymen, while providing just enough identity to make each fellow count.

A favorite nineteenth-century theme pitted brutal Nature against innocent Mankind. Sir Edwin Landseer, the period's best-loved animal painter, depicted polar bears patrolling icy shipwrecks, seeking tasty human victims. What makes Crane's account so everlastingly contemporary? His natural world is not personified—not moralistically adjudged "red in tooth and claw" as Tennyson, Queen Victoria's favorite poet, quaintly described nature's simple ruthlessness. Instead, Crane's ocean seems amoral, as terrifyingly cool and neutral as cyberspace itself. His castaways might be unmoored shuttle astronauts—spun past voice range of any Mission Control—strangers adrift in some nebula unmapped. Their only true relation now is to themselves and to each other. The whole harsh universe seems abruptly masterminded as a great single theological test.

(Hemingway's telegraphic style and man-of-action stance is so prefigured in Crane, it looks cribbed. Hemingway's entire technique and subject matter might be summarized in one sentence written two years before his birth: "A night on the sea in an open boat is a long night.")

Crane's narrative, set down three years before 1900, prophesied and helped found the twentieth century's great theme: how the human psyche, having conquered so much of nature, finally settles into cannibalizing itself. How can sharks ever really scare a species that invented the Holocaust?

As if to predict twentieth-century powerlessness by eliminating the nineteenth century's pride in capacity, Stephen Crane deletes from the record his actual personal heroism.

When the real dinghy, sweeping ashore off Daytona, Florida, capsized, it crushed the first mate. Crane, trying to swim and save this man, sacrificed to the Atlantic his own heavy money belt; it had been laden with gold enough to see him through a long stay in Cuba. Despite his efforts, the other sailor drowned. Next day's newspaper, bearing all the vainglory of its age, read, "YOUNG NEW YORK WRITER ASTONISHED THE SEA DOGS BY HIS COURAGE IN THE FACE OF DEATH." This headline sounds as dated and comically old-fashioned as Crane's fiction still feels briny and immediate, as adaptable and oddly futuristic as the Bible itself.

What twenty-six-year-old man could bear—in his own tale of high-sea adventure—to hide his singular and noble acts? Answer: A great artist.

Crane neutralizes his own crazy physical courage to make room in his open boat for the rest of us sensible cowards. He admits mainly to his solidarity with others and his own quiet terror. Our narrator finally accepts the "serenity of nature amid the struggle of the individual. . . . She did not seem cruel to him then, nor beneficent, nor treacherous, nor wise. But she was indifferent, flatly indifferent."

How to lend heroism to an undifferentiated, carpooling weekday ashore? And how to render as natural, psychological, almost routine, some event harrowing and extreme as a shipwreck?

For all writers and readers, these constitute literature's twin capitals. What percentage of the mundane, how much of the heroic, can we honorably cargo from one into the other, and back and forth all day? Great works of art make peril at sea feel familiar as flossing; they can reveal one mom's carpooling to be headline worthy, brave, and pirate fierce.

Between these harbors, Port Heroic and Bay Mundane, we all commute. Scared to death ourselves, we still guard and reassure each another. Like Crane, we make a mainsail of our overcoat. And somehow—in our art and our acts—we briefly outwit the depths' indifference. Through almost any setback, we somehow tell, tell, tell ourselves to go ahead and row, row, row our little boat.

## BARRY HANNAH

### *Joseph Conrad's* Heart of Darkness

There were plenty of nineteenth-century authors to study but just a handful of real writers, among whom Joseph Conrad stood tallest, to my mind. High adventure, high art, high wisdom. In fact, he belongs to the Modernists of our times, with their tentative connection to this earth and its events. The narrator of Modernist fiction is characteristically sick, diminished, or shocked, barely able to express the special grief and ecstasies of our century, which Milan Kundera has aptly described as one of "massacres and optimism." He might have been speaking directly of "Heart of Darkness," which sounds often like an organ played by a malaria victim—fulsome, shrill, then muffled, then suddenly lucid. Marlow's conclusions on Kurtz seem fevered and strange, very. For he calls Kurtz's final insight "a victory." Would we speak of Hitler, Stalin, or Pol Pot as *victorious* had they uttered "the horror, the horror"—at last seeing it all clear—at the end of their lives? How happy for them as they move on in their growth.

T. S. Eliot, the High Modernist, might enlist "Mistah Kurtz—he dead" as a rubric for the Hollow Man, but the horror was that Kurtz was *not* hollow. He was cultured (he painted), efficient, a man of "ideas." Conrad tells us all Europe had gone into his making. And he becomes a genocidal, homicidal maniac, once threatening to kill even his young ragtag Russian sycophant but settling for merely driving him mad—"He showed me love!" (cf. the Hale-Bopp comet cult in San Diego at the end of the twentieth century).

The best of Modernism's tales seem fuller than rational linear discourse. Conrad's best forms proceed from the gut and head, as all good experimental writing does (see Samuel Beckett, who told Harold Pinter that the only form in his work was that of a *scream*). They are not brain work merely, as post-Modernists might have it. Conrad hardly ever told a tale that didn't seem urgent and necessary. In this he ranks with Twain and Dostoevsky, two other great natural writers of the nineteenth century. His themes were honor, sacrifice, grace, duty, shame, greed, and redemption. A Pole, he was a ship's captain who began writing at age thirty-two, in his third language, English. His parents perished in revolutionary action for Poland when he was a child, and he experienced dark depressions all his life. In his early twenties he had a brush with suicide. We might think of him finding family on the seas. The sea is solid and sweet: "The voice of the surf heard now and then was a positive pleasure, like the speech of a brother." But the riverside Congo is vicious and grim: "The air was warm, thick, heavy, sluggish. There was no joy in the brilliance of sunshine." He reports from a trip that almost killed him, a journey into the heart of the land the Belgians "settled" at a cost of three million native lives. He, like Marlow, changed from a young adventurer to the Ancient Mariner, unable to quit his tale, even though—ever the gentleman—Marlow lies about its end to the heartbroken fiancée of Kurtz. Women, Marlow says, "can't handle the truth." The deeper fact is Marlow is not certain yet what his tale means either. He himself is stricken with contagious moral sickness, and behaves like a fever patient wandering the halls of London. Elliptical, oblique, nearly opaque often, his measured raving reveals only glances of the truth, which is what the Modernist claims is all we ever get.

Rimbaud, the proto-Modernist, surrendered his talent to posterity and quit poetry at age twenty-one, then plunged into North Africa, a money belt constantly around his ribs, and sank into vilest commerce, dying early of fever. A bundle of poems of Rimbaud, "Heart of Darkness," *The Sound and the Fury, The Stranger*—one could claim a pocket education in Modernism with knowledge of these four works. It is significant, though probably not deeply important, that Africa figures as a source in all of the prose. (Dilsey in Faulkner's work, transported from Africa to no paradise in Oxford, Mississippi, is the Christian ballast for the degenerate white Compsons.) Marlow may have found Rimbaud in the person of the raving harlequin who is the acolyte of Kurtz. Conrad disliked Russians, but this young man has Marlow's sympathy. He worshiped England and English, lucky for us. But better for the world, his Africa, almost silent, always dark, was revealed as a holocaust brought in by Europe, the results of which continue in modern Rwanda at century's end. Conrad may not be the fullest humanitarian required by contemporary black intellectuals, but he was the best artist of his day to even glance at the Heart of Darkness that lurked in Western Colonial powers.

We recall the little French ship lobbing shells into the continent of Africa, as Marlow reports early on in the adventure. A silly and ridiculous and puny exercise for the viewer—say we on the television side of the "conflict"—but not to the target of the shells in, and for whom they are all the Armageddon ever predicted. As we get in close to the country, down the sick regions and past the bodies, Conrad gives us one of the most memorable hells of our era.

## EDWARD P. JONES
### *Frank O'Connor's "Guests of the Nation"*

I discovered "Guests of the Nation" some twenty-five years ago at a time when I was—in a creative and just about every other way—young and naive enough to hope that Frank O'Connor would manage some literary sleight of hand to prevent what even the first pages of the story conveyed to me was inevitable. I was never so naive, however, as not to understand that I had come upon a treasure, a small guide of five pages or so to the way I wanted eventually to begin crafting things.

Stories, that me-of-twenty-five-years-ago was beginning to learn, should strive to illuminate that moment or those moments, however grand, however seemingly insignificant, in a character's life when the earth shifts and the world is forever different: Humpty Dumpty falls off the wall reaching for a butterfly and the inconsolable king forsakes his queen and ultimately exhausts all his power in a hopeless effort to put his best friend back together again. . . . I had read very good stories before "Guests of the Nation," but nothing had for a while—and few stories since have—showed what I was coming to believe stories should be.

I go back to the story at least once each year to rediscover the wonders I was able to appreciate after that first, breathless reading: the way, for example, O'Connor seems to dash through the events in the first three sections, then slows down in the last section—which is about twice as long as each of the previous sections—to a nearly minute-by-minute telling of the last hours in the Englishmen's lives.

There is, as well, an appreciation of the things it was almost too easy to overlook with the thunder of the ending: the way O'Connor, in a few strokes, aims to humanize Jeremiah Donovan, who undeservedly lives in some read- ers' minds as the villain. "He reddened when you talked to him, . . . looking down at his big farmer's feet. Noble and me used to make fun of his broad accent, because we were from the town." The narrator is pulled down just a bit here. And Bonaparte, doing his "duty," falls even farther when he puts the second bullet in his friend's head.

But perhaps the most important reason I am compelled to reread "Guests of the Nation" is that sense of being a witness as the earth shifts for Bonaparte and he is being re-created, even as his friends, in Noble's words, are "stiffening" in that "little patch of bog." Even twenty-five years later, the story continues to unfold for me with a monstrous inevitability that begins with the coziness of the first paragraph when Belcher "shifts his long legs out of the ashes." Even twenty-five years and dozens of readings later, the story continues to amaze and move me, perhaps because, given the world I grew into, it is so inevitable.

## C. C. LOOMIS JR.

### Structure and Sympathy in Joyce's "The Dead"[5]

James Joyce's "The Dead" culminates in Gabriel Conroy's timeless moment of almost supreme vision. The fragments of his life's experience, of the epitomizing experiences of one evening in particular, are fused together into a whole: "self-bounded and self-contained upon the immeasurable background of space and time."[6] Initiated by a moment of deep, if localized, sympathy, his vision and his sympathy expand together to include not only himself, Gretta, and his aunts, but all Ireland, and, with the words "all the living and the dead," all humanity.

Gabriel's epiphany manifests Joyce's fundamental belief that true, objective perception will lead to true, objective sympathy; such perception and such sympathy, however, ultimately defy intellectual analysis. Joyce carefully avoids abstract definition of Gabriel's vision by embodying it within the story's central symbol: the snow, which becomes paradoxically warm in the moment of vision, through which Gabriel at long last feels the deeply unifying bond of common mortality.

Gabriel's experience is intellectual only at that level on which intellect and emotional intuition blend, and the full power of the story can be apprehended by the reader only if he sympathetically shares the experience with Gabriel. As understanding of himself, then of his world, then of humanity floods Gabriel, so understanding of Gabriel, his world, and humanity in terms of the story floods the reader. The understanding in both cases is largely emotional and intuitive; intellectual analysis of the snow symbol, however successful, leaves a large surplus of emotion unexplained.

Therefore, Joyce had to generate increasing reader-sympathy as he approached the vision, but this sympathy could not be generated by complete reader-identification with Gabriel. If the reader identifies himself unreservedly with Gabriel in the first ninety per cent of the story, he will lose that critical insight into him which is necessary for full apprehension of his vision. It is, after all, Gabriel's vision, and there is no little irony in this fact. The vision is in sharp contrast with his previous view of the world: in fact, it literally opens a new world to him. If the reader identifies himself uncritically with Gabriel at any point in the story, he is liable to miss those very shortcomings which make the vision meaningful. Yet, in the actual moments of vision, the reader must share Gabriel's view; in a real sense, he must identify himself with Gabriel: "feel with" him.

Joyce, therefore, had to create sympathy without encouraging the reader to a blind, uncritical identification. One aspect of his solution to this problem is a monument to his genius. In the main body of the story, while he is constantly dropping meaningful, often semi-symbolic details which deepen the gulf between the reader and Gabriel, he is also generating what can best be called "aesthetic sympathy"; by the very structure of the story, he increasingly pulls the reader into the story.

---

5. From *PMLA*, March 1960.   6. James Joyce, *A Portrait of the Artist as a Young Man* (New York: Modern Library, 1928), p. 249. See also Irene Hendry, "Joyce's Epiphanies" in *Critiques and Essays on Modern Fiction*, ed. John W. Aldridge (New York: Ronald Press, 1952), p. 129.

"The Dead" can be divided, not arbitrarily, into five sections: the *musicale*, the dinner, the farewells and the drive to the hotel, the scene between Gabriel and Gretta in their room, and, finally, the vision itself. A few of these sections are separated by a time lapse, a few flow smoothly into one another; in all cases, however, the reader is aware of a slight "shifting of gears" between sections.

These sections become shorter as the story progresses. The effect of this constant shortening of scenes, together with a constant speeding up in the narrative line, is an almost constant increase of pace. Within each of the sections, Joyce carefully builds up to a climax, then slackens the pace slightly at the beginning of the next section as he begins to build up to a new climax. The pace in the sections is progressively more rapid, however, partially because of the cumulative effect of the narrative. As the story progresses, more things happen in less time.

The effect of increasing pace is complemented and strengthened by another structural aspect of the story. As the pace increases, the focus narrows. The constantly narrowing focus and the constantly increasing pace complement one another and act to pull the reader into the story. He is caught up in a whirlpool movement, ever-narrowing, ever-faster.

There is much activity in the first part of "The Dead," but the activity is diffuse and the effect is not of great pace. We are given a slightly confused, overall picture of activity: dancing, drinking, singing, chatter. Characters are introduced one after another: Lily, Gabriel, Gretta, the Misses Morkan, Mary Jane, Mr. Browne, Freddy Malins and his mother, Miss Ivors, and so on. Our scope is broad and general. Increasingly, Gabriel becomes our mode of consciousness, but he himself cannot assimilate all the activity. He retreats, isolates himself within his deep but insecure egotism. Rationalizing that "their grade of culture differed from his," he bides his time until dinner, when he knows he will be the center of all eyes.

In this first section, it is interesting to note how Joyce gives us Gabriel's point of view without compromising his own fundamental objectivity; even though we see largely through Gabriel's "delicate and restless" eyes, we nevertheless become increasingly aware of his character, of his defensive feelings of intellectual and social superiority in particular. His eyes are offended by the glittering, waxed floors, his ears by the "indelicate clattering" of the dancers, his intellect by all those present, particularly Miss Ivors, who "has a crow to pluck" with him, and constitutes a threat to his shaky feelings of superiority. His attitude can best be summed up by his reflection, ironic and revealing in view of the toast to come, that his aunts are "only two ignorant old women." Such comments are introduced quietly, but they serve to keep the reader from identifying himself too wholeheartedly with Gabriel. We feel with him to a degree even in these early sections of the story, but our sympathy is seriously reserved and qualified.[7]

In the second section, our focus narrows to the dinner table, and to a few characters at it; the others are blurred in the background. Tension about Gabriel's toast has been built up in the first section; now the pace increases as this particular tension is relieved. The toast, hypocritical and condescending, makes us further aware of Gabriel's isolation from those around him.

---

7. For an enlightening discussion of the problem of reader-identification and "extraordinary perspective" in 19th- and 20th-century literature, see R. W. Langbaum, *The Poetry of Experience* (New York: Random House, 1957).

The pace in this scene is considerably more rapid than in the first. It builds up to the climax, the toast, in a few brief pages; then there is a slackening with the applause and singing.

There is a time-lapse between the conclusion of the toast and the next section; Joyce seems to shift to a higher range. From this point to the moment of vision, the pace increases and the focus narrows almost geometrically.

The shouts and laughter of the departure signal the end of the party, but are counter-balanced by the fine, almost silent tableau of Gabriel watching Gretta on the staircase. Our focus is beginning to narrow down to these two main characters. Gretta has been deliberately held in the background until this moment; now she emerges.

The repeated goodnights and the noisy trip through silent, snow-blanketed Dublin are given increased pace through Gabriel's increasing lust; the pace becomes the pace of "the blood bounding along his veins" and the "thoughts rioting through his brain." The fires of this lust begin to thaw the almost life-deep frost of his self-consciousness. The superiority and self-delusion are still dominant: there is much irony in his remembering "their moments of ecstasy," for his lust is far from ecstatic love. It is, however, the first step toward the moment of objective vision.

We are now approaching the still center of the increasingly rapid, increasingly narrow whirlpool. The scene in the hotel room between Gabriel and Gretta takes up only a few brief minutes, but in these minutes much happens. Gabriel "discovers" Gretta: suddenly she becomes more than a mere appendage to his ego. He discovers himself, in a mirror. His lust turns to anger, then his anger to humility. Gretta, caught up in her memories of the "boy in the gasworks," Michael Furey, is not even aware of his presence. "A shameful consciousness of his own person assailed him. He saw himself as a ludicrous figure, acting as a pennyboy for his aunts, a nervous well-meaning sentimentalist, orating to vulgarians and idealising his own clownish lusts, the pitiable fatuous fellow he had caught a glimpse of in the mirror."

The peak of intensity is reached with Gretta's "O, the day I heard that, that he was dead." She collapses on the bed, sobbing, and Gabriel, quietly, shyly, retires to the window. At this moment, Joyce creates another time-lapse to lead into the vision itself.

Until this moment, the pace has increased and the focus has narrowed almost constantly. Now Joyce does something remarkable and effective: he reverses the process. In doing so, he makes the structure of the story not only useful as a means of generating an "aesthetic sympathy" (perhaps "empathy" with its impersonal connotations would be a more accurate word), but also makes it reinforce the ultimate emotional-intellectual meaning of the vision itself.[8]

---

8. William T. Noon, S.J., in *Joyce and Aquinas* (New Haven: Yale University Press, 1957), pp. 84–85, places Gabriel's epiphany at "the moment when the full impact of Gretta's disclosure of her secret strikes him": before the snow image of the closing paragraphs. Father Noon separates Gabriel's moment of vision from the reader's, and seems to state that the snow image is for the reader's enlightenment, not Gabriel's. I agree with Father Noon that the reader cannot possibly apprehend the depth of Gabriel's sudden sympathy with Gretta until Joyce gives him the closing image, but I do not believe that Gabriel's own vision is complete until this final image; the epiphany begins with his sympathy for Gretta, but is not complete, because not universal, until he "heard the snow falling faintly through the universe."

Pace simply ceases to exist in the vision, and, of course, this is fitting. We are in an essentially timeless world at this point; true, the vision involves time and mortality, but it is timeless time and eternal mortality, man's endless fate as man. The snow "falling faintly through the universe" measures absolute, not relative time. The impact of this sudden cessation of pace on the reader is great; in fact, it parallels the impact on Gabriel himself. With this sudden structural change, we share Gabriel's vision; we do not merely analyze it.

Gabriel's vision begins with Gretta; it is narrow in focus. The whole story has led us down to this narrow focus. Now, as he does with pace, Joyce reverses the process. As the vision progresses toward the ultimate image of the snow falling through the universe, the focus broadens, from Gretta, to his aunts, to himself, to Ireland, to "the universe." Time and space are telescoped in the final words of the story: The snow falls on "all the living and the dead."

"The Dead" follows a logical pattern; we move from the general to the particular, then to a final universal. We see Gabriel's world generally; then we focus down to the particular, and from the combination of the general and particular we are given a universal symbol in the vision itself.

The logic of "The Dead," however, is not the logic of mere intellect; it is the logic which exists on a plane where intellectual perception and emotional intuition, form and content, blend.


### LEO MARX

#### Melville's Parable of the Walls[9]

> Dead,
> 25. Of a wall . . . : Unbroken, unrelieved by breaks or
> interruptions; absolutely uniform and continuous.
> —*New English Dictionary*

In the spring of 1851, while still at work on *Moby Dick*, Herman Melville wrote his celebrated "dollars damn me" letter to Hawthorne:

> In a week or so, I go to New York, to bury myself in a third-story room, and work and slave on my "Whale" while it is driving through the press. *That* is the only way I can finish it now—I am so pulled hither and thither by circumstances. The calm, the coolness, the silent grass-growing mood in which a man *ought* always to compose,—that, I fear, can seldom be mine. Dollars damn me. . . . My dear Sir, a presentiment is on me,—I shall at last be worn out and perish. . . . What I feel most moved to write, that is banned,—it will not pay. Yet, altogether, write the *other* way I cannot.

He went on and wrote the "Whale" as he felt moved to write it; the public was apathetic and most critics were cool. Nevertheless Melville stubbornly refused to return to the *other* way, to his more successful earlier modes, the South Sea

---

**9.** First published in the *Sewanee Review* 61.4 (Autumn 1953).

romance and the travel narrative. In 1852 he published *Pierre*, a novel even more certain not to be popular. And this time the critics were vehemently hostile. Then, the following year, Melville turned to shorter fiction. "Bartleby, the Scrivener," the first of his stories, dealt with a problem unmistakably like the one Melville had described to Hawthorne.

There are excellent reasons for reading "Bartleby" as a parable having to do with Melville's own fate as a writer. To begin with, the story *is* about a kind of writer, a "copyist" in a Wall Street lawyer's office. Furthermore, the copyist is a man who obstinately refuses to go on doing the sort of writing demanded of him. Under the circumstances there can be little doubt about the connection between Bartleby's dilemma and Melville's own. Although some critics have noted the autobiographical relevance of this facet of the story, a close examination of the parable reveals a more detailed parallel with Melville's situation than has been suggested.[1] In fact the theme itself can be described in a way which at once establishes a more precise relation. "Bartleby" is not only about a writer who refuses to conform to the demands of society, but it is, more relevantly, about a writer who foresakes conventional modes because of an irresistible preoccupation with the most baffling philosophical questions. This shift of Bartleby's attention is the symbolic equivalent of Melville's own shift of interest between *Typee* and *Moby Dick*. And it is significant that Melville's story, read in this light, does not by any means proclaim the desirability of the change. It was written in a time of deep hopelessness, and as I shall attempt to show, it reflects Melville's doubts about the value of his recent work.

Indeed, if I am correct about what this parable means, it has immense importance, for it provides the most explicit and mercilessly self-critical statement of his own dilemma that Melville has left us. Perhaps it is because "Bartleby" reveals so much of his situation that Melville took such extraordinary pains to mask its meaning. This may explain why he chose to rely upon symbols which derive from his earlier work, and to handle them with so light a touch that only the reader who comes to the story after an immersion in the other novels can be expected to see how much is being said here. Whatever Melville's motive may have been, I believe it may legitimately be accounted a grave defect of the parable that we must go back to *Typee* and *Moby Dick* and *Pierre* for the clues to its meaning. It is as if Melville had decided that the only adequate test of a reader's qualifications for sharing so damaging a self-revelation was a thorough reading of his own work.

• • •

Among the countless imaginative statements of the artist's problems in modern literature, "Bartleby" is exceptional in its sympathy and hope for the average man, and in the severity of its treatment of the artist. This is particularly remarkable when we consider the seriousness of the rebuffs Melville had so recently been given by his contemporaries. But nothing, he is saying, may

1. The most interesting interpretations of the story are those of Richard Chase and Newton Arvin. Chase stresses the social implications of the parable in his *Herman Melville, A Critical Study* (New York, 1949), pp. 143–149. Arvin describes "Bartleby" as a "wonderfully intuitive study in what would now be called schizophrenia . . ." in his *Herman Melville* (New York, 1950), pp. 240–242. Neither Chase nor Arvin makes a detailed analysis of the symbolism of the walls. E. S. Oliver has written of the tale as embodying Thoreau's political ideas in "A Second Look at 'Bartleby'," *College English* (May, 1945), 431–439.

be allowed to relieve the writer of his obligations to mankind. If he forgets humanity, as Bartleby did, his art will die, and so will he. The lawyer, realizing this, at the last moment couples Bartleby's name with that of humanity itself. The fate of the artist is inseparable from that of all men. The eerie story of Bartleby is a compassionate rebuke to the self-absorption of the artist, and so a plea that he devote himself to keeping strong his bonds with the rest of mankind.

• • •

"Bartleby the Scrivener" is a counter-statement to the large and ever-growing canon of "ordealist" interpretations of the situation of the modern writer.

GARY SAUL MORSON

*The Reader as Voyeur: Tolstoi and the Poetics of Didactic Fiction*[2]

> Of course, I myself have made up just now all the things you say . . . can you really be so credulous as to think that I will print all this and give it to you to read, too? . . . I shall never have readers.
>
> *Notes from Underground*

Readers of Russian fiction accede with special haste to Stendhal's dictum that "politics in a work of literature is like a pistol shot in the middle of a concert, something loud and vulgar, and yet a thing to which it is not possible to refuse one's attention."[3] There are countless histories of Russian literature that divide its authors and critics into two irreconcilable camps, those who judge art "in its own terms" and those who insist on a moralistic or political framework external to art. The nihilist's assertion that boots are more important than Shakespeare, Maiakovskii's self-destructive pledge to step on the throat of his song, Turgenev's plea to Tolstoi to remain a belles-lettrist and leave religion to the church—these are the usual landmarks in the history of Russian literature. Attempts to save radical critics like Belinskii from opprobrium usually take the form of arguing that he was not so Stalinist as the Stalinists say; when we praise the late Tolstoi we marvel at the great art he was able to produce *in spite of* his moralistic strictures.

It is an account on which the new critics and the Soviets can agree, although their values are reversed. And yet it is possible that both sides misstate the question. It is simply inappropriate to ask whether great art *can be* didactic; the fact is, that it often is. I do not know many scholars, whether formalists or new critics, who would deny *The Possessed* and *The Death of Ivan Il'ich* the status of "great literature"; and to argue that they are such despite their didacticism is simply to force reality into a theoretical mold. I simply cannot imagine what would be left of *The Death of Ivan Il'ich* or *The Kreutzer Sonata* without their moralism: perhaps something like the *War and Peace* Percy Lubbock wished Tolstoi had written—without the lectures on history and the polemical story

**2.** From *Canadian-American Slavic Studies*, 12. No. 4 (Winter 1978), 465–480.   **3.** I am not so much citing Stendhal as Irving Howe citing Stendhal, in *Politics and the Novel* (New York: Avon, 1970), p. 17. Howe asks shrewdly: "Once the pistol is fired, what happens to the music? Can the noise of the interruption ever become part of the performance? When is the interruption welcome and when is it resented?"

of Napoleon. The right question, however, should not be *whether* great art can be didactic, but *how* it can be didactic; what we need (and what formalism and new criticism have prevented us from finding) is a poetics of instruction. Only then can we begin to appreciate Russian literature on its own terms.

## EDGAR ALLAN POE

### Review of Hawthorne's Twice-Told Tales[4]

Were we called upon however to designate that class of composition which, next to a poem [of moderate length], should best fulfil the demands of high genius—should offer it the most advantageous field of exertion—we should unhesitatingly speak of the prose tale, as Mr. Hawthorne has here exemplified it. We allude to the short prose narrative, requiring from a half-hour to one or two hours in its perusal. The ordinary novel is objectionable, from its length, for reasons already stated in substance. As it cannot be read at one sitting, it deprives itself, of course, of the immense force derivable from *totality*. Worldly interests intervening during the pauses of perusal, modify, annul, or counteract, in a greater or less degree, the impressions of the book. But simple cessation in reading would, of itself, be sufficient to destroy the true unity. In the brief tale, however, the author is enabled to carry out the fulness of his intention, be it what it may. During the hour of perusal the soul of the reader is at the writer's control. There are no external or extrinsic influences—resulting from weariness or interruption.

A skilful literary artist has constructed a tale. If wise, he has not fashioned his thoughts to accommodate his incidents; but having conceived, with deliberate care, a certain unique or single *effect* to be wrought out, he then invents such incidents—he then combines such events as may best aid him in establishing this preconceived effect. If his very initial sentence tend not to be outbringing of this effect, then he has failed in his first step. In the whole composition there should be no word written, of which the tendency, direct or indirect, is not to the one pre-established design. And by such means, with such care and skill, a picture is at length painted which leaves the mind of him who contemplates it with a kindred art, a sense of the fullest satisfaction. The idea of the tale has been presented unblemished, because undisturbed; and this is an end unattainable by the novel. Undue brevity is just as exceptionable here as in the poem; but undue length is yet more to be avoided.

We have said that the tale has a point of superiority even over the poem. In fact, while the *rhythm* of this latter is an essential aid in the development of the poem's highest idea—the idea of the Beautiful—the artificialities of this rhythm are an inseparable bar to the development of all points of thought or expression which have their basis in *Truth*. But Truth is often, and in very great degree, the aim of the tale. Some of the finest tales are tales of ratiocination. Thus the field of this species of composition, if not in so elevated a region on the mountain of Mind, is a table-land of far vaster extent than the domain of the mere poem. Its products are never so rich, but infinitely more

---

4. Originally appeared in *Graham's Magazine* (May 1842): 298–300.

numerous, and more appreciable by the mass of mankind. The writer of the prose tale, in short, may bring to his theme a vast variety of modes or inflections of thought and expression—(the ratiocinative, for example, the sarcastic or the humorous) which are not only antagonistical to the nature of the poem, but absolutely forbidden by one of its most peculiar and indispensable adjuncts; we allude of course, to rhythm. It may be added, here, *par parenthèse*,[5] that the author who aims at the purely beautiful in a prose tale is laboring at great disadvantage. For Beauty can be better treated in the poem. Not so with terror, or passion, or horror, or a multitude of such other points. And here it will be seen how full of prejudice are the usual animadversions against those *tales of effect* many fine examples of which were found in the earlier numbers of Blackwood. The impressions produced were wrought in a legitimate sphere of action, and constituted a legitimate although sometimes an exaggerated interest. They were relished by every man of genius: although there were found many men of genius who condemned them without just ground. The true critic will but demand that the design intended be accomplished, to the fullest extent, by the means most advantageously applicable.

We have very few American tales of real merit—we may say, indeed, none with the exception of "The Tales of a Traveller" of Washington Irving, and these "Twice-Told Tales" of Mr. Hawthorne. Some of the pieces of Mr. John Neal abound in vigor and originality; but in general, his compositions of this class are excessively diffuse, extravagant, and indicative of an imperfect sentiment of Art. Articles at random are, now and then, met with in our periodicals which might be advantageously compared with the best effusions of the British Magazines; but, upon the whole, we are far behind our progenitors in this department of literature.

Of Mr. Hawthorne's Tales we would say, emphatically, that they belong to the highest region of Art—an Art subservient to genius of a very lofty order. We had supposed, with good reason for so supposing, that he had been thrust into his present position by one of the impudent *cliques* which beset our literature, and whose pretensions it is our full purpose to expose at the earliest opportunity; but we have been most agreeably mistaken. We know of few compositions which the critic can more honestly commend [than] these "Twice-Told Tales." As Americans, we feel proud of the book.

Mr. Hawthorne's distinctive trait is invention, creation, imagination, originality—a trait which, in the literature of fiction, is positively worth all the rest. But the nature of originality, so far as regards its manifestation in letters, is but imperfectly understood. The inventive or original mind as frequently displays itself in novelty of *tone* as in novelty of matter. Mr. Hawthorne is original at *all* points.

In the way of objection we have scarcely a word to say of these tales. There is, perhaps, a somewhat too general or prevalent *tone*—a tone of melancholy and mysticism. The subjects are insufficiently varied. There is not so much of *versatility* evinced as we might well be warranted in expecting from the high powers of Mr. Hawthorne. But beyond these trivial exceptions we have really none to make. The style is purity itself. Force abounds. High imagination gleams from every page. Mr. Hawthorne is a man of the truest genius. We

---

5. Parenthetically (French).

only regret that the limits of our Magazine will not permit us to pay him that full tribute of commendation, which, under other circumstances, we should be so eager to pay.

## C. P. SARVAN

### *Racism and the* Heart of Darkness[6]

As I have shown elsewhere,[7] Conrad's setting, themes, and his triumph in writing major literature in his third language, have won him a special admiration in the non-European world. "The African writer and Joseph Conrad share the same world and that is why Conrad's world is so familiar. Both have lived in a world dominated by capitalism, imperialism, colonialism."[8] But African readers are also checked by, and disconcerted at, works such as *The Nigger of the "Narcissus"* and *Heart of Darkness*. The case against the latter was most strongly made by Chinua Achebe in the course of a lecture titled "An Image of Africa," delivered at the University of Massachusetts on the 18th of February 1975.[9] He argued that Conrad sets up Africa "as a foil to Europe, a place of negations . . . in comparison with which Europe's own state of spiritual grace will be manifest." Africa is "the other world," "the antithesis of Europe and therefore of civilization, a place where man's vaunted intelligence and refinement are finally mocked by triumphant bestiality." Achebe commented on Conrad's comparison of the Congo and the Thames, and also alleged that the contrast made between the two women who loved Kurtz, one African, the other European, is highly prejudiced. Any sympathy expressed for the sufferings of the black African under colonialism, argued Achebe, is a sympathy born of a kind of liberalism which, whilst acknowledging distant kinship, repudiates equality. Conrad, continued Achebe, is a "racist"—and great art can only be "on the side of man's deliverance and not his enslavement; for the brotherhood and unity of all mankind and not for the doctrines of Hitler's master races or Conrad's 'rudimentary souls.'" Achebe concluded his attack on *Heart of Darkness* by describing it as "a book which parades in the most vulgar fashion prejudices and insults from which a section of mankind has suffered untold agonies and atrocities in the past and continues to do so in many ways and many places today. I am talking about a story in which the very humanity of black people is called in question. It seems to me totally inconceivable that great art or even good art could possibly reside in such unwholesome surroundings."

**6.** From *The International Fiction Review* 7 (1980): 6–10.  **7.** "Under African Eyes," *Conradiana,* 8 (1976), 233–239.  **8.** Ngũgĩ wa Thiong'o, "Writers in Politics," *Busara,* 8, No. 1 (1976), 5. Previously known as James Ngugi, he is the author of four novels (*Weep Not, Child,* 1964; *The River Between,* 1965; *A Grain of Wheat,* 1967; *Petals of Blood,* 1977), a play (*The Black Hermit,* 1968) and a collection of essays (*Homecoming,* 1972).  **9.** *The Chancellor's Lecture Series: 1974–75,* University of Massachusetts at Amherst, pp. 31–43. Chancellor Bromery in introducing Achebe said *inter alia,* "The Scottish Arts Council has this year awarded him their second annual Neil Gunn International Fellowship. The Modern Language Association of America has voted Professor Achebe an honourary fellowship in their Association. . . . His first novel, *Things Fall Apart,* brought him to world-wide attention and acclaim. . . . His works have now been translated into twenty languages and his literary reputation is secure" (p. 29). I am grateful to Professor Achebe for sending me a copy of his lecture.

I shall in the following pages attempt to narrowly limit myself to an examination of the charge of racism brought against Conrad's *Heart of Darkness*. Let us begin with the fictional Marlow, whose story was once heard and is now related by a fictional narrator. "It might be contended ... that the attitude to the African. ... is not Conrad's but that of his fictional narrator, Marlow. ... [But] Marlow seems to me to enjoy Conrad's complete confidence." Marlow's portrait is drawn with quiet irony and, at times, a mocking humor which denotes "distance" between creator and character. For example, he is described as resembling an idol and he sits like a European Buddha without the lotus. Marlow claims to be deeply, almost pathologically averse to telling lies but we find that he prevaricates at least twice within this tale. He condemns the Roman conquest and contrasts it with the "superior" European colonialism:

> What saves us is efficiency—the devotion to efficiency. But these chaps were not much account really. They were no colonists, their administration was merely a squeeze. ... They were conquerors, and for that you only want brute force— nothing to boast of, when you have it, since your strength is just an accident arising from the weakness of others. They grabbed what they could. ... It was just robbery with violence, aggravated murder on a great scale. ... The conquest of the earth, which mostly means the taking it away from those who have a different complexion or slightly flatter noses than ourselves, is not a pretty thing when you look into it too much. What redeems it is the idea only. An idea at the back of it, not a sentimental pretence but an idea; and an unselfish belief in the idea. ...

A long quotation but necessary in that it again separates author from character. Significantly, this "idea" is presented in ambiguous "pagan" terms as "something you can set up, and bow down before, and offer a sacrifice to." What is more, the rest of the story shows that the European colonial conquest, contrary to Marlow's claims, was much worse than that of the Romans. One remembers that harrowing description of men waiting to die: "Black shapes crouched, lay, sat between the trees, leaning against the trunks, clinging to the earth, half coming out ... in all the attitudes of pain, abandonment, and despair. ... They were not enemies, they were not criminals. ..." Immediately after this description, Marlow meets the elegant, perfumed, "hairdresser's dummy" and confesses that he "respected his collars," the collars of a man who comes out "to get a breath of fresh air," indifferent to the despair and death by which he is surrounded. It may be argued that Marlow is here speaking with irony and the description "hairdresser's dummy" may appear to make Marlow's attitude to the dummy as clear and unequivocal. But Marlow continues with unmistakable admiration that "in the great demoralisation of the land he kept up his appearance. That's backbone." He kept up *appearances*, and that points to one of the important thematic significances of this work, namely, the discrepancy between appearance and reality; between assumption and fact; between illusion and truth. Thus it is not correct to say that Marlow has Conrad's complete confidence, and even more incorrect to say that Conrad believed Europe to be in a state of grace. The glorious sailors proudly cited by Marlow were pirates and plunderers. This ironic distance between Marlow and Conrad should not be overlooked, though the narrative method makes it all too easy. Nor can Conrad's very forceful criticisms of colonialism be lightly passed over as weak liberalism. What ships unload in Africa are soldiers and customhouse clerks: the one to conquer and the other to administer and efficiently exploit. The cannon pounds a continent and "the merry dance of death and trade goes on." This "rapacious and pitiless folly" attempts to pass itself off as philanthropy, and to hypocritically hide its true nature under words such as *enemies, criminals,* and *rebels.* The counterparts of enemies, criminals, and rebels are the emissaries of light, such as Kurtz!

As a critic has pointed out, "Africa *per se* is not the theme of *Heart of Darkness,* but is used as a locale symbol for the very core of an 'accursed inheritance'."[1] At the risk of oversimplification, the story may be seen as an allegory, the journey ending with the sombre realization of the darkness of man's heart. But it may prove emotionally difficult for some to follow the allegory when it is thought that Conrad, casting about for an external parallel, for a physical setting to match the inner darkness, chose Africa. An argument may be constructed as follows: to the Romans, the people of Britain were barbarians; now when the Europeans come to Africa, the Africans in comparison seem savage, but deep down in the European breast there still lurks the old savagery. "It is not the differentness that worries Conrad but the lurking hint of kinship, of common ancestry... if [the Thames] were to visit its primordial relative, the Congo, it would run the terrible risk of hearing grotesque, suggestive echoes of its own forgotten darkness, and falling victim to an avenging recrudescence of the mindless frenzy of the first beginnings." When the Romans looked down upon the people of Britain, and the Europeans upon "natives," it was because they felt they had achieved a much higher civilization than the people they were confronting and conquering. The contempt was not on grounds of race itself, and Conrad suggests that Europe's claim to be civilized and therefore superior, needs earnest reexamination. The reference in *Heart of Darkness* is not to a place (Africa), but to the condition of European man; not to a black people, but to colonialism. The crucial question is whether European "barbarism" is merely a thing of the historical past. Surely the contrast between savage African and "civilized" European, in the light of that greedy and inhuman colonialism, is shown to be "appearance" rather than reality. The emphasis, the present writer would suggest, is on continuity, on persistence through time and peoples, and therefore on the fundamental oneness of man and his nature. If a judgment has to be made, then uncomplicated "savagery" is better than the "subtle horrors" manifested by almost all the Europeans Marlow met on that ironic voyage of discovery. When Marlow speaks of the African in European service as one of the "reclaimed," it is grim irony for he has been reclaimed to a worse state of barbarism. Left to itself, Africa has a "greatness" that went "home to one's very heart." As Marlow begins his story, the light changes as though "stricken to death by the touch of that gloom brooding over a crowd of men": yet the gloom is very much over the Thames as well. The Thames as "a waterway

---

1. Robert Lee, *Conrad's Colonialism* (The Hague: Mouton, 1969), p. 49.

leading to the uttermost ends of the earth" is connected with and therefore a part of those uttermost ends. The river signifies what is abiding in nature, in man, and in the nature of man, even as "the sea is always the same" and foreign shores and foreign faces are veiled not by mystery but by ignorance.

The immaculately dressed, fastidious, and sensitive hairdresser's dummy, a representative of civilized Europe and a part of the colonial machinery, is totally insensitive to the suffering he helps to cause and by which he is surrounded. (His extreme cleanliness is perhaps to be seen as compulsive, an attempt to keep clean in the midst of that moral dirt.) Even in the case of Kurtz, one must remember that all Europe had "contributed" to his making. As for pagan rites and savage dances, the Europeans with "imbecile rapacity" were "praying" to ivory, that is, to materialism, and one red-haired man "positively danced," bloodthirsty at the thought that he and the others "must have made a glorious slaughter" of the Africans in the bush.[2] The alleged primitiveness of the boilerman only serves to show the similarity between his *appearance* and the *actions* of the "civilized."

Achebe also noted that Kurtz's African mistress is the "savage counterpart to the refined, European woman." But the European woman is pale and rather anemic whilst the former, to use Conrad's words, is gorgeous, proud, superb, magnificent, tragic, fierce, and filled with sorrow. She is an impressive figure and, importantly, her human feelings are not denied. The contrast, however, is not simply between these two, but between Kurtz's African mistress on the one hand, and Marlow's aunt and Kurtz's "Intended" on the other. The aunt glibly believes that he who goes to the Congo is "a lower sort of apostle": "She talked about 'weaning those ignorant millions from their horrid ways.'" The hairdresser's dummy, we recall, was first taken to be "a sort of vision." The same ignorance and the same illusions are found at the end, in Kurtz's Intended. After all, he was also one of those apostles. The darkness which is often mentioned refers not only to the darkness within man, to the mysterious and the unpredictable, but also to ignorance and illusions: it is significant that as Marlow talks with Kurtz's Intended, the "darkness deepened." The African woman faces the truth and endures the pain of her dereliction, whilst the illusions of the two European women are also the fond illusions of European society.

This is not to claim that Conrad was free of all prejudice, nor to deny that he has wholly resisted the temptation to use physical appearance and setting as indicators of nonphysical qualities.[3] Conrad reflects to some degree the attitudes of his age, and his description of the fireman as a dog in a parody of breeches, is cruel. On the one hand, in terms of technological progress, the gap between London and the Congo was immense; on the other, though it is extreme to say that Conrad called into question the very humanity of the African, one's perspective and evaluation of this work need alteration.

---

2. Compare Mark Twain, *More Tramps Abroad*, London, 1897, pp. 137–138: "There are many humorous things in the world; among them, the white man's notion that he is less savage than the other savages." 3. Compare Shiva Naipaul, "Zambia's Compromise with the West," *Spectator*, 11 June 1977, p. 11: "Now and then, in a clearing in the bush, there is the fleeting apparition of a village of mud huts. Women, squatting in the shade, look up expressionlessly from their labours; squads of naked children, shouting, arms flailing, come rushing over the beaten brown earth to wave.... The wilderness closes in again.... Nothing indicates that you have made any progress."

In a conversation with me,[4] Ngũgĩ wa Thiong'o accepted some of Achebe's criticisms but felt he had overlooked the positive aspect, namely, Conrad's attack on colonialism. The skulls stuck on poles outside Kurtz's house, wa Thiong'o said, was the most powerful indictment of colonialism. No African writer, he continued, had created so ironic, apt, and powerful an image: ironic when one considers that Kurtz and many others like him had come to "civilize" the non-European world; apt when one recalls what they really did. But wa Thiong'o also observed that though Conrad (having experienced the evils of Czarist imperialism) castigates Belgian atrocities, he is much milder in his criticisms of British imperialism. This ambivalence, concluded Professor wa Thiong'o, compromised Conrad's otherwise admirable stand. Leonard Kibera (Kenyan novelist, short story writer, critic, and teacher) wrote informally to me as follows: "I study *Heart of Darkness* as an examination of the West itself and not as a comment on Africa. Many Africans do get turned off Conrad because they feel he used the Third World so totally as a background against which he examined Western values and conduct that the people in Africa and Asia are no more than caricatures. I do not object to this and appreciate the fact that in Conrad there is not that Joyce Cary, Graham Greene pretension of understanding the Third World."[5] Nadine Gordimer writing on another famous European in Africa states that Livingstone, reassessed, emerges as a fallible human being.[6] Conrad too was not entirely immune to the infection of the beliefs and attitudes of his age, but he was ahead of most in trying to break free.

## CHARLES C. WALCUTT

### [Stephen Crane: Naturalist][7]

The works of Stephen Crane (1871–1900) are an early and unique flowering of pure naturalism. It is naturalism in a restricted and special sense, and it contains many non-naturalistic elements, but it is nevertheless entirely consistent and coherent. It marks the first entry, in America, of a deterministic philosophy not confused with ethical motivation into the structure of the novel. Ethical judgment there is, in plenty. To define Crane's naturalism is to understand one of the few perfect and successful embodiments of the theory in the American novel. It illustrates the old truth that literary trends often achieve their finest expressions very early in their histories. *Mutatis mutandis*,[8] Crane is the Christopher Marlowe of American naturalism—and we have had no Shakespeare.

Crane's naturalism is to be found, first, in his attitude toward received values, which he continually assails through his naturalistic method of showing that the traditional concepts of our social morality are shams and the motivations presumably controlled by them are pretenses; second, in his impressionism, which fractures experiences into disordered sensation in a way that shatters the old moral "order" along with the old orderly processes of reward and punishment; third, in his obvious interest in a scientific or

**4.** University of Nairobi, 19 July 1977. **5.** Letter dated 7 April 1977. **6.** *Contrast* 30(1973): 82. **7.** From *American Literary Naturalism, A Divided Stream* (Minneapolis: University of Minnesota Press, 1956), pp. vii–viii, 66–67, 74–82. **8.** Duly noting the differences between them (Latin).

deterministic accounting for events, although he does not pretend or attempt to be scientific in either the tone or the management of his fables. Crane's naturalism does not suffer from the problem of the divided stream because each of his works is so concretely developed that it does not have a meaning apart from what happens in it. The meaning is always the action; there is no wandering into theory that runs counter to what happens in the action; and nowhere does a character operate as a genuinely free ethical agent in defiance of the author's intentions. Crane's success is a triumph of style: manner and meaning are one.

•  •  •

Crane's naturalism is descriptive: he does not pretend to set forth a proof, like a chemical demonstration, that what happened must have happened, inevitably. This is what Zola was forever saying he did, and it is for these pretensions of scientific demonstration and proof that he has been chided by later critics. Crane simply shows how a sequence of events takes place quite independently of the wills and judgments of the people involved. The reader is convinced that it happened that way, and he sees that the ordinary moral sentiments do not adequately judge or account for these happenings. The writer does not have to argue that he has proved anything about causation or determinism: he has absolutely shown that men's wills do not control their destinies.

## RICHARD WILBUR

### The House of Poe[9]

A few weeks ago, in the *New York Times Book Review,* Mr. Saul Bellow expressed impatience with the current critical habit of finding symbols in everything. No self-respecting modern professor, Mr. Bellow observed, would dare to explain Achilles' dragging of Hector around the walls of Troy by the mere assertion that Achilles was in a bad temper. That would be too drearily obvious. No, the professor must say that the circular path of Achilles and Hector relates to the theme of circularity which pervades *The Iliad.*

In the following week's *Book Review,* a pedantic correspondent corrected Mr. Bellow, pointing out that Achilles did not, in Homer's *Iliad,* drag Hector's body around the walls of Troy; this perhaps invalidates the Homeric example, but Mr. Bellow's complaint remains, nevertheless, a very sensible one. We are all getting a bit tired, I think, of that laboriously clever criticism which discovers mandalas in Mark Twain, rebirth archetypes in Edwin Arlington Robinson, and fertility myths in everybody.

Still, we must not be carried away by our impatience, to the point of demanding that no more symbols be reported. The business of the critic, after all, is to divine the intention of the work, and to interpret the work in the light of that intention; and since some writers are intentionally symbolic, there is nothing for it but to talk about their symbols. If we speak of Melville, we must speak of symbols. If we speak of Hawthorne, we must speak of symbols. And as for Edgar Allan Poe, whose sesquicentennial year we are

9. Originally presented as a lecture at the Library of Congress under the auspices of the Gertrude Clarke Whittall Poetry and Literature Fund in 1959.

met to observe, I think we can make no sense about him until we consider his work—and in particular his prose fiction—as deliberate and often brilliant allegory.

Not everyone will agree with me that Poe's work has an accessible allegorical meaning. Some critics, in fact, have refused to see any substance, allegorical or otherwise, in Poe's fiction, and have regarded his tales as nothing more than complicated machines for saying "boo." Others have intuited undiscoverable meanings in Poe, generally of an unpleasant kind: I recall one Freudian critic declaring that if we find Poe unintelligible we should congratulate ourselves, since if we *could* understand him it would be proof of our abnormality.

It is not really surprising that some critics should think Poe meaningless, or that others should suppose his meaning intelligible only to monsters. Poe was not a wide-open and perspicuous writer; indeed, he was a secretive writer both by temperament and by conviction. He sprinkled his stories with sly references to himself and to his personal history. He gave his own birthday of January 19 to his character William Wilson; he bestowed his own height and color of eye on the captain of the phantom ship in "Ms. Found in a Bottle"; and the name of one of his heroes, Arthur Gordon Pym, is patently a version of his own. He was a maker and solver of puzzles, fascinated by codes, ciphers, anagrams, acrostics, hieroglyphics, and the Kabbala. He invented the detective story. He was fond of aliases; he delighted in accounts of swindles; he perpetrated the famous Balloon Hoax of 1844; and one of his most characteristic stories is entitled "Mystification." A man so devoted to concealment and deception and unraveling and detection might be expected to have in his work what Poe himself called "undercurrents of meaning."

And that is where Poe, as a critic, said that meaning belongs: not on the surface of the poem or tale, but below the surface as a dark undercurrent. If the meaning of a work is made overly clear—as Poe said in his "Philosophy of Composition"—if the meaning is brought to the surface and made the upper current of the poem or tale, then the work becomes bald and prosaic and ceases to be art. Poe conceived of art, you see, not as a means of giving imaginative order to earthly experience, but as a stimulus to unearthly visions. The work of literary art does not, in Poe's view, present the reader with a provisional arrangement of reality; instead, it seeks to disengage the reader's mind from reality and propel it toward the ideal. Now, since Poe thought the function of art was to set the mind soaring upward in what he called "a wild effort to reach the Beauty above," it was important to him that the poem or tale should not have such definiteness and completeness of meaning as might contain the reader's mind within the work. Therefore Poe's criticism places a positive value on the obscuration of meaning, on a dark suggestiveness, on a deliberate vagueness by means of which the reader's mind may be set adrift toward the beyond.

Poe's criticism, then, assures us that his work does have meaning. And Poe also assures us that this meaning is not on the surface but in the depths. If we accept Poe's invitation to play detective, and commence to read him with an eye for submerged meaning, it is not long before we sense that there *are* meanings to be found, and that in fact many of Poe's stories, though superficially dissimilar, tell the same tale. We begin to have this sense as we notice Poe's repeated use of certain narrative patterns; his repetition of certain words and phrases; his use, in story after story, of certain scenes and properties. We notice, for instance, the recurrence of the *spiral* or *vortex*. In "Ms. Found in a Bottle," the story ends with a plunge into a whirlpool; the "Descent into the Maelström" also concludes in a watery vortex; the house of Usher, just before it plunges into the tarn, is swaddled in a whirlwind; the hero of "Metzengerstein," Poe's first published story, perishes in "a whirlwind of chaotic fire"; and at the close of "King Pest," Hugh Tarpaulin is cast into a puncheon of ale and disappears "amid a whirlpool of foam." That Poe offers us so many spirals or vortices in his fiction, and that they should always appear at the same terminal point in their respective narratives, is a strong indication that the spiral had some symbolic value for Poe. And it did: What the spiral invariably represents in any tale of Poe's is the loss of consciousness, and the descent of the mind into sleep.

I hope you will grant, before I am through, that to find spirals in Poe is not so silly as finding circles in Homer. The professor who finds circles in Homer does so to the neglect of more important and more provable meanings. But the spiral or vortex is a part of that symbolic language in which Poe said his say, and unless we understand it we cannot understand Poe.

# Author in Depth: William Faulkner

Faulkner's fiction touched on a wide range of concerns, but a strong current running through much of his work was a mediation of the Old South's influence on an emerging New South. In the stories collected in this anthology, we see the powerful influence of days gone by on the living, but equally so, the flow of fundamental concerns across generations and classes, "the old verities and truths of the heart," as he put it in his Nobel Address.

Collected here are remarks by Faulkner on the ways he went about his work and his ambitions for it; Sherwood Anderson's provocative analysis of the grotesque—useful for understanding not just Faulkner's fiction, but that of O'Connor, Hemingway, Poe, and others; as well as scholarly critiques of the intersection of past, present, and eternal in the two stories collected in this anthology: "Barn Burning" and "A Rose for Emily."

## WILLIAM FAULKNER

### An Interview[1]

Q. Mr. Faulkner, could I ask you how important you think a college education is to a writer?

A. Well that's—is too much like trying to decide how important is a warm room to a writer. To some writers, some people, the college education might be of great importance, just like some of us couldn't work in a cold room. So that's a question I just wouldn't attempt to answer, and then I'm more or less out of bounds because I didn't have one myself.

Q. I was reading a book . . . yesterday which said that English teachers had gotten a body of American literature and stored it away in musty basements and had sort of stifled the creative impulse in America . . . Do you think that's true?

A. No sir, I do not. I do not. I think that people read into the true meaning of college lots of things that are not there. I think that there's an importance in college that is—adumbrates a specialty like—of being a writer, that is, the college is to produce first a human being, a humanitarian, and no man can write who is not first a humanitarian, and if the college can supply that to him, then the college is of infinite importance. If he has managed to acquire that outside of college, then he doesn't need the college. But you can't—I don't think you can say that the college makes or mars an artist.

Q. If he has it in him, it'll come out.

A. Yes. I would say that the college would help anyone, but it wouldn't make a writer that wouldn't have made himself—that is, I've never held with the mute inglorious Milton.

---

1. From *Faulkner in the University, Class Conferences at the University of Virginia, 1957–58,* ed. by Frederick L. Gwynn and Joseph L. Blotner.

• • •

... Q. I thought I might ask you, Mr. Faulkner, because somebody was speaking of it the other day to me, how you went about writing, how stories came to you. I have a friend, a writer, who has told me sometimes that she will think about her stories for quite a long time and then suddenly they'll be there, and they can be written down without perhaps a great deal of revision or fumbling, that they are there in the mind and they get down on paper that way. Do you have experience of that sort when you write or do you have different things happen?

A. That's sometimes true. I don't think you can make a hard and fast statement about the method of writing, of the conception of a story. It—of course the first thing, the writer's got to be demon-driven. He's got to have to write, he don't know why, and sometimes he will wish that he didn't have to, but he does. The story can come from an anecdote, it can come from a character. With me it never comes from an idea because I don't know too much about ideas and ain't really interested in ideas, I'm interested in people, so what I speak from my experience is probably a limited experience. But I'm interested primarily in people, in man in conflict with himself, with his fellow man, or with his time and place, his environment. So I think there's really no rule for how to begin to write.

.... Q. Mr. Faulkner, do you think that a writer can teach young writers?

A. I don't think anybody can teach anybody anything. I think that you learn it, but the young writer that is as I say demon-driven and wants to learn and has got to write he don't know why, he will learn from almost any source that he finds. He will learn from older people who are not writers, he will learn from writers, but he learns it—you can't teach it. Then I think too that the writer who's actually hot to say something hasn't got time to be taught. He's too busy learning—he knows what he wants—his instinct says to take this from this man or that from that man. That he's not—he hasn't got time to sit under a mentor and listen to try to learn.

• • •

Q. ... Do you feel a necessity to ... tell all the truth about that character that you feel needs to be told regardless ...?

A. No, I think that after about ten books, I had learned enough of judgment to where I could pick and choose the facet of the character which I needed at that particular time to move the story I was telling, so that I can take a facet of one character in one story and another facet of that character in another story. To me it's the same character, though sometimes to the reader it may seem as though the character had changed or had developed more—to me he hasn't. That I used my editorial prerogative of choosing what I needed from that particular character at that particular time.

... Q. Mr. Faulkner, how much do you feel that the writer's being involved with people in his writings is dependent upon his being actively involved with real people in the real world?

A. I think that that has nothing to do with the writing. That he can be involved with people, he can be involved with alcohol, or with gambling or anything and it's not going to affect the writer. Now, I have no patience and I don't hold with the mute inglorious Miltons. I think that if he's demon-driven, with something to be said, then he's going to write it, he can blame his—the fact that he's not turning out the work on lots of things. I've heard lots of people say, Well, if I were not married and had children I would be a writer. I've heard people say, If I could just stop doing this I would be a writer. I don't agree with that. I think if you're going to write, you're going to write and nothing will stop you. If you can be involved, and probably the more you're involved, it may be better for you. That maybe it's bad to crawl off into the ivory tower and stay there—maybe you do need to be involved, to get the edges beaten off of you a little every day—may be good for the writer.

• • •

Q. Sir, in your novels, you said in one of the other classes that you begin with a character in mind or more than one character. In your short stories, do they—do you conceive of them the same way? Do you start with a person or do you—?

A. Sometimes with a person, sometimes with an anecdote, but the short story is conceived in the same terms that the book is. The first job the craftsman faces is to tell this as quickly and as simply as I can, and if he's good, if he's of the first water, like Chekhov, he can do it every time in two or three thousand words, but if he's not that good, sometimes it takes him eighty thousand words. But they are similar, and he is simply trying to tell something which was true and moving in the shortest time he can, and then if he has sense enough stop. That is, I don't believe the man or the woman sits down and says, Now I'm going to write a short story, or Now I'm going to write a novel. It's an idea that begins with the thought, the image of a character, or with an anecdote, and even in the same breath, almost like lightning, it begins to take a shape that he can see whether it's going to be a short story or a novel. Sometimes, not always. Sometimes he thinks it'll be a short story and finds that he can't. Sometimes it looks like it's to be a novel and then after he works on it, he sees that it's not, that he can tell it in two thousand or five thousand words. No rule to it.

• • •

Q. Mr. Faulkner, do you think an author has his prerogative to create his own language? In other words, to go against what the people create, vernacular? Do you think an author has the right to create his own—I believe Joyce and Eliot have done it—have tried to create, they found that language was not—did not suit their purposes, so they had to go beyond and make a—

A. He has the right to do that provided he don't insist on anyone understanding it. That is—what I'm trying to say is—that I believe I'm paraphrasing Whitman, didn't he say, "To have good poets we must have good readers, too," something like that? Who knows?

Q. Whitman, "great audiences."

A. Well, the writer, actually, that's an obligation that he assumes with his vocation, that he's going to write it in a way that people can understand it. He doesn't have to write it in the way that every idiot can understand it—every imbecile in the third grade can understand it, but he's got to use a language which is accepted and in which the words have specific meanings that every-body agrees on. I think that *Finnegans Wake* and *Ulysses* were justified, but then it's hard to say on what terms they were justified. That was a case of a genius who was electrocuted by the divine fire.

Q. Mr. Faulkner, it's often been said about great novels or great short stories that they wouldn't pass muster in a freshman English composition course. Now I was wondering, since this is your first stay at a university, if you had any comments on the traditional or the apparently traditional conflict between the creative writer and the schoolman.

A. Well, as an old veteran sixth-grader, that question is I think outside of my province, because I never got to freshman English. I don't know how much it would conflict. Maybe before I've left the University I will be able to pass freshman English.

• • •

Q. Sir, I think you said that you haven't yet achieved your own personal goal as a writer. What is that goal and is it likely that you will succeed in achiev-ing it?

A. That's difficult to say. It's when I have done something that, to use Heming-way's phrase, makes me feel good, that is completely satisfactory, maybe that will be the goal, and I hope just a little that I'll never quite do that because if I do there won't be any reason to go on writing, and I'm too old to take up another hobby. It's—I think that a writer wants to make something that he knows that a hundred or two hundred or five hundred, a thousand years later will make people feel what they feel when they read Homer, or read Dickens or Balzac, Tolstoy, that that's probably his goal. I don't think that he bothers until he gets old like this and has a right to spend a lot of time talking about it to put that into actual words. But probably that's what he wants, that really the writer doesn't want success, that he knows he has a short span of life, that the day will come when he must pass through the wall of oblivion, and he wants to leave a scratch on that wall—Kilroy was here—that somebody a hun-dred, a thousand years later will see.

• • •

Q. Sir, a few minutes ago you mentioned that people in your home town were looking into your books for familiar characters. Realizing that you've got a rich legacy in your experiences, but it seems to me that nowadays the modern novelist is writing merely thinly disguised autobiography. Which do you think is really more valuable from the sense of the artist, the disguised auto-biography, or making it up from whole cloth, as it were?

A. I would say that the writer has three sources, imagination, observation, and experience. He himself doesn't know how much of which he uses at any given moment because each of the sources themselves are not too important to him. That he is writing about people, and he uses his material from the three sources as the carpenter reaches into his lumber room and finds a board that fits the particular corner he's building. Of course, any writer, to begin with, is writing his own biography because he has discovered the world and then suddenly discovered that the world is important enough or moving enough or tragic enough to put down on paper or in music or on canvas, and at that time all he knows is what has happened to him because he has not developed his capacity to perceive, to draw conclusions, to have an insight into people. His only insight in it is into himself, and it's a biography because that's the only gauge he has to measure—is what he has experienced himself. As he gets older and works more, imagination is like any muscle, it improves with use. Imagination develops, his observation gets shrewder as he gets older, as he writes, so that when he reaches his peak, his best years, when his work is best, he himself doesn't know and doesn't have time to bother and doesn't really care how much of what comes from each of these sources, that then he is writing about people, writing about the aspirations, the troubles, the anguishes, the courage, and the cowardice, the baseness and the splendor of man, of the human heart.

• • •

Q. Mr. Faulkner, you may have touched on this previously, but could you give some advice to young writers? What advice would you give to young writers?

A. At one time I thought the most important thing was talent. I think now that the young man or the young woman must possess or teach himself, train himself, in infinite patience, which is to try and to try and to try until it comes right. He must train himself in ruthless intolerance—that is, to throw away anything that is false no matter how much he might love that page or that paragraph. The most important thing is insight, that is, to be— curiosity—to wonder, to mull, and to muse why it is that man does what he does, and if you have that, then I don't think the talent makes much difference, whether you've got that or not.

Q. How would you suggest that he get this insight? Through experience?

A. Yes, and then the greatest part of experience is in the books, to read. To read and to read and to read and to read. To watch people, to have—to never judge people. To watch people, what they do, without intolerance. Simply to learn why it is they did what they did. . . .

• • •

Q. I have heard you use the word "fun" several times, and I'd like to know your idea of fun.

A. Well—fun—let's see if I can define that. In my own case it is to accomplish something which makes me feel good, which may make somebody else feel good, which won't hurt anybody. Fun is to accomplish something which I thought that perhaps I couldn't. That I might not be brave enough or strong enough, and then I do it and I'm successful. I suppose that everyone has a different notion of what "fun" means, so I can tell you only what it means to me, and when I say that, to write for fun, it's to take man's dilemma, the old familiar things in which there's nothing new and can't be anything new, and by the light of my own experience and imagination and a great deal of hard work, to make something which was a little different, which wasn't here yesterday. People write about the same stories because there're so few to write about, but to take one—human beings in the old familiar dilemma and predicament—and by the imagination and the hard work to show them in some new, interesting, tragic, or comical instance of the struggle within the dilemma, that to me is fun. But then so is getting a horse over a fence that I wasn't too sure he could get over or that I would still be on him is fun.

## WILLIAM FAULKNER

### Nobel Prize Address[2]

I feel that this award was not made to me as a man, but to my work—a life's work in the agony and sweat of the human spirit, not for glory and least of all for profit, but to create out of the materials of the human spirit something which did not exist before. So this award is only mine in trust. It will not be difficult to find a dedication for the money part of it commensurate with the purpose and significance of its origin. But I would like to do the same with the acclaim too, by using this moment as a pinnacle from which I might be listened to by the young men and women already dedicated to the same anguish and travail, among whom is already that one who will some day stand here where I am standing.

Our tragedy today is a general and universal physical fear so long sustained by now that we can even bear it. There are no longer problems of the spirit. There is only the question: When will I be blown up? Because of this, the young man or woman writing today has forgotten the problems of the human heart in conflict with itself which alone can make good writing because only that is worth writing about, worth the agony and the sweat.

He must learn them again. He must teach himself that the basest of all things is to be afraid; and, teaching himself that, forget it forever, leaving no room in his workshop for anything but the old verities and truths of the heart, the old universal truths lacking which any story is ephemeral and doomed—love and honor and pity and pride and compassion and sacrifice. Until he does so, he labors under a curse. He writes not of love but of lust, of defeats in which nobody loses anything of value, of victories without hope and, worst of all, without pity or compassion. His griefs grieve on no universal bones, leaving no scars. He writes not of the heart but of the glands.

Until he relearns these things, he will write as though he stood among and watched the end of man. I decline to accept the end of man. It is easy enough to say that man is immortal simply because he will endure: that when the last dingdong of doom has clanged and faded from the last worthless rock hanging tideless in the last red and dying evening, that even then there will still be one more sound: that of his puny inexhaustible voice, still talking.

I refuse to accept this. I believe that man will not merely endure: he will prevail. He is immortal, not because he alone among creatures has an inexhaustible voice, but because he has a soul, a spirit capable of compassion and sacrifice and endurance. The poet's, the writer's, duty is to write about these things. It is his privilege to help man endure by lifting his heart, by reminding him of the courage and honor and hope and pride and compassion and pity and sacrifice which have been the glory of his past. The poet's voice need

---

**2.** From *Nobel Lectures, Literature 1901–1967*, ed. Horst Frenz, Elsevier Publishing Company, Amsterdam, 1969.

not merely be the record of man, it can be one of the props, the pillars to help him endure and prevail.

## EDMOND L. VOLPE
### "A Rose for Emily"[3]

One of Faulkner's greatest stories, "A Rose for Emily" is a brilliantly wrought, emotionally charged, haunting portrait of the Southern psyche—a psyche tormented by conflicting feelings, impulses, and needs. It is the first story to deal with the village of Jefferson and its community. Publication in *Forum* in 1930 distinguishes it as the first story Faulkner was able to market. Written sometime toward the end of the 1920s, it also dramatically indicates the writer's mastery of the short story form. Faulkner's own ambivalent feelings of love and hate for the South inform every aspect of this story, from its narrative technique to its title. The community's sense of a past, which no winter touches, is countered by the images of death with which Faulkner enshrouds the past. The morbid atmosphere of decay that prepares for the story's macabre ending—revelation of Emily Grierson's necrophilia—is offset by the affectionate tribute of the story's title. The title does not derive from any incident or even image in the story; it is superimposed, Faulkner's expression of affection for what he hates.

What he hates is not so much the South's morbid, pathological attachment to the dead glory of the past but the ghoulish power of the past on the consciousness of the South. And what he loves is the tragic figure of the Southerner, trapped by his pride in his heritage and tormented by conflicting needs to conform and to defy, struggling vainly and helplessly to escape from the past and exist in the present.

"A Rose for Emily" has two major characters: Emily Grierson and the community. They are complementary rather than antagonistic characters; Emily's personal history mirrors the community's collective history. Faulkner provides us three dominant images of Emily, each reflecting a different stage in her history. We catch a brief glimpse of her as a young woman in the tableau the community remembers: Emily's "slender figure in white in the background . . . his [her father's] back to her and clutching a horsewhip, the two of them framed by the back-flung front door" (*CS*, 123). After her father's death, Emily, over thirty, her hair cut short, rides around town in Homer Barron's rented yellow-wheeled buggy to an increasing chorus of disapproval by the community. And after the disappearance of Homer, she becomes the "idol in a niche" (*CS* 128), the small obese figure, looking "bloated, like a body long submerged in motionless water, and of that pallid hue" (*CS*, 121). These three images trace Emily's tragic history: the fearful hold of the past upon her during her youth, her vain attempt to defy "that which had robbed her" of her chance for life, and finally her defeat and regression until she becomes the embodiment of the dead past (*CS*, 124). Faulkner portrays Emily with sufficient: psychological realism to make her a unique, vivid character, but "A Rose for Emily" has two protagonists, and Emily's sick attachment for her father, her affair with Homer Barron, her motivation for murdering her

---

3. From *A Reader's Guide to William Faulkner: The Short Stories* (2004).

lover, and her necrophilia are meaningful only in the contact in which Faulkner presents them: the context of the community's relationship with Emily.

Faulkner, ingeniously, makes the community a living entity, a character with a past, a personality, a memory, and feelings by means of the ubiquitous narrator who refers to the community as "we" and who spans the several generations of Emily's lifetime. This narrative voice ranges freely through time. The entire story is narrated in the past tense, but present action occurs after the death of Emily. The story opens with the announcement of her death and the attendance of "our whole town" at her funeral (*CS,* 119). It ends with the town's examination, after her burial, of that room that "we knew . . . no one had seen in forty years, and which would have to be forced" (*CS,* 129). Between the opening paragraph and the short closing scene, the narrator presents historical data about Emily and the town, focusing upon various episodes covering some fifty years of Emily's seventy-four years, without regard to chronology. Scenes separated by thirty years are juxtaposed. The narrator moves from scene to scene by association of thought. The narrative technique and the narrative structure convey a sense of temporal continuity, a sense of the past, to use Faulkner's own image, not as "a diminishing road but, instead, a huge meadow which no winter ever quite touches," in the collective consciousness of the community (*CS,* 129). "Alive," the narrator says, "Miss Emily had been a tradition, a duty, and a care; a sort of hereditary obligation upon the town" (*CS,* 119).

"Miss Emily," however, is only a symbol of the community's sense of "hereditary obligation" (*CS,* 119). Emily dies sometime in the second decade of the twentieth century, but the old men come to her funeral dressed in Confederate uniforms. The values of antebellum society continue to exert a very powerful influence upon the community in spite of Appomattox, governing its attitudes toward blacks and toward women. In this story, which is centered upon a woman, the past is appropriately evoked by the tradition of Southern chivalry. There are three paternal figures in the story: Colonel Sartoris, Judge Stevens, and Mr. Grierson. Sartoris and Stevens function in the consciousness of the community in the same way that Mr. Grierson functions in the consciousness of Emily. The episodes in which Sartoris and Stevens figure are two of the major scenes in the narrative, and they establish a link between the community's involvement with the past and with Emily's involvement.

Colonel Sartoris, the narrator informs us parenthetically, fathered an edict that no Negro woman should appear on the streets without an apron. It is this representative of the continuing power of the antebellum world who, in 1894, remits Emily Grierson's taxes with a tale that only a "man of Colonel Sartoris' generation and thought could have invented . . . and only a woman could have believed" (*CS,* 120).

The next generation "with its more modern ideas," refuses to accept this dictum from the past, and it decides to collect the taxes (*CS,* 120). The new generation has the power to enforce its will, but the past has too strong a hold upon it. The delegation that calls upon Miss Emily and confronts her in that dust-filled, mausoleum-like front parlor where Mr. Grierson is enshrined, retreats into inactivity and silence when Miss Emily tells them to see Colonel Sartoris, ten years dead.

And just as this generation's attempt to defy the dead falls, so their fathers had been "vanquished ... thirty years before about the smell" (*CS,* 121). The eighty-year-old Judge Stevens is mayor when complaints about the smell from the Grierson house begin to come in. The whole town knows, of course, that the druggist had sold, with much trepidation, arsenic to Miss Emily, just as it knows that Homer Barron entered Emily's kitchen door one evening and disappeared from sight. At first, Judge Stevens tries to fend off the complaints, but finally he calls a meeting of the board of alderman, which consists of "three graybeards and one younger man, a member of the rising generation" (*CS,* 122). This younger man insists that all they need do is order Miss Emily to clean up her place, " 'and if she don't. . . .' 'Dammit, sir,' Judge Stevens said, 'will you accuse a lady to her face of smelling bad?' "(*CS,* 122). That evocation of the old code of Southern chivalry is apparently too much for the member of the rising generation, and the following night all four slink around Miss Emily's yard sprinkling lime.

## SHERWOOD ANDERSON

### The Book of the Grotesque[4]

The writer, an old man with a white mustache, had some difficulty in getting into bed. The windows of the house in which he lived were high and he wanted to look at the trees when he awoke in the morning. A carpenter came to fix the bed so that it would be on a level with the window.

Quite a fuss was made about the matter. The carpenter, who had been a soldier in the Civil War, came into the writer's room and sat down to talk of building a platform for the purpose of raising the bed. The writer had cigars lying about and the carpenter smoked.

For a time the two men talked of the raising of the bed and then they talked of other things. The soldier got on the subject of the war. The writer, in fact, led him to that subject. The carpenter had once been a prisoner in Andersonville prison and had lost a brother. The brother had died of starvation, and whenever the carpenter got upon that subject he cried. He, like the old writer, had a white mustache, and when he cried he puckered up his lips and the mustache bobbed up and down. The weeping old man with the cigar in his mouth was ludicrous. The plan the writer had for the raising of his bed was forgotten and later the carpenter did it in his own way and the writer, who was past sixty, had to help himself with a chair when he went to bed at night.

In his bed the writer rolled over on his side and lay quite still. For years he had been beset with notions concerning his heart. He was a hard smoker and his heart fluttered. The idea had got into his mind that he would some time die unexpectedly and always when he got into bed he thought of that. It did not alarm him. The effect in fact was quite a special thing and not easily explained. It made him more alive, there in bed, than at any other time. Perfectly still he lay and his body was old and not of much use any more, but something inside him was altogether young. He was like a pregnant woman, only that the thing inside him was not a baby but a youth. No, it wasn't a

4. From *Winesburg, Ohio* (1919).

youth. It was a woman, young, and wearing a coat of mail like a knight. It is absurd, you see to try to tell what was inside the old writer as he lay on his high bed and listened to the fluttering of his heart. The thing to get at is what the writer, or the young thing within the writer, was thinking about.

The old writer, like all of the people in the world, had got, during his long life, a great many notions in his head. He had once been quite handsome and a number of women had been in love with him. And then, of course, he had known people, many people, known them in a peculiarly intimate way that was different from the way in which you and I know people. At least that is what the writer thought and the thought pleased him. Why quarrel with an old man concerning his thoughts?

In the bed the writer had a dream that was not a dream. As he grew somewhat sleepy but was still conscious, figures began to appear before his eyes. He imagined the young indescribable thing within himself was driving a long procession of figures before his eyes.

You see the interest in all this lies in the figures that went before the eyes of the writer. They were all grotesques. All of the men and women the writer had ever known had become grotesques.

The grotesques were not all horrible. Some were amusing, some almost beautiful, and one, a woman all drawn out of shape, hurt the old man by her grotesqueness. When she passed he made a noise like a small dog whimpering. Had you come into the room you might have supposed the old man had unpleasant dreams or perhaps indigestion.

For an hour the procession of grotesques passed before the eyes of the old man, and then, although it was a painful thing to do, he crept out of bed and began to write. Some one of the grotesques had made a deep impression on his mind and he wanted to describe it.

At his desk the writer worked for an hour. In the end he wrote a book which he called "The Book of the Grotesque." It was never published, but I saw it once and it made an indelible impression on my mind. The book had one central thought that is very strange and has always remained with me. By remembering it I have been able to understand many people and things that I was never able to understand before. The thought was involved but a simple statement of it would be something like this:

> That in the beginning when the world was young there were a great many thoughts but no such thing as a truth. Man made the truths himself and each truth was a composite of a great many vague thoughts. All about in the world were the truths and they were all beautiful.

> The old man had listed hundreds of the truths in his book. I will not try to tell you of all of them. There was the truth of virginity and the truth of passion, the truth of wealth and of poverty, of thrift and of profligacy, of carelessness and abandon. Hundreds and hundreds were the truths and they were all beautiful. And then the people came along. Each as he appeared snatched up one of the truths and some who were quite strong snatched up a dozen of them.

> It was the truths that made the people grotesques. The old man had quite an elaborate theory concerning the matter. It was his notion that the moment one of the people took one of the truths to himself, called it his truth, and tried to

live his life by it, he became a grotesque and the truth he embraced became a falsehood.

You can see for yourself how the old man, who had spent all of his life writing and was filled with words, would write hundreds of pages concerning this matter. The subject would become so big in his mind that he himself would be in danger of becoming a grotesque. He didn't, I suppose, for the same reason that he never published the book. It was the young thing inside him that saved the old man.

Concerning the old carpenter who fixed the bed for the writer, I only mentioned him because he, like many of what are called very common people, became the nearest thing to what is understandable and lovable of all the grotesques in the writer's book.

## JOEL WILLIAMSON

### From *William Faulkner and Southern History*[5]

Beat Two was notorious in Lafayette County for the fierce independence of its white farmers. They were a proud, hard-working, common-sensical, usually poor, and sometimes violent people who frequently came into conflict with the town-dwelling authorities. In 1938 and 1939, Faulkner fell in love with his role as a working farmer, and he came to identify deeply with these "plain folk" of the South. "These are my kind of people," he said to his mother. The people out in Beat Two were very much in his mind as he got into writing the first volume of the Snopes trilogy in those years. It was then that he created his beloved V.K. Radliff, a man squarely out of the plain farmer tradition, a person of high intelligence, deep morality, and great wisdom who had capacities both for seeing the world as it is and for working effectively toward making it what it ought to be. He also elaborated his depiction of the hardy peasantry as represented by Varners, McCallums, Armstids, Bookrights, and Tulls. And, finally, he began to evolve the story of the Snopeses, first conceived a dozen years before.

The Snopeses were people who had begun somewhere in the middling range of the Southern social order before the Civil War. By the turn of the century, however, they were being ground down from farm owning to farm tenanting for a share of the crop, heading toward farm laboring, working sporadically for whatever they could get, drifting, and wintering on sufferance in outbuildings. In the case of Ab Snopes, Flem's father, it was a powerlessness that he countered with a tactic that slaves had favored—the threat to burn the master's barn under the cover of darkness. Arson, it seems, has always been a favored form of retaliation by the powerless of the world. One might begin with the master's barn, and end with the master's house—in extreme cases, at night with the master and his family sleeping in the house. A wise owner would never push his laborers over the edge.

In reality, the people in Beat Two that Faulkner so loved were the direct descendents of what Vanderbilt University historian Frank W. Owsley described as "the plain folk of the Old South." During the last generation of slavery, they

5. Joel Williamson, *William Faulkner and Southern History* (1993).

had shared generally in the prosperity of the cotton economy. During the war they had supplied, either willingly or by draft, the great majority of the soldiers in the rank and file of the Confederate armies. In the decades after the war, however, they found it increasingly difficult to maintain their middling status in the economy. While the whole of the white South was reduced considerably in the decades after the war, a minority of these yeoman folk lost out altogether, first by losing their farms, then by losing out as tenants for good farms, then by losing out in the competition to tenant any farms at all and becoming day laborers (the worst case scenario), as such to be used to advantage cheaply when needed and discarded when not. In all of this, after 1865, they faced effective competition from black farmers, who at least had the advantage of seeing themselves as rising up from slavery rather than heading down toward it.

Historically, two things were happening to produce this sad state. First, the South had lost power politically by attempting a rebellion and losing. Economic reduction was one of the prices it had to pay as a result of its miscalculation. Secondly, the Industrial Revolution was in full swing, and it fell to the lot of the South to produce raw materials cheaply, especially cotton, for that system while paying dearly to consume its finished products. In the new order, industrial and commercial elements were several steps ahead of farmers everywhere in controlling production and prices. In the turn-of-the-century years, large combinations such as U.S. Steel, Standard Oil, American Tobacco, and several large railroad corporations were able to balance out supply and demand to promote their own interests while farmers perennially produced all that soil, climate, and unrelenting labor could yield regardless of price. In the 1880s, they attempted to organize Farmers Alliances to gain some control over their economic lives both as to production and consumption. These failed dismally and in 1892 they formed the so-called Populist Party in an effort to achieve by political action what they could not do by economic means. That, too, foundered after the elections of 1896, but there were politicians like James K. Vardaman who carried forward the Populist purpose under the Democratic name. At last, in an American prosperity derived from World War I, 1914–1918, they achieved a modicum of success.

By the time Faulkner was a young man in the 1920s, these plain folk had moved into the third postwar generation. The early twenties brought economic reversal and a deep and dispiriting agricultural depression, well before the general depression ushered in by the crash of 1929. The result of this was a wave of migration by Southern whites to the towns and cities, a forced dislocation that still reverberates through Southern culture. When the Great Depression came to the South in the 1930s, it was not news; it was simply more of the same and deeper. Apparently, Faulkner never used the term "depression" in his fiction, and properly so. Nor did he call the New Deal by name, probably because he so hated it for undermining, as he saw it, the individuality and the freedom of his plain folk by its various "doles."

# Author in Depth: Alice Munro

Though Alice Munro often writes that she resists simple one-to-one connections between her biography and her short stories, the interplay between fact and her fiction is irresistible to many readers and critics. The interesting part to Munro herself isn't that her work is rooted in experience, but how her art transforms the experience into something else, something bigger. In the following documents, we catch a glimpse of the method by which Munro crafts her stories out of the details of her upbringing in the small town of Windsor, Ontario, as well as appreciations of the Nobel laureate's work by Margaret Atwood, Russell Banks, and critic Brad Hooper, who argues Munro has permanently expanded the possibilities of the short story.

## ALICE MUNRO

### What Is Real?[1]

Whenever people get an opportunity to ask me questions about my writing, I can be sure that some of the questions asked will be these:
"Do you write about real people?"
"Did those things really happen?"
"When you write about a small town are you really writing about Wingham?" (Wingham is the small town in Ontario where I was born and grew up, and it has often been assumed, by people who should know better, that I have simply "fictionalized" this place in my work. Indeed, the local newspaper has taken me to task for making it the "butt of a soured and cruel introspection.")

The usual thing, for writers, is to regard these either as very naïve questions, asked by people who really don't understand the difference between autobiography and fiction, who can't recognize the device of the first-person narrator, or else as catch-you-out questions posed by journalists who hope to stir up exactly the sort of dreary (and to outsiders, slightly comic) indignation voiced by my home-town paper. Writers answer such questions patiently or crossly according to temperament and the mood they're in. They say, no, you must understand, my characters are composites; no, those things didn't happen the way I wrote about them; no, of course not, that isn't Wingham (or whatever other place it may be that has had the queer unsought-after distinction of hatching a writer). Or the writer may, riskily, ask the questioners what is real, anyway? None of this seems to be very satisfactory. People go on asking these same questions because the subject really does interest and bewilder them. It would seem to be quite true that they don't actually know what fiction is.

And how could they know, when what it is, is changing all the time, and we differ among ourselves, and we don't really try to explain because it is too difficult?

What I would like to do here is what I can't do in two or three sentences at the end of a reading. I won't try to explain what fiction is, and what short

1. From *Making It New: Contemporary Canadian Stories*, ed. John Metcalf (1982).

stories are (assuming, which we can't, that there is any fixed thing that it is and they are), but what short stories are to me, and how I write them, and how I use things that are "real." I will start by explaining how I read stories written by other people. For one thing, I can start reading them anywhere; from beginning to end, from end to beginning, from any point in between in either direction. So obviously I don't take up a story and follow it as if it were a road, taking me somewhere, with views and neat diversions along the way. I go into it, and move back and forth and settle here and there, and stay in it for a while. It's more like a house. Everybody knows what a house does, how it encloses space and makes connections between one enclosed space and another and presents what is outside in a new way. This is the nearest I can come to explaining what a story does for me, and what I want my stories to do for other people.

So when I write a story I want to make a certain kind of structure, and I know the feeling I want to get from being inside that structure. This is the hard part of the explanation, where I have to use a word like "feeling," which is not very precise, because if I attempt to be more intellectually respectable I will have to be dishonest. "Feeling" will have to do.

There is no blueprint for the structure. It's not a question of, "I'll make this kind of house because if I do it right it will have this effect." I've got to make, I've got to build up, a house, a story, to fit around the indescribable "feeling" that is like the soul of the story, and which I must insist upon in a dogged, embarrassed way, as being no more definable than that. And I don't know where it comes from. It seems to be already there, and some unlikely clue, such as a shop window or a bit of conversation, makes me aware of it. Then I start accumulating the material and putting it together. Some of the material I may have lying around already, in memories and observations, and some I invent, and some I have to go diligently looking for (factual details), while some is dumped in my lap (anecdotes, bits of speech). I see how this material might go together to make the shape I need, and I try it. I keep trying and seeing where I went wrong and trying again.

I suppose this is the place where I should talk about technical problems and how I solve them. The main reason I can't is that I'm never sure I do solve anything. Even when I say that I see where I went wrong, I'm being misleading. I never figure out how I'm going to change things, I never say to myself, "That page is heavy going, that paragraph's clumsy, I need some dialogue and shorter sentences." I feel a part that's wrong, like a soggy weight; then I pay attention to the story, as if it were really happening somewhere, not just in my head, and in its own way, not mine. As a result, the sentences may indeed get shorter, there may be more dialogue, and so on. But though I've tried to pay attention to the story, I may not have got it right; those shorter sentences may be an evasion, a mistake. Every final draft, every published story, is still only an attempt, an approach, to the story.

I did promise to talk about using reality. "Why, if Jubilee isn't Wingham, has it got Shuter Street in it?" people want to know. Why have I described somebody's real ceramic elephant sitting on the mantelpiece? I could say I get momentum from doing things like this. The fictional room, town, world, needs a bit of starter dough from the real world. It's a device to help the writer—at least it helps me—but it arouses a certain baulked fury in the people who really do live on Shuter Street and the lady who owns the ceramic elephant. "Why do you put in something true and then go and tell lies?" they say, and anybody who has been on the receiving end of this kind of thing knows how they feel.

"I do it for the sake of my art and to make this structure that encloses the soul of my story, which I've been telling you about," says the writer. "That is more important than anything."

Not to everybody, it isn't.

So I can see there might be a case, once you've written the story and got the momentum, for going back and changing the elephant to a camel (though there's always a chance the lady might complain that you made a nasty camel out of a beautiful elephant), and changing Shuter Street to Blank Street. But what about the big chunks of reality, without which your story can't exist? In the story "Royal Beatings," I use a big chunk of reality: the story of the butcher, and of the young men who may have been egged on to "get" him. This is a story out of an old newspaper; it really did happen in a town I know. There is no legal difficulty about using it because it has been printed in a newspaper, and besides, the people who figure in it are all long dead. But there is a difficulty about offending people in that town who would feel that use of this story is a deliberate exposure, taunt, and insult. Other people who have no connection with the real happening would say, "Why write about anything so hideous?" And lest you think that such an objection could only be raised by simple folk who read nothing but Harlequin Romances, let me tell you that one of the questions most frequently asked at universities is, "Why do you write about things that are so depressing?" People can accept almost any amount of ugliness if it is contained in a familiar formula, as it is on television, but when they come closer to their own place, their own lives, they are much offended by a lack of editing.

There are ways I can defend myself against such objections. I can say, "I do it in the interests of historical reality. That is what the old days were really like." Or, "I do it to show the dark side of human nature, the beast let loose, the evil we can run up against in communities and families." In certain countries I could say, "I do it to show how bad things were under the old system when there were prosperous butchers and young fellows hanging around livery stables and nobody thought about building a new society." But the fact is, the minute I say *to show* I am telling a lie. I don't do it to show anything. I put this story at the heart of my story because I need it there and it belongs there. It is the black room at the centre of the house with all other rooms leading to and away from it. That is all. A strange defence. Who told me to write this story? Who feels any need of it before it is written? I do. I do, so that I might grab off this piece of horrid reality and install it where I see fit, even if Hat Nettleton and his friends were still around to make me sorry.

The answer seems to be as confusing as ever. Lots of true answers are. Yes and no. Yes, I use bits of what is real, in the sense of being really there and really happening, in the world, as most people see it, and I transform it into something that is really there and really happening, in my story. No, I am not concerned with using what is real to make any sort of record or prove any sort of point, and I am not concerned with any methods of selection but my own, which I can't fully explain. This is quite presumptuous, and if writers are not allowed to be so—and quite often, in many places, they are not—I see no point in the writing of fiction.

## ALICE MUNRO

### *Introduction*[2]

Like many writers, I get letters from people who would like some brass-tacks information. Should I consider writing as my career? some ask. How much yearly income can I expect as a writer? How much education should a writer have? Is it necessary to work on a computer? Have an agent? Associate with other writers?

Some clarifying statements about my work are requested by others. What do you consider to be your basic themes? Your major strengths/weaknesses? Why do you choose to write short stories instead of novels? Do you write from a feminist perspective, and if not, why not? How do yon feel that you contribute to the view of Canada held by a reader inside/outside the country? How has your fiction grown or progressed during your career? Do you prefer to write about relationships between people rather than important events, and if so, why? Do you prefer to write about rural and small-town people rather than sophisticated people, and if so, why? Are you a regional writer?

All this is rather flattering because it assumes that I am a person of brisk intelligence, exercising steady control on a number of fronts. I make advantageous judgments concerning computers and themes, I chart a course which is called a career and expect to make progress in it. I know what I am up to. Short stories, yes. Novels, no. I accept that rural folk are never sophisticated and sophisticates are never rural, and I make my choice. Also I keep an eye on feminism and Canada and try to figure out my duty to both.

This isn't exactly the kind of writer I'd like to be, but I wouldn't mind being a little more that way. In control, and pretty certain about what is going on, when I sit down with a pen and scribbler to do a first draft. Of course, if I was that kind of writer I might not know what a scribbler was, and I would pick up a pen only to write checks and autographs.

I am forced, in writing this introduction, to give the whole matter some thought, and I might as well start by answering a question.

I did not "choose" to write short stories. I hoped to write novels. When you are responsible for running a house and taking care of small children, particularly in the days before disposable diapers or ubiquitous automatic washing machines, it's hard to arrange for large chunks of time. A child's illness, relatives coming to stay, a pileup of unavoidable household jobs, can swallow a work-in-progress as surely as a power failure used to destroy a piece of work in the computer. You're better to stick with something you can keep in mind

2. From "Introduction to the Vintage Edition," *Selected Stories* (1997).

and hope to do in a few weeks, or a couple of months at most. I know that there are lots of women who have written novels in the midst of domestic challenges, just as there are men (and women) who have written them after coming home at night from exhausting jobs. That's why I thought I could do it too, but I couldn't. I took to writing in frantic spurts, juggling my life around until I could get a story done, then catching up on other responsibilities. So I got into the habit of writing short stories.

In later years my short stories haven't been so short. They've grown longer, and in a way more disjointed and demanding and peculiar. I didn't choose for that to happen, either. The only choice I make is to write about what interests me in a way that interests me, that gives me pleasure. It may not look like pleasure, because the difficulties can make me morose and distracted, but that's what it is—the pleasure of telling the story I mean to tell as wholly as I can tell it, of finding out in fact what that story is, by working around the different ways of telling it.

• • •

In "Miles City, Montana" and "The Moons of Jupiter" I have used, with some alteration, incidents and emotions from my own family life.

• • •

In "Royal Beatings" I turned to unacknowledged history again. Not exactly unofficial history, because the anecdote of father and daughter, the vigilante punishment handed out for suspected incest, comes right out of a nineteenth-century newspaper. But the town in which this happened, and where I grew up, now claims that no untoward incidents ever took place within its boundaries, and that prostitutes, bootleggers, and unhappy families were pretty much unknown—all being, according to an editorial in the local paper, products of my own "soured introspection."

This is all about beginnings. But that, in fact, is the easy part. Endings are another matter. When I've shaped the story in my head, before starting to put it on paper, it has, of course, an ending. Often this ending will stay in place right through the first draft. Sometimes it stays in place for good. Sometimes not. The story, in the first draft, has put on rough but adequate clothes, it is "finished" and might be thought to need no more than a lot of technical adjustments, some tightening here and expanding there, and the slipping in of some telling dialogue and chopping away of flabby modifiers. It's then, in fact, that the story is in the greatest danger of losing its life, of appearing so hopelessly misbegotten that my only relief comes from abandoning it. It doesn't do enough. It does what I intended, but it turns out that my intention was all wrong. Quite often I decide to give up on it. (This was the point at which, in my early days as a writer, I did just chuck everything out and get started on something absolutely new.) And now that the story is free from my controlling hand a change in direction may occur. I can't ever be sure this will happen, and there are bad times, though I should be used to them. I'm no good at letting go, I am thrifty and tenacious now, no spendthrift and addict of fresh starts as in my youth. I go around glum and preoccupied, trying to think of ways to fix the problem. Usually the right way pops up in the middle of this.

A big relief, then. Renewed energy. Resurrection.

Except that it isn't the right way. Maybe a way *to* the right way. Now I write pages and pages I'll have to discard. New angles are introduced, minor characters brought center stage, lively and satisfying scenes are written, and it's all a mistake. Out they go. But by this time I'm on the track, there's no backing out. I know so much more than I did, I know what I want to happen and where I want to end up and I just have to keep trying till I find the best way of getting there.

### SHEILA MUNRO

### From *Lives of Mothers & Daughters*[3]

As she got older, young Alice felt constantly that she was being judged as bad, that she was always in conflict with her mother. At least once a month, she got into serious trouble of some kind. And it wasn't just with her mother. "I didn't know an adult who wasn't critical of me all the time." At school she was getting in trouble for being "inept, stupid, and terribly messy." Her handwriting was so bad that one teacher called her "Uncle Wiggly." Remember how Del is shaking so badly she starts the treadle sewing machine accidentally and is exempted from sewing? That was my mother. Of course neatness and skill at needlework were more important in a girl than almost anything else in those days, though the letters from my great-grandmother do refer to my mother's triumphs at school, so it couldn't have been all bad.

At home she kept getting in trouble for those things and for everything else, for being sarcastic, for being nasty. "I always talked back. I wasn't a nice child, at that time lots of girls were nice, but being nice meant such a terrible abdication of self." (I don't want her to say this. Surely she *was* nice. I was nice. I wanted to please her. Did I abdicate *my* self?) Her earliest strategy in life was one of protecting herself, thinking her survival depended on it. She often lied and hoped not to be found out, though of course lying was considered a terrible sin.

At the time when Anne[4] was starting to get sick, overtaken by mysterious attacks of lethargy, but before she had any inkling that she was in the early stages of Parkinson's disease, she and her daughter had terrible rows, which culminated in my mother being beaten by her father, in much the same way Rose is punished in "Royal Beatings" in *Who Do You Think You Are?* The arguments between mother and daughter would escalate. My mother would refuse to back down, daring to "talk back" rather than capitulate. Finally her father would be called in from the barn, and Anne would tell her version of events. What my mother found most painful was her perception that "a story was being told on me that wasn't true" and that she was never allowed to tell her side of the story. When things got really bad, which happened two or three times a year, her father would go get his leather belt and beat her with it, exactly the way Rose's father does after Flo calls him in from the barn when she has had enough of Rose's flippancy. "'All right,' says Flo. 'You've done it this time. All right'... Rose tries to butt in, to say it isn't true." But by then it

---

**3.** Sheila Munro, *Lives of Mothers & Daughters: Growing Up with Alice Munro* (2001).  **4.** Anne Laidlaw, Alice's mother.

is too late. She could not write that story, another of her "breakthrough" stories, until after her father had died.

I was surprised when my mother told me about how very puritanical her family life was, and how puritanical she was herself; surprised because that isn't how I have ever seen my mother, and that is not at all what it was like in our household when I was growing up. In her home, any mention of sex was taboo, of course, and so was swearing. Alcohol was "a badge of sin." When my mother saw a bottle of whisky sitting on the kitchen counter in someone's house, she was shocked. Anyone who drank was a "scoundrel" and a "wastrel."

She was also quite a "churchmouse" who attended the Anglican Church with a friend, and found it aesthetically much more appealing than her own United Church (as Del does in *Lives*). She lost her faith when she was about twelve; every time she asked for a "sign" from God and no sign was forthcoming her faith "went down a notch." It didn't matter much because at about this time "art took over." Art became her religion.

According to my mother, Anne "was a very controlling person but her control was not just a personal control, it was the control of a moral order she believed in and projected on to others. She was full of self-assertion; she had no self-doubt and naturally she would clash with a daughter who questioned everything, who resisted any form of control." Anne's values were based on a model of gentility that came from the Victorian period. My mother considers that rural, small-town Ontario was essentially Victorian up until the Second World War, and that she grew up in the last remnants of that age.

## ROBERT THACKER

### From *Alice Munro: Writing Her Lives*[5]

Both "Miles City, Montana" and "Progress of Love," each drafted in the same notebook and finished about this same time, are stories close to Munro's own life. The near-drowning incident at the centre of the first is virtually memoir, the four family members who were there remembering it as narrated. Munro and her father rescuing turkeys from drowning is a memory too, but Steve Gauley, his drowning, and his funeral were imagined, though Munro recalls knowing boys who later drowned. "The Progress of Love" draws on the lives of her great-grandmother, her grandmother, and her mother while Phemie (or Fame), its narrator, includes elements of Munro herself. She is given some of Munro's own memories, certainly, but Fame is also a character offering what might have become of Munro herself had she never got away from Wingham. The narrator's perspective, like Munro's, is that of a middle-aged native. All this admitted, Munro is nevertheless right about these two stories: "not one is as close [to her life] as people seem to think." This is so because of Munro's "energy and devotion and secret pains" — they transform whatever had been remembered, whatever is "real," into the different reality that is the story's world. The story, an artifice, is able to affect its readers on its own terms by way of the words she arranges, those words that she thinks never serve her well enough.

5. Robert Thacker, *Alice Munro: Writing Her Lives* (2005).

"Miles City, Montana" and "The Progress of Love" demonstrate just how Munro's writing during this time began in actual experiences but then, through her art, became something considerably more than experience transcribed. "Miles City" seems to have begun when Munro was working on "The Beggar Maid" during 1976–77; a draft of the Miles City incident includes a courtship for the narrator and her husband Hugh similar to Rose and Patrick's. About this time too there was also the draft story, "Shoebox Babies," which Munro worked on during the late 1970s but never published and which drew from the circumstances of Catherine Munro's birth and death in July 1955. It moved into a notebook draft called just "Miles City," which contains a fairly complete rendering of the near-drowning episode and the family's trip; but rather than just the recollected dead deer the family saw when playing "I Spy" in the finished story, the older daughter recalls Elizabeth, the baby who died. This draft also includes the image of the drowned Steve Gauley being carried by the narrator's father, although it appears just at the story's end where it is connected to the narrator's misgivings about their vulnerability. Its narrator is explicitly Munro herself in 1961: "During those years I was trying to be a writer. I could say that I was trying to write — short stories, and, once, a novel — but it would be more accurate to say that I was trying to be a writer, because I felt as if I had to assemble distant parts of myself and hold them together, before I could start the actual writing. This was my job – this assembling — and it was a tricky business." Neither version includes the narrator and her father saving turkeys from drowning, an experience in the finished story that confirms the narrator's role as daughter and allows her to appreciate his hard-working way of life.

Munro's own "assembling" of "Miles City, Montana" was indeed a tricky business. It takes her memoir — the near-drowning and its circumstances — and marries it to the imagined drowning and funeral of Steve Gauley. Human helplessness in the face of death, and her parents' attitudes toward it, are felt as the narrator and Andrew talk in the aftermath. It is then she imagines what it would have been like if Meg had not been saved. "Who is ready to be a father, a mother, who is fit?" the narrator asks in the draft, just before she shifts back to Steve Gauley's drowning and his funeral, asking the central unanswerable question of "Miles City, Montana." And though Munro omitted any direct reference to Catherine Munro's death in the final version, it is felt on the page, created there in Munro's sensed and mediated human vulnerability.

So while it is possible to see Jenny Munro's near-drowning in 1961 in Miles City, Montana, at the centre of the story, to insist on that incident's recounting as the story's core misses the point of any fiction, and of Munro's in particular. What she creates on the page is the feeling of being, the feeling of authentic experience captured through words. This writing has a kind of purity when it works — as it most certainly does in "Miles City, Montana" and in "The Progress of Love." Yet any created purity is not just in the story's details, since those may be grafted on from anywhere (the swimming pool in Miles City, Montana, for example, was not a swimming pool but a man-made body called Scanlon Lake). Their connection to Munro's own life, while real, is secondary to anyone reading a story that emerges from such connections. For Munro, and for her readers too, the significance of any autobiographical connection comes back to the image of Cynthia and Meg, still in their back seat, still headed to Ontario, still expecting to return home to Vancouver: "So we went on, with the two in the back seat trusting us, because of no choice, and we ourselves trusting to be forgiven, in time, for everything that had first to be seen and condemned by those children: whatever was flippant, arbitrary, careless, callous — all our natural, and particular, mistakes."

## MARGARET ATWOOD

### *An Appreciation*[6]

The fifties were a very male period of writing in the United States. America didn't have a tradition of women writers. Who, among women, were admired? Eudora Welty, Katherine Anne Porter. Among poets? Emily Dickinson. How many others? In Canada, you didn't get points off for being a woman. The challenge wasn't so much being female as it was being Canadian. Embroidery, oil painting, writing, it was all considered a hobby. Writing wasn't important. There was hardly a market for new novels. The writing community up here was so small at that time. Because of readings and little magazines, poets knew one another's work, but it was different for prose writers in Canada.

When we were growing up the idea of being a writer was so alien. Just to think you could do it was an act of major hubris. Talent was discouraged. Yet as a child, Alice had read L. M. Montgomery's *Anne of Green Gables* and *Emily of New Moon*, about a young girl growing up on Prince Edward Island who wants to be a writer. Alice has written an afterword for the latter book.

Two other early influences on her were *Wuthering Heights* and *Pride and Prejudice*. In *Wuthering Heights* you never hear the story directly from the most powerful people in it. You hear it from the observers: a gentleman named Lockwood, who rents Thrushcross Grange, and Nelly, the housekeeper. This is a very interesting way of putting a book together. Also, there are the two houses. There are the Lintons, who are genteel—not forceful and not sexy. And then there's Heathcliff. *Pride and Prejudice* is another very well put together book that draws on the emotions we love so much, and there's Mr. Darcy, another rude man with lots of money underneath. And economics is such a big factor in Alice's work. Who's got money, who hasn't, who needs money, who's making it, and who's paying for things.

Her other influences were writers of stories set in small towns. Alice read Sherwood Anderson—who made her feel that maybe she could do this kind of thing—as well as Eudora Welty, Flannery O'Connor, and Carson McCullers. Having grown up in a small town herself, Alice knows them well—specifically, small towns in southwestern Ontario. Why are there so many crazy, demented people in a small town? It's just that everyone knows everyone and one another's background. Like a big, dysfunctional family. It's that way in cities, too, but you don't necessarily know about all of it, because you may not know the people across the street, or even next door. In small towns people are con-

---

**6.** From "Appreciations of Alice Munro," *Virginia Quarterly Review*, Summer 2006.

scious of gossip, rumor, the keeping up of pretenses, and the varying gradations of social level. It can be confining.

That's why Alice's stories are so place- and time-specific. What people eat,
what they wear, what appliances they are using, are all important to her. She
is interested in questions of authenticity; she looks at her characters' fronts
and pretensions, at what effect they are trying to achieve, and then she examines what lies underneath. Maybe the characters see through each other, and
so they have social lies, such as, "You look terrific." Sometimes they mean it
benignly; sometimes they don't.

She writes about the difficulties faced by people who are bigger or smaller
than they are expected to be. When her protagonists look back, from later
points of view, the older people they have become possess within them all of
the people that they have been. She's very good on what people expect, and
then on the letdown.

One of the many things Alice does so well is to contrast how people thought
something would be, compared to how it turned out. We depend on a certain
amount of fulfilled expectation. The sun will rise in the morning. Mr. Brown
will be at the corner store at 8 A.M. and sell milk. In Alice Munro stories, people
go into a house and find out that someone has been murdered. Every expectation is met; and then, there is an event, a surprise—and that's the story.

## RUSSELL BANKS

### An Appreciation[7]

There is nothing exotic or off-putting in the opening paragraph or two of an
Alice Munro story. The author puts her hand on your shoulder and invites
you into her fictional world. She is friendly, and there is a neighborly quality
to her narrative prose. She starts in a small place and universalizes characters
and lives that we might otherwise overlook. It is as if you are sitting at a table,
and she's going to tell you a story of what happened a while back, down the
street. Her intimate tone is interesting and immediate, and she is relaxed,
calm, even inactive, almost seductive. Then, once you are in this fictional world,
it becomes more threatening.

You realize there are issues of life and death going on, and Munro's fiction
takes hard swerves abruptly. She is able to break off narrative then start it up
later, and it's still connected. We can travel through time and space and point
of view, shifting our relation to time and space, so we're closer in, or further
away. Most contemporary short fiction writers capture moments in time, but
Munro telescopes backward and forward. Usually this is only seen in novels.

What this does for us is to stretch the range of the dramatic possibility
of the short story, which in the hands of US writers has gone minimalist,
become reductive and compressed. Munro's fiction expands outward, and it
shows us that while the short story form can be as compressed and hard as a
diamond, it can also be as expansive as a novel.

She is almost a cubist. That's the way memory works and storytelling
goes. It's not mathematics, it's not logic. It's remembering and recounting
through memory what happened. This is also the way dreams work. Often

---

7. From "Appreciations of Alice Munro," *Virginia Quarterly Review*, Summer 2006.

good fiction corresponds closely to the structure of dreams, but it is aesthetically and morally purposeful. Munro has the great moral force and intelligence to refuse to judge or idealize her characters, which would be easy to do, and she won't allow her readers to do so either. Alice Munro's writing casts her as someone who dares to speak the truth about the world, to say the things that we are ashamed or afraid to tell.

## BRAD HOOPER

### An Appreciation[8]

Munro has modified the short story to suit her own interests, needs, and capabilities, and the short-story genre will remain modified from her efforts. There will always be, now, the Munro-type of short story; and it will be referred to as such. And I do not mean a brand of short story that is simply idiosyncratic to her, which was exercised by her alone. No, I mean a permanent opening of the genre to possibilities—expansion possibilities, primarily—that authors after her can explore for their own purposes.

Munro has not simply taken care of the short story; it has not been up to her, nor has she been inclined to shoulder the responsibility, to maintain its conventions, set them down again intact, after her use of them is done, and send the short story on its way in a healthy condition but still in a traditional form. She has broadened the scope of what defines a short story but by following only the strictest procedures in opening the story form while *keeping* it the short-story form, not calling her product short stories when they are in fact underdeveloped novels. I insist upon this: she writes short stories, not short novels.

It is the resonance of what is on the page that gives her stories the experience of a novel; there is nothing condensed in her stories, only expanded by the universalities she touches upon in the particulars of her stories. That is the essence of a Munro short story, the fundamental process of her technique and the gist of her reader's appeal.

Many instances have been cited in the course of my analysis of her work of her use of first-person narrative; one finds, particularly in the first half of her oeuvre, this is almost exclusively her narrative technique. It is a choice for a reason; it makes no difference whether the narrator proves prejudiced, naive, uninformed, or one-sided, for the point of this narrative technique is to eliminate detachment, to make her stories as personal as possible, to bring her characters to the reader as real as they can be. But not only has Munro claimed the first-person narrative voice as her own, but she has also, as she has adapted the short-story structure to her own needs and interests, adapted it well to suit her purposes. She often uses the technique of first-person narrator narrating from the perspective of many years after the events being recalled as her way of having the narrator reconcile his or her (most often the latter, of course) past to his or her present: not only to see it through the clarifying lens of many years standing between the past and present, but also to help read the past as meaningful provenance of the present.

---

**8.** From *The Fiction of Alice Munro: An Appreciation* (2008).

Of course, no adequately comprehensive discussion of Munro's fiction can fail to bring into the light her use of, her abiding interest in, the past: not so much the historical past, although that occasionally does play a role, at least as a backdrop to her characters' *personal* past. To be specific—to be accurate— her stories are not so much set in the past as they are remembrance pieces "about" the past, glances backward functioning to explore the present. Conversely, very little in a Munro story is about *just* the present; the past is always present in her stories, which, of course is a main reason for the depths to which her fiction goes in exploration of character. The result is her fiction's intense resonance, the profound analysis of a character that at once defines the character as an individual, yet binds that character to the general human condition with whom all readers can connect.

A corollary theme to the theme of the influence of the past on the present, around which many of her stories are constructed, is the "outsider" consciousness. As observed on numerous occasions, Munro's stories, protagonists frequently feel, are outside the mainstream in socioeconomic and, in the case of schoolgirls, "coolness" terms. The outsider theme is often played out in gender situations: girls and women who don't want to practice/perform traditional female roles. They are not so much in rebellion against accepted practices as simply uninterested. They stand outside, looking in, but not willing to be part of the accepted "crowd." A sub theme, a logical extension of it, or even a refinement of it, is the functioning of the adolescent female narrator as a bridge between the traditional male and female spheres of interest and endeavor; these situations—these that spring from this particular sub theme—offer some of the most intriguing, resonant, reader-appealing stories in all her oeuvre, for who cannot identify with an adolescent lack of desire to fit into neat and tidy boxes? Or, better stated: who, even if they did not experience such lack of interest in resisting the traces of tradition when they were adolescents, cannot understand Munro's characters going through such a psychological process? That is a strong testament to her ability to create characters perfectly comprehensible even to readers with whom they share not much in terms of gender, background, or life pursuits.

That brings us to the major conclusion that must be drawn—given the course that this critical survey has taken—about Munro as a fiction writer. She has moved the boundaries, the dimensions, the techniques in composing the short story beyond traditional methods and expectations, yes. But as I stated in the Introduction, all of that was in service to a higher, more personal objective for her: to achieve a deeper understanding of her characters. Her "invention," if you will, of the Munro short story was not intentional as a goal unto itself; it simply was the by-product of her magnificently achieved goal of building a character within the parameters of the short-story form.

# Author in Depth: Flannery O'Connor

Flannery O'Connor wrote that the "writer's business is to contemplate experience, not to be merged with it." Lupus, the painful autoimmune disease that cut short her life, circumscribed her movements—O'Connor spent most of her writing life on her mother's farm in Milledgeville, Georgia—but it did not stop the hard work of contemplation, a process she explained in several essays on her approach to writing fiction, excerpted below. The documents included here also explore the influence of certain experiences in O'Connor's life, as well as her perspective as a Southern writer, and her deeply held religious beliefs, with commentaries by Alice Walker, Lee Smith, and Thomas Merton, among others. The section ends with moving excerpts from O'Connor's prayer journal.

## FLANNERY O'CONNOR

### The Nature and Aim of Fiction[1]

If you go to a school where there are classes in writing, these classes should not be to teach you how to write, but to teach you the limits and possibilities of words and the respect due them. One thing that is always with the writer—no matter how long he has written or how good he is—is the continuing process of learning how to write. As soon as the writer "learns to write," as soon as he knows what he is going to find, and discovers a way to say what he knew all along, or worse still, a way to say nothing, he is finished. If a writer is any good, what he makes will have its source in a realm much larger than that which his conscious mind can encompass and will always be a greater surprise to him than it can ever be to his reader.

I don't know which is worse—to have a bad teacher or no teacher at all. In any case, I believe the teacher's work should be largely negative. He can't put the gift into you, but if he finds it there, he can try to keep it from going in an obviously wrong direction. We can learn how not to write, but this is a discipline that does not simply concern writing itself but concerns the whole intellectual life. A mind cleared of false emotion and false sentiment and egocentricity is going to have at least those roadblocks removed from its path. If you don't think cheaply, then there at least won't be the quality of cheapness in your writing, even though you may not be able to write well. The teacher can try to weed out what is positively bad, and this should be the aim of the whole college. Any discipline can help your writing: logic, mathematics, theology, and of course and particularly drawing. Anything that helps you to see, anything that makes you look. The writer should never be ashamed of staring. There is nothing that doesn't require his attention.

We hear a great deal of lamentation these days about writers having all taken themselves to the colleges and universities where they live decorously

1. From *Mystery and Manners: Occasional Prose,* ed. Robert and Sally Fitzgerald (1969).

instead of going out and getting firsthand information about life. The fact is that anybody who has survived his childhood has enough information about life to last him the rest of his days. If you can't make something out of a little experience, you probably won't be able to make it out of a lot. The writer's business is to contemplate experience, not to be merged in it.

Everywhere I go I'm asked if I think the universities stifle writers. My opinion is that they don't stifle enough of them. There's many a best-seller that could have been prevented by a good teacher. The idea of being a writer attracts a good many shiftless people, those who are merely burdened with poetic feelings or afflicted with sensibility. Granville Hicks, in a recent review of James Jones' novel, quoted Jones as saying, "I was stationed at Hickham Field in Hawaii when I stumbled upon the works of Thomas Wolfe, and his home life seemed so similar to my own, his feelings about himself so similar to mine about myself, that I realized I had been a writer all my life without knowing it or having written." Mr. Hicks goes on to say that Wolfe did a great deal of damage of this sort but that Jones is a particularly appalling example.

Now in every writing class you find people who care nothing about writing, because they think they are already writers by virtue of some experience they've had. It is a fact that if, either by nature or training, these people can learn to write badly enough, they can make a great deal of money, and in a way it seems a shame to deny them this opportunity; but then, unless the college is a trade school, it still has its responsibility to truth, and I believe myself that these people should be stifled with all deliberate speed.

Presuming that the people left have some degree of talent, the question is what can be done for them in a writing class. I believe the teacher's work is largely negative, that it is largely a matter of saying "This doesn't work because..." or "This does work because..." The *because* is very important. The teacher can help you understand the nature of your medium, and he can guide you in your reading. I don't believe in classes where students criticize each other's manuscripts. Such criticism is generally composed in equal parts of ignorance, flattery, and spite. It's the blind leading the blind, and it can be dangerous. A teacher who tries to impose a way of writing on you can be dangerous too. Fortunately, most teachers I've known were too lazy to do this. In any case, you should beware of those who appear overenergetic.

In the last twenty years the colleges have been emphasizing creative writing to such an extent that you almost feel that any idiot with a nickel's worth of talent can emerge from a writing class able to write a competent story. In fact, so many people can now write competent stories that the short story as a medium is in danger of dying of competence. We want competence, but competence by itself is deadly. What is needed is the vision to go with it, and you do not get this from a writing class.

### FLANNERY O'CONNOR

### *The Grotesque in Southern Fiction*[2]

In nineteenth-century American writing, there was a good deal of grotesque literature which came from the frontier and was supposed to be funny; but

2. From *Mystery and Manners* (1969).

our present grotesque characters, comic though they may be, are at least not primarily so. They seem to carry an invisible burden; their fanaticism is a reproach, not merely an eccentricity. I believe that they come about from the prophetic vision peculiar to any novelist whose concerns I have been describing. In the novelist's case, prophecy is a matter of seeing near things with their extensions of meaning and thus of seeing far things close up. The prophet is a realist of distances, and it is this kind of realism that you find in the best modern instances of the grotesque.

Whenever I'm asked why Southern writers particularly have a penchant for writing about freaks, I say it is because we are still able to recognize one. To be able to recognize a freak, you have to have some conception of the whole man, and in the South the general conception of man is still, in the main, theological. That is a large statement, and it is dangerous to make it, for almost anything you say about Southern belief can be denied in the next breath with equal propriety. But approaching the subject from the standpoint of the writer, I think it is safe to say that while the South is hardly Christ-centered, it is most certainly Christ-haunted. The Southerner, who isn't convinced of it, is very much afraid that he may have been formed in the image and likeness of God. Ghosts can be very fierce and instructive. They cast strange shadows, particularly in our literature. In any case, it is when the freak can be sensed as a figure for our essential displacement that he attains some depth in literature.

There is another reason in the Southern situation that makes for a tendency toward the grotesque and this is the prevalence of good Southern writers. I think the writer is initially set going by literature more than by life. When there are many writers all employing the same idiom, all looking out on more or less the same social scene, the individual writer will have to be more than ever careful that he isn't just doing badly what has already been done to completion. The presence alone of Faulkner in our midst makes a great difference in what the writer can and cannot permit himself to do. Nobody wants his mule and wagon stalled on the same track the Dixie Limited is roaring down.

The Southern writer is forced from all sides to make his gaze extend beyond the surface, beyond mere problems, until it touches that realm which is the concern of prophets and poets.

### FLANNERY O'CONNOR
### From *Writing Short Stories*[3]

In good fiction, certain of the details will tend to accumulate meaning from the action of the story itself, and when this happens they become symbolic in the way they work. I once wrote a story called "Good Country People," in which a lady Ph.D. has her wooden leg stolen by a Bible salesman whom she has tried to seduce. Now I'll admit that, paraphrased in this way, the situation is simply a low joke. The average reader is pleased to observe anybody's wooden leg being stolen. But without ceasing to appeal to him and without making any statements of high intention, this story does manage to operate at another level of experience, by letting the wooden leg accumulate meaning.

3. From *Mystery and Manners* (1969).

Early in the story, we're presented with the fact that the Ph.D. is spiritually as well as physically crippled. She believes in nothing but her own belief in nothing, and we perceive that there is a wooden part of her soul that corresponds to her wooden leg. Now of course this is never stated. The fiction writer states as little as possible. The reader makes this connection from things he is shown. He may not even know that he makes the connection, but the connection is there nevertheless and it has its effect on him. As the story goes on, the wooden leg continues to accumulate meaning. The reader learns how the girl feels about her leg, how her mother feels about it, and how the country woman on the place feels about it; and finally, by the time the Bible salesman comes along, the leg has accumulated so much meaning that it is, as the saying goes, loaded. And when the Bible salesman steals it, the reader realizes that he has taken away part of the girl's personality and has revealed her deeper affliction to her for the first time.

If you want to say that the wooden leg is a symbol, you can say that. But it is a wooden leg first, and as a wooden leg it is absolutely necessary to the story. It has its place on the literal level of the story, but it operates in depth as well as on the surface. It increases the story in every direction, and this is essentially the way a story escapes being short.

Now a little might be said about the way in which this happens. I wouldn't want you to think that in that story I sat down and said, "I am now going to write a story about a Ph.D. with a wooden leg, using the wooden leg as a symbol for another kind of affliction." I doubt myself if many writers know what they are going to do when they start out. When I started writing that story, I didn't know there was going to be a Ph.D. with a wooden leg in it. I merely found myself one morning writing a description of two women that I knew something about, and before I realized it, I had equipped one of them with a daughter with a wooden leg. As the story progressed, I brought in the Bible salesman, but I had no idea what I was going to do with him. I didn't know he was going to steal that wooden leg until ten or twelve lines before he did it, but when I found out that this was what was going to happen, I realized that it was inevitable. This is a story that produces a shock for the reader, and I think one reason for this is that it produced a shock for the writer.

Now despite the fact that this story came about in this seemingly mindless fashion, it is a story that almost no rewriting was done on. It is a story that was under control throughout the writing of it, and it might be asked how this kind of control comes about, since it is not entirely conscious.

I think the answer to this is what Maritain calls "the habit of art." It is a fact that fiction writing is something in which the whole personality takes part—the conscious as well as the unconscious mind. Art is the habit of the artist; and habits have to be rooted deep in the whole personality. They have to be cultivated like any other habit, over a long period of time, by experience; and teaching any kind of writing is largely a matter of helping the student develop the habit of art. I think this is more than just a discipline, although it is that; I think it is a way of looking at the created world and of using the senses so as to make them find as much meaning as possible in things.

• • •

There are two qualities that make fiction. One is the sense of mystery and the other is the sense of manners. You get the manners from the texture of existence that surrounds you. The great advantage of being a Southern writer is that we don't have to go anywhere to look for manners; bad or good, we've got them in abundance. We in the South live in a society that is rich in contradiction, rich in irony, rich in contrast, and particularly rich in its speech. And yet here are six stories by Southerners in which almost no use is made of the gifts of the region.

Of course the reason for this may be that you have seen these gifts abused so often that you have become self-conscious about using them. There is nothing worse than the writer who doesn't *use* the gifts of the region, but wallows in them. Everything becomes so Southern that it's sickening, so local that it is unintelligible, so literally reproduced that it conveys nothing. The general gets lost in the particular instead of being shown through it.

However, when the life that actually surrounds us is totally ignored, when our patterns of speech are absolutely overlooked, then something is out of kilter. The writer should then ask himself if he is not reaching out for a kind of life that is artificial to him.

An idiom characterizes a society, and when you ignore the idiom, you are very likely ignoring the whole social fabric that could make a meaningful character. You can't cut characters off from their society and say much about them as individuals. You can't say anything meaningful about the mystery of a personality unless you put that personality in a believable and significant social context. And the best way to do this is through the character's own language.

## BRAD GOOCH

### From *The Bible Salesman*[4]

One spring afternoon in late April 1953, a striking-looking young man appeared at the front door. Tall and blond, described by Caroline Gordon as "a Dane with eyes like blue marbles," Erik Langkjaer was a twenty-six-year-old college textbook salesman for Harcourt Brace, Flannery's publisher. As his recently assigned territory was the entire South east of the Mississippi, he had been visiting with professors at Georgia State College for Women. Among them was Helen Greene, whose English history textbook was published by Harcourt. "After checking out his current offerings in that field, I asked him if he would like to meet one of his company's published authors," Greene has written. As she was his last appointment of the day, the history professor was pleased to take him "out to Andalusia to meet Mary Flannery and Miss Regina."

While Helen Greene remembered Erik's response as an enthusiastic "Of course!" he felt, in truth, puzzled. "She was sure that Flannery would be interested in meeting me," says Langkjaer, "and I must say I couldn't imagine why, because I hadn't read the novel, and I hadn't even been told that she was living in Milledgeville, and why would anyone want to meet a perfect stranger on such a flimsy pretext. But the professor said that she doesn't see too many people, living as she does with her mother. I went along with that idea. Some time in the afternoon, we rang the doorbell of Andalusia." Helen Greene judged the introduction a success: "He and Mary Flannery liked each other a great deal, and, as

4. From *Flannery: A Life of Flannery O'Connor* (2009).

I recall, she guided him on a tour of Baldwin County in his car. . . . He was happily surprised to find such interesting and attractive people in the area."

• • •

They discussed more on this first visit than Day's[5] social activism, or the ecumenical mission of his "aunt" in reuniting the Russian Orthodox Church with Rome. Erik was quite open about his life situation, "that I had come to the U.S., that I was now traveling somewhat rootlessly in the South, and that I had all these religious concerns and problems." Flannery was tickled by a traveling salesman carrying "The Bible," a joke term in publishing for his standard loose-leaf binder of promotional materials and tables. "It amused her very much that something that was not a bible should have been called a bible," says Langkjaer. And she responded with tenderness to his rootless search. Writing to Erik two years later, Flannery recalled a first rush of empathy with his homelessness: "You wonder how anybody can be happy in his home as long as there is one person without one. I never thought of this so much until I began to know you and your situation and I will never quite have a home again on acct. of it."

• • •

That first afternoon, Mrs. O'Connor served Erik and Flannery tea and then withdrew to take care of various business matters. Erik immediately picked up on the wide gap in sensibility between Flannery and her mother. Not "the saint everyone thinks she was, she was rather rebellious," says Langkjaer of the young woman who struck him as still far from reconciled to her fate. "I did sense that Flannery had a tense relationship with her mother. I got the impression that she was quite dependent on her mother now that she had come down with this disease, but that she was not an easy person for Flannery to talk to. I mean they were really not of one mind, to put it mildly.

• • •

Erik had not read a word by the writer with whom he established such sudden intimacy, but she soon gave him *Wise Blood*, with the inscription "For Erik who has wise blood too," and "A Good Man Is Hard to Find," which she was completing when they met. Holding on to his impression of Mrs. O'Connor as "pleasant," yet "rather restrictive, very much focused on the practical aspects of running the farm," he continued later in life to interpret the grandmother of the story—wearing her white cotton gloves and blue navy straw hat so that "anyone seeing her dead on the highway would know at once that she was a lady"—as a version of Regina, or others of Flannery's female relatives. "This woman represented perhaps the essence of members of Flannery's own family that she distilled into this one character," says Langkjaer. "Here was a very, very limited person. . . . The grandmother is a completely banal, superficial woman."

Erik was stimulated enough by the remarkable new friendship to schedule regular visits to Milledgeville on weekends, often needing to rearrange his itinerary and travel a hundred miles or more out of his way. As Regina made clear to Flannery that she considered his staying overnight improper, he rented a room in a local motel, and then made his "calls" to Andalusia. Textbook orders were placed seasonally, clustered over the next fall and spring, so

---

5. Dorothy Day, founder of the Catholic Worker movement.

there were ten or twelve such visits. Erik and Flannery would take long walks, go for rides, or have lunch at Sanford House, talking all the while. "Was he ever handsome," recalls Mary Jo Thompson. "Flannery reserved the table on the porch to have lunch with Erik. It was perfect for a couple." Flannery was invested enough that when Betty Hester mentioned Helene Iswolsky a few years later, she confided, with unusual candor and spunk, "I used to go with her nephew."

### TONY MAGISTRALE

From *"I'm Alien to a Great Deal": Flannery O'Connor and the Modernist Ethic*[6]

O'Connor's particular brand of Roman Catholicism is rooted in the church's pre-Vatican II siege mentality; its strict adherence to doctrine, ecclesiastical government, and an apocalyptic cosmology make it a modern illustration of direct medieval influence. Christianity's flame has always burned brightest for purists, and it was the unadulterated traditionalism of the Catholic church before its liberalization in Pope John XXIII's ecumenical movement of the 1960s that is most similar to Flannery O'Connor's fiction.

• • •

Many readers of O'Connor's fiction claim that her tales are too bleak and despairing, that her conclusions are not filled with the light of transcendence, but rather the darkness of loss. Indeed, her Southerners attain moral development and self-knowledge only through experiencing the devastating realities of human tragedy: widows losing sons through a misplaced sense of charity, grandmothers who uncover the true nature of spirituality at the end of a rifle, fanatics who must kill themselves to atone for their failure to recognize Christ, and intelligent rationalists who discover the inadequacies of their guiding philosophies only after it is too late to save the lives of mothers and sons. Perhaps what is most difficult for modern readers to accept is O'Connor's refusal to equate physical suffering and death with evil. True "rising" is possible in her world only at a severe price, and that expense bears little in common with what we have typically come to regard as a sense of improvement.

I am afraid that those who bemoan the violent and tragic circumstances of O'Connor's fiction tend to confuse her absolute lack of sentimentality with callousness. O'Connor is too intelligent to be sentimental; she is romantic, in the very best sense of the word, which is one of the indulgences of the intelligence. To see something romantically is to "assume the full range of its possibilities that it deserves all its implications, its analogies, its symbolism, its metaphysics." If she is hard on her characters, introducing them to tragic situations, it is because she wanted them to be both recognizable and inspirational in an age of cynicism and disbelief. As a writer in what she labelled the "romance tradition," O'Connor was always:

> interested in what we don't understand rather than what we do . . . interested in possibility rather than probability . . . interested in characters who are forced

---

6. "'I'm Alien to a Great Deal': Flannery O'Connor and the Modernist Ethic." *Journal of American Studies*, Vol. 24, No. 1 (April 1990).

to meet evil and grace and who act on a trust beyond themselves—whether they know very clearly what it is they are upon or not. To the modern mind, this kind of character, and his creator are typical Don Quixotes, tilting at what is not there.

O'Connor's stories are about people struggling with one another, trying to wrest victories from the recalcitrance of love and fate. They are about the triumph and failure of the will, the divine and the human, and about the tragic consequences of our flawed perceptivity, which quietly stalk us all, like age and death. In spite of the brutal fates that so often befall her characters, O'Connor possesses a genuine sympathy for them, even as she modelled the majority after the secular humanists and materialists she so vehemently decried. This sympathy is born from a common humanity, the awareness on O'Connor's part that all of us share in concert the fundamental condition of sin and the possibility for spiritual advancement once we recognize the devil's hand within our own.

Flannery O'Connor remains one of the most difficult writers of the modern period, not because her tales are necessarily more complex than another's, but because her sensibilities and values are so foreign to her era. O'Connor's literary vision comes burning out of a distant time and place; it slashes like a demon's talon, repudiating modernity's complacent conviction that God had died a Victorian. To appreciate fully O'Connor's art, we must accept it in the religious context from which it was written.

## LEE SMITH

### *Flannery O'Connor's "A Good Man Is Hard to Find"*

"A Good Man Is Hard to Find" first hit me like a revelation. I was a college student trying to learn to write fiction myself; somehow I had got the idea that a short story should follow a kind of recipe, like a Lady Baltimore cake. Conflict, suspense, resolution; a clear theme; an ending that tied it all up in a neat little bow. Yet when I read that famous line of "A Good Man Is Hard to Find," I realized that *nothing* was wrapped up here—instead, a whole world opened out before my astonished eyes, a world as wild and scary as life itself. I turned back to the beginning and read it straight through again. I felt like the grandmother in the story, clinging desperately to her outworn beliefs: "I know you're a good man . . . You're not a bit common . . . I know you wouldn't shoot a lady . . . I know you come from nice people!" The gun went off in my own head as surely as it went off in those Georgia pines, and a number of my own ideas died instantly along with the grandmother. A story does *not* have to be resolved in the end, I realized. It is enough to glimpse something, momentarily, before it slips back into the dark woods.

Furthermore, a story can be both very funny and deadly serious at the same time. Though she drew a steady bead on salvation and kept it always in her sights, Flannery O'Connor had time for the gross world, too, and for people with all their comic posturing and blundering. The mix of menace and hilarity is evident early on in "A Good Man Is Hard to Find"; the ominous foreshadowing in the line "this fellow that calls himself The Misfit is aloose from the Federal pen and headed toward Florida and you read here what it says he did to these people" is immediately undercut by the humorous description of the children's mother, "whose face was as broad and innocent as a cabbage and was tied around with a green headkerchief that had two points on top like rabbit's ears." This kind of juxtaposition continues throughout the story—in the image of Bobby Lee and Hiram ambling back from the woods, for instance, dragging Bailey's ridiculous yellow shirt with blue parrots on it, just after killing him, or in those children screaming, "We've had an ACCI-DENT!" in a frenzy of delight. The world has always struck me as both funny and awful, too, and reading "A Good Man Is Hard to Find" for the first time, I realized that I didn't have to *pick*. What a relief!

The older I get, the more profound this story seems to me. Perhaps the constant presence of death in Flannery O'Connor's life allowed her to see beyond her own years. I never read it now without that deep shock of recognition at the bone, and wonder, and pity for us all.

ALICE WALKER

From *Beyond the Peacock: The Reconstruction of Flannery O'Connor*[7]

It was after a poetry reading I gave at a recently desegregated college in Georgia that someone mentioned that in 1952 Flannery O'Connor and I had lived within minutes of each other on the same Eatonton-to-Milledgeville road. I was eight years old in 1952 (she would have been 28) and we moved away from Milledgeville after less than a year. Still, since I have loved her work for many years, the coincidence of our having lived near each other intrigued me, and started me thinking of her again.

As a college student in the sixties I read her books endlessly, scarcely conscious of the difference between her racial and economic background and my own, but put them away in anger when I discovered that, while I was reading O'Connor—Southern, Catholic, and white—there were other women writers—some Southern, some religious, all black—I had not been allowed to know. For several years, while I searched for, found, and studied black women writers, I deliberately shut O'Connor out, feeling almost ashamed that she had reached me first. And yet, even when I no longer read her, I missed her, and realized that though the rest of America might not mind, having endured it so long, I would never be satisfied with a segregated literature.

• • •

I discovered O'Connor when I was in college in the North and took a course in Southern writers and the South. The perfection of her writing was so dazzling I never noticed that no black Southern writers were taught. The other writers we studied—Faulkner, McCullers, Welty—seemed obsessed with a racial past that would not let them go. They seemed to beg the question of their characters' humanity on every page. O'Connor's characters—whose humanity if not their sanity is taken for granted, and who are miserable, ugly, narrow-minded, atheistic, and of intense racial smugness and arrogance, with not a graceful, pretty one anywhere who is not, at the same time, a joke—shocked and delighted me.

7. From *Critical Essays on Flannery O'Connor* (1985).

It was for her description of Southern white women that I appreciated her work at first, because when she set her pen to them not a whiff of magnolia hovered in the air (and the tree itself might never have been planted), and yes, I could say, yes, these white folks without the magnolia (who are indifferent to the tree's existence), and these black folks without melons and superior racial patience, these are like Southerners that I know.

She was for me the first great modern writer from the South, and was, in any case, the only one I had read who wrote such sly, demythifying sentences about white women as: "The woman would be more or less pretty—yellow hair, fat ankles, muddy-colored eyes."

Her white male characters do not fare any better—all of them misfits, thieves, deformed madmen, idiot children, illiterates, and murderers, and her black characters, male and female, appear equally shallow, demented, and absurd. That she retained a certain distance (only, however, in her later, mature work) from the inner workings of her black characters seems to me all to her credit, since, by deliberately limiting her treatment of them to cover their observable demeanor and actions, she leaves them free, in the reader's imagination, to inhabit another landscape, another life, than the one she creates for them. This is a kind of grace many writers do not have when dealing with representatives of an oppressed people within a story, and their insistence on knowing everything, on being God, in fact, has burdened us with more stereotypes than we can ever hope to shed.

In her life, O'Connor was more casual. In a letter to her friend Robert Fitzgerald in the mid-fifties she wrote, "as the niggers say, I have the misery." He found nothing offensive, apparently, in including this unflattering (to O'Connor) statement in his Introduction to one of her books. O'Connor was then certain she was dying, and was in pain; one assumes she made this comment in an attempt at levity. Even so, I do not find it funny. In another letter she wrote shortly before she died she said: "Justice is justice and should not be appealed to along racial lines. The problem is not abstract for the Southerner, it's concrete: he sees it in terms of persons, not races—which way of seeing does away with easy answers." Of course this observation, though grand, does not apply to the racist treatment of blacks by whites in the South, and O'Connor should have added that she spoke only for herself.

But *essential* O'Connor is not about race at all, which is why it is so refreshing, coming, as it does, out of such a *racial* culture. If it can be said to be "about" anything, then it is "about" prophets and prophecy, "about" revelation, and "about" the impact of supernatural grace on human beings who don't have a chance of spiritual growth without it.

• • •

She was an artist who thought she might die young, and who then knew for certain she would. Her view of her characters pierces right through to the skull. Whatever her characters' color or social position she saw them as she saw herself, in the light of imminent mortality.

• • •

It mattered to her that she was a Catholic. This comes as a surprise to those who first read her work as that of an atheist. She believed in all the mysteries of her faith. And yet, she was incapable of writing dogmatic or formulaic stories. No religious tracts, nothing haloed softly in celestial light, not even any happy endings. It has puzzled some of her readers and annoyed the Catholic church that in her stories not only does good not triumph, it is not usually present. Seldom are there choices, and God never intervenes to help anyone win. To O'Connor, in fact, Jesus was God, and he won only by losing. She perceived that not much has been learned by his death by crucifixion, and that it is only by his continual, repeated dying—touching one's own life in a direct, searing way—that the meaning of that original loss is pressed into the heart of the individual.

### THOMAS MERTON

#### Flannery O'Connor: A Prose Elegy[8]

Now Flannery is dead and I will write her name with honor, with love for the great slashing innocence of that dry-eyed irony that could keep looking the South in the face without bleeding or even sobbing. Her South was deeper than mine, crazier than Kentucky, but wild with no other madness than the crafty paranoia that is all over the place, including the North! Only madder, craftier, hung up in wilder and more absurd legends, more inventive of more outrageous lies! And solemn! Taking seriously the need to be respectable when one is an obsolescent and very agile fury.

The key word to Flannery's stories probably is "respect." She never gave up examining its ambiguities and its decay. In this bitter dialectic of half-truths that have become endemic to our system, she probed our very life—its conflicts, its falsities, its obsessions, its vanities. Have we become an enormous complex organization of spurious reverences? Respect is continually advertised, and we are still convinced that we respect "everything good"—when we know too well that we have lost the most elementary respect even for ourselves. Flannery saw this and saw, better than others, what it implied.

She wrote in and out of the anatomy of a word that became genteel, then self-conscious, then obsessive, finally dying of contempt, but kept calling itself "respect." Contempt for the child, for the stranger, for the woman, for the Negro, for the animal, for the white man, for the farmer, for the country, for the preacher, for the city, for the world, for reality itself. Contempt, contempt, so that in the end the gestures of respect they kept making to themselves and to each other and to God became desperately obscene.

But respect had to be maintained. Flannery maintained it ironically and relentlessly with a kind of innocent passion long after it had died of contempt—as if she were the only one left who took this thing seriously. One would think (if one put a Catholic chip on his shoulder and decided to make a problem of her) that she could not look so steadily, so drily and so long at so much false respect without herself dying of despair. She never made any funny faces. She never said: "Here is a terrible thing!" She just looked and said what they said and how they said it. It was not she that invented their despair, and perhaps her only way out of despair herself was to respect the way they announced the gospel of contempt. She patiently recorded all they had got themselves into. Their world was a big, fantastic, crawling, exploding junk pile of despair. I will write her name with honor for seeing it so clearly and

**8.** From *Critical Essays on Flannery O'Connor* (1985).

looking straight at it without remorse. Perhaps her way of irony was the only possible catharsis for a madness so cruel and so endemic. Perhaps a dry honesty like hers can save the South more simply than the North can ever be saved.

Flannery's people were two kinds of very advanced primitives: the city kind, exhausted, disillusioned, tired of imagining, perhaps still given to a grim willfulness in the service of doubt, still driving on in fury and ill will, or scientifically expert in nastiness; and the rural kind: furious, slow, cunning, inexhaustible, living sweetly on the verge of the unbelievable, more inclined to prefer the abyss to solid ground, but keeping contact with the world of contempt by raw insensate poetry and religious mirth: the mirth of a god who himself, they suspected, was the craftiest and most powerful deceiver of all. Flannery saw the contempt of primitives who admitted that they would hate to be saved, and the greater contempt of those other primitives whose salvation was an elaborately contrived possibility, always being brought back into question. Take the sweet idiot deceit of the fury grandmother in "A Good Man Is Hard to Find" whose respectable and catastrophic fantasy easily destroyed her urban son with all his plans, his last shred of trust in reason, and his insolent children.

The way Flannery O'Connor made a story: she would put together all these elements of unreason and let them fly slowly and inexorably at one another. Then sometimes the urban madness, less powerful, would fall weakly prey to the rural madness and be inexorably devoured by a superior and more primitive absurdity. Or the rural madness would fail and fall short of the required malice and urban deceit would compass its destruction, with all possible contempt, cursing, superior violence and fully implemented disbelief. For it would usually be wholesome faith that left the rural primitive unarmed. So you would watch, fascinated, almost in despair, knowing that in the end the very worst thing, the least reasonable, the least desirable, was what would have to happen. Not because Flannery wanted it so, but because it turned out to *be* so in a realm where the advertised satisfaction is compounded of so many lies and of so much contempt for the customer. She had seen too clearly all that is sinister in our commercial paradise, and in its rural roots.

Flannery's people were two kinds of trash, able to mix inanity with poetry, with exuberant nonsense, and with the most profound and systematic contempt for reality. Her people knew how to be trash to the limit, unabashed, on purpose, out of self-contempt that has finally won out over every other feeling and turned into a parody of freedom in the spirit. What spirit? A spirit of ungodly stateliness and parody—the pomp and glee of arbitrary sports, freaks not of nature but of blighted and social willfulness, rich in the creation of respectable and three-eyed monsters. Her beings are always raising the question of *worth*. Who is a good man? Where is he? He is "hard to find." Meanwhile you will have to make out with a bad one who is so respectable that he is horrible, so horrible that he is funny, so funny that he is pathetic, but so pathetic that it would be gruesome to pity him. So funny that you do not dare to laugh too loud for fear of demons.

And that is how Flannery finally solved the problem of respect: having peeled the whole onion of respect layer by layer, having taken it all apart with admirable patience, showing clearly that each layer was only another kind of contempt, she ended up by seeing clearly that it was funny, but not merely funny in a way that you could laugh at. Humorous, yes, but also uncanny, inexplicable, demonic, so you could never laugh at it as if you understood. Because if you pretended to understand, you, too, would find yourself among her demons practicing contempt. She respected all her people by searching for some sense in them, searching for truth, searching to the end and then suspending judgment. To have condemned them on moral grounds would have been to connive with their own crafty arts and their own demonic imagination. It would have meant getting tangled up with them in the same machinery of unreality and of contempt. The only way to be saved was to stay out of it, not to think, not to speak, just to record the slow, sweet, ridiculous verbalizing of Southern furies, working their way through their charming lazy hell.

That is why when I read Flannery I don't think of Hemingway, or Katherine Anne Porter, or Sartre, but rather of someone like Sophocles. What more can be said of a writer? I write her name with honor, for all the truth and all the craft with which she shows man's fall and his dishonor.

## FLANNERY O'CONNOR

### A Prayer Journal[9]

Dear God, I am so discouraged about my work. I have the feeling of discouragement that is. I realize I don't know what I realize. Please help me dear God to be a good writer and to get something else accepted. That is so far from what I deserve, of course, that I am naturally struck with the nerve of it. Contrition in me is largely imperfect. I don't know if I've ever been sorry for a sin because it hurt You. That kind of contrition is better than none but it is selfish. To have the other kind, it is necessary to have knowledge, faith extraordinary. All boils down to grace, I suppose. Again asking God to help us be sorry for having hurt Him. I am afraid of pain and I suppose that is what we have to have to get grace. Give me the courage to stand the pain to get the grace, Oh Lord. Help me with this life that seems so treacherous, so disappointing.

Dear God, tonight it is not disappointing because you have given me a story. Don't let me ever think, dear God, that I was anything but the instrument for Your story—just like the typewriter was mine. Please let the story, dear God, in its revisions, be made too clear for any false & low interpretation because in it, I am not trying to disparage anybody's religion although when it was coming out, I didn't know exactly what I was trying to do or what it was going to mean. I don't know now if it is consistent. Please don't let me have to scrap the story because it turns out to mean more wrong than right—or any wrong. I want it to mean that the good in man sometimes shows through his commercialism but that it is not the fault of the commercialism that it does.

Perhaps the idea would be that good can show through even something that is cheap. I don't know, but dear God, I wish you would take care of making it a sound story because I don't know how, just like I didn't know how to write it but it came. Anyway it all brings me to thanksgiving, the third thing

**9.** From *A Prayer Journal* (2013).

to include in prayer. When I think of all I have to be thankful for I wonder that You don't just kill me now because You've done so much for me already & I haven't been particularly grateful. My thanksgiving is never in the form of self sacrifice—a few memorized prayers babbled once over lightly. All this disgusts me in myself but does not fill me with the poignant feeling I should have to adore You with, to be sorry with, or to thank You with. Perhaps the feeling I keep asking for, is something again selfish—something to help me to feel that everything with *me* is all right. And yet it seems only natural but maybe being thus natural is being thus selfish. My mind is a most insecure thing, not to be depended on. It gives me scruples at one minute & leaves me lax the next. If I must know all these things thru the mind, dear Lord, please strengthen mine. Thank you, dear God, I believe I do feel thankful for all You've done for me. I want to. I do. And thank my dear Mother whom I do love, Our Lady of Perpetual Help.

# Glossary of Critical Terms

**action** Most simply, what happens to, or what is done by, the characters in a story. A somewhat more technical usage—in which "action" is nearly synonymous with **plot**[1]—makes the term signify a unified sequence of events with a beginning, middle, and end.

**allegory** A literary work in which the characters and their situations clearly represent general qualities and types—as, in an animal fable, each animal may represent a type of human personality. Often the characters of an allegory represent abstract vices or virtues such as avarice, charity, innocence, or prudery. See **symbol**.

**ambiguity** Any story or element in a story that can be plausibly interpreted in different ways is said to be ambiguous. Ambiguity can be a fault that obstructs clear communication, but it can also provide enrichment by clustering associated and complementary meanings. See **irony** and **paradox**.

**atmosphere** The enveloping spirit or mood of a story. Used in the same sense as in actual life, it might describe the feeling that prevails at a family reunion, a funeral, or the beginning of a vacation. See also **mood** and **tone**.

**authorial intrusion** Explanations or statements that go beyond a rendering of the situation to make an interpretive comment about it. The author seems to address the reader directly, abandoning the illusion of his or her tale, to deliver an opinion.

**character** 1. One of the people who has a role in the story. 2. The quality or the sum of the qualities of such a person. In most stories we can easily distinguish between central characters—on whom most of the author's attention is focused—and the minor characters—who play some part in the development of the situation. *Round characters* are those presented as having the complex or contradictory qualities that we note in most human beings. *Flat characters* are those who display only a small fraction of normal human complexity. Most good stories will show examples of both flat and round characters according to the requirements of the **focus of interest**.

**chronology** The timeline or calendar of events presented in a story. Chronology may be straightforward—with the narrative beginning at the earliest and running uninterruptedly to the latest point in time—or complicated—with the narrative opening somewhere in the middle and leapfrogging backward or forward. Faulkner's "A Rose for Emily" provides an excellent example for study of complicated chronology. See **flashback**.

**climax** The outcome of the main **action** of a story. That point at which the reader can see what the complications were leading to. Often the climax is a decisive encounter between characters who have been in **conflict**.

**coherence** The consistency of various parts of a story. We expect a character's speech and actions to be consistent with his nature. We expect certain consequences to follow from a particular act, certain feelings to arise from disappointments or rewards. Certain kinds of language will be in keeping with the material described. See **unity** and **style**.

**complication** The emergence of a problem out of the interaction between char-

---

**1.** Words in boldface type are defined in this glossary.

acters and the situation that prevails as the story begins. See **exposition** and **resolution**.

**concreteness** Joseph Conrad wrote: "All art...appeals primarily to the senses.... My task ... is, by the power of the written word, to make you hear, to make you feel—it is, before all, to make you *see*." Fiction renders those concrete details of sensuous experience from which moral and emotional interpretations can be made. Fiction *shows* an action in progress. See **credibility, illusion, setting**.

**conflict** The active opposition of characters, ideas, or ways of life. A dynamic test of the capacities of one thing or person to overcome adversity. Conflict is often considered the soul of fiction, because it gives rise to suspense, drama, and the emotional tension that sharpens our intuitions about characters and their values.

**convention** Any aspect of the literary art that has been established by earlier and repeated usage as part of the way in which language represents experience. Punctuation, syntax, and even the alphabet itself are conventions. So are such things as the use of a narrator, the freedom of the author to substitute his or her language for that of the characters, and the use of paragraphs in dialogue passages.

**conventional** This term frequently has a pejorative meaning—though it derives directly from **convention**, without which no communication would be possible. When used disparagingly, *conventional* means that the writer has tried to find approval by clinging to familiar narrative types and procedures, and uncontroversial values.

**credibility** Is the author telling you something that is unbelievable because it is impossible? Even if it is possible, is it probable? There are degrees of credibility in all reports of human events, and we measure the plausibility of what we read in fiction much as we measure it in history or the daily news. Just because a report is credible it need not be interest-

ing, emotionally convincing, or intuitively comprehensible. See **concreteness** and **illusion**.

**denouement** A synonym for **resolution**.

**description** Those passages devoted to a presentation of the appearance of characters or the setting. Descriptions may appear in passages of dialogue, but they are usually provided by the author or narrator.

**dialogue** The speech of characters in a story, usually punctuated with quotation marks. See **illusion** and **immediacy**.

**diction** The choice and arrangement of words. By disciplining their vocabulary to a degree of conformity with the passions and actions of the story, writers enhance their power to convince. See **illusion** and **unity**.

**didactic** A story is said to be didactic if it deliberately teaches some lesson about the way people should behave. Such teaching was one of the traditional justifications for fiction. Most modern fiction tends to show humanity as it is rather than as it should be, but even modern stories point to general values and distinguish between admirable and contemptible behavior. See **moral** and **parable.**

**distance** Like many other valuable terms that are now conventionally used to discuss fiction, this one is both metaphorical and ambiguous. It may mean the distinction authors preserve between themselves and their central characters (also called **objectivity**). It may refer to a use of language that separates the adventure described from the experience of the reader. It may mean a lack of **immediacy.** The author may choose to let crucial events take place offstage. In such a case they seem to be taking place at a greater distance than events presented directly.

**dramatic** This term is most useful in fictional criticism when it is taken to mean "like something presented on the stage of a theater." The modern writer of fiction tries, most of the time, to *show* us an action rather than simply to *tell* us about it. The writer sets a stage and peoples it. However, the term *dramatic* is also used as a synonym for *exciting* or *suspenseful*. See **concreteness** and **objectivity**.

**effaced narrator** In third-person narration we frequently find that part of the description and narrative is given in a language attributable to the character whose point of view has been assumed by the author, while other parts are in a language that must be attributed to the author's own understanding and observations. The latter is said to come from the effaced narrator, the speaker standing hidden behind his or her character.

**episode** A single part, often a scene, in the continuing action of a story.

**episodic** Usually signifies a loosely constructed or incoherent series of actions. See **coherence**.

**exposition** That part of a story—frequently at or near the beginning—which gives information about the characters and their situation before the action begins to change them.

**first- and third-person narration** In first-person narration the story is told by a character who habitually refers to himself or herself with the pronoun *I*. In third-person all characters are referred to by third-person pronouns and the story is told directly by the author.

**flashback** A break in the chronological sequence of a story to deal with earlier events. See **chronology**.

**focus of interest** Whatever the author tries to make most prominent in his or her narration. May be **plot, setting, characters,** situation, a social problem, or a moral enigma.

**foreshadowing** Hints of things to come. A foolish, impulsive judgment on a small matter hints that a character may be similarly susceptible in the great crises of life. Sometimes foreshadowing is accomplished by a prophetic episode, sometimes by the author's language or by the dialogue.

**form** A term so broad that it sums up all the others in this glossary. The totality of conventions exploited and modified by an author in his or her creative act. See **convention**.

**illusion** Sensory experiences can only be evoked by language; they cannot be duplicated. Nevertheless, in varying degrees, stories can provide the sense that one is morally and emotionally involved in a situation shared with fictional characters. *They* smell the roses and feel the pain of a stab wound, but the reader appreciates the former experience and sympathizes with the latter, much as he or she would if the experiences were real. See **credibility**.

**imagery** 1. Figures of speech, such as similes and metaphors. 2. More generally, all descriptions that prompt the reader to visualize characters in their setting. These visualizations, in turn, set off imaginative analogies that extend the implications of the story beyond its literal limits.

**immediacy** The effect or illusion of sharing the characters' experience. An author may gear all the devices of language, including dialogue and use of the present tense, to promote this effect. It may be enhanced by a deliberate choice of subject matter that will play on the reader's enthusiasms or apprehensions. See **illusion**.

**interior monologue** Sometimes—more popularly—called **stream of consciousness**.

**irony** A discrepancy between what is expected and what is revealed. It may be found either in language usage or in the working out of the action of a story. Surprise endings always depend on some sort of irony, often crude. Irony may appear in the difference between a character's understanding of his or her situation and the reader's estimate of it. See **paradox**.

**milieu** The political, social, cultural, economic, and intellectual aspects of the **setting**. Milieu is to setting as Greek culture is to Greek geography. See **setting**.

**mood** The prevailing feeling of a story, generated by language, **setting,** and the quality of the action. The term is naturally analogous to the moods of our experience—grim, gay, solemn, remorseful, angry, ecstatic, melancholy, anxious, etc. See **atmosphere.**

**moral** The instructive point of a story. (See **didactic.**) The lesson to be drawn from the outcome of the action. While modern taste inclines away from the pat and clear morals that once adorned a lot of stories, a shrewd and important moral in fiction will have the same worth as a shrewd and important axiom delivered without fictional illustration. Handsome is as handsome does.

**motivation** The internal and external forces that compel a **character** to take **action.** Sometimes these forces may be chiefly psychological, sometimes sociological, and sometimes a matter of hostility or opportunity in the physical environment. For **credibility,** motivation should be consistent with **character.**

**narration** 1. A synonym for storytelling, whether the story is told by literary means, by the cinema, or in pantomime. 2. In fiction, narrative passages are to be distinguished from *descriptions* and *scenes.* In narrative passages the **chronology** is condensed so that relatively few words will encompass the events of an extended period of time. Most writers of short stories use narrative passages to fill in the links between events given a scenic treatment.

**narrator** In **first-person narration,** the character tells the story in his or her own words. It is not uncommon in third-person narration for one of the characters to tell an extended story. In such a case it is quite proper to refer to him or her as a narrator.

**novella** (or sometimes **novelette**) Flexible term referring to a piece of fiction intermediate in length between a short story (up to about twelve thousand words) and a novel (thirty thousand words or more). Because some complexities beyond mere length are involved, it is probably best to

think of this class of fiction as being defined by notable examples—as in this text: "Heart of Darkness," "The Death of Ivan Ilych," and "Death in Venice."

**objectivity** Telling a story without bias; telling a story without the interpretive comment to be expected from a partisan or sympathetic observer.

**omniscience** A **convention** in which the author speaks directly to the reader about events that will come in the future and other matters beyond the knowledge of the central character or of all the characters. This contrasts with the discipline of adhering to the **point of view** of a single character and is little used in modern practice.

**pace** The speed at which writers develop any given part of a story. Usually they will hasten over unimportant things, and slow to give a detailed view of what is essential.

**parable** A story told to convey a **moral** or teach a lesson.

**paradox** A statement that appears to be contradictory or inconsistent with common sense—though it may be quite true.

**parody** Mimicry of a work or a style of expression. Sometimes the mimicry is undertaken to make fun of what is parodied; sometimes it is done in a sincere effort to gain the understanding that comes from painstaking imitation. Parody is akin to paraphrase; the translation of a work into your own language to make sure you have grasped it.

**pathos** The pity roused by the situation or the misfortunes of the characters in a story.

**pattern** Like **distance,** a metaphorical and ambiguous term. It is generally taken to refer to changes in the relative position of the characters—as if they were pieces on a game board, shifted, developed, and sometimes sacrificed by the progress of the **action.** Thus if Character A is happy and prosperous in the beginning and becomes poor and wretched while

Character B moves out of poverty and achieves happiness, there is said to be a *crossing pattern*. The term may also refer to the way the author lays out blocks of material. If the author provides a number of small episodes not linked with transitional passages, he or she has made a *mosaic pattern*.

**plot**  Consists of the phases of action in a story that are linked together by a chain of causal relationships. Event A causes or provides motivation for event B, B causes C, etc. Where this chain of causality is not apparent, the story is said to be **episodic.** A well-made plot leads from the potentialities revealed in the **exposition** directly to the situation left in the wake of the **resolution.** Plot may be subordinated to some other **focus of interest** in many stories, but it is one of the most important aspects of fiction, for we understand things best when we are shown what caused them to be as they are.

**point of view**  The events of a story may be told as they appear to one or more participants or observers. In **first-person narration** the point of view is automatically that of the **narrator.** More variation is possible in third-person narration, by which the author may choose to limit his or her report to what could have been observed or known by one of the characters at any given point in the action—or may choose to report the observations and thoughts of several characters. The author might also choose to intrude his or her own point of view. See **omniscience.**

**protagonist**  Chief **character.**

**realism**  An interest in and emphasis on life as it is. In literature this does not mean that writers copy what they see and hear. (Perhaps that is impossible, anyhow.) It means that they will select from their observations the material suitable for constructing a story that faithfully represents what they have understood.

**resolution**  The point in a story at which the **conflict** is decided one way or another and the struggle concluded. The

expectations of the reader and of the characters have, at this point, been confirmed or refuted.

**satire**  The satirist aims to correct, by an exposure to ridicule, deviations from desirable conduct or reasonable opinion. The chief tool of satire is to exaggerate deformities to the point at which their absurdity is unmistakably apparent.

**sentimentality**  An author's attempt to produce an emotional response greater than is warranted by what he or she has to tell. While the student should not be fooled by sentimentality, it is well to remember that the symmetrical and equal fault is hardheartedness, a cold insensitivity to the trouble and joys of the human condition.

**setting**  The physical and cultural environment within which **action** takes place. The stage that serves to demonstrate the qualities of a **protagonist.** An arena suitable for the **conflict.** Weather, urban uproar, the majesty and menace of the ocean can signal moods of human characters. See **concreteness** and **milieu.**

**short-short story**  (also called for convenience simply a "short-short") In recent years there has been a growing interest in stories of a length less than that typical of short stories in general. Writers, critics, and readers at all levels have become more sharply aware of the effects obtained in pieces of minimal length, and they are more and more frequently published in collections. Fables, moral **parables,** epiphanies, prose poems, and thin slices of life may be usefully considered as examples of this general type.

**stream of consciousness**  A fictional device or **convention** in which the author undertakes an imitation of a mind responding to exterior experiences. Frequently it involves a free association of ideas in which normal syntax and logical coherence are suspended. It is usually intended to shortcut the processes of reflection and reconsideration that stand between raw experience and logical statement. See **convention, immediacy, interior monologue.**

**style** A writer's habitual way of expressing himself or herself is his or her style. Examination of it requires consideration of vocabulary, sentence patterns, and other compositional elements. More generally, the appreciation of an author's style comes with a recognition of the way his or her mind plays with experience and literary form.

**symbol** An act, a person, a thing, or a spectacle that represents something else, usually something less palpable than the named symbol. The relationship between the symbol and its referent is not often one of simple equivalence. Allegorical symbols usually express a neater equivalence with what they represent than the symbols found in modern realistic fiction. See **allegory.**

**tension** The emotional and intellectual force generated by disparate potentials within a literary work. In every **ambiguity** there is a tension between the primary meaning and the secondary meanings of a word, phrase, or larger unit of expression. There may be tension between a comic tone and pathetic subject matter. See **ambiguity** and **tone.**

**theme** The unifying point or meaning of a story. Often the theme is implicit in the outcome of the action. It is rarely directly stated, though often it is closely paraphrased by an author's observation or by a statement made by one of the characters.

**tone** A wide-ranging, metaphorical term that usually invites analogy to the tone of voice in which a speaker relates an episode. For example, the speaker might be trying to make light of something that frightened him or her. If we conclude he or she is doing so, the fear will seem magnified by the attempt to disguise it. Tone reveals a storyteller's attitude toward the material.

**understatement** The technique of playing down or underemphasizing a statement. It is a rhetorical trick intended to bring the imagination of the reader into play with a resulting magnification of emotional response. The style of Ernest Hemingway offers some of the best modern examples of this device.

**unity** The shape and consistency of a story. When all the elements and devices of storytelling have been harmonized and nothing extraneous has been included in the text, we speak of it as unified. See **action, coherence, diction, point of view.**

**voice** May be the characteristic mode of expression of a first-person narrator. (See **diction.**) Sometimes the term refers to the total, individualistic effect of all the devices a writer habitually employs, the combination of tactics that distinguishes his or her work from other fiction. (See **style** and **tone.**)

# Permissions Acknowledgments

PHOTOGRAPHS

# Index of Titles